THREE GREAT NOVELS

Also by Michael Connelly

The Black Echo
The Black Ice
The Concrete Blonde
The Poet
Trunk Music
Blood Work
Angels Flight
Void Moon
A Darkness More Than Night
City of Bones
Chasing the Dime
Lost Light
The Narrows

MICHAEL CONNELLY

THREE GREAT NOVELS

THE LAST COYOTE
TRUNK MUSIC
ANGELS FLIGHT

ORION

www.orionbooks.co.uk

CONTENTS

THE LAST COYOTE

This is for Marcus Grupa

1

'Any thoughts that you'd like to start with?'

'Thoughts on what?'

'Well, on anything. On the incident.'

'On the incident? Yes, I have some thoughts.'

She waited but he didn't continue. He had decided before he even got to Chinatown that this would be the way he would be. He'd make her have to pull every single word out of him.

'Could you share them with me, Detective Bosch?' she finally asked. 'That is the purpose of –'

'My thoughts are that this is bullshit. Total bullshit. That's the purpose. That's all.'

'No, wait. How do you mean, bullshit?'

'I mean, okay, I pushed the guy. I guess I hit him. I'm not sure exactly what happened but I'm not denying anything. So, fine, suspend me, transfer me, take it to a Board of Rights, whatever. But going this way is bullshit. ISL is bullshit. I mean, why do I have to come here three times a week to talk to you like I'm some kind of – you don't even know me, you don't know anything about me. Why do I have to talk to you? Why do you have to sign off on this?'

'Well, the technical answer is right there in your own statement. Rather than discipline you the department wants to treat you. You've been placed on involuntary stress leave, which means –'

'I know what it means and that's what's bullshit. Somebody arbitrarily decides I'm under stress and that gives the department the power to keep me off the job indefinitely, or at least until I jump through enough hoops for you.'

'Nothing about this was arbitrary. It was predicated on your actions, which I think clearly show –'

'What happened had nothing to do with stress. What it was about was . . . never mind. Like I said, it's bullshit. So why don't we just cut through it and get to the point. What do I have to do to get back to my job?'

He could see the anger flare behind her eyes. His total disavowal of her science and skill cut to her pride. Quickly the anger was gone, though. Dealing with cops all the time, she had to be used to it.

'Can't you see that all of this is for your own welfare? I have to assume the top managers of this department clearly see you as a valued asset or you wouldn't be here. They'd have put you on a disciplinary track and you'd be

3

on your way out. Instead, they are doing what they can to preserve your career and its incumbent value to the department.'

'Valued asset? I'm a cop, not an asset. And when you're out there on the street nobody's thinking about incumbent value. What does that mean, anyway? Am I going to have to listen to words like that in here?'

She cleared her throat before speaking sternly.

'You have a problem, Detective Bosch. And it goes far beyond the incident that resulted in your being placed on leave. That's what these sessions are going to be all about. Do you understand? This incident is not unique. You have had problems before. What I am trying to do, what I have to do before I can sign off on your return to duty in any capacity, is get you to take a look at yourself. What are you doing? What are you about? Why do these problems happen to you? I want these sessions to be an open dialogue where I ask a few questions and you speak your mind, but with a purpose. Not to harass me and my profession or the leadership of the department. But to talk about you. This is about you in here, no one else.'

Harry Bosch just looked at her silently. He wanted a cigarette but would never ask her if he could smoke. He would never acknowledge in front of her that he had the habit. If he did, she might start talking about oral fixations or nicotine crutches. He took a deep breath instead and looked at the woman on the other side of the desk. Carmen Hinojos was a small woman with a friendly face and manner. Bosch knew she wasn't a bad person. He'd actually heard good things about her from others who had been sent to Chinatown. She was just doing her job here and his anger was not really directed at her. He knew she was probably smart enough to know that, too.

'Look, I'm sorry,' she said. 'I should not have started with that kind of open question. I know that this is an emotional subject with you. Let's try to start again. By the way, you can smoke if you'd like.'

'Is that in the file, too?'

'It's not in the file. It didn't need to be. It's your hand, the way you keep bringing it up to your mouth. Have you been trying to quit?'

'No. But it's a city office. You know the rules.'

It was a thin excuse. He violated that law every day at the Hollywood Station.

'That's not the rule in here. I don't want you to think of this as being part of Parker Center or part of the city. That's the chief reason these offices are away from that. There are no rules like that here.'

'Doesn't matter where we are. You're still working for the LAPD.'

'Try to believe that you are away from the Los Angeles Police Department. When you are in here, try to believe that you're just coming to see a friend. To talk. You can say anything here.'

But he knew she could not be seen as a friend. Never. There was too much at stake here. Just the same, he nodded once to please her.

'That's not very convincing.'

He hiked his shoulders as if to say it was the best he could do, and it was.

'By the way, if you want I could hypnotize you, get rid of your dependency on nicotine.'

'If I wanted to quit, I could do it. People are either smokers or they're not. I am.'

'Yes. It's perhaps the most obvious symptom of a self-destructive nature.'

'Excuse me, am I on leave because I smoke? Is that what this is about?'

'I think you know what it's about.'

He said nothing else, remembering his decision to say as little as possible.

'Well, let's continue then,' she said. 'You've been on leave ... let's see, Tuesday a week?'

'Right.'

'What have you been doing with your time?'

'Filling out FEMA forms mostly.'

'FEMA?'

'My house was red-tagged.'

'The earthquake was three months ago. Why have you waited?'

'I've been busy. I've been working.'

'I see. Did you have insurance?'

'Don't say "I see," because you don't. You couldn't possibly see things the way I do. The answer is no, no insurance. Like most everybody else, I was living in denial. Isn't that what you people call it? I bet you had insurance.'

'Yes. How bad was your house hit?'

'Depends on who you ask. The city inspectors say it's totaled and I can't even go inside. I think it's fine. Just needs some work. They know me by name at Home Depot now. And I've had contractors do some of it. It'll be done soon and I'll appeal the red tag. I've got a lawyer.'

'You're living there still?'

He nodded.

'Now that's denial, Detective Bosch. I don't think you should be doing that.'

'I don't think you have any say about what I do outside my job with the department.'

She raised her hands in a hands-off manner.

'Well, while I don't condone it, I suppose it serves its purpose. I think it's good that you have something to keep you occupied. Though I'd much rather it be a sport or a hobby or maybe plans for a trip out of town, I think it's important to keep busy, to keep your mind off the incident.'

Bosch smirked.

'What?'

'I don't know. Everybody keeps calling it the incident. It kind've reminds me of how people called it the Vietnam conflict, not the war.'

'Then what would you call what happened?'

'I don't know. But incident . . . it sounds like . . . I don't know. Antiseptic. Listen, Doctor, let's go back a minute. I don't want to take a trip out of town, okay? My job is in homicide. It's what I do. And I'd really like to get back to it. I might be able to do some good, you know.'

'If the department lets you.'

'If you do. You know it's going to be up to you.'

'Perhaps. Do you notice that you speak of your job as if it's a mission of some sort?'

'That's about right. Like the Holy Grail.'

He said it with sarcasm. This was getting intolerable and it was only the first session.

'Is it? Do you believe your mission in life is to solve murders, to put bad people in jail?'

He used the shoulder hike to say he didn't know. He stood up and walked to the window and looked down on Hill Street. The sidewalks were crowded with pedestrians. Every time he had been down here they were crowded. He noticed a couple of Caucasian women walking along. They stood out in the sea of Asian faces like raisins in rice. They passed the window of a Chinese butcher shop and Bosch saw a row of smoked ducks hanging whole, by their necks.

Farther up the road he saw the Hollywood Freeway overpass, the dark windows of the old sheriff's jail and the Criminal Courts building behind it. To the left of that he could see the City Hall tower. Black construction tarps hung around the top floors. It looked like some kind of mourning gesture but he knew the tarps were to hold debris from falling while earthquake repairs were made. Looking past City Hall, Bosch could see the Glass House. Parker Center, police headquarters.

'Tell me what your mission is,' Hinojos said quietly from behind him. 'I'd like to hear you put it in words.'

He sat back down and tried to think of a way to explain himself but finally just shook his head.

'I can't.'

'Well, I want you to think about that. Your mission. What is it really? Think about that.'

'What's your mission, Doctor?'

'That's not our concern here.'

'Of course it is.'

'Look, Detective, this is the only personal question I will answer. These dialogues are not to be about me. They are about you. My mission, I believe, is to help the men and women of this department. That's the narrow focus. And by doing that, on a grander scale I help the community, I help the people of this city. The better the cops are that we have out on the street, the better we all are. The safer we all are. Okay?'

'That's fine. When I think about my mission, do you want me to shorten it to a couple sentences like that and rehearse it to the point that it sounds like I'm reading out of the dictionary?'

'Mr – uh, Detective Bosch, if you want to be cute and contentious the whole time, we are not going to get anywhere, which means you are not going to get back to your job anytime soon. Is that what you're looking for here?'

He raised his hands in surrender. She looked down at the yellow legal pad on the desk. With her eyes off him, he was able to study her. Carmen Hinojos had tiny brown hands she kept on the desk in front of her. No rings on either hand. She held an expensive-looking pen in her right hand. Bosch always thought expensive pens were used by people overly concerned with image. But maybe he was wrong about her. She wore her dark brown hair tied back. She wore glasses with thin tortoiseshell frames. She should have had braces when she was a kid but didn't. She looked up from the pad and their eyes locked.

'I am told this inci – this . . . situation coincided with or was close to the time of the dissolving of a romantic relationship.'

'Told by who?'

'It's in the background material given to me. The sources of this material are not important.'

'Well, they are important because you've got bad sources. It had nothing to do with what happened. The dissolving, as you call it, was almost three months ago.'

'The pain of these things can last much longer than that. I know this is personal and may be difficult but I think we should talk about this. The reason is that it will help give me a basis for your emotional state at the time the assault took place. Is that a problem?'

Bosch waved her on with his hand.

'How long did this relationship last?'

'About a year.'

'Marriage?'

'No.'

'Was it talked about?'

'No, not really. Never out in the open.'

'Did you live together?'

'Sometimes. We both kept our places.'

'Is the separation final?'

'I think so.'

Saying it out loud seemed to be the first time Bosch acknowledged that Sylvia Moore was gone from his life for good.

'Was this separation by mutual agreement?'

He cleared his throat. He didn't want to talk about this but he wanted it over with.

'I guess you could say it was mutual agreement, but I didn't know about it until she was packed. You know, three months ago we were holding each other in bed while the house was shaking apart on the pad. You could say she was gone before the aftershocks ended.'

'They still haven't.'

'Just a figure of speech.'

'Are you saying the earthquake was the cause of the breakup of this relationship?'

'No, I'm not saying that. All I'm saying is that's when it happened. Right after. She's a teacher up in the Valley and her school got wrecked. The kids were moved to other schools and the district didn't need as many teachers. They offered sabbaticals and she took one. She left town.'

'Was she scared of another earthquake or was she scared of you?'

She looked pointedly at him.

'Why would she be scared of me?'

He knew he sounded a little too defensive.

'I don't know. I'm just asking questions. Did you give her a reason to be scared?'

Bosch hesitated. It was a question he had never really touched on in his private thoughts about the breakup.

'If you mean in a physical way, no, she wasn't scared and I gave her no reason to be.'

Hinojos nodded and wrote something on her pad. It bothered Bosch that she would make a note about this.

7

'Look, it's got nothing to do with what happened at the station last week.'

'Why did she leave? What was the real reason?'

He looked away. He was angry. This was how it was going to be. She would ask whatever she wanted. Invade him wherever there was an opening.

'I don't know.'

'That answer is not acceptable in here. I think you do know, or at least have your own beliefs as to why she would leave. You must.'

'She found out who I was.'

'She found out who you were, what does that mean?'

'You'd have to ask her. She said it. But she's in Venice. The one in Italy.'

'Well, then what do you think she meant by it?'

'It doesn't matter what I think. She's the one who said it and she's the one who left.'

'Don't fight me, Detective Bosch. Please. There is nothing I want more than for you to get back to your job. As I said, that's my mission. To get you back there if you can go. But you make it difficult by being difficult.'

'Maybe that's what she found out. Maybe that's who I am.'

'I doubt the reason is as simplistic as that.'

'Sometimes I don't.'

She looked at her watch and leaned forward, dissatisfaction with the session showing on her face.

'Okay, Detective, I understand how uncomfortable you are. We're going to move on, but I suspect we will have to come back to this issue. I want you to give it some thought. Try to put your feelings into words.'

She waited for him to say something but he didn't.

'Let's try talking about what happened last week again. I understand it stemmed from a case involving the murder of a prostitute.'

'Yes.'

'It was brutal?'

'That's just a word. Means different things to different people.'

'True, but taking its meaning to you, was it a brutal homicide?'

'Yes, it was brutal. I think almost all of them are. Somebody dies, it's brutal. For them.'

'And you took the suspect into custody?'

'Yes, my partner and I. I mean, no. He came in voluntarily to answer questions.'

'Did this case affect you more than, say, other cases have in the past?'

'Maybe, I don't know.'

'Why would that be?'

'You mean why did I care about a prostitute? I didn't. Not more than any other victim. But in homicide there is one rule that I have when it comes to the cases I get.'

'What is that rule?'

'Everybody counts or nobody counts.'

'Explain it.'

'Just what I said. Everybody counts or nobody counts. That's it. It means I bust my ass to make a case whether it's a prostitute or the mayor's wife. That's my rule.'

'I understand. Now, let's go to this specific case. I'm interested in hearing your description of what happened after the arrest and the reasons you may have for your violent actions at the Hollywood Division.'

'Is this being taped?'

'No, Detective, whatever you tell me is protected. At the end of these sessions I will simply make a recommendation to Assistant Chief Irving. The details of the sessions will never be divulged. The recommendations I make are usually less than half a page and contain no details from the dialogues.'

'You wield a lot of power with that half page.'

She didn't respond. Bosch thought for a moment while looking at her. He thought he might be able to trust her but his natural instinct and experience was that he should trust no one. She seemed to know his dilemma and waited him out.

'You want to hear my side of it?'

'Yes, I do.'

'Okay, I'll tell you what happened.'

2

Bosch smoked along the way home but realized that what he really wanted was not a cigarette, but a drink to deaden his nerves. He looked at his watch and decided it was too early to stop at a bar. He settled for another cigarette and home.

After negotiating the drive up Woodrow Wilson, he parked at the curb a half block from the house and walked back. He could hear gentle piano music, something classical, coming from the home of one of his neighbors but he couldn't tell which house. He didn't really know any of his neighbors or which one might have a piano player in the family. He ducked under the yellow tape strung in front of the property and entered through the door in the carport.

This was his routine, to park down the street and hide the fact that he lived in his own house. The house had been red-tagged as uninhabitable after the earthquake and ordered demolished by a city inspector. But Bosch had ignored both orders, cut the lock on the electric box, and had been living in it for three months.

It was a small house with redwood siding that stood on steel pylons anchored in the sedimentary bedrock folded and formed as the Santa Monica Mountains rose out of the desert during the Mesozoic and Cenozoic eras. The pylons had held true in their moorings during the quake, but the overlying house had shifted atop them, breaking partially free of the pylons and seismic bolts. It slid. All of about two inches. Still, it was enough. Though short on distance the slide was long on damage. Inside, the woodframe house flexed and window and door frames lost their square. The glass shattered, the front door became terminally closed, frozen in a frame that had canted to the north with the rest of the house. If Bosch wanted to open that door, he would probably need to borrow the police tank with the battering ram. As it was, he'd had to use a crowbar to open the carport door. Now that door served as the main entrance to his home.

Bosch had paid a contractor five thousand dollars to jack the house up and then over the two inches it had moved. It was then put down in its proper space and rebolted to the pylons. After that, Bosch was content to work as time allowed on reframing windows and interior doors himself. The glass came first and in the months after that he reframed and rehung the interior doors. He worked from books on carpentry and often had to do individual projects two and three times until he had them reasonably correct. But he found the work enjoyable and even therapeutic. Working

10

with his hands became a respite from his job in homicide. He left the front door as it was, thinking that somehow it was fitting, that it was a salute to the power of nature. And he was content to use the side door.

All of his efforts did not save the house from the city's list of condemned structures. Gowdy, the building inspector who had been assigned to this section of the hills, kept it red-tagged as condemned, despite Bosch's work, and so began the hiding game in which Bosch made his entrances and exits as surreptitiously as a spy's to a foreign embassy. He tacked black plastic tarps over the inside of the front windows so they would emit no telltale light. And he always watched for Gowdy. Gowdy was his nemesis.

In the meantime, Bosch hired a lawyer to appeal the inspector's edict.

The carport door granted entry directly into the kitchen. After he came in, Bosch opened the refrigerator and retrieved a can of Coca-Cola, then stood in the doorway of the aging appliance letting its breath cool him while he studied its contents for something suitable for dinner. He knew exactly what was on the shelves and in the drawers but still he looked. It was as if he hoped for the surprise appearance of a forgotten steak or chicken breast. He followed this routine with the refrigerator often. It was the ritual of a man who was alone. He knew this also.

On the back deck Bosch drank the soda and ate a sandwich consisting of five-day-old bread and slices of meat from plastic packages. He wished he had potato chips to go with it because he would undoubtedly be hungry later after having only the sandwich for dinner.

He stood at the railing looking down at the Hollywood Freeway, near capacity now with the Monday-evening commute. He had gotten out of downtown just before the crest of the rush-hour wave had broken. He would have to guard against going overtime on the sessions with the police psychologist. They were scheduled for 3:30 p.m. on Mondays, Wednesdays and Fridays. Did Carmen Hinojos ever let a session go over? he wondered. Or was hers a nine-to-five mission?

From his vantage on the mountain, he could see almost all northbound lanes of the freeway as it cut through the Cahuenga Pass to the San Fernando Valley. He was reviewing what had been said during the session, trying to decide whether it was a good or bad session, but his focus drifted and he began to watch the point where the freeway came into view as it crested the pass. Absentmindedly, he would choose two cars that came over about even with each other and follow them through the mile-long segment of the freeway that was visible from the deck. He'd pick one or the other and follow the race, unknown to its drivers, until the finish line, which was the Lankershim Boulevard exit.

After a few minutes of this he realized what he was doing and spun around, away from the freeway.

'Jesus,' he said out loud.

He knew then that keeping his hands busy would not be enough while he was away from his job. He went back inside and got a bottle of Henry's from the refrigerator. Right after he opened the beer the phone rang. It was his partner, Jerry Edgar, and the call was a welcome distraction from the silence.

'Harry, how's things in Chinatown?'

Because every cop secretly feared that he or she might one day crack from

11

the pressures of the job and become a candidate for therapy sessions at the department's Behavioral Sciences Section, the unit was rarely spoken of by its formal name. Going to BSS sessions was more often referred to as 'going to Chinatown' because of the unit's location there on Hill Street, several blocks from Parker Center. If it became known about a cop that he was going there, the word would spread that he had the Hill Street blues. The six-story bank building where the BSS was located was known as the 'Fifty-One-Fifty' building. This was not its address. It was the police radio code number for describing a crazy person. Codes like this were part of the protective structure used to belittle and, therefore, more easily contain their own fears.

'Chinatown was great,' Bosch said sarcastically. 'You ought to try it some day. It's got me sitting here counting cars on the freeway.'

'Well, at least you won't run out.'

'Yeah. What's going on with you?'

'Pounds finally did it.'

'Did what?'

'Stuck me with somebody new.'

Bosch was silent a moment. The news gave him a sense of finality. The thought that maybe he would never get his job back began to creep into his mind.

'He did?'

'Yeah, he finally did. I caught a case this morning. So he stuck one of his suckups with me. Burns.'

'Burns? From autos? He's never worked homicide. Has he ever even worked CAPs?'

Detectives usually followed one of two paths in the department. One was property crimes and the other was crimes against persons. The latter included specializing in homicide, rape, assault and robbery. CAPs detectives had the higher-profile cases and usually viewed property crime investigators as paper pushers. There were so many property crimes in the city that the investigators spent most of their time taking reports and processing the occasional arrest. They actually did little detective work. There was no time to.

'He's been a paper guy all the way,' Edgar said. 'But with Pounds that doesn't matter. All he cares about is having somebody on the homicide table who isn't going to give his shit back to him. And Burns is just the guy. He probably started lobbying for the job the minute the word went out about you.'

'Well, fuck him. I'm gonna get back to the table and then he goes back to autos.'

Edgar took his time before answering. It was as if Bosch had said something that made no sense to him.

'You really think that, Harry? Pounds ain't going to stand for you coming back. Not after what you did. I told him when he told me I was with Burns that, you know, no offense but I'd wait until Harry Bosch came back and he said if I wanted to handle it that way, then I'd be waitin' until I was an old man.'

'He said that? Well, fuck him, too. I still got a friend or two in the department.'

'Irving still owes you, doesn't he?'

'I guess maybe I'll find out.'

He didn't go further with it. He wanted to change the subject. Edgar was his partner but they had never gotten to the point where they completely confided in each other. Bosch played the mentor role in the relationship and he trusted Edgar with his life. But that was a bond that held fast on the street. Inside the department was another matter. Bosch had never trusted anyone, never relied on anyone. He wasn't going to start now.

'So, what's the case?' he asked, to divert the conversation.

'Oh, yeah, I wanted to tell you about it. This was weird, man. First the killing's weird, then what happened after. The call out was to a house on Sierra Bonita. This is about five in the a.m. The citizen reports he heard a sound like a gunshot, only muffled-like. He grabs his deer rifle out of the closet and goes outside to take a look. This is a neighborhood that's been picked clean lately by the hypes, you know? Four B and Es on his block alone this month. So, he was ready with the rifle. Anyway, he goes down his driveway with the gun – the garage is in the back – and he sees a pair of legs hanging out of the open door of his car. It was parked in front of the garage.'

'He shoots him?'

'No, that's the crazy thing. He goes up with his gun but the guy in his car is already dead. Stabbed in the chest with a screwdriver.'

Bosch didn't get it. He didn't have enough of the facts. But he said nothing.

'The air bag killed him, Harry.'

'What do you mean, the air bag killed him?'

'The air bag. This goddamn hype was stealing the air bag out of the steering wheel and somehow the thing went off. It inflated instantly, like it was supposed to, and drove the screwdriver right into his heart, man. I've never seen anything like it. He must've been holding the screwdriver backwards or he was using the butt-end to bang on the wheel. We haven't exactly figured out that part yet. We talked to a guy at Chrysler. He says that you take the protective cover off, like this dude had, and even static electricity can set the thing off. Our dead guy was wearing a sweater. I don't know, could've been it. Burns says it's the first death by static cling.'

While Edgar chuckled at his new partner's humor, Bosch thought about the scenario. He remembered a department info bulletin going out on air bag thefts the year before. They had become a hot commodity in the underground market, with thieves getting as much as three hundred dollars apiece for air bags from unscrupulous body shops. The body shops would buy them for three hundred and turn around and charge a customer nine hundred to install one. That was double the profit derived when ordering from the manufacturer.

'So it goes down as accidental?' Bosch asked.

'Yeah, accidental death. But the story ain't over. Both doors of the car were open.'

'The dead guy had a partner.'

'That's what we figure. And so if we find the fucker we can charge him. Under the felony homicide law. So we had SID laser the inside of the car and pull all the prints they could. I took 'em down to Latents and talked one of the techs into scanning them and running them on the AFIS. And bingo.'

'You got the partner?'

'Dead bang. That AFIS computer has got a long reach, Harry. One of the nets is the US Military Identification Center in St Louis. We got a match on our guy outta there. He was in the Army ten years ago. We got his ID from that, then got an address from the DMV and picked him up today. He copped on the ride in. He's gonna go away for a while.'

'Sounds like a good day, then.'

'Didn't end there, though. I haven't told you the weird part yet.'

'Then tell me.'

'Remember I said we lasered the car and took all the prints?'

'Right.'

'Well, we got another match, too. This one on the crime indexes. A case outta Mississippi. Man, all days should be like this one was.'

'What was the match?' Bosch asked. He was growing impatient with the way Edgar was parceling out the story.

'We matched prints put on the net seven years ago by something called the Southern States Criminal Identification Base. It's like five states that don't add up in population to half of LA. Anyway, one of the prints we put through today matched the doer on a double homicide in Biloxi all the way back in 'seventy-six. Some guy the papers there called the Bicentennial Butcher on account he killed two women on the Fourth of July.'

'The car's owner? The guy with the rifle?'

'Damn right. His fingerprints were on the cleaver left in one girl's skull. He was a bit surprised when we came back to his house this afternoon. We said, "Hey, we caught the partner of the guy who died in your car. And by the way, you're under arrest for a two-bagger, motherfucker." I think it blew his mind, Harry. You shoulda been there.'

Edgar laughed loudly into the phone and Bosch knew, after only one week of being grounded, how much he missed the job.

'Did he cop?'

'No, he kept quiet. You can't be that stupid and get away with a double murder for almost twenty years. That's a nice run.'

'Yeah, what's he been doing?'

'Looks like he's just been laying low. Owns a hardware on Santa Monica. Married and has a kid and a dog. A total reform case. But he's going back to Biloxi. I hope he likes southern cooking 'cause he won't be coming back here anytime soon.'

Edgar laughed again. Bosch said nothing. The story was depressing because it was a reminder of what he was no longer doing. It also reminded him about what Hinojos had asked about defining his mission.

'Got a couple of Mississippi state troopers comin' out tomorrow,' Edgar said. 'Talked to them a little while ago and they are happy campers.'

Bosch didn't say anything for a while.

'Harry, you still there?'

'Yeah, I was just thinking about something . . . Well, it sounds like a hell of a day of crime fighting. How's the fearless leader taking it?'

'Pounds? Jesus, he's got a hard-on over this the size of a Louisville slugger.

You know what he's doing? He's trying to figure out a way to take credit for all three clearances. He's trying to put the Biloxi cases on our rate.'

It didn't surprise Bosch. It was a widespread practice among department managers and statisticians to add positive credit to crime clearance levels whenever and wherever possible. In the air bag case, there was no actual murder. It was an accident. But because the death occurred during the commission of a crime, California law held that an accomplice to the crime could be charged with his partner's death. Bosch knew that based on the partner's arrest for murder, Pounds intended to add a case to the murder clearance chart. He would not balance this by adding a case to the murder occurrence chart because the death by air bag was an accident. This little statistical two-step would result in a nice little boost for the Hollywood Division's overall homicide clearance rate, which in recent years had continually threatened to dip below fifty percent.

But unsatisfied with the modest jump this accounting deception would provide, Pounds intended to boldly add the two Biloxi murders to the clearance chart as well. After all, it could be argued, his homicide squad did clear two more cases. Adding a total of three cleared cases to one side of the chart without adding any to the other would likely give a tremendous boost to the overall clearance rate – as well as to the image of Pounds as a detective bureau commander. Bosch knew that Pounds was probably delighted with himself and the accomplishments of the day.

'He said our rate would jump six points,' Edgar was saying. 'He was a very pleased man, Harry. And my new partner was very pleased he had pleased his man.'

'I don't want to hear any more.'

'I didn't think so. So what are you doing to keep busy, besides counting cars on the freeway? You must be bored stiff, Harry.'

'Not really,' Bosch lied. 'Last week I finished fixing the deck. This week I'll –'

'Harry, I'm telling you, you're wasting your time and money. The inspectors are going to find you in there and kick you out on your ass. Then they'll tear the place down themselves and hand you the bill. Your deck and the whole house will be in the back of a dump truck then.'

'I hired a lawyer to work on it.'

'What's he gonna do?'

'I don't know. I want to appeal the red tag. He's a land use guy. He said he can work it out.'

'I hope so. I still think you ought to tear it down and start over.'

'I didn't win the lotto yet.'

'The feds've got disaster loans. You could get one and –'

'I've applied, Jerry, but I like my house the way it is.'

'Okay, Harry. I hope your lawyer works it out. Anyway, I gotta go. Burns wants to have a beer over at the Short Stop. He's there waiting.'

The last time Bosch had been at the Short Stop, a hole-in-the-wall cop bar near the academy and Dodger Stadium, it had still had I SUPPORT CHIEF GATES bumper stickers on the wall. For most cops, Gates was a dying ember of the past, but the Short Stop was a place where old-liners went to drink and remember a department that no longer existed.

'Yeah, have fun over there, Jerry.'

15

'Take care, man.'

Bosch leaned against a counter and drank his beer. He came to the conclusion that Edgar's call had been a cleverly disguised way of telling Bosch that he was choosing sides and cutting him loose. That was okay, Bosch thought. Edgar's first allegiance was to himself, to surviving in a place that could be treacherous. Bosch couldn't hold that against him.

Bosch looked at his reflection in the glass of the oven door. The image was dark but he could see his eyes in the shadow and the line of his jaw. He was forty-four years old and in some ways looked older. He still had a full head of curly brown hair but both the hair and the mustache were going to gray. His black-brown eyes seemed to him tired and used up. His skin had the pallor of a night watchman's. Bosch was still leanly built but sometimes his clothes hung on him as if they had been issued at one of the downtown missions or he had recently been through a bad illness.

He broke away from his reflection and grabbed another beer out of the refrigerator. Outside on the deck, he saw the sky was now brightly lit with the pastels of dusk. It would be dark soon, but the freeway below was a bright river of moving lights, its current never ebbing for a moment.

Looking down on the Monday night commute, he saw the place as an anthill with the workers moving along in lines. Someone or some force would soon come along and kick the hill again. Then the freeways would fall, the houses would collapse and the ants would just rebuild and get in line again.

He was bothered by something but was not quite sure what it was. His thoughts swirled and mixed. He began to see what Edgar had told him about his case in the context of his dialogue with Hinojos. There was some connection there, some bridge, but he couldn't get to it.

He finished his beer and decided that two would be enough. He went to one of the lounge chairs and sat down with his feet up. What he wanted to do was give everything a rest. Mind and body. He looked up and saw the clouds had now been painted orange by the setting sun. They looked like molten lava moving slowly across the sky.

Just before he dozed off a thought pushed through the lava. Everybody counts or nobody counts. And then, in the last moment of clarity before sleep, he knew what the connecting ribbon that had run through his thoughts had been. And he knew what his mission was.

3

In the morning Bosch dressed without showering so he could immediately begin work on the house and blank out the lingering thoughts from the night before with sweat and concentration.

But clearing the thoughts away was not easy. As he dressed in old lacquer-stained jeans, he caught a glimpse of himself in the cracked mirror over the bureau and saw that his T-shirt was on backward. Printed across his chest on the white shirt was the homicide squad's motto.

OUR DAY BEGINS WHEN YOUR DAY ENDS

It was supposed to be on the back of the shirt. He pulled it off, turned it and put it back on. Now in the mirror he saw what he was supposed to see. A replica of a detective's badge on the left breast of the shirt and the smaller printing that said LAPD HOMICIDE.

He brewed a pot of coffee and took it and a mug out to the deck. Next he lugged out his toolbox and the new door he had bought at Home Depot for the bedroom. When he was finally ready and had the mug filled with steaming black coffee, he sat on the footrest of one of the lounge chairs and placed the door on its side in front of him.

The original door had splintered at the hinges during the quake. He had tried to hang the replacement a few days earlier but it was too large to fit the door jamb. He figured he needed to shave no more than an eighth of an inch off the opening side to make the fit. He set to work with the plane, moving the instrument slowly back and forth along the edge as the wood peels fell away in paper-thin curls. Occasionally he would stop and study his progress and run his hand along the area of his work. He liked being able to see the progress he was making. Few other tasks in life seemed that way to him.

But still, he could not concentrate for long. His focus on the door was interrupted by the same intrusive thought that had haunted him the night before. Everybody counts or nobody counts. It was what he had told Hinojos. It was what he had told her he believed. But did he? What did it mean to him? Was it merely a slogan like the one on the back of his shirt or was it something he lived by? These questions mingled with the echoes of the conversation he'd had the night before with Edgar. And with a deeper thought that he knew he had always had.

He took the plane off the door edge and ran his hand along the smooth wood again. He thought he had it right and carried it inside. Over a drop cloth in an area of the living room he had reserved for woodworking, he ran a sheet of small-grain sandpaper over the door edge until it was perfectly smooth to his touch.

Holding the door vertically and balancing it on a block of wood, he eased it into the hinges and then dropped the pins in. He tapped them home with a hammer and they went in easily. He had oiled the pins and hinges earlier and so the bedroom door opened and closed almost silently. Most important, though, was that it closed evenly in the jamb. He opened and closed it several more times, just staring at it, pleased with his accomplishment.

The glow of his success was short-lived, for having completed the project left his mind open to wander. Back out on the deck the other thoughts came back as he swept the wood shavings into a small pile.

Hinojos had told him to stay busy. Now he knew how he would do it. And in that moment he realized that no matter how many projects he found to take his time, there was one job he still had to do. He leaned the broom against the wall and went inside to get ready.

4

The LAPD storage facility and aerosquad headquarters known as Piper Tech was on Ramirez Street in downtown, not far from Parker Center. Bosch, in a suit and tie, arrived shortly before eleven at the gate. He held his LAPD identification card out the window and was quickly waved in. The card was all he had. The card, along with his gold badge and gun, had been taken from him when he was placed on leave the week before. But it was later returned so that he could gain entry to the BSS offices for the stress therapy sessions with Carmen Hinojos.

After parking, he walked to the beige-painted storage warehouse that housed the city's history of violence. The quarter-acre building contained the files of all LAPD cases, solved or unsolved. This was where the case files came when nobody cared anymore.

At the front counter a civilian clerk was loading files onto a cart so that they could be wheeled back into the expanse of shelves and forgotten. By the way she studied Bosch, he knew it was rare that anyone ever showed up here in person. It was all done by telephones and city couriers.

'If you're looking for city council minutes, that's building A, across the lot. The one with brown trim.'

Bosch held up his ID card.

'No, I want to pull a case.'

He reached into his coat pocket while she walked up to the counter and bent forward to read his card. She was a small black woman with graying hair and glasses. The name tag affixed to her blouse said her name was Geneva Beaupre.

'Hollywood,' she said. 'Why didn't you just ask for it to be sent out in dispatch? There ain't no hurry on these cases.'

'I was downtown, over at Parker . . . I wanted to see it as soon as I could, anyway.'

'Well, you got a number?'

From his pocket he pulled a piece of notebook paper with the number 61–743 written on it. She bent to study it and then her head jerked up.

'Nineteen sixty-one? You want a case from – I don't know where nineteen sixty-one is.'

'It's here. I've looked at the file before. I guess there was someone else clerking here back then, but it was here.'

'Well, I'll look. You're going to wait?'

'Yeah, I'll wait.'

This seemed to disappoint her but Bosch smiled at her in the most friendly way he could muster. She took the paper with her and disappeared into the stacks. Bosch walked around the small waiting area by the counter for a few minutes and then stepped outside to smoke a cigarette. He was nervous for a reason he could not exactly place. He kept moving, pacing.

'Harry Bosch!'

He turned and saw a man approaching him from the helicopter hangar. He recognized him but couldn't immediately place him. Then it hit him: Captain Dan Washington, a former Hollywood patrol skipper who was now commander of the aerosquadron. They shook hands cordially and Bosch immediately hoped Washington did not know of his ISL situation.

'Howzit going in the 'wood?'

'Same old same old, Captain.'

'You know, I miss that place.'

'You're not missing much. How is it with you?'

'Can't complain. I like the detail but it's more like being an airport manager than a cop, I guess. It's as good a place to lay low as any other.'

Bosch recalled that Washington had gotten into a political scrap with the department weight and taken the transfer as a means of survival. The department had dozens of out-of-the-way jobs like Washington's, where you could lay up and wait for your political fortunes to change.

'What're you doing over here?'

There it was. If Washington knew Bosch was on leave, then admitting he was pulling an old case file would be admitting he was violating the leave order. Still, as his position in the aerosquad attested, Washington was not a straight-line company man. Bosch decided to run the risk.

'I'm just pulling an old case. I got some free time and thought I'd check a few things.'

Washington narrowed his eyes and Bosch knew that he knew.

'Yeah . . . well, listen, I gotta run, but hang in there, man. Don't let the book men get you down.'

He winked at Bosch and moved on.

'I won't, Captain. You either.'

Bosch felt reasonably sure Washington wouldn't mention their meeting to anybody. He stepped on his cigarette and went back inside to the counter, privately chastising himself anyway for having gone outside and advertised that he was there. Five minutes later he started hearing a squeaking sound coming from one of the aisles between the stacks. In a moment Geneva Beaupre appeared pushing a cart with a blue three-ring binder on it.

It was a murder book. It was at least two inches thick, dusty, and with a rubber band around it. The band held an old green checkout card to the binder.

'Found it.'

There was a note of triumph in her voice. It would be the major accomplishment of her day, Bosch guessed.

'Great.'

She dropped the heavy binder on the counter.

'Marjorie Lowe. Homicide, 1961. Now . . .' She took the card off the binder and looked at it. 'Yes, you were the last to take this out. Let's see, that was five years ago. You were with Robbery-Homicide then . . .'

'Yes. And now I'm in Hollywood. You want me to sign for it again?'

She put the card down in front of him.

'Yes. Put your ID number there, too, please.'

He quickly did as he was told and he could tell she was studying him as he wrote.

'A lefty.'

'Yeah.'

He slid the card back across the counter to her.

'Thanks, Geneva.'

He looked at her, wanting to say something else, but decided it might be a mistake. She looked back at him and a grandmotherly smile formed on her face.

'I don't know what you're doing, Detective Bosch, but I wish you good luck. I can tell it's important, you coming back to this after five years.'

'It's been longer than that, Geneva. A lot longer.'

5

Bosch cleared all the old mail and carpentry books off the dining room table and placed the binder and his own notebook on top of it. He went to the stereo and loaded a compact disc, 'Clifford Brown with Strings.' He went to the kitchen and got an ashtray, then he sat down in front of the blue murder book and looked at it for a long time without moving. The last time he'd had the file, he had barely looked at it as he skimmed through its many pages. He hadn't been ready then and had returned it to the archives.

This time, he wanted to be sure he was ready before he opened it, so he sat there a long time just studying the cracked plastic cover as if it held some clue to his preparedness. A memory crowded into his mind. A boy of eleven in a swimming pool clinging to the steel ladder at the side, out of breath and crying, the tears disguised by the water that dripped out of his wet hair. The boy felt scared. Alone. He felt as if the pool were an ocean that he must cross.

Brownie was working through 'Willow Weep for Me,' his trumpet as gentle as a portrait painter's brush. Bosch reached for the rubber band he had put around the binder five years earlier and it broke at his touch. He hesitated only another moment before opening the binder and blowing off the dust.

The binder contained the case file on the October 28, 1961, homicide of Marjorie Phillips Lowe. His mother.

The pages of the binder were brownish yellow and stiff with age. As he looked at them and read them, Bosch was initially surprised at how little things had changed in nearly thirty-five years. Many of the investigative forms in the binder were still currently in use. The Preliminary Report and the Investigating Officer's Chronological Record were the same as those presently used, save for word changes made to accommodate court rulings and political correctness. Description Boxes marked NEGRO had sometime along the line been changed to BLACK and then AFRICAN-AMERICAN. The list of motivations on the Preliminary Case Screening chart did not include DOMES-TIC VIOLENCE or HATRED/PREJUDICE classifications as they did now. Interview summary sheets did not include boxes to be checked after Miranda warnings had been given.

But aside from those kinds of changes, the reports were the same and Bosch decided that homicide investigation was largely the same now as back then. Of course, there had been incredible technological advances in the past thirty-five years but he believed there were some things that were always the same and always would remain the same. The legwork, the art of interviewing and listening, knowing when to trust an instinct or a hunch. Those were things that didn't change, that couldn't.

The case had been assigned to two investigators on the Hollywood homicide table. Claude Eno and Jake McKittrick. The reports they filed were in chronological order in the binder. On their preliminary reports the victim was referred to by name, indicating she had immediately been identified. A narrative on these pages said the victim was found in an alley behind the north side of Hollywood Boulevard between Vista and Gower. Her skirt and undergarments had been ripped open by her attacker. It was presumed that she had been sexually assaulted and strangled. Her body had been dropped into an open trash bin located next to the rear door of a Hollywood souvenir store called Startime Gifts & Gags. The body was discovered at 7:35 a.m. by a foot patrol officer who walked a beat on the Boulevard and usually checked the back alleys at the beginning of each shift. The victim's purse was not found with her but she was quickly identified because she was known to the beat officer. On the continuation sheet it was made clear why she was known to him.

> Victim had a previous history of loitering arrests in the Hollywood. (See AR 55–002, 55–913, 56–111, 59–056, 60–815 and 60–1121) Vice Detective Gilchrist and Stano described victim as a prostitute who periodically worked in the Hollywood area and had been repeatedly warned off. Victim lived at El Rio Efficiency Apts located two blocks northerly of crime scene. It was believed that the victim had been currently involved in call girl prostitution activities. R/O 1906 was able to make identification of the victim because of familiarity of having seen victim in the area in previous years.

Bosch looked at the reporting officer's serial number. He knew that 1906 belonged to a patrolman then who was now one of the most powerful men in the department. Assistant Chief Irvin S. Irving. Once Irving had confided to Bosch that he had known Marjorie Lowe and had been the one who found her.

Bosch lit a cigarette and read on. The reports were sloppily written, perfunctory, and filled with careless misspellings. In reading them, it was clear to Bosch that Eno and McKittrick did not invest much time in the case. A prostitute was dead. It was a risk that came with her job. They had other fish to fry.

He noticed on the Death Investigation Report a box for listing the next of kin. It said;

> Hieronymus Bosch (Harry), son, age 11, McClaren Youth Hall. Notification made 10/28–1500 hrs. Custody of Department of Public Social Services since 7/60 – UM. (See victim's arrest reports 60–815 and 60–1121) Father unknown. Son remains in custody pending foster placement.

Looking at the report, Bosch could easily decipher all of the abbreviations and translate what was written. UM stood for unfit mother. The irony was not lost on him even after so many years. The boy had been taken from a presumably unfit mother and placed in an equally unfit system of child protection. What he remembered most was the noise of the place. Always loud. Like a prison.

Bosch remembered McKittrick had been the one who came to tell him. It was during the swimming period. The indoor pool was frothing with waves as a hundred boys swam and splashed and yelled. After being pulled from the water, Harry wore a white towel that had been washed and bleached so many times that it felt like cardboard over his shoulders. McKittrick told him the news and he returned to the pool, his screams silenced beneath the waves.

Quickly leafing through the supplemental reports on the victim's prior arrests, Bosch came to the autopsy report. He skipped most of it, not needing the details, and settled on the summary page, where there were a couple of surprises. The time of death was placed at seven to nine hours before discovery. Near midnight. The surprise was in the official cause of death. It was listed as blunt-force trauma to the head. The report described a deep contusion over the right ear with swelling but no laceration that caused fatal bleeding in the brain. The report said the killer might have believed he strangled the victim after knocking her unconscious but it was the coroner's conclusion that she was already dead when the killer wrapped Marjorie Lowe's own belt around her neck and tied it off. The report stated further that while semen was recovered from the vagina there were no other injuries commonly associated with rape.

Rereading the summary with an investigator's eyes, Bosch could see the autopsy conclusions only muddied the waters for the original two detectives. The initial assumption based on the appearance of the body was that Marjorie Lowe was the victim of a sex crime. That raised the specter of a random encounter – as random as the couplings of her profession – leading to her death. But the fact that strangulation occurred after death and that there was no convincing physical evidence of rape raised another possibility as well. They were factors from which it could also be speculated that the victim had been murdered by someone who then attempted to disguise his involvement and motivation in the randomness of a sex crime. Bosch could think of only one reason for such misdirection, if that had been the case. The killer knew the victim. As he moved on, he wondered if McKittrick and Eno had made any of the same conclusions he had made.

There was an eight-by-ten envelope next in the file which was marked as containing crime scene and autopsy photos. Bosch thought about it a long moment and then put the envelope aside. As with the last time he had pulled the murder book out of the archives, he couldn't look.

Next was another envelope with an evidence inventory list stapled to it. It was almost blank.

EVIDENCE RECOVERED
Case 61–743
Latent fingerprints taken from leather belt with silver sea shells.
SID report no. 1114 11/06/61
Murder weapon recovered – black leather belt with sea shells attached. Property of victim.
Victim's clothing, property. Filed w/ evidence custodian – Locker 73B

LAPDHQ
1 blouse, white – blood stain
1 black skirt – torn at seam
1 pair black high heel shoes
1 pair black sheer stockings, torn
1 pair undergarments, torn
1 pair gold colored earrings
1 gold colored hoop bracelet
1 gold chain necklace w/cross

That was it. Bosch studied the list for a long time before jotting the particulars down in his notebook. Something about it bothered him but he couldn't draw it out. Not yet. He was taking in too much information and he would have to let it settle some before the anomalies floated to the surface.

He dropped it for the moment and opened the evidence envelope, breaking the seal of a red tape that had cracked with age. Inside was a yellowed print card on which two complete fingerprints, from a thumb and an index finger, and several partials had been taped after being lifted with black powder from the belt. Also in the envelope was a pink check card for the victim's clothes, which had been placed in an evidence locker. The clothes had never been retrieved because a case had never been made. Bosch put both items aside, wondering what would have happened to the clothing. In the mid-sixties Parker Center had been built and the department moved out of the old headquarters. It was long gone now, falling to the wrecking ball. What happened to the evidence from unsolved cases?

Next in the file was a group of summary reports on interviews conducted during the first days of the investigation. Most of these were of people with peripheral knowledge of the victim or the crime. People like other residents in the El Rio Apartments and other women in the same profession as the victim. There was one short summary that caught Bosch's eye. It was from an interview conducted three days after the murder with a woman named Meredith Roman. She was described in the report as an associate and sometime roommate of the victim. At the time of the report she also lived in the El Rio, one floor up from the victim. The report had been typed up by Eno, who seemed to be the clear-cut winner in illiteracy when comparing the reports of the two investigators assigned to the case.

Meredith Roman (10–9–30) was interviewed at length this date at her apartment in the El Rio Efficiencies where she lived one floor above the victim's apartment. Miss Roman was able to provide this detective with very little useful information in relation to the activities of Marjorie Lowe during the period of the last week of live.

Miss Roman acknowledged that she has engaged in prostitutional acts while in the company of the victim on numrus occassion in the previous eight years but she has no booking record to date. (later confirmed) She told the undersigned detective that such engagements were skeduled by a man named Johnny Fox, (2–2–33) who resides at 1110 Ivar in Hollywood. Fox, age 28, has no records of arrests but vice intelligence confirms he has

25

been a suspect previously in cases of pandering, malicious assault and sales of heroin.

Miss Roman states that the last time she saw the victim was at a party on second floor of the Roosevelt Hotl on 10/21. Miss Roman did not attend party with victim but saw her there momentarily for a short conversation.

Miss Roman states that she now has plans to retire from the business of prostitution and leave Los Angeles. She stated that she will provide detectives with a forwarding adress and telephone number so that she can be contacted if necessary. Her demenor was corperative with the under-signed.

Bosch immediately looked through the summaries again for the report on Johnny Fox. There was none there. He flipped to the front of the binder to the Chronological Record and looked for an entry that would indicate whether they had even talked to Fox. The CR was just a log of one-line entries with references to other reports. On the second page he found a single notation.

11–3 800–2000 Watched Fox apt. No show.

There was no other mention of Fox in the record. But as Bosch read through the CR to the end, another entry caught his eye.

11–5 940 A. Conklin called to skedule meeting.

Bosch knew the name. Arno Conklin had been a Los Angeles district attorney in the 1960s. As Bosch remembered it, 1961 was too early for Conklin to have been DA, but he would still have been one of the office's top prosecutors. His interest in a prostitute's murder seemed curious to Bosch. But there was nothing in the binder that held an answer. There was no summary report of a meeting with Conklin. Nothing.

He noted that the misspelling of the word *schedule* in the CR entry had been made earlier in the summary of the Roman interview typed by Eno. Bosch concluded from this that Conklin had called Eno to set the meeting. However, the significance of this, if any, he didn't know. He wrote Conklin's name down at the top of a page in his notebook.

Getting back to Fox, Bosch could not understand why he was not located and interviewed by Eno and McKittrick. It seemed that he was a natural suspect – the victim's pimp. Or, if Fox had been interviewed, Bosch could not understand why there was no report in the murder book on such a key part of the investigation.

Bosch sat back and lit a cigarette. Already, he was tense with the suspicion that things were amiss with the case. He felt the stirring of what he knew was outrage. The more he read the more he believed the case had been mishandled from the start.

He leaned back over the table and continued flipping through the pages of the binder while he smoked. There were more meaningless interview summaries and reports. It was all just filler. Any homicide cop worth his badge could churn out reports like these by the dozens if he wanted to fill a binder and make it look like he'd done a thorough investigation. It

Past crimes come back to haunt in this tense and twisting psychological thriller.

A few days before the summer solstice a 92 year old woman is found burned to death in her home. On the same day a man's mutilated corpse is discovered in a field, his arms ripped from their sockets, a Tarot card depicting the fool inserted in his mouth. When the victim is identified as someone for whom the police have been looking for almost a year, detectives Anderson and Costello find themselves caught up in a case where nothing is as it seems. Was the dead man really responsible for three child murders? And what is the connection with the death of the elderly woman? The investigation leads to the tranquil shores of Loch Lomond where Anderson and Costello will finally uncover the shocking truth.

CARO RAMSAY

THE TEARS OF ANGELS

AN ANDERSON & COSTELLO THRILLER

'Creepy, chilling, bizarre, and utterly compelling'
Booklist Starred Review of The Night Hunter

Praise For
Caro Ramsay

"Well-drawn characters and great sense of place set this series head and shoulders above most of the competition."
The Times

"Brilliant in twisting the tension tauter with each page."
The Times

"Many shivers in store for the readers, followed by a shattering climax."
The Guardian

"Ramsay's insights into tortured psyches makes for compelling, if often painful, reading."
The Times

"Bleak, black and brilliant."
Publishers Weekly

"If you enjoy clever, well plotted, fast moving crime thrillers (and who doesn't?) Then you'll love The Night Hunter."
The Guardian

"Ramsay handles her characters with aplomb, the dialogue crackles and the search for the killer has surprising twists and turns."
Crimeworm

"This book is definitely one chiller of a thriller."
Observer

Netgalley

Follow Caro on:
'Murder is Everywhere'
Every Friday

For more information, please visit the author's website:
www.caroramsay.co.uk

appeared that McKittrick and Eno were as skilled at it as the best. But any homicide cop worth his badge could also tell filler when he saw it. And that's what Bosch saw here. The hollow feeling in his stomach grew more pronounced.

Finally, he came to the first Follow-Up Homicide Investigation Report. It was dated one week after the murder and written by McKittrick.

Homicide of Marjorie Phillips Lowe remains open at this time, no suspects identified.

Investigation at this time has determined that victim was engaged in prostitution in the Hollywood area and may have fallen victim to a customer who committed the homicide.

Preliminary suspect John Fox denied involvement in the incident and has been cleared at this time through fingerprint comparison and confirmation of alibi through witnesses.

No suspects at this time have been identified. John Fox states that on Friday, 11/30 at approximately 2100 hours the victim left her residence at the El Rio Apts to go to an unknown location for the purposes of prostitution. Fox states the arrangement was made by victim and he was not made privy to it. Fox said it was not unusual practice for victim to make arrangements for liaissons without his knowledge.

Victim's undergarment was found with body in ripped condition. Noted, however, a pair of stockings also belonging to the victim showed no tears and were believed to possibly have been removed voluntarily.

Experience and instinct of investigators leads to the conclusion that the victim met with foul play at the unknown location after voluntarily arriving and possibly removing some clothing. The body was then transported to the trash bin in the alleyway between Vista and Gower, where it was discovered the following morning.

Witness Meredith Roman was reinterviewed this date and asked to amend her earlier statement. Roman informed this investigator that it was her belief that the victim had gone to a party in Hancock Park the night previous to the discovery of her body. She could provide no address or name of party at the location. Miss Roman said her plan was to attend with victim but on the previous evening she was assaulted by John Fox in a dispute over money. She could not attend the party because she believed a bruise on her face made her unpresentable. (Fox readily acknowledged striking Roman in subsequent telephone interview. Roman refused charges.)

Investigation is termed at standstill as no further leads have been provided at this time. Investigators are currently seeking the aid of vice section officers in regard to knowledge of similar incidents and/or possible suspects.

Bosch read the page again and tried to interpret what was really being said about the case. One thing that was clear from it was that regardless of whether there was an interview summary report in the binder, Johnny Fox had obviously been interviewed by Eno and McKittrick. He had been cleared. The question Bosch now had was, why did they not type up a summary report, or had it been typed up and later removed from the murder book? And if so, who removed it and why?

Lastly, Bosch was curious about the lack of any mention of Arno Conklin in the summary or any other report save for the investigative chronology. Maybe, Bosch thought, more than just the Fox interview summary had been lifted from the binder.

Bosch got up and went to his briefcase, which he kept on the counter near the kitchen door. From it he took his personal phone book. He didn't have a number for LAPD archives so he called the regular records number and was transferred. A woman answered after nine rings.

'Uh, Mrs Beaupre? Geneva?'

'Yes?'

'Hello, this is Harry Bosch. I was there earlier today to pick up a file.'

'Yes, from Hollywood. The old case.'

'Yes. Could you tell me, do you still have the checkout card there at the counter?'

'Hold the line. I already filed it.'

A moment later she was back.

'Yes, I have it here.'

'Could you tell me, who else has checked this binder out in the past?'

'Why would you need to know that?'

'There are pages missing from the file, Mrs Beaupre. I'd like to know who might have them.'

'Well, you checked it out last. I mentioned that be –'

'Yes, I know. About five years ago. Is there any listing of it being taken out before that or since then? I didn't notice when I signed the card today.'

'Well, hold the line and let me see.' He waited and she was back quickly. 'Okay, I've got it. According to this card, the only other time that file was ever taken out was in 1972. You're talking way back.'

'Who checked it out back then?'

'It's scribbled here. I can't – it looks like maybe Jack . . . uh, Jack McKillick.'

'Jake McKittrick.'

'Could be.'

Bosch didn't know what to think. McKittrick had the file last but that was more than ten years after the murder. What did it mean? Bosch felt confusion ambush him. He didn't know what he had been expecting but he'd hoped there would have been something other than a name scribbled more than twenty years ago.

'Okay, Mrs Beaupre, thanks very much.'

'Well, if you've got missing pages I'm going to have to make a report and give it to Mr Aguilar.'

'I don't think that will be necessary, ma'am. I may be wrong about the missing pages. I mean, how could there be missing pages if nobody's looked at it since the last time I had it?'

He thanked her again and hung up, hoping his attempt at good humor would persuade her to do nothing about his call. He opened the refrigerator and looked inside while he thought about the case, then closed it and went back out to the table.

The last pages in the murder book were a due diligence report dated

November 3, 1962. The department's homicide procedures called for all unsolved cases to be reviewed after a year by a new set of detectives with an eye toward looking for something that the first set of investigators might have missed. But, in practice, it was a rubber stamp process. Detectives didn't relish the idea of finding the mistakes of their colleagues. Additionally, they had their own case loads to worry about. When assigned DDs, as they were called, they usually did little more than read through the file, make a few calls to witnesses and then send the binder to archives.

In this case, the DD report by the new detectives, named Roberts and Jordan, drew the same conclusions as the reports by Eno and McKittrick. After two pages detailing the same evidence and interviews already conducted by the original investigators, the DD report concluded that there were no workable leads and the prognosis for 'successful conclusion' of the case was hopeless. So much for due diligence.

Bosch closed the murder book. He knew that after Roberts and Jordan had filed their report, the binder had been shipped to archives as a dead case. It had gathered dust there until, according to the checkout card, McKittrick pulled it out for unknown reasons in 1972. Bosch wrote McKittrick's name under Conklin's on the page in the notebook. Then he wrote the names of others he thought it would be useful to interview. If they were still alive and could be found.

Bosch leaned back in his chair, realizing that the music had stopped and he hadn't even noticed. He checked his watch. It was two-thirty. He still had most of the afternoon but he wasn't sure what to do with it.

He went to the bedroom closet and took the shoebox off the shelf. It was his correspondence box, filled with letters and cards and photos he had wished to keep over the course of his life. It contained objects dated as far back as his time in Vietnam. He rarely looked in the box but his mind kept an almost perfect inventory of what was in it. Each piece had a reason for being saved.

On top was the latest addition to the box. A postcard from Venice. From Sylvia. It depicted a painting she had seen in the Palace of the Doges. Hieronymus Bosch's 'The Blessed and the Damned.' It showed an angel escorting one of the blessed through a tunnel to the light of heaven. They both floated skyward. The card was the last he had heard from her. He read the back.

Harry, thought you'd be interested in this piece of your namesake's work. I saw it in the Palace. It's beautiful. By the way, I love Venice! I think I could stay forever! S.

But you don't love me, Bosch thought as he put the card aside and began to dig through the other pieces in the box. He wasn't distracted again. About halfway through the box he found what he was looking for.

6

The midday drive out to Santa Monica was long. Bosch had to take the long way, the 101 to the 405 and then down, because the 10 was still a week away from being reopened. By the time he got into Sunset Park it was after three. The house he was looking for was on Pier Street. It was a small Craftsman bungalow set on the crest of a hill. It had a full porch with red bougainvillea running along the railing. He checked the address painted on the mailbox against the envelope that contained the old Christmas card on the seat next to him. He parked at the curb and looked at the card once more. It had been addressed to him five years earlier, care of the LAPD. He had never responded to it. Not until now.

As he got out he could smell the sea and guessed that there might be a limited ocean view from the house's western windows. It was about ten degrees cooler than it had been at his home and so he reached back into his car for the sport coat. He walked to the front porch while putting it on.

The woman who answered the white door after one knock was in her mid-sixties and looked it. She was thin, with dark hair, but the gray roots were beginning to show and she was ready for another dye job. She wore thick red lipstick, a white silk blouse with blue seahorses on it over navy blue slacks. She readily smiled a greeting and Bosch recognized her, but he could see that his own image was completely alien to her. It had been almost thirty-five years since she had seen him. He smiled back anyway.

'Meredith Roman?'

She lost her smile as quickly as she had found it before.

'That's not my name,' she said in a clipped tone. 'You have the wrong place.'

She moved to close the door but Bosch put his hand on it to stop her. He tried to be as unthreatening about it as he could. But he could see panic starting in her eyes.

'It's Harry Bosch?' he said quickly.

She froze and looked Bosch in the eyes. He saw the panic go away. Recognition and memories flooded her eyes like tears. The smile came back.

'Harry? Little Harry?'

He nodded.

'Oh, darling, c'mere.' She drew him into a tight hug and talked in his ear. 'Oh, so good to see you after – let me look at you.'

She pushed him back and held her hands wide as if appraising a roomful of paintings at once. Her eyes were animated and sincere. It made Bosch feel

30

good and sad at the same time. He shouldn't have waited so long. He should have visited for reasons other than the one that brought him here now.

'Oh, come in, Harry. Come in.'

Bosch entered a nicely furnished living room. The floor was red oak and the stucco walls were clean and white. The furniture was mostly matching white rattan. The place was light and bright but Bosch knew he was there to bring darkness.

'Meredith is no longer your name?'

'No, Harry, not for a long time.'

'What do I call you?'

'My name is Katherine. With a K. Katherine Register. Spelled like the cash register but you pronounce it *ree* as in reefer. That's what my husband used to say. Boy, he was so straight. Outside of me the closest that man ever came to something illegal was to say the word.'

'He *used* to say that?'

'Have a seat, Harry, for crying out loud. Yes, used to. He passed away five years ago last Thanksgiving.'

Bosch sat down on the couch and she took the chair across the glass coffee table.

'I'm sorry.'

'It's okay, you didn't know. You never even knew him and I've been a different person for a long time. Can I get you something? Some coffee or maybe something stronger?'

It occurred to him that she had sent him the card on the Christmas soon after her husband's death. He was hit with another wave of guilt for not having responded.

'Harry?'

'Oh, uh, no, I'm fine. I . . . do you want me to call you by your new name?'

She started laughing at the ridiculousness of the situation and he joined in.

'Call me any damn thing you want.' She laughed girlishly, a laugh he remembered from a long time before. 'It's great to see you. You know, to see how, uh . . .'

'I turned out?'

She laughed again.

'I guess so. You know, I knew you were with the police because I had read your name in some of the news stories.'

'I know you knew. I got the Christmas card you sent to the station. That must have been right after your husband died. I, uh, I'm sorry I never wrote back or visited. I should have.'

'That's okay, Harry, I know you're busy with the job and a career and all . . . I'm glad you got my card. Do you have a family?'

'Uh, no. How about you? Any children?'

'Oh, no. No children. You have a wife, don't you, a handsome man like you?'

'No, I'm alone right now.'

She nodded, seeming to sense that he wasn't here to reveal his personal history to her anyway. For a long moment they just both looked at each other and Bosch wondered what she really thought of his being a cop. The initial delight in seeing each other was descending into the uneasiness that comes when old secrets come close to the surface.

'I guess . . .'

He didn't finish the thought. He was grappling for a way into the conversation. His interviewing skills had deserted him.

'You know, if it's not too much trouble, I'd take a glass of water.'

It was all he could think of.

'Be right back.'

She got up quickly and went to the kitchen. He heard her getting ice out of a tray. It gave him time to think. It had taken him an hour to drive to her house but he hadn't given one thought to what this would be like or how he would get to what he wanted to say and ask. She came back in a few minutes with a glass of ice water. She handed it to him and put a round coaster made of cork on the glass-topped coffee table in front of him.

'If you're hungry, I can bring out some crackers and cheese. I just didn't know how much time you –'

'No, I'm fine. This is great, thanks.'

He saluted her with the glass and drank half of it, then put it down on the table.

'Harry, use the coaster. Getting rings out of the glass is murder.'

Bosch looked down at what he had done.

'Oh, sorry.'

He corrected the placement of his glass.

'You're a detective.'

'Yes. I work in Hollywood now . . . Uh, but I'm not really working right now. I'm on sort of a vacation.'

'Oh, that must be nice.'

Her spirits seemed to lift, as if she knew there was a chance he was not here on business. Bosch knew it was time to get to the point.

'Uh, Mer – uh, Katherine, I need to ask you about something.'

'What is it, Harry?'

'I look around here and I see you have a very nice home, a different name, a different life. You're no longer Meredith Roman and I know you don't need me to tell you that. You've got . . . I think what I'm saying is the past may be a difficult thing to talk about. I know it is for me. And, believe me, I don't want to hurt you in any way.'

'You're here to talk about your mother.'

He nodded and looked down at the glass on the cork coaster.

'Your mother and I were best friends. Sometimes I think I had almost as much a hand in raising you as she did. Until they took you away from her. From us.'

He looked back up at her. Her eyes were looking hard at distant memories.

'I don't think a day goes by that I don't think about her. We were just kids. Having a good time, you know. We never thought either of us could get hurt.'

She suddenly stood up.

'Harry, come here. I want to show you something.'

He followed her down a carpeted hallway and into a bedroom. There was a four-poster bed with light blue coverings, an oak bureau and matching bedside tables. Katherine Register pointed to the bureau. There were several photos in ornate stand-up frames on top. Most of them were of Katherine and a man who seemed much older than she was in the photos. Her husband, Bosch guessed. But she pointed to one that was to the right side of the grouping. The photo was old, its color faded. It was a picture of two young women with a tiny boy of three or four.

'I've always had that there, Harry. Even when my husband was alive. He knew my past. I told him. It didn't matter. We had twenty-three great years together. You see, the past is what you make of it. You can use it to hurt yourself or others or you can use it to make yourself strong. I'm strong, Harry. Now, tell me why you came to visit me today.'

Bosch reached for the framed photo and picked it up.

'I want . . .' He looked up from the photo to her. 'I'm going to find out who killed her.'

An undecipherable look froze on her face for a moment and then she wordlessly took the frame out of his hands and put it back on the bureau. Then she pulled him into another deep embrace, her head against his chest. He could see himself holding her in the mirror over the bureau. When she pulled back and looked up at him he saw the tears were already down her cheeks. There was a slight tremor in her lower lip.

'Let's go sit down,' he said.

She pulled two tissues out of a box on the bureau and he led her back to the living room and to her chair.

'Do you want me to get you some water?'

'No, I'm fine. I'll stop crying, I'm sorry.'

She wiped at her eyes with the tissues. He sat back down on the couch.

'We used to say we were the two musketeers, both for one and one for both. It was stupid, but it was because we were so young and so close.'

'I'm starting from scratch with it, Katherine. I pulled the old files on the investigation. It –'

She made a dismissing sound and shook her head.

'There was no investigation. It was a joke.'

'That's my sense of it, too, but I don't understand why.'

'Look, Harry, you know what your mother was.' He nodded and she continued. 'She was a party girl. We both were. I'm sure you know that's the polite way of saying it. And the cops really didn't care that one of us ended up dead. They just wrote the whole damn thing off. I know you're a policeman now, but that's the way it was then. They just didn't care about her.'

'I understand. Things probably are not too much different now, believe it or not. But there has to have been more to it than that.'

'Harry, I don't know how much you want to know about your mother.'

He looked at her.

'The past made me strong, too. I can handle it.'

'I'm sure it did . . . I remember that place where they put you. McEvoy or something like –'

'McClaren.'

'That's it, McClaren. What a depressing place. Your mother would come home from visiting you and just sit down and cry her eyes out.'

'Don't change the subject, Katherine. What is it I should know about her?'

She nodded but hesitated for a moment before continuing.

'Mar knew some policemen. You understand?'

He nodded.

'We both did. It was the way it worked. You had to get along to go along. That's what we called it anyway. And when you have that situation and she ends up dead, it's usually best for the cops to just sweep it under the rug. Let sleeping dogs lie, as they say. You pick the cliché. They just didn't want anyone embarrassed.'

'Are you saying you think it was a cop?'

'No. I'm not saying that at all. I have no idea who did it, Harry. I'm sorry. I wish I did. But what I'm saying is, I think those two detectives that were assigned to investigate this knew where it could lead. And they weren't going to go that way because they knew what was good for them in the department. They weren't stupid in that way and like I said, she was a party girl. They didn't care. Nobody did. She got killed and that was that.'

Bosch looked around the room, not sure what to ask next.

'Do you know who the policemen she knew were?'

'It was a long time ago.'

'You knew some of the same policemen, didn't you?'

'Yes. I had to. That was the way it worked. You used your contacts to keep you out of jail. Everybody was for sale. Back then, at least. Different people wanted different forms of payment. Some of them, money. Some of them, other things.'

'It said in the mur – the file that you never had a record.'

'Yes, I was lucky. I was picked up a few times but never booked once. They always turned me loose once I could make a call. I kept a clean record because I knew a lot of policemen, honey. You understand?'

'Yes, I understand.'

She didn't look away when she said it. All these years in the straight life and she still had a whore's pride. She could talk about the low points of her life without flinching or batting an eye. It was because she had made it through and there was dignity in that. Enough to last the rest of her life.

'Do you mind if I smoke, Harry?'

'No, not if I can.'

They took out cigarettes and Bosch got up to light them.

'You can use that ashtray on the side table. Try not to get ashes on the rug.'

She pointed to a small glass bowl on the table at the other end of the couch. Bosch reached over for it and then held it with one hand while he smoked with the other. He looked down into it as he spoke.

'The policemen you knew,' he said, 'and who she probably knew, you don't remember any names?'

'I said it was a long time ago. And I doubt they had anything to do with this, with what happened to your mother.'

'Irvin S. Irving. Do you remember that name?'

She hesitated a moment as the name rolled around in her mind.

'I knew him. I think she did, too. He was on the beat on the Boulevard. I think it would have been hard for her not to know him . . . but I don't know. I could be wrong.'

Bosch nodded.

34

'He was the one who found her.'

She hiked her shoulders in a what's-that-prove gesture.

'Well, somebody had to find her. She was left out there in the open like that.'

'What about a couple of vice guys, Gilchrist and Stano?'

She hesitated before answering.

'Yes, I knew them . . . they were mean men.'

'Would my mother have known them? In that way?'

She nodded.

'What do you mean that they were mean? In what way?'

'They just . . . they just didn't care about us. If they wanted something, whether it was a little piece of information you might have picked up on a date or something more . . . personal, they just came and took it. They could be rough. I hated them.'

'Did they –'

'But could they have been killers? My feeling at the time, and now, is no. They weren't killers, Harry. They were cops. True, they were bought and paid for, but it seemed everybody was. But it wasn't like it is today where you read the paper and you see some cop on trial for killing or beating or whatever. It's – sorry.'

'It's okay. Anybody else you can think of?'

'No.'

'No names?'

'I put that all out of my mind a long time ago.'

'Okay.'

Bosch wanted to take out his notebook but he didn't want to make this seem like an interview. He tried to remember what else he had read in the murder book that he could ask about.

'What about this guy Johnny Fox?'

'Yes, I told those detectives about him. They got all excited but then nothing ever happened. He was never arrested.'

'I think he was. But then he was let go. His fingerprints didn't match the killer's.'

She raised her eyebrows.

'Well, that's news to me. They never told me anything about any fingerprints.'

'On your second interview – with McKittrick, you remember him?'

'Not really. I just remember that there were police, you know? Two detectives. One was smarter than the other, that's what I remember. But I don't remember which one was which. It seemed like the dumber one was in charge and that was par for the course in those days.'

'Well, anyway, McKittrick talked to you the second time. In his report he said you changed your story and you told about this party in Hancock Park.'

'Yes, the party. I didn't go because that . . . Johnny Fox hit me the night before and I had a bruise on my cheek. It was gorgeous. I played around with makeup but I couldn't do anything about the swelling. Believe me there wasn't much business in Hancock Park for a party girl with a knot on her face.'

'Who was having the party?'

'I don't remember. I don't know if I even knew whose party it was.'

Something about the way she answered bothered Bosch. Her tone had changed and it came across as almost a rehearsed answer.

'Are you sure you don't remember?'

'Of course, I'm sure.' Katherine stood up. 'I think I'm going to get some water now.'

She took his glass to refill and left the room again. Bosch realized that his familiarity with the woman, his emotion in seeing her again after so long, had blocked most of his investigative instincts. He had no feel for the truth. He could not tell whether there was more to what she was telling him or not. He decided he had to somehow steer the conversation back to the party. He thought she knew more than she had said all those years ago.

She came back with two glasses filled with ice water and placed his back down on the cork coaster. Something about the way she was so careful about putting the glass down gave him a knowledge about her that had not come through in her spoken words. It was simply that she had worked hard to attain the level she was at in life. That position and the material things it brought with it – like glass coffee tables and plush carpets – meant a lot to her and were to be taken care of.

She took a long drink from her glass after sitting down.

'Let me tell you something, Harry,' she said. 'I didn't tell them everything. I didn't lie, but I didn't tell them everything. I was afraid.'

'Afraid of what?'

'I became afraid on the day they found her. You see, I'd gotten a call that morning. Before I even knew what had happened to her. It was a man, but a voice I didn't recognize. He told me if I said anything I would be next. I remember, he said, "My advice to you, little lady, is to get the hell out of Dodge." Then, of course, I heard the police were in the building and had gone to her apartment. Then I heard she was dead. So I did what I was told. I left. I waited about a week until the police said they were done with me, then I moved to Long Beach. I changed my name, changed my life. I met my husband down there and then years later we moved here. . . . You know, I've never been back to Hollywood, not even to drive through. It's an awful place.'

'What was it that you didn't tell Eno and McKittrick?'

Katherine looked down at her hands as she spoke.

'I was afraid, you see, so I didn't tell everything . . . but I knew who she was going to see there, at the party. We were like sisters. Lived in the same building, shared clothes, secrets, everything. We talked every morning, had our coffee together. We had no secrets between us. And we were going to go to the party together. Of course, after that . . . after Johnny hit me, she had to go alone.'

'Who was she going to meet there, Katherine?' Bosch prompted.

'You see that is the right question but the detectives never asked that. They only wanted to know whose party it was and where it was. That didn't matter. What was important was who was she going to meet there and they never asked that.'

'Who was it?'

She looked away from her hands and to the fireplace. She stared at the cold, blackened logs left from an old fire the way some people stare mesmerized by a burning fire.

36

'It was a man named Arno Conklin. He was a very important man in the –'

'I know who he was.'

'You do?'

'His name came up in the records. But not that way. How could you not tell the cops this?'

She turned and looked at him sharply.

'Don't you look at me that way. I told you I was scared. I'd been threatened. And they wouldn't have done anything with it anyway. They were bought and paid for by Conklin. They wouldn't go near him on just the word of a . . . call girl who didn't see anything but knew a name. I had to think of myself. Your mother was dead, Harry. There was nothing I could do about it.'

He could see the sharp edges of anger in her eyes. He knew it was directed at him but more toward herself. She could list all her reasons out loud but inside Bosch thought she paid a price every day for not having done the right thing.

'You think Conklin did it?'

'I don't know. All I know is that she'd been with him before and there was never anything violent. I don't know the answer to that.'

'Any idea now who called you?'

'No, none.'

'Conklin?'

'I don't know. I didn't know his voice anyway.'

'Did you ever see them together, my mother and him?'

'Once, at a dance at the Masonic. I think it was the night they met. Johnny Fox introduced them. I don't think Arno knew . . . anything about her. At least, then.'

'Could it have been Fox who called you?'

'No. I would've recognized his voice.'

Bosch thought a moment.

'Did you ever see Fox again after that morning?'

'No. I avoided him for a week. It was easy because I think he was hiding from the cops. But after that I was gone. Whoever called me, he put the fear of God in me. I left town for Long Beach the day the cops said they were done with me. Packed one suitcase and took the bus . . . I remember, your mother had some of my clothes in her apartment. Things that she had borrowed. I didn't even bother to try to get them. I just took what I had and left.'

Bosch was silent. He had nothing else to ask.

'I think about those days a lot, you know,' Katherine said. 'We were in the gutter, your mother and I, but we were good friends and we had fun in spite of it all.'

'You know, all my memories . . . you're in a lot of them. You were always there with her.'

'We had a lot of laughs in spite of everything,' she said wistfully. 'And you, you were the highlight of it all. You know, when they took you away from her, it nearly killed her right then . . . She never stopped trying to get you back, Harry. I hope you know that. She loved you. I loved you.'

'Yes, I know that.'

'But after you were gone, she wasn't the same. Sometimes I think what happened to her was sort of inevitable. Sometimes I think it was like she had been heading toward that alley for a long time beforehand.'

Bosch stood up, looking at the sorrow in her eyes.

'I better go. I'll let you know what happens.'

'I'd like that. I'd like to stay in touch.'

'I'd like that, too.'

He headed toward the door knowing that they wouldn't stay in touch. Time had eroded the bond between them. They were strangers who shared the same story. On the outside step he turned and looked back at her.

'The Christmas card you sent. You wanted me to look into this back then, didn't you?'

She brought out the faraway smile again.

'I don't know. My husband had just died and I was taking stock, you know? I thought about her. And you. I'm proud of how I turned out, Little Harry. So I think about what there could have been for her and you. I'm still mad. Whoever did this should . . .'

She didn't finish but Bosch nodded.

'Good-bye, Harry.'

'You know, my mother, she had a good friend.'

'I hope so.'

7

Back in his car Bosch took his notebook out and looked at the list.

> Conklin
> McKittrick & Eno
> Meredith Roman
> Johnny Fox

He drew a line through Meredith Roman's name and studied those left on it. He knew that the way he had ordered the names was not the same order in which he would attempt to interview them. He knew that before he could approach Conklin, or even McKittrick and Eno, he needed more information.

He took his phone book out of his coat pocket and his portable from his briefcase. He dialed the Department of Motor Vehicles law enforcement line in Sacramento and identified himself to the clerk as Lieutenant Harvey Pounds. He gave Pounds's serial number and asked for a license check on Johnny Fox. After checking his notebook, he gave the appropriate date of birth. As he did this he ran the numbers and figured that Fox was now sixty-one years old.

As he continued to wait he smiled because Pounds would have some explaining to do in about a month. The department had recently begun to audit use of the DMV trace service. Because the *Daily News* had reported that cops all over the department were secretly doing the traces for friendly reporters and private detectives with liberal expense accounts, the new chief had cracked down by requiring all calls and computer link-ups to DMV to be documented on the newly implemented DMVT form, which required attribution of traces to a specific case or purpose. The forms were sent to Parker Center and then audited against the list of traces provided each month by the DMV. When the lieutenant's name showed up on the DMV list in the next audit and there was no corresponding DMVT form, he'd get a call from the auditors.

Bosch had gotten the lieutenant's serial number off his ID card one day when Pounds had left it clipped to his jacket on the coatrack outside his office. He'd written it down in his phone book on a hunch that one day it would come in handy.

The DMV clerk finally came back on the line and said there was no driver's license presently issued to a Johnny Fox with the birth date Bosch had provided.

'Anything close?'

'No, honey.'

'That's Lieutenant, miss,' Bosch said sternly. 'Lieutenant Pounds.'

'That's Ms, Lieutenant. Ms Sharp.'

'And I bet you are. Tell me, Ms Sharp, how far back does that computer run go?'

'Seven years. Anything else?'

'How do I check the years before that?'

'You don't. If you want a hand records search you drop us a letter, Looten-ANT. It will take ten to fourteen days. In your case, count on the fourteen. Anything else?'

'No, but I don't like your demeanor.'

'That makes us even. Good-bye.'

Bosch laughed out loud after flipping the phone closed. He was sure now that trace wouldn't get lost in the process. Ms. Sharp would see to that. The name Pounds would probably be on the top of the list when it came in to Parker Center. He dialed Edgar's number on the homicide table next and caught him before he had left the bureau for the day.

'Harry, what's up?'

'You busy?'

'No. Nothing new.'

'Can you run a name for me? I already did DMV but I need somebody to do the computer.'

'Uh ...'

'Look, can you or can't you? If you're worried about Pounds, then –'

'Hey, Harry, cool it. What's wrong with you, man? I didn't say I couldn't do it. Just give me the name.'

Bosch couldn't understand why Edgar's attitude enraged him. He took a breath and tried to calm down.

'The name's John Fox. Johnny Fox.'

'Shit, there's going to be a hundred John Foxes. You got a DOB?'

'Yeah, I got a DOB.'

Bosch checked his notebook again and gave it to him.

'What'd he do to you? Say, how you doing?'

'Funny. I'll tell you later. You going to run it?'

'Yes, I said I'll do it.'

'Okay, you got my portable number. If you can't get through, leave me a message at home.'

'When I can get to it, Harry.'

'What, you said nothing's happening.'

'Nothing is, but I'm working, man. I can't be running around doing shit for you all the time.'

Bosch was stunned into a short moment of silence.

'Hey, Jerry, fuck you, I'll do it myself.'

'Look, Harry, I'm not saying I'm –'

'No, I mean it. Never mind. I don't want to compromise you with your new partner or your fearless leader. I mean after all, that's what it's about, isn't it? So don't give me this shit about working. You're not working.

40

You're about to go out the door for home and you know it. Or wait a minute, maybe it's drinks with Burnsie again tonight.'

'Harry –'

'Take care, man.'

Bosch flipped the phone closed and sat there letting the anger work out of him like heat from the grill of a radiator. The phone rang while it was still in his hand and he immediately felt better. He flipped it open.

'Look, I'm sorry, okay?' he said. 'Forget it.'

There was a long silence.

'Hello?'

It was a woman's voice. Bosch felt immediately embarrassed.

'Yes?'

'Detective Bosch?'

'Yes, I'm sorry, I thought it was someone else.'

'Like who?'

'Who is this?'

'It's Dr Hinojos.'

'Oh.' Bosch closed his eyes and the anger came back. 'What can I do for you?'

'I was just calling to remind you that we have a session tomorrow. Three-thirty. You will be there?'

'I don't have a choice, remember? And you don't have to call to remind me about our sessions. Believe it or not, I have an appointment calendar, a watch, an alarm clock, all of that stuff now.'

He immediately thought he had gone over the top with the sarcasm.

'Sounds like I caught you at a bad time. I'll let –'

'You did.'

'– you go. See you tomorrow, Detective Bosch.'

'Good-bye.'

He snapped the phone closed again and dropped it on the seat. He started the car. He took Ocean Park out to Bundy and then up toward the 10. As he approached the freeway overpass he saw the eastbound cars on top weren't moving and the on ramp was jammed with cars waiting to wait.

'Fuck it,' he said out loud.

He went by the freeway ramp without turning and then under the overpass. He took Bundy up to Wilshire and then headed west into downtown Santa Monica. It took him fifteen minutes to find street parking near the Third Street Promenade. He had been avoiding multilevel parking garages since the quake and didn't want to start using them now.

What a walking contradiction, Bosch thought as he prowled for a parking spot along the curb. You live in a condemned house the inspectors claim is ready to slide down the hill but you won't go into a parking garage. He finally found a spot across from the porno theater about a block from the Promenade.

Bosch spent the rush hours walking up and down the three-block stretch of outdoor restaurants, movie theaters and shops. He went into the King George on Santa Monica, which he knew was a hangout for some of the detectives out of West LA Division, but didn't see anybody he knew. After that, he ate pizza from a to-go joint and people-watched. He saw a street

41

performer juggling five butcher knives at once. And he thought he might know something about how the man felt.

He sat on a bench and watched the droves of people pass him by. The only ones who stopped and paid attention to him were the homeless, and soon he had no change or dollar bills left to give them. Bosch felt alone. He thought about Katherine Register and what she had said about the past. She had said she was strong but he knew that comfort and strength could come from sadness. That was what she had.

He thought about what she had done five years ago. Her husband dead, she had taken stock of her life and found the hole in her memories. The pain. She had sent him the card in hopes he might do something then. And it had almost worked. He had pulled the murder book from the archives but hadn't had the strength, or maybe it was the weakness, to look at it.

After it got dark he walked down Broadway to Mr B's, found a stool at the bar and ordered a draft with a Jack Daniels depth charge. There was a quintet playing on the small stage in the back, the lead on tenor saxophone. They were finishing up 'Do Nothing Till You Hear from Me' and Bosch got the idea he had come in at the end of a long set. The sax was draggy. It wasn't a clean sound.

Disappointed, he looked away from the group and took a large swallow of beer. He checked his watch and knew he'd have clear driving if he left now. But he stayed. He picked the shot up and dropped it into the mug and drank deeply from the brutal mix. The group moved into 'What a Wonderful World.' No one in the band stepped up to sing the words but, of course, nobody could touch Louis Armstrong's vocals if they tried. It was okay, though. Bosch knew the words.

> I see trees of green
> Red roses, too
> I see them bloom
> For me and you
> And I think to myself
> What a wonderful world

The song made him feel lonely and sad but that was okay. Loneliness had been the trash can fire he huddled around for most of his life. He was just getting used to it again. It had been that way for him before Sylvia and it could be that way again. It would just take time and the pain of letting her go.

In the three months since she had left, there had been the one postcard and nothing else. Her absence had fractured the sense of continuity in his life. Before her, his job had always been the iron rails, as dependable as the sunset over the Pacific. But with her he had attempted to switch tracks, the bravest jump he had ever made. But somehow he had failed. It wasn't enough to keep her and she was gone. And now he felt he had run clear off the tracks. Inside, he felt as fragmented as his city. Broken, it seemed at times, at every level.

He heard a female voice from nearby singing the words of the song. He turned to see a young woman a few stools away, her eyes closed as she sang very softly. She sang only to herself but Bosch could hear.

I see skies of blue
And clouds of white
The bright blessed day
The dark sacred night
And I think to myself
What a wonderful world

She wore a short white skirt, a T-shirt and a brightly colored vest. Bosch guessed she wasn't older than twenty-five and he liked the idea that she even knew the song. She sat straight, her legs crossed. Her back swayed with the music of the saxophone. Her face was framed by brown hair and was turned upward, her lips slightly apart, almost angelic. Bosch thought she was quite beautiful, so totally lost in the majesty of the music. Clean or not, the sound took her away and he admired her for letting it. He knew that what he saw in her face was what a man would see if he made love to her. She had what other cops called a getaway face. So beautiful it would always be a shield. No matter what she did or what was done to her, her face would be her ticket. It would open doors in front of her, close them behind her. It would let her get away.

The song ended and she opened her eyes and clapped. No one else had applauded until she began. Then everyone in the bar, Bosch included, joined in. Such was the power of the getaway face. Bosch turned and flagged the bartender for another shot and beer. When it was down in front of him he took a glance over at the woman, but she was gone. He turned and checked the bar's door and saw it closing. He'd missed her.

8

On the way home he worked his way up to Sunset and took that all the way into the city. Traffic was sparse. He had stayed out later than he had planned. He smoked and listened to the all-news channel on the radio. There was a report about Grant High finally reopening in the Valley. It was where Sylvia had taught. Before going to Venice.

Bosch was tired and guessed that he probably wouldn't pass a breath test if stopped. He dropped his speed to below the limit as Sunset cut through Beverly Hills. He knew the cops in BH wouldn't cut him a break and that would be all he'd need on top of the involuntary stress leave.

He turned left at Laurel Canyon and took the winding road up the hill. At Mulholland he was about to turn right on red when he checked the traffic from the left and froze. He saw a coyote step out of the brush of the arroyo to the left of the roadway and take a tentative look around the intersection. There were no other cars. Only Bosch saw this.

The animal was thin and ragged, worn by the struggle to sustain itself in the urban hills. The mist rising from the arroyo caught the reflection of the street lights and cast the coyote in almost a dim blue light. And it seemed to study Bosch's car for a moment, its eyes catching the reflection of the stoplight and glowing. For just a moment Bosch believed that the coyote might be looking directly at him. Then the animal turned and moved back into the blue mist.

A car came up behind him and honked. Bosch had the green light. He waved and made the turn onto Mulholland. But then he pulled to the side. He put the car in park and got out.

It was a cool evening and he felt a chill as he walked across the intersection to the spot where he had seen the blue coyote. He wasn't sure what he was doing but he wasn't afraid. He just wanted to see the animal again. He stopped at the edge of the drop-off and looked down into the darkness below. The blue mist was all around him now. A car passed behind him and when the noise receded he listened and looked intently. But there was nothing. The coyote was gone. He walked back to his car and drove on Mulholland to Woodrow Wilson Drive to home.

Later, as he lay in his bed after more drinks and with the light still on, he smoked the last cigarette of the night and stared up at the ceiling. He'd left the light on but his thoughts were of the dark, sacred night. And the blue coyote. And the woman with the getaway face. Soon all of those thoughts disappeared with him into the dark.

9

Bosch got little sleep and was up before the sun. The last cigarette of the night before had nearly been his last for all time. He had fallen asleep with it between his fingers, only to be jolted awake by the searing pain of the burn. He dressed the wounds on two fingers and tried to return to sleep, but it wouldn't take him. His fingers throbbed and all he could think of was how many times he had investigated the deaths of hapless drunks who had fallen asleep and self-immolated. All he could think of was what Carmen Hinojos would have to say about such a stunt. How was that for a symptom of self-destruction?

Finally, as dawn's light began to leak into the room he gave up on sleep and got up. While coffee brewed in the kitchen he went into the bathroom and rebandaged the burns on his fingers. As he taped the fresh gauze on, he glanced at himself in the mirror and saw the deep lines under his eyes.

'Shit,' he said to himself. 'What's going on?'

He had black coffee on the back deck while watching the silent city come awake. There was a crisp chill in the air and the earthy smell of eucalyptus was rising from the tall trees down in the pass. The marine fog layer had filled the pass and the hills were just mysterious silhouettes in the mist. He watched the morning begin for nearly an hour, fascinated by the show he had from his deck.

It wasn't until he went back inside for a second cup that he noticed the red light flashing on his phone machine. He had two messages that had probably been left the day before and that he hadn't noticed after coming in last night. He pressed the play button.

'Bosch, this is Lieutenant Pounds calling on Tuesday at three thirty-five. I have to inform you that while you are on leave and until your, uh, status with the department is decided, you will be required to return your vehicle to the Hollywood Division garage. I have here that it is a four-year-old Chevrolet Caprice, tag number one-adam-adam-three-four-zero-two. Please make arrangements immediately to have the car turned in and checked out. This order is per *Standard Practices Manual* citation three dash thirteen. Violation could result in suspension and/or dismissal. Again, this is an order from Lieutenant Pounds, now three thirty-six on Tuesday. If there is any part of this message that you do not understand, feel free to contact me at the office.'

The machine reported the message had actually been left at 4 P.M.

45

Tuesday, probably right before Pounds had gone home for the day. Fuck him, Bosch thought. The car's a piece of shit anyway. He can have it.

The second message was from Edgar.

'Harry, you there? It's Edgar . . . Okay, listen, let's forget about today, okay? I mean it. Let's just say I was a prick and you were a prick and we're both pricks and forget it. Whether it turns out you are my partner or you were my partner, I owe you a lot, man. And if I ever act like I forgot that, hit me alongside the head like you did today. Now, to the bad news. I checked everything on this Johnny Fox. I got exactly nothing, man. That's from the NCIC, DOJ, DPP, Corrections, National Warrants, everything. I ran the works on him. Looks like this guy is clean, if he's alive. You say he doesn't even have a DL so that makes me think maybe you got a phony name there or maybe this guy ain't among the living. So, that's that. I don't know what you're up to but if you want anything else, give a call . . . Oh, and hang in there, buddy. I'm ten-seven after this so you can reach me at home if –'

The message cut off. Edgar had run out of time. Bosch rewound the tape and poured his coffee. Back on the deck he mulled over the whereabouts of Johnny Fox. When he had gotten nothing on the DMV trace, Bosch had assumed Fox might be in prison, where driver's licenses weren't issued or needed. But Edgar had not found him there nor had he found his name on any national computer that tracks criminals. Now Bosch guessed that Johnny Fox had either gone straight or, as Edgar had suggested, was dead. If Bosch was betting, he'd take the latter. Men like Johnny Fox didn't go straight.

Bosch's alternative was to go down to the Los Angeles County Hall of Records and look for a death certificate but without a date of death it would be a needle in the haystack search. It might take him days. Before he'd do that, he decided, he'd try an easier way, the *LA Times*.

He went back inside to the phone and dialed a reporter named Keisha Russell. She was new on the cop beat and still struggling to find her way. She had made a subtle attempt to recruit Bosch as a source a few months earlier. The way reporters usually did that was to write an inordinate number of stories on a crime that did not merit such intense attention. But the process put them in constant contact with the detectives on the case and that allowed them the chance to ingratiate themselves and hopefully procure the investigators as future sources.

Russell had written five stories in a week about one of Bosch's cases. It was a domestic violence case in which a husband had disregarded a temporary restraining order and gone to his separated wife's new apartment on Franklin. He carried her to the fifth-floor balcony and threw her off. He went over next. Russell had talked to Bosch repeatedly during the stretch of stories. The resultant dispatches were thorough and complete. It was good work and she began to earn Bosch's respect. Still, he knew that she hoped that the stories and her attention would be the building blocks of a long reporter/investigator relationship. Since then not a week had gone by that she didn't call Bosch once or twice to bullshit, pass along departmental gossip she had picked up from other sources, and ask the one question all reporters live and die by: 'Anything going on?'

She answered on the first ring and Bosch was a little surprised she was in so early. He was planning on leaving a message on her voice mail.

'Keisha, it's Bosch.'

'Hey, Bosch, how you doing?'

'Okay, I guess. I guess you heard about me.'

'Not everything, but I heard you went on temporary leave. But nobody would tell me why. You want to talk about it?'

'No, not really. I mean, not now. I have a favor to ask. If it works out, I'll give you the story. That's the deal I've made in the past with other reporters.'

'What do I have to do?'

'Just walk over to the morgue.'

She groaned.

'I mean the newspaper morgue, right there at the *Times*.'

'Oh, that's better. What do you need?'

'I've got a name. It's old. I know the guy was a dirtbag in the fifties and at least the early sixties. But I've lost track of him after that. Thing is, my hunch is that he's dead.'

'You want an obit?'

'Well, I don't know if this is the type of guy the *Times* would write an obituary on. He was strictly small time, near as I can tell. I was thinking that there might be a story, you know, if his death was sort of untimely.'

'You mean like if he got his shit blown away.'

'You got it.'

'Okay, I'll take a look.'

She seemed eager, Bosch sensed. He knew that she thought that by doing this favor she would be cementing their relationship in place and it would only pay dividends in the future. He said nothing that would dissuade her of this.

'What's the name?'

'His name is John Fox. He went by Johnny. Last I have a trace on him is 1961. He was a pimp, general piece of trash.'

'White, black, yellow or brown?'

'General piece of white trash, you could say.'

'You have a birth date? It will help narrow it down if there's more than one Johnny Fox in the clips.'

He gave it to her.

'Okay, where you going to be?'

Bosch gave her his portable phone number. He knew that would set the hook. The number would go right onto the source list she kept in her computer like gold earrings in a jewelry box. Having the number where he could be reached at almost any time was worth the search in the morgue.

'Okay, listen, I've got a meeting with my editor – that's the only reason I'm in this early. But after, I'll go take a look. I'll call you as soon as I have something.'

'If there is something.'

'Right.'

After Bosch hung up he ate some Frosted Flakes from a box he took out of the refrigerator and turned on the news radio. He had discontinued the newspaper after the earthquake in case Gowdy, the building inspector, happened by early and saw it out front, a clue that someone was inhabiting the uninhabitable. There was nothing much in the top of the news

47

summary that interested him. No homicides in Hollywood, at least. He wasn't missing out on anything.

There was one story after the traffic report that caught his attention. An octopus on display at a city aquarium in San Pedro had apparently killed itself by pulling a water circulation tube out of its tank fitting with one of its tentacles. The tank emptied and the octopus died. Environmental groups were calling it suicide, a desperate protest by the octopus against its captivity. Only in LA, Bosch thought as he turned the radio off. A place so desperate even the marine life was killing itself.

He took a long shower, closing his eyes and holding his head directly under the spray. As he was shaving in front of the mirror after, he couldn't help but study the circles under his eyes again. They seemed even more pronounced than earlier and fit nicely with the eyes cracked with red from his drinking the night before.

He put the razor down on the edge of the sink and leaned closer to the mirror. His skin was as pale as a recycled paper plate. As he appraised himself, the thought he had was that he had once been considered a handsome man. Not anymore. He looked beaten. It seemed that age was gripping him, beating him down. He thought that he resembled some of the old men he'd seen after they were found dead in their beds. The ones in the rooming houses. The ones living in refrigerator boxes. He reminded himself more of the dead than the living.

He opened the medicine cabinet so the reflection would go away. He looked among the various items on the glass shelves and chose a squeeze bottle of Murine. He put in a heavy dose of the eye drops, wiped the excess spill off his face with a towel and left the bathroom without closing the cabinet and having to look at himself again.

He put on his best clean suit, a gray two-piece, and a white button-down shirt. He added his maroon tie with gladiator helmets on it. It was his favorite tie. And his oldest. One edge of it was fraying but he wore it two or three times a week. He'd bought it ten years earlier when he was first assigned to homicide. He pegged it in place on his shirt with a gold tie tack that formed the number 187 – the California penal code for homicide. As he did this, he felt a measure of control come back to him. He began to feel good and whole again, and to feel angry. He was ready to go out into the world, whether or not it was ready for him.

10

Bosch pulled the knot of his tie tight against his throat before pulling open the back door of the station. He took the hallway to the rear of the detective bureau and then the aisle between the tables toward the front, where Pounds sat in his office behind the glass windows that separated him from the detectives he commanded. Heads at the burglary table bobbed up as he was noticed, then at the robbery and homicide tables. Bosch did not acknowledge anyone, though he almost lost a step when he saw someone sitting in his seat at the homicide table. Burns. Edgar was there at his own spot, but his back was to Bosch's path and he didn't see Harry coming through the room.

But Pounds did. Through the glass wall he saw Bosch's approach to his office and he stood up behind his desk.

The first thing Bosch noticed as he got closer was that the glass panel that he had broken just a week before in the office had already been replaced. He thought it was strange that this could happen so quickly in a department where more vital repairs – such as replacing the bullet-riddled windshield of a patrol car – normally took a month of red tape and paper pushing. But those were the priorities of this department.

'Henry!' Pounds barked. 'Come in here.'

An old man who sat at the front counter and took calls on the public line and gave general directions jumped up and doddered into the glass office. He was a civilian volunteer, one of several who worked in the station, mainly retirees that most cops referred to collectively as members of the Nod Squad.

Bosch followed the old man in and put his briefcase down on the floor.

'Bosch!' Pounds yelped. 'There's a witness here.'

He pointed to old Henry, then out through the glass.

'Witnesses out there as well.'

Bosch could see that Pounds still had deep purple remnants of broken capillaries under each eye. The swelling was gone, though. Bosch walked up to the desk and reached into the pocket of his coat.

'Witnesses to what?'

'To whatever you're doing here.'

Bosch turned to look at Henry.

'Henry, you can leave now. I'm just going to talk to the lieutenant.'

'Henry, you stay,' Pounds commanded. 'I want you to hear this.'

'How do you know he'll remember it, Pounds? He can't even transfer a call to the right table.'

Bosch looked back at Henry again and fixed him with a stare that left no doubt who was in charge in the glass room.

'Close the door on your way out.'

Henry made a timid glance back at Pounds but then quickly headed out the door, closing it as instructed. Bosch turned back to Pounds.

The lieutenant slowly, like a cat sneaking past a dog, lowered himself into his seat, perhaps thinking or knowing from experience that there might be more safety in not being at a face-to-face level with Bosch. Harry looked down and saw that there was a book open on the desk. He reached down and turned the cover to see what it was.

'Studying for the captain's exam, Lieutenant?'

Pounds shrank back from Bosch's reach. Bosch saw it was not the captain's exam manual but a book on creating and honing motivational skills in employees. It had been written by a professional basketball coach. Bosch had to laugh and shake his head.

'Pounds, you know, you're really something. I mean, at least you're entertaining. I gotta give you that.'

Pounds grabbed the book back and shoved it in a drawer.

'What do you want, Bosch? You know you're not supposed to be in here. You're on leave.'

'But you called me in, remember?'

'I did not.'

'The car. You said you wanted the car.'

'I said turn it in at the garage. I didn't say come in here. Now get out!'

Bosch could see the rosy spread of anger on the other man's face. Bosch remained cool and took that as a sign of a declining level of stress. He brought his hand out of his pocket with the car keys in them. He dropped them on the desk in front of Pounds.

'It's parked out by the drunk tank door. You want it back, you can have it. But you take it through the checkout at the garage. That's not a cop's job. That's a job for a bureaucrat.'

Bosch turned to leave and picked up his briefcase. He then opened the door to the office with such force that it swung around and banged against one of the glass panels of the office. The whole office shook but nothing broke. He walked around the counter, saying, 'Sorry about that, Henry,' without looking at the old man, and then headed down the front hall.

A few minutes later he was standing on the curb on Wilcox, in front of the station, waiting for the cab he had called with his portable. A gray Caprice, almost a duplicate of the car he had just turned in, pulled up in front of him and he bent down to look in. It was Edgar. He was smiling. The window glided down.

'You need a ride, tough guy?'

Bosch got in.

'There's a Hertz on La Brea near the Boulevard.'

'Yeah, I know it.'

They drove in silence for a few minutes, then Edgar laughed and shook his head.

'What?'

'Nothing . . . Burns, man. I think he was about to shit his pants when you were in there with Pounds. He thought you were gonna come outta there and throw his ass outta your chair at the table. He was pitiful.'

'Shit. I should've. I didn't think of it.'

Silence came back again. They were on Sunset coming up to La Brea.

'Harry, you just can't help yourself, can you?'

'I guess not.'

'What happened to your hand?'

Bosch held it up and studied the bandage.

'Ah, I hit it last week when I was working on the deck. Hurt like a son of a bitch.'

'Yeah, you better be careful or Pounds is going to be on you like a son of a bitch.'

'He already is.'

'Man, he's nothing but a bean counter, a punk. Why can't you just leave it alone? You know you're just –'

'You know, you're beginning to sound like the shrink they're sending me to. Maybe I should just sit with you for an hour today, what you say?'

'Maybe she's talking some sense to you.'

'Maybe I should've taken the cab.'

'I think you should figure out who your friends are and listen to them for once.'

'Here it is.'

Edgar slowed in front of the rental car agency. Bosch got out before the car was even stopped.

'Harry, wait a minute.'

Bosch looked back in at him.

'What's going on with this Fox thing? Who is the guy?'

'I can't tell you now, Jerry. It's just better this way.'

'You sure?'

Bosch heard the phone in his briefcase start to ring. He looked down at it and then back at Edgar.

'Thanks for the ride.'

He closed the car door.

11

The call was from Keisha Russell at the *Times*. She said she'd found one small story in the morgue under Fox's name but she wanted to meet with Bosch to give it to him. He knew it was part of the game, part of making the pact. He looked at his watch. He could wait to see what the story said. He told her he'd buy her lunch at the Pantry in downtown.

Forty minutes later she was already in a booth near the cashier's cage when he got there. He slipped into the opposite side of the booth.

'You're late,' she said.

'Sorry, I was renting a car.'

'They took your car, huh? Must be serious.'

'We're not going to talk about that.'

'I know. You know who owns this place?'

'Yeah, the mayor. Doesn't make the food bad.'

She curled her lip and looked around as if the place were crawling with ants. The mayor was a Republican. The *Times* had gone with the Democrat. What was worse, for her, at least, was that the mayor was a supporter of the Police Department. Reporters didn't like that. That was boring. They wanted City Hall infighting, controversy, scandal. It made things more interesting.

'Sorry,' he said. 'I guess I could've suggested Gorky's or some more liberal establishment.'

'Don't worry about it, Bosch. I'm just funnin' with ya.'

She wasn't more than twenty-five, he guessed. She was a dark-complected black woman who had a beautiful grace about her. Bosch had no idea where she was from but he didn't think it was LA. She had the touch of an accent, a Caribbean lilt, that maybe she had worked on smoothing out. It was still there, though. He liked the way she said his name. In her mouth, it sounded exotic, like a wave breaking. He didn't mind that she was little more than half his age and addressed him only by his last name.

'Where you from, Keisha?'

'Why?'

'Why? Because I'm interested is all. You're on the beat. I wanna know who I'm dealing with.'

'I'm from right here, Bosch. I came from Jamaica when I was five years old. I went to USC. Where are you from?'

'Right here. Been here all my life.'

He decided not to mention the fifteen months he spent fighting in the tunnels in Vietnam and the nine in North Carolina training for it.

52

'What happened to your hand?'

'Cut it working on my house. Been doing odd jobs while I'm off. So, what's it been like taking Bremmer's place on the cop beat? He'd been there a long time.'

'Yeah, I know. It's been difficult. But I'm making my way. Slowly. I'm making friends. I hope you'll be one of my friends, Bosch.'

'I'll be your friend. When I can. Let's see what you got.'

She brought a manila file up onto the table but the waiter, an old bald man with a waxed mustache, arrived before she could open it. She ordered an egg salad sandwich. He ordered a well-done hamburger and fries. She frowned and he guessed why.

'You're vegetarian, right?'

'Yes.'

'Sorry. Next time you pick the place.'

'I will.'

She opened the file and he noticed she had several bracelets on her left wrist. They were made of braided thread in many bright colors. He looked in the file and saw a photocopy of a small newspaper clipping. Bosch could tell by the size of the clip that it was one of the stories that gets buried in the back of the paper. She passed it over to him.

'I think this is your Johnny Fox. The age is right but it does not describe him like you did. White trash, you said.'

Bosch read the story. It was dated September 30, 1962.

CAMPAIGN WORKER VICTIM OF HIT AND RUN
By Monte Kim, *Times* Staff Writer

A 29-year-old campaign worker for a candidate for the district attorney's office was killed Saturday when he was struck by a speeding car in Hollywood, the Los Angeles police reported.

The victim was identified as Johnny Fox, who lived in an apartment on Ivar Street in Hollywood. Police said Fox had been distributing campaign literature supporting district attorney hopeful Arno Conklin at the corner of Hollywood Boulevard and La Brea Avenue when he was cut down by the speeding car as he crossed the street.

Fox was crossing the southbound lanes of La Brea about 2 P.M. when the car struck him. Police said it appeared Fox was killed on impact and his body was dragged for several yards by the car.

The car that hit Fox slowed momentarily after the collision but then sped away, police said. Witnesses told investigators the car proceeded south on La Brea at a high rate of speed. Police have not located the vehicle and witnesses could not provide a clear description of the make and model year. Police said an investigation is continuing.

Conklin campaign manager Gordon Mittel said Fox had joined the campaign only a week ago.

Reached at the district attorney's office, where he is in charge of the special investigation branch under retiring DA John Charles Stock, Conklin said he had not yet met Fox but regretted the death of the man working for his election. The candidate declined further comment.

Bosch studied the clip for a long moment after reading it.

53

'This Monte Kim, is he still at the paper?'

'Are you kidding? That's like a millennium ago. Back then the newsroom was a bunch of white guys sitting around in white shirts and ties.'

Bosch looked down at his own shirt, then at her.

'Sorry,' she said. 'Anyway, he's not around. And I don't know about Conklin. A little before my time. Did he win?'

'Yeah. I think he had two terms, then I think he ran for attorney general or something and got his ass handed to him. Something like that. I wasn't here then.'

'I thought you said you've been here all your life.'

'I went away for a while.'

'Vietnam, right?'

'Right.'

'Yeah, a lot of cops your age were there. Must've been a trip. Is that why you all became cops? So you could keep carrying guns?'

'Something like that.'

'Anyway, if Conklin's still alive, he's probably an old man. But Mittel's still around. Obviously, you know that. He's probably in one of these booths eating with the mayor.'

She smiled and he ignored it.

'Yeah, he's a big shot. What's the story on him?'

'Mittel? I don't know. First name on a big downtown law firm, friend of governors and senators and other powerful people. Last I heard, he's running the financing behind Robert Shepherd.'

'Robert Shepherd? You mean that computer guy?'

'More like computer magnate. Yeah, don't you read the paper? Shepherd wants to run but doesn't want to use up his own money. Mittel is doing the fund-raising for an exploratory campaign.'

'Run for what?'

'Jesus, Bosch, you don't read the paper or watch TV.'

'I've been busy. Run for what?'

'Well, like any egomaniac I guess he wants to run for president. But for now he's looking at the Senate. Shepherd wants to be a third-party candidate. Says the Republicans are too far right and the Democrats too left. He's right down the middle. And from what I hear, if anybody can get the money together for him to do the third-candidate dance, it's Mittel.'

'So Mittel wants to make himself a president.'

'I guess. But what are you asking me about him for anyway? I'm a cop reporter. You're a cop. What's this have to do with Gordon Mittel?'

She pointed to the photocopy. Bosch became aware that he might have asked too many questions.

'I'm just trying to catch up,' he said. 'Like you said, I don't read the papers.'

'That's *paper*, not papers,' she said smiling. 'I better not catch you reading or talking to the *Daily Snews*.'

'Hell hath no fury like a reporter scorned, right?'

'Something like that.'

He felt assured that he had deflected her suspicions. He held up the photocopy.

'There was no follow-up to this? They never caught anybody?'

'I guess not or there would be a story.'

'Can I keep this?'

'Sure.'

'You feel like taking another walk back to the morgue?'

'For what?'

'Stories about Conklin.'

'There will be hundreds, Bosch. You said he was DA for two terms.'

'I only want stories from before he was elected. And if you have the time, throw in stories on Mittel, too.'

'You know, you're asking a lot. I could get in trouble if they knew I was doing clip searches for a cop.'

She put on a fake pout and he ignored that, too. He knew what she was driving at.

'You want to tell me what this is about, Bosch?'

He still didn't say anything.

'I didn't think so. Well, look, I've got two interviews to do this afternoon. I'm going to be gone. What I can do is get an intern to get the clips together and leave it all for you with the guard in the globe lobby. It will be in an envelope so nobody will know what it is. Would that be okay?'

He nodded. He'd been to Times Square before on a handful of occasions, usually meetings with reporters. It was a block-sized building with two lobbies. The centerpiece of the lobby at the First and Spring entrance was a huge globe that never stopped rotating, just as the news never stopped happening.

'You'll just leave it under my name? Won't that get you in trouble? You know, like you said, being too friendly with a cop. That's got to be against the rules over there.'

She smiled at his sarcasm.

'Don't worry. If an editor or somebody asks, I'll just say it's an investment in the future. You better remember that, Bosch. Friendship is a two-way street.'

'Don't worry. I never forget that.'

He leaned forward across the table so he was up close to her face.

'I want you to remember something, too. One of the reasons I'm not telling you why I need this stuff is because I'm not sure what it means. If anything. But don't you get too curious. Don't you go making any calls. You do that, and you might mess things up. I might get hurt. You might get hurt. Got it?'

'Got it.'

The man with the waxed mustache appeared at the side of the table with their plates.

12

'I noticed you arrived early today. Am I to take that as a sign that you want to be here?'

'Not especially. I was downtown having lunch with a friend, so I just came over.'

'Well, it's good to hear you were out with a friend. I think that is good.'

Carmen Hinojos was behind her desk. The notebook was out and open but she sat with her hands clasped together in front of her. It was as if she was going out of her way to make no move that could be construed as threatening to the dialogue.

'What happened to your hand?'

Bosch held it up and looked at the bandages on his fingers.

'I hit it with a hammer. I was working on my house.'

'That's too bad. I hope it's okay.'

'I'll live.'

'Why are you so dressed up? I hope you don't feel you have to do that for these sessions.'

'No. I . . . I just like following my routine. Even if I'm not going to work, I got dressed like I was.'

'I understand.'

After she made an offer of coffee or water and Bosch declined, she got the session going.

'Tell me, what would you like to talk about today?'

'I don't care. You're the boss.'

'I'd rather that you not look at the relationship in that way. I'm not your boss, Detective Bosch. I'm just a facilitator, someone to help you talk about whatever you want, whatever you want to get off your chest.'

Bosch was silent. He couldn't think of anything to volunteer. Carmen Hinojos drummed her pencil on her yellow tablet for a few moments before taking up the slack.

'Nothing at all, huh?'

'Nothing comes to mind.'

'Then why don't we talk about yesterday. When I called you, to remind you of our session today, you obviously seemed upset about something. Was that when you hit your hand?'

'No, that wasn't it.'

He stopped but she said nothing and he decided to give in a little bit. He had to admit to himself that there was something about her that he liked.

She was not threatening and he believed she was telling the truth when she said she was there only to help him.

'What happened when you called was that I had found out earlier that my partner, you know, my partner before all of this, had been paired up with a new man. I've been replaced already.'

'And how'd that make you feel?'

'You heard how I was. I was mad about it. I think anybody would be. Then I called my partner up later and he treated me like yesterday's news. I taught that guy a lot and . . .'

'And what?'

'I don't know. It hurt, I guess.'

'I see.'

'No, I don't think you do. You'd have to be me to see it the way I did.'

'I guess that's true. But I can sympathize. Let's leave it at that. Let me ask you this. Shouldn't you have expected your partner to be paired up again? After all, isn't it a department rule that detectives work in pairs? You are on leave for a so-far-unknown period of time. Wasn't it a given that he'd get a new partner, whether permanent or otherwise?'

'I suppose.'

'Isn't it safer to work in pairs?'

'I suppose.'

'What is your own experience? Did you feel safer the times you were with a partner on the job as opposed to those times when you were alone?'

'Yes, I felt safer.'

'So what happened was inevitable and inarguable, yet still it made you angry.'

'It wasn't that it happened that brought it on. I don't know, it was the way he told me and then the way he acted when I called. I really felt left out. I asked him for a favor and he . . . I don't know.'

'He what?'

'He hesitated. Partners don't do that. Not with each other. They're supposed be there for each other. It's supposedly a lot like a marriage, but I've never been married.'

She paused to write some notes, which made Bosch wonder what had just been said that was so important.

'You seem,' she said while still writing, 'to have a low threshold for the toleration of frustrations.'

Her statement immediately made him angry but he knew that if he showed it then he would be confirming her statement. He thought maybe it was a trick designed to elicit such a response. He tried to calm himself.

'Doesn't everybody?' he said in a controlled voice.

'I suppose, to a degree. When I reviewed your records I saw that you were in the Army during the Vietnam War. Did you see any combat?'

'Did I *see* any combat? Yes, I saw combat. I was in the middle of combat, too. I was even under it. Why do people always ask, did you *see* combat, like it was a goddamn movie they took you to over there?'

She was quiet for a long time, holding the pen but doing no writing. It seemed like she was simply waiting for the sails of his anger to lose the wind. He waved his hand in a gesture he hoped told her that he was sorry, that it was behind him, that they should move on.

'Sorry,' he said, just to make sure.

She still didn't say anything and her stare was beginning to weigh on him. He looked away from her to the bookshelves along one wall of the office. They were filled with heavy, leather-bound psychiatry texts.

'I am sorry to intrude on such an emotionally sensitive area,' she finally said. 'The reason –'

'But that's what this is all about, right? What you have is a license to intrude and I can't do anything about it.'

'So, then, accept it,' she said sternly. 'We've been over this before. To help you we have to talk about you. Accept it and maybe we can move on. Now, as I was saying, the reason I mentioned the war was that I wanted to ask you if you are familiar with post-traumatic stress syndrome. Have you ever heard of it?'

He looked back at her. He knew what was coming.

'Yes, of course. I've heard of it.'

'Well, Detective, in the past it's primarily been associated with service-men returning from the war but it's not just a war or post-war problem. It can happen in any kind of stressful environment. Any kind. And I have to say I think that you are a walking, talking example of this disorder's symtoms.'

'Jesus . . .,' he said, shaking his head. He turned in his seat so he wasn't looking at her or her bookcase. He stared at the sky through the window. It was cloudless. 'You people sit up here in these offices and have no idea . . .'

He didn't finish. He just shook his head. He reached to his neck and loosened his tie. It was like he couldn't get enough air into his chest.

'Hear me out, Detective, okay? Just look at the facts here. Can you think of anything more stressful to be in this city during the last few years than a police officer? Between Rodney King and the scrutiny and villainy that brought, the riots, fires, floods and earthquakes, each officer on this force has had to write the book on stress management and, of course, mismanagement.'

'You left out killer bees.'

'I'm being serious.'

'So am I. It was on the news.'

'With all that's happened and gone on in this city, with every one of these calamities, who is in the middle every time? The police officers. The ones who have to respond. The ones who can't stay at home, duck down and wait until it's over. So let's go from that generalization to the individual. You, Detective. You have been a front-line contender with all of these crises. At the same time you've had your real job to contend with. Homicide. It's one of the highest-stress jobs in the department. Tell me, how many murders have you investigated in the last three years?'

'Look, I'm not looking for an excuse. I told you before that I did what I did because I wanted to. It had nothing to do with riots or –'

'How many dead bodies have you looked at? Just answer my question, please. How many dead bodies? How many widows did you break the news to? How many mothers did you tell about their dead children?'

He brought his hands up and rubbed his face. All he knew was that he wanted to hide from her.

'A lot,' he finally whispered.

'More than a lot . . .'

He exhaled loudly.

'Thank you for answering. I'm not trying to corner you. The point of my questions and the treatise on the social, cultural and even geologic fragmentation of this city is that what I'm saying here is that you've been through more than most, okay? And this doesn't even include the baggage you might still have from Vietnam or the loss of the romantic relationship. But whatever the reasons, the symptoms of stress are showing. They are there, plain as day. Your intolerance, your inability to sublimate frustrations, most of all your assault on your commanding officer.'

She paused but Bosch didn't say anything. He had a feeling she wasn't finished. She wasn't.

'There are other signs as well,' she continued. 'Your refusal to leave your damaged home can be perceived as a form of denial of what is happening around you. There are physical symptoms. Have you looked at yourself in the mirror lately? I don't think I need to ask to know that you're drinking too much. And your hand. You didn't hurt yourself with a hammer. You fell asleep with a cigarette in your hand. That is a burn and I'd bet my state license on it.'

She opened a drawer and took out two plastic cups and a bottle of water. She filled the cups and pushed one across the desk to him. A peace offering. He watched her silently. He felt exhausted, unrepairable. He also couldn't help but be amazed by her at the same time she was so expertly cutting him open. After she took a sip of water she continued.

'These things are all indicative of a diagnosis of post-traumatic stress syndrome. However, we have one problem with that. The word *post* when used in such a diagnosis indicates the time of stress has passed. That's not the case here. Not in LA. Not with your job. Harry, you are in a nonstop pressure cooker. You owe yourself some breathing room. That's what this leave is all about. Breathing room. Time to recoup and recover. So don't fight it. Grab it. That's the best advice I can give you. Grab it and use it. To save yourself.'

Bosch breathed out heavily and held up his bandaged hand.

'You can keep your state license.'

'Thank you.'

They rested a moment until she continued in a voice meant to soothe him.

'You also have to know you are not alone. This is nothing to be embarrassed about. There has been a sharp increase in incidents of officer stress in the last three years. Behavioral Sciences Services just made a request to the City Council for five more psychologists. Our caseload went from eighteen hundred counseling sessions in 1990 to more than double that last year. We've even got a name for what's going on here. The blue angst. And you have it, Harry.'

Bosch smiled and shook his head, still clinging to what denial he had left.

'The blue angst. Sounds like the name of a Wambaugh novel, doesn't it?'

She didn't answer.

'So what you're saying is that I'm not going to get my job back.'

'No, I'm not saying that at all. All I am saying is that we have a lot of work ahead of us.'

'I feel like I've been broken down by the world champ. You mind if I call you sometime when I'm trying to get a confession out of a hump who won't talk to me?'

'Believe me, just saying that is a start.'

'What do you want me to do?'

'I want you to want to come here. That's all. Don't look at it as a punishment. I want you to work with me, not against me. When we talk I want you to talk about everything and nothing. Anything that comes to mind. Hold back nothing. And one other thing. I'm not telling you to completely cut it out, but you have to cut back on the drinking. You have to have a clear mind. As you obviously know, the effects of alcohol stay with an individual long after the night they were consumed.'

'I'll try. All of it. I'll try.'

'That's all I ask. And since you suddenly seem so willing, I have another thought. I have a cancelation of a session tomorrow at three. Can you make it?'

Bosch hesitated, didn't say anything.

'We seem to finally be working well and I think it will help. The sooner we get through with our work, the sooner you should be able to get back to your work. What do you say?'

'Three?'

'Yes.'

'Okay, I'll be here.'

'Good. Let's get back to our dialogue. Why don't you start? Whatever you want to talk about.'

He leaned forward and reached for the cup of water. He looked at her as he drank from it, then put the cup back on the desk.

'Just say anything?'

'Anything. Whatever is happening in your life or mind that you want to talk about.'

He thought for a long moment.

'I saw a coyote last night. Near my house. I . . . I was drunk, I guess, but I know I saw him.'

'Why was that significant to you?'

He tried to compose the proper answer.

'I'm not sure . . . I guess there's not too many left in the hills in the city – least near where I live. So whenever I see one, I get this feeling that it might be the last one left out there. You know? The last coyote. And I guess that would bother me if it ever turned out to be true, if I never saw one again.'

She nodded as if he had scored some point in a game he wasn't sure how to play.

'There used to be one that lived in the canyon below my house. I'd see him down there and –'

'How do you know it was a he? And I think you called the one you saw last night a he. How are you sure?'

'I'm not sure. I guess I don't even know. It's just a guess.'

'Okay. Go on.'

'Um, he – it – lived down there below my house and I used to see him from time to time. After the earthquake it was gone. I don't know what happened to it. Then I saw this one last night. Something about the mist

60

and the light out there . . . it looked like its coat was blue. He looked hungry. There is something . . . they're kind of sad and threatening at the same time. You know?'

'Yes, I do.'

'Anyway, I thought about him when I got in bed after I got home. That was when I burned my hand. I fell asleep with the cigarette. But before I woke up I had this dream. I mean, I think it was a dream. Maybe like a daydream, like I was still kind of awake. And in it, whatever it was, the coyote was there again. But it was with me. And we were in the canyon or on a hill or something and I wasn't really sure.'

He held up his hand.

'And then I felt the fire.'

She nodded but didn't say anything.

'So what do you think?' he asked.

'Well, interpretation of dreams is not something I do often. Frankly, I'm not sure of its value. The real value I think I see in what you just told me was the willingness to tell me. It shows me a one-eighty-degree turn in your approach to these sessions. For what it's worth, I think it's clear you identify with the coyote. Perhaps, there are not many policemen like you left and you feel the same threat to your existence or your mission. I don't really know. But look at your own words. You called them sad and threatening at the same time. Could that be you also?'

He drank from his cup before answering.

'I've been sad before. But I've found comfort in it.'

They sat in silence for a while, digesting what had been said. She looked at her watch.

'We still have some time. Is there anything else you want to talk about? Maybe something related to this story?'

He contemplated the question for a while and took out a cigarette.

'How much time do we have?'

'As long as you want. Don't worry about the time. I want to do this.'

'You've talked about my mission. You told me to think about my mission. And you said the word again just a minute ago.'

'Yes.'

He hesitated.

'What I say here is protected, right?'

She furrowed her brow.

'I'm not talking about anything illegal. What I mean is, whatever I tell you in here, you're not going to tell people, right? It won't get back to Irving.'

'No. What you tell me stays right here. That's an absolute. I told you, I make a single, narrowly focused recommendation for or against return to duty that I give to Assistant Chief Irving. That's it.'

He nodded, hesitated again and then made his decision. He would tell her.

'Well, you were talking about my mission and your mission and so on and, well, I think I've had a mission for a long time. Only I didn't know it, or I mean . . . I didn't accept it. I didn't acknowledge it. I don't know how to explain it right. Maybe I was afraid or something. I put it off. For a lot of years. Anyway, what I'm telling you is that I've accepted it now.'

61

'I'm not sure I'm following you. Harry, you have to come out and tell me what you're talking about.'

He looked down at the gray rug in front of him. He spoke to it because he didn't know how to say it to her face.

'I'm an orphan . . . I never knew my father and my mother was murdered in Hollywood when I was a kid. Nobody . . . there never was any arrest made.'

'You're looking for her killer, aren't you?'

He looked up at her and nodded.

'That's my mission right now.'

She showed no shock on her face, which in turn surprised him. It was as if she expected him to say what he had just said.

'Tell me about it.'

13

Bosch sat at his dining room table with his notebook out and the newspaper clips that Keisha Russell had had a *Times* intern gather for him sitting in front of him in two separate stacks. One stack for Conklin stories and one for Mittel stories. There was a bottle of Henry's on the table and through the evening he had been nursing it like cough syrup. The one beer was all he would allow himself. The ashtray, however, was loaded and there was a pall of blue smoke around the table. He had placed no limit on cigarettes. Hinojos had said nothing about smoking.

She'd had plenty to say about his mission, though. She'd flatly counseled him to stop until he was better emotionally prepared to face what he might find. He told her that he was too far down the road to stop. Then she said something that he kept thinking about as he drove home and it intruded even now.

'You better think about this and make sure it's what you want,' she said. 'Subconsciously or not, you may have been working toward this all your life. It could be the reason you are who you are. A policeman, a homicide investigator. Resolving your mother's death could also resolve your need to be a policeman. It could take your drive, your mission, away from you. You have to be prepared for that or you should turn back.'

Bosch considered what she had said to be true. He knew that all his life it had been there. What had happened to his mother had helped define everything he did after. And it was always there in the dark recesses of his mind. A promise to find out. A promise to avenge. It was never anything that had been spoken aloud or even thought about with much focus. For to have done that was to plan and this was no part of a grand agenda. Still, he was crowded with the feeling that what he was doing was inevitable, something scheduled by an unseen hand a long time ago.

His mind put Hinojos aside and focused on a memory. He was under the surface of the water, eyes open and looking up toward the light above the pool. Then, the light was eclipsed by a figure standing above, the image murky, a dark angel hovering above. Bosch kicked off the bottom and moved toward the figure.

Bosch picked up the bottle of beer and finished it in one pull. He tried to concentrate again on the newspaper clips in front of him.

He had initially been surprised at how many stories there were about Arno Conklin prior to his ascendance to the throne of the district attorney's office. But as he started to read through them he saw most of the stories were mundane dispatches from trials in which Conklin was the prosecuting attorney. Still, Bosch got somewhat of a feel for the man through the cases he tried and his style as a prosecutor. It was clear that his star rose both in the office and the public's eyes with a series of highly publicized cases.

The stories were in chronological order and the first dealt with the successful prosecution in 1953 of a woman who poisoned both her parents and then stored their bodies in trunks in the garage until neighbors complained about the smell to the police a month later. Conklin was quoted at length in several articles on the case. One time he was described as the 'dashing deputy district attorney.' The case was one of the early forerunners of the insanity defense. The woman claimed diminished capacity. But judging by the number of articles, there was a public furor over the case and the jury only took a half hour to convict. The defendant received the death penalty and Conklin's place in the public arena as a champion of public safety, a seeker of justice, was secured. There was a photo of him talking to the reporters after the verdict. The paper's earlier description of him had him down perfectly. He was a dashing man. He wore a dark three-piece suit, had short blond hair and was cleanshaven. He was lean and tall and had the ruddy, All-American look that actors pay surgeons thousands for. Arno was a star in his own right.

There were more stories about more murder cases in the clips after that first one. Conklin won every one of them. And he always asked for – and got – the death penalty. Bosch noticed that in the stories from the later fifties, he had been elevated in title to senior deputy district attorney and then by the end of the decade to assistant, one of the top jobs in the office. It was a meteoric rise to have taken place in only a decade.

There was one report on a press conference in which DA John Charles Stock announced he was placing Conklin in charge of the Special Investigations Unit and charging him with cleaning up the myriad vice problems that threatened the social fabric of Los Angeles County.

'I've always gone to Arno Conklin with the toughest jobs,' the DA said. 'And I go to him again. The people of the Los Angeles community want a clean community and, by God, we will have it. To those who know we are coming for you, my advice is, move out. San Francisco will have you. San Diego will have you. But the City of Angels won't have you!'

Following that there were several stories spread over a couple of years with splashy headlines about crackdowns on gambling parlors, pipe dens, whorehouses and the street prostitution trade. Conklin worked with a task force of forty cops comprised of loaners from all departments in the county. Hollywood was the main target of 'Conklin's Commandos,' as the *Times* dubbed the squad, but the scourge of the law came down on wrongdoers all over the county. From Long Beach to the desert, all those who labored for the wages of sin were running scared – at least according to the newspaper articles. Bosch had no doubt that the vice lords Conklin's Commandos were targeting operated business as usual and that it was only the bottom feeders, the replaceable employees, that were getting the hook.

The last Conklin story in the stack was on his February 1, 1962, announcement that he would run for the top spot in the district attorney's office on a campaign of renewed emphasis on ridding the county of the vices that threatened any great society. Bosch noted that part of the stately speech he delivered on the steps of the old downtown courthouse was a well-known police philosophy that Conklin, or his speechwriter, had apparently appropriated as original thought.

> People sometimes say to me, 'What's the big deal, Arno? These are victimless crimes. If a man wants to place a bet or sleep with a woman for money, what's wrong with that? Where's the victim?' Well, my friends, I'll tell you what's wrong with that and who the victim is. We're the victim. All of us. When we allow this kind of activity to occur, when we simply look the other way, then it weakens us all. Every one of us.
>
> I look at it this way. These so-called little crimes are each like a broken window in an abandoned house. Doesn't seem like a big problem, right? Wrong. If nobody fixes that window, pretty soon kids come along and think nobody cares. So they throw a few rocks and break a few more windows. Next, the burglar drives down the street and sees the house and thinks nobody around there cares. So he sets up shop and starts breaking into houses while the owners are at work.
>
> Next thing you know, another miscreant comes along and steals cars right off the street. And so on and so on. The residents start to see their own neighborhood with different eyes then. They think, Nobody cares anymore, so why should I? They wait an extra month before cutting the grass. They don't tell the boys hanging on the corner to put the cigarettes out and go back to school. It's gradual decay, my friends. It happens all across this great country of ours. It sneaks in like weeds in our yard. Well, when I'm district attorney the weeds are coming out by the roots.

The story ended by reporting that Conklin had chosen a young 'firebrand' from his office to manage his campaign. He said that Gordon Mittel would resign from the DA's office and begin work immediately. Bosch reread the story and immediately became transfixed by something that hadn't registered during his first read. It was in the second paragraph.

> For the well-known and not-press-shy Conklin, it will be his first run for public office. The 35-year-old bachelor and Hancock Park resident said he has planned the run for a long time and has the backing of retiring DA John Charles Stock, who also appeared at the press conference.

Bosch turned the pages of his notebook back to the list of names he had written before and wrote 'Hancock Park' after Conklin's name. It wasn't much but it was a little piece of verification of Katherine Register's story. And it was enough to get Bosch's juices going. It made him feel that at least he had a line in the water.

'Fucking hypocrite,' he whispered to himself.

He drew a circle around Conklin's name in the notebook. He absentmindedly kept circling it as he tried to decide what he should do next.

Marjorie Lowe's last known destination was a party in Hancock Park. According to Katherine Register, she was more specifically going to meet Conklin. After she was dead, Conklin had called the detectives on the case to make an appointment but any record of the interview, if any occurred, was missing. Bosch knew it was all a general correlation of facts but it served to deepen and solidify the suspicion he had felt from the night he had first looked through the murder book. Something was not right about the case. Something didn't fit. And the more he thought about it, the more he believed Conklin was the wrong piece.

He reached into his jacket, which was on the chairback behind him, and took out his small phone book. He took it into the kitchen, where he dialed the home line of Deputy District Attorney Roger Goff.

Goff was a friend who shared Bosch's affection for the tenor saxophone. They'd spent many days in court sitting side by side during trials and many nights in jazz bars side by side on stools. Goff was an old-line prosecutor who had been with the office nearly thirty years. He had no political aspirations inside or outside of the office. He just liked his job. He was a rarity because he never tired of it. A thousand deputies had come in, burned out, and gone on to corporate America during Goff's watch, but he stayed. He now labored in the criminal courts building with prosecutors and public defenders twenty years his junior. But he was still good at it and, more important, still had the fire in his voice when he stood before a jury and called down the outrage of God and society against those in the defendant's chair. His mixture of tenacity and plain fairness had made him a legend in downtown legal and law enforcement circles. And he was one of the few prosecutors Bosch had unconditional respect for.

'Roger, Harry Bosch.'

'Hey, goddamnit, how you doing?'

'I'm fine. What are you up to?'

'Watching the tube like everybody else. What're you doing?'

'Nothing. I was just thinking, you remember Gloria Jeffries?'

'Glo – shit, of course I do. Let's see. She's … yeah, she's the one with the husband got quaded in the motorcycle accident, right?'

Recalling the case, it sounded as if he were reading it off one of his yellow tablets.

'She got tired of caring for him. So one morning he's in bed and she sits on his face until she smothers him. It was about to go by as a natural but a suspicious detective named Harry Bosch wouldn't let it go. He came up with a witness who Gloria had told everything to. The clincher, the thing that got the jury, was that she told the wit that when she smothered him, it was the first orgasm the poor devil had ever been able to give her. How is that for a memory?'

'Damn, you're good.'

'So what about her?'

'She's raising up at Frontera. Getting ready to. I was wondering if you'd have time to write a letter.'

'Fuck, already? What was that, three, four years ago?'

'Almost five. I hear she's got the book now and goes to the board next month. I'll write a letter but it'd be good if there was one from the prosecutor, too.'

'Don't worry about it, I got a standard in my computer. All I do is change the name and the crime, throw in a few of the gruesome details. The basic line is that the crime was too heinous for parole to be considered at this time. It's a good letter. I'll send it out tomorrow. It usually works charms.'

'Good. Thanks.'

'You know, they gotta stop giving the book to those women. They all get religion when they're coming up. You ever go to one of those hearings?'

'A couple.'

'Yeah, sit through a half a day of them if you have the time and aren't feeling particularly suicidal sometime. They sent me out to Frontera once when one of the Manson girls was up. See, with the big ones like that they send a body out instead of a letter. So, I went out and I sat through about ten of these things waiting for my girl to come up. And let me tell you, everybody's quoting Corinthians, they're quoting Revelations, Matthew, Paul, John three-sixteen, John this, John that. And it works! It goddamn works. These old guys on the board eat that shit up. Plus I guess they're all sitting up there getting thick in their pants having all these women groveling in front of them. Anyway, you got me started, Harry. It's your fault, not mine.'

'Sorry about that.'

'It's okay. So what else is new? Haven't seen you in the building. You got anything coming my way?'

It was the question Bosch had been waiting for Goff to get to so he could nonchalantly steer the conversation toward Arno Conklin.

'Ah, nothing much. It's been slow. But, hey, let me ask you, did you know Arno Conklin?'

'Arno Conklin? Sure, I knew him. He hired me. What are you asking about him for?'

'Nothing. I was going through some old files, making room in one of the cabinets, and I came across some old newspapers. They were pushed into the back. There were some stories about him and I thought of you, thought it was about when you started.'

'Yeah, Arno, tried to be a good man. A little high and mighty for my taste, but I think he was a decent man overall. Especially considering he was both a politician and a lawyer.'

Goff laughed at his own line but Bosch was silent. Goff had used the past tense. Bosch felt a heavy presence push into his chest and he only realized then how strong the desire to avenge could be.

'He's dead?'

He closed his eyes. He hoped Goff wouldn't detect the urgency he had let slip into his voice.

'Oh, no, he's not dead. I meant, you know, when I knew him. He was a good man then.'

'He's still practicing law somewhere?'

'Oh, no. He's an old man. Retired. Once a year they wheel him out at the annual prosecutors banquet. He personally hands out the Arno Conklin Award.'

'What's that?'

'Some piece of wood with a brass plate on it that goes to the administrative prosecutor of the year, if you can believe that. That's the guy's legacy, an annual award to a so-called prosecutor who doesn't set foot inside a courtroom all year. It always goes to one of the division heads. I don't know how they decide which one. Prob'ly whoever got his or her nose farthest up the DA's ass that year.'

67

Bosch laughed. The line wasn't that funny but he was also feeling the relief of learning that Conklin was still alive.

'It's not funny, Bosch. It's fucking sad. Administrative prosecutor, whoever heard of such a thing? An oxymoron. Like Andrew and his screenplays. He deals with these studio people called, get this, creative executives. There's your classic contradiction. Well, there you go, Bosch, you got me going again.'

Bosch knew Andrew was Goff's roommate but he had never met him.

'Sorry, Roger. Anyway, what do you mean, they wheel him out?'

'Arno? Well, I mean they wheel him out. He's in a chair. I told you, he's an old man. Last I heard he was in some full-care retirement home. One of the classy ones in Park La Brea. I keep saying I'm going to see him one day, thank him for hiring me way back when. Who knows, maybe I could put in a word for that award or something.'

'Funny guy. You know, I heard that Gordon Mittel used to be his frontman.'

'Oh, yeah, he was the bulldog outside the door. Ran his campaigns. That's how Mittel got started. Now that's one mean – I'm glad he got out of criminal law and into politics, he'd be a motherfucker to come up against in court.'

'Yeah, I've heard,' Bosch said.

'Whatever you've heard, you can double it.'

'You know him?'

'Not now and not then. I just knew to keep clear. He was already out of the office by the time I came in. But there were stories. Supposedly in those early days, when Arno was the heir apparent and everybody knew it, there was a lot of maneuvering. You know, to get next to him. There was one guy, Sinclair I think his name was, that was set to run Arno's campaign. Then one night the cleaning lady found some porno shots under his blotter. There was an internal investigation and the photos proved to be stolen from another prosecutor's case files. Sinclair was dumped. He always claimed he was set up by Mittel.'

'Think he was?'

'Yes. It was Mittel's style . . . But who knows.'

Bosch sensed that he had said and asked enough to pass it off as conversation and gossip. Anything further and Goff might get suspicious about the call.

'So what's the deal?' he asked. 'You zipped up for the night or you want to go by the Catalina? I heard Redman's in town to do Leno. I'd bet you the cover charge that he and Branford drop by to sit in on the late set.'

'Sounds tempting, Harry, but Andrew's making a late dinner now and I think we're just going to stay at home tonight. He's counting on it. You mind?'

'Not at all. Anyway, I'm trying not to bend the elbow so much lately. I need to give it a rest.'

'Now that, sir, is quite admirable. I think you deserve a piece of wood with a brass plate on it.'

'Or a shot of whiskey.'

After hanging up Bosch sat back down at the desk and wrote notes on the highlights of the conversation with Goff into his notebook. Next he pulled the stack of clips on Mittel in front of him. These were more recent clips than those on Conklin because Mittel had not made a name for himself until much later. Conklin had been his first step up the ladder.

Most of the stories were just mentions of Mittel as being in attendance at various galas in Beverly Hills or as host of various campaign or charity dinners. From the start he was a money man, a man politicians and charities went to when they wanted to cast their nets into the rich enclaves of the Westside. He worked both sides, Republican, Democrat, it didn't seem to matter. His profile grew, though, when he started working for candidates on a larger scale. The current governor was a client. So, too, were a handful of congressman and senators from other western states.

A profile written several years earlier – and apparently without his cooperation – ran under the headline THE PRESIDENT'S MAIN MONEY MAN. It said Mittel had been tapped to round up California contributors for the president's reelection war chest. It said the state was one of the cornerstones of the national campaign's funding plan.

The story also noted the irony that Mittel was a recluse in the high-profile world of politics. He was a backstage man who abhorred the spotlight. So much so that he had repeatedly turned down patronage jobs from those he'd helped elect.

Instead, Mittel elected to stay in Los Angeles, where he was the founding partner of a powerful financial district law firm, Mittel, Anderson, Jennings & Rountree. Still, it seemed to Bosch that what this Yale-educated lawyer did had little to do with law as Bosch knew it. He doubted Mittel had been inside a courtroom in years. That made Harry think of the Conklin award and he smiled. Too bad Mittel had quit the DA's office. He might've been in line for it someday.

There was a photo that ran with the profile. It showed Mittel at the bottom of the steps of Air Force One greeting the then president at LAX. Though the article had been published years earlier, Bosch was nevertheless startled by how young Mittel was in the photo. He looked at the story again and checked the man's age. Doing the arithmetic, he realized that currently Mittel was barely sixty years old.

Bosch pushed the newspaper clips aside and got up. For a long time he stood at the sliding glass door to the deck and stared at the lights across the pass. He began to consider what he knew about circumstances thirty-three years old. Conklin, according to Katherine Register, knew Marjorie Lowe. It was clear from the murder book that he had somehow reached into the investigation of her death for reasons unknown. His reach was then apparently covered up for reasons unknown. This had occurred only three months before he announced his candidacy for district attorney and less than a year before a key figure in the investigation, Johnny Fox, died while in his political employ.

Bosch thought that it was obvious that Fox would have been known to Mittel, the campaign manager. Therefore, he further concluded, whatever it was that Conklin did or knew, it was likely that Mittel, his frontman and the architect of his political run, had knowledge of it as well.

Bosch went back to the table and turned to the list of names in his notebook. Now he picked up the pen and circled Mittel's name as well. He felt like having another beer but he settled for a cigarette.

14

In the morning Bosch called the LAPD personnel office and asked them to check whether Eno and McKittrick were still current. He doubted they were still around but knew he had to make the check. It would be embarrassing if he went through a search for them only to find one or both still on the payroll. The clerk checked the roll and told him no such officers were currently on the force.

He decided he would have to put on his Harvey Pounds pose after that. He dialed the DMV in Sacramento, gave the lieutenant's name and asked for Ms Sharp again. By the tone she inflected in the single word 'Hello' after picking up the phone, Bosch had no doubt that she remembered him.

'Is this Ms Sharp?'

'That's who you asked for, isn't it?'

'I did, indeed.'

'Then it's Ms Sharp. What can I do for you?'

'Well, I wanted to mend our fences, so to speak. I have a few more names I need driver's license addresses for and I thought that directly working with you would expedite the matter and perhaps repair our working relationship.'

'Honey, we don't have a working relationship. Hold the line, please.'

She punched the button before he could say anything. The line was dead for so long that he began to believe his scam to burn Pounds wasn't worth it. Finally, a different clerk picked up and said Ms Sharp had instructed her to help. Bosch gave her Pounds's serial number and then the names Gordon Mittel, Arno Conklin, Claude Eno and Jake McKittrick. He said he needed the home addresses on their licenses.

He was put on hold again. During the time he waited he held the phone to his ear with his shoulder and fried an egg over easy in a pan on the stove. He made a sandwich out of it with two slices of white toast and cold salsa from a jar he kept in the refrigerator. He ate the dripping sandwich while leaning over the sink. He had just wiped his mouth and poured himself a second cup of coffee when the clerk finally picked back up.

'Sorry it took so long.'

'No problem.'

He then remembered he was Pounds and wished he hadn't said that.

The clerk explained that she had no addresses or license information on Eno or McKittrick, then gave him addresses for Conklin and Mittel. Goff had been right. Conklin lived in Park La Brea. Mittel lived above Hollywood on Hercules Drive in a development called Mount Olympus.

Bosch was too preoccupied at that point to continue the Pounds charade. He thanked the clerk without further confrontation and hung up. He thought about what his next move should be. Eno and McKittrick were either dead or out of state. He knew he could get their addresses through the department's personnel office but that might take all day. He picked up the phone again and called Robbery-Homicide, asking for Detective Leroy Ruben. Ruben had put nearly forty years in on the department, half of it in RHD. He might know something about Eno and McKittrick. He might also know Bosch was on stress leave.

'Ruben, can I help you?'

'Leroy, it's Harry Bosch. What do you know?'

'Not much, Harry. Enjoying the good life?'

Right away he was telling Bosch he knew of his situation. Bosch knew now that his only alternative was to be straight with him. To a point.

'It ain't bad. But I'm not sleeping late every day.'

'No? What're you getting up for?'

'I'm kind've freelancing on an old case, Leroy. That's why I called. I want to try to track down a couple of old dicks. Thought maybe you'd know of them. They were out of Hollywood.'

'Who are they?'

'Claude Eno and Jake McKittrick. Remember them?'

'Eno and McKittrick. No . . . I mean, yeah, I think I remember McKittrick. He checked out . . . it must've been ten, fifteen years ago. He went back to Florida, I think. Yeah, Florida. He was here in RHD for a year or so. At the end there. The other one, Eno, I don't remember any Eno.'

'Well, it was worth a try. I'll see what I can find in Florida. Thanks, Leroy.'

'Hey, Harry, what gives anyway?'

'It's just an old case I had in my desk. It's giving me something to do while I see what happens.'

'Any word?'

'Not yet. They got me talking to the shrink. If I can talk my way past her, I'll get back to the table. We'll see.'

'Okay, well, good luck. You know, me and some of the boys here, when we heard that story we laughed our asses off. We heard about that guy Pounds. He's an asshole. You done good, kid.'

'Well, let's hope I didn't do so good that I lost my job.'

'Ah, you'll be all right. They send you to Chinatown a few times, brush you off and send you back into the ring. You'll be okay.'

'Thanks, Leroy.'

After hanging up, Bosch got dressed for the day, putting on a fresh shirt and the same suit as the day before.

He headed downtown in his rented Mustang and spent the next two hours in a bureaucratic maze. He first went to the Personnel Office at Parker Center, told a clerk what he wanted and then waited half an hour for a supervisor to tell him all over again. The supervisor told him he had wasted his time and that the information he sought was at City Hall.

· He walked across the street to the City Hall annex, took the stairs up and then crossed on the tramway over Main Street into the white obelisk of City

71

Hall. He took the elevator up to the Finance Department, on nine, showed his ID card to another counter clerk and told her that, in the interest of streamlining the process, maybe he should talk to a supervisor first.

He waited on a plastic chair in a hallway for twenty minutes before he was ushered into a small office cramped with two desks, four file cabinets and several boxes on the floor. An obese woman with pale skin and black hair, sideburns and the slight hint of a mustache sat behind one of the desks. On her calendar blotter Bosch noticed a food stain from some prior mishap. There was also a reusable plastic quart soda container with a screw-on top and straw on her desk. A plastic name plate on the desk said Mona Tozzi.

'I'm Carla's supervisor. She said you are a police officer?'

'Detective.'

He pulled the chair away from the empty desk and sat down in front of the fat woman.

'Excuse me, but Cassidy is probably going to need her chair when she gets back. That's her desk.'

'When's she coming back?'

'Anytime. She went up for coffee.'

'Well, maybe if we hurry we'll be done by then and I'll be out of here.'

She gave a short who-do-you-think-you-are laugh that sounded more like a snort. She said nothing.

'I've spent the last hour and a half trying to get just a couple addresses from the city and all I get are a bunch of people who want to send me to someone else or make me wait out in the hall. And what's funny about that is that I work for the city myself and I'm trying to do a job for the city and the city isn't giving me the time of day. And, you know, my shrink tells me I've got this post-traumatic stress stuff and should take life easier. But, Mona, I gotta tell you, I'm getting pretty fucking frustrated with this.'

She stared at him a moment, probably wondering if she could possibly make it out the door if he decided to go nuts on her. She then pursed her lips, which served to change her mustache from a hint to an announcement, and took a hard pull on the straw of her soda container. Bosch saw a liquid the color of blood go up through the straw into her mouth. She cleared her throat before talking in a comforting tone.

'Tell you what, Detective, why don't you tell me what it is you are trying to find?'

Bosch put on his hopeful face.

'Great. I knew there was somebody who cared. I need to get the addresses where pension checks for two different retired officers are sent each month.'

Her eyebrows mated as she frowned.

'I'm sorry, but those addresses are strictly confidential. Even within the city. I couldn't give –'

'Mona, let me explain something. I'm a homicide investigator. Like you, I work for the city. I have leads on an old unsolved murder that I am following up on. I need to confer with the original case detectives. We're talking about a case more than thirty years old. A woman was killed, Mona. I can't find the two detectives that originally worked the case and the police personnel people sent me over here. I need the pension addresses. Are you going to help me?'

'Detective – is it Borsch?'

'Bosch.'

'Detective Bosch, let me explain something to you. Just because you work for the city does not give you access to confidential files. I work for the city but I don't go over to Parker Center and say let me see this or let me see that. People have a right to privacy. Now, this is what I can do. And it is all I can do. If you give me the two names, I will send a letter to each person asking them to call you. That way, you get your information, I protect the files. Would that work for you? They'll go out in the mail today. I promise.'

She smiled but it was the phoniest smile Bosch had seen in days.

'No, that wouldn't work at all, Mona. You know, I'm really disappointed.'

'I can't help that.'

'But you can, don't you see?'

'I have work to do, Detective. If you want me to send the letter, give me the names. If not, that's your decision.'

He nodded that he understood and brought his briefcase up from the floor to his lap. He saw her jump when he angrily unsnapped the locks. He opened it and took out his phone. He flipped it open and dialed his home number, then waited for the machine to pick up.

Mona looked annoyed.

'What are you doing?'

He held his hand up for silence.

'Yes, can you transfer me to Whitey Springer?' he said to his tape.

He watched her reaction while acting like he wasn't. He could tell, she knew the name. Springer was the City Hall columnist for the *Times*. His specialty was writing about the small bureaucratic nightmares, the little guy against the system. Bureaucrats could largely create these nightmares with impunity, thanks to civil service protections, but politicians read Springer's column and they wielded tremendous power when it came to patronage jobs, transfers and demotions at City Hall. A bureaucrat vilified in print by Springer might be safe in his or her job but there likely would never be advancement, and there was nothing stopping a city council member from calling for an audit on an office or a council observer to sit in the corner. The word to the wise was to stay out of Springer's column. Everybody knew that, including Mona.

'Yeah, I can hold,' Bosch said into the phone. Then to Mona, he said, 'He's gonna love this one. He's got a guy trying to solve a murder, the victim's family waiting for thirty-three years to know who killed her, and some bureaucrat sitting in her office sucking on a quart of fruit punch isn't giving him the addresses he needs just to talk to the other cops who worked the case. I'm not a newspaper man but I think that's a column. He'll love it. What do you think?'

He smiled and watched her face flush almost as red as her fruit punch. He knew it was going to work.

'Okay, hang up the phone,' she said.

'What? Why?'

'HANG UP! Hang up and I'll get the information.'

Bosch flipped the phone closed.

'Give me the names.'

He gave her the names and she got up angrily and silently to leave the room. She could barely fit around the desk but made the maneuver like a ballerina, the pattern instilled in her body's memory by repeated practice.

'How long will this take?' he asked.

'As long as it takes,' she answered, regaining some of her bureaucratic bluster at the door.

'No, Mona, you got ten minutes. That's all. After that, you better not come back 'cause Whitey's gonna be sitting here waiting for you.'

She stopped and looked at him. He winked.

After she left he got up and went around the side of the desk. He pushed it about two inches closer to the opposite wall, narrowing her path back to her chair.

She was back in seven minutes, carrying a piece of paper. But Bosch could see it was trouble. She had a triumphant look on her face. He thought of that woman who had been tried a while back for cutting off her husband's penis. Maybe it was the same face she had when she ran out the door with it.

'Well, Detective Borsch, you've got a little problem.'

'What is it?'

She started around the desk and immediately rammed her thick thigh into its Formica-topped corner. It looked more embarrassing than painful. She had to flail her arms for balance and the impact of the collision shook the desk and knocked her container over. The red liquid began leaking out of the straw onto the blotter.

'Shit!'

She quickly moved the rest of the way around the desk and righted the container. Before sitting down she looked at the desk, suspicious that it had been moved.

'Are you all right?' Bosch asked. 'What is the problem with the addresses?'

She ignored his first question, forgot her embarrassment and looked at Bosch and smiled. She sat down. She spoke as she opened a desk drawer and took out a wad of napkins stolen from the cafeteria.

'Well, the problem is you won't be talking to former detective Claude Eno anytime soon. At least, I don't think you will.'

'He's dead.'

She started wiping up the spill.

'Yes. The checks go to his widow.'

'What about McKittrick?'

'Now McKittrick is a possibility. I have his address here. He's over in Venice.'

'Venice? So what's the problem with that?'

'That's Venice, Florida.'

She smiled, delighted with herself.

'Florida,' Bosch repeated.

He had no idea there was a Venice in Florida.

'It's a state, over on the other side of the country.'

'I know where it is.'

'Oh, and one other thing. The address I have is only a P.O. box. Sorry about that.'

'Yeah, I bet. What about a phone?'

She tossed the wet napkins into a trash can in the corner of the room.

'We have no phone number. Try information.'

'I will. Does it say there when he retired?'

'You didn't ask me to get that.'

'Then give me what you've got.'

Bosch knew he could get more, that they'd have to have a phone number somewhere, but he was handicapped because this was an unauthorized investigation. If he pushed things too far, then he'd only succeed in having his activities discovered and then halted.

She floated the paper across the desk to him. He looked at it. It had two addresses on it, the P.O. box for McKittrick and the street address in Las Vegas for Eno's widow. Her name was Olive.

Bosch thought of something.

'When do the checks go out?'

'Funny you should ask.'

'Why?'

'Because today's the last day of the month. They always go out the last day of the month.'

That was a break and he felt like he deserved it, that he had worked for it. He picked up the paper she had given him and slipped it into his briefcase, then he stood up.

'Always a pleasure to do work with the public servants of the city.'

'Likewise. And, uh, Detective? Could you return the chair to the place you found it? As I said, Cassidy will need it.'

'Of course, Mona. Pardon my forgetfulness.'

15

After the bout with bureaucratic claustrophobia, Bosch decided he needed some air to recover. He took the elevator down to the lobby and out the main doors to Spring Street. As he walked out, he was directed by a security officer to walk down the right side of the wide-staired entrance to the great building because there was a film location shoot taking place on the left side. Bosch watched what they were doing as he stepped down the stairs and then decided to take a break and have a smoke.

He sat down on one of the concrete sidings along the stairs and lit a cigarette. The film shoot involved a group of actors posing as reporters who rushed down the stairs of City Hall to meet and question two men getting out of a car at the curb. They rehearsed it twice and then shot it twice while Bosch sat there and smoked two cigarettes. Each time, the reporters all yelled the same thing at the two men.

'Mr Barrs, Mr Barrs, did you do it? Did you do it?'

The two men refused to answer and pushed through the pack and up the stairs with the reporters backtracking. On one of the takes one of the reporters stumbled as he moved backwards, fell on his back on the stairs and was partially trampled by the others. The director kept the scene going, perhaps thinking that the fall added a touch of realism to the scene.

Bosch figured that the filmmakers were using the steps and front facade of City Hall as a courthouse setting. The men coming from the car were the defendant and his high-priced lawyer. He knew that City Hall was frequently used for such shots because it actually looked more like a courthouse than any real courthouse in the city.

Bosch was bored after the second take, though he guessed there would be many more. He got up and walked down to First and then over to Los Angeles Street. He took that back to Parker Center. Along the way he was asked for spare change only four times, which he thought was a low count for downtown and possibly a sign of improving economic times. In the lobby of the police building he passed the bank of pay phones and on a whim stopped, picked one of the phones off the hook and dialed 305–555–1212. He had dealt with Metro-Dade Police in Miami several times over the years and 305 was the only Florida area code that readily came to mind. When the operator came on he asked for Venice and she informed him that 813 was the proper area code.

He then redialed and got information in Venice. First he asked the operator what the nearest large city to Venice was. She told him that was

Sarasota and he asked what the nearest large city was to that. When she said St Petersburg, he finally started getting his bearings. He knew where St Petersburg was on a map – the west coast of Florida – because he knew the Dodgers occasionally played spring training games there and he had looked it up once.

He finally gave the operator McKittrick's name and promptly got a tape recording saying the number was unlisted at the customer's request. He wondered if any of the detectives he had dealt with by phone at Metro-Dade could get the number for him. He still had no idea exactly where Venice was or how far it was from Miami. Then he decided to leave it alone. McKittrick had taken steps to make it difficult to be contacted. He used a P.O. box and had an unlisted phone. Bosch didn't know why a retired cop would take such steps in a state three thousand miles away from where he had worked but he felt sure that the best approach to McKittrick was going to have to be in person. A telephone call, even if Bosch got the number, was easy to avoid. Someone standing right at your door was different. Besides, Bosch had caught a break; he knew McKittrick's pension check was in the mail to his P.O. box. He was sure he could use it to find the old cop.

He clipped his ID card to his suit and went up to the Scientific Investigation Division. He told the woman behind the counter that he had to talk to someone in Latent Prints and pushed through the half door and down the hall to the print lab like he always did, without waiting for her go-ahead.

The lab was a large room with two rows of work tables with overhead fluorescent lights. At the end of the room were two desks with AFIS computer terminals on them. Behind them was a glass-walled room with the mainframes inside. There was condensation on the glass because the mainframe room was kept cooler than the rest of the lab.

Because it was lunch time there was only one technician in the lab and Bosch didn't know him. He was tempted to turn around and come back later when someone else might be there, but the tech looked up from one of the computer terminals and saw him. He was a tall, skinny man with glasses and a face that had been ravaged by acne when he was younger. The damage gave him a permanently sullen expression.

'Yes?'

'Yeah, hi, howya doin'?'

'I'm doing fine. What can I do for you?'

'Harry Bosch, Hollywood Division.'

He put out his hand and the other man hesitated, then shook it tentatively.

'Brad Hirsch.'

'Yeah, I think I've heard your name. We've never worked together but that probably won't last. I work homicide so it seems I basically get around to working with everybody in here eventually.'

'Probably.'

Bosch sat down on a chair to the side of the computer module and pulled his briefcase onto his lap. He noticed that Hirsch was looking into his blue computer screen. He seemed more comfortable looking there than at Bosch.

'Reason I'm here is, at the moment, it's kind of slow out in Tinseltown.

77

And so I've been going through some old cases. I came across this one from nineteen sixty-one.'

'Nineteen sixty-one?'

'Yeah, it's old. A female . . . cause of death blunt force trauma, then he made it look like a strangulation, a sex crime. Anyway, nobody was ever popped for it. It never went anywhere. In fact, I don't think anyone's really looked at it since the due diligence in sixty-two. A long time. Anyway, the thing is, the reason I'm here, is that back then the cops on this pulled a decent set of prints at the crime scene. They got a bunch of partials and some full rounds. And I've got them here.'

Bosch took the yellowed print card out of the briefcase and held it out to the man. Hirsch looked at it but didn't take it. He looked back at the computer screen and Bosch placed the print card down on the keyboard in front of him.

'And, well, as you know, that was before we had these fancy computers and all of this technology you got here. All they did with this back then was use it to compare these to a suspect's prints. They got no match, they let the guy go and then they just shoved these in an envelope. They've been sitting in the case file ever since. So what I was thinking was, we could –'

'You want to run them through AFIS.'

'Yeah, right. You know, take a shot at it. Spin the dice, maybe we get lucky and pick up a hitchhiker on the information highway. It's happened before. Edgar and Burns out on the Hollywood table nailed an old one this week with an AFIS run. I was talking to Edgar and he said one of you guys down here – I think it was Donovan – said the computer has access to millions of prints from all across the country.'

Hirsch nodded unenthusiastically.

'And that's not just criminal print files, right?' Bosch asked. 'You've got military, law enforcement, civil service, everything. That right?'

'Yes, that's right. But, look, Detective Bosch, we –'

'Harry.'

'Okay, Harry. This is a great tool that's getting better all the time. You're correct about that but there still are human and time elements here. The comparison prints have to be scanned and coded and then those codes have to be entered into the computer. And right now we have a backup that's running twelve days.'

He pointed to the wall above the computer. There was a sign with changeable numbers on it. Like the signs in the union office that said X number of days since the last death in the line of duty.

AUTOMATED FINGERPRINT IDENTIFICATION SYSTEM
Search Requests Will Take 12 Days To Process
No Exception!

'So, you see, we can't take everybody who walks in here and put them at the front of the pack, okay? Now if you want to fill out a search request form, I can –'

'Look, I know there are exceptions. Especially in homicide cases. Somebody made that run for Burns and Edgar the other day. They didn't wait twelve days. They were put through right away and they cleared three homicides just like that.'

Bosch snapped his fingers. Hirsch looked at him and then back to the computer.

'Yes, there are exceptions. But that comes from on high. If you want to talk to Captain LeValley, maybe she'll approve it. If you –'

'Burns and Edgar didn't talk to her. Somebody just did it for them.'

'Well, then that was against the rules. They must have known somebody who did it for them.'

'Well, I know you, Hirsch.'

'Why don't you just fill out a request and I'll see what –'

'I mean, what's it take, ten minutes?'

'No. In your case much longer. This print card you have is an antique. It's obsolete. I'd have to run it through the Livescan machine, which would then assign codes to the prints. Then I'd have to hand-enter the codes it gives me. Then depending on the restrictions on the run you want, it could take –'

'I don't want any restrictions. I want it compared to all data bases.'

'Then the computer time can run as long as thirty, forty minutes.'

With a finger Hirsch punched his glasses back up his nose as if punctuating his resolve not to break the rules.

'Well, Brad,' Bosch said, 'the problem is I don't know how much time I've got on this. Certainly not twelve days. No way. I'm working on it now because I have the time, but the next time I get a fresh call that will be it, I'll be off it. That's the nature of homicide, you know? So, are you sure there isn't something we can do right now?'

Hirsch didn't move. He just stared at the blue screen. It reminded Bosch of the youth hall, when kids would literally shut down like a computer on standby when the bullies taunted them.

'What are you doing now, Hirsch? We could do it right now.'

Hirsch looked at him for a long moment before talking.

'I'm busy. And look, Bosch, I know who you are, okay? That's an interesting story about pulling old cases but I know it's a lie. I know you're on a stress leave. The story's getting around. And you shouldn't even be here and I shouldn't be talking to you. So, could you please leave me alone? I don't want to get into trouble. I don't want people to get the wrong idea, you know?'

Bosch looked at him but Hirsch's eyes had moved back onto the computer screen.

'Okay, Hirsch, let me tell you a real story. One –'

'I really don't want any more stories, Bosch. Why don't you just –'

'I'm going to tell you this story, then I'm leaving, okay? Just this one story.'

'Okay, Bosch, okay. You tell the story.'

Bosch looked at him silently and waited for Hirsch to make eye contact but the latent print technician's eyes remained on the computer screen as if it were his security blanket. Bosch told the story anyway.

'One time, a long time ago, I was almost twelve and I'm swimming in this pool, you see, and I'm under the water but I've got my eyes open. And I look up and I see up through the water up to the edge of the pool. I see this dark figure. You know, it was hard to figure out what it was, all wavy and all. But I could tell it was a man and there wasn't supposed to be a man up there. So I came up for air at the side of the pool and I was right. It was a man. He was wearing this dark suit. And he reached down and grabbed me by the wrist. I was just a scrawny little runt. It was easy for him to do. He pulled me out and he gave me this towel to put on my shoulders and he led me over to a chair and he told me . . . he told me that my mother was dead. Murdered. He said they didn't know who did it, but whoever he was, he left his fingerprints. He said, "Don't worry, son, we got the fingerprints and they're as good as gold. We'll get him." I remember those words exactly. "We'll get him." Only they never did. And now I'm going to. That's my story, Hirsch.'

Hirsch's eyes dropped down to the yellowed print card on the keyboard.

'Look, man, it's a bad story, but I can't be doing this. I'm sorry.'

Bosch stared at him a moment and then slowly stood up.

'Don't forget the card,' Hirsch said.

He picked it up and held it up to Bosch.

'I'll leave it here. You're going to do the right thing, Hirsch. I can tell.'

'No, don't. I can't do –'

'I'm leaving it here!'

The power of his voice shocked even Bosch and it seemed to have scared Hirsch. The print tech replaced the card on the keyboard. After a few seconds of silence Bosch leaned down and spoke quietly.

'Everybody wants the chance to do the right thing, Hirsch. It makes them feel good inside. Even if doing it doesn't exactly fit inside the rules, sometimes you have to rely on the voice inside that tells you what to do.'

Bosch stood back up and took out his wallet and a pen. He pulled out a business card and wrote some numbers on it. He put it down on the keyboard next to the print card.

'That's got my portable and my home on it. Don't bother calling the office, you know I won't be there. I'll be waiting to hear from you, Hirsch.'

He walked slowly out of the lab.

16

Waiting for the elevator, Bosch guessed that his effort to persuade Hirsch had fallen on deaf ears. Hirsch was the type of guy whose exterior scars masked deeper interior wounds. There were a lot in the department like him. Hirsch had grown up intimidated by his own face. He'd probably be the last person to dare go outside the bounds of his job or the rules. Another department automaton. For him, doing the right thing was ignoring Bosch. Or turning him in.

He punched at the elevator button with his finger again and contemplated what else he could do. The AFIS search was a long shot but he still wanted it done. It was a loose end and any thorough investigation took care of loose ends. He decided he would give Hirsch a day and then he'd make another run at him. If that didn't work, he'd try another tech. He'd try them all until he got the killer's prints into that machine.

The elevator finally opened and he squeezed on. That was one of the only things you could rely on inside Parker Center. Cops would come and go, chiefs, even political power structures, but the elevators would always move slowly and always be crowded when they got to you. Bosch pushed the unlighted button marked B as the doors slowly closed and the square room started to descend. While everyone stood and stared blankly at the lighted numbers over the door, Bosch looked down at his briefcase. No one in the small space spoke. Until, as the car slowed to its next stop, Bosch heard his first name spoken from behind. He turned his head slightly, not sure if it had been someone speaking to him or the name had been directed toward someone else.

His eyes fell on Assistant Chief Irvin S. Irving standing in the rear of the elevator. They exchanged nods just as the doors opened on the first floor. Bosch wondered if Irving had seen him push the button for the basement. There was no reason for a man on involuntary stress leave to be going to the basement.

Bosch decided the car was too crowded for Irving to have seen what button he had pushed. He stepped off the elevator into the alcove off the main lobby and Irving followed him out and caught up with him.

'Chief.'

'What brings you all the way in, Harry?'

It was said casually but the question signaled that there was more than passing interest from Irving. They started walking toward the exit, Bosch quickly putting a story together.

'I have to go over to Chinatown anyway, so I dropped by to go to payroll. I wanted to see about them sending my check to my house instead of out to Hollywood, since I'm not sure when I'll be back.'

Irving nodded and Bosch was pretty sure he had bought it. He was about Bosch's size but had the stand-out feature of a completely shaved head. That feature and his reputation for intolerance for corrupt cops got him the nickname within the department of Mr Clean.

'You're in Chinatown today? I thought you were Monday, Wednesday, Friday. That was the schedule I approved.'

'Yes, that's the schedule. But she had an opening come up today and wanted me to come in.'

'Well, I'm glad to hear you being so cooperative. What happened to your hand?'

'Oh, this?' Bosch held up his hand as if it were someone else's that he had just noticed at the end of his arm. 'I've been using some of my free time to do some work around the house and I cut it on a piece of broken glass. I'm still doing clean-up from the quake.'

'I see.'

Bosch guessed that he didn't buy that one. But he didn't really care.

'I'm getting a quick lunch in the federal plaza,' Irving said. 'You want to come along?'

'Thanks just the same, Chief. I already ate.'

'Okay, well, take care of yourself. I mean that.'

'I will. Thanks.'

Irving started off and then stopped.

'You know, we're handling this situation with you a little differently because I hope to get you back in there at Hollywood homicide without any change in grade or position. I'm waiting to hear from Dr Hinojos but I understand it will be a few more weeks, at least.'

'That's what she tells me.'

'You know, if you're willing to do it, an apology in the form of a letter to Lieutenant Pounds could be beneficial. When push comes to shove, I'm going to have to sell him on letting you back in there. That will be the hard part. I think getting you a clean bill from the doctor won't be a problem. I can simply issue the order and Lieutenant Pounds will have to accept it, but that won't ease the pressure there. I would rather work it that he accepts your return and everybody's happy.'

'Well, I heard he already's got a replacement for me.'

'Pounds?'

'He paired my partner with somebody off autos. Doesn't sound to me like he's expecting or planning on me coming back, Chief.'

'Well, that's news to me. I'll talk to him about that. What do you think about this letter? It could go a long way toward helping your situation.'

Bosch hesitated before answering. He knew Irving wanted to help him. The two of them shared an unspoken bond. Once they had been complete enemies in the department. But contempt had eroded into a truce which now was more a line of wary mutual respect.

'I'll think about the letter, Chief,' Bosch finally said. 'I'll let you know.'

'Very well. You know, Harry, pride gets in the way of a lot of the right decisions. Don't let that happen to you.'

'I'll think about it.'

Bosch watched him bound off around the fountain memorial to officers killed in the line of duty. He watched until Irving got to Temple and started to cross Los Angeles Street to the federal plaza, where there was an array of fast-food emporiums. Then Bosch figured it was safe and turned to go back inside.

He skipped waiting for the elevator again and went down the stairs to the basement.

Most of the underground floor of Parker Center was taken up by the Evidence Storage Division. There were a few other offices, like the Fugitives Division, but it was generally a quiet floor. Bosch found no pedestrian traffic on the long yellow linoleum hallway and was able to get to the steel double doors of ESD without running into anyone else he knew.

The police department held physical evidence on investigations that had not yet gone to the district attorney or city attorney for filing. Once that happened, the evidence usually stayed with the prosecutor's office.

Essentially, that made ESD the city's temple of failure. What was behind the steel doors Bosch opened was the physical evidence from thousands of unsolved crimes. Crimes that had never resulted in prosecution. It even smelled of failure. Because it was in the basement of the building, there was a damp odor here that Bosch always believed was the rank stink of neglect and decay. Of hopelessness.

Bosch stepped into a small room that was essentially a wire-mesh cage. There was another door on the other side but there was a sign on it that said ESD STAFF ONLY. There were two windows cut in the mesh. One was closed and a uniform officer sat behind the other working on a crossword puzzle. Between the two windows was another sign that said DO NOT STORE LOADED FIREARMS. Bosch walked up to the open window and leaned on the counter. The officer looked up after filling in a word on the puzzle. Bosch saw the name tag on his uniform said Nelson. Nelson read Bosch's ID card so Bosch didn't have to bother to introduce himself, either. It worked out nicely.

'Her . . . on – how you say that?'

'Hieronymus. Rhymes with anonymous.'

'Hieronymus. Isn't there a rock and roll band named that?'

'Maybe.'

'What can I do for you, Hieronymus from Hollywood?'

'I got a question.'

'Shoot.'

Bosch put the pink evidence check slip on the counter.

'I want to pull the box on this case. It's pretty old. Would it still be around anywhere?'

The cop took the slip, looked at it and whistled when he saw the year. While writing the case number down on a request log, he said, 'Should be here. Don't see why not. Nothing gets tossed, you know. You want to look at the Black Dahlia case, we got that. That's what, fifty-something years old. We got 'em going back even further. If it ain't solved, it's here.'

He looked up at Bosch and winked.

'Be right back. Why don't you fill out the form.'

Nelson pointed with his pen out the window to a counter on the back wall where the standard request forms were. He got up and disappeared from the window. Bosch heard him yell to someone else in the back.

'Charlie! Hey, Char-LEE!'

A voice from somewhere in the back yelled a response that was unintelligible.

'Take the window,' Nelson called back. 'I'm taking the time machine.'

Bosch had heard about the time machine. It was a golf cart they used to get back to the deep recesses of the storage facility. The older the case, the farther back in time it went, the farther away it was from the front windows. The time machine got the window cops back there.

Bosch walked over to the counter and filled out a request form, then reached in the window and put it on the crossword puzzle. While he was waiting, he looked around and noticed another sign on the back wall. NARCOTICS EVIDENCE NOT RELEASED WITHOUT 492 FORM. Bosch had no idea what that form was. Somebody came through the steel doors then carrying a murder book. A detective, but Bosch didn't recognize him. He opened it on the counter, got a case number and then filled out a form. He then went to the window. There was no sign of Charlie. After a few minutes, the detective turned to Bosch.

'Anybody working back there?'

'Yeah, one guy went to get me a box. He told another guy to watch. I don't know where he is.'

'Shit.'

He rapped sharply with his knuckles on the counter. In a few minutes another uniform cop came to the window. He was an old horse, with white hair and a pear shape. Bosch guessed he'd been working in the basement for years. His skin was as white as a vampire's. He took the other detective's evidence request slip and was gone. Then both Bosch and the other detective were left waiting. Bosch could tell the other man had started looking at him but was acting like he wasn't.

'You're Bosch, right?' he finally asked. 'From Hollywood?'

Bosch nodded. The other man put out his hand and smiled.

'Tom North, Pacific. We've never met.'

'No.'

Bosch shook his hand but didn't act enthusiastic about the introduction.

'We never met but listen, I worked Devonshire burglary for six years before I got my homicide gig in Pacific. Know who my CO was up there back then?'

Bosch shook his head. He didn't know and he didn't care but North didn't seem to realize that.

'Pounds. Lieutenant Harvey "Ninety-eight" Pounds. The fuck. He was my CO. So, anyway, I heard through the network, you know, what you did to his ass. Put his face right through the fuckin' window. That's great, man, fuckin' great. More power to you. I laughed my ass off when I heard that.'

'Well, I'm glad it entertained you.'

'No, really, I know you're getting piped for it. I heard about that, too. But I just wanted to let you know you made my day and a lot of people are with you, man.'

'Thanks.'

'So what are you doing down here? I heard they had you on the Fifty-One-Fifty list.'

It annoyed Bosch to realize that there were those in the department whom he didn't even know who knew what had happened to him and what his situation was. He tried to keep calm.

'Listen, I –'

'Bosch! You gotta box!'

It was the time traveler, Nelson. He was at the window, pushing a light blue box through the opening. It was about the size of a boot box and was held closed with red tape that was cracking with age. It looked like the box was powdered with dust. Bosch didn't bother finishing his sentence. He waved off North and went to the box.

'Sign here,' Nelson said.

He put a yellow slip down on top of the box. It kicked up a small dust cloud, which he waved away with his hand. Bosch signed the paper and took the box in two hands. He turned and saw North looking at him. North just nodded once. He seemed to know it wasn't the right time to ask questions. Bosch nodded back and headed to the door.

'Uh, Bosch?' North said. 'I didn't mean anything about what I said. About the list. No offense, okay?'

Bosch stared at him as he pushed through the door with his back. But he didn't say anything. He then proceeded down the hall carrying the box with two hands, as if it contained something precious.

17

Carmen Hinojos was in her waiting room when Bosch got there a few minutes late. She ushered him in and waved off his apology for lateness as if it was unnecessary. She wore a dark blue suit and as he passed her in the doorway he smelled a light soapy fragrance. He took the seat on the right side of the desk near the window again.

Hinojos smiled and Bosch wondered why. There were two chairs on the other side of the desk from her. So far, in three meetings, he had taken the same one each time. The one closest to the window. He wondered if she had taken note of this and what, if anything, it meant.

'Are you tired?' she asked. 'You don't look like you got much sleep last night.'

'I guess I didn't. But I'm fine.'

'Have you changed your mind about anything we discussed yesterday?'

'No, not really.'

'You are continuing this private investigation?'

'For now.'

She nodded in a way that told him she expected his reply.

'I want to talk about your mother today.'

'Why? It's got nothing to do with why I'm here, why I'm on leave.'

'I think it's important. I think it will help us get to what is happening with you, what has made you take on this private investigation of yours. It might explain a lot about your recent actions.'

'I doubt it. What do you want to know?'

'When you spoke yesterday, you made several references to her lifestyle, but you never really came out and said what she did, what she was. Thinking about it after the session, I was wondering if you have trouble accepting what she was. To the point of not being able to say she –'

'Was a prostitute? There, I said it. She was a prostitute. I'm a grown man, Doctor. I accept the truth. I accept the truth in anything as long as it's the truth. I think you're going far afield here.'

'Perhaps. What do you feel about her now?'

'What do you mean?'

'Anger? Hatred? Love?'

'I don't think about it. Certainly not hate. I loved her at the time. After she was gone that didn't change.'

'What about abandonment?'

'I'm too old for that.'

86

'What about back then? Back when it happened.'

Bosch thought a moment.

'I'm sure there was some of that. Her lifestyle, her line of work, got her killed. And I was left behind the fence. I guess I was mad about that and felt abandoned. I was also hurt. The hurt was the worst part. She loved me.'

'What do you mean, left behind the fence?'

'I told you yesterday. I was in McClaren, the youth hall.'

'Right. So her death prevented you from leaving there, correct?'

'For a while.'

'How long?'

'I was there on and off until I was sixteen. I lived a few months two different times with some fosters but I always got sent back. Then, when I was sixteen, another couple took me. I was with them until I was seventeen. I found out later that they kept getting the DPSS checks for a year after I'd split.'

'DPSS?'

'Department of Public Social Services. Now they call it the Division of Youth Services. Anyway, when you took a kid into your home as foster parents, you got a monthly support payment. A lot of people took kids in just for those checks. I'm not saying these people did, but they never told DPSS I wasn't in their home anymore after I left.'

'I understand. Where were you?'

'Vietnam.'

'Wait a minute, let's go back. You said that two different times before this you lived with foster parents but were then sent back. What happened? Why were you sent back?'

'I don't know. They didn't like me. They said it wasn't working out. I went back into the dorms behind the fence and waited. I think getting rid of a teenage boy was about as easy as selling a car with no wheels. The fosters always wanted the younger ones.'

'Did you ever run away from the hall?'

'A couple times. I always got caught in Hollywood.'

'If placing teenagers was so difficult, how did it happen to you the third time, when you were even older, sixteen?'

Bosch laughed falsely and shook his head.

'You'll get a kick out of this. I was chosen by this guy and his wife because I was left-handed.'

'Left-handed? I don't follow.'

'I was a lefty and I could throw a pretty good fastball.'

'What do you mean?'

'Ah, Jesus, it was – see, Sandy Koufax was with the Dodgers then. He was a lefty and I guess they were paying him about a zillion bucks a year to pitch. This guy, the foster, his name was Earl Morse, he had played semipro baseball or something and never really made it. So, he wanted to *create* a left-handed major league prospect. Good left-handers were pretty rare back then, I guess. Or he thought that. Anyway, they were the hot commodity. Earl thought he'd grab some kid with some potential, slap him into shape and then be his manager or agent or something when it came to contract time. He saw it as his way back into the game. It was crazy. But I guess he'd seen his own big league dream crash and burn. So he came out to McClaren and took a bunch of us into the field for a catch. We had a team, we played other halls, sometimes the schools in the Valley let us play them. Anyway, Earl took us out to throw the ball around and it was a tryout but none of us knew it at the time. It didn't even enter my mind what was going on until later. Anyway, he glommed on to me when he saw I was a lefty and could throw. He forgot the others like they were last season's program.'

Bosch shook his head again at the memory.

'What happened? You went with him?'

'Yeah. I went with him. There was a wife, too. She never said much to me or him. He used to make me throw a hundred balls a day at a tire hanging in the backyard. Then every night he'd have these coaching sessions. I put up with it for about a year and then I split.'

'You ran away?'

'Sort of. I joined the Army. I had to get Earl to sign for me, though. At first he wouldn't do it. He had major league plans for me. But then I told him I was never going to pick up another baseball as long as I lived. He signed. Then he and the wife kept cashing those DPSS checks while I was overseas. I guess the extra money helped make up for losing the prospect.'

She was quiet for a long time. It looked to Bosch like she was reading her notes but he had not seen her write anything during this session.

'You know,' he said into the silence, 'about ten years later, when I was still in patrol, I pulled over a drunk driver coming off the Hollywood Freeway onto Sunset. He was all over the place. When I finally got him over and got up there to the window, I bent over to look in and it was Earl. It was a Sunday. He was coming home from the Dodgers. I saw the program on the seat.'

She looked at him but didn't say anything. He was looking at the memory still.

'I guess he'd never found that lefty he was looking for . . . Anyway, he was so drunk he didn't recognize me.'

'What did you do?'

'Took his keys and called his wife . . . I guess it was the only break I ever gave the guy.'

She looked back down at the pad while asking her next question.

'What about your real father?'

'What about him?'

'Did you ever know who he was? Did you have any relationship at all?'

'I met him once. I was never curious about it until I came back from overseas. Then I traced it down. Turned out he was my mother's lawyer. He had a family and all of that. He was dying when I met him, looked like a skeleton . . . So I never really knew him.'

'His name was Bosch?'

'No. My name was just something she came up with. The painter, you know. She thought LA was a lot like his paintings. All the paranoia, the fear. Once she gave me a book that had his paintings in it.'

More silence followed as she thought about this one, too.

'These stories, Harry,' she finally said, 'these stories that you tell are heartbreaking in their own way. It makes me see the boy who became the man. It makes me see the depth of the hole left by your mother's death. You know, you would have a lot to blame her for and no one would blame you for doing it.'

He looked at her pointedly while composing a response.

'I don't blame her for anything. I blame the man who took her from me. See, these are stories about me. Not her. You can't get the feel for her. You can't know her like I did. All I know is that she did all she could to get me out of there. She never stopped telling me that. She never stopped trying. She just ran out of time.'

She nodded, accepting his answer. A few moments passed.

'Did there come a time when she told you what she did . . . for a living?'

'Not really.'

'How did you know?'

'I can't remember. I think I really didn't know for sure what she did until she was gone and I was older. I was ten when they took me away. I didn't really know why.'

'Did she have men stay with her while you were together?'

'No, that never happened.'

'But you must have had some idea about this life she was leading, that you both were leading.'

'She told me she was a waitress. She worked nights. She used to leave me with a lady who had a room at the hotel. Mrs DeTorre. She watched four or five kids whose mothers were doing the same thing. None of us knew.'

He finished there but she didn't say anything and he knew he was expected to continue.

'One night I snuck out when the old lady fell asleep and I walked down to the Boulevard to the coffee shop where she said she worked. She wasn't in there. I asked and they didn't know what I was talking about . . .'

'Did you ask your mother about it?'

'No . . . The next night I followed her. She left in her waitress uniform and I followed her. She went to her best friend's place upstairs. Meredith Roman. When they came out, they were both wearing dresses, makeup, the whole thing. Then they both left in a cab and I couldn't follow them.'

'But you knew.'

'I knew something. But I was like nine or something. How much could I know?'

'What about the charade she followed, dressing every night like a waitress, did that anger you?'

'No. The opposite. I thought that was . . . I don't know, there was something noble about her doing that for me. She was protecting me, in a way.'

Hinojos nodded that she saw his point.

'Close your eyes.'

'Close my eyes?'

'Yes, I want you to close your eyes and think back to when you were a boy. Go ahead.'

'What is this?'

'Indulge me. Please.'

Bosch shook his head as if annoyed but did as she asked. He felt stupid.

'Okay.'

'Okay, I want you to tell me a story about your mother. Whatever image or episode with her that you have the clearest in your mind, I want you to tell it to me.'

He thought hard. Images of her passed through and disappeared. Finally, he came to one that stayed.

'Okay.'

'Okay, tell it.'

'It was at McClaren. She had come to visit and we were out at the fence at the ballfield.'

'Why do you remember this story?'

'I don't know. Because she was there and that always made me feel good, even though we always ended up crying. You should have seen that place on visiting day. Everybody crying . . . And I remember it, too, because it was near the end. It wasn't too long after that she was gone. Maybe a few months.'

'Do you remember what you talked about?'

'A lot of stuff. Baseball, she was a Dodgers fan. I remember one of the older kids had taken my new sneakers that she had given me for my birthday. She noticed I didn't have 'em on and she got pretty mad about it.'

'Why did the older boy take your sneakers?'

'She asked the same thing.'

'What did you tell her?'

'I told her the kid took my shoes because he could. You see, they could call that place whatever they wanted but basically it was a prison for kids and it had the same societies as a prison has. Your dominant cliques, your submissives, everything.'

'What were you?'

'I don't know. I pretty much kept to myself. But when some older, bigger kid took my shoes, I was a submissive. It was a way of surviving.'

'Your mother was unhappy about this?'

'Well, yeah, but she didn't know the score. She wanted to go complain or something. She didn't know that if she did that it would only make it worse for me there. Then she suddenly did realize what the deal was. She started crying.'

Bosch was silent, picturing the scene perfectly in his mind. He remembered the dampness in the air and the smell of the orange blossoms from the nearby groves.

Hinojos cleared her throat before breaking into his memory.

'What did you do when she started crying?'

'I probably started crying, too. I usually did. I didn't want her to feel bad but there was a comfort in knowing she knew what was happening to me. Only mothers can do that, you know? Make you feel good when you're sad . . .'

Bosch still had his eyes closed and was seeing only the memory.

'What did she tell you?'

'She . . . she just told me she was going to get me out. She said that her lawyer was going to go to court soon to appeal the custody ruling and the unfit mother finding. She said there were other things she could do, too. The point was, she was getting me out.'

'That lawyer was your father?'

'Yes, but I didn't know it . . . Anyway, what I'm saying is that the courts were wrong about her. That's the thing that bothers me. She was good to me and they didn't see that . . . anyway, I remember she promised me that she would do what she had to do, but she would get me out.'

'But she never did.'

'No. Like I said, she ran out of time.'

'I'm sorry.'

Bosch opened his eyes and looked at her.

'So am I.'

18

Bosch had parked in a public lot off Hill Street. It cost him twelve dollars for his car. He then got onto the 101 and headed north toward the hills. As he drove, he occasionally looked over at the blue box on the seat next to him. But he didn't open it. He knew that he had to but he would wait for home.

He turned the radio on and listened as the DJ introduced a song by Abbey Lincoln. Bosch had never heard it before but he immediately liked the words and the woman's smoky voice.

> Bird alone, flying high
> Flying through a clouded sky
> Sending mournful, soulful sounds
> Soaring over troubled grounds

After he got to Woodrow Wilson and followed his usual routine of parking a half block away from his home, Bosch brought the box inside and placed it on the dining room table. He lit a cigarette and paced the room, looking down occasionally at the box. He knew what was in it. He had the evidence list from the murder book. But he couldn't overcome a feeling that by opening the box he was invading some secret privacy, committing a sin that he didn't understand.

Finally, he took his keys out. There was a small pen knife on the ring and he used it to slice through the red tape that sealed the box. He put the knife down and without thinking about it any further lifted the top off the box.

The victim's clothes and other belongings were wrapped individually in plastic bags, which Bosch took out of the box one by one and placed on the table. The clear plastic was yellowed but he could see through it. He did not remove anything from the bags but instead just held each piece of evidence up and studied it in its sterile covering.

He opened the murder book to the evidence list and made sure nothing was missing. It was all there. He held the small bag containing the gold earrings up to the light. They were like frozen tear drops. He put the bag back down and at the bottom of the box he saw the blouse, folded neatly in plastic, the spot of blood exactly where the evidence sheet said it was, on the left breast, about two inches from the center button.

Bosch ran his finger over the plastic where the spot was. It was then that he realized something. There was no other blood. He knew that it was the thing that had bothered him as he read the murder book but he had been unable to get ahold of the thought then. Now he had it. The blood. No blood on the undergarments, the skirt or the stockings, or pumps. Only on the blouse.

Bosch also knew the autopsy had described a body with no lacerations. Then where had the blood come from? He wanted to look at the crime scene and autopsy photos but knew that he couldn't. There was no way he would open that envelope.

Bosch pulled the bag containing the blouse from the box and read the evidence tag and other markings. Nowhere did it mention or give any reference code for any analysis ever being done on the blood.

This invigorated him. There was a good chance that the blood spot came from the killer, not the victim. He had no idea whether blood that old could still be typed or even submitted for DNA analysis but he intended to find out. The problem, he knew, was comparison. It didn't matter if the blood could still be analyzed if there was nothing to compare it to. To get blood from Conklin or Mittel or anyone, for that matter, he would need a court order. And to get that, he needed evidence. Not just suspicions and hunches.

He had gathered the evidence bags together to replace in the box when he stopped to study one he had not considered closely before. It contained the belt that had been used to strangle the victim.

Bosch studied it a few moments as if it were a snake he was trying to identify before cautiously reaching into the box and picking it up. He could see the evidence tag tied through one of the belt holes. On the smooth silver sea shell buckle there was black powder. He could see that part of the ridge lines from a thumbprint were still there.

He held the belt up to the light. It pained him to look at it but he did. The belt was an inch in width, made of black leather. The sea shell buckle was the largest ornamentation but smaller silver shells were attached along its length. Looking at it brought back the memory. He hadn't really chosen it. Meredith Roman had taken him to the May Co. on Wilshire. She had seen the belt on a rack with many others and told him his mother would like it. She paid for it and allowed him to give it to his mother as a birthday present. Meredith had been right. His mother wore the belt often, including every time she visited him after the court took him away. And including the night she was murdered.

Bosch read the evidence tag but all it said was the case number and McKittrick's name. On the tongue he noticed that the second and fourth holes were imperfect circles, distended by the spoke of the buckle during wear. He guessed that maybe his mother wore it tighter at times, maybe to impress someone, or looser at times, over bulkier clothing. He now knew everything about the belt except who had used it last to kill her.

He realized then that whoever had held this belt, this weapon, before the police had been responsible for taking a life and indelibly changing his own. He carefully replaced it in the box and put the other clothing in on top of it. He then put the lid back on top.

Bosch couldn't stay in the house after that. He felt he had to get out. He didn't bother changing his clothes. He just got in the Mustang and started driving. It was dark now and he took Cahuenga down into Hollywood. He told himself he didn't know or care where he was going but that was a lie. He knew. When he got to Hollywood Boulevard he turned east.

The car took him to Vista, where he turned north and then cut into the first alley. The headlights sliced through the darkness and he saw a small homeless encampment. A man and woman huddled under a cardboard lean-to. Two other bodies, wrapped in blankets and newspapers, lay nearby. A small glow from dying flames came from the rim of a trash can. Bosch cruised by slowly, his eyes further down the alley, to the spot he knew from the crime scene drawing that was in the murder book.

The Hollywood souvenir store was now an adult book and video store. There was an alley entrance for shy customers and several cars were parked alongside the rear of the building. Bosch stopped near the door and killed the lights. He just sat in the car, feeling no need to get out. He had never been to the alley, to the spot, before. He just wanted to sit and watch and feel for a few moments.

He lit a cigarette and watched as a man carrying a bag walked quickly out the door of the adult shop to a car parked at the end of the alley.

Bosch thought about a time when he was a small boy and still with his mother. They'd had a small apartment on Camrose then and during the summer they'd sit in the back courtyard on the nights she wasn't working or on Sunday afternoons and listen to the music coming over the hill from the Hollywood Bowl. The sound was bad, attacked by traffic and the white noise of the city before it got to them, but the high notes were clear. What he liked about it wasn't the music but that she was there. It was their time together. She always told him that she would take him one day to the bowl to hear 'Scheherazade.' It was her favorite. They never got the chance. The court took him away from her and she was dead before she could get him back.

Bosch finally heard the philharmonic perform 'Scheherazade' the year he spent with Sylvia. When she saw tears welling in the corners of his eyes, she thought it was because of the pure beauty of the music. He never got around to telling her it was something else.

A blur of motion caught his attention and someone banged a fist on the driver's side window. Bosch's left hand instinctively went under his jacket to his waist, but there was no gun there. He turned and looked into the face of an old woman whose years were etched like hash marks on her face. It looked like she was wearing three sets of clothes. When she was done knocking on the window, she opened her palm and held it out. Still startled, Bosch quickly reached into his pocket and pulled out a five. He started the car so he could put the window down and handed the money out to her. She said nothing. She just took it and walked away. Bosch watched her go and wondered how had she ended up in this alley. How had he?

Bosch drove out of the alley and back out to Hollywood Boulevard. He started cruising again. At first aimlessly but soon he found his purpose. He wasn't yet ready to confront Conklin or Mittel but he knew where they were and he wanted to see their homes, their lives, the places they had ended up.

He stayed on the Boulevard until Alvarado and then took that down to Third, where he started west. The drive took him from the Third World poverty of the area known as Little Salvador past the faded mansions of Hancock Park and then to Park La Brea, a huge complex of apartments, condominiums and attendant rest homes.

Bosch found Ogden Drive and cruised slowly down it until he saw the Park La Brea Lifecare Center. There's another irony, he thought. Lifecare. The only thing the place probably cared about was when you were going to die, so your space could be sold to the next one.

It was a nondescript twelve-story building of concrete and glass. Through the glass facade of the lobby Bosch could see a security guard at a post. In this town, even the elderly and infirm weren't safe. He glanced up the front of the building and saw most of the windows were dark. Only nine o'clock and the place was already dead. Someone honked at him from behind and he sped up and away, thinking about Conklin and what his life might be like. He wondered if the old man in his room up there ever gave a thought to Marjorie Lowe after so many years.

Bosch's next stop was Mount Olympus, the gaudy outcropping of modern Roman-style homes above Hollywood. The look was supposed to be neoclassical but he had heard it referred to more than once as neo*crassical*. The huge, expensive homes were jammed side by side as close as teeth. There were ornate columns and statues but the only thing that seemed classic about most of the place was the kitsch. Bosch took Mount Olympus Drive off Laurel Canyon, turned on Electra and then went to Hercules. He was driving slowly, looking for addresses on curbs to match the one he had written in his notebook that morning.

When he found Mittel's house, he stopped on the street, stunned. It was a house that he knew. He had never been inside it, of course, but everyone knew it. It was a circular mansion that sat atop one of the most recognizable promontories in the Hollywood Hills. Bosch looked at the place with awe, imagining its interior size and its exterior ocean-to-mountain views. Its rounded walls lit from the outside with white lights, it looked like a spaceship that had alighted on a mountaintop and was poised to take to the air once again. Classic kitsch it wasn't. This was a home that bespoke its owner's power and influence.

An iron gate guarded a long driveway that went up a hill to the house. But tonight the gate was open and Bosch could see several cars and at least three limousines parked along one side of the drive. Other cars were parked in the circle at the top. It only dawned on Bosch that there was a party underway at the house when a red blur passed the car window and the door was suddenly sprung open. Bosch turned and looked into the face of a swarthy Latino man in a white shirt and red vest.

'Good evening, sir. We will take your car here. If you could walk up the drive on the left side, the greeters will find you.'

Bosch stared at the man unmoving, thinking.

'Sir?'

Bosch tentatively stepped out of the Mustang and the man in the vest gave him a slip of paper with a number on it. He then slipped into the car and drove away. Bosch stood there, aware that he was about to let events control him, something he knew he should avoid. He hesitated and looked back at the tail lights of the Mustang gliding away. He let the temptation take him.

Bosch fastened his top button and pulled his tie back into place as he walked up the driveway. He passed a small army of men in red vests and as he came all the way up past the limousines, a startling view of the lighted city came into view. He stopped and just looked for a moment. He could see from the moonlit Pacific in one direction to the towers of downtown in the other. The view alone was worth the price of the house, no matter how many millions that was.

The sound of soft music, laughter and conversation came from his left. He followed it down a stone path that curved along the form of the house. The drop-off to the houses down the hill was steep and deadly. He finally came to a flat yard that was lighted and full of people milling about beneath a tent as white as the moon. Bosch guessed there were at least a hundred and fifty well-dressed people sipping cocktails and taking small hors d'oeuvres off trays carried by young women wearing short black dresses, sheer stockings and white aprons. He wondered where the red vests were putting all the cars.

Bosch immediately felt underdressed and was sure he would be identified in seconds as a gate-crasher. But there was something so otherworldly about the scene that he held his ground.

A surfer in a suit approached him. He was about twenty-five, with short, sun-bleached hair and a dark tan. He wore a custom-fitted suit that looked as if it had cost more than every piece of clothing Bosch owned combined. It was light brown but the wearer probably described it as cocoa. He smiled the way enemies smile.

'Yes, sir, how are we doing tonight?'

'I'm doing fine. I don't know about you, yet.'

The surfer in a suit smiled a little more brightly at that.

'I'm Mr Johnson and I'm providing security for the benefit tonight. Might I inquire if you brought your invitation with you?'

Bosch hesitated for only a moment.

'Oh, I'm sorry. I didn't realize I needed to bring that along. I didn't think Gordon would need security at a benefit like this.'

He hoped dropping Mittel's first name would give the surfer pause before he did anything rash. The surfer frowned for only a moment.

'Then could I ask you just to sign in for me?'

'Of course.'

Bosch was led to a table to the side of the entrance area. Taped across the front of it was a red, white and blue banner that said ROBERT SHEPHERD NOW! It told Bosch all he needed to know about the affair.

There was a guest registry on the table and a woman sat behind it in a black crushed-velvet cocktail dress that did little to camouflage her breasts. Mr Johnson seemed more intent on these two items than on Bosch as he signed the name Harvey Pounds in the registry.

As he signed, Bosch noticed a stack of pledge cards and a champagne goblet filled with pencils on the table. He picked up an information sheet and started to read about the unannounced candidate. Johnson finally pulled his eyes away from the table hostess and checked the name Bosch had written.

'Thank you, Mr Pounds. Enjoy yourself.'

He disappeared into the crowd then, probably to check on whether a

Harvey Pounds was on the list of invitees. Bosch decided he'd stay a few minutes, see if he could spot Mittel and then leave before the surfer came looking for him.

He stepped away from the entrance and out from beneath the tent. After crossing a short lawn to a retainer wall, he tried to act like he was just enjoying the view. And it was a view; the only higher one would have been from a jet coming in to LAX. But on the jet you wouldn't have the breadth of vision, the cool breeze, or the sounds from the city below.

Bosch turned around and looked back at the crowd under the tent. He studied the faces but could not spot Gordon Mittel. There was no sign of him. There was a large knot of people beneath the center of the tent and Bosch realized that it was a grouping of people trying to reach their hands toward the unannounced candidate, or at least the man Bosch assumed was Shepherd. Harry noticed that while the crowd seemed to exhibit solidarity in terms of wealth, it cut across all age lines. He guessed that many were there to see Mittel as much as Shepherd.

One of the women in black-and-white came out from under the white canopy and toward him with a tray of champagne glasses. He took one, thanked her, and turned back to the view. He sipped at it and supposed that it was top quality, but he wouldn't be able to tell the difference. He decided he should gulp it and go when a voice from his left interrupted.

'Wonderful view, isn't it? Better than a movie. I could stand here for hours.'

Bosch turned his head to acknowledge the speaker but didn't look at him. He didn't want to get involved.

'Yeah, it's nice. But I'll take the mountains I have.'

'Really? Where is that?'

'The other side of the hill. On Woodrow Wilson.'

'Oh, yes. There are some very nice properties there.'

Not mine, Bosch thought. Unless you like neoearthquake classic.

'The San Gabriels are brilliant in the sun,' the conversationalist said. 'I looked there but then I bought here.'

Bosch turned. He was looking at Gordon Mittel. The host put out his hand.

'Gordon Mittel.'

Bosch hesitated but then figured Mittel was used to people losing a step or stuttering in his presence.

'Harvey Pounds,' Bosch said, taking his hand.

Mittel was wearing a black tuxedo. He was as overdressed for the crowd as Bosch was underdressed. His gray hair was cropped short and he had a smooth machine tan. He was as trim and tight as a rubber band stretched around a stack of hundreds and looked at least five to ten years younger than he was.

'Glad to meet you, glad you could come,' he said. 'Did you meet Robert yet?'

'No, he's kind of in the middle of the pack there.'

'Yes, that's true. Well, he'll be happy to meet you when he gets the chance.'

'I guess he'll be happy to take my check as well.'

'That, too.' Mittel smiled. 'Seriously, though, I hope you can help us out. He's a good man and we need people like him in office.'

His smile seemed so phony that Harry wondered if Mittel had already pegged him as a crasher. Bosch smiled back and patted the right breast of his jacket.

'I've got the checkbook right here.'

Doing that, Bosch remembered what he really had in his pocket and got an idea. The champagne, though only a single glass, had emboldened him. He suddenly realized he wanted to spook Mittel and maybe get a look at his real colors.

'Tell me,' he said, 'is Shepherd the one?'

'I don't quite follow.'

'Is he going all the way to the White House someday? Is he the one that's going to take you?'

Mittel sloughed off a frown or maybe it was a glimmer of annoyance.

'I guess we shall see. We've got to get him into the Senate first. That's the important thing.'

Bosch nodded and made a show of scanning the crowd.

'Well, it looks like you have the right people here. But, you know, I don't see Arno Conklin. Are you still tight with him? He was your first, wasn't he?'

Mittel's forehead creased with a deep furrow.

'Well . . .' Mittel seemed to be uncomfortable, but then it quickly passed. 'To tell the truth, we haven't spoken in a long time. He's retired now, an old man in a wheelchair. Do you know Arno?'

'Never spoken to him in my life.'

'Then tell me, what prompts a question about ancient history?'

Bosch hiked his shoulders.

'I guess I'm just a student of history, that's all.'

'What do you do for a living, Mr Pounds? Or are you a full-time student?'

'I'm in law.'

'We have something in common then.'

'I doubt it.'

'I'm a Stanford man. How about you?'

Bosch thought a moment.

'Vietnam.'

Mittel frowned again and Bosch saw the interest go out of his eyes like water down a drain.

'Well, I tell you, I ought to mingle a little more. Watch the champagne, and if you decide you don't want to drive, one of the boys on the driveway can get you home. Ask for Manuel.'

'The one in the red vest?'

'Uh, yes. One of them.'

Bosch held up his glass.

'Don't worry, this is only my third.'

Mittel nodded and disappeared back into the crowd. Bosch watched him cross beneath the tent, stop to shake a few hands, but eventually make it to the house. He entered through a wall of French doors into what looked like a living room or some sort of viewing area. Mittel walked to a couch and bent down to speak quietly to a man in a suit. This man looked to be about the same age as Mittel but with a harder appearance. He had a sharp face and, though sitting, clearly had a much heavier body. As a younger man he had probably used his strength, not his brain. Mittel straightened up and the other man just nodded. Mittel then disappeared into the further recesses of his house.

Bosch finished his glass of champagne and started moving through the crowd under the tent toward the house. As he got near the French doors, one of the black-and-white women asked if he needed help finding something. He said he was looking for the bathroom and she directed him to another door to the left. He went where he was told and found the door was locked. He waited for a few moments and the door finally opened, emitting a man and a woman. They giggled when they saw Bosch waiting and headed back to the tent.

Inside the bathroom Bosch opened his jacket and took a folded piece of paper from the inside pocket on the left. It was the photocopy of the Johnny Fox story that Keisha Russell had given him. He unfolded it and took out a pen. He circled the names Johnny Fox, Arno Conklin and Gordon Mittel, then, under the story, wrote, 'What prior work experience got Johnny the job?'

He refolded the page twice and ran his fingers tightly over the creases. Then, on the outside, he wrote, 'For Gordon Mittel Only!'

Back under the tent, Bosch found a black-and-white woman and gave her the folded paper.

'You have to find Mr Mittel right away,' he told her. 'Give him this note. He's waiting on it.'

He watched her go and then made his way back out through the crowd to the sign-in table at the entry area. He quickly bent over the guest registry and wrote his mother's name down. The table hostess protested that he had already signed in.

'This is for somebody else,' he said.

For an address, he wrote Hollywood and Vista. He left the line for a telephone number blank.

Bosch scanned the crowd again and saw neither Mittel nor the woman he had given the note to. Then he looked into the room beyond the French doors and Mittel appeared with the note in his hand. He walked slowly into the room, studying it. Bosch could tell by the direction of his eyes that he was studying the note scribbled on the bottom. Even with his phony tan, he seemed to Bosch to go pale.

Bosch took a step back into the entrance alcove and watched. He could feel his heart beating at a quicker pace. He felt like he was watching some secret play on a stage.

There was a look of perplexed anger on Mittel's face now. Bosch saw him hand the page to the rough man who still sat in the cushioned chair. Then Mittel turned to the glass panels and looked out at the people under the tent. He said something and Bosch thought he could read his lips.

'Son of a bitch.'

Then he started talking more quickly, barking orders. The man on the chair rose and Bosch knew instinctively that it was his cue to leave. He walked quickly back out to the driveway and trotted down to the group of men in red vests. He handed his valet ticket and a ten-dollar bill to one of them and said in Spanish that he was in a great hurry.

Still, it seemed to take forever. As he waited nervously, Bosch kept his eyes on the house, waiting for the rough man to appear. He had watched which direction the valet had gone for his car and he was ready to bolt that way if necessary. He began to wish he had his gun. Whether he really needed it or not did not matter. In this moment he knew it gave him a sense of security that he felt naked without.

The surfer in a suit appeared at the top of the driveway and strode down toward Bosch. At the same time, Bosch saw his Mustang approaching. He walked out into the street, ready to take it. The surfer got to him first.

'Hey, buddy, hold on a sec –'

Bosch turned from his approaching car and hit him in the jaw, sending him backward onto the driveway. He moaned and rolled onto his side, both hands clutching his jaw. Bosch was sure the jaw was dislocated if not broken. He shook away the pain in his hand as the Mustang screeched to a stop.

The man in the red vest was slow in getting out. Bosch pulled him away from the open door and jumped in. As he settled in behind the wheel he looked up the driveway and saw the rough man was now coming. When he saw the surfer on the ground, he started running but his steps were unsteady on the downgrade of the driveway. Bosch saw his heavy thighs pressing the fabric of his pants and suddenly he slipped and fell. Two of the red vests went to help him up but he angrily shoved them away.

Bosch gunned the car and sped away. He worked his way up to Mulholland and turned east toward home. He could feel adrenaline surging through him. Not only had he gotten away, but it was clear he had struck a nerve with a hammer. Let Mittel think about that for a while, he thought. Let him sweat. Then he yelled out loud in the car, though no one could hear except himself.

'Spooked ya, didn't I, you fuck!'

He banged his palm triumphantly on the steering wheel.

19

He dreamed of the coyote again. The animal was on a mountain path where there were no homes, no cars, no people. It was moving very quickly through the dark as if it was trying to get away. But the path and place were his. He knew the land and knew he would escape. What it was he fled from was never clear, never seen. But it was there, behind him in the dark. And the coyote knew by instinct it must get away.

The phone woke Bosch, breaking into the dream like a knife stabbed through paper. Bosch pulled the pillow off his head, rolled to his right and his eyes were immediately assaulted by the light of dawn. He had forgotten to close the blinds. He reached for the phone on the floor.

'Hold on,' he said.

He put the phone down on the bed, sat up and rubbed a hand across his face. He squinted at the clock. It was ten minutes after seven. He coughed and cleared his throat, then picked the phone back up.

'Yeah.'

'Detective Bosch?'

'Yeah.'

'It's Brad Hirsch. I'm sorry to call so early.'

Bosch had to think a moment. Brad Hirsch? He had no idea who it was.

'Yeah, it's okay,' he said while he continued to search his mind for the name.

A silence followed.

'I'm the one ... In Latents? Remember, you –'

'Hirsch? Yeah, Hirsch. I remember. What's up?'

'I wanted to tell you I made the AFIS run you wanted. I came in early and ran it with another search I'm doing for Devonshire Homicide. I don't think anybody will know.'

Bosch kicked his legs over the side of the bed, opened a drawer in the bed table and took out a pad and a pencil. He noticed that he had taken the pad from the Surf and Sand Hotel in Laguna Beach. He remembered he had spent a few days with Sylvia there the year before.

'Yeah, you made the run? What'd you get?'

'Well, that's the thing. I'm sorry but I got nothing.'

Bosch threw the pad back into the open drawer and threw himself backward on the bed.

'No hits?'

'Well, the computer came up with two candidates. I then did a visual comparison and it was no good. No matches. I'm sorry. I know this case means …'

He didn't finish.

'You took it through all the data bases?'

'Every one on our network.'

'Let me ask you something. All those data bases, do they include DA's employees and LAPD personnel?'

There was silence as Hirsch must have been mulling over what the question might mean.

'You there, Hirsch?'

'Yes. The answer is yes.'

'How far back? You know what I mean? These bases have prints going how far back?'

'Well, each data base is different. The LAPD's is extensive. I'd say we have prints on everybody who's worked here since World War II.'

Well, that clears Irving and the rest of the cops, Bosch thought. But that didn't bother him much. His sights were definitely somewhere else.

'What about people working for the DA?'

'The DA's office would be different,' Hirsch said. 'I don't think they started printing employees until the middle sixties.'

Conklin had been there during that time, Bosch knew, but he would already have been elected DA. It would seem that he would not have submitted his own prints, especially if he knew there was a print card in a murder book somewhere that could possibly be matched to him.

He thought of Mittel. He would have been out of the DA's office by the time employees' prints were taken as a matter of course.

'What about the federal base?' he asked. 'What if some guy worked for a president and got the kind of clearance you need to go visit the White House, would those prints be in that base?'

'Yes, they'd be in twice. In the federal employees base and in the FBI's. They keep prints on record of everyone they do background investigations on, if that's what you mean. But remember, just because somebody visits the president, it doesn't mean they get printed.'

Well, Mittel isn't a scratch but it's close, Bosch thought.

'So what you're saying,' Bosch said, 'is that whether or not we have complete data files going back to 1961, whoever belongs to those prints I gave you hasn't been printed since then?'

'That's not one hundred percent but it's close. The person who left these prints probably hasn't been printed – at least by any contributor to the data banks. We can only reach so far with this. One way or another we can pull prints on one out of about every fifty or so people in the country. But I just didn't get anything this time. Sorry.'

'That's okay, Hirsch, you tried.'

'Well, I guess I'll be getting back to work now. What do you want me to do with the print card?'

Bosch thought a moment. He wondered if there was any other avenue to chase down.

'Tell you what, can you just hold on to it? I'll come by the lab and pick it up when I can. Probably be by later today.'

'Okay, I'll put it in an envelope for you in case I'm not here. Good-bye.'

'Hey, Hirsch?'

'Yeah?'

'It feels good, don't it?'

'What's that?'

'You did the right thing. You didn't get a match but you did the right thing.'

'Yeah, I guess.'

He was acting like he didn't understand because he was embarrassed, but he understood.

'Yeah, I'll see you Hirsch.'

After hanging up, Bosch sat on the side of the bed, lit a cigarette and thought about what he was going to do with the day. The news from Hirsch was not good but it wasn't daunting. It certainly didn't clear Arno Conklin. It might not even have cleared Gordon Mittel. Bosch wasn't sure whether Mittel's work for presidents and senators would have required a fingerprint check. He decided his investigation was still intact. He wasn't changing any plans.

He thought about the night before and the wild-ass chance he had taken confronting Mittel the way he had. He smiled at his own recklessness and thought about what Hinojos might make of it. He knew she'd say it was a symptom of his problem. She wouldn't see it as a tactful way of flushing the bird from the bush.

He got up and started the coffee and then showered, shaved and got ready for the day. He took his coffee and the box of cereal from the refrigerator out to the deck, leaving the sliding door open so he could hear the stereo. He had KFWB news on.

It was cool and crisp outside but he could tell it would get warmer later. Blue jays were swooping in and out of the arroyo below the deck and he could see black bees the size of quarters working in the yellow flowers of the primrose jasmine.

There was a story on the radio about a building contractor making a fourteen-million-dollar bonus for completing the rebuilding of the 10 freeway three months ahead of schedule. The officials who gathered to announce the engineering feat likened the fallen freeway to the city itself. Now that it was back upright, so, too, was the city. The city was on the move again. They had a lot to learn, Bosch thought.

Afterward, he went in and got out the yellow pages and started working the phone in the kitchen. He called the major airlines, shopped around and made arrangements to fly to Florida. But flying on one day's notice, the best deal he could get was still seven hundred dollars, a shocking amount to him. He put it on a credit card so that he could pay it off over time. He also reserved a rental car at Tampa International Airport.

When he had that finished he went back out to the deck and thought about the next project he had to tackle:

He needed a badge.

For a long time he sat on the deck chair and contemplated whether he needed it for his own sense of security or because it was a bona fide necessity to his mission. He knew how naked and vulnerable he had felt this week without the gun and the badge, extremities he had carried on his body for more than twenty years. But he had avoided the temptation to carry the backup gun that he knew was in the closet next to the front door. That he could do, he knew. But the badge was different. More so than the gun, the badge was the symbol of what he was. It opened doors better than any key, it gave him more authority than any words, than any weapon. He decided the badge was a necessity. If he was going to Florida and was going to scam McKittrick, he had to look legit. He had to have a badge.

He knew his badge was probably in a desk drawer in Assistant Chief Irvin S. Irving's office. There was no way he could get to it and not be discovered. But he knew where there was another one that would work just as well.

Bosch looked at his watch. Nine-fifteen. It was forty-five minutes until the daily command meeting at Hollywood Station. He had plenty of time.

20

Bosch pulled into the rear parking lot of the station at five minutes after ten. He was sure that Pounds, who was punctual about everything he did, would already have gone down the front hall to the captain's office with the overnight logs. The meeting was held every morning and included the station's CO, patrol captain, watch lieutenant and detective commander, who was Pounds. They were routine affairs and never lasted longer than twenty minutes. The members of the station's command staff simply drank coffee and went through the overnight reports and ongoing problems, complaints or investigations of particular note.

Bosch went in the back door by the drunk tank and then up the hallway to the detective bureau. It had been a busy morning. There were already four men handcuffed to benches in the hallway. One of them, a drug hype Bosch had seen in the station before and used as an unreliable informant on occasion, asked Bosch for a smoke. It was illegal to smoke in any city-owned building. Bosch lit a cigarette anyway and put it in the man's mouth because both his needle-scarred arms were cuffed behind his back.

'What is it this time, Harley?' Bosch asked.

'Shit, a guy leaves his g'rage open, he's asking me to come in. Isn't that right?'

'Tell that one to the judge.'

As Bosch walked away one of the other lockdowns yelled at him from down the hallway.

'What about me, man? I need a smoke.'

'I'm out,' Bosch said.

'Fuck you, man.'

'Yeah, that's what I thought.'

He came into the detective bureau through the rear door. The first thing he did was confirm that Pounds's glass office was empty. He was at the command meeting. Then he checked the coatrack up at the front and saw he was in business. As he walked down the aisle formed by the separation of the investigation tables, he exchanged nods with a few of the other detectives.

Edgar was at the homicide table sitting across from his new partner, who was in Bosch's old chair. Edgar heard one of the 'Hi, Harry' greetings and turned around.

'Harry, wassup?'

'Hey, man, just came in to get a couple things. Hang on a sec, it's hot outside.'

Bosch walked to the front of the bureau, where old Henry of the Nod Squad sat at the desk behind the counter. He was working on a crossword puzzle and Bosch could see several erasure marks had turned the grid gray.

'Henry, howzit hanging? You getting anywhere with that?'

'Detective Bosch.'

Bosch slipped his sport coat off and hung it on a hook on the rack next to a jacket with a gray cross-hatch pattern. It was on a hanger and Bosch knew it belonged to Pounds. As he put his coat on the hook with his back to Henry and the rest of the bureau, he snaked his left hand inside the other coat, felt for the interior pocket and then pulled out Pounds's badge wallet. He knew it would be there. Pounds was a creature of habit and Bosch had seen the badge wallet in the suit coat once before. He put the wallet into his pants pocket and turned around as Henry continued talking. Bosch had only a momentary tinge of hesitation at the seriousness of what he was doing. Taking another cop's badge was a crime, but Bosch looked at Pounds as being the reason he did not have his own badge. In the inventory of his morality, what Pounds had done to him was equally wrong.

'If you want to see the lieutenant, he's down the hall at a meeting,' Henry said.

'No, I don't want to see the lieutenant, Henry. In fact, don't even tell him I was here. I don't want his blood pressure to go up, you know. I'm just going to get a few things and get out of here, okay?'

'That's a deal. I don't want him cranky, either.'

Bosch didn't have to worry about anyone else in the bureau telling Pounds he had been in. He gave Henry a friendly clasp on the shoulder as he walked behind him, sealing the agreement. He went back to the homicide table and as he approached, Burns began to rise from Bosch's old spot.

'You need to get in here, Harry?' he asked.

Bosch thought he could detect nervous energy in the other man's voice. He understood his predicament and wasn't going to make it a difficult time for him.

'Yeah, if you don't mind,' he said. 'I figured I'd get my personal stuff out of there so you can move in the right way.'

Bosch came around and opened the drawer at the table. There were two boxes of Junior Mints on top of old paperwork that had been shoved in long ago.

'Oh, those are mine, sorry,' Burns said.

He reached in for the two boxes of candy and stood next to the table, holding them like a big kid in a suit while Bosch went through the paperwork.

It was all a show. Bosch took some of the paperwork and dumped it in a manila file and then pointed with his hand, signaling to Burns he could put his candy back.

'Be careful, Bob.'

'It's Bill. Careful of what?'

'Ants.'

Bosch went to the bank of file cabinets that ran along the wall to the side of the table and opened one of the drawers with his business card taped to it. It was three up from the bottom, waist-high, and it was one he knew was almost empty. With his back to the table again, he pulled the badge wallet out of his pocket and put it in the drawer. Then, with his hands in the drawer and out of sight, he opened the wallet and took out the gold badge. He then put it in one pocket and the wallet back in the other. For good measure, he pulled a file out of the drawer and closed it.

He turned around and looked at Jerry Edgar.

'Okay, that's it. Just some personal stuff I might need. Anything going on?'

'Nah, quiet.'

Back at the coatrack, Bosch turned his back on the bureau again and used one hand to reach for his coat while using the other to take the badge wallet from his pocket and slip it back into Pounds's coat. He then put his coat on, said good-bye to Henry and went back to the homicide table.

'I'm outta here,' he said to Edgar and Burns while picking up the two files he had pulled. 'I don't want Ninety-eight to see me and throw a fit. Good luck, boys.'

On the way out, Bosch stopped and gave the hype another cigarette. The lockdown who had complained before was no longer on the bench or Bosch would have given him one, too.

Back in the Mustang, he dumped the files on the backseat and took his empty badge wallet out of his briefcase. He slipped Pounds's badge into place next to his own ID card. It would work, he decided, as long as no one looked too closely at it. The badge said LIEUTENANT across it. Bosch's ID card identified him as a detective. It was a minor discrepancy and Bosch was happy with it. Best of all, he thought, there was a good chance Pounds would not notice that the badge was missing for some time. He rarely left the station to go to crime scenes and so rarely had to open the wallet or show his badge. There was a good chance its disappearance would go unnoticed. All he had to do was get it back into place when he was done with it.

21

Bosch ended up outside the door of Carmen Hinojos's office early for his afternoon session. He waited until exactly three-thirty and knocked. She smiled as he entered her office and he noticed that the late-afternoon sun came through the window and splashed light directly across her desk. He moved toward the chair he usually took but then stopped himself and sat on the chair to the left of the desk. She noticed this and frowned at him as if he were a schoolboy.

'If you think I care which chair you sit in, you are wrong.'

'Am I? Okay.'

He got up and moved to the other chair. He liked being near the window.

'I might not be here for Monday's session,' he said after settling in.

She frowned again, this time more seriously.

'Why not?'

'I'm going away. I'll try to be back.'

'Away? What happened to your investigation?'

'It's part of it. I'm going to Florida to track down one of the original investigators. One's dead, the other one's in Florida. So I've got to go to him.'

'Couldn't you just call?'

'I don't want to call. I don't want to give him the chance to put me off.'

She nodded.

'When do you leave?'

'Tonight. I'm taking a red-eye to Tampa.'

'Harry, look at you. You practically look like the walking dead. Can't you get some sleep and take a plane in the morning?'

'No, I've gotta get out there before the mail arrives.'

'What's that mean?'

'Nothing. It's a long story. Anyway, I wanted to ask you something. I need your help.'

She contemplated this for several seconds, apparently weighing how far she wanted to go into the pool without knowing how deep it was.

'What is it you want?'

'Do you ever do any forensic work for the department?'

She narrowed her eyes, not seeing where this was going.

'A little. From time to time somebody will bring me something, or maybe ask me to do a little profiling of a suspect. But mostly the department uses outside contractors. Forensic psychiatrists who have experience with this.'

108

'But you've been to crime scenes?'

'Actually, no. I've only looked at photos brought to me and worked from them.'

'Perfect.'

Bosch pulled his briefcase onto his lap and opened it. He took out the envelope of crime scene and autopsy photos that had been in the murder book and gently placed them on her desk.

'Those are from this case. I don't want to look at them. I can't look at them. But I need someone to do it and tell me what's there. There's probably nothing but I'd like another opinion. The investigation these two guys did on this case was ... well, it was almost like there was no investigation.'

'Oh, Harry.' She shook her head. 'I'm not sure this is wise. Why me?'

'Because you know what I'm doing. And because I trust you. I don't think I can trust anybody else.'

'Would you trust me if there was no ethical constraint on me telling others about what we've talked about here?'

Bosch studied her face.

'I don't know,' he finally said.

'I thought so.'

She slid the envelope to the side of the desk.

'Let's put these aside for now and go on with the session. I really have to think about this.'

'Okay, you can take them. But let me know, okay? I just want your feel for them. As a psychiatrist and as a woman.'

'We'll see.'

'What do you want to talk about?'

'What is happening with the investigation?'

'Is that a professional question, Dr Hinojos? Or are you just curious about the case?'

'No, I'm curious about you. And I'm worried about you. I'm still not convinced that what you are doing is safe – either psychologically or physically. You're mucking around in the lives of powerful people. And I'm caught in the middle. I know what you're doing but am almost powerless to make you stop. I'm afraid you tricked me.'

'Tricked you?'

'You pulled me into this. I bet you've wanted to show me these pictures since you told me what you're doing.'

'You're right, I have. But there was no trick. I thought this was a place where I could talk about anything. Isn't that what you said?'

'Okay, I wasn't tricked, just led down the path. I should've seen it coming. Let's move on. I want to talk more about the emotional aspect of what you are doing. I want to know more about why finding this killer is so important to you after so many years?'

'It should be obvious.'

'Make it more obvious for me.'

'I can't. I can't put it into words. All I know is that everything changed for me after she was gone. I don't know how things would have been if she hadn't been taken away but ... everything changed.'

'Do you understand what you're saying and what it means? You're looking at your life in two parts. The first part is with her, which you seem to have imbued with a happiness I'm sure was not always there. The second part is your life after, which you acknowledge has not met expectations or is in some way unsatisfactory. I think you've been unhappy for a long time, possibly all of that time. This recent relationship you had may have been a highlight but you were still and, I think, have always been, an unhappy man.'

She rested a moment but Bosch didn't speak. He knew she wasn't done.

'Now, maybe the traumas of the last few years – both personally for you and for your community at large – have made you take stock of yourself. And I fear that you believe, whether subconsciously or not, that by going back and bringing some form of justice to what happened to your mother, you will be righting your life. And there's the problem. Whatever happens with this private investigation of yours, it's not going to change things. It just can't be done.'

'You're saying that I can't blame what happened then for what I am now?'

'No, listen to me, Harry. All I'm saying is you are the sum of many parts, not the sum of one. It's like dominoes. Several different blocks must click together for you to arrive at the end, at the point you are at now. You don't jump from the first domino to the last.'

'So I should just give it up? Just let it go?'

'I'm not saying that. But I am finding it hard to see the emotional benefit or healing you will get from this. In fact, I think there is the possibility that you may do yourself more damage than repair. Does that make any sense?'

Bosch stood up and went to the window. He stared out but didn't compute what he saw. He felt the warmth of the sun on him. He didn't look at her as he spoke.

'I don't know what makes sense. All I know is that on every level it seems to make sense that I do this. In fact, I feel . . . I don't know what the word is, maybe ashamed. I feel ashamed that I haven't done this long before now. A lot of years have gone by and I just let them go. I feel like I let her down somehow . . . that I let myself down.'

'That's understa –'

'Remember what I told you the first day? Everybody counts or nobody counts. Well, for a long time she didn't count. Not with this department, this society, not even with me. I have to admit that, not even with me. Then I opened that file this week and I could see that her death was just put away. It was buried, just like I had buried it. Somebody put the fix in because she didn't count. They did it because they could. And then when I think about how long I've let it go . . . it makes me want to . . . I don't know, just hide my face or something.'

He stopped, unable to put into words what he wanted to say. He looked down and noticed there were no ducks in the butcher shop window.

'You know,' he said, 'she might've been what she was but sometimes I feel like I didn't even deserve that . . . I guess I got what I deserved in life.'

He stayed at the window, not looking at her. It was several moments before Hinojos spoke.

'I guess this is the point where I should tell you that you're being too hard on yourself, but I don't think that would help much.'

110

'No, it wouldn't.'

'Could you come back here and sit down? Please?'

Bosch did as he was asked. Finally, after he was seated, his eyes met hers. She spoke first.

'What I want to say is that you are mixing things up. Putting the cart before the horse. You can't take the blame because this case may have been covered up. First of all, you had nothing to do with that, and secondly, you didn't even realize that until you read through the file this week.'

'But don't you see? Why didn't I look at it before? I'm not new here. I've been a cop twenty years. I should've been there before this. I mean, so what that I didn't know the details. I knew she was killed and nothing was ever done about it. That was enough.'

'Look, Harry, think about this, okay? On the plane over tonight, just give it some thought. You've engaged yourself in a noble pursuit but you have to safeguard against damaging yourself further. The bottom line is that it is not worth that. It's not worth the toll you may have to pay.'

'Not worth it? There's a killer out there. He thinks he made it away free. For years, he has thought that. Decades. And I'm going to change that.'

'You're not understanding what I'm saying. I don't want any guilty person to get away, especially with murder. But what I am talking about here is you. You are my only concern here. There is a basic rule of nature. No living thing sacrifices itself or hurts itself needlessly. It's the will of survival and I fear the circumstances of your life may have blunted your own survival skills. You may be throwing it to the wind, not caring what happens to you emotionally, physically, in every way, in this pursuit. I don't want to see you hurt.'

She took a breather. He said nothing.

'I have to say,' she continued quietly, 'I'm very nervous about this. I've never had this situation come up before and I've counseled a lot of cops in nine years here.'

'Well, I got bad news for you.' He smiled. 'I went and crashed a party last night at Mittel's. I think I may have spooked him. At least, I spooked myself.'

'Shit!'

'Is that some new psychiatric term? I'm not familiar with it.'

'This isn't funny. Why'd you do that?'

Bosch thought a moment.

'I don't know. It was kind of a whim type of thing. I was just driving by his house and there was a party. It kind of . . . it just made me angry for some reason. Him having a party and my mother . . .'

'Did you speak to him about the case?'

'No. I didn't even tell him my name. We just kind've sparred around for a few minutes but then I left him something. Remember that newspaper clip I showed you Wednesday? I left that for him. I saw him read it. I think it struck a nerve.'

She exhaled loudly.

'Now, step outside yourself and look as an uninvolved observer at what you did. If you can. Was that a smart thing to do, going there like that?'

'I already have thought about it. No, it wasn't smart. It was a mistake.

He'll probably warn Conklin. They'll both know somebody's out there, coming for them. They'll close ranks.'

'You see, you are proving my point for me. I want you to promise me you won't do anything foolish like that again.'

'I can't.'

'Well, then I have to tell you that a patient-doctor relationship can be broken if the therapist believes the patient is endangering himself or others. I told you I was almost powerless to stop you. Not completely.'

'You'd go to Irving?'

'I will if I believe you are being reckless.'

Bosch felt anger as he realized she had ultimate control over him and what he was doing. He swallowed the anger and held up his hands, surrendering.

'All right. I won't go crashing any parties again.'

'No. I want more than that. I want you to stay away from these men that you think may have been involved.'

'What I'll promise you is that I won't go to them until I have the whole thing in the bag.'

'I mean it.'

'So do I.'

'I hope so.'

They were silent for nearly a minute after that. It was a cooling-off period. She turned slightly in her chair, not looking at him, probably thinking what to say next.

'Let's move on,' she finally said. 'You understand that this whole thing, this pursuit of yours, has eclipsed what we're supposed to be doing here?'

'I know.'

'So we're prolonging my evaluation.'

'Well, that doesn't bother me as much anymore. I need the time off the job for this other thing.'

'Well, as long as you are happy,' she said sarcastically. 'Okay, then I want to go back to the incident that brought you to me. The other day you were very general and very short in your description of what happened. I understand why. I think we were both feeling each other out at that point. But we are far past that now. I'd like a fuller story. You said the other day that Lieutenant Pounds set things into motion?'

'That's right.'

'How?'

'First of all, he's a commander of detectives who has never been a detective himself. Oh, technically, he probably spent a few months on a table somewhere along the line so he'd have it on his résumé, but basically he's an administrator. He's what we call a Robocrat. A bureaucrat with a badge. He doesn't know the first thing about clearing cases. The only thing he knows about it is how to draw a line through the case on this little chart he keeps in his office. He doesn't know the first thing about the differences between an interview and an interrogation. And that's fine, the department is full of people like him. I say let them do their job and let me do mine. The problem is Pounds doesn't realize where he's good and where he's bad. It's led to problems before. Confrontations. It finally led to the incident, as you keep calling it.'

'What did he do?'

'He touched my suspect.'

'Explain what that means.'

'When you've got a case and you bring someone in, he's all yours. Nobody goes near him, understand? The wrong word, the wrong question and it could spoil a case. That's a cardinal rule; don't touch somebody else's suspect. It doesn't matter if you're a lieutenant or the damn chief, you stay clear until you check first with the guys with the collar.'

'So what happened?'

'Like I told you the other day, my partner Edgar and I brought in this suspect. A woman had been killed. One of these ones who puts ads in the sex tabs you can buy on the Boulevard. She gets called to one of those shithole motel rooms on Sunset, has sex with the guy and ends up stabbed to death. That's the short story. The stab wound's to the upper right chest. The john, he plays it cool, though. He calls the cops and says it was her knife and she tried to rob him with it. He says he turned her arm and put it into her. Self-defense. Okay, so that's when me and Edgar show up and right away we see some things don't fit with that story.'

'Like what?'

'First of all, she's a lot smaller than he is. I don't see her coming at him with a knife. Then there's the knife itself. It's a serrated steak knife, 'bout eight inches long, and she had one of those little purses without a strap.'

'A clutch.'

'Yeah, I guess. Anyway, that knife wouldn't've fit in it, so how'd she bring it in? As they say on the street, her clothes fit tighter than the rubbers in her purse, so she wasn't hiding it on her, either. And there was more. If her purpose was to rip the guy off, why have sex first? Why not pull the knife, take his shit and go? But that didn't happen. His story was that they did it first, then she came at him, which explained why she was still naked. Which, of course, raised another question. Why rob the guy when you're naked? Where you going to run like that?'

'The guy was lying.'

'Seemed obvious. Then we got something else. In her purse – the clutch – was a piece of paper on which she had written down the motel's name and the room number. It was consistent with a right-handed person. Like I said, the stab was to the upper right chest of the victim. So it doesn't add up. If she came at him, the chances are the knife would be in her right hand. If the john then turns it into her, it's likely the wound would be on the left side of the chest, not the right.'

Bosch made a motion of pulling his right hand toward his chest, showing how awkward it would be for it to stab his right side.

'There was all kinds of stuff that wasn't right. It was a downward-grade wound, also inconsistent with it being in her hand. That would have been upward-grade.'

Hinojos nodded that she understood.

'The problem was, we had no physical evidence contradicting his story. Nothing. Just our feeling that she wouldn't have done it the way he said. The wound stuff wasn't enough. And then, in his favor, was the knife. It was on the bed, we could see it had fingerprints in the blood. I had no doubt they'd be hers. That's not hard to do once she's dead. So while it didn't impress me, that didn't matter. It's what the DA would think and then what a jury would think after that. Reasonable doubt is a big black hole that swallows cases like this. We needed more.'

'So what happened?'

'It's what we call a he-said-she-said. One person's word against the other, but only the other is dead in this case. Makes it even harder. We had nothing but his story. So what you do in a case like that is you sweat the guy. You turn him. And there's a lot of ways to do it. But, basically, you gotta break him down in the rooms. We –'

'The rooms?'

'The interrogation rooms. In the bureau. We took this guy into a room. As a witness. We didn't formally arrest him. We asked if he'd come down, said that we had to straighten a few things out about what she did, and he said sure. You know, Mr Cooperative. Still cool. We stuck him in a room and then Edgar and I went down to the watch office to get some of the good coffee. They've got good coffee there, one of those big urns that was donated by some restaurant that got wrecked in the quake. Everybody goes in there to get coffee. Anyway, we're takin' our time, talkin' about how we're going to go at this guy, which one of us wanted him first, and so on. Meantime, fuckin' Pounds – excuse me – sees the guy in the room through the little window and goes in and informs him. And –'

'What do you mean, informs him?'

'Reads him his rights. This is our goddamn witness and Pounds, who doesn't know what the hell he's doing, thinks he's gotta go in there and give the guy the spiel. He thinks like we forgot or something.'

Bosch looked at her with outrage on his face but immediately saw she didn't understand.

'Wasn't that the right thing to do?' she asked. 'Aren't you required by law to inform people of their rights?'

Bosch struggled to contain his anger, reminding himself that Hinojos might work for the department, but she was an outsider. Her perceptions of police work were likely based more on the media than on the actual reality.

'Let me give you a quick lesson on what's the law and what's real. We – the cops – have the deck stacked against us. What *Miranda* and all the other rules and regs amount to is that we have to take some guy we know is, or at least think is, guilty and basically say, 'Hey, look, we think you did it and the Supreme Court and every lawyer on the planet would advise you not to talk to us, but, how about it, will you talk to us?' It just doesn't work. You gotta get around that. You gotta use guile and some bluffing and you gotta be sneaky. The rules of the courts are like a tightrope that you're walking on. You have to be very careful but there is a chance you can walk on it to get to the other side. So when some asshole who doesn't know shit walks in on your guy and informs him, it can pretty much ruin your whole day, not to mention the case.'

He stopped and studied her. He still saw skepticism. He knew then that she was just another citizen who would be scared shitless if she ever got a dose of the way things really were on the street.

'When someone is informed, that's it,' he said. 'It's over. Me and Edgar came back in from coffee and the john sits there and says he thinks he wants his lawyer. I said, "What lawyer, who's talking about lawyers? You're

114

a witness, not a suspect," and he tells us that the lieutenant just read him his rights. I don't know at that moment who I hated more, Pounds for blowing it or this guy for killing the girl.'

'Well, tell me this, what would have happened if Pounds had not done what he did?'

'We would've made friendly with the guy, asked him to tell his story in as much detail as possible and hoped there would be inconsistencies when compared to what he'd told the uniforms. Then we would have said, "The inconsistencies in your statements make you a suspect." *Then* we would have informed him and hopefully clubbed the shit out of him with the inconsistencies and the problems we found with the scene. We would have tried, and maybe succeeded, in finessing a confession. Most of what we do is just get people to talk. It's not like the stuff on TV. It's a hundred times harder and dirtier. But just like you, what we do is get people to talk ... Anyway, that's my view. But we'll never know now what could've happened because of Pounds.'

'Well, what did happen after you found out he'd been informed?'

'I left the room and walked straight into where Pounds was in his office. He knew something was wrong because he stood up. I remember that. I asked him if he'd informed my guy and when he said yes, we got into it. Both of us, screaming . . . then I don't really remember how it happened. I'm not trying to deny anything. I just don't remember the details. I must've grabbed him and pushed him. And his face went through the glass.'

'What did you do when that happened?'

'Well, some of the guys came running in and pulled me out of there. The station commander sent me home. Pounds had to go to the hospital to fix his nose. IAD took a statement from him and I was suspended. And then Irving stepped in and changed it to ISL. Here I am.'

'What happened with the case?'

'The john never talked. He got his lawyer and waited it out. Edgar went with what we had to the DA last Friday and they kicked it. They said they weren't going into court with a no-witness case with a few minor inconsistencies . . . Her prints were on the knife. Big surprise. What it came down to is that she didn't count. At least not enough for them to take the chance of losing.'

Neither of them spoke for a few moments. Bosch guessed that she was thinking about the corollaries between this case and his mother's.

'So what we've got,' he finally said, 'is a murderer out there on the street and the guy who allowed him to go free is back behind his desk, the broken glass already replaced, business as usual. That's our system. I got mad about it and look what it got me. Stress leave and maybe the end of my job.'

She cleared her throat before going into her appraisal of the story.

'As you have set down the circumstances of what happened, it is quite easy to see your rage. But not the ultimate action you took. Have you ever heard the phrase, "a mad minute?" '

Bosch shook his head.

'It's a way of describing a violent outburst that has its roots in several pressures on an individual. It builds up and is released in a quick moment – usually violently, often against a target not wholly responsible for the pressure.'

'If you need me to say Pounds was an innocent victim, I'm not going to say it.'

'I don't need that. I just need you to look at this situation and how it could happen.'

'I don't know. Shit just happens.'

'When you physically attack someone, don't you feel that you lower yourself to the same level as the man who was set free?'

'Not by a long shot, Doctor. Let me tell you something, you can look at all parts of my life, you can throw in earthquakes, fires, floods, riots and even Vietnam, but when it came down to just me and Pounds in that glass room, none of that mattered. You can call it a mad minute or whatever you want. Sometimes, the moment is all that matters and in that moment I was doing the right thing. And if these sessions are designed to make me see I did something wrong, forget it. Irving buttonholed me the other day in the lobby and asked me to think about an apology. Fuck that. I did the right thing.'

She nodded, adjusted herself in her seat and looked more uncomfortable than she had through his long diatribe. Finally, she looked at her watch and he looked at his. His time was up.

'So,' he said, 'I guess I've set the cause of psychotherapy back a century, huh?'

'No, not at all. The more you know of a person and the more you know of a story, the more you understand how things happen. It's why I enjoy my job.'

'Same here.'

'Have you spoken to Lieutenant Pounds since the incident?'

'I saw him when I dropped off the keys to my car. He had it taken away. I went into his office and he practically got hysterical. He's a very small man and I think he knows it.'

'They usually do.'

Bosch leaned forward, ready to get up and leave, when he noticed the envelope she had pushed to the side of her desk.

'What about the photos?'

'I knew you'd bring that up one more time.'

She looked at the envelope and frowned.

'I need to think about it. On several levels. Can I keep them while you go to Florida? Or will you need them?'

'You can keep 'em.'

22

At four-forty in the morning California time the air carrier landed at Tampa International Airport. Bosch leaned bleary-eyed against a window in the coach cabin, watching the sun rising in the Florida sky for the first time. As the plane taxied, he took off his watch and moved the hands ahead three hours. He was tempted to check into the nearest motel for some real sleep but knew he didn't have the time. From the AAA map he had brought with him, it looked like it was at least a two-hour drive down to Venice.

'It's nice to see a blue sky.'

It was the woman next to him in the aisle seat. She was leaning over toward him, looking out the window herself. She was in her mid-forties with prematurely gray hair. It was almost white. They had talked a bit in the early part of the flight and Bosch knew she was heading back to Florida rather than visiting as he was. She had given LA five years but had had enough. She was going home. Bosch didn't ask who or what she was coming home to, but had wondered if her hair was white when she had first landed in LA five years before.

'Yeah,' he replied. 'These night flights take forever.'

'No, I meant the smog. There is none.'

Bosch looked at her and then out the window, studying the sky.

'Not yet.'

But she was right. The sky had a quality of blue he rarely saw in LA. It was the color of swimming pools, with billowing white cumulus clouds floating like dreams in the upper atmosphere.

The plane cleared out slowly. Bosch waited until the end, got up and rolled his back to relieve the tension. The joints of his backbone cracked like dominoes going down. He got his overnighter out of the compartment above and headed out.

As soon as he stepped off the plane into the jetway, the humidity surrounded him like a wet towel with an incubating warmth. He made it into the air-conditioned terminal and decided to scratch his plan to rent a convertible.

A half hour later he was on the 275 freeway crossing Tampa Bay in another rented Mustang. He had the windows up and the air conditioning on but he was sweating as his body still had not acclimated to the humidity.

What struck him most about Florida on this first drive was its flatness. For forty-five minutes not a hillrise came in sight until he reached the concrete-and-steel mountain called the Skyway Bridge. Bosch knew that the steeply

117

graded bridge over the mouth of the bay was a replacement for one that had fallen but he drove across it fearlessly and above the speed limit. After all, he came from postquake Los Angeles, where the unofficial speed limit *under* bridges and overpasses was on the far right side of the speedometer.

After the skyway the freeway merged with the 75 and he reached Venice two hours after landing. Cruising along the Tamiami Trail, he found the small pastel-painted motels inviting as he struggled with fatigue, but he drove on and looked for a gift shop and a pay phone.

He found both in the Coral Reef Shopping Plaza. The Tacky's Gifts and Cards store wasn't due to open until ten and Bosch had five minutes to waste. He went to a pay phone on the outside wall of the sand-colored plaza and looked up the post office in the book. There were two in town so Bosch took out his notebook and checked Jake McKittrick's zip code. He called one of the post offices listed in the book and learned that the other one catered to the zip code Bosch had. He thanked the clerk who had provided the information and hung up.

When the gift shop opened, Bosch went to the cards aisle and found a birthday card that came with a bright red envelope. He took it to the counter without even reading the inside or the outside of the card. He picked a local street map out of a display next to the cash register and put that on the counter as well.

'That's a nice card,' said the old woman who rang up the sale. 'I'm sure she'll just love it.'

She moved as if she were underwater and Bosch wanted to reach over the counter and punch in the numbers himself, just to get it going.

In the Mustang, Bosch put the card in the envelope without signing it, sealed it and wrote McKittrick's name and post office box number on the front. He then started the car and got back on the road.

It took him fifteen minutes working with the map to find the post office on West Venice Avenue. When he got inside, he found it largely deserted. An old man was standing at a table slowly writing an address on an envelope. Two elderly women were in line for counter service. Bosch stood behind them and realized that he was seeing a lot of senior citizens in Florida and he'd only been here a few hours. It was just like he had always heard.

Bosch looked around and saw the video camera on the wall behind the counter. He could tell by its positioning it was there more for recording customers and possible robbers than for surveilling the clerks, though their workstations were probably fully in view as well. He was undeterred. He took a ten-dollar bill out of his pocket, folded it cleanly and held it with the red envelope. He then checked his loose change and came up with the right amount. It seemed like an excruciatingly long time as the one clerk waited on the women.

'Next in line.'

It was Bosch. He walked up to the counter where the clerk waited. He was about sixty and had a perfect white beard. He was overweight and his skin seemed too red to Bosch. As if he was mad or something.

'I need a stamp for this.'

Bosch put down the change and the envelope. The ten-dollar bill was folded on top of it. The postman acted like he didn't see it.

'I was wondering, did they put the mail out yet in the boxes?'

'They're back there doin' it now.'

He handed Bosch a stamp and swiped the change off the counter. He didn't touch the ten or the red envelope.

'Oh, really?'

Bosch picked up the envelope, licked the stamp and put it on. He then put the envelope back down on top of the ten. He was sure the postman had observed this.

'Well, jeez, I really wanted to get this to my Uncle Jake. It's his birthday today. Any way somebody could run it back there? That way he'd get it when he came in today. I'd deliver it in person but I've got to get back to work.'

Bosch slid the envelope with the ten underneath it across the counter, closer to white beard.

'Well,' he said, 'I'll see what I can do.'

The postman shifted his body to the left and turned slightly, shielding the transaction from the video camera. In one fluid motion he took the envelope and the ten off the counter. He quickly transferred the ten to his other hand and it dove for cover in his pocket.

'Be right back,' he called to the people still in line.

Out in the lobby, Bosch found Box 313 and looked through the tiny pane of glass inside. The red envelope was there along with two white letters. One of the white envelopes was upside down and its return address was partially visible.

City of

Departm

P.O. Bo

Los Ang

90021–3

Bosch felt reasonably sure the envelope carried McKittrick's pension check. He had beaten the mail to him. He walked out of the post office, bought two cups of coffee and a box of doughnuts in the convenience store next door and then returned to the Mustang to wait in the day's growing heat. It wasn't even May yet. He couldn't imagine what a summer must be like here.

Bored with watching the post office door after an hour, Bosch turned on the radio and found it tuned to a channel featuring a southern evangelical ranter. It took several seconds before Harry realized that the speaker's subject was the Los Angeles earthquake. He decided not to change the station.

'And ah ask, is it a coincidence that this cata-clysmic calamity was centered in the very heart of the ind'stry that poe-loots this entarh nation with the smut of pone-ography? I think not! I believe the Lahd struck a mighty blow to the infidels engaged in this vile and mul-tie-billyon-dollah trade when he cracked the uth asundah. It is a sign, mah frens, a sign of things that ah to come. A sign that all is not right in –'

Bosch turned it off. A woman had just come out of the post office holding a red envelope among other pieces of mail. Bosch watched her cross the

119

parking lot to a silver Lincoln Town Car. Bosch instinctively jotted the plate number down, though he had no law enforcement contact in this part of the state who would run it for him. The woman was in her mid-sixties, Bosch guessed. He had been waiting for a man, but her age made her fit. He started the Mustang and waited for her to pull out.

She drove north on the main highway toward Sarasota. Traffic moved slowly. After about fifteen minutes and maybe two miles, the Town Car took a left on Vamo Road and then almost immediately took a right on a private road camouflaged by tall trees and green growth. Bosch was only ten seconds behind her. As he came up to the drive, he slowed but didn't turn in. He saw a sign set back in the trees.

WELCOME TO

PELICAN COVE

Condominium Homes, Dockage

The Town Car passed by a guard shack with a red-and-white-striped gate arm coming down behind it.

'Shit!'

Bosch hadn't anticipated anything like a gated community. He assumed that such things were rare outside of Los Angeles. He looked at the sign again, then turned around and headed out to the main road. He remembered seeing another shopping plaza right before he had turned on to Vamo.

There were eight homes in Pelican Cove listed in the For Sale section of the *Sarasota Herald-Tribune*, but only three were for sale by owner. Bosch went to a pay phone in the plaza and called the first one. He got a tape. On the second call the woman who answered said her husband was golfing for the day and she felt uncomfortable showing the property without him. On the third call, the woman who answered invited Bosch to come over right away and even said she'd have fresh lemonade prepared when he got there.

Bosch felt a momentary pang of guilt about taking advantage of a stranger who was just trying to sell her home. But it passed quickly as he considered that the woman would never know she had been used in such a way, and he had no other alternative for getting to McKittrick.

After he was cleared at the gate and got directions to the lemonade lady's unit, Bosch drove through the densely wooded complex, looking for the silver Town Car. It didn't take him long to see that the complex was mostly a retirement community. He passed several elderly people in cars or on walks, almost all of them with white hair and skin browned by the sun. He quickly found the Town Car, checked his location against the map given to him at the guard shack and was about to make a cursory visit to the lemonade lady to avoid suspicion. But then he saw another silver Town Car. It was a popular car with the older set, he guessed. He took out his notebook and checked the plate number he had written down. Neither car had been the one he had followed earlier.

He drove on and finally found the right Town Car in a secluded spot in the far reaches of the complex. It was parked in front of a two-story building of dark wood siding surrounded by oak and paper trees. It looked to Bosch as if there were six units in the building. Easy enough, he thought. He

120

consulted the map and got back on course to the lemonade lady. She was on the second floor of a building on the other side of the complex.

'You're young,' she said when she answered the door.

Bosch wanted to say the same thing back to her but held his tongue. She looked like she was in her mid- to late thirties, which put her three decades behind anyone Bosch had seen around the complex so far. She had an attractive and evenly tanned face framed in brown shoulder-length hair. She wore blue jeans, a blue oxford shirt and a black vest with a colorful pattern in the front. She didn't bother with much makeup, which Bosch liked. She had serious green eyes, which he also didn't disagree with.

'I'm Jasmine. Are you Mr Bosch?'

'Yes. Harry. I just called.'

'That was quick.'

'I was nearby.'

She invited him in and started the rundown.

'It's three bedrooms, like the paper said. Master suite has a private bath. Second bath off the main hall. The view is what makes the place, though.'

She pointed Bosch toward a wall of sliding glass doors that looked out on a wide expanse of water dotted with mangrove islands. Hundreds of birds perched in the branches of these otherwise untouched islands. She was right, the view was beautiful.

'What is that?' Bosch asked. 'The water.'

'That's – you're not from around here, are you? That's Little Sarasota Bay.'

Bosch nodded while computing the mistake he had made by blurting out the question.

'No, I'm not from around here. I'm thinking of moving here though.'

'Where from?'

'Los Angeles.'

'Oh, yes, I've heard. A lot of people are bailing out. Because the ground won't stop shaking.'

'Something like that.'

She led him down a hallway to what must have been the master suite. Bosch was immediately struck by how the room didn't seem to fit this woman. It was all dark and old and heavy. A mahogany bureau that looked like it weighed a ton, matching bedside tables with ornate lamps and brocaded shades. The place smelled old. It couldn't be where she slept.

He turned and noticed on the wall next to the door an oil painting that was a portrait of the woman standing next to him. It was a younger likeness of her, the face much gaunter, more severe. Bosch was wondering what kind of person hangs a painting of herself in her bedroom when he noticed that the painting was signed. The artist's name was Jazz.

'Jazz. Is that you?'

'Yes. My father insisted on hanging that in here. I actually should have taken it down.'

She went to the wall and began to lift the painting off.

'Your father?'

He moved to the other side of the painting to help her.

'Yes. I gave this to him a long time ago. At the time I was thankful he didn't hang it out in the living room where his friends would see it but even here is a little too much.'

She turned the painting so the back faced outward and leaned it against the wall. Bosch put together what she had been saying.

'This is your father's place.'

'Oh, yes. I've just been staying here while the ad ran in the paper. You want to check out the master bath? It has a Jacuzzi tub. That wasn't mentioned in the ad.'

Bosch moved closely by her to the bathroom door. He looked down at her hands, a natural instinct, and saw no rings on any of her fingers. He could smell her as he passed and the scent he picked up was the same as her name: Jasmine. He was beginning to feel some kind of attraction to her but wasn't sure if it was the titillation of being there under false pretenses or an honest pull. He was exhausted, he knew, and decided that was it. His defenses were down. He gave the bathroom a quick once-over and stepped out.

'Nice. Did he live here alone?'

'My father? Yes, alone. My mother died when I was little. My father passed away over Christmas.'

'I'm sorry.'

'Thank you. What else can I tell you?'

'Nothing. I was just curious about who had been living here.'

'No. I mean, what else can I tell you about the condo?'

'Oh, I . . . nothing. It's very nice. I'm still in the looking-around stage, I guess, not sure what I'm going to do. I –'

'What are you really doing?'

'Excuse me?'

'What are you doing here, Mr Bosch? You're not looking to buy a condo in here. You're not even looking at the place.'

There was no anger in her voice. It was a voice full of the confidence she had in reading people. Bosch felt himself turning red. He had been found out.

'I'm just . . . I'm just here to look at places.'

It was a terribly weak comeback and he knew it. But it was all he could think of to say. She sensed his predicament and let him off the hook.

'Well, I'm sorry if I embarrassed you. Do you want to see the rest of the place?'

'Yes – uh, well, did you say it was three bedrooms? That's really too big for what I'm looking for.'

'Yes, three. But it said that in the newspaper ad, too.'

Luckily, Bosch knew he probably couldn't get any redder than he already was.

'Oh,' he said. 'I must've missed that. Uh, thanks for the tour, though. It's a very nice place.'

He moved quickly through the living room toward the door. As he opened it he looked back at her. She spoke before he could say anything.

'Something tells me it's a good story.'

'What's that?'

'Whatever it is you're doing. If you ever feel like telling it, the number's in the paper. But you already know that.'

Bosch nodded. He was speechless. He stepped through the door and closed it behind him.

23

By the time he drove back to where he had seen the Town Car, his face had returned to its normal color but he still felt embarrassed about being cornered by the woman. He tried to dismiss it and concentrate on the task at hand. He parked and went to the first-floor door that was nearest the Town Car and knocked. Eventually, an old woman opened the door and stared at him with frightened eyes. One hand clasped the handle of a small two-wheeled cart that carried an oxygen bottle. Two clear plastic tubes snaked over her ears and across both cheeks to her nose.

'I'm sorry to disturb you,' he said quickly. 'I was looking for the McKittricks.'

She raised a frail hand, formed a fist with the thumb out and jerked it up toward the ceiling. Her eyes went up that way, too.

'Upstairs?'

She nodded. He thanked her and headed for the stairs.

The woman who had picked up the red envelope answered the next door he knocked on and Bosch exhaled as if he had spent a lifetime looking for her. It almost felt that way.

'Mrs McKittrick?'

'Yes?'

Bosch pulled out his badge case and flipped it open. He held the wallet so that his first two fingers crossed most of the badge, obscuring the LIEUTENANT.

'My name's Harry Bosch. I'm a detective with the LAPD. I was wondering if your husband was here. I'd like to talk to him.'

An immediate concern clouded her face.

'LAPD? He hasn't been out there in twenty years.'

'It's about an old case. I was sent out to ask him about it.'

'Well, you could've called.'

'We didn't have a number. Is he here?'

'No, he's down with the boat. He's going fishing.'

'Where's that? Maybe I can catch him.'

'Well, he doesn't like surprises.'

'I guess it will be a surprise whether you tell him or I tell him. Doesn't make any difference to me. I just have to talk to him, Mrs McKittrick.'

Maybe she was used to the no-debate tone that cops can put into their voice. She gave in.

'You walk around the building here and go straight back past the next three buildings. Go left, you'll see the docks after that.'

'Where's his boat?'

'It's slip six. It says *Trophy* in big letters on the side. You can't miss it. He hasn't left yet because I'm supposed to bring his lunch down.'

'Thanks.'

He had started away from the door to the side of the building when she called after him.

'Detective Bosch? Are you going to be a while? Should I make you a sandwich, too?'

'I don't know how long I'll be but that would be nice of you.'

As he headed toward the docks, he realized that the woman named Jasmine had never offered him the lemonade she had promised.

24

It took Bosch fifteen minutes to find the little inlet where the docks were. After that, McKittrick was easy enough to spot. There were maybe forty boats in slips but only one of them was occupied. A man with a deep tan set off by his white hair stood in the stern bending over the outboard engine. Bosch studied him as he got closer but saw nothing recognizable about the man. He did not fit with the image Bosch had in his mind's eye of the man who had pulled him from the pool so long ago.

The cover was off the boat engine and the man was doing something with a screwdriver. He wore khaki shorts and a white golf shirt that was too old and stained for golf but was fine for boating. The boat was about twenty feet long, Bosch guessed, and had a small cabin near the bow, where the helm was. There were fishing rods erected in holders along the sides of the boat, two rods per side.

Bosch stopped on the dock at the bow of the boat on purpose. He wanted to be at a distance from McKittrick when he showed the badge. He smiled.

'Never thought I'd see somebody from the Hollywood homicide table so far away from home,' he said.

McKittrick looked up but showed no surprise. He showed nothing.

'Nope, you're wrong. This is home. When I was over there, that's when I was far away.'

Bosch gave a that's-fair-enough nod and showed the badge. He held it the same way as when he'd showed it to McKittrick's wife.

'I'm Harry Bosch, from Hollywood homicide.'

'Yeah, that's what I heard.'

Bosch was the one who showed surprise. He could not think of who in LA would have tipped McKittrick to his arrival. No one knew. He had only told Hinojos and he could not fathom that she would betray him.

McKittrick relieved him by gesturing to the portable phone on the dashboard of the boat.

'The wife called.'

'Oh.'

'So what's this all about, Detective Bosch? When I used to work there, we did things in pairs. It was safer that way. You folks that understaffed, you're going singleton?'

'Not really. My partner's chasing down another old case. These are such long shots, they're not wasting money sending two.'

'I assume you're going to explain that.'

'Yeah. As a matter of fact, I am. Mind if I come down there?'

'Suit yourself. I'm fixing to shove off as soon as the wife comes with the food.'

Bosch began walking along the finger dock to the side of McKittrick's boat. He then stepped down into the craft. It wobbled on the water with the added weight but then steadied. McKittrick lifted the engine cover and began snapping it back in place. Bosch felt grossly out of place. He wore street shoes with black jeans, an Army green T-shirt and a black light-weight sport jacket. And he was still hot. He took the jacket off and folded it over one of the two chairs in the cockpit.

'What are you going for?'

'Whatever's biting. What are you going for?'

He looked directly at Bosch when he asked this and Harry saw that his eyes were brown like beer-bottle glass.

'Well, you heard about the earthquake, didn't you?'

'Sure, who didn't? You know, I've been through quakes and 'canes and you can keep the quakes. At least with a hurricane, you see it coming. You take Andrew, he left a lot of devastation, but think how much it woulda been if nobody knew he was about to hit. That's what you get with your earthquakes.'

It took Bosch a few moments to place Andrew, the hurricane that had slammed the South Florida coast a couple of years earlier. It was hard to keep track of all the disasters in the world. There were enough just in LA. He looked out across the inlet. He saw a fish jump and its reentry create a stampede of jumping among the others in the school. He looked at McKittrick and was about to tell him when he realized it was probably something McKittrick saw every day of his life.

'When'd you leave LA?'

'Twenty-one years ago. I got my twenty in and *pffft*, I was gone. You can have LA, Bosch. Shit, I was out there for the Sylmar quake in seventy-one. Knocked down a hospital and a couple freeways. At the time we were living in Tujunga, a few miles from the epicenter. I'll always remember that one. It was like God and the devil meetin' in the room and you were there with 'em playin' referee. Goddamn . . . So what's the quake got to do with you being here?'

'Well, it's kind of a strange phenomenon but the murder rate's fallen off. People are being more civil, I guess. We –'

'Maybe there's nothing left there worth killing for.'

'Maybe. Anyway, we're usually running seventy, eighty murders a year in the division, I don't know what it was like when you –'

'We'd do less than half that. Easy.'

'Well, we're running way below the average this year. It's given us time to go back through some of the old ones. Everybody on the table's taken a share. One of the ones I've got has your name on it. I guess you know your partner from back then passed away and –'

'Eno's dead? Goddamn, I didn't know that. I thought I would've heard about that. Not that it would've mattered a whole hell of a lot.'

'Yeah, he's dead. His wife gets the pension checks. Sorry, you hadn't heard.'

'That's okay. Eno and me . . . well, we were partners. That's about it.'

126

'Anyway, I'm here because you're alive and he isn't.'

'What's the case?'

'Marjorie Lowe.' He waited a moment for a reaction from McKittrick's face and got none. 'You remember it? She was found in the trash in an alley off –'

'Vista. Behind Hollywood Boulevard between Vista and Gower. I remember them all, Bosch. Cleared or not, I remember every goddamn one of them.'

But you don't remember me, Bosch thought but didn't say.

'Yeah, that's the one. Between Vista and Gower.'

'What about it?'

'It was never cleared.'

'I know that,' McKittrick said, his voice rising. 'I worked sixty-three cases during seven years on the homicide table. I worked Hollywood, Wilshire, then RHD. Cleared fifty-six. I'll put that up against anybody. Today they're lucky if they clear half of 'em. I'll put it up against you blind.'

'And you'd win. That's a good record. This isn't about you, Jake. It's about the case.'

'Don't call me Jake. I don't know you. Never seen you before in my life. I – wait a minute.'

Bosch stared at him, astonished that he might actually remember the pool. But then he realized that McKittrick had stopped because of his wife's approach along the dock. She was carrying a plastic cooler. McKittrick waited silently for her to put it down on the dock near the boat and he hoisted it aboard.

'Oh, Detective Bosch, you'll be way too hot in that,' Mrs McKittrick said. 'Do you want to come back up and borrow a pair of Jake's shorts and a white T-shirt?'

Bosch looked at McKittrick, then up at her.

'No, thanks, ma'am, I'm fine.'

'You are going fishing, aren't you?'

'Well, I haven't exactly been invited and I –'

'Oh, Jake, invite him fishing. You're always looking for somebody to go out with you. Besides, you can catch up on all that blood-and-guts stuff you used to love in Hollywood.'

McKittrick looked up at her and Bosch could see the horses fighting against the restraints. He was able to get it under control.

'Mary, thanks for the sandwiches,' he said calmly. 'Now, could you go back up to the house and leave us be?'

She threw him a frown and shook her head as if he were a spoiled boy. She went back the way she had come without another word. The two of them left on the boat let some time go by before Bosch finally spoke and tried to recover the situation.

'Look, I'm not here for any reason other than to ask you a few questions about this case. I'm not trying to suggest there was anything wrong with the way it was handled. I'm just taking another look at it. That's all.'

'You left something out.'

'What's that?'

'That you're full of shit.'

Bosch could feel the horses rearing up in himself. He was angry at this

127

man's questioning his motives, even though he was right to do so. He was on the verge of shedding the nice-guy skin and going at him. But he knew better. He knew that for McKittrick to act this way, there must be a reason. Something about the old case was like a pebble in his shoe. He had worked it over to the side where it didn't hurt when he walked. But it was still in there. Bosch had to make him want to take it out. He swallowed his own anger and tried to stay level.

'Why am I full of shit?' he said.

McKittrick's back was to him. The former cop was reaching down under the steering console. Bosch couldn't see what he was trying to do, except he guessed he was maybe looking for a hidden set of boat keys.

'Why are you full of shit?' McKittrick answered as he turned around. 'I'll tell you why. Because you come here flashing that bullshit badge around when we both know you don't have a badge.'

McKittrick was pointing a Beretta twenty-two at Bosch. It was small but it would do the job at this distance, and Bosch had to believe that McKittrick knew how to use it.

'Jesus, man, what's the problem with you?'

'I had no problem until you showed up.'

Bosch held his hands chest-high in a nonthreatening pose.

'Just take it easy.'

'You take it easy. Put your fucking hands down. I want to see that badge again. Take it out and toss it over here. Slowly.'

Bosch complied, all the while trying to look around the docks without turning his head more than a few inches. He didn't see anyone. He was alone. And unarmed. He threw the badge wallet down on the deck near McKittrick's feet.

'Now I want you to walk around the bridge to the bow up there. Stand against the bow rail where I can see you. I knew somebody would try to fuck with me someday. Well, you picked the wrong guy and the wrong day.'

Bosch did as instructed and went up to the bow. He grabbed the railing for support and turned around to face his captor. Without taking his eyes off Bosch, McKittrick bent and picked up the wallet. Then he moved into the cockpit and put the gun down on top of the console. Bosch knew if he tried for it McKittrick would get there first. McKittrick reached down and turned something and the engine kicked over.

'What are you doing, McKittrick?'

'Oh, now it's McKittrick. What happened to the friendly "Jake"? Well, what's doing is, we're going fishing. You wanted to fish, that's what we'll do. You try to jump and I'll shoot you in the water. I don't care.'

'I'm not going anywhere. Just take it easy.'

'Now, reach down to that cleat and unhook that line. Throw it up on the dock.'

When Bosch had finished completing the order, McKittrick picked up the gun and stepped back three paces into the stern. He untied the other line and pushed off from a pylon. He returned to the helm and gently put the boat in reverse. It glided out of the slip. McKittrick then put it in forward and they started moving through the inlet toward the mouth of the canal. Bosch could feel the warm salt breezes drying the sweat on his skin. He decided he would jump as soon as they got to some open water, or where there were other boats with people on them.

'Kind of surprised you're not carrying. What kind of guy says he's a cop, then doesn't carry a piece?'

'I am a cop, McKittrick. Let me explain.'

'You don't have to, boy, I already know. Know all about you.'

McKittrick flipped open the badge wallet and Bosch watched him study the ID card and the gold lieutenant's badge. He threw it on the console.

'What do you know about me, McKittrick?'

'Don't worry, I still have a few teeth left, Bosch, and I still have a few friends in the department. After the wife called, I made a call. One of my friends. He knew all about you. You're on leave, Bosch. Involuntary. So I don't know about this bullshit story about earthquakes you were spinning. Makes me think maybe you picked up a little freelance work while you're off the job.'

'You got it wrong.'

'Yeah, well, we'll see. Once we get out into some open water, you're gonna tell me who sent you or you're gonna be fish food. Makes no difference to me.'

'Nobody sent me. I sent myself.'

McKittrick slapped his palm against the red ball on the throttle lever and the boat surged forward. Its bow rose and Bosch grabbed the railing to hold on.

'Bullshit!' McKittrick yelled above the engine noise. 'You're a liar. You lied before, you're lying now.'

'Listen to me,' Bosch yelled. 'You said you remember every case.'

'I do, goddamnit! I can't forget them.'

'Cut it back!'

McKittrick pulled the throttle back and the boat evened off and the noise reduced.

'On the Marjorie Lowe case you pulled the dirty work. You remember that? Remember what we call the dirty work? You had to tell the next of kin. You had to tell her kid. Out at McClaren.'

'That was in the reports, Bosch. So –'

He stopped and stared at Bosch for a long moment. Then he flipped open the badge case and read the name. He looked back at Bosch.

'I remember that name. The swimming pool. You're the kid.'

'I'm the kid.'

25

McKittrick let the boat drift in the shallows of Little Sarasota Bay while Bosch told the story. He asked no questions. He simply listened. At a moment where Bosch paused, he opened the cooler his wife had packed and took out two beers, handing one to Bosch. The can felt ice-cold in Bosch's hand.

Bosch didn't pull the tab on his beer until he finished the story. He had told everything he knew to McKittrick, even the nonessential part about his run-in with Pounds. He had a hunch, based on McKittrick's anger and bizarre behavior, that he had been wrong about the old cop. He had flown out to Florida believing he was coming to see either a corrupt or a stupid cop and he wasn't sure which he would dislike more. But now he believed that McKittrick was a man who was haunted by memories and the demons of choices made badly many years ago. Bosch thought that the pebble still had to come out of the shoe and that his own honesty was the best way to get to it.

'So that's my story,' he said at the end. 'I hope she packed more than two of these.'

He popped the beer and drank nearly a third of it. It tasted delicious going down his throat in the afternoon sun.

'Oh, there's plenty more where that came from,' McKittrick replied. 'You want a sandwich?'

'Not yet.'

'No, what you want is my story now.'

'That's what I came for.'

'Well, let's get out there to the fish.'

He restarted the engine and they followed a trail of channel markers south through the bay. Bosch finally remembered he had sunglasses in the pocket of his sport coat and put them on.

It seemed like the wind was cutting in on him from all directions and on occasion its warmth would be traded for a cool breeze that would come up off the surface of the water. It was a long time since Bosch had been on a boat or had even been fishing. For a man who had had a gun pointed at him twenty minutes earlier, he realized he felt pretty good.

As the bay tapered off into a canal, McKittrick pulled back on the throttle and cut their wake. He waved to a man on the bridge of a giant yacht tied up outside a waterside restaurant. Bosch couldn't tell if he knew the man or was just being neighborly.

'Take it on a line even with the lantern on the bridge,' McKittrick said.

'What?'

'Take it.'

McKittrick stepped away from the wheel and into the stern of the boat. Bosch quickly stepped behind the wheel, sighted the red lantern hanging at center point beneath the span of a drawbridge a half mile ahead and adjusted the wheel to bring the boat into line. He looked back and saw McKittrick pull a plastic bag of small dead fish out of a compartment in the deck.

'Let's see who we've got here today,' he said.

He went to the side of the boat and leaned well over the gunwale. Bosch saw him start slapping an open palm on the side of the boat. McKittrick then stood up, surveyed the water for about ten seconds and repeated the banging.

'What's going on?' Bosch asked.

Just as he said it, a dolphin crested the water off the port stern and reentered no more than five feet from where McKittrick was standing. It was a slippery gray blur and Bosch wasn't exactly sure at first what had happened. But the dolphin quickly resurfaced next to the boat, its snout out of the water and chattering. It sounded like it was laughing. McKittrick dropped two of the fish into its open mouth.

'That's Sergeant, see the scars?'

Bosch took a quick look back at the bridge to make sure they were still reasonably on line and then stepped back to the stern. The dolphin was still there. McKittrick pointed down into the water beneath its dorsal fin. Bosch could see three white stripes slashed across its smooth gray back.

'He got too close to a prop one time and it cut him up. The people up at Mote Marine took care of him. But he was left with those sergeant's stripes.'

Bosch nodded as McKittrick fed the dolphin again. Without looking up to see if they were off course, McKittrick said, 'You better get the wheel.'

Bosch turned and saw that they had drifted far off line. He went back to the wheel and corrected the course. He stayed there while McKittrick remained in the back, throwing fish to the dolphin, until they passed under the bridge. Bosch decided he could wait him out. Whether it was while they were going out or coming in didn't matter. He was going to get McKittrick's story. He was not going to leave without it.

Ten minutes after the bridge they came to a channel that took them out to the Gulf of Mexico. McKittrick dropped lures from two of the poles into the water and put out about a hundred yards of line on each one. He took the wheel back from Bosch then, yelling into the wind and engine noise.

'I want to take it out to the reefs. We'll troll until we're there and then we'll do some drift fishing in the shallows. We'll talk then.'

'Sounds like a plan,' Bosch yelled back.

Nothing hit either of the lures, and about two miles from the shore McKittrick killed the engines and told Bosch to bring in one line while he handled the other. It took Bosch, who was left handed, a few moments to get himself coordinated on the right-handed reel but then he started smiling.

'I don't think I've done this since I was a kid. At McClaren every now and then they'd put us on a bus and take us out to the Malibu Pier.'

'Jesus, that pier still there?'

'Yeah.'

'Must be like fishing in a cesspool by now.'

'I guess.'

McKittrick laughed and shook his head.

'Why do you stay there, Bosch? Doesn't sound like they particularly want you.'

Bosch thought a moment before answering. The comment was on point but he wondered if it was on point from McKittrick or whoever the source was he had called.

'Who'd you call back there about me?'

'I'm not telling you. That's why he talked to me, because he knew I wouldn't tell you.'

Bosch nodded, signaling he'd let it go.

'Well, you're right,' he said. 'I don't think they particularly want me back there. But I don't know. It's kind've like the more they push one way, the more I push the other. I feel like if they'd stop asking or trying to make me leave, then I'd probably want to do it.'

'I guess I know what you mean.'

McKittrick stowed the two rods they had used and set to work outfitting the other two with hooks and buckshot weights.

'We're going to use mullet.'

Bosch nodded. He didn't know the first thing about it. But he watched McKittrick closely. He thought it might be a good time to start.

'So you punched out after your twenty in LA. What'd you do after that?'

'You're looking at it. I moved back here – I'm from Palmetto, up the coast, originally. I bought a boat and became a fishing guide. Did that another twenty, retired and now I fish for my own damned self.'

Bosch smiled.

'Palmetto? Isn't that the name of those big cockroaches?'

'No. Well, yeah, but it's also the name of a scrub palm. That's what the town's named for, not the bug.'

Bosch nodded and watched as McKittrick opened a bag of mullet strips and hooked pieces on each line. After opening fresh beers, they cast on separate sides of the boat and then sat on the gunwales, waiting.

'Then how'd you end up in LA?' Bosch asked.

'What was that somebody said about going west young man? Well, after Japan surrendered I passed through LA on my way back home and I saw those mountains going all the way up from the sea to the sky ... Damn, I ate dinner at the Derby my first night in town. I was going to blow my whole wallet and you know who saw me there in uniform and picked up the tab? Goddamn Clark Gable. I'm not kidding you. I fuckin' fell in love with that place and it took me almost thirty years to see the light . . . Mary's from LA, you know. Born and raised. She likes it out here fine.'

He nodded to reassure himself. Bosch waited a few moments and McKittrick was still looking off at distant memories.

'He was a nice guy.'

'Who's that?'

'Clark Gable.'

Bosch crunched the empty beer can in his hand and got another.

132

'So tell me about the case,' he said after popping it. 'What happened?'

'You know what happened if you read the book. It was all in there. It got dumped. One day we had an investigation, the next we were writing 'No leads at this time.' It was a joke. That's why I remember the case so well. They shouldn't've done what they did.'

'Who's they?'

'You know, the big shots.'

'What did they do?'

'They took it away from us. And Eno let them. He cut some deal with them himself. Shit.'

He shook his head bitterly.

'Jake,' Bosch tried. He got no protest this time over using the first name. 'Why don't you start at the beginning. I need to know everything I can from you.'

McKittrick was quiet while he reeled in. His bait hadn't been touched. He recast it, put the rod in one of the gunwale pipes and got another beer. From beneath the console he grabbed a Tampa Bay Lightning cap and put it on. He leaned on the gunwale with his beer and looked at Bosch.

'Okay, kid, listen, I got nothin' against your mother. I'm just gonna tell you this the way it fell, okay?'

'That's all I want.'

'You want a hat? You're gonna get burned.'

'I'm fine.'

McKittrick nodded and finally started.

'Okay, so we got the call out from home. It was a Saturday morning. One of the footbeat guys had found her. She hadn't been killed in that alley. That much was clear. She'd been dropped off. By the time I got down there from Tujunga, the crime scene investigation was already underway. My partner was there, too. Eno. He was the senior man, he was there first. He took charge of it.'

Bosch put his rod in a pipe and went to his jacket.

'You mind if I take notes?'

'No, I don't mind. I guess I've been waiting for somebody to care about this one since I walked away from it.'

'Go ahead. Eno was in charge.'

'Yeah, he was the man. You've got to understand something. We'd been a team maybe three, four months at that time. We weren't tight. After this one, we'd never be tight. I switched off after about a year. I went in for the transfer. They moved me to Wilshire dicks, homicide table. Never had much to do with him after that. He never had much to do with me.'

'Okay, what happened with the investigation?'

'Well, it was like anything else that you'd expect. We were going through the routine. We had a list of her KAs – got it mostly from the vice guys – and were working our way through it.'

'The known associates, did they include clients? There was no list in the murder book.'

'I think there were a few clients. And the list didn't go into the book because Eno said so. Remember, he was the lead.'

'Okay. Johnny Fox was on the list?'

'Yeah, he was at the top of it. He was her . . . uh, manager and –'

133

'Her pimp, you mean.'

McKittrick looked at him.

'Yeah. That's what he was. I wasn't sure what you, uh –'

'Forget it. Go on.'

'Yeah, Johnny Fox was on the list. We talked to about everybody who knew her and this guy was described by everybody as one mean guy. He had a history.'

Bosch thought of Meredith Roman's report that he had beaten her.

'We'd heard that she was trying to get away from him. I don't know, either to go out on her own or maybe go straight. Who knows? We heard –'

'She wanted to be a straight citizen,' Bosch interrupted. 'That way she could get me out of the hall.'

He felt foolish for saying it, knowing his saying it was not convincing.

'Yeah, whatever,' McKittrick said. 'Point is, Fox was none too happy about that. That put him at the top of our list.'

'But you couldn't find him. The chrono says you watched his place.'

'Yeah. He was our man. We had prints we had taken off the belt – the murder weapon – but we had no comparisons from him. Johnny had been pulled in a few times in the past but never booked. Never printed. So we really needed to bring him in.'

'What did it tell you, that he'd been picked up but never booked?'

McKittrick finished his beer, crunched it in his hand and walked the empty over to a large bucket in the corner of the deck and dropped it.

'To be honest, at the time it didn't hit me. Now, of course, it's obvious. He had an angel watching over him.'

'Who?'

'Well, on one of the days we were watching Fox's place, waiting for him to show up, we got a message on the radio to call Arno Conklin. He wanted to talk about the case. ASAP. Now this was a holy shit kind of call. For two reasons. One, Arno was going great guns then. He was running the city's moral commandos at the time and had a lock on the DA's office, which was coming open in a year. The other reason was that we'd only had the case a few days and hadn't come near the DA's office with anything. So now all of a sudden the most powerful guy in the agency wants to see us. I'm thinking . . . I don't really know what I was thinking. I just knew it – hey, you got one!'

Bosch looked at his pole and saw it bend from a violent jerk on the line. The reel started spinning as the fish pulled against the drag. Bosch grabbed the pole out of the pipe and jerked it back. The hook was set well. He started reeling but the fish had a lot of fight and was pulling out more line than he was reeling in. McKittrick came over and tightened the drag dial, which immediately put a more pronounced bend in the pole.

'Keep the pole up, keep the pole up,' McKittrick counseled.

Bosch did as he was told and spent five minutes battling the fish. His arms started to ache. He felt a strain on his lower back. McKittrick put on gloves and when the fish finally surrendered and Bosch had it alongside the boat, he bent over and hooked his fingers into the gills and brought it on board. Bosch saw a shiny blue-black fish that looked beautiful in the sunlight.

'Wahoo,' McKittrick said.

'What?'

McKittrick held the fish up horizontally.

'Wahoo. Over there in your fancy LA restaurants I think they call it Ono. Here, we just call it wahoo. Meat cooks up white as halibut, you wanna keep it?'

'No, put it back. It's beautiful.'

McKittrick roughly pulled the hook from the gulping mouth of the fish and then held the catch out to Bosch.

'You want to hold it? Must be twelve, thirteen pounds.'

'Nah, I don't need to hold it.'

Bosch stepped closer and ran his finger along the slick skin of the fish. He could almost see himself in the reflection of its scales. He nodded to McKittrick and the fish was thrown back into the water. For several seconds it remained motionless, about two feet below the surface. Post-traumatic stress syndrome, Bosch thought. Finally, the fish seemed to come out of it and darted down into the depths. Bosch put the hook through one of the eyelets on his pole and put the pole back in its pipe. He was done fishing. He got another beer out of the cooler.

'Hey, you want a sandwich, go ahead,' McKittrick said.

'No. I'm fine.'

Bosch wished the fish hadn't interrupted them.

'You were saying that you guys got the call from Conklin.'

'Yeah, Arno. Only I had it wrong. The request for a meeting was only for Claude. Not me. Eno went alone.'

'Why only Eno?'

'I never knew and he acted like he didn't know, either. I just assumed it was because he and Arno had a prior relationship of some kind.'

'But you don't know what.'

'No. Claude Eno was about ten years older than me. He'd been around.'

'So what happened?'

'Well, I can't tell you what happened. I can only tell you what my partner said happened. Understand?'

He was telling Bosch that he didn't trust his own partner. Bosch had known that feeling himself at times and nodded that he understood.

'Go ahead.'

'He came back from the meeting saying Conklin asked him to lay off Fox because Fox was clear on this case and Fox was working as an informant on one of the commando investigations. He said Fox was important to him and he didn't want him compromised or roughed up, especially over a crime he didn't commit.'

'How was Conklin so sure?'

'I don't know. But Eno told me that he told Conklin that assistant DAs, no matter who they are, didn't decide whether someone was clear or not for the police, and that we weren't backing off until we talked to Fox for ourselves. Faced with that, Conklin said he could deliver Fox to be interviewed and fingerprinted. But only if we did it on Conklin's turf.'

'Which was . . . ?'

'His office in the old courthouse. That's gone now. They built that big square thing right before I left. Horrible-looking thing.'

'What happened in the office? Were you there for that?'

135

'Yeah, I was there but nothing happened. We interviewed him. Fox was there with Conklin, so was the Nazi.'

'The Nazi?'

'Conklin's enforcer, Gordon Mittel.'

'He was there?'

'Yup. I guess he was sort of watching out for Conklin while Conklin was watching out for Fox.'

Bosch showed no surprise.

'Okay, so what did Fox tell you?'

'Like I said, not much. At least, that's how I remember it. He gave us an alibi and the names of the people who could verify it. I took his prints.'

'What'd he say about the victim?'

'He said pretty much what we'd already heard from her girlfriend.'

'Meredith Roman?'

'Yeah, I think that's it. He said she went to a party, was hired as kind of a decoration to be on some guy's arm. He said it was in Hancock Park. He didn't have the address. He said he had nothing to do with setting it up. That didn't make sense to us. You know, a pimp not knowing where . . . not knowing where one of his girls was. It was the one thing we had and when we started leaning on him about it, Conklin stepped in like a referee.'

'He didn't want you leaning on him.'

'Craziest thing I ever saw. Here was the next DA – everybody knew he was going to run. Here he was taking this bastard's side against us . . . Sorry about that bastard comment.'

'Forget it.'

'Conklin was trying to make it seem like we were out of line, while all the time this big-piece-of-shit Fox was sitting there smiling with a toothpick in the side of his mouth. It's what, thirty-somethin' years ago and I can still remember that toothpick. Galled the Jesus out of me. So to make a long story short, we never did get to brace him on having set up the date she went on.'

The boat rocked on a high wake and Bosch looked around and didn't see any other boat. It was weird. He looked out across the water and for the first time realized how different it was from the Pacific. The Pacific was a cold and forbidding blue, the Gulf a warm green that invited you.

'We left,' McKittrick continued. 'I figured we'd have another shot at him. So we left and started to work on his alibi. It turned out to be good. And I don't mean it was good because his own witnesses said it was. We did the work. We found some independent people. People that didn't know him. As I remember it, it was rock solid.'

'You remember where he was?'

'Spent part of the night in a bar over there on Ivar, place a lot of the pimps hung around. Can't remember the name of it. Then later he drove out to Ventura, spent most of the rest of the night in a card room until he got a phone call, then he split. The other thing about this was that it didn't smack of an alibi set up for this particular night. This was his routine. He was well known in all of these places.'

'What was the phone call?'

'We never knew. We didn't know about it until we started checking his alibi and somebody mentioned it. We never got to ask Fox about it. But to be honest, we didn't care too much at that point. Like I said, his alibi was solid and he didn't get the call until later in the morning. Four, five o'clock. The vic – your mother had been dead a good long while by then. TOD was midnight. The call didn't matter.'

Bosch nodded but it was the kind of detail he would not have left open if it had been his investigation. It was too curious a detail. Who calls a poker room that early in the morning? What kind of call would make Fox up and leave the game?

'What about the prints?'

'I had 'em checked anyway and they didn't match those on the belt. He was clean. The dirtbag was clear.'

Bosch thought of something.

'You did check the prints on the belt against the victim's, right?'

'Hey, Bosch, I know you highfalutin' guys think you're the cat's ass now but we were known for having a brain or two back in those days.'

'Sorry.'

'There were a few prints on the buckle that were the victim's. That's it. The rest were definitely the killer's because of their location. We got good direct lifts and partials on two other spots where it was clear the belt had been grasped by the full hand. You don't hold a belt that way when you're putting it on. You hold it that way when you're putting it around someone's neck.'

They were both silent after that. Bosch couldn't figure out what McKittrick was telling him. He felt deflated. He had thought that if he got McKittrick to open up, the old cop would point the finger at Fox or Conklin or somebody. But he was doing none of that. He really wasn't giving Bosch anything.

'How come you remember so many details, Jake? It's been a long time.'

'I've had a long time to think about it. When you finish up, Bosch, you'll see, there'll always be one. One case that stays with you. This is the one that stayed with me.'

'So what was your final take on it?'

'My final take? Well, I never got over that meeting at Conklin's office. I guess you had to be there but it just … it just seemed that the one that was in charge of that meeting was Fox. It was like he was calling the shots.'

Bosch nodded. He could see that McKittrick was struggling for an explanation of his feelings.

'You ever interview a suspect with his lawyer there jumpin' in and out of the conversation?' McKittrick asked. 'You know, "Don't answer this, don't answer that." Shit like that.'

'All the time.'

'Well, it was like that. It was like Conklin, the next DA for Chrissake, was this shitheel's lawyer, objecting all the time to our questions. What it came down to was that if you didn't know who he was or where we were, you'd've sworn he was working for Fox. Both of them, Mittel, too. So, I felt pretty sure Fox had his hooks into Arno. Somehow he did. And I was right. It was all confirmed later.'

'You mean when Fox died?'

'Yeah. He got killed in a hit and run while working for the Conklin campaign. I remember the newspaper story on it didn't say nothin' about

137

his background as a pimp, as a Hollywood Boulevard hoodlum. No, he was just this guy who got run down. Joe Innocent. I tell ya, that story must've cost Arno a few dollars and made a reporter a little richer.'

Bosch could tell there was more so he said nothing.

'I was in Wilshire dicks by then,' McKittrick continued. 'But I got curious when I heard about it. So I called over to Hollywood to see who was on it. It was Eno. Big surprise. And he never made a case on anybody. So that about confirmed what I was thinking about him, too.'

McKittrick stared off across the water to where the sun was getting low in the sky. He threw his empty beer can at the bucket. It missed and bounced over the side into the water.

'Fuck it,' he said. 'I guess we should head in.'

He started reeling in his line.

'What do you think Eno got out of all of this?'

'I don't know exactly. He might've just been trading favors, something like that. I'm not saying he got rich, but I think he got something out of the deal. He wouldn't do it for nothing. I just don't know what it was.'

McKittrick started taking the rods out of the pipes and stowing them on hooks along the sides of the stern.

'In 1972 you checked the murder book out of archives, how come?'

McKittrick looked at him curiously.

'I signed the same checkout slip a few days ago,' Bosch explained. 'Your name was still on it.'

McKittrick nodded.

'Yeah, that was right after I put in my papers. I was leaving, going through my files and stuff. I'd hung on to the prints we took off the belt. Kept the card. Also hung on to the belt.'

'Why?'

'You know why. I didn't think it would be safe in that file or in the evidence room. Not with Conklin as DA, not with Eno doing him favors. So I kept the stuff. Then a bunch of years went by and it was there when I was cleaning shit out and going to Florida. So right before I decided to punch out, I put the print card back in the murder book and went down and put the belt back in the evidence box. Eno was already in Vegas, retired. Conklin had crashed and burned, was out of politics. The case was long forgotten. I put the stuff back. I guess maybe I hoped someday somebody like you would take a look at it.'

'What about you? Did you look at the book when you put the card back?'

'Yeah, and I saw I had done the right thing. Somebody had gone through it, stripped it. They pulled the Fox interview out of it. Probably was Eno.'

'As the second man on the case you had to do the paper, right?'

'Right. The paperwork was mine. Most of it.'

'What did you put on the Fox interview summary that would have made Eno need to pull it?'

'I don't remember anything specific, just that I thought the guy was lying and that Conklin was out of line. Something like that.'

'Anything else you remember that was missing?'

'Nah, nothing important, just that. I think he just wanted to get Conklin's name out of it.'

'Yeah, well, he missed something. You'd noted his first call on the Chronological Record. That's how I knew.'

'Did I? Well, good for me. And here you are.'

'Yeah.'

'All right, we're heading in. Too bad they weren't really biting today.'

'I'm not complaining. I got my fish.'

McKittrick stepped behind the wheel and was about to start the engine when he thought of something.

'Oh, you know what?' He moved to the cooler and opened it. 'I don't want Mary to be disappointed.'

He pulled out the plastic bags that contained the sandwiches his wife had made.

'You hungry?'

'Not really.'

'Me neither.'

He opened the bags and dumped the sandwiches over the side. Bosch watched him.

'Jake, when you pulled out that gun, who'd you think I was?'

McKittrick didn't say anything as he neatly folded the plastic bags and put them back in the cooler. When he straightened up, he looked at Bosch.

'I didn't know. All I knew was that I thought I might have to take you out here and dump you like those sandwiches. Seems like I've been hiding out here all my life, waiting for them to send somebody.'

'You think they'd go that far over time and distance?'

'I don't have any idea. The more time that goes by, the more I doubt it. But old habits die hard. I always keep a gun nearby. Doesn't matter that most times I don't even remember why.'

They rode in from the Gulf with the engine roaring and the soft spray of the sea in their faces. They didn't talk. That was done with. Occasionally, Bosch glanced over at McKittrick. His old face fell under the shadow of his cap brim. But Bosch could see his eyes in there, looking at something that had happened a long time before and no longer could be changed.

26

After the boat trip Bosch felt the onset of a headache from the combination of too much beer and too much sun. He begged off an invitation to dinner from McKittrick, saying he was tired. Once in his car, he took a couple of Tylenol caplets out of his overnighter, downed them without any liquid chaser and hoped they would do the job. He took out his notebook and reviewed some of the things he had written about McKittrick's story.

He had come to like the old cop by the end of the fishing trip. Maybe he saw some of himself in the older man. McKittrick was haunted because he had let the case go. He had not done the right thing. And Bosch knew he was guilty of the same during all the years he had ignored the case that he knew was there waiting for him. He was making up for that now, and so was McKittrick by talking to him. But both of them knew it might be too little too late.

Bosch wasn't sure what he would do next when he got back to Los Angeles. It seemed to him that his only move was to confront Conklin. He was reluctant to do this because he knew he would go into such a confrontation soft, with only his suspicions and no hard evidence. Conklin would have the upper hand.

A wave of desperation came over him. He did not want the case to come to this. Conklin hadn't flinched in almost thirty-five years. He wouldn't with Bosch in his face now. Harry knew he needed something else. But he had nothing.

He started the car but left it in Park. He turned the air conditioner on high and added what McKittrick had told him into the stew of what he already knew. He began formulating a theory. For Bosch, this was one of the most important components of homicide investigation. Take the facts and shake them down into hypothesis. The key was not to become beholden to any one theory. Theories changed and you had to change with them.

It seemed clear from McKittrick's information that Fox had a hold on Conklin. What was it? Well, Bosch thought, Fox dealt in women. The theory that emerged was that Fox had gotten a hook into Conklin through a woman, or women. The news clips at the time reported Conklin was a bachelor. The morals of the time would have dictated then as now that as a public servant and soon-to-be candidate for top prosecutor, Conklin needed not necessarily to be celibate but, at least, not to have succumbed privately to the very vices he was publicly attacking. If he had done that and was exposed, he could kiss his political career good-bye, let alone his position as commander of the DA commandos. So, Bosch concluded, if this was Conklin's flaw and it was through Fox that such dalliances were arranged, then Fox would hold an almost unbeatable hand when it came to having juice with Conklin. It would explain the unusual circumstances of the interview McKittrick and Eno conducted with Fox.

The same theory, Bosch knew, would work to an even greater degree if Conklin had done more than succumb to the vice of sex but had gone further: if he had killed a woman Fox had sent to him, Marjorie Lowe. For one thing, it would explain how Conklin knew for sure that Fox was in the clear on the murder – because he was the killer himself. For another, it would explain how Fox got Conklin to run interference for him and why he was later hired as a Conklin campaign worker. The bottom line was, if Conklin was the killer, Fox's hook would be set even deeper and it would be set for good. Conklin would be like that wahoo at the end of the line, a pretty fish unable to get away.

Unless, Bosch knew, the man at the other end of the line and holding the rod were to go away somehow. He thought about Fox's death and saw how it fit. Conklin let some time separate one death from the other. He played like a hooked fish, even agreeing to Fox's demand for a straight job with the campaign, and then, when all seemed clear, Fox was run down in the street. Maybe a payoff to a reporter kept the victim's background quiet – if the reporter even knew it, and a few months later Conklin was crowned district attorney.

Bosch considered where Mittel would fit into the theory. He felt it was unlikely that all of this had transpired in a vacuum. It was Bosch's guess that Mittel, as Conklin's right-hand man and enforcer, would know what Conklin knew.

Bosch liked his theory but it angered him, largely because that was all it was, theory. He shook his head as he realized he was back to ground zero. All talk, no evidence of anything.

He grew weary thinking about it and decided to put the thoughts aside for a while. He turned the air down because it was too cool against his sunburned skin and put the car in gear. As he slowly cruised through Pelican Cove toward the gatehouse, his thoughts drifted to the woman who was trying to sell her dead father's condo. She had signed the name Jazz on the self-portrait. He liked that.

He turned the car around and drove toward her unit. It was still daylight and no lights shone from behind the building's windows when he got there. He couldn't tell if she was there or not. Bosch parked nearby and watched for a few minutes, debating what he should do, if anything at all.

Fifteen minutes later, when it seemed that indecisiveness had paralyzed him, she stepped out the front door. He was parked nearly twenty yards away, between two other cars. His paralytic affliction eased enough for him to slide down in his seat to avoid detection. She walked out into the parking lot and behind the row of cars which included Bosch's rental. He didn't move or turn to follow her movement. He listened. He waited for the sound of a car starting. Then what, he wondered. Follow her? What are you doing?

He jerked upright at the sound of sharp rapping on the window next to him. It was her. Bosch was flustered but managed to turn the key so he could lower the window.

'Yes?'

'Mr Bosch, what are you doing?'

'What do you mean?'

'You've been sitting out here. I saw you.'

'I . . .'

He was too humiliated to finish.

'I don't know whether to call security or not.'

'No, don't do that. I, uh, I was just – I was going to go to your door. To apologize.'

'Apologize? Apologize for what?'

'For today. For earlier, when I was inside. I – you were right, I wasn't looking to buy anything.'

'Then what were you doing?'

Bosch opened the car door and stepped out. He felt disadvantaged with her looking down at him in the car.

'I'm a cop,' he said. 'I needed to get in here to see someone. I used you and I'm sorry. I am. I didn't know about your father and all of that.'

She smiled and shook her head.

'That's the dumbest story I've ever heard. What about LA, was that part of the story?'

'No. I'm from LA. I'm a cop there.'

'I don't know if I'd go around admitting that if I were you. You guys've got some bad PR problems.'

'Yeah, I know. So . . .' He felt his courage rising. He told himself he was flying out in the morning and it didn't matter what happened because he'd never see her or this state again. 'You said something before about lemonade but I never got any. I was thinking, maybe I could tell you the story, apologize and have some lemonade or something.'

He looked over toward the door of the condo.

'You LA cops are pushy,' she said but she was smiling. 'One glass and the story better be good. After that, we both gotta go. I'm driving up to Tampa tonight.'

They started walking toward the door and Bosch realized he had a smile on his face.

'What's in Tampa?'

'It's where I live and I miss it. I've been down here more than up there since I put the condo on the market. I want to spend a Sunday at my own place and in my own studio.'

'That's right, a painter.'

'I try to be.'

She opened the door for him and allowed him in first.

'Well, that's okay by me. I have to get to Tampa sometime tonight. I fly out in the morning.'

While nursing a tall glass of lemonade, Bosch explained his scam of using her to get into the complex to see another resident and she didn't seem upset. In fact, he could tell she admired the ingenuity of it. Bosch didn't tell her how it had backfired anyway when McKittrick had pulled a gun on him. He gave her a vague outline of the case, never mentioning its personal connection to himself and she seemed intrigued by the whole idea of solving a murder that happened thirty-three years earlier.

The one glass of lemonade turned into four and the last two were spiked nicely with vodka. They took care of what was left of Bosch's headache and put a nice bloom on everything. Between the third and the fourth she asked if he would mind if she smoked and he lit cigarettes for both of them. And as the sky darkened over the mangroves outside, he finally turned the conversation toward her. Bosch had sensed a loneliness about her, a mystery of some sort. Behind the pretty face there were scars. The kind that couldn't be seen.

Her name was Jasmine Corian but she said that friends called her Jazz. She spoke of growing up in the Florida sun, of never wanting to leave it. She had married once but it was a long time ago. There was nobody in her life now and she was used to it. She said she concentrated most of her life on her art and, in a way, Bosch understood what she meant. His own art, though few would call it that, took most of his life as well.

'What do you paint?'

'Portraits mostly.'

'Who are they?'

'Just someone I know. Maybe I'll paint you, Bosch. Someday.'

He didn't know what to say to that so he made a clumsy transition to safer ground.

'Why don't you give this place to a realtor to sell? That way you could stay in Tampa and paint.'

'Because I wanted the diversion. I also didn't want to give a realtor the five percent. This is a nice complex. These units sell pretty well without realtors. A lot of Canadian investment. I think I'll sell it. This was only the first week I've run the ad.'

Bosch just nodded and wished he had kept the conversation on her painting instead of realtors. The clumsy change seemed to have clogged things up a bit.

'I was thinking, you want to have dinner?'

She looked at him solemnly, as if the request and her answer had far deeper implications. They probably did. At least, he thought they did.

'Where would we go?'

That was a stall but he played along.

'I don't know. It's not my town. Not my state. You could pick a place. Around here or on the way up to Tampa. I don't care. I'd like your company, though, Jazz. If you want to.'

'How long has it been since you were with a woman? I mean on a date.'

'On a date? I don't know. A few months, I guess. But, look, I'm not a hard-luck case. I'm just in town and alone and thought maybe you'd –'

'It's okay, Harry. Let's go.'

'To eat?'

'Yes, to eat. I know a place on the way up. It's above Longboat. You'll have to follow me.'

He smiled and nodded.

She drove a Volkswagen Beetle convertible that was powder blue with one red fender. He couldn't lose her in a hailstorm let alone the slow-moving Florida highways.

Bosch counted two drawbridges that they had to stop for before they got to Longboat Key. From there they headed north for the length of the island, crossed a bridge onto Anna Maria Island and finally stopped at a place called the Sandbar. They walked through the bar and sat on a deck overlooking the Gulf. It was cool and they ate crabs and oysters chased with Mexican beer. Bosch loved it.

They didn't talk much but didn't need to. It was always in the silences that Bosch felt most comfortable with the women who had moved through his life. He felt the vodka and beer working on him, warming him toward her, sanding off any sharp edges to the evening. He felt a desire for her growing and tugging at him. McKittrick and the case had somehow been pushed into the darkness at the back of his mind.

'This is good,' he said when he was finally nearing his capacity for food and drink. 'It's great.'

'Yeah, they do it right. Can I tell you something, Bosch?'

'Go ahead.'

'I was only kidding about what I was saying about LA cops before. But I have known some cops before . . . and you seem different. I don't know what it is but it's like you've got too much of yourself left, you know?'

'I guess.' He nodded. 'Thanks. I think.'

They both laughed and then in a hesitant move, she leaned over and kissed him quickly on the lips. It was nice and he smiled. He could taste garlic.

'I'm glad you're already sunburned or you'd be turning red again.'

'No, I wouldn't. I mean, that was a nice thing to say.'

'You want to come home with me, Bosch?'

Now he hesitated. Not because there was any deliberation in his answer. But he wanted her to have the chance to withdraw it in case she had spoken too quickly. After a moment of silence from her he smiled and nodded.

'Yes, I would like that.'

They left then and cut inland to the freeway. Bosch wondered as he tailed the Volkswagen if she would change her mind as she drove alone. He got his answer at the Skyway bridge. As he pulled up to the tollbooth with his dollar already in hand, the tolltaker shook his head and waved off the money.

'Nope. That lady in the bug got ya covered.'

'Yeah?'

'Yeah. You know her?'

'Not yet.'

'I think you're goin' to. Good luck.'

'Thanks.'

27

Now Bosch couldn't lose her in a blizzard. As the drive grew longer, he found himself in a growing sense of an almost adolescent euphoria of anticipation. He was captured by the directness of this woman and he was wondering how and what that would translate to when they were making love.

She led him north to Tampa and then into an area called Hyde Park. Overlooking the bay, the neighborhood consisted of old Victorian and Craftsman-style houses with sweeping front porches. Her home was an apartment above the three-car garage set behind a gray Victorian with green trim.

As they got to the top of the steps and she was putting the key into the knob, Bosch thought of something and didn't know what to do. She opened the door and looked at him. She read him.

'What's wrong?'

'Nothing. But I was thinking, maybe I should go find a drugstore or something and then come back.'

'Don't worry, I've got what you'll need. But can you stand out here for a second? I just want to make a mad dash inside and clean up a few things.'

He looked at her.

'I don't care about that.'

'Please?'

'Okay. Take your time.'

He waited for about three minutes and then she opened the door and pulled him in. If she had cleaned up, she had done it in the dark. The only light came from what Bosch could see was the kitchen. She took his hand and led him away from the light to a darkened hallway that gave way to her bedroom. Here she turned on the light, revealing a sparely furnished room. A wrought-iron bed with a canopy was the centerpiece. There was a night table of unfinished wood next to it, a matching unfinished bureau and an antique Singer sewing machine table on which stood a blue vase with dead flowers in it. There was nothing hung on any of the walls, though Bosch saw a nail protruding from the plaster above the vase. Jasmine noticed the flowers and quickly took the vase off the table and headed out the door.

'I have to go dump this. I haven't been here in a week and forgot to change them.'

Moving the flowers raised a slightly acrid smell in the room. While she was gone Bosch looked at the nail again and thought he could see the delineation of a rectangle on the wall. Something had hung there, he decided. She hadn't come in to clean up. If she had, she would have gotten rid of the flowers. She'd come in to take down a painting.

When she came back into the room, she put the empty vase back on the table.

'Would you like another beer? I have some wine, too.'

Bosch moved toward her, intrigued even more by her mysteries.

'No, I'm fine.'

Without further word they embraced. He could taste beer and garlic and cigarette smoke as he kissed her but didn't care. He knew she was getting the same from him. He pressed his cheek against hers and with his nose he came across the spot on her neck where she had dabbed perfume. Night-blooming jasmine.

They moved onto the bed, each taking pieces of clothing off between hard kisses. Her body was beautiful, the tan lines distinct. He kissed her lovely small breasts and gently pushed her back on the bed. She told him to wait and she rolled to the side and from the drawer of the bed table extracted a strip of three condom packages and handed it to him.

'Is this wishful thinking?' he asked.

They both burst out laughing and it seemed to make things all the better.

'I don't know,' she said. 'We'll see.'

For Bosch, sexual encounters had always been a question of timing. The desires of two individuals rose and subsided on their own courses. There were emotional needs separate from physical needs. And sometimes all of those things clicked together in a person and then clicked in tandem with those of the other person. Bosch's encounter with Jasmine Corian was one of those times. The sex created a world without intrusion. One so vital that it could have lasted an hour or maybe only a few minutes and he wouldn't have known the difference. At the end, he was above her, looking into her open eyes, and she clutched his upper arms as if she were holding on for her life. Both of their bodies shuddered in unison and then he lay still on top of her, catching his breath from the hollow between her neck and shoulder. He felt so good he had the urge to laugh out loud but he didn't think she'd understand. He stifled it and made it sound like a muffled cough.

'Are you okay?' she asked softly.

'I've never felt better.'

Eventually, he moved off her, backing down over her body. He kissed both of her breasts, then sat up with her legs on either side of him. He removed the condom while using his body to shield her view of the process.

He got up and walked to the door he hoped was the bathroom and found it was a closet. The next door he tried was the bathroom and he flushed the condom down the toilet. He absentmindedly wondered if it would end up somewhere in Tampa Bay.

When he came back from the bathroom she was sitting up with the sheet bunched around her waist. He found his sport coat on the floor and got out his cigarettes. He gave her one and lit it. Then he bent over and kissed her breasts again. Her laugh was infectious and it made him smile.

'You know, I like it that you didn't come equipped.'

'Equipped? What are you talking about?'

146

'You know, that you offered to go to the drugstore. It shows what kind of man you are.'

'What do you mean?'

'If you had come over here from LA with a condom in your wallet, that would've been so . . . I don't know, premeditated. Like some guy just on the make. The whole thing would have had no spontaneity. I'm glad you weren't like that, Harry Bosch, that's all.'

He nodded, trying to follow her line of thought. He wasn't sure he understood. And he wondered what he should think of the fact that she *was* equipped. He decided to drop it and lit his cigarette.

'How'd you hurt your hand like that?'

She had noticed the marks on his fingers. Bosch had taken the Band-Aids off while flying over. The burns had healed to the point that they looked like red welts on two of his fingers.

'Cigarette. I fell asleep.'

He felt he could tell her the truth about everything about himself.

'God, that's scary.'

'Yeah. I don't think it will happen again.'

'Do you want to stay with me tonight?'

He moved closer to her and kissed her on the neck.

'Yes,' he whispered.

She reached over and touched the zipper scar on his left shoulder. The women he was with in bed always seemed to do this. It was an ugly mark and he never understood why they were drawn to touch it.

'You got shot?'

'Yeah.'

'That's even scarier.'

He hiked his shoulders. It was history and he never really thought about it anymore.

'You know, what I was trying to say before is that you're not like most cops I've known. You've got too much of your humanity left. How'd that happen?'

He shook his shoulders again like he didn't know.

'Are you okay, Bosch?'

He stubbed out his cigarette.

'Yeah, I'm fine. Why?'

'I don't know. You know what that guy Marvin Gaye sang about, don't you? Before he got killed by his own dad? He sang about sexual healing. Said it's good for the soul. Something like that. Anyway, I believe it, do you?'

'I suppose.'

'I think you need healing in your life, Bosch. That's the vibe I'm getting.'

'You want to go to sleep now?'

She lay down again and pulled the sheet up. He walked around the room naked, turning out the lights. When he was under the sheet in the dark, she turned on her side so her back was to him and told him to put his arm around her. He moved up close behind her and did. He loved her smell.

'How come people call you Jazz?'

'I don't know. They just do. Because it goes with the name.'

After a few moments she asked him why he had asked that.

'Because. You smell like both your names. Like the flower and the music.'

'What does jazz smell like?'

'It smells dark and smoky.'

They were silent for a long while after that and eventually Bosch thought she was asleep. But he still could not make it down. He lay with his eyes open, looking at the shadows of the room. Then she spoke softly to him.

'Bosch, what's the worst thing you've ever done to yourself?'

'What do you mean?'

'You know what I mean. What's the worst thing? What's the thing that keeps you awake at night if you think about it too hard?'

He thought for a few moments before answering.

'I don't know.' He forced an uneasy and short laugh. 'I guess I've done a lot of bad things. I suppose a lot of them are to myself. At least I think about them a lot . . .'

'What's one of them? You can tell me.'

And he knew that he could. He thought he could tell her almost anything and not be judged harshly.

'When I was a kid – I grew up mostly in a youth hall, like an orphanage. When I was new there, one of the older kids took my shoes, my sneakers. They didn't fit him or anything but he did it because he knew he could do it. He was one of the rulers of the roost and he took 'em. I didn't do anything about it and it hurt.'

'But you didn't do it. That's not what I –'

'No, I'm not done. I just told you that because you had to know that part. See, when I got older and I was one of the big shots in the place, I did the same thing. I took this new kid's shoes. He was smaller, I couldn't even put 'em on. I just took them and I . . . I don't know, I threw them out or something. But I took them because I could. I did the same thing that was done to me ... And sometimes, even now, I think about it and I feel bad.'

She squeezed his hand in a way he thought was meant to be comforting but said nothing.

'Is that the kind of story you wanted?'

She just squeezed his hand again. After a while he spoke.

'I think the one thing I did that I regret the most, though, was maybe letting a woman go.'

'You mean like a criminal?'

'No. I mean like we lived – we were lovers and when she wanted to go, I didn't really . . . do anything. I didn't put up a fight, you know. And when I think about it, sometimes I think that maybe if I had, I could've changed her mind . . . I don't know.'

'Did she say why she was leaving?'

'She just got to know me too well. I don't blame her for anything. I've got baggage. I guess maybe I can be hard to take. I've lived alone most of my life.'

Silence filled the room again and he waited. He sensed that there was something more she wanted to say or be asked. But when she spoke he wasn't sure if she was talking about him or herself.

'They say when a cat is ornery and scratches and hisses at everybody, even somebody who wants to comfort it and love it, it's because it wasn't held enough when it was a kitten.'

'I never heard that before.'

'I think it's true.'

He was quiet a moment and moved his hand up so that it was touching her breasts.

'Is that what your story is?' he asked. 'You weren't held enough.'

'Who knows.'

'What was the worst thing you ever did to yourself, Jasmine? I think you want to tell me.'

He knew she wanted him to ask it. It was true confessions time and he began to believe that the whole night had been directed by her to arrive at this one question.

'You didn't try to hold on to someone you should have,' she said. 'I held on to someone I shouldn't have. I held on too long. Thing is, I knew what it was leading to, deep down I knew. It was like standing on the tracks and seeing the train coming at you but being too mesmerized by the bright light to move, to save yourself.'

He had his eyes open in the dark still. He could barely see the outline of her shoulder and cheek. He pulled himself closer to her, kissed her neck and in her ear whispered, 'But you got out. That's what's important.'

'Yeah, I got out,' she said wistfully. 'I got out.'

She was silent for a while and then reached up under the covers and touched his hand. It was cupped over one of her breasts. She held her hand on top of it.

'Good night, Harry.'

He waited a while, until he heard the measured breathing of her sleep, and then he was finally able to drift off. There was no dream this time. Just warmth and darkness.

28

In the morning Bosch awoke first. He took a shower and borrowed Jasmine's toothbrush without asking. Then he dressed in the clothes he'd worn the day before and went out to his car to retrieve his overnight bag. Once he was dressed in fresh clothes he ventured into the kitchen to see about coffee. All he found was a box of tea bags.

Leaving the idea behind, he walked around the apartment, his steps creaking on the old pine floors. The living room was as spare as the bedroom. A sofa with an off-white blanket spread on it, a coffee table, an old stereo with a cassette but no CD player. No television. Again, nothing on the walls but the telltale indication that there had been. He found two nails in the plaster. They weren't rusted or painted over. They hadn't been there very long.

Through a set of French doors the living room opened up to a porch enclosed in windows. There was rattan furniture out here and several potted plants, including a dwarf orange tree with fruit on it. The entire porch was redolent with its smell. Bosch stepped close to the windows and by looking south down the alley behind the property, he could see the bay. The morning sun's reflection on it was pure white light.

He walked back across the living room to another door on the wall opposite the French doors. Immediately upon opening this door, he could smell the sharp tang of oils and turpentine. This was where she painted. He hesitated but only for a moment, then walked in.

The first thing he noticed was that the room had a window that gave a direct view of the bay across the backyards and garages of three or four houses down the alley. It was beautiful and he knew why she chose this room for her art. At center on a paint-dappled drop cloth was an easel but no stool. She painted standing. He saw no overhead lamp or artificial light source anywhere else in the room. She painted only by true light.

He walked around the easel and found the canvas on it had been untouched by the painter. Along one of the side walls was a high work counter with various tubes of paint scattered about. There were palette boards and coffee cans with brushes stacked in them. At the end of the counter was a large laundry sink for washing up.

Bosch noticed more canvases leaning against the wall under the counter. They were faced inward and appeared to be unused pieces like the one on the easel, waiting for the artist's hand. But Bosch suspected otherwise. Not with the exposed nails in the walls in the other rooms of the apartment. He reached under the counter and slid a few of the canvases out. As he did this he almost felt as if he was on some case, solving some mystery.

The three portraits he pulled out were painted in dark hues. None were signed though it was obvious all were the work of one hand. And that hand was Jasmine's. Bosch recognized the style from the painting he had seen at her father's house. Sharp lines, dark colors. The first one he looked at was of a nude woman with her face turned away from the painter and into the shadows. The sense Bosch felt was that the darkness was taking the woman, rather than her turning to the darkness. Her mouth was completely in shadow. It was as if she was mute. The woman, Bosch knew, was Jasmine.

The second painting seemed to be part of the same study as the first. It was the same nude in shadow, though she was now facing the viewer. Bosch noted that in the portrait Jasmine had given herself fuller breasts than in reality and he wondered if this was done on purpose and had some meaning, or was perhaps a subliminal improvement made by the painter. He noticed that beneath the veneer of gray shadow over the painting there were red highlights on the woman. Bosch knew little about the art, but he knew this was a dark portrait.

Bosch looked at the third painting he had pulled out and found this to be unattached to the first two, save for the fact that again it was a nude portrait of Jasmine. But this piece he clearly recognized as a reinterpretation of 'The Scream' by Edvard Munch, a painting that had always fascinated Bosch but that he had only seen in books. In the piece before him, the figure of the frightened person was Jasmine. The location had been transferred from Munch's horrific, swirling dreamscape, to the Skyway bridge. Bosch clearly recognized the bright yellow vertical piping of the bridge's support span.

'What are you doing?'

He jumped as if stabbed in the back. It was Jasmine, at the door of the studio. She wore a silk bathrobe she held closed with her arms. Her eyes were puffy. She had just woken up.

'I'm looking at your work, is that okay?'

'This door was locked.'

'No, it wasn't.'

She reached to the doorknob and turned it, as if that could disprove his claim.

'It wasn't locked, Jazz. I'm sorry. I didn't know you didn't want me in here.'

'Could you put those back under there, please?'

'Sure. But why'd you take them off the walls?'

'I didn't.'

'Was it because they're nudes, or is it because of what they mean?'

'Please don't ask me about this. Put them back.'

She left the doorway and he put the paintings back where he found them. He left the room and found her in the kitchen filling a tea kettle with water from the sink. Her back was to him and he walked in and lightly put a hand on her back. Even so, she started slightly at his touch.

'Jazz, look, I'm sorry. I'm a cop. I get curious.'

'It's okay.'

'Are you sure?'

'Yes, I'm sure. You want some tea?'

She had stopped filling the kettle but did not turn around or make a move to put it on the stove.

'No. I was thinking maybe I could take you out for breakfast.'

'When do you leave? I thought you said the plane's this morning.'

'That was the other thing I was thinking about. I could stay another day, leave tomorrow, if you want me to. I mean, if you'll have me. I'd like to stay.'

She turned around and looked at him.

'I want you to stay, too.'

They embraced and kissed but she quickly pulled back.

'It's not fair, you brushed your teeth. I have monster breath.'

'Yeah, but I used your toothbrush, so it evens out.'

'Gross. Now I have to get a new one.'

'That's right.'

They smiled and she gave him a tight hug around the neck, his trespass in her studio seemingly forgotten.

'You call the airline and I'll get ready. I know where we can go.'

When she pulled away he held her in front of him. He wanted to bring it up again. He couldn't help it.

'I want to ask you something.'

'What?'

'How come those paintings aren't signed?'

'They're not ready to be signed.'

'The one at your father's was signed.'

'That was for him, so I signed it. Those others are for me.'

'The one on the bridge. Is she going to jump?'

She looked at him a long time before answering.

'I don't know. Sometimes when I look at it, I think she is. I think the thought is there, but you never know.'

'It can't happen, Jazz.'

'Why not?'

'Because it can't.'

'I'll get ready.'

She broke away from him then and left the kitchen.

He went to the wall phone next to the refrigerator and dialed the airline. While making the arrangements to fly out Monday morning, he decided on a whim to ask the airline agent if it was possible to route his new flight back to Los Angeles through Las Vegas. She said not without a three-hour-and-fourteen-minute layover. He said he'd take it. He had to pay fifty dollars on top of the seven hundred they already had from him in order to make the needed changes. He put it on his credit card.

He thought about Vegas as he hung up. Claude Eno might be dead but his wife was still cashing his checks. She might be worth the fifty-dollar layover.

'Ready?'

It was Jasmine calling from the living room. Bosch stepped out of the kitchen and she was waiting for him in cut-off jeans and a tank top beneath a white shirt she left open and tied above her waist. She already had on sunglasses.

She took him to a place where they poured honey on top of the biscuits and served the eggs with grits and butter. Bosch hadn't had grits since basic training at Benning. The meal was delicious. Neither of them spoke much. The paintings and the conversation they had before falling asleep the night before were not mentioned. It seemed that what they had said was better left for the dark shadows of night, and maybe her paintings, too.

When they were done with their coffee, she insisted on picking up the check. He got the tip. They spent the afternoon cruising in her Volkswagen with the top down. She took him all over the place, from Ybor City to St Petersburg Beach, burning up a tank of gas and two packs of cigarettes. By late in the afternoon they were at a place called Indian Rocks Beach to look at the sunset over the Gulf.

'I've been a lot of places,' Jasmine told him. 'I like the light here the best.'

'Ever been out to California?'

'No, not yet.'

'Sometimes the sunset looks like lava pouring down on the city.'

'That must be beautiful.'

'It makes you forgive a lot, forget a lot . . . That's the thing about Los Angeles. It's got a lot of broken pieces to it. But the ones that still work, really do work.'

'I think I know what you mean.'

'I'm curious about something.'

'Here we go again. What?'

'If you don't show your paintings to anybody, how do you make a living?' It was from out of left field but he had been thinking about it all day.

'I have money from my father. Even before he died. It's not a lot but I don't need a lot. It's enough. If I don't feel the need to sell my work when it is finished, then as I am doing it, it won't be compromised. It will be pure.'

It sounded to Bosch like a convenient way of explaining away the fear of exposing oneself. But he let it go. She didn't.

'Are you always a cop? Always asking questions?'

'No. Only when I care about someone.'

She kissed him quickly and walked back to the car.

After stopping by her place to change, they had dinner in a Tampa steak house where the wine list was actually a book so thick it came on its own pedestal. The restaurant itself seemed to be the work of a slightly delusional Italian decorator, a dark blend of gilded rococo, garish red velvet and classical statues and paintings. It was the kind of place he would expect her to suggest. She mentioned that this meateater's palace was actually owned by a vegetarian.

'Sounds like somebody from California.'

She smiled and was quiet for a while after that. Bosch's mind wandered to the case. He had spent the entire day without giving it a thought. Now a pang of guilt thrummed in his mind. It was almost as if he felt he was shunting his mother aside to pursue the selfish pleasure of Jasmine's company. Jasmine seemed to read him and to know he was privately debating something.

'Can you stay another day, Harry?'

He smiled but shook his head.

'I can't. I gotta go. But I'll be back. As soon as I can.'

Bosch paid for dinner with a credit card he guessed was reaching its limit and they headed back to her apartment. Knowing their time together was drawing to a close, they went right to the bed and made love.

The feel of her body, its taste and its scent seemed perfect to Bosch. He didn't want the moment to end. He'd had immediate attractions to women before in his life and had even acted on them. But never one that felt so fully engaging and complete. He guessed that it was because of all he did not know about her. That was the hook. She was a mystery. Physically, he could not get any closer than he was to her during these moments, yet there was so much of her hidden, unexplored. They made love in gentle rhythm and held each other in a deep, long kiss at the end.

Later, he lay on his side, next to her, his arm across the flatness of her belly. One of her hands traced circles in his hair. The true confessions began.

'Harry, you know, I haven't been with a lot of men in my life.'

He didn't respond because he didn't know what the proper response could be. He was well past caring about a woman's sexual history for anything other than health reasons.

'What about you?' she asked.

He couldn't resist.

'I haven't been with a lot of men, either. In fact, none, as far as I know.'

She punched him on the shoulder.

'You know what I mean.'

'The answer is no. I haven't been with a lot of women in my life. Not enough, at least.'

'I don't know, the men that I've been with, most of them, it's like they wanted something from me I didn't have. I don't know what it was but I just didn't have it to give. Then I either left too soon or stayed too long.'

He propped himself up on one elbow and looked at her.

'Sometimes I think that I know strangers better than I know anybody else, even myself. I learn so much about people in my job. Sometimes I think I don't even have a life. I only have their life . . . I don't know what I'm talking about.'

'I think you do. I understand. Maybe everybody's like this.'

'I don't know. I don't think so.'

They were quiet for a while after that. Bosch leaned down and kissed her breasts, holding a nipple between his lips for a long moment. She brought her hands up and held his head to her chest. He could smell the jasmine.

'Harry, have you ever had to use your gun?'

He pulled his head up. The question seemed out of place. But through the darkness he could see her eyes on him, watching and waiting for an answer.

'Yes.'

'You killed someone.'

It wasn't a question.

'Yes.'

She said nothing else.

'What is it, Jazz?'

'Nothing. I was just wondering how that would be. How you would go on.'

'Well, all I can tell you is that it hurts. Even when there was no choice and they had to go down, it hurts. You just have to go on.'

154

She was silent. Whatever she had needed to hear from him he hoped she had gotten. Bosch was confused. He didn't know why she had asked such questions and wondered if she was testing him in some way. He lay back on his pillow and waited for sleep but confusion kept it away from him. After a while she turned on the bed and put her arm over him.

'I think you are a good man,' she whispered close to his ear.

'Am I?' he whispered back.

'And you will come back, won't you?'

'Yes. I'll come back.'

29

Bosch went to every rental counter in McCarran International Airport in Las Vegas but none had a car left. He silently chastised himself for not making a reservation and walked outside the terminal into the dry crisp air to catch a cab. The driver was a woman and when Bosch gave the address, on Lone Mountain Drive, he could clearly see her disappointment in the rearview mirror. The destination wasn't a hotel, so she wouldn't be picking up a return fare.

'Don't worry,' Bosch said, understanding her problem. 'If you wait for me, you can take me back to the airport.'

'How long you gonna be? I mean, Lone Mountain, that's way out there in the sand pits.'

'I might be five minutes, I might be less. Maybe a half hour. I'd say no longer than a half hour.'

'You waiting on the meter?'

'On the meter or you. Whatever you want to do.'

She thought about it a moment and put the car in drive.

'Where are all the rental cars, anyway?'

'Big convention in town. Electronics or something.'

It was a thirty-minute ride out into the desert northwest of the strip. The neon-and-glass buildings retreated and the cab passed through residential neighborhoods until these, too, became sparse. The land was a ragged brown out here and dotted unevenly with scrub brush. Bosch knew the roots of every bush spread wide and sucked up what little moisture was in the earth. It made for a terrain that seemed dying and desolate.

The houses, too, were few and far between, each one an outpost in a no-man's-land. The streets had been gridded and paved long ago but the boomtown of Las Vegas hadn't quite caught up yet. It was coming, though. The city was spreading like a patch of weeds.

The road began to rise toward a mountain the color of cocoa mix. The cab shook as a procession of eighteen-wheel dump trucks thundered by with loads of sand from the excavation pits the driver had mentioned. And soon the paved roadway gave way to gravel and the cab sent up a tail of dust in its wake. Bosch was beginning to think the address the smarmy supervising clerk at City Hall had given him was a phony. But then they were there.

The address to which Claude Eno's pension checks were mailed each month was a sprawling ranch-style house of pink stucco and dusty white tile roof. Looking past it, Bosch could see where even the gravel road ended just past it. It was the end of the line. Nobody had lived farther away than Claude Eno.

'I don't know about this,' the driver said. 'You want me to wait? This is like the goddamn moon out here.'

She had pulled into the driveway behind a late 1970s-model Olds Cutlass. There was a carport where another car was parked hidden beneath a tarp that was blue in the further recesses of the carport but bleached nearly white along the surfaces sacrificed to the sun.

Bosch took out his fold of money and paid the driver thirty-five dollars for the ride out. Then he took two twenties, ripped them in half and handed one side of each over the seat to her.

'You wait, you get the other half of those.'

'Plus the fare back to the airport.'

'Plus that.'

Bosch got out, realizing it would probably be the quickest forty bucks ever lost in Las Vegas if nobody answered the door. But he was in luck. A woman who looked to be in her late sixties opened the door before he could knock. And why not, he thought. In this house, you could see visitors coming for a mile.

Bosch felt the blast of air conditioning escaping through the open door.

'Mrs Eno?'

'No.'

Bosch pulled out his notebook and checked the address against the black numbers tacked on the front wall next to the door. They matched.

'Olive Eno doesn't live here?'

'You didn't ask that. I'm not Mrs Eno.'

'Can I please speak with Mrs Eno then?' Annoyed with the woman's preciseness, Bosch showed the badge he had gotten back from McKittrick after the boat ride. 'It's police business.'

'Well, you can try. She hasn't spoken to anybody, at least anybody outside her imagination, in three years.'

She motioned Bosch in and he stepped into the cool house.

'I'm her sister. I take care of her. She's in the kitchen. We were in the middle of lunch when I saw the dust come up on the road and heard you arrive.'

Bosch followed her down a tiled hallway toward the kitchen. The house smelled like old age, like dust and mold and urine. In the kitchen a gnome-like woman with white hair sat in a wheelchair, barely taking up half of the space it gave for an occupant. There was a slide-on tray in front of it and the woman's gnarled pearl-white hands were folded together on top of it. There were milky blue cataracts on both eyes and they seemed dead to the world outside the body. Bosch noticed a bowl of applesauce on the nearby table. It only took him a few seconds to size up the situation.

'She'll be ninety in August,' said the sister. 'If she makes it.'

'How long has she been like this?'

'Long time. I've been taking care of her for three years now.' She then bent into the gnome's face and loudly added, 'Isn't that right, Olive?'

The loudness of the question seemed to kick a switch and Olive Eno's jaw started working but no sound that was intelligible issued. She stopped the effort after a while and the sister straightened up.

157

'Don't worry about it, Olive. I know you love me.'

She wasn't as loud with that sentence. Maybe she feared Olive might actually muster a denial.

'What's your name?' Bosch asked.

'Elizabeth Shivone. What's this about? I saw that badge of yours says Los Angeles, not Las Vegas. Aren't you off the beat here a bit?'

'Not really. It's about her husband. One of his old cases.'

'Claude's been dead going on five years now.'

'How did he die?'

'Just died. His pump went out. Died right there on the floor, about where you're standing.'

They both looked down at the floor as if maybe his body was still there.

'I came to look through his things,' Bosch said.

'What things?'

'I don't know. I was thinking maybe he kept files from his time with the police.'

'You better tell me what you're doing here. This doesn't sound right to me.'

'I'm investigating a case he worked back in 1961. It's still open. Parts of the file are missing. I thought maybe he'd taken it. I thought maybe there might be something important that he kept. I don't know what. Anything. I just thought it was worth a try.'

He could see that her mind was working and her eyes suddenly froze for a second when her memory snagged on something.

'There is something, isn't there?' he said.

'No. I think you should go.'

'It's a big house. Did he have a home office?'

'Claude left the police thirty years ago. He built this house in the middle of nowhere just to be away from all of that.'

'What did he do when he moved out here?'

'He worked casino security. A few years at the Sands, then twenty at the Flamingo. He was getting two pensions and took good care of Olive.'

'Speaking of which, who's signing those pension checks these days?'

Bosch looked at Olive Eno to make his point. The other woman was silent a long moment, then went on the offense.

'Look, I could get power of attorney. Look at her. It wouldn't be a problem. I take care of her, mister.'

'Yeah, you feed her applesauce.'

'I have nothing to hide.'

'You want somebody to make sure or do you want to let it end right here? I don't really care what you're doing, lady. I don't really care if you're even her sister or not. If I was betting, I'd say you're not. But I don't really care right now. I'm busy. I just want to look through Eno's things.'

He stopped there and let her think about it. He looked at his watch.

'No warrant then, right?'

'I don't have a warrant. I've got a cab waiting. You make me get a warrant and I'm going to stop being such a nice guy.'

Her eyes went up and down his body as if to measure how nice and how not nice he could be.

'The office is this way.'

She said the words as if they were bites out of wood planks. She swiftly led him down the hall again and then off to the left into a study. There was an old steel desk as the room's centerpiece, a couple of four-drawer file cabinets, an extra chair and not much else.

'After he died, Olive and I moved everything into those file cabinets and haven't looked at it since.'

'They're all full?'

'All eight. Have at it.'

Bosch reached his hand into his pocket and took out another twenty-dollar bill. He tore it in half and gave one side to Shivone.

'Take that out to the cab driver. Tell her I'm going to be a little longer than I thought.'

She exhaled loudly, snatched the half and left the room. After she was gone Bosch went to the desk and opened each of the drawers. The first two he tried were empty. The next contained stationery and office supplies. The fourth drawer contained a checkbook that he quickly leafed through and saw it was an account covering household expenses. There was also a file containing recent receipts and other records. The last drawer in the desk was locked.

He started with the bottom file drawers and worked his way up. Nothing in the first few seemed even remotely connected with what Bosch was working on. There were files labeled with the names of different casinos and gaming organizations. The files in another drawer were labeled by people's names. Bosch looked through a few of these and determined they were files on known casino cheats. Eno had built a library of home intelligence files. By this time, Shivone had come back from her errand and had taken the seat opposite the desk. She was watching Bosch and he threw a few idle questions at her while he looked.

'So what did Claude do for the casinos?'

'He was a bird dog.'

'What's that?'

'Kind've an undercover thing. He mingled in the casinos, gambled with house chips, watched people. He was good at picking out the cheats and how they did it.'

'Guess it takes one to know one, right?'

'What's that crack supposed to mean? He did a good job.'

'I'm sure he did. Is that how he met you?'

'I'm not answering any of your questions.'

'Okay by me.'

He had only the two top drawers left. He opened one and found it contained no files at all. Just an old, dust-covered Rolodex and other items that had probably sat on the top of the desk at one point. There was an ashtray, a clock and a pen holder made of carved wood that had Eno's name carved on it. Bosch took the Rolodex out and put it on top of the cabinet. He blew the dust off it and then began turning it until he came to the Cs. He looked through the cards but found no listing for Arno Conklin. He met with similar failure when he tried to find a listing for Gordon Mittel.

'You're not going to look through that whole thing, are you?' Shivone asked in exasperation.

'No, I'm just going to take it with me.'

159

'Oh, no you don't. You can't just come in here and –'

'I'm taking it. If you want to make a complaint about it, be my guest. Then I'll make a complaint about you.'

She went quiet after that. Bosch went on to the next drawer and found it contained about twelve files on old LAPD cases from the 1950s and early 1960s. Again, he didn't have the time to study them, but he checked all the labels and none was marked Marjorie Lowe. By randomly pulling out a few of the files it became clear to him that Eno had made copies of files on some of his cases to take with him when he left the department. Of the random selections, all were murders, including two of prostitutes. Only one of the cases was closed.

'Go get me a box or a bag or something for these files,' Bosch said over his shoulder. When he sensed the woman in the room had not moved, he barked, 'Do it!'

She got up and left. Bosch stood gazing at the files and thinking. He had no idea if these were important or not. He had no idea what they meant. He only knew he should take them in case they turned out to be important. But what bothered him more than what the files that were in the drawer could mean was the feeling that something was certainly missing. This was based on his belief in McKittrick. The retired detective was sure his former partner, Eno, had some kind of hold on Conklin, or at the very least, some kind of deal with him. But there was nothing here about that. And it seemed to Bosch that if Eno was holding something on Conklin, it would still be here. If he kept old LAPD files, then he kept whatever he had on Conklin. In fact, he would have kept it in a safe place. Where?

The woman came back and dropped a cardboard box on the floor. It was the kind a case of beer had come in. Bosch put a foot-thick stack of files in it along with the Rolodex.

'You want a receipt?' he asked.

'No, I don't want anything from you.'

'Well, there is still something I need from you.'

'This doesn't end, does it?'

'I hope it does.'

'What do you want?'

'When Eno died, did you help the old lady – uh, your sister, that is – did you help her clear out his safe deposit box?'

'How'd –'

She stopped herself but not soon enough.

'How'd I know? Because it's obvious. What I'm looking for, he would have kept in a safe place. What did you do with it?'

'We threw everything away. It was meaningless. Just some old files and bank statements. He didn't know what he was doing. He was old himself.'

Bosch looked at his watch. He was running out of time if he was going to make his plane.

'Get me the key for this desk drawer.'

She didn't move.

'Hurry up, I don't have a lot of time. You open it or I'll open it. But if I do it, that drawer isn't going to be much use to you anymore.'

She reached into the pocket of her house dress and pulled out the house

160

keys. She reached down and unlocked the desk drawer, pulled it open and then stepped away.

'We didn't know what any of it was, or what it meant.'

'That's fine.'

Bosch moved to the drawer and looked in. There were two thin manila files and two packs of envelopes with rubber bands holding them together. The first file he looked through contained Eno's birth certificate, passport, marriage license and other personal records. He put it back in the drawer. The next file contained LAPD forms and Bosch quickly recognized them as the pages and reports that had been removed from the Marjorie Lowe murder book. He knew he had no time to read them at the moment and put the file in the beer box with the other files.

The rubber band on the first package of envelopes snapped when he tried to remove it and he was reminded of the band that had been around the blue binder that contained the case files. Everything about this case was old and ready to snap, he thought.

The envelopes were all from a Wells Fargo Bank branch in Sherman Oaks and each one contained a statement for a savings account in the name of McCage Inc. The address of the corporation was a post office box, also in Sherman Oaks. Bosch randomly took envelopes from different spots in the pack and studied three of them. Though separated by years in the late 1960s, each statement was basically the same. A deposit of one thousand dollars was made in the account on the tenth of each month and on the fifteenth a transfer of an equal amount was made to an account with a Nevada Savings and Loan branch in Las Vegas.

Without looking further, Bosch concluded that the bank statements might be the records of some kind of payoff account Eno kept. He quickly looked through the envelopes at the postmarks looking for the most recent one. He found none more recent than the late 1980s.

'What about these envelopes? When did he stop getting them?'

'What you see is what you get. I have no idea what they mean and Olive didn't know either back when they drilled his box.'

'Drilled his box?'

'Yeah, after he died. Olive wasn't on the safe deposit box. Only him. We couldn't find his key. So we had to have it drilled.'

'There was money, too, wasn't there?'

She waited a moment, probably wondering if he was going to demand that, too.

'Some. But you're too late, it's already spent.'

'I'm not worried about that. How much was there?'

She pinched her lips and acted like she was trying to remember. It was a bad act.

'C'mon. I'm not here for the money and I'm not from the IRS.'

'It was about eighteen thousand.'

Bosch heard a horn honk from outside. The cabdriver was getting restless. Bosch looked at his watch. He had to go. He tossed the envelope packs into the beer box.

'What about his account at Nevada Savings and Loan? How much was in it?'

It was a scam question based on his guess that the account that the money from Sherman Oaks was transferred to was Eno's. Shivone hesitated again. A delay punctuated by another horn blast.

'It was about fifty. But most of that's gone, too. Taking care of Olive, you know?'

'Yeah, I bet. Between that and the pensions, it's gotta be rough,' Bosch said with all the sarcasm he could put into it. 'I bet your accounts aren't too thin, though.'

'Look, mister, I don't know who you think you are but I'm the only one in the world that she has and who cares about her. That's worth something.'

'Too bad she doesn't get to decide what it's worth instead of you. Answer one question for me and then I'm out of here and you can go back to taking whatever you can off her ... Who are you? You're not her sister. Who are you?'

'It's none of your business.'

'That's right. But I could make it my business.'

She put on a look that showed Bosch what an affront he was to her delicate sensibilities but then seemed to gain a measure of self-esteem. Whoever she was, she was proud of it.

'You want to know who I am? I was the best woman he ever had. I was with him for a long time. She had his wedding band but I had his heart. Near the end, when they were both old and it didn't matter, we dropped the pretension and he brought me in here. To live with them. Take care of them. So don't you dare tell me I don't deserve something out of it.'

Bosch just nodded. Somehow, as sordid as the story seemed, he found a measure of respect for her for just having told the truth. And he felt sure it was.

'When did you meet?'

'You said one question.'

'When did you meet?'

'When he was at the Flamingo. We both were. I was a dealer. Like I said, he was a bird dog.'

'He ever talk about LA, about any cases, any people from back there?'

'No, never. He always said that was a closed chapter.'

Bosch pointed to the envelope stacks in the box.

'Does the name McCage mean anything?'

'Not to me.'

'What about these account statements?'

'I never saw any of those things until the day we opened that box. Didn't know he even had an account over at Nevada Savings. Claude had secrets. He even kept secrets from me.'

30

At the airport Bosch paid off the cabdriver and struggled into the main terminal with his overnighter and the beer box full of files and other things. In one of the stores along the main terminal mall he bought a cheap canvas satchel and transferred the items he had taken from Eno's office into it. It was small enough so he didn't have to check it. Printed on the side of the bag was LAS VEGAS – LAND OF SUN AND FUN! There was a logo depicting the sun setting behind a pair of dice.

At his gate he had a half hour before they loaded the plane, so he found a section of open seats as far away as possible from the cacophony of the rows of slot machines set in the center of the circular terminal.

He began going through the files in the satchel. The one he was most interested in was the one containing records stolen from the Marjorie Lowe murder book. He looked through the documents and found nothing unusual or unexpected.

The summary of the McKittrick-Eno interview of Johnny Fox with Arno Conklin and Gordon Mittel present was here and Bosch could sense the contained outrage at the situation in McKittrick's writing. In the last paragraph it was no longer contained.

> Interview with suspect was regarded by the undersigned as fruitless because of the intrusive behavior of A. Conklin and G. Mittel. Both 'prosecutors' refused to allow 'their' witness to answer questions fully or in the undersign's opinion with the whole truth. J. Fox remains suspect at this time until verification of his alibi and fingerprint analysis.

Nothing else in the documents was of note and Bosch realized that they were probably removed from the file by Eno solely because they mentioned Conklin's involvement in the case. Eno was covering up for Conklin. When Bosch asked himself why Eno was doing this, he immediately thought of the bank statements that had been in the safe deposit box with the stolen documents. They were records of the deal.

Bosch took out the envelopes and, going by the postmarks, began putting them in chronological order. The earliest one he could find was mailed to the McCage Inc. postal drop in November 1962. That was one year after the death of Marjorie Lowe and two months after the death of Johnny Fox. Eno had been on the Lowe case and then, according to McKittrick, he had investigated the Fox killing.

Bosch felt in his gut that he was right. Eno had squeezed Conklin. And maybe Mittel. He somehow knew what McKittrick didn't, that Conklin had been involved with Marjorie Lowe. Maybe he even knew Conklin had killed her. He had enough to put Conklin on the line for a thousand bucks a month for life. It wasn't a lot. Eno wasn't greedy, though a thousand a month in the early sixties probably more than matched what he was making on the job. But the amount didn't matter to Bosch. The payment did. It was an admission. If it could be traced to Conklin, it was hard evidence. Bosch felt himself getting excited. The records hoarded by a corrupt cop dead five years now might be all he needed to go head to head with Conklin.

He thought of something and looked around for the usual bank of phones. He checked his watch and looked over at the gate. People were milling about, ready to board and getting anxious. Bosch put the file and envelopes back into the satchel and carried his things to the phone.

Using his AT&T card, he dialed information in Sacramento and then dialed the state offices and asked for the corporate records unit. In three minutes he knew that McCage Inc. was not a California corporation and never was, at least in records going back to 1971. He hung up and went through the same process again, this time calling the Nevada state offices in Carson City.

The phone clerk told him the incorporation of McCage Inc. was defunct and asked if he was still interested in what information the state had. He excitedly said yes and was told by the clerk that she had to switch to microfiche and it would take a few minutes. While he waited, Bosch got out a notebook and got ready to take notes. He saw the gate door had been opened and people were just starting to board the plane. He didn't care, he'd miss it if he had to. He was too juiced to do anything but hang on to the phone.

Bosch studied the rows of slot machines in the center of the terminal. They were crowded with people trying their last chance at luck before leaving or their first chance after stepping off planes from all over the country and the world. Gambling against the machines had never appealed much to Bosch. He didn't understand it.

As he watched those milling about, it was easy to pick who was winning and who wasn't. It didn't take a detective to study the faces and know. He saw one woman with a stuffed teddy bear clamped under her arm. She was working two machines at once and Bosch could see that all she was doing was doubling her losses. To her left was a man in a black cowboy hat who was filling the machine with coins and pulling the arm back as quickly as he could. Bosch could see he was playing a dollar machine and was going to the five-dollar max on every roll. Bosch figured that, in the few minutes he watched, the man had spent sixty dollars with no return. At least he wasn't carrying a stuffed animal.

Bosch turned back to check the gate. The line of boarders had thinned to a few stragglers. Bosch knew he was going to miss it. But that was okay. He hung on and stayed calm.

Suddenly there was a shout and Bosch looked over and saw the man with the cowboy hat waving it as his machine was paying off a jackpot. The woman with the stuffed animal stepped back from her machines and solemnly watched the payoff. Each metallic *ching* of the dollars dropping in the tray must have been like a hammer pounding in her skull. A steady reminder that she was losing.

'Take a look at me now, baby!' the cowboy whooped.

It didn't appear that the exclamation was directed at anyone in particular. He stooped down and started scooping the coins into his hat. The woman with the teddy bear went back to work on her machines.

Just as the gate door was being closed, the clerk came back on the phone. She told Bosch the immediately available records showed McCage was incorporated in November 1962 and was dissolved by the state twenty-eight years later when a year went by without renewal fees or taxes being paid to keep the incorporation current. Bosch knew this had occurred because Eno had died.

'Do you want the officers?' the clerk asked.

'Yes, I do.'

'Okay, president and chief executive officer is Claude Eno. That's E-N-O. Vice president is Gordon Mittel with two Ts. And the treasurer is listed as Arno Conklin. That first name's spelled –'

'I got it. Thanks.'

Bosch hung up the phone, grabbed his overnighter and the satchel and ran to the gate.

'Just in time,' the attendant said with a tone of annoyance. 'Couldn't leave those one-armed bandits alone, huh?'

'Yeah,' Bosch said, not caring.

She opened the door and he went down the hallway and onto the plane. It was only half filled. He ignored his seat assignment and found an empty row. While he was pushing his luggage into the overhead storage bin, he thought of something. Once in his seat he took out his notebook and opened it to the page where he had just written the notes of his conversation with the incorporation clerk. He looked at the abbreviated notations.

Prez., CEO – C.E.
VP – G.M.
Treas. – A.C.

He then wrote only the initials in a line.

CE GM AC

He looked at the line for a moment and then smiled. He saw the anagram and wrote it on the next line.

MC CAGE

Bosch felt the blood jangling through his body. It was the feeling of knowing he was close. He was on a roll those people out there at the slot machines and all the casinos in the desert could never understand. It was a high they would never feel, no matter how many sevens came up on the dice or how many black jacks they were dealt. Bosch was getting close to a killer and that made him as juiced as any jackpot winner on the planet.

31

Driving the Mustang out of LAX an hour later, Bosch rolled the windows down and bathed his face in the cool, dry air. The sound of the breeze through the grove of eucalyptus trees at the airport gateway was always there like a welcome home. Somehow, he always found it reassuring when he came back from his trips. It was one of the things he loved about the city and he was glad it always greeted him.

He caught the light at Sepulveda and used the time to change the time on his watch. It was five minutes after two. He decided that he would have just enough time to get home, change into fresh clothes and grab something to eat before heading to Parker Center and his appointment with Carmen Hinojos.

He drove quickly under the 405 overpass and then took the curving on-ramp up onto the crowded freeway. As he turned the wheel to negotiate the turn, he realized that his upper arms ached deep in the biceps and he wasn't sure if it was from his fight with the fish on Saturday or from the way Jasmine had gripped his arms while they made love. He thought about her for a few more minutes and decided he would call her at the house before heading downtown. Their parting that morning already seemed long ago to him. They had made promises to meet again as soon as possible and Bosch hoped the promises would be kept. She was a mystery to him, one in which he knew he had not yet even begun to scratch the surface.

The 10 wasn't set to reopen until the following day, so Bosch bypassed the exit and stayed on the 405 until it rose over the Santa Monica Mountains and dropped into the Valley. He took the long way because he bet it would be faster, and because he had a mail drop in Studio City that he had been using since the post office refused to deliver mail to a red-tagged structure.

He transferred onto the 101 and promptly hit a wall of traffic inching its way along the six lanes. He stayed with it until impatience got the better of him. He exited Coldwater Canyon Boulevard and started taking surface streets. On Moorpark Road he passed several apartment buildings that still hadn't been demolished or repaired, the red tags and yellow tape bleached near-white by the months in the sun. Many of the condemned buildings still had signs like $500 MOVES YOU IN! and NEWLY REMODELED. On one red-tagged structure with the telltale crisscross stress fractures running along its entire length, someone had spray-painted a slogan that many took as the epitaph of the city in the months since the earthquake.

Somedays it was hard not to believe it. But Bosch tried to keep the faith. Somebody had to. The newspaper said more people were leaving than coming. But no matter, Bosch thought, I'm staying.

He cut over to Ventura and stopped at the private mailbox office. There was nothing but bills and junk mail in his box. He stopped at a deli next door and ordered the special, turkey on wholewheat with avocado and bean sprouts, to go. After that, he stayed on Ventura until it became Cahuenga and then took the turn off to Woodrow Wilson Drive and the climb up the hill to home. On the first curve he had to slow on the narrow road to squeeze by an LAPD squad car. He waved but he knew they wouldn't know him. They would be out of North Hollywood Division. They didn't wave back.

He followed his usual practice of parking a half block away from his house and then walking back. He decided to leave the satchel in the trunk because he might need the files downtown. He headed down the street to his house with his overnighter in one hand and the sandwich bag in the other.

As he got to the carport, he noticed a patrol car coming up the road. He watched it and noticed it was the same two patrolmen he had just passed. They had turned around for some reason. He waited at the curb to see if they would stop to ask him for directions or maybe an explanation of his wave, and because he didn't want them to see him enter the condemned house. But the car drove by with neither of the patrolmen even looking at him. The driver had his eyes on the road and the passenger was talking into the radio microphone. It must be a call, Bosch thought. He waited until the car had gone around the next curve and then headed into the carport.

After opening the kitchen door, Bosch stepped in and immediately felt that something was amiss. He took two steps in before placing it. There was a foreign odor in the house, or at least the kitchen. It was the scent of perfume, he realized. No, he corrected, it was cologne. A man wearing cologne had either recently been in the house or was still there.

Bosch quietly placed his overnighter and the sandwich bag on the kitchen floor and reached to his waist. Old habits died hard. He still had no gun and he knew his backup was on the shelf in the closet near the front door. For a moment he thought about running out to the street in hopes of catching the patrol car but he knew it was long gone.

Instead, he opened a drawer and quietly withdrew a small paring knife. There were longer blades in there but the small knife would be easier to handle. He stepped toward the archway that led from the kitchen to the house's front entry. At the threshold, still hidden from whoever might be out there, he stopped, tilted his head forward and listened. He could hear the low hiss of the freeway down the hill behind the house, but nothing from within. Nearly a minute of silence passed. He was about to step out of the kitchen when he heard a sound. It was the slight whisper of cloth moving. Maybe the crossing or uncrossing of legs. He knew someone was in the living room. And he knew by now that they would know that he knew.

'Detective Bosch,' a voice said from the silence of the house. 'It is safe for you. You can come out.'

Bosch knew the voice but was operating at such an acute level of intensity, he couldn't immediately compute it and place it. All he knew was that he had heard it before.

'It's Assistant Chief Irving, Detective Bosch,' the voice said. 'Could you please step out? That way you don't get hurt and we don't get hurt.'

Yes, that was the voice. Bosch relaxed, put the knife down on the counter, the sandwich bag in the refrigerator and stepped out of the kitchen. Irving was there, sitting in the living room chair. Two men in suits whom Bosch didn't recognize sat on the couch. Looking around, Bosch could see his box of letters and cards from the closet sitting on the coffee table. He saw the murder book that he had left on the dining room table was sitting on the lap of one of the strangers. They had been searching his house, going through his things.

Bosch suddenly realized what had happened outside.

'I saw your lookout. Anybody want to tell me what's going on?'

'Where've you been, Bosch?' one of the suits asked.

Bosch looked at him. Not a single glimmer of recognition hit him.

'Who the fuck are you?'

He bent down and picked the box of cards and letters up off the coffee table, where it had been in front of the man.

'Detective,' Irving said, 'This is Lieutenant Angel Brockman and this is Earl Sizemore.'

Bosch nodded. He recognized one of the names.

'I've heard of you,' he said, looking at Brockman. 'You're the one who sent Bill Connors to the closet. That must've been good for IAD man of the month. Quite an honor.'

The sarcasm in Bosch's voice was unmistakable, as he intended it to be. The closet was where most cops kept their guns while off duty; going to the closet was department slang for a cop killing himself. Connors was an old beat cop in Hollywood Division who had killed himself the year before while he was under IAD investigation for trading dime bags of heroin to runaway girls for sex. After he was dead, the runaways had admitted making up the complaints because Connors was always hassling them to move off his beat. He had been a good man but saw everything stacked against him and decided to go to the closet.

'That was his choice, Bosch. And now you've got yours. You want to tell us where you've been the last twenty-four?'

'You want to tell me what this is about?'

He heard a clunking sound coming from the bedroom.

'What the hell?' He walked to the door and saw another suit in his bedroom, standing over the open drawer of the night table. 'Hey, fuckhead, get out of there. Get out now!'

Bosch stepped in and kicked the drawer closed. The man stepped back, raised his hands like a prisoner and walked out to the living room.

'And this is Jerry Toliver,' Irving added. 'He's with Lieutenant Brockman, IAD. Detective Sizemore has joined us here from RHD.'

'Fantastic,' Bosch said. 'So everybody knows everybody. What's going on?'

He looked at Irving as he said this, believing if he was going to get a straight answer from anyone here, it would be him. Irving was generally a straight shooter when it came to his dealings with Bosch.

'De – Harry, we have got to ask you some questions,' Irving said. 'It would be best if we explain things later.'

Bosch could tell this one was serious.

'You got a warrant to be in here?'

'We'll show it to you later,' Brockman said. 'Let's go.'

'Where are we going?'

'Downtown.'

Bosch had had enough run-ins with the Internal Affairs Division to know things were being handled differently here. Just the fact that Irving, the second-highest-ranking officer in the department, was with them was an indication of the gravity of the situation. He guessed it was more than their simply finding out about his private investigation. If it was just that, Irving wouldn't have been here. There was something terribly wrong.

'All right,' Bosch said, 'who's dead?'

All four looked at him with faces of stone, confirming that in fact someone was dead. Bosch felt his chest tighten and for the first time he began to be scared. The names and faces of people he had involved flashed through his mind. Meredith Roman, Jake McKittrick, Keisha Russell, the two women in Las Vegas. Who else? Jazz? Could he have possibly put her in some kind of danger? Then it hit him. Keisha Russell. The reporter had probably done what he told her not to. She had gone to Conklin or Mittel and asked questions about the old clip she had pulled for Bosch. She had walked in blindly and was now dead because of her mistake.

'Keisha Russell?' he asked.

He got no reply. Irving stood up and the others followed. Sizemore kept the murder book in his hand. He was going to take it. Brockman went into the kitchen, picked up the overnighter and carried it to the door.

'Harry, why don't you ride with Earl and I?' Irving said.

'How 'bout I meet you guys down there.'

'You ride with me.'

It was said sternly. It invited no further debate. Bosch raised his hands, acknowledging he had no choice, and moved toward the door.

Bosch sat in the back of Sizemore's LTD, directly behind Irving. He looked out the window as they went down the hill. He kept thinking of the young reporter's face. Her eagerness had killed her but Bosch couldn't help but share the blame. He had planted the seed of mystery in her mind and it had grown until she couldn't resist it.

'Where'd they find her?' he asked.

He was met only with silence. He couldn't understand why they said nothing, especially Irving. The assistant chief had led him to believe in the past that they had an understanding, if not a liking, between each other.

'I told her not to do anything,' he said. 'I told her to sit on it a few days.'

Irving turned his body so that he could partially see Bosch behind him.

'Detective, I don't know who or what you're talking about.'

'Keisha Russell.'

'Don't know her.'

He turned back around. Bosch was puzzled. The names and faces went through his mind again. He added Jasmine but then subtracted her. She knew nothing about the case.

'McKittrick?'

'Detective,' Irving said and again struggled to turn around to look at Bosch. 'We are involved in the investigation of the homicide of Lieutenant Harvey Pounds. These other names are not involved. If you think they are people that should be contacted, please let me know.'

Bosch was too stunned to answer. Harvey Pounds? That made no sense. He had nothing to do with the case, didn't even know about it. Pounds never left the office, how could he have gotten into danger? Then it came to him, washing over him like a wave of water that brought with it a chill. He understood. It made sense. And in the moment that he saw that it did, he also saw his own responsibility as well as his own predicament.

'Am I . . . ?'

He couldn't finish.

'Yes,' Irving said. 'You are currently considered a suspect. Now maybe you will be quiet until we can set up a formal interview.'

Bosch leaned his head against the window glass and closed his eyes.

'Ah, Jesus . . .'

And in that moment he realized he was no better than Brockman was for having sent a man to the closet. For Bosch knew in the dark part of his heart that he was responsible. He didn't know how or when it had happened but he knew.

He had killed Harvey Pounds. And he carried Pounds's badge in his pocket.

32

Bosch was numb to most of what was going on around him. After they reached Parker Center he was escorted up to Irving's office on the sixth floor and then placed in a chair in the adjoining conference room. He was in there alone for a half hour before Brockman and Toliver came in. Brockman sat directly across from Bosch, Toliver to Harry's right. It was obvious to Bosch by their being in Irving's conference room instead of an IAD interview room that Irving wanted to keep a tight control on this one. If it turned out to be a cop-killed-cop case, he'd need all the control he could muster to contain it. It could be a publicity debacle to rival those of the Rodney King days.

Through his daze and the jarring images of Pounds being dead, a pressing thought finally got Bosch's attention: he was in serious trouble himself. He told himself he couldn't retreat into a shell. He must be alert. The man sitting across from him would like nothing better than to hang a killing on Bosch and he was willing to go to any extreme to do it. It wasn't good enough that Bosch knew in his own mind that he had not, at least physically, killed Pounds. He had to defend himself. And so he resolved that he would show Brockman nothing. He would be just as tough as anybody in the room. He cleared his throat and began before Brockman got the chance.

'When did it happen?'

'I'm asking the questions.'

'I can save you time, Brockman. Tell me when it happened and I'll tell you where I was. We'll get this over with. I understand why I'm a suspect. I won't hold it against you but you're wasting your time.'

'Bosch, don't you feel anything at all? A man is dead. You worked with him.'

Bosch stared at him a long moment before answering in an even voice.

'What I feel doesn't matter. Nobody deserves to be killed, but I'm not going to miss him and I certainly won't miss working for him.'

'Jesus.' Brockman shook his head. 'The man had a wife, a kid in college.'

'Maybe they won't miss him, either. You never know. The guy was a prick at work. No reason to expect him to be anything else at home. What's your wife think about you, Brockman?'

'Save it, Bosch. I'm not falling for any of your –'

'Do you believe in God, Brickman?'

Bosch used Brockman's nickname in the department, awarded to him for

172

his methodical way of building cases against other cops, like the late Bill Connors.

'This isn't about me or what I believe in, Bosch. We're talking about you.'

'That's right, we're talking about me. So, I'll tell you what I think. I'm not sure what I believe. My life's more than half over and I still haven't figured it out. But the theory I'm leaning toward is that everybody on this planet has some kind of energy that makes them what they are. It's all about energy. And when you die, it just goes somewhere else. And Pounds? He was bad energy and now it's gone somewhere else. So I don't feel too bad about him dying, to answer your question. But I'd like to know where that bad energy went. Hope you didn't get any, Brickman. You already have a lot.'

He winked at Brockman and saw the momentary confusion in the IAD detective's face as he tried to interpret what the jibe had meant. He seemed to shake it off and go on.

'Enough of the bullshit. Why did you confront Lieutenant Pounds in his office on Thursday? You know that was off limits while you are on leave.'

'Well, it was kind've like one of those Catch-22 situations. I think that's what they call 'em. It was off limits to go there but then Pounds, my commanding officer, called me up and told me I had to turn in my car. See, it was that bad energy working. I was already on involuntary leave but he couldn't leave well enough alone. He had to take my car, too. So I brought him in the keys. He was my supervisor and it was an order. So going there broke one of the rules but not going would have broken one, too.'

'Why'd you threaten him?'

'I didn't.'

'He filed an addendum to the assault complaint of two weeks earlier.'

'I don't care what he filed. There was no threat. The guy was a coward. He probably felt threatened. But there was no threat. There is a difference.'

Bosch looked over at the other suit. Toliver. It looked as if he was going to be silent the whole time. That was his role. He just stared at Bosch as if he were a TV screen.

Bosch looked around the rest of the room and for the first time noticed the phone on the banquette to the left of the table. The green light signaled a conference call was on. The interview was being piped out of the room. Probably to a tape recorder. Probably to Irving in his office next door.

'There is a witness,' Brockman said.

'To what?'

'The threat.'

'I'll tell you what, Lieutenant, why don't you tell me exactly what the threat was so I know what we're talking about. After all, if you believe I made it, what's wrong with me knowing what it was I said?'

Brockman gave it some thought before answering.

'Very simple, as most are, you told him if he ever, quote, fucked with you again, you'd kill him. Not too original.'

'But damning as hell, right? Well, fuck you, Brockman, I never said that. I don't doubt that that asshole wrote up an addendum, that was just his style, but whoever this wit is you got, they're full of shit.'

'You know Henry Korchmar?'

'Henry Korchmar?'

Bosch had no idea whom he was talking about. Then he realized

Brockman meant old Henry of the Nod Squad. Bosch had never known his last name and so hearing it in this context had confused him.

'The old guy? He wasn't in the room. He's no witness. I told him to get out and he did. Whatever he told you, he probably backed Pounds because he was scared. But he wasn't there. You go ahead with it, Brockman. I'll be able to pull twelve people out of that squadroom who watched the whole thing through the glass. And they'll say Henry wasn't in there, they'll say Pounds was a liar and everybody knew it, and then where's your threat?'

Brockman said nothing into the silence so Bosch continued.

'See, you didn't do your work. My guess is that you know everybody who works in that squadroom thinks people like you are the bottom feeders of this department. They've got more respect for the people they put in jail. And you know that, Brickman, so you were too intimidated to go to them. Instead, you rely on some old man's word and he probably didn't even know Pounds was dead when you talked to him.'

Bosch could tell by the way Brockman's eyes darted away that he had nailed him. Empowered with the victory, he stood up and headed toward the door.

'Where are you going?'

'To get some water.'

'Jerry, go with him.'

Bosch paused at the door and looked back.

'What, do you think I'm going to run, Brockman? You think that and you don't know the first thing about me. You think that and you haven't prepared for this interview. Why don't you come over to Hollywood one day and I'll teach you how to interview murder suspects. Free of charge.'

Bosch walked out, Toliver following. At the water fountain down the hall, he took a long drink of water and then wiped his mouth with his hand. He felt nervous, frayed. He didn't know how long it would be before Brockman could see through the front he was putting up.

As he walked back to the conference room, Toliver stayed a silent three paces behind him.

'You're still young,' Bosch said over his shoulder. 'There might be a chance for you, Toliver.'

Bosch stepped back into the conference room just as Brockman stepped through a door from the other side of the room. Bosch knew it was a direct entrance to Irving's office. He had once worked an investigation of a serial killer out of this room and under Irving's thumb.

Both men sat down across from each other again.

'Now, then,' Brockman started. 'I'm going to read you your rights, Detective Bosch.'

He took a small card from his wallet and proceeded to read to Bosch the Miranda warning. Bosch knew for sure the phone line was going to a tape recorder. This was something they would want on tape.

'Now,' Brockman said when he was finished. 'Do you agree to waive those rights and talk to us about this situation?'

'It's a situation now, huh? I thought it was a murder. Yeah, I'll waive.'

'Jerry, go get a waiver, I don't have one here.'

Jerry got up and left through the hallway door. Bosch could hear his feet moving quickly on the linoleum, then a door open. He was taking the stairs down to IAD on the fifth.

'Uh, let's start by –'

'Don't you want to wait until you have your witness back? Or is this being secretly recorded without my knowledge?'

This immediately flustered Brockman.

'Yes, Bosch it's being sec – it's being recorded. But not secretly. We told you before we started that we'd be taping.'

'Good cover-up, Lieutenant. That last line, that was a good one. I'll have to remember that one.'

'Now, let's start with –'

The door opened and Toliver came in with a sheet of paper. He handed it to Brockman, who studied it a moment, made sure it was the correct form and slid it across the table to Bosch. Harry grabbed it and quickly scribbled a signature on the appropriate line. He was familiar with the form. He slid it back and Brockman put it off to the side of the table without looking at it. So he didn't notice the signature Bosch had written was 'Fuck You.'

'All right, let's get this going. Bosch, give us your whereabouts over the last seventy-two hours.'

'You don't want to search me first, do you? How 'bout you, Jerry?'

Bosch stood up, opening his jacket so they could see he was not armed. He thought by taunting them like this they would do the exact opposite and not search him. Carrying Pounds's badge was a piece of evidence that would probably put him in the ground if they discovered it.

'Siddown, Bosch!' Brockman barked. 'We're not going to search you. We're trying to give you every benefit of the doubt but you make it damn hard.'

Bosch sat back down, relieved for the time being.

'Now, just give us your whereabouts. We don't have all day.'

Bosch thought about this. He was surprised by the window of time they wanted. Seventy-two hours. He wondered what had happened to Pounds and why they hadn't narrowed time of death to a shorter span.

'Seventy-two hours ago. Well, about seventy-two hours ago it was Friday afternoon and I was in Chinatown at the Fifty-One-Fifty building. Which reminds me, I'm due over there in ten minutes. So, boys, if you'll excuse me . . .'

He stood up.

'Siddown, Bosch. That's been taken care of. Sit down.'

Bosch sat down and said nothing. He realized, though, that he actually felt disappointed he would miss the session with Carmen Hinojos.

'Come on, Bosch, let's hear it. What happened after that?'

'I don't remember all the details. But I ate over at the Red Wind that night, also stopped at the Epicentre for a few drinks. Then I got to the airport about ten. I took a red-eye to Florida, to Tampa, spent the weekend there and got back about an hour and a half before I found you people illegally inside my home.'

'It's not illegal. We had a warrant.'

'I've been shown no warrant.'

'Never mind that, what do you mean you were in Florida?'

'I guess I mean I was in Florida. What do you think it means?'

'You can prove this?'

Bosch reached into his pocket, took out his airline folder with the ticket receipt and slid it across the table.

'For starters there's the ticket receipt. I think there's one in there for a rental car, too.'

Brockman quickly opened the ticket folder and started reading.

'What were you doing there?' he asked without looking up.

'Dr Hinojos, that's the company shrink, said I should try to get away. And I thought, how 'bout Florida? I'd never been there and all my life I've liked orange juice. I thought, what the hell? Florida.'

Brockman was flustered again. He wasn't expecting something like this. Bosch could tell. Most cops never realized how important the initial interview with a suspect or witness was to an investigation. It informed all other interviews and even court testimony that followed. You had to be prepared. Like lawyers, you had to know most of the answers before you asked the questions. The IAD relied so much on its presence as an intimidating factor that most of the detectives assigned to the division never really had to prepare for interviews. And when they hit a wall like this, they didn't know what to do.

'Okay, Bosch, uh, what did you do in Florida?'

'You ever heard that song Marvin Gaye sang? Before he got killed? It's called –'

'What are you talking about?'

'– "Sexual Healing." It says it's good for the soul.'

'I've heard it,' Toliver said.

Both Brockman and Bosch looked at him.

'Sorry,' he offered.

'Again, Bosch,' Brockman said. 'What are you talking about?'

'I'm talking about that I spent most of the time with a woman I know there. Most of the other time I spent with a fishing guide on a boat in the Gulf of Mexico. What I'm talking about, asshole, is that I was with people almost every minute. And the times I wasn't weren't long enough for me to fly back here and kill Pounds. I don't even know when he was killed but I'll tell you right now you don't have a case, Brockman, because there is no case. You're looking in the wrong direction.'

Bosch had chosen his words carefully. He was unsure what, if anything, they knew about his private investigation and he wasn't going to give them anything if he could help it. They had the murder book and the evidence box but he thought that he might be able to explain all of that away. They also had his notebook because he had stuffed it into his overnighter at the airport. In it were the names, numbers and addresses of Jasmine and McKittrick, the address of the Eno house in Vegas, and other notes about the case. But they might not be able to put together what it all meant. Not if he was lucky.

Brockman pulled a notebook and pen from the inside pocket of his jacket.

'Okay, Bosch, give me the name of the woman and this fishing guide. I need their numbers, everything.'

'I don't think so.'

Brockman's eyes widened.

'I don't care what you think, give me the names.'

176

Bosch said nothing, just stared down at the table in front of him.

'Bosch, you've told us your whereabouts, now we need to confirm them.'

'I know where I was at, that's all I need.'

'If you're in the clear, as you claim, let us check it out, clear you and move on to other things, other possibilities.'

'You've got the airlines and the car rental right there. Start with that. I'm not dragging people into this who don't need to be. They're good people and unlike you, they like me. I'm not going to let you spoil that by having you come in with your concrete block feet and step all over the relationships.'

'You don't have a choice, Bosch.'

'Oh, yes, I do. Right now, I do. You want to try to make a case against me, do it. If it gets to that point, I'll bring these people out and they'll blow your shit away, Brockman. You think at the moment you've got PR problems in the department over sending Bill Connors to the closet? You'll end this case with worse PR than Nixon had. I'm not giving you the names. If you want to write something down there in your notebook, just write that I said "Fuck you." That ought to cover it.'

Brockman's face got kind of blotchy with pinks and whites. He was quiet a moment before speaking.

'Know what I think? I still think you did it. I think you hired somebody to do it and you went waltzing off to Florida so you'd be nowhere near here. A fishing guide. If that doesn't sound like a conjured-up piece of shit I don't know what does. And the woman? Who was she, some hooker you picked up in a bar? What was she, a fifty-dollar alibi? Or did you go a hundred?'

In one explosive move, Bosch shoved the table toward Brockman, catching him completely by surprise. It slid under his arms and crashed into his chest. His chair tipped back against the wall behind him. Bosch kept the pressure on his end and pinned Brockman against the wall. Bosch pushed back on his own chair until it was against the wall behind him. He raised his left leg and put his foot against the table to keep the pressure on it. He saw the blotches of color on Brockman's face become more pronounced as he went without air. His eyes bugged. But he had no leverage and couldn't move the table off himself.

Toliver was slow to react. Stunned, he seemed to look at Brockman for a long moment as if awaiting orders before jumping up and moving toward Bosch. Bosch was able to fend off his first effort, shoving the younger man back into a potted palm tree that was in the corner of the room. While Bosch did this, he saw in his peripheral vision a figure enter the room through the other door. Then his chair was abruptly knocked over and he was on the ground with a heavy weight on top of him. By turning his head slightly he could see it was Irving.

'Don't move, Bosch!' Irving yelled in his ear. 'Settle down right now!'

Bosch went limp to signify his compliance and Irving got off him. Bosch stayed still for a few moments and then put a hand up on the table to pull himself up. As he got up, he saw Brockman hacking and trying to get air into his lungs while holding both hands against his chest. Irving held one hand out to Bosch's chest as a calming gesture and a means of stopping him from taking another run at Brockman. With his other hand, he pointed at

Toliver, who was trying to right the potted palm. It had become uprooted and wouldn't stand up. He finally just leaned it against the wall.

'You,' Irving snapped at him. 'Out.'

'But, sir, the –'

'Get out!'

Toliver quickly left through the hallway door as Brockman was finally finding his voice.

'Buh . . . Bosch, you sonova bitch, you . . . you're going to jail. You –'

'Nobody's going to jail,' Irving said sternly. 'Nobody's going to jail.'

Irving stopped to gulp down some air. Bosch noticed that the assistant chief seemed just as winded as anybody in the room.

'There will be no charges on this,' Irving finally continued. 'Lieutenant, you baited him and got what you got.'

Irving's tone invited no debate. Brockman, his chest still heaving, put his elbows on the table and began running his fingers through his hair, trying to look as if he still had some composure but all he had was defeat. Irving turned to Bosch, anger bunching the muscles of his jaw into hard surfaces.

'And you. Bosch, I don't know how to help you. You're always the loose cannon. You knew what he was doing, you've done it yourself. But you couldn't sit there and take it. What kind of man are you?'

Bosch didn't say anything and he doubted Irving wanted a spoken answer. Brockman started coughing and Irving looked back at him.

'Are you all right?'

'I think.'

'Go across the street, have one of the paramedics check you out.'

'No, I'm all right.'

'Good, then go down to your office, take a break. I have someone else I want to have talk to Bosch.'

'I want to continue the inter –'

'The interview is over, Lieutenant. You blew it.' Then, looking at Bosch, he added, 'You both did.'

33

Irving left Bosch alone in the conference room and in a few moments Carmen Hinojos walked in. She took the same seat that Brockman had sat in. She looked at Bosch with eyes that seemed filled with equal parts anger and disappointment. But Bosch didn't flinch under her gaze.

'Harry, I can't believe –'

He held a finger up to his mouth, silencing her.

'What is it?'

'Are our sessions still supposed to be private?'

'Of course.'

'Even in here?'

'Yes. What is it?'

Bosch got up and walked to the phone on the counter. He pushed the button that disconnected the conference call. He returned to his seat.

'I hope that was left on unintentionally. I'm going to speak to Chief Irving about that.'

'You're probably speaking to him right now. The phone was too obvious. He's probably got the room wired.'

'C'mon, Harry, this isn't the CIA.'

'No, it's not. Sometimes it's even worse. All I'm saying is Irving, the IAD, they still might be listening somehow. Be careful what you say.'

Carmen Hinojos looked exasperated.

'I'm not paranoid, Doctor. I've been through this before.'

'All right, never mind. I really don't care who's listening or not. I can't believe what you just did. It makes me very sad and disappointed. What have our meetings been about? Nothing? I'm sitting in there hearing you resort to the same type of violence that brought you to me in the first place. Harry, this isn't some joke. This is real life. And I have to make a decision that could very well decide your future. This makes it all the more difficult to do.'

He waited until he was sure she was done.

'You were in there with Irving the whole time?'

'Yes, he called and explained the situation and asked me to come over and sit in. I have to say –'

'Wait a minute. Before we go any further. Did you talk to him? Did you tell him about our sessions?'

'No, of course not.'

179

'Okay, for the record, I just want to reiterate that I do not give up any of my protections under the patient-doctor relationship. We okay on that?'

For the first time she looked away from him. He could see her face turning dark with anger.

'Do you know what an insult that is for you to tell me that? What, do you think I'd tell him about our sessions just because he may have ordered me to?'

'Did he?'

'You don't trust me at all, do you?'

'Did he?'

'No, he didn't.'

'That's good.'

'It's not just me. You don't trust anyone.'

Bosch realized that he had been out of line. He could see, though, that there was more hurt than anger in her face.

'I'm sorry, you're right, I shouldn't have said that. I'm just ... I don't know, I've got my back to the corner here, Doctor. When that happens, sometimes you forget who's on your side and who isn't.'

'Yes, and as a matter of course you respond with violence against those who you perceive are not on your side. This is not good to see. It's very, very disappointing.'

He looked away from her and over to the potted palm in the corner. Before leaving the room, Irving had replanted it, getting his hands dirty with black soil. Bosch noticed it was still slightly tilted to the left.

'So what are you doing up here?' he asked. 'What does Irving want?'

'He wanted me to sit in his office and listen to your interview on the conference line. He said he was interested in my evaluation of your answers as to whether I believed you could have been responsible for the death of Lieutenant Pounds. Thanks to you and your attack on your interviewer, he didn't need any evaluation from me. It's clear at this point you are prone to and quite capable of violence against fellow police officers.'

'That's bullshit and you know it. Damn it, what I did in here to that guy masquerading as a cop was a lot different than what they think I did. You're talking about things that are worlds apart and if you don't see that, you're making your living in the wrong business.'

'I'm not so sure.'

'Have you ever killed anyone, Doctor?'

Saying the question reminded him of his true confessions conversation with Jasmine.

'Of course not.'

'Well, I have. And believe me it's a lot different than roughing up some pompous ass in a suit with a shine on its ass. A lot different. If you or they think that doing one means you can do the other, you all have a lot to learn.'

They were both quiet for a long while, letting their anger ebb away.

'All right,' he finally said. 'So what happens now?'

'I don't know. Chief Irving just asked me to sit in with you, to calm you. I guess he's figuring out what to do next. I guess I'm not doing a very good job of calming you.'

'What did he say when he first asked you to come up here and listen?'

'He just called me and explained what happened and said he wanted my take on the interview. You have to understand something, despite your problems with authority, he is one person who I think is in your court on this. I don't think he honestly believes you're involved in the death of your lieutenant – at least directly. But he realizes that you are a viable suspect who needs to be questioned. I think if you had held your temper during the interview this all might've been over for you soon. They would've checked your story in Florida and that would have been the end of it. I even told them that you told me you were going to Florida.'

'I don't want them checking my story. I don't want them involved.'

'Well, it's too late. He knows you're up to something.'

'How?'

'When he called to ask me to come over he mentioned the file on your mother's case. The murder book. He said it was found at your house. He also said they found the stored evidence from the case there . . .'

'And?'

'And he asked if I knew what you were doing with all of it.'

'So he did ask you to reveal what we've talked about in our sessions.'

'In an indirect way.'

'Sounds pretty direct to me. Did he say specifically that it was my mother's case?'

'Yes, he did.'

'What did you tell him?'

'I told him that I was not at liberty to discuss anything that was talked about in our sessions. It didn't satisfy him.'

'I'm not surprised.'

Another wave of silence washed between them. Her eyes wandered the room. His stayed on hers.

'Listen, what do you know about what happened to Pounds?'

'Very little.'

'Irving must have told you something. You must've asked.'

'He said Pounds was found in the trunk of his car Sunday evening. I guess he had been there a while. A day maybe. The chief said he . . . the body showed signs of torture. Particularly sadistic mutilation, he said. He didn't go into detail. It had happened before Pounds was dead. They do know that. He said that he'd been in a lot of pain. He wanted to know if you were the type of man who could've done that.'

Bosch said nothing. He was imagining the crime scene in his mind. His guilt came crushing back down on him and for a moment he thought he might even get nauseous.

'For what it's worth, I said no.'

'What?'

'I told him you weren't the type of man who could've done that.'

Bosch nodded. But his thoughts were already a great distance away again. What had happened to Pounds was becoming clear and Bosch carried the guilt of having set things in motion. Though legally innocent, he knew he was morally culpable. Pounds was a man he despised, had less respect for than some of the murderers he had known. But the weight of the guilt was bearing down on him. He ran his hands hard over his face and through his hair. He felt a shudder move through his body.

'Are you all right?' Hinojos asked.

'I'm fine.'

Bosch took out his cigarettes and started to light one with his Bic.

'Harry, you better not. This isn't my office.'

'I don't care. Where was he found?'

'What?'

'Pounds! Where was he found?'

'I don't know. You mean where was the car? I don't know. I didn't ask.'

She studied him and he noticed the hand that held his cigarette was shaking.

'All right, Harry, that's it. What's the matter? What is going on?'

Bosch looked at her for a long moment and nodded.

'Okay, you want to know? I did it. I killed him.'

Her face immediately reacted as if perhaps she had seen the killing firsthand, so close that she had been spattered with blood. It was a horrible face. Repulsed. And she moved back in her chair as if even a few more inches of separation from him were needed.

'You . . . you mean this story about Florida was –'

'No. I don't mean I killed him. Not with my hands. I mean what I've done, what I've been doing. It got him killed. I got him killed.'

'How do you know? You can't know for sure that –'

'I know. Believe me, I know.'

He looked away from her to a painting on the wall over the banquette. It was a generic depiction of a beach scene. He looked back at Hinojos.

'It's funny . . . ,' he said but didn't finish. He just shook his head.

'What is?'

He got up and reached to the potted palm and stubbed the cigarette out in the dark soil.

'What is funny, Harry?'

He sat back down and looked at her.

'The civilized people in the world, the ones who hide behind culture and art and politics . . . and even the law, they're the ones to watch out for. They've got that perfect disguise goin' for them, you know? But they're the most vicious. They're the most dangerous people on earth.'

34

It seemed to Bosch that the day would never end, that he would never get out of the conference room. After Hinojos left, it was Irving's turn. He came in silently, took the Brockman seat and folded his hands on the table and said nothing. He looked irritated. Bosch thought maybe he smelled the smoke. Bosch didn't care about that but he found the silence discomforting.

'What about Brockman?'

'He's gone. You heard me tell him, he blew it. So did you.'

'How's that?'

'You could've talked your way out of it. Could've let him check your story and be done with it. But you had to make another enemy. You had to be Harry Bosch.'

'That's where you and I differ, Chief. You oughta get out of the office and come out on the street again sometime. I didn't make Brockman an enemy. He was my enemy before I even met him. They all are. And, you know, I'm really getting tired of everybody analyzing me and sticking their noses up my ass. It's getting real old.'

'Somebody's got to do it. You don't.'

'You don't know a thing about it.'

Irving waved Bosch's pale defense away like cigarette smoke.

'So what now?' Bosch continued. 'Why are you here? You going to try to break my alibi now? Is that it? Brockman's out and you're in?'

'I don't need to break your alibi. It's been checked and it looks like it holds. Brockman and his people have already been instructed to follow other avenues of investigation.'

'What do you mean, it's been checked?'

'Give us some credit here, Bosch. The names were in your notebook.'

He reached into his coat and pulled out the notebook. He tossed it across the table to Bosch.

'This woman that you spent some time with over there, she told me enough to the point that I believed it. You might want to call her yourself, though. She certainly seemed confused by my call. I was rather circumspect in my explanation.'

'I appreciate that. So, then, I guess I'm free to split?'

Bosch stood up.

'In a technical sense.'

'And the other senses?'

'Sit down for a minute, Detective.'

183

Bosch held his hands up. He'd gone this far. He decided he might as well go all the way and hear it all. He sat back down in his chair with a meager protest.

'My butt's getting sore from all this sitting.'

'I knew Jake McKittrick,' Irving said. 'Knew him well. We worked Hollywood together many years ago. But you know that already. As nice as it is to touch base with an old colleague, I can't say I enjoyed anything about the conversation I had with my old friend Jake.'

'You called him, too.'

'While you were in here with the doctor.'

'So then what do you want from me? You got the story from him, what's left?'

Irving drummed his fingers on the tabletop.

'What do I want? What I want is for you to tell me that what you are doing, what you have been doing, is in no way connected to what has happened to Lieutenant Pounds.'

'I can't, Chief. I don't know what happened to him, other than that he's dead.'

Irving studied Bosch for a long moment, contemplating something, deciding whether to treat him as an equal and tell him the story.

'I guess I expected an immediate denial. Your answer already suggests that you think there might be a correlation. I can't tell you how much that bothers me.'

'Anything is possible, Chief. Let me ask you this. You said Brockman and his crew were out chasing other leads – I guess avenues is what you said. Are any of these avenues viable? I mean, did Pounds have a secret life or are they just out there chasing their tails?'

'There's nothing that stands out. I'm afraid you were the best lead. Brockman still thinks so. He wants to pursue the theory that you hired a hitman of some sort and then flew to Florida to establish an alibi.'

'Yeah, that's a good one.'

'I think it stretches credibility some. I told him to drop it. For the moment. And I'm telling you to drop what you are doing. This woman in Florida sounds like the kind of person you could spend some time with. I want you to get on a plane and go back to her. Stay a couple weeks. When you come back, we'll talk about going back on the homicide table at Hollywood.'

Bosch was unsure whether there was a threat in all that Irving had just said. If not a threat, then maybe a bribe.

'And if I don't?'

'If you don't, then you are stupid. And you deserve whatever happens to you.'

'What is it that you think I'm doing, Chief?'

'I don't *think*, I *know* what you're doing. It's easy. You pulled the book on your mother's homicide. Why at this particular point in time you've done this, I don't know. But you're out running a freelance investigation and that's a problem for us. You have to stop it, Harry, or I'll stop you. I'll shut you down. Permanently.'

'Who are you protecting?'

184

Bosch saw the anger move into Irving's face as his skin turned from pink to an intense red. His eyes seemed to grow smaller and darker with fury.

'Don't you ever suggest such a thing. I've dedicated my life to this depart –'

'It's yourself, isn't it? You knew her. You found her. You're afraid of being dragged into this if I put something together on it. I bet you already knew everything McKittrick told you on the phone.'

'That's ridiculous, I –'

'Is it? Is it? I don't think so. I've already talked to one witness who remembers you from those days on the Boulevard beat.'

'What witness?'

'She said she knew you. She knows my mother knew you, too.'

'The only person I am protecting is you, Bosch. Can't you see that? I'm *ordering* you to stop this investigation.'

'You can't. I don't work for you anymore. I'm on leave, remember? Involuntary leave. That makes me a citizen now, and I can do whatever I goddamn want to do as long as it's legal.'

'I could charge you with possession of stolen documents – the murder book.'

'It wasn't stolen. Besides, what if you bullshit a case, what's that, a misdemeanor? They'll laugh you out of the city attorney's office on your ass with that.'

'But you'd lose your job. That would be it.'

'You're a little late with that one, Chief. A week ago that would've been a valid threat. I'd have to consider it. But it doesn't matter anymore. I'm free of all of that bullshit now and this is all that matters to me and I don't care what I have to do, I'm doing it.'

Irving was silent and Bosch guessed that the assistant chief was realizing that Bosch had moved beyond his reach. Irving's hold over Bosch's job and future had been his leverage before. But Bosch had finally broken free. Bosch began again in a low, calm voice.

'If you were me, Chief, could you just walk away? What does doing what I do for the department matter if I can't do this for her ... and for me?'

He stood up and put the notebook into his jacket pocket.

'I'm going. Where's the rest of my stuff?'

'No.'

Bosch hesitated. Irving looked up at him and Bosch saw the anger was gone now.

'I did nothing wrong,' Irving said quietly.

'Sure you did,' Bosch said just as quietly. He leaned over the table until he was only a few feet away. 'We all did, Chief. We let it go. That was our crime. But not anymore. At least, not with me. If you want to help, you know how to reach me.'

He headed toward the door.

'What do you want?'

Bosch looked back at him.

'Tell me about Pounds. I need to know what happened. It's the only way I'll know if it's connected.'

'Then sit down.'

Bosch took the chair by the door and sat down. They both took some time to calm down before Irving finally spoke.

'We started looking for him Saturday night. We found his car Sunday noon in Griffith Park. One of the tunnels closed after the quake. It was like they knew we'd be looking from the air, so they put the car in a tunnel.'

'Why'd you start looking before you knew he was dead?'

'The wife. She started calling Saturday morning. She said he'd gotten a call Friday night at home, she didn't know who. But whoever it was managed to convince Pounds to leave the house and meet him. Pounds didn't tell his wife what it was about. He said he'd be back in an hour or two. He left and never came back. In the morning she called us.'

'Pounds is unlisted, I assume.'

'Yes. That gives rise to the probability it was someone in the department.'

Bosch thought about this.

'Not necessarily. It just had to be someone with connections to people in the city. People that could get his number with a phone call. You ought to put out the word. Grant amnesty to anyone who comes forward and says they gave up the number. Say you'll go light in exchange for the name of the person they gave it to. That's who you want. Chances are whoever gave out the number didn't know what was going to happen.'

Irving nodded.

'That's an idea. Within the department there are hundreds who could get his number. There may be no other way to go.'

'Tell me more about Pounds.'

'We went to work right there in the tunnel. By Sunday the media had wind that we were looking for him, so the tunnel worked to our advantage. No helicopters flying over, bothering us. We just set up lights in the tunnel.'

'He was in the car?'

Bosch was acting like he knew nothing. He knew that if he expected Hinojos to respect his confidences, he must in turn respect hers.

'Yes, he was in the trunk. And, my God, was it bad. He ... He'd been stripped of his clothes. He'd been beaten. Then – then there was the evidence of torture ...'

Bosch waited but Irving had stopped.

'What? What did they do to him?'

'They burned him. The genitals, nipples, fingers ... My God.'

Irving ran his hand over his shaven scalp and closed his eyes while he did it. Bosch could see that he could not get the images out of his mind. Bosch was having trouble with it, too. His guilt was like a palpable object in his chest.

'It was like they wanted something from him,' Irving said. 'But he couldn't give it. He didn't have it and ... and they kept at him.'

Suddenly, Bosch felt the slight tremor of an earthquake and reached for the table to steady himself. He looked at Irving for confirmation and realized there was no tremor. It was himself, shaking again.

'Wait a minute.'

The room tilted slightly then righted itself.

'What is it?'

'Wait a minute.'

Without another word Bosch stood up and went out the door. He quickly went down the hall to the men's room by the water fountain. There was someone in front of one of the sinks shaving but Bosch didn't take the time to look at him. He pushed through one of the stall doors and vomited into the toilet, barely making it in time.

He flushed the toilet but the spasm came again and then again until he was empty, until he had nothing left inside but the image of Pounds naked and dead, tortured.

'You okay in there, buddy?' a voice said from outside the stall.

'Just leave me alone.'

'Sorry, just asking.'

Bosch stayed in the stall a few more minutes, leaning against the wall. Eventually, he wiped his mouth with toilet paper and then flushed it down. He stepped out of the stall unsteadily and went to the sink. The other man was still there. Now he was putting on a tie. Bosch glanced at him in the mirror but didn't recognize him. He bent over the sink and rinsed his face and mouth out with cold water. He then used paper towels to dry off. He never looked at himself once in the mirror.

'Thanks for asking,' he said as he left.

Irving looked as if he hadn't moved while Bosch was gone.

'Are you all right?'

Bosch sat down and took out his cigarettes.

'Sorry, but I'm gonna smoke.'

'You already have been.'

Bosch lit up and took a deep drag. He stood up and walked to the trash can in the corner. There was an old coffee cup in it and he took it to use as an ashtray.

'Just one,' he said. 'Then you can open the door and air the place out.'

'It's a bad habit.'

'In this town so is breathing. How did he die? What was the fatal injury?'

'The autopsy was this morning. Heart failure. The strain on him was too much, his heart gave way.'

Bosch paused a moment. He felt the beginning of his strength coming back.

'Why don't you tell me the rest of it?'

'There is no rest of it. That's it. There was nothing there. No evidence on the body. No evidence in the car. It had been wiped clean. There was nothing to go on.'

'What about his clothes?'

'They were there in the trunk. No help. The killer kept one thing, though.'

'What?'

'His shield. The bastard took his badge.'

Bosch just nodded and averted his eyes. They were both silent for a long time. Bosch couldn't get the images out of his mind and he guessed Irving was having the same problem.

'So,' Bosch finally said, 'looking at what had been done to him, the torture and everything, you immediately thought of me. That's a real vote of confidence.'

'Look, Detective, you had put the man's face through a window two weeks earlier. We had gotten an added report from him that you had threatened him. What –'

'There was no threat. He –'

'I don't care if there was or wasn't. He made the report. That's the point. True or false, he made the report, therefore, he felt threatened by you. What were we supposed to do, ignore it? Just say, "Harry Bosch? Oh, no, there's no way our own Harry Bosch could do this," and go on? Don't be ridiculous.'

'All right, you're right. Forget it. He didn't say anything at all to his wife before leaving?'

'Only that someone called and he had to go out for an hour to a meeting with a very important person. No name was mentioned. The call came in about nine Friday night.'

'Is that exactly how she said he said it?'

'I believe so. Why?'

'Because if he said it in that way, then it sounds like two people may be involved.'

'How so?'

'It just sounds as though one person called him to set up a meeting with a second person, this very important person. If that person had made the call, then he would have told the wife that so and so, the big important guy, just called and I have to go meet him. See what I mean?'

'I do. But whoever called could have also used the name of an important person as bait to draw Pounds out. That actual person may not have been involved at all.'

'That's also true. But I think that whatever was said, it would have to have been convincing to get Pounds out at night, by himself.'

'Maybe it was someone he already knew.'

'Maybe. But then he probably would have told his wife the name.'

'True.'

'Did he take anything with him? A briefcase, files, anything?'

'Not that we know of. The wife was in the TV room. She didn't see him actually go out the door. We've been over all of this with her, we've been all over the house. There's nothing. His briefcase was in his office at the station. He didn't even take it home with him. There's nothing to go on. To be honest, you were the best candidate and you're clear now. It brings me back to my question. Could what you've been doing have had anything to do with this?'

Bosch could not bring himself to tell Irving what he thought, what he knew in his gut had happened to Pounds. It wasn't the guilt that stopped him, though. It was the desire to keep his mission to himself. In that moment he realized that vengeance was a singular thing, a solo mission, something never to be spoken of out loud.

'I don't know the answer,' he said. 'I told Pounds nothing. But he wanted me to go down. You know that. The guy's dead but he was an asshole and he wanted me to go down. So he'd have had his ear to the ground for anything about me. A couple people have seen me around in the last week. Word could've gotten back to him and he could've blundered into something. He wasn't much of an investigator. He could've made a mistake. I don't know.'

Irving looked at him through dead eyes. Bosch knew he was trying to determine how much was true and how much was bullshit. Bosch spoke first.

'He said he was going to meet someone important.'

'Yes.'

'Look, Chief, I don't know what McKittrick told you about the conversation I had out there with him, but you know there were important people involved back . . . you know, with my mother. You were there.'

'Yes, I was there, but I wasn't part of the investigation, not after the first day.'

'Did McKittrick tell you about Arno Conklin?'

'Not today. But back then. I remember once when I asked him what was happening with the case, he told me to ask Arno. He said Arno was running interference for someone on it.'

'Well, Arno Conklin was an important person.'

'But now? He's an old man if he's even still alive.'

'He's alive, Chief. And you have to remember something. Important men surround themselves with important men. They're never alone. Conklin may be old but there could be someone else who isn't.'

'What are you telling me, Bosch?'

'I'm telling you to leave me alone. I have to do this. I'm the only one who can. I'm telling you to keep Brockman and everybody else away from me.'

Irving stared at him a long moment and Bosch could tell he didn't know which way to go with this. Bosch stood up.

'I'll keep in touch.'

'You're not telling me everything.'

'It's better that way.'

He stepped through the door into the hallway, remembered something and then stepped back into the room with Irving.

'How am I going to get home? You brought me here.'

Irving reached over to the phone.

35

Bosch went through the fifth-floor door to the Internal Affairs Division and found no one behind the counter. He waited a few moments for Toliver to show up since Irving had just ordered him to drive Bosch home, but the young IAD detective never showed. Bosch figured it was just one more mind game they were trying to play with him. He didn't want to walk around the counter and have to find Toliver so he just yelled his name out. Behind the counter was a door that was slightly ajar and he was reasonably sure Toliver heard the call.

But the person who stepped through the door was Brockman. He stared at Bosch for a long moment without saying anything.

'Look, Brockman, Toliver is supposed to run me home,' Bosch said to him. 'I don't want anything else to do with you.'

'Yeah, well, that's too bad.'

'Just get Toliver.'

'You better watch out for me, Bosch.'

'Yeah, I know. I'll be watching.'

'Yeah, and you won't see me coming.'

Bosch nodded and looked past him to the door where he expected Toliver to step out any moment. He just wanted to diffuse the situation and get his ride home. He considered walking out and catching a cab, but he knew in rush hour it would probably cost him fifty bucks. He didn't have it on him. Plus, he liked the idea of having an IAD shine chauffeur him home.

'Hey, killer?'

Bosch looked back at Brockman. He was getting tired of this.

'What's it like to fuck another killer? Must really be something, to go all the way to Florida for it.'

Bosch tried to stay cool but he felt his face betray himself. For he suddenly knew who and what Brockman was talking about.

'What are you talking about?'

Brockman's face lit up with a bully's delight as he read Bosch's surprised look.

'Oooh, baby! She didn't even bother telling you, did she?'

'Tell me what?'

Bosch wanted to reach over the counter and drag Brockman across it but at least outwardly he maintained his cool.

'Tell you what? I'll tell you what. I think your whole story stinks and I'm going to bust it open. Then Mr Clean upstairs isn't going to be able to protect you.'

'He said you were told to leave me alone, that I was clear.'

'Fuck him and fuck you. When I come in with your alibi in a bag, he's not going to have a choice but to cut you loose.'

Toliver stepped through the doorway behind the counter. He was holding a set of car keys in his hands. He stood silently behind Brockman with his eyes down.

'First thing I did was run her on the computer,' Brockman said. 'She's got a record, Bosch. You didn't know that? She's a killer, just like you. Takes one to know one, I guess. Nice couple.'

Bosch wanted to ask a thousand questions but he wouldn't ask any of this man. He felt a deep void opening inside as he began jettisoning his feelings for Jazz. He realized that she had left all the signs out for him but he hadn't read them. Even so, the feeling that descended on him with the strongest grip was one of betrayal.

Bosch pointedly ignored Brockman and looked at Toliver.

'Hey, kid, you going to give me a ride or what?'

Toliver moved around the counter without answering.

'Bosch, I already got you on an association beef,' Brockman said. 'But I'm not satisfied.'

Bosch went to the hallway door and opened it. It was against LAPD regulations to associate with known criminals. Whether Brockman could make a charge like that stick was the least of Bosch's worries. He headed out the door with Toliver following. Before it closed Brockman yelled after them.

'Give her a kiss for me, killer.'

36

At first, Bosch sat silently next to Jerry Toliver on the ride back to his house. He had a waterfall of thoughts dropping through his mind and decided to simply ignore the young IAD detective. Toliver left the police scanner on and the sporadic chatter was the only thing resembling conversation in the car. They had caught the crest of the evening commute out of downtown and were moving at an excruciatingly slow pace toward the Cahuenga pass.

Bosch's guts ached from the wracking convulsions of nausea of an hour earlier and he kept his arms crossed in front of him as if he were cradling a baby. He knew he had to compartmentalize his thoughts. As much as he was confused and curious about what Brockman had alluded to in regard to Jasmine, he knew he had to put it aside. At the moment, Pounds and what had happened to him were more important.

He tried to piece together the chain of events and the conclusion he drew was obvious. His stumbling into the party at Mittel's and delivery of the photocopy of the *Times* clip had set off a reaction that ended with the murder of Harvey Pounds, the man whose name he had used. Though he had given Mittel only the name at the party, it was somehow traced back to the real Pounds, who was then tortured and killed.

Bosch guessed that it was the DMV calls that had doomed Pounds. Fresh from receiving the threatening news clip at the fund-raiser from a man who had introduced himself as Harvey Pounds, Mittel likely would have put his lengthy arm out to find out who this man was and what his purpose was. Mittel had connections from LA to Sacramento to Washington, DC. He could have quickly found out that Harvey Pounds was a cop. Mittel's campaign financing work had put a good number of legislators in seats in Sacramento. He would certainly have the connections in the capital city to find out if anyone was running traces on his name. And if he had that done, then he would have learned that Harvey Pounds, an LAPD lieutenant, had inquired not only about him but about four other men who would be of vital interest to him as well. Arno Conklin, Johnny Fox, Jake McKittrick and Claude Eno.

True, all the names were involved in a case and conspiracy almost thirty-five years old. But Mittel was at the center of that conspiracy and the snooping around by Pounds would be more than enough, Bosch believed, for someone of his position to take some kind of action to find out what Pounds was doing.

Because of the approach the man he thought was Pounds had made at the party, Mittel had probably concluded he was being set upon by a chiseler, an extortionist. And he knew how to eliminate the problem. Like Johnny Fox had been eliminated.

That was the reason Pounds had been tortured, Bosch knew. For Mittel to make sure the problem went no further than Pounds, he had to know who else knew what Pounds knew. The problem was that Pounds didn't know anything himself. He had nothing to give. He was tormented until his heart could take it no longer.

A question that remained unanswered in Bosch's mind was what Arno Conklin knew of all this. He had not yet been contacted by Bosch. Did he know of the man who approached Mittel? Did he order the hit on Pounds or was it solely Mittel's reaction?

Then Bosch saw a bump in his theory that needed refining. Mittel had come face to face with him posing as Harvey Pounds at the fund-raiser. The fact that Pounds was tortured before he died indicated that Mittel was not present at the time, or he would have seen that they were brutalizing the wrong man. Bosch wondered now if they understood that they had, in fact, killed the wrong man, and if they would be looking for the right one.

He mulled over the point that Mittel could not have been there and decided that it fit. Mittel was not the type to get involved in the blood work. He'd have no problem calling the shots, he just wouldn't want to see them fired. Bosch realized the surfer in a suit had also seen him at the party and, therefore, could not have been directly involved in the killing of Harvey Pounds, either. That left the man Bosch had seen through the French doors at the house. The man with the wide body and thick neck whom he had seen Mittel show the newspaper clip to. The man who had slipped and fallen while coming down the driveway for Bosch.

Bosch realized that he didn't know how close he had come to being where Pounds was now. He reached into his jacket pocket for his cigarettes and started to light one.

'Do you mind not smoking?' Toliver asked, his first words of the thirty-minute journey.

'Yeah, I do mind.'

Bosch finished lighting the smoke and put his Bic away. He lowered the window.

'There. You happy? The exhaust fumes are worse than the smoke.'

'It's a nonsmoking vehicle.'

Toliver tapped his finger on a plastic magnet that was on the dashboard ashtray cover. It was one of the little doodads that were distributed when the city passed a widespread antismoking law that forbade the practice in all city buildings and allowed for half of the department's fleet to be declared nonsmoking vehicles. The magnet showed a cigarette in the middle of a red circle with a slash through it. Beneath the circle it said THANK YOU FOR NOT SMOKING. Bosch reached over, peeled the magnet off and threw it out the open window. He saw it bounce once on the pavement and stick on the door of a car one lane over.

'Now it's not. Now it's a smoking car.'

'Bosch, you're really fucked, you know that?'

'Write me up, kid. Add it to the association beef your boss is working on. I don't care.'

They were silent for a few moments and the car crept further away from Hollywood.

'He's bluffing you, Bosch. I thought you knew that.'

'How so?'

He was surprised that Toliver was turning.

'He's just bluffing, that's all. He's still hot about what you did with that table. But he knows it won't stick. It's an old case. Voluntary manslaughter. A domestic violence case. She walked on five years probation. All you have to do is say you didn't know and it gets shitcanned.'

Bosch could almost guess what the case was about. She had practically told him during true confessions. She stayed too long with someone. That was what she had said. He thought of the painting he had seen in her studio. The gray portrait with the highlights red like blood. He tried to pull his mind away from it.

'Why're you telling me this, Toliver? Why are you going against your own?'

'Because they're not my own. Because I want to know what you meant by what you said to me in the hallway.'

Bosch couldn't even remember what he said.

'You told me it wasn't too late. Too late for what?'

'Too late to get out,' Bosch said, recalling the words he had thrown as a taunt. 'You're still a young guy. You better get yourself out of IAD before it's too late. You stay too long and you'll never get out. Is that what you want, spend your career busting cops for trading hookers dime bags?'

'Look, I want to work out of Parker and I don't want to wait ten years like everybody else. It's the easiest and fastest way for a white guy to get in there.'

'It's not worth it, is what I'm telling you. Anybody stays in IAD more than two, three years, they're there for life because nobody else wants 'em, nobody else trusts 'em. They're lepers. You better think about it. Parker Center isn't the only place in the world to work.'

A few moments of silence passed as Toliver tried to muster a defense.

'Somebody's got to police the police. A lot of people don't seem to understand that.'

'That's right. But in this department nobody polices the police who police the police. Think about that.'

The conversation was interrupted by the sharp tone he recognized as his mobile phone. On the back seat of the car were the items the searchers had taken from his apartment. Irving had ordered it all returned. Among them was his briefcase and inside it he heard his phone. He reached back, flipped the briefcase open and grabbed the phone.

'Yeah. It's Bosch.'

'Bosch, it's Russell.'

'Hey, I got nothing to tell you yet, Keisha. I'm still working on it.'

'No, I have something to tell you. Where are you?'

'I'm in the soup. The 101 coming up to Barham, my exit.'

'Well, I have to talk to you, Bosch. I'm writing a story for tomorrow. You will want to comment, I think, if only in your defense.'

'My defense?'

A dull thud went through him and he felt like saying, What now? But he held himself in check.

'What are you talking about?'

'Did you read my story today?'

'No, I haven't had the time. What –'

'It's about the death of Harvey Pounds. Today I have a follow ... It concerns you, Bosch.'

Jesus, he thought. But he tried to keep calm. He knew that if she detected any panic in his voice she would gain confidence in whatever it was she was about to write. He had to convince her she had bad information. He had to undermine that confidence. Then he realized Toliver was sitting next to him and would hear everything he said.

'I have a problem talking now. When is your deadline?'

'Now. We have to talk now.'

Bosch looked at his watch. It was twenty-five minutes until six.

'You can go to six, right?'

He'd worked with reporters before and knew that was the deadline for the *Times*'s first edition.

'No, I can't go to six. If you want to say something, say it now.'

'I can't. Give me fifteen minutes and then call back. I can't talk now.'

There was a pause and then she said, 'Bosch, I can't push it far past then. You better be able to talk then.'

They were at the Barham exit now and they'd be up to his house in ten minutes.

'Don't worry about it. In the meantime, you go warn your editor that you might be pulling the story.'

'I will not.'

'Look, Keisha, I know what you're going to ask me about. It's a plant and it's wrong. You have to trust me. I'll explain in fifteen minutes.'

'How do you know it's a plant?'

'I know. It came from Angel Brockman.'

He flipped the phone closed and looked over at Toliver.

'See, Toliver? Is that what you want to do with your job? With your life?'

Toliver said nothing.

'When you get back, you can tell your boss that he can shove tomorrow's *Times* up his ass. There isn't going to be any story. See, even the reporters don't trust IAD guys. All I had to do was mention Brockman. She'll start backpedaling when I tell her I know what's going on. Nobody trusts you guys, Jerry. Get out of it.'

'Oh, and like *everybody* trusts you, Bosch.'

'Not everybody. But I can sleep at night and I've been on the job twenty years. Think you'll be able to? What have you got in, five, six years? I'll give you ten, Jerry. That's all for you. Ten and out. But you'll look like one of these guys who puts in thirty.'

His prediction was met with a stony silence from Toliver. Bosch didn't know why he even cared. Toliver was part of the team trying to put him in the dirt. But something about the young cop's fresh face gave him the benefit of the doubt.

They made the last curve on Woodrow Wilson and Bosch could see his house. He could also see a white car with a yellow plate parked in front of it and a man wearing a yellow construction helmet standing in front holding a toolbox. It was the city building inspector. Gowdy.

'Shit,' Bosch said. 'This one of IAD's tricks, too?'

'I don't – if it is, I don't know anything about it.'

'Yeah, sure.'

Without a further word Toliver stopped in front of the house and Bosch got out with his returned property. Gowdy recognized him and immediately came over as Toliver pulled away from the curb.

'Listen, you're not living in this place, are ya?' Gowdy asked. 'It's been red-tagged. We gotta call said somebody bootlegged the electric.'

'I gotta call, too. See anybody? I was just going to check it out.'

'Don't bullshit me, Mr Bosch. I can see you've made some repairs. You gotta know something, you can't repair this place, you can't even go in. You gotta demolition order and it's overdue. I'm gonna put in a work order and have a city contractor do it. You'll get the bill. No use waitin' any longer. Now, you might as well get out of here because I'm going to pull the electric and padlock it.'

He bent down to put the toolbox on the ground and proceeded to open it up and retrieve a set of stainless steel hinges and hasp locks he would apply to the doors.

'Look, I've got a lawyer,' Bosch said. 'He's trying to work it out with you people.'

'There's nothing to work out. I'm sorry. Now if you go in there again, you're subject to arrest. If I find these locks have been tampered with, you're also subject to arrest. I'll call North Hollywood Division. I'm not fooling with you anymore.'

For the first time it occurred to Bosch that it might be a show, that the man might want money. He probably didn't even know Bosch was a cop. Most cops couldn't afford to live up here and wouldn't want to if they could. The only reason Bosch could afford it was he had bought the property with a chunk of money he had made years earlier on a TV movie deal based on a case he had solved.

'Look, Gowdy,' he said, 'just spell it out, okay? I'm slow about these things. Tell me what you want and you've got it. I want to save the house. That's all I care about.'

Gowdy looked at him for a long moment and Bosch realized he had been wrong. He could see the indignation in Gowdy's eyes.

'You keep talking like that and you could go to jail, son. I'll tell you what I'm going to do. I'm going to forget what you just said. I –'

'Look, I'm sorry . . .' Bosch looked back at the house. 'It's just like, I don't know, the house is the only thing I've got.'

'You've got more than that. You just haven't thought about it. Now, I'm going to cut you a break here. I'll give you five minutes to go inside and get what you need. After that, I'm putting the locks on it. I'm sorry. But that's the way it is. If that house goes down the hill on the next one, maybe you'll thank me.'

Bosch nodded.

'Go on. Five minutes.'

Bosch went inside and grabbed a suitcase from the top shelf of the hallway closet. First he put his second gun in it, then he dumped in as

196

much of the clothing from the bedroom closet as he could. He walked the overstuffed suitcase out to the carport, then came back inside for another load. He opened the drawers of his bureau and dumped them on the bed, then wrapped everything in the bedclothes and carried that out as well.

He went past the five-minute mark but Gowdy didn't come in after him. Bosch could hear him working with a hammer on the front door.

After ten minutes he had a large stack of belongings gathered in the carport. Included there was the box in which he kept his keepsakes and photos, a fireproof box containing his financial and personal records, a stack of unopened mail and unpaid bills, the stereo and two boxes containing his collection of jazz and blues LPs and CDs. Looking at the pile of belongings, he felt forlorn. It was a lot to fit into a Mustang, but he knew it wasn't much to show for almost forty-five years on the planet.

'That it?'

Bosch turned around. It was Gowdy. He was holding a hammer in one hand and a steel latch in the other. Bosch saw a keyed lock was hooked through one of the belt loops on his pants.

'Yeah,' Bosch said. 'Do it.'

He stepped back and let the inspector go to work. The hammering had just begun when his phone rang. He had forgotten about Keisha Russell.

He had the phone in his jacket pocket instead of his briefcase now. He took it out and flipped it open.

'Yeah, it's Bosch.'

'Detective, it's Dr Hinojos.'

'Oh … Hi.'

'Something wrong?'

'No, uh, yeah, I was expecting somebody else. I've got to keep this line open for a few minutes. I've got a call coming in. Can I call you back?'

Bosch looked at his watch. It was five minutes until six.

'Yes,' Hinojos said. 'I'll be at the office until six-thirty. I want to talk to you about something, and to see how you fared on the sixth floor after I left.'

'I'm fine, but I'll call you back.'

As soon as he flipped the phone closed, it rang again in his hand.

'Bosch.'

'Bosch, I'm up against it and don't have time for bullshit.' It was Russell. She also didn't have time to identify herself. 'The story is that the investigation into the killing of Harvey Pounds has turned inward and detectives spent several hours with you today. They searched your home and they believe you are the prime suspect.'

'Prime suspect? We don't even use those words, Keisha. Now I *know* you're talking to one of those squints in IAD. They wouldn't know how to run a homicide investigation if the doer came up and bit them on their shiny ass.'

'Don't try to deflect what we're talking about here. It's really simple. Do you or don't you have a comment on the story for tomorrow's paper? If you want to say something, I have just enough time to get it in the first run.'

'On the record, I have no comment.'

'And off?'

'Off the record, not for attribution or any use at all, I can tell you that

197

you're full of shit, Keisha. Your story is wrong. Flat-out wrong. If you run it as you have just summarized it for me, you will have to write another one tomorrow correcting it. It will say I am not a suspect at all. Then, after that, you'll have to find another beat to cover.'

'And why is that?' she asked haughtily.

'Because this is a smear orchestrated by Internal Affairs. It's a plant. And when it is read tomorrow by everybody else in the department they'll know it is and they'll know you fell for it. They won't trust you. They'll think you're just a front for people like Brockman. No one that it is important for you to have a source relationship with will want to have that relationship with you. Including me. You'll be left covering the police commission and rewriting the press releases out of media relations. And then, of course, whenever Brockman wants to cream somebody else, he'll pick up the phone and call.'

There was silence on the line. Bosch looked up at the sky and saw it turning pink with the start of sunset. He looked at his watch. It was one minute until her deadline.

'You there, Keisha?'

'Bosch, you're scaring me.'

'You should be scared. You got about a minute to make a big decision.'

'Let me ask you this. Did you attack Pounds two weeks ago and throw him through a window?'

'On or off the record?'

'It doesn't matter. I just need an answer. Quick!'

'Off the record, that's more or less accurate.'

'Well, that would seem to make you a suspect in his death. I don't see –'

'Keisha, I've been out of the state for three days. I got back today. Brockman brought me in and talked to me for less than an hour. My story checked and I was kicked free. I'm not a suspect. I'm talking to you from the front of my house. You hear that hammering? That's my house. I've got a carpenter here. Are prime suspects allowed to go home at night?'

'How can I confirm all of this?'

'Today? You can't. You've got to pick. Brockman or me. Tomorrow, you can call Assistant Chief Irving and he'll confirm – if he is willing to talk to you.'

'Shit! Bosch, I can't believe this. If I go to my editor at deadline and tell him a story that they had budgeted for the front page since the three o'clock meeting is not a story . . . I might be looking for a new beat and a new paper to cover it for.'

'There's other news in the world, Keisha. They can find something for the front page. This will pay off for you in the long run, anyway. I'll spread the word about you.'

There was a brief silence while she made her decision.

'I can't talk. I have to get in there and grab him. Good-bye, Bosch. I hope I'm still working here the next time we talk.'

She was gone before he could say good-bye.

He walked up the street to the Mustang and drove it down to the house. Gowdy had finished with the latches and both doors now had locks on them. The inspector was out at his car using the front hood as a desk. He was writing on a clipboard and Bosch guessed he was moving slowly so as to make sure Bosch left the property. Bosch started loading his pile of belongings into the Mustang. He didn't know where he was going to take himself.

He put the thought of his homelessness aside and began thinking about Keisha Russell. He wondered if she would be able to stop the story so late in the game. It had probably taken on a life of its own. Like a monster in the newspaper's computer. And she, its Dr Frankenstein, would likely have little power over stopping it.

When he had everything in the Mustang, he waved a salute to Gowdy, got in and drove down the hill. Down at Cahuenga he didn't know which way to turn because he still didn't know where he should go. To the right was Hollywood. To the left was the Valley. Then he remembered the Mark Twain. In Hollywood, only a few blocks from the station on Wilcox, the Mark Twain was an old residence hotel with efficiencies that were generally clean and neat – a lot more so than the surrounding neighborhood. Bosch knew this because he had stashed witnesses there on occasion. He also knew that there were a couple of units that were two-room efficiencies with private baths. He decided he would go for one of them and turned right. The phone rang almost as soon as he had made the decision. It was Keisha Russell.

'You owe me big time, Bosch. I killed it.'

He felt relief and annoyance at the same time. It was typical thinking for a reporter.

'What are you talking about?' he countered. 'You owe me big time for saving your ass.'

'Well, we'll see about that. I'm still going to check this out tomorrow. If it falls the way you said, I'm going to Irving to complain about Brockman. I'll burn him.'

'You just did.'

Realizing she had just confirmed Brockman as the source, she laughed uneasily.

'What did your editor say?'

'He thinks I'm an idiot. But I told him there's other news in the world.'

'Good line.'

'Yeah, I'm going to keep that one in my computer. So what's going on? And what's happening with those clips I got you?'

'The clips are still percolating. I can't really talk about anything yet.'

'Figures. I don't know why I keep helping you, Bosch, but here goes. Remember you asked about Monte Kim, the guy who wrote that first clip I gave you?'

'Yeah. Monte Kim.'

'I asked about him around here and one of the old rewrite guys told me he's still alive. Turns out that after he left the *Times* he worked for the DA's office for a while. I don't know what he's doing now but I got his number and his address. He's in the Valley.'

'Can you give it to me?'

'I guess so, since it was in the phonebook.'

'Damn, I never thought of that.'

'You might be a good detective, Bosch, but you wouldn't make much of a reporter.'

She gave him the number and address, said she'd be in touch and hung up. Bosch put the phone down on the seat and thought about this latest piece of information as he drove into Hollywood. Monte Kim had worked for the district attorney. Bosch had a pretty good idea which one that would be.

37

The man behind the front desk at the Mark Twain didn't seem to recognize Bosch, though Harry was reasonably sure he was the same man he had dealt with before while renting rooms for witnesses. The counterman was tall and thin and had the hunched-over shoulders of someone carrying a heavy burden. He looked like he'd been behind the desk since Eisenhower.

'You remember me? From down the street?'

'Yeah, I remember. I didn't say anything 'cause I didn't know if this was an undercover job or not.'

'No. No undercover. I wanted to know if you have one of the big rooms in the back open. One with a phone.'

'You want one?'

'That's why I'm asking.'

'Who you going to put in there this time? I don't want no gangbangers again. Last time, they –'

'No, no gangbangers. Only me. I want the room.'

'You want the room?'

'That's right. And I won't paint on the walls. How much?'

The desk man seemed nonplussed by the fact that Bosch wanted to stay there himself. He finally recovered and told Bosch he had his choice: thirty dollars a day, two hundred a week or five hundred a month. All in advance. Bosch paid for a week with his credit card and waited anxiously while the man checked to make sure the charge would clear.

'Now, how much for the parking space in the loading zone out front?'

'You can't rent that.'

'I want to park out front, make it harder for one of your other tenants to rip my car off.'

Bosch took out his money and slid fifty dollars across the counter.

'If parking enforcement comes by, tell them it's cool.'

'Yeah.'

'You the manager?'

'And owner. Twenty-seven years.'

'Sorry.'

Bosch went out to get his things. It took him three trips to bring everything up to room 214. The room was in the back and its two windows looked across an alley to the back of a one-story building that housed two bars and an adult film and novelties store. But Bosch had known all along it would be no garden spot. It wasn't the kind of place where he would find a terry cloth robe in the closet and mints on the pillow at night. It was just a couple of notches up from the places where you slid your money to the clerk through a slot in the bulletproof glass.

One room had a bureau and a bed, which had only two cigarette burns in the bedspread, and a television mounted in a steel frame that was bolted to the wall. There was no cable, no remote and no courtesy *TV Guide.* The other room had a worn green couch, a small table for two and a kitchenette that had a half refrigerator, a bolted-down microwave and a two-coil electric range. The bathroom was off the hallway that connected the two rooms and came complete with white tile that had yellowed like old men's teeth.

Despite the drab circumstances and his hopes that his stay would be temporary, Bosch tried his best to transform the hotel room into a home. He hung some clothes in the closet, put his toothbrush and shaving kit in the bathroom and set the answering machine up on the phone, though nobody knew his number. He decided that in the morning he'd call the telephone company and have a forwarding tape put on his old line.

Next he set up the stereo on the bureau. For the time being he just placed the speakers on the floor on either side of the bureau. He then rummaged through his box of CDs and came across a Tom Waits recording called 'Blue Valentine.' He hadn't listened to it in years so he put it on.

He sat down on the bed near the phone and listened and thought for a few minutes about calling Jazz in Florida. But he wasn't sure what he could say or ask. He decided it might be better to just let it go for now. He lit a cigarette and went to the window. There was nothing happening in the alley. Across the tops of the buildings he could see the ornate tower of the nearby Hollywood Athletic Club. It was a beautiful building. One of the last in Hollywood.

He closed the musty curtains, turned around and studied his new home. After a while he yanked the spread off the bed along with the other covers and then remade it with his own sheets and blanket. He knew it was a small gesture of continuity but it made him feel less lonely. It also made him feel a little bit as though he knew what he was doing with his life at that point and it made him forget for a few more moments about Harvey Pounds.

Bosch sat on the newly made bed and leaned back on the pillows propped against the headboard. He lit another cigarette. He studied the wounds on his two fingers and saw that the scabs had been replaced with hard pink skin. They were healing nicely. He hoped the rest of him would, too. But he doubted it. He knew he was responsible. And he knew he had to pay. Somehow.

He absentmindedly pulled the phone off the bed table and placed it on his chest. It was an old one with a rotary dial. Bosch lifted the receiver and looked at the dial. Who was he going to call? What was he going to say? He replaced the receiver and sat up. He decided he had to get out.

38

Monte Kim lived on Willis Avenue in Sherman Oaks in the midst of a ghost town of apartment buildings red-tagged after the quake. Kim's apartment building was a gray-and-white Cape Cod affair that sat between two empties. At least they were supposed to be empty. As Bosch pulled up he saw lights go out in one of the buildings. Squatters, he guessed. Like Bosch had been, always on alert for the building inspector.

Kim's building looked as though it had been either completely spared by the quake or already completely repaired. Bosch doubted it was the latter. He believed the building was more a testament to the serendipitous violence of nature, and maybe a builder who didn't cut corners. The Cape Cod had stood up while the buildings around it cracked and slid.

It was a common, rectangular building with apartment entrances running down each side of it. But to get to one of the doors, you had to be buzzed through a six-foot-tall electronic gate. The cops called them 'feel good' gates because they made the dwellers inside feel safer, but they were worthless. All they did was put up a barrier for legitimate visitors to the building. Others could simply climb over, and they did, all over the city. Feel good gates were everywhere.

He said only that it was the police when Kim's voice sounded on the intercom and he was buzzed in. He took the badge wallet out of his pocket as he walked down to apartment eight. When Kim opened up, Bosch shoved the open badge wallet through the door and about six inches from his face. He held it so his finger was across the badge and obscured the marking that said LIEUTENANT. He then pulled the wallet back quickly and put it away.

'I'm sorry, I didn't catch the name on there,' Kim said, still blocking the way.

'Hieronymus Bosch. But people call me Harry.'

'You're named for the painter.'

'Sometimes I feel old enough that I think he was named for me. Tonight's one of those nights. Can I come in? This shouldn't take long.'

Kim led him into the living room with a confused look on his face. It was a decent-sized and neat room with a couch and two chairs and a gas fireplace next to the TV. Kim took one of the chairs and Bosch sat on the end of the couch. He noticed a white poodle sleeping on the carpet next to Kim's chair. Kim was an overweight man with a wide, florid face. He wore glasses that pinched his temples and what was left of his hair was dyed brown. He wore a red cardigan sweater over a white shirt and old khakis. Bosch guessed Kim wasn't quite sixty. He had been expecting an older man.

'I guess this is where I ask, "What's this all about?" '

'Yeah, and I guess this is where I tell you. Problem is I'm not sure how to begin. I'm investigating a couple of homicides. You can probably help. But I wonder if you'd indulge me and let me ask you some questions going a while back? Then, when we're done, I'll explain why.'

'Seems unusual but . . .,'

Kim raised his hands and waved off any problems. He made a movement in his chair as if to get more comfortable. He checked the dog and then squinted his eyes as if that might better help him understand and answer the questions. Bosch could see a film of sweat developing in the defoliated landscape that had once been his scalp.

'You were a reporter for the *Times*. How long did that last?'

'Oh, boy, that was just a few years in the early sixties. How do you know that?'

'Mr Kim, let me ask these questions first. What kind of reporting did you do?'

'Back then they called us cub reporters. I was on the crime beat.'

'What do you do now?'

'Currently, I work out of my home. I'm in public relations. I have an office upstairs in the second bedroom. I had an office in Reseda but the building was condemned. You could see daylight through the cracks.'

He was like most people in LA. He didn't have to preface his remarks by saying he was talking about earthquake damage. It was understood.

'I have several small accounts,' he continued. 'I was a local spokesman for the GM plant in Van Nuys until they closed it down. Then I went out on my own.'

'What made you quit the *Times* back in the sixties?'

'I got – Am I a suspect in something?'

'Not at all, Mr Kim. I'm just trying to get to know you. Indulge me. I'll get to the point. You were saying why you quit the *Times*.'

'Yes, well, I got a better job. I was offered the position of press spokesman for the district attorney at the time, Arno Conklin. I took it. Better pay, more interesting than the cop beat and a brighter future.'

'What do you mean, brighter future?'

'Well, actually I was wrong about that. When I took the job I thought the sky would be the limit with Arno. He was a good man. I figured I'd eventually – you know, if I stayed with him – ride with him to the governor's mansion, maybe the Senate in Washington. But things didn't turn out. I ended up with an office in Reseda with a crack in the wall I could feel the wind come through. I don't see why the police would be interested in all –'

'What happened with Conklin? Why didn't things turn out?'

'Well, I'm not the expert on this. All I know is that in sixty-eight he was planning on running for attorney general and the office was practically his for the taking. Then he just . . . dropped out. He quit politics and went back to practice law. And it wasn't to harvest the big corporate bucks that sit out there when these guys go into private practice. He opened a one-man law firm. I admired him. As far as I heard, sixty percent or better of his practice was pro bono. He was working for free most of the time.'

'Like he was serving a penance or something?'

'I don't know. I guess.'

'Why'd he drop out?'

'I don't know.'

'Weren't you part of the inner circle?'

'No. He didn't have a circle. He had one man.'

'Gordon Mittel.'

'Right. You want to know why he didn't run, ask Gordon.' Then it clicked in Kim's brain that Bosch had introduced the name Gordon Mittel to the conversation. 'Is this about Gordon Mittel?'

'Let me ask the questions first. Why do you think Conklin didn't run? You must have some idea.'

'He wasn't officially in the race in the first place, so he didn't have to make any public statement about dropping out. He just didn't run. There were a lot of rumors, though.'

'Like what?'

'Oh, lots of stuff. Like he was gay. There were others. Financial trouble. Supposedly there was a threat from the mob that if he won, they'd kill him. Just stuff like that. None of it was ever more than backroom talk amongst the town politicos.'

'He was never married?'

'Not as far as I know. But as far as him being gay, I never saw anything like that.'

Bosch noted that the top of Kim's head was slick now with sweat. It was already warm in the room but he kept the cardigan on. Bosch made a quick change of tracks.

'Okay, tell me about the death of Johnny Fox.'

Bosch saw the quick glimmer of recognition pass behind the glasses but then it disappeared. But it was enough.

'Johnny Fox, who's that?'

'C'mon, Monte, it's old news. Nobody cares what you did. I just need to know the story behind the story. That's why I'm here.'

'You're talking about when I was a reporter? I wrote a lot of stories. That was thirty-five years ago. I was a kid. I can't remember everything.'

'But you remember Johnny Fox. He was your ticket to that brighter future. The one that didn't happen.'

'Look, what are you doing here? You're not a cop. Did Gordon send you? After all these years, you people think I . . .'

He stopped.

'I am a cop, Monte. And you're lucky I got here before Gordon did. Something's coming undone. The ghosts are coming back. You read in the paper today about that cop found in his trunk in Griffith Park?'

'I saw it on the news. He was a lieutenant.'

'Yeah. He was my lieutenant. He was looking into a couple old cases. Johnny Fox was one of them. Then he ended up in his trunk. So you'll have to excuse me if I'm a little nervous and pushy, but I need to know about Johnny Fox. And you wrote the story. You wrote the story after he got killed that made him out to be an angel. Then you end up on Conklin's team. I don't care what you did, I just want to know what you did.'

'Am I in danger?'

Bosch hiked his shoulders in his best who-knows-and-who-cares gesture.

'If you are, then we can protect you. You don't help us, we can't help you. You know how it goes.'

'Oh my God! I knew this – What other cases?'

'One of Johnny's girls who got killed about a year before him. Her name was Marjorie Lowe.'

Kim shook his head. He didn't recognize the name. He ran his hand over his scalp, using it like a squeegee to move the sweat into the thicker hair. Bosch could tell he had perfectly primed the fat man to answer the questions.

'So what about Fox?' Bosch asked. 'I don't have all night.'

'Look, I don't know anything. All I did was a favor for a favor.'

'Tell me about it.'

He composed himself for a long moment before speaking.

'Look, you know who Jack Ruby was?'

'In Dallas?'

'Yeah, the guy who killed Oswald. Well, Johnny Fox was the Jack Ruby of LA, okay? Same era, same kind of guy. Fox ran women, was a gambler, knew which cops could be greased and greased them when he needed to. It kept him out of jail. He was a classic Hollywood bottom feeder. When he ended up dead on the Hollywood Division blotter, I saw it but was going to pass. He was trash and we didn't write about trash. Then a source I had in the cop shop told me Johnny had been on Conklin's payroll.'

'That made it a story.'

'Yeah. So I called up Mittel, Conklin's campaign manager, and ran it by him. I wanted a response. I don't know how much you know about that time, but Conklin had this squeaky-clean image. He was the guy attacking every vice in the city and here he had a vice hoodlum on the payroll. It was a great story. Though Fox didn't have a record, I don't think, there were intel files on him and I had access to them. The story was going to do damage and Mittel knew it.'

He stopped there at the edge of the story. He knew the rest but to speak of it out loud he had to be pushed over the edge.

'Mittel knew it,' Bosch said. 'So he offered you a deal. He'd make you Conklin's flak if you cleaned up the story.'

'Not exactly.'

'Then what? What was the deal?'

'I'm sure any kind of statute has passed ...'

'Don't worry about it. Just tell me and only me, you and your dog will ever know it.'

Kim took a deep breath and continued.

'This was mid-campaign so Conklin already had a spokesman. Mittel offered me a job as deputy spokesman after the election. I'd work out of the office in the Van Nuys Courthouse, handle the Valley stuff.'

'If Conklin won.'

'Yeah, but that was a given. Unless this Fox story caused a problem. But I held out, used some leverage. I told Mittel I wanted to be the main spokesman after Arno's election or forget it. He got back to me later and agreed.'

'After he talked to Conklin.'

'I guess. Anyway, I wrote a story that left out the details of Fox's past.'

'I read it.'

'That's all I did. I got the job. It was never mentioned again.'

Bosch sized Kim up for a moment. He was weak. He didn't see that being a reporter was a calling just the same as being a cop. You took an oath to yourself. Kim had seemingly had no difficulty breaking it. Bosch could not imagine someone like Keisha Russell acting the same way under the same circumstances. He tried to cover his distaste and move on.

'Think back now. This is important. When you first called up Mittel and told him about Fox's background, did you get the impression that he already knew the background?'

'Yes, he knew. I don't know if the cops had told him that day or he had known all along. But he knew Fox was dead and he knew who he was. I think he was a little surprised that I knew and he became eager to make a deal to keep it out of the paper . . . It was the first time I ever did anything like that. I wish I hadn't done it.'

Kim looked down at the dog and then to the beige rug and Bosch knew it was a screen on which he saw how his life diverged sharply the moment he took the deal. It went from where it was going to where it eventually was.

'Your story didn't name any cops,' Bosch said. 'Do you remember who handled it?'

'Not really. It was so long ago. It would have been a couple guys from the Hollywood homicide table. Back then, they handled fatal accidents. Now there's a division for that.'

'Claude Eno?'

'Eno? I remember him. It might've been. I think I remember that it ... Yes, it was. Now I remember. He was on it alone. His partner had transferred or retired or something and he was working alone, waiting for his next partner to transfer in. So they gave him the traffic cases. They were usually pretty light, as far as any investigation went.'

'How do you remember so much of this?'

Kim pursed his lips and struggled for an answer.

'I guess . . . Like I said, I wish I never did what I did. So, I guess, I think about it a lot. I remember it.'

Bosch nodded. He had no more questions and was already thinking of the implications of how Kim's information fit with his own. Eno had worked both cases, Lowe and Fox, and later retired, leaving behind a mail-drop corporation with Conklin's and Mittel's name on it that collected a thousand dollars a month for twenty-five years. He realized that compared to Eno, Kim had settled for too little. He was about to get up when he thought of something.

'You said that Mittel never mentioned the deal you made or Fox again.'

'That's right.'

'Did Conklin ever say anything about either one?'

'No, he never mentioned a thing, either.'

'What was your relationship like? Didn't he treat you as a chiseler?'

'No, because I wasn't a chiseler,' Kim protested but the indignation in his voice was hollow. 'I did a job for him and I did it well. He was always very nice to me.'

'He was in your story on Fox. I don't have it here but in it he said he had never met Fox.'

'Yeah, that was a lie. I made that up.'

Bosch was confused.

'What do you mean? You mean, you made up the lie?'

'In case they went back on the deal. I put Conklin in the story saying he didn't know the guy because I had evidence he did. They knew I had it. That way, if after the election they reneged on the deal, I could dredge up the story again and show Conklin said he didn't know Fox but he did. I could then make the inference that he also knew Fox's background when he hired him. It wouldn't have done much good because he'd have already been elected, but it would do some PR damage. It was my little insurance policy. Understand?'

Bosch nodded.

'What was the evidence you had that Conklin knew Fox?'

'I had photos.'

'What photos?'

'They were taken by the society photographer for the *Times* at the Hollywood Masonic Lodge's St Patrick's Day dance a couple of years before the election. There's two of them. Conklin and Fox are at a table. They were scratches but one day I was –'

'What do you mean, scratches?'

'Photos never published. Outtakes. But, see, I used to look at the society stuff in the photo lab, so I could learn who the big shots in the city were and who they were out with and so on. It was useful information. One day I saw these photos of Conklin and some guy that I recognized but wasn't sure from where. It was because of the social background. This wasn't Fox's turf so at the time I didn't recognize him. Then, when Fox got killed and I was told he worked for Conklin, I remembered the photos and who the other man was. Fox. I went back to the scratch files and pulled them out.'

'They were just sitting there together at this dance?'

'In the photos? Yeah. And they were smiling. You could tell they knew each other. These weren't posed shots. In fact, that's why each was a scratch. They weren't good photos, not for the society page.'

'Anybody else with them?'

'A couple women, that was it.'

'Go get the photos.'

'Oh, I don't have them anymore. I tossed them after I didn't need them anymore.'

'Kim, don't bullshit me, okay? There was never a time you didn't need them. Those photos are probably why you are alive today. Now go get them or I'll take you downtown for withholding evidence, then I'll come back with a warrant and tear this place apart.'

'All right! Jesus! Wait here. I have one of them.'

He got up and went up the stairs. Bosch just stared at the dog. It was wearing a sweater that matched Kim's. He heard a closet door being moved on rollers, then a heavy thud. He guessed a box had been taken off the shelf and dropped to the floor. In a few more moments, Kim's heavy steps were coming down the stairs. As he passed the couch, he handed Bosch a black-and-white eight-by-ten that was yellowed around the edges. Bosch stared at it for a long time.

'I have the other in a safe deposit box,' Kim said. 'It's a clearer shot of the two of them. You can tell it's Fox.'

Bosch didn't say anything. He was still looking at the photo. It was a flashbulb shot. Everybody's face was lit up white as snow. Conklin sat across a table from the man Bosch assumed was Fox. There were a half dozen drink glasses on the table. Conklin was smiling and heavy-lidded – that was probably why the photo was a scratch – and Fox was turned slightly away from the camera, his features indistinguishable. Bosch guessed you would have had to know him to recognize him. Neither of them seemed aware of the photographer's presence. Flashbulbs were probably going off all over the place.

But more so than the men, Bosch studied the two women in the photo. Standing next to Fox and bending over to whisper in his ear was a woman in a dark one-piece dress that was tight around the middle. Her hair was swirled on top of her head. It was Meredith Roman. And sitting across the table and next to Conklin, mostly obscured by him, was Marjorie Lowe. Bosch guessed that if you didn't already know her, she wouldn't have been recognizable. Conklin was smoking and had his hand up to his face. His arm blocked off half of Bosch's mother's face. It almost looked as if she was peeking around a corner at the camera.

Bosch turned the photo over and there was a stamp on the back that said TIMES PHOTO BY BORIS LUGAVERE. It was dated March 17, 1961, seven months before his mother's death.

'Did you ever show this to Conklin or Mittel?' Bosch finally asked.

'Yeah. When I made my case for head spokesman. I gave Gordon a copy. He saw that it was proof the candidate knew Fox.'

Mittel must also have seen that it was proof that the candidate knew a murder victim, Bosch realized. Kim didn't know what he had. But no wonder he got the head spokesman's job. You're lucky you're alive, he thought but didn't say.

'Did Mittel know it was only a copy?'

'Oh yeah, I made that clear. I wasn't stupid.'

'Did Conklin ever mention it to you?'

'Not to me. But I assume Mittel told him about it. Remember, I said he had to get back to me about the job I wanted. Who would he have to clear it with, he was campaign manager? So he must've talked to Conklin.'

'I'm going to keep this.'

Bosch held up the photo.

'I've got the other.'

'Have you stayed in touch with Arno Conklin over the years?'

'No. I haven't spoken to him in, I don't know, twenty years.'

'I want you to call him now and I –'

'I don't even know where he is.'

'I do. I want you to call him and tell him you want to see him tonight. Tell him it has to be tonight. Tell him it's about Johnny Fox and Marjorie Lowe. Tell him not to tell anyone you are coming.'

'I can't do that.'

'Sure you can. Where's your phone? I'll help you.'

'No, I mean, I can't go see him tonight. You can't make –'

'You're not going to see him tonight, Monte. I'm going to be you. Now where's your phone?'

39

At Park La Brea Lifecare, Bosch parked in a visitor's space in the front lot and got out of the Mustang. The place looked dark; few windows in the upper stories had lights on behind them. He checked his watch – it was only nine-fifty – and moved toward the glass doors of the lobby.

He felt a slight pull in his throat as he made the walk. Deep down he had known as soon as he finished reading the murder book that his sights were set on Conklin and that it would come to this. He was about to confront the man he believed had killed his mother and then used his position and the people he surrounded himself with to walk away from it. To Bosch, Conklin was the symbol of all that he never had in his life. Power, home, contentment. It didn't matter how many people had told him on the trail that Conklin was a good man. Bosch knew the secret behind the good man. His rage grew with each step he took.

Inside the door a uniformed guard sat behind a desk working on a crossword puzzle torn from the *Times Sunday Magazine*. Maybe he had been working on it since then. He looked up at Bosch as if he was expecting him.

'Monte Kim,' Bosch said. 'One of the residents is expecting me. Arno Conklin.'

'Yeah, he called down.' The guard consulted a clipboard, then turned it around and handed the pen to Bosch. 'Been a long time since he's had any visitors. Sign here, please. He's up in nine-oh-seven.'

Bosch signed and dropped the pen on the clipboard.

'It's kind of late,' the guard said. 'Visitation is usually over by nine.'

'What's that mean? You want me to leave? Fine.' He held his briefcase up. 'Mr Conklin can just roll his wheelchair down to my office tomorrow to pick this stuff up. I'm the one making a special trip here, buddy. For him. Let me up or not, I don't care. He cares.'

'Whoah, whoah, whoah, hold on there, partner. I was just saying it was late and you didn't let me finish. I'm going to let you go up. No problem. Mr Conklin specifically requested it and this ain't no prison. I'm just saying all the visitors are gone, okay? People are sleeping. Just keep it down, is all. No reason to blow a gasket.'

'Nine-oh-seven, you said?'

'That's right. I'll call him and tell him you're on your way up.'

'Thanks.'

Bosch moved past the guard toward the elevators without apology. He

211

was forgotten as soon as he was out of Bosch's sight. Only one thing, one person, occupied his mind now.

The elevator moved about as quickly as the building's inhabitants. When he finally got to the ninth floor, Bosch walked past a nurses' station but it was empty, the night nurse apparently tending to a resident's needs. Bosch headed the wrong way down the hall, then corrected himself and headed back the other way. The paint and linoleum in the hallway were fresh but even top-dollar places like this couldn't completely eliminate the lingering smell of urine, disinfectant and the sense of closed lives behind the closed doors. He found the door to nine-oh-seven and knocked once. He heard a faint voice telling him to enter. It was more like a whimper than a whisper.

Bosch was unprepared for what he saw when he opened the door. There was a single light on in the room, a small reading lamp to the side of the bed. It left most of the room in shadow. An old man sat on the bed propped against three pillows, a book in his frail hands, bifocals on the bridge of his nose. What Bosch found so eerie about the tableau before him was that the bedcovers were bunched around the old man's waist but were flat on the remainder of the bed. The bed was flat. There were no legs. Compounding this shock was the wheelchair to the right of the bed. A plaid blanket had been thrown over the seat. But two legs in black pants and loafers extended from beneath it and down to the chair's footrests. It looked as if half the man was in his bed but he had left his other half in the chair. Bosch's face must have shown his confusion.

'Prosthesis,' said the raspy voice from the bed. 'Lost my legs . . . diabetes. Almost nothing of me left. Except an old man's vanity. I had the legs made for public appearances.'

Bosch stepped closer to the light. The man's skin was like the back of peeled wallpaper. Yellowish, pale. His eyes were deep in the shadows of his skeletal face, his hair just a whisper around his ears. His thin hands were ribbed with blue veins the size of earthworms under his spotted skin. He was death, Bosch knew. Death certainly had a better grip on him than life did.

Conklin put the book on the table near the lamp. It seemed to be a labor for him to make the reach. Bosch saw the title. *The Neon Rain.*

'A mystery,' Conklin said, a small cackle following. 'I indulge myself with mysteries. I've learned to appreciate the writing. I never did before. Never took the time. Come in, Monte, no need to be afraid of me. I'm a harmless old man.'

Bosch stepped closer until the light was on his face. He saw Conklin's watery eyes study him and conclude that he was not Monte Kim. It had been a long time but Conklin seemed to be able to tell.

'I came in Monte's place,' he whispered.

Conklin turned his head slightly and Bosch saw his eyes fall on the emergency call button on the bed table. He must have figured he had no chance and no strength for another reach. He turned back to Bosch.

'Who are you, then?'

'I'm working on a mystery, too.'

'A detective?'

'Yes. My name's Harry Bosch and I want to ask you about . . .'

He stopped. There was a change in Conklin's face. Bosch could not tell if it was fear or maybe recognition but something had changed. Conklin brought his eyes up to Bosch's and Bosch realized the old man was smiling.

'Hieronymus Bosch,' he whispered. 'Like the painter.'

Bosch nodded slowly. He now realized he was as shocked as the old man. 'How do you know that?'

'Because I know of you.'

'How?'

'Through your mother. She told me about you and your special name. I loved your mother.'

It was like getting hit in the chest with a sandbag. Bosch felt the air go out of him and he put a hand down on the bed to hold himself steady.

'Sit. Please. Sit.'

Conklin held out a shaky hand, motioning Bosch onto the bed. He nodded when Bosch did as he had been told.

'No!' Bosch said loudly as he rose off the bed almost as soon as he had sat down on it. 'You used her and you killed her. Then you paid off people to bury it with her. That's why I'm here. I came for the truth. I want to hear you tell it and I don't want to hear any bullshit about loving her. You're a liar.'

Conklin had a pleading look in his eyes, then he turned them away, toward the dark side of the room.

'I don't know the truth,' he said, his voice like dried leaves blown along the sidewalk. 'I take responsibility and therefore, yes, it could be said I killed her. The only truth I know is that I loved her. You can call me a liar but that is the truth. You could make an old man whole again if you believed that.'

Bosch couldn't fathom what was happening, what was being said.

'She was with you that night. In Hancock Park.'

'Yes.'

'What happened? What did you do?'

'I killed her . . . with my words, my actions. It took me many years to realize that.'

Bosch moved closer until he was hovering over the old man. He wanted to grab him and shake some sense out of him. But Arno Conklin was so frail that he might shatter.

'What are you talking about? Look at me. What are you talking about?'

Conklin turned his head on a neck no wider than a glass of milk. He looked at Bosch and nodded solemnly.

'You see, we made plans that night. Marjorie and I. I had fallen for her against all better judgment and advice. My own and others. We were going to get married. We'd decided. We were going to get you out of that youth hall. We had many plans. That was the night we made them. We were both so happy that we cried. The next day was Saturday. I wanted to go to Las Vegas. Take the car and drive through the night before we could change our minds or have them changed for us. She agreed and went home to pick up her things . . . She never came back.'

'That's your story? You expect me –'

'You see, after she had left, I made one call. But that was enough. I called my best friend to tell him the good news and to ask him to stand with me as my best man. I wanted him to go with us to Las Vegas. Do you know what he said? He declined the honor of being my best man. He said that if I

213

married that . . . that woman, I'd be finished. He said he wouldn't let me do that. He said he had great plans for me.'

'Gordon Mittel.'

Conklin nodded sadly.

'So what are you saying, Mittel killed her? You didn't know?'

'I didn't know.'

He looked down at his feeble hands and balled them into tiny fists on the blanket. They looked completely powerless. Bosch only watched.

'I did not realize it for many years. It was beyond the pale to consider that he had done it. And then, of course, I must admit I was thinking of myself at the time. I was a coward, thinking only of my escape.'

Bosch was not tracking what he was saying. But it didn't seem that Conklin was talking to him, anyway. The old man was really telling himself the story. He suddenly looked up from his reverie at Bosch.

'You know, I knew someday you would come.'

'How?'

'Because I knew you would care. Maybe no one else. But I knew you would. You had to care. You were her son.'

'Tell me about what happened that night. Everything.'

'I need you to get me some water. For my throat. There's a glass there on the bureau, a fountain in the hallway. Don't let it run too long. It gets too cold and hurts my teeth.'

Bosch looked at the glass on the bureau and then back at Conklin. He was seized with a fear that if he left the room for even a minute the old man might die and take the story with him. Bosch would never hear it.

'Go. I'll be fine. I certainly can't go anywhere.'

Bosch glanced at the call button. Again, Conklin knew his thoughts.

'I am closer to hell than heaven for what I've done. For my silence. I need to tell my story. I think you'd be a better confessor than any priest could be.'

As Bosch stepped into the hallway with the glass, he saw a figure of a man turn the corner at the end of the hall and disappear. He thought the man was wearing a suit. It wasn't the guard. He saw the fountain and filled the glass. Conklin smiled weakly as he took the glass and murmured a thanks before drinking. Bosch then took the glass back and put it on the night table.

'Okay,' Bosch said. 'You said she left that night and never came back. How did you find out what happened?'

'By the next day, I was afraid something had happened. I finally called my office and made a routine check to see what had come in on the overnight reports. Among the things they told me was that there had been a homicide in Hollywood. They had the victim's name. It was her. It was the most horrible day of my life.'

'What happened next?'

Conklin rubbed a hand on his forehead and continued.

'I learned that she had been found that morning. She – I was in shock. I couldn't believe this could have happened. I had Mittel make some inquiries but there was nothing useful coming out. Then the man who had . . . introduced me to Marjorie called.'

'Johnny Fox.'

'Yes. He called and he said he had heard the police were looking for him.

He said he was innocent. He threatened me. He said if I did not protect him, he would reveal to the police that Marjorie was with me that last night. It would be the end of my career.'

'So you protected him.'

'I turned it over to Gordon. He investigated Fox's claim and confirmed his alibi. I cannot remember it now but it was confirmed. He had been in a card game or somewhere where there had been many witnesses. Since I was confident that Fox was not involved, I called the detectives assigned to the case and arranged for him to be interviewed. In order to protect Fox and thereby protect myself, Gordon and I concocted a story in which we told the detectives that Fox was a key witness in a grand jury investigation. The plan was successful. The detectives turned their attention elsewhere. At one point I spoke to one of them and he told me he believed that Marjorie was the victim of some sort of a sex killer. You see, they were quite rare back then. The detective said the outlook on the case was not good. I'm afraid that I never suspected . . . Gordon. Such a horrible thing to do to an innocent person. It was right there in front of my face but I didn't see it for so long. I was a fool. A puppet.'

'You're saying that it wasn't you and that it wasn't Fox. You're saying that Mittel killed her to eliminate a threat to your political career. But that he didn't tell you. It was all his idea and he just went out and did it.'

'Yes, I say that. I told him, I told him that night when I called, I said that she meant more to me than all of the plans he had for me, that I had for myself. He said it would mean the end of my career and I accepted it. I accepted it as long as I started the next part of my life with her. I believe those minutes were the most peaceful of my life. I was in love and I had made a stand.'

He softly pounded a fist onto the bed, an impotent gesture.

'I told Mittel I didn't care what he thought the damage to my career would be. I told him we were going to move away. I didn't know where. La Jolla, San Diego, I threw a few places out. I didn't know where we were going to go but I was defiant. I was mad at him for not sharing the joy of our decision. And in doing so I provoked him, I know now, and I hastened your mother's death.'

Bosch studied him a long moment. His agony seemed sincere. Conklin's eyes looked as haunted as the portholes on a sunken ship. There was only blackness behind them.

'Did Mittel ever admit this to you?'

'No, but I knew. I guess it was a subconscious knowledge but then something he said years later brought it out. It confirmed it in my mind. And that was the end of our relationship.'

'What did he say? When?'

'Many years later. It was at the time I was preparing for a run for attorney general. Do you believe such a charade occurred? Me the liar, the coward, the conspirator being groomed for the office of the state's top law enforcement officer. Mittel came to me one day and said that I needed to take a wife before the election year. He was that blunt about it. He said there were rumors about me that could cost me votes. I said that was preposterous and that I wouldn't take a wife just to assuage some rednecks out in

Palmdale or the desert somewhere. Then he made a comment, just a flippant, offhand comment as he was leaving my office.'

He broke off to reach for the glass of water. Bosch helped him and he slowly drank. Bosch noticed the medicinal smell about him. It was horrible. It reminded him of dead people and the morgue. Bosch took the glass when Conklin was done and put it back.

'What was the comment?'

'As he was leaving my office, he said, and I remember it word for word, he said, "Sometimes I wish I hadn't saved you from that whore scandal. Maybe if I hadn't, we wouldn't have this problem now. People would know you aren't queer." Those were his words.'

Bosch just stared at him for a moment.

'It might've been just a figure of speech. He could have just meant that he had saved you from the scandal of knowing her by taking the steps to keep you out of it. It's not evidence that he killed her or had her killed. You were a prosecutor, you know that's not enough. It wasn't direct evidence of anything. Didn't you ever directly confront him?'

'No. Never. I was too intimidated by him. Gordon was becoming a powerful man. More powerful than I. So I said nothing to him. I simply dismantled my campaign and folded my tent. I left the public life and haven't spoken to Gordon Mittel since that time. More than twenty-five years.'

'You went into private practice.'

'Yes. I took up pro bono work as my self-imposed penance for what I was responsible for. I wish I could say it helped suture the wounds of my soul but it did not. I'm a helpless man, Hieronymus. So tell me, did you come here to kill me? Don't let my story dissuade you from believing I deserve it.'

The question at first startled Bosch into silence. Finally, he shook his head and spoke.

'What about Johnny Fox? He had his hooks into you after that night.'

'Yes, he did. He was very capable as extortionists go.'

'What happened with him?'

'I was forced to hire him as a campaign employee, paying him five hundred dollars a week for practically nothing. You see what a farce my life had become? He was killed in a hit and run before picking up his first paycheck.'

'Mittel?'

'I would assume that he was responsible, though I must admit he's a rather convenient scapegoat for all the bad deeds I've been involved in.'

'You didn't think that it was just a little too coincidental that he got killed?'

'Things are so much clearer in hindsight.' He shook his head sadly. 'At the time I remember being thrilled with my luck. The one thorn in my side had been removed by serendipity. You have to remember, at the time I had no inkling that Marjorie's death was in any way connected to me. I simply saw Fox as being a man on the make. When he was removed through the luck of an automobile mishap, I was pleased. A deal was made with a reporter to keep Fox's background on the QT and everything was fine . . . But, of course, it wasn't. It never was. Gordon, genius that he was, didn't plan on me not being able to get over Marjorie. And I'm still not.'

'What about McCage?'

'Who?'

'McCage Incorporated. Your payoffs to the cop. Claude Eno.'

Conklin was quiet a moment while he composed an answer.

'Of course, I knew Claude Eno. I didn't care for him. And I never paid him a dime.'

'McCage was incorporated in Nevada. It was Eno's company. You and Mittel are both listed as corporate officers. It was a payoff scam. Eno was getting a grand a month from somewhere. You and Mittel.'

'No!' Conklin said as forcefully as he could. The word came out as little more than a cough. 'I don't know about McCage. Gordon could have set it up, even signed for me or made me sign unwittingly. As district attorney he took care of things for me. I signed when he told me to sign.'

He said it while looking directly at Bosch and Harry believed him. Conklin had admitted to far worse deeds. Why would he lie about paying off Eno?

'What did Mittel do when you folded your tent, when you told him you were through?'

'By then he was already quite powerful. Politically. His law firm represented the city's upper tier and his political work was branching out, growing. Still, I was the centerpiece. The plan was to take the attorney general's office and then the governor's mansion. Who knows what after that. So Gordon . . . he was unhappy. I refused to see him but we talked on the phone. When he could not convince me to change my mind, he threatened me.'

'How?'

'He told me that if I ever attempted to assault his reputation, he would see to it that I was indicted for Marjorie's death. And I had no doubt that he could have done it.'

'From best man to greatest enemy. How'd you ever get hooked up with him?'

'I guess he slipped in the door while I wasn't looking. I never saw the real face until it was too late . . . I don't think in my life I've come across anyone as cunningly focused as Gordon. He was – is – a dangerous man. I'm sorry I ever brought your mother into his path.'

Bosch nodded. He had no more questions and didn't know what else to say. After a few moments during which Conklin seemed to be lost in thought, the old man spoke up.

'I think, young man, that you only run into a person that is a perfect fit once in your life. When you find the one that you think fits, then grab on for dear life. And it's no matter what she's done in the past. None of that matters. Only the holding on matters.'

Bosch nodded again. It was all he could think of to do.

'Where did you meet her?'

'Oh . . . I met her at a dance. She was introduced and, of course, she was younger than me so I didn't think there would be any interest from her. But I was wrong . . . We danced. We dated. And I fell in love.'

'You didn't know about her past?'

'At the time, no. But she told me eventually. By then I didn't care.'

'What about Fox?'

'Yes, he was the liaison. He introduced us. I didn't know who he was, either. He said he was a business man. You see, for him, it was a business move. Introduce the girl to the prosecutor, sit back and see what happens. I never paid her and she never asked me for money. All the while we fell in love, Fox must have been weighing his options.'

Bosch wondered if he should take the photo from Monte Kim out of his case and show it to Conklin, but he decided not to tempt the old man's memory with the reality of a photo. Conklin spoke while Bosch was still thinking about it.

'I'm very tired now and you never answered my question.'

'What question?'

'Did you come here to kill me?'

Bosch looked at his face and his useless hands and realized he felt the stirring of sympathy.

'I didn't know what I was going to do. I just knew I was coming.'

'You want to know about her?'

'My mother?'

'Yes.'

Bosch thought about the question. His own memories of his mother were dim and fading farther all the time. And he had few recollections about her that came from others.

'What was she like?' he said.

Conklin thought for a moment.

'She is hard for me to describe. I felt a great attraction to her . . . that crooked smile . . . I knew she had secrets. I suppose all people do. But hers ran deep. And despite all of that, she was full of life. And, you see, I didn't think I was at the time we met. That's what she gave to me.'

He drank from the glass of water again, emptying it. Bosch offered to get more but Conklin waved off the offer.

'I had been with other women and they wanted to show me off like a trophy,' he said. 'Your mother wasn't like that. She'd rather stay at home or take a picnic basket to Griffith Park than go to the clubs on the Sunset Strip.'

'How did you find out about . . . what she did?'

'She told me. The night she told me about you. She said she needed to tell me the truth because she needed my help. I have to admit . . . the shock was . . . I initially thought of myself. You know, protecting myself. But I admired her courage in telling me and I was in love by then. I couldn't turn away.'

'How did Mittel know?'

'I told him. I regret it to this day.'

'If she . . . If she was as you described her, why did she do what she did? I've never . . . understood.'

'I haven't, either. As I told you, she had her secrets. She didn't tell me them all.'

Bosch looked away from him and out the window. The view was to the north. He could see the lights of the Hollywood Hills glimmering in the mist from the canyons.

'She used to tell me that you were a tough little egg,' Conklin said from behind him. His voice was almost hoarse now. It was probably more talking than he had done in months. 'She once told me that she knew it didn't matter what happened to her because you were tough enough to make it through.'

Bosch said nothing. He just looked through the window.

'Was she right?' the old man asked.

Bosch's eyes followed the crestline of the hills directly north. Somewhere up there the lights glowed from Mittel's spaceship. He was up there somewhere waiting for Bosch. He looked back at Conklin, who was still waiting for an answer.

'I think maybe the jury's still out.'

40

Bosch leaned against the stainless steel wall of the elevator as it descended. He realized how different his feelings were from those that he held while the elevator had been carrying him up. He had ridden up with hatred pounding in his chest like a cat in a burlap bag. He didn't even know the man he carried it for. Now he looked upon that man as a pitiful character, a half of a man who lay with his frail hands folded on the blanket, waiting, maybe hoping, for death to come and end his private misery.

Bosch believed Conklin. There was something about his story and his pain that seemed too genuine to be dismissed as an act. Conklin was far beyond posing. He was facing his grave. He had called himself a coward and a puppet and Bosch could think of nothing much harsher that a man could put on his own tombstone.

In realizing that Conklin spoke the truth, Bosch knew that he had already met the real enemy face to face. Gordon Mittel. The strategist. The fixer. The killer. The man who held the strings to the puppet. Now they would meet again. But this time, Bosch planned to make it on his terms.

He pushed the L button again as if that might coax the elevator to descend faster. He knew it was a useless gesture but he did it again.

When the elevator finally opened, the lobby seemed empty and sterile. The guard was there, behind his desk, working on his word puzzle. There wasn't even the sound of a far-off TV. Only the silence of old people's lives. He asked the guard if he needed him to sign out and he was waved off.

'Look, sorry I was an asshole before,' Bosch offered.

'Don't worry about it, partner,' the guard replied. 'It gets to the best of us.'

Bosch wondered what the 'it' was he was talking about but said nothing. He nodded solemnly, as if he got most of his life lessons from security guards. He pushed through the glass doors and headed down the steps into the parking lot. It was getting cool and he turned up the collar of his jacket. He saw the sky was clear and the moon as sharp as a sickle. As he approached the Mustang he noticed the trunk of the car next to it was open and a man was bent over, attaching a jack to the rear bumper. Bosch picked up his pace and hoped he wouldn't be asked to help out. It was too cold and he was tired of talking to strangers.

He passed the crouched man and then, not used to the rental car keys, he fumbled as he tried to get the proper key into the Mustang's door lock. Just as he got the key in the slot, he heard a shoe scuff along the pavement behind him and a voice said, 'Excuse me, fella.'

Bosch turned, trying to quickly think of an excuse for why he couldn't help the man. But all he saw was the blur of the other man's arm coming down. Then he saw an explosion of red the color of blood.

Then all he saw was black.

41

Bosch followed the coyote again. But this time the animal did not take him on the path through the mountain brush. The coyote was out of his element. He led Bosch up a steep incline of pavement. Bosch looked around and realized he was on a tall bridge over a wide expanse of water that his eyes followed to the horizon. Bosch became panicked as the coyote got too far ahead of him. He chased the animal but it crested the rise of the bridge and disappeared. The bridge was now empty, except for Bosch. He struggled to the top and looked around. The sky was blood red and seemed to be pulsing with the sound of a heartbeat.

Bosch looked in all directions but the coyote was gone. He was alone.

But suddenly he wasn't alone. The hands of someone unseen grabbed him from behind and pushed him toward the railing. Bosch struggled. He swung his elbows wildly and dug his heels in and tried to stop his movement to the edge. He tried to speak, to yell for help, but nothing came from his throat. He saw the water shimmering like the scales of a fish below him.

Then, as quickly as they had taken hold of him, the hands were gone and he was alone. He spun around and no one was there. From behind he heard a door close sharply. He turned again and there was no one. And there was no door.

42

Bosch woke up in darkness and pain to the sound of muffled shouting. He was lying on a hard surface and at first it was a struggle just to move. Eventually, he slid his hand across the ground and determined it was carpet. He knew he was inside somewhere, lying on a floor. Across the expanse of darkness he saw a small line of dim light. He stared at it for some time, using it as a focal point, before realizing that it was the crack of light emitted at the bottom edge of a door.

He pulled himself up into a sitting position and the movement made his interior world slide and melt like a Dalí painting. A feeling of nausea came over him and he closed his eyes and waited for several seconds until equilibrium returned. He raised his hand to the side of his head where the pain came from and found the hair matted with a stickiness he knew by smell was blood. His fingers carefully traced the matted hair to a two-inch-long gash in his scalp. He touched it gingerly and determined that the blood had clotted for now. The wound was no longer bleeding.

He didn't think he could stand so he crawled toward the light. The dream of the coyote broke into his mind and then disappeared in a flash of red pain.

He found the door knob was locked. That didn't surprise him. But the effort exhausted him. He leaned back against the wall and closed his eyes. Inside, his instinct to seek a means of escape and his desire to lay up and mend fought for his attention. The battle was interrupted only by the start of the voices again. Bosch could tell they did not come from the room on the other side of the door. They were farther away, yet near enough to be understood.

'Stupid fuck!'

'Look, I tol' you, you didn't say anything about any briefcase. You –'

'There had to have been one. Use your common sense.'

'You said bring the man. I brang the man. You want, I go back to the car and look for a briefcase. But you dint say nothin' about –'

'You can't go back, you fool! The place will be crawling with cops. They probably have his car and the briefcase already.'

'I didn't see any briefcase. Maybe he didn't have one.'

'And maybe I should have depended on someone else.'

Bosch realized that they were talking about him. He also recognized the angry voice as belonging to Gordon Mittel. It had the crisp delivery and haughtiness of the man Bosch had met at the fund-raiser. The other voice

Bosch didn't recognize, though he had a good idea who it was. Though defensive and submissive, it was a gruff voice full of the timbre of violence. Bosch guessed it was the man who had hit him. And he imagined that to be the man he had seen Mittel with inside the house during the fund-raiser.

It took Bosch several minutes to consider the content of what they were arguing about. A briefcase. His briefcase. It wasn't in the car, he knew. Then he realized he must have forgotten it, left it in Conklin's room. He had brought it up with him so he could take out the photo Monte Kim had given him and the bank statements from Eno's safe deposit box and confront the old man with his lies. But the old man hadn't lied. He hadn't denied Bosch's mother. And so the photo and statements weren't necessary. The briefcase lay at the foot of the bed, forgotten.

He thought about the last exchange he had heard. Mittel told the other man he could not go back, that the police would be there. This made no sense to him. Unless someone had witnessed the attack on him. Maybe the security guard. It gave him hope, then he dashed it himself when he thought of another possibility. Mittel was taking care of all the loose ends and Conklin had to be one of them. Bosch slumped against the wall. He knew he was now the last loose end. He sat there in silence until he heard Mittel's voice once more.

'Go get him. Bring him outside.'

As quickly as he could, not yet formulating a plan, Bosch crawled back toward the spot where he thought he had been when he woke up. He rammed into something heavy, put his hands on it and determined it was a pool table. He quickly found the corner and reached into the pocket. His hand closed on a billiard ball. He pulled it out, quickly trying to think of a way to conceal it. Finally, he shoved it inside his sport coat so that it rolled down the inside of the left sleeve to the crook in his elbow. There was more than enough room. Bosch liked large jackets because they gave him room to grab his gun. That made the sleeves baggy. He believed that by cocking his arm he could conceal the heavy ball in the folds of the sleeve.

As he heard a key hit the door knob, he moved to his right and sprawled on the carpet, closed his eyes and waited. He hoped he was in or close to the spot on the carpet where he had been dropped by his captors. In moments, he heard the door open and then light burned through his eyelids. There was nothing after that. No sound or movement. He waited.

'Forget it, Bosch,' the voice said. 'That only works in movies.'

Bosch didn't move.

'Look, your blood is all over the carpet. It's on the door knob here.'

Bosch realized he must have left a trail to the door and back. His half-hatched plan to surprise his captor and overtake him had no chance now. He opened his eyes. There was a light on the ceiling directly overhead.

'All right,' he said. 'What do you want?'

'Get up. Let's go.'

Bosch slowly got up. It was an actual struggle but he added to it, ad libbing a bit. And when he was all the way up, he saw blood on the green felt bumper of the pool table. He quickly stumbled and grabbed the spot for support. He hoped the man in the room had not seen the blood was already there.

'Get away from there, goddamnit. That's a five-thousand-dollar table. Look at the blood . . . shit.'

'Sorry. I'll pay for it.'

'Not where you're going. Let's go.'

Bosch recognized him. It was the man he guessed it would be. Mittel's man from the party. And his face matched his voice. Gruff, strong, he had broken a few boards with it. He had a ruddy complexion set off by two small brown eyes that never seemed to blink.

He wore no suit this time. At least that Bosch could see. He was dressed in a bulky blue jumpsuit that looked brand-new. It was a splatter suit. Bosch knew that professional killers often used them. It was easier to clean up after a job and you didn't mess up your suit. Just zip off the splatter suit, dump it, and you're on your way.

Bosch stood on his own and took a step but immediately bent over and folded his arms across his stomach. He thought this was the best way to conceal the weapon he had.

'You really hit me, man. My balance is shot. I think I might get sick or something.'

'You get sick and I'll make you clean it up with your tongue. Like a fuckin' cat.'

'I guess I won't get sick then.'

'You're a funny guy. Let's go.'

The man backed away from the door and into the room. He then signaled Bosch out. For the first time Bosch saw that he carried a gun. It looked like a Beretta twenty-two and was held down low at his side.

'I know what you're thinking,' he said. 'Only a twenty-two. You think you could take maybe two, three shots and still get to me. Wrong. I got hollow points in here. I'll put you down with one shot. Tear a hole the size of a soup bowl outta your back. Remember that. Walk ahead a'me.'

He was playing it smart, Bosch noticed, not coming closer than five or six feet even though he had the gun. Once Bosch was through the door, the man issued directions. They walked down a hallway, through what looked like a living room and then through another room that Bosch thought would also qualify as a living room. This one Bosch recognized by the French doors and windows. It was the room off the party lawn at Mittel's mansion on Mount Olympus.

'Go out the door. He's waiting for you out there.'

'What did you hit me with, man?'

'Tire iron. Hope it put a splinter in your skull, but it don't matter if it did or didn't.'

'Well, I think it did anyway. Congratulations.'

Bosch stopped at one of the French doors as if he expected it to be opened for him. Outside the party tent was gone. And out near the edge of the overhang he saw Mittel standing with his back turned to the house. He was silhouetted by the lights of the city extending out into infinity from below.

'Open it.'

'Sorry, I thought . . . never mind.'

'Yeah, never mind. Just get out there. We don't have all night.'

Out on the lawn, Mittel turned around. Bosch could see he was holding the badge wallet with his ID in one hand and the lieutenant's badge in the

225

other. The gunman stopped Bosch with a hand on his shoulder, then moved back to his six-foot distance.

'So, then, Bosch is the real name?'

Bosch looked at Mittel. The former prosecutor turned political backdoor man smiled.

'Yes. That's the real name.'

'Well, then, how do you do, Mr Bosch?'

'It's Detective, actually.'

'Detective, actually. You know, I was wondering about that. Because that's what this ID card says but then this badge says something completely different. It says lieutenant. And that's curious. Wasn't that a lieutenant I read about in the papers? The one who was found dead and without his badge? Yes, I'm sure it was. And wasn't his name, Harvey Pounds, the same name that you used when you were parading around here the other night? Again, I think so, but correct me if I am wrong, Detective Bosch.'

'It's a long story, Mittel, but I am a cop. LAPD. If you want to save yourself a few years in prison, you'll get this old fuck with the gun away from me and call me an ambulance. I've got a concussion, at least. It might be worse.'

Before speaking, Mittel put the badge in one of the pockets of his jacket and the ID wallet in the other.

'No, I don't think we'll be making any calls on your behalf. I think things have gone a little too far for humanitarian gestures like that. Speaking of the human existence, it's a shame that your play here the other night cost an innocent man his life.'

'No. It's a fucking crime *you* killed an innocent man.'

'Well, I was thinking more along the lines that it was you who killed him. I mean, of course, you are ultimately responsible.'

'Just like a lawyer, passing the buck. Should've stayed out of politics, Gordie. Stuck to the law. You'd probably have your own TV commercials by now.'

Mittel smiled.

'And what? Given up all of this?'

He spread his arms to take in the house and the magnificent view. Bosch followed the arc of his arm to look at the house but he was really trying to get a bead on the other man, the one with the gun. He spotted him standing five feet directly behind him, the gun at his side. He was still too far away for Bosch to risk making a move. Especially in his condition. He moved his arm slightly and felt the billiard ball nesting in the crook of his elbow. It was reassuring to him. It was all he had.

'The law is for fools, Detective Bosch. But I must correct you. I don't really consider myself to be in politics. I consider myself to be just a fixer. A solver of problems of any kind for anyone. Political problems just happen to be my forte. But now, you see, I have to fix a problem that is neither political nor someone else's. This one is my own.'

He raised his eyebrows as though he could hardly believe it himself.

'And that's why I have invited you here. Why I asked Jonathan to bring you along. You see, I had an idea that if we watched Arno Conklin, our mystery party crasher of the other night would eventually show up. And I wasn't disappointed.'

'You're a clever man, Mittel.'

Bosch turned his head slightly so that he could see Jonathan in his peripheral vision. He was still out of reach. Bosch knew he had to draw him closer.

'Hold your ground, Jonathan,' Mittel said. 'Mr Bosch is not one to get excited about. Just a minor inconvenience.'

Bosch looked back at Mittel.

'Just like Marjorie Lowe, right? She was just a minor inconvenience. Just a nobody who didn't count.'

'Now, that's an interesting name to bring up. Is that what this is about, Detective Bosch?'

Bosch stared at him, too angry to speak.

'Well, the only thing I can admit to is that I did use her death to my advantage. I saw it as an opportunity, you could say.'

'I know all about it, Mittel. You used her to get control of Conklin. But eventually even he saw through your lies. It's over now. It doesn't matter what you do to me here, my people will be coming. You can count on it.'

'The old give-up-the-place-is-surrounded ploy. I don't think so. This badge business . . . something tells me that you've exceeded your bounds on this one. I think maybe this is what they call an unofficial investigation and the fact that you used a false name before and were carrying a dead man's badge tends to bear me out . . . I don't think anyone is coming. Are they?'

Bosch's mind raced but he drew a blank and remained silent.

'I think you're just a small-time extortionist who stumbled onto something somehow and wants a payoff to go away. Well, we're going to give you a payoff, Detective Bosch.'

'There are people who know what I know, Mittel,' Bosch blurted. 'What are you going to do, go out and kill them all?'

'I'll take that suggestion under advisement.'

'What about Conklin? He knows the whole story. Anything happens to me, I guarantee he'll go right to the cops.'

'As a matter of fact, you could say Arno Conklin is with the police right now. But I don't think he's saying much.'

Bosch dropped his head and slumped a little. He had guessed that Conklin was dead but had hoped he was wrong. He felt the billiard ball move in his sleeve and he folded his arms again to cover up.

'Yes. Apparently, the former district attorney threw himself from his window after your visit.'

Mittel stepped aside and pointed out into the lights below. Far off Bosch could see the cluster of lighted buildings that were Park La Brea. And he could see blue and red lights flashing at the base of one of the buildings. It was Conklin's building.

'Must have been a truly traumatic moment,' Mittel continued. 'He chose death rather than give in to extortion. A principled man to the end.'

'He was an old man!' Bosch yelled angrily. 'Goddamnit, why?'

'Detective Bosch, keep your voice down or Jonathan will have to lower it for you.'

'You're not getting away this time,' Bosch said in a lower, tighter, controlled voice.

'As far as Conklin goes, I assume the final declaration will be suicide. He was very sick, you know.'

227

'Right, a guy with no legs walks over to the window and decides to throw himself out.'

'Well, if the authorities don't believe that, then maybe they will come up with an alternate scenario when they find your fingerprints in the room. I'm sure you obliged us by leaving a few.'

'Along with my briefcase.'

That hit Mittel like a slap across the face.

'That's right. I left it there. And there's enough in it to bring them up this mountain to see you, Mittel. They'll come for you!'

Bosch yelled the last line at him as a test.

'Jon!' Mittel barked.

Almost before the word was out of Mittel's mouth, Bosch was clubbed from behind. The impact came on the right side of the neck and he went down to his knees, careful to keep his arm bent and the heavy ball in place. He slowly, more slowly than was needed, got up. Since the impact had been on the right, he assumed that Jonathan had hit him with his gun hand.

'By providing me with the location of the briefcase, you have answered the most important question I had,' Mittel said. 'The other, of course, was what was in the briefcase and how it would concern me. Now, the problem I have is that without the briefcase or the ability to get it I have no way of checking the veracity of what you tell me here.'

'So I guess you're fucked.'

'No, Detective, I think that would more accurately describe your situation. However, I have one other question before you go off. Why, Detective Bosch? Why were you bothering with something so old and so meaningless?'

Bosch looked at him for a long time before answering.

'Because everybody counts, Mittel. Everybody.'

Bosch saw Mittel nod in the direction of Jonathan. The meeting was over. He had to make his play.

'Help!'

Bosch yelled it as loudly as he could. And he knew the gunman would make his move toward him immediately. Anticipating the same swing of the gun to the right side of the neck, Bosch spun to his right. As he moved he straightened his left arm and used the centrifugal force of the move to let the billiard ball roll down his sleeve into his hand. In continuing the move, he swung his arm up and out. And as he turned his face he saw Jonathan inches behind him, swinging his own hand down, the fingers laced around the Beretta. He also saw the surprise on Jonathan's face as he realized his swing would surely miss and that his momentum prevented him from correcting the course.

After Jonathan's arm went by harmlessly and he was vulnerable, Bosch's arm arced downward. Jonathan made a last-second lunge to his left but the billiard ball in Bosch's fist still caught him with a glancing blow to the right side of his head. It made a sound like a lightbulb popping and Jonathan's body followed the momentum of his falling arm. He fell face first on the grass, his body on top of the gun.

Almost immediately, the man tried to get up and Bosch delivered a vicious kick to his ribs. Jonathan rolled off the gun and Bosch came down on his body with his knees, swinging his fist into the back of his head and neck two more times before realizing that he still gripped the billiard ball and that he had hurt the man enough.

Breathing as if he had just come up for air, Bosch glanced around and saw the gun. He quickly grabbed it up and looked for Mittel. But he was gone.

The slight sound of running on grass caught his attention and he looked to the far northern line of the lawn. He caught a glimpse of Mittel then, just as he disappeared into the darkness at the spot where the flat, manicured grass gave way to the rugged brush of the hilltop.

'Mittel!'

Bosch jumped up and followed. At the point where he had last seen Mittel, he found a path worn into the brush. He realized it was an old coyote trail that had been widened over time by human feet. He raced down it, the yawning drop-off to the city below no more than two feet on his right.

He saw no sign of Mittel and followed the trail along the edge of the drop-off until the house was no longer in sight behind him. Finally he stopped after coming across nothing that indicated Mittel was even near or had taken this path.

Breathing heavily, his head pounding where he was wounded, Bosch came upon a steep bluff rising off the side of the trail and saw that it was ringed with old beer bottles and other debris. The bluff was a popular lookout spot. He put the gun in his waistband and then used his hands for balance and purchase as he climbed ten feet to its top. He did a slow three-sixty-degree turn while on top of the bluff but saw nothing. He listened but the hiss of the city's traffic precluded any chance of his hearing Mittel moving in the brush. He decided to give it up, to get back to the house and call out an air unit before Mittel could get away. They'd find him with a spotlight if the chopper could get out here quickly enough.

As he gingerly slid back down the bluff, Mittel suddenly came at him from the darkness to the right. He had been hiding behind a thick growth of brush and Spanish sword plants. He dove into Bosch's midsection, knocking him down onto the trail, his weight on top of him. Bosch felt the man's hands going for the gun still in his waistband. But Bosch was younger and stronger. The surprise attack was Mittel's last card. Bosch closed his arms around him and rolled to his left. Suddenly, the weight was off and Mittel was gone.

Bosch sat up and looked about, then pulled himself over to the edge. He pulled the gun out of his waistband and then leaned over and looked down. There was only darkness when he looked directly down the side of the rugged hill. He could see the rectangular roofs of houses about a hundred and fifty yards down. He knew they were built along the twisting roads that fed off Hollywood Boulevard and Fairfax Avenue. He did another complete turn and then looked down again. He didn't see Mittel anywhere.

Bosch surveyed the scene beneath him in its entirety until his eyes caught the backyard lights flicking on behind one of the houses directly below. He watched as a man came out of the house carrying what looked like a rifle. The man slowly approached a round backyard spa platform, the rifle pointed ahead of him. The man stopped at the edge of the spa and reached to what must have been the outdoor electrical box.

The tub light came on, silhouetting the body of a man floating in a circle of blue. Even from on top of the hill Bosch could see the swirls of blood seeping from Mittel's body. Then the voice of the man with the rifle came up the hillside intact.

'Linda, don't come out! Just call the police. Tell them we got a body in our hot tub.'

Then the man looked up the hillside and Bosch moved back away from the edge. Immediately, he wondered why he'd had the instinctive reaction to hide.

He got up and slowly made his way back to Mittel's house along the path. As he walked, he looked out across the city at the lights shimmering in the night and thought it was beautiful. He thought about Conklin and Pounds and then pushed the guilt out of his mind with thoughts about Mittel, about how his death finally closed the circle begun so long ago. He thought of the image of his mother in Monte Kim's photo. Her looking timidly around the edge of Conklin's arm. He waited for the feeling of satisfaction and triumph that he knew was supposed to come with vengeance accomplished. But none of it ever came to him. He only felt hollow and tired.

When he got back to the perfect lawn behind the perfect mansion, the man called Jonathan was gone.

43

Assistant Chief Irvin S. Irving stood in the open doorway of the examination suite. Bosch was sitting on the side of the padded table holding an ice pack to his head. The doctor had given it to him after putting in the stitches. He noticed Irving when he adjusted the bag in his hand.

'How do you feel?'

'I'll live, I guess. That's what they tell me, at least.'

'Well, that's better than you can say for Mittel. He took the high dive.'

'Yeah. What about the other one?'

'Nothing on him. We got his name, though. You told the uniforms Mittel called him Jonathan. So that means he's probably Jonathan Vaughn. He's worked for Mittel for a long time. They're working on it, checking the hospitals. Sounds like you might've hurt him enough that he'd come in.'

'Vaughn.'

'We're trying to do a background on him. So far, not much. He's got no record.'

'How long was he with Mittel?'

'That we're not sure of. We've talked to Mittel's people at the law firm. Not what you'd call cooperative. But they say Vaughn has been around forever. He was described by most people as Mittel's personal valet.'

Bosch nodded and put the information away.

'There's also a driver. We picked him up but he isn't saying much. A little surfer punk. He couldn't talk if he wanted to anyway.'

'What do you mean?'

'His jaw is broken. Wired shut. He won't talk about that, either.'

Bosch just nodded again and looked at him. There didn't seem to be anything hidden in what he had said.

'The doctor said you have a severe concussion but the skull is not fractured. Minor laceration.'

'Could've fooled me. My head feels like the Goodyear blimp with a hole in it.'

'How many stitches?'

'I think he said eighteen.'

'He said you'll probably have headaches and keep the knot up there and the eye hemorrhages for a few days. It'll look worse than it is.'

'Well, nice to know he's telling somebody what's going on. I haven't heard anything from him. Just the nurses.'

'He'll be in in a minute. He was probably waiting for you to come out of it a little more.'

'Come out of what?'

'You were a little dazed when we got up there to you, Harry. You sure you want to talk about this now? It can wait. You're hurt and need to take it –'

'I'm okay. I want to talk. You been by the scene at Park La Brea?'

'Yes, I was there. I was there when we got the call from Mount Olympus. I've got your briefcase in the car, by the way. You left it there, didn't you? With Conklin?'

He started to nod but stopped because it made things swirl.

'Good,' he said. 'There's something there I want to keep.'

'The photo?'

'You looked through it?'

'Bosch! You must be groggy. It was found at the scene of a crime.'

'Yeah, I know, sorry.'

He waved off his objection. He was tired of fighting.

'So, the crew working the scene up on the hill already told me what happened. At least, the early version based on the physicals. What I'm not clear about is what got you up there. You know, how all of this figures. You want to run it down for me or wait until maybe tomorrow?'

Bosch nodded once and waited a moment for his mind to clear. He hadn't tried to collect the story into one cohesive thought yet. He thought about it some more and finally gave it a shot.

'I'm ready.'

'Okay, I want to read you your rights first.'

'What, again?'

'It's just a procedure so it doesn't look like we're cutting any slack to one of our own. You've got to remember, you were at two places tonight and at both somebody took a big fall. It doesn't look good.'

'I didn't kill Conklin.'

'I know that and we have the security guard's statement. He says you left before Conklin took the dive. So you're gonna be okay. You're clear but I have to follow procedure. Now, you still want to talk?'

'I waive my rights.'

Irving read them to him from a card anyway and Bosch waived them again.

'Okay, then, I don't have a waive form. You'll have to sign that later.'

'You want me to tell the story?'

'Yes, I want you to tell the story.'

'Okay, here we go.'

But then he stopped as he tried to put it into words.

'Harry?'

'Okay, here it is. In 1961 Arno Conklin met Marjorie Lowe. He was introduced by local scumbucket Johnny Fox, who made his living off making such introductions and arrangements. Usually for money. This initial meeting between Arno and Marjorie was at the St Pat's party at the Masonic Lodge on Cahuenga.'

'That's the photo in the briefcase, right?'

'Right. Now, at that first meeting, according to Arno's story, which I believe, he didn't know that Marjorie was a pro and Fox was a pimp. Fox arranged the introduction because he probably saw the opportunity and had one eye on the future. See, if Conklin knew it was a pay-to-play sort of thing, he would have walked away. He was the top county vice commando. He would have walked away.'

'So he didn't know who Fox was either?' Irving asked.

'That's what he said. He just said he was innocent. If you find that hard to take, the alternative is harder; that this prosecutor would openly consort with these types of people. So, I'm going with Arno's story. He didn't know.'

'Okay, he didn't know he was being compromised. So what was in it for Fox and . . . your mother?'

'Fox is easy. Once Conklin went with her, Fox had a nice hook into him and he could reel him in whenever he wanted. Marjorie is something else and I've been thinking about it but it still isn't clear. But you can say this, most women in that situation are looking for a way out. She could have played along with Fox's plan because she had her own plan. She was looking for a way out of the life.'

Irving nodded and added to the hypothesis.

'She had a boy in the youth hall and wanted to get him out. Being with Arno could only help.'

'That's right. The thing of it was, Arno and Marjorie did something none of the three of them expected. They fell in love. Or at least Conklin did. And he believed she did, too.'

Irving took a chair in the corner, crossed his legs and stared thoughtfully at Bosch. He said nothing. Nothing about his demeanor indicated he was anything else but totally interested and believing in Bosch's story. Bosch's arm was getting tired of holding the ice pack up and he wished he could lie down. But there was only the table in the examination suite. He continued the story.

'So they fall in love and their relationship continues and somewhere along the line she tells him. Or maybe Mittel did some checking and told him. It doesn't matter. What matters is that at some point Conklin knew the score. And again, he surprises everybody.'

'How?'

'On October twenty-seven, nineteen sixty-one, he proposes marriage to Marj –'

'He told you this? Arno told you this?'

'He told me tonight. He wanted to marry her. She wanted to marry him. On that night back then, he finally decided to chuck it all, to risk losing everything he had to gain the one thing he wanted most.'

Bosch reached into his jacket on the table and took out his cigarettes. Irving spoke up.

'I don't think this is a – nothing, never mind.'

Bosch lit a smoke with his lighter.

'It was the bravest act of his life. You realize that? That took balls to be willing to risk everything like that . . . But he made a mistake.'

'What?'

'He called his friend Gordon Mittel to ask him to go with them to Vegas to be best man. Mittel refused. He knew it would be the end of a promising political career for Conklin, maybe even his own career, and he wanted no part of it. But then he went further than just refusing to be best man. See, he saw Conklin as the white horse on which he would be able to ride into the castle. He had big plans for himself and Conklin and he wasn't going to sit back and let some ... some Hollywood whore ruin it. He knew from Conklin's call that she had gone home to pack. So Mittel went there and intercepted her somehow. Maybe told her that Conklin had sent him. I don't know.'

'He killed her.'

Bosch nodded and this time he didn't go dizzy.

'I don't know where, maybe in his car. He made it look like a sex crime by tying the belt around her neck and tearing up her clothes. The semen ... it was already there because she had been with Conklin ... After she was dead, Mittel took the body to the alley near the Boulevard and put her in the trash. The whole thing stayed a secret for a lot of years after that.'

'Until you came along.'

Bosch didn't answer. He was savoring his cigarette and the relief of the end of the case.

'What about Fox?' Irving asked.

'Like I said, Fox knew about Marjorie and Arno. And he knew they were together the night before Marjorie was found dead in that alley. That knowledge gave Fox a powerful piece of leverage over an important man, even if the man was innocent. Fox used it. In who knows how many ways. Within a year he was on Arno's campaign payroll. He was hooked on him like a bloodsucking leech. So Mittel, the fixer, finally stepped in. Fox died in a hit and run while supposedly handing out Conklin campaign fliers. Would've been easy to set up, make it look like it was an accident and the driver just fled. But that's no surprise. The same guy who worked the Marjorie Lowe case worked the hit and run. Same result. Nobody ever arrested.'

'McKittrick?'

'No. Claude Eno. He's dead now. Took his secrets with him. But Mittel was paying him off for twenty-five years.'

'The bank statements?'

'Yeah, in the briefcase. You look, you'll probably find records somewhere linking Mittel to the payments. Conklin said he didn't know about them and I believe him ... You know, somebody ought to check all the elections Mittel worked on over the years. They'll probably find out he was a rat fucker that could've held his own in the Nixon White House.'

Bosch ground his cigarette out on the side of a trash can next to the table and dropped the butt in. He started to feel very cold and put his jacket back on. It was smudged with dirt and dried blood.

'You look like a mess in that, Harry,' Irving said. 'Why don't you –'

'I'm cold.'

'Okay.'

'You know, he didn't even scream.'

'What?'

'Mittel. He didn't even scream when he went down that hill. I can't figure that out.'

'You don't have to. It's just one of those –'

'And I didn't push him. He jumped me in the brush and when we rolled, he went over. He didn't even scream.'

'I understand. No one is saying –'

'All I did was start to ask questions about her and people started dying.'

Bosch was staring at an eye chart on the far wall of the room. He could not figure out why they would have such a thing in an emergency room examination suite.

'Christ . . . Pounds . . . I –'

'Yes, I know what happened,' Irving interrupted.

Bosch looked over at him.

'You do?'

'We interviewed everyone in the squad. Edgar told me that he made a computer run for you on Fox. My only conclusion is that Pounds either overheard or somehow got wind of it. I think he was monitoring what your close associates were doing after you went on ISL. Then he must've taken it a step further and stumbled into Mittel and Vaughn. He ran DMV traces on the parties involved. I think it got back to Mittel. He had the connections that would have warned him.'

Bosch was silent. He wondered if Irving really believed that scenario or if he was signaling to Bosch that he knew what had really happened and was letting it go by. It didn't matter. Whether or not Irving blamed him or took departmental action against him, Bosch's own conscience would be the hardest thing to live with.

'Christ,' he said again. 'He got killed instead of me.'

His body started shuddering then. As if saying the words out loud had started some kind of exorcism. He threw the ice pack into the trash can and wrapped his arms around himself. But the shuddering wouldn't stop. It seemed to him that he would never be warm again, that his shaking was not a temporary affliction but a permanent part of him now. He had the warm salty taste of tears in his mouth and he realized then that he was crying. He turned his face away from Irving and tried to tell him to leave but he couldn't say anything. His jaw was locked as tight as a fist.

'Harry?' he heard Irving say. 'Harry, you okay?'

Bosch managed to nod, not understanding how Irving could not see his body shaking. He moved his hands into the pockets of his jacket and pulled it closed around him. He felt something in his left pocket and started absentmindedly pulling it out.

'Look,' Irving was saying, 'the doctor said you could get emotional. This knock on the head . . . they do weird things to you. Don't wor – Harry, are you sure you're okay? You're turning blue, son. I'm gonna – I'll go get the doctor. I'll –'

He stopped as Bosch managed to remove the object from his jacket. He held his palm upright. Clasped in his shaking hand was a black eight ball. Much of it was smeared with blood. Irving took it from him, having to practically pry his fingers off it.

'I'll go get somebody,' was all he said.

Then Bosch was alone in the room, waiting for someone to come and the demon to leave.

44

Because of the concussion, Bosch's pupils were dilated unevenly and purple hemorrhages bulged below them. He had a hell of a headache and a one-hundred-degree temperature. As a precaution, the emergency room physician ordered that he be admitted and monitored, not allowed to sleep until four in the morning. He tried to pass the time by reading the newspaper and watching the talk shows but they only seemed to worsen the pain. Finally, he just stared at the walls until a nurse came in, checked on him and told him he could sleep. After that, nurses kept coming into his room and waking him at two-hour intervals. They checked his eyes and temperature and asked if he was okay. They never gave him anything for the headache. They told him to go back to sleep. If he dreamed of the coyote during the short sleep cycles, or anything else, he didn't remember it.

Finally, at noon, he got up for good. He was unsteady on his feet at first but equilibrium quickly came back to him. He made his way into the bathroom and studied his image in the mirror. He burst out laughing at what he saw, though it was not that funny. It was just that he seemed to be about to laugh or cry or do both at any given moment.

He had a small shaved spot on his skull where there was an L-shaped seam of stitches. It hurt when he touched the wound but he laughed about that, too. He managed to comb hair over it with his hand, fairly well camouflaging the injury.

The eyes were another matter. Still dilated unevenly and now cracked with red veins, they looked like the bad end of a two-week bender. Below them, deep purple triangles pointed to the corners of the eyes. A double shiner. Bosch didn't think he'd ever had one before.

Stepping back into the room he saw that his briefcase had been left by Irving next to the bed table. He bent to pick it up and almost lost his balance, grabbing on to the table at the last moment. He got back into bed with the briefcase and began examining its contents. He had no purpose in mind, he just wanted to be doing something.

He leafed through his notebook, finding it hard to concentrate on the words. He then reread the five-year-old Christmas card from Meredith Roman, now Katherine Register. He realized he needed to call her, that he wanted to tell her what happened before she read about it in the paper or heard it on the news. He found her number in his notebook and dialed on the room's phone. He got her answering machine and left a message.

'Meredith, uh, Katherine . . . this is Harry Bosch. I need to talk to you today when you get a minute. Some things have happened and I think you'll, uh, feel better about things when you hear from me. So, give me a call.'

Bosch left a variety of numbers on the tape, including his mobile, the Mark Twain and the hospital room and then hung up.

He opened the accordion pocket in the lid of the briefcase and slipped out the photo Monte Kim had given him. He studied his mother's face for a long time. The thought that eventually poked through was a question. Bosch had no doubt from what Conklin had said that he had loved her. But he wondered if she really loved Conklin back. Bosch remembered a time when she had visited him at McClaren. She had promised to get him out. At the time, the legal effort was going slowly and he knew that she had no faith in courts. When she made the promise, he knew she wasn't thinking about the law, only ways to get around it, to manipulate it. And he believed she would have found a way to do it if her time hadn't been taken away.

He realized, looking at the photo, that Conklin might simply have been part of the promise, part of the manipulation. Their marriage plan was her way of getting Harry out. From unwed mother with an arrest record to wife of an important man. Conklin would be able to get Harry out, to win back Marjorie Lowe's custody of her son. Bosch considered that love may have had nothing to do with it on her part, that it was only opportunity. In all the visits to McClaren, she had never spoken of Conklin or any man in particular. If she had truly been in love, wouldn't she have told him?

And in considering that question, Bosch realized that his mother's effort to save him was what might ultimately have led to her death.

'Mr Bosch, are you okay?'

The nurse moved quickly into the room and put the food tray down on the table with a rattle. Bosch didn't answer her. He barely noticed her. She took the napkin off the tray and used it to wipe the tears off his cheeks.

'It's okay,' she soothed. 'It's okay.'

'Is it?'

'It's the injury. Nothing to be embarrassed about. Head injuries jumble the emotions. One minute you're crying, the next you're laughing. Let me open these curtains. Maybe that will cheer you up.'

'I think I just want to be left alone.'

She ignored him and opened the curtains and Bosch had a view of another building twenty yards away. It did cheer him up, though. The view was so bad it made him laugh. It also reminded him he was in Cedars. He recognized the other medical tower.

The nurse then closed his briefcase so she could roll the table over the bed. On the tray was a plate containing Salisbury steak, carrots and potatoes. There was a roll that looked as hard as the eight ball he had found in his pocket the night before and some kind of red dessert wrapped in plastic. The tray and its smell made him feel the onset of nausea.

'I'm not going to eat this. Is there any Frosted Flakes?'

'You have to eat a full meal.'

'I just woke up. You people kept me up all night. I can't eat this. It's making me sick.'

She quickly picked up the tray and headed to the door.

'I'll see what I can do. About the Frosted Flakes.'

She looked back at him and smiled before heading out the door.

'Cheer up.'

'Yeah, that's the prescription.'

Bosch didn't know what to do with himself but wait for time to pass. He started thinking about his encounter with Mittel, about what was said and what was meant. There was something about it that bothered him.

He was interrupted by a beeping sound coming from the side panel of the bed. He looked down and found it was the phone.

'Hello?'

'Harry?'

'Yes.'

'It's Jazz. Are you okay?'

There was a long silence. Bosch didn't know if he was ready for this yet, but now it was unavoidable.

'Harry?'

'I'm fine. How'd you find me?'

'The man who called me yesterday. Irving something. He –'

'Chief Irving.'

'Yes. He called and told me you were hurt. He gave me the number.'

That annoyed Bosch but he tried not to show it.

'Well, I'm fine, but I can't really talk.'

'Well, what happened?'

'It's just a long story. I don't want to go through it now.'

Now she was quiet. It was one of those moments when both people try to read the silence, pick up each other's meanings in what they weren't saying.

'You know, don't you?'

'Why didn't you tell me, Jasmine?'

'I . . .'

More silence.

'Do you want me to tell you now?'

'I don't know . . .'

'What did he tell you?'

'Who?'

'Irving.'

'It wasn't from him. He doesn't know. It was somebody else. Somebody trying to hurt me.'

'It was a long time ago, Harry. I want to tell you what happened … but not on the phone.'

He closed his eyes and thought for a minute. Just hearing her voice had renewed his sense of connection to her. But he had to question whether he wanted to get into this.

'I don't know, Jazz. I've got to think about –'

'Look, what was I supposed to do? Wear a sign or something to warn you away from the start? You tell me, when was a good time for me to tell you? Was it right after that first lemonade? Should I have said, "Oh, by the way, six years ago I killed the man I was living with when he tried to rape me for the second time in the same night?" Would that have been proper?'

'Jazz, don't . . .'

'Don't what? Look, the cops didn't believe my story here, what should I expect from you?'

He could tell she was crying now, not so that he was supposed to hear. But he could tell it in her voice, full of loneliness and pain.

'You said things to me,' she said. 'I thought . . .'

'Jazz, we spent a weekend together. You're putting too much –'

'Don't you dare! Don't you tell me it didn't mean anything.'

'You're right. I'm sorry . . . Look, this isn't the right time. I've got too much going on. I gotta call you back . . .'

She didn't say anything.

'Okay?'

'Okay, Harry, you call me.'

'Okay, good-bye, Jazz.'

He hung up and kept his eyes closed for a while. He felt the numbness of disappointment that comes from broken hopes and wondered if he would ever talk to her again. In analyzing his thoughts he realized how much they seemed to be the same. And so his fear was not of what she had done, whatever the details were. His fear was that he would indeed call her and that he would become entwined with someone with more baggage than himself.

He opened his eyes and tried to put the thoughts aside. But he came back to her. He found himself marveling at the randomness of their meeting. A newspaper want ad. It might as well have said Single White Killer Seeks Same. He laughed out loud but it wasn't funny.

He turned the television on as a distraction. There was a talk show on and the host was interviewing women who stole their best friends' men. The best friends were also on and every question devolved into a verbal cat fight. Bosch turned the sound down and watched for ten minutes in silence, studying the contortions of the women's angry faces.

After a while he turned it off and rang the nurses' station on the intercom to inquire about his cereal. The nurse he spoke to knew nothing about his request for breakfast at lunch time. He tried Meredith Roman's number again but hung up when he got the tape.

Just as Bosch was getting hungry enough to be tempted to call for the return of the Salisbury steak, a nurse finally came back in with another food tray. This one contained a banana, a small glass of orange juice, a plastic bowl with a little box of Frosted Flakes in it and a pint-size carton of milk. He thanked her and began eating the cereal out of the box. The other stuff he didn't want.

He picked up the phone and dialed the main number at Parker Center and asked for Assistant Chief Irving's office. The secretary who eventually answered said Irving was in conference with the police chief and could not be disturbed. Bosch left his number.

Next he dialed Keisha Russell's number at the paper.

'It's Bosch.'

'Bosch, where have you been? You turn your phone off?'

Bosch reached into his briefcase and took the phone out. He checked the battery.

'Sorry, it's dead.'

'Great. That doesn't help me any, does it? The two biggest names in that clip I gave you end up dead last night and you don't even call. Some deal we made.'

239

'Hey, this is me on the phone, right?'

'So what've you got for me?'

'What've you got already? What are they saying about it?'

'They're not saying jack. I've been waiting on you, man.'

'But what are they really saying?'

'I mean it, nothing. They're saying both deaths are being investigated and that there is no clear connection. They're trying to pass it off as a big coincidence.'

'What about the other man? Did they find Vaughn?'

'Who's Vaughn?'

Bosch couldn't figure out what was happening, why there was a cover-up. He knew he should wait to hear from Irving but the anger was growing in his throat.

'Bosch? You there? What other man?'

'What are they saying about me?'

'You? They're not saying anything.'

'The other man's name is Jonathan Vaughn. He was there, too. Up at Mittel's last night.'

'How do you know?'

'I was there, too.'

'Bosch, you were there?'

Bosch closed his eyes but his mind couldn't penetrate the shroud being thrown over the case by the department. He didn't get it.

'Harry, we had a deal. Tell me the story.'

He noted that it was the only time she had ever used his first name. He continued to say nothing while he tried to figure out what was happening and weighed the consequences of talking to her.

'Bosch?'

Back to normal.

'All right. You got your pencil? I'm going to give you enough to get started. You'll have to go to Irving to get the rest.'

'I've been calling him. He won't even take my calls.'

'He will when he knows you have the story. He'll have to.'

By the time he was done telling her the story he was fatigued and his head was hurting again. He was ready to go to sleep, if it would have him. He wanted to forget everything and just sleep.

'That's an incredible story, Bosch,' she said when he was done. 'I'm sorry, you know, about your mother.'

'Thanks.'

'What about Pounds?'

'What about him?'

'Is it connected? Irving was honchoing that investigation. Now he's doing this one.'

'You'll have to ask him.'

'If I can get him on the line.'

'When you call over there, tell the adjutant to tell Irving you're calling on behalf of Marjorie Lowe. He'll call you back when he gets the message. I guarantee it.'

'Okay, Bosch, last thing. We didn't talk about this at the start like we should have. Can I use your name as a source?'

Bosch thought about it but only for a few moments.

'Yeah, you can use it. I don't know what my name's worth anymore but you can use it.'

'Thanks. I'll see you. You're a pal.'

'Yeah, I'm a pal.'

He hung up and closed his eyes. He dozed off but wasn't sure for how long. He was interrupted by the phone. It was Irving and he was angry.

'What did you do?'

'What do you mean?'

'I just got a message from a reporter. She says she's calling because of Marjorie Lowe. Have you talked to reporters about this?'

'I talked to one.'

'What did you tell her?'

'I told her enough so that you won't be able to let this one blow away.'

'Bosch . . .'

He didn't finish. There was a long silence and then Bosch spoke first.

'You were going to cover it all up, weren't you? Shove it in the trash with her. You see, after everything that's happened, she still doesn't count, does she?'

'You don't know what you're talking about.'

Bosch sat up. Now he was angry. Immediately, he was hit with vertigo. He closed his eyes until it passed.

'Well, then why don't you tell me what I don't know? Okay, Chief? You're the one who doesn't know what you're talking about. I heard what you people put out. That there may be no connection between Conklin and Mittel. What kind of – you think I'm going to sit here for that? And Vaughn. Not even a mention of him. A fucking mechanic in a splatter suit, he throws Conklin out the window and is ready to put me in the dirt. He's the one who did Pounds and he doesn't even rate a mention by you people. So, Chief, why don't you tell me what the fuck I don't know, okay?'

'Bosch, listen to me. *Listen* to me. Who did Mittel work for?'

'I don't know and I don't care.'

'He was employed by very powerful people. Some of the most powerful in this state, some of the most powerful in the country. And –'

'I don't give a shit!'

'– a majority of the city council.'

'So? What are you telling me? The council and the governor and the senators and all of those people, what, are they all involved now, too? You covering their asses, too?'

'Bosch, would you calm down and make sense? Listen to yourself. Of course, I'm not saying that. What I am trying to explain to you is that if you taint Mittel with this, then you taint many very powerful people who associated with him or who used his services. That could come back to haunt this department as well as you and me in immeasurable ways.'

That was it, Bosch saw. Irving the pragmatist had made a choice, probably along with the police chief, to put the department and themselves ahead of the truth. The whole deal stunk like rotting garbage. Bosch felt exhaustion roll over him like a wave. He was drowning in it. He'd had enough of this.

'And by covering it up, you are helping them in immeasurable ways, right? And I'm sure you and the chief have been on the phone all morning

241

letting each of those powerful people know just that. They'll all owe you, they'll all owe the department a big one. That's great, Chief. That's a great deal. I guess it doesn't matter that the truth is nowhere to be found in it.'

'Bosch, I want you to call her back. Call that reporter and tell her that you took this knock on the head and you –'

'No! I'm not calling anybody back. It's too late. I told the story.'

'But not the whole story. The whole story is just as damaging to you, isn't it?'

There it was. Irving knew. He either outright knew or had made a pretty good guess that Bosch had used Pounds's name and was ultimately responsible for his death. That knowledge was now his weapon against Bosch.

'If I can't contain this,' Irving added, 'I may have to take action against you.'

'I don't care,' Bosch said quietly. 'You can do whatever you want to me, but the story is coming out, Chief. The truth.'

'But is it the truth? The whole truth? I doubt it and deep in inside I know you doubt it, too. We'll never know the whole truth.'

A silence followed. Bosch waited for him to say more and when there was only more silence, he hung up. He then disconnected the phone and finally went to sleep.

45

Bosch awoke at six the next morning with dim memories of his sleep having been interrupted by a horrible dinner and the visits of nurses through the night. His head felt thick. He gently touched the wound and found it not as tender as the day before. He got up and walked around the room a bit. His balance seemed back to normal. In the bathroom mirror his eyes were still a colorful mess but the dilation of the pupils had evened out. It was time to go, he knew. He got dressed and left the room, briefcase in hand and carrying his ruined jacket over his arm.

At the nurses' station he pushed the elevator button and waited. He noticed one of the nurses behind the counter eyeing him. She apparently didn't readily recognize him, especially with his street clothes on.

'Excuse me, can I help you?'

'No, I'm fine.'

'Are you a patient?'

'I was. I'm leaving. Room four-nineteen. Bosch.'

'Wait a moment, sir. What are you doing?'

'I'm leaving. Going home.'

'What?'

'Just send me the bill.'

The elevator doors opened and he stepped in.

'You can't do that,' the nurse called. 'Let me get the doctor.'

Bosch raised his hand and waved good-bye.

'Wait!'

The doors closed.

He bought a newspaper in the lobby and caught a cab outside. He told the driver to take him to Park La Brea. Along the way, he read Keisha Russell's story. It was on the front page and it was pretty much an abbreviated account of what he had told her the day before. Everything was qualified with the caveat that it was still under investigation, but it was a good read.

Bosch was mentioned throughout by name as a source and main player in the story. Irving was also a named source. Bosch figured the assistant chief must have decided in the end to throw in with the truth, or a close approximation of it, once Bosch had already let it out. It was the pragmatic thing to do. This way it seemed like he had a handle on things. He was the voice of conservative reason in the story. Bosch's statements were usually followed by those from Irving cautioning that the investigation was still in its infancy and no final conclusions had been made.

The part Bosch liked best about the story were the statements from several statesmen, including most of the city council, expressing shock both at the deaths of Mittel and Conklin and at their involvement in and/or cover-up of murders. The story also mentioned that Mittel's employee, Jonathan Vaughn, was being sought by police as a murder suspect.

The story was most tenuous in regard to Pounds. It contained no mention that Bosch was suspected or known to have used the lieutenant's name or that his using it had led to Pounds's death. The story simply quoted Irving as saying the connection between Pounds and the case was still under investigation but that it appeared that Pounds might have stumbled onto the same trail Bosch had been following.

Irving had held back when he talked to Russell even after threatening Bosch. Harry could only believe it was the assistant chief's desire not to see the department's dirty laundry in print. The truth would hurt Bosch but could damage the department as well. If Irving was going to make a move against him, Bosch knew it would be inside the department. It would remain private.

Bosch's rented Mustang was still in the La Brea Lifecare parking lot. He had been lucky; the keys were in the door lock where he had left them a moment before being attacked by Vaughn. He paid the driver and went to the Mustang.

Bosch decided to take a cruise up Mount Olympus before going to the Mark Twain. He plugged his phone into the cigarette lighter so it would recharge and headed up Laurel Canyon Boulevard.

On Hercules Drive, he slowed outside the gate in front of Mittel's grounded spaceship. The gate was closed and there was yellow police-line tape still hanging from it. Bosch saw no cars in the driveway. It was quiet and peaceful. And soon he knew that a FOR SALE sign would be erected and the next genius would move in and think he was master of all he surveyed.

Bosch drove on. Mittel's place wasn't what he really wanted to see, anyway.

Fifteen minutes later Bosch came around the familiar turn on Woodrow Wilson but immediately found things unfamiliar. His house was gone, its disappearance as glaring in the landscape as a tooth missing from a smile.

At the curb in front of his address were two huge construction waste bins filled with splintered wood, mangled metal and shattered glass, the debris of his home. A mobile storage container had also been placed at the curb and Bosch assumed – hoped – it contained the salvageable property removed before the house was razed.

He parked and walked over to the flagstone path that formerly had led to his front door. He looked down and all that was left were the six pylons that poked out of the hillside like tombstones. He could rebuild upon these. If he wanted.

Movement in the acacia trees near the footings of the pylons caught his eye. He saw a flash of brown and then the head of a coyote moving slowly through the brush. It never heard Bosch or looked up. Soon it was gone. Harry lost sight of it in the brush.

He spent another ten minutes there, smoking a cigarette and waiting, but he saw nothing else. He then said a silent good-bye to the place. He had the feeling he wouldn't be back.

46

When Bosch got to the Mark Twain, the city's morning was just starting. From his room he heard a garbage truck making its way down the alley, taking away another week's debris. It made him think of his house again, fitted nicely into two dumpsters.

Thankfully, the sound of a siren distracted him. He could identify it as a squad car as opposed to a fire engine. He knew he'd get a lot of that with the police station just down the street. He moved about his two rooms and felt restless and out of it, as if life was passing by while he was stuck here. He made coffee with the machine he had brought from home and it only served to make him more jittery.

He tried the paper again but there was nothing of real interest to him except the story he had already read on the front page. He paged through the thin Metro section anyway and saw a report that the county commission chambers were being outfitted with bulletproof desk blotters that the commissioners could hold up in front of them in the event a maniac came in spraying bullets. He threw the section aside and picked up the front section again.

Bosch reread the story about his investigation and couldn't escape a growing feeling that something was wrong, that something was left out or incomplete. Keisha Russell's reporting had been fine. That wasn't the problem. The problem was in seeing the story in words, in print. It didn't seem as convincing to him as it had been when he recounted it for her or for Irving or even for himself.

He put the newspaper aside, leaned back on the bed and closed his eyes. He went over the sequence of events once more and in doing so finally realized the problem that gnawed at him was not in the paper but in what Mittel had said to him. Bosch tried to recall the words exchanged between them on the manicured lawn behind the rich man's house. What had really been said there? What had Mittel admitted to?

Bosch knew that at that moment on the lawn, Mittel was in a position of seeming invulnerability. He had Bosch captured, wounded and doomed before him. His attack dog, Vaughn, stood ready with a gun to Bosch's back. In that situation, Bosch believed there would be no reason for a man of Mittel's ego to hold back. And, in fact, he had not held back. He had boasted of his scheme to control Conklin and others. He had freely, though indirectly, admitted that he had caused the deaths of Conklin and Pounds.

But despite those admissions, he had not done the same when it came to the killing of Marjorie Lowe.

Through the fragmented images of that night, Bosch tried to recall the exact words said and couldn't quite get to them. His visual recollection was good. He had Mittel standing in front of the blanket of lights. But the words weren't there. Mittel's mouth moved but Bosch couldn't get the words. Then, finally, after working at it for a while, it came to him. He had it. Opportunity. Mittel had called her death an opportunity. Was that an acknowledgement of culpability? Was he saying he killed her or had her killed? Or was he simply admitting that her death presented an opportunity for him to take advantage of?

Bosch didn't know and not knowing felt like a heavy weight in his chest. He tried to put it out of his mind and eventually started drifting off toward sleep. The sounds of the city outside, even the sirens, were comforting. He was at the threshold of unconsciousness, almost there, when he suddenly opened his eyes.

'The prints,' he said out loud.

Thirty minutes later he was shaved, showered and in fresh clothes heading downtown. He had his sunglasses on and he checked himself in the mirror. His battered eyes were hidden. He licked his fingers and pressed his curly hair down to better cover the shaved spot and the stitches in his scalp.

At County-USC Medical Center, he drove through the back lot to the parking slots nearest the rear garage bays of the Los Angeles County medical examiner's office. He walked in through one of the open garage doors and waved to the security guard, who knew him by sight and nodded back. Investigators weren't supposed to go in the back way but Bosch had been doing it for years. He wasn't going to stop until someone made a federal case out of it. The minimum-wage guard was an unlikely candidate to do that.

He went up to the investigators' lounge on the second floor, hoping not only that there would be someone there he knew but, more important, someone Bosch hadn't alienated over the years.

He swung the door open and immediately was hit with the smell of fresh coffee. But the room was bad news. Only Larry Sakai was in the room, sitting at a table with newspapers spread across it. He was a coroner's investigator Bosch had never really liked and the feeling was mutual.

'Harry Bosch,' Sakai said after looking up from the newspaper he held in his hands. 'Speak of the devil, I'm reading about you here. Says here you're in the hospital.'

'Nah, I'm here, Sakai. See me? Where's Hounchell and Lynch? Either of them around?'

Hounchell and Lynch were two investigators who Bosch knew would do him a favor without having to think about it too long. They were good people.

'Nah, they're out baggin' and taggin'. Busy morning. Guess things are picking up again.'

Bosch had heard a rumor through the grapevine that while removing victims from one of the collapsed apartment buildings after the earthquake, Sakai had gone in with his own camera and taken photos of people dead in their beds – the ceilings crushed down on top of them. He then sold the prints to the tabloid newspapers under a false name. That was the kind of guy he was.

'Anybody else around?'

'No, Bosch, jus' me. Whaddaya want?'

'Nothing.'

Bosch turned back to the door, then hesitated. He needed to make the print comparison and didn't want to wait. He looked back at Sakai.

'Look, Sakai, I need a favor. You want to help me out? I'll owe you one.'

Sakai leaned forward in his chair. Bosch could see just the point of a toothpick poking out between his lips.

'I don't know, Bosch, having you owe me one is like having the old whore with AIDS say she'll give me a free one if I pay for the first.'

Sakai laughed at the comparison he had created.

'Okay, fine.'

Bosch turned and pushed through the door, keeping his anger in check. He was two steps down the hall when he heard Sakai call him back. Just as he had hoped. He took a deep breath and went back into the lounge.

'Bosch, c'mon, I didn't say I wouldn't help you out. Look, I read your story here and I feel for what you're going through, okay?'

Yeah, right, Bosch thought but didn't say.

'Okay,' he said.

'What do you need?'

'I need to get a set of prints off one of the customers in the cooler.'

'Which one?'

'Mittel.'

Sakai nodded toward the paper, which he had thrown back onto the table.

'That Mittel, huh?'

'Only one I know of.'

Sakai was quiet while he considered the request.

'You know, we make prints available to investigating officers assigned to homicides.'

'Cut the crap, Sakai. You know I know that and you know, if you read the paper, that I'm not the IO. But I still need the prints. You going to get them for me or am I just wasting my time here?'

Sakai stood up. Bosch knew that Sakai knew that if he backed down now after making the overture, then Bosch would gain a superior position in the netherworld of male interaction and in all their dealings that would follow. If Sakai followed through and got the prints, then the advantage would obviously go to him.

'Cool your jets, Bosch. I'm gonna get the prints. Why don't you get yourself a cup of coffee and sit down? Just put a quarter in the box.'

Bosch hated the idea of being beholden to Sakai for anything but he knew this was worth it. The prints were the one way he knew to end the case. Or tear it open again.

Bosch had a cup of coffee and in fifteen minutes the coroner's investigator was back. He was still waving the card so the ink would dry. He handed it to Bosch and went to the counter to get another cup of coffee.

'This is from Gordon Mittel, right?'

'Right. That's what it said on the toe tag. And, man, he got busted up pretty good in that fall.'

'Glad to hear it.'

'You know, it sounds to me like that story in the newspaper ain't as solid as you LAPD guys claim if you're sneaking around here gettin' the guy's prints.'

'It's solid, Sakai, don't worry about it. And I better not get any calls from any reporters about me picking up prints. Or I'll be back.'

'Don't give yourself a hernia, Bosch. Just take the prints and leave. Never met anybody who tried so hard to make the person doin' him a favor feel bad.'

Bosch dumped his coffee cup in a trash can and started out. At the door he stopped.

'Thanks.'

It burned him to say it. The guy was an asshole.

'Just remember, Bosch, you owe me.'

Bosch looked back at him. He was stirring cream into his cup. Bosch walked back, sticking his hand in his pocket. When he got to the counter he pulled out a quarter and dropped it into the slotted tin box that was the coffee fund.

'There, that's for you,' Bosch said. 'Now we're even.'

He walked out and in the hallway he heard Sakai call him an asshole. To Bosch that was a sign that all might be right in the world. His world, at least.

When Bosch got to Parker Center fifteen minutes later, he realized he had a problem. Irving had not returned his ID tag because it was part of the evidence recovered from Mittel's jacket in the hot tub. So Bosch loitered around the front of the building until he saw a group of detectives and administrative types walking toward the building from the City Hall annex. When the group moved inside and around the entry counter, Bosch stepped up behind them and got by the duty officer without notice.

Bosch found Hirsch at his computer in the Latent Fingerprint Unit and asked him if he still had the Lifescan from the prints off the belt buckle.

'Yeah, I've been waiting for you to pick them up.'

'Well, I got a set I want you to check against them first.'

Hirsch looked at him but hesitated only a second.

'Let's see 'em.'

Bosch got the print card Sakai had made out of his briefcase and handed it over. Hirsch looked at it a moment, turning the card so it reflected the overhead light better.

'These are pretty clean. You don't need the machine, right? You just want to compare these to the prints you brought in before.'

'That's right.'

'Okay, I can eyeball it right now if you want to wait.'

'I want to wait.'

Hirsch got the Lifescan card out of his desk and took it and the coroner's card to the work counter, where he looked at them through a magnifying lamp. Bosch watched his eyes going back and forth between the prints as if he were watching a tennis ball go back and forth across a net.

Bosch realized as he watched Hirsch work that more than anything else in the world he wanted the print man to look up at him and say that the prints from the two cards in front of him matched. Bosch wanted this to be over. He wanted to put it away.

After five minutes of silence, the tennis match was over and Hirsch looked up at him and gave him the score.

47

When Carmen Hinojos opened her waiting room door she seemed pleasantly surprised to see Bosch sitting on the couch.

'Harry! Are you all right? I didn't expect to see you here today.'

'Why not? It's my time, isn't it?'

'Yes, but I read in the paper you were at Cedars.'

'I checked out.'

'Are you sure you should have done that? You look . . .'

'Awful?'

'I didn't want to say that. Come in.'

She ushered him in and they took their usual places.

'I actually look better than I feel right now.'

'Why? What is it?'

'Because it was all for nothing.'

His statement put a confused look on her face.

'What do you mean? I read the story today. You solved the murders, including your mother's. I thought you'd be quite different than this.'

'Well, don't believe everything you read, Doctor. Let me clarify things for you. What I did on my so-called mission was cause two men to be murdered and another to die by my own hands. I solved, let's see, I solved one, two, three murders, so that's good. But I didn't solve the murder I set out to solve. In other words, I've been running around in circles causing people to die. So, how did you expect me to be during our session?'

'Have you been drinking?'

'I had a couple beers with lunch but it was a long lunch and I think that a minimum of two beers is required considering what I just told you. But I am not drunk, if that is what you want to know. And I'm not working, so what's the difference?'

'I thought we agreed to cut back on –'

'Oh, fuck that. This is the real world here. Isn't that what you called it? The real world? Between now and the last time we talked, I've killed someone, Doc. And you want to talk about cutting back on booze. Like it means anything anymore.'

Bosch took out his cigarettes and lit one. He kept the pack and the Bic on the arm of the chair. Carmen Hinojos watched him for a long time before speaking again.

'You're right. I'm sorry. Let's go to what I think is the heart of the problem. You said you didn't solve the murder you set out to solve. That, of course, is your mother's death. I am only going by what I read, but today's *Times* attributes her killing to Gordon Mittel. Are you telling me that you now know that to be incontrovertibly wrong?'

'Yes. I now know that to be incontrovertibly wrong.'

'How?'

'Simple. Fingerprints. I went down to the morgue, got Mittel's prints and had them compared to those on the murder weapon, the belt. No match. He didn't do it. Wasn't there. Now, I don't want you to get the wrong idea. I'm not sitting here with a guilty conscience over Mittel. He was a man who decided to kill people and then had them killed. Just like that. At least two times I'm sure of, then he was going to have me killed, too. So I say fuck him. He got what he had coming. But I'll carry Pounds and Conklin around with me for a long time. Maybe forever. And one way or another, I'll pay for it. It's just that it would make that weight easier to carry if there had been a reason. Any good reason. Know what I mean? But there isn't a reason. Not anymore.'

'I understand. I don't – I'm not sure how to proceed with this. Do you want to talk some about your feelings in regard to Pounds and Conklin?'

'Not really. I've thought about it enough already. Neither man was innocent. They did things. But they didn't have to die like they did. Especially Pounds. Jesus. I can't talk about it. I can't even think about it.'

'Then how will you go on?'

'I don't know. Like I said, I have to pay.'

'What is the department going to do, any idea?'

'I don't know. I don't care. It's bigger than the department to decide. I have to decide my penance.'

'Harry, what does that mean? That concerns me.'

'Don't worry, I'm not going to the closet. I'm not that type.'

'The closet?'

'I'm not going to stick a gun in my mouth.'

'Through what you've said here today, it is already clear you have accepted responsibility for what happened to these two men. You're facing it. In effect, you are denying denial. That is a foundation you can build on. I am concerned about this talk about penance. You have to go on, Harry. No matter what you do to yourself, it doesn't bring them back. So the best you can do is go on.'

He didn't say anything. He suddenly grew tired of all the advice, of her intervention in his life. He was feeling resentful and frustrated.

'Do you mind if we cut the session short today?' he asked. 'I'm not feeling so hot.'

'I understand. It's no problem. But I want you to promise me something. Promise me we will talk again before you make any decisions.'

'You mean about my penance?'

'Yes, Harry.'

'Okay, we'll talk.'

He stood up and attempted a smile but it came out more like a frown. Then he remembered something.

'By the way, I apologize for not getting back to you the other night when you called. I was waiting on a call and couldn't talk and then I just kind of forgot. I hope you were just checking on me and it wasn't too important.'

'Don't worry about it. I forgot myself. I was just calling to see how you made it through the rest of the afternoon with Chief Irving. I also wanted to see if you wanted to talk about the photos. It doesn't matter now.'

'You looked at them?'

'Yes. I had a couple of comments but –'

'Let's hear them.'

Bosch sat back down. She looked at him, weighing his suggestion, and decided to go ahead.

'I have them here.'

She bent down to get the envelope out of one of the lower drawers of the desk. She almost disappeared from Bosch's view. Then she was up and placed the envelope on the desk.

'I guess you should take these back.'

'Irving took the murder book and the evidence box. He's got it all now except for those.'

'You sound like you're unhappy about that, or that you don't trust him with it. That's a change.'

'Aren't you the one who said I don't trust anyone?'

'Why don't you trust him?'

'I don't know. I just lost my suspect. Gordon Mittel's clear and I'm starting from ground zero. I was just thinking about the percentages . . .'

'And?'

'Well, I don't know the numbers but a significant number of homicides are reported by the actual doer. You know, the husband who calls up crying, saying his wife is missing. More often than not, he's just a bad actor. He killed her and thinks calling the cops helps convince everybody he's clean. Look at the Menendez brothers. One of 'em calls up boohooing about mom and dad being dead. Turns out he and the brother were the ones who shotgunned them. There was a case up in the hills a few years back. This little girl was missing. It was Laurel Canyon. It made the papers, TV. So the people up there organized search parties and all of that and a few days later one of the searchers, a teen-aged boy who was one of the girl's neighbors, found her body under a log near Lookout Mountain. It turned out he was the killer. I got him to confess in fifteen minutes. The whole time of the search I was just waiting for the one who would find the body. It was percentages. He was a suspect before I even knew who it was.'

'Irving found your mother's body.'

'Yes. And he knew her before that. He told me once.'

'It seems like a stretch to me.'

'Yeah. Most people probably thought that about Mittel, too. Right up until they fished him out of the hot tub.'

'Isn't there an alternative scenario? Isn't it possible that maybe the original detectives were correct in their assumption back then that there was a sex killer out there and that tracking him was hopeless?'

'There's always alternative scenarios.'

'But you always seem drawn toward finding someone of power, a person of the establishment, to blame. Maybe that's not the case here. Maybe it's a symptom of your larger desire to blame society for what happened to your mother . . . and to you.'

Bosch shook his head. He didn't want to hear this.

'You know, all this psychobabble . . . I don't . . . Can we just talk about the photos?'

'I'm sorry.'

She looked down at the envelope as if she was seeing right through it to the photos inside it.

'Well, it was very difficult for me to look at them. As far as their forensic value goes, there wasn't a lot there. The photos show what I would call a statement homicide. The fact that the ligature, the belt, was still wrapped around her neck seems to indicate that the killer wanted police to know exactly what he did, that he had been deliberate, that he had had control over this victim. I also think the choice of placement is significant as well. The trash bin had no top. It was open. That suggests that placing the body there may not have been an effort to hide it. It was also a –'

'He was saying she was trash.'

'Right. Again, a statement. If he was just getting rid of a body, he could've put it anywhere in that alley, but he chose the open dumpster. Subconsciously or not, he was making a statement about her. So to make a statement such as that about a person, he would have to have known her to some degree. Known about her. Known she was a prostitute. Known enough to judge her.'

Irving came to Bosch's mind again but he said nothing.

'Well,' he said instead, 'couldn't it have been a statement about all women? Could it be some sick fuck who – excuse me – some nut who hated all women and thought all women were trash? That way he wouldn't have to have known her. Maybe somebody who simply wanted to kill a prostitute, any prostitute, to make a statement about them.'

'Yes, that's a possibility, but like you I'm going with the percentages. The kind of sick fuck you are talking about – which, incidentally, in psychobabble we call a sociopath – is much rarer than the one who keys on specific targets, specific women.'

Bosch shook his head dismissively and looked out the window.

'What is it?'

'It's just frustrating, that's all. There wasn't much in the murder book about them taking a hard look at anybody in her circle, any of the neighbors, nothing like that. To do it now is impossible. It makes me feel like it's hopeless.'

He thought of Meredith Roman. He could go to her to ask about his mother's acquaintances and customers, but he didn't know if he had the right to reawaken that part of her life.

'You have to remember,' Hinojos said, 'in 1961 a case like this would probably have seemed impossible to solve. They wouldn't even have known how to start. It just didn't happen as often as today.'

'They're almost impossible to solve today, too.'

They sat in silence for a few moments. Bosch thought about the possibility that the killer was some hit-and-run nut. A serial killer who was long gone into the darkness of time. If that was the case, then his private investigation was over. It was a failure.

'Do you have anything else on the photos?'

'That's really all I had – no, wait. There was one thing. And you may already have this.'

She picked the envelope up and opened it. She reached in and began sliding out a photo.

'I don't want to look at that,' Bosch said quickly.

'It's not a photo of her. Actually, it's her clothing, laid out on a table. Is that okay to look at?'

She paused, her hand holding the photo half in and half out of the envelope. Bosch waved his hand, telling her to go ahead.

'I've already seen the clothes.'

'Then you've probably already considered this.'

She slid the photo to the edge of the desk and Bosch leaned forward to study it. It was a color photo that had yellowed with age, even inside the envelope. The same items of clothing he had found in the evidence box were spread out on a table in a formation that outlined a body, in the way a woman might put them out on a bed before dressing. It reminded Bosch of cutouts for paper dolls. Even the belt with the sea shell buckle was there, but it was between the blouse and the black skirt, not at the imaginary neck.

'Okay,' she said. 'What I found odd here was the belt.'

'The murder weapon.'

'Yes. Look, it has the large silver shell as the buckle and there are smaller silver shells as ornamentation. It's rather showy.'

'Right.'

'But the buttons on the blouse are gold. Also, the photos of the body, they show she was wearing gold teardrop earrings and a gold neck chain. Also a bracelet.'

'Right, I know that. They were in the evidence box, too.'

Bosch didn't understand what she was getting at.

'Harry, this is not a universal rule or anything, that's why I hesitate to bring it up. But usually people – women – don't mix and match gold and silver. And it appears to me your mother was well dressed on this evening. That she had jewelry on that matched the buttons of her blouse. She was coordinated and she had style. What I am saying is that I don't think she would have worn this belt with those other items. It was silver and it was showy.'

Bosch said nothing. Something was poking its way into his mind and its point was sharp.

'And lastly, this skirt buttons on the hip. It's a style that is still around and I even have something similar to it myself. What's so functional about it is that because of the wide waistband it can be worn with or without a belt. There are no loops.'

Bosch stared at the photo.

'No loops.'

'Right.'

'So what you're saying is . . .'

'This might not have been her belt. It might have –'

'But it was. I remember it. The sea shell belt. I gave it to her for her birthday. I identified it for the cops, for McKittrick the day he came to tell me.'

'Well . . . then that shoots down everything I was going to say. I guess maybe when she came into the apartment the killer was already waiting with it.'

254

'No, it didn't happen in her apartment. They never found the crime scene. Listen, never mind whether it was her belt or not, what were you going to say?'

'Oh, I don't know, just a theory about it possibly being the property of another woman who may have been the motivating factor behind the killer's action. It's called aggression transference. It doesn't make sense now with this evidence but there are examples of what I was going to suggest. A man takes his ex-girlfriend's stockings and strangles another woman with them. In his mind, he's strangling the girlfriend. Something like that. I was going to suggest it could have happened in this case with the belt.'

But Bosch was no longer listening. He turned and looked out the window but wasn't seeing anything either. In his mind, he was seeing the pieces falling together. The silver and gold, the belt with two of the punch holes worn, two friends as close as sisters. One for both and both for one.

But then one was leaving the life. She'd found a white knight.

And one was staying behind.

'Harry, are you okay?'

He looked over at Hinojos.

'You just did it. I think.'

'Did what?'

He reached for his briefcase and from it withdrew the photo taken at the St Patrick's Day dance more than three decades before. He knew it was a long shot but he needed to check. This time he didn't look at his mother. He looked at Meredith Roman, standing behind the sitting Johnny Fox. And for the first time he saw that she wore the belt with the silver sea shell buckle. She had borrowed it.

It dawned on him then. She had helped Harry pick the belt out for his mother. She had coached him and she chose it not because his mother would like it but because she liked it and knew she would get to use it. Two friends who shared everything.

Bosch shoved the photo back into the briefcase and shut it. He stood up.

'I gotta go.'

48

Bosch used the same ruse he had earlier to get back into Parker Center. Coming out of the elevator on the fourth floor, he practically ran into Hirsch, who was waiting to go down. He grabbed hold of the young print tech's arm and held him in the hallway as the elevator doors closed.

'You going home?'

'I was trying to.'

'I need one more favor. I'll buy you lunch, I'll buy you dinner, I'll buy you whatever you want if you do it for me. It's important and it won't take long.'

Hirsch looked at him. Bosch could see he was beginning to wish he'd never gotten involved.

'What's that saying, Hirsch? "In for a penny, in for a pound." Whaddaya say?'

'I've never heard it.'

'Well, I have.'

'I'm having dinner with my girlfriend tonight and I –'

'That's great. This won't take that long. You'll make it to your dinner.'

'All right. What is it you need?'

'Hirsch, you're my goddamn hero, you know that?'

Bosch doubted he even had a girlfriend. They went back to the lab. It was deserted, since it was almost five on a slow day. Bosch put his briefcase on one of the abandoned desks and opened it. He found the Christmas card and took it out by holding a corner between two fingernails. He held it up for Hirsch to see.

'This came in the mail five years ago. You think you can pull a print off it? A print from the sender? My prints are going to be on there, too, I'm sure.'

Hirsch furrowed his brow and studied the card. His lower lip jutted outward as he contemplated the challenge.

'All I can do is try. Prints on paper are usually pretty stable. The oils last long and sometimes leave ridge patterns in the paper even when they evaporate. Has it been in its envelope?'

'Yeah, for five years, until last week.'

'That helps.'

Hirsch carefully took the card from Bosch and walked over to the work counter, where he opened the card and clipped it to a board.

'I'm going to try the inside. It's always better. Less chance of you having

256

touched it inside. And the writer always touches the inside. Is it all right if this gets kind of ruined?'

'Do what you have to do.'

Hirsch studied the card with a magnifying glass, then lightly blew over the surface. He reached to a rack of spray bottles over the work table and took down one marked NINHYDRIN. He sprayed a light mist over the surface of the card and in a few minutes it began to turn purple around the edges. Then light shapes began to bloom like flowers on the card. Fingerprints.

'I've got to bring this out some,' Hirsch said, more to himself than Bosch.

Hirsch looked up at the rack and his eyes followed the row of chemical reagents until he found what he was looking for. A spray bottle marked ZINC CHLORIDE. He sprayed it on the card.

'This should bring the storm clouds in.'

The prints turned the deep purple shade of heavy rain clouds. Hirsch then took down a bottle labeled PD, which Bosch knew meant physical developer. After the card was misted with PD, the prints turned a grayish black and were more defined. Hirsch looked them over with his magnifying lamp.

'I think this is good enough. We won't need the laser. Now, look at these here, Detective.'

Hirsch pointed to a print that appeared to have been left by a thumb on the left side of Meredith Roman's signature and two smaller finger marks above it.

'These look like marks left by someone trying to hold the card steady while it was being written on. Any chance that you might've touched it this way?'

Hirsch held his fingers in place an inch over the card in the same position that the hand that left the prints would have been in. Bosch shook his head.

'All I ever did was open it and read it. I think those are the prints we want.'

'Okay. Now what?'

Bosch went to his briefcase and pulled out the print cards Hirsch had returned to him earlier in the day. He found the card containing the lifts from the belt with the sea shell buckle.

'Here,' he said. 'Compare this to what you got on the Christmas card.'

'You got it.'

Hirsch pulled the magnifying glass with the ringed light attachment in front of him and once again began his tennis match eye movement as he compared the prints.

Bosch tried to envision what had happened. Marjorie Lowe was going to Las Vegas to get married to Arno Conklin. The very thought of it must have been absurdly wonderful to her. She had to go home and pack. The plan was to drive through the night. If Arno was planning to bring along a best man, perhaps Marjorie was to bring a maid of honor. Maybe she would have gone upstairs to ask Meredith to come. Or maybe she would have gone to her to borrow back the belt that her son had given her. Maybe she would have gone to say good-bye.

But something happened when she got there. And on her happiest night Meredith killed her.

Bosch thought about the interview reports that had been in the murder book. Meredith told Eno and McKittrick that Marjorie's date on the night she died had been arranged by Johnny Fox. But she didn't go to the party herself because she said Fox had beaten her the night before and she was not presentable. The detectives noted in the report that she had a bruise on her face and a split lip.

Why didn't they see it then, Bosch wondered. Meredith had sustained those injuries while killing Marjorie. The drop of blood on Marjorie's blouse had come from Meredith.

But Bosch knew why they hadn't seen it. He knew the investigators dismissed any thought in that direction, if they ever even had any, because she was a woman. And because Fox backed her story. He admitted he beat her.

Bosch now saw what he believed was the truth. Meredith killed Marjorie and then hours later called Fox at his card game to give him the news. She asked him to help her get rid of the body and hide her involvement.

Fox must have readily agreed, even to the point of his willingness to say he beat her, because he saw the larger picture. He lost a source of income when Marjorie was killed but that would have been tempered by the increased leverage the murder would give him over Conklin and Mittel. Keeping it unsolved would make it even better. He'd always be a threat to them. He could walk into the police station at any time to tell what he knew and lay it on Conklin.

What Fox didn't realize was that Mittel could be as cunning and vicious as he was. He learned that a year later on La Brea Boulevard.

Fox's motivation was clear. Bosch still wasn't sure about Meredith's. Could she have done it for the reasons Bosch had set out in his mind? Would the abandonment of a friend have led to the rage of murder? He began to believe there was still something left out. He still didn't know it all. The last secret was with Meredith Roman and he would have to go get it.

An odd thought pushed through these questions to Bosch. The time of death of Marjorie Lowe was about midnight. Fox didn't get his call and leave his card game until roughly four hours later. Bosch now assumed that the murder scene was Meredith's apartment. Now he wondered, what did she do in that place for four hours with the body of her best friend lying there?

'Detective?'

Bosch looked away from his thoughts to Hirsch, who was sitting at the desk nodding his head.

'You got something?'

'Bingo.'

Bosch just nodded.

It was confirmation of more than just the match of fingerprints. He knew it was a confirmation that all the things he had accepted as the truths of his life could be as false as Meredith Roman.

49

The sky was the color of a ninhydrin bloom on white paper. It was cloudless and growing dark purple with the aging of dusk. Bosch thought of the sunsets he had told Jazz about and realized that even that was a lie. Everything was a lie.

He stopped the Mustang at the curb in front of Katherine Register's home. There was another lie. The woman who lived here was Meredith Roman. Changing her name didn't change what she had done, didn't change her from guilty to innocent.

There were no lights on that he could see from the street, no sign of life. He was prepared to wait but didn't want to deal with the thoughts that would intrude as he sat alone in the car. He got out, crossed the lawn to the front porch and knocked on the door.

While he waited, he got out a cigarette and was lighting it when he suddenly stopped. He realized that what he was doing was his reflex of smoking at death scenes where the bodies were old. His instincts had reacted before he had consciously registered the odor from the house. Outside the door it was barely noticeable, but it was there. He looked back out to the street and saw no one. He looked back at the door and tried the knob. It turned. As he opened it, he felt a rush of cool air and the odor came out to meet him.

The house was still, the only sound the hum of the air conditioner in the window of her bedroom. That was where he found her. He could tell right away that Meredith Roman had been dead for several days. Her body was in the bed, the covers pulled up to her head on the pillow. Only her face, what was left of it, was visible. Bosch's eyes did not linger on the image. The deterioration had been extensive and he guessed that maybe she had been dead since the day he had visited.

On the table next to the bed were two empty glasses, a half-gone fifth of vodka and an empty bottle of prescription pills. Bosch bent down to read the label and saw the prescription was for Katherine Register, one each night before bed. Sleeping pills.

Meredith had faced her past and administered her own penance. She had taken the blue canoe. Suicide. Bosch knew it wasn't for him to decide but it looked that way. He turned to the bureau because he remembered the Kleenex box and he wanted to use a tissue to cover his tracks. But there on the top, near the photos in gilded frames, was an envelope that had his name on it.

He picked it up, took some tissues and left the room. In the living room, a bit farther away from the source of the horrible odor but not far enough, he turned the envelope over to open it and noticed the flap was torn. The envelope had been opened already. He guessed maybe Meredith had reopened it to read again what she had written. Maybe she'd had second thoughts about what she was doing. He dismissed the question and took the note out. It was dated a week earlier. Wednesday. She had written it the day after his visit.

Dear Harry,
If you are reading this then my fears that you would learn the truth were well founded. If you are reading this then the decision I have made tonight was the correct one and I have no regrets as I make it. You see, I would rather face the judgment of afterlife than have you look at me while knowing the truth.

I know what I have taken from you. I have known all my life. It does no good to say I am sorry or to try to explain. But it still amazes me how one's life can change forever in a few moments of uncontrolled rage. I was angry at Marjorie when she came to me that night so full of hope and happiness. She was leaving me. For a life with you. With him. For a life we had only dreamed was possible.

What is jealousy but a reflection of your own failures? I was jealous and angry and I struck at her. I then made a feeble effort to cover what I had done. I am sorry, Harry, but I took her from you and with that took any chance you ever had. I've carried the guilt every day since then and I take it with me now. I should have paid for my sin a long time ago but someone convinced me otherwise and helped me get away. There is no one left to convince me now.

I don't ask for your forgiveness, Harry. That would be an insult. I guess all I want is for you to know my regrets and to know that sometimes people who get away don't really get away. I didn't. Not then, not now. Good-bye.
Meredith

Bosch reread the note and then stood there thinking about it for a long time. Finally, he folded it and put it back in its envelope. He walked over to the fireplace, lit the envelope on fire with his Bic and then tossed it onto the grate. He watched the paper bend and burn until it bloomed like a black rose and went out.

He went to the kitchen and lifted the receiver off the phone after wrapping his hand in tissue. He put it on the counter and dialed nine-one-one. As he walked toward the front door, he could hear the tiny voice of the Santa Monica police operator asking who was there and what the problem was.

He left the door unlocked and wiped the exterior knob with the tissue after stepping out onto the porch. He heard a voice from behind him.

'She writes a good letter, don't she?'

Bosch turned around. Vaughn was sitting on the rattan love seat on the porch. He was holding a new twenty-two in his hand. It looked like another Beretta. He looked none the worse for wear. He didn't have the black eyes that Bosch had, or the stitches.

'Vaughn.'

Bosch couldn't think of anything else to say. He couldn't imagine how he had been found by him. Could Vaughn have been daring enough to hang around Parker Center and follow Bosch from there? Bosch looked out into the street and wondered how long it would take the police operator to dispatch a car to the address the computer gave her for the 911 call. Even though Bosch had said nothing on the line, he knew they would eventually send a car to check it out. He had wanted them to find Meredith. If they took their time about it, they would probably find him as well. He had to stall Vaughn for as long as possible.

'Yeah, nice note,' the man with the gun said. 'But she left something out, don't you think?'

'What's left out?'

Vaughn seemed not to have heard him.

'It's funny,' he said. 'I knew your mother had a kid. But I never met you, never even saw you. She kept you away from me. I wasn't good enough, I guess.'

Bosch continued to stare as things began to fall together.

'Johnny Fox.'

'In the flesh.'

'I don't understand. Mittel . . .'

'Mittel had me killed? No, not really. I killed myself, I guess you could say. I read that story you people put in the paper today. But you had it wrong. Most of it, at least.'

Bosch nodded. He knew now.

'Meredith killed your mother, kid. Sorry about that. I just helped her take care of it after the fact.'

'And then you used her death to get to Conklin.'

Bosch didn't need any confirmation from Fox. He was just trying to chew up time.

'Yeah, that was the plan, to get to Conklin. Worked pretty good, too. Got me out of the sewer. Only I found out pretty fast that the real power was Mittel. I could tell. Between the two of them, Mittel could go the distance. So I threw in with him, you could say. He wanted a better hold on the golden boy. He wanted an ace up his own sleeve. So I helped.'

'By killing yourself? I don't get it.'

'Mittel told me that supreme power over someone is the power they don't know you have until you need to use it. You see, Bosch, Mittel always suspected that Conklin was really the one who did your mother.'

Bosch nodded. He saw where the story was going.

'And you never told Mittel that Conklin wasn't the killer.'

'That's right. I never told him about Meredith. So knowing that, look at it from his side. Mittel figured that if Conklin was the doer and he believed I was dead, then he'd think he was home free. See, I was the only loose end, the one who could tie him in. Mittel wanted him to think he was clear. He wanted it because he wanted Conklin at ease. He didn't want him to lose his drive, his ambition. Conklin was going places and Mittel didn't want him to even hesitate. But he also wanted to keep an ace up his sleeve, something that he could always pull out if Conklin tried to step out of line. That was me. I was the ace. So we arranged that little hit and run, me and Mittel.

Thing is, Mittel never had to play the ace with Conklin. Conklin gave Mittel a lot of good years after that. By the time he backed out on that attorney general thing, Mittel was well diversified. By then he had a congressman, a senator, a quarter of the local pols on his client list. You could say by then he had already climbed on Conklin's shoulders to the higher ground. He didn't need Arno anymore.'

Bosch nodded again and thought a moment about the scenario. All those years. Conklin believed it had been Mittel who killed her and Mittel believed it had been Conklin. It was neither.

'So who was the one you ran over?'

'Oh, just somebody. It doesn't matter. He was just a volunteer, you could say. I picked him up on Mission Street. He thought he was handing out Conklin fliers. I planted my ID in the bottom of the satchel I gave him. He never knew what hit him or why.'

'How'd you get away with it?' Bosch asked, though he thought he already knew the answer to that as well.

'Mittel had Eno on the line. We set it up so that it happened when he was next up on call. He took care of everything and Mittel took care of him.'

Bosch could see that the setup also gave Fox a share of power over Mittel. And he'd ridden along with him ever since. A little plastic surgery, a nicer set of clothes, and he was Jonathan Vaughn, aid to the wunderkind political strategist and rainmaker.

'So how'd you know I'd show up here?'

'I'd kept tabs on her over the years. I knew she was here. Alone. After our little run-in on the hill the other night, I came here to hide, to sleep. You gave me a headache – what the hell you hit me with?'

'The eight ball.'

'I guess I should have thought of that when I put you in there. Anyway, I found her like that in the bed. I read the note and knew who you were. I figured you'd be back. Especially after you left that message on the phone yesterday.'

'You've been here all this time with . . .'

'You get used to it. I put the air on high, closed the door. You get used to it.'

Bosch tried to imagine it. Sometimes he believed that he was used to the smell, but he knew he wasn't.

'What did she leave out of the note, Fox?'

'That was the part about her wanting Conklin for herself. See, I tried her with Conklin first. But it didn't take. Then I set him up with Marjorie and got the fireworks. Nobody expected that he'd want to end up marrying her, though. Least of all Meredith. There was only room on the horse with the white knight for one rider. That was Marjorie. Meredith couldn't handle that. Must've been a hell of a cat fight.'

Bosch said nothing. But the truth stung his face like a sunburn. That's what it had all come down to, a cat fight between whores.

'Let's go to your car now,' Fox said.

'Why?'

'We need to go to your place now.'

'For what?'

262

Fox never answered. A Santa Monica squad car stopped in front of the house just as Bosch asked his question. Two officers started getting out.

'Be cool, Bosch,' Fox said quietly. 'Be cool if you want to live a little longer.'

Bosch saw Fox turn the aim of his gun toward the approaching officers. They could not see it because of the thick bougainvillea running along the front of the porch. One of them started to speak.

'Did someone here call nine –'

Bosch took two steps and launched himself over the railing to the lawn. As he did it, he yelled a warning.

'He's got a gun! He's got a gun!'

On the ground, Bosch heard Fox start running on the wood decking of the porch. He guessed he was going for the door. Then came the first shot. He was sure it came from behind him, from Fox. Then the two cops opened up like the Fourth of July. Bosch couldn't count all the shots. He stayed on the grass with his arms spread wide and his hands up, just hoping they wouldn't send one his way.

It was over in no more than eight seconds. When the echoes died and silence returned, Bosch yelled again.

'I'm unarmed! I'm a police officer! I am no threat to you! I am an unarmed police officer!'

He felt the end of a hot gun barrel pressed against his neck.

'Where's the ID?'

'Right inside coat pocket.'

Then he remembered he still didn't have it. The cop's hands grasped him by the shoulders.

'I'm going to roll you over.'

'Wait a minute. I don't have it.'

'What is this? Roll over.'

Bosch complied.

'I don't have it with me. I've got other ID though. Left inside pocket.'

The cop started going through his jacket. Bosch was scared.

'I'm not going to do anything wrong here.'

'Just be quiet.'

The cop got Bosch's wallet out and looked at the driver's license that was behind a clear plastic window.

'Whaddaya got, Jimmy?' the other cop yelled. Bosch couldn't see him. 'He legit?'

'Says he's a cop, got no badge. Got a DL here.'

Then he hunched back down over Bosch and patted the rest of his body in a search for weapons.

'I'm clean.'

'All right, turn back over.'

Bosch did so and his hands were cuffed behind his back. He then heard the man above him call in for backup and an ambulance on his radio.

'All right, get up.'

Bosch did as he was told. For the first time he could see the porch. The other cop stood with his handgun pointing down at Fox's crumpled body at the front door. Bosch was led up the steps to the porch. He could see Fox was still alive. His chest was heaving, he had wounds in both legs and the stomach and it looked like one slug had gone through both cheeks. His jaw hung open. But his eyes seemed even wider as he stared at death coming for him.

'I knew you'd fire, you fuck,' Bosch said to him. 'Just die now.'

'Shut up,' the one called Jimmy ordered. 'Right now.'

The other cop pulled him away from the front door. Out in the street, Bosch could see neighbors joining together in little knots or watching from their own porches. Nothing like gunshots in suburbia for getting people together, he thought. The smell of spent gunpowder in the air does it better than a barbecue any day.

The young cop got right up in Bosch's face. Harry could see that his name plate identified him as D. Sparks.

'Okay, what the fuck's going on here? If you're a cop, tell us what's going on.'

'You two are a couple of heroes, that's what's going on.'

'Tell the story, man. I don't have time for bullshit.'

Bosch could hear approaching sirens now.

'My name's Bosch. I'm with LAPD. This man you shot is the suspect in the killing of Arno Conklin, the former district attorney of this county, and LAPD Lieutenant Harvey Pounds. I'm sure you've heard about these cases.'

'Jim, you hear that?' He turned back to Bosch. 'Where's your badge?'

'Stolen. I can give you a number to call. Assistant Chief Irvin Irving. He'll tell you about me.'

'Never mind that. What's he doing here?'

He pointed to Fox.

'He told me he was hiding out. Earlier today I got a call to come to this address and he was here waiting to ambush me. See, I could identify him. He had to take me out.'

The cop looked down at Fox wondering if he should believe such an incredible story.

'You got here right in time,' Bosch said. 'He was going to kill me.'

D. Sparks nodded. He was beginning to like the sound of this story. Then concern creased his brow.

'Who called 911?' he asked.

'I did,' Bosch said. 'I came here, found the door open and went in. I was calling 911 when he got the jump on me. I just dropped the phone because I knew you people would come.'

'Why call 911 if he hadn't grabbed you yet?'

'Because of what's in the back bedroom.'

'What?'

'There's a woman in the bed. She looks like she's been dead about a week.'

'Who is she?'

Bosch looked at the young cop's face.

'I don't know.'

264

50

'Why didn't you reveal that you knew she was your mother's killer? Why did you lie?'

'I don't know. I haven't figured it out. It's just that there was something about what she wrote and what she did at the end that . . . I don't know, I just felt like that was enough. I just wanted to let it go.'

Carmen Hinojos nodded her head as if she understood but Bosch wasn't sure he did himself.

'I think that's a good decision, Harry.'

'You do? I don't think anybody else would think it was a good decision.'

'I'm not talking about on a procedural or criminal justice level. I'm just talking about on a human level. I think you did the right thing. For yourself.'

'I guess . . .'

'Do you feel good about it?'

'Not really . . . You were right, you know.'

'I was? About what?'

'About what you said about me finding out who did it. You warned me. Said it might do me more harm than good. Well, that was an understatement . . . Some mission I gave myself, right?'

'I'm sorry if I was right. But as I said in the last session, the deaths of those men can't be –'

'I'm not talking about them anymore. I'm talking about something else. You see, I know now that my mother was trying to save me from that place I was at. Like she had promised me that day out by the fence that I told you about. I think that whether she loved Conklin or not, she was thinking of me. She had to get me out and he was the way to do it. So, ultimately, you see, it was because of me that she died.'

'Oh, please, don't tell yourself that, Harry. That's ridiculous.'

Bosch knew that the anger in her voice was real.

'If you are going to take that form of logic,' she continued, 'you can come up with any reason why she was killed, you can argue that your own birth set circumstances in motion that led to her death. You see how silly that is?'

'Not really.'

'It's the same argument you made the other day about people not taking responsibility. Well, the inverse of that is people who take too much responsibility. And you are becoming one of them. Let that go, Harry. Let it go. Let someone else take some responsibility for some things. Even if that someone else is dead. Being dead does not absolve them of everything.'

He was cowed by the forcefulness of her admonition. He just looked at her for a long moment. He could tell her outburst would signal a natural break in the session. The discussion of his guilt was done. She had ended it and he had his instructions.

'I'm sorry to have raised my voice.'

'No problem.'

'Harry, what do you hear from the department?'

'Nothing. I'm waiting on Irving.'

'What do you mean?'

'He kept my . . . culpability out of the paper. Now it's his move. He's either going to come at me with IAD – if he can make a case against me impersonating Pounds – or he's going to let it go. I'm betting he's going to let it go.'

'Why?'

'The one thing about the LAPD is that it is not into self-flagellation. Know what I mean? This case is very public and if they do something to me, they know there's always the danger it will get out and it will be one more black eye for the department. Irving sees himself as the protector of the department's image. He'll put that ahead of taking me down. Besides, he'll have leverage on me now. I mean, he thinks he will.'

'You seem to know Irving and the department well.'

'Why?'

'Chief Irving called me this morning and asked me to forward a positive RTD evaluation to his office as soon as possible.'

'He said that? He wants a positive return-to-duty report?'

'Yes, those were his words. Do you think you are ready for that?'

He thought a few moments but didn't answer the question.

'Has he done that before? Told you how to evaluate somebody?'

'No. It's a first time and I'm very concerned about it. It undermines my position here if I simply accede to his wishes. It's quite a dilemma because I don't want you caught in the middle.'

'What if he didn't tell you which way to go, what would your evaluation be? Positive or negative?'

She played with a pencil on the desktop for a few moments while considering the question.

'It's very close, Harry, but I think you need more time.'

'Then don't do it. Don't give in to him.'

'That's quite a change. Only a week ago all you could talk about was getting back to the job.'

'That was a week ago.'

There was a palpable sadness in his voice.

'Stop beating yourself to death with it,' she said. 'The past is like a club and you can only hit yourself in the head with it so many times before there is serious and permanent damage. I think you're at your limit. For what it's worth, I think you are a good and clean and ultimately kind man. Don't do this to yourself. Don't ruin what you have, what you are, with this kind of thinking.'

266

He nodded as if he understood but he had dismissed her words as soon as he heard them.

'I've been doing a lot of thinking the last couple of days.'

'About what?'

'Everything.'

'Any decisions on anything?'

'Almost. I think I'm going to pull the pin, leave the department.'

She leaned forward and folded her arms on the desk. A serious look creased her brow.

'Harry, what are you talking about? This is not like you. Your job and your life are the same. I think it's good to have some distance but not total separation. I –' She stopped when she seemed to come upon an idea. 'Is this your idea of penance, of making up for what happened?'

'I don't know . . . I just . . . For what I did, something has to be paid. That's all. Irving's not going to do anything. I will.'

'Harry, you made a mistake. A serious mistake, yes. But for that you are giving up your career, the one thing that even you readily admit you do well? You're going to throw it all away?'

He nodded.

'Did you pull the papers yet?'

'Not yet.'

'Don't do it.'

'Why not? I can't do this anymore. It's like I'm walking around handcuffed to a chain of ghosts.'

He shook his head. They were having the same debate that he had been having in his mind for the last two days, since the night at Meredith Roman's house.

'Give it some time,' Hinojos said. 'All I'm saying is, think about it. You're on paid leave now. Use it. Use the time. I'll tell Irving he's not getting an RTD from me yet. Meantime, you just give it some time and think hard on it. Go away somewhere, sit on the beach. But think about it before you turn in your papers.'

Bosch raised his hands in surrender.

'Please, Harry. I want to hear you say it.'

'All right. I'll do some more thinking.'

'Thank you.'

She let some silence underline his agreement.

'Remember what you said about seeing the coyote on the street last week?' she asked quietly. 'About it being the last coyote?'

'I remember.'

'I think I know how you felt. I'd hate to think that I was seeing the coyote for the last time, too.'

49

From the airport Bosch took the freeway to the Armenia exit and then south to Swann. He found that he didn't even need the rent-a-car map. He went east on Swann into Hyde Park and then down South Boulevard to her place. He could see the bay shimmering in the sun at the end of the street.

At the top of the stairs the door was open but the screen door was closed. Bosch knocked.

'Come in. It's open.'

It was her. Bosch pushed through the screen into the living room. She wasn't there but the first thing he noticed was a painting on the wall where before there had been only the nail. It was a portrait of a man in shadows. He was sitting at a table alone. The figure's elbow was on the table and the hand was up against his cheek, obscuring the face and making the deep set of the eyes the focal point of the painting. Bosch stared at it a moment until she called again.

'Hello? I'm in here.'

He saw the door to her studio was open a half foot. He stepped over and pushed it open. She was there, standing in front of the easel, dark earth-tone oils on the palette in her hand. There was a single errant slash of ocher on her right cheek. She immediately smiled.

'Harry.'

'Hello, Jasmine.'

He moved in closer to her and stepped around the side of the easel. The portrait had only just been started. But she had begun with the eyes. The same eyes in the portrait that hung on the wall in the other room. The same eyes he saw in the mirror.

She hesitantly came closer to him. There was not a glimmer of embarrassment or unease in her face.

'I thought that if I painted you, you would come back.'

She dropped her brush into an old coffee can bolted to the easel and came even closer. She embraced him and they kissed silently. At first it was a gentle reunion, then he put his hand against her back and pulled her tightly against his chest as if she were a bandage that could stop his bleeding. After a while she pulled back, brought her arms up and held his face in her hands.

'Let me see if I got the eyes right.'

She reached up and took off his sunglasses. He smiled. He knew the purple below his eyes was almost gone but they were still red-rimmed and shot with swollen capillaries.

'Jesus, you took the red-eye.'

'It's a long story. I'll tell you later.'

'God, put these back on.'

She hooked the glasses back on and laughed.

'It's not that funny. It hurt.'

'Not that. I got paint on your face.'

'Well, then I'm not alone.'

He traced the slash on her face. They embraced again. Bosch knew they could talk later. For now he just held her and smelled her and looked over her shoulder to the brilliant blue of the bay. He thought of something the old man in the bed had told him. When you find the one that you think fits, then grab on for dear life. Bosch didn't know if she was the one, but for the moment he held on with everything he had left.

TRUNK MUSIC

I

As he drove along Mulholland Drive toward the Cahuenga Pass, Bosch began to hear the music. It came to him in fragments of strings and errant horn sequences, echoing off the brown summer-dried hills and blurred by the white noise of traffic carrying up from the Hollywood Freeway. Nothing he could identify. All he knew was that he was heading toward its source.

He slowed when he saw the cars parked off to the side of a gravel turn-off road. Two detective sedans and a patrol car. Bosch pulled his Caprice in behind them and got out. A single officer in uniform leaned against the fender of the patrol car. Yellow plastic crime-scene tape – the stuff used by the mile in Los Angeles – was strung from the patrol car's sideview mirror across the gravel road to the sign posted on the other side. The sign said, in black-on-white letters that were almost indistinguishable behind the graffiti that covered the sign:

L.A.F.D. FIRE CONTROL

MOUNTAIN FIRE DISTRICT ROAD

NO PUBLIC ADMITTANCE – NO SMOKING!

The patrol cop, a large man with sun-reddened skin and blond bristly hair, straightened up as Bosch approached. The first thing Bosch noted about him other than his size was the baton. It was holstered in a ring on his belt and the business end of the club was marred, the black acrylic paint scratched away to reveal the aluminum beneath. Street fighters wore their battle-scarred stick proudly, as a sign, a not so subtle warning. This cop was a headbanger. No doubt about it. The plate above the cop's breast pocket said his name was Powers. He looked down at Bosch through Ray-Bans, though it was well into dusk and a sky of burnt orange clouds was reflected in his mirrored lenses. It was one of those sundowns that reminded Bosch of the glow the fires of the riots had put in the sky a few years back.

'Harry Bosch,' Powers said with a touch of surprise. 'When did you get back on the table?'

Bosch looked at him a moment before answering. He didn't know Powers but that didn't mean anything. Bosch's story was probably known by every cop in Hollywood Division.

'Just did,' Bosch said.

He didn't make any move to shake hands. You didn't do that at crime scenes.

'First case back in the saddle, huh?'

Bosch took out a cigarette and lit it. It was a direct violation of department policy but it wasn't something he was worried about.

'Something like that.' He changed the subject. 'Who's down there?'

'Edgar and the new one from Pacific, his soul sister.'

'Rider.'

'Whatever.'

Bosch said nothing further about that. He knew what was behind the contempt in the uniform cop's voice. It didn't matter that he knew Kizmin Rider had the gift and was a top-notch investigator. That would mean nothing to Powers, even if Bosch told him it was so. Powers probably saw only one reason why he was still wearing a blue uniform instead of carrying a detective's gold badge: that he was a white man in an era of female and minority hiring and promotion. It was the kind of festering sore better left undisturbed.

Powers apparently registered Bosch's nonresponse as disagreement and went on.

'Anyway, they told me to let Emmy and Sid drive on down when they get here. I guess they're done with the search. So you can drive down instead of walking, I guess.'

It took a second for Bosch to register that Powers was referring to the medical examiner and the Scientific Investigation Division tech. He'd said the names as if they were a couple invited to a picnic.

Bosch stepped out onto the pavement, dropped the half cigarette and made sure he put it out with his shoe. It wouldn't be good to start a brush fire on his first job back with the homicide table.

'I'll walk it,' he said. 'What about Lieutenant Billets?'

'Not here yet.'

Bosch went back to his car and reached in through the open window for his briefcase. He then walked back to Powers.

'You the one who found it?'

'That was me.'

Powers was proud of himself.

'How'd you open it?'

'Keep a slim jim in the car. Opened the door, then popped the trunk.'

'Why?'

'The smell. It was obvious.'

'Wear gloves?'

'Nope. Didn't have any.'

'What did you touch?'

Powers had to think about it for a moment.

'Door handle, the trunk pull. That'd be about it.'

'Did Edgar or Rider take a statement? You write something up?'

'Nothing yet.'

Bosch nodded.

'Listen, Powers, I know you're all proud of yourself, but next time don't open the car, okay? We all want to be detectives but not all of us are. That's how crime scenes get fucked up. And I think you know that.'

Bosch watched the cop's face turn a dark shade of crimson and the skin go tight around his jaw.

'Listen, Bosch,' he said. 'What I know is that if I just called this in as a suspicious vehicle that *smells* like there's a stiff in the trunk, then you people would've said, "What the fuck does Powers know?" and left it there to rot in the sun until there was nothing left of your goddamn crime scene.'

'That might be true but, see, then that would be our fuckup to make. Instead, we've got you fucking us up before we start.'

Powers remained angry but mute. Bosch waited a beat, ready to continue the debate, before dismissing it.

'Can you lift the tape now, please?'

Powers stepped back to the tape. He was about thirty-five, Bosch guessed, and had the long-practiced swagger of a street veteran. In L.A. that swagger came to you quickly, as it had in Vietnam. Powers held the yellow tape up and Bosch walked under. As he passed, the cop said, 'Don't get lost.'

'Good one, Powers. You got me there.'

The fire road was one lane and overgrown at its sides with brush that came as high as Bosch's waist. There was trash and broken glass strewn along the gravel, the trespasser's answer to the sign at the gate. Bosch knew the road was probably a favorite midnight haunt for teenagers from the city below.

The music grew louder as he went further in. But he still could not identify it. About a quarter mile in, he came to a gravel-bedded clearing that he guessed was a staging point for fire-fighting apparatus in the event that a brush fire broke out in the surrounding hills. Today it would serve as a crime scene. On the far side of the clearing Bosch saw a white Rolls-Royce Silver Cloud. Standing near it were his two partners, Rider and Edgar. Rider was sketching the crime scene on a clipboard while Edgar worked with a tape measure and called out measurements. Edgar saw Bosch and gave an acknowledging wave with a latex-gloved hand. He let the tape measure snap back into its case.

'Harry, where you been?'

'Painting,' Bosch said as he walked up. 'I had to get cleaned up and changed, put stuff away.'

As Bosch stepped closer to the edge of the clearing, the view opened below him. They were on a bluff rising above the rear of the Hollywood Bowl. The rounded music shell was down to the left, no more than a quarter mile. And the shell was the source of the music. The L.A. Philharmonic's end-of-the-season Labor Day weekend show. Bosch was looking down at eighteen thousand people in concert seats stretching up the opposite side of the canyon. They were enjoying one of the last Sunday evenings of the summer.

'Jesus,' he said out loud, thinking of the problem.

Edgar and Rider walked over.

'What've we got?' Bosch asked.

Rider answered.

'One in the trunk. White male. Gunshots. We haven't checked him out much further than that. We've been keeping the lid closed. We've got everybody rolling, though.'

Bosch started walking toward the Rolls, going around the charred remnants of an old campfire that had burned in the center of the clearing. The other two followed.

'This okay?' Bosch asked as he got close to the Rolls.

'Yeah, we did the search,' Edgar said. 'Nothing much. Got some leakage under the car. That's about it, though. Cleanest scene I've been at in a while.'

Jerry Edgar, called in from home like everybody else on the team, was wearing blue jeans and a white T-shirt. On the left breast of the shirt was a drawing of a badge and the words LAPD Homicide. As he walked past Bosch, Harry saw that the back of the shirt said Our Day Begins When Your Day Ends. The tight-fitting shirt contrasted sharply with Edgar's dark skin and displayed his heavily muscled upper body as he moved with an athletic grace toward the Rolls. Bosch had worked with him on and off for six years but they had never become close outside of the job. This was the first time it had dawned on Bosch that Edgar actually was an athlete, that he must regularly work out.

It was unusual for Edgar not to be in one of his crisp Nordstrom's suits. But Bosch thought he knew why. His informal dress practically guaranteed he would avoid having to do the dirty work, next-of-kin notification.

They slowed their steps when they got close to the Rolls, as if perhaps whatever was wrong here might be contagious. The car was parked with its rear end facing south and visible to the spectators in the upper levels of the Bowl across the way. Bosch considered their situation again.

'So you want to pull this guy out of there with all those people with their wine and box lunches from the Grill watching?' he asked. 'How do you think that's going to play on the TV tonight?'

'Well,' Edgar replied, 'we thought we'd kind of leave that decision to you, Harry. You being the three.'

Edgar smiled and winked.

'Yeah, right,' Bosch said sarcastically. 'I'm the three.'

Bosch was still getting used to the idea of being a so-called team leader. It had been almost eighteen months since he had officially investigated a homicide, let alone headed up a team of three investigators. He had been assigned to the Hollywood Division burglary table when he returned to work from his involuntary stress leave in January. The detective bureau commander, Lieutenant Grace Billets, had explained that his assignment was a way of gradually easing him back into detective work. He knew that explanation was a lie and that she had been told where to put him, but he took the demotion without complaint. He knew they would come for him eventually.

After eight months of pushing papers and making the occasional burglary arrest, Bosch was called into the CO's office and Billets told him she was making changes. The division's homicide clearance rate had dipped to its lowest point ever. Fewer than half of the killings were cleared. She had taken over command of the bureau nearly a year earlier, and the sharpest decline, she struggled to admit, had come under her own watch. Bosch could have told her that the decline was due in part to her not following the same statistical deceptions practiced by her predecessor, Harvey Pounds, who had always found ways of pumping up the clearance rate, but he kept that to himself. Instead, he sat quietly while Billets laid out her plan.

The first part of the plan was to move Bosch back to the homicide table as of the start of September. A detective named Selby, who barely pulled his weight, would go from homicide to Bosch's slot on the burglary table. Billets would also be adding a young and smart detective transfer she had previously worked with in the Pacific Division detective bureau, Kizmin Rider. Next, and this was the radical part, Billets was changing the traditional pairing of detectives. Instead, the nine homicide detectives assigned to Hollywood would be grouped into three teams of three. Each of the three teams would have a detective third grade in charge. Bosch was a three. He was named team leader of squad one.

The reasoning behind the change was sound – at least on paper. Most homicides are solved in the first forty-eight hours after discovery or they aren't solved at all. Billets wanted more solved so she was going to put more detectives on each one. The part that didn't look so good on paper, especially to the nine detectives, was that previously there had been four pairs of partners working homicide cases. The new changes meant each detective would be working every third case that came up instead of every fourth. It meant more cases, more work, more court time, more overtime, and more stress. Only the overtime was considered a positive. But Billets was tough and didn't care much for the complaints of the detectives. And her new plan quickly won her the obvious nickname.

'Anybody talk to Bullets yet?' Bosch asked.

'I called,' Rider said. 'She was up in Santa Barbara for the weekend. Left a number with the desk. She's coming down early but she's still at least an hour and a half from us. She said she was going to have to drop the hubby off first and would probably just roll to the bureau.'

Bosch nodded and stepped to the rear of the Rolls. He picked up the smell right away. It was faint but it was there, unmistakable. Like no other. He nodded to no one in particular again. He placed his briefcase on the ground, opened it and took a pair of latex gloves from the cardboard box inside. He then closed the case and placed it a few feet behind him and out of the way.

'Okay, let's take a look,' he said while stretching the gloves over his hands. He hated how they felt. 'Let's stand close, we don't want to give the people in the Bowl more of a show than they paid for.'

'It ain't pretty,' Edgar said as he stepped forward.

The three of them stood together at the back end of the Rolls to shield the view from the concertgoers. But Bosch knew that anybody with a decent pair of field glasses would know what was going on. This was L.A.

Before opening the trunk, he noticed the car's personalized license plate. It said TNA. Before he could speak, Edgar answered his unasked question.

'Comes back to TNA Production. On Melrose.'

'T and A?'

'No, the letters, T-N-A, just like on the plate.'

'Where on Melrose?'

Edgar took a notebook out of his pocket and looked through the page. The address he gave was familiar to Bosch but he couldn't place it. He knew it was down near Paramount, the sprawling studio that took up the entire north side of the fifty-five-hundred block. The big studio was surrounded by smaller production houses and ministudios. They were like sucker fish that swam around the mouth of the big shark, hoping for the scraps that didn't get sucked in.

'Okay, let's do it.'

He turned his attention back to the trunk. He could see that the lid had been lightly placed down so it would not lock closed. Using one rubber-coated finger, he gently lifted it.

As the trunk was opened, it expelled a sickeningly fetid breath of death. Bosch immediately wished he had a cigarette but those days were through. He knew what a defense lawyer could do with one ash from a cop's smoke at a crime scene. Reasonable doubts were built on less.

He leaned in under the lid to get a close look, careful not to touch the bumper with his pants. The body of a man was in the trunk. His skin was a grayish white and he was expensively dressed in linen pants sharply pressed and cuffed at the bottom, a pale blue shirt with a flowery pattern and a leather sport coat. His feet were bare.

The dead man was on his right side in the fetal position except his wrists were behind him instead of folded against his chest. It appeared to Bosch that his hands had been tied behind him and the bindings then removed, most likely after he was dead. Bosch looked closely and could see a small abrasion on the left wrist, probably caused by the struggle against the bindings. The man's eyes were closed tightly and there was a whitish, almost translucent material dried in the corners of the sockets.

'Kiz, I want you taking notes on appearance.'

'Right.'

Bosch bent further into the trunk. He saw a froth of purged blood had dried in the dead man's mouth and nose. His hair was caked with blood which had spread over the shoulders and to the trunk mat, coating it with a coagulated pool. He could see the hole in the floor of the trunk through which blood had drained to the gravel below. It was a foot from the victim's head and appeared to be evenly cut in the metal underlining in a spot where the floor mat was folded over. It was not a bullet hole. It was probably a drain or a hole left by a bolt that had vibrated loose and fallen out.

In the mess that was the back of the man's head, Bosch could see two distinct jagged-edged penetrations to the lower rear skull – the occipital protuberance – the scientific name popping easily into his mind. Too many autopsies, he thought. The hair close to the wounds was charred by the gases that explode out of the barrel of a gun. The scalp showed stippling from gunpowder. Point-blank shots. No exit wounds that he could see. Probably twenty-twos, he guessed. They bounce around inside like marbles dropped into an empty jelly jar.

Bosch looked up and saw a small spray of blood splattered on the inside of the trunk lid. He studied the spots for a long moment and then stepped back and straightened up. He appraised the entire view of the trunk now, his mind checking off an imaginary list. Because no blood drips had been found on the access road into the clearing, he had no doubts that the man had been killed here in the trunk. Still, there were other unknowns. Why here? Why no shoes and socks? Why were the bindings taken off the wrists? He put these questions aside for the time being.

'You check for the wallet?' he asked without looking at the two others.

'Not yet,' Edgar replied. 'Recognize him?'

For the first time Bosch looked at the face as a face. There was still fear etched on it. The man had closed his eyes. He had known what was coming. Bosch wondered if the whitish material in the eyes was dried tears.

'No, do you?'

'Nope. It's too messy, anyway.'

Bosch gingerly lifted the back of the leather coat and saw no wallet in the back pockets of the dead man's pants. He then opened the jacket and saw the wallet was there in an inside pocket that carried a Fred Haber men's shop label on it. Bosch could also see a paper folder for an airline ticket in the pocket. With his other hand he reached into the jacket and removed the two items.

'Get the lid,' he said as he backed away.

Edgar closed it over as gently as an undertaker closing a coffin. Bosch then walked over to his briefcase, squatted down and put the two items down on it.

He opened the wallet first. There was a full complement of credit cards in slots on the left side and a driver's license behind a plastic window on the right. The name on the license said Anthony N. Aliso.

'Anthony N. Aliso,' Edgar said. 'Tony for short. TNA. TNA Productions.'

The address was in Hidden Highlands, a tiny enclave off Mulholland in the Hollywood Hills. It was the kind of place that was surrounded by walls and had a guard shack manned twenty-four hours a day, mostly by off-duty or retired LAPD cops. The address went well with the Rolls-Royce.

Bosch opened the billfold section and found a sheaf of currency. Without taking the money out, he counted two one-hundred-dollar bills and nine twenties. He called the amount out so that Rider could make a note of it. Next he opened the airline folder. Inside was the receipt for a one-way ticket on an American Airlines flight departing Las Vegas for LAX at 10:05 Friday night. The name on the ticket matched the driver's license. Bosch checked the back flap of the ticket folder, but there was no sticker or staple indicating that a bag had been checked by the ticket holder. Curious, Bosch left the wallet and the ticket on the case and went to look into the car through the windows.

'No luggage?'

'None,' Rider said.

Bosch went back to the trunk and raised the lid again. Looking in at the body, he hooked a finger up the left sleeve of the jacket and pulled it up. There was a gold Rolex watch on the wrist. The face was encircled with a ring of tiny diamonds.

'Shit.'

Bosch turned around. It was Edgar.

'What?'

'You want me to call OCID?'

'Why?'

'Wop name, no robbery, two in the back of the head. It's a whack job, Harry. We oughta call OCID.'

'Not yet.'

'I'll tell you right now that's what Bullets is gonna wanna do.'

'We'll see.'

Bosch appraised the body again, looking closely at the contorted, bloodied face. Then he closed the lid.

Bosch stepped away from the car and to the edge of the clearing. The spot offered a brilliant view of the city. Looking east across the sprawl of

Hollywood, he could easily pick up the spires of downtown in the light haze. He saw the lights of Dodger Stadium were on for the twilight game. The Dodgers were dead even with Colorado with a month to go and Nomo due to pitch the game. Bosch had a ticket in his inside coat pocket. But he knew bringing it along had been wishful thinking. He wouldn't get anywhere near the stadium tonight. He also knew Edgar was right. The killing had all the aspects of a mob hit. The Organized Crime Intelligence Division should be notified – if not to take over the investigation entirely, then at least to offer advice. But Bosch was delaying that notification. It had been a long time since he'd had a case. He didn't want to give it up yet.

He looked back down at the Bowl. It looked like a sellout to him, the crowd seated in an elliptical formation going up the opposite hill. The seating sections furthest away from the music shell were the highest up the hill and at an almost even level with the clearing where the Rolls was parked. Bosch wondered how many of the people were watching him at that moment. Again he thought of the dilemma he faced. He had to get the investigation going. But he knew that if he pulled the body out of the trunk with such an audience watching, there likely would be hell to pay for the bad public relations such a move would cause the city and the department.

Once again Edgar seemed to know his thoughts.

'Hell, Harry, they won't care. At the jazz festival a few years back, there was a couple up on this spot doing the nasty for half an hour. When they were done, they got a standing ovation. Guy stands up buck naked and takes a little bow.'

Bosch looked back at him to see if he was serious.

'I read it in the *Times*. The "Only in L.A." column.'

'Well, Jerry, this is the Philharmonic. It's a different crowd, know what I mean? And I don't want this to end up in "Only in L.A.," okay?'

'Okay, Harry.'

Bosch looked at Rider. She hadn't said much of anything yet.

'What do you think, Kiz?'

'I don't know. You're the three.'

Rider was small, five feet and no more than a hundred pounds with her gun on. She would never have made it before the department relaxed the physical requirements to attract more women. She had light brown skin. Her hair was straightened and kept short. She wore jeans and a pink oxford shirt beneath a black blazer. On her small body, the jacket did not do much to disguise a 9mm Glock 17 holstered on her right hip.

Billets had told him that she had worked with Rider in Pacific. Rider had worked robbery and fraud cases but was called out on occasion to work homicides in which there were overlying financial aspects. Billets had said Rider could break a crime scene down as well as most veteran homicide detectives. She had pulled strings to get Rider's transfer approved but was already resigned to the fact that she wouldn't stay long in the division. Rider was marked for travel. Her double minority status coupled with the facts that she was good at what she did and had a guardian angel – Billets wasn't sure who – at Parker Center practically guaranteed her stay in Hollywood would be short. It was a bit of final seasoning before she headed downtown to the Glass House.

'What about the OPG?' Bosch asked.

'Held up on that,' Rider said. 'Thought we'd be here a while before we moved the car.'

Bosch nodded. It was what he expected her to say. The official police garage was usually last on the call-out list. He was just stalling, trying to make a decision while asking questions he already knew the answers to.

Finally he made his decision on what to do.

'Okay, go ahead and call,' he said. 'Tell them to come now. And tell them to bring a flatbed. Okay? Even if they've got a hook in the neighborhood, make 'em turn around. Tell 'em it's gotta be a flat. There's a phone in my briefcase.'

'Got it,' Rider said.

'Why the flatbed, Harry?' Edgar asked.

Bosch didn't answer.

'We're moving the whole show,' Rider said.

'What?' Edgar said.

Rider went to the briefcase without answering. Bosch held back a smile. She knew what he was doing, and he began to see some of the promise Billets had talked about. He got out a cigarette and lit it. He put the burnt match into the cellophane around the pack and replaced it in the pocket of his coat.

He noticed as he smoked that the sound at the edge of the clearing, where he could look directly down into the Bowl, was much better. After a few moments he was even able to identify the piece being played.

'*Sheherazade*,' he said.

'What's that, Harry?' Edgar asked.

'The music. It's called *Sheherazade*. Ever heard it?'

'I'm not sure I'm hearing it now. All the echoes, man.'

Bosch snapped his fingers. Out of the blue a thought had pushed through. In his mind he saw the studio's arched gate, the replica of the Arc de Triomphe in Paris.

'That address on Melrose,' Bosch said. 'That's near Paramount. One of those feeder-fish studios right nearby. I think it's Archway.'

'Yeah? I think you're right.'

Rider walked up then.

'We got a flat on the way,' she said. 'ETA is fifteen. I checked on SID and ME. Also on the way. SID has somebody just wrapped up a home invasion in Nichols Canyon, so they should be right over.'

'Good,' Bosch said. 'Either of you go over the story with the swinging stick, yet?'

'Not since the preliminary,' Edgar said. 'Not our type. Thought we'd leave him for the three.'

The unspoken meaning of this was that Edgar had sensed the racist animosity Powers radiated toward himself and Rider.

'Okay, I'll take him,' Bosch said. 'I want you two to finish the charting, then do another sweep of the immediate area. Take different areas this time.'

He realized he had just told them things he didn't need to tell them.

'Sorry. You know what to do. All I'm saying is let's take this one by the numbers. I've got a feeling it's going eight by ten on us.'

'What about OCID?' Edgar asked.

'I told you, not yet.'

'Eight by ten?' Rider said, a confused expression on her face.

'Eight by ten case,' Edgar told her. 'Celebrity case. Studio case. If that's a hotshot from the industry in the trunk, somebody from Archway, we're going to get some media on this. More than some. A dead guy in the trunk of his Rolls is news. A dead industry guy in the trunk of his Rolls is bigger news.'

'Archway?'

Bosch left them there as Edgar filled her in on the facts of life when it came to murder, the media and the movie business in Hollywood.

Bosch licked his fingers to put the cigarette out and then put it with the used match in the cellophane wrapper. He slowly began walking the quarter mile back to Mulholland, once again searching the gravel road in a back-and-forth manner. But there was so much debris on the gravel and in the nearby brush that it was impossible to know if anything – a cigarette butt, a beer bottle, a used condom – was related to the Rolls or not. The one thing he looked closest for was blood. If there was blood on the road that could be linked to the victim, it could indicate that he was killed elsewhere and left in the clearing. No blood probably meant the killing had taken place right there.

He realized as he made the fruitless search that he was feeling relaxed, maybe even happy. He was back on the beat and following his mission once again. Mindful that the man in the trunk had to have perished for him to feel this way, Bosch quickly wrote that guilt off. The man would have ended up in the trunk whether Bosch had ever made it back to the homicide table or not.

When Bosch got to Mulholland he saw the fire trucks. There were two of them and a battalion of firefighters standing around them, seemingly waiting for something. He lit another cigarette and looked at Powers.

'You've got a problem,' the uniform cop said.

'What?'

Before Powers answered, one of the firefighters stepped up. He wore the white helmet of a battalion chief.

'You in charge?' he asked.

'That's me.'

'Chief Jon Friedman,' he said. 'We've got a problem.'

'That's what I hear.'

'The show down in the Bowl is supposed to end in ninety minutes. After that we've got the fireworks. Problem is this fellow says you got yourself a dead body up there and a crime scene. That's the problem. If we can't get up there to set up a safety position for the fireworks, there isn't going to be any fireworks. We can't allow it. If we're not in position, we could see the whole down slope of these hills go up with one errant missile. Know what I mean?'

Bosch noticed Powers smirking at his dilemma. Bosch ignored him and returned his attention to Friedman.

'Chief, how long do you need to set up?'

'Ten minutes max. We just got to be there before the first one goes up.'

'Ninety minutes?'

'About eighty-five now. There's gonna be a lot of angry people down there if they don't get their fireworks.'

Bosch realized he wasn't as much making decisions as having them made for him.

'Chief, hold here. We'll be out in an hour and fifteen. Don't cancel the show.'

'You sure about that?'

'Count on it.'

'Detective?'

'What, Chief?'

'You're breaking the law with that cigarette.'

He nodded toward the graffiti-covered sign.

'Sorry, Chief.'

Bosch walked out to the road to stamp out the smoke while Friedman headed back to his people to radio in that the show would go on. Bosch realized the danger and caught up to him.

'Chief, you can say the show will go on, but don't put anything out on the air about the body. We don't need the media out here, helicopters swooping over.'

'I gotcha.'

Bosch thanked him and turned his attention to Powers.

'You can't clear a scene in an hour and fifteen,' Powers said. 'The ME isn't even here.'

'Let me worry about that, Powers. You write something up yet?'

'Not yet. Been dealing with these guys. Would've helped if one of you folks had a two-way with you up there.'

'Then why don't you run it down for me from the start.'

'What about them?' Powers asked, nodding in the direction of the clearing. 'Why isn't one of them talking to me? Edgar and Rider?'

'Because they're busy. You want to run it down for me or not?'

'I already told you.'

'From the start, Powers. You told me what you did once you checked the car out. What made you check it?'

'There's nothin' much to tell. I usually make a pass by here each watch, chase away the dirtbags.'

He pointed across Mulholland and up to the crest of the hill. There was a line of houses, most on cantilevers, clinging to the crestline. They looked like mobile homes suspended in air.

'People up there call the station all the time, say they got campfires going down here, beer parties, devil worship, who knows what. Guess it ruins their view. And they don't want nothin' to spoil that million-dollar view. So I come up and sweep out the trash. Mostly bored little pissants from the Valley. Fire Department used to have a lock on the gate here, but a deuce plowed through it. That was six months ago. Takes the city at least a year to repair anything 'round here. Shit, I requisitioned batteries for my Mag three weeks ago and I'm still waiting for them. If I didn't buy them myself, I'd be working the fuckin' night watch without a flashlight. City doesn't care. This ci—'

'So what about the Rolls, Powers? Let's stay on the subject.'

285

'Yeah, well, I usually make it by after dark, but because of the show in the Bowl I swung by early today. Saw the Rolls then.'

'You came on your own? No complaint from up the hill?'

'No. Today I just cruised it on my own. On account of the show. I figured there might be some trespassers.'

'Were there?'

'A few – people waiting to hear the music. Not the usual crowd, though. That's refined music, I guess you'd call it. I chased 'em out anyway, and when they were gone, the Rolls was what was left. But there was no driver for it.'

'So you checked it out.'

'Yeah, and I know the smell, man. Popped it with the slim and there he was. The stiff. Then I backed out and called the pros.'

There was a note of sarcasm in the way he said the last word. Bosch ignored it.

'The people you chased, you get any names?'

'No, like I told you, I chased them, then noticed that nobody got in and drove away in the Rolls. It was too late by then.'

'What about last night?'

'What about it?'

'Did you make it by here?'

'I was off. I'm on Tuesday–Saturday but I switched with a buddy last night 'cause he had something to do tonight.'

'So then what about Friday night?'

He shook his head.

'Three watch is always busy Friday. I had no time for free cruising and we didn't get a complaint as far as I know . . . so I never made it by.'

'Just chasin' the radio?'

'I had calls backed up on me all night. I didn't even get a ten-seven.'

'No dinner break, that's dedication, Powers.'

'What's that supposed to mean?'

Bosch saw he had made a mistake. Powers was consumed by job frustrations and he had pushed him too far. Powers turned crimson again and slowly took off his Ray-Bans before speaking.

'Let me tell you something, big shot. You got in while the getting was good. The rest of us? We get shit. We – I've been trying for so many years I can't count to get a gold shield and I've got about as much chance of getting one as whoever's in the trunk of that Rolls-Royce. But I'm not laying down. I'm still out here five nights a week chasin' the radio. Says "Protect and Serve" on the car door and I'm doin' it, man. So don't give me any shit about dedication.'

Bosch hesitated until he was sure Powers was done.

'Look, Powers, I didn't mean to give you shit. Okay? You want a cigarette?'

'I don't smoke.'

'Okay, let's try this again.' He waited a beat while Powers put the mirrors back on his eyes and seemed to calm down. 'You always work alone?'

'I'm the Z car.'

Bosch nodded. Zebra unit. An officer of many stripes, meaning he handled a variety of calls, usually trash calls, while cars with two officers

286

abroad handled the hotshots – the prime, possibly dangerous, calls. Zebra worked patrol alone and often had free rein of the entire division. They were in the supervisory level between the sergeants and the grunts who were assigned to patrol geographic slices of the division known as basic car areas.

'How often you chase people outta here?'

'Once or twice a month. Can't say what happens on the other shifts or with the basic cars. But shit calls like this usually go to the Z car.'

'You got any shakes?'

Shakes were three-by-five cards formally called field interview, or FI, cards. Cops filled them out when they stopped suspicious people but did not have enough evidence to arrest them, or when making such an arrest – in this case, for trespassing – would be a waste of time. The American Civil Liberties Union called such stops shakedowns and an abuse of police powers. The name stuck, even with the cops.

'I've got some, yeah, at the station.'

'Good. We'd like to have a look if you could dig them out. Also, think you could ask the cops in the basic car if they've noticed the Rolls here the last few days?'

'Is this where I'm supposed to thank you for letting me have a part in the big bad investigation and ask you to put in a good word for me with the deputy chief of dicks?'

Bosch stared at him a few moments before answering.

'No, this is where I tell you to have the cards ready for us by nine tonight or I'll put in a word about that with the patrol skipper. And never mind the basic car people. We'll go ahead and talk to them ourselves. Don't want you to miss your ten-seven two shifts in a row, Powers.'

Bosch started back toward the crime scene, moving slowly again and checking the other side of the gravel road. Twice he had to step off the gravel and into the brush to let the official police garage truck pass and then the Scientific Investigation Division van.

By the time he got to the clearing, he again had come up with nothing during his search and was sure the victim had been murdered in the trunk while the Rolls was parked in the clearing. He saw Art Donovan, the SID tech, and Roland Quatro, the photographer who came with him, starting their work. Bosch walked up to Rider.

'Anything?' she asked.

'No. You?'

'Nothing. I think the Rolls must've been driven in with our guy in the trunk. Then the doer gets out, opens the lid and pops him twice. He closes the trunk and walks out. Somebody picks him up out on Mulholland. Clean scene back here.'

Bosch nodded.

'Him?'

'Well, I'm going with the percentages for now.'

Bosch walked over to Donovan, who was bagging the wallet and airline ticket in a clear plastic evidence envelope.

'Art, we've got a problem.'

'You're telling me. I was just thinking I can rig some tarps over light

287

tripods, but I don't think you'll be able to block the view for everybody in the Bowl. Some of them are going to get a show all right. I guess it will make up for canceling the fireworks. That is, unless you're just planning to sit tight with it until after the show.'

'Nah, we do that and some defense lawyer will tear us new assholes in court for delaying things. Every lawyer went to school on O.J., Art. You know that.'

'So then what do we do?'

'Just do what you've got to do here with some speed and then we'll take the whole thing to the print shed. You know if anybody's in there right now?'

'No, it should be free,' Donovan said slowly. 'You mean you're talking about the whole thing? The body, too?'

Bosch nodded.

'Besides, you can do a better job with it in the shed, right?'

'Absolutely. But what about the ME? They've got to sign off on something like this, Harry.'

'I'll deal with that. Before we put it on the flatbed, though, make sure you guys have got stills and video in case things shift during transit. Also, run a print card off the guy and give it to me.'

'You got it.'

While Donovan went to Quatro to explain the drill, Bosch huddled with Edgar and Rider.

'Okay, for now we're going to run with this one. If you had plans for the rest of the night, make your calls. It's going to be a long one. This is how I want to break it up.'

He pointed up to the homes on the crestline.

'First, Kiz, I want you to go up there and do a house-to-house. You know the routine. See if anybody remembers seeing the Rolls or knows how long it's been here. Maybe somebody heard the shots. They might've echoed up the side of the hill. We want to try to pin down the time this happened. After that, I – you got a phone?'

'No. I have a rover in the car.'

'No. I want to keep everything about this off the air.'

'I can use a phone in somebody's house.'

'Okay, call me when you're done or I'll page you when I'm done. Depending on how things shake out, you and I will either do next of kin or his office after that.'

She nodded. Bosch turned to Edgar.

'Jerry, you go in and work from the station. You've got the paper on this one.'

'She's the rookie.'

'Well, then, next time don't show up in a T-shirt. You can't go knocking on doors dressed like that.'

'I got a shirt in the car. I'll change.'

'Next time. You're on the paper on this one. But before you start, I want you to put Aliso through the box and see what you get on him. He's got a DL issued last year, so they've got his thumb print on file through DMV. See if you can get somebody from prints to compare it to the print card Art's getting for you right now. I want the ID confirmed as soon as possible.'

288

'There ain't going to be anybody in prints t'night. Art's the guy on call. He should do this.'

'Art's going to be tied up. See if you can shake somebody at home loose. We need the ID.'

'I'll try but I can't prom—'

'Good. After that, I want you to call everybody who works a basic car in this area and see if anyone's seen the Rolls. Powers – the guy up at the road – is going to pull shake cards on the kids who hang out here. I want you to start running them down, too. After that you can start the paper going.'

'Shit, with all this, I'll be lucky if I start typing before *next* Monday.'

Bosch ignored his whining and appraised both his partners.

'I'll stay with the body. If I get tied up, Kiz, you go on to check out the office address and I'll handle next of kin. Okay, everybody know what's what?'

Rider and Edgar nodded. Bosch could tell Edgar was still annoyed about something.

'Kiz, you head out now.'

She walked away and Bosch waited until she was out of earshot before speaking.

'Okay, Jerry, what's the problem?'

'I just want to know if that's how it's going to be on this team. Am I going to get the shit work while the princess skates?'

'No, Jerry, it's not going to be like that, and I think you know me well enough not to ask. What's the real problem?'

'I don't like your choices on this, Harry. We should be on the phone with Organized Crime right now. If anything looks like an OC case, this is it. I think you should call 'em, but I think 'cause you're fresh back on the table and been waiting for a case so long, you're not making the call. That's the problem.'

Edgar held his hands out as if to indicate how obvious this was.

'You know, you've got nothing to prove here, Harry. And there's never going to be a shortage of bodies to come along. This is Hollywood, remember? I think we should just turn this one over and wait for the next one.'

Bosch nodded.

'You may be right,' he said. 'You probably are. About all of it. But I'm the three. So we do it my way for now. I'm going to call Bullets and tell her what we've got, then I'm going to call OCID. But even if they roll out, we're going to keep a part of this. You know that. So let's do it good. Okay?'

Edgar nodded reluctantly.

'Look,' Bosch said, 'your objection is noted for the record, okay?'

'Sure, Harry.'

Bosch saw the blue ME's van pull into the clearing then. The tech behind the wheel was Richard Matthews. It was a break. Matthews wasn't as territorial as some of the others, and Bosch figured he could convince him to go along with the plan to move the whole package to the print shed. Matthews would understand that it was the only choice.

'Stay in touch,' Bosch said as Edgar walked off.

Edgar sullenly waved without looking back.

For the next few moments Bosch stood alone in the midst of the activities of the crime scene. He realized he truly reveled in his role. The start of a case always seemed to jazz him this way, and he knew how much he had missed it and craved it during the last year and a half.

Finally, he put his thoughts aside and walked toward the ME's van to talk to Matthews. There was a burst of applause from the Bowl as *Sheherazade* ended.

The print shed was a World War II Quonset hut that sat in the City Services equipment yard behind the police headquarters at Parker Center. It had no windows and a double-wide garage door. The interior was painted black and every crack or crevice where light might come in was taped over. There were thick black curtains that could be pulled closed after the garage door was shut. When they were pulled, the interior was as black as a loan shark's heart. The techs who worked there even referred to the place as 'the cave'.

While the Rolls was being unloaded from the OPG truck, Bosch took his briefcase to a workbench inside the shed and got the phone out. The Organized Crime Investigation Division was a secret society within the greater closed society of the department. Bosch knew very little about OCID and was acquainted with few detectives assigned to the unit. The OCID was a mysterious force, even to those within the department. Not many knew exactly what it did. And this, of course, bred suspicions and jealousies.

Most OCID detectives were known in Detective Services as big-footers. They swooped down to take investigations away from detectives like Bosch, but they didn't often make cases in return. Bosch had seen many investigations disappear under their door with not many prosecutions of OC wise guys resulting. They were the only division in the department with a black budget – approved in closed session by the chief and a police commission that largely followed his lead. From there, the money disappeared into the dark, to pay for informants, investigations and high-tech equipment. Many of their cases disappeared in that netherworld as well.

Bosch asked the communications operator to connect his call to the OCID supervisor on call for the weekend. As he waited for the patch through, he thought again about the body in the trunk. Anthony Aliso – if that was who it was – had seen it coming and closed his eyes. Bosch hoped it wouldn't be that way for himself. He didn't want to know.

'Hello,' a voice said.

'Yes, this is Harry Bosch. I'm the D-three on a homicide call out in Hollywood. Who am I speaking with?'

'Dom Carbone. I've got the weekend call out. You going to spoil it?'

'Maybe.' Bosch tried to think. The name was vaguely familiar but he could not place it. He was sure they had never worked together. 'That's why I'm calling. You might want to take a look at this.'

'Run it down for me.'

'Sure. White male found in the trunk of his Silver Cloud with two in the back of the head. Probably twenty-twos.'

'What else?'

'Car was on a fire road off Mulholland. Doesn't look like a straight robbery. At least, not a personal robbery. I got cards and cash in the wallet and a Presidential on his wrist. Diamonds at every hour on the hour.'

'You're not telling me who the stiff is. Who's the stiff?'

'Nothing confirmed yet but—'

'Just give it to me.'

Bosch had trouble not being able to put a face with the voice over the phone.

'It looks like the ID is going to be Anthony N. Aliso, forty-eight years old. Lives up in the hills. Looks like he has some kind of company with an office at one of the studios down on Melrose near Paramount. TNA Productions is the name of his outfit. I think it's over at Archway Studios. We'll know more in a little while.'

He only got silence in return.

'Mean anything?'

'Anthony Aliso.'

'Yeah, right.'

'Anthony Aliso.'

Carbone repeated the name slowly, as if it were a fine wine he was tasting before deciding whether to accept the bottle or spit it out. He was then quiet for another long moment.

'Nothing hits me right away, Bosch,' he finally said. 'I can make a couple calls. Where you going to be?'

'The print shed. He's here with us and I'll be here a while.'

'What do you mean, you got the guy's body there in the shed?'

'It's a long story. When do you think you can get back to me?'

'As soon as I make the calls. You been over to his office?'

'Not yet. We'll get there sometime tonight.'

Bosch gave him the number of his cellular phone, then closed it and put it in his coat pocket. For a moment he thought about Carbone's reaction to the victim's name. He finally decided he could not read anything into it.

After the Cloud was rolled into place in the shed and the doors shut, Donovan pulled the curtains closed. There was fluorescent lighting overhead which he left on while he got his equipment ready. Matthews, the coroner's tech, and his two assistants – the body movers – huddled over a workbench getting the tools they would need out of a case.

'Harry, I'm going to take my time with this, okay? First I'll laser the trunk with the guy in it. Then we take him out. Then we glue it and laser it again. Then we worry about the rest of it.'

'Your show, man. Whatever time you need.'

'I'll need your help with the wand when I shoot pictures. Roland had to go to shoot another scene.'

Bosch nodded and watched as the SID tech screwed an orange filter onto a Nikon camera. He put the camera strap over his head and turned on the laser. It was a box about the size of a VCR with a cable attachment that led to a footlong wand with a hand grip on it. From the end of the wand a strong orange beam was emitted.

Donovan opened a cabinet and took out several pairs of orange-tinted safety glasses which he handed to Bosch and the others. He put the last pair on himself. He gave Bosch a pair of latex gloves to put on as well.

'I'll do a quick run around the outside of the trunk and then open her up,' Donovan said.

Just as Donovan moved to the switch box to cut off the overheads, the phone in Bosch's pocket buzzed. Donovan waited while Bosch answered. It was Carbone.

'Bosch, we're taking a pass.'

Harry didn't say anything for a moment and neither did Carbone. Donovan hit the light switch and the room plunged into complete blackness.

'You're saying you don't have this guy.' Bosch finally spoke into the dark.

'I checked around, made some calls. Nobody seems to know this guy. Nobody's working him . . . Clean, as far as we know . . . You said he was put in his trunk and capped twice, huh? . . . Bosch, you there?'

'Yeah, I'm here. Yeah, capped twice in the trunk.'

'Trunk music.'

'What?'

'It's a wise guy saying outta Chicago. You know, when they whack some poor slob they say, "Oh, Tony? Don't worry about Tony. He's trunk music now. You won't see him no more." But the thing is, Bosch, this doesn't seem to fit. We don't know this guy. People I talked to, they think maybe somebody's trying to make you think it's OC connected, know what I mean?'

Bosch watched as the laser beam cut through the blackness and bombarded the rear of the trunk with searing light. With the glasses on, the orange was filtered out and the light was a bright, intense white. Bosch was ten feet away from the Rolls, but he could see glowing patterns on the trunk lid and the bumper. This always reminded him of those National Geographic shows in which a submersible camera moved through the ocean's black depths, putting its light on sunken ships or aircraft. It was somehow eerie.

'Look, Carbone,' he said, 'you aren't even interested in coming out to take a look?'

'Not at this time. Of course, give me a call back if you come across anything, you know, that shows different than what I told you. And I'll do some more checking tomorrow. I got your number.'

Bosch was secretly pleased that he wasn't going to get bigfooted by the OCID, but he was also surprised at the brush-off. The quickness with which Carbone had dismissed the case seemed unusual.

'Any other details you want to give me, Bosch?'

'We're just starting. But let me ask you, you ever hear of a hitter takes the vic's shoes with him? Also, he unties the body afterward.'

'Takes his shoes . . . unties him. Uh, not offhand, no. Nobody specific. But like I said, I'll ask around in the morning and I'll put it on our box. Anything else cute about this one?'

Bosch didn't like what was happening. Carbone seemed too interested while saying he wasn't. He said Tony Aliso wasn't connected, yet he still wanted the details. Was he just trying to be helpful or was there something more to it?

'That's about all we got at the moment,' Bosch said, deciding not to give up anything else for free. 'Like I said, we're just getting going here.'

'Okay, then, give me the morning and I'll do some more checking. I'll call if I come up with anything, okay?'

'Right.'

'Check you later. But you know what I think you have there, Bosch? You've got a guy, he was probably making sandwiches with somebody's wife. Lotta times things look like pro hits that aren't, you know what I mean?'

'Yeah, I know what you mean. I'll talk to you later.'

Bosch walked to the rear of the Rolls. Up close he could see the pattern swirls he had noticed in the laser light before appeared to be swipe marks made with a cloth. It looked like the whole car had been wiped down.

But when Donovan moved the wand over the bumper, the laser picked up a partial shoe print on the chrome.

'Did anybody—'

'No,' Bosch said. 'Nobody put their foot there.'

'Okay, then. Hold the wand on the print.'

Bosch did so while Donovan bent over and took several photos, bracketing the exposure settings to make sure he had at least one clear shot. It was the forward half of the foot. There was a circle pattern at the ball of the foot with lines extending from it like the rays of a sun. There was a cross-cut pattern through the arch and then the print was cut off by the edge of the bumper.

'Tennis shoe,' Donovan said. 'Maybe a work shoe.'

After he photographed it, he moved the wand around the trunk again, but there was nothing but wipe marks.

'Okay,' Donovan said. 'Open it.'

Using a penlight to guide his way, Bosch made it to the driver's door and bent in to pull the trunk release. Shortly afterward, the smell of death flooded the shed.

It looked to Bosch as though the body had not shifted during the transport. But the victim took on a ghoulish look under the harsh examination of the laser, his face almost skeletal, like the monsters painted in Day-Glo in fun-house hallways. The blood seemed blacker and the bone chips in the jagged wound were luminescent in bright counterpoint.

On his clothes, small strands of hair and tiny threads glowed. Bosch moved in with a pair of tweezers and a plastic vial like the kind made to hold a stack of silver half dollars. He carefully picked these pieces of potential evidence off the clothing and collected them in the vial. It was painstaking work and there was nothing much there. He knew this kind of material could be found on anybody at anytime. It was common.

When he was done he said to Donovan, 'The tail of the jacket. I flipped it up to check for a wallet.'

'Okay, pull it back down.'

Bosch did so, and there on Aliso's hip was another footprint. It matched the footprint on the bumper but was more complete. On the heel was another circle pattern with off-shooting lines. In the lower arch was what looked like a brand name but it was unreadable.

Regardless of whether they could identify the shoe, Bosch knew it was a good find. It meant that a careful killer had made a mistake. At least one. If nothing else, it gave rise to the hope that there might be other mistakes, that they might eventually lead him to the killer.

'Take the wand.'

Bosch did so and Donovan did his thing with the camera again.

'I'm just shooting this to document it, but we'll take the jacket off before the body goes,' he said.

Next Donovan moved the laser up around the inside of the trunk lid. Here the laser illuminated numerous fingerprints, mostly thumbprints, where a hand would have been placed to prop the lid open while loading things in or out. Many of the prints overlapped each other, a sign that they were old, and Bosch knew right away they probably belonged to the victim himself.

'I'll shoot these, but don't count on anything,' Donovan said.

'I know.'

When he was done, Donovan put the wand and the camera on top of the laser box and said, 'Okay, why don't we take this fellow out of there, lay 'im out and scan 'im real quick before he's outta here?'

Without waiting for an answer, he flipped the fluorescents back on and everybody put their hands to their eyes as the harsh light blinded them. A few moments later the body movers and Matthews went to the trunk and started transferring the corpse to a black plastic body bag they had unfolded on a gurney.

'This guy is loose,' Matthews said as they put the corpse down.

'Yeah,' Bosch said. 'What do you think?'

'Forty-two to forty-eight hours. But let me do some stuff and see what we've got.'

But first Donovan put out the lights again and moved the wand over the body, from the head down. The tear pools in the eye sockets glowed white in the light. There were a few hairs and fibers on the dead man's face and Bosch dutifully collected them. There was also a slight abrasion high on the right cheekbone, which had been hidden when the body was lying on its right side in the trunk.

'He could've been hit or it mighta been from being shoved into the trunk,' Donovan said.

As the beam moved down over the chest, Donovan got excited.

'Well lookee here.'

Glowing in the laser light were what looked like a complete handprint on the right shoulder of the leather jacket and two smudged thumbprints, one on each of the lapels. Donovan bent down very close to look.

'This is treated leather, it doesn't absorb the acids in the prints. We caught a major break here, Harry. This guy wears anything else and forget it. The hand is excellent. These thumbs didn't take . . . I think we can raise them up with some glue. Harry, bend one of the lapels over.'

Bosch reached for the left lapel and carefully turned the cloth over. There on the inside of the crease were four more fingerprints. He turned the right lapel and saw four more there. It appeared that someone had grabbed Tony Aliso by the lapels.

Donovan whistled.

'This looks like two different people. Look at the size of the thumbs on the lapel and the hand on the shoulder. I'd say the hand is smaller, Harry. Maybe a woman. I don't know. But the hands that grabbed this guy by the lapels were big.'

Donovan got scissors from a nearby toolbox and carefully cut the sport coat off the body. Bosch then held it as Donovan went over it with the laser wand. Nothing else came up besides the shoe print and the fingerprints they had already sighted. Bosch carefully hung the jacket over a chair at the counter and came back to the body. Donovan was moving the laser over the lower extremities.

'What else?' Donovan said to no one except maybe the body. 'Come on now, tell us a story.'

There were more fibers and some old stains on the pants. Nothing that stood out as possibly significant until they reached the cuffs. Bosch pulled open the cuff on the right leg and in the crease was a large buildup of dust and fibers. Also, five tiny pieces of gold glitter glowed in the laser beam. Bosch carefully tweezered these into a separate plastic vial. From the left cuff, he recovered two more similar pieces.

'What is it?' he asked.

'Got me. Looks like glitter or something.'

Donovan moved the wand over the bare feet. They were clean, which indicated to Bosch that the victim's shoes had probably been removed after he was forced into the trunk of the Rolls.

'Okay, that's it,' Donovan said.

The lights came back on and Matthews went to work with the corpse, rotating joints, opening the shirt to look at the lividity level of the blood, opening the eyes and swiveling the head. Donovan paced around, waiting for the coroner's tech to finish so he could continue the laser show. He walked over to Bosch.

'Harry, you want the swag on this?'

'Swag?'

'Scientific wild ass guess.'

'Yeah,' Bosch said, amused. 'Give me the swag.'

'Well, I think somebody gets the drop on this guy. Ties him up, dumps him in the trunk and drives him to that fire road. He's still alive, okay? Then our doer gets out, opens the trunk, puts his foot on the bumper ready to do the job but can't get all the way in there to put the muzzle against the bone, you know? That was important to him. To do the job right. So he sticks his big foot on this poor guy's hip, leans further in and bam, bam, out go the headlights. What do you think?'

Bosch nodded.

'I think you are on to something.'

He had already been thinking along the same lines but was past those deductions to the problem.

'Then how does he get back?' he asked.

'Back to where?'

'If this guy was in the trunk the whole time, then the doer drove the Rolls. If he drove there in the Rolls, then how'd he get back to wherever he intercepted Tony?'

'The other one,' Donovan said. 'We've got two different prints on the jacket. Somebody could've followed behind the Rolls. The woman. The one who put her hand on the vic's shoulder.'

Bosch nodded. He had already been puzzling with this but didn't like something about the scenario Donovan had woven. He wasn't sure what it was.

'Okay, Bosch,' Matthews interrupted. 'You want to hear this tonight or you want to wait for the report?'

'T'night,' Bosch said.

'Okay then, listen up. Lividity was fixed and unchanged. The body was never moved once the heart stopped pumping.' He referred to a clipboard. 'Let's see, what else. We've got ninety percent rigor mortis resolution, cornea clouding and we've got skin slippage. I think you take all of that and it's forty-eight hours, maybe a couple hours less. Let us know if you come up with any markers and we might do better.'

'Will do,' Bosch said.

By markers he knew Matthews meant that if he traced the victim's last day and found out what he had eaten last and when, the ME could get a better fix on time of death by studying the digestion of food in the stomach.

'He's all yours,' Bosch said to Matthews. 'Any idea on the post?'

'You caught the tail end of a holiday weekend. That's bad luck for you. Last I heard, we've run on twenty-seven homicides in the county so far. We probably won't cut this one until Wednesday, if you're lucky. Don't call us, we'll call you.'

'Yeah, I've heard that one before.'

But the delay didn't really bother Bosch this time. In cases like this, the autopsy usually held few surprises. It was pretty clear how the victim died. The mystery was why and by whom.

Matthews and his assistants wheeled the corpse out, leaving Bosch and Donovan alone with the Rolls. Donovan stared at the car silently, contemplating it the way a matador looks at the bull he is going to fight.

'We're going to get her secrets, Harry.'

Bosch's phone buzzed then and he fumbled getting it out of his jacket and open. It was Edgar.

'We got the ID, Harry. It is Aliso.'

'You got this off the prints?'

'Yeah. Mossler's got a fax at home. I sent him everything and he eyeballed it.'

Mossler was one of the SID's latent-print men.

'This is with the DL thumbprint?'

'Right. Also, I pulled a full set of Tony's prints from an old pop for soliciting. Mossler had those to look at, too. It's Aliso.'

'Okay, good work. What else you got?'

'Like I said, I ran this guy. He's pretty clean. Just the soliciting arrest back in seventy-five. Few other things, though. His name comes up as a victim on a burglary up at his house in March. And on the civil indexes I've got a few civil actions against the guy. Breach-of-contract stuff, it looks like. A trail of broken promises and pissed-off people, Harry, good motive stuff.'

'What were the cases about?'

'That's all I've got for now, just the abstracts in the civil index. I'll have to pull the actual cases when I can get into the courthouse.'

'Okay. Did you check Missing Persons?'

'Yeah, I did. He was never reported. You got anything there?'

'Maybe. We might've gotten lucky. Looks like we are going to get some prints off the body. Two sets.'

'Off the body? That's very cool.'

'Off the leather jacket.'

Bosch could tell Edgar was excited. Both detectives knew that if the prints were not those of a suspect, then they would surely be fresh enough to belong to people who had seen the victim in the time shortly before his death.

'You call OCID?'

Bosch was waiting for him to ask.

'Yeah. They're taking a pass.'

'What?'

'That's what they said. At least for now. Until we find something they might be interested in.'

Bosch wondered if Edgar even believed he had made the call.

'That doesn't figure, Harry.'

'Yeah, well, all we can do is our job. You hear from Kiz?'

'Not yet. Who'd you talk to over at Organized Crime?'

'Guy named Carbone. He was on call.'

'Never heard of him.'

'Well, neither had I. I gotta go, Jerry. Let me know what you know.'

As soon as Bosch hung up, the door to the shed opened and in stepped Lieutenant Grace Billets. She quickly scanned the room and saw Donovan working in the car. She asked Bosch to step outside and that was when he knew she was unhappy.

She closed the door after he stepped out. She was in her forties and had as many years on the job as Bosch, give or take a couple, but they had never worked together before her assignment as his commanding officer. She was of medium build, with reddish-brown hair she kept short. She wore no makeup. She was dressed entirely in black – jeans, T-shirt and blazer. She also wore black cowboy boots. Her only concession to femininity was the pair of thin gold hoop earrings. Her manner was no concession to anything.

'What's going on, Harry? You moved the body *in* the car?'

'Had to. It was either that or dump it out of the car with about ten thousand people watching us instead of the fireworks they were supposed to see.'

Bosch explained the situation in detail and Billets listened silently. When he was done, she nodded.

'I'm sorry,' she said. 'I didn't know the details. It looks like it was your only choice.'

Bosch liked that about her. She wasn't always right and she was willing to admit it.

'Thanks, Lieutenant.'

'So what do we have?'

When Bosch and Billets stepped back into the shed, Donovan was at one of the worktables working with the leather jacket. He had hung it on a wire inside an empty one-hundred-gallon aquarium and then dropped in a Hard Evidence packet. The packet, when broken open, emitted cyanoacrylate fumes which would attach to the amino acids and oils of fingerprints and crystallize, thereby raising the ridges and whorls and making them more visible and photo-ready.

'How's it look?' Bosch asked.

'Real good. We're going to get something off this. Howdy, Lieutenant.'

'Hello there,' Billets said.

Bosch could tell she didn't remember Donovan's name.

'Listen, Art,' he said, 'when you get those together, get them over to the print lab and then call me or Edgar and tell us. We'll get somebody over there to do them code three.'

Code three was a patrol response code meaning lights and siren authorized. Bosch needed the prints to be handled quickly. So far, they were the best lead.

'Will do, Harry.'

'What about the Rolls? Can I get in it yet?'

'Well, I'm not quite through with it. You can go in. Just be careful.'

Bosch began searching the interior of the car, checking the door and seat pockets first and finding nothing. He checked the ashtray and found it empty, not even an ash. He made a mental note that the victim apparently didn't smoke.

Billets stood nearby, watching but not helping. She had risen to detective bureau commander primarily on the success of her skills as an administrator, not as an investigator. She knew when to watch and not get in the way.

Bosch checked under the seats and found nothing of interest. He opened the glove compartment last and a small square piece of paper fell out. It was a receipt for an airport valet company. Holding it by the corner, Bosch walked it over to the workbench and told Donovan to check it for prints when he got the chance.

He went back to the glove compartment and found the lease agreement and registration of the car, its service records and a small tool kit with a flashlight. There was also a half-used tube of Preparation H, a hemorrhoid medication. It seemed like an odd place to keep it, but Bosch guessed that maybe Aliso kept the tube handy for long drives.

He bagged all of the items from the compartment separately and while doing so noticed an extra battery in the tool kit. It struck him as odd because the flashlight obviously took two batteries. Having one extra would not do much good.

He pressed the flashlight's on/off switch. It was dead. He unscrewed the cap and one battery slid out. Looking into the barrel, Bosch saw a plastic bag. He used a pen to reach in and pull the bag out. It contained about two dozen brown capsules.

Billets stepped closer.

'Poppers,' Bosch said. 'Amyl nitrate. Supposed to help you get it up and keep it there. You know, improve your orgasm.'

He suddenly felt the need to explain his knowledge was not based on personal experience.

'It's come up in other cases before.'

She nodded. Donovan walked over with the valet ticket in a clear plastic envelope.

'A couple smudges. Nothing we can work with.'

Bosch took it back. He then carried the various plastic evidence bags he had to the counter.

'Art, I'm taking the receipt, the poppers and the car's service records, okay?'

'You got it.'

'I'll leave you the plane ticket and the wallet. You are also going to put some speed on the prints from the jacket and what else? Oh yeah, those sparkles. What do you think?'

'Hopefully tomorrow. The rest of the fiber stuff I'll take a look at, but it's probably going to be exclusionary.'

That meant most of the material they had collected would sit in storage after a quick examination by Donovan, and come into play only if a suspect was identified. It would then be used either to tie that suspect to the crime scene or to exclude him.

Bosch took a large envelope off a shelf over the counter, put all the pieces of evidence he was taking into it, then put it in his briefcase and snapped it closed. He headed for the curtain with Billets.

'Good to see you again, Art,' she said.

'Likewise, Lieutenant.'

'You want me to call OPG to come get the car?' Bosch asked.

'Nah, I'm going to be here a while,' Donovan said. 'Gotta use the vac and I might think of something else to do. I'll take care of it, Harry.'

'Okay, man, later.'

Bosch and Billets stepped through the curtain and then through the door. Outside he lit a cigarette and looked up at the dark, starless sky. Billets lit one of her own.

'Where to?' she asked.

'Next of kin. You want to come? It's always a fun thing.'

She smiled at his sarcasm.

'No, I think I'll pass on that. But before you leave, what's your gut on this, Harry? I mean, OCID passing without taking a look, that kind of bothers me.'

'Me, too.' He took a long drag and exhaled. 'My gut is that this one's going to be tough. Unless something good comes out of those prints. That's our only real break so far.'

'Well, tell your people that I want everybody in at eight for a roundtable on what we've got so far.'

'Let's make it nine, Lieutenant. I think by then we should have something back from Donovan on the prints.'

'Okay, nine then. I'll see you then, Harry. And from now on, when we're talking like this, you know, informally, call me Grace.'

'Sure, Grace. Have a nice night.'

She expelled her smoke in a short burst that sounded like the start of a laugh.

'You mean, what's left of it.'

On the way up to Mulholland Drive and Hidden Highlands Bosch paged Rider and she called back from one of the houses she was visiting. She said it was the last of the houses overlooking the clearing where the Rolls was parked. She told him the best she could come up with was a resident who

299

remembered seeing the white Rolls-Royce from the back deck of his home on Saturday morning about ten. The same resident also believed the car was not there on Friday evening when he was out on the deck to watch the sunset.

'That fits with the time frame the ME's looking at and the plane ticket. I think we're zeroing in on Friday night, sometime after he got in from Vegas. Probably on his way home from the airport. Nobody heard any shots?'

'Not that I've found. There's two houses where I got no answer. I was going to go back and try them now.'

'Maybe you can catch them tomorrow. I'm heading up to Hidden Highlands. I think you should go with me.'

They made arrangements to meet outside the entrance to the development where Aliso had lived, and Bosch closed the phone. He wanted Kiz along when he told Aliso's next of kin he was dead because it would be good for her to learn the grim routine and because the percentages called for whoever that next of kin was to be considered a possible suspect. It was always good to have a witness with you when you first spoke to the person who later could become your quarry.

Bosch looked at his watch. It was nearly ten. Taking care of the notification meant they probably wouldn't be getting to the victim's office until midnight. He called the communications center and gave the operator the address on Melrose and had her look it up in the cross directory. It came back to Archway Pictures, as Bosch had guessed. He knew they had caught a bit of a break. Archway was a midsize studio that largely rented offices and production facilities to independent filmmakers. As far as Bosch knew, it hadn't made its own films since the 1960s. The break was that he knew someone in security over there. Chuckie Meachum was a former Robbery-Homicide bull who had retired a few years earlier and taken a job as assistant director of security at Archway. He would be useful in smoothing their way in. Bosch considered calling ahead and arranging for Chuckie Meachum to meet them at the studio but decided against it. He decided he didn't want anyone to know he was coming until he got there.

He got to Hidden Highlands fifteen minutes later. Rider's car was parked on the shoulder off Mulholland. Bosch pulled up and she got in his car. Then he pulled into the entrance lane next to the gatehouse. It was a small brick structure with a single guard inside. Hidden Highlands was maybe a little richer but not that different from many of the other small, wealthy and scared enclaves nestled in the hills and valleys around Los Angeles. Walls and gates, guardhouses and private security forces were the secret ingredients of the so-called melting pot of southern California.

A guard in a blue uniform stepped out of the gatehouse carrying a clipboard and Bosch had his badge wallet out and open. The guard was a tall, thin man with a worn, gray face. Bosch didn't recognize him, though he had heard in the station that most of the guards working here were off-duty uniforms from Hollywood Division. In the past he had seen postings for part-time jobs on the bulletin board outside the roll call room.

The guard gave Bosch a once-over in a laconic manner, avoiding a look at the badge on purpose.

'Kenahepyou?' he finally said.

'I need to go to the home of Anthony Aliso.'

He gave the address on Hillcrest that had been on the victim's driver's license.

'Your names?'

'Detective Harry Bosch, LAPD. Says it right here. This is Detective Kizmin Rider.'

He proffered the badge wallet, but it was still ignored. The guard was writing on his clipboard. Bosch saw his name tag said Nash. He also saw that the tin badge said CAPTAIN across it.

'They expecting you at the Aliso place?'

'I don't think so. It's police business.'

'Okay, but I've got to call ahead. It's the development's rules, you know.'

'I prefer you didn't do that, Captain Nash.'

Bosch hoped his use of the security guard's title would win him over. Nash thought a moment.

'Tell you what,' he said. 'You go on ahead and I'll come up with a reason for delaying making the call a few minutes. I'll just say I'm up here by myself t'night and I got kind of busy, if there's a complaint.'

He stepped back and reached in the open door of the gatehouse. He pressed a button on the inside wall and the crossguard went up.

'Thanks, Captain. You work out of Hollywood?'

Bosch knew he didn't. He could tell Nash wasn't even a cop. He didn't have the cold eyes of a cop. But Bosch was playing to him, just in case he became a useful source of information later on.

'Nah,' Nash said. 'I'm full-time. That's why they made me captain of the watch. Everybody else is part-time out of Hollywood or West Hollywood sheriffs. I run the schedule.'

'Then how'd you get stuck on the night shift on Sunday night?'

'Everybody can use some OT now and then.'

Bosch nodded.

'You're right about that. Hillcrest, where's that?'

'Oh, yeah, forgot. Take your second left. That's Hillcrest. The Aliso place is about the sixth house on the right. Nice view of the city from the pool.'

'Did you know him?' Rider asked, leaning down so she could see Nash through Bosch's window.

'Aliso?' Nash said, bending further to look in at her. He thought a moment. 'Not really. Just like I know people when they come through here. I'm just the same to them as the pool man, I guess. I notice you asked *did* I know him. Am I not going to get the chance?'

'Smart man, Mr Nash,' Rider said.

She straightened up, finished with the conversation. Bosch nodded his thanks and drove through the gate to Hillcrest. As he passed the broad, manicured lawns surrounding houses the size of apartment buildings, he filled Rider in on what he had learned at the print shed and from Edgar. He also admired the properties they were passing. Many of them were surrounded by walls or tall hedges that looked as though they were trimmed into sharp edges every morning. Walls within walls, Bosch thought. He wondered what the owners did with all of their space besides fearfully guard it.

It took them five minutes to find the Aliso house on a cul-de-sac at the top of the hill. He passed through the open gates of an estate with a Tudor-style mansion set behind a circular driveway made of gray paver stones. Bosch got out with his briefcase and looked up at the place. It was intimidating in its size, but its style was not much to speak of. He wouldn't want it, even if he had the money.

After getting to the door and pushing the doorbell button, he looked at Rider.

'You ever done this before?'

'No. But I grew up in South L.A. A lot of drive-bys. I was around when people got the news.'

Bosch nodded.

'Not to belittle that experience, but this is different. What is important is not what you hear said, it's what you observe.'

Bosch pushed the lighted button again. He could hear the bell sound from inside the house. He looked at Rider and could tell she was about to ask a question, when the door was opened by a woman.

'Mrs Aliso?' Bosch asked.

'Yes?'

'Mrs Aliso, I'm Detective Harry Bosch with the LAPD. This is my partner, Detective Kizmin Rider. We need to speak with you concerning your husband.'

He held out his badge wallet and she took it from his hand. Usually, they didn't do that. Usually, they recoiled from it or looked at it like it was some strange and fascinating object not to be touched.

'I don't under—'

She stopped when the sound of a phone ringing began somewhere behind her in the big house.

'Would you excuse me a moment. I have to—'

'That's probably Nash at the gate. He said he had to call ahead, but there was a lineup of cars behind us. I guess we beat him here. We need to come in to talk to you, ma'am.'

She stepped back in and opened the door wide for him. She looked about five to ten years younger than her husband had been. She was about forty, attractive, with dark straight hair and a trim build. She wore a lot of makeup on a face Bosch guessed had been sculpted at times by the surgeon's knife. Still, through the makeup she looked tired, worn. He could see her face was flushed pink, as though she might have been drinking. She wore a light blue dress that showed off her legs. They were tan and the muscles still taut. Bosch could see she had been considered very beautiful at one time but was sliding into that stage when a woman believes her beauty may be leaving – even if it isn't. Maybe that was why she had all the makeup on, Bosch guessed. Or maybe it was because she was still expecting her husband to show up.

Bosch closed the door after they entered and they followed the woman into a large living room with an incongruous mix of modern prints on the walls and French antiques on the thick white carpet. The phone was still ringing. She told Bosch and Rider to sit down and then walked through the living room into another hallway, which she crossed to what looked like a den. He heard her answer the phone, tell Nash that the delay was all right and hang up.

She came back into the living room then and sat on a couch with a muted flower print. Bosch and Rider took nearby chairs with a matching pattern. Bosch took a quick look around and saw no photographs in frames. Only the artwork. It was always one of the first things he looked for when he had to quickly judge a relationship.

'I'm sorry,' he said. 'I didn't get your name.'

'Veronica Aliso. What about my husband, Detective? Is he hurt?'

Bosch leaned forward in his chair. No matter how many times he did this, he never got used to it and he was never sure he was doing it the right way.

'Mrs Aliso . . . I am very sorry, but your husband is dead. He was the victim of a homicide. I am sorry to have to tell you this.'

He watched her closely and she said nothing at first. She instinctively crossed her arms in front of her and brought her face down in a pained grimace. There were no tears. Not yet. In his experience, Bosch had seen them come either right away – as soon as they opened the door and saw him and knew – or much later, when it sank in that the nightmare was reality.

'I don't . . . How did this happen?' she asked, her eyes staring down at the floor.

'He was found in his car. He'd been shot.'

'In Las Vegas?'

'No. Here. Not far. It looks like he was coming home from the airport when . . . when he was somehow stopped by somebody. We're not sure yet. His car was found off Mulholland Drive. Down by the Bowl.'

He watched her a little more. She still had not looked up. Bosch felt a sense of guilt pass over him. Guilt because he was not watching this woman with sympathy. He had been in this place too many times for that. Instead, he watched her with an eye for false mannerisms. In these situations his suspicion outweighed his compassion. It had to.

'Can I get you anything, Mrs Aliso?' Rider asked. 'Water? Do you have coffee? Do you want something stronger?'

'No. I'm fine. Thank you. It's just a terrible shock.'

'Do you have any children in the house?' Rider asked.

'No, we . . . no children. Do you know what happened? Was he robbed?'

'That's what we're trying to find out,' Bosch said.

'Of course . . . Can you tell me, was there much pain?'

'No, there was no pain,' Bosch said.

He thought of the tears welled in Tony Aliso's eyes. He decided not to tell her about that.

'It must be hard, your job,' she said. 'Telling people this sort of thing.'

He nodded and looked away. For a moment he thought of the old squad room joke about the easiest way to do next-of-kin notification. When Mrs Brown opens the door, you say, 'Are you the widow Brown?'

He looked back at the widow Aliso.

'Why did you ask if it happened in Las Vegas?'

'Because that was where he was.'

'How long was he supposed to be there?'

'I don't know. He never scheduled it with a return. He always bought open-ended tickets so he could come back when he wanted to. He always said he'd be back when his luck changed. For the worse.'

'We have reason to believe he came back to Los Angeles on Friday night.

His car wasn't found until this evening. That's two days, Mrs Aliso. Did you try to call him in Las Vegas during that time?'

'No. We usually didn't speak when he was over there.'

'And how often was it that he went?'

'Once or twice a month.'

'For how long each time?'

'Anywhere from two days to once he spent a week. Like I said, it all depended on how he was doing.'

'And you never called him there?' Rider asked.

'Rarely. Not at all this time.'

'Was it business or pleasure that took him there?' Bosch asked.

'He always told me it was both. He said he had investors to see. But it was an addiction. That's what I believed. He loved to gamble and could afford to do it. So he went.'

Bosch nodded but didn't know why.

'This last time, when did he go?'

'He went Thursday. After leaving the studio.'

'You saw him last then?'

'Thursday morning. Before he went to the studio. He left for the airport from there. It's closer.'

'And you had no idea when to expect him back.'

He said it as a statement. It was out there for her to challenge if she wanted to.

'To be honest, I was just beginning to wonder tonight. It usually doesn't take long for that place to separate a man from his money. I thought it was a little long, yes. But I didn't try to track him down. And then you came.'

'What did he like to play over there?'

'Everything. But poker the most. It was the only game where you weren't playing against the house. The house took a cut, but you were playing against the other players. That's how he explained it to me once. Only he called the other players schmucks from Iowa.'

'Was he always alone over there, Mrs Aliso?'

Bosch looked down at his notebook and acted as if he was writing something important and that her answer wasn't. He knew it was cowardly.

'I wouldn't know.'

'Did you ever go with him at all?'

'I don't like to gamble. I don't like that city. That city is a horrible place. They can dress it up all they want, it's still a city of vices and whores. Not just the sexual kind.'

Bosch studied the cool anger in her dark eyes.

'You didn't answer the question, Mrs Aliso,' Rider said.

'What question?'

'Did you ever go to Las Vegas with him?'

'At first, yes. But I found it boring. I haven't been in years.'

'Was your husband in any kind of serious debt?' Bosch asked.

'I don't know. If he was, he didn't tell me. You can call me Veronica.'

'You never asked if he was getting into trouble?' Rider asked.

'I just assumed that he would tell me if he was.'

She turned the hard dark eyes on Rider now, and Bosch felt a weight lift off him. Veronica Aliso was challenging them to disagree.

'I know this probably makes me some kind of a suspect, but I don't care,' she said. 'You have your job to do. It must be obvious to you that my husband and I . . . let's just say we coexisted here. So as to your questions about Nevada, I couldn't tell you whether he was a million up or a million down. Who knows, he could've beaten the odds. But I think he would have bragged about it if he had.'

Bosch nodded and thought about the body in the trunk. It didn't seem like that of a man who had beaten any odds.

'Where did he stay in Las Vegas, Mrs Aliso?'

'Always at the Mirage. I do know that. You see, not all of the casinos have poker tables. The Mirage has a classy one. He always said that if I needed to call, call there. Ask for the poker pit if there is no answer in the room.'

Bosch took a few moments to write this down. He found that often silence was the best way to get people to talk and reveal themselves. He hoped Rider realized that he was leaving holes of silence in the interview on purpose.

'You asked if he went there alone.'

'Yes?'

'Detectives, in the course of your investigation I believe you will undoubtedly learn that my husband was a philanderer. I ask only one thing of you, please do your best to keep that information from me. I simply don't want to know.'

Bosch nodded and was silent a moment while he composed his thoughts. What kind of woman wouldn't want to know, he wondered. Maybe one who already did. He looked back at her and their eyes connected again.

'Aside from gambling, was your husband in any other kind of trouble as far as you know?' he asked. 'Work-related, financial?'

'As far as I know he wasn't. But he kept the finances. I could not tell you what our situation is at the moment. When I needed money I asked him, and he always said cash a check and tell him the amount. I have a separate account for household expenses.'

Without looking up from the notebook, Bosch said, 'Just a few more and we'll leave you alone for now. Did your husband have any enemies that you know of? Anybody who would want to harm him?'

'He worked in Hollywood. Back stabbing is considered an art form there. Anthony was as skilled at it as anyone else who has been in the industry twenty-five years. Obviously that means there could always be people who were unhappy with him. But who would do this, I don't know.'

'The car . . . the Rolls-Royce is leased to a production company over at Archway Studios. How long had he worked there?'

'His office was there, but he didn't work for Archway per se. TNA Productions is his . . . was his own company. He simply rented an office and a parking spot on the Archway lot. But he had about as much to do with Archway as you do.'

'Tell us about his production company,' Rider said. 'Did he make films?'

'In a manner of speaking. You could say he started big and ended small. About twenty years ago he produced his first film. *The Art of the Cape*. If you saw it, you were one of the few. Bullfight movies are not popular. But it was critically acclaimed, played the film festival circuit and then the art houses and it was a good start for him.'

She said that Aliso had managed to make a couple more films for general release. But after that his production and moral values steadily declined, until he was producing a procession of exploitative dreck.

'These films, if you want to call them that, are notable only for the number of exposed breasts in them,' she said. 'In the business, it's called straight-to-video stock. In addition to that Tony was quite successful in literary arbitrage.'

'What is that?'

'He was a speculator. Mostly scripts, but he did manuscripts, books on occasion.'

'And how would he speculate on them?'

'He'd buy them. Wrap up the rights. Then when they became valuable or the author became hot, he'd go to market with them. Do you know who Michael St John is?'

The name sounded familiar but Bosch could not place it. He shook his head. Rider did the same.

'He's one of the screenwriters of the moment. He'll be directing studio features within a year or so. He's the flavor-of-the-month, so to speak.'

'Okay.'

'Well, eight years ago when he was in the USC film school and was hungry and was trying to find an agent and trying to catch the attention of the studios, my husband was one of the vultures who circled overhead. You see, my husband's films were so low-budget that he'd get students to shoot them, direct them, write them. So he knew the schools and he knew talent. Michael St John was one he knew had talent. Once when he was desperate, he sold Anthony the rights to three of his student screenplays for two thousand dollars. Now, anything with St John's name on it goes for at least six figures.'

'What about these writers, how do they take this?'

'Not well. St John was trying to buy his scripts back.'

'You think he could have harmed your husband?'

'No. You asked me what he did and I told you. If you are asking who would kill him, I don't know.'

Bosch jotted a couple of notes down.

'You mentioned that he said that he saw investors when he went to Las Vegas,' Rider said.

'Yes.'

'Can you tell us who they were?'

'Schmucks from Iowa, I would assume. People he would meet and persuade to invest in a movie. You'd be surprised how many people jump at a chance to be part of a Hollywood movie. And Tony was a good salesman. He could make a two-million budget flick sound like the sequel to *Gone With the Wind*. He convinced me.'

'How so?'

'He talked me into being in one of his movies once. That's how I met him. Made it sound like I was going to be the new Jane Fonda. You know, sexy but smart. It was a studio picture. Only the director was a coke addict and the writer couldn't write and the movie was so bad it was never released. That was it for my career and Tony never made a studio picture again. He spent the rest of his life making video garbage.'

Looking around the tall-ceilinged room at the paintings and furniture, Bosch said, 'Doesn't look like he did too badly at it.'

'No, he didn't,' she responded. 'I guess we have those people from Iowa to thank for that.'

Her bitterness was stifling. Bosch looked down at his notebook just so he could avert his eyes from her.

'All this talk,' she said then. 'I need some water. Do either of you want something?'

'Water would be fine,' Bosch said. 'We're not going to be much longer.'

'Detective Rider?'

'I'm fine, thank you.'

'I'll be right back.'

While she was gone Bosch stood up and looked around the living room in a manner that suggested he wasn't really interested. He said nothing to Rider. He was standing near a side table looking at a carved glass figurine of a nude woman when Veronica Aliso came back in with two glasses of ice water.

'I just want to ask you a few more questions about this past week,' Bosch said.

'Fine.'

He sipped from his glass and remained standing.

'What would your husband have taken with him to Las Vegas as far as luggage went?'

'Just his overnighter.'

'What did it look like?'

'It was a hanging bag that, you know, folded over. It was green with brown leather trim and straps. He had a name tag on it.'

'Did he take a briefcase or any work with him?'

'Yes, his briefcase. It was one of those aluminum shell kind. You know, they are lightweight but impossible to break into or something. Is the luggage missing?'

'We're not sure. Do you know where he kept the key to the briefcase?'

'On his key chain. With the car keys.'

There had been no car keys in the Rolls or on Aliso's body. Bosch realized that the reason they might have been taken was to open the briefcase. He put the glass down next to the figurine and looked at it again. He then began writing the descriptions of the briefcase and hanging bag in his notebook.

'Did your husband wear a wedding ring?'

'No. He did wear quite an expensive watch, though. It was a Rolex. I gave it to him.'

'The watch was not taken.'

'Oh.'

Bosch looked up from his notebook.

'Do you remember what your husband was wearing on Thursday morning? When you last saw him?'

'Um, just clothes . . . uh, he had on his white pants and a blue shirt and his sport coat.'

'His black leather sport coat?'

'Yes.'

'Mrs Aliso, do you remember if you hugged him or kissed him good-bye?'

This seemed to fluster her, and Bosch immediately regretted the way he had phrased the question.

'I'm sorry. What I meant was that we found some fingerprints on the jacket. On the shoulder. And if you might have touched him there on the day he left, it could explain this piece of evidence.'

She was quiet a moment and Bosch thought that she was finally going to begin to cry. But instead, she said, 'I might have but I don't remember . . . I don't think I did.'

Bosch opened his briefcase and looked for a print screen. He found one in one of the pockets. It looked like a photo slide but the center was a double-sided screen with ink between the screens. A thumb could be pressed on the A side and a fingerprint would be imprinted on a card held against the B side.

'I want to take your thumbprint so we can compare it to the print taken off the jacket. If you did not touch him there, then it might be a good lead for us.'

She stepped over to him and he pressed her right thumb down on the print screen. When he was done she looked at her thumb.

'No ink.'

'Yes, that's nice. No mess. We just started using these a few years ago.'

'The print on the jacket, did it belong to a woman?'

He looked at her and held her eyes for a moment.

'We won't know for sure until we get a match.'

As he put the card and the print screen back in the briefcase, he noticed the evidence bag containing the poppers. He took it out and held it up for her to look at.

'Do you know what these are?'

She narrowed her eyes and shook her head no.

'Amyl nitrate poppers. Some people use them to enhance sexual performance and satisfaction. Do you know if your husband ever used these?'

'You found them with him?'

'Mrs Aliso, I'd rather that you'd just answer my questions. I know this is difficult, but there are some things I can't tell you yet. I will when I can. I promise.'

'No, he didn't use them . . . with me.'

'I'm sorry that I have to be so personal, but we want to catch the person who did this. We both want that. Now, your husband was about ten or twelve years older than you.' He was being charitable here. 'Did he have problems performing sexually? Is there any chance he might have been using poppers without your knowledge?'

She turned to go back to her chair. When she was seated again she said, 'I wouldn't know.'

Now Bosch narrowed his eyes. What was she trying to say? His silence worked. She answered before he had to ask, but as she spoke she looked directly at Rider, the unspoken message being that as a woman Rider might sympathize.

'Detective, I haven't had . . . I guess, sexual relations is the way it is said in these matters. My husband and I . . . not in almost two years.'

Bosch nodded and looked down at his notebook. The page was blank but he couldn't bring himself to write this latest piece of information down with her watching them. He folded the notebook closed and put it away.

'You want to ask me why, don't you?'

He just looked at her and she answered with a measure of defiance in her face and voice.

'He had lost interest.'

'Are you sure?'

'He told me that to my face.'

Bosch nodded.

'Mrs Aliso, I'm sorry for the loss of your husband. I'm also sorry for the intrusion and the personal questions. I'm afraid, though, that there will be more as the investigation progresses.'

'I understand.'

'There is one other thing I'd like to cover.'

'Yes, what is it?'

'Did your husband have a home office?'

'Yes.'

'Could we take a quick look at it?'

She stood up and they followed her down the second hallway to the office. They both stepped into the room and Bosch looked around. It was a small room with a desk and two file cabinets. There was a TV on a cart in front of a wall of shelves. Half were filled with books and the rest stacked with scripts, the titles written with Magic Markers on the edges of the pages. There was a golf bag leaning in the corner.

Bosch walked over and studied the desk. It was spotless. He came around and saw that the desk contained two file drawers. He opened these and found one empty and one containing several files. He quickly looked through the file tabs and saw that they apparently were files containing personal finance records and tax documents. He closed the drawers, deciding that a search of the office could probably keep.

'It's late,' he said. 'This is not the time. I want you to understand, though, that investigations like this often shoot off into many directions. But we have to follow up on everything. We're going to need to come in here tomorrow and go through your husband's things. We'll probably take a lot with us. We'll have a warrant so everything will be perfectly legal.'

'Yes. Of course. But can't I just give you permission to take what you need?'

'You could, but it would be better this way. I'm talking about check books, savings account records, credit card statements, insurance, everything. We'll probably need the records on your household account, too.'

'I understand. What time?'

'I don't know yet. I'll call first. Or someone will. Do you know, did your husband leave a will?'

'Yes. Both of us made wills. They're with our attorney.'

'How long ago was that?'

'The will? Oh, a long time. Years.'

'In the morning, I'd like you to call the attorney and tell him we'll need a copy of it. Are you up to doing that?'

'Of course.'

'What about insurance?'

'Yes, we have policies. The attorney, Neil Denton in Century City, will have them also.'

'Okay, we'll worry about that tomorrow. I need to seal this room now.'

They stepped back into the hallway and Bosch closed the door. From his briefcase he took a sticker that said

CRIME SCENE

DO NOT ENTER PREMISES

CALL LAPD 213 485–4321

Bosch pressed the sticker across the door jamb. If anyone entered the room now, they would have to cut the sticker or peel it off. Bosch would know.

'Detective?' Veronica Aliso said quietly from behind him.

Bosch turned around.

'I am the suspect, aren't I?'

Bosch put the two papers he had peeled off the back of the sticker in his pocket.

'I suppose everyone and no one is a suspect at this point. We're looking at everything. But, yes, Mrs Aliso, we're going to be looking at you.'

'I guess I shouldn't have been so candid before, then.'

Rider said, 'If you've got nothing to hide, the truth shouldn't hurt you.'

Bosch knew from long experience never to say such a thing. He knew the words were false before they were out of her mouth. Judging by the small, thin smile on Veronica Aliso's face, she knew it as well.

'Are you new at this, Detective Rider?' she asked while looking at Bosch with that smile.

'No, ma'am, I've been a detective for six years.'

'Oh. And I guess I don't have to ask Detective Bosch.'

'Mrs Aliso?' Bosch asked.

'Veronica.'

'There is one last thing you could clear up for us tonight. We do not know yet exactly when your husband was killed. But it would help us concentrate on other matters if we could quickly eliminate routine avenues of—'

'You want to know if I have an alibi, is that it?'

'We just want to know where you were the last few days and nights. It's a routine question, nothing else.'

'Well, I hate to bore you with my life's details, because I'm afraid that's what they are, boring. But other than a trip to the mall and supermarket Saturday afternoon, I haven't left the house since I had dinner with my husband Wednesday night.'

'You've been here alone?'

'Yes . . . but I think you can verify this with Captain Nash at the gate. They keep records of who comes in as well as out of Hidden Highlands. Even the residents. Also, on Friday our pool man was here in the afternoon. I gave him his check. I can get you his name and number.'

'That won't be necessary right now. Thank you. And again, I'm sorry for your loss. Is there anything we can do for you right now?'

She seemed to be withdrawing into herself. He was not sure she had heard his question.

'I'm fine,' she finally said.

He picked up his briefcase and headed down the hallway with Rider. It ran behind the living room and took them directly to the front door. All the way along the hallway there were no photographs on the wall. It didn't seem right to him, but he guessed nothing had been right in this house for a while. Bosch studied dead people's rooms the way scholars studied dead people's paintings at the Getty. He looked for the hidden meanings, the secrets of lives and deaths.

At the door Rider went out first. Bosch then stepped out and looked back down the hall. Veronica Aliso was framed at the other end in the light. He hesitated for a beat. He nodded and walked out.

They drove in silence, digesting the conversation, until they got to the gatehouse and Nash came out.

'How'd it go?'

'It went.'

'He's dead, isn't he? Mr Aliso.'

'Yeah.'

Nash whistled quietly.

'Captain Nash, you keep records here of when cars come in and out?' Rider asked.

'Yes. But this is private property. You'd need a—'

'Search warrant,' Bosch said. 'Yes, we know. But before we go to all that trouble, tell me something. Say I come back with a warrant, are your gate records going to tell me when exactly Mrs Aliso came in and out of here the last few days?'

'Nope. It'll only tell you when her car did.'

'Gotcha.'

Bosch dropped off Rider at her car and they drove separately down out of the hills to the Hollywood Division station on Wilcox. On the way Bosch thought about Veronica Aliso and the fury she seemed to hold in her eyes for her dead husband. He didn't know how it fit or if it even fit at all. But he knew they would be coming back to her.

Rider and Bosch stopped briefly in the station to update Edgar and pick up cups of coffee. Bosch then called Archway and arranged for the security office to call in Chuckie Meachum from home. Bosch did not tell the duty officer who took the call what it was about or what office inside the studio they would be going to. He just told the officer to get Meachum there.

At midnight they went out the rear door of the station house, past the fenced windows of the drunk tank and to Bosch's car.

'So what did you think of her?' Bosch finally asked as he pulled out of the station lot.

'The embittered widow? I think there wasn't much to their marriage. At least at the end. Whether that makes her a killer or not, I don't know.'

'No pictures.'

'On the walls? Yeah, I noticed that.'

Bosch lit a cigarette and Rider didn't say anything about it, although it was a violation of department policy to smoke in the detective car.

'What do you think?' Rider asked.

'I'm not sure yet. There's what you said. The bitterness you could almost put in a glass if you ever ran out of ice. Couple other things I'm still thinking about.'

'Like what?'

'Like all the makeup she had on and the way she took my badge out of my hand. Nobody's ever done that before. It's like . . . I don't know, like maybe she was waiting for us.'

When they got to the entrance of Archway Pictures, Meachum was standing under the half-size replica of the Arc de Triomphe smoking a cigarette and waiting. He was wearing a sport coat over a golf shirt and had a bemused smile on his face when he recognized Bosch pulling up. Bosch had spent time with Meachum in the Robbery-Homicide Division ten years before. Never partnered, but they worked a few of the same task forces. Meachum had gotten out when the getting out was good. He pulled the pin a month after the Rodney King tape hit the news. He knew. He told everybody it was the beginning of the end. Archway hired him as the assistant director of security. Nice job, nice pay, plus he was pulling in the twenty-year pension of half pay. He was the one they talked about when they talked about smart moves. Now, with all the baggage the LAPD carried – the King beating, the riots, the Christopher Commission, O. J. Simpson and Mark Fuhrman – a retiring dick would be lucky if a place like Archway hired him to work the front gate.

'Harry Bosch,' Meachum said, leaning down to look in. 'What it is, what it is?'

The first thing Bosch had noticed was that Meachum had gotten his teeth capped since he'd last seen him.

'Chuckie. Long time. This is my partner, Kiz Rider.'

Rider nodded and Meachum nodded and studied her a moment. Black female detectives were a rarity in his day, even though he hadn't been off the job more than five years.

'So what's shaking, Detectives? Why'd you want to go and pull me out of the hot tub?'

He smiled, showing off the teeth. Bosch guessed he knew that they had been noticed.

'We got a case. We want to take a look at the vic's office.'

'It's here? Who's the stiff?'

'Anthony N. Aliso. TNA Productions.'

Meachum crinkled his eyes. He had the deep tan of a golfer who never misses his Saturday morning start and usually gets away for at least nine once or twice during the week.

'Doesn't do anything for me, Harry. You sure he—'

'Look it up, Chuck. He's here. Was.'

'All right, tell you what, park the car over in the main lot and we'll go back to my office, grab a cup and look this guy up.'

He pointed toward a lot directly through the gate and Bosch did as instructed. The lot was almost empty and was next to a huge soundstage with an outside wall painted powder blue with puffs of white clouds. It was used for shooting exteriors when the real sky was too brown with smog.

They followed Meachum on foot to the studio security offices. Entering the suite, they passed by a glass-walled office in which a man in a brown Archway Security outfit sat at a desk surrounded by banks of video monitors. He was reading the *Times* sports page, which he quickly dropped into a trash can next to the desk when he saw Meachum.

Bosch saw that Meachum didn't seem to notice because he had been holding the door open for them. When he turned, he casually saluted the man in the glass office and led Bosch and Rider back to his office.

Meachum slid in behind his desk and turned to his computer. The monitor screen depicted an intergalactic battle among assorted space ships. Meachum hit one key and the screen saver disappeared. He asked Bosch to spell Aliso's name and he punched it into the computer. He then tilted the monitor so Bosch and Rider couldn't see the screen. Bosch was annoyed by this but he didn't say anything. After a few moments, Meachum did.

'You're right. He was here. Tyrone Power Building. Had one of the little cubbyholes they rent to nonplayers. Three-office suite. Three losers. They share a secretary who comes with the rent.'

'How long's he been here? That say?'

'Yeah. Almost seven years.'

'What else you got there?'

Meachum looked at the screen.

'Not much. No record of problems. He complained once about somebody dinging his car in the parking lot. Says here he drove a Rolls-Royce. Probably the last guy in Hollywood who hadn't traded in his Rolls on a Range Rover. That's tacky, Bosch.'

'Let's go take a look.'

'Well, I'll tell you what, why don't you and Detective Riley go out there and grab a cup of joe while I make a call about that. I'm not sure what our procedure is for this.'

'First of all, Chuck, it's Rider, not Riley. And second, we're running a homicide investigation here. Whatever your procedures are, we are expecting you to allow us access.'

'You're on private property here, buddy. You've got to keep that in mind.'

'I will.' Bosch stood up. 'And when you make your call, the thing you should keep in mind is that so far the media haven't gotten wind of any of this. I didn't think it would be good to pull Archway into this sort of thing, especially since we don't know for sure what's involved here. You can tell whoever you're calling that I'll try to keep it that way.'

Meachum smirked and shook his head.

'Still the same old Bosch. Your way or the highway.'

'Something like that.'

While waiting, Bosch had time to gulp down a cup of lukewarm coffee from a pot that had been on a warmer in the outer office for the better part of the night. It was bitter, but he knew the cup he'd had at the station would not take him through the night. Rider passed on the coffee, instead drinking water from a dispenser in the hallway.

After nearly ten minutes Meachum came out of his office.

'Okay, you got it. But I'll tell you right now that me or one of my people gotta be in there the whole time as observers. That going to be a problem for you, Bosch?'

'No problem.'

'Okay, let's go. We'll take a cart.'

313

On the way out he opened the door to the glass room and stuck his head in.

'Peters, who's roving?'

'Uh, Serrurier and Fogel.'

'Okay, get on the air and tell Serrurier to meet us at Tyrone Power. He's got keys, right?'

'Right.'

'Okay, do it.' Meachum made a motion to close the door but stopped. 'And Peters? Leave the sports page in the trash can.'

They took a golf cart to Tyrone Power Building because it was on the other side of the lot from the security offices. Along the way Meachum waved to a man dressed entirely in black who was coming out of one of the buildings they passed.

'We've got a shoot on New York Street tonight, otherwise I'd take you through there. You'd swear you were in Brooklyn.'

'Never been,' Bosch said.

'Me neither,' Rider added.

'Then it doesn't matter, unless you wanted to see them shooting.'

'The Tyrone Power Building will be just fine.'

'Fine.'

When they got there, another uniformed man was waiting. Serrurier. At Meachum's instructions he first unlocked a door to a reception area that served the three separate offices of the suite, then the door to the office Aliso had used. Meachum then told him to go back out on roving patrol of the studio.

Meachum's calling it a closet was not too far off. Aliso's office was barely large enough for Bosch, Rider and Meachum to stand in together without having to smell each other's breath. It contained a desk with a chair behind it and two more close in front of it. Against the wall behind the desk was a four-drawer file cabinet. The left wall was hung with framed one-sheets advertising two classic films: *Chinatown* and *The Godfather*, both of which had been made down the street at Paramount. Aliso had countered these on the right wall with framed posters of his own efforts, *The Art of the Cape* and *Casualty of Desire*. There were also smaller frames of photos depicting Aliso with various celebrities, many of the shots taken in the same office with Aliso and the celebrity of the moment standing behind the desk smiling.

Bosch first studied the two posters. Each one carried the imprimatur along the top *Anthony Aliso Presents*. But it was the second poster, for *Casualty of Desire*, that caught his attention. The artwork beneath the title of the film showed a man in a white suit carrying a gun down at his side, a desperate look on his face. In larger scale, a woman with flowing dark hair that framed the image looked down on him with sultry eyes. The poster was a rip-off of the scene depicted in the *Chinatown* poster on the other wall. But there was something entrancing about it. The woman, of course, was Veronica Aliso, and Bosch knew that was one reason why.

'Nice-looking woman,' Meachum said from behind him.

'His wife.'

'I see that. Second billing. Only I never heard of her.'

Bosch nodded at the poster.

'I think this was her shot.'

314

'Well, like I said, nice-looking gal. I doubt she looks like that anymore.'

Bosch studied the eyes again and remembered the woman he had seen just an hour ago. The eyes were still as dark and gleaming, a little cross of light at the center of each.

Bosch looked away and began to study the framed photos. He immediately noticed that one of them was of Dan Lacey, the actor who had portrayed Bosch eight years earlier in a mini-series about the search for a serial killer. The studio that had produced it had paid Bosch and his then partner a lot of money to use their names and technical advice. His partner took the money and ran, retired to Mexico. Bosch bought a house in the hills. He couldn't run. He knew the job was his life.

He turned and took in the rest of the small office. There were shelves against the wall near the door and these were piled with scripts and videotapes, no books save for a couple of directories of actors and directors.

'Okay,' Bosch said. 'Chuckie, you stand back by the door and observe like you said. Kiz, why don't you start with the desk and I'll start with the files.'

The files were locked and it took Bosch ten minutes to open them with the picks he got out of his briefcase. It then took an hour just to make a cursory study of the files. The drawers were stocked with notes and financial records regarding the development of several films that Bosch had never heard of. This did not seem curious to him after what Veronica Aliso had said and because he knew little about the film business anyway. But it seemed from his understanding of the files he was quickly scanning that large sums of money had been paid to various film services companies during the production of the films. And what struck Bosch the most was that Aliso seemed to have financed a hell of a nice lifestyle from this little office.

After he was finished going through the fourth and bottom drawer, Bosch stood and straightened his back, his vertebrae popping like dominoes clicking together. He looked at Rider, who was still going through the drawers of the desk.

'Anything?'

'A few things of interest but no smoking gun, if that's what you mean. Aliso's got a flag here from the IRS. His corporation was going to be audited next month. Other than that, there is some correspondence between Tony Aliso and St John, the flavor-of-the-month Mrs Aliso mentioned. Heated words but nothing overtly threatening. I've still got one drawer to go.'

'There's a lot in the files. Financial stuff. We're going to have to go through it all. I'd like you to be the one. You going to be up for it?'

'No problem. What I'm seeing so far is a lot of routine, if not sloppy, business records. It just happens to be the movie business here.'

'I'm going outside to catch a smoke. When you're done there, why don't we switch and you take the files, I'll take the desk.'

'Sounds like a plan.'

Before going out he ran his eyes along the shelves by the door and read the titles of the videotapes. He stopped when he came to the one he was looking for. *Casualty of Desire*. He reached up and took it down. The cover carried the same artwork as the movie poster.

He stepped back and put it on the desk so it would be gathered with things they would be taking. Rider asked what it was.

'It's her movie,' he said. 'I want to watch it.'

'Oh, me too.'

Outside, Bosch stood in the small courtyard by a bronze statue of a man he guessed was Tyrone Power and lit a cigarette. It was a cool night and the smoke in his chest warmed him. The studio grounds were very quiet now.

He walked over to a trash can next to a bench in the courtyard and used it to tip his ashes. He noticed a broken coffee mug at the bottom of the can. There were several pens and pencils scattered in the can as well. He recognized the Archway insignia, the Arc de Triomphe with the sun rising in the middle of the arch, on one of the fragments. He was about to reach into the trash can to pick out what looked like a gold Cross pen when he heard Meachum's voice and turned around.

'She's going places, isn't she? I can tell.'

He was lighting his own cigarette.

'Yeah, that's what I hear. It's our first case together. I don't really know her, and from what I hear I shouldn't try. She's going to the Glass House as soon as the time is right.'

Meachum nodded and flicked his ashes onto the pavement. Bosch watched him glance up toward the roofline above the second floor and give another one of his casual salutes. Bosch looked up and saw the camera moored to the underside of the roof eave.

'Don't worry about it,' Bosch said. 'He can't see you. He's reading about the Dodgers last night.'

'S'pose you're right. Can't get good people these days, Harry. I get guys who like driving around in the carts all day, hoping they're going to be discovered like Clint Eastwood or something. Had a guy run into a wall the other day 'cause he was so intent on talking with a couple of creative execs walking by. There's one of them oxymorons for you. Creative executive . . .'

Bosch was silent. He didn't care about anything that Meachum had just said.

'You ought to come work here, Harry. You've gotta have your twenty in by now. You should pull the pin and then come work for me. Your lifestyle will rise a couple of notches. I guarantee it.'

'No thanks, Chuck. Somehow I just don't see myself tooling around in one of your golf carts.'

'Well, the offer's there. Anytime, buddy. Anytime.'

Bosch put his cigarette out on the side of the trash can and dropped the dead butt inside. He decided that he didn't want to go picking through the can with Meachum watching. He told Meachum he was heading back in.

'Bosch, I gotta tell you something.'

Bosch looked back at him and Meachum raised his hands.

'We're going to have a problem if you want to take anything out of that office without a warrant. I mean, I heard what you said about that tape and now she's in there stacking stuff on the desk to go. But I can't let you take anything.'

'Then you are going to be here all night, Chuck. There are a lot of files in there and a lot of work to do. It'd be a lot easier for us to haul it all back to the bureau now.'

'I know that. I've been there. But this is the position I've been instructed to take. We need the warrant.'

Bosch used the phone on the receptionist's desk to call Edgar, who was still in the detective bureau just beginning the paperwork the case would generate. Bosch told him to drop that work for the moment and start drawing up search warrants for all financial records in Aliso's home and the Archway offices and any being held by his attorney.

'You want me to call the duty judge tonight?' Edgar asked. 'It's almost two in the morning.'

'Do it,' Bosch said. 'When you have 'em signed, bring them out here to Archway. And bring some boxes.'

Edgar groaned. He was getting all the shit work. Nobody liked waking up a judge in the middle of the night.

'I know, I know, Jerry. But it's got to be done. Anything else going on?'

'No. I called the Mirage, talked to a guy in security. The room Aliso used was rebooked over the weekend. It's open now and he's got a hold on it, but it's spoiled.'

'Probably . . . Okay, man, next time you'll eat the bear. Get on those warrants.'

In Aliso's office, Rider was already looking through the files. Bosch told her Edgar was working on a warrant and that they would have to draw up an inventory for Meachum. He also told her to take a break if she wanted but she declined.

Bosch sat down behind the desk. It had the usual clutter. There was a phone with a speaker attachment, a Rolodex, a blotter, a magnetic block that held paper clips to it and a wood carving that said TNA Productions in script. There was also a tray stacked with paperwork.

Bosch looked at the phone and noticed the redial button. He lifted the handset and pushed the button. He could tell by the quick procession of tones that the last call made on the phone had been long distance. After two rings it was answered by a female voice. There was loud music in the background.

'Hello?' she said.

'Yes, hello, who's this?'

She giggled.

'I don't know, who's this?'

'I might have the wrong number. Is this Tony's?'

'No, it's Dolly's.'

'Oh, Dolly's. Okay, uh, then where are you located?'

She giggled again.

'On Madison, where do you think? How do you think we got the name?'

'Where's Madison?'

'We're in North Las Vegas. Where are you coming from?'

'The Mirage.'

'Okay, just follow the boulevard out front to the north. You go all the way past downtown and past a bunch of cruddy areas and into North Las Vegas. Madison is your third light after you go under the overpass. Take a left and we're a block down on your left. What's your name again?'

'It's Harry.'

'Well, Harry, I'm Rhonda. As in . . .'

Bosch said nothing.

317

'Come on, Harry, you're supposed to say, "Help me, Rhonda, help, help me, Rhonda." '

She sang the line from the old Beach Boys song.

'Actually, Rhonda, there *is* something you can help me with,' Bosch said. 'I'm looking for a buddy of mine. Tony Aliso. He been in there lately?'

'Haven't seen him this week. Haven't seen him since Thursday or Friday. I was wondering how you got the dressing room number.'

'Yeah, from Tony.'

'Well, Layla isn't here tonight, so Tony wouldn't be coming in anyway, I don't think. But you can come on out. He don't have to be here for you to have a good time.'

'Okay, Rhonda, I'll try to swing by.'

Bosch hung up. He took a notebook out of his pocket and wrote down the name of the business he had just called, the directions to it and the names Rhonda and Layla. He drew a line under the second name.

'What was that?' Rider asked.

'A lead in Vegas.'

He recounted the call and the inference made about the person named Layla. Rider agreed that it was something to pursue, then went back to the files. Bosch went back to the desk. He studied the things on top of it before going to the things in it.

'Hey, Chuckie?' he asked.

Meachum, leaning against the door with his arms folded in front of him, raised his eyebrows by way of response.

'He's got no phone tape. What about when the receptionist isn't out there? Do phone calls go to the operator or some kind of a phone service?'

'Uh, no, the whole lot's on voice mail now.'

'So Aliso had voice mail? How do I get into it?'

'Well, you've got to have his code. It's a three-digit code. You call the voice mail computer, punch in the code and you pick up your messages.'

'How do I get his code?'

'You don't. He programmed it himself.'

'There's no master code I can break in with?'

'Nope. It's not that sophisticated a system, Bosch. I mean, what do you want, it's phone messages.'

Bosch took out his notebook again and checked the notes for Aliso's birthday.

'What's the voice mail number?' he asked.

Meachum gave him the number and Bosch called the computer. After a beep he punched in 721 but the number was rejected. Bosch drummed his fingers on the desk, thinking. He tried 862, the numbers corresponding with TNA, and a computer voice told him he had four messages.

'Kiz, listen to this,' he said.

He put the phone on speaker and hung up. As the messages were played back Bosch took a few notes, but the first three messages were from men reporting on technical aspects of a planned film shoot, equipment rental and costs. Each call was followed by the electronic voice which reported when on Friday the call had come in.

The fourth message made Bosch lean forward and listen closely. The voice belonged to a young woman and it sounded like she was crying.

318

'Hey, Tone, it's me. Call me as soon as you get this. I almost feel like calling your house. I need you. That bastard Lucky says I'm fired. And for no reason. He just wants to get his dick into Modesty. I'm so . . . I don't want to have to work at the Palomino or any of those other places. The Garden. Forget it. I want to come out there to L.A. Be with you. Call me.'

The electronic voice said the call had come in at 4 a.m. on Sunday – long after Tony Aliso was dead. The caller had not given her name. It was therefore obviously someone Aliso would have known. Bosch wondered if it was the woman Rhonda had mentioned, Layla. He looked at Rider and she just shook her shoulders. They knew too little to judge the significance of the call.

Bosch sat in the desk chair contemplating things a few moments. He opened a drawer but didn't start through it. His eyes traveled up the wall to the right of the desk and roamed across the photos of the smiling Tony Aliso posed with celebrities. Some of them had written notes on the photos but they were hard to read. Bosch studied the photo of his celluloid alter ego, Dan Lacey, but couldn't read the small note scrawled across the bottom of the photo. Then he looked past the ink and realized what he was looking at. On Aliso's desk in the photo was an Archway mug crammed with pens and pencils.

Bosch took the photo off the wall and called Meachum's name. Meachum came over.

'Somebody was in here,' Bosch told him.

'What are you talking about?'

'When was the trash can emptied outside?'

'How the hell would I know? What are—'

'The surveillance camera out there on the roof, how long you keep the tapes?'

Meachum hesitated a second but then answered.

'We roll 'em over every week. We'd have seven days off that camera. It's all stop action, ten frames a minute.'

'Let's go take a look.'

Bosch didn't get home until four. That left him only three hours to sleep before an agreed-upon breakfast meeting with Edgar and Rider at seven-thirty, but he was too strung out on coffee and adrenaline to even think about shutting his eyes.

The house had the sour tang of a fresh-paint smell and he opened the sliders onto the back deck to let in the cool night air. He checked out the Cahuenga Pass below and watched the cars on the Hollywood Freeway cutting through. He was always amazed at how there were always cars on the freeway, no matter what the hour. In L.A. they never stopped.

He thought about putting on a CD, some saxophone music, but instead just sat down on the couch in the dark and lit a cigarette. He thought about the different currents running through the case. Going by the preliminary take on the victim, Anthony Aliso had been a financially successful man. That kind of success usually brought with it a thick insulation from violence and murder. The rich were seldom murdered. But something had gone wrong for Tony Aliso.

Bosch remembered the tape and went to his briefcase, which he had left on the dining room table. Inside it there were two video cassettes, the Archway surveillance tape and the copy of *Casualty of Desire*. He turned on the TV and put the movie in the video player. He began watching in the dark.

After viewing the tape it was obvious to Bosch that the movie deserved the fate it had received. It was badly lit and in some frames the end of a boom microphone hovered above the players. This was particularly jarring in scenes shot in the open desert where there should have been nothing above but blue sky. It was basic filmmaking gone wrong. And added to the amateurish look of the film were the poor performances of the players. The male lead, an actor Bosch had never seen before, was woodenly ineffective in portraying a man desperate to hold on to his young wife, who used sexual frustration and taunting to coerce him into committing crimes, eventually including murder, all for her morbid satisfaction. Veronica Aliso played the wife and was not much better an actor than the male lead.

When lighted well, she was stunningly beautiful. There were four scenes in which she appeared partially nude and Bosch watched these with a voyeuristic fascination. But overall it was not a good role for her, and Bosch also understood why her career, like her husband's, had not moved forward. She might blame her husband and harbor resentment toward him, but the bottom line was that she was like thousands of beautiful women who came to Hollywood every year. Her looks could put a pause in your heart, but she could not act to save her life.

In the climactic scene of the film, in which the husband was apprehended and the wife cut him loose with the cops, she delivered her lines with the conviction and weight of a blank page of typing paper.

'It was him. He's crazy. I couldn't stop him until it was too late. Then I couldn't tell anyone because it . . . it would look like I was the one who wanted them all dead.'

Bosch watched all the way through the credits and then rewound the tape by using the remote. He never got off the couch. He then turned the TV off and put his feet up on the couch. Looking through the open sliders he could see the light of dawn etching the ridgeline across the Pass. He still wasn't tired. He kept thinking about the choices people make with their lives. He wondered what would have happened if the performances had been at least passable and the film had found a distributor. He wondered if that would have changed things now, if it would have kept Tony Aliso out of that trunk.

The meeting at the station with Billets didn't start until nine-thirty. Though the squad room was deserted because of the holiday, they all rolled chairs into the lieutenant's office and closed the door. Billets started things off by saying that members of the local media, apparently having picked up on the case by checking the coroner's over-night log, were already beginning to take a more than routine interest in the Aliso murder. Also, she said, the department weight all the way up the line was questioning whether the investigation should be turned over to the elite Robbery-Homicide Division. This, of course, grated on Bosch. Earlier in his career he had been assigned to RHD. But then a questionable on-duty shooting resulted in his demotion to Hollywood. And so it was particularly upsetting to him to think of turning over the case to the big shots downtown. If OCID had been interested, that would have been easier to accept. But Bosch told Billets that he could not accept turning the case over to RHD after his team had spent almost an entire night without sleep on it and had produced some viable leads. Rider jumped in and agreed with him. Edgar, still riding his sulk over being put on the paperwork, remained silent.

'Your point is well taken,' Billets said. 'But when we're done here, I have to call Captain LeValley at home and convince her we've got a handle on this. So let's go over what we have. You convince me, I'll convince her. She'll then let them know how we feel about it downtown.'

Bosch spent the next thirty minutes talking for the team and carefully recounting the night's investigation. The detective squad's only television/VCR was kept in the lieutenant's office because it wasn't safe to leave it unlocked, even in a police station. He put in the tape Meachum had dubbed off the Archway surveillance tape and queued up the part that included the intruder.

'The surveillance camera this was shot from turns a frame every six seconds, so it's pretty quick and jerky but we've got the guy on it,' Bosch said.

He hit the play button and the screen depicted a grainy black and white view of the courtyard and front of the Tyrone Power Building. The lighting made it appear to be late dusk. The time counter on the bottom of the screen showed the time and date to be eight-thirteen the evening before.

Bosch put the machine on slow motion, but still the sequence he wanted to show Billets was over very quickly. In six quick frames they showed a man go to the door of the building, hunch over the knob and then disappear inside.

'Actual time at the door was about thirty to thirty-five seconds,' Rider said. 'It may look from the tape like he had a key, but that's too long to open a door with a key. The lock was picked. Somebody good and fast.'

'Okay, here he comes back out,' Bosch said.

When the time counter hit eight-seventeen, the man was captured on the video emerging from the doorway. The video jumped and the man was in the courtyard heading toward the trash can, then it jumped and the man was walking away from the trash can. Then he was gone. Bosch backed the tape up and froze it on the last image of the man as he walked from the trash can. It was the best image. It was dark and the man's face was blurred but still possibly recognizable if they ever found someone to compare it to. He was white, with dark hair and a stocky, powerful build. He wore a golf shirt with short sleeves, and the watch on his right wrist, visible just above one of the black gloves he wore, had a chrome band that glinted with the reflection of the courtyard light. Above the wrist was the dark blur of a tattoo on the man's forearm. Bosch pointed these things out to Billets and added that he would be taking the tape to SID to see if this last frame, the best of those showing the intruder, could be sharpened in any way by computer enhancement.

'Good,' Billets said. 'Now, what do you think he was doing in there?'

'Retrieving something,' Bosch said. 'From the time he goes in until he comes out, we've got less than four minutes. Not a lot of time. Plus he had to pick the interior door to Aliso's office. Whatever he is doing in there, he knocks an Archway mug off the desk and it breaks on the floor. He does what he was there to do, then gathers up the broken mug and the pens and dumps them in the trash can on his way out. We found the broken mug and the pens in the can last night.'

'Any prints?' Billets asked.

'Once we figured there was a break-in, we backed out and had Donovan come on out when he was done with the Rolls. He got prints but nothing we can use. He got Aliso's and mine and Kiz's. As you can see on the video, the guy wore gloves.'

'Okay.'

Bosch involuntarily yawned and Edgar and Rider followed suit. He drank from the cup of stale coffee he had brought into the office with him. He had long had the caffeine jitters but knew if he stopped feeding the beast now he would quickly crash.

'And the theory on what this intruder was retrieving?' Billets asked.

'The broken mug puts him at the desk rather than the files,' Rider said. 'Nothing in the desk seemed disturbed. No empty files, nothing like that. We think it was a bug. Somebody put a bug in Aliso's phone and couldn't afford to let us find it. The phone was right next to the mug in the pictures on Aliso's walls. The intruder somehow knocked it over. Funny thing is, we never checked the phone for a bug. If whoever this guy was had left well enough alone, we probably would have never tumbled to it.'

'I've been to Archway,' Billets said. 'It's got a wall around it. It's got its own private security force. How's this guy get in? Or are you suggesting an inside job?'

'Two things,' Bosch said. 'There was a film shooting in progress at the studio on the New York Street set. That meant a lot of people in and out of the front gate. Maybe this guy was able to slip through with part of the shooting crew. The direction in which he walks off in the video is to the north. That's where New York Street is. The gate is to the south. Also, the north side of the studio butts up against the Hollywood Cemetery. You're right, there is a wall. But at night, after the cemetery is closed, it's dark and secluded. Our guy could've climbed the wall there. Whatever way he did it, he had practice.'

'What do you mean?'

'If he was taking a bug out of Tony Aliso's phone, it had to have been planted there in the first place.'

Billets nodded.

'Who do you think he was?' she asked quietly.

Bosch looked at Rider to see if she wanted to answer. When she didn't speak, he did.

'Hard to say. The timing is the catch. Aliso's probably been dead since Friday night, his body's not found till about six last night. Then this break-in comes at eight-thirteen. That's after Aliso's been found and after people start finding out about it.'

'But eight-thirteen, that's before you talked to the wife?'

'Right. So that kind of threw a wrench into it. I mean, I was all set to say let's go full speed on the wife and see what we get. Now, I'm not so sure. See, if she's involved, this break-in doesn't make sense.'

'Explain.'

'Well, first you've got to figure out why he was being bugged. And what's the most likely answer? The wife put a PI or somebody on Tony to see if he was screwing around. Okay?'

'Okay.'

'Now, saying that's the case, if the wife was involved in putting her husband down into that trunk, why would she or her PI or whoever wait until last night – this is after the body's been found – to pull the bug out of there? It doesn't make sense. It only makes sense if the two things were not related, if the killing and the bug are separate. Understand?'

'I think so.'

'And that's why I'm not ready to chuck everything and just look at the wife. Personally, I think she might be good for this. But there's too much we don't know right now. It doesn't feel right to me. There's something else running through all of this, and we don't know what yet.'

Billets nodded and looked at all the investigators.

'This is good. I know there isn't a lot that is solid yet, but it's still good work. Anything else? What about the prints Art Donovan pulled off the victim's jacket last night?'

'For now we've struck out. He put them on AFIS, NCIC, the whole works, and got blanked.'

'Damn.'

'They're still valuable. We come up with a suspect, the prints could be a clincher.'

'Anything else from the car?'

'No,' Bosch said.

'Yes,' Rider said.

Billets raised her eyebrows at the contradiction.

'One of the prints Donovan found on the inside lip of the trunk lid,' Rider said. 'It came back to Ray Powers. He's the P-3 who found the body. He overstepped when he popped the trunk. He obviously left his print when he opened it. We caught it and no harm, no foul, but it was sloppy work and he should have never opened the trunk in the first place. He should've called us.'

Billets glanced at Bosch and he guessed she was wondering why he hadn't brought this to her attention. He looked down at her desk.

'Okay, I'll take care of it,' Billets said. 'I know Powers. He's been around and he should certainly know procedure.'

Bosch could have defended Powers with the explanation the cop had given the day before but he let it go. Powers wasn't worth it. Billets went on.

'So where do we go from here?'

'Well, we've got a lot of ground to cover,' Bosch said. 'I once heard this story about a sculptor and somebody asked him how he turned a block of granite into a beautiful statue of a woman. And he said that he just chips away everything that isn't the woman. That's what we have to do now. We've got this big block of information and evidence. We've got to chip away everything that doesn't count, that doesn't fit.'

Billets smiled and Bosch suddenly felt embarrassed about the analogy, though he believed it was accurate.

'What about Las Vegas?' she asked. 'Is that part of the statue or the part we need to chip away?'

323

Now Rider and Edgar were smiling.

'Well, we've got to go there, for one thing,' Bosch said, hoping he didn't sound defensive. 'Right now all we know is that this victim went there and was dead pretty soon after he came back. We don't know what he did there, whether he won, lost, whether somebody tailed him back here from there. For all we know, he could've hit a jackpot there and was followed back here and ripped off. We've got a lot of questions about Las Vegas.'

'Plus, there's the woman,' Rider said.

'What woman?' Billets asked.

'Right,' Bosch said. 'The last call made on Tony Aliso's office line was to a club in North Las Vegas. I called it and got the name of a woman I think he was seeing over there. Layla. There was—'

'Layla? Like that song?'

'I guess. There also was a message from an unnamed woman on his office line. I think it might have been this Layla. We've got to talk to her.'

Billets nodded, made sure Bosch was done and then laid down the battle plan.

'All right,' Billets said. 'First off, all media inquiries are to be directed to me. The best way to control information on this is to have it come from one mouth. For the moment, we'll tell the reporters it is obviously under investigation and we are leaning toward a possible carjacking or robbery scenario. It's innocuous enough and will probably appease them. Everyone okay with that?'

The three detectives nodded.

'Okay, I'm going to make a case with the captain to keep the case here with us. It looks to me like we have three or four avenues which need to be pursued vigorously. Granite that we have to chip away at, as Harry would say.

'Anyway, it will also help me with the captain if we are already scrambling on these things. So, Harry, I want you to get on a plane as soon as possible and get to Vegas. I want you on that end of it. But if there's nothing there, I want you to get in and get out. We'll need you back here. Okay?'

Bosch nodded. It would have been his choice if he were the one making the decisions, but he felt a pang of discomfort that she was doing it.

'Kiz, you stick with the financial trail. I want to be in a position of knowing everything about this guy Anthony Aliso by tomorrow morning. You're also going to have to go up to the house with the search warrant, so while you are there, take another shot at the wife, see what else you can get about the marriage when you're picking up the records. I don't know, if you get a chance, sit down with her, try to get a heart-to-heart.'

'I don't know,' Rider said. 'I think we're past the heart-to-heart. She's a smart woman, smart enough to already know we're taking a look at her. I almost think that to be safe we've got to advise her next time any of us talk to her. It was pretty close last night.'

'Use your judgment on that,' Billets said. 'But if you advise, she's probably going to call her lawyer.'

'I'll see what I can do.'

'And Jerry, you—'

'I know, I know, I've got the paper.'

324

It was the first time he had spoken in fifteen minutes. Bosch thought he was carrying his sulk to the limit.

'Yes, you have the paper. But I also want you on the civil cases and this screenwriter guy who was having the dispute with Aliso. It sounds to me to be the longest shot, but we've got to cover everything. Get that cleared up and it will help narrow our focus.'

Edgar mock-saluted her.

'Also,' she said, 'while Harry's putting together the trail in Vegas, I want you to put it together from the airport here. We've got his parking stub. I think you should start there. When I talk to the media I'll also give a detailed description of the car – can't be that many white Clouds around – and say we're looking for anyone who might've seen it Friday night. I'll say we're trying to re-create the victim's ride from the airport. Maybe we'll get lucky and get some help from the John Qs out there.'

'Maybe,' Edgar said.

'Okay then, let's do it,' Billets said.

The three of them stood up while Billets stayed seated. Bosch took his time taking the tape out of the VCR so that the other two were out of the office when he was done, and he was alone with Billets.

'I'd heard that you didn't have any actual time on a homicide table while you were coming up,' he said to her.

'That's true. My only job as an actual detective was working sexual crimes in Valley Bureau.'

'Well, for what it's worth, I would have assigned things just the way you just did.'

'But did it annoy you that I did it instead of you?'

Bosch thought a moment.

'I'll get over it.'

'Thank you.'

'No problem. Listen, that thing about Powers leaving his print, I probably would have told you about it, but I didn't think this meeting was the right time. I chewed him out for opening the car yesterday. He said if he hadn't opened it and waited for us to check it out, the car would probably still be sitting out there. He is an asshole but he makes a point.'

'I understand.'

'You pissed at me for not telling you?'

Billets thought a moment.

'I'll get over it.'

Bosch fell asleep a few minutes after belting himself into a window seat on the Southwest shuttle from Burbank to Las Vegas. It was a deep, dreamless sleep and he didn't wake until the clunk of the landing gear hitting the tarmac jolted him forward. As the plane taxied to its gate he came out of the fog and felt himself re-energized by the hour-long rest.

It was high noon and 104 degrees when he walked out of the terminal. As he headed toward the garage where his rental car was waiting, he felt his newfound energy being leached away by the heat. After finding his car in its assigned parking stall, he put the air-conditioning on high and headed toward the Mirage.

Bosch had never liked Las Vegas, though he came often on cases. It shared a kinship with Los Angeles; both were places desperate people ran to. Often, when they ran from Los Angeles, they came here. It was the only place left. Beneath the veneer of glitz and money and energy and sex beat a dark heart. No matter how much they tried to dress her up with neon and family entertainment, she was still a whore.

But if any place could sway him from that opinion it was the Mirage. It was the symbol of the new Las Vegas, clean, opulent, legit. The windows of its tower glinted gold in the sun. And inside no money had been spared in its rich casino design. As Bosch walked through the lobby he was first mesmerized by the white tigers in a huge glassed-in environment that any zookeeper in the world would salivate over. Next, as he waited in line to check in, he eyed the huge aquarium behind the front desk. Sharks lazily turned and moved back and forth behind the glass. Just like the white tigers.

When it was Bosch's turn to check in, the desk clerk noticed a flag on his reservation and called security. A dayshift supervisor named Hank Meyer appeared and introduced himself. He said that Bosch would have the complete cooperation of the hotel and casino.

'Tony Aliso was a good and valued customer,' he said. 'We want to do what we can to help. But it's highly unlikely that his death had anything to do with his stay here. We run the cleanest ship in the desert.'

'I know that, Hank,' Bosch said. 'And I know it is a reputation you don't want blemished. I'm not expecting to find anything inside the Mirage, but I need to go through the motions. So do you, right?'

'Right.'

'Did you know him?'

'No, I didn't. I've been on day shift the entire three years I've been here. From what I understand, Mr Aliso primarily gambled at night.'

Meyer was about thirty and had the clean-cut image that the Mirage, and now all of Las Vegas, wanted to present to the world. He went on to explain that the room Aliso had last stayed in at the hotel was sealed and was being held that way for Bosch's inspection. He gave Bosch the key and asked that he return it as soon as he was finished with the room. He also said the poker pit dealers and sports book clerks who worked the night shift would be made available for interviews. All of them knew Aliso because of his regular visits.

'You have an eye in the sky over the poker tables?'

'Uh, yes, we do.'

'You have video from Thursday going into Friday? I'd like to see it if you do.'

'That won't be a problem.'

Bosch made arrangements to meet Meyer at the second-floor security office at four. That was when the casino shifts changed and the dealers who knew Aliso would report for work. He could look at the surveillance tape from the poker pit's overhead camera then as well.

A few minutes later, alone in his room, Bosch sat on the bed and looked around. The room was smaller than he had expected but it was very nice, by far the most comfortably appointed room he had ever seen in Las Vegas. He pulled the phone off the side table onto his lap and called the Hollywood Division to check in. Edgar picked up the line.

'It's Bosch.'

'Well, the Michelangelo of murder, the Rodin of homicide.'

'Funny. So what's going on over there?'

'Well, for one thing, Bullets won the battle,' Edgar said. 'Nobody from RHD has come around to snatch the case.'

'That's good. What about you? You making any progress?'

'I almost have the murder book up to speed. I have to put it aside now, though. The screenwriter is coming in at one-thirty for a sit-down. Says he doesn't need a lawyer.'

'Okay, I'll leave you to it. Tell the lieutenant I checked in.'

'Yeah, and by the way, she wants another confab on how things are going at six. You should call in and we'll put you on the speaker.'

'Will do.'

Bosch sat on the bed a few moments wishing he could lie back on it and sleep. But he knew he couldn't. He had to drive the case forward.

He got up and unpacked his overnighter, hanging his two shirts and one pair of pants in the closet. He put his extra underwear and socks on the closet shelf, then left the room and took an elevator to the top floor. The room Aliso had used was at the end of the corridor. The card key Meyer had given him worked without a problem and he stepped into a room about twice the size of his own. It was a combination bedroom and sitting room and had an oval Jacuzzi next to the windows that looked out across the expanse of the desert and the smooth cocoa-colored mountain chain to the northwest of the city. Directly below was a view of the pool and the hotel's porpoise-habitat attraction. Looking down, he could see one of the gray fish

330

moving beneath the shimmering water. It looked as out of place as Bosch felt in the suite he stood in.

'Dolphins in the desert,' he said out loud.

The room was plush by any standards in any city and obviously was kept for high rollers. Bosch stood by the bed for a few moments and just looked around. There was nothing that seemed out of place and the thick carpet had the uniformed waves left by a recent vacuuming. He guessed that if there had been anything of evidentiary value in the room it was gone now. But still he went through the motions. He looked under the bed and in the drawers. Behind the bureau he found a matchbook from a local Mexican restaurant called La Fuentes, but there was no telling how long it had been there.

The bathroom was tiled in pink marble floor to ceiling. The fixtures were polished brass. Bosch looked around for a moment but saw nothing of interest. He opened the glass door to the shower stall and looked in and also found nothing. But as he was closing the door his eyes caught on something on the drain. He reopened the door and looked down, then pressed his finger on the tiny speck of gold caught in the rubber sealant around the drain fitting. He raised his finger and found the tiny piece of glitter stuck to his finger. He guessed that it was a match to the pieces of glitter found in the cuffs of Tony Aliso's pants. Now all he needed was to figure out what they were and where they had come from.

The Metro Police Department was on Stewart Street in downtown. Bosch stopped at the front desk and explained he was an out-of-town investigator wanting to make a courtesy check-in with the homicide squad. He was directed to the third-floor detective bureau, where a desk man escorted him through a deserted squad room to the commander's office. Captain John Felton was a thick-necked, deeply tanned man of about fifty. Bosch figured he had probably given the welcome speech to at least a hundred cops from all over the country in the last month alone. Las Vegas was that kind of place. Felton asked Bosch to sit down and he gave him the standard spiel.

'Detective Bosch, welcome to Las Vegas. Lucky for you I decided to come in on the holiday to take care of some of this paperwork that haunts me. Otherwise, there'd be nobody here. Anyway, I hope you find your stay enjoyable and productive. If there is anything you need, don't hesitate to call. I can promise you nothing, but if you request something that is within my power to provide, I will be more than happy to provide it. So, that out of the way, why don't you tell me what brings you here?'

Bosch gave him a quick rundown on the case. Felton wrote down the name Tony Aliso and the last days he was known to have stayed in Las Vegas and where.

'I'm just trying to run down his activities on the days he was here.'

'You think he was followed from here and then taken off in L.A.?'

'I don't think anything at the moment. We don't have evidence of that.'

'And I hope you won't find any. That's not the kind of press we want to get in L.A. What else you got?'

Bosch pulled his briefcase onto his lap and opened it.

'I've got two sets of prints taken off the body. We—'

'The body?'

'He was wearing a treated leather jacket. We got the prints with the laser. Anyway, we ran them on AFIS, NCIC, California DOJ, the works, but got nothing. I thought maybe you'd run them through your own computer, see what happens.'

While the Automated Fingerprint Identification System used by the LAPD was a computer network of dozens of fingerprint databases across the country, it didn't connect them all. And most big-city police departments had their own private databases. In Vegas they would be prints taken from people who applied for jobs for the city or the casinos. They were also prints taken from people on the sly, prints the department shouldn't legally have because their owners had simply fallen under the suspicion of the department but had never been arrested. It was against this database that Bosch was hopeful Felton would check the sets from the Aliso case.

'Well, let me see what you have,' Felton said. 'I can't promise anything. We've probably gotta few that the national nets don't, but it's a long shot.'

Bosch handed over print cards Art Donovan had prepared for him.

'So you are starting at the Mirage?' the captain asked after he put the cards to the side of his desk.

'Yeah. I'll show his picture around, go through the motions, see what I can come up with.'

'You're telling me everything you know, right?'

'Right,' Bosch lied.

'Okay.' Felton opened a desk drawer and took out a business card and handed it over to Bosch. 'That's got my office and pager on it. Call me if anything comes up. I've got the pager with me at all times. Meantime, I'll get back to you about the prints, one way or the other, by tomorrow morning.'

Bosch thanked him and left. In the lobby of the police station he called the SID office at LAPD and asked Donovan if he'd had time to check out the tiny pieces of glitter they had found in the cuffs of Tony Aliso's pants.

'Yeah, but you aren't going to like it,' Donovan said. 'It's just glitter. Tinted aluminum. You know, like they use in costuming and in celebrations. Your guy probably went to a party or something, they were throwing this stuff around, maybe popping it out of party favors or something, and some of it got on him. He could brush off what he could see, but he didn't see the particles that fell into the cuffs of his pants. They stayed.'

'Okay. Anything else?'

'Uh, no. Not on the evidence at least.'

'Then on what?'

'Well, Harry, you know the guy from OCID that you were talking on the phone with last night while we were in the shed?'

'Carbone?'

'Yeah, Dominic Carbone. Well, he dropped by the lab today. He was asking questions about what we found last night.'

Bosch's vision darkened. He said nothing and Donovan continued.

'He said he was here on something else and was just acting curious. But, Harry, I don't know. It seemed more than just a passing interest, if you know what I mean.'

'Yeah, I know what you mean. How much did you tell him?'

'Well, before I caught on and started wondering what was going on, I sort of let slip we pulled prints off the jacket. Sorry, Harry, but I was proud. It's rare that we pull righteous prints off a dead guy's jacket, and I guess I was sort of braggin' about it.'

'It's okay. You tell him we didn't get anything with them?'

'Yeah, I said they came back clean. But then . . . then he asked for a copy of the set, said he might be able to do something with them, whatever that means.'

'What did you do?'

'What do you think, I gave him a set.'

'You what?'

'Just kidding, Harry. I told him to call you if he wanted a set.'

'Good. What else you tell him?'

'That's it, Harry.'

'Okay, Art, it's cool. I'll check you later.'

'See you, Harry. Hey, where are you, anyway?'

'Vegas.'

'Really? Hey, put down a five for me on seven on the roulette wheel. Do it one time. I'll pay you when you get back. Unless I win. Then you pay me.'

Bosch got back to his room forty-five minutes before his appointment with Hank Meyer. He used the time to shower, shave and change into one of his fresh shirts. He felt refreshed, ready to go back into the desert heat.

Meyer had arranged to have the sports book clerks and dealers who worked the poker pit on the previous Thursday and Friday evening shifts to be interviewed one at a time in his office. There were six men and three women. Eight were dealers and one was the clerk Aliso always placed his sports bets with. During any shift, the poker dealers rotated around the casino's six poker tables every twenty minutes. This meant that all eight had dealt cards to Aliso during his last visit to Las Vegas, and by virtue of his regular trips to the casino, they readily recognized him and knew him.

With Meyer sitting by watching, Bosch quickly moved through the interviews with the poker dealers in an hour. He was able to establish that Aliso usually played the five-to-ten table. This meant each hand started with a five-dollar ante and each deal carried a minimum bet of five dollars and a maximum of ten. Three raises were allowed per deal. Since the game was seven card stud, that meant there were five deals per hand. Bosch quickly realized that if a table was full with eight players, each hand could easily result in several hundred dollars being at stake in the pot. Aliso was playing in a league far removed from the Friday night poker games Bosch had participated in with the dicks from the detective bureau.

According to the dealers, Aliso had played for about three hours on Thursday night and had come out about even. He played another two hours early Friday evening, and it was estimated that he left the tables a couple thousand short. None of them recalled Aliso ever being a big winner or loser during previous visits. He always came out a few thousand light or heavy. He seemed to know when to quit.

The dealers also noted that Aliso was quick with the gratuity. His standard tip was ten dollars in chips for every win, a twenty-five chip on particularly big pots. It was that practice more than anything else that endeared him to their memories. He always played alone, drank gin and tonic and small-talked with the other players. In recent months, the dealers said, Aliso had been in the company of a young blond woman, barely into her twenties. She never played but would work the slots nearby and come back to Tony when she needed more money. Tony never introduced her to anybody and none of the dealers ever overheard her name. In his notebook, where Bosch jotted this down, he wrote 'Layla?' after this entry.

After the dealers came Aliso's favorite sports book clerk. She was a mousy-looking bottle-blonde named Irma Chantry. She lit a cigarette as soon as she sat down and talked in a voice that indicated she had never gone long without a smoke. She said that on both of the last two nights Aliso had been in town he had bet on the Dodgers.

'He had a system,' she said. 'He always doubled up until he won.'

'How do you mean?'

'Well, that first night he put a grand down on the Dodgers to win. They lost. So the next day he comes in and puts down two big ones on them again. They won. So after you take out the casino vig, he was almost a grand up for the trip. Except he never picked it up.'

'He didn't collect?'

'Nope. But that's not unusual. His chit was good as long as he kept it. He could come in anytime and we'd stick it in the computer. It'd happened before. He'd win but he wouldn't collect until the next time he was in town.'

'How do you know he didn't take it to another clerk?'

'Tony wouldn't do that. He always cashed out with me, that way he could tip me. He always said I was his lucky charm.'

Bosch thought a moment. He knew the Dodgers had played at home Friday night and Aliso's plane left Las Vegas at ten. Therefore, it was a pretty safe bet that Aliso had to be at McCarran International or already on his plane heading back to L.A. before the game was over. But there was no betting receipt found in his wallet or on his person. Harry considered the missing briefcase again. Would it have been in there? Could a betting slip worth four thousand dollars minus the vig be motive for his murder? It seemed unlikely, but still, it was something to pursue. He looked at Irma, who was drawing so hard on her cigarette that he could see the outline of her teeth on her cheeks.

'What if somebody else cashed the bet? With another clerk. Is there any way to tell that?'

Irma hesitated and Meyer broke in.

'There's a good chance,' he said. 'Each receipt is coded with a clerk number and time the bet was placed.'

He looked at Irma.

'Irma, you remember taking very many two-thousand-dollar bets on the Dodgers on Friday?'

'Nope, not a one, other than Tony's.'

'We'll get on it,' Meyer said to Bosch. 'We'll start going through the cashed receipts going back to Friday night. If Mr Aliso's bet was cashed, then we'll know when it was cashed and we'll have video of who cashed it.'

Bosch looked at Irma again. She was the only one of the casino employees he had talked to who had referred to Aliso by his first name. He wanted to ask her if there was something more than a gambling relationship between them. But he knew that it was likely that employees were forbidden by the casino to date or fraternize with the guests. He couldn't ask her in front of Meyer and expect a straight reply. He made a mental note to track Irma down later and then excused her from the interview.

Bosch looked at his watch and saw he had forty minutes until the conference call with Billets and the others. He asked Meyer if he'd had a chance to get the surveillance tapes from the eye in the sky over the poker pit for Thursday and Friday.

'I just want to see the guy gambling,' he said. 'I want to get a feel for him in life.'

'I understand and, yes, the tapes are ready for viewing. I told you we wanted to cooperate completely.'

They left the office and walked down a corridor to a tech room. The room was dimly lit and very quiet except for the thrum of an air conditioner. There were six consoles arranged in two lines where men in gray blazers sat and watched banks of six video monitors per console. On the video screens Bosch could see various overhead views of gambling tables. Each console had an electronic control board that allowed the operator to change focus or magnification of a particular camera view.

'If they wanted to,' Meyer whispered, 'they could tell you what cards a player is holding at any black jack table in the house. It's amazing.'

Meyer led Bosch to a supervisor's office off the tech room. There was more video equipment as well as a bank of tape storage units. There was a small desk and another man in a gray blazer sat behind it. Meyer introduced him as Cal Smoltz, the supervisor.

'Cal, are we set up?'

'This screen here,' Smoltz said, pointing to one of the fifteen-inch monitors. 'We'll start with Thursday. I had one of the dealers come in and ID your guy. He shows up at eight-twenty on Thursday and plays until eleven.'

He started the tape. It was grainy black and white, similar to the quality of the Archway surveillance tape, but this one was filmed in real time. No jerking movements. It began with the man Bosch recognized as Aliso being led to an open chair at a table by a pit boss. The pit boss carried a rack of chips which he put down on the table in front of Aliso's spot. Aliso nodded and exchanged smiles with the dealer, a woman Bosch had interviewed earlier, and began to play.

'How much in the rack?' Bosch asked.

'Five hundred,' Smoltz said. 'I've already gone through this on fast speed. He never buys another rack and at the end when he cashes out, he looks like he's just shy of a full rack. You want it on real time or fast speed?'

'Speed it up.'

Bosch watched closely as the tape sped through the hours. He saw Aliso take four gin and tonics, fold early on most of the deals, win five big pots and lose six others. It was pretty uneventful. Smoltz slowed the tape down when the time counter neared eleven, and Bosch watched as Aliso called for the pit boss, cashed out and left the frame of the camera.

'Okay,' Smoltz said. 'On Friday, we have two tapes.'

'How come?' Bosch asked.

'He played at two tables. When he first showed up, there wasn't a seat open at the five-and-dime table. We only have one because there aren't that many customers who want to play for those stakes. So he played on a one-to-five until something came open. This tape is the one-to-five, the cheaper table.'

Another video began and Bosch watched as Aliso went through the same motions as in the other tape. This time, Bosch noticed, Aliso was wearing the leather sports jacket. He also noticed that while Aliso exchanged the routine nod and smile with the dealer, he thought he saw Aliso nod at a player across the table. It was a woman and she nodded back. But the angle of the camera was bad and Bosch could not see her face. He told Smoltz to keep it on real-time play and he watched the tape for a few minutes, waiting to see if any other acknowledgment would pass between the two players.

It appeared that no further communication was occurring between the two. But five minutes into the tape a dealer rotation occurred, and when the new dealer sat down, also a woman Bosch had interviewed an hour earlier, she acknowledged both Aliso and the woman across the table from him.

'Can you freeze it there?' Bosch asked.

Without answering, Smoltz froze the image on the screen.

'Okay,' Bosch said. 'Which dealer is that?'

'That's Amy Rohrback. You talked to her.'

'Right. Hank, could you bring her back up here?'

'Uh, sure. Can I ask why?'

'This player,' Bosch said, pointing on the screen to the woman across from Aliso. 'She acknowledged Aliso when he sat down. Amy Rohrback just acknowledged her. She must be a regular. She knew Aliso and Rohrback. I might want to talk to her and your dealer might know her name.'

'Okay, I'll go get her, but if she's in the middle of a dealing rotation I'll have to wait.'

'That's fine.'

While Meyer went down to the casino, Bosch and Smoltz continued to review the tapes on fast speed. Aliso played for twenty-five minutes at the one-to-five table before the pit boss came around, picked up his rack of chips and moved him to the more expensive five-to-ten table. Smoltz put in the tape for that table and Aliso played there, losing miserably, for two more hours. Three times he bought five-hundred-dollar racks of chips and each time he quickly lost them. Finally, he put the few remaining chips he had left down as a tip for the dealer and got up and left the table.

The tape was finished and Meyer still hadn't returned with Rohrback. Smoltz said he would spool up the tape with the mystery woman on it so it would be ready. When it was, Bosch told him to fast-forward it to see if there was ever a moment when her face was visible. Smoltz did so and after five minutes of straining to watch the quick movements of the people on the tape, Bosch saw the mystery woman look up at the camera.

'There! Back it up and slow it down.'

Smoltz did so and Bosch watched the screen as the woman took out a cigarette, lit it and leaned her head back, her face toward the ceiling camera, and exhaled. The discharged smoke blurred her image. But before it had done so, Bosch thought he had recognized her. He was frozen to silence. Smoltz backed the tape up to the moment her face was most clearly visible and froze the image on the screen. Bosch just stared silently.

Smoltz was saying something about the image being the best they could hope for when the door opened and Meyer came back in. He was alone.

'Uh, Amy had just started a deal set, so it's going to be another ten minutes or so. I gave her the message to come back up.'

'You can call down there and tell her never mind,' Bosch said, his eyes still on the screen.

'Really? How come?'

'I know who she is.'

'Who is she?'

Bosch was silent a moment. He didn't know if it was seeing her light the cigarette or some pang of deeper anxiety, but he dearly wanted a cigarette.

'Just somebody. I knew her a long time ago.'

Bosch sat on the bed with the phone on his lap, waiting for the conference call. But his mind was far off. He was remembering a woman he had long believed was out of his life. What had it been now, four, five years? His mind was such a rush of thoughts and emotions, he couldn't remember for sure. It had been long enough, he realized. It should be no surprise that she was out of prison by now.

'Eleanor Wish,' he said out loud.

He thought of the jacaranda trees outside her townhouse in Santa Monica. He thought of them making love and the small crescent scar barely visible on her jawline. He remembered the question she had asked him so long ago, when they were making love. 'Do you believe you can be alone and not be lonely?'

The phone rang. Bosch jerked out of his reverie and answered. It was Billets.

'Okay, Harry, we're all here. Can you hear me all right?'

'It's not good but it probably won't get any better.'

'Right, city equipment. Okay, let's start by everybody kind of reporting on the day's events. Harry, you want to go first?'

'All right. There's not a lot to tell.'

He went over the details of what he had done so far, stressing the missing betting receipt as something to watch for. He told of his review of the surveillance tapes but left out mention of his recognizing Eleanor Wish. He had decided that there was no definitive sign of a connection between her and Aliso and that for the time being he would keep it to himself. He ended his summary by telling the others of his plans to check out Dolly's, the place Aliso had last called from his office line at Archway, and the woman named Layla who was mentioned when Bosch called there.

Next it was Edgar's turn. He announced the flavor-of-the-month screenwriter had been cleared through alibi and Edgar's own gut instinct that the young man might have rightfully hated Aliso but was not of the personality type that would act on that hate with a twenty-two.

Edgar said he had also interviewed the employees at the garage where Aliso had his car washed and waxed while he went to Las Vegas. Part of the service was airport pickup, and Edgar said the man who picked Aliso up said that Tony was alone, relaxed and in no hurry.

'It was a routine pickup,' Edgar said. 'Aliso took his car and went home. Gave the guy a twenty-buck tip. So whoever put him down, they intercepted him on the way home. My guess is it was somewhere up there on Mulholland. Lot of deserted curves. You could stop a guy if you did it quick. Probably two people.'

'What did the valet say about luggage?' Bosch asked.

'Oh, yeah,' Edgar said. 'He said that as near as he could remember, Tony had the two bags the wife described, a silver briefcase and one of those hanging bags. He hadn't checked either one for the flight.'

Bosch nodded, though he was alone.

'What about the media?' Bosch said. 'We put anything out yet?'

'It's being handled,' Billets said. 'Media relations is putting out a release first thing tomorrow. It will have a picture of the Rolls. They'll also make the car available at the OPG for video. And I'll be available for sound bites. I'm hoping the stations will pick it up. Anything else, Jerry?'

Edgar concluded by saying he had the murder book up to speed and that he was halfway through the list of plaintiffs from the various lawsuits against Aliso. He said he would be setting up interviews for the next day with others who had allegedly been wronged by Aliso. Lastly, he said he had called the coroner's office and the autopsy on Aliso had not yet been scheduled.

'Okay,' Billets said. 'Kiz, what do you have?'

Rider broke her report into two parts. The first was on her interview with Veronica Aliso, which she covered quickly, saying the woman had been extremely close-mouthed during their morning interview in comparison to the night before when Bosch and Rider brought her the news of her husband's death. The morning session consisted mostly of yes and no answers and a few added details. The couple had been married seventeen years. They had no children. Veronica Aliso had been in two of her husband's films and never worked again.

'You think she talked to a lawyer about talking to us?' Bosch asked.

'She didn't say so, but I think that's exactly what's going on,' Rider said. 'Just getting what I got was like pulling teeth.'

'Okay, what else?' Billets said, trying to keep the discussion moving.

Rider went on to the second part of her day's investigation, which was the focus on the financial records of Anthony Aliso. Even listening on the poor conference line connection, Bosch could tell Kiz was excited about what she had learned so far.

'Basically, this guy's financial portfolio shows an extremely comfortable standard of living. He's got high-five-figure sums in his personal bank accounts, zeroed-out credit cards, that house that has a seven-hundred-thousand mortgage against a value of a million one. That's it, though, as far as what I could find. The Rolls is leased, his wife's Lincoln is leased, and the office we know is leased.'

She paused a moment before going on.

'Incidentally, Harry, if you have the time, here's something you might want to check out over there. Both the cars are leased to his company, TNA Productions, through a dealership over there in Vegas. You might want to check it out if there's time. It's called Ridealong – one word – Incorporated. The address is two thousand and two Industrial Drive, suite three-thirty.'

Bosch's jacket, with his notebook inside it, was on a chair on the other side of the room. He wrote the name and address down on a little pad that was on the night table.

'Okay,' Rider said, 'so now we go on to his business, and this is where it gets pretty interesting. I'm really only halfway through the records we pulled out of his office, but so far it looks like this guy was into a class A scam. And I'm not talking about ripping off some schmuck's student screenplays. I think that was just his side hobby. I'm talking about him running a laundry. I think he was a front for somebody.'

She waited a beat before going on. Bosch moved to the edge of the bed, excitement tickling the back of his neck.

'We've got tax returns, production orders, equipment rentals, pays and owes from the making of several films – more than a dozen. All of it straight-to-video stuff. Like Veronica said, it's just this side of porno. I looked at some of the tapes he had in his office and it was all pretty awful stuff. Not much in the way of narrative unless you count the buildup of tension waiting for the female lead to get naked.

'The only problem is that the ledgers don't match what's on the film and most of the big checks paid by TNA Productions went to mail drops and companies that I'm finding out don't exist anywhere but on paper.'

'How do you mean?' Billets asked.

'I'm saying his business records show a million to a million five going into each of these so-called movies, and you look at the tapes and, I'm telling you, there can't be more than a hundred, maybe two hundred thousand involved. My brother works in the business as an editor, and I know enough to know that the kind of money Aliso's books show being spent on these movies is not being spent on these movies. I think that what he was doing was using these flicks to launder money, lots of money.'

'Run it down, Kiz,' Billets said. 'Just how would he do it?'

'Okay, start with his source. We'll call him Mr X for now. Mr X has a million bucks he shouldn't have. Whether it's from drugs or whatever, he needs to clean it up, legitimize it so he can put it in the bank and spend it without drawing attention. He gives it to Tony Aliso – invests it in Tony's production company. Aliso then makes a cheap movie with it, spending less than a tenth of it.

'But when it comes to keeping the books, he makes it look like he's used all of the money for production costs. He's got checks going out almost weekly to various production companies, prop companies, movie equipment companies. All the checks are in the eight- to nine-thousand range, just under the government reporting limit.'

Bosch listened carefully as she spoke. He had his eyes closed and concentrated. He admired Rider's ability to cull all of this out of the records.

'Okay, then at the end of production, Tony probably dubs a few thousand copies of the flick, sells them or tries to sell them to independent video stores and distributors – because the chains wouldn't touch this crap – and that's that, end of show. But what he has done is turned around and given back to Mr X, his original investor, about eighty cents on the dollar in the form of payments to these dummy companies. It's a shell game. Whoever is behind these companies is being paid with his own money for services *not* rendered. But now the money's legit. It's clean and he can walk into any bank in America and deposit it, pay taxes on it, then spend it. Meantime,

Tony Aliso takes a nice production fee for his end of it and goes on to the next flick. It looks like he was handling two or three of these productions a year and clearing half a million in fees himself.'

They were all silent for a few moments before Rider spoke again.

'There's only one problem,' Rider said.

'He's got the IRS on him,' Bosch said.

'Riiiiiight,' she responded, and he could visualize the smile on her face. 'It's a nice scam but it was about to go down the toilet. The IRS was going to take a look at Tony's books later this month, and there is a good chance that if I could come up with this in just one day, the feds would pick up on it in an hour.'

'That would make Tony a danger to Mr X,' Edgar said.

'Especially if he was going to cooperate with the audit,' Rider added.

Someone on the other end of the line whistled, but Bosch couldn't tell who it was. He guessed it was Edgar.

'So what's next, find Mr X?' Bosch asked.

'For starters,' Rider replied. 'I'm working up a request I'll fax to the state department of corporations tomorrow morning. It's got all the dummy companies on it. Maybe, whoever he is, he was foolish enough to put a real name or address on the incorporation forms. I'm also working on another search warrant. I have the canceled checks from Tony's company. I want the records of the accounts the checks were deposited to, maybe find out where the money went after Tony cleaned it up.'

'What about the IRS?' Bosch asked. 'Have you talked to them?'

'They're closed for the holiday. But according to the notice Aliso got in the mail, there is a criminal prefix on the audit number. That makes me think this wasn't a random audit. They were tipped somehow. There's an agent assigned to it and I'll be on the phone to him first thing in the morning.'

'You know,' Edgar said, 'this whole thing about OCID taking a pass is beginning to stink. Whether Tony was hooked up with the Eye-talians or not, this shit is as organized as organized crime can get. And I'd bet my last button that they'd heard somewhere along the line, whether it was from the IRS or not, about our guy here.'

'I think you're right,' Billets said.

'I forgot to mention something,' Bosch threw in. 'Today I was talking with Art Donovan. He said the guy I talked to at OCID last night, a supe named Carbone, well he just happens to show up over at SID today and starts asking Art about the case. Art says the guy's acting like he's not interested, but he's very interested, you know what I mean?'

Nobody said anything for a long moment.

'So what do we do?' Edgar asked.

Bosch closed his eyes again and waited. Whatever Billets said would determine the course of the case as well as affect his regard for her. Bosch knew what her predecessor would have done. He would have made sure the case was dumped on OCID.

'We don't do anything,' Billets finally said. 'It's our case, we work it. But be careful. If OCID is sniffing around after taking a pass, then there is something going on here we don't know about yet.'

Another silence passed and Bosch opened his eyes. He was liking Billets better all the time.

'Okay,' Billets said. 'I think we should be focusing on Tony's company as a priority. I want to shift most of our attention there. Harry, can you wrap up Vegas quickly and get back here?'

'Unless I find something, I should be out of here before lunch tomorrow. But remember this, last night Mrs Aliso told us that Tony always told her he came to Vegas to see investors. Maybe our Mr X is right here.'

'Could be,' Billets said. 'Okay then, again, people, it's been good work. Let's stay on it.'

They said their good-byes and Bosch put the phone back on the side table. He felt invigorated by the advances of the investigation. He just sat there a moment and reveled in the feeling of the adrenaline jazzing through his body. It had been a long time coming. He squeezed his hands into fists and banged them together.

Bosch stepped out of the elevator and began moving through the casino. It was quieter than most casinos he had been in – there wasn't any yelling or whooping from the craps table, no begging of the dice to come up seven. The people who gambled here were different, Bosch thought. They came with money and they'd leave with money no matter how much they lost. The smell of desperation wasn't here. This was the casino for the well-heeled and thick-walleted.

He passed by a crowded roulette wheel and remembered Donovan's bet. He squeezed between two smoking Asian women, put down a five and asked for a chip but was told it was a twenty-five-dollar-minimum table. One of the Asians pointed with her cigarette across the casino to another roulette table.

'They'll take your five over there,' she said with distaste.

Bosch thanked her and headed over to the cheap table. He put a five chip down on the seven and watched the wheel turn, the little metal ball bouncing over the numbers. It did nothing for him. He knew that true-blue gamblers said it wasn't the winning and losing, it was the anticipation. Whether it was the next card, the fall of the dice or the number the little ball stopped on, it was those few seconds of waiting and hoping and wishing that charged them, that addicted them. But it did nothing for Bosch.

The ball stopped on five and Donovan owed Bosch five. Bosch turned and started looking for the poker pit. He saw a sign and headed that way. It was early, not yet eight, and there were several chairs open at the tables. He checked the faces and did not see Eleanor Wish, though he wasn't really expecting to. Bosch recognized many of the dealers he had interviewed earlier, including Amy Rohrback. He was tempted to take one of the empty chairs at her table and ask how she had recognized Eleanor Wish but figured it wouldn't be cool to question her while she worked.

While he considered what to do, the pit boss stepped up to him and asked if he was waiting to play. Bosch recognized him as the one from the video who had led Tony Aliso to his place at the tables.

'No, I'm just watching,' Bosch said. 'You got a minute while it's slow?'

'A minute for what?'

'I'm the cop who's been interviewing your people.'

'Oh, yeah. Little Hank told me about that.'

He introduced himself as Frank King and Bosch shook his hand.

'Sorry, I couldn't come up. But I don't work on rotation. I had to be here. This is about Tony A, right?'

'Yeah, you knew him, right?'

'Sure, we all knew him. Good guy. Too bad about what happened.'

'How do you know what happened?'

Bosch had specifically not told any of the dealers about Aliso's demise during the interviews.

'Little Hank,' King said. 'He said he got shot up or something in L.A. What do you want, I mean you live in L.A. you take your chances.'

'I guess. How long have you known him?'

'We go back years, me and Tony. I used to be at the Flamingo before the Mirage opened. Tony stayed there back then. He's been coming out here a long time.'

'You ever socialize with him? Outside the casino?'

'Once or twice. But that was usually by accident. I'd be some place and Tony'd just happen to come in or something. We'd have a drink, be cordial, but that was about it. I mean, he was a guest of the hotel and I'm an employee. We weren't buddies, if you know what I mean.'

'I get it. What places did you run into him?'

'Oh, Jesus, I don't know. You're talking – hold on a sec.'

King cashed out a player who was leaving Amy Rohrback's table. Bosch had no idea how much the man had started with, but he was leaving with forty dollars and a frown. King sent him away with a better-luck-next-time salute and then came back to Bosch.

'Like I was saying, I saw him in a couple of bars. You're talking a long time ago. One was the round bar at the Stardust. One of my buddies was the barkeep and I used to drop by there after work time to time. I saw Tony there and he sent over a drink. This was probably three years ago, at least. I don't know what good it does you.'

'Was he alone?'

'No, he was with some broad. Young piece of fluff. Nobody I recognized.'

'All right, what about the other time, when was that?'

'That was maybe last year sometime. I was with a bachelor party – it was for Marty, who runs the craps here – and we all went to get straightened out at Dolly's. It's a strip club on the north side. And Tony was in there, too. He was by hisself and he came over and had a drink. In fact, he bought the whole table a drink. Must've been eight of us. He was a nice guy. That was it.'

Bosch nodded. So Aliso had been a regular at Dolly's going back at least a year. Bosch was planning to go there, to get a line on the woman named Layla. She was probably a dancer, Bosch guessed, and Layla was more than probably not her real name.

'You seen him more recently with anybody?'

'You mean a broad?'

'Yeah, some of the dealers said there was a blonde recently.'

'Yeah, I think I saw him a couple, three times with the blonde. He was giving her the dough to play the machines while he played cards. I don't know who it was, if that's what you mean.'

Bosch nodded.

'That it?' King asked.

'One more thing. Eleanor Wish, you know her? She was playing the cheap table on Friday night. Tony played for a while at the same table. It looked like they knew each other.'

'I know a player named Eleanor. I never knew her last name. She the looker, brown hair, brown eyes, still in nice shape despite, as they say, the encroachment of time?'

King smiled at his clever use of words. Bosch didn't.

'That sounds like her. She a regular?'

'Yeah, I see her in here maybe once a week, maybe less. She's a local, as far as I know. The local players run a circuit. Not all the casinos have live poker, see. It doesn't earn a lot for the house. We have it as a courtesy to our customers, but we hope they play a little poker and a lot of black jack. Anyway, the locals run a circuit so they don't play against the same faces all the time. So they maybe play here one night, over to Harrah's the next, then it's the Flamingo, then maybe they work the downtown casinos a few nights. You know, like that.'

'You mean she's a pro?'

'No, I mean she's a local and she plays a lot. Whether she's got a day job or lives off poker I don't know. I don't think I ever cashed her out for more than two bills. That's not a lot. The other thing is I heard she tips the dealers too well. The pros don't do that.'

Bosch asked King to list all the casinos in the city that he knew offered live poker, then thanked him.

'You know, I doubt you're going to find anything other than Tony knowin' her to say hello to, that's all.'

'Why's that?'

'Too old. She's a nice lookin' gal, but she was too old for Tony. He liked 'em young.'

Bosch nodded and let him go. He then wandered through the casino in a quandary. He didn't know what to do about Eleanor Wish. He was intrigued by what she was doing and King's explanation about her being a once-a-week regular seemed to make her recognition of Aliso innocent enough. But while she most likely had nothing to do with the case, Bosch felt the desire to talk to her. To tell her he was sorry for the ways things had turned out, for the way he had made them turn out.

He saw a bank of pay phones near the front desk and used one to call information. He asked for a listing for Eleanor Wish and got a recording saying the phone number was unlisted at the customer's request. Bosch thought a moment and then dug through the pocket of his jacket. He found the card that Felton, the Metro detectives captain, had given him and paged him. He waited with his hand on the phone so no one else could use it for four minutes before it rang.

'Felton?'

'Yeah, who's this?'

'Bosch. From earlier today?'

'Right. L.A. I still haven't gotten the prints back. I'm expecting to hear something first thing.'

'No, I'm not calling about that. I was wondering if you or any of your people have enough juice with the phone company to get me a listing, number and address.'

'It's unlisted?'

Bosch felt like telling him that he wouldn't be calling if the account was listed but let it go.

'Yeah, unlisted.'

'Who is it?'

'A local. Somebody who was playing poker with Tony Aliso on Friday night.'

'So?'

'So, Captain, they knew each other and I want to talk to her. If you can't help me, fine. I'll find her some other way. I was calling because you told me to call if I needed something. This is what I need. Can you do it or not?'

There was silence for a few moments before Felton came back.

'Okay, give it to me. I'll see what I can get. Where you going to be?'

'I'm mobile. Can I ring you back?'

Felton gave him his home number and told him to call back in a half hour.

Bosch used the time to walk across the Strip to Harrah's to check out the poker room. Eleanor Wish wasn't there. He then went back out onto the Strip and headed down to the Flamingo. He took his jacket off because it was still very warm out. It would be dark soon and he hoped it would cool off then.

In the Flamingo casino he found her. She was playing at a one-to-four table with five men. The seat on her left was open but Bosch didn't take it. Instead, he hung back with the crowd around a roulette table and watched her.

Eleanor Wish's face showed total concentration on the cards as she played. Bosch watched as the men she was playing against stole looks at her, and it gave Bosch a weird thrill to know they secretly coveted her. In the ten minutes he watched, she won one hand – he was too far away to see what she won with – and bailed out early on five others. It looked as though she was well ahead. She had a full rack in front of her and six stacks of chips on the blue felt.

After he watched her win a second hand – this time a massive pot – and the dealer began to push the pile of blue chips to her spot, Bosch looked around for a pay phone. He called Felton at home and got Wish's home phone and address. The captain told him that the address, on Sands Avenue, was not far off the strip in an area of apartment buildings mostly inhabited by casino employees. Bosch didn't tell him that he had already found her. Instead, he thanked him and hung up.

When Bosch got back to the poker room she was gone. The five men were still there, but there was a new dealer and no Eleanor Wish. Her chips were gone. She had cashed out and he had lost her. Bosch cursed to himself.

'You looking for someone?'

Bosch turned around. It was Eleanor. There was no smile on her face, just a slight look of irritation or maybe defiance. His eyes fell to the small white scar on her jawline.

'I, uh . . . Eleanor . . . yeah, I was looking for you.'

'You were always so obvious. I picked you out one minute after you were there. I would've gotten up then but I was bringing that guy from Kansas along. He thought he knew when I was bluffing. He didn't know shit. Just like you.'

Bosch was tongue-tied. This was not how he had envisioned this happening and he didn't know how to proceed.

'Look, Eleanor, I, uh, just wanted to see how you were doing. I don't know, I just . . .'

'Right. So you just flew out to Vegas to look me up? What's going on, Bosch?'

Bosch looked around. They were standing in a crowded section of the casino. Players passing on both sides of them, the cacophony of the slot machine din and whoops of success and failure created a blur of sight and sound around him.

'I'll tell you. Do you want to get a drink or something, maybe something to eat?'

'One drink.'

'You know a place that's quiet?'

'Not here. Follow me.'

They left through the front doors of the casino and walked out into the dry heat of the night. The sun was all the way down now and it was neon that lit the sky.

'There's a bar in Caesar's that's quiet. It doesn't have any machines.'

She led him across the street and onto the people mover that delivered them to the front door of Caesar's Palace. They walked past the front desk and into a circular bar where there were only three other customers. Eleanor had been right. It was an oasis with no poker or slot machines. Just the bar. He ordered a beer and she ordered scotch and water. She lit a cigarette.

'You didn't used to smoke before,' he said. 'In fact, I remember you were—'

'That was a long time ago. Why are you here?'

'I'm on a case.'

During the walk over he'd had time to compose himself and put his thoughts in order.

'What case and what does it have to do with me?'

'It's got nothing to do with you, but you knew the guy. You played poker with him on Friday at the Mirage.'

Curiosity and confusion creased her brow. Bosch remembered how she used to do that and remembered how attractive he'd found it. He wanted to reach over and touch her but he didn't. He had to remind himself that she was different now.

'Anthony Aliso,' he said.

He watched the surprise play on her face and believed instantly that it was real. He wasn't a poker player from Kansas who couldn't read a bluff. He had known this woman and believed from the look on her face she clearly did not know Aliso was dead until he told her.

'Tony A . . .,' she said and then let it trail off.

'Did you know him well or just to play against?'

She had a distant look in her dark eyes.

'Just when I'd see him there. At the Mirage. I've been playing there on Fridays. A lot of fresh money and faces come in. I'd see him there a couple times a month. For a while I thought he was a local, too.'

'How'd you find out he wasn't?'

'He told me. We had a drink together a couple months ago. There were no seats at the tables. We put our names in and told Frank, he's the night man, to come get us at the bar when there was an opening. So we had a drink and that's when he told me he was from L.A. He said he was in the movie business.'

'That's it, nothing else?'

'Well, yeah, he said other things. We talked. Nothing that stands out, though. We were passing the time until one of our names came up.'

'You didn't see him again outside of playing?'

'No, and what's it to you? Are you saying I'm a suspect because I had a drink with the guy?'

'No, I'm not saying that, Eleanor. Not at all.'

Bosch got out his own cigarettes and lit one. The waitress in a white-and-gold toga brought their drinks, and they settled into a silence for a long moment. Bosch had lost his momentum. He was back to not knowing what to say.

'Looked like you were doing pretty good tonight,' he tried.

'Better than most nights. I got my quota and I got out.'

'Quota?'

'Whenever I get two hundred up I cash out. I'm not greedy and I know luck doesn't last for long on any given night. I never lose more than a hundred, and if I'm lucky enough to get two hundred ahead, then I'm done for the night. I got there early tonight.'

'How'd you—'

He stopped himself. He knew the answer.

'How'd I learn to play poker well enough to live off it? You spend three and a half years inside and you learn to smoke and play poker and other things.'

She looked directly at him as if daring him to say anything about it. After another long moment she broke away and got out another cigarette. Bosch lit it for her.

'So there's no day job? Just the poker?'

'That's right. I've been doing this almost a year now. Kind of hard to find a straight job, Bosch. You tell 'em you're a former FBI agent and their eyes light up. Then you tell them you just got out of federal prison and they go dead.'

'I'm sorry, Eleanor.'

'Don't be. I'm not complaining. I make more than enough to get by, every now and then I meet interesting people like your guy Tony A, and there's no state income tax here. What do I have to complain about, except maybe that it gets to be over a hundred degrees in the shade about ninety times a year too many?'

The bitterness was not lost on him.

'I mean I'm sorry about everything. I know it doesn't do you any good now, but I wish I had it to do all over again. I've learned things since then, and I would've played it all differently. That's all I wanted to tell you. I saw you on the surveillance tape playing with Tony Aliso and I wanted to find you to tell you that. That's all I wanted.'

She stubbed her half-finished smoke out in the glass ashtray and took a strong pull on her glass of scotch.

'I guess I should be going, then,' she said.

She stood up.

'Do you need a ride anywhere?'

'No, I actually have a car, thank you.'

She started out of the bar in the direction of the front doors but after a few yards stopped and came back to the table.

'You're right, you know.'

'About what?'

'About it not doing me any good now.'

With that she left. Bosch watched her push through the revolving doors and disappear into the night.

Following the directions he had written down when he spoke with Rhonda over the phone in Tony Aliso's office, Bosch found Dolly's on Madison in North Las Vegas. It was strictly an upper-crust club: twenty-dollar cover, two-drink minimum and you were escorted to your seat by a large man in a tuxedo with a starched collar that cut into his neck like a garrote. The dancers were upper-crust, too. Young and beautiful, they probably were just shy of having enough coordination and talent to work the big room shows on the Strip.

Bosch was led by the tuxedo to a table the size of a dinner plate about eight feet from the main stage, which was empty at the moment.

'A new dancer will be on stage in a couple of minutes,' the man in the tuxedo told Bosch. 'Enjoy the show.'

Bosch didn't know if he was supposed to tip the guy for seating him at such a close-up location as well as putting up with the tuxedo, but he let it go and the man didn't hang around with his hand out. Bosch had barely gotten his cigarettes out when a waitress in a red silk negligee, high heels and black fishnet stockings floated over and reminded him of the two-drink minimum. Bosch ordered beer.

While he waited for his two beers, Bosch took a look around. Business seemed slow, it being the Monday night tail-end of a holiday weekend. There were maybe twenty men in the place. Most of them were sitting by themselves and not looking at each other while they waited for the next nude woman to entertain them.

There were full-length mirrors on the side and rear walls. A bar ran along the left side of the room, and cut into the wall in the back was an arched entrance above which a red neon sign that glowed in the darkness announced PRIVATE DANCERS. The front wall was largely taken up by a shimmering curtain and the stage. A runway projected from the stage through the center of the room. The runway was the focus of several bright lights attached to a metal gridwork on the ceiling. Their brightness made the runway almost glow in contrast to the dark and smoky atmosphere of the seating area.

347

A disk jockey in a sound booth at the left side of the stage announced the next dancer would be Randy. An old Eddie Money song, 'Two Tickets to Paradise,' started blaring over the sound system as a tall brunette wearing blue jeans cut off to expose the lower half of her bottom and a neon pink bikini top charged through the shimmering curtain and started moving to the beat of the music.

Bosch was immediately mesmerized. The woman was beautiful and the first thought he had was to question why she was doing this. He had always believed that beauty helped women get away from many of the hardships of life. This woman, this girl, was beautiful and yet here she was. Maybe that was the real draw for these men, he thought. Not the glimpse of a naked woman, but the knowledge of submission, the thrill of knowing another one had been broken. Bosch began to think he had been wrong about beautiful women.

The waitress put down two beers on the little table and told Bosch he owed fifteen dollars. He almost asked her to repeat the price but then figured it came with the territory. He handed her a twenty, and when she started digging through the stack of bills on her tray for his change he waved it off.

She clutched at his shoulder and bent down to his ear, making sure that she was at an angle that afforded him a look at her full cleavage.

'Thank you, darlin'. I 'preciate that. Let me know if you need anything else.'

'There is one thing. Is Layla here tonight?'

'No, she's not here.'

Bosch nodded. And the waitress straightened up.

'How about Rhonda then?' Bosch asked.

'That's Randy up there.'

She pointed to the stage and Bosch shook his head and signaled her to come closer.

'No, Rhonda, like help, help me Rhonda. She working tonight? She was here last night.'

'Oh, that Rhonda. Yeah, she's around. You just missed her set. She's probably in the back changing.'

Bosch reached into his pocket for his money and put a five on her bar tray.

'Will you go back and tell her the friend of Tony's she talked to last night wants to buy her a drink?'

'Sure.'

She squeezed his shoulder again and went off. Bosch's attention was drawn to the stage, where Randy's first song had just ended. The next song was 'Lawyers, Guns and Money' by Warren Zevon. Bosch hadn't heard it in a while and he remembered how it had been an anthem among the uniforms back when he had worked patrol.

The dancer named Randy soon slipped out of her outfit and was nude except for a garter stretched tightly around her left thigh. Many of the men got up and met her as she danced her way slowly down the runway. They slid dollar bills under the garter. And when a man put a five under the strap, Randy bent down over him, using his shoulder to steady herself, and did an extra wiggle and kissed his ear.

Bosch watched this and was thinking that he now had a pretty good idea how Tony Aliso ended up with the small handprint on his shoulder, when a petite blond woman slid into the seat next to him.

'Hi. I'm Rhonda. You missed my show!'

'I heard that. I'm sorry.'

'Well, I go back on in a half hour and do it all over again. I hope you'll stay. Yvonne said you wanted to buy me a drink?'

As if on cue Bosch saw the waitress heading their way. Bosch leaned over to Rhonda.

'Listen, Rhonda, I'd rather take care of you than give my money to the bar. So do me a favor and don't go exorbitant on me.'

'Exorbitant . . .'

She crinkled her face up in a question.

'Don't go ordering champagne.'

'Oh, I gotcha.'

She ordered a martini and Yvonne floated back into the darkness.

'So, I didn't catch your name.'

'Harry.'

'And you're a friend of Tony's from L.A. You make movies, too?'

'No, not really.'

'How do you know Tony?'

'I just met him recently. Listen, I'm trying to find Layla to get a message to her. Yvonne tells me she's not on tonight. You know where I can find her?'

Bosch noticed her stiffen. She knew something wasn't right.

'First of all, Layla doesn't work here anymore. I didn't know that when I talked to you last night, but she's gone and won't be back. And secondly, if you're a friend of Tony's, then how come you're asking me how to find her?'

She wasn't as dumb as Bosch had thought. He decided to go direct.

'Because Tony got himself killed, so I can't ask him. I want to find Layla to tell her and maybe warn her.'

'*What?*' she shrieked.

Her voice cut through the loud music like a bullet through a slice of bread. Everybody in the place, including the naked Randy on the stage, looked in their direction. Bosch had no doubt that everyone in the place must think he had just propositioned her, offering an insulting fee for an equally insulting act.

'Keep it down, Randy,' he quickly said.

'It's Rhonda.'

'Rhonda then.'

'What happened to him? He was just here.'

'Somebody shot him in L.A. when he got back. Now, do you know where Layla is or not? You tell me and I'll take care of you.'

'Well, what are you? Are you really his friend or not?'

'In a way I'm his only friend right now. I'm a cop. My name's Harry Bosch and I'm trying to find out who did it.'

Her face took on a look that seemed even more horrified than when he told her Aliso was dead. Sometimes telling people you were a cop did that.

'Save your money,' she said. 'I can't talk to you.'

She got up then and moved quickly away toward the door next to the stage. Bosch threw her name out after her but it was crushed by the sound of the music. He casually took a look around and noticed behind him that the tuxedo man was eyeing him through the darkness. Bosch decided he wasn't going to stick around for Rhonda's second show. He took one more gulp of beer – he hadn't even touched his second glass – and got up.

As he neared the exit the tuxedo leaned back and knocked on the mirror behind him. It was then that Bosch realized there was a door cut into the glass. It opened and the tuxedo stepped to the side to block Bosch's exit.

'Sir, could you step into the office, please?'

'What for?'

'Just step in. The manager would like a word with you.'

Bosch hesitated but through the door he could see a lighted office where a man in a suit sat behind a desk. He stepped in and the tuxedo came in behind him and shut the door.

Bosch looked at the man behind the desk. Blond and beefy. Bosch wouldn't know whom to bet on if a fight broke out between the tuxedoed bouncer and the so-called manager. They were both brutes.

'I just got off the phone with Randy in the dressing room, she says you were asking about Tony Aliso.'

'It was Rhonda.'

'Rhonda, whatever, never-the-fuck-mind. She said you said he was dead.'

He spoke with a midwestern accent. Sounded like southside Chicago, Bosch guessed.

'Was and still is.'

The blond nodded to the tuxedo and his arm came up in a split second and hit Bosch with a backhand in the mouth. Bosch went back against the wall, banging the back of his head. Before his mind cleared, the tuxedo twirled him around until he was face-against-the-wall and leaned his weight against him. He felt the man's hands begin patting him down.

'Enough of the wiseass act,' the blond said. 'What are you doing talking to the girls about Tony?'

Before Bosch could say anything the hands running over his body found his gun.

'He's strapped,' the tuxedo said.

Bosch felt the gun being jerked out of his shoulder holster. He also tasted blood in his mouth and felt rage building in his throat. The hands then found his wallet and his cuffs. Tuxedo threw them on the desk in front of the blond and held Bosch pinned against the wall with one hand. By straining to turn his head Bosch could watch the blond open the wallet.

'He's a cop, let him go.'

The hand came off his neck and Bosch gruffly pulled away from the tuxedo.

'An L.A. cop,' the blond said. 'Hieronymus Bosch. Like that painter, huh? He did some weird stuff.'

Bosch just looked at him and he handed the gun and cuffs and wallet back.

'Why'd you have him hit me?'

'That was a mistake. See, most cops what come in here, they announce themselves, they tell us their business and we help 'em if we can. You were sneaking around, Anonymous Hieronymus. We have a business to protect here.'

He opened a drawer and pulled out a box of tissues and proffered it to Bosch.

'Your lip's bleeding.'

Bosch took the whole box.

'So this is true what she says you told her. Tony's dead.'

'That's what I said. How well did you know him?'

'See, that's good. You assume I knew him and put that assumption in your question. That's good.'

'So then answer it.'

'He was a regular in here. He was always trying to pick off girls. Told 'em he'd put 'em in the movies. Same old stuff. But, hell, they keep falling for it. Last two years he cost me three of my best girls. They're in L.A. now. He left 'em high and dry once he got them there and did what he wanted with 'em. They never learn.'

'Why'd you let him keep coming in if he was picking off your girls?'

'He spent a lot of bread in here. Besides, there's no shortage of quiff here in Vegas. No shortage at all.'

Bosch headed in another direction.

'What about Friday? Was he here?'

'No, I don't – yes, yes he was. He stopped by for a short while. I saw him out there.'

With his hand he indicated a panel of video monitors showing every angle of the club and front entrance. It was equally as impressive as the setup Hank Meyer had shown Bosch at the Mirage.

'You remember seeing him, Gussie?' the blond asked the tuxedo.

'Yeah, he was here.'

'There you go. He was here.'

'No problems? He just came and went?'

'Right, no problems.'

'Then why'd you fire Layla?'

The blond pinched his lips tight for a moment.

'Now I get it,' he said. 'You're one of those guys what likes to weave a web with words, get somebody caught in it.'

'Maybe.'

'Well, nobody's caught anywhere. Layla was Tony's latest fuck, that's true, but she's gone now. She won't be back.'

'Yeah, and what happened to her?'

'Like you heard, I fired her. Saturday night.'

'For what?'

'For any number of infractions of the rules. But it doesn't really matter because it's none of your business, now is it?'

'What did you say your name is?'

'I didn't.'

'Then how 'bout if I just call you asshole, how would that be?'

'People 'round here call me Lucky. Can we get on with this, please?'

'Sure, we can get on with it. Just tell me what happened to Layla.'

'Sure, sure. But I thought you were here to talk about Tony, least that's what Randy said.'

351

'Rhonda.'

'Rhonda, right.'

Bosch was losing his patience but managed to just stare at him and wait him out.

'Layla, right. Well, Saturday night she got into a beef with one of the other girls. It got a little nasty and I had to make a choice. Modesty is one of my best girls, best producers. She gave me an ultimatum: either Layla goes or she goes. I had to let Layla go. Modesty, man, she sells ten, twelve splits of champagne a night to those suckers out there. I had to back her over Layla. I mean, Layla's good and she's a looker but she ain't no Modesty. Modesty's our top girl.'

Bosch just nodded. So far his story jibed with the phone message Layla had left for Aliso. By drawing it out of the blond man, Bosch was getting a sense of how much he could be believed.

'What was the trouble between Layla and the other girl about?' he asked.

'I don't know and don't really care. Just your typical catfight. They didn't like each other since day one. See, Bosch, every club has its top girl. And here, it's Modesty. Layla was trying to move in on that and Modesty didn't want to be moved in on. But I have to say, Layla was trouble since she came here. None of the girls liked her act. She stole songs from the other girls, wouldn't stop with the pussy dust even when I told her, we just had a lot of trouble with her. I'm glad she's gone. I gotta business to run here. I can't be babysitting a bunch of spoiled cunts.'

'Pussy dust?'

'Yeah, you know, she put that sparkly stuff on her snatch, made it sparkle in the dark and twinkled in the lights. Only problem is those sparkles come off and get on the suckers. She does a lap dance on you and *you* end up with a crotch that glitters. Then you go home and the wife figures it out and raises holy hell. I lose customers. I can't have that shit, Bosch. If it hadn't been Modesty, it would have been something else. I got rid of Layla when I got the chance.'

Bosch thought about the story for a few moments.

'Okay,' he said. 'Just give me her address and I'll be on my way.'

'I would but I can't.'

'Don't start that shit now. I thought we were having a conversation. Let me see your payroll records. There's got to be an address.'

The man called Lucky smiled and shook his head.

'Payroll? We don't pay these broads a dime. They ought to pay us. Comin' in here, it's a license to make money.'

'You must have a phone number or an address. You want your man Gussie here to go down to Metro on an assaulting-a-police-officer clip?'

'We don't have her address, Bosch, what can I tell you? Or her phone number.'

He held his hands out, palms up.

'I mean, I don't have addresses on any of the girls. I set a schedule and they come in and dance. They don't show, they aren't allowed back. See, it's nice and simple, streamlined, that way. It's the way we do it. And as far as the assault thing goes with Gussie, if you want to do that dance we'll do it. But remember you're the guy what came in here by hisself, never said who you were or what you wanted to nobody, had four beers in less than an hour and insulted one of the dancers before we asked you to leave. We can have affidavits to that effect in an hour.'

He raised his arms again, this time in a hands-off manner as if to say it was Bosch's call. Bosch had no doubt that Yvonne and Rhonda would tell the story they were told to tell. He decided to cut his losses. He smiled glibly.

'Have a good night,' he said and turned to the door.

'You, too, Officer,' Lucky said to his back. 'Come back when you have time and can enjoy the show.'

The door opened by some unseen electronic means apparently controlled from the desk. Gussie allowed Bosch to leave first. He then followed behind as Bosch went through the main door to the valet stand. Bosch gave a Mexican man with a face like a crumpled paper lunch bag his parking stub. He and Gussie then waited in silence for the car to be brought up.

'No hard feelings, right?' Gussie finally said as the car was approaching. 'I didn't know you was a cop.'

Bosch turned to face him.

'No, you just thought I was a customer.'

'Yeah, right. And I had to do what the boss told me to do.'

He put his hand out. In his peripheral vision Bosch could see his car still coming. He took Gussie's hand and in a sharp move pulled the big man toward him at the same time he raised his knee and drove it into his groin. Gussie let out an *oomph* and doubled over. Bosch let go of his hand and quickly jerked the tail of the man's jacket up over his head, pinning his arms in the tangle. Finally, he brought his knee up into the jacket and felt it connect solidly with Gussie's face. The big man fell forward onto the hood of a black Corvette parked near the door just as the valet jumped out of Bosch's rental car and came scrambling around to defend his boss. The man was older and smaller than Bosch. This one wouldn't even be close and Bosch wasn't interested in any innocent bystanders. He held his finger up to stop the man.

'Don't,' he said.

The man considered his situation while Gussie groaned through his tuxedo jacket. Finally, the valet raised his hands and stepped back, allowing Bosch a path to the car door.

'At least somebody around here makes the right choices,' Bosch said as he slid in.

He looked through the windshield and saw Gussie's body slide down the slope of the Corvette's hood and fall to the pavement. The valet ran to his side.

As Bosch pulled out onto Madison, he checked the rearview mirror. The valet was pulling the jacket back over Gussie's head. Bosch could see blood on the bouncer's white shirt.

Bosch was too keyed up to go back to the hotel to sleep. He also had a bad mix of emotions weighing on him. Seeing the naked woman dancing still bothered him. He didn't even know her but thought he had invaded some private world of hers. He also felt angry at himself for lashing out at the brute, Gussie. But most of all, what bothered him was that he had played the whole scene wrong. He had gone to the strip club to try to get a line on

Layla and he got nothing. At best, all he had come up with was the probable explanation for what the specks of glitter found in the cuffs of Tony Aliso's pants and the shower drain were and where they came from. It wasn't enough. He had to go back to L.A. in the morning and he had nothing.

When he got to a traffic light at the beginning of the Strip, he lit a cigarette, then took out his notebook and opened it to the page on which he had written down the address Felton had given him earlier in the night.

At Sands Boulevard he turned east and within a mile he came to the apartment complex where Eleanor Wish lived. It was a sprawling development with numbered buildings. It took him a while until he found hers and then figured out which unit was hers. He sat in his car and smoked and watched her lighted windows for a while. He wasn't sure what he was doing or what he wanted.

Five years earlier Eleanor Wish had done the worst and the best to him. She had betrayed him, put him in danger and she had also saved his life. She had made love to him. And then it all went bad. Still, he had often thought about her, the old what-might-have-been blues. She had a hold on him through time. She had been cold to him this night but he thought for sure the hold went both ways. She was his reflection, he had always been sure of that.

He got out of the car, dropped his dead cigarette and went to her door. She answered his knock quickly, almost as if she was expecting him. Or someone.

'How'd you find me? Did you follow me?'

'No. I made a call, that's all.'

'What happened to your lip?'

'It's nothing. Are you going to ask me in?'

She backed up to allow him to enter. It was a small place with spare furnishings. It looked as though she was adding things over time, as she could afford them. He first noticed the print of Hopper's *Nighthawks* on the wall over the couch. It was a painting that always struck a chord with him. He had once had the same print on his own wall. It had been a gift from her five years before. A good-bye gift.

He looked from the painting to her. Their eyes met and he knew everything she had said earlier had been a front. He stepped closer to her and touched her, put his hand on her neck and ran a thumb along her cheek. He looked closely at her face. It was resolute, determined.

'This time it's been a long time for me,' she whispered.

And he remembered that he had told her the same on the night they'd first made love. That was a lifetime ago, Bosch thought. What am I doing now? Can you pick up after so long and so many changes?

He pulled her close and they held each other and kissed for a long moment and then she wordlessly led him to the bedroom, where she quickly unbuttoned her blouse and dropped her jeans to the floor. She pressed herself to him again and they kissed while she worked her hands up his shirt, opening it and pressing her skin to his. Her hair smelled of smoke from the tables, but there was an underlying scent of perfume that reminded him of a night five years before. He remembered the jacaranda trees outside her window and how they put a violet snow on the ground.

They made love with an intensity that Bosch had forgotten that he had. It was a bruising, huffing physical act devoid of love, invigorated and driven solely, it seemed, by lust and maybe a memory. When he was done she pulled him toward her, into her, in rhythmic thrusts until she, too, reached her moment and subsided. Then, with the clarity of thought that always comes after, they became embarrassed about their nakedness, about how they had coupled with the ferocity of animals and now looked at each other as human beings.

'I forgot to ask,' she said. 'You're not married now, are you?'

She giggled. He reached to the floor to where his jacket had been thrown and pulled out the cigarettes.

'No,' he said. 'I'm alone.'

'I should've known. Harry Bosch, the loner. I should've known.'

She was smiling at him in the darkness. He saw it when the match flared. He lit the cigarette and then offered it to her. She shook her head no.

'How many women have there been since me? Tell me.'

'I don't know, just a few. There was one, we were together about a year. That was the most serious one.'

'What happened to her?'

'She went to Italy.'

'For good?'

'Who knows?'

'Well, if you don't know, then she isn't coming back. At least to you.'

'Yeah. I know. That one's been over a while.'

He was silent for a moment and then she asked him who else there had been.

'There was a painter I met in Florida on a case. That didn't last long. After that, there's you again.'

'What happened to the painter?'

Bosch shook his head as if to dismiss the inquiry. He didn't really enjoy reviewing his ill-fated romantic record.

'Distance, I guess,' he said. 'It just didn't work. I couldn't leave L.A., she couldn't leave where she was.'

She moved closer to him and kissed him on the chin. He knew he needed a shave.

'What about you, Eleanor? Are you alone?'

'Yes . . . The last man to make love to me was a cop. He was gentle but very strong. I don't mean in a physical way. In a life way. It was a long time ago. At the time we both needed healing. We gave it to each other . . .'

They looked at each other in the darkness for a long moment and then she came closer. Just before their mouths met she whispered, 'A lot of time gone past.'

He thought about those words as she kissed him and then pushed him back on the pillows. She straddled him and started a gentle rocking motion with her hips. Her hair hung down around his face until he was in a perfect darkness. He ran his hands along her warm skin from her hips to her shoulders and then underneath to touch her breasts. He could feel her wetness on him but it was too soon for him.

'What's the matter, Harry?' she whispered. 'You want to rest a while?'

'I don't know.'

355

He kept thinking of those words. A lot of time gone past. Maybe too much time. She kept rocking.

'I don't know what I want,' he said. 'What do you want, Eleanor?'

'All I want is the moment. We've fucked everything else up, it's all we've got left.'

After a while he was ready and they made love again. She was very silent, her movements steady and gentle. She stayed on top of him, her face above him, breathing in short rhythmic clips. Near the end, when he was just trying to hang on, waiting for her, he felt a teardrop hit his cheek. He reached up and smeared the tears on her face with his thumbs.

'It's all right, Eleanor, it's all right.'

She put one of her hands on his face, feeling it in the dark as if she were a blind woman. In a short while they met at the moment when nothing in the world can intrude. Not words or even memories. It was just them together. They had the moment.

He slept on and off in her bed until nearly dawn. She slept soundly with her head on his shoulder but when he was lucky enough to doze off, it never lasted long. For the most part he lay there staring into the gray darkness, smelling their sweat and sex, wondering what road he was on now.

At six he extricated himself from her unconscious embrace and got dressed. When he was ready he kissed her awake and told her he must go.

'I go back to L.A. today but I want to come back to you as soon as I can.'

She nodded sleepily.

'Okay, Bosch, I'll be waiting.'

It was finally cool outside. He lit his first smoke of the day as he walked to his car. When he pulled onto Sands to head up to the Strip, he saw the sun was throwing a golden light on the mountains west of town.

The Strip was still lit by a million neon lights, though the crowds on the sidewalk had greatly decreased by this hour. Still, Bosch was awed by the spectacle of light. In every imaginable color and configuration, it was a megawatt funnel of enticement to greed that burned twenty-four hours a day. Bosch felt the same attraction that all the other grinders felt tug at them. Las Vegas was like one of the hookers on Sunset Boulevard in Hollywood. Even happily married men at least glanced their way, if only for a second, just to get an idea what was out there, maybe give them something to think about. Las Vegas was like that. There was a visceral attraction here. The bold promise of money and sex. But the first was a broken promise, a mirage, and the second was fraught with danger, expense, physical and mental risk. It was where the real gambling took place in this town.

When he got to his room, he noticed the message light was blinking. He called the operator and was told that someone named Captain Felton had called at one and then again at two and then someone named Layla at four. There were no messages or numbers left by either of the callers. Bosch put the phone down and frowned. He figured it was too early to call Felton. But it was the call from Layla that most interested him. If it had been the real Layla who had called, then how did she know where to reach him?

He decided that it had probably been through Rhonda. The night before when he had called from Tony Aliso's office in Hollywood, he had asked

Rhonda for directions from the Mirage. She could have passed that on to Layla. He wondered why she had called. Maybe she hadn't heard about Tony until Rhonda had told her.

Still, he decided to put Layla on a back burner for the moment. With the financial probe Kizmin Rider had opened up in L.A., the focus of the case seemed to be shifting. It was important for them to talk to Layla but his priority was to get back to L.A. He picked the phone back up and called Southwest and booked a 10:30 flight to L.A. He figured that would give him time to check in with Felton, then check out the dealership where Rider said Tony Aliso had leased his cars and still make it back to the Hollywood Division by lunchtime.

Bosch stripped off his clothes and took a long hot shower, washing the sweat of the night away. When he was done he wrapped a towel around himself and used another to wipe the fog off the mirror so he could shave. He noticed that his lower lip had swollen on one side to the size of a marble and his mustache did little to hide it. His eyes were red-rimmed and bloodshot. He wondered as he got the bottle of Visine drops out of his shaving bag if Eleanor had found a single thing about him attractive.

When he stepped back into the room to get dressed, he was greeted by a man he had never seen before sitting in the chair by the window. He was holding a newspaper, which he put down when he noticed Bosch step into the room clad only in the towel.

'It's Bosch, right?'

Bosch looked to the bureau and saw his gun was still sitting there. It was closer to the man in the chair but Bosch thought he might be able to get to it first.

'Easy now,' the man said. 'We're in this together. I'm a cop. With Metro. Felton sent me.'

'What the fuck you doing in my room?'

'I came up, got no answer. I could hear the shower. I had a friend from downstairs slip me in. I didn't want to wait around in the hall. Go ahead, get dressed. Then I'll tell you what we got.'

'Let me see some ID.'

The man got up and approached Bosch, pulling a wallet from his inside coat pocket and putting a bored look on his face. He opened the wallet, flashing the badge and ID card.

'Iverson. From Metro. Captain Felton sent me.'

'What's so important that Felton had to send somebody to break into my room?'

'Look, I didn't break in, okay? We've been calling all night and got no answer. We first of all wanted to make sure you were all right. And, secondly, the captain wants you to be in on the arrest, so he sent me over to try to find you. We gotta get going. Why don't you get dressed?'

'What arrest?'

'That's what I'm trying to tell you if you'd get dressed and we could get going. You hit the jackpot with those prints you flew in here with.'

Bosch looked at him for a moment and then went to the closet to grab a pair of pants and some underwear. He then went into the bathroom to put them on. When he came back out, he said one word to Iverson.

'Talk.'

357

Bosch quickly finished dressing as Iverson began.

'You know the name Joey Marks?'

Bosch thought a moment and then said it sounded familiar but he couldn't place it.

'Joseph Marconi. They call him Joey Marks. Used to, before he tried to put on legitimate airs. Now, it's Joseph Marconi. Anyway, he got the name Joey Marks 'cause that's what he did, he left marks on anybody who crossed him, got in his way.'

'Who is he?'

'He's the Outfit's guy in Vegas. You know what the Outfit is, right?'

'The Chicago Mafia family. They control or have the say, at least, on everything west of the Mississippi. That includes Vegas and L.A.'

'Hey, you took some geography, didn't you? I probably won't have to school you too much then on what's what out here. You already've got a score card.'

'You're saying the prints on my vic's jacket came from Joey Marks?'

'In your dreams. But they did come back to one of his top guys and, Bosch, that's like manna from heaven. We're taking this guy down today, pulling him right the fuck out of bed. We're going to turn him, Bosch, make him our boy and through him we'll finally get Joey Marks. He's been a thorn in our side going on near a decade now.'

'Aren't you forgetting something?'

'No, I don't think – oh, yeah, of course you and the LAPD have our undivided thanks for this.'

'No, you're forgetting it's my case. It's not your case. What the fuck you people think you're doing taking this guy down without even talking to me?'

'We tried to call. I told you that.'

Iverson sounded hurt.

'So? You don't get me and you just go ahead with the plan?'

Iverson didn't answer. Bosch finished tying his shoes and stood up ready to go.

'Let's go. Take me to Felton. I can't believe you guys.'

On the elevator down Iverson said that while Bosch's exception to the plan was noted, it was too late to stop anything. They were heading out to a command post in the desert and from there they would move in on the suspect's house, which was out near the mountains.

'Where's Felton?'

'He's out there at the CP.'

'Good.'

Iverson was silent during most of the ride out, which was good because it allowed Bosch to think about this latest development. He realized suddenly that Tony Aliso might have been washing money for Joey Marks. Marks was Rider's Mr X, he guessed. But something went wrong. The IRS audit was endangering the scheme and thereby endangering Joey Marks. Marks had responded by eliminating the washer.

The story felt good to Bosch, but there were still things that didn't jibe. The break-in at Aliso's office two days after he was dead. Why did whoever that was wait until then, and why didn't they take all the financial records? The records – if connections between the dummy corporations and Joey

Marks could be made – might be just as dangerous to Marks as Aliso was. Bosch found himself wondering if the hitter and the B&E man were the same person. It didn't seem so.

'What's this guy's name, the one the prints matched?'

'Luke Goshen. We only had his prints on file because he had to give 'em to get the entertainment license for one of Joey's strip clubs. The license is in Goshen's name. It keeps Joey out of it. Nice and clean. Only not anymore. The prints tie Goshen to a murder and that means Joey isn't far behind.'

'Wait a minute, what's the name of the club?'

'Dolly's. It's in—'

'North Las Vegas. Son of a bitch.'

'What, I say something?'

'This Goshen guy, do they call him Lucky?'

'Probably not after today. His luck's about to run out. Sounds like you know of him.'

'I met the prick last night.'

'You're shitting me.'

'At Dolly's. The last phone call from Aliso's office in L.A. was to Dolly's. I found out he was coming out here and spending time with one of the dancers at that place. I went to check it out last night and fucked up. Goshen had one of his guys give me this.'

Bosch touched the bump on his lip.

'I was wondering where you got that. Which one give you that?'

'Gussie.'

'Fucking Big John Flanagan. We'll be bringing his lard ass in today, too.'

'John Flanagan? How they get Gussie out of that?'

'It's on account he's the best-dressed bouncer in the country. You know, the tuxedo. He gets all gussied up to go to work. That's how he got that one. I hope you didn't let him get away with puttin' that knot on your lip.'

'We had a little discussion in the parking lot before I left.'

Iverson laughed.

'I like you, Bosch. You're a tough nut.'

'I'm not sure I like you yet, Iverson. I'm still not happy about you people trying to take over my case.'

'It'll work out for all of us. You're going to clear your case and we're going to take a couple of major douche bags out of the picture. City fathers are going to be smiling all around.'

'We'll see.'

'There's one other thing,' Iverson said. 'We were already working a tip on Lucky when you showed up.'

'What are you talking about?'

'We got a tip. It was anonymous. Came in Sunday to the bureau. Guy won't give his name but says he was in a strip club the night before and hears a couple of big guys talking about a hit. He heard one call the other Lucky.'

'What else?'

'Just something about the guy being put in the trunk and then getting capped.'

'Felton know this when I talked to him yesterday?'

'No, it hadn't filtered up to him. It came up last night after he found out the prints you brought matched Goshen. One of the guys in the bureau had taken the tip and was going to check it out. Put out a flier on it. It would've eventually gotten over there to L.A. and you woulda come calling. You're just here sooner rather than later.'

They had completely left the urban sprawl of the city and the chocolate-brown mountain chain rose in front of them. There were sporadic patches of neighborhoods. Homes that were built way out and were waiting for the city to catch up. Bosch had been out this way once before on an investigation, going to a retired cop's house. It had reminded him of no-man's-land then and it still did now.

'Tell me about Joey Marks,' Bosch said. 'You said he's trying to go legitimate?'

'No, I said he's trying to give the appearance of legitimacy. That's two different things. Guy like that, he'll never be legitimate. He can clean up his act, but he's always going to be a grease spot on the road.'

'What's he into? If you believe the media, the mob was run out of town to make way for all the All-American family.'

'Yeah, I know the tune. It's true, though. Vegas has changed in ten years. When I first made it to the bureau, you could practically take your pick of the casinos and go to work. They all had connections. If it wasn't the front office, then it was the supplies, the unions, whatever. Now it's cleaned up. It's gone from sin city to fuckin' Disneyland. We got more water slides than whorehouses now. I think I liked it the old way. Had more of an edge, know what I mean?'

'Yeah, I know what you mean.'

'Anyway, the important thing is we ninety-nine percent have the mob out of the casinos. That's the good thing. But there's still a lot of what we call ancillary action around. That's where Joey fits in. He runs a string of high-rent strip bars, mostly in North Vegas because nudity and alcohol are allowed there and the money is in alcohol. Very hard to watch, that money. We figure he's siphoning a couple mil a year off the top on the clubs alone. We've had the IRS go after his books but he does too good a job.

'Let's see, we think he also has a piece of some of the brothels up north. Then he's got the usual, your standard loan-sharking and fencing operations. He runs a book and has the street tax on almost anything that moves in town. You know, the escort services, peep shows, all of that. He's the king. He can't go in any of the casinos 'cause he's in the commission's black book but it doesn't matter. He's the king.'

'How does he have a betting book in a town where you can walk into any casino and bet on any game, any race, anywhere?'

'You gotta have money to do that. Not with Joey. He'll take your bet. And if you are unlucky enough to lose, then you better come up with the money quick or you're one sorry motherfucker. Remember how he got his name. Well, suffice it to say his employees carry on the tradition. See, that's how he gets his hooks into people. He gets them to owe him and then they have to give him a piece of what they have, whether it's a company that makes paint in Dayton or something else.'

'Maybe a guy who makes cheap movies in L.A.'

'Yeah, like that. That's how it works. They open up to him or they get two broken knees or worse. People still disappear in Vegas, Bosch. It might look like it's all volcanoes and pyramids and pirate ships on the outside, but on the inside it's still dark enough for people to disappear in.'

Bosch reached over and turned the air up a notch. The sun was already all the way up and the desert was beginning to bake.

'This is nothing,' Iverson said. 'Wait till about noon. If we're out here then, forget about it. We'll be over one-ten easy.'

'What about Joey's air of legitimacy?'

'Yeah, well, like I said, he's got holdings all over the country. Pieces of the legitimate world he got through these various scams. He also reinvests. He cleans up all the cash he's pulling out of his various enterprises and then puts it into legit stuff, even charities. He's got car dealerships, a country club on the east side, a goddamn wing of a hospital named after one of his kids who died in a swimming pool. His picture gets in the paper at ribbon cuttings, Bosch. I tell you, we've either got to fucking take the guy down or give him the key to the city and I don't know which would be more appropriate.'

Iverson shook his head.

After a few minutes of silence they were there. Iverson pulled into a county fire station and drove around back, where there were several more detective cars and several men standing around them holding paper cups of coffee. One of them was Captain Felton.

Bosch had forgotten to take a bulletproof vest with him from Los Angeles and had to borrow one from Iverson. He was also given a plastic raid jacket that said LVPD in bright yellow letters across the chest when it was zipped closed.

They were standing around Felton's Taurus, going over the plan and waiting for the uniform backup. Execution of the warrant was going to be done by Vegas rules, the captain said. That meant at least one uniform team had to be there when they kicked the door.

By this time Bosch had already had his 'friendly' exchange with Felton. The two had gone into the fire station to get Bosch some coffee, and Bosch had given the police captain an earful for the way he had handled the discovery that the prints Bosch had brought with him belonged to Lucky Luke Goshen. Felton feigned contrition and told Bosch he'd be involved in calling the shots from that moment on. Bosch had to back down after that. He'd gotten what he wanted, at least in the captain's words. Now he just had to watch that Felton walked the talk.

Besides Felton and Bosch, there were four others standing around the car. They were all from Metro's Organized Crime Unit. It was Iverson and his partner, Cicarelli, and then another pair, Baxter and Parmelee. The OCU was part of Felton's domain in the department, but it was Baxter who was running the show. He was a black man who was balding, with gray hair lightly powdered around the sides of his head. He was heavily muscled and had a countenance that said I want no hassles. He seemed to Bosch to be a man accustomed to both the violent and violence. There was a difference.

Luke Goshen's home was known to them. From their banter Bosch figured that they had watched the place before. It was about a mile further

361

west from the station, and Baxter had already made a drive-by and determined that Goshen's black Corvette was in the carport.

'What about a warrant?' Bosch asked.

He could just envision the whole thing getting kicked out of court because of a warrantless entry into the suspect's house.

'The prints were more than enough for a warrant to search the premises and arrest your man,' Felton said. 'We took it to a judge first thing this morning. We also had our own information, which I think Iverson told you about.'

'Look, his prints were on the guy but it doesn't mean he did it. It doesn't make a case. We're acting too quickly here. My guy was put down in L.A. I've got nothing putting Luke Goshen there. And your own information? That's a joke. You've got an anonymous call, that's it. It doesn't mean shit.'

They all looked at Bosch as if he had just belched at the debutante ball.

'Harry, let's get another cup,' Felton said.

'I'm fine.'

'Let's get one anyway.'

He put his arm on Bosch's shoulder and led him back toward the station. Inside at the kitchen counter, where there was a coffee urn, Felton poured himself another cup before speaking.

'Look, Harry, you gotta go with this. This is a major opportunity for us and for you.'

'I know that. I just don't want to blow it. Can't we hold off on this until we're sure of what we've got? It's my case, Captain, and you're still running the show.'

'I thought we had that all straightened out.'

'I thought we did, too, but I might as well be pissing in the wind.'

'Look, Detective, we're going to go up the road and take this guy down, search his place and put him in a little room. I guarantee that if he isn't your man, he's going to give him to you. And he's going to give us Joey Marks along the way. Now, come on, get with the program and get happy.'

He cuffed Bosch on the shoulder and headed back out to the lot. Bosch followed in a few moments. He knew that he was whining over nothing. You find somebody's prints on a body, you bring him in. That's a given. You sweat the details later. But Bosch didn't like being a bystander. That was the real rub and he knew it. He wanted to run the show. Only out here in the desert, he was a fish out of water, flopping on the sand. He knew he should call Billets, but it was too late for her to do anything and he didn't like the idea of telling her he had let this one get away from him.

The patrol car with the two uniforms was there when Bosch stepped out of the fire station and back into the oven.

'All right,' Felton said. 'We're all here. Mount up and let's go get this fucker.'

They were there in five minutes. Goshen lived in a house that rose out of the scrubland on Desert View Avenue. It was a large house but not one that looked particularly ostentatious. The one thing that looked out of the ordinary was the concrete-block wall and gate that surrounded the half-acre property. The house was in the middle of nowhere but its owner needed to put a security wall around it.

They all stopped their cars on the shoulder of the road and got out. Baxter had come prepared. From the trunk of his Caprice he pulled out two stepladders that they would use to scale the wall next to the driveway gate. Iverson was the first to go over. When he got to the top of the wall, he put the other ladder in place on the other side but hesitated before climbing down into the front yard.

'Anybody see any dogs?'

'No dogs,' Baxter said. 'I checked this morning.'

Iverson went down and the others followed him over. While he waited for his turn, Bosch looked around and could just see the neon demarcation of the Strip several miles to the east. Above this the sun was a neon red ball. The air had gone from warm to hot and was as dry and rough as sandpaper. Bosch thought of the cherry-flavored Chap Stick in his pocket that he had bought at the hotel gift shop. But he didn't want to use it in front of the local boys.

After Bosch had scaled the wall and was approaching the house behind the others, he looked at his watch. It was now almost nine but the house seemed dead. No movement, no sound, no lights, nothing. Curtains were closed across every window.

'You sure he's here?' Bosch whispered to Baxter.

'He's here,' Baxter replied without lowering his voice. 'I jumped the wall about six and touched the hood of the Vette. It was warm. He hadn't been home long. He's in there asleep, I guarantee it. Nine o'clock to this guy is like four in the morning for normal people.'

Bosch looked over at the Corvette. He remembered it from the night before. As he looked around further, he realized the confines within the walls of the compound were carpeted in lush, green grass. It must have cost a fortune to plant and another one to keep it watered. The property sat in the desert like a towel on the beach. Bosch was drawn from his wonder by the sound of Iverson hitting the front door with his foot.

With weapons drawn, Bosch and the others followed Iverson into the dark opening to the house. They went in screaming the usual identifiers – *Police!* and *Don't Move!* – and quickly moved down a hallway to the left. Bosch followed the sharp slashes of light from their flashlights. Almost immediately he heard female screams and then a light came on in a room at the end of the hall.

By the time he got in there, he saw Iverson kneeling on a king-size bed, holding his Smith & Wesson short barrel six inches from the face of Luke Goshen. The big man Bosch had encountered the night before was wrapped in the bed's black silk sheets and looked as calm about the situation as Magic Johnson used to look while shooting free throws with the game on the line. He even took the time to glance up at the ceiling to view the reflection of the scene in the mirror.

It was the women who weren't calm. Two of them, both nude, stood on either side of the bed, oblivious to their nakedness but fully in the latter stages of fright. Finally, Baxter quieted them with a loud shout of 'Shut up!'

It took a few moments for the silence to sink in. Nobody moved. Bosch never took his eyes off Goshen. He was the only danger in the room. He sensed that the other cops, who had branched off to search the house, had now moved into the room behind him along with the two uniform cops.

'On your face, Luke,' Iverson finally ordered. 'You girls get some clothes on. Now!'

One of the women said, 'You can't just—'

'Shut up!' Iverson cut her off. 'Or you go in to town like that. Your choice.'

'I'm not go—'

'Randy!' Goshen boomed with a voice as deep as a barrel. 'Shut the fuck up and get dressed. They're not taking you anywhere. You, too, Harm.'

All the men but Goshen instinctively looked at the woman he had called Harm. She looked like she weighed about ninety pounds. She had soft blond hair, breasts she could hide in a child's tea cups and a gold hoop piercing one of the folds of her vagina. There was a look of fright etched on her face that had completely crowded out any hint of beauty.

'Harmony,' she whispered, understanding their dilemma.

'Well, get dressed, Harmony,' Felton said. 'Both of you. Turn to the wall and get dressed.'

'Just get 'em their clothes and get 'em out of here,' Iverson said.

Harmony was stepping into a pair of jeans when she stopped and looked at the men giving conflicting orders.

'Well, which is it?' Randy asked in an irritated voice. 'You people got your shit together or what?'

Bosch recognized her as the woman who had been dancing in Dolly's the night before.

'Get 'em out of here!' Iverson yelled. 'Now.'

The uniforms moved in to usher the naked women out.

'We're going,' Randy yelped. 'Don't touch me.'

Iverson yanked the sheets off Goshen and began cuffing his hands behind his back. Goshen's blond hair ran in a thin and tightly braided ponytail down his back. Bosch hadn't noticed that the night before.

'Whatsa matter, Iverson?' he said, his face against the mattress. 'You got a problem with a little poon hangin' around? You a little punk or something?'

'Goshen, do yourself a favor, shut your fuckin' hole.'

Goshen laughed off the threat. He was a deeply tanned man who seemed even larger than Bosch recalled from the night before. He was completely buffed, his arms the size of hams. For a short moment, Bosch thought he understood Goshen's desire to sleep with two women. And why they willingly went with him in twos.

Goshen faked a yawn to make sure everyone knew he wasn't the least bit threatened by what was happening. He wore only black bikini underwear that matched the sheets. There were tattoos on his back. A one percent sign on the left shoulder blade, a Harley Davidson insignia on the right. On the upper left arm there was another tattoo. The number eighty-eight.

'What's this, your IQ?' Iverson said as he sharply slapped the arm.

'Fuck you, Iverson, and the phony fuckin' warrant you rode in on.'

Bosch knew what the tattoo meant. He had seen it enough in L.A. The eighth letter of the alphabet was H. Eight-eight meant HH, short for Heil Hitler. It means Goshen had spent some time with white supremacists. But most of the assholes Bosch came across with similar tattoos had gotten them in prison. It was amazing to him that Goshen apparently had no criminal record and had spent no time in stir. If he had, his name would have come up when the prints from Tony Aliso's jacket had been run through the AFIS computer. He put thoughts of this contradiction aside when Goshen managed to turn his head so that he was looking at Bosch.

'You,' he said. 'You're the one they should be arresting. After what you did to Gussie.'

Bosch bent over the bed to reply.

'This ain't about last night. This is about Tony Aliso.'

Iverson roughly turned Goshen over on the bed.

'What the fuck are you talking about?' Goshen asked angrily. 'I'm clean on that, man. What are you—'

He tried to pull himself up into a sitting position but Iverson pushed him back down hard.

'Just sit tight,' Iverson said. 'We'll hear your sorry side of things. But we're going to have a look around first.'

He took the warrant out of his pocket and dropped it on Goshen's chest.

'There's your warrant.'

'I can't read it.'

'Not my fault you didn't stay in school.'

'Just hold it up for me.'

Iverson ignored him and looked at the others.

'Okay, let's split up and see what we've got here. Harry, you take this room, okay, keep our friend here company?'

'Right.'

Iverson then addressed the two uniforms.

'I want one of you guys in here. Just stand out of the way and keep your eyes on douche bag here.'

One of the uniforms nodded and the others left the room. Bosch and Goshen looked at each other.

'I can't read this thing,' Goshen said.

'I know,' Bosch said. 'You said that.'

'This is bullshit. It's just a roust. You couldn't possibly have anything on me because I didn't do it.'

'Then who'd you have do it? Gussie?'

'No, man, nobody. There's no way you'll be able to pin this on me. No fucking way. I want my lawyer.'

'As soon as you're booked.'

'Booked for what?'

'For murder, Lucky.'

Goshen continued his denials and demands for a lawyer while Bosch ignored him and started looking around the room, checking the drawers of the dresser. He glanced back at Goshen every few seconds. It was like walking around a lion's cage. He knew he was safe but that didn't stop him from checking. He could tell Goshen was watching him in the mirror over the bed. When the big man finally quieted, Bosch waited a few moments and then started asking questions. He did it casually while he continued the search, as if he didn't really care about the answers.

'So where were you Friday night?'

'Fuckin' your mother.'

'She's dead.'

'I know it. It wasn't all that good.'

Bosch stopped what he was doing and looked at him. Goshen wanted him to hit him. He wanted the violence. It was the playing field he understood.

'Where were you, Goshen? Friday night.'

'Talk to my lawyer.'

'We will. But you can talk, too.'

'I was working the club. I have a fucking job, you know.'

'Yeah, I know. When did you work till?'

'I don't know. Four. I go home after that.'

'Yeah, right.'

'It's the truth.'

'Where were you, in that office?'

'That's right.'

'Anybody see you? You ever come out before four?'

'I don't know. Talk to my lawyer.'

'Don't worry. We will.'

Bosch went back to the search and opened the closet door. It was a walk-in but it was only a third lined with clothes. Goshen lived light.

'Fuckin' A it's right,' Goshen called from the bed. 'You go check. Check it out.'

The first thing Bosch did was to turn over the two pairs of shoes and the Nikes that were lined on the floor. He studied the sole patterns and none of them appeared even remotely like the pattern found on the bumper of the Rolls and Tony Aliso's hip. He glanced back out at Goshen to make sure the big man wasn't moving. He wasn't. Bosch next reached to the shelf above the clothes rod. He took a box down and found it full of photos. They were eight by ten publicity shots of dancers. They weren't nudes. Each young woman was posed provocatively in a skimpy costume. Each one's name was printed in the white border below the photo, accompanied by the name and number of Models A Million, which Bosch guessed was a local agency that provided dancers to clubs. He looked through the box until he found a photo with the name Layla on it.

He studied the photo of the woman he had been looking for the previous night. She had long flowing brown hair with blond highlights, a full figure, dark eyes and bee sting lips. In the photo they were parted just enough to show a hint of white teeth. She was a beautiful woman and there was something familiar about her but he couldn't place it. He decided that maybe the familiarity was the sexual malice that all the women in the photos and those whom he had seen the night before in the club seemed to convey.

Bosch took the box out of the closet and dropped it on the bureau. He held the picture of Layla out of it.

'What's with the pictures, Lucky?'

'They're all the girls I've been with. How 'bout you, cop? You had that many? I bet the ugliest one in there is better than the best one you've ever had.'

'So what do you want to do, compare pricks, too? I'm glad you've had your fill of women, Lucky, 'cause there aren't going to be any more. I mean, sure, you'll be able to fuck or be fucked. It just won't be with women is all I'm saying.'

Goshen was quiet while he contemplated this. Bosch put the photo of Layla on the bureau next to the box.

'Look, Bosch, just tell me what you guys've got and I'll tell you what I know so we can get this straightened out. You're wrong on this. I didn't do anything, so let's get this over with, stop wasting each other's time.'

Bosch didn't answer. He went back into the closet and hiked up on his toes to see if there was anything else on the shelf. There was. A small cloth folded like a handkerchief. He took it down and unfolded it. It was soiled with oil. He smelled it and recognized it.

Bosch came out of the closet, tossed the rag so it hit Goshen in the face and fell onto the bed.

'What's this?'

'I don't know. What is it?'

'It's a rag with gun oil on it. Where's the gun?'

'I don't have a gun and that isn't mine, either. Never saw it before.'

'Okay.'

'What do you mean, okay? I never fuckin' saw it before.'

'I mean, okay, Goshen. That's all. Don't get nervous.'

'It's hard with you people sticking your nose up my ass.'

Bosch bent over the night table. He opened the top drawer, found an empty cigarette box, a set of pearl earrings and an unopened box of condoms. Bosch threw the box at Goshen. It bounced off his huge chest and fell to the floor.

'You know, Goshen, just buying them ain't safe sex. You gotta put 'em on.'

He opened the bottom drawer. It was empty.

'How long you lived here, Goshen?'

'Moved in right after I kicked your sister out on her ass. Put her on the street. Last I seen, she was selling it over on Fremont outside the Cortez.'

Bosch straightened up and looked at him. Goshen was smiling. He wanted to provoke something. He wanted to control things, even handcuffed on the bed. Even if it cost him some blood.

'My mother, now my sister, who's next, my wife?'

'Yeah, I got something planned for her. I'll—'

'Shut up, would you? It's not working, understand? You're not getting to me. You can't get to me. So save your strength.'

'Everybody can be gotten to, Bosch. Remember that.'

Bosch looked at him and then stepped into the master bathroom. It was a large room with a separate shower and tub, almost in the same configuration as the room Tony Aliso had used at the Mirage. The toilet was in a small closet-size room behind a door with a slatted grill. Bosch started there. He quickly lifted the top of the water tank and found nothing unusual. Before putting the porcelain top back in place he leaned over the toilet and looked down the wall behind the tank. What he saw made him immediately call for the uniform in the bedroom.

'Yes, sir?' the cop said.

He looked like he wasn't yet twenty-five. His black skin had almost a bluish tint to it. He kept his hands on his equipment belt in a relaxed mode, his right just a few inches from his gun. It was the standard pose. Bosch saw that the nameplate above his breast pocket said Fontenot.

'Fontenot, take a look down here behind the tank.'

The cop did as he was asked without even taking his hands off his belt.

'What is it?' he asked.

'I think it's a gun. Why don't you step back and let me pull it out.'

Bosch flattened his hand and reached it down into the two-inch space between the wall and the tank. His fingers closed on a plastic bag attached to the back of the tank with gray duct tape. He managed to pull it free and get the bag out. He held it up for Fontenot to see. The bag contained a blue metal pistol equipped with a three-inch screw-on silencer.

'A twenty-two?' Fontenot asked.

'Oh, yeah,' Bosch said. 'Go get Felton and Iverson, would you?'

'Right away.'

Bosch followed Fontenot out of the bathroom. He was holding the bag containing the gun the way a fisherman holds a fish by its tail. When he stepped into the bedroom he couldn't help but smile at Goshen, whose eyes noticeably widened.

'That ain't mine,' Goshen immediately protested. 'That's a plant, you fuck! I don't be – Get me my goddamned lawyer, you son of a bitch!'

Bosch let the words go by but studied the look. He saw something flash in Goshen's eyes. It was there for only a second and then he covered up. It wasn't fear. He didn't think that was something Goshen would let slip into his eyes. Bosch believed he had seen something else. But what? He looked at Goshen and waited a moment for the look to return. Was it confusion? Disappointment? Goshen's eyes showed nothing now. But Bosch believed he knew the look. What he had seen had been surprise.

Iverson, Baxter and Felton then filed into the room. They saw the gun and Iverson yelped in triumph.

'Sayonara, *bay-bee!*'

His glee showed on his face. Bosch explained how and where he had found the weapon.

'These fuckhead gangsters,' Iverson said, looking at Goshen. 'Think the cops never saw *The Godfather?* Who'd you put it there for, Goshen? Michael Corleone?'

'I said get me my fucking lawyer!' Goshen yelled.

'You'll get your lawyer,' Iverson said. 'Now get up, you piece of shit. You gotta get dressed for the ride in.'

Bosch held him at gunpoint while Iverson took one of the cuffs off. Then they both pointed guns at him while he got dressed in black jeans, boots and T-shirt – the shirt manufactured for a much smaller man.

'You guys are always tough in numbers,' Goshen said as he went about putting the clothes on. 'You ever come up against me alone, then it's going to be wet ass time.'

'Come on, Goshen, we don't have all day,' Iverson said.

When he was done, they cuffed him and stuffed him into the back of Iverson's car. Iverson locked the gun in the trunk, then they went back inside the house. In a short meeting inside the front hallway it was decided that Baxter and two of the other detectives would stay behind to finish the search of the house.

'What about the women?' Bosch asked.

'The uniforms will watch them until these boys are done,' Iverson said.

'Yeah, but as soon as they leave they'll be on the phone. We'll have Goshen's lawyer down our throat before we even get started.'

'I'll take care of that. Goshen's got one car here, right? Where's the keys?'

'Kitchen counter,' one of the other detectives said.

'Okay,' Iverson said. 'We're out of here.'

Bosch followed him through the kitchen, watching him pocket the keys that were on the counter, and then out into the carport by the Corvette. There was a little workroom here with tools hanging on a peg board. Iverson selected a shovel and then stepped out of the carport and around to the back yard.

Bosch followed and watched as Iverson found the spot where the telephone line came in from a pole at the street and connected to the house. He swung the shovel up and with one strike disconnected the line.

'Amazing how strong the wind can get out here in the open desert,' he said.

He looked around behind the house.

'Those girls have no car and no phone,' he said. 'Nearest house is a half mile, city's about five. My guess is they'll stay put a while. That'll give us time. All we need.'

Iverson took a baseball swing with the shovel and launched it out over the property wall and into the scrub brush. He started walking toward the front of the house and his car.

'What do you think?' Bosch asked.

'I think the bigger they are, the harder they fall. Goshen's ours, Harry. Yours.'

'No. I mean about the gun.'

'What about it?'

'I don't know . . . It seems too easy.'

'Nobody said criminals gotta be smart. Goshen's not smart. He's just been lucky. But not anymore.'

Bosch nodded but he still didn't like it. It wasn't really a question of being smart or not. Criminals followed routines, instincts. This didn't make sense.

'I saw something in his eyes when he saw the gun. Like he was just as surprised to see it as we were.'

'Maybe. Maybe he's just a good actor. And maybe it's not even the right gun. You'll have to take it back with you to run tests. Find out if it's the gun, Harry, then worry about if it's too easy.'

Bosch nodded. He took out a cigarette and lit it.

'I don't know. I feel like I'm missing something.'

'Look, Harry, you want to make a case or not?'

'I want a case.'

'Then let's take him in and put him in a room, see what he has to say.'

They were at the car. Bosch realized he had left the photo of Layla inside. He told Iverson to start the car and he'd be right back. When he came back with the photo and got in, he checked Goshen in the back and saw a trickle of blood running down from the corner of his mouth. Bosch looked at Iverson, who was smiling.

'I don't know, he must've bumped his face getting in. Either that or he did it on purpose to make it look like I did it.'

Goshen said nothing and Bosch just turned around. Iverson pulled the

369

car out onto the road and they headed back toward the city. The temperature was climbing rapidly and Bosch could already feel the sweat sticking his shirt to his back. The air conditioner labored to overcome the heat that had built up in the car while they were inside the house. The air was as dry as old bones. Bosch finally took out the Chap Stick and rolled it across his sore lips. He didn't care what Iverson or Goshen thought about it.

They took Goshen up to the detective bureau in a back elevator in which Goshen audibly farted. Then Bosch and Iverson walked him down a hallway off the squad room and into an interview room barely larger than a rest-room stall. They handcuffed him to a steel ring bolted to the center of the table and locked him in. Then they left him there. As Iverson closed the door, Goshen called after him that he wanted to make his phone call.

Bosch noticed that the squad room was almost deserted as they walked back toward Felton's office.

'Somebody die?' Bosch asked. 'Where is everybody?'

'They're out picking up the others.'

'What others?'

'The captain wanted to bring in your pal, Gussie, throw a scare at him. They're bringing in the girl, too.'

'Layla? They found her?'

'No, not her. The one you had us run last night. The one that played with your victim at the Mirage. Turns out she's got a jacket.'

Bosch reached over and yanked Iverson's arm to stop him.

'Eleanor Wish? You're bringing in Eleanor Wish?'

He didn't wait for Iverson's reply. He broke away from the man and charged into Felton's office. The captain was on the phone and Bosch paced anxiously in front of the desk waiting for him to hang up. Felton pointed at the door but Bosch shook his head. He could see Felton's eyes start to smolder as he told whoever was on the other end of the line he had to go.

'I can't talk right now,' he said. 'You don't have to worry, it's under control. I'll talk to you.'

He hung up and looked at Bosch.

'What is it now?'

'Call your people. Tell them to leave Eleanor Wish alone.'

'What are you talking about?'

'She had nothing to do with this. I checked her out last night.'

Felton leaned forward and clasped his hands together as he thought.

'When you say you checked her out, what does that mean?'

'I interviewed her. She had a passing acquaintance with the victim, that's it. She's clean.'

'Do you know who she is, Bosch? I mean, do you know her history?'

'She was an FBI agent assigned to the L.A. bank robbery squad. She went to prison five years ago on a conspiracy charge stemming from a series of burglaries involving bank safe deposit vaults. It doesn't matter, Captain, she's clean on this.'

'I think it might be good to sweat her a little bit and take another go at her with one of my guys. Just to be sure.'

'I'm already sure. Look, I—'

Bosch looked back at the office door and saw Iverson hanging around, trying to listen in. Bosch walked over and closed the door, then pulled a chair away from the wall and sat right in front of Felton's desk and leaned across to him.

'Look, Captain, I knew Eleanor Wish in L.A. I worked that case with the bank vaults. I . . . we were more than just partners on it. Then it all turned to shit and she went away. I hadn't seen her in five years until I saw her on the surveillance tape at the Mirage. That's why I called you last night. I wanted to talk to her but not because of the case. She's clean. She did her time and she's clean. Now call your people.'

Felton was quiet. Bosch could see the wheels turning.

'I've been up most of the night working on this. I called your room a half dozen times to bring you in on it but you weren't there. I don't suppose you want to tell me where you were?'

'No, I don't.'

Felton thought some more and then shook his head.

'I can't do it. I can't cut her loose yet.'

'Why not?'

'Because there is something about her you apparently don't know.'

Bosch closed his eyes for a moment like a boy expecting to get slapped by an angry mother but steadying himself to take it.

'What don't I know?'

'She might've only had a passing acquaintance with your victim, but she's got more than that with Joey Marks and his group.'

It was worse than he expected.

'What are you talking about?'

'I put her name up for discussion with some of my people last night after you called. We've got her in a file. On numerous occasions she has been seen in the company of a man named Terrence Quillen who works for Goshen who works for Marks. Numerous times, Detective Bosch. In fact, I've got a team out looking for Quillen now. See what he has to say.'

'In the company of, what does that mean?'

'Looked like strictly business, according to the reports.'

Bosch felt like he'd been punched. This was impossible. He had spent the night with the woman. The sense of betrayal was building in him but a deeper gut sense told him she was true, that this was all some huge mix-up.

There was a knock on the door and Iverson poked his head in.

'FYI, the others are back, boss. They're puttin' them in the interview rooms.'

'Okay.'

'You need anything?'

'No, we're fine. Close the door.'

After Iverson left, Bosch looked at the captain.

'Is she arrested?'

'No, we asked her to come in voluntarily.'

'Let me talk to her first.'

'I don't think that would be wise.'

'I don't care if it's wise. Let me go talk to her. If she'll tell anybody, she'll tell me.'

Felton thought a moment and then finally nodded his head.

'Okay, go ahead. You get fifteen minutes.'

Bosch should have thanked him but didn't. He just got up quickly and went to the door.

'Detective Bosch?' Felton said.

Harry looked back from the door.

'I'll do what I can for you on this. But this cuts us in in a big way, you understand that?'

Bosch stepped out without answering. Felton had no finesse. It was understood without being said that Bosch was now beholden to him. But Felton had to say it anyway.

In the hallway, Bosch passed the first interview room, where they had placed Goshen, and opened the door to the second. Sitting there handcuffed to the table was Gussie Flanagan. His nose was misshapen and looked like a new potato. He had cotton jammed into the nostrils. He looked at Bosch with bloodshot eyes and recognition showed on his face. Bosch backed out and closed the door without saying a word.

Eleanor Wish was behind door number three. She was disheveled, obviously dragged from sleep by the Metro cops. But her eyes had the alert and wild quality of a cornered animal and that cut Bosch to the bone.

'Harry! What are they doing?'

He closed the door and moved quickly into the tiny room, touching her shoulder in a consoling manner and taking the seat across from her.

'Eleanor, I'm sorry.'

'What? What did you do?'

'Yesterday when I saw you on the tape at the Mirage I asked Felton, he's the captain here, to get me your number and address because you were unlisted. He did. But then without my knowledge he ran your name and pulled up your package. Then on his own he had his people get you this morning. It's all part of this Tony Aliso thing.'

'I told you. I didn't know him. I had one drink with him once. Just because I happened by chance to be at the same table with him they bring me in?'

She shook her head and looked away, the distress written on her face. This was the way it would always be, she now knew. The criminal record she carried would guarantee it.

'I've got to ask you something. I want to get this cleared up and get you out of here.'

'What?'

'Tell me about this man Terrence Quillen.'

He saw the shock in her eyes.

'Quillen? What does he – is he the suspect?'

'Eleanor, you know how this works. I can't tell you things. You tell me. Just answer the question. Do you know Terrence Quillen?'

'Yes.'

'How do you know him?'

'He came up to me about six months ago when I was leaving the Flamingo. I had been out here four or five months. I was settling in, playing six nights a week by then. He came up to me and in his words told me what's what. He somehow knew about me. Who I was, that I'd just gotten out. He said there was a street tax. He said I had to pay it, that all the locals paid it, and that if I didn't there'd be trouble. He said that if I did pay it, he'd watch out for me. Be there if I ever got in a jam. You know how it goes, extortion plain and simple.'

She broke then and started to cry. It took all of Bosch's will not to get up and try to hold her and comfort her in some way.

'I was alone,' she said. 'Scared. I paid. I pay him every week. What was I supposed to do. I had nothing and nowhere to go.'

'Fuck it,' Bosch said under his breath.

He got up and squeezed around the end of the table and grabbed hold of her. He pulled her to his chest and kissed the top of her head.

'Nothing's going to happen,' he whispered. 'I promise you that, Eleanor.'

He held her there in silence for a few moments, listening to her quiet crying, until the door opened and Iverson stood there. He had a toothpick in his mouth.

'Get the fuck out of here, Iverson.'

The detective slowly closed the door.

'I'm sorry,' Eleanor said. 'I'm getting you in trouble.'

'No, you're not. It's all on me. Everything is on me.'

A few minutes later he walked back into Felton's office. The captain looked up at him wordlessly.

'She was paying off Quillen to leave her alone. Two hundred a week. That was all it was. The street tax. She doesn't know anything about anything. She happened by chance to be at the same table as Aliso for about an hour Friday. She's clean. Now kick her loose. Tell your people.'

Felton leaned back and started tapping his lower lip with the end of a pen. He was showing Bosch his deep-thinking pose.

'I don't know,' he said.

'Okay, this is the deal. You let her go and I make a call to my people.'

'And what'll you tell 'em?'

'I'll tell them I've gotten excellent cooperation from Metro out here and that we ought to run this as a joint operation. I'll say we're going to put the squeeze on Goshen here and go for the two-for-one sale. We're going to go for Goshen and Joey Marks because Marks was the one who would've ultimately pushed the button on Tony Aliso. I'll say it's highly recommended that Metro take the lead out here because they know the turf and they know Marks. Do we have a deal?'

Felton tapped out another code message on his lip, then reached over and turned the phone on his desk so Bosch could have access to it.

'Make the call now,' he said. 'After you talk to your CO, put me on the line. I want to talk to him.'

'It's a her.'

'Whatever.'

A half hour later Bosch was driving a borrowed unmarked Metro car with Eleanor Wish sitting crumpled in the passenger seat. The call to Lieutenant Billets had gone over well enough for Felton to keep his end of the deal. Eleanor was kicked loose, though the damage was pretty much done. She had been able to eke out a new start and a new existence, but the underpinnings of confidence and pride and security had all been kicked out from beneath her. It was all because of Bosch and he knew it. He drove in silence, unable to even fathom what to say or how to make it better. And it cut him deeply because he truly wanted to. Before the previous night he had not seen her in five years, but she had never been far from his deepest thoughts, even when he had been with other women. There had always been a voice back there that whispered to him that Eleanor Wish was the one. She was the match.

'They're always going to come for me,' she said in a small voice.

'What?'

'You remember that Bogart movie where the cop says, "Round up the usual suspects," and they go out and do it? Well, that's me now. They are going to mean me. I guess I never realized that until now. I'm one of the usual suspects. I guess I should thank you for slapping me in the face with reality.'

Bosch said nothing. He didn't know how to respond because her words were true.

In a few minutes they were at her apartment and Bosch walked her in and sat her on the couch.

'You okay?'

'Fine.'

'When you get a chance, look around and make sure they didn't take anything.'

'I didn't have anything to take.'

Bosch looked at the *Nighthawks* print on the wall above her. It was a painting of a lonely coffee shop on a dark night. A man and a woman sitting together, another man by himself. Bosch used to think he was the man alone. Now he stared at the couple and wondered.

'Eleanor,' he said. 'I have to go back. I'll come back here as soon as I can.'

'Okay, Harry, thanks for getting me out.'

'You going to be okay?'

'Sure.'

'Promise?'

'Promise.'

Back at Metro, Iverson was waiting for Bosch before they took their first shot at Goshen. Felton had acceded to leaving Goshen for Bosch. It was still his case.

In the hallway outside the interview room, Iverson tapped Bosch on the arm to stop him before going in.

'Listen, Bosch, I just want to say I don't know what you got going on with that woman and I guess it's nobody's business anymore since the captain let her go, but since we're going to be working together on Lucky here, I thought I'd clear the air. I didn't appreciate the way you spoke to me, telling me to get the fuck out and all.'

Bosch looked at him a minute. The detective still had a toothpick in his mouth and Bosch wondered if it was the same one from before.

'You know, Iverson, I don't even know your first name.'

'It's John, but people call me Ivy.'

'Well, Iverson, I didn't appreciate the way you were sneaking around the captain's office or the interview room. In L.A. we've got a name for cops who sneak around and eavesdrop and are assholes on general principle. We call 'em squints. And I don't really care if you're offended by me or not.

374

You're a squint. And you make any trouble for me from here on out and I'll go right to Felton and make trouble for you. I'll tell him about finding you in my room today. And if that's not enough, I'll tell 'im that I won six hundred bucks on the wheel in the casino last night but the money disappeared off the bureau after you were there. Now, you want to do this interview or not?'

Iverson grabbed Bosch by the collar and shoved him against the wall.

'Don't you fuck with me, Bosch.'

'Don't you fuck with me, *Ivy*.'

A smile slowly cracked across Iverson's face and he released his grip and stepped back. Bosch straightened his tie and shirt.

'Then let's do it, cowboy,' Iverson said.

When they squeezed into the interview room, Goshen was waiting for them with his eyes closed, his legs up on the table and his hands laced behind his head. Bosch watched Iverson look down at the torn metal where the cuff ring had been attached to the table. Red flares of anger burst on his cheeks.

'Okay, asshole, get up,' Iverson ordered.

Goshen stood up and brought his cuffed hands up. Iverson got out his keys and took the cuff off one wrist.

'Let's try this again. Sit down.'

When Goshen was back down, Iverson cuffed his wrists behind his back, looping the chain through one of the steel slats of the chair back. Iverson then kicked out a chair and sat to the side of the gangster. Bosch sat across from him.

'Okay, Houdini, you also've got destroying public property on your list now,' Iverson said.

'Wow, that's bold, Iverson. Really bold. That's like the time you came into the club and took Cinda into the fantasy booth. I think you called it interrogation. She called it something else. What's this going to be?'

Iverson's face now glowed with anger. Goshen puffed his chest up proudly and smirked at the detective's embarrassment.

Bosch shoved the table into Goshen's midsection and the big man doubled over it as his breath burst out. Bosch was up quickly and around the table. As he went, he pulled his keychain from his pocket. Then, using his elbow to keep Goshen's chest down on the table, he flicked open the blade of his pocket knife and sawed off the big man's ponytail. He went back to his seat and when Goshen lifted up, threw the six-inch length of hair on the table in front of him.

'Ponytails went out of style at least three years ago, Goshen. You probably didn't hear about it.'

Iverson burst out in uproarious laughter. Goshen looked at Bosch with pale blue eyes that seemed as soulless as buttons on a machine. He didn't say a word. He was showing Bosch he could take it. He was stand-up. But Bosch knew even he couldn't stand up forever. Nobody can.

'You've got a problem, Lucky,' Iverson said. 'Big problems. You—'

'Wait a minute, wait a minute. I don't want to talk to you, Iverson. I don't want you to talk to me. You're a runt. I've got no respect for you. Understand? Anybody talks, let him talk.'

Goshen nodded to Bosch. There was a silence during which Bosch looked from him to Iverson and then back.

'Go get a cup,' Bosch said, without looking at Iverson. 'We'll be fine in here.'

'No, you—'

'Go get a cup.'

'You sure?'

Iverson looked as if he were being kicked out of the college fraternity because the boys didn't think he fit in.

'Yeah, I'm sure. You got a rights form on you?'

Iverson got up. He took a folded piece of paper out of his coat pocket and tossed it on the table.

'I'll be right outside the door.'

When Goshen and Bosch were alone they studied each other for a moment before Bosch spoke.

'You want a smoke?'

'Don't play the good guy with me. Just tell me what's what.'

Bosch shrugged off the rebuke and got up. He moved behind Goshen and took his keys out again. This time he unlocked one of the cuffs. Goshen brought his hands up and began rubbing the wrists to get circulation going. He noticed the length of hair on the table and slapped it onto the floor.

'Let me tell you something, Mr L.A. I've been to a place where it doesn't matter what they do to you, where nothing can hurt you. I've been there and back.'

'Everybody's been to Disneyland, so what?'

'I'm not talking about fuckin' Disneyland, asshole. I spent three years in the penta down in Chihuahua. They didn't break me then, you aren't going to do it now.'

'Let me tell you something then. In my life I've killed a lot of people. Just wanted you to know that up front. Time comes again, there won't be any hesitation. None. This isn't about good guy cops and bad guy cops, Goshen. That's the movies. The movies where the bad guys have ponytails, I guess. But this is real life. You are nothing to me but meat. And I'm gonna put you down. That's a given. It's just up to you how hard and how far you want to go down.'

Goshen thought a moment.

'All right, so now we know each other. Talk to me. And I'll take that smoke now.'

Bosch put his cigarettes and matches on the table. Goshen got one out and lit it. Bosch waited until he was done.

'I gotta advise you first. You know the routine.'

Bosch opened the piece of paper Iverson had left and read Goshen his rights. He then had the man sign his name on it.

'This is being taped, isn't it?'

'Not yet.'

'Okay then, what've you got?'

'Your fingerprints were on Tony Aliso's body. The gun we found behind the toilet will be going back to L.A. today. The prints are good to have, real good. But if the bullets they pick out of Tony's gourd match that gun, then it's all over. I don't care what kind of alibi you line up or what your explanation will be or if your lawyer's Johnny fucking Cochran, you won't just be meat, you'll be one hundred percent grade A dead meat.'

'That gun ain't mine. It's a plant, goddamn it. You know it and I know it. And it's not going to fly, Bosch.'

Bosch looked at him a moment and felt his face getting hot.

'You're saying I put that there?'

'I'm saying I watched the O.J. show. Cops out here are no different. I'm saying I don't know if it was you or Iverson or whoever, but that gun's a fuckin' plant, goddammit. That's what I'm saying.'

Bosch traced a finger along the top of the table, waiting for the anger to dissipate to the point where he could control his voice.

'You hang on to that bullshit story, Goshen, and you'll go far with it. You'll go about ten years and then they'll strap you down and stick a needle in your arm. At least it's not the gas chamber anymore. They make it easy on you guys now.'

Bosch leaned back but there wasn't a lot of room. The back of the chair hit the wall. He took out the Chap Stick and reapplied it.

'We own you now, Goshen. All you have left is one small window of opportunity. Call it a little piece of destiny still in your grasp.'

'And what window's that?'

'You know what window, you know what I'm talking about. Guy like you doesn't move an inch without the okay. Give us the guy you worked the hit with and the guy who told you to put Tony in the trunk. You don't make a deal and there's no light at the end of the tunnel.'

Goshen let out his breath and shook his head.

'Look, I did not do this. I did not!'

Bosch didn't expect him to say anything different. It wasn't that easy. He had to wear him down. He leaned across the table conspiratorially.

'Listen, I'm going to tell you something so that you know that I'm not bullshitting you. Maybe save some time, so you can decide where to go from here.'

'Go ahead, but it's not going to change anything.'

'Anthony Aliso was wearing a black leather jacket Friday night. Remember that? One with the two-inch lapels. It—'

'You're wasting your—'

'You grabbed him there, Goshen. Just like this.'

Bosch reached across the table and demonstrated, using both hands to grab an imaginary set of lapels on a jacket Goshen wasn't wearing.

'Remember that? Tell me I'm wasting my time now. Remember, Goshen? You did it, you grabbed him like that. Now who is bullshitting who?'

Goshen shook his head but Bosch knew he had scored. The pale blues were looking inward at the memory.

'Kind've a freaky thing. Processed leather like that holds the amino acids from the prints. That's what the tech tells me. We got some nice ones. Enough to take to the DA or the grand jury. Enough for me to come out here. Enough for us to come right into your fucking house and hook you up.'

He hesitated a moment until Goshen was looking at him.

'And now this gun turns up in your house. I guess we'll just have to wait

377

on the ballistics if you don't want to talk anymore. But I've got a hunch about it. I like my chances.'

Goshen slammed two open palms down on the steel table. It made a sound like a shot and echo.

'This is a setup. You people put—'

Iverson burst through the door, his gun out and aimed at Goshen. He jerked the weapon up like a TV cop.

'You okay?'

'Yeah,' Bosch said. 'Lucky here is just a little mad, is all. Give us a few more minutes.'

Iverson went back out without a word.

'Nice play, but that's all it was,' Goshen said. 'Where's my phone call?'

Bosch leaned back across the table.

'You can make the call now. But you make the call and it's over right here. Because that won't be your lawyer. That will be Joey's lawyer. He'll be here to represent you, but we both know the one he'll be watching out for is Joey Marks.'

Bosch stood up.

'I guess then we'll just have to settle for you. We'll go the distance on you.'

'Yeah, but you don't have me, you prick. Fingerprints? You need more than that. That gun's a plant and everybody's going to know it.'

'Yeah, you keep saying it. I'll know what I need to know from ballistics by tomorrow morning.'

It was hard for Bosch to tell if that had registered because Goshen didn't give it much time to.

'I've got a fuckin' alibi! You can't pin this on me, man!'

'Yeah? What's your fuckin' alibi? How do you even know when he got hit?'

'You asked me about Friday night, right? That's the night.'

'I didn't say that.'

Goshen sat silent and motionless for a half minute. Bosch could see the eyes going to work. Goshen knew he had crossed one line with what he had said. Bosch guessed he was considering how far he should cross. Bosch pulled the chair out and sat back down.

'I got an alibi, so I'm in the clear.'

'You're not in the clear till we say you are. What's your story?'

'No. I'm gonna tell my lawyer what it is.'

'You're hurting yourself, Goshen. You've got nothing to lose telling me.'

'Except my freedom, right?'

'I could go out, verify your story. Maybe then I'd start listening to your story about the gun being planted.'

'Yeah, right, that's like puttin' the inmates in charge of the prison. Talk to my lawyer, Bosch. Now get me a fucking phone.'

Bosch stood up and signaled for him to put his arms behind his back. He did so and Bosch cuffed him again, then left the room.

After Bosch filled them in on how Goshen had won round one, Felton told Iverson to take a phone into the interview room and allow the suspect to call his lawyer.

'I guess we'll let him stew,' Felton said when he and Bosch were alone. 'See how he likes his first taste of incarceration.'

'He told me he did three years down in Mexico.'

'He tells that to a lot of people he's trying to impress. Like the tattoos. When we were backgrounding him after he showed up a couple years ago, we never found anything about a Mexican prison and as far as we know, he's never ridden a Harley, let alone with any motorcycle gang. I think a night in county might soften him up. Maybe by round two we'll have the ballistics back.'

Bosch said he had to use a phone to call his CO to check on what the plan was for the gun.

'Just pick an empty desk out there,' Felton said. 'Make yourself at home. Listen, I'll tell you how this most likely will go and you can tell your Lieutenant Billets. The lawyer he calls is most likely going to be Mickey Torrino. He's Joey Marks's top guy. He's going to object to extradition and meantime try to get bail. Any bail will do. All they want to do is get him out of our hands and into their hands and then they can make their decision.'

'What decision?'

'Whether or not to whack him. If Joey thinks Lucky might flip, he'll just take him out to the desert somewhere and we'll never see him again. Nobody will.'

Bosch nodded.

'So you go make your call and I'll call over to the prosecutor's office, see if we can't get an X hearing scheduled. I think the sooner the better. If you can get Lucky to L.A., he's going to be even more likely to start thinking about cutting a deal. That is, if we don't break him first.'

'It'd be nice to have the ballistics before the extradition hearing. If we get a ballistics match, it will seal it. But things don't move so quickly in L.A., if you know what I mean. I doubt there's even been an autopsy.'

'Well, make your call and then we'll reconnoiter.'

Bosch used an empty desk next to Iverson's to make his call. He got Billets at her desk and he could tell she was eating. He quickly updated her on his failed effort to scam Goshen into talking and the plans to have the prosecutor's office in Las Vegas handle the extradition hearing.

'What do you want to do about the gun?' he asked when he was done.

'I want it back here as soon as possible. Edgar talked somebody over at the coroner's office into doing the cut this afternoon. We should have the bullets by tonight. If we have the gun, we can take the whole thing over to ballistics tomorrow morning. Today's Tuesday. I doubt there'd be an extradition hearing before Thursday. We'd have an answer from ballistics by then.'

'Okay, I'll grab a plane.'

'Good.'

Bosch sensed something off about her tone. She was preoccupied by something other than ballistics and what she was eating.

'Lieutenant,' he said. 'What's up? Is there something I don't know about?'

She hesitated a moment and Bosch waited her out.

'Actually, something's come up.'

Bosch's face flashed warm. He guessed that Felton had screwed him and told Billets about the Eleanor Wish situation.

'What is it?'

'I've made an ID on the guy who was in Tony Aliso's office.'

'That's great,' Bosch said, relieved but confused by her somber tone. 'Who?'

'No, it's not great. It was Dominic Carbone from OCID.'

Bosch was stunned into silence for a long moment.

'Carbone? What the . . . ?'

'I don't know. I've got some feelers out. I'd like you back here until we figure out what to do with this. Goshen will keep until the extradition hearing. He's not going to be talking to anyone but his lawyer. If you can get back, I'd like us all to get together and hash this around. I haven't talked to Kiz and Jerry yet today. They're still working the financial trail.'

'How'd you make the ID on Carbone?'

'Pure luck. Things were kind of slow after I talked to you and the captain out there this morning. I took a drive downtown and stopped by Central. I've got a friend, she's a lieutenant, too, up in OC. Lucinda Barnes, you know her?'

'No.'

'Anyway, I went up to see her. I wanted to kind of feel around, maybe get an idea why they took the pass on this one. And, lo and behold, we're sitting there talking and this guy walks through the squad and I think I recognize him but I'm not sure from where. I ask who he is and she tells me that's Carbone. And that's when I remembered. He's the guy on the tape. He had his suit jacket off and his sleeves rolled up. I even saw the tattoo. It's him.'

'You tell all this to your friend?'

'Hell no. I just acted natural and got the hell out of there. I tell you, Harry, I don't like this inside stuff. I don't know what to do.'

'We'll figure something. Look, I'm going to go. I'll be there as soon as I can. What you might want to do in the meantime, Lieutenant, is try to use some juice with ballistics. Tell them we'll be coming in with a code three in the morning.'

Billets said she would do what she could on that.

After making arrangements to fly back to L.A., Bosch barely had time to take a cab back to the Mirage and check out and still make it by Eleanor's apartment to say good-bye. But his knock on her door went unanswered. He didn't know what kind of car she had, so it was impossible for him to check the lot to make sure she was gone. He went back to his rental and sat inside and waited as long as he could, until he was at risk of missing his flight. He then scribbled a message on a page from his notebook saying he would call her and went back to the door. He folded the page up tight and stuck it in the crack of the door jamb so that it would fall and be noticed the next time she opened the door.

He wanted to wait around longer and talk to her in person but he couldn't. Twenty minutes later he was leaving the security office of the airport. The gun from Goshen's house was wrapped in an evidence bag and safely in his briefcase. Five minutes later he was aboard a jet headed for the city of angels.

Billets had a weighted and worried look on her face when Bosch stepped into her office.

'Harry.'

'Lieutenant. I dropped the gun at ballistics. They're waiting on the bullets. Whoever it was you talked to over there, they snapped to.'

'Good.'

'Where is everybody?'

'They're both over at Archway. Kiz spent the morning at the IRS and then went over to help Jerry with the interviews with Aliso's associates. I also borrowed a couple of people from Major Fraud to help with the books. They're tracing down these dummy corporations. They're going to go after the bank accounts. Search and seizure. When we freeze the money, then maybe some real live people will come out of the woodwork and claim it. My theory is that this Joey Marks was not the only one Aliso was washing money for. There's too much involved – if Kiz's numbers are right. Aliso was probably working for every mob combine west of Chicago.'

Bosch nodded.

'Oh, by the way,' she continued, 'I told Jerry that you'd take the autopsy so he can stay at Archway. Then I want everybody back here at six to talk about what we have.'

'Okay, when's the autopsy?'

'Three-thirty. That going to be a problem?'

'No. Can I ask you something, why'd you call Major Fraud in instead of OCID?'

'For obvious reasons. I don't know what to do about Carbone and OCID. I don't know whether to bring in Internal Affairs, look the other way or what.'

'Well, we can't look the other way. They have something we need. And if you call in IAD, then forget it. That will freeze everything up down there and that will be that.'

'What do they have that we need?'

'It stands to reason that if Carbone was pulling a bug out of that office, then—'

'There's tapes. Jesus, I forgot about that.'

They dropped into silence for a few moments. Bosch pulled the chair out across from her desk and finally sat down.

'Let me take a run at Carbone, see if I can figure out what they were doing and get the tapes,' he said. 'We've got the leverage.'

'This may have something to do with the chief and Fitzgerald, you know.'

'Maybe.'

She was referring to the intradepartmental skirmish between Deputy Chief Leon Fitzgerald, commander of OCID for more than a decade, and the man who was supposed to be his boss, the chief of police. In the time Fitzgerald had run the OCID, he had taken on an aura akin to J. Edgar Hoover's at the FBI, a keeper of secrets who would use them to protect his position, his division and his budget. It was believed by many that Fitzgerald had his minions investigate and keep tabs on more honest citizens, cops and elected officials of the city than the mobsters his division was charged with rooting out. And it was no secret within the department that there was an ongoing power struggle between Fitzgerald and the police chief. The chief wanted to rein in OCID and its deputy chief but Fitzgerald didn't want to be reined in. In fact, he wanted his domain to broaden. He wanted to be police chief. The struggle was largely at a name-calling standstill. The chief could not fire Fitzgerald outright because of civil service protections; and he could not get backing to simply gut and overhaul OCID from the police commissions, mayor or city council members because it was believed that Fitzgerald had thick files on all of them, including the chief. These elected and appointed officials did not know what was in those files but they had to assume that the worst things they had ever done were duly recorded. And therefore they would not back the chief's move against Fitzgerald unless they and the chief were in a guaranteed no-lose position.

Most of this was department legend or rumor, but Bosch knew even legend and rumor usually have some basis in reality. He was reluctant to step behind this curtain and possibly into this fight, as Billets clearly was, but offered to do so because he saw no alternative. He had to know what OCID had been doing and what it was that Carbone was trying to protect by breaking into the Archway office.

'Okay,' Billets said after some long thought. 'But be careful.'

'Where's the video from Archway?'

She pointed to the safe on the floor behind her desk. It was used to secure evidence.

'It will be safe,' she said.

'It better be. It will probably be the only thing that keeps them off me.'

She nodded. She knew the score.

The OCID offices were on the third floor of Central Division in downtown. The division was located away from police headquarters at Parker Center because the work of the OCID involved many undercover operations and it would not be wise to have so many undercovers going in and out of a place as public as the so-called Glass House, Parker Center. But it was that separation that helped foster the deepening gulf between Leon Fitzgerald and the police chief.

On the drive over from Hollywood, Bosch thought about a plan and knew just how he was going to play it by the time he got to the guard shack and flipped his ID to the rookie assigned parking lot duty. He read the name off the tag above the cop's breast pocket and drove into the lot and over toward the back doors of the station, then put the car in park and got out his phone. He called the OCID's main number and a secretary answered.

'Yeah, this is Trindle down on the parking lot,' Bosch said. 'Is Carbone there?'

'Yes, he is. If you hold a—'

'Just tell him to come down. Somebody busted into his car.'

Bosch hung up and waited. In three minutes one of the doors at the rear of the station house opened and a man hurried out. Bosch recognized him from the Archway surveillance tape. Billets had been right on. Bosch put the car in drive and followed along behind the man. Eventually, he pulled up alongside him and lowered the window.

'Carbone.'

'Yeah, what?'

He kept walking, barely giving Bosch a glance.

'Slow down. Your car's all right.'

Carbone stopped and now looked closely at Bosch.

'What? What are you talking about?'

'I made the call. I just wanted to get you out here.'

'Who the fuck are you?'

'I'm Bosch. We talked the other night.'

'Oh, yeah. The Aliso caper.'

Then it dawned on him that Bosch could have just taken the elevator up to the third floor if he wanted to see him.

'What is this, Bosch? What's going on?'

'Why don't you get in? I want to take a little ride.'

'I don't know, man. I don't like the way you're doing this.'

'Get in, Carbone. I think you better.'

Bosch said it in a tone and with an accompanying stare that invited no choice but compliance. Carbone, who was about forty with a stocky build, hesitated a moment, then walked around the front of the car. He was wearing a nice dark blue suit like most mob cops liked to wear and he filled the car with the smell of a brisk cologne. Right away Bosch didn't like him.

They drove out of the parking lot and Bosch went north toward Broadway. There was a lot of traffic and pedestrians and they moved slowly. Bosch said nothing, waiting for Carbone.

'Okay, so what's so important you have to kidnap me away from the station?' he finally asked.

Bosch drove another block without answering. He wanted Carbone to sweat a little.

'You've got problems, Carbone,' he finally said. 'I just thought I should tell you. See, I want to be your friend, Carbone.'

Carbone looked at Bosch with caution.

'I know I got problems,' he said. 'I'm paying two different women child support, my house still has cracks in the walls from the earthquake and the union ain't going to get us a raise again this year. So fuckin' what?'

'Those aren't problems, man. Those are inconveniences. I'm talking about real problems. About the break-in you did the other night over at Archway.'

Carbone was silent for a long moment and Bosch wasn't sure but he thought the man was holding his breath.

'I don't know what you're talking about. Take me back.'

'No, Carbone, see, that's the wrong answer. I'm here to help you, not hurt you. I'm your friend. And that goes for your boss, Fitzgerald, too.'

'I still don't know what you're talking about.'

'Okay, then I'll tell you what I'm talking about. I called you Sunday night and asked you about my stiff named Aliso. You call me back and tell me not only is OCID taking a pass, but you never heard of the guy. But as soon as you hang up the phone, you get over to Archway, break into the guy's office and pop the bug you people planted in his phone. That's what I'm talking about.'

Bosch looked over at him for the first time and he saw the face of a man whose mind is racing to find a way out. Bosch knew he had him now.

'Bullshit, that's what you're talking about.'

'Yeah, you dumb fuck? Next time you decide to do a little breaking and entering, look up. Check for cameras. Rodney King Rule Number One, don't get caught on tape.'

He waited a moment to let that sink in and then put the final nails in the coffin.

'You knocked the mug off the desk and broke it. You then dumped it outside hoping nobody would notice anything. And one last thing about the rules. If you're going to do a B&E in short sleeves, then you ought to get yourself a Band-Aid or somethin' and cover up that tattoo on your arm, know what I mean? That's a slam-bang identifier when you got it on tape. And, Carbone, you're on tape, lots of tape.'

Carbone wiped a hand across his face. Bosch turned on Third and they went into the tunnel that runs under Bunker Hill. In the darkness that shrouded the car, Carbone finally spoke.

'Who knows about this?'

'For the moment, just me. But don't get any ideas. Anything happens to me and the tape will get known by a lot of people. But for the moment, I can probably contain it.'

'What do you want?'

'I want to know what was going on and I want all the tapes you took off his phone.'

'Impossible. Can't do it. I don't have those tapes. It wasn't even my file. I just did what . . . '

'What Fitz told you to do. Yeah, I know. But I don't care about that. You go to Fitz or whoever's file it was and get it. I'll go with you if you want or I'll wait out in the car. But we're going back now to get them.'

'I can't do it.'

What Bosch knew he meant was that he couldn't get the tapes without going to Fitzgerald and telling him how he had so badly messed up the break-in.

'You're going to have to, Carbone. I don't give a shit about you. You lied to me and fucked with my case. You either get me the tapes and an explanation or this is what I do. I dub off three copies of the surveillance tape. One goes to the chief's office in the Glass House, one goes to Jim Newton at the *Times* and the last goes over to Stan Chambers at Channel 5. Stan's a good man, he'll know what to do with it. Do you know he's the one who got the Rodney King tape first?'

386

'Jesus, Bosch, you're killing me!'

'You've got your choice.'

The autopsy was being conducted by a deputy coroner named Salazar. He had already started by the time Bosch got to the coroner's office at County–USC Medical Center. They said their perfunctory hellos and Bosch, garbed in the protective paper body suit and plastic mask, leaned back against one of the stainless counters and just watched. He wasn't expecting much from the autopsy. He had really only come for the bullets and his hope was that one of them would be usable for comparison purposes. It was well known that one reason hitters preferred to use twenty-twos on the job was that the soft bullets often became so misshapen after bouncing around in the brain case that they were worthless for ballistic comparison.

Salazar kept his long black hair in a ponytail that he then wrapped in a larger paper cap. Because he was in a wheelchair, he worked at an autopsy table that was lowered to accommodate him. This gave Bosch an unusually clear vantage point in viewing what was happening to the body.

In years past, Bosch would have maintained an ongoing banter with Salazar while the autopsy proceeded. But since his motorcycle accident, his nine-month medical leave and his return in a wheelchair, Salazar was no longer a cheerful man and rarely engaged in small talk.

Bosch watched as Salazar used a dulled scalpel to scrape a sample of the whitish material from the corners of Aliso's eyes. He placed the material in a paper bindle and put it in a petri dish. He placed the dish on a tray that held a small stand containing the test tubes filled with blood, urine and other samples of body materials to be scanned and tested.

'Think it was tears?' Bosch asked.

'I don't think so. Too thick. He had something in his eyes or on his skin. We'll find out what.'

Bosch nodded and Salazar proceeded to open the skullcap and examine the brain.

'The bullets mushed this puppy,' he said.

After a few minutes he used a pair of long tweezers to pick out two bullet fragments and drop them in a dish. Bosch stepped over and looked at them and frowned. At least one of the bullets had fragmented upon impact. The pieces were probably worthless for comparison purposes.

Then Salazar pulled out a complete bullet and dropped it in the tray.

'You might be able to work with this one,' he said.

Bosch took a look. The bullet had mushroomed on impact but about half the shaft was still intact, and he could see the tiny scratches made when it was fired through the barrel of a gun. He felt a twinge of encouragement.

'This might work,' he said.

The autopsy wrapped up in about ten more minutes. Overall, Aliso had gotten fifty minutes of Salazar's time. It was more than most. Bosch checked a clipboard that was on the counter and saw that it was the eleventh autopsy of the day for Salazar.

Salazar cleaned the bullets and put them in an evidence envelope. As he handed it to Bosch, he told the detective that he would be informed of the results of the analysis of the samples retrieved from the body as soon as it was completed. The only other thing that he thought was worth mentioning was that the bruise on Aliso's cheek was antemortem by four or five hours. This Bosch found to be very curious. He didn't know how it fit in. It would mean that someone had roughed Aliso up while he was in Las Vegas, yet he had been killed here in L.A. He thanked Salazar, calling him Sally as many people did, and headed out. He was in the hallway before he remembered something and went back to the door of the autopsy suite. When he stuck his head in, he saw Salazar tying the sheet around the body, making sure the toe tag hung free and could be read.

'Hey, Sally, the guy had hemorrhoids, right?'

Salazar looked back at him with a quizzical look on his face.

'Hemorrhoids? No. Why do you ask?'

'I found a tube of Preparation H in his car. In the glove box. It was half used.'

'Hmmm . . . well, no hemorrhoids. Not on this one.'

Bosch wanted to ask him if he was sure but knew that would be insulting. He let it go for the moment and left.

Details fueled any investigation. They were important and not to be misplaced or forgotten. As he headed toward the glass exit doors of the coroner's office, Bosch found himself bothered by the detail of the tube of Preparation H found in the glove box of the Silver Cloud. If Tony Aliso hadn't suffered from hemorrhoids, then whom did the tube belong to and why was it in his car? He could dismiss it as probably being unimportant, but that wasn't his way. Everything had its place in an investigation, Bosch believed. Everything.

His deep concentration on this problem caused Bosch to go through the glass doors and down the stairs to the parking lot before he saw Carbone standing there smoking a cigarette and waiting. When Bosch had dropped him off earlier, the OCID detective had begged for a couple of hours to get the tapes together. Bosch had agreed but hadn't told him that he was heading to an autopsy. So he now assumed that Carbone had called the bureau in Hollywood and been told by Billets or someone else that he was at the coroner's office. Bosch wouldn't check this with Carbone because he didn't want to show any kind of concern that the OCID detective had so easily found him.

'Bosch.'

'Yeah.'

'Somebody wants to talk.'

'Who? When? I want the tapes, Carbone.'

'Cool your jets for a couple minutes. Over here in the car.'

He led Bosch to the second parking row, where there was a car with its engine running and its dark-tinted windows all the way up.

'Hop in the back,' Carbone said.

Bosch nonchalantly walked to the door, still showing no concern. He opened it and ducked in. Leon Fitzgerald was sitting in the back. He was a tall man – more than six and a half feet – and his knees were pressed hard against the back of the driver's seat. He wore a beautiful suit of blue silk and held the stub of a cigar between his fingers. He was almost sixty and his hair was a jet-black dye job. His eyes, behind steel-rimmed glasses, were pale gray. His skin was pasty white. He was a night man.

'Chief,' Bosch said, nodding.

He had never met Fitzgerald before but had seen him often enough at cop funerals and on television news reports. He was the embodiment of the OCID. No one else from the secretive division ever went on camera.

'Detective Bosch,' Fitzgerald said. 'I know of you. Know of your exploits. Over the years you have been suggested to me more than once as a candidate for our unit.'

'Why didn't you call?'

Carbone had come around and gotten in the driver's seat. He started moving the car slowly through the lot.

'Because like I said, I know of you,' Fitzgerald was saying. 'And I know you would not leave homicide. Homicide is your calling. Am I correct?'

'Pretty much.'

'Which brings us to the current homicide case you are pursuing. Dom?'

With one hand, Carbone passed a shoebox over the seat. Fitzgerald took it and put it on Bosch's lap. Bosch opened it and found it full of audiocassette tapes with dates written on tape stuck to the cases.

'From Aliso's phone?' he asked.

'Obviously.'

'How long were you on it?'

'We'd only been listening for nine days. It hadn't been productive, but the tapes are yours.'

'And what do you want in return, Chief?'

'What do I want?'

Fitzgerald looked out the window, down at the railroad switching yard in the valley below the parking lot.

'What do I want?' he asked again. 'I want the killer, of course. But I also want you to be careful. The department's been through a lot these past few years. No need to hang our dirty laundry in public once again.'

'You want me to bury Carbone's extracurricular activities.'

Neither Fitzgerald nor Carbone said anything but they didn't have to. Everybody in the car knew that Carbone did what he did on orders. Probably orders from Fitzgerald himself.

'Then you've got to answer some questions.'

'Of course.'

'Why was there a bug on Tony Aliso's phone?'

'Same reason there's a bug on anyone's phone. We heard things about the man and set about finding out if they were true.'

'What did you hear?'

'That he was dirty, that he was a scumbag, that he was a launderer for the mob in three states. We opened a file. We had just begun when he was killed.'

'Then when I called, why did you pass on it?'

Fitzgerald took a long pull on his cigar and the car filled with its smell.

'There's a complicated answer to that question, Detective. Suffice it to say that we thought it best if we remained uninvolved.'

'The tap was illegal, wasn't it?'

'It is extremely difficult under state law to gather the required information needed for a wiretap. The feds, they can get it done on a whim. We can't and we don't want to work with the feds all the time.'

'It still doesn't explain why you passed. You could've taken the case from

389

us and then controlled it, buried it, done whatever you wanted with it. No one would have known about illegal wiretaps or anything else.'

'Perhaps. Perhaps it was a wrong choice.'

Bosch realized they had underestimated himself and his crew. Fitzgerald had believed the break-in would go unnoticed and therefore his unit's involvement would not be discovered. Bosch understood the tremendous leverage he held over Fitzgerald. Word about the illegal wiretap would be all the police chief would need to rid himself of Fitzgerald.

'So what else do you have on Aliso?' he asked. 'I want everything. If I hear at any point you held something back, then your little-black-bag job is going to get known. You know what I mean? It will get known.'

Fitzgerald turned from the window and looked at him.

'I know exactly what you mean. But you are making a mistake if you are going to smugly sit there and believe you have all the high cards in this game.'

'Then put whatever cards you have on the table.'

'Detective, I am about to fully cooperate with you, but know this. If you seek to hurt me or anyone in my division with the information you get here, I will hurt you more. For example, there's this matter of your keeping company last night with a convicted felon.'

He let that hang in the air with his cigar smoke. Bosch was stunned and angry but managed to swallow down his urge to throttle Fitzgerald.

'There is a department prohibition against any officer knowingly associating with criminals. I'm sure you know that, Detective, and understand the need for such a safeguard. If this were to become known about you, then your job could be in jeopardy. Then where would you and your mission be?'

Bosch didn't answer. He looked straight ahead, over the seat and out the front window. Fitzgerald leaned over so that he was almost whispering in his ear.

'This is what we know about you in just one hour,' he said. 'What if we spend a day? A week? And it's not just you, my friend. You can tell your lieutenant that there is a glass ceiling in the department for lesbians, especially if something like that should get out. Now her girlfriend, she could go further, her being black. But the lieutenant, she'd have to get used to Hollywood, you ask me.'

He leaned back to his spot and returned his voice to normal modulation.

'Do we have an understanding here, Detective Bosch?'

Bosch turned and finally looked at him.

'We have an understanding.'

After dropping the bullets retrieved from Tony Aliso's head at the ballistics lab in Boyle Heights, Bosch made it back to the Hollywood Division just as the investigators were gathering in Billets's office for the six o'clock meeting. Bosch was introduced to Russell and Kuhlken, the two fraud investigators, and everybody sat down. Also sitting in was a deputy district attorney. Matthew Gregson was from Special Prosecutions, a unit that handled organized crime cases as well as the prosecution of police officers and other delicate matters. Bosch had never met him.

Bosch gave his report first and concisely brought the others up to date on the occurrences in Las Vegas as well as the autopsy and his swing by the department's gun shop. He said he'd been promised that the ballistics comparison would be done by ten the following morning. But Bosch made no mention of his meetings with Carbone and Fitzgerald. Not because of the threat Fitzgerald had made – or so Bosch told himself. But because the information he had gleaned from those meetings was best not discussed with such a large group in general and a prosecutor in particular. Apparently, feeling the same way, Billets asked him no questions in this regard.

When Bosch was finished, Rider went next. She said she had talked to the IRS auditor assigned to the TNA Productions case and gotten very little information.

'Basically, they have a whistle-blowing program,' she said. 'You blow the whistle on a tax scofflaw and you get a share of whatever taxes the IRS finds it's been cheated out of. That's how this started. Only problem is, according to Hirschfield, he's the IRS guy, this tip came in anonymously. Whoever blew the whistle didn't want a share. He said they got a three-page letter outlining Tony Aliso's money-washing scam. He would not show it to me because he claimed, anonymous or not, the guidelines of the program call for strict confidence and the specific language of the letter could lead to identification of the author. He—'

'That's bullshit,' Gregson said.

'Probably,' Rider said. 'But there was nothing I could do about it.'

'Afterwards, give me the guy's name and I'll see what I can do.'

'Sure. Anyway, they got this letter, did some preliminary looking at TNA's corporate filings over the years and decided the letter had merit. They sent the audit letter to Tony on August 1 and were going to do him at the end of this month. That was it with him – oh, the one thing he would tell me about the letter was that it was mailed from Las Vegas. It was on the postmark.'

Bosch almost nodded involuntarily because that last bit of information fit with something Fitzgerald had told him.

'Okay, now for Tony Aliso's associates. Jerry and I spent the better part of the day interviewing the core group of people he used when making this trash he called film. He basically raided the local film schools, low-rent acting schools and strip bars for the so-called artistic talent for these shoots, but there were five men that he repeatedly worked with to get them off the ground. We took them all one by one and it appears they were not privy to financing of the movies or the books Tony kept. We think they were in the dark. Jerry?'

'That's right,' Edgar said. 'I personally think Tony picked these guys because they were stupid and didn't ask questions about that sort of stuff. He just sent them out, you know, over to USC or UCLA to grab some kid who'd want to direct or write one of these things. They'd go over to the Star Strip on La Cienega and talk girls into taking the bimbo parts. On and on, you know how it goes. Our conclusion is that this little money washing scam was Tony's. Only he and his customers knew.'

'Which leads us to you guys,' Billets said, looking at Russell and Kuhlken. 'You got anything to tell us, yet?'

Kuhlken said they were still waist-deep in the financial records but they had so far traced money from TNA Productions to dummy corporations in

California, Nevada and Arizona. The money went into the corporation bank accounts and was then invested in other, seemingly legitimate, corporations. He said when the trail was fully documented they would be in a position to use the IRS and federal statutes to seize the money as the illegal funds of a racketeering enterprise. Unfortunately, Russell said, the documentation period was long and difficult. It would be another week before they could move.

'Keep at it and take the time you need,' Billets said, then she looked at Gregson. 'So then, how are we doing? What should we be doing?'

Gregson thought a moment.

'I think we are doing fine. First thing tomorrow I'll call Vegas and find out who's handling the extradition hearing. I'm thinking that I possibly should go out there to babysit that. I'm not that comfortable at the moment with all of us here and Goshen over there with them. If we are lucky enough to pull a match out of ballistics, I think you and I, Harry, should go over there and not leave until we have Goshen with us.'

Bosch nodded his agreement.

'After hearing all of these reports, I really have just one question,' Gregson continued. 'Why isn't there someone from OCID sitting in this room right now?'

Billets looked at Bosch and almost imperceptibly nodded. The question was being passed to him.

'Initially,' Bosch said, 'OCID was informed of the murder and the victim's ID and they passed. They said they didn't know Tony Aliso. As recently as two hours ago I had a conversation with Leon Fitzgerald and told him what it looked like we had. He offered whatever expertise his people had but felt we were too far along now to have fresh people come in. He wished us best of luck with it.'

Gregson stared at him a long moment and then nodded. The prosecutor was in his mid-forties with short-cropped hair already completely gray. Bosch had never worked with him but he'd heard the name. Gregson had been around – long enough to know there was more to what Bosch had said. But he had also been around long enough to let it go for the time being. Billets didn't give him a lot of time to make something of it anyway.

'Okay, so why don't we brainstorm a little bit before we call it a night?' she said. 'What do we think happened to this man? We're gathering a lot of information, a lot of evidence, but do we know what happened to him?'

She looked at the faces gathered in the room. Finally, Rider spoke up.

'My guess is that the IRS audit brought it all about,' she said. 'He got the notice in the mail and he made a fatal mistake. He told this guy in Vegas, Joey Marks, that the government was going to look at his books and his cheap movies and the scam was likely going to come out. Joey Marks responded the way you expect these guys to respond. He whacked him. He had his man Goshen follow Tony back home from Vegas so it would happen far away from him and Goshen puts him in the trunk.'

The others nodded their heads in agreement. This included Bosch. The information he'd received from Fitzgerald fit with this scenario as well.

'It was a good plan,' Edgar said. 'Only mistake was the fingerprints Artie Donovan got off the jacket. That was pure luck and if we didn't have that, we probably wouldn't have any of this. That was the only mistake.'

'Maybe not,' Bosch said. 'The prints on the jacket just hurried things along, but Metro in Vegas was already working a tip from an informant who overheard Lucky Goshen talking about hitting somebody and putting them in a trunk. It would've gotten back to us. Eventually.'

'Well, I'd rather be already on it than waiting for eventually,' Billets said. 'Any alternative theories we should also be chasing? Are we clear on the wife, the angry screenwriter, his other associates?'

'Nothing that sticks out,' Rider said. 'There definitely was no love lost between the victim and the wife but she seems clean so far. I pulled the gatehouse log up there with a warrant and her car never left Hidden Highlands on Friday night. She seems clean.'

'What about the letter to the IRS?' Gregson asked. 'Who sent it? Obviously, someone with pretty good knowledge of what this man was doing, but who would that be?'

'This could all be part of a power play within the Joey Marks group,' Bosch said. 'Like I said before, something about the look on Goshen's face when he saw that gun and his claims later that it was a plant . . . I don't know, maybe somebody tipped the IRS knowing it would get Tony whacked and that they could then possibly lay it off on Goshen. With Goshen gone, this person moves up.'

'You're saying Goshen didn't do it?' Gregson asked, his eyebrows arched.

'No. I think Goshen is probably good for it. But I don't think he was counting on that gun showing up behind the toilet. It doesn't make sense, anyway, to keep it around. So say he whacks out Tony Aliso on orders from Joey Marks. He gives the gun to somebody in his crew to get rid of. Only that person goes and plants it at the house – this is the same person who sent the letter to the IRS in the first place to get the whole thing going. Now we come along and wrap Goshen up in a bow. The guy who stashed the gun and sent the letter, he's in a position to move up.'

Bosch looked at their faces as they tried to follow the logic.

'Maybe Goshen isn't the intended target,' Rider said.

Everyone looked at her.

'Maybe there's one more play. Maybe it's someone who wants Goshen and Joey Marks out of the way so he can move in.'

'How will they get Marks now?' Edgar asked.

'Through Goshen,' she said.

'If those ballistics come back a match,' Bosch said, 'then you can stick a fork in Goshen because he'll be done. He'll be looking at the needle or life without possibility. Or a reduced sentence if he gives us something.'

'Joey Marks,' Gregson and Edgar said at the same time.

'So who is the letter writer?' Billets asked.

'Who knows?' Bosch answered. 'I don't know enough about the organization over there. But there's a lawyer who was mentioned by the cops there. A guy who handles everything for Marks. He'd know about Aliso's scam. He could pull this off. There's probably a handful of people close to Marks capable of doing it.'

They all were silent for a long moment, each one thinking the story through and seeing that it could work. It was a natural conclusion to the meeting and Billets stood up to end it.

'Let's keep up the good work,' she said. 'Matthew, thanks for coming out. You'll be the first one I call when we get the ballistics in the morning.'

Everyone else started standing up.

'Kiz and Jerry, flip a coin,' Billets said. 'One of you will have to go to Vegas to work the extradition escort with Harry. It's regulations. Oh, and Harry, could you wait a minute? There's something I need to discuss with you about another case.'

After the others left, Billets told Bosch to close the door. He did so and then sat down in one of the chairs in front of her desk.

'So what happened?' she asked. 'Did you really talk to Fitzgerald?'

'Well, I guess it was more that he talked to me, but, yeah, I met with him and Carbone.'

'What's the deal?'

'Basically, the deal is that they didn't know Tony Aliso from a hole in the ground until they, too, got a letter, probably the same one that went to the IRS. I've got a copy of it. It has details. It was from somebody with knowledge, just like Kiz said. The letter OCID got also was postmarked in Las Vegas and it was addressed specifically to Fitzgerald.'

'So their response was to bug his office phone.'

'Right, illegal bug. They had just started – I have nine days' worth of tapes to listen to – when I call up and say Tony got whacked. They panicked. You know his situation with the chief. If it came out that first of all they illegally put the bug on Tony and second of all might have somehow been the cause of his death because Joey Marks found out, then the chief would pretty much have all he'd need to move Fitzgerald out and reestablish controls on OCID.'

'So Fitzgerald sends Carbone in to get the bug and they play dumb about Tony.'

'Right. Carbone didn't see the camera or we wouldn't know any of this.'

'That prick. When this is over, the first thing I'm going to do is give it all to the chief.'

'Uh . . .'

Bosch wasn't sure how to say it.

'What is it?'

'Fitzgerald could see that coming. I cut a deal with him.'

'What?'

'I cut a deal. He gave me everything, the tapes, the letter. But their activities go no further than you and me. The chief never knows.'

'Harry, how could you? You had no—'

'He's got something on me, Lieutenant. He's got something on you, too . . . and Kiz.'

A long silence followed and Bosch watched the anger flush her cheeks.

'That arrogant bastard,' she said.

Bosch told her what it was Fitzgerald had come up with. Since Bosch now was privy to her secret, he thought it was only fair that he tell her about Eleanor. Billets just nodded. She was clearly thinking more about her own secret and the consequences of Fitzgerald having knowledge of it.

'Do you think he actually put people on me? A tail?'

'Who knows? He's the kind of guy who sees opportunities and acts on them. He keeps information like money in a bank. In case of a rainy day. This was a rainy day for him and he pulled it out. I made the deal. Let's forget about it and move on with the case.'

She was silent a moment and Bosch watched her for any sign of embarrassment. There was none. She looked directly at Bosch, her eyes searching him for any sign of judgment. There was none. She nodded.

'What else did they do after the letter came?'

'Not much. They put Aliso on a loose surveillance. I have the logs. But they weren't watching him Friday night. They knew he'd gone to Las Vegas, so they were planning to pick him up again after the holiday if he was back. They were really just getting started when it all went down.'

She nodded again. Her mind wasn't on the subject. Bosch stood up.

'I'll listen to the tapes tonight. There's about seven hours but Fitzgerald said it's mostly Aliso talking to his girlfriend in Vegas. Nothing much else. But I'll listen anyway. You need anything else, Lieutenant?'

'No. Let's talk in the morning. I want to know about the ballistics as soon as you know.'

'You got it.'

Bosch headed to the door but she stopped him.

'It's weird, isn't it, when sometimes you can't tell the good guys from the bad.'

He looked back at her.

'Yeah, it's weird.'

The house still smelled of fresh paint when Bosch finally got home. He looked at the wall he had started to paint three days before and it seemed long ago. He didn't know when he'd finish now. The house had been a ground-up rebuilding job after the earthquake. He'd only been back a few weeks after more than a year of living in a residence hotel near the station. The earthquake, too, seemed long ago. Things happened fast in this city. Everything but the moment seemed like ancient history.

He got out the number Felton had given him for Eleanor Wish and called it but there was no answer, not even a machine picking up. He hung up and wondered if she had gotten the note he left for her. His hope was that they would somehow be together after this case was over. But if it came to that, he realized, he wasn't sure how he'd deal with the department's prohibition against associating with a convicted felon.

His thoughts about this spun into the question of how Fitzgerald had found out about her and the night they had spent together in her apartment. It seemed to him it was likely that Fitzgerald would maintain contacts with Metro, and he guessed that maybe Felton or Iverson had informed the deputy chief about Eleanor Wish.

Bosch made two sandwiches of lunch meat from the refrigerator and then took them, two bottles of beer and the box of tapes Fitzgerald had given him over to the chair next to his stereo. As he ate, he arranged the tapes in chronological order and then started playing them. There was a photocopy of a log and pen register with entries showing what time of day Aliso either received or made the calls and what number he had called.

More than half the calls were between Aliso and Layla, either placed to the club – Bosch could tell because of the background music and noise – or a number he assumed was her apartment. She never identified herself on any of the calls, but on the occasions Tony called her at the club he asked for her by her stage name, Layla. Other than that, he never used her name. Most of their conversations were about the minutiae of daily life. He called her most often at home in the midafternoon. In one call to her home, Layla was angry at Aliso for waking her up. He complained that it was already noon and she reminded him that she had worked until four at the club. Like a chastened boy, he apologized and offered to call back. He did, at two.

In addition to the conversations with Layla there were calls to other women involving the timing of a scene that needed to be reshot for one of Tony's movies and various other film-related business calls. There were two calls placed by Aliso to his home but both of his conversations with his wife were quick and to the point. One time he said he was coming home and the other time he said he was going to be held up and wouldn't be home for dinner.

When Bosch was done it was after midnight and he had counted only one of the conversations as being of even marginal interest. It was a call placed to the dressing room at the club on the Tuesday before Aliso was murdered. In the midst of their rather boring, innocuous conversation, Layla asked him when he was coming out next.

'Comin' out Thursday, baby,' Aliso replied. 'Why, you miss me already?'

'No – I mean, yeah, sure, I miss you and all, Tone. But Lucky was asking if you were coming. That's why I asked.'

Layla had a soft, little-girl voice that seemed unpracticed or fake.

'Well, tell him I'll be in Thursday night. You working then?'

'Yeah, I'm working.'

Bosch turned off the stereo and thought about the one call that mattered. It meant Goshen knew, through Layla, that Aliso was coming out. It wasn't much, but it could probably be used by a prosecutor as part of an argument for premeditation. The problem was that it was tainted evidence. In legal terms, it did not exist.

He looked at his watch. It was late but he decided to call. He took the number off the log where Layla's number had been recorded by a pen register which read the tones that sounded when a number was punched into a phone. After four rings it was answered by a woman with a slow voice laced with practiced sexual intent.

'Layla?'

'No, this is Pandora.'

Bosch almost laughed but he was too tired.

'Where's Layla?'

'She isn't here.'

'This is a friend of hers. Harry. She tried to call me the other night. You know where she is or where I could reach her?'

'No. She hasn't been around for a couple days. I don't know where she is. Is this about Tony?'

'Yeah.'

'Well, she's pretty upset. I guess if she wants to talk to you, she'll call you again. You in town?'

'Not right now. Where d'you guys live?'

'Uh, I don't think I'm going to tell you that.'

396

'Pandora, is Layla scared of something?'

'Of course she is. Her old man gets killed. She thinks people might think she knows something, but she doesn't. She's just scared.'

Bosch gave Pandora his home number and told her to have Layla call if she checked in.

After he hung up he looked at his watch and took out the little phone book he kept in his jacket. He called Billets's number and a man answered. Her husband. Bosch apologized for the late call, asked for the lieutenant and wondered while he waited what the husband knew about his wife and Kizmin Rider. When Billets picked up, Bosch told her about his review of the tapes and how little value they had.

'The one call establishes Goshen's knowledge of Aliso's trip to Vegas, as well as his interest in it. But that's about it. I think it's kind of marginal and we'll be okay without it. When we find Layla, we should be able to get the same information from her. Legally.'

'Well, that makes me feel better.'

Bosch heard her exhale. Her unspoken worry had obviously been that if the tapes contained any vital information, they would have to have been brought forward to prosecutors, thereby alienating Fitzgerald and ending her own career.

'Sorry for the late call,' Bosch said, 'but I thought you might want to know as soon as I knew.'

'Thanks, Harry. I'll see you in the morning.'

After he hung up he tried Eleanor Wish's line once more and again there was no answer. Now the slight worry he'd had in his chest bloomed into a full-fledged concern. He wished he was still in Vegas so he could go to her apartment to see if she was there and just not answering or if it was something worse.

Bosch got himself another beer from the refrigerator and went out to the back deck. The new deck was larger than its predecessor and offered a deeper view into the Pass. It was dark and peaceful out. The usual hiss of the Hollywood Freeway far below was easily tuned out. He watched the spotlights from Universal Studios cut across the starless sky and finished his beer, wondering where she was.

On Wednesday morning, Bosch got to the station at eight and typed out reports detailing his moves and investigation in Las Vegas. He made copies and put them in the lieutenant's mailbox and then clipped the originals into the already inch-thick murder book that Edgar had started. He filed no report on his conversations with Carbone and Fitzgerald or his review of the tapes OCID had made off Aliso's office phone. His work was only interrupted by frequent walks to the watch office for coffee.

He had completed these chores by ten o'clock but waited another five minutes before calling the department's gun shop. He knew from experience that he should not call before the time the report on the bullet comparisons was to be finished. He threw in the extra five minutes just to make sure. It was a long five minutes.

As he called, Edgar and Rider gravitated toward his spot at the homicide table so that they could immediately get the comparison results. It was a make-or-break point in the investigation and they all knew it. Bosch asked for Lester Poole, the gun tech assigned the case. They had worked together before. Poole was a gnomish man whose whole life revolved around guns, though as a civilian employee of the department he did not carry one himself. But there was no one more expert at the gun shop than he. He was a curious man in that he would not acknowledge anyone who called him Les. He insisted on being called Lester or even just Poole, never the diminutive of Lester. Once he confided to Bosch that this was because he feared that if he became known as Les Poole, it would only be a matter of time before some smartass cops started calling him Cess Poole. It was his intention never to let that happen.

'Lester, it's Harry,' Bosch said when the tech picked up. 'You're the man this morning. What have you got for me?'

'I've got good and bad news for you, Harry.'

'Give me the bad first.'

'Just finished with your case. Haven't written the report yet but this is what I can tell you. The gun has been wiped clean of prints and is not traceable. Your doer used acid on the serial and I couldn't bring it up with any of my magic tricks. So that's that.'

'And the good?'

'I *can* tell you that you've got yourself a match between the weapon and the bullets extracted from your victim. It's a definite match.'

Bosch looked up at Edgar and Rider and gave the thumbs-up. They exchanged a high five and then Bosch watched as Rider gave Lieutenant Billets the thumbs-up through the glass of her office. Bosch then saw Billets pick up her phone. Bosch presumed she was calling Gregson at the DA's office.

Poole told Bosch that the report would be finished by noon and shipped through intradepartmental courier. Bosch thanked him and hung up. He stood up smiling and then walked with Edgar and Rider into the lieutenant's office. Billets spent another minute on the phone and Bosch could tell she was talking to Gregson. She then hung up.

'That's a very happy man there,' she said.

'He should be,' Edgar said.

'All right, so now what?' Billets asked.

'We go over there and drag that desert dirtbag's ass back here,' Edgar said.

'Yes, that's what Gregson said. He's going to go over to babysit the hearing. It's tomorrow morning, right?'

'Supposed to be,' Bosch said. 'I'm thinking of heading over there today. There are a couple loose ends I want to square away, maybe take another shot at finding the girlfriend, and then I want to make the arrangements so we can get out of there with him as soon as the judge says go.'

'Fine,' Billets said. Then to Edgar and Rider, she asked, 'Did you two decide who is going with Harry?'

'Me,' Edgar said. 'Kiz is more plugged in on the financial stuff. I'll go with Harry to get this sucker.'

'Okay, fine. Anything else?'

Bosch told them about the gun being untraceable, but this didn't seem to dent the euphoria engendered by the ballistics match. The case was looking more and more like a slam dunk.

They left the office after a few more self-congratulatory statements and

Bosch went back to his phone. He dialed Felton's office at Metro. The captain picked up right away.

'Felton, it's Bosch in L.A.'

'Bosch, what's up?'

'Thought you might want to know. The gun checks out. It fired the bullets that killed Tony Aliso.'

Felton whistled into the phone.

'Damn, that's nice and neat. Lucky ain't going to feel so lucky when he hears about that.'

'Well, I'm coming out in a little while to tell him.'

'Good. When you going to be here?'

'Haven't set it up yet. What about the extradition hearing? We still on for tomorrow morning?'

'Absolutely, as far as I know. I'll have somebody double-check to make sure. His lawyer might be trying to make waves but that won't work. This added piece of evidence will help, too.'

Bosch told him that Gregson would be coming out in the morning to aid the local prosecutor if needed.

'That's probably a wasted trip but he's welcome just the same.'

'I'll tell him. Listen, if you've got a spare body, there's still one loose end bugging me.'

'What?'

'Tony's girlfriend. She was a dancer at Dolly's till she got fired by Lucky on Saturday. I still want to talk to her. She goes by the name of Layla. That's all I have. That and her phone number.'

He gave Felton the number and the captain said he'd have somebody check into it.

'Anything else?'

'Yeah, one other thing. You know Deputy Chief Fitzgerald out here, don't you?'

'Sure do. We've worked cases together.'

'You talked to him lately?'

'Uh, no . . . no. Not in – it's been a while.'

Bosch thought he was lying but decided to let it go. He needed the man's cooperation for at least another twenty-four hours.

'Why do you ask, Bosch?'

'No reason. Just thought I'd ask. He's been advising us from this end, that's all.'

'Good to hear that. He's a very capable individual.'

'Capable. Yeah, that he is.'

Bosch hung up and then immediately set about making travel arrangements for himself and Edgar. He booked two rooms at the Mirage. They were above the department's maximum allowance for hotel rooms but he was sure Billets would approve the vouchers. Besides, Layla had called him once at the Mirage. She might try again.

Last, he reserved round-trip tickets for himself and Edgar out of Burbank. On the Thursday afternoon return he reserved one more seat for Goshen.

Their flight out left at three-thirty and got them into Las Vegas an hour later. He figured that would give them plenty of time to do what they had to do.

Nash was in the gatehouse and came out to greet Bosch with a smile. Harry introduced Edgar.

'Looks like you guys've got yourself a real whodunit, eh?'

'Looks that way,' Bosch said. 'You got any theories?'

'Not a one. I gave your girl the gate log, she tell you that?'

'She's not my girl, Nash. She's a detective. Pretty good one, too.'

'I know. I didn't mean nothing.'

'So, is Mrs Aliso home today?'

'Let's take a look.'

Nash slid the door of the gatehouse back open, went inside and picked up a clipboard. He scanned it quickly and flipped back to the prior page. After scanning it he put the clipboard down and came back out.

'She should be there,' he said. 'Hasn't been out in two days.'

Bosch nodded his thanks.

'I gotta call her, you know,' Nash said. 'Rules.'

'No problem.'

Nash raised the gate and Bosch drove through.

Veronica Aliso was waiting at the open door of her house when they got there. She was wearing tight gray leggings beneath a long loose T-shirt with a copy of a Matisse painting on it. She had on a lot of makeup again. Bosch introduced Edgar and she led them to the living room. They declined an offer for something to drink.

'Well, then, what can I do for you men?'

Bosch opened his notebook and tore out a page he had already written on. He handed her the page.

'That's the number of the coroner's office and the case number,' he said. 'The autopsy was completed yesterday and the body can be released to you now. If you are already working with a funeral home, just give that case number to them and they'll take care of it.'

She looked at the page for a long moment.

'Thank you,' she finally said. 'You came all the way up here to give me this?'

'No. We also have some news. We've arrested a man for your husband's murder.'

Her eyes widened.

'Who? Did he say why he did this?'

'His name is Luke Goshen. He's from Las Vegas. Have you ever heard of him?'

Confusion spread across her face.

'No, who is he?'

'He's a mobster, Mrs Aliso. And your husband knew him pretty well, I'm afraid. We're going to Las Vegas now to get him. If all goes well, we will be coming back with him tomorrow. Then the case will proceed through the courts. There will be a preliminary hearing in municipal court, and then if Goshen is bound over for trial as we assume he will be, there will be a trial in Los Angeles Superior Court. It is likely you will have to testify briefly during the trial. Testify for the prosecution.'

She nodded, her eyes far off.

'Why did he do it?'

'We're not sure yet. We're working on that. We do know that your husband was involved in business dealings with this man's, uh, employer. A man named Joseph Marconi. Do you recall if your husband ever mentioned Goshen or Joseph Marconi?'

'No.'

'What about the names Lucky or Joey Marks?'

She shook her head in the negative.

'What business dealings?' she asked.

'He was cleaning money for them. Washing it through his film business. You sure you did not know anything about this?'

'Of course not. Do I need my lawyer? You know he already told me not to talk to you people.'

Bosch gave an easy smile and held his hands up.

'No, Mrs Aliso, you don't need your lawyer. We're just trying to get to the facts of the case. If you knew something about your husband's business dealings, it might help us build a case against this man Goshen and possibly his employer. You see, right now we've got this Goshen character pretty well tied up for this. We're not sweating that. We've got ballistics, fingerprints, hard evidence. But he wouldn't have done what he did if Joey Marks didn't tell him to. Joey Marks is who we'd really like to get. And the more information I have about your husband and his business, the better the chance we have of getting to Joey Marks. So if there is anything you can help us with, now is the time to tell us.'

He was silent and waited. She looked down at the now folded piece of paper in her hand. She finally nodded to herself and looked at him.

'I know nothing about his business,' she said. 'But there was a call last week. It came here on Wednesday night. He took it in the office and closed the door but . . . I went to the door and listened. I could hear his side of it.'

'What did he say?'

'He called the caller Lucky. I know that. He did a lot of listening and then he said he'd be out there by the end of the week. He then said he'd see the caller at the club. And that was it.'

Bosch nodded.

'Why didn't you tell us this before?'

'I didn't think it was important. I . . . you see, I thought he was talking to a woman. The name Lucky, I thought it was a woman's name.'

'Was that why you were listening through the door?'

She averted her eyes and nodded her head.

'Mrs Aliso, have you ever hired a private investigator to follow your husband?'

'No. I thought about it but I didn't.'

'But you suspected he was having an affair?'

'Affairs, Detective. I not only suspected, I knew. A wife can tell.'

'Okay, Mrs Aliso. Do you remember anything else about the telephone conversation? Anything else that was said?'

'No. Just what I told you.'

'It might help us with the court case, as far as questions of premeditation go, if we could isolate this call. Are you sure it was Wednesday?'

'Yes, because he left the next day.'

'What time did the call come in?'

'It was late. We were watching the news on Channel 4. So it was after eleven and before eleven-thirty. I don't think I can narrow it down any further.'

'Okay, Mrs Aliso, that's good.'

Bosch looked over at Edgar and raised his eyebrows. Edgar just nodded. He was ready to go. They stood up and Veronica Aliso led them to the door.

'Oh,' Bosch said before he got to the door. 'There was a question that came up about your husband. Do you know, did he have a regular doctor that he went to?'

'Yes, on occasion. Why?'

'Well, I wanted to check to see if he suffered from hemorrhoids.'

She looked like she was about to laugh.

'Hemorrhoids? I don't think so. I think Tony would've complained loud and often if he did.'

'Really?'

Bosch was standing in the doorway now.

'Yes, really. Besides, you just told me that the autopsy was completed, wouldn't that doctor be able to tell you the answer to that question?'

Bosch nodded. She had him there.

'I guess so, Mrs Aliso. The only reason I ask is that we found a tube of Preparation H in his car. I was wondering why it was there if, you know, he didn't need it.'

She smiled this time.

'Oh, that's an old performer's trick.'

'A performer's trick?'

'You know, actresses, models, dancers. They use that stuff.'

Bosch looked at her, waiting for more. She didn't say anything.

'I don't get it,' he said. 'Why do they use it?'

'Under their eyes, Detective Bosch. You know, shrinks the swelling? Well, you put it under your eyes and the bags from all that hard living get shrunk, too. Probably half the people who buy that stuff in this town use it under their eyes, not what it's supposed to be used for. My husband . . . he was a vain man. If he was going to Las Vegas to be with some young girl, I think he would have done this. It was just like him.'

Bosch nodded. He thought of the unidentified substance under Tony Aliso's eyes. You learn something new every day, he thought. He would have to call Salazar.

'How do you think he would have known about that?' he asked.

She was about to answer but hesitated, then she just hiked her shoulders.

'It's a not-so-secret Hollywood secret,' she said. 'He could've learned it anywhere.'

Including from you, Bosch thought but didn't say. He just nodded and stepped through the door.

'Oh, one last thing,' he said before she closed it. 'This arrest is probably going to hit the media today or tomorrow. We'll try to contain it as much as possible. But in this town, nothing's ever sacred or secret for long. You should be prepared for that.'

'Thank you, Detective.'

'You might want to think about a small funeral. Something inside. Tell the director not to give information out over the phone. Funerals always make good video.'

She nodded and closed the door.

On the way out of Hidden Highlands, Bosch lit a cigarette and Edgar didn't object.

'She's a cold piece of work,' Edgar said.

'That she is,' Bosch answered. 'What do you think of the phone call from Lucky?'

'It's just one more piece. We got Lucky by the balls. As far as he's concerned, it's over.'

Bosch took Mulholland along the crest of the mountains until it wound down to the Hollywood Freeway. They passed without comment the fire road down which Tony Aliso had been found. At the freeway, Bosch turned south so he could pick up the 10 in downtown and head east.

'Harry, what's up?' Edgar asked. 'I thought we were leavin' outta Burbank.'

'We're not flying. We're driving.'

'What are you talking about?'

'I only reserved the flights in case somebody checked. When we get to Vegas, we let on that we flew in and that we're flying out right after the hearing with Goshen. Nobody has to know we're driving. You okay with that?'

'Yeah, sure, fine. I get it. Precautions, settin' a smoke screen in case somebody checks. I can dig it. You never know with the mobsters, do you?'

'Or with the cops.'

Averaging over ninety miles an hour, including a fifteen-minute stop at a McDonald's, they got to Las Vegas in four hours. They drove to McCarran International Airport, parked in the garage and took their briefcases and overnighters out of the trunk. While Edgar waited outside, Bosch went into the terminal and rented a car at the Hertz counter.

It was almost four-thirty by the time they got to the Metro building. As they walked through the detective bureau, Bosch saw Iverson sitting at his desk and talking to Baxter, who stood nearby. A thin smile played on Iverson's face but Bosch ignored it and went straight to Felton's office. The police captain was behind his desk doing paperwork. Bosch knocked on the open door and then entered.

'Bosch, where ya been?'

'Taking care of details.'

'This your prosecutor?'

'No, this is my partner, Jerry Edgar. The prosecutor isn't coming out until the morning.'

Edgar and Felton shook hands but Felton continued to look at Bosch.

'Well, you can call him and tell him not to bother.'

Bosch looked at him a moment. He knew now why Iverson had smiled. Something was going on.

'Captain, you're always full of surprises,' he said. 'What is it this time?'

Felton leaned back in his chair. He had an unlit cigar, one end soggy with saliva, on the edge of the desk. He picked it up and clenched it between two fingers. He was playing it out, obviously trying to get a rise out of Bosch. But Bosch didn't bite and the captain finally spoke.

'Your boy, Goshen, is packing his bags.'

'He's waiving extradition?'

'Yeah, he got smart.'

Bosch took the chair in front of the desk and Edgar took one to the right. Felton continued.

'Fired that mouthpiece Mickey Torrino and got his own guy. Not that much of an improvement, but at least the new guy's got Lucky's best interest in mind.'

'And how did he get smart?' Bosch asked. 'You tell him about the ballistics?'

'Sure, I told him. Brought him over, told him the score. I also told him how we broke his alibi down to shit.'

Bosch looked at him but didn't ask the question.

'Yeah, that's right, Bosch. We haven't been exactly sitting over here on our asses. We went to work on this guy and we're helping to pound him into the ground for you. He said he never left his office Friday night until it was time to go home at four. Well, we went over and checked that office out. There's a back door. He could've come in and gone out. Nobody saw him from the time Tony Aliso left until four, when he came out to close the club. That gave him plenty of time to go out there, take down Tony and hop the last flight back. And here's the kicker. Girl that works over there goes by the name of Modesty. She got into it with another dancer and went to the office to complain to Lucky. She said nobody answered when she knocked. So she tells Gussie she wants to see the boss and he tells her the boss ain't in. That was about midnight.'

Felton nodded and winked.

'Yeah, and what did Gussie say about that?'

'He isn't saying shit. We don't expect him to. But if he wants to get on the stand and back up Lucky's alibi, you can tear him apart easy. He's got a record goin' back to the seventh grade.'

'All right, never mind him. What about Goshen?'

'Like I said, we brought him over this morning and told him what we got and that he was running out of time right quick. He had to make a decision and he made it. He switched lawyers. That's about as clear a sign as you're going to get. He's ready to deal, you ask me. That means you'll get him and Joey Marks, a few of the other douche bags in town. We'll take the biggest bite out of the outfit in ten years. Everybody's happy.'

Bosch stood up. Edgar followed suit.

'This is the second time you've done this to me,' Bosch said, his voice measured and controlled. 'You're not going to get a third. Where is he?'

'Hey, cool down, Bosch. We're all working for the same thing.'

'Is he here or not?'

'He's in interview room three. Last I checked, Weiss was in there with him, too. Alan Weiss, he's the new lawyer.'

'Has Goshen given you any statement?'

'No, of course not. Weiss gave us the particulars. No negotiating until you get him to L.A. In other words, he'll waive and you take him home. Your people will have to work out the deal over there. We're out of it after today. Excepting when you come back to pick up Joey Marks. We'll help with that. I've been waiting for that day for a long time.'

Bosch left the office without further word. He walked through the squad room without looking at Iverson and made his way to the rear hallway that led to the interview rooms. He lifted the flap that covered the door's small window and saw Goshen in blue jail overalls sitting at the small table, a much smaller man in a suit across from him. Bosch knocked on the glass, waited a beat and opened the door.

'Counselor? Could we speak for a moment outside?'

'Are you from L.A.? It's about time.'

'Let's talk outside.'

As the lawyer got up, Bosch looked past him at Goshen. The big man was handcuffed to the table. It was barely thirty hours since Bosch had seen him last but Luke Goshen was a different man. His shoulders seemed slumped, as if he was closing in on himself. His eyes had a hollow look, the kind of stare that comes from a night of looking at the future. He didn't look at Bosch. After Weiss stepped out, Bosch closed the door.

Weiss was about Bosch's age. He was trim and deeply tanned. Bosch wasn't sure but thought he wore a hairpiece. He wore glasses with thin gold frames. In the few seconds he had to size the lawyer up, Bosch decided that Goshen had probably done well for himself.

After introductions Weiss immediately got down to business.

'My client is willing to waive any challenge to extradition. But, Detectives, you need to act quickly. Mr Goshen does not feel comfortable or safe in Las Vegas, even in Metro lockup. My hope was that we would have been able to go before a judge today but it's too late now. But at nine a.m. tomorrow, I'll be in court. It's already arranged with Mr Lipson, the local prosecutor. You'll be able to take him to the airport by ten.'

'Slow down a second, Counselor,' Edgar said. 'What's the hurry all of a sudden? Is it 'cause Luke in there heard about the ballistics we got or because maybe Joey Marks has heard, too, and figures he better cut his losses?'

'I guess maybe it's easier for Joey to put the hit out on him in Metro than all the way over in L.A., right?' Bosch added.

Weiss looked at them as if they were some form of life he had not previously encountered.

'Mr Goshen doesn't know anything about a hit and I hope that statement is just part of the usual intimidation tactics you employ. What he does know is he is being set up to take the fall for a crime he did not commit. And he feels the best way to handle this is to cooperate fully in a new environment. Someplace away from Las Vegas. Los Angeles is his only choice.'

'Can we talk to him now?'

Weiss shook his head.

'Mr Goshen won't be saying a word until he's in Los Angeles. My brother will take the case from there. He has a practice there. Saul Weiss, you may have heard of him.'

Bosch had but shook his head in the negative.

'I believe he has already contacted your Mr Gregson. So, you see, Detective, you're just a courier here. Your job is to get Mr Goshen on a plane tomorrow morning and get him safely to Los Angeles. It will most likely be out of your hands after that.'

'Most likely not,' Bosch said.

He stepped around the lawyer and opened the door to the interview room. Goshen looked up. Bosch stepped in and moved to the table. He leaned over it and put his hands flat on the table. Before he could speak, Weiss had moved into the room and was talking.

'Luke, don't say a word to this man. Don't say a word.'

Bosch ignored Weiss and looked only at Goshen.

'All I want, Lucky, is a show of faith. You want me to take you to L.A., get you there safe, then give me something. Just answer one question. Where—'

'He has to take you anyway, Luke. Don't fall for this. I can't represent you if you don't listen to me.'

'Where's Layla?' Bosch asked. 'I'm not leaving Vegas until I talk to her. If you want to get out of here in the morning, I've got to talk to her tonight.

409

She's not at her place. I talked to her roommate, Pandora, last night and she says Layla's been gone a couple of days. Where is she?'

Goshen looked from Bosch to Weiss.

'Don't say a word,' Weiss said. 'Detective, if you step out, I'd like to confer with my client. I think, actually, that might be something I won't have a problem with him answering.'

'Hope not.'

Bosch went back into the hallway with Edgar. He put a cigarette in his mouth but didn't light it.

'Why's Layla so important?' Edgar asked.

'I don't like loose ends. I want to know how she fits.'

Bosch didn't tell him that he knew from the illegal tapes that Layla had called Aliso and asked, at Goshen's request, when he'd be coming out to Vegas. If they found her, he would have to draw it out of her during the interview without giving away that he already knew it.

'It's also a test,' he did tell Edgar. 'To see how far we can get Goshen to go with us.'

The lawyer stepped out then and closed the door behind him.

'If you try that again, talking to him when I specifically said he would not respond, then we will have no relationship whatsoever.'

Bosch felt like asking what relationship they already had but let it go.

'Is he going to tell us?'

'No. I am. He said that when this person Layla first came to work at the club, he gave her a ride home a few nights. On one of those nights she asked him to drop her at a different place because she was trying to avoid somebody she was dating at the time and she thought he might be waiting at her apartment. Anyway, it was a house in North Las Vegas. She told him it was where she grew up. He doesn't have the exact address but said the place was at the corner of Donna Street and Lillis. The northeast corner. Try there. That's all he had.'

Bosch had his notebook out and wrote the street names down.

'Thank you, Counselor.'

'While you have the notebook out, write down courtroom ten. That's where we will be tomorrow at nine. I trust you will make secure arrangements for my client's safe delivery?'

'That's what a courier is for, right?'

'I'm sorry, Detective. Things are said in the heat of the moment. No offense.'

'None taken.'

Bosch went out to the squad room and used the phone at an empty desk to call Southwest and change the reservations on the return flight from three in the afternoon to a ten-thirty morning flight. Bosch didn't look at Iverson but could tell the detective was watching him from a desk fifteen feet away.

When he was done Bosch stuck his head in Felton's office. The captain was on the phone. Bosch just mock-saluted him and was gone.

Back in the rental car, Edgar and Bosch decided to go over to the jail and make arrangements for the custody transfer before trying to find Layla.

The jail was next to the courthouse. A discharge sergeant named Hackett gave the detectives a rudimentary rundown on how and where Goshen would be delivered to them. Since it was after five and the shifts had changed, Bosch and Edgar would be dealing with a different sergeant in the morning. Still, it made Bosch feel more comfortable seeing the routine ahead of time. They would be able to put Goshen into their car in an enclosed and safe loading-dock area. He felt reasonably sure that there wouldn't be trouble. At least not there.

With directions from Hackett, they drove into a middle-class neighborhood in North Las Vegas and found the house where Goshen had once dropped Layla off. It was a small bungalow-style house with an aluminum awning over each window. There was a Mazda RX7 parked in the carport.

An older woman answered the door. She was mid-sixties and well preserved. Bosch thought he could see some of the photo of Layla in her face. Bosch held his badge up so she could see it.

'Ma'am, my name is Harry Bosch and this is Jerry Edgar. We're over from Los Angeles and we are looking for a young woman we need to talk to. She's a dancer and goes by the name Layla. Is she here?'

'She doesn't live here. I don't know what you're talking about.'

'I think you do, ma'am, and I'd appreciate it if you'd help us out.'

'I told you, she's not here.'

'Well, we heard she's staying here with you. Is that right? Are you her mother? She's tried to contact me. There's no reason for her to be afraid or to not want to talk to us.'

'I'll tell her that if I see her.'

'Can we come in?'

Bosch put his hand on the door and firmly but slowly started to push it open before she could reply.

'You can't just . . .'

She didn't finish. She knew what she was going to say would be meaningless. In a perfect world the cops couldn't just push their way in. She knew it wasn't a perfect world.

Bosch looked around after he entered. The furnishings were old, having to last a few more years than they were intended to and she probably thought they would have to when she bought them. It was the standard couch and matching chair setup. There were patterned throws on each, probably to cover the wear. There was an old TV, the kind with a dial to change the channels. There were gossip magazines spread on a coffee table.

'You live here alone?' he asked.

'Yes, I do,' she said indignantly, as if his question was an insult.

'When was the last time you saw Layla?'

'Her name's not Layla.'

'That was my next question. What is her name?'

'Her name's Gretchen Alexander.'

'And you are?'

'Dorothy Alexander.'

'Where is she, Dorothy?'

'I don't know and I didn't ask.'

'When'd she leave?'

'Yesterday morning.'

Bosch nodded to Edgar and he took a step back, turned and headed down a hallway leading to the rear of the house.

411

'Where's he going?' the woman asked.

'He's just going to take a look around, that's all,' Bosch said. 'Sit down here and talk to me, Dorothy. Faster we get this over with, the faster we're out of here.'

He pointed to the chair and remained standing until she finally sat. He then moved around the coffee table and sat on the couch. Its springs were shot. He sank so low in it that he had to lean forward and even then it felt like his knees were halfway up to his chest. He got out his notebook.

'I don't like him messing around in my things,' Dorothy said, looking back over her shoulder toward the hallway.

'He'll be careful.' Bosch took out his notebook. 'You seemed to know we were coming. How'd you know that?'

'I know what she told me, is all. She said the police might come. She didn't say anything about them coming all the way from Los Angeles.'

She said *Angeles* with a hard G.

'And you know why we're here?'

'Because of Tony. She said he went and got himself killed over there.'

'Where did Gretchen go, Dorothy?'

'She did not tell me. You can ask me all the times you like but my answer's always going to be the same. I don't know.'

'Is that her sports car in the carport?'

'Sure is. She bought it with her own money.'

'Stripping?'

'I always said money was the same whether it was made one way or the next.'

Edgar came in then and looked at Bosch. Harry nodded for him to report.

'Looks like she was here. There's a second bedroom. Ashtray on the nightstand's full. There's a space on the rod in the closet where it looks like somebody had hung up some clothes. They're gone now. She left this.'

He held his hand out and cradled in his palm was a small oval picture frame with a photograph of Tony Aliso and Gretchen Alexander. They had their arms around each other and were smiling at the camera. Bosch nodded and looked back at Dorothy Alexander.

'If she left, why'd she leave her car here?'

'Don't know. A taxi came for her.'

'Did she fly?'

'How could I know that if I don't know where she was going?'

Bosch pointed a finger at her like a gun.

'Good point. Did she say when she'd be back?'

'No.'

'How old is Gretchen?'

'She'll be twenty-three.'

'How'd she take the news about Tony?'

'Not well. She was in love and now her heart's broken. I'm worried about her.'

'You think she might do something to hurt herself?'

'I don't know what she might do.'

'Did she tell you she was in love, or did you just think that?'

'I just didn't think it up, she told me. She confided in me and it was the truth. She said they were going to get married.'

'Did she know Tony Aliso was already married?'

'Yes, she knew. But he told her, he said that it was over and it was just a matter of time.'

Bosch nodded. He wondered if it was the truth. Not the truth that Gretchen might have believed, but the truth that Tony Aliso believed. He looked down at the blank page of his notebook.

'I'm trying to think if there is anything else,' he said. 'Jerry?'

Edgar shook his head, then spoke.

'I guess I'd just like to know why a mother would let her daughter do that for a living. Taking her clothes off like that.'

'Jerry, I—'

'She has a talent, mister. Men came from all over the country and when they see her they keep coming back. Because of her. And I'm not her mother. I might as well have been, her own went and left her with me a long time ago. But she has a talent and I'm not talking to you two anymore. Get out of my house.'

She stood up, as if ready to physically enforce her edict if she needed to. Bosch decided to let her have her say and stood up, putting his notebook away.

'I'm sorry for the intrusion,' he said as he dug a business card out of his wallet. 'If you hear from her, would you give her this number? And tonight she can get me at the Mirage again.'

'I'll tell her if I hear from her.'

She took the card and followed them to the door. On the front step Bosch looked back at her and nodded.

'Thanks, Mrs Alexander.'

'For what?'

They were quiet for a while driving back to the Strip. Eventually, Bosch asked Edgar what he thought of the interview.

'She's a crusty old bitch. I had to ask that question. Just to see how she'd react. Other than that, I think this Layla or Gretchen is just a dead end. Just some stupid girl Tony was leading on. You know, it's usually the strippers that are working the angles. But this time I think it was Tony.'

'Maybe.'

Bosch lit a cigarette and dropped back into silence. He was no longer thinking of the interview. As far as he was concerned, the work for the day was over and he was now thinking about Eleanor Wish.

When he got to the Mirage, Bosch swung the car into the circle in front and pulled to a stop near the front doors.

'Harry, man, what are you doing?' Edgar said. 'Bullets might pop for the Mirage, but she isn't going to dig into the company wallet for valet parking.'

'I'm just dropping you off. I'm going to go switch the cars tonight. I don't want to go anywhere near that airport tomorrow.'

'That's cool, but I'll go with you, man. Nothin' to do here but lose money on the machines.'

Bosch reached over and opened the glove box and pushed the trunk-release button.

'No, Jed, I'm going on my own. I want to think about some things. Grab your stuff outta the trunk.'

413

Edgar looked at him a long moment. Bosch had not called him Jed in a long time. Edgar was about to say something but apparently thought better of it. He opened the door.

'Okay, Harry. You want to grab dinner or something later?'

'Yeah, maybe. I'll call you in your room.'

'You're the man.'

After Edgar slammed the trunk, Bosch drove back out onto Las Vegas Boulevard and then north to Sands. It was dusk and the day's dying light was being replaced with the neon glow of the city. In ten minutes he pulled into a parking space in front of Eleanor Wish's apartment building. He took a deep breath and got out of the car. He had to know. Why had she not answered his calls? Why had she not responded to his message?

When he got to the door, he felt his guts seize as if gripped in a huge fist. The note he had carefully folded and squeezed into the doorjamb two nights before was still there. Bosch looked down at the worn doormat and then squeezed his eyes shut. He felt a tremendous wave of the guilt he had worked so hard to bury come forth from inside. He had once made a phone call that got an innocent man killed. It had been a mistake, something he could not possibly have seen coming, but it happened just the same and he had worked hard to put it not behind him but, at least, in a place where he could live with it. But now Eleanor. Bosch knew what he would find behind the door. Asking Felton for her number and address had sent things into motion, a terrible motion that ended with her being hauled into Metro and her fragile dignity and belief that bad things were behind her being crushed.

Bosch kicked over the doormat on the off chance she had left a key. There was none. His lock picks were in the glove compartment of the car parked at the airport. He hesitated a moment, focused on a spot over the doorknob, then stepped back, raised his left leg and drove his heel into the door. It splintered along the jamb and flew open. Bosch slowly stepped into the apartment.

He noticed nothing amiss in the living room. He moved quickly into the hallway and then down into the bedroom. The bed was unmade and empty. Bosch stood there for a moment, taking it all in. He realized he hadn't taken a breath since he had kicked in the door. He slowly exhaled and began breathing normally. She was alive. Somewhere. At least he thought so. He sat down on the bed, took out a cigarette and lit it. His feeling of relief was quickly crowded by other doubts and nagging questions. Why hadn't she called? Hadn't there been something real about what they had shared?

'Hello?'

A man's voice came from the front of the apartment. Bosch assumed it was someone who had heard him pop the door. He stood up and headed out of the bedroom.

'Yeah,' he said. 'I'm back here. I'm with the police.'

He stepped into the living room and saw a man impeccably dressed in a black suit with a white shirt and black tie. It wasn't what Bosch expected.

'Detective Bosch?'

Bosch tensed and didn't answer.

'There's someone outside who would like to talk to you.'

'Who?'

'He'll tell you who he is and what his business is.'

The man walked out the front door, leaving it up to Bosch whether to follow. He hesitated a moment and did.

There was a stretch limousine in the parking lot, its engine running. The man in the black suit walked around and got into the driver's seat. Bosch watched this for a moment and then walked toward the limo. He brought his arm up instinctively and brushed it against his coat until he felt the reassuring shape of his gun beneath it. As he did this, the rear door closest to him opened and a man with a rough, dark face beckoned to him. Bosch showed no hesitation. It was too late now.

Bosch ducked into the big car and took a seat facing the rear. There were two men sitting on the plushly padded backseat. One was the rough-faced man, who was casually dressed and slouching in his luxurious spot, and the other an older man in an expensive three-piece suit, the tie pulled tight to his neck. Sitting between the two men on a padded armrest was a small black box with a green light glowing on it. Bosch had seen such a box before. It detected electronic radio waves emitted by eavesdropping devices. As long as that green light glowed they could talk and be reasonably assured they wouldn't be overheard and recorded.

'Detective Bosch,' the rough-faced man said.

'Joey Marks, I presume.'

'My name is Joseph Marconi.'

'What can I do for you, Mr Marconi?'

'I thought we'd have a little conversation, that's all. You, me and my attorney here.'

'Mr Torrino?'

The other man nodded.

'Heard you lost a client today.'

'That's what we want to talk to you about,' Marconi said. 'We've got a problem here. We—'

'How did you know where I was?'

'I've had some fellows watching it for me. We kind of figured you'd be back. Once you left that note, especially.'

They had obviously followed him and he wondered when that had started. His mind then jumped to another conclusion and he suddenly knew what the meeting was all about.

'Where's Eleanor Wish?'

'Eleanor Wish?' Marconi looked at Torrino and then back at Harry. 'I don't know her. But I suppose she'll turn up.'

'What do you want, Marconi?'

'I just wanted this chance to talk, that's all. Just a little calm conversation. We've got a problem here and maybe we can work it out. I want to work with you, Detective Bosch. Do you want to work with me?'

'Like I said, what do you want?'

'What I want is to straighten this out before it gets too far out of hand. You are going down the wrong road here, Detective. You are a good man. I had you checked out. You've got ethics and I appreciate that. Whatever you do in life, you need a code of ethics. You have that. But you are on the wrong road here. Tony Aliso, I had nothing to do with that.'

Bosch smirked and shook his head.

'Look, Marconi, I don't want your alibi. I'm sure it's airtight but I couldn't care less. You can still pull a trigger from three hundred fifty miles away. It's been done from farther away, know what I mean?'

'Detective Bosch, there is something wrong here. Whatever that rat bastard is telling you, it's a lie. I'm clean on Tony A., my people are clean on Tony A., and I'm simply giving you this opportunity to make it right.'

'Yeah, and how do I do that? Just kick Lucky loose so you can pick him up outside the jail in your limo here, take him for a ride out into the desert? Think we'll ever see Lucky again?'

'You think you'll ever see that lady ex-FBI agent again?'

Bosch stared at him a moment, letting his anger build up until he felt a slight tremor tick in his neck. Then, in one quick move, he pulled his gun and leaned across the space between the seats. He grabbed the thick gold braided chain around Marconi's neck and jerked him forward. He pressed the barrel deep into Marconi's cheek.

'Excuse me?'

'Easy now, Detective Bosch,' Torrino said then. 'You don't want to do something rash.'

He put a hand on Bosch's arm.

'Take your hand off me, you asshole.'

Torrino removed his hand and raised it along with his other one in a surrendering gesture.

'I just want to calm things down a little here, that's all.'

Bosch leaned back into his seat but kept his gun in his hand. The muzzle had left a ring of skin indentation and gun oil on Marconi's cheek. He wiped it away with his hand.

'Where is she, Marconi?'

'I just heard she wanted to get away for a few days, Bosch. No need to overreact like that. We're friends here. She'll be back. In fact, now that I know you're so, uh, attached to her, I'll personally guarantee she'll be back.'

'In exchange for what?'

Hackett was still on duty at the Metro jail. Bosch told him he had to talk to Goshen for a couple of minutes in regard to a security issue. Hackett hemmed and hawed about it being against regulations to set up an after-hours visit but Bosch knew it was done on occasion for the locals, against the rules or not. Eventually Hackett gave way and took Bosch to a room lawyers used to interview clients and told him to wait. Ten minutes later, Hackett waltzed Goshen into the room and cuffed one wrist to the chair he was placed in. Hackett then folded his arms and stood behind the suspect.

'Sergeant, I need to talk to him alone.'

'Can't do it. It's a security issue.'

'We're not going to talk anyway,' Goshen interjected.

'Sergeant,' Bosch said. 'What I tell this man, whether he chooses to talk to me or not, could put you in danger if it becomes known you have this knowledge. Know what I mean? Why add that potential danger to your list? Five minutes. It's all I want.'

Hackett thought a moment and without a word left them alone.

'Pretty smooth, Bosch, but I'm not talking to you. Weiss said you might try a backdoor run. He said you'd want to try to get into the candy jar before it's time. I'm not playing with you. Get me to L.A., sit me in front of the people who can deal, and then we'll deal. Everybody will get what they want then.'

'Shut up and listen, you stupid fuck. I don't give a shit about any deal anymore. The only deal I'm worried about now is whether to keep you alive or not.'

Bosch saw he had his attention now. He waited a few moments to turn the squeeze up and then began.

'Goshen, let me explain something to you. In all of Las Vegas there is exactly one person I care about. One. You take her out of the picture and the whole place could dry up and blow away and I really wouldn't worry about it. But there's that one person I care about. And out of all the people in this place, she's the one that your employer decides to grab and hold against me.'

Goshen's eyes narrowed in concern. Bosch was talking about his people. Goshen knew exactly what was coming.

'So the deal I'm talking about is this,' Bosch said. 'You for her. Joey Marks said if you never get to L.A., then my friend comes back. And vice versa. You understand what I'm telling you?'

Goshen looked down at the table and slowly nodded.

'Do you?'

Bosch pulled his gun and pointed it three inches from the big man's face. Goshen went cross-eyed looking at the barrel's black hole.

'I could blow your shit away right here. Hackett would come in here and I'd tell him you made a move for my gun. He'd go along. He set the meeting up here. It's against the rules. He'd have to go along.'

Bosch withdrew the gun.

'Or tomorrow. This is how it goes tomorrow. At the airport we're waiting for our flight. There's a commotion over at the machines. Somebody's won a big fucking jackpot and my partner and I make the mistake of looking over there. Meantime, somebody – maybe it's your pal Gussie – puts a six-inch stiletto in your neck. End of you, my friend comes home.'

'What do you want, Bosch?'

Bosch leaned across to him.

'I want you to give me the reason not to do it. I don't give a shit about you, Goshen, dead or alive. But I'm not going to let any harm befall her. I've made mistakes in my life, man. I once got somebody killed that shouldn't have been killed. You understand that? It's not going to happen again. This is redemption, Goshen. And if I have to give a piece of shit like you up to get it, I'll do it. There's only one alternative. You know Joey Marks, where would he have her?'

'Oh, Jesus, I don't know.'

Goshen rubbed a hand over his scalp.

'Think, Goshen. He's done this kind of thing before. It's routine for you people. Where would he hold somebody he doesn't want anyone to find?'

'There was . . . there's a couple of safe houses he uses. He'd, uh, . . . I think for this he'd use the Samoans.'

'Who are they?'

'These two big fuckers he uses. Samoans. They're brothers. Their names are too hard to say. We call them Tom and Jerry. They've got one of the safe houses. Joey would use their place for this. The other place is mostly for counting cash, putting up people from Chicago.'

'Where is the house with the Samoans?'

'It's in North Vegas, not too far from Dolly's, actually.'

On a piece of notebook paper Bosch gave him, Goshen drew a crude map with directions to the house.

'You've been there, Goshen?'

'A few times.'

Bosch turned the piece of paper over on the table.

'Draw the layout of the house.'

Bosch pulled the dusty detective car he had picked up at the airport into the valet circle at the Mirage and jumped out. A valet approached but Bosch walked past him.

'Sir, your keys?'

'I'll only be a minute.'

The valet was protesting that he couldn't just leave the car there when Bosch disappeared through the revolving door. As he crossed through the casino toward the lobby, Bosch scanned the players for Edgar, his eyes stopping on every tall black man, of whom there were few. He didn't see Edgar.

On a house phone in the lobby he asked for Edgar's room and then breathed an almost audible sigh of relief when his partner picked up the phone.

'Jerry, it's Bosch. I need your help.'

'What's up?'

'Meet me out front at the valet.'

'Now? I just got room service. When you didn't call I—'

'Right now, Jerry. And did you bring your vest from L.A.?'

'My vest? Yeah. What's—'

'Bring your vest with you.'

Bosch hung up before Edgar could ask any questions.

As he turned to head back to the car, he came face to face with someone he knew. At first, because the man was well dressed, Bosch thought it was one of Joey Marks's men, but then he placed him. Hank Meyer, Mirage security.

'Detective Bosch, I didn't expect to see you here.'

'Just got in tonight. Came to pick somebody up.'

'You got your man then?'

'We think so.'

'Congratulations.'

'Listen, Hank, I gotta go. I've got a car blocking traffic in the front circle.'

'Oh, that's your car. I just heard that on the security radio. Yes, please move it.'

'I'll talk to you later.'

Bosch made a move to pass him.

'Oh, Detective? Just wanted you to know we still haven't had that betting slip come in.'

Bosch stopped.

'What?'

'You asked if we'd check to see if anyone cashed the bet your victim put down Friday night. On the Dodgers?'

'Oh, yeah, right.'

'Well, we went through the computer tapes and located the sequence number. I then checked the number on the computer. No one has collected on it yet.'

'Okay, thanks.'

'I called your office today to let you know but you weren't there. I didn't know you were coming here. We'll keep an eye out for it.'

'Thanks, Hank. I gotta go.'

Bosch started walking away but Meyer kept talking.

'No problem. Thank *you*. We look forward to opportunities to cooperate with and hopefully help our law enforcement brethren.'

Meyer smiled broadly. Bosch looked back at him and felt like he had a weight tied to his leg. He couldn't get away from him. Bosch just nodded and kept going, trying to remember the last time he had heard the phrase *law enforcement brethren*. He was almost across the lobby when he glanced back and saw that Meyer was still behind him.

'One more thing, Detective Bosch.'

Bosch stopped but lost his patience.

'Hank, what? I've got to get out of here.'

'It will just take a second. A favor. I assume your department will go to the press with this arrest. I'd appreciate it if you kept any mention of the Mirage out of it. Even our help, if you don't mind.'

'No problem. I won't say a word. Talk to you later, Hank.'

Bosch turned and walked away. It was unlikely the Mirage would have been mentioned in any press release anyway, but he understood the concern. Guilt by association. Meyer was mixing public relations with casino security. Or maybe they were the same thing.

Bosch got to the car just as Edgar came out, carrying his bullet-proof vest in his hand. The valet looked at Bosch balefully. Bosch took out a five and handed it to him. It didn't do much to change his disposition. Then Bosch and Edgar jumped in the car and took off.

The safe house Goshen told Bosch about looked deserted when they drove by. Bosch pulled the car to a stop a half block away.

'I still don't know about this, Harry,' Edgar said. 'We should be calling in Metro.'

'I told you. We can't. Marks has to have somebody inside Metro. Or else he wouldn't have known to snatch her in the first place. So we call Metro, he finds out and she's dead or moved somewhere else before Metro even makes a move. So we go in and we call Metro afterward.'

'If there is an afterward. Just what the hell are we going to do? Go in blasting? This is cowboy shit, Harry.'

'No, all you're going to do is get behind the wheel, turn the car around and be ready to drive. We might have to leave in a hurry.'

Bosch had hoped to use Edgar as a backup but after he'd told him the situation on the way over, it was clear that Edgar wasn't going to be solid. Bosch went to plan B, where Edgar was simply a wheel man.

Bosch opened his door and looked back at Edgar before getting out.

'You're going to be here, right?'

'I'll be here. Just don't get killed. I don't want to have to explain it.'

'Yeah, I'll do my best. Let me borrow your cuffs and pop the trunk.'

Bosch put Edgar's cuffs into his coat pocket and went to the trunk. At the trunk, he took out his vest and put it on over his shirt and then put his coat back on to hide his holster. He pulled up the trunk liner and lifted up the spare tire. Below it was a Glock 17 pistol wrapped in an oily rag. Bosch popped the clip on it, checked the top bullet for corrosion and then put the weapon back together. He put it in his belt. If there was going to be any shooting on this mission, he wasn't going to use his service gun.

He came up alongside the driver's window, saluted Edgar and headed down the street.

The safe house was a small concrete-block-and-plaster affair that blended in with the neighborhood. After jumping a three-foot fence Bosch took the gun from his belt and held it at his side as he walked along the side of the house. He saw no light emitted from any of the front or side windows. But he could hear the muffled sound of television. She was here. He could feel it. He knew Goshen had told the truth.

When he got to the rear corner, he saw there was a pool in the backyard as well as a covered porch. There was a concrete slab with a satellite dish anchored to it. The modern Mafia crash pad, Bosch thought. You never knew how long you'd have to hole up, so it was good to have five hundred channels.

The backyard was empty but as Bosch turned the corner he saw a lighted window. He crept down the back of the house until he was close. The blinds were drawn on the window, but by getting close and looking between the cracks he could see them in there. Two huge men he immediately assumed were the Samoans. And Eleanor. The Samoans sat on a couch in front of a television. Eleanor sat on a kitchen chair next to the couch. One wrist and one ankle were handcuffed to the chair. Because the shade of a floor lamp was in the way, he could not see her face. But he recognized her clothes as those she had worn on the day they had dragged her into Metro. The three of them were sitting there watching a rerun of a Mary Tyler Moore show. Bosch felt the anger building in his throat.

Bosch crouched down and tried to think of a way to get her out of there. He leaned his back against the wall and looked across the yard and the shimmering pool. He got an idea.

After taking one more glimpse through the blind and seeing that no one had moved, Bosch went back to the corner of the house to the slab where the satellite dish sat. He put his gun back in his belt, studied the equipment for a few moments and then simply used two hands to turn the dish out of alignment and point its focus toward the ground.

It took about five minutes. Bosch figured most of this must have been spent with one or the other of the Samoans fiddling with the TV and trying to get the picture back. Finally, an outdoor floodlight came on, the back door opened and one of them stepped out onto the porch. He wore a Hawaiian shirt as big as a tent and had long dark hair that flowed over his shoulders.

When the big man got to the dish, he clearly wasn't sure how to proceed.

He looked at it for a long moment, then came around to the other side to see if this afforded him a better angle. He now had his back to Bosch.

Bosch stepped away from the corner of the house and came up behind the man. He placed the muzzle of the Glock against the small of the man's back, though even the small of his back wasn't small.

'Don't move, big man,' he said in a low, calm voice. 'Don't say a word, 'less you want to spend the rest of your life in a wheelchair with your piss sloshing around in a bag.'

Bosch waited. The man did not move and said nothing.

'Which are you, Tom or Jerry?'

'I'm Jerry.'

'Okay, Jerry, we're going to walk over to the porch. Let's go.'

They moved to one of two steel supporter beams that held up the porch roof. Bosch kept the gun pressed against the man's shirt the whole time. He then reached into his pocket and pulled out Edgar's cuffs. He handed them around the girth of the man and held them up.

'Okay, take 'em. Cuff yourself around the beam.'

He waited until he heard both cuffs click, then came around and checked them, clicking them tightly around the man's thick wrists.

'Okay, that's good, Jerry. Now, do you want me to kill your brother? I mean I could just walk in there and waste him and get the girl. That's the easy way. You want me to do it that way?'

'No.'

'Then do exactly what I tell you. If you fuck up, he dies. Then you die 'cause I can't afford to leave a witness. Got it?'

'Yes.'

'Okay, without saying his name, because I don't trust you, just call to him and ask if the picture's back on the TV. When he says no, tell him to come out here and help. Tell him she'll be fine, she's handcuffed. Do it right, Jerry, and everybody lives. Do it wrong and some people aren't going to make it.'

'What do I call him?'

'How 'bout "Hey, Bro?" That oughta work.'

Jerry did as he was told and did it right. After some back-and-forth banter, the brother stepped out onto the porch, where he saw Jerry with his back to him. Just as he realized something wasn't right, Bosch came from the blind spot to his right rear and put the gun on him. Using his own cuffs this time, he locked the second brother, who he guessed was slightly larger than the first and had on a louder shirt, to the porch's other support beam.

'Okay, take five, boys. I'll be back in a minute. Oh, who has the key to the cuffs on the woman?'

They both said, 'He does.'

'That's not smart, guys. I don't want to hurt anybody. Now who has the cuff key?'

'I do.'

The voice came from behind him, from the porch door. Bosch froze.

'Slowly, Bosch. Toss the gun into the pool and turn around real slow like.'

Bosch did what he was told and turned around. It was Gussie. And Bosch could see the delight and hate in his eyes, even in the dark. He stepped onto the porch and Bosch could see the shape of a gun in his right hand. Bosch immediately became angry with himself for not casing the house further or even asking Jerry if there was anyone other than his brother and Eleanor in the house. Gussie raised the gun and pressed its barrel against Bosch's left cheek, just below the eye.

'See how it feels?'

'Been talking to the boss, huh?'

'That's right. And we're not stupid, man, you're stupid. We knew you might try something like this. Now we gotta call him and see what he wants to do. But first off, what you're gonna do is unhook Tom and Jerry. Right the fuck now.'

'Sure, Gussie.'

Bosch was contemplating reaching into his coat and going for his other gun but knew it was suicide as long as Gussie held his gun at point-blank range. He started slowly reaching into his pocket for his keys when he saw the movement to his left and heard the shout.

'Freeze it up, asshole!'

It was Edgar. Gussie didn't move an inch. After a few moments of this stand-off, Bosch reached into his coat, pulled his own gun and pushed the muzzle up into Gussie's neck. They stood there staring at each other for a long moment.

'What do you think?' Bosch finally said. 'You want to try it? See if we both get one off?'

Gussie said nothing and Edgar moved in. He put the muzzle of his gun against Gussie's temple. A smile broke across Bosch's face and he reached up and took Gussie's gun from him and threw it into the pool.

'I didn't think so.'

He looked over at Edgar and nodded his thanks.

'You got him? I'll go get her.'

'I got him, Harry. And I'm hoping he does something stupid, the big fat fuck.'

Bosch checked Gussie for another weapon and found none.

'Where's the cuff key?' he asked.

'Fuck you.'

'Remember the other night, Gussie? You want a repeat performance? Tell me where the fucking key is.'

Bosch figured his own cuff key would fit but he wanted to make sure he got one away from Gussie. The big man finally blew out his breath and told Bosch the key was on the kitchen counter.

Bosch went inside the house, his gun out, his eyes scanning for more surprises. There was nobody. He grabbed the cuff key off the kitchen counter and went into the back den where Eleanor was. When he stepped into the room and her eyes rose to his, he saw something that he knew he would always cherish. It wasn't something he believed he could ever put into words. The giving way of fear, the knowledge of safety. Maybe thanks. Maybe that was how people looked at heroes, he thought. He rushed to her and knelt in front of her chair so that he could unlock the cuffs.

'You okay, Eleanor?'

'Yes, yes. I'm fine. I knew, Harry. I knew you would come.'

He had the cuffs off and he just looked up at her face. He nodded and pulled her into a quick hug.

422

'We gotta go.'

They went out the back, where the scene did not look as if it had changed at all.

'Jerry, you got him? I'm going to find a phone and call Felton.'

'I got—'

'No,' Eleanor said. 'Don't call them. I don't want that.'

Bosch looked at her.

'Eleanor, what are you talking about? These guys, they abducted you. If we hadn't come here, there's a good chance they would've taken you out into the desert tomorrow and planted you.'

'I don't want the cops. I don't want to go through all of that. I just want this to end.'

Bosch looked at her a long moment.

'Jerry, you got him?' he asked.

'I got him.'

Bosch went to Eleanor and grabbed her arm and led her back into the house. When they were in the alcove by the kitchen and far enough away that the men outside could not hear them, he stopped and looked at her.

'Eleanor, what's going on?'

'Nothing. I just don't want—'

'Did they hurt you?'

'No, I'm—'

'Did they rape you? Tell me the truth.'

'No, Harry. It is nothing like that. I just want this to end here.'

'Listen to me, we can take down Marks, his lawyer and those three assholes out on the porch. That's why I'm here. Marks told me he had you.'

'Don't kid yourself, Harry. You can't touch Marks on this. What did he really tell you? And who's your witness going to be? Me? Look at me. I'm a convicted felon, Harry. Not only that, I used to be one of the good guys. Just think what a mob lawyer can do with that.'

Bosch didn't say anything. He knew she was right.

'Well, I'm not going to put myself through that,' she said. 'I got a dose of reality when they jerked me out of my home and took me down to Metro. I'm not going to go to bat for them on this. Now can you get me out of here?'

'As long as you are sure. You can't change your mind once we're out of here.'

'I'm as sure as I'll ever be.'

Bosch nodded and let her out to the porch.

'It's your lucky day, boys,' he said to the three thugs. Then to Edgar he said, 'We're pulling out of here. We'll talk about it later.'

Edgar just nodded. Bosch went one by one to the Samoans and put their own cuffs on their wrists and then took off the others. When he was done, he held the key up in front of the smaller of the two giants and then tossed it into the pool. He went over to the fence that ran behind the pool and took down a long pole with a net attached to the end of it. He fished his gun off the bottom and handed it to Eleanor to hold. He then returned to Gussie, who was dressed completely in black. Edgar was still standing to his right, holding the gun against his temple.

'Almost didn't recognize you without the tux, Gussie. Will you give Joey Marks a message?'

'Yeah. What?'

'Fuck you. Just tell him that.'

'He's not going to like that.'

'I don't really care. He's lucky I don't leave him three bodies here as a message.'

Bosch looked over at Eleanor.

'Anything you want to say or do?'

She shook her head.

'Then we're outta here. Only thing is, Gussie, we're one set of cuffs short. That's too bad for you.'

'There's rope in the—'

Bosch hit him on the bridge of the nose with the butt end of his gun, crushing whatever bone had not been broken in their earlier scuffle. Gussie dropped heavily to his knees, then pitched forward, his face making a thud on the porch tile.

'Harry! Jesus!'

It was Edgar. He looked shocked by the sudden violence.

Bosch just looked at him a moment and said, 'Let's go.'

When they got to Eleanor's apartment, Bosch backed the car up nearly to the door and popped the trunk.

'We don't have a lot of time,' he said. 'Jerry, you stay out here, watch for anybody coming. Eleanor, you can fill the trunk with whatever you can fit in there. That's about all you can take.'

She nodded. She understood. Las Vegas was over for her. She could no longer stay, not with what had happened. Bosch wondered if she also understood that it was all because of him. Her life would still be as it had been if he had not wanted to reach out to her.

They all got out of the car and Bosch followed Eleanor into the apartment. She studied the broken door for a moment until he told her he had done it.

'Why?'

'Because when I didn't hear from you I thought . . . I thought something else.'

She nodded again. She understood that, too.

'There's not a lot,' she said, looking around the place. 'Most of this stuff I don't care about. I probably won't even need the whole trunk.'

She went into the bedroom, took an old suitcase out of the closet and started filling it with clothes. When it was full, Bosch took it out and put it in the trunk. When he came back in, she was filling a box from the closet with her remaining clothes and other personal belongings. He saw her put a photo album in the box and then she went to the bathroom to clear the medicine cabinet.

In the kitchen all she took was a wine bottle opener and a coffee mug with a picture of the Mirage hotel on it.

'Bought this the night I won four hundred sixty-three dollars there,' she said. 'I was playing the big table and I was way in over my head but I won. I want to remember that.'

424

She put that in the top of the full box and said, 'That's it. That's all I have to show for my life.'

Bosch studied her a moment and then took the box out to the car. He struggled a bit, getting it to fit in next to the suitcase. When he was done, he turned around to call to Eleanor that they must go and she was already standing there, holding the framed print of *The Nighthawks*, the Edward Hopper painting. She was holding it in front of her like a shield.

'Will this fit?'

'Sure. We'll make it fit.'

At the Mirage, Bosch pulled into the valet circle again and saw the chief valet frown as he recognized the car. Bosch got out, showed the man his badge quickly so that he might not notice it wasn't a Metro badge, and gave him twenty dollars.

'Police business. I'll be twenty-thirty minutes tops. I need the car here because when we leave we're going to have to really book.'

The man looked at the twenty in his hand as if it were human feces. Bosch reached into his pocket, pulled out another twenty and gave it to him.

'Okay?'

'Okay. Leave me the keys.'

'No. No keys. Nobody touches the car.'

Bosch had to take the picture out of the trunk to get to Eleanor's suitcase and a gun kit he kept there. He then repacked the trunk and lugged the suitcase inside, waving off an offer of help from a doorman. In the lobby, he put the case down and looked at Edgar.

'Jerry, thanks a lot,' he said. 'You were there, man. Eleanor's going to change and then I'm going to shoot her out to the airport. I probably won't be back until late. So let's just meet here at eight o'clock tomorrow and we'll go to court.'

'Sure you don't need me for the airport run?'

'No, I think we're fine. Marks won't try anything now. And if we're lucky, Gussie won't be waking up for another hour or so anyway. I'm going to go check in.'

He left Eleanor there with him and went to the desk. There was no wait. It was late. After giving the clerk his credit card, he looked back at Eleanor saying her good-bye to Edgar. He put out his hand and she shook it but then she pulled him into an embrace. Edgar disappeared into the crowd of the casino.

Eleanor waited until they were in his room before she spoke.

'Why am I going to the airport tonight? You said you doubted they would do anything.'

'Because I want to make sure you're safe. And tomorrow I won't be able to worry about it. I've got court in the morning and then I'm driving Goshen to L.A. I have to know you're safe.'

'Where am I going to go?'

'You could go to a hotel but I think my place would be better, safer. You remember where it is?'

'Yes. Up off Mulholland?'

425

'Yeah. Woodrow Wilson Drive. I'll give you the key. Take a cab from the airport and I'll be there by tomorrow night.'

'Then what?'

'I don't know. We'll figure it out.'

She sat down on the edge of the bed and Bosch came around and sat next to her. He put his arms around her shoulders.

'I don't know if I could live in L.A. again.'

'We'll figure it out.'

He leaned in and kissed her on the cheek.

'Don't kiss me. I need to take a shower.'

He kissed her again and then pulled her back onto the bed. They made love differently this time. They were more tender, slower. They found each other's rhythm.

After, Bosch took the first shower and then while Eleanor bathed he used oil and a rag from his gun kit to clean the Glock that had been thrown into the pool. He worked the action and trigger several times to make sure the weapon was working properly. Then he filled the clip with fresh ammunition. He went to the closet and took a plastic laundry bag off the shelf, put the gun inside it and shoved it beneath a stack of clothes in Eleanor's suitcase.

After her shower Eleanor dressed in a yellow cotton summer dress and twined her hair into a French braid. Bosch liked watching her do it with such skill. When she was ready, he closed the suitcase and they left the room. The head valet came up to Bosch as he was putting the suitcase into the trunk.

'Next time, thirty minutes is thirty minutes. Not an hour.'

'Sorry 'bout that.'

'Sorry doesn't cut it. I could've lost my job, man.'

Bosch ignored him and got in the car. On the way to the airport he tried to compose his thoughts into articulate sentences that he could recite to her but it wasn't working. His emotions were too much of a jumble.

'Eleanor,' he finally said. 'Everything that's happened, it's my fault. And I want to try to make it up to you.'

She reached over and put her hand on his thigh. He put his hand on top of hers. She didn't say anything.

At the airport, Bosch parked in front of the Southwest terminal and got her suitcase out of the trunk. He locked his own gun and badge in the trunk so he could go through the airport's metal detector without a problem.

There was one last flight to L.A., leaving in twenty minutes. Bosch bought her a ticket and checked her bag. The gun would cause no problem as long as the bag was checked. He then escorted her to the terminal, where there was already a line of people making their way down the jetway.

Bosch took the key to his house off his keychain, gave it to her and told her the exact address.

'It's not the same as you might remember it,' he said. 'The old place got wrecked in the earthquake. It's been rebuilt and it's not all the way done. But it will be all right. The sheets, uh, I probably should've washed them a few days ago but didn't have time. There's fresh ones in the hallway closet.'

She smiled.

'Don't worry, I'll figure everything out.'

'Uh, listen, like I said before, I don't think that you've got anything to worry about anymore but just in case, you've got the Glock in your suitcase. That's why I checked it.'

'You cleaned it while I was in the shower, didn't you? I thought I smelled the oil when I came out.'

He nodded.

'Thanks but I don't think I'll need it anyway.'

'Probably not.'

She looked over at the line. The last people were boarding. She had to go.

'You're being very good to me, Harry. Thank you.'

He frowned.

'Not good enough. Not enough to make up for everything.'

She went up on her toes and kissed him on the cheek.

'Good-bye, Harry.'

'Good-bye, Eleanor.'

He watched her hand in her ticket and go through the door to the jetway. She didn't look back and there was a whisper in the back of his mind telling him he might never see her again. But he shut it off and walked back through the nearly deserted airport. Most of the slot machines stood mute and ignored. Bosch felt a deep sense of loneliness engulf him.

The only hitch in Thursday morning's court proceedings occurred before they started, when Weiss came out of lockup after conferring with his client and quickly went into the hall to find Bosch and Edgar conferring with Lipson, the local prosecutor who would handle the extradition hearing. Gregson had not made the trip from the L.A. County DA's office. Weiss and Lipson had given him their assurances that Luke Goshen was going to waive any objection to being brought back to California.

'Detective Bosch?' Weiss said. 'I was just in with my client and he asked me to get him some information before the hearing. He said he wanted an answer before he gave any waiver. I don't know what it's about, but I hope you haven't been in contact with my client.'

Bosch put a concerned yet puzzled look on his face.

'What's he want to know?'

'He just wanted to know how last night worked out, whatever that means. I'd like to know what is going on here.'

'Just tell him everything is fine.'

'What is fine, Detective?'

'If your client wants to tell you, he can tell you. Just deliver the message.'

Weiss stalked away, heading back toward the lockup door.

Bosch looked at his watch. It was five till nine and he figured the judge wouldn't come out to the bench at the crack of nine. None of them ever did. He reached into his pocket for his cigarettes.

'I'm going outside to have a smoke,' he told Edgar.

Bosch took the elevator down and went out to the front of the courthouse to have his cigarette. It was warm out and he thought the day would probably be another scorcher. With Las Vegas in September it was pretty much guaranteed. He was glad he'd be leaving soon. But he knew the ride through the desert during the heat of the day would be rough.

He didn't notice Mickey Torrino until the lawyer was a few feet away from him. He, too, was smoking a cigarette before going in to handle the day's business of mob-related legal work. Bosch nodded his greeting as did Torrino.

'I guess you heard by now. No deal.'

Torrino looked around to see if they were being watched.

'I don't know what you're talking about, Detective.'

'Yeah, I know. You guys never know anything.'

'I do know one thing and that's that you are making a mistake on this one. In case you care about things like that.'

'I don't think so. At least not in the big picture. We might not have the real shooter but we have the guy who set it up. And we're going to get the guy who ordered it. Who knows, maybe we'll get the whole crew. Who you going to work for then, Counselor? That is, if we don't get you, too.'

Torrino smirked and shook his head as if he were dealing with a foolish child.

'You don't know what you're dealing with here. It's not going to play. You'll be lucky if you get to keep Goshen. At best you've got only him. That's all.'

'You know, Lucky keeps making noises about being set up. He, of course, thinks it's us putting him in the frame and I know that's bullshit. But I keep thinking, "What if there is a frame?" I mean, I have to admit that him keeping that gun is hard to figure, though I've seen even dumber moves in my time. But if there is a frame and we didn't do it, who did? Why would Joey Marks frame his own guy when that guy's just going to roll over and put the finger back on Joey? Doesn't make sense. At least, from Joey's point of view. But then I started thinking, What if you were Joey's righthand man, say his lawyer, and you wanted to be the big shot, the one who makes the calls? See what I'm talking about here? This'd be a nice little way of getting rid of your nearest competitor and Joey at the same time. How would that play, Counselor?'

'If you ever repeat that bullshit story to anyone, you will be very, very sorry.'

Bosch took a step toward him so that their faces were only a foot apart.

'If you ever threaten me again, *you* will be very, very sorry. If anything ever happens to Eleanor Wish again, I will hold you personally responsible, asshole, and sorry is not the right word for how you will be then.'

Torrino stepped back, loser in the staring contest. Without another word he walked away from Bosch and toward the courthouse doors. As he opened the heavy glass door, he looked back at Bosch, then disappeared inside.

When Bosch got back to the third floor, he met Edgar as he was coming quickly out of the courtroom, followed by Weiss and Lipson. Bosch looked at the hallway clock. It was five after nine.

'Harry, whereya been, smokin' a whole pack?' Edgar asked.

'What happened?'

'It's over. He waived. We've got to bring the car around and get over to the release desk. We'll have him in fifteen minutes.'

'Detectives?' Weiss said. 'I want to know every detail of how my client will be moved and what security measures you're taking.'

Bosch put his arm on Weiss's shoulders and leaned into him in a confidential manner. They had stopped at the bank of elevators.

'The very first security measure we are taking is that we aren't telling anyone how or when we're getting back to L.A. That includes you, Mr Weiss. All you need to know is that he'll be in L.A. Municipal Court for arraignment tomorrow morning.'

'Wait a minute. You can't—'

'Yes, we can, Mr Weiss,' Edgar said as an elevator opened. 'Your client waived his opposition to extradition and in fifteen minutes he'll be in our custody. And we're not going to divulge any information about security, here or there or on the way there. Now, if you'll excuse us.'

They left him there and loaded onto the elevator. As the doors closed, Weiss shouted something about them not being allowed to talk to his client until his Los Angeles counsel had met with him.

A half hour later the Strip was in the rearview mirror and they were driving into the open desert.

'Say good-bye, Lucky,' Bosch said. 'You won't be back.'

When Goshen didn't say anything, Bosch checked him in the mirror. The big man was sitting sullenly in the back with his arms cuffed to a heavy chain that went around his waist. He returned Bosch's stare and for a brief moment Bosch thought he saw the same look he had let loose for a moment in his bedroom before he managed to drag it back inside like a naughty child.

'Just drive,' he said after he had recovered his demeanor. 'We're not having a conversation here.'

Bosch looked back at the road ahead and smiled.

'Maybe not now, but we will. We'll be talking.'

V

As Bosch and Edgar were leaving the Men's Central Jail in downtown Los Angeles, Bosch's pager sounded and he checked the number. He didn't recognize it but the 485 exchange told him the person paging him was in Parker Center. He took the phone out of his briefcase and returned the call. Lieutenant Billets answered.

'Detective, where are you?'

Her use of his rank instead of his name told him she probably wasn't alone. The fact that she was calling from Parker Center rather than the bureau in Hollywood told him that something had gone wrong.

'At Men's Central. What's up?'

'Do you have Luke Goshen with you?'

'No, we just dropped him off. Why, what is it?'

'Give me the booking number.'

Bosch hesitated a moment but then held the phone under his chin while he reopened his briefcase and got the number from the booking receipt. He gave Billets the number and once again asked what was going on. She once again ignored the question.

'Detective,' she said, 'I want you to come over to Parker right away. The sixth-floor conference room.'

The sixth floor was administration level. It was also where the Internal Affairs offices were. Bosch hesitated again before finally answering.

'Sure, Grace. You want Jerry, too?'

'Tell Detective Edgar to go back to Hollywood Division. I'll contact him there.'

'We've only got the one car.'

'Then tell him to take a cab and put it on his expense account. Hurry it up, Detective. We are waiting for you here.'

'We? Who's waiting?'

She hung up then and Bosch just stared at the phone for a moment.

'What is it?' Edgar asked.

'I don't know.'

Bosch stepped off the elevator into the deserted sixth-floor hallway and proceeded toward the conference room he knew was behind the last door before the entrance to the police chief's office at the end of the hall. The yellowed linoleum had been recently polished. As he walked toward his destiny with his head down, he saw his own dark reflection moving just in front of his steps.

The door to the conference room was open and as Bosch stepped in all eyes in the room were on him. He looked back at Lieutenant Billets and Captain LeValley from the Hollywood Division and the recognizable faces of Deputy Chief Irvin Irving and an IAD squint named Chastain. But the four remaining men gathered in chairs around the long conference table were strangers to Bosch. Nevertheless, he guessed from their conservative gray suits that they were feds.

'Detective Bosch, have a seat,' Irving said.

Irving stood up, ramrod straight in a tight uniform. The dome of his shaven head shone under the ceiling fluorescents. He motioned to the empty seat at the head of the table. Bosch pulled the chair out and sat down slowly as his mind raced. He knew that this kind of showing of brass and feds was too big to have been caused by his affair with Eleanor Wish. There was something else going on and it involved only him. Otherwise, Billets would have told him to bring Edgar along.

'Who died?' Bosch asked.

Irving ignored the question. When Bosch's eyes traveled across the table to his left and up to Billets's face, the lieutenant glanced away.

'Detective, we need to ask you some questions pertaining to your investigation of the Aliso case,' Irving said.

'What are the charges?' Bosch responded.

'There are no charges,' Irving replied calmly. 'We need to clear some things up.'

'Who are these people?'

Irving introduced the four strangers. Bosch had been right, they were feds: John Samuels, an assistant U.S. Attorney assigned to the organized crime strike force, and three FBI agents from three different field offices. They were John O'Grady from L.A., Dan Ekeblad from Las Vegas and Wendell Werris from Chicago.

Nobody offered to shake Bosch's hand, nobody even nodded. They just stared at Bosch with looks that transmitted their contempt for him. Since they were feds, their dislike of the LAPD was standard issue. Bosch still couldn't figure out what was going on here.

'Okay,' Irving said. 'We're going to get some things cleared up first. I'm going to let Mr Samuels take it from here.'

Samuels wiped a hand down his thick black mustache and leaned forward. He was in the chair at the opposite end of the table from Bosch. He had a yellow legal tablet on the table in front of him but it was too far away for Bosch to be able to read what was on it. He held a pen in his left hand and used it to hold his place in his notes. Looking down at the notes, he began.

'Let's start with your search of Luke Goshen's home in Las Vegas,' Samuels said. 'Exactly who was it who found the firearm later identified as the weapon used in the killing of Anthony Aliso?'

Bosch narrowed his eyes. He tried looking at Billets again, but her eyes were focused on the table in front of her. As he scanned the other faces, he caught the smirk on Chastain's face. No surprise there. Bosch had hooked up with Chastain before. He was known as Sustained Chastain by many in the department. When departmental charges are brought against an officer, an Internal Affairs investigation and Board of Rights hearing result in one of two findings: the allegations are either sustained or ruled unfounded. Chastain had a high ratio of sustained to unfounded cases – thus the departmental moniker which he wore like a medal.

'If this is the subject of a department investigation, I think I'm entitled to representation,' Bosch said. 'I don't know what this is about but I don't have to tell you people anything.'

'Detective,' Irving said. He slid a sheet of paper across the table to Bosch. 'That is a signed order from the chief of police telling you to cooperate with these gentlemen. If you choose not to, you will be suspended without pay forthwith. And you'll be assigned your union rep then.'

Bosch looked down at the letter. It was a form letter and he had received them before. It was all part of the department's way of backing you into the corner, to the point that you had to talk to them or you didn't eat.

'I found the gun,' Bosch said without looking up from the order. 'It was in the master bathroom, wrapped in plastic and secreted between the toilet tank and the wall. Somebody said the mobsters in *The Godfather* did that. The movie. But I don't remember.'

'Were you alone when you supposedly found the weapon there?'

'Supposedly? Are you saying it wasn't there?'

'Just answer the question, please.'

Bosch shook his head in disgust. He didn't know what was going on but it was looking worse than he had imagined.

'I wasn't alone. The house was full of cops.'

'Were they in the master bathroom with you?' O'Grady asked.

Bosch just looked at O'Grady. He was at least ten years younger than Bosch, with the clean-cut looks the bureau prized.

'I thought Mr Samuels was going to handle the questioning,' Irving said.

'I am,' Samuels said. 'Were any of these cops in that bathroom with you when you located this weapon?'

'I was by myself. As soon as I saw it, I called the uniform in the bedroom in to take a look before I even touched it. If this is about Goshen's lawyer making some beef to you people about me planting the gun, it's bullshit. The gun was there, and besides, we've got enough on him without the gun. We've got motive, prints . . . why would I plant a gun?'

'To make it a slam dunk,' O'Grady said.

Bosch blew out his breath in disgust.

'It's typical of the bureau to drop everything and come after an L.A. cop just because some sleazeball gangster drops a dime. What, are they givin' annual bonuses now if you guys nail a cop? Double if it's an L.A. cop? Fuck you, O'Grady. Okay?'

'Yeah, fuck me. Just answer the questions.'

'Then ask them.'

Samuels nodded as if Bosch had scored a point and moved his pen a half inch down his pad.

'Do you know,' he asked, 'did any other police officer enter that bathroom before you entered to search it and subsequently found the gun?'

Bosch tried to remember, picturing the movements of the Metro cops in

435

the room. He was sure no one had gone into the bathroom other than to take a quick look to make sure no one was in there hiding.

'I don't know for sure about that,' he said. 'But I doubt it. If somebody did go in, there wasn't enough time to plant the gun. The gun was already there.'

Samuels nodded again, consulted his legal pad and then looked at Irving.

'Chief Irving, I think that's as far as we want to take it for the moment. We certainly appreciate your cooperation in this matter and I expect we'll be talking again soon.'

Samuels made a move to stand up.

'Wait a minute,' Bosch said. 'That's it? You're just going to get up and leave? What the fuck is going on here? I deserve an explanation. Who made the complaint, Goshen's lawyer? Because I'm going to make a complaint right back at him.'

'Your deputy chief can discuss this with you, if he chooses to.'

'No, Samuels. You tell me. You're asking the questions, now you answer a few.'

Samuels drummed his pen on his pad for a moment and looked at Irving. Irving opened his hands to show it was his choice. Samuels then leaned forward and looked balefully at Bosch.

'If you insist on an explanation, I'll give you one,' he said. 'I'm limited, of course, in what I can say.'

'Jesus, would you just tell me what the hell is going on?'

Samuels cleared his throat before going on.

'About four years ago, in a joint operation involving the FBI offices in Chicago, Las Vegas and Los Angeles, the strike force instituted what we called Operation Telegraph. Personnel-wise it was a small operation but it had a large goal. Our goal was Joseph Marconi and the remaining tentacles of the mob's influence in Las Vegas. It took us more than eighteen months but we managed to get someone inside. An agent on the inside. And in the two years since that was accomplished, that agent was able to rise to a level of prominence in Joseph Marconi's organization, one in which he had the intended target's complete confidence. Conservatively, we were four to five months from closing the operation and going to a grand jury to seek indictments for more than a dozen high-ranking members of the Cosa Nostra in three cities, not to mention an assortment of burglars, casino cheats, bust-out artists, cops, judges, lawyers and even a few Hollywood fringe players such as Anthony N. Aliso. This is not to mention that, largely through the efforts of this undercover agent and the wiretaps authorized with probable cause gathered through him, we now have a greater understanding of the sophistication and reach of organized crime entities such as Marconi's.'

Samuels was talking as if he were addressing a press conference. He let a moment pass as he caught his breath. But he never took his eyes off Bosch.

'That undercover agent's name is Roy Lindell. Remember it, because he's going to be famous. No other agent was underground for so long and with such important results. You notice that I said *was*. He's no longer under, Detective Bosch. And for that we can thank you. The name Roy used undercover was Luke Goshen. Lucky Luke Goshen. So I want to thank you for fucking up the end of a wonderful and important case. Oh, we'll still get

Marconi and all the others with what Roy's good work got us, but now it's all been marred by a . . . by you.'

Bosch felt anger backing up in his throat but tried to remain calm and he managed to speak in an even voice.

'Your suggestion then is – no, your accusation is – that I planted that gun. Well, you are wrong about that. Dead wrong. I should be angry and offended, but given the situation I understand how you made the mistake. But instead of pointing at me, maybe you folks ought to take a look at your man Goshen or whatever the hell his name is. Maybe you should question whether you left him under too long. Because that gun wasn't planted. You—'

'Don't you dare!' O'Grady blurted out. 'Don't you dare say a word about him. You, you're nothing but a fucking rogue cop! We know about you, Bosch, all your baggage. This time you went too far. You planted evidence on the wrong man this time.'

'I take it back,' Bosch said, still calm. 'I am offended. I am angry. So fuck you, O'Grady. You say I planted the gun, prove it. But first I guess you gotta prove that I was the one who put Tony Aliso in his trunk. Because how the hell else would I have the gun to plant?'

'Easy. You could've found it there in the bushes off the goddamned fire road. We already know you searched it by yourself. We—'

'Gentlemen,' Irving interjected.

'—will put you down for this, Bosch.'

'Gentlemen!'

O'Grady closed his mouth and everyone looked at Irving.

'This is getting out of hand. I'm ending this meeting. Suffice it to say, an internal investigation will be conducted and—'

'We are doing our own investigation,' Samuels said. 'Meantime, we have to figure out how to salvage our operation.'

Bosch looked at him incredulously.

'Don't you understand?' he said. 'There is no operation. Your star witness is a murderer. You left him in too long, Samuels. He turned, became one of them. He killed Tony Aliso for Joey Marks. His prints were on the body. The gun was found in his house. Not only that, he's got no alibi. Nothing. He told me he spent all night in the office, but I know he wasn't there. He left and he had time to get over here, do the job and get back.'

Bosch shook his head sadly and finished in a low voice.

'I agree with you, Samuels. Your operation is tainted now. But not because of me. It was you who left the guy in the oven too long. He got cooked. You were his handler. You fucked up.'

This time Samuels shook his head and smiled sadly. That was when Bosch realized the other shoe hadn't dropped. There was something else. Samuels angrily flipped up the top page of his pad and read a notation.

'The autopsy concludes time of death was between eleven p.m. Friday and two a.m. Saturday. Is that correct, Detective Bosch?'

'I don't know how you got the report, since I haven't seen it myself yet.'

'Was the death between eleven and two?'

'Yes.'

'Do you have those documents, Dan?' Samuels asked Ekeblad.

Ekeblad took several pages folded lengthwise from the inside of his jacket and handed them to Samuels. Samuels opened the packet and glanced at its contents and then tossed it across the table to Bosch. Bosch picked it up but didn't look at it. He kept his eyes on Samuels.

'What you have there are copies of a page from an investigative log as well as an interview report prepared Tuesday morning by Agent Ekeblad here. There are also two sworn affidavits from agents Ekeblad and Phil Colbert, who will be with us here shortly. What you'll find if you look at those is that on Friday night at midnight, Agent Ekeblad was sitting behind the wheel of his bureau car in the back parking lot at Caesar's, just off Industrial Road. His partner Colbert was there next to him and in the back seat, Agent Roy Lindell.'

He waited a beat and Bosch looked down at the papers in his hands.

'It was Roy's monthly meeting. He was being debriefed. He told Ekeblad and Colbert that just that night he had put four hundred and eighty thousand dollars cash from Marconi's various enterprises into Anthony Aliso's briefcase and sent him back to L.A. to have it put in the wash. He also, by the way, mentioned that Tony had been in the club drinking and got a little out of line with one of the girls. In his role as enforcer for Joey Marks and manager of the club, he had to get tough with Tony. He cuffed him once and jerked him around by his collar. This, I think, you might agree, would account for the fingerprints recovered from the deceased's jacket and the antemortem facial bruising noted in the autopsy.'

Bosch still refused to look up from the documents.

'Other than that, there was a lot to talk about, Detective Bosch. Roy stayed for ninety minutes. And there is no fucking way in the world he could have gotten to Los Angeles to kill Tony Aliso before two a.m., let alone three a.m. And just so you don't leave here thinking all three of these agents were involved in the murder, you should know that the meeting was monitored by four additional agents in a chase car also parked in the lot for security reasons.'

Samuels waited a beat before delivering his closing argument.

'You don't have a case. The prints can be explained and the guy you said did it was sitting with two FBI agents three hundred and fifty miles away when the shooting went down. You've got nothing. No, actually, that's wrong. You do have one thing. A planted gun, that's what you've got.'

As if on cue the door behind Bosch opened and he heard footsteps. Keeping his eyes on the documents in front of him, Bosch didn't turn around to see who it was until he felt a hand grip his shoulder and squeeze. He looked up into the face of Special Agent Roy Lindell. He was smiling, standing next to another agent who Bosch assumed was Ekeblad's partner, Colbert.

'Bosch,' Lindell said, 'I owe you a haircut.'

Bosch was dumbfounded to see the man he had just locked up standing there but quickly assimilated what had happened. Irving and Billets had already been told about the meeting in the parking lot behind Caesar's, had read the affidavits and believed the alibi. They had authorized Lindell's release. That was why Billets had asked for the booking number when Bosch had returned her page.

Bosch looked away from Lindell to Irving and Billets.

'You believe this, don't you? You think I found the gun out there in the weeds and planted it just to make the case a slam.'

There was a hesitation while each one left space for the other to answer. Finally, it was Irving.

'The only thing we know for sure is that it wasn't Agent Lindell. His story is solid. I'm reserving judgment on everything else.'

Bosch looked at Lindell, who was still standing.

'Then why didn't you tell me you were federal when we were in that room together at Metro?'

'Why do you think? For all I knew, you had already put a gun in my bathroom. You think I'm just going to tell you I'm an agent and everything would be cool after that? Yeah, right.'

'We had to play along, Bosch, to see what moves you'd make and to make sure Roy got out of the Metro jail in one piece,' O'Grady said. 'After that, we were two thousand feet above you and two thousand behind you all the way across the desert. We were waiting. Half of us were betting you made a deal with Joey Marks. You know, in for a pinch, in for a pound?'

They were taunting him now. Bosch shook his head. It seemed to be the only thing he could do.

'Don't you people see what is happening?' he said. 'You're the ones who made a deal with Joey Marks. Only you don't know it. He is playing you like a symphony. Jesus! I can't believe I'm sitting here and this is actually happening.'

'How is he playing us?' Billets asked, the first indication that she might not have gone all the way across to the other side on him.

Bosch answered, looking at Lindell.

'Don't you see? They found out about you. They knew you were an agent. So they set this all up.'

Ekeblad snorted in derision.

'They don't set things up, Bosch,' Samuels said. 'If they thought Roy was an informant, they'd just take him out to the desert and put him under three feet of sand. End of threat.'

'No, because we're not talking about an informant. I'm talking about them knowing specifically he was an agent and knowing that because of that they couldn't just take him out to the desert. Not an FBI agent. If they did that, they'd have more heat on them than the Branch Davidians ever felt. No, so what they did was make a plan. They know he's been around a couple years and knows more than enough to take them all down hard. But they can't just kill him. Not an agent. So they've got to neutralize him, taint him. Make him look like he crossed, like he's just as bad as they are. So when he testifies, they can take him apart with Tony Aliso's hit. Make a jury think that he'd carry out a hit to maintain his cover. They sell a jury that and they could all walk away.'

Bosch thought he had planted the seeds of a pretty convincing story, even having pulled it together on the fly. The others in the room looked at him in silence for a few moments, but then Lindell spoke up.

'You give them too much credit, Bosch,' he said. 'Joey's not that smart. I know him. He's not that smart.'

'What about Torrino? You going to tell me he couldn't come up with this? I just thought of it sitting here. Who knows how long he had to come up with something. Answer one question, Lindell. Did Joey Marks know that Tony Aliso had the IRS on his back, that an audit was coming?'

Lindell hesitated and looked to Samuels to see if he could answer. Bosch felt the sweat of desperation breaking on his neck and back. He knew he had to convince them or he wouldn't walk out of the room with his badge. Samuels nodded to Lindell.

'If he knew, he didn't tell me,' Lindell said.

'Well maybe that's it,' Bosch said. 'Maybe he knew but he didn't tell you. Joey knew he had a problem with Aliso and somehow he knew he had a bigger problem with you. And he and Torrino put their heads together and came up with this whole thing so they could kill two birds with the one stone.'

There was another pause, but Samuels shook his head.

'It doesn't work, Bosch. You're stretching. Besides we've got seven hundred hours of tapes. There's enough on them to put Joey away without Roy even testifying one word.'

'First of all, they might not have known there were tapes,' Billets said. 'And secondly, even if they did, it's fruit of the poison tree. You wouldn't have the tapes without Agent Lindell. You want to introduce them in court, you have to introduce him. They destroy him, they destroy the tapes.'

Billets had clearly shifted to Bosch's side of the equation and that gave him hope. It also made Samuels see that the meeting was over. He gathered up his pad and stood up.

'Well,' he said, 'I can see we aren't going any further with this. Lieutenant, you're listening to a desperate man. We don't have to. Chief Irving, I don't envy you. You have a problem and you have to do something about it. If on Monday I find out that Bosch is still carrying his badge, then I'm going to go to the sitting grand jury and get an indictment against him for evidence tampering and violating the civil rights of Roy Lindell. I will also ask our civil rights unit to look into every arrest this man has made in the last five years. A bad cop never plants evidence once, Chief. It's a habit.'

Samuels made his way around the table toward the door. The others got up and were following. Bosch wanted to jump up and throttle him but he remained outwardly calm. His dark eyes followed Samuels as the federal attorney moved to the door. He never looked back at Bosch. But before stepping out, he took one last shot at Irving.

'The last thing I want to have to do is air your dirty laundry, Chief. But if you don't take care of this, you'll leave me no choice.'

With that, the federals filed out and those remaining sat in silence for a long moment, listening to the sound of the steps tracking down the polished linoleum in the hallway. Bosch looked at Billets and nodded.

'Thanks, Lieutenant.'

'For what?'

'Sticking up for me at the end there.'

'I just don't believe you'd do it, is all.'

'I wouldn't plant evidence on my worst enemy. If I did that I'd be lost.'

Chastain shifted in his seat while a small smile played on his face, but not small enough to pass Bosch's notice.

'Chastain, you and I have hooked up a couple times before and you missed me both times,' Bosch said. 'You don't want to strike out, do you? You better sit this one out.'

'Look, Bosch, the chief asked me to sit in on this and I did that. It's his call, but I think you and that story you just wove out of thin air are full of shit. I agree with the feds on this one. If it was my choice, I wouldn't let you out of this room with a badge.'

'But it's not your choice, is it?' Irving said.

When Bosch got to his house, he carried a bag of groceries to the door and knocked but there was no answer. He kicked over the straw mat and found the key he had given Eleanor there. A feeling of sadness came over him as he bent to pick it up. She was not there.

Upon entering he was greeted by the strong smell of fresh paint, which he thought was odd because it had now been four days since he had painted. He went directly into the kitchen and put away the groceries. When he was finished, he took a bottle of beer from the refrigerator and leaned against the counter drinking it slowly, making it last. The smell of paint reminded him that now he would have plenty of time to finish all the work the house needed. He was strictly a nine-to-fiver at the moment.

He thought of Eleanor again and decided to look to see if there was a note from her or whether her suitcase might be in the bedroom. But he went no further than the living room, where he stopped and looked at the wall he had left half-painted after getting the call to the crime scene on Sunday. The wall was now completely painted. Bosch stood there a long moment, appraising the work as though it were a masterpiece in a museum. Finally he stepped to the wall and lightly touched it. It was fresh but dry. Painted just a few hours before, he guessed. Though no one was there to see it, a broad smile broke across his face. He felt a jolt of happiness break through the gray aura surrounding him. He didn't need to look for her suitcase in the bedroom. He took the painted wall as a sign, as her note. She'd be back.

An hour later, he had unpacked his overnighter and the rest of her belongings from the car and was standing in the darkness on the rear deck. He held another bottle of beer and watched the ribbon of lights moving along the Hollywood Freeway at the bottom of the hill. He had no idea how long she had stood in the frame of the sliding door to the deck and watched him. When he turned around, she was just there.

'Eleanor.'

'Harry . . . I thought you wouldn't be back until later.'

'Neither did I. But I'm here.'

He smiled. He wanted to go to her and touch her, but a cautious voice told him to move slowly.

'Thanks for finishing.'

He gestured toward the living room with his bottle.

'No problem. I like to paint. It relaxes me.'

'Yeah. Me, too.'

They looked at each other a moment.

'I saw the print,' she said. 'It looks good there.'

Bosch had taken her print of Hopper's *Nighthawks* out of the trunk and hung it on the freshly painted wall. He knew that how she reacted to seeing

441

it there would tell him a lot about where they were and where they might be headed.

'Good,' he said, nodding and trying not to smile.

'What happened to the one I sent you?'

That had been a long time ago.

'Earthquake,' he said.

She nodded.

'Where'd you just come from?'

'Oh, I went and rented a car. You know, until I can figure out what I'm going to do. I left my car in Vegas.'

'I guess we could go over and get it, drive it back. You know, get in and out, not hang around.'

She nodded.

'Oh, I got a bottle of red wine, too. You want something? Or another beer?'

'I'll have what you're having.'

'I'm going to have a glass of wine. You sure you want that?'

'I'm sure. I'll open it.'

He followed her into the kitchen and opened the wine and took down two glasses from a cabinet and rinsed them. He hadn't had anyone who liked wine over in a long time. She poured and they touched glasses before drinking.

'So how's the case going?' she asked.

'I don't have a case anymore.'

She creased her brow and frowned.

'What happened? I thought you were bringing your suspect back.'

'I did. But it's no longer my case. Not since my suspect turned out to be a bureau agent with an alibi.'

'Oh, Harry.' She looked down. 'Are you in trouble?'

Bosch put his glass on the counter and folded his arms.

'I'm on a desk for the time being. I've got the squints investigating me. They think – along with the bureau – that I planted evidence against the agent. The gun. I didn't. But I guess somebody did. When I figure out who, then I'll be okay.'

'Harry, how did this—'

He shook his head, and moved toward her and put his mouth on hers. He gently took the glass out of her hand and put it on the counter behind her.

After they made love, Bosch went into the kitchen to open a bottle of beer and make dinner. He peeled an onion and chopped it up along with a green pepper. He then cleared the cutting board into a frying pan and sautéed the mixture with butter, powdered garlic and other seasonings. He added two chicken breasts and cooked them until the meat was easy to shred and pull away from the bone with a fork. He added a can of Italian tomato sauce, a can of crushed tomatoes and more seasonings. He finished by pouring a shot of red wine from Eleanor's bottle in. While it all simmered, he put a pot of water on to boil for rice.

It was the best dinner he knew how to cook in a kitchen. He would have preferred grilling something on the deck, but the grill had been hauled away when the original house was demolished after the earthquake. While he had replaced the house, he had not yet gotten around to getting a new grill. He decided as he mixed rice into the boiling water that if Eleanor chose to stay for a while, he would get the grill.

'Smells good.'

He turned and she was standing in the doorway. She was dressed in blue jeans and a denim shirt. Her hair was damp from the shower. Bosch looked at her and felt the desire to make love to her again.

'I hope it tastes good,' he said. 'This is a new kitchen, but I don't really know how to use it yet. Never did much cooking.'

She smiled.

'I can tell already it will be good.'

'Tell you what, will you stir this every few minutes while I take a shower?'

'Sure. I'll set the table.'

'Okay. I was thinking we'd eat out on the deck. It doesn't smell like paint out there.'

'Sorry.'

'No, I mean it will be nice out there. I'm not complaining about the paint. In fact, that was all a ruse, you know, to leave the wall half painted like that. I knew you wouldn't be able to resist.'

She smiled.

'A regular Tom Sawyer, detective third grade.'

'Maybe not for long.'

His comment ruined the moment and she stopped smiling. He silently chastised himself on the way back to the bedroom.

After his shower, Bosch put the last part of his recipe into the frying pan. He took a handful of frozen peas and mixed them into the simmering chicken-and-tomato stew. As he brought the food and wine out to the picnic table on the deck, he told Eleanor, who was standing at the railing, to have a seat.

'Sorry,' he said as they settled in. 'I forgot about a salad.'

'This is all I need.'

They started the meal in silence. He waited.

'I like it a lot,' she finally said. 'What do you call this?'

'I don't know. My mother just called it Chicken Special. I think that's what it was called in a restaurant where she first had it.'

'A family recipe.'

'The only one.'

They ate quietly for a few minutes during which Bosch surreptitiously tried to watch her to see if she really enjoyed the food. He was pretty sure she did.

'Harry,' Eleanor said after a while, 'who are the agents involved in this?'

'They're from all over; Chicago, Vegas, L.A.'

'Who from L.A.?'

'Guy named John O'Grady? You know him?'

It had been more than five years since she had worked in the bureau's L.A. field office. FBI agents moved around a lot. He doubted she would know O'Grady and she said she didn't.

'What about John Samuels? He's the AUSA on it. He's from the OC strike force.'

'Samuels I know. Or knew. He was an agent for a while. Not a particularly good one. Had the law degree and when he figured out he wasn't much of an investigator, he decided he wanted to prosecute.'

She started laughing and shook her head.

'What?'

'Nothing. Just something they used to say about him. It's kind of gross.'

'What?'

'Does he still have his mustache?'

'Yeah.'

'Well, they used to say that he could sure put a case together for prosecution, but as far as investigating it out on the street went, he couldn't find shit if it was in his own mustache.'

She laughed again – a little too hard, Bosch thought. He smiled back.

'Maybe that's why he became a prosecutor,' she added.

Something occurred to Bosch then and he quickly withdrew into his thoughts. Eventually he heard Eleanor's voice.

'What?'

'You disappeared. I asked what you were thinking. I didn't think it was that bad a joke.'

'No, I was just thinking about what a bottomless hole I'm in. About how it doesn't really matter whether Samuels actually believes I'm dirty on this. He needs me to be dirty.'

'How so?'

'They've got cases to make with their undercover guy against Joey Marks and his crew. And they've got to be ready and able to explain how a murder weapon got to be in their guy's house. Because if they can't explain it, then Joey's lawyers are going to shove it down their throats, make it look like their guy is tainted, is a killer worse than the people he was after. That gun has reasonable doubt written all over it. So the best way to explain away the gun is to blame it on the LAPD. On me. A bad cop from a bad department who found the gun in the weeds and planted it on the guy he thought did it. The jury will go along. They'll make me out to be this year's Mark Fuhrman.'

He saw the humor was long gone from her face now. There was obvious concern in her eyes but he thought there was also sadness. Maybe she understood, too, how well he was boxed in.

'The alternative is to prove that Joey Marks or one of his people planted the gun because they somehow knew Luke Goshen was an agent and needed to discredit him. Though that's the likely truth, it's a harder road to follow. It's easier for Samuels just to throw the mud on me.'

He looked down at his half-finished dinner and put his knife and fork on the plate. He couldn't eat anymore. He took a long drink of wine and then kept the glass in his hand, ready.

'I think I'm in big trouble, Eleanor.'

The gravity of his situation was finally beginning to weigh on him. He'd been operating on his faith that the truth would win out and now clearly saw how little truth would have to do with the outcome. He looked up at her. Their eyes connected and he saw that she was about to cry. He tried to smile.

'Hey, I'll think of something,' he said. 'I might be riding a desk for the time being, but I'm not taking both oars out of the water. I'm going to figure this out.'

She nodded but her face still looked distraught.

'Harry, remember when you found me in the casino that first night and we went to the bar at Caesar's and you tried to talk to me? Remember what you said about doing things differently if you had the chance to go back?'

'Yes, I remember.'

She wiped her eyes with her palms, before any tears could show.

'I have to tell you something.'

'You can tell me anything, Eleanor.'

'What I told you about me paying Quillen and the street tax and all of that . . . there's more to it.'

She looked at him with intensity now, trying to read his reaction before going further. But Bosch sat stone still and waited.

'When I first went to Vegas after getting out of Frontera, I didn't have a place or a car and I didn't know anyone. I just thought I'd give it a shot. You know, playing cards. And there was a girl I knew from Frontera. Her name was Patsy Quillen. She told me to look up her uncle – that was Terry Quillen – and that he'd probably stake me after he checked me out and saw me play. Patsy wrote him and gave me an introduction.'

Bosch sat silently, listening. He now had an idea where this was going but couldn't figure out why she was telling him.

'So he staked me. I got the apartment and some money to play with. He never said anything about Joey Marks, though I should have known the money came from somewhere. It always does. Anyway, later, when he finally told me who had really staked me, he said I shouldn't worry because the organization he worked for didn't want me to pay the nut back. What they wanted was just the interest. Two hundred a week. The tax. I didn't think I had a choice. I'd already taken the money. So I started paying. In the beginning it was tough. I didn't have it a couple times and it was double the next week plus that week's regular tax. You get behind and there's no way out.'

She looked down at her hands and clasped them on the table.

'What did they make you do?' Bosch asked quietly, also averting his eyes.

'It's not what you're thinking,' she said. 'I was lucky . . . they knew about me. I mean, that I had been an agent. They figured they could use my skills, as dormant as they were. So they had me just watch people. Mostly in casinos. But there were a few times I followed them outside. Most of the time I didn't even know exactly who they were or why they wanted the information, but I just watched, sometimes played at the same tables, and reported to Terry what the guy was winning or losing, who he was talking to, any nuances of his game . . . you know, things like that.'

She was just rambling now, putting off the meat of what she had to tell him, but Bosch didn't say anything. He let her go on.

'A couple days I watched Tony Aliso for them. They wanted to know how much he was dropping at the tables and where he was going, the usual stuff. But as it turned out, he wasn't losing. He actually was quite good at cards.'

'Where did you watch him go?'

'Oh, he'd go out to dinner, to the strip club. He'd run errands, things like that.'

445

'You ever see him with a girl?'

'One time. I followed him on foot from the Mirage into Caesar's and then into the shopping arcade. He went to Spago for a late lunch. He was alone and then the girl showed up. She was young. I thought at first it was like an escort thing, but then I could tell, he knew her. After lunch they went back to his hotel room for a while and when they came out, they took his rental and he took her to get a manicure and to buy cigarettes and to a bank while she opened an account. Just errands. Then they went to the strip club in North Vegas. When he left, he was alone. I figured then she was a dancer.'

Bosch nodded.

'Were you watching Tony last Friday night?' Bosch asked.

'No. That was just coincidence that we ended up at the same table. It was because he was waiting to go to the high-stakes table. I actually hadn't done anything for them in a month or so, other than pay the weekly tax, until . . . Terry . . .'

Her voice trailed off. They were finally at the point of no return.

'Until Terry what, Eleanor?'

She looked toward the fading horizon. The lights across the Valley were coming on and the sky was pink neon mixed with gray paint. Bosch kept his eyes on her. She spoke while still watching the end of the day.

'Quillen came to my apartment after you took me home from Metro. He took me to the house where you found me. They wouldn't tell me why and they told me not to leave. They said nobody would get hurt if I just did what I was told. I sat around that place for two days. They only put the handcuffs on me that last night. It was like they knew you'd be coming then.'

She let a beat of silence follow. It was there if Bosch wanted to use it but he didn't say a word.

'I guess what I'm trying to tell you is that the whole thing was something less than an abduction.'

She looked back down at her hands now.

'And that's obviously why you didn't want us to call out Metro,' Bosch said quietly.

She nodded.

'I don't know why I didn't tell you everything before. I'm really sorry, Harry. I . . .'

Now Bosch felt his own words sticking in his throat. Her story was understandable and believable. He even felt for her and understood that she was in her own bottomless pit. He saw how she had believed she had no choices. What he couldn't see, and what hurt him, was why she couldn't tell him everything from the start.

'Why couldn't you tell me, Eleanor?' he managed to get out. 'I mean right away. Why didn't you tell me that night?'

'I don't know,' she said. 'I wanted . . . I guess I hoped it would just go away and you would never have to know.'

'Then why are you telling me now?'

She looked right at him.

'Because I hated not telling you everything . . . and because while I was there at that house I heard something that you need to know now.'

Bosch closed his eyes.

446

'I'm sorry, Harry. Very sorry.'

He nodded. He was, too. He washed his hands over his face. He didn't want to hear this but knew he had to. His mind raced, jumping between feelings of betrayal and confusion and sympathy. One moment his thoughts were of Eleanor and the next they were on the case. They knew. Someone had told Joey Marks about Eleanor and him. He thought of Felton and Iverson, then Baxter and every cop he had seen at Metro. Someone had fed Marks the information and they used Eleanor as bait for him. But why? Why the whole charade? He opened his eyes and looked at Eleanor with a blank stare.

'What was it that you heard and that I need to know?'

'It was the first night. I was kept in that back room, where the TV was, where you came and got me. I was kept in there and the Samoans were there, in and out. But from time to time there were people in other parts of the house. I heard them talking.'

'Gussie and Quillen?'

'No, Quillen left. I know his voice and it wasn't him. And I don't think it was Gussie. I think it was Joey Marks and someone else, probably the lawyer, Torrino. Whoever it was, I heard the one man call the other Joe at one point. That's how come I think it was Marks.'

'Okay. Go on, what did they say?'

'I couldn't hear all of it. But one man was telling the other, the one he called Joe, what he had learned about the police investigation. About the Metro side of things, I think. And I heard the one called Joe get very angry when he was told the gun had been found at Luke Goshen's house. And I remember his words. Very clearly. He was yelling. He said, "How the hell did they find the gun there when we didn't do the goddamned hit?" And then he said some more things about the cops planting the gun and he said, "You tell our guy that if this is some kind of shakedown, then he can fuck off, he can forget it." I didn't hear much after that. They lowered their voices and the first guy was just trying to calm the other guy down.'

Bosch stared at her for a few moments, trying to analyze what she had overheard.

'Do you think it was a show?' he asked. 'You know, put on for your benefit because they figured you'd turn around and tell me what you heard?'

'I did at first, and that's another reason I didn't tell you this right away,' she said. 'But now I'm not so sure. When they first took me, when Quillen was driving me out there and I was asking a lot of questions, he wouldn't answer them. But he did say one thing. All he would tell me was that they needed me for a day or two to run a test on somebody. He would explain no further. A test, that's all he said.'

'A test?'

Bosch looked confused.

'Listen to me, Harry. I've done nothing but think about this since you got me out of there.'

She held up a finger.

'Let's start with what I overheard. Let's say it was Joey Marks and his lawyer, and let's say it wasn't a show but what they said was true. They didn't put the hit on Tony Aliso, okay?'

447

'Okay.'

'Look at it from their perspective. They had nothing to do with this, but one of their in-close guys gets picked up for it. And from what they hear from their source in Metro, it's looking like a slam-bang case. I mean, the cops have fingerprints and the murder weapon found right there in Goshen's bathroom. Joey Marks has to be thinking either it's all been planted by the cops or maybe Goshen went and did this on his own for some unknown reason. Either way, what do you think his immediate concern would be?'

'Damage control.'

'Right. He has to figure out what is going on with Goshen and what's the damage. But he can't because Goshen has gone and gotten himself his own attorney. Torrino has no access to him. So what Joey does instead is he and Torrino set up a test to see if the reason Goshen's gotten his own attorney is because he's going to talk.'

'Make a deal.'

'Right. Now, let's say that from their source in Metro they know that the lead cop on the case has a relationship with someone they know of and have their hooks in. Me.'

'So they just take you to the safe house and wait. Because they know that if I find out where the safe house is and show up to get you, or if I call up Metro and say I know where you are, then they know Goshen is the only one who could have told me. It means he's talking. That was the test Quillen was talking about. If I don't show, they're cool. It means Goshen is standing up. If I *do* show up, then they know they've got to get to Goshen in Metro right quick and put a hit on him.'

'Right, before he can talk. That's how I figured it, too.'

'So that would mean that Aliso wasn't really a hit – at least by Marks and his people – and that they had no idea Goshen was an agent.'

She nodded. Bosch felt the surge of energy that comes with making a huge step through the murky darkness of an investigation.

'There was no trunk music,' he said.

'What?'

'The whole Las Vegas angle, Joey Marks, all of that, it was all a diversion. We went completely down the wrong path. It had to be engineered by someone very close to Tony. Close enough to know what he was doing, to know about the money washing, and to know how to make his killing look mob connected. To pin it on Goshen.'

She nodded.

'And that's why I had to tell you everything. Even if it meant we . . .'

Bosch looked at her. She didn't finish the line and neither did he.

Bosch took a cigarette out of his pocket and put it in his mouth but didn't light it. He leaned across the table and picked up her plate and his own. He spoke to her as he slid off the bench.

'I don't have any dessert, either.'

'That's okay.'

He took the plates into the kitchen and rinsed them and put them into the dishwasher. He had never used the new appliance before and spent some time leaning over it and trying to figure out how to operate it. Once he got it going, he started cleaning the frying pan and the pot in the sink.

The simple work began to relax him. Eleanor came into the kitchen with her wineglass and watched him for a few moments before speaking.

'I'm sorry, Harry.'

'It's okay. You were in a bad situation and you did what you had to do, Eleanor. Nobody can be blamed for that. I probably would have done everything you did.'

It was a few moments before she spoke again.

'Do you want me to go?'

Bosch turned off the water and looked into the sink. He could make out his dark image reflected in the new stainless steel.

'No,' he said. 'I don't think so.'

Bosch arrived at the station at seven Friday morning with a box of glazed doughnuts from the Fairfax Farmers Market. He was the first one in. He opened the box and put it on the counter near the coffee machine. He took one of the doughnuts and put it on a napkin and left it at his spot on the homicide table while he went up to the watch office to get coffee from the urn. It was much better than what came out of the detective bureau's machine.

Once he had his coffee, he took his doughnut and moved to the desk that was behind the bureau's front counter. His assignment to desk duty meant that he would handle most of the walk-ins as well as the sorting and distribution of overnight reports. The phones he wouldn't have to worry about. They were answered by an old man from the neighborhood who donated his time to the department.

Bosch was alone in the squad room for at least fifteen minutes before the other detectives started to trickle in. Six different times he was asked by a new arrival why he was at the front desk, and each time he told the detective who asked that it was too complicated to get into but that the word would be out soon enough. Nothing remained a secret for long in a police station.

At eight-thirty the lieutenant from the a.m. watch brought the morning reports in before going off shift and smiled when he saw Bosch. His name was Klein and he and Bosch had known each other in a surface way for years.

'Who'd you beat up this time, Bosch?' he kidded.

It was well known that the detective who sat at the desk where Bosch now sat was either there by fate of the bureau rotation or on a desk duty assignment while the subject of an internal investigation. More often than not it was the latter. But Klein's sarcasm revealed that he had not yet heard that Bosch actually was under investigation. Bosch played off the question with a smile but didn't answer. He took the two-inch-thick stack of reports from Klein and gave him a mock salute back.

The stack Klein had given him constituted nearly all crime reports filed by Hollywood Division patrol officers in the last twenty-four hours. There would be a second, smaller delivery of stragglers later in the morning, but the stack in his hands constituted the bulk of the day's work in the bureau.

Keeping his head down and ignoring the buzz of conversations around him, it took Bosch a half hour to sort all the reports into piles according to crimes. Next he had to scan them all, using his experienced eye to possibly make connections between robberies and burglaries or assaults and so on, and then deliver the individual piles to the detective tables assigned to that particular classification of crime.

When he looked up from his work, he saw that Lieutenant Billets was in her office on the phone. He hadn't noticed that she had come in. Part of his desk job would be to give her a morning briefing on the reports, informing her of any significant or unusual crimes or anything else she should be aware of as the detective bureau commander.

He went back to work and weeded through the auto-theft reports first because they made up the largest pile he had culled from the stack of reports. There had been thirty-three cars reported stolen in Hollywood in the last twenty-four hours. Bosch knew that this was probably a below-average tally. After reading the summaries in the reports and checking for other similarities, he found nothing of significance and took the pile to the detective in charge of the auto-theft table. As he was heading back to the front of the squad room, he noticed that Edgar and Rider were standing at the homicide table putting things into a cardboard box. As he approached, he realized they were packing up the murder book and the ancillary files and evidence bags relating to the Aliso case. It was all being sent to the feds.

'Morning, guys,' Bosch said, unsure of how to start.

'Harry,' Edgar said.

'How are you doing, Harry?' Rider said, genuine concern in her voice.

'I'm hangin' in . . . Uh, listen, I just . . . I just want to say that I'm sorry you guys have been pulled into this, but I wanted you to know there is no way I—'

'Forget it, Harry,' Edgar said. 'You don't have to say one damn thing to us. We both know the whole thing is bullshit. In all my years on the job you are the most righteous cop I know, man. All the rest is bullshit.'

Bosch nodded, touched by Edgar's words. He didn't expect such sentiments from Rider because it had been their first case together. But she spoke anyway.

'I haven't worked with you long, Harry, but from what I do know I agree with what Jerry says. You watch, this will blow over and we'll be back at it again.'

'Thanks.'

Bosch was about to head back to his new desk when he looked down into the box they were packing. He reached in and pulled out the two-inch-thick murder book that Edgar had been charged with preparing and keeping up to date on the Aliso case.

'Are the feds coming here or you just sending it out?'

'S'posed to have somebody come pick it up at ten,' Edgar said.

Bosch looked up at the clock on the wall. It was only nine.

'Mind if I copy this? Just so we have something in case the whole thing drops into that black hole they keep over there at the bureau.'

'Be my guest,' Edgar said.

'Did Salazar ever send over a protocol?' Bosch asked.

'The autopsy?' Rider asked. 'No, not yet. Unless it's in dispatch.'

Bosch didn't tell them that if it was in transit, then the feds had somehow intercepted it. He took the murder book to the copy machine, unhooked the three rings and removed the stack of reports. He set the machine to

450

copy both sides of the original documents and put the stack into the automatic feed tray. Before starting he checked to make sure the paper tray was filled with three-hole paper. It was. He pressed the start button and stood back to watch. There was a copying franchise chain in town that had donated the machine and regularly serviced it. It was the one thing in the bureau that was modern and could be counted on to work most of the time. Bosch finished the job in ten minutes. He put the original binder back together and returned it to the box on Edgar's desk. He then took a fresh binder from the supply closet, put his copies of the reports on the rings and dropped it into a file cabinet drawer that had his business card taped to it. He then told his two partners where it was if they needed it.

'Harry,' Rider said in a low voice, 'you're thinking of doing a little freelancing on it, aren't you?'

He looked at her a moment, unsure of how to answer. He thought about her relationship with Billets. He had to be careful.

'If you are,' she said, perhaps sensing his indecision, 'I'd like to be in on it. You know the bureau isn't going to work it with any due diligence. They're going to let it drop.'

'Count me in, too,' Edgar added.

Bosch hesitated again, looked from one to the other and then nodded.

'How 'bout we meet at Musso's at twelve-thirty?' he said. 'I'm buying.'

'We'll be there,' Edgar said.

When he got back to the front of the bureau, he saw through the glass window of her office that Billets was off the phone and looking at some paperwork. Her door was open and Bosch stepped in, knocking on the doorjamb as he entered.

'Good morning, Harry.' There was a wistfulness to her voice and demeanor, as if maybe she was embarrassed that he was her front-desk man. 'Anything happening I should know about right away?'

'I don't think so. It looks pretty tame. Uh, there's a hot prowler working the strip hotels again, though. At least it looks like one guy. Did one at the Chateau and another at the Hyatt last night. People never woke up. Looks like the same MO on both.'

'Were the vics anybody we should know and care about?'

'I don't think so but I don't read *People* magazine. I might not recognize a celebrity if they came up and bit me.'

She smiled.

'How much were the losses?'

'I don't know. I'm not done with that pile yet. That's not why I came in. I just wanted to say thanks again for sticking up for me like you did yesterday.'

'That was hardly sticking up for you.'

'Yes it was. In those kinds of circumstances what you said and did was sticking your neck way out. I appreciate it.'

'Well, like I said, I did it because I don't believe it. And the sooner IAD and the bureau get on with it, the sooner they won't believe it. When's your appointment, by the way?'

'Two.'

'Who is your defense rep going to be?'

'Guy I know from RHD. Name's Dennis Zane. He's a good guy and he'll know what to do for me. You know him?'

'No. But listen, let me know if there is anything else I can do.'

'Thanks, Lieutenant.'

'Grace.'

'Right. Grace.'

When Bosch went back to his desk he thought about his appointment with Chastain. In accordance with department procedures, Bosch would be represented by a union defense rep who was actually a fellow detective. He would act almost as an attorney would, counseling Bosch on what to say and how to say it. It was the first formal step of the internal investigation and disciplinary process.

When he looked up, he saw a woman standing at the counter with a young girl. The girl had red-rimmed eyes and a marble-sized swelling on her lower lip that looked like it might have been the result of a bite. She was disheveled and stared at the wall behind Bosch with a distance in her eyes that suggested that a window was there. But there wasn't.

Bosch could have asked how he could help them without moving from his desk, but it didn't take a detective to guess why they were there. He got up, came around the desk and approached the counter so they could speak confidentially. Rape victims were the people who evoked the most sadness in Bosch. He knew he wouldn't be able to last a month on a rape squad. Every victim he had ever seen had that stare. It was a sign that all things in their lives were different now and forever. They would never get back to what they had had before.

After speaking briefly to the mother and daughter, Bosch asked if the girl needed immediate medical attention and the mother said she didn't. He opened the half door in the counter and ushered them both back to one of the three interview rooms off the hallway to the rear of the bureau. He then went to the sex crimes table and approached Mary Cantu, a detective who had been handling for years what Bosch knew he couldn't handle for a month.

'Mary, you've got a walk-in back in room three,' Bosch said. 'She's fifteen. Happened last night. She got too curious about the pusher who works the nearby corner. He grabbed her and sold her and a rock to his next customer. She's with her mother.'

'Thanks, Bosch. Just what I needed on a Friday. I'll go right back. You ask if she needed medical?'

'She said no, but I think the answer is yes.'

'Okay, I'll handle it. Thanks.'

Back at the front desk, it took Bosch a few minutes to clear his thoughts about the girl from his mind and another forty-five to finish reading through the reports and deliver them to the appropriate detective squads.

When he was done, he checked on Billets through the window and saw she was on the phone with a pile of paperwork in front of her. Bosch got up and went to his file cabinet and took out the copy of the murder book he had put there earlier. He lugged the thick binder back to his desk at the front counter. He had decided that in his free time between his duties at the front desk he would begin reviewing the murder book. The case had taken off so quickly earlier in the week that he had not had the time he usually liked to spend reviewing the paperwork. He knew from experience that command of the details and the nuances of an investigation was often the key to closing it out. He had just started turning through the pages in a cursory review when a vaguely familiar voice addressed him from the counter.

'Is that what I think it is?'

Bosch looked up. It was O'Grady, the FBI agent. Bosch felt his face burn with embarrassment that he'd been caught red-handed with the file and with his growing dislike for the agent.

'Yeah, it's what you think it is, O'Grady. You were supposed to be here a half hour ago to pick it up.'

'Yeah, well, I don't run on your time. I had things to do.'

'Like what, get your buddy Roy a new ponytail?'

'Just give me the binder, Bosch. And all the rest.'

Bosch still had not gotten up and made no move to now.

'What do you want it for, O'Grady? We all know you're going to let the thing drop. You people don't care who killed Tony Aliso and you don't want to know.'

'That's bullshit. Give me the file.'

O'Grady reached over the counter and was reaching around blindly for the release button on the half door.

'Hold your fucking horses, man,' Bosch said as he stood up. 'Just wait there. I'll get it all.'

Carrying the binder, Bosch walked back to the homicide table and, using his back to shield O'Grady's view, placed the binder on the table and picked up the box containing the original binder and the ancillary reports and evidence bags that Edgar and Rider had put in with it. He carried it back and dropped it on the counter in front of O'Grady.

'You gotta sign for it,' he said. 'We're extra careful about how we handle evidence and who gets to handle it.'

'Yeah, right. The whole world knows that from the O.J. case, don't they?'

Bosch grabbed O'Grady's tie and jerked his upper body down over the counter. The agent could not find a purchase with his hands that would give him the leverage to pull back. Bosch bent down so that he was talking directly into his ear.

'Excuse me?'

'Bosch you—'

'Harry!'

Bosch looked up. Billets was standing in the door of her office. Bosch let go of the tie and O'Grady's body sprang backward as he straightened up. His face was crimson with embarrassment and anger. As he jerked his tie loose from around his neck he yelled, 'You're certifiable, you know that? You're a fucking asshole!'

'I didn't know you agents used that kind of language,' Bosch said.

'Harry, just sit down,' Billets commanded. 'I'll take care of this.'

She had come up to the counter now.

'He's got to sign the receipt.'

'I don't care! I'll handle it!'

Bosch went back to his desk and sat down. He stared dead-eyed at O'Grady while Billets dug through the box until she found the inventory list and receipt Edgar had prepared. She showed O'Grady where to sign and then told him to go.

'You better watch him,' he said to Billets as he picked the box up off the counter.

'You better watch yourself, Agent O'Grady. If I hear anything else about this little disagreement here, I'll file a complaint against you for inciting it.'

'He's the one who—'

'I don't care. Understand? I don't care. Now leave.'

'I'm leaving. But you watch your boy there. Keep him away from this.' O'Grady pointed to the contents of the box. Billets didn't answer. O'Grady picked the box up and made a move to step away from the counter but stopped and looked once more at Bosch.

'Hey, Bosch, by the way, I got a message from Roy.'

'Agent O'Grady, would you please leave!' Billets said angrily.

'What is it?' Bosch said.

'He just wanted to ask, who's the meat now?'

With that he turned around and headed down the hall to the exit. Billets watched him until he was gone and then turned around and looked at Bosch with anger in her eyes.

'You just don't know how to help yourself, do you?' she said. 'Why don't you grow up and quit these little pissing wars?'

She didn't wait for his reply because he didn't have one. She walked quickly back into her office and shut the door. She then closed the blinds over the interior window. Bosch leaned back with his hands laced behind his neck, looked up at the ceiling and exhaled loudly.

After the O'Grady incident Bosch almost immediately became busy with a walk-in case involving an armed robbery. At the time, the entire robbery crew was out on a carjacking that had involved a high-speed chase, and that meant Bosch, as the desk man, had to interview the walk-in victim and type up a report. The victim was a young Mexican boy whose job it was to stand on the corner of Hollywood Boulevard at Sierra Bonita and sell maps to the homes of movie stars up in the hills. At ten that morning, shortly after he had set up his plywood sign and begun waving down cars, an old American-made sedan had pulled up with a man driving and a woman in the passenger seat. After asking how much the maps cost and whether he had sold very many of them, the woman had pointed a gun at the boy and robbed him of thirty-eight dollars. He had come in to report the crime with his mother. As it turned out, he had sold only one map that day before the robbery, and nearly all of the money taken from him was his own – he had brought it with him to make change. His loss was about what he made for a whole day of standing on the corner and waving his arm like a windmill.

Because of the small take and sloppy method used by the robbers, Bosch immediately thought the suspects were a couple of hypes looking for a quick score to buy their next balloon of heroin. They had not even bothered to hide the car's license plate, which the boy had spotted and memorized as they drove away.

After he was finished with the boy and his mother, he went to the teletype machine and put out a wanted on the car with a description of the suspects. He found when he did this that there was already a wanted out on the vehicle for its use in two prior robberies in the last week. A lot of good that did the kid who lost a day's pay, Bosch thought. The robbers should have been picked up before they got to the boy. But this was the big city, not a perfect world. Disappointments like that didn't stay long with Bosch.

By this time the squad room had pretty much cleared out for lunch. Bosch saw only Mary Cantu at the sex crimes table, probably working on the paper from that morning's walk-in job.

Edgar and Rider were gone, apparently having decided it would be better to go separately to Musso's. As Bosch got up to leave, he noticed that the blinds were still drawn over the window to the lieutenant's office. Billets was still in there, he knew. He went to the homicide table and put the copy of the murder book into his briefcase and then went and knocked on her door. Before she could answer, he opened the door and stuck his head in.

'I'm going to go catch some lunch and then go downtown for the IAD thing. You won't have anybody out on the counter.'

'Okay,' she said. 'I'll put Edgar or Rider up there after lunch. They're just waiting around for a case, anyway.'

'Okay then, I'll see you.'

'Uh, Harry?'

'Yes?'

'I'm sorry for what happened earlier. Not for what I said. I meant what I said, but I should have taken you in here and spoken to you. Doing it out there in front of the others was wrong. I apologize.'

'Don't worry about it. Have a nice weekend.'

'You, too.'

'I'll try, Lieutenant.'

'Grace.'

'Grace.'

Bosch got to Musso and Frank's Restaurant on Hollywood Boulevard at exactly twelve-thirty and parked in the back. The restaurant was a Hollywood landmark, having been on the Boulevard since 1924. In its heyday it had been a popular destination for Hollywood's elite. Fitzgerald and Faulkner held forth. Chaplin and Fairbanks once raced each other down Hollywood Boulevard on horseback, the loser having to pick up the dinner tab. The restaurant now subsisted mostly on its past glory and faded charm. Its red leather padded booths still filled every day for lunch and some of the waiters looked and moved as if they had been there long enough to have served Chaplin. The menu hadn't changed in all the years Bosch had been eating there – this in a town where the hookers out on the Boulevard lasted longer than most restaurants.

Edgar and Rider were waiting in one of the prized round booths, and Bosch slid in after they were pointed out by the maître d' – he was apparently too old and tired to walk Bosch over himself. They were both drinking iced tea and Bosch decided to go along with that, though privately he lamented that they were in the place that made the best martini in the city. Only Rider was looking at the menu. She was new in the division and hadn't been to Musso's enough times to know what the best thing was to order for lunch.

'So what are we doing?' Edgar asked while she looked.

'We've got to start over,' Bosch said. 'The Vegas stuff was all misdirection.'

Rider glanced over the top of the menu at Bosch.

'Kiz, put that down,' he said. 'If you don't get the chicken pot pie you're making a mistake.'

She hesitated, nodded and put the menu aside.

'What do you mean, misdirection?' she asked.

'I mean whoever killed Tony wanted us to go that way. And they planted the gun out there to make sure we stayed out there. But they screwed up. They didn't know the guy they planted the gun on was a fed who would have a bunch of other feds as an alibi. That was the screwup. Now, once I learned that our suspect was an agent, I thought Joey Marks and his people must have figured out he was a fed and set the whole thing up to taint him.'

'I still think that sounds good,' Edgar said.

'It does, or it did until last night,' Bosch said as an ancient waiter in a red coat came to the table.

'Three chicken pot pies,' Bosch said.

'Do you want something to drink?' the waiter asked.

Hell with it, Bosch decided.

'Yeah, I'll have a martini, three olives. You can bring them some more iced tea. That's it.'

The waiter nodded and slowly glided away without writing anything on his pad.

'Last night,' Bosch continued, 'I learned from a source that Joey Marks did not know the man he thought was named Luke Goshen was a plant. He had no idea he was an informant, let alone an agent. In fact, once we picked Goshen up, Joey was engaged in a plan to try to find out whether Goshen was going to stand up or talk. This was because he had to decide whether to put a contract on him in the Metro jail.'

He waited a moment to let them think about this.

'So, you can see with that information in the mix now, the second theory no longer works.'

'Well, who's the source?' Edgar asked.

'I can't tell you that, guys. But it's solid. It's the truth.'

He watched their eyes float down to the table. He knew they trusted him, but they also knew how informants were often the most skilled liars in the game. It was a tough call to base everything from here on out on an informant.

'Okay, then you know who she is. She overheard all of what I told you while they had her in that house. Before we got there, both Joey and the lawyer, Torrino, were there. She overheard them and from what she heard, they didn't know about Goshen. See, that whole abduction was part of the test. They knew the only way I could find out where the safe house was would be to get it from Goshen. That was the test, to see if he was talking or not.'

They sat in silence for a few minutes while Edgar and Rider digested this.

'Okay,' Edgar finally said. 'I see what you're saying. But if Vegas was one big fucking red herring, how does the gun get over there in the agent's house?'

'That's what we have to figure out. What if there was someone outside of Tony's mob connections but close enough to him to know he was washing money and the reason why he made all the trips to Vegas? Someone who either had personal knowledge or maybe followed Tony to Vegas and watched how he worked, how he picked up the money from Goshen, everything? Someone who knew exactly how he did it, who knew Goshen could be set up to take the fall, and that Tony'd be coming back on Friday with a lot of money in his briefcase?'

'They would be able to set the whole thing up, as long as they could get into the agent's house to plant the gun,' Edgar answered.

'Right. And getting into the house would be no problem. It's out in the middle of nowhere. He was away at the club for long stretches at a time. Anybody could get in, plant the gun, and get out. The question is who?'

'You're talking about either his wife or his girlfriend,' Edgar said. 'Both could have had that kind of access.'

Bosch nodded.

'So which one do we set up on? The three of us can't do both, not on a freelance like this.'

'We don't need to,' Bosch said. 'I think the choice is obvious.'

'Which?' Edgar said. 'The girlfriend?'

Bosch looked at Rider, giving her the chance to answer. She saw his look and then her eyes narrowed as she went to work.

'It . . . it can't be the girlfriend because . . . because she called Tony on Sunday morning. On the voice mail. Why would she call the guy if she knew he was dead?'

Bosch nodded. She was good.

'Could have been part of a setup,' Edgar said. 'Another mis-direction.'

'Could be but I doubt it,' Bosch said. 'Plus, we know she worked Friday night. That would make it kind of tough for her to be over here whacking Tony.'

'So then it's the wife,' Edgar said. 'Veronica.'

'Right,' Bosch said. 'I think she was lying to us, acting like she didn't know anything about her husband's business when she knew everything. I think this whole thing was her plan. She wrote the letters to the IRS and to the OCID. She wanted to get something going against Tony, then when he ended up dead it would point toward a mob hit. Trunk music. Planting the gun on Goshen was just icing. If we found it, fine. If we didn't, then we'd be sniffing around Vegas until we shelved the case.'

'You're saying she did this all on her own?' Edgar asked.

'No,' Bosch said. 'I'm just saying I think this was her plan. But she had to have had help. An accomplice. It took two to do the actual hit and she sure didn't take the gun to Vegas. After the kill, she stays at the house and waits while the accomplice goes to Vegas and plants the gun while Luke Goshen's at the club.'

'But wait a minute,' Rider said. 'We're forgetting something. Veronica Aliso had it very cushy in her existing life. Tony was raking in the bread with his washing machine. They had the big house in the hills, the cars . . . why would she want to kill the cash cow? How much was in that briefcase?'

'According to the feds, four hundred and eighty thousand,' Bosch said.

Edgar whistled softly. Rider shook her head.

'I still don't see it,' she said. 'That's a hell of a lot of money, but Tony was making at least that much a year. In business terms, killing him was a short-term gain/long-term loss for her. Doesn't make sense.'

457

'Then there is something else running through all of this that we don't know about yet,' Bosch said. 'Maybe he was about to dump her. Maybe that old lady in Vegas who said Tony was going to go away with Layla was telling the truth. Or maybe there's money somewhere we don't know about. But for now I can't see anybody else fitting into this picture but her.'

'But what about the gatehouse?' Rider said. 'The log shows she never left Friday, the whole night. And she had no visitors.'

'Well, we've got to work on that,' Bosch said. 'There had to have been a way for her to get in and out.'

'What else?' Edgar asked.

'We start over,' Bosch said. 'I want to know everything about her. Where'd she come from, who are her friends, what does she do in that house all day long and what did she do and who did she do it with all those times Tony was away?'

Rider and Edgar nodded.

'There's got to be an accomplice. And my guess is that it's a man. And I'll bet we'll find him through her.'

The waiter came up with a tray and put it down on a folding cart. They watched silently as he prepared the meal. There were three separate chicken pot pies on the tray. The waiter used a fork and spoon to take the top crust off each and put it on a plate. Next he scooped the contents of each pie out and put it on the crust, served the three cops their dishes and put down fresh glasses of iced tea for Edgar and Rider. He then poured Bosch's martini from a small glass carafe and floated away without a word.

'Obviously,' Bosch said, 'we have to do this quietly.'

'Yeah,' Edgar said, 'and Bullets also put us on the top of the rotation. Next call comes in, me and Kiz get it. And we hafta work it without you. That's going to take us away from this.'

'Well, do what you can. If you get a body you get a body, nothing we can do about that. Meantime, this is what I propose. You two work on Veronica's background, see what you can find. You got any sources at the *Times* or the trades?'

'I know a couple at the *Times*,' Rider said. 'And there's a woman I once had a case with – she was a vic – who's a receptionist or something at *Variety*.'

'You trust 'em?'

'I think I can.'

'See if they'll pull a search on Veronica for you. She had a brief flash of fame a while back. Her fifteen minutes. Maybe there were some stories about her, stories that would have names of people we could talk to.'

'What about talking to her again?' Edgar asked.

'I don't think we should do it yet. I want to have something to talk to her about.'

'What about neighbors?'

'You can do that. Maybe she'll look out the window and see you, give her something to think about. If you go up there, see if you can take another look at the gate log. Talk to Nash. I'm sure you can turn him without needing another search warrant. I'd like to take a look at the whole year, know who has been going in to see her, especially while Tony was out of town. We have Tony's credit records and can construct his travel history. You'll be able to know when she was in that house alone.'

Bosch raised his fork. He hadn't had a bite of food yet, but his mind was too full of the case and what needed to be done.

'The other thing is we need as much of the case file as we can get. All we've got is the copy of the murder book. I'm going down to Parker Center for my little chat with the IAD. I'll swing by USC and get a copy of the autopsy. The feds already have it. I'll also go talk to Donovan in SID and see if he came up with anything we pulled out of the car. Also, he's got the shoe prints. I'll get copies, hopefully before the feds come in and take everything. Anything else I'm missing?'

The other two shook their heads.

'You want to see what we get and then put our heads together after work?'

They nodded.

'Cat and Fiddle, about six?'

They nodded again. They were too busy eating to talk. Bosch took his first bite of food, which was already getting cold. He joined them in their silence, thinking about the case.

'It's in the details,' he said after a few moments.

'What?' Rider asked.

'The case. When you get one like this, the answer is always in the details. You watch, when we break it, the answer will have been sitting in the files, in the book. It always happens.'

The interview with Chastain at Internal Affairs began as Bosch expected it would. He sat with Zane, his defense rep, at a gray government table in one of the IAD interview rooms. An old Sony cassette player was turned on and everything said in the room was recorded. In police parlance, Chastain was locking up Bosch's story. Getting his words and explanation in as much detail as possible down on tape. Chastain really wouldn't begin his investigation until after Bosch's story was locked in. He would then hunt for flaws in it. All he had to do was catch Bosch in a single lie and he could take him to a Board of Rights hearing. Depending on the size and import of the lie, he could seek a penalty ranging from suspension to dismissal.

In a dull and laborious drone, Chastain read prepared questions from a legal pad and Bosch slowly and carefully answered them with as few words as possible. It was a game. Bosch had played it before. In the fifteen minutes they had before reporting to IAD, Zane had counseled Bosch on how it would go and how they should proceed. Like a good criminal defense lawyer, he never directly asked Harry if he had planted the gun. Zane didn't really care. He simply looked at IAD as the enemy, as a group of bad cops with the sole purpose of going after good cops. Zane was part of the old school who thought all cops were inherently good and though sometimes the job turned them bad, they should not be persecuted by their own.

Everything was routine for a half hour. But then Chastain threw an unexpected pitch at them.

'Detective Bosch, do you know a woman named Eleanor Wish?'

Zane reached out a hand in front of Bosch to stop him from answering.

'What is this shit, Chastain?'

459

'Who have you been talking to, Chastain?' Bosch added.

'Wait a minute, Harry,' Zane said. 'Don't say anything. Where's this going, Chastain?'

'It's very clear from the orders from the chief. I'm investigating Bosch's conduct during this investigation. As far as who I have been talking to or where I get my information, you are not privy to that at this point in the process.'

'This is supposed to be about a supposedly planted gun that we all know is bullshit. That's what we are here to answer.'

'Do you wish to read the order from the chief again? It's quite clear.'

Zane looked at him a moment.

'Give us five minutes so we can talk about this. Why don't you go get the points of your teeth filed?'

Chastain stood up and reached over and turned the tape recorder off. As he stepped to the door, he looked back at them with a smile.

'This time I got you both. You won't get out from under this one, Bosch. And Zane, well, I guess you can't win them all, can you?'

'You ought to know that better than me, you sanctimonious asshole. Get out of here and leave us alone.'

After Chastain was gone, Zane bent over the tape recorder to make sure it was off. He then got up and checked the thermostat on the wall to make sure it wasn't a secret listening device. After he was satisfied their conversation was private, he sat back down and asked Bosch about Eleanor Wish. Bosch told him about his encounters with Eleanor over the past few days but left out mention of the abduction and her subsequent confession.

'One of those cops over there in Metro must've told him you shacked up with her,' Zane said. 'That's all he's got. He's going for an associating beef. If you admit it here, then he's got you. But if that's all he gets, then it's a slap on the wrist at best. As long as he gets nothing else. But if you lie about it and say you weren't with her when you were, and he can prove you were, then you've got a problem. So my advice is that you tell him, yeah, you know her and you've been with her. Fuck it, it's nothing. Tell him it's over, and if that's all he's got, then he's a chickenshit asshole.'

'I don't know if it is or it isn't.'

'What?'

'Over.'

'Well, don't tell him nothin' about that unless he asks for it. Then use your best judgment. Ready?'

Bosch nodded and Zane opened the door. Chastain was sitting outside at a desk.

'Where ya been, Chastain?' Zane complained. 'We're waiting in here.'

Chastain didn't answer. He came in, turned the recorder back on and continued the Q and A.

'Yes, I know Eleanor Wish,' Bosch said. 'Yes, I've spent time with her over the last few days.'

'How much time?'

'I don't know exactly. A couple of nights.'

'While you were conducting the investigation?'

'Not *while* I was conducting it. At night, when I was done for the day. We all don't work around the clock like you, Chastain.'

Bosch smiled at him without humor.

'Was she a witness in this case?' Chastain asked with a tone that denoted that he was shocked that Bosch would cross that line.

'Initially, I thought she might be a witness. After I located her and talked to her, I learned pretty quickly that she was not an evidentiary witness of any kind.'

'But you did initially encounter her while you were in your capacity as an investigator on this case.'

'That's correct.'

Chastain consulted his pad for a long moment before asking the next question.

'Is this woman, that's the convicted felon Eleanor Wish I am still talking about, is she living in your home at this time?'

Bosch felt the bile rising in his throat. The personal invasion and Chastain's tone were getting to him. He struggled to remain calm.

'I don't know the answer to that,' he said.

'You don't *know* if someone is *living* in your house or not?'

'Look, Chastain, she was there last night, okay? Is that what you want to hear? She was there. But whether she'll be there tonight I don't know. She's got her own place in Vegas. She may have gone back today, I don't know. I didn't check. You want me to call and ask her if she is officially *living* in my home at this time, I will.'

'I don't think that's necessary. I think I have everything I need for the time being.'

He then went directly into the standard IAD end-of-interview spiel.

'Detective Bosch, you will be informed of the results of the ongoing investigation into your conduct. If departmental charges are filed, you will be informed of the scheduling of a Board of Rights hearing in which three captains will hear evidence. You will be allowed to choose one of those captains, I will select a second and the third will be chosen at random. Any questions?'

'Just one. How can you call yourself a cop when all you do is sit up here and conduct these bullshit investigations into bullshit?'

Zane reached over and put a hand on Bosch's forearm to quiet him.

'No, that's okay,' Chastain said, waving off Zane's effort to calm things. 'I don't mind answering. In fact, I get that question a lot, Bosch. Funny, but it always seems I get it from the cops I happen to be investigating. Anyway, the answer is that I take pride in what I do because I represent the public, and if there is no one to police the police then there is no one to keep the abuse of their wide powers in check. I serve a valuable purpose in this society, Detective Bosch. I'm proud of what I do. Can you say the same?'

'Yeah, yeah, yeah,' Bosch said. 'I'm sure that sounds great on tape for whoever listens to it. I get the feeling you probably sit alone at night and listen to it yourself. Over and over again. After a while, you believe it. But let me ask you this, Chastain. Who polices the police who police the police?'

Bosch stood up and Zane followed. The interview was over.

After leaving IAD and thanking Zane for his help, Bosch went down to the SID lab on the third floor to see Art Donovan. The criminologist had just come back from a crime scene and was sorting through evidence bags and checking the material against an evidence list. He looked up as Bosch was approaching.

'How'd you get in here, Harry?'

'I know the combination.'

Most detectives who worked RHD knew the door-lock combo. Bosch hadn't worked RHD in five years and they still hadn't changed it.

'See,' Donovan said. 'That's how the trouble starts.'

'What trouble?'

'You coming in here while I'm handling evidence. Next thing you know some wiseass defense lawyer says it got tainted and I look like an asshole on national TV.'

'You're paranoid, Artie. Besides, we're not due for another trial of the century for at least a few years.'

'Funny. What do you want, Harry?'

'You're the second guy who said I was funny today. What happened with my shoe prints and all the rest of the stuff?'

'The Aliso case?'

'No, the Lindbergh case. What do you think?'

'Well, I heard that Aliso wasn't yours anymore. I'm supposed to have everything ready for the FBI to pick up.'

'When is that?'

Donovan looked up from what he was doing for the first time.

'They just said they'd send somebody by five.'

'Then it's still my case until they show up. What about the shoe prints you pulled?'

'There's nothing about them. I sent copies to the bureau's crime lab in DC to see if they could ID the make and model.'

'And?'

'And nothing. I haven't heard back. Bosch, every department in the country sends shit to them. You know that. And last I heard, they don't drop everything they're doing when a package from the LAPD comes in. It will probably be next week sometime before I hear back. If I'm lucky.'

'Shit.'

'It's too late to call the East Coast now, anyway. Maybe Monday. I didn't know they suddenly became so important to you. Communication, Harry, that's the secret. You ought to try it sometime.'

'Never mind that, do you still have a set of copies?'

'Yup.'

'Can I get a set?'

'Sure can, but you're going to have to wait about twenty minutes or so till I'm done with this.'

'Come on, Artie, it's probably just sitting in a file cabinet or something. It'll take you thirty seconds.'

'Would you leave me alone?' Donovan said with exasperation. 'I'm serious, Harry. Yes, it's sitting in a file and it would only take me half a minute to get it for you. But if I leave what I'm doing here, I could get crucified when I testify in *this* case. I can see it now, some shyster all righteous and angry and saying, "You are telling this jury that while in the middle of handling evidence from this case you got up and handled evidence from *another*?" And you don't have to be F. Lee Bailey anymore to make it sound good to a jury. Now leave me alone. Come back in a half hour.'

'Fine, Artie, I'll leave you alone.'

'And buzz me when you come back. Don't just come in. We gotta get that combination changed.'

The last line he said more to himself than to Bosch.

Bosch left the way he had come in and took the elevator down to go outside and have a smoke. He had to walk out to the curb and light up because it was now against departmental rules to stand outside the front door of Parker Center and smoke. So many cops working there were addicted to cigarettes that there had often been a crowd outside the building's main doors and a permanent haze of blue smoke had begun to hang over the entrance. The chief thought this was unsightly and instituted the rule that if you left the building to smoke, you had to leave the property as well. Now the front sidewalk along Los Angeles Street often looked like the scene of a labor action, with cops, some even in uniform, pacing back and forth in front of the building. The only thing missing from the scene was picket signs. The word was that the police chief had consulted with the city attorney to see if he could outlaw smoking on the sidewalk as well, but he was told that the sidewalk was beyond the bounds of his control.

As Bosch was lighting a second cigarette off the first, he saw the huge figure of FBI agent Roy Lindell waltzing leisurely out of the glass doors of the police headquarters. When he got to the sidewalk, he turned right and headed toward the federal courthouse. He was coming directly toward Bosch. Lindell didn't see Bosch until he was a few feet away. It startled him.

'What is this? Are you waiting for me?'

'No, I'm having a cigarette, Lindell. What are you doing?'

'None of your business.'

He made a move to pass but Bosch stopped him with the next line.

'Have a nice chat with Chastain?'

'Look, Bosch, I was asked to come over and give a statement and I obliged. I told the truth. Let the chips fall.'

'Trouble is you don't know the truth.'

'I know you found that gun and I didn't put it there. That's the truth.'

'Part of it, at least.'

'Well, it's the only part I know, and that's what I told him. So have a good day.'

He passed by Bosch and Harry turned around to watch him go. Once again he stopped him.

'You people might be satisfied with only part of the truth. But I'm not.'

Lindell turned around and stepped back to Bosch.

'What's that supposed to mean?'

'Figure it out.'

'No, you tell me.'

'We were all used, Lindell. I'm going to find out by who. When I do, I'll be sure to let you know.'

'Look, Bosch, you don't have the case anymore. We're working it and you better stay the fuck away from it.'

'Yeah, you guys are working the case, all right,' Bosch said sarcastically.

'I'm sure you're pounding the pavement on this one. Let me know when you figure it out.'

'Bosch, it's not like that. We care about it.'

'Give me one answer, Lindell.'

'What?'

'In the time you were under, did Tony Aliso ever bring his wife over there to make a pickup?'

Lindell was quiet a moment while he decided whether to answer. He finally shook his head.

'Not once,' he said. 'Tony always said she hated the place. Too many bad memories, I guess.'

Bosch tried to remain cool.

'Memories of Vegas?'

Lindell smiled.

'For somebody who supposedly has all the answers, you don't know much, do you, Bosch? Tony met her in the club something like twenty years ago. Long before my time. She was a dancer and Tony was going to make her a movie star. Same story he was using on 'em to the end. Only, after her I guess he got wise and learned not to marry every one of them.'

'Did she know Joey Marks?'

'Your one question is now up to three, Bosch.'

'Did she?'

'I don't know.'

'What was her name back then?'

'That's another one I don't know. I'll see you around, Bosch.'

He turned and walked away. Bosch threw his cigarette into the street and walked back toward the Glass House. A few minutes later, after being properly buzzed through the door into the SID offices, Bosch found Donovan at his desk again. The criminalist lifted a thin file from the desk and handed it to Harry.

'You got copies in there,' he said. 'Same thing I sent the bureau. What I did was shoot a copy of the negative and then shot the new negative and printed it in black-and-white contrast for comparison purposes. I also blew it up to actual size.'

Bosch didn't understand what Donovan had just said except for the last part. He opened the file. There were two pages of copy paper with the shoe prints in black. Both were partial prints of the same right shoe. But between the two partials almost all of the shoe was there. Donovan got up and looked at the open file. He pointed to a tread ridge on one of the copies. It was a curving line on the heel. But the line was broken.

'Now, if you find the shooter and he still has the shoes, this is where you'll get him. See how that line is broken there? That does not appear to be a manufacturer's design. This guy stepped on glass or something at some point and it cut the tread there. It's either that or a flaw in manufacturing. But if you find the shoe, we'll be able to make an ID match that should send the boy away.'

'Okay,' Bosch said, still looking at the copies. 'Now, did you get anything even preliminary from the bureau on this?'

'Not really. I've got a guy I go to pretty regularly with this kind of stuff. I know him, seen him at a couple of the SID conventions. Anyway, he called just to let me know he got the package and he'd get on it as soon as he could. He said that off the top of his head he thought it was one of those lightweight boots that are popular now. You know, they're like work boots but they're comfortable and wear like a pair of Nikes.'

'Okay, Artie, thanks.'

Bosch drove over to the County-USC Medical Center and around to the parking lot by the railroad yard. The coroner's office was located at the far end of the medical center property, and Bosch went in through the back door after showing his badge to a security guard.

He checked Dr Salazar's office first but it was empty. He then went down to the autopsy floor and looked in the first suite, where the lowered table that Salazar always used was located. Salazar was there, working on another body. Bosch stepped in and Salazar looked up from the open chest cavity of what looked like the remains of a young black man.

'Harry, what are you doing here? This is a South Bureau case.'

'I wanted to ask about the Aliso case.'

'Kind of got my hands full at the moment. And you shouldn't be in here without a mask and gown.'

'I know. You think you could have your assistant dub off a copy of the protocol for me?'

'No problem. I heard the FBI took an interest in the case, Harry. Is that true?'

'That's what I hear.'

'Funny thing, those agents didn't bother talking to me. They just came in and got a copy of the protocol. The protocol only has conclusions, none of the ruminating we doctors like to do.'

'So what would you have ruminated about with them if they had talked to you?'

'I would have told them my hunch, Harry.'

'Which is?'

Salazar looked up from the body but kept his rubber-gloved and bloody hands over the open chest so they wouldn't drip on anything else.

'My hunch is that you're looking for a woman.'

'Why's that?'

'The material in and below the eyes.'

'Preparation H?'

'What?'

'Nothing, never mind. What did you find?'

'The substance was analyzed and it came back oleo capsicum. Found it on the nasal swabs, too. Know what oleo capsicum is better known as, Harry?'

'Pepper spray.'

'Shit, Harry, you ruin my fun.'

'Sorry. So somebody sprayed him with pepper spray?'

'Right again. That's why I think it's a woman. Someone who was either having problems controlling him or afraid of problems. That makes me think it's a woman. Besides, all these women around here, they all carry that stuff in their purses.'

Bosch wondered if Veronica Aliso was one of those women.

'That's good, Sally. Anything else?'

465

'No surprises. Tests came back clean.'

'No amyl nitrate?'

'Nope, but that has a short retention. We don't find it that often. Did you get anywhere with the slugs?'

'Yeah, we did all right. Can you call your guy?'

'Take me to the intercom.'

While Salazar held his hands up in front of himself so they wouldn't touch anything, Bosch pushed his wheelchair to the nearby counter, where there was a phone with an intercom attachment. Salazar told Bosch which button to push and then ordered someone to make a copy of the protocol immediately for Bosch.

'Thanks,' Bosch said.

'No problem. Hope it helps. Remember, look for a woman who carried pepper spray in her purse. Not mace. Pepper spray.'

'Right.'

The end-of-the-week traffic was intense and it took Bosch nearly an hour to get out of downtown and back to Hollywood. When he got to the Cat & Fiddle pub on Sunset it was after six, and as he walked through the gate he saw Edgar and Rider already sitting at a table in the open-air courtyard. There was a pitcher of beer on their table. And they weren't alone. Sitting at the table with them was Grace Billets.

The Cat & Fiddle was a popular drinking spot with the Hollywood cops because it was only a few blocks from the station on Wilcox. So Bosch didn't know as he approached the table whether Billets happened to be there by coincidence or because she knew of their freelance operation.

'Howdy, folks,' Bosch said as he sat down.

There was one empty glass on the table and he filled it from the pitcher. He then held the glass up to the others and toasted to the end of another week.

'Harry,' Rider said, 'the lieutenant knows what we've been doing. She's here to help.'

Bosch nodded and slowly looked at Billets.

'I'm disappointed that you didn't come to me first,' she said. 'But I understand what you are doing. I agree that it might be in the bureau's best interest to let this lie and not endanger their case. But a man was murdered. If they're not going to look for the killer, I don't see why we shouldn't.'

Bosch nodded. He was almost speechless. He'd never had a boss who wasn't a rigid by-the-book man. Grace Billets was a major change.

'Of course,' she said, 'we have to be very careful. We screw this up and we'll have more than just the FBI mad at us.'

The unspoken message was that their careers were at stake here.

'Well, my position's already pretty much shot,' Bosch said. 'So if anything goes wrong, I want you all to lay it on me.'

'That's bullshit,' Rider said.

'No, it's not. You all are going places. I'm not going anywhere. Hollywood is it for me and all of us here know it. So if this thing hits the fan, back out. I'll take the heat. If you can't agree to that, I want you to back out now.'

There was silence for a few moments, and then one by one the other three nodded.

'Okay, then,' he said, 'you may have told the lieutenant what you've been doing, but I'd like to hear it myself.'

'We've come up with a few things, not a lot,' Rider said. 'Jerry went up the hill to see Nash while I worked the computer and talked to a friend at the *Times*. First off, I ran Tony Aliso's TRW credit report and got Veronica's Social Security computer to try and get a work history and found out that Veronica is not her real name. The Social comes back to Jennifer Gilroy, born forty-one years ago in Las Vegas, Nevada. No wonder she said she hated Vegas. She grew up there.'

'Any work history?'

'Nothing until she came out here and worked for TNA Productions.'

'What else?'

Before she could answer, there was a loud commotion near the glass door to the interior bar. The door opened and a large man in a bartender's jacket pushed a smaller man through. The smaller man was disheveled and drunk and yelling something about the lack of respect he was getting. The bartender roughly walked him to the courtyard gate and pushed him through. As soon as the bartender turned to go back to the bar, the drunk spun around and started back in. The bartender turned around and pushed him so hard he fell backward onto the seat of his pants. Now embarrassed, he threatened to come back and get the bartender. A few people at some of the outside tables snickered. The drunk got up and staggered out to the street.

'They start early around here,' Billets said. 'Go ahead, Kiz.'

'Anyway, I did an NCIC run. Jennifer Gilroy got picked up twice in Vegas for soliciting. This is going back more than twenty years. I called over there and had them ship us the mugs and reports. It's all on fiche and they have to dig it out, so we won't get it till next week. There probably won't be much there, anyway. According to the computer, neither case went to court. She pleaded out and paid a fine each time.'

Bosch nodded. It sounded like a routine disposal of routine cases.

'That's all I've got on that. As far as the *Times* goes, there was nothing on the search. And my friend at *Variety* didn't do much better. Veronica Aliso was barely mentioned in the review of *Casualty of Desire*. Both she and the movie were panned, but I'd like to see it anyway. Do you still have the tape, Harry?'

'On my desk.'

'Does she get naked in it?' Edgar asked. 'If she does, I'd like to see it, too.' He was ignored.

'Okay, what else?' Rider said. 'Uh, Veronica also got a couple mentions in stories about movie premieres and who attended. It wasn't a lot. When you said she had fifteen minutes, I think you confused minutes with seconds. Anyway, that's it from me. Jerry?'

Edgar cleared his throat and explained that he had gone up to the gatehouse at Hidden Highlands and run into a problem when Nash insisted on a new search warrant to look at the complete gate log. Edgar said he then spent the afternoon typing up the search warrant and hunting for a judge who hadn't left early for the weekend. He eventually was successful and had a signed warrant which he planned to deliver the next morning.

'Kiz and I are goin' up there in the morning. We'll get a look at the gate log and then we're probably going to hit some of the neighbors, do some interviews. Like you said, we're hopin' the widow will look out her window and catch our act, maybe get a little spooked. Maybe panic, make a mistake.'

It was then Bosch's turn, and he recounted his afternoon efforts, including his run-in with Roy Lindell and the agent's recollection that Veronica Aliso had started her show business career as a stripper in Vegas. He also discussed Salazar's finding that Tony Aliso had been hit in the face with a blast of pepper spray shortly before his death and shared the deputy coroner's hunch that it might have been a woman who sprayed him.

'Does he think she could have pulled this off by herself after hitting him with the pepper spray?' Billets asked.

'It doesn't matter, because she wasn't alone,' Bosch answered.

He pulled his briefcase onto his lap and took out the copies of the shoe prints Donovan had recovered from the body and the bumper of the Rolls. He slid the pages to the middle of the table so the three others could look.

'That's a size eleven shoe. It belongs to a man, Artie says. A big man. So the woman, if she was there, could have sprayed him with the pepper, but this guy finished the job.'

Bosch pointed to the shoe prints.

'He put his foot right on the victim so he could lean in close and do the job point-blank. Very cool and very efficient. Probably a pro. Maybe someone she knew since her Vegas days.'

'Probably the one who planted the gun in Vegas?' Billets asked.

'That's my guess.'

Bosch had been keeping his eye on the front gate of the courtyard, just in case the drunk who had been tossed out decided to come back and make his point. But when he glanced over now, he didn't see the drunk. He saw Officer Ray Powers, wearing mirrored glasses despite the lateness of the day, entering the courtyard and being met halfway across by the bartender. Waving his arms in an animated fashion, the bartender told the big cop about the drunk and the threats. Powers glanced around at the tables and saw Bosch and the others. When he had disengaged from the bartender he sauntered over.

'So, the detective bureau brain trust takes five,' he said.

'That's right, Powers,' Edgar said. 'I think the guy you're looking for is out there pissing in the bushes.'

'Yes, suh, I'll jus' go out there 'n' fetch him, boss.'

Powers looked around the table at the others with a satisfied smirk on his face. He saw the copies of the shoe prints on the table and pointed at them with his chin.

'Is this what you dicks call an investigative strategy session? Well, I'll give you a tip. Those there are what they call shoe prints.'

He smiled at his remark, proud of it.

'We're off duty, Powers,' Billets said. 'Why don't you go do your job and we'll worry about ours.'

Powers saluted her.

'Somebody's got to do the job, don't they?'

He walked away and out through the gate without waiting for a reply.

'He's got one hell of a bug up his ass,' Rider said.

'He's just mad because I told his lieutenant about the fingerprint he left on our car,' Billets said. 'I think he got his ass chewed. Anyway, back to business. What do you think, Harry? Do we have enough to take a hard run at Veronica?'

'I think we almost do. I'm going to go up there with these guys tomorrow, see what's on the gate log. Maybe we'll pay her a visit. I just wish we had something concrete to talk to her about.'

Billets nodded.

'I want to be kept informed tomorrow. Call me by noon.'

'Will do.'

'The more time that goes by on this, the harder it will be to keep this investigation among just us. I think by Monday we're going to have to take stock and decide whether to turn what we have over to the bureau.'

'I don't see that,' Bosch said, shaking his head. 'Whatever we give them, they're just going to sit on. If you want to clear this, you've got to let us alone, keep the bureau off us.'

'I will try, Harry, but there will come a point where that will be impossible. We're running a full-scale investigation off the books here. Word's going to get out. It has to. And all I'm saying is that it will be better if that word comes from me and can be controlled.'

Bosch nodded reluctantly. He knew she was right but he had to fight her suggestion. The case belonged to them. It was his. And all that had happened to him in the last week made it all the more personal. He didn't want to give it up.

He gathered up the copies of the shoe prints and put them back in his briefcase. He finished the last of his glass of beer and asked who and what he owed for it.

'It's on me,' Billets said. 'The next one, after we clear this, is on you.'

'It's a deal.'

When Bosch got to his house he found the door locked, but the key he had given Eleanor Wish was under the front mat. The first thing he checked when he got inside was the Hopper print. It was still there on the wall. But she was gone. He made a quick scan of the rooms and found no note. He checked the closet and her clothes were gone. So was her suitcase.

He sat on the bed and thought about her leaving. That morning they had left things open. He had risen early and, while she was still in bed, watching him get ready for the day, he'd asked her what she was going to do during the day. She had told him she didn't know.

Now she was gone. He rubbed a hand over his face. He was already beginning to feel the loss of her and he replayed in his mind their conversations of the night before. He had played it wrong, he decided. It had cost her something to tell him of her complicity. And he had only evaluated it in terms of what it meant to him and to his case. Not to her. Not to them.

Bosch leaned back until he was lying across the bed. He spread his arms and stared up at the ceiling. He could feel the beer working inside him, making him tired.

'Okay,' he said out loud.

He wondered if she would call or if another five years would go by before he saw her again by happenstance. He thought about how much had happened to him in the past five years and how long a wait that had been. His body ached. He closed his eyes.

'Okay.'

He fell asleep and dreamed about being alone in a desert with no roads and miles of open, desolate country ahead of him in every direction he looked.

VI

Bosch picked up two containers of coffee and two glazed doughnuts from Bob's in the farmers market at seven Saturday morning, then drove to the clearing where Tony Aliso's body had been found in the trunk of his car. As he ate and drank, he looked out on the marine layer shrouding the quiet city below. The sun rising behind the towers of downtown cast them as opaque monoliths in the haze. It was beautiful but Bosch felt as though he were the only one in the world seeing it.

When he had finished eating, he used a napkin he had wet in the water fountain at the farmers market to clean the sticky residue of sugar off his fingers. He then stuffed all the papers and the first empty coffee cup back into the doughnut bag and started the car.

Bosch had fallen asleep early Friday evening and awakened in his clothes before sunrise. He felt the need to get out of the house and do something. He had always believed that you could make things happen in an investigation by staying busy and with hard work. He decided that he would use the morning to try to find the spot where Tony Aliso's Rolls-Royce was intercepted and pulled over by his killers.

He concluded for a couple of reasons that the abduction had to have taken place on Mulholland Drive near the entrance to Hidden Highlands. First, the clearing where the car had been found was off Mulholland. If the abduction had taken place near the airport, it was likely the car would have been dumped near the airport, not fifteen miles away. And second, the abduction could be done more easily and quietly up on Mulholland in the dark. The airport and the surrounding area were always congested with traffic and people and would have presented too much of a risk.

The next question was whether Aliso had been followed from the airport or his killers simply waited for him at the abduction spot on Mulholland. Bosch decided on the latter, figuring that it was a small operation – two people, tops – and a tail and vehicle stop would be too iffy a proposition, particularly in Los Angeles, where every owner of a Rolls-Royce would be acutely aware of the danger of carjackings. He thought that they had waited on Mulholland and somehow created a trap or scene that made Aliso stop his car, even though he was carrying $480,000 in cash in his briefcase. And Bosch guessed that the only way Aliso would make such a stop was if that scenario involved his wife. In his mind Bosch saw the headlights of the Rolls-Royce sweeping around a curve and illuminating a frantically waving Veronica Aliso. Tony would stop for that.

Bosch knew that the waiting spot had to be on a place on Mulholland they were sure Tony would pass. There were only two logical routes from the airport to Mulholland Drive and then to the gatehouse at Hidden Highlands. One way would be to go north on the 405 freeway and simply take the Mulholland Drive exit. The other way would have been to take La Cienega Boulevard from the airport north to Laurel Canyon and up the hill to Mulholland.

The two routes had only a one-mile stretch of Mulholland in common. And since there was no way of knowing for sure which route Aliso would take home that night, it seemed obvious to Bosch that the car stop and abduction would have been somewhere along that one mile of road. It was here that Bosch came, and for nearly an hour he drove back and forth along the stretch, finally settling on the spot he would have chosen for the abduction if it had been his plan. The location was at the bend in a hairpin curve a half mile from the Hidden Highlands gatehouse. It was in an area with few homes and those that were there were built on the south side on a promontory well above the road. On the north side, the undeveloped land dropped steeply away from the road into a heavily wooded arroyo where eucalyptus and acacia trees crowded one another. It was the perfect spot. Secluded, out of sight.

Once again Bosch envisioned Tony Aliso coming around the curve and the lights of his Rolls coming upon his own wife in the road. Aliso stops, confused – what is she doing there? He gets out and from the north side of the road her accomplice goes to the Rolls and pops the trunk. Aliso's hands are clawing at his eyes when he is roughly thrown into the trunk and his hands tied behind him. All they had to worry about was a car coming around the curve and throwing its lights on them. But at that late hour on Mulholland, it didn't seem likely. The whole thing could have been done in fifteen seconds. That's why the spray was used. Not because it was a woman, but because it would make it fast.

Bosch pulled off the road, got out and looked around. The spot had the right feel to him. It was as quiet as death. He decided that he would come back that night to see it in darkness, to further confirm what he felt in his gut to be true.

He crossed the street and looked down into the arroyo where her accomplice would have hidden and waited. Looking down he tried to find a spot just off the road where a man could have ducked down and been concealed. He noticed a dirt trail going into the woods and stepped down to it, looking for shoe prints. There were many prints and he squatted down to study them. The ground here was dusty and some of the prints were fully recognizable. He found prints from two distinctly different sets of shoes, an old pair of shoes with worn heels and a much newer pair with heels that left sharp lines in the dirt. Neither pair was what he was looking for, the work-shoe pattern with the cut in the sole that Donovan had noticed.

Bosch's eyes looked up from the ground and followed the trail into the brush and trees. He decided to take a few more steps in, lifted a branch of an acacia and ducked under it. After his eyes adjusted to the darkness under the canopy of foliage, they were drawn to a blue object he could see but not identify about twenty yards further into the dense growth. He would have to leave the trail to get to it, but he decided to investigate.

After slowly moving ten feet into the brush, he could see that the blue object was part of a plastic tarp, the kind you saw on roofs all over the city after an earthquake knocked down chimneys and opened up the seams of buildings. Bosch stepped closer and saw that two corners of the tarp were tied to trees and it was hung over the branch of a third, creating a small shelter on a level portion of the hillside. He watched for a few moments but saw no movement.

It was impossible to come up on the shelter quietly. The ground was covered with a thick layer of dead and dried leaves and twigs that crackled under Bosch's feet. When he was ten feet from the canvas tarp, a man's hoarse voice stopped him.

'I've got a gun, you fuckers!'

Bosch stood stock-still and stared at the tarp. Because it was draped over the long branch of an acacia tree, he was in a blind spot. He could not see whoever it was who had yelled. And the man who yelled probably couldn't see him. Bosch decided to take a chance.

'I've got one, too,' he called back. 'And a badge.'

'Police? I didn't call the police!'

There was a hysterical tinge to the voice now, and Bosch suspected he was dealing with one of the homeless wanderers who were dumped out of mental institutions during the massive cutbacks in public assistance in the 1980s. The city was teeming with them. They stood at almost every major intersection holding their signs and shaking their change cups, they slept under overpasses or burrowed like termites into the woods on the hillsides, living in makeshift camps just yards from million-dollar mansions.

'I'm just passing through,' Bosch yelled. 'You put down yours, I'll put down mine.'

Bosch guessed that the man behind the scared voice didn't even have a gun.

'Okay. It's a deal.'

Bosch unsnapped the holster under his arm but left his gun in place. He walked the final few steps and came slowly around the trunk of the acacia. A man with long gray hair and beard flowing over a blue silk Hawaiian shirt sat cross-legged on a blanket under the tarp. There was a wild look in his eyes. Bosch quickly scanned the man's hands and the surroundings within his immediate reach and saw no weapon. He eased up a bit and nodded at the man.

'Hello,' he said.

'I didn't do nothin'.'

'I understand.'

Bosch looked around. There were folded clothes and towels under the shelter of the tarp. There was a small folding card table with a frying pan on it along with some candles and Sterno cans, two forks and a spoon, but no knife. Bosch figured the man had the knife under his shirt or maybe hidden in the blanket. There was also a bottle of cologne on the table, and Bosch could tell that it had been liberally sprinkled about the shelter. Also under the tarp were an old tar bucket filled with crushed aluminum cans, a stack of newspapers and a dog-eared paperback copy of *Stranger in a Strange Land*.

He stepped to the edge of the man's clearing and squatted like a baseball catcher so they could face each other on the same level. He took a look around the outer edge of the clearing and saw that this was where the man discarded what he didn't need. There were bags of trash and remnants of clothing. By the base of another acacia there was a brown-and-green suit bag. It was unzipped and lying open like a gutted fish. Bosch looked back at the man. He could see he wore two other Hawaiian shirts beneath the blue one on top, which had a pattern of hula girls on surfboards. His pants were dirty but had a sharper crease in them than a homeless man's pants would usually have. His shoes were too well polished for a man of the woods. Bosch guessed that the pair he wore had made some of the prints up on the trail, the ones with the sharp-edged heels.

'That's a nice shirt,' Bosch said.

'It's mine.'

'I know. I just said it was nice. What's your name?'

'Name's George.'

'George what?'

'George whatever the hell you want it to be.'

'Okay, George whatever the hell you want it to be, why don't you tell me about that suit bag over there and those clothes you're wearing? The new shoes. Where did it all come from?'

'It was delivered. It's mine now.'

'What do you mean by delivered?'

'Delivered. That's what I mean. Delivered. They gave it all to me.'

Bosch took out his cigarettes, took one and offered the pack to the man. He waved them away.

'Can't afford it. Take me half a day to find enough cans to buy a pack of smokes. I quit.'

Bosch nodded.

'How long you been livin' up here, George?'

'All my life.'

'When did they kick you out of Camarillo?'

'Who told you that?'

It had been an educated guess, Camarillo being the nearest state institution.

'They did. How long ago was that?'

'If they told you about me, then they would've told you that. I'm not stupid, you know.'

'You got me there, George. About the bag and the clothes, when was it all delivered?'

'I don't know.'

Bosch got up and went over to the suit bag. There was an identification tag attached to the handle. He turned it over and read Anthony Aliso's name and address. He noticed the bag was lying on top of a cardboard box that was damaged from a tumble down the hill. Bosch tipped the box with his foot and read the markings on the side.

Scotch standard HS/T-90 VHS 96-count

He left the box and the suit bag there and went back to the man and squatted again.

'How's last Friday night sound for the delivery?'

'Whatever you say is good.'

'It's not what I say, George. Now if you want me to leave you alone and

476

you want to stay here, you've got to help me. If you go into your nut bag, you're not helping me. When was it delivered?'

George tucked his chin down on his chest like a boy who'd been chastised by a teacher. He brought a thumb and forefinger up and pressed them against his eyes. His voice came out as if it were being strangled with piano wire.

'I don't know. They just came and dropped it off for me. That's all I know.'

'Who dropped it off?'

George looked up, his eyes bright, and pointed upward with one of his dirty fingers. Bosch looked up and saw a patch of blue sky through the upper limbs of the trees. He blew out his breath in exasperation. This wasn't going anywhere.

'So little green men dropped it down from their spaceship, is that right, George? Is that your story?'

'I didn't say that. I don't know if they were green. I didn't see them.'

'But you saw the spaceship?'

'Nope. I didn't say that, neither. I didn't see their craft. Only the landing lights.'

Bosch looked at him a moment.

'Perfect size,' George said. 'They got an invisible beam that measures you from up there, you don't even know it, then they send down the clothes.'

'That's great.'

Bosch's knees were beginning to ache. He stood up and they painfully cracked.

'I'm getting too old for this shit, George.'

'That's a policeman's line. I watched "Kojak" when I had the house.'

'I know. Tell you what, I'm going to take this suit bag with me, if you don't mind. And the box of videotapes.'

'Help yourself. I'm not going anywhere. And I don't have no video machine, either.'

Bosch walked toward the box and bag, wondering why they had been discarded and not just left in the Rolls. After a moment he decided they must have been in the trunk. And in order to make room for Aliso in there, the killers had yanked them out and thrown them down the hill out of sight. They were in a hurry. It was the kind of decision made in haste. A mistake.

He picked up the suit bag by a corner, careful not to touch the handle, though he doubted there would be any prints on it other than George's. The box was light but bulky. He would have to make a second trip for it. He turned and looked at the homeless man. He decided not to ruin his day yet.

'George, you can keep the clothes for now.'

'Okay, thanks.'

'You're welcome.'

As he climbed back up the hill to the road, Bosch was thinking about how he should declare the area a crime scene and call out SID to process everything. But he couldn't do that. Not without announcing he had been continuing an investigation he had been ordered away from.

It didn't bother him, however, because by the time he got up to the road, he knew he had a new direction. A plan was coming together. Quickly.

Bosch was jazzed. When he stepped onto level ground he punched his fist in the air and walked quickly to his car.

Bosch worked out the details in his head while he was driving to Hidden Highlands. The Plan. He had been like a cork floating in a great wide ocean that was the case. Bouncing with the currents, not in control of anything. But now he had an idea, a plan that would hopefully draw Veronica Aliso into the box.

Nash was in the gatehouse when Bosch pulled up. He stepped out and leaned down on Bosch's door.

'Morning, Detective Bosch.'

'Howzit going, Captain Nash?'

'It's going. I gotta say your people are creating a bit of a stir already this morning.'

'Yeah, well, that can happen. Whaddaya gonna do?'

'Go with the flow, I guess. You going in to catch up with them or you heading to Mrs Aliso's?'

'I'm going to see the lady.'

'Good. Maybe that'll get her off my back. I gotta call, you know.'

'Why's she on your back?'

'She's just been calling up wondering why you people have been talkin' to the neighbors all morning.'

'What did you tell her?'

'I told her they got a job to do and a murder investigation requires them to talk to a lot of people.'

'That's good. I'll see you.'

Nash waved him off and opened the gate. Bosch drove to the Aliso house, but before he got there he saw Edgar walking from the front door of the home next door to his car. Bosch stopped and waved him over.

'Harry.'

'Jerry. Get anything yet?'

'Nah, not really. Thing about these rich neighborhoods, it's like working a shooting in South Central. Nobody ever wants to talk, nobody saw nothing. I get tired of these people.'

'Where's Kiz?'

'She's working the other side of the street. We met at the station and took one car. She's on foot down there somewhere. Hey, Harry, what do you think about her?'

'Kiz? I think she's good.'

'No, I don't mean as a cop. You know . . . what do you think?'

Bosch looked at him.

'You mean like you and her? What do I think?'

'Yeah. Me and her.'

Bosch knew Edgar was six months divorced and starting to pull his head out of the sand again. But he also knew something about Kiz that he didn't have the right to tell him.

'I don't know, Jerry. Partners shouldn't get involved.'

'I suppose. So you going to see the widow now?'

'Yeah.'

478

'Maybe I better go with you. You never know, if she figures out we think she's it, then she's liable to wig out, maybe try to take you out.'

'I doubt it. She's too cool for that. But let's go find Kiz. I think both of you should come. I've got a plan now.'

Veronica Aliso was waiting for them at her door.

'I've been waiting for you people to come by to explain just what is going on.'

'Sorry, Mrs Aliso,' Bosch said. 'We've been kind of busy.'

She ushered them in.

'Can I get you something?' she asked over her shoulder as she led them in.

'I think we're fine.'

Part of the plan was for Bosch to do all the talking, if possible. Rider and Edgar were to intimidate her with their silence and their cold-eyed stares.

Bosch and Rider sat where they had sat before and so did Veronica Aliso. Edgar remained standing on the periphery of the seating section of the living room. He put his hand on the mantel of the fireplace and the look on his face said he would rather be anywhere else on the planet on this Saturday morning.

Veronica Aliso was wearing blue jeans, a light blue Oxford shirt and dirty work boots. Her hair was pulled back and pinned up in the back. She was still very attractive though obviously dressing down. Through her open collar Bosch could see a scattering of freckles that he knew from her video went all the way down her chest.

'Are we interrupting something?' Bosch asked. 'Were you about to go out?'

'I wanted to go to the Burbank stables sometime today if I could. I keep a horse there. My husband's body was cremated and I want to take his ashes up the trail into the hills. He loved the hills . . .'

Bosch somberly nodded.

'Well, this won't take too long. First off, you've seen us in the neighborhood this morning. We're just conducting a routine canvass. You never know, maybe someone saw something, maybe somebody watching the house or a car here that shouldn't have been here. You never know.'

'Well, I think I'd be the one who would know about any car that shouldn't be here.'

'Well, I mean if you weren't here. If you were out and someone was here, you probably wouldn't know.'

'How could they get in past the gate?'

'It's a long shot, we know, Mrs Aliso. It's all we've got right now.'

She frowned.

'There's nothing else? What about what you told me the other day? About this man in Las Vegas?'

'Well, Mrs Aliso, I hate to tell you this, but we went down the wrong path on that. We gathered a lot of information about your husband and initially it looked like that was the way to go. But it didn't work out. We do think we're moving in the right direction now, and we're going to make up for the lost time.'

She seemed genuinely stunned.

'I don't understand. The wrong path?'

'Yes, well, I can explain it to you, if you want to hear it. But it involves your husband and some unsavory things.'

'Detective, I've prepared myself over the last few days for anything. Tell me.'

'Mrs Aliso, as I think I indicated to you on our last visit, your husband was involved with some very dangerous people in Las Vegas. I think I mentioned them, Joey Marks and Luke Goshen?'

'I don't recall.'

She kept the look of bewilderment on her face. She was good. Bosch had to give that to her. She might not have made it in the film business but she could act when she needed to.

'To put it bluntly, they're mobsters,' Bosch said. 'Organized crime. And it looks like your husband had been working for them for a long time. He took mob money from Vegas and put it into his films. Laundered it through. Then he gave it back to them, after taking out a fee. It was a lot of money and that's where we went down the wrong path. Your husband was about to get audited by the IRS. Did you know that?'

'Audited? No. He didn't tell me anything about an audit.'

'Well, we found out about the audit, which likely would have revealed his illegal activities, and we thought maybe these people he did business with became aware of it, too, and had him killed so he wouldn't be able to talk about their business. Only we don't think that anymore.'

'I don't understand. Are you sure of this? It seems obvious to me that these people had some involvement.'

She faltered a little bit there. Her voice was a little too urgent.

'Well, like I said, we thought that, too. We haven't fully dropped it, but so far it doesn't check out. The man we arrested over there in Vegas, this Goshen fellow I mentioned, he looked pretty good for it, I have to say. But then his alibi turned out to be a rock we couldn't break. It couldn't have been him, Mrs Aliso. It looks as though somebody went to great lengths to make it look like it was him, even planted a gun in his house, but we know it wasn't.'

She looked at him with dull eyes for a moment and then shook her head. Then she made her first real mistake. She should have said that if it wasn't Goshen, then it was probably the other one Bosch had mentioned or some other mobster associate. But she said nothing and that instinctively told Bosch that she knew of the setup on Goshen. She now knew the plan hadn't worked and her mind was probably scrambling.

'So then what will you do?' she finally asked.

'Oh, we already had to let him go.'

'No, I mean about the investigation. What's next?'

'Well, we're sort of starting from scratch. Looking at it like maybe it was a planned robbery.'

'You said his watch wasn't taken.'

'Right. It wasn't. But the Las Vegas angle wasn't a total waste. We found out that your husband was carrying a lot of money with him when he landed here that night. He was taking it back here to run through his company. To clean it up. It was a lot of money. Nearly a million dollars. He was carrying it for—'

'A *million* dollars?'

That was her second mistake. To Bosch, her emphasis on *million* and her shock betrayed her knowledge that there had been far less than that in Tony Aliso's briefcase. Bosch watched as her eyes stared blankly and all her movement was interior. He guessed – and hoped – she was now wondering where the rest of the money was.

'Yes,' he said. 'See, the man who gave your husband the money, the one we first thought was a suspect, is an FBI agent who infiltrated the organization your husband worked for. That is why his alibi is so solid. Anyway, he told us that your husband was carrying a million dollars. It was all in cash and there was so much that he couldn't fit it all into his briefcase. He had to put about half of it in his suit bag.'

He paused for a few moments. He could tell the story was playing in her internal theater. Her eyes had that faraway look in them. He remembered that look from her movie. But this time it was for real. He hadn't even finished the interview, but she was already making plans. He could see it.

'Was the money marked by the FBI?' she asked. 'I mean, could they trace it that way?'

'No, unfortunately their agent did not have it long enough to do that. There was too much of it, frankly. But the transaction did take place in an office with a hidden video camera. There is no doubt, Tony left there with a million dollars. Uh . . .'

Bosch paused to open his briefcase and quickly consult a page from a file.

' . . . actually, it was a million, seventy-six thousand. All in cash.'

Veronica's eyes went down to the floor as she nodded. Bosch studied her but his concentration was interrupted when he thought he heard a sound from somewhere in the house. It suddenly occurred to him that maybe there was someone else there. They had never asked.

'Did you hear that?' Bosch asked.

'What?'

'I thought I heard something. Are you alone in the house?'

'Yes.'

'I thought I heard a bump or something.'

'You want me to look around?' Edgar offered.

'Oh, no,' Veronica said quickly, ' . . . uh, it probably was just the cat.'

Bosch didn't remember seeing any sign of a cat when he had been in the house before. He glanced at Kiz and saw her almost imperceptibly turn her head to signal she didn't remember a cat either. He decided to let it go for the time being.

'Anyway,' he said, 'that's why we're canvassing and that's why we're here. We need to ask you some questions. They might go over some of the same ground we've covered before but, like I said, we're kind of starting over. It won't take too much longer. Then you'll be able to go to the stables.'

'Fine. Go ahead.'

'Would you mind if I have a drink of water first?'

'No, of course not. I'm sorry, I should have asked. Anybody else want something?'

'I'll pass,' Edgar said.

'I'm fine,' Rider said.

Veronica Aliso stood up and headed toward the hallway. Bosch gave her a head start and then stood up and followed.

'You did ask,' he said to her back. 'But I turned it down. I didn't think I'd get thirsty.'

He followed her into the kitchen, where she opened a cabinet and took down a glass. Bosch looked around. It was a large kitchen with stainless-steel appliances and black granite countertops. There was a center island with a sink in it.

'Tap water'd be fine for me,' he said, taking the glass from her and filling it at the island.

He turned and leaned against the counter and drank from it. He then poured the rest out and put the glass on the counter.

'That's all you want?'

'Yes. Just needed something to wash the dust down, I guess.'

He smiled and she didn't.

'Well then, should we go back to the living room?' she asked.

'That'd be fine.'

He followed her out of the kitchen. Just before he entered the hallway, he turned back and his eyes swept across the gray-tiled floor. He didn't see what he thought should be there.

Bosch spent the next fifteen minutes asking mostly questions that had been asked six days earlier and that had little bearing on the case now. He was going through the motions, the finishing touches. The trap was baited and this was his way of quietly stepping back from it. Finally, when he thought he had said and asked enough, Bosch closed the notebook in which he had been scribbling notes he'd never look at again and stood up. He thanked her for her time and Veronica Aliso walked the three detectives to the door. Bosch was the last one out, and as he stepped over the threshold she spoke to him. He somehow knew that she would. There were parts to her act that had to be played as well.

'Keep me informed, Detective Bosch. Please keep me informed.'

Bosch turned and looked back at her.

'Oh, I will. If anything happens, you'll be the first to know.'

Bosch drove Edgar and Rider back to their car. He didn't speak about the interview until he pulled in behind it.

'So what do you think?' he asked as he got out his cigarettes.

'I think we sunk the hook but good,' Edgar said.

'Yeah,' Rider said. 'It's going to be interesting.'

Bosch lit a cigarette.

'What about the cat?' he asked.

'What?' Edgar asked.

'The noise in the house. She said it was the cat. But in the kitchen there were no food bowls on the floor.'

'Maybe they were outside,' Edgar offered.

Bosch shook his head.

'I think people who keep cats inside feed them inside,' he said. 'In the hills you're supposed to keep 'em in. Coyotes. Anyway, I don't like cats. I get allergic to them. I can usually tell when somebody has a cat. I don't think she has a cat. Kiz, you didn't see a cat in there, did you?'

'I spent all Monday morning in there and I never saw a cat.'

'You think maybe it was the guy then?' Edgar asked. 'Whoever she worked this with?'

'Maybe. I think somebody was in there. Maybe her lawyer.'

'Nah, lawyers don't hide like that. They come out and confront.'

'True.'

'Should we watch the place, see who comes out?' Edgar asked.

Bosch thought a moment.

'No,' Bosch said. 'They spot us and they'll know the money thing is just bait. Better we let it go. Better just to get out of here, go get set up. We gotta get ready.'

VII

During his time in Vietnam, Bosch's primary assignment had been to fight the war in the tunnel networks that ranged beneath the villages in the Cu Chi province, to go into the darkness they called the black echo and to come back alive. But the tunnel work was done quickly, and between those missions he spent days in the bush, fighting and waiting under the jungle canopy. One time he and a handful of others got cut off from their unit and Bosch spent a night sitting in the elephant grass, his back pressed against the back of an Alabama boy named Donnel Fredrick, listening as a company of VC fighters moved through. They sat there and waited for Charlie to stumble onto them. There was nothing else they could do and there were too many to fight. So they waited and the minutes went by like hours. They all made it through, though Donnel was later killed in a foxhole by a direct mortar hit – friendly fire. Bosch always thought that night in the elephant grass was the closest he'd ever come to experiencing a miracle.

Bosch remembered that night sometimes when he was alone on a stakeout or in a tight spot. He thought about it now as he sat cross-legged against the base of a eucalyptus tree ten yards from the tarp the homeless man, George, had erected. Over his clothes, he wore a green plastic poncho he always kept in the trunk of his work car. The candy bars he had with him were Hershey's chocolate with almonds, the same kind he had taken with him into the bush so long ago. And like that night in the tall grass, he had not moved for what seemed like hours. It was dark, with only a glimmer of moonlight making it down through the overhead canopy, and he was waiting. He wanted a cigarette but couldn't afford to open a flame in the blackness. Every now and then he thought he could hear Edgar make a move or readjust himself twenty yards to his right, but he couldn't be sure that it was his partner and not a deer or maybe a coyote passing through.

George had told him there were coyotes. When he had put the old man into the back of Kiz's car for the ride to the hotel they were putting him up in, he had warned Bosch. But Bosch wasn't afraid of coyotes.

The old man had not gone easily. He was sure they were there to take him back to Camarillo. And the truth was, he should have been going back there but the institution wouldn't have him, not without a government-punched ticket. Instead he was going to be treated to a couple of nights at the Mark Twain Hotel in Hollywood. It wasn't a bad place. Bosch had lived there for more than a year while his house was being rebuilt. The worst room there beat a tarp in the woods hands down. But Bosch knew George might not see it that way.

By eleven-thirty the traffic up on Mulholland had thinned down to a car every five minutes or so. Bosch couldn't see them because of the incline and the thickness of the brush, but he could hear them and see the lights wash through the foliage above him as the cars made the curve. He was alert now because a car had slowly gone by twice in the last fifteen minutes, once each way. Bosch had sensed that it was the same car because the engine was over-throttled to compensate for the skip in the engine stroke.

And now it was back for a third time. Bosch listened intently as he heard the familiar engine, and this time there was the added sound of tires turning on gravel. The car was pulling off the road. In a few moments the engine stopped and the following silence was punctuated only by the sound of a car door being opened and then closed. Bosch slowly got up on his haunches, as painful as it was on his knees, and got ready. He looked into the darkness to his right, toward Edgar's position, and saw nothing. He then looked up the incline, toward the edge, and waited.

In a few moments he could see the beam of a flashlight cut through the brush. The light was pointed downward and was moving in a back-and-forth sweeping pattern as its holder slowly descended the hill toward the tarp. Under his poncho Bosch held his gun in one hand and a flashlight in the other, his thumb paused on the switch and ready to turn it on.

The movement of the light stopped. Bosch guessed that its holder had found the spot where the suit bag should have been. After a moment of seeming hesitation the beam was lifted and it swept through the woods, flicking across Bosch for a fraction of a second. But it didn't come back to him. Instead, it held on the blue tarp as Bosch guessed it probably would. The light began advancing, its holder stumbling once as he or she went toward George's home. A few moments later, Bosch saw the beam moving behind the blue plastic. He felt another charge of adrenaline begin to course through his body. Again, his mind flashed on Vietnam. This time it was the tunnels that he thought of. Coming upon an enemy in the darkness. The fear and thrill of it. It was only after he had left that place safely that he acknowledged to himself there had been a thrill to it. And in looking to replace that thrill, he had joined the cops.

Bosch slowly raised himself, hoping his knees wouldn't crack, as he watched the light. They had placed the suit bag in underneath the shelter after stuffing it first with crumpled newspaper. Bosch began to move as quietly as he could in behind the tarp. He was coming from the left. According to the plan, Edgar would be coming from the right, but it was still too dark for Bosch to see him.

Bosch was ten feet away now and could hear the excited breathing of the person under the tarp. Then there was the sound of a zipper being pulled open followed by the sharp cut-off of breath.

'Shit!'

Bosch moved in after hearing the curse. He realized he recognized the man's voice just as he came around the open side of the tarp and raised both his weapon and his flashlight from beneath his poncho.

'*Freeze! Police!*' Bosch yelled at the same moment he put on his light. 'All right, come out of there, Powers.'

Almost immediately Edgar's light came on from Bosch's right.

'What the . . . ?' Edgar started to say.

Crouched there in the crossing beams of light was Officer Ray Powers. In full uniform, the big patrol cop held a flashlight in one hand and a gun in the other. A look of utter surprise played across his face. His mouth dropped open.

'Bosch,' he said. 'What the fuck are you doing here?'

'That's our line, Powers,' Edgar said angrily. 'Don't you know what the fuck you just did? You walked right into a – what are *you* doing here, man?'

Powers lowered his gun and slid it back into his holster.

'I was – there was a report. Somebody must've seen you guys sneaking in here. They said they saw two men sneaking around.'

Bosch stepped back from the tarp, keeping his gun raised.

'Come out of there, Powers,' he said.

Powers did as he was commanded. Bosch put the beam from his light right in the man's face.

'What about this report? Who called it in?'

'Just some guy driving by up on the road. Must've seen you going in here. Can you get the light out of my face?'

Bosch didn't move the focus of the light an inch.

'Then what?' he asked. 'Who'd he call?'

Bosch knew that after Rider had dropped them off, her job was to park on a nearby street and keep her scanner on. If there had been such a radio call, she would have heard it and called off the patrol response, telling the dispatcher it was a surveillance operation.

'He didn't call it in. I was cruising by and he waved me down.'

'You mean he claimed he just saw two guys going into the woods?'

'Uh, no. No, he waved me down earlier. I just didn't get a chance to check it out until now.'

Bosch and Edgar had gone into the woods at two-thirty. It was full daylight then and Powers hadn't even been on duty yet. And the only car that had been in the area at the time was Rider's. Bosch knew Powers was lying, and it was all beginning to fall into place. His finding the body, his fingerprint on the trunk, the pepper spray on the victim, the reason the bindings were taken off the wrists. It was already there, in the details.

'How much earlier?' Bosch asked.

'Uh, it was right after I came on duty. I can't remember the time.'

'Daylight?'

'Yeah, daylight. Can you put the fuckin' light down?'

Bosch ignored him again.

'What was the citizen's name?'

'I didn't get it. Just some guy in a Jag, he waved me down at Laurel Canyon and Mulholland. Told me what he saw and I said I'd check it when I got the chance. So I was checking it out and saw the bag here. I figured it belonged to the guy in the trunk. I saw the bulletin you people put out about the car and the luggage, so I knew you were looking for it. Sorry I blew it, but you people should've let the watch commander know what you were doing. Jesus, Bosch I'm going blind here.'

'Yeah, it's blown all right,' Bosch said, finally lowering the light. He lowered his gun to his side also but didn't put it away. He kept it ready there, under the poncho. 'Might as well pack it in now. Powers, go on up the hill to your car. Jerry, grab the bag.'

Bosch climbed up the hill behind Powers, careful to keep the light up and back on the patrol cop. He knew that if they had cuffed Powers down by the tarp, they'd never get him up the hill because of the steep terrain and because Powers might fight them. So he had to scam him. He let him think he was clear.

At the top of the hill, Bosch waited until Edgar came up behind them before making a move.

'Know what I don't get, Powers?' he said.

'What, Bosch?'

'I don't get why you waited until dark to check out a complaint you got during the day. You're told that two suspicious-looking characters went into the woods and you decide to wait until it's late and it's dark to check it out by yourself.'

'I told you. Didn't have the time.'

'You're full of shit, Powers,' Edgar said.

He had either just caught on or had played along with Bosch perfectly.

Bosch saw Powers's eyes go dead as he went inside to try to figure out what to do. In that instant Bosch raised his gun again and aimed it at a spot between those two vacant portals.

'Don't think so much, Powers,' he said. 'It's over. Now stand still. Jerry?'

Edgar moved in behind the big cop and yanked his gun out of its holster. He dropped it on the ground and jerked one of Powers's hands behind his back. He cuffed the hand and then he did the other. When he was done, he picked up the gun. It seemed to Bosch that Powers was still inside, still staring blankly at nothing. Then he came back.

'You people, you have just fucked up big time,' he said, controlled rage in his voice.

'We'll see about that. Jerry, you got him? I want to call Kiz.'

'Go ahead. I got his ass. I hope he does make a move. Go ahead, Powers, do something stupid for me.'

'Fuck you, Edgar! You don't know what you've just done. You're goin' down, bro. You're going *down!*'

Edgar remained silent. Bosch took the Motorola two-way out of his pocket, turned it on and keyed the mike.

'Kiz, you there?'

'Here. I'm here.'

'Come on over. Hurry.'

'On my way.'

Bosch put the two-way back and they stood there in silence for a minute until they saw the flashing blue light lead Rider's car around the bend. When it pulled up, the lights swept repeatedly through the tops of the trees on the incline. Bosch realized that from below, down in George's shelter, the lights on the trees might look as if they were coming from the sky. It all came to Bosch then. George's spacecraft had been Powers's patrol car. The abduction had been a traffic stop. The perfect way to get a man carrying nearly a half million in cash to stop. Powers had simply waited for Aliso's white Rolls, probably at Mulholland and Laurel Canyon, then followed and put the lights on when they approached the secluded curve. Tony probably thought he had been speeding. He pulled over.

Rider pulled off the road behind the patrol car. Bosch came over and opened the back door and looked in at her.

'Harry, what is it?' she asked.

'Powers. Powers is it.'

'Oh my God.'

'Yeah. I want you and Jerry to take him in. I'll follow with his car.'

He walked back over to Edgar and Powers.

'Okay, let's go.'

'You people have all lost your jobs,' Powers said. 'You fucked yourselves up.'

'You can tell us about it at the station.'

Bosch jerked him by the arm, feeling its thickness and strength. He and Edgar then hustled him into the back of Rider's car. Edgar went around and got in the other side next to him.

Looking in through the open rear door, Bosch went over what would be the procedure.

'Take all his shit away and lock him in one of the interview rooms,' he said. 'Make sure you get his cuff key. I'll be right behind you.'

Bosch slammed the door and knocked twice on the roof. He then went to the patrol car, put the suit bag in the back seat and got in. Rider pulled out and Bosch followed. They sped west toward Laurel Canyon.

It took Billets less than an hour to come in. When she got there, the three of them were sitting at the homicide table. Bosch was going through the murder book with Rider while she took notes on a legal pad. Edgar was at the typewriter. Billets walked in with a force and look on her face that clearly showed the situation. Bosch hadn't talked to her yet. It had been Rider who had called her in from home.

'What are you doing to me?' Billets asked, her piercing eyes clearly fixed on Bosch.

What she was really saying to him was that he was the team leader and the responsibility for this potential fuckup rested squarely on him. That was okay with Bosch, because not only was that right and fair, but in the half hour he'd had to go through the murder book and the other evidence, his confidence had grown.

'What am I doing to you? I'm bringing in your killer.'

'I told you to conduct a quiet and careful investigation,' Billets responded. 'I didn't tell you to conduct some kind of half-assed sting operation and then drag a cop in here! I can't believe this.'

Billets was now pacing behind Rider's back without looking at them. The squad room was deserted except for the three of them and the angry lieutenant.

'It's Powers, Lieutenant,' Bosch said. 'If you'd calm down, we—'

'Oh, it's him, is it? You have the evidence of that? Great! I'll call a DA in here right now and we'll write up the charges then. Because you really had me worried there for a minute that you three jerked this guy off the street with just enough probable cause to charge him with jaywalking.'

Now she was looking at Bosch with the angry eyes again. She had even

491

stopped her pacing to level them at him. He responded as calmly as he could.

'First of all, it was my decision to take him off the street. And you're right, we don't have enough to call out a DA yet. But we'll get it. There's no doubt in my mind he's the man. It's him and the widow.'

'Well, I'm glad there's no doubt in *your* mind but you're not the DA or the goddamned jury.'

He didn't respond. It was no use. He had to wait for her anger to ebb and then they could talk sensibly.

'Where is he?' Billets asked.

'Room three,' Bosch said.

'What did you tell the watch commander?'

'Nothing. It happened at the end of shift. Powers was going to grab the suit bag and then go punch out. We were able to bring him in while most everybody else was still up in roll call. I parked his car and dropped the key at the watch office. I told the watch lieutenant we were using Powers for a little while on a warrant, that we wanted a uniform with us when we knocked on a door. He said fine and then I expect he went off shift. As far as I know, nobody knows we have him back there.'

Billets thought for a moment. When she spoke, she was calmer and more like the person who normally sat behind the desk in the glass office.

'Okay, I'm going to go back there and get some coffee, see if I get asked about him. When I come back, we'll go over all of this in detail and see what we have.'

She walked slowly to the hallway at the rear of the squad room that led to the watch office. Bosch watched her go and then picked up the phone and dialed the number of the security office of the Mirage hotel and casino. He told the officer who answered who he was and that he needed to speak with Hank Meyer immediately. When the officer mentioned that it was after midnight, Bosch told him it was an emergency and that he was sure that if Meyer was informed who needed to speak with him, he would return the call. Bosch gave him all the numbers he could be reached at, beginning with his number at the homicide table, and hung up. He went back to his work with the murder book.

'Did you say he's in three?'

Bosch looked up. Billets was back, a cup of steaming coffee in her hand. He nodded.

'I want to have a look,' she said.

Bosch got up and walked with her down the hallway to the four doors leading to the interview rooms. Doors marked one and two were on the left, three and four on the right. But there was no fourth interview room. The room marked four was actually a small cubicle with a one-way glass window that allowed for observation of room three. In three, the other side of the glass was a mirror. Billets entered four and looked through the glass at Powers. He sat ramrod straight at a table in a chair directly opposite the mirror. His hands were cuffed behind his back. He still wore his uniform but his equipment belt had been removed. He stared straight ahead at his own reflection in the mirror. This created an eerie effect in the fourth room because it appeared that he was looking right at them, as if there were no mirror or glass between them.

Billets said nothing. She just looked back at the man staring at her.

'There is a lot hanging in the balance tonight, Harry,' she said quietly.

'I know,' he said.

They stood there silently for a few moments until Edgar opened the door and told Bosch that Hank Meyer was on the phone. Bosch headed back, picked up the phone and told Meyer what he needed. Meyer said he was at home and that he'd have to go into the hotel, but he would call back as soon as possible. Bosch thanked him and hung up. Billets had now taken one of the empty seats at the homicide table.

'Okay,' she said, 'one of you tell me exactly how this went down tonight.'

Bosch remained in the lead and took the next fifteen minutes to recount how he found Tony Aliso's suit bag, set up the sting through Veronica Aliso and then waited in the woods off Mulholland until Powers showed up. He explained how the story Powers had offered for his being there did not make sense.

'What else did he say?' Billets asked at the end.

'Nothing. Jerry and Kiz put him in the room and that's where he's been ever since.'

'What else have you got?'

'For starters, we have his print on the inside of the trunk lid. We also have a record of association with the widow.'

Billets raised her eyebrows.

'That's what we were working on when you came in. On Sunday night when Jerry ran the victim's name through the computer, we got a hit on a burglary report from back in March. Somebody hit the Aliso house. Jerry pulled the report but it looked unconnected. Just a routine burglary. And it was, except the officer who took the initial report from Mrs Aliso was Powers. We think the relationship started with the burglary. That's when they met. After that, we have the gate records. Police patrols of Hidden Highlands are recorded on the gate logs by the car's roof number. The logs show the car assigned to Powers – the Zebra car – has been going in there two, three nights a week on patrol, always on the nights we know from credit card records that Tony was out of town. I think he was poppin' over there to see Veronica.'

'What else?' the lieutenant asked. 'So far all you've got is a bunch of coincidences strung together.'

'There are no coincidences,' Bosch said. 'Not like this.'

'Then what else have you got?'

'Like I said, his story about why he came down into the woods doesn't check out. He came down looking for the suit bag and the only way he would have known that it was worth coming back for was through Veronica. It's him, Lieutenant. It's him.'

Billets thought about this. Bosch believed the facts he was giving her were beginning to have a cumulative effect in convincing her. He had one thing left with which to nail her down.

'There's one other thing. Remember our problem with Veronica? If she was involved in this, how did she get out of Hidden Highlands and not have it noted on the gate log?'

'Right.'

'Well, the gate log shows that on the night of the murder, the Zebra car cruised through on patrol. Twice. He was in and out both times. First time he was logged in at ten and out at ten-ten. Then back in at eleven-forty-eight and out four minutes later. It was noted as just routine patrol.'

'Okay, so?'

'So on the first time, he cruises in and picks her up. She gets down on the floor in the back. It's dark out, the gate guy only sees Powers heading back out. They go and wait for Tony, do the deed and then Powers takes her back home – the second set of entries on the log.'

'It works,' Billets said, nodding her approval. 'The actual abduction, how do you see it?'

'We've figured all along it took two people to do this job. First off, Veronica had to know from Tony what flight he was taking. So that set the time frame. Powers picks her up that night and they go to Laurel Canyon and Mulholland and wait for the white Rolls to go by. We figure that happens about eleven or so. Powers follows until Tony is close to the curve through the woods. He puts on the lights and pulls him over, like a routine traffic stop. Only he tells Tony to step out and go to the back of the car. Maybe he makes him open the trunk, maybe he does that himself after he cuffs him. Either way, the trunk is opened and Powers has a problem. Tony's suit bag and a box of videos are in the trunk and that doesn't leave much room for him. Powers doesn't have much time. A car could come around the bend any moment and light up the whole thing. So he takes the suit bag and the box out and throws them down the hill into the woods. He then tells Tony to get in the trunk. Tony says no or maybe he struggles a bit. Either way, Powers takes out his pepper spray and gives him a shot in the face. Tony is then real manageable, easy to throw into the trunk. Maybe Powers pulled his shoes off then to stop him from kicking around in there, making noise.'

'That's when Veronica pops out,' Rider said, picking up the story. 'She drives the Rolls while Powers follows in the squad car. They knew where they were going. They needed a spot where the car wouldn't be found for a couple days, giving Powers time to get over to Vegas on Saturday, plant the gun and lay down a few more clues like the anonymous call to Metro. That call was what was supposed to put the finger on Luke Goshen. Not the fingerprints. That was just luck for them. Anyway, that's getting ahead of the story. Veronica drives the Rolls and Powers follows. To the clearing over the Bowl. She pops the trunk and Powers leans in and does the job. Or maybe he puts one cap in Tony and he makes Veronica do the second. That way they're partners for good, partners in blood.'

Billets nodded, a serious look on her face.

'It seems kind of risky. What if he had to take a radio call? The whole plan would go down the drain.'

'We thought of that and Jerry checked with the watch office. Gomez was the CO Friday night. He says he remembers that Powers had such a busy shift he didn't take a dinner break until ten. He doesn't recall hearing from him until just before end of the watch.'

Billets nodded again.

'What about the shoe prints recovered? Are they his?'

'Powers got lucky there,' Edgar said. 'He's wearing brand-new boots in there. Looks like he maybe just bought 'em today.'

'Shit!'

'Yeah,' Bosch said. 'We figure he saw the shoe prints on the table last night at the Cat and Fiddle. He went out and got new ones today.'

'Oh man . . .'

'Well, maybe there's still a chance he didn't get rid of the old ones. We're working on a search warrant for his place. Oh, and our luck ain't so bad, either. Jerry, tell her about the spray.'

Edgar leaned forward on the table.

'I went back to the supply post, took a look at the sheet. On Sunday Powers signed out an OC cartridge. Only I then went and looked at the fifty-one list in the watch loo's office. No use-of-force reported by Powers in this deployment period.'

'So,' Billets said, 'he somehow used his pepper spray, because he had to get a refill cartridge but he never reported using the spray to his watch commander.'

'Right.'

Billets thought about things for a few moments before speaking again.

'Okay,' she said, 'what you've come up with quickly is all good stuff. But it's not enough. It's a circumstantial case and most of this can be explained away. Even if you could prove he and the widow have been meeting, it doesn't prove murder. The fingerprint on the trunk can be explained by sloppy work at the crime scene. Who knows, maybe that's all it really was.'

'I doubt it,' Bosch said.

'Well, your doubts aren't good enough. Where do we go from here?'

'We still have some things in the fire. Jerry's going for a warrant based on what we've got so far. If we get inside Powers's house, maybe we find the shoes, maybe we find something else. We'll see. I also have an angle in Vegas working. We figure that for them to have pulled this off, Powers had to have followed Tony over there once or twice, you know, to know about Goshen and pick him to hang it all on. If we're lucky, Powers would've wanted to stay right on Tony. That would mean staying at the Mirage. You can't stay there without a trail. You can pay cash but you've got to give a legit credit card imprint to cover room charges, phone calls, things like that. In other words, you can't register under any name you don't have on a credit card. I've got a guy checking.'

'Okay, it's a start,' Billets said.

She nodded her head, cupped a hand over her mouth and lapsed into a contemplative silence for a long moment.

'What it all comes down to is that we need to break him, don't we?' she finally asked.

Bosch nodded.

'Probably. Unless we get lucky with the warrant.'

'You're not going to break him. He's a cop, he knows the angles, he knows the rules of evidence.'

'We'll see.'

She looked at her watch. Bosch looked at his and saw it was now one o'clock.

'We're in trouble,' Billets said solemnly. 'We won't be able to contain this much past dawn. After that I will have to make proper notification of what we've done and what we've got going. If that happens, you can count on us not being involved, and worse.'

Bosch leaned forward.

'Go back home, Lieutenant,' he said. 'You were never here. Let us have the night. Come back in at nine tomorrow. Bring a DA back with you if you want. Make sure it's somebody who will go to the edge with you. If you don't know one, I can call somebody. But give us till nine. Eight hours. Then you come in and we either have the complete package tied up for you or you go ahead and do what you have to do.'

She looked carefully at each one of them, took a deep breath and exhaled slowly.

'Good luck,' she said.

She nodded, got up and left them there.

Outside the door to interview room three, Bosch paused and composed his thoughts. He knew that everything would turn on what happened inside the room. He had to break Powers and that would be no easy task. Powers was a cop. He knew all the tricks. But somehow Bosch had to find a weakness he could exploit until the big man went down. He knew it was going to be a brutal match. He blew out his breath and opened the door.

Bosch stepped into the interview room, took the chair directly across from Powers and spread out the two sheets of paper he carried with him in front of Powers.

'Okay, Powers, I'm here to tell you what's what.'

'You can save it, asshole. The only one I want to talk to is my lawyer.'

'Well, that's what I'm here for. Why don't you take it easy and we'll talk about it?'

'Take it easy? You people arrest me, hook me up like a goddamn criminal and then leave me in here for a fucking hour and a half while you sit out there and figure out how fucked up this is, and you want me to take it easy? What planet are you on, Bosch? I'm not taking anything easy. Now cut me loose or give me the goddamn phone!'

'Well, that's the problem, isn't it? Deciding whether to book you or cut you loose. That's why I came in, Powers. I thought maybe you could help us out on that.'

Powers didn't appear to pick up on that. His eyes dropped to the center of the table and they were working – small, quick movements, looking for the angles.

'This is what is what,' Bosch said. 'If I book you now, then we call the lawyer and we both know that is going to be that. No lawyer is gonna let his client talk to the cops. We'll just have to go to court and you know what that means. You'll be suspended, no pay. We'll go for no bail and you'll sit in the can nine, ten months and then maybe it gets straightened out in your favor. And maybe not. Meantime, you're all over the front page. Your mother, father, neighbors . . . well, you know how it goes.'

Bosch took out a cigarette and put it in his mouth. He didn't light it and he didn't offer one to Powers. He remembered offering one to the big cop at the crime scene and being turned down.

'The alternative to that,' he continued, 'is that we sit here and try to get this straightened out right now. You've got two forms there in front of you.

The good thing about dealing with a cop like this is I don't really need to explain this stuff to you. The first one's a rights form. You know what that is. You sign that you understand your rights and then you make your choice. Talk to me or call your lawyer after we book you. The second form is the attorney waiver.'

Powers stared silently down at the pages and Bosch put a pen down on the table.

'I'll take the cuffs off when you're ready to sign,' Bosch said. 'See, now the bad thing about dealing with a cop is that I can't bluff you. You know the game. You know if you sign that waiver and talk to me, you'll either talk yourself out of this or right into it . . . I can give you more time to think about it, if you want.'

'I don't need any more time,' he said. 'Take off the cuffs.'

Bosch got up and went around behind Powers.

'You right or left?'

'Right.'

There was barely enough room between the back of the big man and the wall to work on the cuffs. It was a dangerous position to be in with most suspects. But Powers was a cop and he probably knew that the moment he became violent was the moment he lost any chance of getting out of this room and back to his life. He also had to assume someone was watching and ready behind the glass in room four. Bosch unhooked the right cuff and closed it around one of the metal slats of the chair.

Powers scribbled signatures across both forms. Bosch tried to give no indication of his excitement. Powers was making a mistake. Bosch took the pen from him and put it in his pocket.

'Put your arm behind you.'

'Come on, Bosch. Treat me like a human. If we're going to talk, let's talk.'

'Put your arm behind you.'

Powers did as he was told and blew out his breath in frustration. Bosch recuffed his wrists through the metal slat at the back of the chair and then took his seat again. He cleared his throat, going over the last details in his mind. He knew his mission here. He had to make Powers believe he had the edge, that he had a chance to get out. If he believed that, then he might start talking. If he started talking, Bosch thought he could win the fight.

'Okay,' Bosch said. 'I'm going to lay it out for you. If you can convince me that we have it wrong, then you'll be out of here before the sun's up.'

'That's all I want.'

'Powers, we know you have a relationship with Veronica Aliso predating her husband's death. We know you followed him to Vegas on at least two occasions prior to the killing.'

Powers kept his eyes on the table in front of him. But Bosch was able to read them like the needles of a polygraph machine. There had been a slight tremor in the pupils when Bosch mentioned Las Vegas.

'That's right,' Bosch said. 'We've got the records from the Mirage. That was careless, Powers, leaving a record like that. We can put you in Vegas with Tony Aliso.'

'So I like goin' to Vegas, big deal. Tony Aliso was there? Wow, what a coincidence. From what I heard, he went there a lot. What else you got?'

'We've got your print, Powers. Fingerprint. Inside the car. You got a refill of pepper spray on Sunday, but you never filed a use-of-force report explaining how you used it.'

'Accidental discharge. I didn't file a use-of-force because there wasn't any. You haven't got shit. My fingerprint? You're right, you've probably got prints. But I was in that car, asshole. I'm the one who found the body, remember? This is a joke, man. I'm thinking I better just get my lawyer in here and take my chances. No DA is going to touch this bullshit with a ten-foot pole.'

Bosch ignored the baiting and went on.

'And last but not least, we have your little climb down the hill tonight. Your story is for shit, Powers. You went down there to look for Aliso's suit bag because you knew it was there and you thought it had something you and the widow overlooked before. About a half million dollars. The only question I really have is whether she called you up and told you or if that was you in her house this morning when we dropped by.'

Bosch saw the pupils jump again slightly but then they went flat.

'Like I said, I'll take that lawyer now.'

'I guess you're just the errand boy, right? She told you to go and get the money while she waited at the mansion.'

Powers started laughing in a fake way.

'I like that, Bosch. Errand boy. Too bad I barely know the woman. But it's a good try. Good try. I like you, too, Bosch, but I gotta tell you something.'

He leaned across the table and lowered his voice.

'I ever run across you again on the outside, you know, when it's just me and you, head to head, I'm going to seriously fuck you up.'

He straightened up again and nodded. Bosch smiled.

'You know, I don't think I was sure until now. But now I'm sure. You did it, Powers. You're the man. And there is never going to be an outside for you. Never. So tell me, whose idea was it? Was she the first one to bring it up or was that you?'

Powers stared sullenly down at the table and shook his head.

'Let me see if I can figure it out,' Bosch said. 'I guess you went up there to that big house and saw all that they had, the money, maybe heard about Tony and his Rolls, and it just went on from there. I'm betting it was your idea, Powers. But I think she knew you would come up with it. See, she's a smart woman. She knew you would come up with it. And she waited . . .

'And you know what? We've got nothing on her. Nothing. She played you perfect, man. Right down the line. She's going to do the walk and *you*' – he pointed at Powers's chest – 'are going to do the time. Is that how you want it?'

Powers leaned back, a bemused smile on his face.

'You don't get it, do you?' Powers said. 'You're the errand boy here, but look at yourself. You've got nothin' to deliver. Look at what you've got. You can't tie me to Aliso. I found the body, man. I opened the car. If you found a print, then that's when I left it. All the rest is a bunch of bullshit adding up to nothing. You go in to see a prosecutor with that, they're going to laugh your ass out onto Temple Street. So go get me the phone, errand boy, and let's get it on. Just go get me the phone.'

'Not yet, Powers,' Bosch said. 'Not just yet.'

Bosch sat at his spot at the homicide table with his head down on his folded arms. An empty coffee cup was near his elbow. A cigarette he had perched on the edge of the table had burned down to the butt, leaving one more scar on the old wood.

Bosch was alone. It was almost six and there was just the hint of dawn's light coming through the windows that ran high along the east wall of the room. He'd gone at it for more than four hours with Powers and had gained no ground. He hadn't even made a dent in Powers's cool demeanor. The first rounds had assuredly gone to the big patrol cop.

Bosch wasn't asleep, though. He was simply resting and waiting and his thoughts remained focused on Powers. Bosch had no doubts. He was sure that he had the right man sitting handcuffed in the interview room. What minimal evidence they had certainly pointed to Powers. But it was more than the evidence that convinced him. It was experience and gut instinct. Bosch believed an innocent man would have been scared, not smug as Powers had been. An innocent man would not have taunted Bosch. And so what still remained now was to take away that smugness and break him. Bosch was tired but still felt up to the task. The only thing that worried him was time. Time was against him.

Bosch raised his head and looked at his watch. Billets would be back in three hours. He picked up the empty cup, used his palm to push the dead cigarette and its ashes into it and dropped it into the trash can under the table. He stood up, lit another cigarette and took a walk down the aisle between the crime tables. He tried to clear his mind, to get ready for the next round.

He thought about paging Edgar to see if he and Rider had found anything yet, anything at all that could help, but decided against it. They knew that time was important. They would have either called or come back if they had something.

As he stood at the far end of the squad room and these thoughts travelled through his mind, his eyes fell on the sex crimes table, and he realized after a moment that he was looking at a Polaroid photo of the girl who had come into the station with her mother on Friday to report that she had been raped. The photo was on the top of a stack of Polaroids that were paper-clipped to the outside of the case envelope. Detective Mary Cantu had left it on the top of her pile for Monday. Without thinking about it, Bosch pulled the stack of photos from beneath the clip and began to look through them. The girl had been badly mistreated and the bruises documented on her body by Cantu's camera were a depressing testament to all that was wrong with the city. Bosch always found it easier to deal with victims who were no longer living. The live ones haunted him because they could never be consoled. Not fully. They were forever left with the question why.

Sometimes Bosch thought of his city as some kind of vast drain that pulled all bad things toward a spot where they swirled around in a deep concentration. It was a place where it seemed the good people were often outnumbered by the bad. The creeps and schemers, the rapists and killers. It was a place that could easily produce someone like Powers. Too easily.

Bosch put the photos back under the clip, embarrassed by his thoughtless voyeurism of the girl's pain. He went back to the homicide table, picked up the phone and dialed his home number. It was nearly twenty-four hours since he had been to his house, and his hope was that Eleanor Wish would answer – he had left the key under the mat – or there might be a message from her. After three rings the line was picked up and he heard his own voice on tape tell himself to leave a message. He punched in his code to check for messages and the machine told him he had none.

He stood there a long moment thinking about Eleanor, the phone still at his ear, when suddenly he heard her voice.

'Harry, is that you?'

'Eleanor?'

'I'm here, Harry.'

'Why didn't you answer?'

'I didn't think it would be for me.'

'When did you get there?'

'Last night. I've been waiting for you. Thanks for leaving the key.'

'You're welcome . . . Eleanor, where'd you go?'

There was a beat of silence before she answered.

'I went back to Vegas. I needed to get my car . . . clear out my bank account, things like that. Where have you been all night?'

'Working. We have a new suspect. We're holding him here. Did you go by your apartment?'

'No. There was no reason to. I just did what I had to do and drove back.'

'I'm sorry if I woke you.'

'That's okay. I was worried about where you were, but I didn't want to call you there in case you were in the middle of something.'

Bosch wanted to ask her what came next for them, but he felt such a sense of happiness that she was there in his home that he didn't dare to ruin the moment.

'I don't know how much longer I'll be tied up,' he said.

Bosch heard the heavy doors in the station's rear hallway open and bang shut. Footsteps were coming toward the squad room.

'Do you have to go?' Eleanor asked.

'Um . . .'

Edgar and Rider walked into the squad room. Rider carried a brown evidence bag with something heavy in it. Edgar carried a closed cardboard box across which someone had stenciled *Xmas* with a Magic Marker. He also had a broad smile on his face.

'Yeah,' Bosch said, 'I think I better go.'

'Okay, Harry, I'll see you.'

'You'll be there?'

'I'll be here.'

'Okay, Eleanor, I'll see you as soon as I can.'

He hung up and looked up at his two partners. Edgar was still smiling.

'We got your Christmas present here, Harry,' Edgar said. 'We got Powers right here in this box.'

'You got the boots?'

'No. No boots. We got better than boots.'

'Show me.'

Edgar lifted the lid off the box. Off the top he took out a manila envelope. He then tilted the box so that Bosch could look in. Bosch whistled.

'Merry Christmas,' Edgar said.

'You count it?' Bosch asked, his eyes still on the stacks of currency with rubber bands around them.

'Each bundle has a number on it,' Rider said. 'You add them all up, it equals four hundred eighty thousand. It looks like it's everything.'

'Not a bad present, eh Harry?' Edgar said excitedly.

'No. Where was it?'

'Attic crawl space,' Edgar said. 'One of the last places we looked. Box was just sitting there in front of me as soon as I stuck my head up.'

Bosch nodded.

'Okay, what else?'

'Found these under the mattress.'

From the envelope Edgar withdrew a stack of photos. They were six by four in size and each had the date of the photograph digitally printed on the bottom left corner. Bosch put them on the table in front of them and looked through them, carefully picking them up by the corners. He hoped Edgar had handled them the same way.

The first photo was of Tony Aliso getting into a car at the valet stand in front of the Mirage. The next was of him walking to the door of Dolly's talking to the man Aliso knew as Luke Goshen. It was dark outside in these shots and they were taken from a distance, but the neon-glutted entrance of the club was lit as brightly as daylight and Aliso and Goshen were easily recognizable.

Then there were photos from the same location but the date at the bottom corner had changed. They showed a young woman leaving the club and walking to Aliso's car. Bosch recognized her. It was Layla. There were also pictures of Tony and Layla poolside at the Mirage. The last shot was of Tony leaning his deeply tanned body over Layla's lounge chair and kissing her on the mouth.

Bosch looked up at Edgar and Rider. Edgar was smiling again. Rider wasn't.

'Just like we thought,' Edgar said. 'He cased this guy over there in Vegas. That shows he had the knowledge to set this whole thing up. Him and the widow. We got 'em, Harry. This shows premeditation, lying in wait, the works. We got 'em both, nine ways to Sunday.'

'Maybe.' He looked at Rider. 'What's up with you, Kiz?'

She shook her head.

'I don't know. It just seems too easy. The place was very clean. No old boots, no sign that Veronica ever even set foot in that place. Then we find these so easy. It was like we were supposed to find it all. I mean, why would he take the time to get rid of the boots but leave the photos under the mattress? I can see him wanting to hang on to the money, but putting it in the attic seems pretty lame.'

She moved her hand toward the photos and the cash in a dismissive gesture. Bosch nodded his agreement and leaned back in his chair.

'I think you're right,' he said. 'He's not that stupid.'

He thought about the similarity to the gun being planted on Goshen. That, too, turned out to be too easy.

'I think it's a setup,' Bosch said. 'Veronica did this. He took the photos for her. He probably told her to destroy them, but she didn't. She hung on to

501

them just in case. She probably snuck them back in under his bed and put the cash up in the attic. Was it easy to get to?'

'Easy enough,' Rider said. 'Fold-down ladder.'

'Wait a minute, why would she set him up?' Edgar asked.

'Not from the start,' Bosch said. 'It was like a fall-back position. If things started to go wrong, if we got too close, she had Powers out there ready to take the fall. Maybe when she sent Powers after the suitcase she went to his place with the photos and the cash. Who knows when it started? But I bet when I tell Powers we found this stuff in his house, his eyes are going to pop. Whaddaya got in the bag, Kiz, the camera?'

She nodded and put the bag on the table without opening it.

'Nikon with a telephoto on it, credit card receipt for his purchase of it.'

Bosch nodded and his thoughts strayed a bit. He was trying to think about how he was going to work the photos and money with Powers. It was their shot at breaking him. It had to be played right.

'Hold on, hold on,' Edgar said, a look of confusion on his face. 'I still don't get this. What makes you say it was a setup? Maybe he was holding the cash and the photos and they were going to split it all after the heat died down. Why does it have to be that she set him up?'

Bosch looked at Rider and then back at Edgar.

''Cause Kiz is right. It's too easy.'

'Not if he thought we didn't have a clue, if he thought he was clear right up to the moment we jumped out of the bushes up there in the woods.'

Bosch shook his head.

'I don't know. I don't think he would have played it the way he did when I was just talking to him. Not if he knew he had this stuff back at his place. I go with it being a setup. She's putting it all on him. We pull her in and she'll feed us some story about the guy being obsessed with her. Maybe, if she's any kind of actress, she tells us, yes, she had an affair with him but then she broke it off. But he wouldn't go away. He killed her old man so he could have her all to himself.'

Bosch leaned back and looked at them, waiting for their response.

'I think it's good,' Rider said. 'It could work.'

'Except we don't believe it,' Bosch said.

'So what's she get out of this?' Edgar asked, refusing to drop his disagreement. 'She's givin' up the money puttin' it in his pad. What's that leave her?'

'The house, the cars, insurance,' Bosch said. 'Whatever's left of the company – and the chance to get away.'

But it was a weak answer and he knew it. A half million dollars was a lot of cash to use to set somebody up. It was the one flaw in the theory he had just spun.

'She got rid of her husband,' Rider said. 'Maybe that was all that was important to her.'

'He'd been screwing around on her for years,' Edgar said. 'Why now? What was different this time?'

'I don't know,' Rider said. 'But there was something different or something else we don't know about. That's what we have to find out.'

'Yeah, well, good luck,' Edgar said.

'I've got an idea,' Bosch said. 'If anyone knows what that something else is, it's Powers. I want to try to scam him and I think I know how. Kiz, you still got that tape, the one with Veronica in it?'

'*Casualty of Desire?* Yeah. It's in my drawer.'

'Go get it and set it up in the lieutenant's office. I'm going to grab some more coffee and I'll meet you there.'

Bosch stepped into interview room three with the box of cash turned so that the side that said *Xmas* on it was held against his chest. He hoped it looked like any common cardboard box. He watched Powers for a sign of recognition and got none. Powers was sitting just as Bosch had left him. Ramrod straight, his arms behind him as if by choice. He looked at Bosch with deadpan eyes that were ready and waiting for the next go-round. Bosch put the box on the floor where it would be shielded from view, pulled out the chair and sat across from him again. He then reached down, opened the box and took out a tape recorder and a file folder. He put them on the table in plain sight.

'I told you, Bosch, no taping. If you got the camera on the other side of the glass going, then you're ripping off my rights, too.'

'No camera, no tape, Powers. This is just to play you something, that's all. Now, where were we?'

'We were to the point of put up or shut up. You cut me loose or you get my lawyer in here.'

'Well, actually, a couple of things have come up. I thought you might want to know about them first. You know, before you make a decision like that.'

'Fuck that. I'm through with this shit. Get me the phone.'

'Do you own a camera, Powers?'

'I said get – a camera? What about it?'

'Do you own a camera? It's a pretty straightforward question.'

'Yes. Everybody owns a camera. What about it?'

Bosch studied him for a moment. He could feel the momentum and control start to maybe shift just a bit. It was coming across the table from Powers. He could feel it. Bosch played a thin smile on his face. He wanted Powers to know that from this point on it was slipping away from him.

'Did you take the camera with you when you went to Vegas last March?'

'I don't know. Maybe. I take it on all my vacations. Didn't know it was a crime. The fucking legislature, what will they think of next?'

Bosch let him have his smile but didn't return it.

'Is that what you called it?' he said quietly. 'A vacation?'

'Yeah, that's exactly what I called it.'

'That's funny, because that's not what Veronica is calling it.'

'I don't know anything about that or her.'

His eyes momentarily looked away from Bosch. It was the first time, and again Bosch felt the balance shifting. He was playing it right. He felt it. Things were shifting.

'Sure you know about it, Powers. And you know her pretty good, too. She just told us all about it. She's in the other room right now. Turns out she was weaker than I thought. My money had been on you. You know the saying, the bigger they are the harder they fall, all of that. I thought you'd be the one but it was her. Edgar and Rider broke her down a little while ago.

Amazing how crime scene photos can work on somebody's guilty conscience. She told us everything, Powers. Everything.'

'You're so full of bullshit, Bosch, and it's getting pretty old. Where's the phone?'

'This is how she tells it. You—'

'I don't want to hear it.'

'You met her when you went up there that night to take the burglary report. One thing led to another and pretty soon you two were having a little romance. An affair to remember. Only she came to her senses and broke it off. She still loved ol' Tony. She knew he travelled a lot, strayed a lot, but she was used to that. She needed him. So she cut you off. Only, and this is according to her, you wouldn't be cut off. You kept after her, calling her, following her when she'd leave the estate up there. It was getting scary. I mean, what could she do? Go to Tony and say this guy I had an affair with is following me all the time? She—'

'This is so much bullshit, Bosch. It's a joke!'

'Then you started following Tony. You see, he was your problem. He was in the way. So you did your homework. You followed him to Vegas and you caught him in the act. You knew just what he was up to and how to put him down in a way that we'd go down the wrong path. Trunk music, they call it. Only you couldn't carry the tune, Powers. We're on to you. With her help, we're going to put you down.'

Powers was looking down at the table. The skin around his eyes and his jawline had drawn tight.

'This is so much crap,' he said without looking up. 'I'm tired of listening to it and to you. She's not in the other room. She's sitting up there in that big house on the hill. This is the oldest trick in the book.'

Powers looked up and a twisted smile cracked his face.

'You try to pull this shit on a cop? I can't believe it. This is really weak, man. You're weak. You're embarrassing yourself here.'

Bosch reached over to the tape recorder and pushed the play button. Veronica Aliso's voice filled the tiny room.

'It was him. He's crazy. I couldn't stop him until it was too late. Then I couldn't tell anyone because it . . . it would look like I—'

Bosch turned it off.

'That's enough,' he said. 'It's out of line for me to even play *that* for you. But I thought, cop to cop, you should know where you stand.'

Bosch silently watched Powers as he did a slow burn. Bosch could see the anger boiling up behind his eyes. He didn't seem to move a muscle, yet he seemed all at once to become as hard as a stack of lumber. He finally was able to hold himself back, though, and compose himself.

'It's just her word,' he said in a quiet voice. 'There's no corroboration of anything. It's a fantasy, Bosch. Her word against mine.'

'It could be. Except we have these.'

Bosch opened the file and threw the stack of photos in front of Powers. Then he reached across and carefully fanned them on the table so they could be seen and recognized.

'That backs up a good part of her story, don't you think?'

Bosch watched as Powers studied the photographs. Once again Powers

504

seemed to go to the edge with an interior rage, but once more he contained it.

'It doesn't back up shit,' he said. 'She could've taken these herself. Anybody could have. Just because she gives you a stack of . . . She's got you people wrapped up, doesn't she? You're buying every line she feeds you.'

'Maybe that would be so, only she didn't give us the photos.'

Bosch reached into the file again and pulled out a copy of the search warrant. He reached over and put it on top of the photos.

'Five hours ago we faxed that to Judge Warren Lambert at his home in the Palisades. He faxed it back signed. Edgar and Rider have been in your little Hollywood bungalow most of the night. Among the items seized was a Nikon camera with telephoto lens. And these photos. They were under your mattress, Powers.'

He paused here to let it all sink in behind Powers's darkening eyes.

'Oh, and one other thing we found.' Bosch reached down and brought the box up. 'This was in the attic with the Christmas stuff.'

He dumped the contents of the box on the table and the stacks of cash tumbled every which way, some falling to the floor. Bosch shook the box to make sure it had all come out and then dropped it to the floor. He looked at Powers. His eyes were wild, darting over the thick bundles. Bosch knew he had him. And he also knew in his gut that he had Veronica Aliso to thank for that.

'Now, personally, I don't think you are this stupid,' Bosch said quietly. 'You know, to keep the pictures and all this cash right in your house. Of course, I've seen crazier things in my time. But if I was betting, I'd bet that you didn't know all of this was there because you didn't put it there. But, hey, either way it works fine for me. We've got you and we'll clear this one, that's all I care about. It would be nice to grab her, too, but that's okay. We'll need her for you. With the photos and her story and all the other stuff we've talked about here, I think we got you for the murder easy. There's also lying-in-wait to tack on. That makes it a special circumstances case, Powers. You're looking at one of two things. The needle or LWP.'

He pronounced the last acronym *el-wop*, knowing that any cop, just as any criminal in the system, would know it meant life without parole.

'Anyway,' Bosch continued, 'I guess I'll go get that phone brought in here so you can call your lawyer. Better make it a good one. And none of those grandstanders from the O.J. case. You need to get yourself a lawyer who does his best work outside of the courtroom. A negotiator.'

He stood up and turned to the door. With his hand on the knob he looked back at Powers.

'You know, I feel bad, Powers. You being a cop and all, I was sort of hoping you'd catch the break instead of her. I feel like we're hitting the wrong person with the hammer. But I guess that's life in the big city. Somebody's got to be hit with it.'

He turned back to the door and opened it.

'*Bitch!*' Powers said with a quiet forcefulness.

Then he whispered something under his breath that Bosch couldn't hear. Bosch looked back at him. He knew enough not to say a word.

'It was her idea,' Powers said. 'All of it. She conned me and now she's conning you.'

505

Bosch waited a beat but there was nothing else.

'Are you saying you want to talk to me?'

'Yeah, Bosch, have a seat. Maybe we can work something out.'

At nine Bosch sat in the lieutenant's office, Billets behind the desk, bringing her up to date. He had an empty Styrofoam cup in his hand, but he didn't drop it in the trash can because he needed something to remind him that he needed more coffee. He was beat tired and the lines beneath his eyes were so pronounced they almost hurt. His mouth tasted sour from all the coffee and cigarettes. He'd eaten nothing but candy bars in the last twenty hours and his stomach was finally protesting. But he was a happy man. He had won the last round with Powers and in this kind of battle the last round was the only one that mattered.

'So,' Billets said, 'he told you everything?'

'His version of it,' Bosch said. 'He lays everything on her and that's to be expected. Remember, he thinks she's in the other room laying everything on him. So he's making her out to be the big bad black widow, like he never had an impure thought in his life until he ran across her.'

He brought the cup up to his mouth but then realized it was empty.

'But once we get her in here and she knows he's talking, we'll probably get her version,' he said.

'When did Jerry and Kiz leave?'

Bosch looked at his watch.

'About forty minutes ago. They should be back with her any time.'

'Why didn't you go up to get her?'

'I don't know. I figured I took Powers, they should have her. Spread it around, you know?'

'Better be careful. You keep acting like that and you'll lose your rep as a hardass.'

Bosch smiled and looked down into his cup.

'So what's the gist of his story?' Billets asked.

'The gist is pretty much how we figured it. He went up there to take a burglary report that day and it went from there. He says she put the moves on him and next thing you know they had a thing going. He started taking more and more patrol swings through the neighborhood and she was stopping by his bungalow in the mornings after Tony went to work or while he was in Vegas. The way he describes, she was reeling him in. The sex was good and exotic. He was hooked up pretty good.'

'Then she asked him to tail Tony.'

'Right. That first trip Powers took to Vegas was a straight job. She asked him to tail Tony. He did and he came back with a bunch of photos of Tony and the girl and a lot of questions about who Tony was meeting with over there and why. He wasn't stupid. He could tell Tony was into something. He says Veronica filled him in, knew every detail, knew all the OC guys by name. She also told him how much money was involved. That was when the plan came together. She told Powers that Tony had to go, that it would be just them afterward, them and a lot of money. She told him Tony had been skimming. Skimming off the skim. For years. There was at least a couple million in the pot plus whatever they took off Tony when they put him down.'

506

Bosch stood up and continued the story while pacing in front of her desk. He was too tired to sit for very long without being overcome with fatigue.

'Anyway, that was what the second trip was for. Powers went over and watched Tony one more time. It was research. He also tailed the guy Tony made the pickups from. Luke Goshen, who he obviously had no idea was an agent. They decided Goshen would be the patsy and worked out the plan to make it look like a mob hit. Trunk music.'

'It's pretty complicated.'

'Yeah, that it is. He says the planning was all hers, and I kind of think he might be telling the truth there. You ask me, Powers is smart but not that smart. This whole thing was Veronica's plan and he became a willing player. Only she had a backdoor built into it that Powers didn't know about.'

'He was the backdoor.'

'Yeah. She set him up to take the fall, but only if we got too close. He said he'd given her a key to his place. It's a bungalow over on Sierra Bonita. She must've gone over there sometime this week, shoved the photos under the mattress and stuck the box of money in the attic. Smart woman. Nice setup. When Jerry and Kiz get her in here, I know just what she'll say. She's going to say it was all him, that he became infatuated with her, that they had an affair and that she broke it off. He went ahead and knocked off her husband. When she realized what had happened, she couldn't say anything. He forced her to go along with it. She had no choice. He was a cop and he told her he could pin it all on her if she didn't go along.'

'It's a good story. In fact, it still might work with a jury. She could walk on this.'

'Maybe. We still have some things to do.'

'What about the skim?'

'Good question. Nothing like the kind of money he's talking about showed up on Aliso's bank accounts. Powers said she said it was in a safe deposit box but she never told him where. It's got to be somewhere. We'll find it.'

'If it exists.'

'I think it does. She planted a half million in Powers's place to put him in the frame. That's a lot of money to spend on setting him up, unless you happen to have a couple million more stashed someplace. That's what we—'

Bosch looked through the glass into the squad room. Edgar and Rider were walking towards the lieutenant's office. Veronica Aliso was not with them. They came into the office with urgent looks on their faces and Bosch knew what they were going to say.

'She's gone,' Edgar said.

Bosch and Billets just stared at them.

'Looks like she split last night,' Edgar said. 'Her cars are still there but there was nobody at the house. We slipped in a back door and it's empty, man.'

'She take her clothes, jewelry?' Bosch asked.

'Doesn't look like it. She's just gone.'

'You check the gate?'

'Yeah, we checked at the gate. She had two visitors yesterday. First was a courier at four-fifteen. Legal Eagle Messenger Service. Guy was there about five minutes, in and out. Then a visitor last night. Late. Guy gave the name John Galvin. She had already called the gate and given the same name and told them to let him through when he showed up. They took his plate down and we ran it. It's Hertz out of Vegas. We'll put a call in. Anyway, Galvin stayed until one this morning. Just about the time we were in the woods hooking up Powers, he split. She probably went with him.'

'We called the guard on duty at the time,' Rider said. 'He couldn't remember if Galvin left alone or not. He doesn't specifically remember seeing Mrs Aliso last night, but she could have been down in the backseat.'

'Do we know who her attorney is?' Billets asked.

'Yes,' Rider said, 'Neil Denton, Century City.'

'Okay, Jerry, you work the trace on the Hertz rental and, Kiz, you try to run down Denton and see if you can find out what was so important that he had to messenger it over to her on Saturday.'

'All right,' Edgar said. 'But I got a bad feeling. I think she's in the wind.'

'Well, then we have to go into the wind to find her,' Billets said. 'Go to it.'

Edgar and Rider went back out to the homicide table and Bosch stood silent for a few moments, thinking about this latest development.

'Should we have put people on her?' Billets asked.

'Well, looking back, it seems that way. But we were off the books. We didn't have the people. Besides, we didn't really have anything on her until a couple hours ago.'

Billets nodded, a pained expression on her face.

'If they don't get a line on her in the next fifteen minutes, put it out on the air.'

'Right.'

'Listen, getting back to Powers, you think he's holding anything back?'

'Hard to say. Probably. There's still the question about why this time.'

'What do you mean?'

'I mean Aliso had been going over to Vegas for years and bringing back suitcases full of money. He'd been skimming for years, according to Powers, and also had been having his share of the women over there. Veronica knew all of this. She had to. So what was it that made her do it now, rather than last year or next year?'

'Maybe she just got fed up. Maybe this was just the right time. Powers came along and it clicked.'

'Maybe. I asked Powers and he said he didn't know. But I think maybe he was holding back. I'm going to take another run at him.'

Billets didn't respond.

'There's still some sort of secret we don't know about,' Bosch continued. 'There's something there. I'm hoping she'll tell it. If we find her.'

Billets dismissed it with a wave of her hand.

'You have Powers on tape?' she asked.

'Audio and video. Kiz was watching in room four. As soon as he said he wanted to talk she started it all rolling.'

'Did you advise him again? On the tape?'

'Yeah, it's all on there. He's sealed up pretty good. You want to watch it, I'll get the tape.'

'No. I don't even want to look at him if I can help it. You didn't promise him anything, did you?'

Bosch was about to answer but stopped. There was the sound of muffled yelling that he could tell was coming from Powers, still sequestered in room three. He looked through the glass of the lieutenant's office and saw Edgar get up from the homicide table and go down the hall to check it out.

'He probably wants his lawyer now,' Bosch said. 'Well, it's a little late for that . . . Anyway, no, I made no promises. I did tell him I'd talk to the DA about dropping special circs, but that's going to be tough. With what he told me in there, we can take our pick. Conspiracy to commit, lying in wait, murder for hire maybe.'

'I guess I should get a DA in here.'

'Yeah. If you don't have anyone in mind or anybody you owe a hot case to, put in a request for Roger Goff. This is his kind of case and I've owed him one for a while. He won't blow it.'

'I know Roger. I'll ask for him . . . I have to call out the brass, too. It's not every day you get to call a deputy chief and tell him not only have your people been running an investigation they were specifically told to stay away from, but that they've arrested a cop to boot. And for murder, no less.'

Bosch smiled. He would not relish having to make such a call.

'It's really going to hit the fan this time,' he said. 'One more black eye for the department. By the way, they didn't seize any of it because it's not related to this case, but Jerry and Kiz found some scary stuff in Powers's place. Nazi paraphernalia, white-power stuff. You might alert the brass about that, so they can do with it what they want.'

'Thanks for telling me. I'll talk to Irving. I'm sure he won't want that to see the light of day.'

Edgar leaned in through the open door.

'Powers says he's got to take a leak and can't hold it any longer.'

He was looking at Billets.

'Well, take him,' she said.

'Keep him hooked,' Bosch added.

'How's he gonna piss, his hands behind his back? Don't be expecting me to be taking it out for him. No way.'

Billets laughed.

'Just move the cuffs to the front,' Bosch said. 'Give me a second to finish in here and I'll be right there.'

'Okay, I'll be in three.'

Edgar left and Bosch watched him through the glass as he walked to the hallway leading to the interview rooms. Bosch looked back at Billets, who was still smiling at Edgar's comical protest. Bosch put a serious look on his face.

'You know, you can use me when you make that call.'

'What do you mean?'

'I mean, if you want to say you didn't know about any of this until I called you this morning with the bad news, that's cool with me.'

'Don't be ridiculous. We cleared a murder and got a killer cop off the street. If they can't see that the good in this outweighs the bad, then . . . well, fuck 'em if they can't take a joke.'

Bosch smiled and nodded.

'You're cool, Lieutenant.'

'Thanks.'

'Anytime.'

'And it's Grace.'

'Right. Grace.'

Bosch was thinking about how much he liked Billets as he walked down the short hallway to the interview rooms and into the open door of room three. Edgar was just closing the cuffs on Powers's wrists. His hands were in front of him now.

'Do me a favor, Bosch,' Powers said. 'Let me use the can in the front hallway.'

'What for?'

'So nobody'll see me in the back. I don't want anybody to see me like this. Besides, you might have a problem if people don't like what they see.'

Bosch nodded. Powers had a point. If they took him to the locker room, then all the cops in the watch office would likely see them and there would be questions, maybe even anger from some of the cops who didn't know what was going on. The bathroom in the front hallway was a public rest room, but this early on a Sunday morning it would likely be empty and they could take Powers in and out of there without being seen.

'Okay, let's go,' Bosch said. 'To the front.'

They walked him past the front counter and down the hallway past the administration offices, which were empty and closed for the day. While Bosch stayed with Powers in the hall, Edgar checked the rest room out.

'It's empty,' he said, holding the door open from inside.

Bosch followed Powers in and the big cop went to the furthest of three urinals. Bosch stayed by the door and Edgar took a position on the other side of Powers by the row of sinks. When Powers was finished at the urinal, he stepped toward one of the sinks. As he walked, Bosch saw that his right shoelace was untied and so did Edgar.

'Tie your shoe, Powers,' Edgar said. 'You trip and fall and break your pretty face, I don't want any cryin' 'bout *po*-lice brutality.'

Powers stopped and looked down at the shoelace on the floor and then at Edgar.

'Sure,' he said.

Powers first washed his hands, used a paper towel to dry them and then brought his right foot up on the edge of the sink to tie his shoe.

'New shoes,' Edgar said. 'Laces on 'em always come undone, don't they?'

Bosch couldn't see Powers's face because the cop's back was turned toward the door. But he was looking up at Edgar.

'Fuck you, nigger.'

It was almost as if he had slapped Edgar, whose face immediately filled with revulsion and anger. He looked over at Bosch, a quick glance to judge whether Bosch was going to do anything about his plan to hit Powers. But it was all the time Powers needed. He sprang away from the sink and threw his body into Edgar, pinning him against the white-tiled wall. His cuffed hands came up and the left one grabbed a handful of the front of Edgar's shirt while the right pressed the barrel of a small gun into the stunned detective's throat.

Bosch had covered half of the distance to them when he saw the gun and Powers began to shout.

'Back off, Bosch. Back off or you got a dead partner. You want that?'

Powers had turned his head so that he was looking back at Bosch. Bosch stopped and raised his hands away from his body.

'That's it,' Powers said. 'Now this is what you're going to do. Take your gun out real slowly and drop it in that first sink there.'

Bosch made no move.

'Do it. Now.'

Powers spoke with measured force, careful to keep his voice low.

Bosch looked at the tiny gun in Powers's hand. He recognized it as a Raven .25, a favored throw-down gun among patrol cops going back to at least his own time in a uniform. It was small – it looked like a toy in Powers's hand – but deadly and it fit snugly into a sock or boot, virtually unseen with the pants leg pulled down. As Bosch came to the realization that Edgar and Rider had not completely searched Powers, he also knew that a shot from the Raven at point-blank range would certainly kill Edgar. It was against all his instincts to give up his weapon, but he saw no alternative. Powers was desperate and Bosch knew desperate men didn't think things out. They went against the odds. They were killers. With two fingers he slowly removed his gun and dropped it into the sink.

'That's real good, Bosch. Now I want you to get on the floor underneath the sinks.'

Bosch did as he was told, never taking his eyes off Powers as he moved.

'Edgar,' Powers said. 'Now your turn. You can just go ahead and drop yours on the floor.'

Edgar's gun hit the tile.

'Now, you get under there with your partner. That's it.'

'Powers, this is crazy,' Bosch said. 'Where're you going to go? You can't run.'

'Who's talking about running, Bosch? Take out your cuffs and put one on your left wrist.'

After Bosch had complied, Powers told him to loop the cuffs through one of the sink trap pipes. He then told Edgar to put the free cuff around his right wrist. He did so and then Powers smiled.

'There, that's good. That ought to hold you guys for a few minutes. Now, give me your keys. Both of you, throw 'em out here.'

Powers picked Edgar's set up off the floor and unlocked the cuffs around his wrists. He quickly massaged them to get the circulation going. He was smiling but Bosch wondered if he even knew it.

'Now, let's see.'

He reached into the sink and grabbed Bosch's gun.

'This is a nice one, Bosch. Nice weight, balance. Beats mine. Mind if I borrow it for a couple minutes?'

Bosch knew then what he was planning to do. He was going for Veronica. Bosch thought of Kiz sitting at the homicide table, her back to the front counter. And Billets in her office. They wouldn't see him until it was too late.

'She's not here, Powers,' he said.

'What? Who?'

'Veronica. It was a scam. We never even picked her up.'

Powers was silent as the smile dropped away and was replaced with a serious look of concentration. Bosch knew what he was thinking.

'The voice came from one of her movies. I taped it off the video-tape. You go back to those interview rooms and it's a dead end. There's nobody back there and no way out.'

Bosch saw the same tightening of skin around Powers's face that he had seen before. His face grew dark with blood and anger, then, inexplicably, the smile suddenly creased across it.

'You smart fucker, Bosch. Is that so? You 'spect me to believe she's not there? Maybe this is the con, and not before. See what I'm saying?'

'It's no con. She isn't there. We were going to pick her up with what you told us. Went up the hill an hour ago but she's not there either. She left last night.'

'If she's not already here, then how . . .'

'That part was no scam. The money and pictures were in your house. If you didn't put them there, then she did. She's setting you up. Why don't you just put the gun down and let's start this over. You apologize to Edgar for what you called him and we drop this little incident.'

'Oh, I see. You drop the escape but I still get hit with the murder.'

'I told you, we're going to talk to the DA. We got one coming in right now. He's a friend. He'll do right by you. She's the one we really want.'

'You fucking asshole!' Powers said loudly. He then brought his voice back into check. 'Don't you see that I want her? You think you beat me? You think you broke me down in there? You didn't win, Bosch. I talked because I wanted to talk. I broke you, man, but you didn't know it. You started trusting me because you needed me. You should've never moved the cuffs, brother.'

He was silent a moment, letting that sink in.

'Now I've got an appointment with that bitch that I'm going to keep no matter what. She ain't here, then I'll go find her.'

'She could be anywhere.'

'So could I, Bosch, and she won't see me coming. I have to go.'

Powers grabbed the plastic bag out of the trash can and emptied it on the floor. He put Bosch's gun into the bag, then turned the faucets in all three sinks on full blast. The cascading water created a cacophony as it echoed off the tile walls. Powers picked up Edgar's gun and put it in the bag. He then wrapped the bag around itself several times, concealing the two guns inside. He put the Raven in his front pocket for easy access, threw the handcuff keys into one of the urinals and flushed each one. Without even looking at the two men handcuffed under the sink, he headed to the door.

'Adios, dipshits,' he threw over his shoulder and then he was gone.

Bosch looked at Edgar. He knew that if they yelled, it was likely they wouldn't be heard. It was a Sunday, the administration wing was empty. And in the bureau there were only Billets and Rider. With the water running, their shouts would probably be unintelligible. Billets and Rider would probably think it was the normal yelling from the drunk tank.

Bosch swiveled around and braced his feet on the wall beneath the sink counter. He grabbed the trap pipe so that he could use his legs as leverage in an attempt to pull the pipe free. But the pipe was burning hot.

'Son of a bitch!' Bosch yelled as he let go. 'He turned the hot water on.'

'What are we going to do? He's getting away.'

'Your arms are longer. See if you can reach up there and turn off the water. It's too hot. I can't grab the pipe.'

With Bosch feeding his arm almost up to the elbow through the pipe loop, Edgar was barely able to touch the faucet. It took him several seconds to turn the water down to a trickle.

'Now turn on the cold,' Bosch said. 'Cool this thing down.'

It took another few seconds, but then Bosch was ready to try again. He grabbed the pipe and pushed against the walls with his legs. As he did this, Edgar squeezed his hands around the pipe and did the same. The added muscle broke the pipe free along the seal beneath the sink. Water sloshed down on them as they threaded the cuffs chain through the pipe break. They got up and slid along the tile to the urinal, where Bosch saw his keys on the bottom grate. He grabbed them up and fumbled with them until he had the cuff off. He handed the keys to Edgar and ran toward the door, sloshing through the water that had completely spread across it.

'Turn off the water,' he yelled as he hit the door.

Bosch ran down the hallway and vaulted over the detective bureau front counter. The squad room was empty and through the glass he saw the lieutenant's office was vacant. He then heard a loud pounding and the muffled shouts of Rider and Billets. He ran down the hallway to the interview rooms and found all the doors open but one. He knew Powers had checked for Veronica Aliso anyway after locking Billets and Rider in room three. He opened the door to three and then quickly ran back through the squad room into the station house's rear hallway. He slammed through the heavy metal door and into the back parking yard. Instinctively reaching to his empty shoulder holster, he scanned the parking lot and the open bays of the garage. There was no sign of Powers, but there were two patrol officers standing near the gas pumps. Bosch focused on them.

'You seen Powers?'

'Yeah,' said the older of the two. 'He just left. With our fucking car. What the fuck's going on?'

Bosch didn't answer. He closed his eyes, bowed his head and cursed silently to himself.

Six hours later, Bosch, Edgar and Rider sat at the homicide table, silently watching the meeting taking place in the lieutenant's office. Huddled in the small office like people on a bus were Billets, Captain LeValley, Deputy Chief Irving, three IAD investigators including Chastain, and the chief of police and his administrative aide. Deputy District Attorney Roger Goff had been consulted on the speaker-phone – Bosch had heard his voice through the open door. But then the door was closed and Bosch was sure the group was deciding the fate of the three detectives sitting outside.

The police chief stood in the middle of the cramped room with his arms folded and his head down. He was the last to arrive, and it looked as if he was getting the run-down from the others. Occasionally he nodded, but it didn't look to Bosch as though he was saying much at all. Bosch knew that the main issue they were discussing was how to handle the problem with Powers. There was a killer cop on the loose. Going to the media with that would be an exercise in self-flagellation, but Bosch saw no way around it.

They had looked in all the likely places for Powers and had not found him. The patrol car he had commandeered had been found abandoned up in the hills on Fareholm Drive. Where he had gone from there was anyone's guess. Surveillance teams stationed outside his bungalow and the Aliso house, as well as the lawyer Neil Denton's house and office, had produced nothing. It was now time to go to the media, to put the rogue cop's picture on the six o'clock news. Bosch guessed that the reason the police chief had showed up was that he planned to call a press conference. Otherwise he would have left the whole thing for Irving to deal with.

Bosch realized Rider had said something.

'Excuse me?'

'I said what are you going to do with your time?'

'I don't know. Depends on how much we get. If it's just one DP, I'll use it to finish work on my house. If it's longer than two, I'll have to see about making some money somehow.'

A DP, or deployment period, was fifteen days. Suspensions were usually handed out in such increments when the offense was serious. Bosch was pretty sure the chief wouldn't be handing out minor suspensions to them.

'He isn't going to fire us, is he, Harry?' Edgar asked.

'Doubt it. But it all depends on how they're telling it to him.'

Bosch looked back at the office window just as the chief was looking out at him. The chief looked away, not a good sign. Bosch had never met him and never expected that he would. He was an outsider brought in to appease the community. Not because of any particular police administrative skills, but because they needed an outsider. He was a large black man with most of his weight around his waist. Cops who didn't like him, and there were many, often referred to him as Chief Mud Slide. Bosch didn't know what cops who liked him called him.

'I just want to say I'm sorry, Harry,' Rider said.

'Sorry about what?' Bosch asked.

'About missing the gun. I patted him down. I ran my hands down his legs but somehow I missed it. I don't understand it.'

'It was small enough that he could fit it in his boot,' Bosch said. 'It's not all on you, Kiz. We all had our chances. Me and Jerry fucked up in the rest room. We should've been watching him better.'

She nodded but Bosch could tell she still felt miserable. He looked up and saw that the meeting in the lieutenant's office was beginning to break up. As the police chief and his aide, followed by LeValley and the IAD dicks, filed out, they left the bureau through the front entrance. It would make for an out-of-the-way walk if their cars were parked in the station lot out back, but it meant they didn't have to walk by the homicide table and acknowledge Bosch and the others. Another bad sign, he thought.

Only Irving and Billets remained in the office after it cleared. Billets then looked out at Bosch and signaled the three of them into her office. They got up slowly and headed in. Edgar and Rider sat down but Bosch stayed on his feet.

'Chief,' Billets said, giving Irving the floor.

'Okay, I'll give it to you the way it was just given to me,' Irving said. He looked down at a piece of paper on which he had taken a few notes. 'For conducting an unauthorized investigation and for failure to follow

514

procedure in searching and transporting a prisoner each of you is suspended without pay two deployment periods and suspended *with* pay for two deployment periods. These are to run consecutively. That's two months. And, of course, a formal reprimand goes into each of your jackets. Per procedure, you can appeal this to a Board of Rights.'

He waited a beat. It was heavier than Bosch had expected, but he showed nothing on his face. He heard Edgar audibly exhale. As far as the appeal went, disciplinary action by the police chief was rarely overturned. It would require two of the three captains on the Board of Rights to vote against their commander in chief. Overruling an IAD investigator was one thing, overruling the chief was political suicide.

'However,' Irving continued, 'the suspensions are being held in abeyance by the chief pending further developments and evaluation.'

There was a moment of silence while the last sentence was computed.

'What does he mean, abeyance?' Edgar asked.

'It means the chief is offering you a break,' Irving said. 'He wants to see how things fall out over the next day or two. Each of you is to come to work tomorrow and proceed with the investigation where you can. We talked with the DA's office. They're willing to file on Powers. Get the paperwork over there tomorrow first thing. We've put the word out and the chief will take it to the media in a couple hours. If we're lucky, we'll get this guy before he finds the woman or does any other damage. And if we're lucky, you three will probably be lucky.'

'What about Veronica Aliso, aren't they going to file on her?'

'Not yet. Not until we have Powers back. Goff said that without Powers, the taped confession is worthless. He won't be able to use it against her without Powers on the stand to introduce it or her being able to confront a witness against her.'

Bosch looked down at the floor.

'So without him, she walks.'

'That's the way it looks.'

Bosch nodded his head.

'What's he going to say?' he asked. 'The chief, I mean.'

'He's going to tell it like it is. You people will come out okay in some parts, not so okay in others. Overall, it's not going to be a good day for this department.'

'Is that why we're getting hit for two months? Because we're the messengers?'

Irving looked at him a long moment, his jaw clenched, before answering.

'I'm not going to dignify that with a reply.'

He looked at Rider and Edgar and said, 'You two can go now. You're finished here. I need to discuss another matter with Detective Bosch.'

Bosch watched them go and prepared for more of Irving's ire about the last comment. He wasn't sure why he had said it. He knew it would bait the deputy chief.

But after Rider closed the door to the office, Irving spoke of another matter.

'Detective, I wanted you to know that I've already talked to the federal people and we're all squared away on that.'

'How is that?'

'I told them that with today's developments it has become pretty clear – make that crystal clear – that you had nothing to do with planting evidence on their man. I told them it was Powers and that we were terminating that particular aspect of our internal investigation of your conduct.'

'Fine, chief. Thanks.'

Thinking that was it, Bosch made a move toward the door.

'Detective, there is one other thing.'

Bosch turned back to him.

'In discussing this matter with the chief of police, there is still one other aspect that bothers him.'

'And what is that?'

'The investigation started by Detective Chastain brought in ancillary information about your association with a convicted felon. It's troubling to me, too. I'd like to be able to get some assurance from you that this is not going to continue. I'd like to take that assurance to the chief.'

Bosch was silent a moment.

'I can't give you that.'

Irving looked down at the floor. He was working the thick muscles of his jaw again.

'You disappoint me, Detective Bosch,' he finally said. 'This department has done a lot by you. So have I. I've stood by you through some tough spots. You've never been easy, but you have a talent that I think this department and this city certainly need. I suppose that makes you worth it. Do you want to possibly alienate me and others in this department?'

'Not particularly.'

'Then take my advice and do the right thing, son. You know what that is. That's all I'm going to say on that.'

'Yes, sir.'

'That's all.'

When Bosch got to his house, he saw a dusty Ford Escort parked at the curb out front. It had Nevada plates. Inside the house, Eleanor Wish was sitting at the table in the small dining room with the classified ads section of the Sunday *Times*. She had a lit cigarette in the ashtray next to the paper and she was using a black marker to circle want ads. Bosch saw all of this and his heart jumped into a higher gear. What it meant to him was that if she was looking for a job, then she might be digging in, staying in L.A. and staying with him. To top it all off, the house was filled with the aroma of an Italian restaurant, heavy on the garlic.

He came around the table and put his hand on her shoulder and tentatively kissed her on the cheek. She patted his hand. As he straightened up, though, he noticed she was looking at ads for furnished apartments in Santa Monica, not the employment section.

'What's cooking?' he asked.

'My spaghetti sauce. You remember it?'

He nodded that he did but he really didn't. His memory of the days he had spent with her five years before were all centered on her, the moments they were intimate, and what happened afterward.

'How was Las Vegas?' he asked, just to be saying something.

'It was Vegas. The kind of place you never miss. If I never go back that will be fine with me.'

'You're looking for a place here?'

'I thought I might as well start looking.'

She had lived in Santa Monica before. Bosch remembered her apartment with the bedroom balcony. You could smell the sea and if you leaned out over the railing, you could look down Ocean Park Boulevard and even see it. He knew she couldn't afford a place like that now. She was probably looking at the listings east of Lincoln.

'You know there's no hurry,' he said. 'You can stay here. Nice view, it's private. Why don't you . . . I don't know, take your time.'

She looked up at him but decided not to say what she was about to say. Bosch could tell.

'Do you want a beer?' she asked instead. 'I bought some more. They're in the fridge.'

He nodded, letting her escape from the moment, and went into the kitchen. He saw a Crock-Pot on the counter and wondered if she had bought it or brought it back with her from Las Vegas. He opened the refrigerator and smiled. She knew him. She had bought bottles of Henry Weinhard's. He took two out and brought them back to the dining room. He opened hers and gave it to her, then his own. They both started to speak at the same time.

'Sorry, go ahead,' she said.

'No, you.'

'You sure?'

'Yeah, what?'

'I was just going to ask how things went today.'

'Oh. Well, they went good and bad. We broke the guy down and he told us the story. He gave up the wife.'

'Tony Aliso's wife?'

'Yeah. It was her plan all along. According to him. The Vegas stuff was just a misdirection.'

'That's great. What's the bad part?'

'Well, first of all, our guy is a cop and—'

'Oh, shit!'

'Yeah, but it's even worse. He got away from us today.'

'Got away? What do you mean got away?'

'I mean he escaped. Right out of the station. He had a pistol, a little Raven, in his boot. We missed it when we hooked him up. Edgar and me took him into the can, and he must've stepped on his shoelace while we were going over. You know, on purpose. Then, when Edgar noticed it and told him to tie his shoe, he came up with the Raven. He got away from us, went into the back lot and just took a squad car. He was still in uniform.'

'Jesus, and they didn't find him yet?'

'That was about eight hours ago. He's in the wind.'

'Well, where could he go in a patrol car and in a uniform?'

'Oh, he dumped the car – they already found that – and I doubt, wherever he is, he's in the uniform. It looks like he was into the far-right, white-supremacy thing. He probably knew people who'd get him clothes, no questions asked.'

'Sounds like a helluva cop.'

'Yeah. It's funny. He was the guy who found the body, you know, last week. It was on his beat. And because he was a cop, I didn't give him a second thought. I knew that day he was an asshole, but I didn't even look at him at all as anything other than the cop who found the stiff. And he must've known that. And he timed it so that we'd be in a rush out there. He was pretty smart about it.'

'Or she was.'

'Yeah. More likely it was her. But, anyway, I feel more, I don't know, upset or disappointed about that first day, that I didn't take a look at him, than I do about letting him get away today. I should've looked at him. More often than not the one who finds the body is the one. His uniform blinded me to that.'

She got up from the table and came over to him. She put her arms around his neck and smiled up at him.

'You'll get him. Don't worry.'

He nodded. They kissed.

'What were you going to say before?' she asked. 'When we both talked at once.'

'Oh . . . I don't remember now.'

'Must not have been important, then.'

'I wanted to tell you to stay here with me.'

She put her head down against his chest so that he couldn't see her eyes. 'Harry . . .'

'Just to see how it works. I feel like . . . it's almost like all this time hasn't gone by. I want – I just want to be with you. I can take care of you. You can feel safe and you can have all the time you need to make a new start here. Find a job, whatever you want to do.'

She stepped back from him and looked up into his eyes. The warning Irving had given him was the furthest thing from his mind. Right now all he cared about was keeping her close and doing whatever it took to accomplish that.

'But a lot of time has gone by, Harry. We just can't jump in like this.'

Bosch nodded and lowered his eyes. He knew she was right but he still didn't care.

'I want you, Harry,' she said. 'Nobody else. But I want to take it slow. So that we're sure. Both of us.'

'I already know I'm sure.'

'You just think you are.'

'Santa Monica is so far away from here.'

She smiled and then laughed and shook her head.

'Then you're just going to have to sleep over when you come visit.'

He nodded again and they embraced for a long moment.

'You can make me forget a lot of things, you know that?' he whispered into her ear.

'You, too,' she said back.

While they made love the phone rang, but whoever was calling did not leave a message when the machine picked up. Later, after Bosch got out of the shower, Eleanor reported that another call had come in but no message was left.

Finally, while Eleanor was boiling water for the pasta, the phone rang a third time and Bosch got it before the machine picked up.

'Hey, Bosch?'

'Yeah, who's this?'

'It's Roy Lindell. Remember me, Luke Goshen?'

'I remember. Was that you who called a couple times before?'

'Yeah, why didn't you pick up?'

'I was busy. What do you need?'

'So, it was the bitch, huh?'

'What?'

'Tony's wife.'

'Yeah.'

'Did you know this guy Powers?'

'Not really. Just to see around.'

Bosch didn't want to tell him anything he didn't already know.

Lindell exhaled in a bored way loudly into the phone.

'Yeah, well, Tony once told me that he was more afraid of his wife than he was of Joey Marks.'

'Yeah?' Bosch said, suddenly interested. 'He said that? When?'

'I don't know. One night we were talking in the club and he just said it. I remember the place was closed. He was waiting for Layla and we were talking.'

'Lindell, thanks a lot for telling me this. What else did he say?'

'Hey, I'm telling you now, Bosch. Anyway, I couldn't before. I was in character, man, and in that character you don't tell the cops shit. And then after, I . . . well, then I thought you were trying to fuck me over. I wasn't going to tell you shit then, either.'

'And now you know better.'

'Yeah, right. Look, Bosch, most guys you would've never heard from. But I'm calling. You think you'll hear from anybody else from the bureau saying maybe we made a mistake about you? No way. But I like your style. I mean, you get pulled off the case and what do you do, you turn around and get right back on it. Then you solve the fucker. That takes balls and style, Bosch. I can dig that.'

'You can dig it. That's great, Roy. What else did Tony Aliso tell you about his wife?'

'Nothing much. He just said she was cold. He said that she had him by the short hairs. Hooked and snooked and that was that. He couldn't get a divorce from her without losing half his wad and then having her running around out there with all that she knew about his business and his business associates. If you know what I mean.'

'Why didn't he just go to Joey Marks and ask for a whack on her?'

'I think on account that she knew Joey from way back and he liked her. It was Joey who introduced her to Tony way back when. I think Tony knew that if he went to Joey, it would get KO'd pretty quick and it might get back to her. And if he went to somebody else, he'd have to answer to Joey. Joey had the final say on that kind of stuff, and he wouldn't want Tony getting involved in a freelance job like that and possibly endangering the wash operation.'

'How well do you think she knew Joey Marks? You think she could've gone back to him now?'

'No way. She killed the golden goose. Tony made Joey legitimate money. His first allegiance is always to the money.'

Bosch was quiet for a few moments and so was Lindell.

'So what happens with you now?' Bosch finally said.

'You mean with my thing? I go back to Vegas tonight. I sit down in front of the grand jury in the morning. I figure I'll be talking to them at least a couple weeks. I've got a pretty good story to tell 'em. We should have Joey and his crew tagged and bagged by Christmas.'

'Hope you're bringing your bodyguards.'

'Oh, yeah. I'm not alone.'

'Well, good luck, Lindell. All the bullshit aside, I like your style, too. Let me ask you something, why'd you tell me about the safe house and the Samoans? That wasn't in keeping with your character.'

'I had to, Bosch. You scared me.'

'You thought I'd actually clip you for them?'

'I wasn't sure, but that didn't really worry me. I had people watching over me that you didn't know about. But I *was* sure that they'd clip her. And I'm an agent, man. It was my duty to try to stop that. So I told you. I was surprised you didn't guess I was undercover right then.'

'Never crossed my mind. You were good.'

'Well, I fooled the people I had to fool. I'll see you around, Bosch.'

'Sure. Oh, Lindell?'

'Yeah.'

'Did Joey Marks ever think that Tony A was skimming off him?'

Lindell laughed.

'You don't give up, do you, Bosch?'

'I guess not.'

'Well, that information would be part of the investigation and I can't talk about it. Officially.'

'What about unofficially?'

'Unofficially you didn't hear it from me and I never talked to you. But to answer your question, Joey Marks thought everybody was skimming off him. He trusted no one. Every time I wore a wire with the guy, I was sweating bullets. Because you never knew when he was going to put his hand down your chest. I was with him more than a year and he was still doin' that every now and then. I had to wear the bug in my armpit, man. You try pulling tape out of your armpit sometime, man. It hurts.'

'What about Tony?'

'That's what I'm getting at. Sure, Joey thought Tony was skimming. He thought I was, too. And you gotta understand, a certain amount of that was permissible. Joey knew everybody had to make a buck to be happy. But he mighta felt Tony was taking more than his share. He never told me that's what he thought, but I know he had the boy followed a couple times over here in L.A. And he got to somebody in Tony's bank in Beverly Hills. Joey was being copied on the monthly statements.'

'Yeah?'

'Yeah. He would've known if there were any deposits that were outta line.'

Bosch thought a moment but couldn't think what else to ask.

'Why'd you ask that, Bosch?'

'Oh, I don't know, something I'm workin' out. Powers said the wife told him Tony had a couple million he skimmed. It's hidden somewhere.'

Lindell whistled over the line.

'Seems like a lot to me. Seems like Joey would've caught that and put the hammer down on Tony pronto. That's not what you call permissible.'

'Well, I think it accrued over the years, you know. He could have piecemealed it. Also, he was washing money for some of Joey's friends in Chicago and Arizona, remember? He could've skimmed them, too.'

'Anything's possible. Listen, Bosch, let me know how it all shakes out. I have to catch a plane.'

'One more thing.'

'Bosch, I gotta get to Burbank.'

'You ever heard of anybody in Vegas named John Galvin?'

Galvin was the name of the man who had last visited Veronica Aliso on the night she disappeared. There was a beat of silence before Lindell finally said the name was not familiar. But that silence was what Bosch really heard.

'You sure?'

'Look, I never heard of the guy, okay? I gotta go.'

After hanging up, Bosch opened his briefcase on the dining room table and took out a notebook so he could write down a few notes about what Lindell had said. Eleanor came out of the kitchen with utensils and napkins in her hands.

'Who was that?'

'Lindell.'

'Who?'

'The agent who was Luke Goshen.'

'What did he want?'

'I guess to apologize.'

'That's unusual. The bureau usually doesn't apologize for anything.'

'It wasn't an official call.'

'Oh. Just one of those macho male bonding calls.'

Bosch smiled because she was so right.

'What's this?' she asked as she put the silverware down and took the tape of *Casualty of Desire* out of his briefcase. 'Oh, was this one of Tony Aliso's movies?'

'Yeah. Part of his Hollywood legacy. It's one of the ones Veronica was in. I was supposed to give it back to Kiz.'

'You already saw it?'

Bosch nodded.

'I would've liked to see it. Did you like it?'

'It was pretty bad, but we can put it on tonight if you want.'

'You sure you wouldn't mind?'

'I'm sure.'

During dinner Bosch updated her in detail about the case. Eleanor asked few questions and eventually they lapsed into a comfortable quiet. The

521

Bolognese sauce and linguini Eleanor had made was fantastic and Bosch broke the silence to tell her so. She had opened a bottle of red wine and that tasted good, too. He told her about that as well.

Afterward, they left the dishes in the sink and went out to the living room to watch the movie. Bosch sat with his arm on the back of the couch, his hand lightly touching Eleanor's neck. He found it boring to watch the film again and his mind quickly drifted away as he thought over the day's events. The money was what held his attention the longest. He wondered if Veronica already had it in her possession or if it was in a place where she had to go to get it. Not a local bank, he decided. They had already checked the local bank accounts.

That left Las Vegas, he concluded. Tony Aliso's travel records showed that in the last ten months he had not been anywhere but Los Angeles and Las Vegas. If he had been operating a skim fund, he'd have to have had access to it. If the money wasn't here, then it was over there. And since Veronica had not left the house before today, Bosch also concluded that she didn't have the money yet.

The phone rang and interrupted these thoughts. Bosch climbed up from the couch and answered the phone in the kitchen so he wouldn't disturb Eleanor's viewing of the movie. It was Hank Meyer calling from the Mirage but it didn't sound like Hank Meyer. It sounded like a scared boy.

'Detective Bosch, can I trust you?'

'Sure you can, Hank, what's the matter?'

'Something's happened. I mean, something's come up. Uh, because of you I know something I don't think I should know. I wish this whole thing . . . I don't know what to—'

'Hold on, hold on, Hank. Just calm down and tell what it is that's wrong. Be calm. Talk to me and we'll fix it. Whatever it is, we'll fix it.'

'I'm at the office. They called me at home because I had a flag on the computer for that betting slip that belonged to your victim.'

'Right.'

'Well, somebody cashed it tonight.'

'Okay, somebody cashed it. Who was it?'

'Well, you see, I put an IRS flag on the computer. Meaning that the cashier was supposed to request a driver's license and get a Social Security number, you know, for tax purposes. Even though this ticket was worth only $4,000 I put the flag on it.'

'Okay, so who cashed the slip?'

'A man named John Galvin. He had a local address.'

Bosch leaned over the counter and pressed the phone tightly to his ear.

'When did this happen?' he asked.

'At eight-thirty tonight. Less than two hours ago.'

'I don't understand, Hank. Why is this upsetting to you?'

'Well, I left instructions on the computer for me to be contacted at home as soon as this slip was cashed. I was contacted. I came in and got the information on who cashed the slip so I could get it to you ASAP and then I went directly to the video room. I wanted to see this John Galvin, you know, if we got a clear picture of him.'

He stopped there. It was like pulling teeth getting the story out of him.

'And?' Bosch said. 'Who was it, Hank?'

'We got a clear picture. It turns out I know John Galvin but not as John Galvin. Uh, as you know, one of my duties is to interface with law enforcement, maintain relations and help when I can whenever there—'

'Yes, Hank, I know. *Who* was it?'

'I looked at the video. It was very clear. John Galvin is a man I know. He's in Metro, a captain. His name is—'

'John Felton.'

'How'd—'

'Because I know him, too. Now listen to me, Hank. You didn't tell me this, okay? We never talked. It's best that way. Safest for you. Understand?'

'Yes, but . . . but what is going to happen?'

'You don't have to worry. I'll take care of it and no one at Metro will ever know about this. Okay?'

'Okay, I guess. I—'

'Hank, I've got to go. Thanks, and I owe you a favor.'

Bosch hung up and called information for the number of Southwest Airlines at the airport in Burbank. He knew Southwest and America West handled most of the flights to Las Vegas and they both flew out of the same terminal. He called Southwest and had them page Roy Lindell. While he waited, he looked at his watch. It had been more than an hour since he had talked to Lindell, but he didn't think the agent was in as much of a hurry as he had intimated on the phone. Bosch thought he had just said that to get off the phone.

A voice came on the line and asked who he was holding for. After Bosch repeated Lindell's name, he was told to hold and after two clicks Lindell's voice was on the line.

'Yeah, this is Roy, who's this?'

'You son of a bitch.'

'Who is this?'

'John Galvin is John Felton and you knew it all the time.'

'Bosch? Bosch, what are you doing?'

'Felton is Joey's man in Metro. You knew that from being on the inside. And when Felton does things for Marks, he uses the name John Galvin. You knew that, too.'

'Bosch, I can't talk about this. It's all part of our in—'

'I don't give a shit about your investigation. You have to figure out whose side you're on, man. Felton has got Veronica Aliso. And that means Joey Marks has got her.'

'What are you talking about? This is crazy.'

'They know about the skim, don't you see? Joey wants his money back and they're going to squeeze it out of her.'

'How do you know all of this?'

'Because I know.'

Bosch thought of something and looked out through the kitchen door to the living room. Eleanor was still watching the movie and she looked over at him and raised her eyebrows in a question. Bosch shook his head to show his dissatisfaction with the person on the other end.

'I'm going to Vegas, Lindell. And I think I know where they'll be. You want to get your people involved? I sure as hell can't call Metro on this.'

'How are you so sure she's even there?'

'Because she sent up a distress signal. Are you in or out?'

'We're in, Bosch. Let me give you a number. You call it when you get over there.'

After Bosch hung up, he went into the living room. Eleanor had already turned off the tape.

'I can't watch any more of that. It's terrible. What's going on?'

'That time you followed Tony Aliso around in Vegas, you said he went to a bank with the girlfriend, right?'

'Right.'

'Which bank? Where?'

'I, uh . . . it was on Flamingo, east of the Strip, east of Paradise Road. I can't remember the name. I think it was Silver State National. Yes, that's it. Silver State.'

'The Silver State on Flamingo, are you sure now?'

'Right, yes.'

'And it looked like she was opening an account?'

'Yes, but I can't be sure. That's the problem with a one-man tail. It's a small branch bank and I couldn't hang around inside too long. It looked like she was signing account papers and Tony was just watching. But I had to go out and wait outside until they were done. Remember, Tony knew me. If he even saw me, the tail would be blown.'

'Okay, I'm going.'

'Tonight?'

'Tonight. I have to make some calls first.'

Bosch went back into the kitchen and called Grace Billets. While filling her in on what he had learned and his hunch about what it all meant, he got a pot of coffee going. After getting her approval to travel, he next called Edgar and then Rider and made arrangements to pick them up at the station in one hour.

He poured himself a cup of coffee and leaned against the counter in deep thought. Felton. There was a contradiction, it seemed to Bosch. If the Metro captain was the Joey Marks organization's inside man, why had he moved so quickly to go after Goshen when he got the match on the fingerprints Bosch had provided? Bosch played with this for a while and finally decided that Felton must have seen an opportunity in moving Goshen out of the way. He must have believed that his position in the Las Vegas underworld would rise if Goshen were out of the picture. Perhaps he even planned to arrange Goshen's assassination, thereby insuring the indebtedness of Joey Marks. Bosch realized that for this plan to work, Felton either didn't know that Goshen knew he was the organization's inside man, or he planned to get rid of Goshen before he got a chance to tell anyone.

Bosch took a sip of the scalding coffee and put these thoughts aside. He went back into the living room. Eleanor was still on the couch.

'Are you going?'

'Yeah. I've got to pick up Jerry and Kiz.'

'Why tonight?'

'Got to be there before the bank opens tomorrow.'

'You think Veronica is going to be there?'

'It's a hunch. I think Joey Marks finally figured out just like we did that if he didn't whack Tony, then somebody else did and that person had to have been close to him. And that that person now has his money. He knew Veronica from way back and would figure she was up to it. I think he sent Felton over to check into it and to get his money back and take care of her if she was dirty on it. But she must've talked him out of it somehow. Probably by mentioning she had two million in skim in a safe deposit box in Vegas. I think that's what stopped Felton from killing her and instead made him take her with him. She's probably only alive until they get into that box. I think she gave Felton her husband's last betting slip because she knew he might cash it and we'd be watching for it.'

'What makes you think it's at the bank where I saw him go?'

'Because we know about everything he had over here, all his accounts. It's not over here. Powers told me Veronica had told him that Tony dropped the skim into a safe deposit box that she wouldn't have access to until he was dead. She wasn't a signatory on it. So my guess is that it's in Vegas. It's the only place he's been outside of L.A. for the last year. And that if one day he was taking his girlfriend to open a bank account somewhere, he'd just go ahead and take her to the same bank he used.'

Eleanor nodded.

'It's funny,' Bosch said.

'What is?'

'That what all of this really came down to was a bank caper. It's not really about Tony Aliso's murder, it's about the money he skimmed and hid. A bank caper with his murder sort of a side effect. And that's how you and I met. On a bank job.'

She nodded, her eyes going far off as she thought about it. Bosch immediately wished he hadn't brought the memory up.

'Sorry,' he said. 'I guess it's not really that funny.'

Eleanor looked up at him from the couch.

'Harry, I'm going with you to Las Vegas.'

VIII

The Silver State National Bank branch where Tony Aliso had taken his girlfriend while Eleanor Wish had watched was in the corner of a small shopping plaza between a Radio Shack and a Mexican restaurant called La Fuentes. The parking lot was largely empty at dawn on Monday morning when the FBI agents and LAPD detectives came to set up. The bank didn't open until nine and the other businesses would follow beginning at ten.

Because the businesses were closed, the agents had a problem in locating their surveillance points. It would be too obvious to stick four government cars in the lot. They would be too noticeable because there were only five other cars in the entire block-long parking lot, four parked on the outer fringes and an old Cadillac parked in the first row nearest the bank. There were no license plates on the Caddy, which had a spider web crack in the windshield, its windows left open and the trunk sprung and held closed by a chain and padlock through one of its many rusted-out spots. It had the sad appearance of having been abandoned, its owner probably another Las Vegas casualty. Like someone lost in the desert and dying of thirst just a few feet from an oasis, the Caddy had stopped for the final time just a few feet from the bank and all the money inside it.

The agents, after cruising by the location a few times to get the lay of the land, decided to use the Caddy as a blind, by popping the hood and sticking an agent in a greasy T-shirt under it and ostensibly working on the dead engine. They complemented this agent with a panel van parked right next to the Caddy. Four agents were in the van. At seven that morning they had taken it to the federal utilities shop and had a painter stencil *La Fuentes Mexican Restaurant – Established 1983* on the side panels in red paint. The paint was still drying when they drove the van into the lot at eight.

Now at nine, the lot was slowly beginning to fill, mostly with employees of the stores and a few Silver State customers who needed to take care of business as soon as the bank opened its doors. Bosch watched all of this from the backseat of a federal car. Lindell and an agent named Baker were in the front seat. They were parked in the service bay of a gas station across Flamingo Road from the shopping center where the bank was located. Edgar and Rider were in another bureau car parked further up Flamingo. There were two other bureau cars in the area, one static and one roving. The plan was for Lindell to move his car into the bank parking lot once it became more crowded with cars and the bureau car would not stand out. This plan included a bureau helicopter making wide arcs around the shopping center.

529

'They're opening up,' a voice from the car radio reported.

'Gotcha, La Fuentes,' Lindell said back.

The bureau cars were each equipped with a radio pedal and overhead mike on the windshield visor, meaning the driver of each car simply depressed the foot pedal and spoke, avoiding having to raise a microphone to his mouth and possibly being noticed and identified as law enforcement. Bosch had heard that the LAPD was finally getting such equipment, but the narcotics units and specialized surveillance teams were getting it first.

'Lindell,' he said, 'you ever go to talk on the radio and slam on the brakes by mistake?'

'Not yet, Bosch. Why?'

'Just curious how all this fancy equipment works.'

'It's only as good as the people who work it.'

Bosch yawned. He couldn't remember the last time he had slept. They had driven through the night to get to Las Vegas and then spent the rest of the time planning for the bank surveillance.

'So what do you think, Bosch?' Lindell asked him. 'Sooner or later?'

'This morning. They'll want their money. They don't want to wait.'

'Yeah, maybe.'

'You think it's later?'

'If it was me, I'd do it later. That way if there were people out there watching and waiting – whether it's the bureau or LAPD or Powers or whoever – they'd get cooked in the sun. Know what I mean?'

'Yeah. We sit out here all day and we aren't going to be very sharp when the time comes.'

Bosch was quiet for a little while after that. From the backseat he studied Lindell. He noticed that the agent had gotten a haircut. There was no sign of the spot where Bosch had hacked off his ponytail.

'You think you're going to miss it?' Bosch asked.

'Miss what?'

'Being under. The life, I mean.'

'No, it was getting old. I'll be happy to go straight.'

'Not even the girls?'

Bosch saw Lindell's eyes take a quick swipe at Baker and then look at Bosch in the rearview mirror. That told Bosch to let that subject go.

'Whaddaya think about the lot now, Don?' Lindell said, changing the subject.

Baker scanned the lot. It was slowly filling up. There was a bagel shop on the far end from the bank, and that was responsible for most of the autos at the moment.

'I think we can take it in, park it by the bagel place,' Baker said. 'There's enough cover now.'

'Okay, then,' Lindell said. He tilted his head slightly so that he was projecting his voice toward the visor. 'Uh, La Fuentes, this is Roy Rogers. We're going to take our position in now. We'll check ya from the bagel shop. That will be to your posterior, I believe.'

'Roger that,' came the return. 'You always wanted to be on my tail end, didn't you, Roy?'

'Funny guy,' Lindell said.

An hour went by while they watched from their new position and nothing happened. Lindell was able to move their car in closer, parking in front of a card-dealing school about half the parking lot's length from the bank. It was class day and several would-be dealers had been pulling in and parking. It was good cover.

'I don't know, Bosch,' Lindell said, breaking a long silence. 'You think they're going to show or not?'

'I never said it was anything more than a hunch. But I still think it all fits. It even fits better since we got here. Last week I found a matchbook in Aliso's room at the Mirage. It was from La Fuentes. Whether they show or not, I say Tony's got a box in that bank.'

'Well, I'm thinking about sending Don here in to ask about that. We might be able to call an end to this and stop wasting our time if we find out there's no box.'

'Well, it's your call.'

'You got that right.'

A couple more minutes of tense silence went by.

'What about Powers?' Lindell asked.

'What about him?'

'I don't see him here, either, Bosch. When you got here this morning, you were all hot and heavy about him comin' out to find her and blast her full of holes. So where is he?'

'I don't know, Lindell. But if we're smart enough to figure this out, so is he. I wouldn't doubt it if he knew from tailing Tony where the box was all along and just left that out of our little conversation.'

'Wouldn't surprise me, either. But I still say it'd be stupid for him to come here. He's got to know we have a fix on this.'

'Stupid isn't the word. It's suicidal. But I don't think he cares. He just wants her to go down. And if he takes a bullet, too, then that's the way it goes. Like I told you before, he was ready to do the kamikaze scene at the station when he thought she was there.'

'Well, let's just hope he's cooled down a little since—'

'There!' Baker barked out.

Bosch followed his pointing finger toward the far corner of the lot, where a white limousine had just pulled in and was moving slowly toward the bank.

'Jesus,' Lindell said. 'Don't tell me he is this stupid.'

All limos looked basically the same to Bosch but somehow Lindell and Baker had recognized the car.

'Is that Joey Marks?'

'It's his limo. He likes those big whitewalls. It's the wop in him. I just can't – he can't be in there. He's not going to waste two years of my fucking life making this pickup, is he?'

The limo stopped in the lane in front of the bank. There was no further movement.

'You got this, La Fuentes?' Lindell asked.

'Yeah, we got it,' came a whispered reply, though there was clearly no way anyone in that van could be overheard by someone in the limo.

'Uh, one, two and three, standby,' Lindell continued. 'Looks like we might have the fox in the henhouse. Air Jordan, you take five until further. I don't want you swinging over and spooking anybody.'

This brought a chorus of rogers from the three other ground units and the helicopter.

'On second thought, three, why don't you come on up by the southwest entrance and stand by there for me,' Lindell said.

'Roger that.'

Finally, the door to the limo opened, but it was on the side blocked from Bosch's view. He waited, not breathing, and after a beat Captain John Felton emerged from the limo.

'Bingo,' the whisper came over the radio.

Felton then leaned back into the open door and reached in. Veronica Aliso now emerged, Felton's hand tightly around her arm. Following her, another man emerged at the same time the trunk opened automatically. While this second man, who was wearing gray pants and a shirt with an oval name tag sewn above the breast pocket, went to the trunk, Felton bent down and said something to someone still inside the limo. He never took his hand off Veronica's arm.

Bosch caught only a glimpse of Veronica's face then. Though he was an easy thirty yards from her, he could see the fear and weariness. It had probably been the longest night of her life.

The second man pulled a heavy red toolbox from the trunk and followed behind as Felton walked Veronica toward the bank, his arm still gripping her and his head swiveling as he looked about. Bosch saw Felton's focus linger on the van and then finally look away. The paint job had probably been the deciding factor. It had been a nice touch.

As they walked alongside the old Cadillac, Felton bent down to look at the man working under the hood. Satisfied he was not a threat, Felton straightened up and went on to the glass doors of the bank. Before they disappeared inside, Bosch saw that Veronica was clutching a cloth bag of some kind. Its dimensions were not discernible because it appeared to be empty and folded over on itself.

Bosch didn't breathe again until they were no longer in sight.

'Okay,' Lindell said to the visor. 'We've got three. Felton, the woman, and the driller. Anbody recognize him?'

The radio was silent for a few seconds and then a lone voice answered.

'I'm too far away but I thought it looked like Maury Pollack. He's a safe-and-lock man who's worked for Joey's crew before.'

'Okay,' Lindell said. 'We'll check him later. I'm sending Baker in now to open a new account. Wait five and then, Conlon, you go in next. Check your sets now.'

They went through a quick check of the radio sets Baker and Conlon were wearing under their clothes with wireless earpieces and wrist mikes. They checked out and Baker got out of the car and walked briskly along the sidewalk in front of the other stores toward the bank.

'Okay, Morris,' Lindell said. 'Take a walk. Try the Radio Shack.'

'Roger.'

Bosch watched as an agent he recognized from the pre-dawn meeting started crossing the lot from a car parked near the southwest entrance to the lot. Morris and Baker crossed paths ten feet apart but didn't acknowledge each other or even glance at the limo, which still sat with its engine idling in the lane in front of the bank.

It took about an hour for the next five minutes to go by. It was hot out but Bosch was mainly sweating from the anxiety of waiting and wondering what was going on. There had been only one transmission from Baker once he was inside. He had whispered that the subjects were in the safe deposit vault.

'Okay, Conlon, go,' Lindell ordered at the five-minute mark.

Bosch soon saw Conlon walking along the storefronts from the direction of the bagel shop. He went into the bank.

And then there was nothing for the next fifteen excruciating minutes. Finally, Lindell spoke just to break the silence.

'How we doin' out there. Everybody chipper?'

There was a chorus of microphone clicks signaling an affirmative response. Just as the radio had gone silent again, Baker's voice came up in an urgent whisper.

'They're coming out, coming out. Something's wrong.'

Bosch watched the bank doors and in a moment Felton and Veronica came out, the police captain's hand still firmly on her arm. The driller followed behind, lugging his red toolbox.

Felton didn't look around this time. He just walked with purpose toward the limo. He carried the bag now and it did not appear to Bosch to have grown in size. If Veronica's face looked fearful and tired before, it now looked even more distorted by fright. It was hard for Bosch to tell at this distance, but it looked like she was crying.

The door to the limo was opened from within as the threesome retraced their path alongside the old Cadillac and were getting near.

'All right,' Lindell said to the listening agents. 'On my call we go in. I'll take the front of the limo, three, you are in behind me. One and two, you got the back. Standard vehicular stop. La Fuentes, I want you people to come up and clear the limo. Do it quick. If there's shooting, everybody watch the cross fire. Watch the cross fire.'

As the rogers were coming in, Bosch was watching Veronica. He could tell she knew she was going to her death. The look on her face was vaguely reminiscent of what Bosch had seen on her husband's face. That certain knowledge that the game was up.

As he watched, he suddenly saw the trunk of the Cadillac spring open behind her. And from it, as if propelled by the same taut steel, jumped Powers. In a loud, wild-animal voice that Bosch heard clearly and would never forget, Powers yelled one word as he hit the ground.

'*Veronica!*'

As she, Felton and the driller turned to the origin of the sound, Powers raised his hands, both of them holding weapons. In that instant Bosch saw the glint of his own gun, the satin-finished Smith & Wesson, in the killer cop's left hand.

'*Gun!*' Lindell yelled. '*Everybody in! Everybody in!*'

He jerked the car into gear and slammed his foot on the gas pedal. The car jerked forward and started screaming toward the limo. But Bosch knew there was nothing they could do. They were too far away. He watched the scene unfold with a grim fascination, as if he were watching a slow-motion scene from a Peckinpah movie.

Powers began firing both guns, the shells ejecting and arcing away over both his shoulders as he stepped toward the limo. Felton made an attempt to go inside his jacket for his own gun but he was cut down in the fusillade, the first to drop. Then Veronica, standing perfectly still, facing her killer and making no move to run or shield herself, was hit and went down, dropping to the pavement, where Bosch couldn't see her because the limo blocked his view.

Powers kept coming and firing. The driller dropped his toolbox, raised his hands and started stepping backward away from the line of fire. Powers apparently ignored him. Bosch couldn't tell if he was shooting at Veronica's fallen body or into the open door of the limo. The limo took off, its tires spinning at first without purchase before it finally started to move, the rear door still open. But almost immediately, its driver failed to negotiate the left turn in the parking lane and the big car crashed into a row of parked cars. The driver jumped out and started running in the direction of the bagel shop.

Powers seemed to pay the fleeing driver no mind. He had reached the spot where Felton had fallen to the ground. He dropped Bosch's gun on the police captain's chest and reached down for the bag, which was on the ground next to Felton's hand.

It seemed that Powers did not realize that bag was empty until he had actually picked it up off the ground and held it. And as he was making this discovery, the doors of the van behind him were opened and four agents carrying shotguns were coming out. The agent in the T-shirt was coming around the side of the Cadillac, the handgun he had hidden in the engine compartment now pointed at Powers.

A squealing tire from one of the approaching bureau cars drew Powers's attention away from the empty duffel bag. He dropped it and turned on the five agents behind him. He raised both his hands again, though he only had one gun this time.

The agents opened fire and Bosch watched as Powers was literally lifted off the ground by the force of the impact and onto the front hood of a full-sized pickup truck that probably belonged to a bank customer. Powers landed on his back. His hand lost its grip on the remaining gun and it clattered off the hood to the ground. As loud as the eight seconds of shooting had been, the silence that followed the gun falling to the ground seemed even louder.

Powers was dead. Felton was dead. Giuseppe Marconi, aka Joseph Marconi, aka Joey Marks, was dead – his body sprawled and awash in blood on the soft leather seats in the back of his limousine.

When they got to Veronica Aliso, she was alive but dying. She had been hit with two rounds in the upper chest, and the bubbles in the froth of blood in her mouth indicated her lungs had been shredded. While the FBI agents ran about securing and containing the scene, Bosch and Rider went to Veronica.

Her eyes were open but losing their moisture. They were moving all around as if searching for someone or something that wasn't there. Her jaw started to work and she said something but Bosch couldn't hear. He crouched down over her and turned his ear to her mouth.

'Can you . . . get me ice?' she whispered.

Bosch turned and looked at her. He didn't understand. She started to speak again and he turned his ear to her mouth again.

' . . . the pavement . . . so hot. I . . . I need ice.'

Bosch looked at her and nodded.

'It's coming. It's coming. Veronica, where's the money?'

He bent over her, realizing that she was right, the pavement was now burning the palms of his hands. He could barely make out her words.

'At least they don't . . . they don't get it.'

She started coughing then, a deep wet cough, and Bosch knew her chest was full of blood and it wouldn't be long before she drowned. He couldn't think of what to do or say to this woman. He realized they were probably his own bullets in her and that she was dying because they had fucked up and let Powers get away. He almost wanted to ask her to forgive him, to say she understood how things could go so wrong.

He looked away from her and across the lot. He could hear sirens approaching. But he had seen enough gunshot wounds to know she wasn't going to need the ambulance. He looked back down at her. Her face was very pale and going slack. Her lips moved once more and he bent to listen. This time her voice was no more than a desperate rasp in his ear. He could not understand her words and he whispered in her ear to say it again.

' . . . et my gergo . . .'

He turned his head to look at her, the confusion in his eyes. He shook his head. An annoyed expression crossed her face.

'Let,' she said clearly, using the last of her strength. 'Let . . . my daughter go.'

Bosch kept his eyes locked on hers as that last line ran through his mind. Then, without thinking about it, he nodded once to her. And as he watched, she died. Her eyes lost their focus and he could tell she was gone.

Bosch stood up and Rider studied his face.

'Harry, what did she say?'

'She said . . . I'm not sure what she said.'

Bosch, Edgar and Rider stood leaning against the trunk of Lindell's car, watching as a phalanx of FBI and Metro people continued to descend on the crime scene. Lindell had ordered the entire shopping center closed and marked off with yellow tape, a move that prompted Edgar to comment, 'When these guys throw a crime scene, they really throw a crime scene.'

Each of them had already given a statement. They were no longer part of the investigation. They were merely witnesses to the event and now observers.

The special agent in charge of the Las Vegas field office was on the scene directing the investigation. The bureau had brought in a motor home that had four separate interview rooms in it and agents were taking statements in them from witnesses to the shooting. The bodies were still there, now covered in yellow plastic on the pavement and in the limo. That splash of bright color made for good video for the news helicopters circling overhead.

Bosch had been able to pick up pieces of information from Lindell on how things stood. The ID number on the Cadillac in which Powers had hidden for at least the four hours it was under observation by the FBI was traced to an owner in Palmdale, California, a desert town northeast of Los Angeles. The owner was already on file with the bureau. He was a white supremacist who had held antigovernment rallies on his land the last two Independence Days. He was also known to have sought to contribute to the defense funds of the men charged with bombing the federal courthouse in Oklahoma City two years before. Lindell told Bosch that the SAIC had ordered an arrest warrant for the owner on charges of conspiracy to commit murder for his role in helping Powers. It had been a nice plan. The trunk of the Caddy was lined with a thick carpet and several blankets. The chain and padlock used to hold it closed could be unhooked from the inside. Through rusted-out spots on the fenders and trunk it had been possible for Powers to watch and wait for the right moment to come out, guns ready.

The driller, who it turned out was indeed Maury Pollack, was only too happy to cooperate with the gents. He was just happy he wasn't one of the ones wearing a yellow plastic blanket. He told Lindell and the others that Joey Marks had picked him up that morning, told him to wear a working-man's outfit and to bring his drill. He didn't know what the situation was because there was little talking in the limo on the ride over. He just knew the woman was scared.

Inside the bank Veronica Aliso had presented a bank officer with a copy of her husband's death certificate, his will and a court order issued Friday in Las Vegas Municipal Court granting her, as sole heir to Anthony Aliso, access to his safe deposit box. Access was approved and the box was drilled because Mrs Aliso said she had not been able to locate her husband's key.

The trouble was, Pollack said, when he drilled the box open, they found it was empty.

'Can you imagine that?' Lindell said as he related this information to Bosch. 'All of this for nothing. I was hoping to get my hands on that two mil. Of course, we'd've split it with L.A. Right down the middle, Bosch.'

'Right,' Bosch said. 'Did you look at the records? When was the last time Tony went into his box?'

'That's another thing. He was just in on Friday. Like twelve hours before they killed him, he went in and cleared the box. He must've had a premonition or something. He knew, man. He knew.'

'Maybe.'

Bosch thought about the matchbook from La Fuentes that he had found in Tony's room at the Mirage. Tony didn't smoke but he remembered the ashtrays at the house where Layla had grown up. He decided that if Tony had cleared his box out on that Friday and eaten at La Fuentes while he was here, the only likely reason he would have ended up with matches from the restaurant in his room was that he had been at the restaurant with someone who needed them.

'Now the question is, where's the money?' Lindell said. 'We can seize it if we can find it. Ol' Joey's not going to need it.'

Lindell looked over at the limo. The door was still open and one of Marconi's legs stuck out from under the yellow plastic. A powder blue pants leg, a black loafer and white sock. That was all Bosch could see of Joey Marks now.

'The bank people, are they cooperating or do you need a warrant for every move you make?' Bosch asked.

'No, they're on board. The manager's in there shaking like a leaf. Not every day you get a massacre outside your front door.'

'Then ask them to check their records and see if there's a box in there under the name Gretchen Alexander.'

'Gretchen Alexander? Who's that?'

'You know her, Roy. It's Layla.'

'Layla? Are you fuckin' kidding me? You think he'd give that bimbo two million duckets while he goes off and gets himself killed?'

'Just check, Roy. It's worth a shot.'

Lindell went off toward the bank doors. Bosch looked at his partners.

'Jerry, you going to want your gun back? We should tell them now so they don't destroy them or file them away forever.'

'My gun?'

Edgar looked at all of the yellow plastic with a pained look on his face.

'No, Harry, I don't think so. That piece is haunted now. I don't ever want it back.'

'Yeah,' Bosch said. 'I was thinking the same thing.'

Bosch brooded about things for a while and then heard his name being called. He turned and saw Lindell beckoning him from the door of the bank. He headed over.

'Bingo,' Lindell said. 'She's got a box.'

They walked back into the bank and Bosch saw several agents conducting interviews with the branch's stunned employees. Lindell led him to a desk where the branch manager sat. She was a woman of about thirty with brown curly hair. The nameplate on her desk said Jeanne Connors. Lindell picked up a file that was on her desk and showed it to Bosch.

'She has a box here and she made Tony Aliso a signatory on it. He pulled the box at the same time he pulled his own on the Friday before he got nailed. You know what I'm thinking? I think he emptied his and put it all in hers.'

'Probably.'

Bosch was looking at the safe deposit entry records in the file. They were handwritten on a three by five card.

'So,' Lindell said, 'what we do is we get a warrant for her box and drill the sucker – maybe get Maury out there to do it, since he's being so cooperative. We seize the money and the federal government is that much ahead. You guys'd get a split, too.'

Bosch looked at him.

'You can drill it, if you've got the probable cause, but there isn't going to be anything in it.'

Bosch pointed to the last entry on the box card. Gretchen Alexander had pulled the box herself five days earlier – the Wednesday after Tony Aliso was killed. Lindell stared at it a long moment before reacting.

'Jesus, you think she cleared it out?'

'Yeah, Roy, I do.'

'She's gone, isn't she? You've been looking for her, haven't you?'

'She's in the wind, man. And I guess so am I.'

'You're leaving?'

'I gave my statement, I'm clear. I'll see you, Roy.'

'Yeah, okay, Bosch.'

Bosch headed to the door of the bank. As he opened it, Lindell came up behind him.

'But why'd he put it all in her box?'

He was still holding the box card and staring at it as if it might suddenly answer all his questions.

'I don't know but I've got a guess.'

'What's that, Bosch?'

'He was in love with her.'

'Him? A girl like that?'

'You never know. People can kill each other for all kinds of reasons. I guess they can fall in love with each other for all kinds of reasons. You gotta take it when it comes, no matter if it's a girl like that or . . . someone else.'

Lindell just nodded and Bosch stepped through the door.

Bosch, Edgar and Rider took a cab to the federal building and picked up their car. Bosch said he wanted to stop by the house in North Las Vegas where Gretchen Alexander had grown up.

'She isn't going to be there, Harry,' Edgar said. 'Are you kidding?'

'I know she won't be there. I just want to talk to the old lady for a minute.'

He found the house without getting lost and pulled into the driveway. The RX7 was still there and didn't look like it had moved.

'This will only take a minute, if you want to stay in the car.'

'I'll go in,' Rider said.

'I'll stay and keep the AC going,' Edgar said. 'In fact, I'll drive the first leg, Harry.'

He got out as Bosch and Rider exited and came around and took Bosch's place behind the wheel.

Bosch's knock on the front door was answered quickly. The woman had heard or seen the car and was ready.

'You,' she said, looking through the two-inch crack she had allowed in the door. 'Gretchen still isn't here.'

'I know, Mrs Alexander. It's you I want to talk to.'

'Me? What on earth for?'

'Would you please let us in? It's hot out here.'

She opened the door with a resigned look on her face.

'Hot in here, too. I can't afford to put the thermostat lower than eighty.'

Bosch and Rider entered and moved into the living room. He introduced Rider and all three of them sat down. This time Bosch sat on the edge of the sofa, remembering how he had sunk in last time.

'All right, what's this about? Why do you want to talk to me?'

'I want to know about your granddaughter's mother,' Bosch said.

The old woman's mouth went slack and Bosch could tell Rider wasn't much less confused.

'Her mother?' Dorothy asked. 'Her mother's long gone. Didn't have the

538

decency to see her own child through. Never mind her mother.'

'When did she leave?'

'Long time ago. Gretchen wasn't even out of diapers. She just left me a note saying good-bye and good luck. She was gone.'

'Where'd she go?'

'I have no earthly idea and I don't want to know. Good riddance, is what I say. She turned her back on that beautiful little girl. Didn't have the decency to ever call or even send for a picture.'

'How did you know she was even alive?'

'I didn't. She could be dead all these years for all I know or care.'

She was a bad liar, the type who got louder and indignant when she lied.

'You know,' Bosch said. 'She sent you money, didn't she?'

The woman looked sullenly down at her hands for a long moment. It was her way of confirming his guess.

'How often?'

'Once or twice a year. It wasn't near enough to make up for what she did.'

Bosch wanted to ask how much would have been enough but let it go.

'How did the money come?'

'Mail. It was in cash. I know it came from Sherman Oaks, California. That was always the postmark. What does this have to do with anything now?'

'Tell me your daughter's name, Dorothy.'

'She was born to me and my first husband. My name was Gilroy back then and that was hers.'

'Jennifer Gilroy,' Rider said, repeating Veronica Aliso's true name.

The old woman looked at Rider with surprise but didn't ask how she knew.

'We called her Jenny,' she said. 'Anyway, you see, when I took over with Gretchen I was remarried and had a new name. I gave it to Gretchen so the kids at school wouldn't bother her about it. Everybody always thought I was her momma and that was fine with the both of us. Nobody needed to know diff'rent.'

Bosch just nodded. It had all come together now. Veronica Aliso was Layla's mother. Tony Aliso had gone from the mother to the daughter. There was nothing else to ask or say. He thanked the old woman and touched Rider on the back so that she would go through the door first. Out on the front step, he paused and looked back at Dorothy Alexander. He waited until Rider was a few steps toward the car before speaking.

'When you hear from Layla – I mean, Gretchen – tell her not to come home. Tell her to stay as far away from here as she can.'

He shook his head.

'She shouldn't ever come home.'

The woman didn't say anything. Bosch waited a couple moments while looking down at the worn welcome mat. He then nodded and headed to the car.

Bosch took the backseat behind Edgar, Rider sat in the front. As soon as they were in the car and Edgar was backing out of the driveway, Rider turned around and looked at Bosch.

'Harry, how did you ever put that together?'

'Her last words. Veronica's. She said, "Let my daughter go." I just sort of knew then. There's a resemblance there. I just didn't place it before.'

'You've never even seen her.'

'I've seen her picture.'

'What?' Edgar said. 'What's going on?'

'Do you think Tony Aliso knew who she was?' Rider asked, ignoring Edgar.

'Hard to say,' Bosch said. 'If he did, it makes what happened to him easier to understand, easier to take. Maybe he was flaunting it with Veronica. Maybe it's what sent her over the edge.'

'And Layla-slash-Gretchen?'

Edgar's head was swiveling back and forth between them and the road, a look of confusion on his face.

'Something tells me she didn't know. I think if she did, she would have told her grandmother and the old lady didn't know.'

'If he was just using her to get to Veronica, why'd he move all the money into her box?'

'He could've been using her but he also could've been in love with her. We'll never know. Might've just been coincidence that it happened on the day he got killed. He could've just transferred the cash because he had the IRS on him. Maybe he was afraid they'd find out about the box and freeze his access to it. It could've been a lot of things. But we'll never know now. Everybody's dead.'

'Except for the girl.'

Edgar made a hard stop, pulling to the side of the road. Coincidentally, they happened to be across the street from Dolly's on Madison.

'Is somebody gonna tell me what the hell is going on?' he demanded. 'I do you people a favor and keep the car cool while you two go inside for a chat and then I'm left in the dark. Now what the hell are you two talking about?'

He was looking at Bosch in the rearview mirror.

'Just drive, Jed. Kiz will tell you when we get to the Flamingo.'

They drove into the front circle of the Hilton Flamingo and Bosch left them there. He moved quickly through the football field-sized casino, dodging rows of slot machines, until he reached the poker room, where Eleanor had said she would be when they were done. They had dropped her at the Flamingo that morning after she had shown them the bank she had once seen Tony Aliso going into with Gretchen Alexander.

There were five tables going in the poker room. Bosch quickly scanned the faces of the players but did not see Eleanor. Then, as he turned to look back across the casino, she was there, just as when she had appeared on the first night he'd gone looking for her.

'Harry.'

'Eleanor. I thought you'd be playing.'

'I couldn't play while thinking about you out there. Is everything okay?'

'Everything is fine. We're leaving.'

'Good. I don't like Las Vegas anymore.'

He hesitated for a moment before saying anything. He almost faltered but then the resolve came back to him.

'There is that one stop I'd still like to make before we leave. The one we talked about. That is, if you've decided.'

She looked at him for a long moment and then a smile broke across her face.

Bosch walked across the polished linoleum on the sixth floor of Parker Center, purposely driving his heels down with each step. He wanted to put scuff marks on the carefully tended finish. He turned into the alcove entrance to the Internal Affairs Division and asked the secretary behind the counter for Chastain. She asked if he had an appointment and Bosch told her he didn't make appointments with people like Chastain. She stared at him a moment and he stared back until she picked up a phone and punched in an extension. After whispering into the line, she held the phone to her chest and looked up at Bosch and then eyed the shoebox and file he held in his hands.

'He wants to know what it's about.'

'Tell him it's about his case against me falling apart.'

She whispered some more and then Bosch was finally buzzed through the counter's half door. He went into the IAD squad room, where several of the desks were occupied by investigators. Chastain stood up from behind one of these.

'What are you doing here, Bosch? You're on suspension for letting that prisoner escape.'

He said it loudly so that the others in the squad room would know that Bosch was a guilty man.

'The chief cut it down to a week,' Bosch said. 'I call that a vacation.'

'Well, that's only round one. I still got your file open.'

'That's why I'm here.'

Chastain pointed to the interview room Bosch had been in the week before with Zane.

'Let's talk in there.'

'No,' Bosch said. 'We're not talking, Chastain. I'm just showing.'

He dropped the file he was carrying on the desk. Chastain remained standing and looked at it without opening it.

'What is this?'

'It's the end of the case. Open it.'

Chastain sat down and opened the file, exhaling loudly, as if he were embarking on a distasteful and worthless chore. On top was a copy of a page from the department's manual of procedure and officer conduct. The manual was to IAD dicks what the state penal code was to the rest of the officers and investigators in the department.

The page in the file pertained to officers associating with known criminals, convicted felons and members of organized crime. Such association was strictly forbidden and punishable by dismissal from the department, according to the code.

'Bosch, you didn't need to bring me this, I've got the whole book,' Chastain said.

He was trying out some light banter because he didn't know what Bosch was doing and was well aware that his peers were watching from their desks while trying to act as if they weren't.

'Yeah? Well, you better get your book out and read the bottom line there, pal. The exception.'

Chastain looked down at the bottom of the page.

'Says, "Exception to this code can be established if the officer can show to the satisfaction of superior officers a family relationship through blood or marriage. If that is established, the officer must—"'

'That's enough,' Bosch said.

He reached down and took the page so that Chastain could see what was in the rest of the file.

'What you have there, Chastain, is a marriage certificate issued in Clark County, Nevada, attesting to my marriage to Eleanor Wish. If that's not good enough for you, beneath it are two affidavits from my partners. They witnessed the marriage. Best man and maid of honor.'

Chastain kept his eyes on the paperwork.

'It's over, man,' Bosch said. 'You lose. So get the fuck out of my life.'

Chastain leaned back. His face was red and he had an uncomfortable smile on his face. Now he was sure the others were watching.

'You're telling me you got married just to avoid an IAD beef?'

'No, asshole. I got married because I love somebody. That's why you get married.'

Chastain didn't have a reply. He shook his head, looked at his watch and shuffled some papers while trying to act as though this was just a minor interruption in his day. He did everything but look at his nails.

'Yeah, I thought you'd run out of things to say,' Bosch said. 'I'll see you around, Chastain.'

He turned to walk away but then turned back to Chastain.

'Oh, and I almost forgot, you can tell your source our deal is done with, also.'

'What source, Bosch? Deal? What are you talking about?'

'I'm talking about Fitzgerald or whoever you get your information from at OCID.'

'I don't—'

'Sure you do. I know you, Chastain. You couldn't have come up with Eleanor Wish on your own. You've got a pipeline over there to Fitzgerald. He told you about her. It was him or one of his people. Doesn't matter to me who. Either way I'm out of a deal I made with him. You can tell him that.'

Bosch held the shoebox up and shook it. The videotape and audiotapes rattled inside it, but he could tell Chastain had no idea what was in the box or what it meant.

'You tell him, Chastain,' he said again. 'See you around.'

He finally left then, pausing only at the counter to give the secretary a thumbs-up sign. In the hallway, rather than turn left toward the elevators, he took a right and headed through the double doors of the chief of police's office suite. The chief's adjutant, a lieutenant in uniform, sat behind the reception desk. Bosch didn't know him, which was good. He walked up and put the shoebox down on the desk.

'Can I help you? What's this?'

'It's a box, Lieutenant. It's got some tapes the chief will want to watch and listen to. Right away.'

Bosch made a move to leave.

'Wait a minute,' the adjutant said. 'Will he know what this is about?'

Bosch left then, not turning around when the adjutant called after him for his name. He slipped through the double doors and headed down to the elevator. He felt good. He didn't know if anything would come of the illegal tapes he had given the police chief, but he felt that all decks were cleared. His show with the box earlier with Chastain would ensure that the word got back to Fitzgerald that this was exclusively Bosch's play. Billets and Rider should be safe from recriminations by the OCID chief. He could come after Bosch if he wanted, but Bosch felt safe now. Fitzgerald had nothing on him anymore. No one did.

It was their first day on the beach after spending two days almost exclusively in their room. Bosch couldn't get comfortable on the chaise longue. He didn't understand how people did this, just sit in the sun and bake. He was covered with lotion and there was sand caked between his toes. Eleanor had bought him a red bathing suit that he thought made him look foolish and that made him feel like a target. At least, he thought, it wasn't one of those slingshot things some of the men on the beach were wearing.

He propped himself up on his elbows and looked around. Hawaii was unbelievable. So beautiful it was like a dream. And the women were beautiful, too. Especially Eleanor. She lay beside him on her own chaise. Her eyes were closed and there was a small smile on her face. She wore a one-piece black bathing suit that was cut high on her hips and showed off her tanned and nicely muscled legs.

'What are you looking at?' she said without opening her eyes.

'Nothing. I just . . . I can't get comfortable. I think I'm going to take a walk or something.'

'Why don't you get a book to read, Harry? You have to relax. That's what honeymoons are about. Sex, relaxation, good food and good company.'

'Well, two out of four isn't bad.'

'What's wrong with the food?'

'The food's great.'

'Funny.'

She reached out and hit him in the arm. Then she, too, propped herself up on her elbows and gazed out at the shimmering blue water. They could see the spine of Molokini rising in the distance.

'It's so beautiful here, Harry.'

'Yes, it is.'

They sat in silence for a few moments, watching the people walking by at the water's edge. Bosch brought his legs up, leaned forward and sat with his elbows on his knees. He could feel the sun burning into his shoulders. It was beginning to feel good.

He noticed a woman walking languidly along the edge. She had the attention of every man on the beach. She was tall and lithe and had long brownish-blond hair that was wet from the sea. Her skin was copper and she wore the smallest of bathing suits, just a few strings and triangles of black cloth.

551

As she passed in front of him, the glare dropped off Bosch's sunglasses and he studied her face. The familiar lines and tilt of the jaw were there. He knew her.

'Harry,' Eleanor whispered then. 'Is that . . . it looks like the dancer. The girl in that photo you had, the one I saw Tony with.'

'Layla,' Bosch said, not answering her but just to say the name.

'It's her, isn't it?'

'I didn't used to believe in coincidences,' he said.

'Are you going to call the bureau? The money's probably right here on the island with her.'

Bosch watched the woman moving away. Her back was to him now and from that angle it was almost as if she were naked. Just a few strings from her suit were visible. The glare came back on his glasses at this angle and his vision of her was distorted. She was disappearing in the glare and the mist coming in from the Pacific.

'No, I'm not calling anybody,' he finally said.

'Why not?'

'She didn't do anything,' he said. 'She let some guy give her money. Nothing wrong with that. Maybe she was even in love with him.'

He watched for another moment, thinking about Veronica's last words to him.

'Anyway, who's going to miss the money?' he said. 'The bureau? The LAPD? Some fat old gangster in a Chicago suburb with a bunch of bodyguards around him? Forget it. I'm not calling anybody.'

He took one last look at her. She was far away now and as she walked she was looking out to sea, the sun holding her face. Bosch nodded to her, but of course she didn't see this. He then lay back down on the chaise and closed his eyes. Almost immediately he felt the sun begin penetrating his skin, doing its healing work. And then he felt Eleanor's hand on top of his. He smiled. He felt safe. He felt like nobody could ever hurt him again.

ANGELS FLIGHT

This is for McCaleb Jane Connelly

1

The word sounded alien in his mouth, as if spoken by someone else. There was an urgency in his own voice that Bosch didn't recognize. The simple hello he had whispered into the telephone was full of hope, almost desperation. But the voice that came back to him was not the one he needed to hear.

'Detective Bosch?'

For a moment Bosch felt foolish. He wondered if the caller had recognized the faltering of his voice.

'This is Lieutenant Michael Tulin. Is this Bosch?'

The name meant nothing to Bosch and his momentary concern about how he sounded was ripped away as an awful dread entered his mind.

'This is Bosch. What is it? What's wrong?'

'Hold please for Deputy Chief Irving.'

'What is—'

The caller clicked off and there was only silence. Bosch now remembered who Tulin was – Irving's adjutant. Bosch stood still and waited. He looked around the kitchen; only the dim oven light was on. With one hand he held the phone hard against his ear, the other he instinctively brought up to his stomach, where fear and dread were twisting together. He looked at the glowing numbers on the stove clock. It was almost two, five minutes past the last time he had looked at it. This isn't right, he thought as he waited. They don't do this by phone. They come to your door. They tell you this face-to-face.

Finally, Irving picked up on the other end of the line.

'Detective Bosch?'

'Where is she? What happened?'

Another moment of excruciating silence went by as Bosch waited. His eyes were closed now.

'Excuse me?'

'Just tell me, what happened to her? I mean . . . is she alive?'

'Detective, I'm not sure what it is you are talking about. I'm calling because I need to muster your team as soon as possible. I need you for a special assignment.'

Bosch opened his eyes. He looked through the kitchen window into the dark canyon below his house. His eyes followed the slope of the hill down toward the freeway and then up again to the slash of Hollywood lights he could see through the cut of the Cahuenga Pass. He wondered if each light meant someone awake and waiting for someone who wasn't going to come. Bosch saw his own reflection in the window. He looked weary. He could make out the deep circles etched beneath his eyes, even in the dark glass.

'I have an assignment, Detective,' Irving repeated impatiently. 'Are you able to work or are you—'

'I can work. I just was mixed up there for a moment.'

'Well, I'm sorry if I woke you. But you should be used to it.'

'Yes. It's no problem.'

Bosch didn't tell him that he hadn't been awakened by the call. That he had been roaming around in his dark house waiting.

'Then get it going, Detective. We'll have coffee down here at the scene.'

'What scene?'

'We'll talk about it when you get here. I don't want to delay this any further. Call your team. Have them come to Grand Street between Third and Fourth. The top of Angels Flight. Do you know where I'm talking about?'

'Bunker Hill? I don't—'

'It will be explained when you get here. Seek me out when you are here. If I am at the bottom come down to me before you speak with anyone.'

'What about Lieutenant Billets? She should—'

'She will be informed about what is happening. We're wasting time. This is not a request. It is a command. Get your people together and get down here. Am I making myself clear to you?'

'You're clear.'

'Then I will be expecting you.'

Irving hung up without waiting for a reply. Bosch stood with the phone still at his ear for a few moments, wondering what was going on. Angels Flight was the short inclined railroad that carried people up Bunker Hill in downtown – far outside the boundaries of the Hollywood Division homicide table. If Irving had a body down there at Angels Flight the investigation would fall under the jurisdiction of Central Division. If Central detectives couldn't handle it because of caseload or personnel problems, or if the case was deemed too important or media sensitive for them, then it would be bumped to the bulls, the Robbery-Homicide Division. The fact that a deputy chief of police was involved in the case before dawn on a Saturday suggested the latter possibility. The fact that he was calling Bosch and his team in instead of the RHD bulls was the puzzle. Whatever it was that Irving had working at Angels Flight didn't make sense.

Bosch glanced once more down into the dark canyon, pulled the phone away from his ear and clicked it off. He wished he had a cigarette but he had made it this far through the night without one. He wouldn't break now.

He turned his back and leaned on the counter. He looked down at the phone in his hand, turned it back on and hit the speed dial button that would connect him with Kizmin Rider's apartment. He would call Jerry Edgar after he talked to her. Bosch felt a sense of relief come over him that he was reluctant to acknowledge. He might not yet know what awaited him at Angels Flight, but it would certainly take his thoughts away from Eleanor Wish.

Rider's alert voice answered after two rings.

'Kiz, it's Harry,' he said. 'We've got work.'

2

Bosch agreed to meet his two partners at the Hollywood Division station to pick up cars before they headed downtown to Angels Flight. On the way down the hill to the station he had punched in KFWB on his Jeep's radio and picked up a breaking news report on a homicide investigation under way at the site of the historical inclined railroad. The newsman on the scene reported that two bodies had been found inside one of the train cars and that several members of the Robbery-Homicide squad were on the scene. But that was the extent of the reporter's information, as he also noted that the police had placed an unusually wide cordon of yellow tape around the crime scene, prohibiting him from getting a closer look. At the station Bosch communicated this thin bit of information to Edgar and Rider while they signed three slickbacks out of the motor pool.

'So it looks like we're gonna be playing sloppy seconds to RHD,' Edgar concluded, showing his annoyance at being rousted from sleep to spend probably the whole weekend doing gofer work for the RHD bulls. 'Our guts, their glory. And we aren't even on call this weekend. Why didn't Irving call out Rice's got-damned team if he needed a Hollywood team?'

Edgar had a point. Team One – Bosch, Edgar and Rider – wasn't even up on call rotation this weekend. If Irving had followed proper call-out procedure he would have called Terry Rice, who headed up Team Three, which was currently on top of the rotation. But Bosch had already figured that Irving wasn't following any procedures, not if the deputy chief had called him directly before checking with his supervisor, Lieutenant Grace Billets.

'Well, Jerry,' Bosch said, more than used to his partner's whining, 'you'll get the chance to ask the deputy chief personally in a little while.'

'Yeah, right, I do that and I'll find my ass down in Harbor the next ten years. Fuck that.'

'Hey, Harbor Division's an easy gig,' Rider said, just to rag Edgar a bit. She knew Edgar lived in the Valley and that a transfer to Harbor Division would mean a miserable ninety-minute commute each way – the pure definition of freeway therapy, the brass's method of unofficially punishing malcontents and problem cops. 'They only pull six, seven homicides a year down there.'

'That's nice but count me the fuck out.'

'Okay, okay,' Bosch said. 'Let's just get going and we'll worry about all of that stuff later. Don't get lost.'

Bosch took Hollywood Boulevard to the 101 and coasted down the freeway in minimal traffic to downtown. Halfway there he checked the mirror and saw his partners cruising in the lanes behind him. Even in the dark and with other traffic he could pick them out. He hated the new detective cars. They were painted black and white and looked exactly like patrol cruisers with the exception that they did not carry emergency lights across the roof. It had been the former chief's idea to replace unmarked detective cars with the so-called slickbacks. The whole thing had been a scam perpetrated to fulfill his promises to put more cops on the street. By changing unmarked cars into clearly marked cars, he was giving the public the erroneous impression that there were more cops patrolling the streets. He also counted the detectives using slickbacks when he addressed community groups and proudly reported that he had increased the number of cops on the street by hundreds.

Meantime, detectives trying to do their jobs drove around like targets. More than once Bosch and his team had sought to serve an arrest warrant or had attempted to come into a neighborhood quietly in the course of an investigation only to have their presence signaled by their own cars. It was stupid and dangerous but it was the chief's edict and it was carried out throughout the department's divisional detective bureaus, even after the chief was not asked back for a second five-year term. Bosch, like many of the department's detectives, hoped the new chief would soon order the detective cars back to normal. Meanwhile, he no longer drove the car assigned to him home from work. It had been a nice detective supervisor's perk having a take-home car but he didn't want the marked car sitting in front of his house. Not in L.A. You never knew what menace that could bring to your door.

They got to Grand Street by two forty-five. As Bosch pulled to a stop he saw an unusually large number of police-related vehicles parked along the curb at California Plaza. He noted the crime scene and coroner's vans, several patrol cars and several more detective sedans – not the slickbacks, but the unmarked cars still used by the RHD bulls. While he waited for Rider and Edgar to pull up he opened his briefcase, took out the cellular phone and called his home. After five rings the machine picked up the call and he heard his own voice telling him to leave a message. He was about to click off but decided to leave a message.

'Eleanor, it's me. I've got a call out . . . but page me or call me on the cell phone when you get in so I know you're okay . . . Um, okay, that's it. Bye – oh, it's about two forty-five right now. Saturday morning. Bye.'

Edgar and Rider had walked up to his door. He put the phone away and got out with his briefcase. Edgar, the tallest, held up the yellow crime scene tape and they crossed under, gave their names and badge numbers to a uniform officer with the crime scene attendance list, and then walked across California Plaza.

The plaza was the centerpiece of Bunker Hill, a stone courtyard formed by the conjoining of two marble office towers, a high-rise apartment building and the Museum of Modern Art. There was a huge fountain and reflecting pool at its center, though the pumps and lights were off at this hour, leaving the water still and black.

Past the fountain was the beaux arts revival-styled station and wheel-house at the top of Angels Flight. It was next to this small structure that most of the investigators and patrol officers milled about as if waiting for something. Bosch looked for the gleaming shaven skull that belonged to Deputy Chief Irvin Irving but didn't see it. He and his partners stepped into the crowd and moved toward the lone rail car sitting at the top of the tracks. Along the way he recognized many faces of Robbery-Homicide detectives. They were men he had worked with years earlier when he had been part of the elite squad. A few of them nodded to him or called him by name. Bosch saw Francis Sheehan, his former partner, standing off by himself smoking a cigarette. Bosch broke from his partners and stepped over.

'Frankie,' he said. 'What's going on?'

'Harry, what are you doing here?'

'Got called out. Irving called us out.'

'Shit. Sorry, partner, I wouldn't wish this one on my enemy.'

'Why, what's going—'

'You better talk to the man first. He's putting the big blanket on this one.'

Bosch hesitated. Sheehan looked worn down but Bosch hadn't seen him in months. He had no idea what had put the dark circles under his hound dog eyes or when they had been cut into his face. For a moment Bosch remembered the reflection of his own face that he had seen earlier.

'You okay, Francis?'

'Never better.'

'Okay, I'll talk to you.'

Bosch rejoined Edgar and Rider, who were standing near the rail car. Edgar nodded slightly to Bosch's left.

'Hey, Harry, you see that?' he said in a low voice. 'That's Sustain Chastain and that bunch over there. What are those pricks doin' here?'

Bosch turned and saw the grouping of men from Internal Affairs.

'Got no idea,' he said.

Chastain and Bosch locked eyes for a moment but Bosch didn't hold it. It wasn't worth the waste of energy to get worked up over just seeing the IAD man. Instead, he focused on trying to put the whole scene together. His curiosity level was at maximum. The number of RHD bulls hanging around, the IAD shines, a deputy chief on the scene – he had to find out what was going on.

With Edgar and Rider behind him in single file, Bosch worked his way to the rail car. Portable lights had been set up inside and the car was lit up like somebody's living room. Inside, two crime scene techs were at work. This told Bosch that he was quite late arriving at the scene. The crime scene techs didn't move in until after the coroner's techs had completed their initial procedures – declaring victims dead, photographing the bodies *in situ*, searching them for wounds, weapons and identification.

Bosch stepped to the rear of the car and looked through the open door. The technicians were at work around two bodies. A woman was sprawled on one of the stepped seats about midway through the car. She was wearing gray leggings and a white thigh-length T-shirt. A large flower of blood had blossomed on her chest where she had been hit dead center with a single bullet. Her head was snapped back against the sill of the window behind her seat. She had dark hair and features, her lineage obviously stretching somewhere south of the border. On the seat next to her body was a plastic bag filled with many items Bosch couldn't see. A folded newspaper protruded from the top of it.

On the steps near the rear door to the car was the facedown body of a black man wearing a dark gray suit. From his viewpoint Bosch could not see the man's face and only one wound was visible – a through-and-through gunshot wound at the center of the victim's right hand. Bosch knew it was what would later be called a defensive wound in the autopsy report. The man had held his hand up in a futile attempt to ward off gunfire. Bosch had seen it often enough over the years and it always made him think about the desperate actions people take at the end. Putting a hand up to stop a bullet was one of the most desperate.

Though the techs were stepping in and out of his line of sight, Bosch could look straight down through the inclined train car and down the track to Hill Street about three hundred feet below. A duplicate train car was down there at the bottom of the hill and Bosch could see more detectives milling about by the turnstiles and the closed doors of the Grand Central Market across the street.

Bosch had ridden the inclined railroad as a kid and had studied how it worked. He still remembered. The two matching cars were counterbalanced. When one went up the side-by-side tracks the other went down, and vice versa. They passed each other at the midpoint. He remembered riding on Angels Flight long before Bunker Hill had been reborn as a slick business center of glass and marble towers, classy condominiums and apartments, museums, and fountains referred to as water gardens. Back then the hill had been a place of once-grand Victorian homes turned into tired-looking rooming houses. Harry and his mother had taken Angels Flight up the hill to look for a place to live.

'Finally, Detective Bosch.'

Bosch turned around. Deputy Chief Irving stood in the open door of the little station house.

'All of you,' he said, signaling Bosch and his team inside.

They entered a cramped room dominated by the large old cable wheels that once moved the train cars up and down the incline. Bosch remembered reading that when Angels Flight was rehabilitated a few years earlier after a quarter century of disuse, the cables and wheels had been replaced with an electric system monitored by computer.

On one side of the wheel display was just enough room for a small lunch table with two folding chairs. On the other side was the computer for operating the trains, a stool for the operator and a stack of cardboard boxes, the top one open and showing stacks of pamphlets on the history of Angels Flight.

Standing against the far wall, in the shadow behind the old iron wheels, his arms folded and his craggy, sun-reddened face looking down at the floor, was a man Bosch recognized. Bosch had once worked for Captain John Garwood, commander of the Robbery-Homicide Division. He knew by the look on his face that he was very put out about something. Garwood didn't look up at them and the three detectives said nothing.

Irving went to a telephone on the lunch table and picked up the loose handset. As he began talking he motioned to Bosch to close the door.

'Excuse me, sir,' Irving said. 'It was the team from Hollywood. They are all here and we are ready to proceed.'

He listened for a few moments, said good-bye and hung up the phone. The reverence in his voice and his use of the word *sir* told Bosch that Irving had been talking to the chief of police. It was one more curiosity about the case.

'All right, then,' Irving said, turning around and facing the three detectives. 'I am sorry to roust you people, especially out of rotation. However, I have spoken with Lieutenant Billets and as of now you have been cut free of the Hollywood rotation until we get this handled.'

'What exactly is *this* that we are handling?' Bosch asked.

'A delicate situation. The homicides of two citizens.'

Bosch wished he would get to the point.

'Chief, I see enough RHD people around here to investigate the Bobby Kennedy case all over again,' he said, glancing at Garwood. 'And that's not to mention the IAD shines hovering around the edges. What exactly are we doing here? What do you want?'

'Simple,' Irving said. 'I am turning the investigation over to you. It is your case now, Detective Bosch. The Robbery-Homicide detectives will be withdrawing as soon as you people are brought up to speed. As you can see, you are coming in late. That's unfortunate but I think you will be able to overcome it. I know what you can do.'

Bosch stared at him blankly for a long moment, then glanced at Garwood again. The captain had not moved and continued to stare at the floor. Bosch asked the only question that could bring understanding to this strange situation.

'That man and woman on the train car, who are they?'

Irving nodded.

'*Were* is probably the more correct word. *Were*. The woman's name was Catalina Perez. Who exactly she was and what she was doing on Angels Flight we do not know yet. It probably does not matter. It appears that she was just in the wrong place at the wrong time. But that will be for you to officially determine. Anyway, the man in there, he is different. That was Howard Elias.'

'The lawyer?'

Irving nodded. Bosch heard Edgar draw in a breath and hold it.

'This is for real?'

'Unfortunately.'

Bosch looked past Irving and through the ticket window. He could see into the train car. The techs were still at work, getting ready to shut off the lights so they could laser the inside of the car to look for fingerprints. His eyes fell to the hand with the bullet wound through it. Howard Elias. Bosch thought about all the suspects there would be, many of them standing around outside at that very moment, watching.

'Shit,' Edgar said. 'Don't suppose we could take a pass on this one, could we, Chief?'

'Watch your language, Detective,' Irving snapped, the muscles of his jaw bulging as he grew angry. 'That is not acceptable here.'

'Look, Chief, all I'm sayin' is if you're looking for somebody to play department Uncle Tom, it ain't going to be—'

'That has nothing to do with this,' Irving said, cutting him off. 'Whether you like it or not, you have been assigned to this case. I expect each of you to do it professionally and thoroughly. Most of all, I expect results, as does the chief of police. Other matters mean nothing. Absolutely nothing.'

After a brief silence, during which Irving's eyes went from Edgar to Rider and then to Bosch, the deputy chief continued.

'In this department there is only one race,' he said. 'Not black or white. Just the blue race.'

3

Howard Elias's notoriety as a civil rights attorney did not come to him because of the clients he served – they could best be described as ne'er-do-wells if not outright criminals. What had made Elias's face and name so well known to the masses of Los Angeles was his use of the media, his skill at probing the inflamed nerve of racism in the city, and the fact that his law practice was built entirely around one particular expertise: suing the Los Angeles Police Department.

For nearly two decades he had made a more than comfortable living filing lawsuit after lawsuit in federal court on behalf of citizens who had collided in some way with the police department. Elias sued patrol officers, detectives, the chief of police, the institution itself. When he filed, he used the shotgun approach, naming as defendants anyone remotely connected with the incident at the heart of the matter. After a fleeing burglary suspect was chewed up by a police dog, Elias had sued on the injured man's behalf, naming the dog, its handler and the line of supervision from the handler up to the chief of police. For good measure, he had sued the handler's academy instructors and the dog's breeder as well.

In his late-night television 'infomercials' and frequent 'impromptu' but cleverly orchestrated press conferences on the steps of the U.S. District Courthouse, Elias always cast himself as a watchdog, a lone voice crying out against the abuses of a fascist and racist paramilitary organization known as the LAPD. To his critics – and they ran from the rank and file of the LAPD to the offices of the city and district attorneys – Elias was a racist himself, a loose cannon who helped widen the fractures in an already divided city. To these detractors he was the scum of the legal system, a courtroom magician who could reach into the deck at any place and still pull out the race card.

Most often Elias's clients were black or brown. His skills as a public speaker and his selective use of facts while employing those skills often turned his clients into community heroes, emblematic victims of a police department out of control. Many in the city's south neighborhoods credited Elias with single-handedly keeping the LAPD from behaving as an occupying army. Howard Elias was one of the few people in the city who could be absolutely hated and fervently celebrated in different quarters at the same time.

Few who revered Elias understood that his entire practice was built around one simple piece of the law. He filed lawsuits only in federal court and under provisions of the U.S. civil rights codes that allowed him to bill the city of Los Angeles for his fees in any case in which he was victorious in court.

The Rodney King beating, the Christopher Commission report excoriating the department in the wake of the King trial and subsequent civil unrest, and the racially divisive O. J. Simpson case created a shadow that stretched over every case Elias filed. And so it was not particularly difficult for the lawyer to win cases against the department, convincing juries to award at least token damages to plaintiffs. Those juries never realized that such verdicts opened the door for Elias to bill the city and its taxpayers, themselves included, hundreds of thousands of dollars in fees.

In the dog bite lawsuit, which became Elias's signature case, the jury found that the rights of the plaintiff had been violated. But since that plaintiff was a burglar with a long track record of prior arrests and convictions, the jury awarded him only one dollar in damages. Their intent was clear, to send a message to the police department rather than to make a criminal wealthy. But that didn't matter to Elias. A win was a win. Under the federal guidelines he then submitted a bill to the city for $340,000 in legal fees. The city screamed and audited it, but still ended up paying more than half. In effect, the jury – and the many before and since – believed they were delivering a rebuke to the LAPD, but they were also paying for Elias's half-hour late-night infomercials on Channel 9, his Porsche and his Italian courtroom suits, his opulent home up in Baldwin Hills.

Elias, of course, was not alone. There were dozens of attorneys in the city who specialized in police and civil rights cases and mined the same federal provision allowing them to extract fees far in excess of the damages awarded their clients. Not all were cynical and motivated by money. Lawsuits by Elias and others had brought about positive change in the department. Even their enemies – the cops – could not begrudge them that. Civil rights cases brought about the end of the department-approved use of the choke hold while subduing suspects – after an inordinately high number of minority deaths. Lawsuits had also improved conditions and protections in local jails. Other cases opened and streamlined means for citizens to file complaints against abusive police officers.

But Elias stood head and shoulders above them all. He had media charm and the speaking skills of an actor. He also seemed to lack any criteria when it came to choosing his clients. He represented drug dealers who claimed to have been abused by their interrogators, burglars who stole from the poor but objected to being beaten by the police who chased them down, robbers who shot their victims but then cried foul when they in turn were shot by police. Elias's favorite line – used as a tagline on his commercials and whenever cameras were pointed at his face – was to say that abuse of power was abuse of power, regardless of whether the victim was a criminal. He was always quick to look into the camera and declare that if such abuse were tolerated when it was aimed at the guilty, it wouldn't be long before the innocent were targeted.

Elias was a sole practitioner. In the last decade he had sued the department more than a hundred times and won jury verdicts in more than half of the cases. His was a name that could freeze a cop's brain when he heard it. In the department, you knew that if Elias sued you, it would not be a small case that would be cleaned up and swept away. Elias didn't settle cases out of court – nothing in the civil rights codes gave an incentive to settle cases. No, you would be dragged through a public spectacle if Elias aimed a lawsuit at you. There would be press releases, press conferences, newspaper headlines, television stories. You'd be lucky to come out of it in one piece, let alone with your badge.

Angel to some, devil to others, Howard Elias was now dead, shot to death on the Angels Flight railroad. Bosch knew as he looked through the small room's window and watched the orange glow of the laser beam move about the darkened train car that he was in the calm before the storm. In just two days what might have been Elias's biggest case was due to begin. The lawsuit against the LAPD that had become known in the media as the 'Black Warrior' case was set for jury selection in U.S. District Court on Monday morning. The coincidence – or, as a wide swath of the public would undoubtedly believe, the lack of coincidence – between Elias's murder and the start of the trial would make the investigation of the attorney's death an easy seven on the media's Richter scale. Minority groups would howl with rage and rightful suspicion. The whites in the West Side would whisper about their fears of another riot. And the eyes of the nation would be on Los Angeles and its police department once more. Bosch at that moment agreed with Edgar, though for different reasons than his black partner's. He wished they could take a pass on this one.

'Chief,' he said, turning his focus back to Irving, 'when it gets out who . . . I mean, when the media find out it was Elias, we're going to—'

'That is not your concern,' Irving said. 'Your concern is the investigation. The chief and I will deal with the media. Not a word comes from anyone on the investigation. Not a word.'

'Forget the media,' Rider said. 'What about South Central? People are going to—'

'That will be handled,' Irving said, interrupting. 'The department will institute the public disorder readiness plan beginning with the next watch. All personnel shift to twelve and twelves until we see how the city reacts. Nobody who saw nineteen ninety-two wants to see that again. But again, that is not your concern. You have one concern here.'

'You didn't let me finish,' Rider said. 'I wasn't going to say they would riot. I actually have faith in the people there. I don't think there will be trouble. What I was going to say was that they will be angry about this and suspicious. If you think you can ignore that or contain it by putting more cops on the—'

'Detective Rider,' Irving said, interrupting again, 'that is not your concern. The *investigation* is your concern.'

Bosch saw that Irving's interruptions and words, telling a black woman not to be concerned about her own community, had incensed Rider. It was on her face and Bosch had seen the look before. He decided to speak before she said something out of line.

'We're going to need more people. With just the three of us, we'll be running down alibis full-time for weeks, maybe a month. Case like this, we need to move fast, not only because of the case but because of the people. We're going to need more than just three of us.'

'That, too, has been taken care of,' Irving said. 'You will have all the help you need. But it won't come from Robbery-Homicide. It's a conflict of interest because of the Michael Harris matter.'

Before speaking, Bosch noted how Irving refused to call it the Black Warrior case, instead using the plaintiff's name.

'Why us?'

'What?'

'I understand why RHD is out. But where are the Central Division teams? We're off our beat and out of rotation here. Why us?'

Irving exhaled audibly.

'The entire Central Division homicide squad is in academy training this week and next. Sensitivity training and then the FBI workshop on new crime scene techniques. Robbery-Homicide was covering their calls. They took this one. Once it was determined who that was with the bullets in his head, I was contacted and in subsequent discussions with the chief of police it was determined that we would reach out to you. You are a good team. One of our best. You have cleared your last four, including that hard-boiled eggs job – yes, I was briefed on it. Plus, the main thing is, none of you were ever sued by Elias.'

He pointed with his thumb over his shoulder in the direction of the crime scene in the train car. As he did this he glanced at Garwood but the captain was still looking down at the floor.

'No conflict of interest,' Irving said. 'Correct?'

The three detectives nodded. Bosch had been sued often enough in his twenty-five years with the department, but somehow he had always avoided tangling with Elias. Still, he didn't believe Irving's explanation was complete. He knew that Edgar had already alluded to a reason for their choice, probably a reason more important than the fact that none of them had been sued by Elias. Bosch's two partners were black. That might come in handy for Irving at some point. Bosch knew Irving's desire that the department have only one face and one race – blue – would go out the window when he needed a black face for the cameras.

'I don't want my people paraded in front of the media, Chief,' Bosch said. 'If we're on the case, we're on the case to work it, not for a show.'

Irving stared at him with angry eyes.

'What did you call me?'

Bosch was momentarily taken aback.

'I called you Chief.'

'Oh, good. Because I was wondering if there was some confusion here over the line of command in this room. Is there, Detective?'

Bosch looked away and out the window again. He could feel his face turning red and it upset him to give himself away.

'No,' he said.

'Good,' Irving said without a trace of tension. 'Then I am going to leave you with Captain Garwood. He will bring you up to speed on what has been accomplished so far. When he is done, we will talk about how we are going to set this case up.'

He turned to the door but Bosch stopped him.

'One more thing, Chief.'

Irving turned back to him. Bosch had recovered his composure now. He looked calmly at the deputy chief.

'You know we are going to be looking hard at cops on this. Lots of them. We'll have to go through all of the lawyer's cases, not just the Black Warrior thing. So I just need to know up front – we all need to – do you and the police chief want the chips to fall where they fall or . . .'

He didn't finish and Irving said nothing.

'I want to protect my people,' Bosch said. 'This kind of case . . . we just need to be clear about everything up front.'

Bosch was taking a gamble saying it in front of Garwood and the others. It would likely anger Irving again. But Bosch took the shot because he wanted Irving to answer him in front of Garwood. The captain was a powerful man in the department. Bosch wanted him to know that his team would be following the directives of the highest command, just in case the chips fell close to some of Garwood's people.

Irving looked at him for a long moment before finally speaking.

'Your insolence is noted, Detective Bosch.'

'Yes, sir. But what's the answer?'

'Let them fall, Detective. Two people are dead that should not be dead. It does not matter who they were. They should not be dead. Do your best work. Use all your skills. And let the chips fall.'

Bosch nodded once. Irving turned and glanced quickly at Garwood before leaving the room.

4

'Harry, you have a smoke?'

'Sorry, Cap, I'm trying to quit.'

'Me, too. I guess all that really means is that you borrow 'em rather than buy 'em.'

Garwood stepped away from the corner and blew out his breath. With his foot he moved a stack of boxes away from the wall and sat down on them. He looked old and tired to Bosch but then he had looked that way twelve years before when Bosch had gone to work for him. Garwood didn't raise any particular feelings in Bosch. He had been the aloof sort of supervisor. Didn't socialize with the squad after hours, didn't spend much time out of his office and in the bullpen. At the time, Bosch thought maybe that was good. It didn't engender a lot of loyalty from Garwood's people, but it didn't create any enmity either. Maybe that was how Garwood had lasted in the spot for so long.

'Well, it looks like we really got our tit in the wringer this time,' Garwood said. He then looked at Rider and added, 'Excuse the saying, Detective.'

Bosch's pager sounded and he quickly pulled it off his belt, disengaged the beep and looked at the number. It was not his own number as he had hoped it would be. He recognized it as the home number of Lieutenant Grace Billets. She probably wanted to know what was going on. If Irving had been as circumspect with her as he had been with Bosch on the phone, then she knew next to nothing.

'Important?' Garwood asked.

'I'll take care of it later. You want to talk in here or should we go out to the train?'

'Let me tell you what we have first. Then it's your scene to do with what you want.'

Garwood reached into the pocket of his coat, took out a softpack of Marlboros and began opening it.

'I thought you asked me for a smoke,' Bosch said.

'I did. This is my emergency pack. I'm not supposed to open it.'

It made little sense to Bosch. He watched as Garwood lit a cigarette and then offered the pack to Bosch. Harry shook his head. He put his hands in his pockets to make sure he wouldn't take one.

'This going to bother you?' Garwood asked, holding up the cigarette, a taunting smile on his face.

'Not me, Cap. My lungs are probably already shot. But these guys . . .'

Rider and Edgar waved it off. They appeared as impatient as Bosch did in getting to the story.

'Okay, then,' Garwood finally said. 'This is what we know. Last run of the night. Man named Elwood . . . Elwood . . . hold on a sec.'

He pulled a small pad from the same pocket he had replaced the cigarette package in and looked at some writing on the top page.

'Eldrige, yeah, Eldrige. Eldrige Peete. He was running the thing by himself – it only takes one person to run the whole operation – it's all computer. He was about to close her down for the night. On Friday nights the last ride is at eleven. It was eleven. Before sending the top car down for the last ride he goes out, gets on it, closes and locks the door. Then he comes back in here, puts the command on the computer and sends it down.'

He referred to the pad again.

'These things have names. The one he sent down is called Sinai and the one he brought up was Olivet. He says they're named after mountains in the Bible. It looked to him when Olivet got up here that the car was empty. So he goes out to lock it up – 'cause then he has to send them one more time and the computer stops them side by side in the middle of the track for overnight. Then he's done and out of here.'

Bosch looked at Rider and made a signal as if writing on his palm. She nodded and took her own pad and a pen out of the bulky purse she carried. She started taking notes.

'Only Elwood, I mean, Eldrige, he comes out to lock up the car and he finds the two bodies onboard. He backs away, comes in here and calls the police. With me?'

'So far. What next?'

Bosch was already thinking of the questions he would have to ask Garwood and then probably Peete.

'So we're covering for Central dicks and the call eventually comes to me. I send out four guys and they set up the scene.'

'They didn't check the bodies for ID?'

'Not right away. But there was no ID anyway. They were going by the book. They talked to this Eldrige Peete and they went down the steps and did a search for casings and other than that held tight until the coroner's people arrived and did their thing. Guy's wallet and watch are missing. His briefcase, too, if he was carrying one. But they got an ID off a letter the stiff had in his pocket. Addressed to Howard Elias. Once they found that, my guys took a real good look at the stiff and could tell it was Elias. They then, of course, called me and I called Irving and he called the chief and then it was decided to call you.'

He had said the last part as if he had been part of the decision process. Bosch glanced out the window. There was still a large number of detectives milling about.

'I'd say those first guys made more than just a call to you, Captain,' Bosch said.

Garwood turned to look out the window as if it had never occurred to him that it was unusual to see as many as fifteen detectives at a murder scene.

'I suppose,' he said.

'Okay, what else?' Bosch said. 'What else did they do before they figured out who it was and that they weren't long for the case?'

'Well, like I said, they talked to this fellow Eldrige Peete and they searched the areas outside the cars. Top and bottom. They—'

'Did they find any of the brass?'

'No. Our shooter was careful. He picked up all the casings. We do know that he was using a nine, though.'

'How?'

'The second victim, the woman. The shot was through and through. The slug hit a steel window bracket behind her, flattened and fell on the floor. It's too mashed for comparison but you can still tell it was a nine. Hoffman said if he was guessing he'd say it was a federal. You'll have to hope for a better lead from the autopsies as far as ballistics go. If you ever get that far.'

Perfect, Bosch thought. Nine was a cop's caliber. And stopping to pick up the shells, that was a smooth move. You didn't usually see that.

'The way they see it,' Garwood continued, 'Elias got it just after he stepped onto the train down there. The guy comes up and shoots him in the ass first.'

'The ass?' Edgar said.

'That's right. The first shot is in the ass. See, Elias is just stepping on so he's a couple steps up from the sidewalk level. The shooter comes up from behind and holds the gun out – it's at ass level. He sticks the muzzle in there and fires off the first cap.'

'Then what?' Bosch asked.

'Well, we think Elias goes down and sort of turns to see who it is. He raises his hands but the shooter fires again. The slug goes through one of his hands and hits him in the face, right between the eyes. That's probably your cause-of-death shot right there. Elias drops back down. He's facedown now. The shooter steps into the car and puts one more in the back of his head, point-blank. He then looks up and sees the woman, maybe for the first time. He hits her from about five feet. One in the chest, through and through, and she's gone. No witness. The shooter gets the wallet and watch off Elias, picks up his shells and is gone. A few minutes later Peete brings the car up and finds the bodies. You now know what I know.'

Bosch and his partners were quiet a long moment. The scenario Garwood had woven didn't sit right with Bosch but he didn't know enough about the crime scene yet to challenge him on it.

'The robbery look legit?' Bosch finally asked.

'It did to me. I know the people down south aren't going to want to hear that but there it is.'

Rider and Edgar were silent stones.

'What about the woman?' Bosch asked. 'Was she robbed?'

'Doesn't look like it. I kind of think the shooter didn't want to come onto the train. Anyway, the lawyer was the one in the thousand-dollar suit. He'd be the target.'

'What about Peete? Did he hear the shots, a scream, anything?'

'He says no. He says the generator for the electric is right below the floor here. Sounds like an elevator running all day long so he wears earplugs. He never heard anything.'

Bosch stepped around the cable wheels and looked at the train operator's station. For the first time he saw that mounted above the cash register was a small video display box with a split screen showing four camera views of Angels Flight – from a camera in each of the train cars and from above each terminus. On one corner of the screen he could see a long shot of the inside of Olivet. The crime scene techs were still working with the bodies.

Garwood came around the other side of the cable wheels.

'No luck there,' he said. 'The cameras are live only, no tape. They are so the operator can check to make sure everyone is aboard and seated before starting the train.'

'Did he—'

'He didn't look,' Garwood said, knowing Bosch's questions. 'He just checked through the window, thought the car was empty and brought it up so he could lock it up.'

'Where is he?'

'At Parker. Our offices. I guess you'll have to come over and talk to him for yourself. I'll keep somebody with him until you make it by.'

'Any other witnesses?'

'Not a one. Eleven o'clock at night down here, the place is pretty dead. The Grand Central Market closes up at seven. There's nothing else down there except some office buildings. A couple of my guys were getting ready to go into those apartments next door here to knock on doors. But then they got the ID and sort of backed away.'

Bosch paced around in a small area of the room and thought. Very little had been done so far and the discovery of the murders was already four hours old. This bothered him even though he understood the reason behind the delay.

'Why was Elias on Angels Flight?' he asked Garwood. 'They figure that out before backing away?'

'Well, he must've wanted to go up the hill, don't you think?'

'Come on, Captain, if you know, why not save us the time?'

'We don't know, Harry. We ran a DMV check, he lives out in Baldwin Hills. That's a long way from Bunker Hill. I don't know why he was coming up here.'

'What about where he was coming from?'

'That's a little easier. Elias's office is just over on Third. In the Bradbury Building. He was probably coming from there. But where he was going . . .'

'Okay, then what about the woman?'

'She's a blank. My guys hadn't even started with her when we were told to pull back.'

Garwood dropped his cigarette to the floor and crushed it with his heel. Bosch took it as a signal that the briefing was about over. He decided to see if he could get a rise out of him.

'You pissed off, Captain?'

'About what?'

'About being pulled off. About your people being on the suspect list.'

A small smile played on Garwood's thin lips.

'No, I'm not angry. I see the chief's point.'

'Are your people going to cooperate with us on this?'

After some hesitation Garwood nodded.

'Of course. The quicker they cooperate, the quicker you will clear them.'

571

'And you'll tell them that?'

'That's exactly what I'll tell them.'

'We appreciate that, Captain. Tell me, which one of your people do you think could have done this?'

The lips curled into a full smile now. Bosch studied Garwood's cigarette-yellowed teeth and for a moment was glad he was trying to quit.

'You're a clever guy, Harry. I remember that.'

He said nothing else.

'Thanks, Captain. But do you have an answer to the question?'

Garwood moved to the door and opened it. Before leaving he turned and looked back at them, his eyes traveling from Edgar to Rider to Bosch.

'It wasn't one of mine, Detectives. I guarantee it. You'll be wasting your time if you look there too long.'

'Thanks for the advice,' Bosch said.

Garwood stepped out, closing the door behind him.

'Jeez,' Rider said. 'It's like Captain Boris Karloff or something. Does that guy only come out at night?'

Bosch smiled and nodded.

'Mr Personality,' he said. 'So, what do you think so far?'

'I think we're at ground zero,' Rider said. 'Those guys didn't do jack before getting the hook.'

'Yeah, well, Robbery-Homicide, what do you want?' Edgar said. 'They aren't known for tap dancing. They back the tortoise over the hare any day of the week. But if you ask me, we're fucked. You and me, Kiz, we can't win on this one. Blue race, my ass.'

Bosch stepped toward the door.

'Let's go out and take a look,' he said, cutting off discussion of Edgar's concerns. He knew they were valid but for the moment they only served to clutter their mission. 'Maybe we'll get a few ideas before Irving wants to talk again.'

5

The number of detectives outside the station had finally begun to decrease. Bosch watched as Garwood and a group of his men crossed the plaza toward their cars. He then saw Irving standing to the side of the train car talking to Chastain and three detectives. Bosch didn't know them but assumed they were IAD. The deputy chief was animated in his discussion but kept his voice so low that Bosch couldn't hear what he was saying. Bosch wasn't sure exactly what the IAD presence was all about, but he was getting an increasingly bad feeling about it.

He saw Frankie Sheehan hanging back behind Garwood and his group. He was about to leave but was hesitating. Bosch nodded at him.

'I see what you mean now, Frankie,' he said.

'Yeah, Harry, some days you eat the bear . . .'

'Right. You taking off?'

'Yeah, the cap told us all to get out of here.'

Bosch stepped over and kept his voice low.

'Any ideas I could borrow?'

Sheehan looked at the train car as if considering for the first time who might have killed the two people inside it.

'None other than the obvious and I think that will be a waste of time. But then again, you have to waste it, right? Cover all the bases.'

'Yeah. Anybody you think I should start with?'

'Yeah, me.' He smiled broadly. 'I hated the douche bag. Know what I'm gonna do? I'm going now to try and find an all-night liquor store and buy the best Irish whiskey they got. I'm going to have a little celebration, Hieronymus. Because Howard Elias was a motherfucker.'

Bosch nodded. With cops the word *motherfucker* was rarely used. It was heard a lot by them but not used. With most cops it was reserved as being the worst thing you could say about someone. When it was said it meant one thing; that the person had crossed the righteous, that the person had no respect for the keepers of the law and therefore the rules and bounds of society. Cop killers were always motherfuckers, no questions asked. Defense lawyers got the call, most of the time. And Howard Elias was on the motherfucker list, too. Right at the top.

Sheehan gave a little salute and headed off across the plaza. Bosch turned his attention toward the interior of the train while he put on rubber gloves. The lights were back on and the techs were finished with the laser. Bosch knew one of them, Hoffman. He was working with a trainee Bosch had

573

heard about but not met. She was an attractive Asian woman with a large bust. He had overheard other detectives in the squad room discussing her attributes and questioning their authenticity.

'Gary, is it cool to come in?' Bosch asked, leaning in through the door.

Hoffman looked up from the tackle box in which he kept his tools. He was organizing things and was about to close it.

'It's cool. We're wrapping up. This one yours, Harry?'

'It is now. Got anything good for me? Gonna make my day?'

Bosch stepped into the car, followed by Edgar and Rider. Since the car was on an incline, the floor was actually a series of steps down to the other door. The seats also were on graduated levels on either side of the center aisle. Bosch looked at the slatted bench seats and suddenly remembered how hard they had been on his skinny behind as a boy.

''Fraid not,' Hoffman said. 'It's pretty clean.'

Bosch nodded and moved down a few more steps to the first body. He studied Catalina Perez the way someone might study a sculpture in a museum. There was no feeling for the object in front of him as human. He was studying details, gaining impressions. His eyes fell to the bloodstain and the small tear the bullet had made in the T-shirt. The bullet had hit the woman dead center. Bosch thought about this and envisioned the gunman in the doorway of the train twelve feet away.

'Hell of a shot, huh?'

It was the tech Bosch didn't know. He looked at her and nodded. He had been thinking the same thing, that the shooter was someone with some expertise in firearms.

'Hi, I don't think we've met. I'm Sally Tam.'

She put out her hand and Bosch shook it. It felt weird. They were both wearing rubber gloves. He told her his name.

'Oh,' she said. 'Somebody was just talking about you. About the hard-boiled eggs case.'

'It was just luck.'

Bosch knew he was getting a longer ride out of that case than he deserved. It was all because a *Times* reporter had heard about it and written a story that exaggerated Bosch's skills to the point where he seemed like a distant relative of Sherlock Holmes.

Bosch pointed past Tam and said he needed to get by to take a look at the other body. She stepped to the side and leaned back and he slid by, careful not to allow himself to rub against her. He heard her introducing herself to Rider and Edgar. He dropped into a crouch so he could study the body of Howard Elias.

'Is this still as is?' he asked Hoffman, who was squatting next to his tackle box near the feet of the dead man.

'Pretty much. We turned him to get into his pockets but then put him back. There are some Polaroids over on that seat behind you if you want to double-check. Coroner's people took those before anybody touched him.'

Bosch turned and saw the photos. Hoffman had been right. The body was in the same position in which it had been found.

He turned back to the body and used both hands to turn the head so that he could study the wounds. Garwood's interpretation had been correct, Bosch decided. The entry wound at the back of the head was a contact wound. Though partially obscured by blood that had matted the hair, there were still powder burns and stippling visible in a circular pattern around the wound. The face shot, however, was clean. This did not refer to the blood – there was a good amount of that. But there were no powder burns on the skin. The bullet to the face had come from a distance.

Bosch picked up the arm and turned the hand so he could study the entry wound in the palm. The arm moved easily. Rigor mortis had not yet begun – the cool evening air was delaying this process. There was no discharge burn on the palm. Bosch did some computing. No powder burns on the palm meant the firearm was at least three to four feet away from the hand when the bullet was discharged. If Elias had his arm extended with his palm out, then that added another three feet.

Edgar and Rider had made their way to the second body. Bosch could feel their presence behind him.

'Six to seven feet away, through the hand and still right between the eyes,' he said. 'This guy can shoot. Better remember that when we take him down.'

Neither of them answered. Bosch hoped they picked up on the confidence in his last line as well as the warning. He was about to place the dead man's hand down on the floor when he noticed the long scratch mark on the wrist and running along the side of the palm. He guessed the wound had occurred when Elias's watch had been pulled off. He studied the wound closely. There was no blood in the track. It was a clean white laceration along the surface of the dark skin, yet it seemed deep enough to have drawn blood.

He thought about this for a moment. There were no shots to the heart, only to the head. The blood displacement from the wounds indicated the heart had continued to pump for at least several seconds after Elias had gone down. It would seem that the shooter would have yanked the watch off Elias's wrist very quickly after the shooting – there was obviously no reason to hang around. Yet, the scratch on the hand had not bled. It was as if it had occurred well after the heart had stopped pumping.

'What do you think about the lead enema?' Hoffman asked, interrupting Bosch's thoughts.

As Hoffman got out of the way, Bosch stood and gingerly stepped around the body until he was down by the feet. He crouched again and looked at the third bullet wound. Blood had soaked the seat of the pants. Still, he could see the tear and tight burn pattern where the bullet went through the cloth and into Howard Elias's anus. The weapon had been pressed in deep at the point where the seams of the pants were joined and then fired. It was a vindictive shot. More than a coup de grâce, it showed anger and hatred. It contradicted the cool skill of the other shots. It also told Bosch that Garwood had been wrong about the shooting sequence. Whether the captain had been intentionally wrong, he didn't know.

He stood up and backed to the rear door of the car so that he was in the spot where the shooter had probably stood. He surveyed the carnage in front of him once more and nodded to no one in particular, just trying to commit it all to memory. Edgar and Rider were still between the bodies and making their own observations.

Bosch turned around and looked down the tracks to the turnstile station

575

below. The detectives he had seen before were gone. Now a lone cruiser sat down there and two patrol officers guarded the lower crime scene.

Bosch had seen enough. He made his way past the bodies and carefully around Sally Tam again and up onto the platform. His partners followed, Edgar moving by Tam more closely than he had to.

Bosch stepped away from the train car so they could huddle together privately.

'What do you think?' he said.

'I think they're real,' Edgar said, looking back toward Tam. 'They've got that natural slope to them. What do you think, Kiz?'

'Funny,' Rider said, not taking the bait. 'Can we talk about the case, please?'

Bosch admired how Rider took Edgar's frequent comments and sexual innuendo without more than a sarcastic remark or complaint fired back at him. Such comments could get Edgar in serious trouble but only if Rider made a formal complaint. The fact that she didn't indicated either she was intimidated or she could handle it. She also knew that if she went formal, she'd get what cops called a 'K-9 jacket,' a reference to the city jail ward where snitches were housed. Bosch had once asked her in a private moment if she wanted him to talk to Edgar. As her supervisor he was legally responsible for resolving the problem but he knew that if he talked to Edgar, then Edgar would know he had gotten to her. Rider knew this as well. She had thought about all of this for a few moments and told Bosch to let things alone. She said she wasn't intimidated, just annoyed on occasion. She could handle it.

'You go first, Kiz,' Bosch said, also ignoring Edgar's comment, even though he privately disagreed with his conclusion about Tam. 'Anything catch your eye in there?'

'Same as everybody else, I guess. Looks like the victims were not together. The woman either got on ahead of Elias or was about to get off. I think it's pretty clear Elias was the primary target and she was just an also-ran. The shot up the ass tells me that. Also, like you said in there, this guy was a hell of a shot. We're looking for someone who's spent some time at the range.'

Bosch nodded.

'Anything else?'

'Nope. It's a pretty clean scene. Nothing much to work with.'

'Jerry?'

'Nada. What about you?'

'Same. But I think Garwood was telling us a story. His sequence was for shit.'

'How?' Rider said.

'The shot up the pipe was the last one, not the first. Elias was already down. It's a contact wound and the entry is in the underside, where all the seams of the pants come together. It would be hard to get a muzzle up there if Elias was standing – even if he was up a step from the shooter. I think he was already down when the shooter popped that cap.'

'That changes things,' Rider said. 'Makes the last one a "fuck you" shot. The shooter was angry at Elias.'

'So he knew him,' Edgar said.

Bosch nodded.

'And you think Garwood knew this and was just trying to steer us wrong by planting the suggestion?' Rider asked. 'Or do you think he just missed it?'

'What I know about Garwood is that he is not a stupid man,' Bosch said. 'He and fifteen of his men were about to be pulled into federal court on Monday by Elias and dragged right through the shit. He knows any one of those boys might possibly be capable of this. He was protecting them. That's what I think.'

'Well, that's bullshit. Protecting a killer cop? He should be—'

'*Maybe* protecting a killer cop. We don't know. He didn't know. I think it was probably a just-in-case move.'

'Doesn't matter. If that's what he was doing, he shouldn't have a badge.'

Bosch didn't say anything to that and Rider wasn't placated. She shook her head in disgust. Like most cops in the department, she was tired of fuck-ups and cover-ups, of the few tainting the many.

'What about the scratch on the hand?'

Edgar and Rider looked at him with arched eyebrows.

'What about it?' Edgar said. 'Prob'ly happened when the shooter pulled off the watch. One of those with the expanding band. Like a Rolex. Knowing Elias, it was prob'ly a Rolex. Makes a nice motive.'

'Yeah, if it was a Rolex,' Bosch said.

He turned and looked out across the city. He doubted Elias wore a Rolex. For all of his flamboyance, Elias was the kind of lawyer who also knew the nuances of his profession. He knew that a lawyer wearing a Rolex might turn jurors off. He wouldn't wear one. He would have a nice and expensive watch, but not one that advertised itself like a Rolex.

'What, Harry?' Rider said. 'What about the scratch?'

Bosch looked back at them.

'Well, whether it was a Rolex or a high-priced watch or not, there's no blood in the scratch.'

'Meaning?'

'There is a lot of blood in there. The bullet wounds bled out, but there was no blood in the scratch. Meaning I don't think the shooter took the watch. That scratch was made after the heart stopped. I'd say long after. Which means it was made after the shooter left the scene.'

Rider and Edgar considered this.

'Maybe,' Edgar finally said. 'But that vascular system shit is hard to nail down. Even the coroner isn't gonna be definitive on that.'

'Yeah,' Bosch said, nodding. 'So call it gut instinct. We can't take it to court but I know the shooter didn't take the watch. Or probably the wallet, for that matter.'

'So what are you saying?' Edgar asked. 'Somebody else came along and took it?'

'Something like that.'

'You think it was the guy who ran the train – the one who called it in?'

Bosch looked at Edgar but didn't answer him. He hiked his shoulders.

'You think it was one of the RHD guys,' Rider whispered. 'Another just-in-case move. Send us down the robbery path, just in case it was one of their own.'

Bosch looked at her a moment, thinking about how to respond and how thin the ice was where they now stood.

'Detective Bosch?'

He turned. It was Sally Tam.

'We're clear and the coroner's people want to bag 'em and tag 'em if that's okay.'

'Fine. Hey, listen, I forgot to ask, did you get anything with the laser?'

'We got a lot. But probably nothing that will help. A lot of people ride that car. We probably got passengers, not the shooter.'

'Well, you'll run them anyway, right?'

'Sure. We'll put everything through AFIS and DOJ. We'll let you know.'

Bosch nodded his thanks.

'Also, did you collect any keys from the guy?'

'We did. They're in one of the brown bags. You want them?'

'Yeah, we're probably going to need them.'

'Be right back.'

She smiled and went back to the train car. She seemed too cheerful to be at a crime scene. Bosch knew that would wear off after a while.

'See what I mean?' Edgar said. 'They gotta be real.'

'Jerry,' Bosch said.

Edgar raised his hands in surrender.

'I'm a trained observer. Just filing a report.'

'Well, you better keep it to yourself,' Bosch whispered. 'Unless you want to file it with the chief.'

Edgar turned just in time to see Irving come up to them.

'Well, initial conclusions, Detectives?'

Bosch looked at Edgar.

'Jerry? What were you just saying you observed?'

'Uh, well, uh, at the moment we're still kind of thinking about all we saw in there.'

'Nothing that doesn't really jibe with what Captain Garwood told us,' Bosch said quickly, before Rider could say anything that would reveal their true conclusions. 'At least, preliminarily.'

'What next, then?'

'We've got plenty to do. I want to talk to the train operator again and we've got to canvass that residential building for wits. We've got next-of-kin notification and we've got to get into Elias's office. When is that help you promised us going to show up, Chief?'

'Right now.'

Irving raised an arm and beckoned Chastain and the three others he stood with. Bosch had known that was probably what they were doing at the scene but seeing Irving waving them over still put a tight feeling in his chest. Irving was well aware of the animosity between IAD and the rank and file, and the enmity that existed between Bosch and Chastain in particular. To put them together on the case told Bosch that Irving wasn't as interested in finding out who killed Howard Elias and Catalina Perez as he had outwardly expressed. This was the deputy chief's way of appearing to be conscientious but actually working to cripple the investigation.

'Are you sure you want to do this, Chief?' Bosch asked in an urgent whisper as the IAD men approached. 'You know Chastain and I don't—'

'Yes, it is how I want to do it,' Irving said, cutting Bosch off without looking at him. 'Detective Chastain headed up the internal review of the Michael Harris complaint. I think he is an appropriate addition to this investigation.'

'What I'm saying is that Chastain and I have a history, Chief. I don't think it's going to work out with—'

'I do not care if you two do not like each other. Find a way to work together. I want to go back inside now.'

Irving led the entourage back into the station house. It was close quarters. No one said anything by way of a greeting to one another. Once inside, they all looked expectantly at Irving.

'Okay, we are going to set some ground rules here,' the deputy chief began. 'Detective Bosch is in charge of this investigation. The six of you report to him. He reports to me. I do not want any confusion about that. Detective Bosch runs this case. Now I have arranged for you to set up an office in the conference room next to my office on the sixth floor at Parker Center. There will be added phones and a computer terminal in there by Monday morning. You men from IAD, I want you to be primarily used in the areas of interviewing police officers, running down alibis, that part of the investigation. Detective Bosch and his team will handle the traditional elements of homicide investigation, the autopsy, witness interviews, that whole part of it. Any questions so far?'

The room went stone silent. Bosch was quietly seething. It was the first time he had thought of Irving as a hypocrite. The deputy chief had always been a hard-ass but ultimately a fair man. This move was different. He was maneuvering to protect the department when the rot they were seeking might be inside it. But what Irving didn't know was that Bosch had accomplished everything in his life by channeling negatives into motivation. He vowed to himself that he would clear the case in spite of Irving's maneuvers. And the chips would fall where they would fall.

'A word of warning about the media. It will be all over this case. You are not to be distracted or deterred. You are not to talk to the media. All such communications will come through my office or Lieutenant Tom O'Rourke in media relations. Understood?'

The seven detectives nodded.

'Good. That means I will not have to fear picking the *Times* up off the driveway in the morning.'

Irving looked at his watch and then back at the group.

'I can control you people but not the coroner's people or anyone else who learns about this through official channels in the next few hours. I figure by ten hundred the media will be all over this with full knowledge of the victims' identities. So I want a briefing in the conference room at ten hundred. After I am up-to-date I will brief the chief of police and one of us will address the media with the bare minimum of information we wish to put out. Any problem with that?'

'Chief, that barely gives us six hours,' Bosch said. 'I don't know how much more we'll know by then. We've got a lot of leg-work to do before we can sit down and start sifting through—'

'That is understood. You are to feel no pressure from the media. I do not care if the press conference is merely to confirm who is dead and nothing else. The media will not be running this case. I want you to run with it full bore, but at ten hundred I want everyone back at my conference room. Questions?'

There were none.

'Okay, then I will turn it over to Detective Bosch and leave you people to it.'

He turned directly to Bosch and handed him a white business card.

'You have all my numbers there. Lieutenant Tulin's as well. Anything comes up that I should know about, you call me forthwith. I do not care what time it is or where you are at. You call me.'

Bosch nodded, took the card and put it in his jacket pocket.

'Go to it, people. As I said before, let the chips fall where they may.'

He left the room and Bosch heard Rider whisper, 'Yeah, right.'

Bosch turned and looked at the faces of the new team, coming to Chastain's last.

'You know what he's doing, don't you?' Bosch said. 'He thinks we can't work together. He thinks we'll be like those fighting fish that you put in the same bowl and they go nuts trying to get at each other. Meantime, the case is never cleared. Well, it's not going to happen. Anything anybody in here's ever done to me or anyone else, forget about it. I let it go. This case is the thing. There are two people in that train that somebody blew away without so much as a second thought. We're going to find that person. That's all I care about now.'

He held Chastain's eyes until he finally saw a slight nod of agreement. Bosch nodded back. He was sure all the others had seen the exchange. He then took out his notebook and opened it to a fresh page. He handed it to Chastain.

'Okay, then,' he said. 'I want everybody to write down their names followed by their home and pager numbers. Cell phones, too, if you got 'em. I'll make a list up and everybody will get copies. I want everybody in communication. That's the trouble with these big gang bangs. If everybody isn't on the same wavelength, something can slip through. We don't want that.'

Bosch stopped and looked at the others. They were all watching him, paying attention. It seemed that for the moment the natural animosities were relaxed, if not forgotten.

'Okay,' he said. 'This is how we're going to break this down from here on out.'

6

One of the men from IAD was a Latino named Raymond Fuentes. Bosch sent him along with Edgar to the address on Catalina Perez's identification cards to notify her next of kin and to handle the questions about her. It was most likely the dead-end part of the investigation – it seemed apparent that Elias was the primary target – and Edgar tried to protest. But Bosch cut him off. The explanation he would share privately with Edgar later was that he needed to spread the IAD men out in order to give him better control of things. So Edgar went with Fuentes. And Rider was sent with a second IAD man, Loomis Baker, to interview Eldrige Peete at Parker Center and then bring him back to the scene. Bosch wanted the train operator at the scene to go over what he had seen and to operate the train as he had before discovering the bodies.

That left Bosch, Chastain and the last IAD man, Joe Dellacroce. Bosch dispatched Dellacroce to Parker Center as well, to draw up a search warrant for Elias's office. He then told Chastain that the two of them would go to Elias's home to make the death notification to his next of kin.

After the group split up, Bosch walked to the crime scene van and asked Hoffman for the keys found on the body of Howard Elias. Hoffman looked through the crate he had placed his evidence bags in and came out with a bag containing a ring with more than a dozen keys on it.

'From the front pants pocket, right side,' Hoffman said.

Bosch studied the keys for a moment. There seemed to be more than enough keys for the lawyer's home, office and cars. He noticed that there was a Porsche key on the ring as well as a Volvo key. He realized that when the investigators finished the current crop of tasks, one assignment he would have to make would be to put someone on locating Elias's car.

'Anything else in the pockets?'

'Yeah. In the left front he had a quarter.'

'A quarter.'

'Costs a quarter to ride Angels Flight. That's probably what that was for.'

Bosch nodded.

'And in the inside coat pocket was a letter.'

Bosch had forgotten that Garwood had mentioned the letter.

'Let's see that.'

Hoffman looked through his crate again and came up with a plastic evidence bag. Inside it was an envelope. Bosch took it from the crime scene tech and studied it without removing it. The envelope had been addressed to Elias's office by hand. There was no return address. On the left lower corner the sender had written PERSONAL & CONFIDENTIAL. Bosch tried to read the postmark but the light was bad. He wished he still carried a lighter.

'It's your neck of the woods, Harry,' Hoffman said. 'Hollywood. Mailed Wednesday. He probably got it Friday.'

Bosch nodded. He turned the bag over and looked at the back of the envelope. It had been cleanly cut open along the top. Elias or his secretary had opened it, probably at his office, before he had put it into his pocket. There was no way of knowing if the contents had been examined since.

'Anybody open it?'

'We didn't. I don't know what happened before we got here. I understand that the first detectives saw the name on there and then recognized the body. But I don't know if they actually looked at the letter.'

Bosch was curious about the contents of the envelope but knew it wasn't the right time or place to open it.

'I'm going to take this, too.'

'You got it, Harry. Let me just get you to sign it out. And the keys, too.'

Bosch waited while Hoffman got a chain-of-evidence form out of his kit. He squatted down and put the envelope and keys into his briefcase. Chastain came over, ready to leave the scene.

'You want to drive or you want me to?' Bosch said as he snapped his case closed. 'I've got a slick. What have you got?'

'I still have a plain jane. Runs like dogshit but at least I don't stand out like dogshit on the street.'

'That's good. You got a bubble?'

'Yes, Bosch, even IAD guys have to respond to calls now and then.'

Hoffman held a clipboard and pen out to Bosch and he signed his initials next to the two pieces of crime scene evidence he was taking with him.

'Then you drive.'

They started walking across California Plaza to where the cars were parked. Bosch pulled his pager off his belt and made sure it was running properly. The battery light was still green. He hadn't missed any pages. He looked up at the tall towers surrounding them, wondering if they could possibly interfere with a page from his wife, but then he remembered the page from Lieutenant Billets had come through earlier. He clipped the pager back to his belt and tried to think about something else.

Following Chastain's lead they came to a beat-up maroon LTD that was at least five years old and about as impressive looking as a Pinto. At least, Bosch thought, it isn't painted black and white.

'It's unlocked,' Chastain said.

Bosch went to the passenger side door and got in the car. He got his cell phone out of his briefcase and called the central dispatch center. He asked for a Department of Motor Vehicles run on Howard Elias and was given the dead man's home address as well as his age, driving record and the plate numbers of the Porsche and Volvo registered in his and his wife's names. Elias had been forty-six. His driving record was clean. Bosch thought that the lawyer was probably the most cautious driver in the city. The last thing Elias probably ever wanted to do was draw the attention of an LAPD patrol cop. It made driving a Porsche seem almost a waste.

'Baldwin Hills,' he said after closing the phone. 'Her name is Millie.'

Chastain started the engine, then plugged the flashing emergency light – the bubble – into the lighter and put it on the dashboard. He drove the car quickly down the deserted streets toward the 10 Freeway.

Bosch was silent at first, not sure how to break the ice with Chastain. The two men were natural enemies. Chastain had investigated Bosch on two different occasions. Both times Bosch was grudgingly cleared of any wrongdoing, but only after Chastain was forced to back off. It seemed to Bosch that Chastain had a hard-on for him that felt close to a vendetta. The IAD detective seemed to take no joy in clearing a fellow cop. All he wanted was a scalp.

'I know what you are doing, Bosch,' Chastain said once they got onto the freeway and started west.

Bosch looked over at him. For the first time he considered how physically similar they were. Dark hair going gray, full mustache beneath dark brown-black eyes, a lean, almost wiry build. Almost mirror images, yet Bosch had never considered Chastain to be the kind of physical threat that Bosch knew he projected himself. Chastain carried himself differently. Bosch had always carried himself like a man afraid of being cornered, like a man who wouldn't allow himself to be cornered.

'What? What am I doing?'

'You're thinning us out. That way you have better control.'

He waited for Bosch to reply but only got silence.

'But eventually, if we're going to do this thing right, you are going to have to trust us.'

After a pause, Bosch said, 'I know that.'

Elias lived on Beck Street in Baldwin Hills, a small section of upper-middle-class homes south of the 10 Freeway and near La Cienega Boulevard. It was an area known as the black Beverly Hills – a neighborhood where affluent blacks moved when they did not wish to have their wealth take them out of their community. As Bosch considered this he thought that if there was anything that he could like about Elias, it was the fact that he didn't take his money and move to Brentwood or Westwood or the real Beverly Hills. He stayed in the community from which he had risen.

With little middle-of-the-night traffic and Chastain cruising on the freeway at ninety, they got to Beck Street in less than fifteen minutes. The house was a large brick colonial with four white columns holding up a two-story portico. It had the feeling of a Southern plantation and Bosch wondered if it was some kind of statement being made by Elias.

Bosch saw no lights from behind any of the windows and the hanging light in the portico was dark as well. This didn't sit right with him. If this was Elias's home, why wasn't a light left on for him?

There was a car in the circular driveway that was neither a Porsche nor a Volvo. It was an old Camaro with fresh paint and chromed wheels. To the right of the house there was a detached two-car garage but its door was closed. Chastain pulled into the drive and stopped behind the Camaro.

'Nice car,' Chastain said. 'Tell you what, I wouldn't leave a car like that out overnight. Even in a neighborhood like this. Too close to the jungle.'

He turned the car off and reached to open his door.

'Let's wait a second here,' Bosch said.

He opened his briefcase, got out the phone and called dispatch again. He asked for a double check on the address for Elias. They had the right place. He then asked the dispatcher to run the plate on the Camaro. It came back registered to a Martin Luther King Elias, age eighteen. Bosch thanked the dispatcher and clicked off.

'We got the right place?' Chastain asked.

'Looks like it. The Camaro must be his son's. But it doesn't look like anyone was expecting dad to come home tonight.'

Bosch opened his door and got out, Chastain doing the same. As they approached the door Bosch saw the dull glow of a bell button. He pushed it and heard the sharp ringing of a chime inside the quiet house.

They waited and pushed the bell button two more times before the portico light came on above them and a woman's sleepy but alarmed voice came through the door.

'What is it?'

'Mrs Elias?' Bosch said. 'We're police. We need to talk to you.'

'Police? What for?'

'It's about your husband, ma'am. Can we come in?'

'I need some identification before I open this door.'

Bosch took out his badge wallet and held it up but then noticed there was no peephole.

'Turn around,' the woman's voice said. 'On the column.'

Bosch and Chastain turned and saw the camera mounted on one of the columns. Bosch walked up to it and held up his badge.

'You see it?' he said loudly.

He heard the door open and turned around. A woman in a white robe with a silk scarf wrapped around her head looked out at him.

'You don't have to yell,' she said.

'Sorry.'

She stood in the one-foot opening of the door but made no move to invite them in.

'Howard is not here. What do you want?'

'Uh, can we come in, Mrs Elias? We want—'

'No, you can't come in my house. My home. No policeman has ever been in here. Howard wouldn't have it. Neither will I. What do you want? Has something happened to Howard?'

'Uh, yes, ma'am, I'm afraid. It would really be better if we—'

'Oh my God!' she shrieked. 'You killed him! You people finally killed him!'

'Mrs Elias,' Bosch started, wishing he had better prepared himself for the assumption he should have known the woman would make. 'We need to sit down with you and—'

Again he was cut off, but this time it was by an unintelligible, animal-like sound from deep in the woman. Its anguish was resonant. The woman bowed her head and leaned into the door jamb. Bosch thought she might fall and made a move to grab her shoulders. The woman recoiled as if he were a monster reaching out to her.

'No! No! Don't you touch me! You – you murderers! Killers! You killed my Howard. Howard!'

The last word was a full-throated scream that seemed to echo through the neighborhood. Bosch looked behind him, half-expecting to see the street

584

lined with onlookers. He knew he had to contain the woman, get her inside or at least quiet. She was moving into a full-fledged wail now. Meantime, Chastain just stood there, paralyzed by the scene unfolding before him.

Bosch was about to make another attempt to touch the woman when he saw movement from behind her and a young man grabbed hold of her from behind.

'Ma! What? What is it?'

The woman turned and collapsed against the young man.

'Martin! Martin, they killed him! Your father!'

Martin Elias looked up over his mother's head and his eyes burned right through Bosch. His mouth formed the horrible *Oh* of shock and pain that Bosch had seen too many times before. He suddenly realized his mistake. He should have made this call with either Edgar or Rider. Rider, probably. She would have been a calming influence. Her smooth demeanor and the color of her skin would have done more than Bosch and Chastain combined.

'Son,' Chastain said, coming out of his inertia. 'We need to settle down a bit here and go inside to talk about this.'

'Don't you call me son. I'm not your goddamn son.'

'Mr Elias,' Bosch said forcefully. Everyone, including Chastain, looked at him. He then continued, in a calmer, softer voice. 'Martin. You need to take care of your mother. We need to tell you both what has happened and to ask you a few questions. The longer we stand here cursing and yelling, the longer it will be before you can take care of your mother.'

He waited a moment. The woman turned her face back into her son's chest and began to cry. Martin then stepped back, pulling her with him, so that there was room for Bosch and Chastain to enter.

For the next fifteen minutes Bosch and Chastain sat with the mother and son in a nicely furnished living room and detailed what was known of the crime and how the investigation would be handled. Bosch knew that to them it was like a couple of Nazis announcing they would investigate war crimes, but he also knew that it was important to go through the routine, to do his best to assure the victim's family that the investigation would be thorough and aggressive.

'I know what you said about it being cops,' Bosch said in summation. 'At the moment we don't know that. It is too early in the investigation to know anything about a motive. We are in a gathering phase at this time. But soon we'll move to the sifting phase and any cop who might have had even a remote reason to harm your husband will be looked at. I know there will be many in that category. You have my word that they will be looked at very closely.'

He waited. The mother and son were huddled together on a couch with a cheerful floral pattern. The son kept closing his eyes like a child hoping to ward off a punishment. He was flagging under the weight of what he had just been told. It was finally hitting home that he would not see his father again.

'Now, we know this is an awful time for you,' Bosch said softly. 'We would like to put off any kind of prolonged questioning so that you have time to yourselves. But there are a few questions that would help us right now.'

He waited for an objection but none came. He continued.

'The main one is that we can't figure out why Mr Elias was on Angels Flight. We need to find out where he was—'

'He was going to the apartment,' Martin said, without opening his eyes.

'What apartment?'

'He kept an apartment near the office so he could just stay over on court days or when he was busy getting ready for trial.'

'He was going to stay there tonight?'

'Right. He'd been staying there all week.'

'He had depos,' the wife said. 'With the police. They were coming in after work so he was staying late at the office. Then he would just go over to the apartment.'

Bosch was silent, hoping either one of them would add something more about the arrangement but nothing else was said.

'Did he call you and tell you he was staying over?' he asked.

'Yes, he always called.'

'When was this? This last time, is what I mean.'

'Earlier today. He said he'd be working late and needed to get back into it on Saturday and Sunday. You know, preparing for the trial on Monday. He said he would try to be home on Sunday for supper.'

'So you weren't expecting him to be home here tonight.'

'That's right,' Millie Elias said, a note of defiance in her voice as if she had taken the tone of Bosch's question to mean something else.

Bosch nodded as if to reassure her that he was not insinuating anything. He asked the specific address of the apartment and was told it was in a complex called The Place, just across Grand Street from the Museum of Modern Art. Bosch took out his notebook and wrote it down, then kept the notebook out.

'Now,' he said, 'Mrs Elias, can you remember more specifically when it was you last spoke to your husband?'

'It was right before six. That is when he calls and tells me, otherwise I have to figure out what's for supper and how many I'm cooking for.'

'How about you, Martin? When did you last speak to your father?'

Martin opened his eyes.

'I don't know, man. Couple days ago, at least. But what's this got to do with anything? You *know* who did it. Somebody with a badge did this thing.'

Tears finally began to slide down Martin's face. Bosch wished he could be somewhere else. Anywhere else.

'If it was a cop, Martin, you have my word, we will find him. He won't get away with it.'

'Sure,' Martin replied, without looking at Bosch. 'The man gives us his word. But who the hell is the man?'

The statement made Bosch pause a moment before continuing.

'A few more questions,' he finally said. 'Did Mr Elias have an office here at home?'

'No,' the son said. 'He didn't do his work here.'

'Okay. Next question. In recent days or weeks, had he mentioned any specific threat or person who he believed wanted to harm him?'

Martin shook his head and said, 'He just always said that it was the cops who would get him someday. It was the cops . . .'

Bosch nodded, not in agreement but in his understanding of Martin's belief.

'One last question. There was a woman who was killed on Angels Flight. It looks like they were not together. Her name was Catalina Perez. Does that name mean anything to either of you?'

Bosch's eyes moved from the woman's face to her son's. Both stared blankly and shook their heads.

'Okay then.'

He stood up.

'We will leave you alone now. But either myself or other detectives will need to speak with you again. Probably later on today.'

Neither the mother nor son reacted.

'Mrs Elias, do you have a spare photo of your husband we could borrow?'

The woman looked up at him, her face showing confusion.

'Why do you want a picture of Howard?'

'We may need to show people in the course of the investigation.'

'Everybody already knows Howard, what he looks like.'

'Probably, ma'am, but we might need a photo in some cases. Do you—'

'Martin,' she said, 'go get me the albums out of the drawer in the den.'

Martin left the room and they waited. Bosch took a business card from his pocket and put it down on the wrought iron-and-glass coffee table.

'There's my pager number if you need me or if there is anything else I can do. Is there a family minister you would like us to call?'

Millie Elias looked up at him again.

'Reverend Tuggins over at the AME.'

Bosch nodded but immediately wished he hadn't made the offer. Martin came back into the room with a photo album. His mother took it and began to turn through the pages. She began to weep silently again at the sight of so many pictures of her husband. Bosch wished he had put off getting the photo until the follow-up interview. Finally, she came upon a close-up shot of Howard Elias's face. She seemed to know it would be the best photo for the police. She carefully removed it from the plastic sleeve and handed it to Bosch.

'Will I get that back?'

'Yes, ma'am, I'll see that you do.'

Bosch nodded and was about to make his way to the door. He was wondering if he could just forget about calling Reverend Tuggins.

'Where's my husband?' the widow suddenly asked.

Bosch turned back.

'His body is at the coroner's office, ma'am. I will give them your number and they will call you when it is time for you to make arrangements.'

'What about Reverend Tuggins? You want to use our phone?'

'Uh, no, ma'am. We'll contact Reverend Tuggins from our car. We can see ourselves out now.'

On the way to the door, Bosch glanced at the collection of framed photographs that hung on the wall in the entrance hallway. They were photos of Howard Elias with every notable black community leader in the city as well as many other celebrities and national leaders. There he was with Jesse Jackson, with Congresswoman Maxine Waters, with Eddie Murphy. There was a shot of Elias flanked by Mayor Richard Riordan on one side and City Councilman Royal Sparks on the other. Bosch knew that Sparks had used outrage over police misconduct to forge his rise in city politics. He would miss having Elias around to keep the fire fanned, though Bosch also knew that Sparks would now use the lawyer's murder to any advantage he could. Bosch wondered how it was that good and noble causes often seemed to bring slick opportunists to the microphones.

There were also family photos. Several depicted Elias and his wife at social functions. There were shots of Elias and his son – one of them on a boat, both holding up a black marlin and smiling. Another photo showed them at a firing range posing on either side of a paper target with several holes shot through it. The target depicted Daryl Gates, a former police chief whom Elias had sued numerous times. Bosch remembered that the targets, created by a local artist, were popular toward the end of Gates's tumultuous stewardship of the department.

Bosch leaned forward to study the photo and see if he could identify the weapons Elias and his son held but the photo was too small.

Chastain pointed to one of the photos, which showed Elias and the chief of police at some formal affair, supposed adversaries smiling at the camera.

'They look cozy,' he whispered.

Bosch just nodded and went out through the door.

Chastain pulled the car out of the driveway and headed down out of the hills and back to the freeway. They were silent, both absorbing the misery they had just brought to a family and how they had received the blame for it.

'They always shoot the messenger,' Bosch said.

'I think I'm glad I don't work homicide,' Chastain replied. 'I can deal with cops being pissed at me. But that, that was bullshit.'

'They call it the dirty work – next-of-kin notification.'

'They ought to call it something. Fucking people. We're trying to find out who killed the guy and they're saying it was us. You believe that shit?'

'I didn't take it literally, Chastain. People in that position are entitled to a little slack. They're hurting, they say things, that's all.'

'Yeah, you'll see. Wait until you see that kid on the six o'clock news. I know the type. You won't have much sympathy then. Where are we going anyway, back to the scene?'

'Go to his apartment first. You know Dellacroce's pager number?'

'Not offhand, no. Look at your list.'

Bosch opened his notebook and looked up the pager number Dellacroce had written down. He punched the number into his phone and made the page.

'What about Tuggins?' Chastain asked. 'You call him, you give him the head start on getting the south end ready to rock and roll.'

'I know. I'm thinking.'

Bosch had been thinking about that decision since the moment Millie Elias had mentioned the name Tuggins. As with many minority communities, pastors carried as much weight as politicians when it came to shaping that community's response to a social, cultural or political cause or event. In the case of Preston Tuggins, he carried even more. He headed a group of associated ministers and together they were a force, a major media-savvy force that could hold the whole community in check – or unleash it like an earthquake. Preston Tuggins had to be handled with utmost care.

Bosch dug through his pocket and pulled out the card Irving had given him earlier. He was about to call one of the numbers on it when the phone rang in his hand.

It was Dellacroce. Bosch gave him the address of Elias's apartment at The Place and told him to draw up an additional search warrant. Dellacroce cursed because he had already wakened a judge to fax him the office search warrant. He would now have to do it again.

'Welcome to homicide,' Bosch said as he clicked off.

'What?' Chastain said.

'Nothing. Just bullshit.'

Bosch punched in Irving's number. The deputy chief answered after one ring, giving his full name and rank. It seemed odd to Bosch that Irving seemed fully alert, as if he had not been asleep.

'Chief, it's Bosch. You said to call if—'

'It's no problem, Detective. What is it?'

'We just made notification. To Elias's wife and son. Uh, she wanted me to call her minister.'

'I don't see the problem.'

'The minister is Preston Tuggins and I thought maybe somebody a little further up the ladder might be better making—'

'I understand. It was good thinking. I will have it taken care of. I think perhaps the chief will want to handle that. I was just about to call him anyway. Anything else?'

'Not at this time.'

'Thank you, Detective.'

Irving hung up. Chastain asked what he said and Bosch told him.

'This case . . . ,' Chastain said. 'I have a feeling things are going to get hairy.'

'Say that again.'

Chastain was about to say something else but Bosch's pager sounded. He checked the number. Again it wasn't a call from home but Grace Billets's second page. He had forgotten to call her earlier. He called now and the lieutenant answered after one ring.

'I wondered if you were going to call me back.'

'Sorry. I sort of got tied up, then I forgot.'

'So what's going on? Irving wouldn't tell me who was dead, just that RHD and Central couldn't handle it.'

'Howard Elias.'

'Oh, shit . . . Harry . . . I'm sorry it's you.'

'It's okay. We'll make out.'

'Everybody will be watching you. And if it's a cop . . . it's a no-win situation. Do you get any sense from Irving, does he want to go at it balls to the wall?'

'Mixed signals.'

'You can't talk freely?'

'Right.'

'Well, I'm getting mixed signals here, too. Irving told me to take your team off the rotation but he said it would only be until Friday. Then I'm supposed to talk to Irving about it. Now that I know who is dead, I think the translation of that is that you have till then before he probably ships you back to Hollywood and you have to take Howard Elias back here with you and work it when you can.'

Bosch nodded but didn't say anything. It went with the other moves Irving had made. The deputy chief had created a large team to work the case, but it looked as though he was only giving them a week to work it full-time. Maybe he hoped that the media glare would drop off to a more manageable level by then and the case could eventually disappear into the unsolved files. But Bosch thought Irving was kidding himself if he thought that.

He and Billets talked for a few minutes more before Billets finally signed off with a warning.

'Watch yourself, Harry. If a cop did this, one of those RHD guys . . .'

'What?'

'Just be careful.'

'I will.'

He closed the phone and looked out the windshield. They were almost to the 110 transition. They would be back at California Plaza soon.

'Your lieutenant?' Chastain asked.

'Yeah. She just wanted to know what was going on.'

'So what's the deal with her and Rider? They still munching each other's pie on the side?'

'It's none of my business, Chastain. And none of yours.'

'Just asking.'

They rode in silence for a while. Bosch was annoyed by Chastain's question. He knew it was the IAD detective's way of reminding Bosch that he knew secrets, that he might be out of his element when it came to straight homicide investigation but he knew secrets about cops and should not be taken lightly. Bosch wished he hadn't made the call to Billets while Chastain was in the car.

Chastain seemed to sense his misstep and broke the silence by trying some harmless banter.

'Tell me about this hard-boiled eggs caper I keep hearing people talk about,' he said.

'It was nothing. Just a case.'

'I missed the story in the paper, I guess.'

'Just a piece of luck, Chastain. Like we could use on this case.'

'Well, tell me. I want to know – especially now that we're partnering up, Bosch. I like stories about luck. Maybe it will rub off.'

'It was just a routine call out on a suicide. Patrol called us to come out and sign off on it. Started when a mother got worried about her daughter because she hadn't shown up at the airport up in Portland. She was supposed to fly up there for a wedding or something and never showed up. The family was left waiting at the airport. Anyway, the mother called up and asked for a drive-by check of the daughter's apartment. A little place over on Franklin near La Brea. So a blue suit went by, got the manager to let him in and they found her. She had been dead a couple of days – since the morning she was supposed to have flown up to Portland.'

'What did she do?'

'It was made to look like she took some pills and then cut her wrists in the bathtub.'

'Patrol said suicide.'

'That's the way it was supposed to look. There was a note. It was torn out of a notebook and it said things about life not being what she expected and about being lonely all the time and stuff. It was kind of a ramble. Very sad, actually.'

'So? How'd you figure it out?'

'Well, we were – Edgar was with me, Rider had court – we were about to close it out. We had looked around the place and found nothing really wrong – except for the note. I couldn't find the notebook that the page had been torn out of. And that didn't sit right. I mean, it didn't mean she didn't kill herself, but it was a loose end, you know? A *what is wrong with this picture* sort of thing.'

'Okay, so you thought somebody was in there and took the notebook?'

'Maybe. I didn't know what to think. I told Edgar to take another look around and this time we switched and searched through things the other guy had searched the first time.'

'And you found something Edgar had missed.'

'He didn't miss it. It just didn't register with him. It did with me.'

'What was it already?'

'In her refrigerator there was a shelf for the eggs. You know, like little indentations that you sit the eggs in?'

'Right.'

'Well, I noticed on some of the eggs she had written a date. All the same date. It was the same day she was flying up to Portland.'

Bosch looked over at Chastain to see if there was a reaction. The IAD man had a confused look on his face. He didn't get it.

'They were hard-boiled eggs. The ones with dates on them had been hard-boiled. I took one over to the sink and cracked it. It was hard-boiled.'

'Okay.'

He still didn't get it.

'The date on the eggs was probably the date she had boiled them,' Bosch said. 'You know, so she could tell the boiled ones from the others and she'd know how old they were. And it just hit me then. You don't boil a bunch of eggs so they're ready for when you want them and then go kill yourself. I mean, what's the point?'

'So it was a hunch.'

'More than that.'

'But you just knew. Homicide.'

'It changed things. We started to look at things differently. We began a homicide investigation. It took a few days but we got it. Friends told us about some guy who was giving her trouble. Harassing her, stalking her because she turned him down on a date. We asked around the apartment and we started looking at the apartment manager.'

'Shit, I shoulda guessed it was him.'

'We talked to him and he fucked up just enough for us to convince a judge to sign a search warrant. In his place we found the notebook that the supposed suicide note had been torn from. It was like a diary where she wrote down her thoughts and things. This guy found a page where she was

591

talking about life being bad and knew he could use it as a suicide note. We found other stuff that was hers.'

'Why'd he keep the stuff?'

'Because people are stupid, that's why, Chastain. You want clever killers, watch TV. He kept the stuff because he never thought we'd think it wasn't a suicide. And because he was in the notebook. She wrote about him stalking her, about how she was sort of flattered and scared of him at the same time. He probably got off on reading it. He kept it.'

'When's the trial?'

'Couple months.'

'Sounds like a slam dunk.'

'Yeah, we'll see. So was O.J.'

'What did he do, drug her somehow, then put her in the tub and cut her?'

'He was letting himself in her apartment when she was out. There was stuff in the diary about her thinking someone had been creepin' her place. She was a runner – did three miles a day. We think that was when he liked to go in. She had prescription painkillers in the medicine cabinet – she got hurt playing racketball a couple years before. We think he took the pills on one of his visits and dissolved them in orange juice. The next time he went in he poured it into the juice bottle in her fridge. He knew her habits, knew that after jogging she liked to sit on the steps out front, drink her juice and cool down. She may have realized she had been drugged and looked around for help. It was him who came. He took her back inside.'

'He rape her first?'

Bosch shook his head.

'He probably tried but he couldn't get it up.'

They drove in silence for a few moments.

'You're cool, Bosch,' Chastain said. 'Nothing gets by you.'

'Yeah, I wish.'

7

Chastain parked the car in the passenger loading zone in front of the modern high-rise building called The Place. Before they were out of the car the night doorman came through the glass entrance to either greet them or tell them to move. Bosch got out and explained that Howard Elias had been murdered less than a block away and that they needed to check his apartment to make sure there were no additional victims or someone needing help. The doorman said no problem but wanted to go along. Bosch told him in a tone that invited no debate to wait in the lobby for other officers who would be arriving.

Howard Elias's apartment was on the twentieth floor. The elevator moved quickly but the silence between Bosch and Chastain made the trip seem longer.

They found their way to 20E and Bosch knocked on the door and rang the doorbell on the wall next to it. After getting no response, Bosch stooped and opened his briefcase on the floor, then took the keys out of the evidence bag Hoffman had given him earlier.

'You think we ought to wait on the warrant?' Chastain asked.

Bosch looked up at him as he closed the briefcase and snapped the locks. 'No.'

'That was a line of bullshit you gave the doorman, that people maybe needed help.'

Bosch stood up and started trying keys in the door's two locks.

'Remember what you said before about me eventually having to trust you? This is where I start to trust you, Chastain. I don't have the time to wait on a warrant. I'm going in. A homicide case is like a shark. It's gotta keep moving or it drowns.'

He turned the first lock.

'You and your fucking fish. First fighting fish, now a shark.'

'Yeah, you keep sticking around, Chastain, you might even learn how to catch something.'

Just as he said the line he turned the second lock. He looked at Chastain and winked, then opened the door.

They entered a medium-sized living room with expensive leather furnishings, cherrywood bookcases, and windows and a balcony with an expansive southern view across downtown and the civic center. The place was neatly kept except for sections of Friday morning's *Times* spread across the black leather couch and an empty coffee mug on the glass-topped coffee table.

'Hello?' Bosch called out, just to be sure the place was empty. 'Police. Anyone home?'

No answer.

Bosch put his briefcase down on the dining room table, opened it and took a pair of latex gloves out of a cardboard box. He asked Chastain if he wanted a pair but the IAD man declined.

'I'm not going to be touching anything.'

They separated and began moving through the apartment on a quick initial survey. The rest of the place was as neat as the living room. It was a two-bedroom and had a master suite with its own balcony facing west. It was a clear night. Bosch could see all the way to Century City. Past those towers the lights dropped off in Santa Monica to the sea. Chastain came into the bedroom behind him.

'No home office,' he said. 'The second bedroom looks like a guest room. Maybe for stashing witnesses.'

'Okay.'

Bosch scanned the contents of the top of the bureau. There were no photos or anything of a strong personal nature. Same with the small tables on either side of the bed. It looked like a hotel room and in a way it was – if Elias only used it for overnight stays while readying cases for court. The bed was made and this stood out to Bosch. Elias was in the middle of preparations for a major trial, working day and night, yet he had stopped to make his bed that morning when supposedly it would just be he returning at the end of the day. No way, Bosch thought. Either he made the bed because there would be someone else in the apartment or someone else made the bed.

Bosch ruled out a maid because a maid would have picked up the strewn newspaper and the empty coffee cup in the living room. No, it was Elias who had made the bed. Or someone who was with him. It was gut instinct based on his long years of delving into human habits, but at that moment Bosch felt reasonably sure that there now was another woman in the mix.

He opened the drawer of the bed table where a phone sat and found a personal phone book. He opened it and flipped through the pages. There were many names he recognized. Most were lawyers Bosch had heard about or even knew. He stopped when he came across one name. Carla Entrenkin. She, too, was an attorney specializing in civil rights cases – or had been until a year earlier, when the Police Commission appointed her inspector general of the Los Angeles Police Department. He noted that Elias had her office and home number listed. The home number was in darker, seemingly more recent, ink. It looked to Bosch as though the home number had been added well after the business number had been recorded in the book.

'Whaddaya got?' Chastain said.

'Nothing,' Bosch answered. 'Just a bunch of lawyers.'

He closed the phone book as Chastain stepped over to look. He tossed it back in the drawer and closed it.

'Better leave it for the warrant,' he said.

They conducted a casual search of the rest of the apartment for the next twenty minutes, looking in drawers and closets, under beds and couch cushions, but not disturbing anything they found. At one point Chastain called out from the bathroom off the master bedroom.

'Got two toothbrushes here.'

'Okay.'

Bosch was in the living room, studying the books on shelves. He saw one he had read years before, *Yesterday Will Make You Cry* by Chester Himes. He felt Chastain's presence and turned around. Chastain stood in the hallway leading to the bedrooms. He was holding a box of condoms up for Bosch to see.

'These were hidden in the back of a shelf under the sink.'

Bosch didn't respond. He just nodded.

In the kitchen there was a wall-mounted telephone with an answering machine. There was a flashing light on it and the digital display showed there was one message waiting to be played. Bosch pushed the playback button. It was a woman's voice on the message.

'Hey, it's me. I thought you were going to call me. I hope you didn't fall asleep on me.'

That was it. After the message, the machine reported that the call had come in at 12:01 A.M. Elias was already dead by then. Chastain, who had come into the kitchen from the living room when he heard the voice, just looked at Bosch and hiked his shoulders after the message was played. Bosch played it again.

'Doesn't sound like the wife to me,' Bosch said.

'Sounds white to me,' Chastain said.

Bosch thought he was right. He played the message one more time, this time concentrating on the tone of the woman's voice. There was a clear sense of intimacy in the voice. The time of the call and the woman's assumption that Elias would know her voice supported this conclusion as well.

'Condoms hidden in the bathroom, two toothbrushes, mystery woman on the phone,' Chastain said. 'Sounds like we got a girlfriend in the works. That could make things interesting.'

'Maybe,' Bosch said. 'Somebody made the bed this morning. Any female stuff in the medicine cabinet?'

'Nothing.'

Chastain went back to the living room. After Bosch was finished in the kitchen, he felt he had seen enough for the time being and slid open the glass door leading from the living room to the balcony. He leaned on the iron railing and checked his watch. It was 4:50. He then pulled the pager off his belt to make sure he hadn't turned it off by mistake.

The pager was on, the battery not dead. Eleanor had not tried to reach him. He heard Chastain come out onto the balcony behind him. Bosch spoke without turning to look at him.

'Did you know him, Chastain?'

'Who, Elias? Yeah, sort of.'

'How?'

'I've worked cases he later went to court on. I got subpoenaed and deposed. Plus, the Bradbury. He's got his office there, we've got offices there. I'd see him every now and then. But if you're asking if I played golf with the guy, the answer is no. I didn't know him like that.'

'The guy made a living suing cops. When he got into court he always seemed to have real good information. Inside stuff. Some say better stuff than he should have had access to through legal discovery. Some say he might've had sources inside—'

'I wasn't a snitch for Howard Elias, Bosch,' Chastain said, his voice tight. 'And I don't know anyone in IAD who was. We investigate cops. *I* investigate cops. Sometimes they deserve it and sometimes it turns out they don't. You know as well as I do that there has to be somebody to police the police. But snitching to the likes of Howard Elias and his bunch, that's the lowest of the low, Bosch. So fuck you very much for asking.'

Bosch looked at him now, studying the way the anger was moving into his dark eyes.

'Just asking,' he said. 'Had to know who I am dealing with.'

He looked back out across the city and then down to the plaza below. He saw Kiz Rider and Loomis Baker crossing toward Angels Flight with a man Bosch assumed was Eldrige Peete, the train operator.

'All right, you asked,' Chastain said. 'Can we get on with it now?'

'Sure.'

They were silent during the elevator ride down. It wasn't until they were in the lobby that Bosch spoke.

'You go on ahead,' he said. 'I'm gonna see if there's a can around here. Tell the others I'll be right there.'

'Sure.'

The doorman had overheard the exchange from his little lobby desk and told Bosch the rest room was around the corner behind the elevators. Bosch headed that way.

In the rest room Bosch put his briefcase on the sink counter and got his phone out. He called his house first. When the machine picked up he punched in the code to play all new messages. Only his own message played back to him. Eleanor hadn't got it.

'Shit,' he said as he hung up.

He then called information and got the number for the Hollywood Park poker room. The last time Eleanor had not come home she had told him she was playing cards there. He called the number and asked for the security office. A man identifying himself as Mr Jardine answered and Bosch gave his name and badge number. Jardine asked him to spell his name and give the number again. He was obviously writing it down.

'Are you in the video room?'

'Sure am. What can I do for you?'

'I'm looking for somebody and there is a good chance she is at one of your tables right now. I was wondering if you could look at the tubes for me.'

'What's she look like?'

Bosch described his wife but could not give any description on clothes because he had not checked the closets at the house. He then waited two minutes while Jardine apparently studied the video screens connected to the surveillance cameras in the poker room.

'Uh, if she's here, I'm not seeing her,' Jardine finally said. 'We don't have very many women in here this time of night. And she doesn't match the ones we've got. I mean, she could have been in here earlier, maybe one or two o'clock. But not now.'

'Okay, thanks.'

'Hey, you got a number? I'll take a walk around the place, call you back if I see anything.'

'I'll give you my pager. But if you see her, don't approach her. Just give me a page.'

'Will do.'

After giving the man his pager number and hanging up, Bosch thought about the card clubs in Gardena and Commerce but decided not to call. If Eleanor was going to stay local she would have gone to Hollywood Park. If she didn't go there she'd go to Vegas or maybe the Indian place in the desert near Palm Springs. He tried not to think about that and focused his mind back on the case.

Bosch next called the district attorney's night switchboard after getting the number out of his phone book. He asked to be connected to the on-call prosecutor and was eventually connected to a sleepy attorney named Janis Langwiser. She happened to be the same prosecutor who had filed charges in the so-called hard-boiled eggs case. She had recently moved over from the city attorney's office and it had been the first time Bosch had worked with her. He had enjoyed her sense of humor and enthusiasm for her job.

'Don't tell me,' she said, 'you've got a scrambled eggs case this time? Or better yet, the western omelet case.'

'Not quite. I hate to pull you out of bed but we're going to need somebody to come out and give us a little guidance on a search we'll be doing pretty soon.'

'Who's dead and where's the search?'

'Dead is Howard Elias, Esquire, and the search is going to be in his office.'

She whistled into the phone and Bosch had to hold it away from his ear.

'Wow,' she said, now fully alert. 'This is going to be . . . well, something. Tell me the general details.'

He did and when he was finished Langwiser, who lived thirty miles north in Valencia, agreed to meet the search team at the Bradbury in one hour.

'Until then, take things very carefully, Detective Bosch, and don't go into the office until I am there.'

'Will do.'

It was a little thing but he liked her calling him by his title. It was not because she was a good deal younger than he was. It was because so often prosecutors treated him and other cops without respect, as simply tools for them to use whatever way they wanted in prosecuting a case. He was sure Janis Langwiser would be no different as she became more seasoned and cynical, but at least for now she outwardly showed him small nuances of respect.

Bosch disconnected and was about to put the phone away when he thought of something else. He called information again and asked for the home listing for Carla Entrenkin. He was connected to a recording that told him the number was unlisted at the customer's request. It was what he had expected to hear.

As he crossed Grand Street and California Plaza to Angels Flight, Bosch again tried not to think of Eleanor and where she might be. But it was hard.

It hurt his heart when he thought about her being out there somewhere alone, searching for something he obviously couldn't give her. He was beginning to feel his marriage would be doomed if he didn't soon figure out what it was she needed. When they had married a year ago, he had found a feeling of contentment and peace that he had never experienced before. For the first time in his life he felt there was someone to sacrifice for – everything if needed. But he had come to the point where he was acknowledging to himself that it was not the same for her. She was not content or complete. And it made him feel awful and guilty and a small bit relieved, all at the same time.

Again he tried to concentrate on other things, on the case. He knew he needed to put Eleanor aside for the time being. He started thinking about the voice on the phone, the condoms hidden in the bathroom cabinet and the bed that had been neatly made. He thought about how Howard Elias could come to have the unlisted home telephone number of Carla Entrenkin in the drawer next to his bed.

8

Rider was standing next to a tall black man with graying hair just outside the door to the Angels Flight station house. They were sharing a smile about something when Bosch walked up.

'Mr Peete, this is Harry Bosch,' Rider said. 'He's in charge of this investigation.'

Peete shook his hand.

'Worst thing I ever saw in m'life. Worst thing.'

'I'm sorry you had to witness this, sir. But I'm glad you are willing to help us out. Why don't you go in and have a seat inside. We'll be with you in a few minutes.'

When Peete was inside Bosch looked at Rider. He didn't have to speak.

'Same as Garwood said. He didn't hear anything and he didn't see a lot until the car came up and he went to lock it up for the night. He didn't see anybody hanging around down there, as if they were waiting for anyone, either.'

'Any chance he's just playing deaf and dumb?'

'My gut says no. I think he's legit. He didn't see it or hear it go down.'

'He touch the bodies?'

'No. You mean the watch and wallet? I doubt it was him.'

Bosch nodded.

'Mind if I ask him a couple follow-ups?'

'Be my guest.'

Bosch walked into the little office and Rider followed. Eldrige Peete was sitting at the lunch table, holding the phone to his ear.

'I gotta go, hon,' he said when he saw Bosch. 'The policeman wants to talk to me.'

He hung up.

'My wife. She's wondering when I'm coming home.'

Bosch nodded.

'Mr Peete, did you go into the train after you saw the bodies in there?'

'No, sir. Uh, they looked pretty dead to me. I saw a lot of blood. I thought I should leave it all alone for the authorities.'

'Did you recognize either of those people?'

'Well, the man I couldn't rightly see, but I thought it might be Mr Elias just on account of the nice suit and how he looked. Now, the woman, I recognized her, too. I mean, I didn't know her name or nothin' but she got on the train a few minutes before and went on down.'

'You mean she went down first?'

'Yes, sir, she went down. She also a regular like Mr Elias. 'Cept she ride maybe only one time a week. On Fridays, like last night. Mr Elias, he ride more.'

'Why do you think she went down the hill but didn't get off the train?'

Peete stared at him blankly, as if surprised by such an easy question.

''Cause she got shot.'

Bosch almost laughed but kept it to himself. He wasn't being clear enough with the witness.

'No, I mean before she was shot. It seems as though she never got up. As if she was on the bench and had been waiting to go back up when the shooter arrived behind the other passenger who was getting on.'

'I surely don't know what she was doing.'

'When exactly did she go down?'

'The ride right before. I sent Olivet down and that lady was on it. This was five, six minutes to 'leven. I sent Olivet down and I just let her sit down there till 'leven and then I brought her up. You know, last ride. When she came up, those people were dead on there.'

Peete's apparent ascribing of the female gender to the train was confusing to Bosch. He tried to make it clear.

'So you sent Olivet down with the woman on it. Then five, six minutes later she is still on the train car when you bring it up. Is that right?'

'Right.'

'And during that five or six minutes that Olivet was sitting down there, you weren't looking down there?'

'No, I was counting the money outta the register. Then when it was 'leven 'clock I went out and locked up Sinai. Then I brought Olivet on up. That's when I found them. They were dead.'

'But you didn't hear anything from down there? No shots?'

'No, like I told the lady – Miss Kizmin – I wear earplugs on account of the noise underneath the station. Also, I was countin' the money. It's mostly all quarters. I run 'em through the machine.'

He pointed to a stainless-steel change counter next to the cash register. It looked like the machine put the quarters into paper rolls containing ten dollars. He then stamped his foot on the wood floor, indicating the machinery below. Bosch nodded that he understood.

'Tell me about the woman. You said she was a regular?'

'Yeah, once a week. Fridays. Like maybe she have a little job up here in the apartments, cleanin' or somethin'. The bus runs down there on Hill Street. I think she caught it down there.'

'And what about Howard Elias?'

'He a regular, too. Two, three times a week, all different times, sometimes late like last night. One time I was locking up and he was down there callin' up to me. I made a 'ception. I brought him up on Sinai. I was bein' nice. At Christmas time he gave me a little envelope. He was a nice man, 'membering me like that.'

'Was he always alone when he rode the train?'

The old man folded his arms and thought about this for a moment.

'Mostly, I think.'

'You remember him ever being with somebody else?'

'I think one or two times I remember him bein' with somebody. I can't rightly remember who it was.'

'Was it a man or woman?'

'I don't know. I think it mighta been a lady but I'm not gettin' a picture, know what I mean?'

Bosch nodded and thought about things. He looked at Rider and raised his eyebrows. She shook her head. She had nothing more to ask.

'Before you go, Mr Peete, can you turn everything on and let us ride down?'

'Sure. Whatever you and Miss Kizmin need.'

He looked at Rider and bowed his head with a smile.

'Thank you,' Bosch said. 'Then let's do it.'

Peete moved to the computer keyboard and began typing in a command. Immediately the floor began to vibrate and there was a low-pitched grinding sound. Peete turned to them.

'Anytime,' he said above the din. Bosch waved and headed out to the train car. Chastain and Baker, the IAD man who had been paired with Kizmin Rider, were standing at the guard rail, looking down the track.

'We're going down,' Bosch called over. 'You guys coming?'

Without a word they fell in behind Rider and the four detectives stepped onto the train car called Olivet. The bodies had long been removed and the evidence technicians cleared out. But the spilt blood was still on the wood floor and the bench where Catalina Perez had sat. Bosch moved down the steps, careful to avoid stepping in the maroon pool that had leaked from Howard Elias's body. He took a seat on the right side. The others sat on benches further up the train, away from where the bodies had fallen. Bosch looked up at the station house window and waved. Immediately the car jerked and began its descent. And immediately Bosch again recalled riding the train as a kid. The seat was just as uncomfortable as he remembered it.

Bosch didn't look at the others as they rode. He kept looking out the lower door and at the track as it went underneath the car. The ride lasted no longer than a minute. At the bottom he was the first off. He turned and looked back up the tracks. He could see Peete's head silhouetted in the station house window by the overhead light inside.

Bosch did not push through the turnstile, as he could see black fingerprint powder on it and didn't want to get it on his suit. The department did not consider the powder a hazard of the job and would not repay a dry cleaning bill if he got it on himself. He pointed the powder out to the others and climbed over the turnstile.

He scanned the ground on the off chance something would catch his eye but there was nothing unusual. He was confident that the area had already been gone over by the RHD detectives anyway. Bosch had primarily come down to get a firsthand look and feel for the place. To the left of the archway was a concrete staircase for when the train wasn't running or for those who were afraid to ride the incline railroad. The stairs were also popular with weekend fitness enthusiasts who ran up and down them. Bosch had read a story about it a year or so back in the *Times*. Next to the stairs a lighted bus stop had been cut into the steep hill. There was a glass fiberglass sunshade over a double-length bench. The side partitions were used to advertise films. On the one Bosch could see there was an ad for an

Eastwood picture called *Blood Work*. The movie was based on a true story about a former FBI agent Bosch was acquainted with.

Bosch thought about whether the gunman could have waited in the bus shelter for Elias to walk up to the Angels Flight turnstile. He decided against it. The shelter was lit by an overhead light. Elias would have had a good view of whoever sat in there as he approached the train. Since Bosch thought it was likely that Elias knew his killer, he didn't think the shooter would have waited out in the open like that.

He looked at the other side of the archway where there was a heavily landscaped ten-yard strip between the train entrance and a small office building. Bushes crowded thickly around an acacia tree. Bosch wished he hadn't left his briefcase up in the station house.

'Anybody bring a flashlight?' he asked.

Rider reached into her purse and brought out a small penlight. Bosch took it and headed into the bushes, putting the light on the ground and studying his pathway in. He found no obvious sign that the killer had waited in here. There was trash and other debris scattered in behind the bushes but none of it appeared to be fresh. It looked like a place where homeless people had stopped to look through trash bags they had picked up from somewhere else.

Rider made her way into the bushes.

'Find anything?'

'Nothing good. I'm just trying to figure out where this guy would have hidden from Elias. This could have been as good a spot as any. Elias wouldn't see him, he'd come out after Elias walked by, move up behind him at the train car.'

'Maybe he didn't need to hide. Maybe they walked here together.'

Bosch looked at her and nodded.

'Maybe. As good as anything I'm coming up with in here.'

'What about the bus bench?'

'Too open, too well lighted. If it was someone Elias had reason to fear, he'd've seen him.'

'What about a disguise? He could have sat in the bus stop in a disguise.'

'There's that.'

'You've already considered all of this but you let me go on talking, saying things you already know.'

He didn't say anything. He handed the flashlight back to Rider and headed out of the bushes. He looked over at the bus stop once more and felt sure he was right in his thinking. The bus stop hadn't been used. Rider came up next to him and followed his gaze.

'Hey, did you know Terry McCaleb over at the bureau?' she asked.

'Yeah, we worked a case once. Why, you know him?'

'Not really. But I've seen him on TV. He doesn't look like Clint Eastwood, if you ask me.'

'Yeah, not really.'

Bosch saw Chastain and Baker had crossed the street and were standing in the hollow created by the closed roll-up doors at the entrance of the huge Grand Central Market. They were looking at something on the ground.

Bosch and Rider walked over.

'Got something?' Rider asked.

'Maybe, maybe not,' Chastain said.

He pointed to the dirty, worn tiles at his feet.

'Cigarette butts,' Baker said. 'Five of them – same brand. Means somebody was waiting here a while.'

'Could have been a homeless,' Rider said.

'Maybe,' Baker replied. 'Could've been our shooter.'

Bosch wasn't that impressed.

'Any of you smokers?' he asked.

'Why?' Baker asked.

'Because then you'd see what this probably is. What is it you see when you go in the front doors at Parker Center?'

Chastain and Baker looked puzzled.

'Cops?' Baker tried.

'Yeah, but cops doing what?'

'Smoking,' Rider said.

'Right. No smoking in public buildings anymore, so the smokers gather round the front doors. This market is a public facility.'

He pointed at the cigarette butts crushed on the tiles.

'It doesn't necessarily mean somebody was waiting there a long time. I think it means somebody in the market came out five times during the day for smokes.'

Baker nodded but Chastain refused to acknowledge the deduction.

'Still could be our guy,' he said. 'Where else did he wait, the bushes over there?'

'He could have. Or like Kiz said, maybe he didn't wait. Maybe he walked right up to the train with Elias. Maybe Elias thought he was with a friend.'

Bosch reached into his jacket pocket and took out a plastic evidence bag. He handed it to Chastain.

'Or maybe I'm all wrong and you're all right. Bag 'em and tag 'em, Chastain. Make sure they get to the lab.'

A few minutes later Bosch was finished with his survey of the lower crime scene. He got on the train, picked up his briefcase where he had left it and moved up the stairs to one of the benches near the upper door. He sat down heavily, almost dropping onto the hard bench. He was beginning to feel fatigue take over and wished he had gotten some sleep before Irving's call had come. The excitement and adrenaline that accompany a new case caused a false high that always wore off quickly. He wished he could have a smoke and then maybe a quick nap. But only one of the two was possible at the moment, and he would have to find an all-night market to get the smokes. Again he decided against it. For some reason he felt that his nicotine fast had become part of his vigil for Eleanor. He thought that if he smoked all would be lost, that he would never hear from her again.

'What are you thinking, Harry?'

He looked up. Rider was in the doorway of the train, coming aboard.

'Nothing. Everything. We're really just getting started on this. There's a lot to do.'

'No rest for the weary.'

'Say that again.'

His pager sounded and he grabbed it off his belt with the urgency of a man who has had one go off in a movie theater. He recognized the number on the display but couldn't remember where he had seen it before. He took the phone out of his briefcase and punched it in. It was the home of Deputy Chief Irvin Irving.

'I spoke with the chief,' he said. 'He'll handle Reverend Tuggins. He's not to be your concern.'

Irving put a sneer into the word *Reverend*.

'Okay. He isn't.'

'So where are we?'

'We're still at the scene, just finishing up. We need to canvass the building over here for witnesses, then we'll clear out. Elias kept an apartment downtown. That was where he was headed. We need to search that and his office as soon as the search warrants are signed.'

'What about next of kin on the woman?'

'Perez should be done by now, too.'

'Tell me how it went at the Elias home.'

Since Irving had not asked before, Bosch assumed he was asking now because the chief of police wanted to know. Bosch quickly went over what had happened and Irving asked several questions about the reaction of Elias's wife and son. Bosch could tell he asked them from the standpoint of public relations management. He knew that, just as with Preston Tuggins, the way in which Elias's family reacted to his murder would have a direct bearing on how the community reacted.

'So it does not at this time sound as though we can enlist the widow or the son in helping us contain things, correct?'

'As of now, that's correct. But once they get over the initial shock, maybe. You also might want to talk to the chief about calling the widow personally. I saw his picture on the wall in the house with Elias. If he's talking to Tuggins, maybe he could also talk to the widow about helping us out.'

'Maybe.'

Irving switched gears and told Bosch that his office's conference room on the sixth floor of Parker Center was ready for the investigators. He said that the room was unlocked at the moment but in the morning Bosch would be given keys. Once the investigators moved in, the room was to remain locked at all times. He said that he would be in by ten and was looking forward to a more expanded rundown of the investigation at the team meeting.

'Sure thing, Chief,' Bosch said. 'We should be in from the canvass and the searches by then.'

'Make sure you are. I'll be waiting.'

'Right.'

Bosch was about to disconnect when he heard Irving's voice.

'Excuse me, Chief?'

'One other matter. I felt because of the identity of one of the victims in this case that it was incumbent upon me to notify the inspector general. She seemed – how do I put this – she seemed acutely interested in the case when I explained the facts we had at that time. Using the word acutely is probably an understatement.'

Carla Entrenkin. Bosch almost cursed out loud but held it back. The inspector general was a new entity in the department: a citizen appointed by the Police Commission as an autonomous civilian overseer with ultimate

authority to investigate or oversee investigations. It was a further politiciz-
ing of the department. The inspector general answered to the Police
Commission which answered to the city council and the mayor. And there
were other reasons Bosch almost cursed as well. Finding Entrenkin's name
and private number in Elias's phone book bothered him. It opened up a
whole set of possibilities and complications.

'Is she coming out here to the scene?' he asked.

'I don't think so,' Irving said. 'I waited to call so that I could say the scene
was clearing. I saved you that headache. But don't be surprised if you hear
directly from her in the daylight.'

'Can she do that? I mean, talk to me without going through you? She's a
civilian.'

'Unfortunately, she can do whatever she wants to. That is how the Police
Commission set up the job. So what it means is that this investigation,
wherever it goes, it better be seamless, Detective Bosch. If it is not, we will be
hearing from Carla Entrenkin about it.'

'I understand.'

'Good, then all we need is an arrest and all will be fine.'

'Sure, Chief.'

Irving disconnected without acknowledging. Bosch looked up. Chastain
and Baker were stepping onto the train.

'There's only one thing worse than having the IAD tagging along on this,'
he whispered to Rider. 'That's the inspector general watching over our
shoulders.'

Rider looked at him.

'You're kidding? Carla I'mthinkin' is on this?'

Bosch almost smiled at Rider's use of the nickname bestowed on
Entrenkin by an editorialist in the police union's *Thin Blue Line* newsletter.
She was called Carla I'mthinkin' because of her tendency toward slow and
deliberate speech whenever addressing the Police Commission and criticiz-
ing the actions or members of the department.

Bosch would have smiled but the addition of the inspector general to the
case was too serious.

'Nope,' he said. 'Now we got her, too.'

9

At the top of the hill they found Edgar and Fuentes had returned from notifying Catalina Perez's family of her death, and Joe Dellacroce had returned from Parker Center with completed and signed search warrants. Court-approved searches were not always needed for the home and business of the victim of a homicide. But it made good sense to get warrants in high-profile cases. Such cases attracted high-profile attorneys if they eventually resulted in arrest. These attorneys invariably created their high profiles by being thorough and good at what they did. They exploited mistakes, took the frayed seams and loose ends of cases and ripped open huge holes – often big enough for their clients to escape through. Bosch was already thinking that far ahead. He knew he had to be very careful.

Additionally, he believed a warrant was particularly necessary to search Elias's office. There would be numerous files on police officers and cases pending against the department. These cases would most likely proceed after being taken on by new attorneys, and Bosch needed to balance the preservation of attorney-client privacy with the need to investigate the killing of Howard Elias. The investigators would no doubt need to proceed carefully while handling these files. It was the reason he had called the district attorney's office and asked Janis Langwiser to come to the scene.

Bosch approached Edgar first, taking him by the arm and nudging him over to the guardrail overlooking the steep drop-off to Hill Street. They were out of earshot of the others.

'How'd it go?'

'It went the way they all go. About a million other places I'd rather be than watching the guy get the news. Know what I mean?'

'Yeah, I know. You just tell him or did you ask him some questions?'

'We asked, but we didn't get very many answers. The guy said his wife was a housecleaner and she had a gig somewhere over here. She took the bus over. He couldn't give an address. Said his wife kept all of that stuff in a little notebook she carried.'

Bosch thought for a moment. He didn't remember any notebook in the evidence inventory. Balancing his briefcase on the guardrail, he opened it and took out the clipboard on which he had the accumulated paperwork from the crime scene. On top was the yellow copy of the inventory Hoffman had given him before he had left. It listed Victim #2's belongings but there was no notebook.

'Well, we'll have to check with him again later on. We didn't get any notebook.'

'Well, send Fuentes back. The husband didn't speak English.'

'All right. Anything else?'

'No. We did the usual checklist. Any enemies, any problems, anybody giving her trouble, anybody stalking her, so on and so forth. Nada. The husband said she wasn't worried about anything.'

'Okay. What about him?'

'He looked legit. Like he got hit in the face with the big frying pan called bad luck. You know?'

'Yeah, I know.'

'Hit hard. And there was as much surprise there as anything else.'

'Okay.'

Bosch looked around to make sure they were not being overheard. He spoke low to Edgar.

'We're going to split up now and go with the searches. I want you to take the apartment Elias kept over at The Place. I was—'

'So that's where he was going.'

'Looks like it. I was just up there with Chastain, did a drive-by. I want you to take your time this time. I also want *you* to start in his bedroom. Go to the bed and take the phone book out of the top drawer of the table with the phone on it. Bag it and seal it so nobody can look at it until we get everything back to the office.'

'Sure. How come?'

'I'll tell you later. Just get to it before anybody else. Also, take the tape from the phone machine in the kitchen. There's a message we want to keep.'

'Right.'

'Okay then.'

Bosch stepped away from the guardrail and approached Dellacroce.

'Any problems with the paper?'

'Not really – except for waking the judge twice.'

'Which judge?'

'John Houghton.'

'He's okay.'

'Well, it didn't sound like he appreciated having to do everything twice.'

'What did he say about the office?'

'Had me add in a line about preserving the sanctity of attorney-client privilege.'

'That's it? Let me see.'

Dellacroce took the search warrants out of the inside pocket of his suit jacket and handed Bosch the one for the office at the Bradbury. Bosch scanned through the stock wording on the first page of the declaration and got to the part Dellacroce had talked about. It looked okay to him. The judge was still allowing the search of the office and the files, but was simply saying that any privileged information gleaned from the files must be germane to the murder investigation.

'What he's saying is that we can't go through the files and turn what we get over to the city attorney's office to help defend those cases,' Dellacroce said. 'Nothing goes outside our investigation.'

'I can live with that,' Bosch said.

He called everybody into a huddle. He noticed Fuentes was smoking and tried not to think about his own desire for a cigarette.

'Okay, we've got the search warrants,' he said. 'This is how we're gonna split it up. Edgar, Fuentes and Baker, you three take the apartment. I want Edgar on lead. The rest of us will go to the office. You guys on the apartment, I also want you to arrange for interviews of all the doormen in the building. All shifts. We need to find out as much about this guy's routines and personal life as we can. We're thinking there may be a girlfriend somewhere. We need to find out who that was. Also, on the key chain there is a key to a Porsche and a Volvo. My guess is Elias drove the Porsche and it's probably in the parking garage at the apartment building. I want you to take a look at that, too.'

'The warrants don't specify a car,' Dellacroce protested. 'Nobody told me about a car when I was sent to work up the warrants.'

'Okay, then just find the car, check it out through the windows and we'll get a search warrant if you see something and think it is necessary.'

Bosch was looking at Edgar as he said this last part. Edgar almost imperceptibly nodded, meaning that he understood that Bosch was telling him to find the car and to simply open it and search it. If anything of value to the investigation was found, then he would simply back out, get a warrant and they would act as if they had never been in the car in the first place. It was standard practice.

Bosch looked at his watch and wrapped it up.

'Okay, it's five-thirty now. We should be done with the searches by eight-thirty max. Take anything that even looks of interest and we'll sift through it all later. Chief Irving has set up the command post for this investigation in the conference room next to his office at Parker. But before we go back there, I want to meet everybody right back here at eight-thirty.'

He pointed up to the tall apartment building overlooking Angels Flight.

'We'll canvass this building then. I don't want to wait until later, have people get out for the day before we can get to them.'

'What about the meeting with Deputy Chief Irving?' Fuentes asked.

'That's set for ten. We should make it. If we don't, don't worry about it. I'll take the meeting and you people will proceed. The case comes first. He'll go along with that.'

'Hey, Harry?' Edgar said. 'If we get done before eight-thirty, all right if we get breakfast?'

'Yes, it's all right, but I don't want to miss anything. Do not hurry the search just so you can get pancakes.'

Rider smiled.

'Tell you what,' Bosch said. 'I'll make sure we have doughnuts here at eight-thirty. If you can, just wait until then. Okay, so let's do it.'

Bosch took out the key ring they had taken from the body of Howard Elias. He removed the keys to the apartment and the Porsche key and gave them to Edgar. He noted that there were still several keys on the ring that were unaccounted for. At least two or three would be to the office and another two or three for his home in Baldwin Hills. That still left four keys and Bosch thought about the voice he had heard on the answering machine. Maybe Elias had keys to a lover's home.

He put the keys back in his pocket and told Rider and Dellacroce to drive cars down the hill and over to the Bradbury. He said he and Chastain would take the train down and walk over, making a check of the sidewalks Elias would have covered between his office building and the lower Angels Flight terminus. As the detectives broke up and headed toward their assignments, Bosch went to the station window and looked in on Eldrige Peete. He was sitting on the chair by the cash register, earplugs in place and his eyes closed. Bosch rapped gently on the window but the train operator was startled anyway.

'Mr Peete, I want you to send us down once more and then you can close up, lock up and go home to your wife.'

'Okay, whatever you say.'

Bosch nodded and turned to head to the train, then he stopped and looked back at Peete.

'There's a lot of blood. Do you have someone who is going to clean up the inside of the train before it opens tomorrow?'

'Don't worry, I'll get that. I've got a mop and bucket back here in the closet. I called my supervisor. Before you got here. He said I gotta clean Olivet up so she's ready to go in the morning. We start at eight Satadays.'

Bosch nodded.

'Okay, Mr Peete. Sorry you have to do that.'

'I like to keep the cars clean.'

'Also, down at the bottom, they left fingerprint dust all over the turnstile. It's nasty stuff if you get that on your clothes.'

'I'll get that, too.'

Bosch nodded.

'Well, thanks for your help tonight. We appreciate it.'

'Tonight? Hell, it's morning already.'

Peete smiled.

'I guess you're right. Good morning, Mr Peete.'

'Yeah, not if you ask them two that were on the train.'

Bosch started away and then once more came back to the man.

'One last thing. This is going to be a big story in the papers. And on TV. I'm not telling you what to do but you might want to think about taking your phone off the hook, Mr Peete. And maybe not answering your door.'

'I gotcha.'

'Good.'

'I'm gonna sleep all day, anyway.'

Bosch nodded to him one last time and got on the train. Chastain was already on one of the benches near the door. Bosch walked past him and again went down the steps to the end where Howard Elias's body had fallen. He was careful again not to step in the pooled and coagulated blood.

As soon as he sat down the train began its descent. Bosch looked out the window and saw the gray light of dawn around the edges of the tall office buildings to the east. He slumped on the bench and yawned deeply, not bothering to raise a hand to cover his mouth. He wished he could turn his body and lie down. The bench was hard, worn wood but he had no doubts that he would quickly fall into sleep and that he would dream about Eleanor and happiness and places where you did not have to step around the blood.

He dropped the thought and brought his hand up and all the way into the pocket of his jacket before he remembered there were no cigarettes to be found there.

10

The Bradbury was the dusty jewel of downtown. Built more than a century before, its beauty was old but still brighter and more enduring than any of the glass-and-marble towers that now dwarfed it like a phalanx of brutish guards surrounding a beautiful child. Its ornate lines and glazed tile surfaces had withstood the betrayal of both man and nature. It had survived earthquakes and riots, periods of abandonment and decay, and a city that often didn't bother to safeguard what little culture and roots it had. Bosch believed there wasn't a more beautiful structure in the city – despite the reasons he had been inside it over the years.

In addition to holding the offices for the legal practice of Howard Elias and several other attorneys, the Bradbury housed several state and city offices on its five floors. Three large offices on the third floor were leased to the LAPD's Internal Affairs Division and used for holding Board of Rights hearings – the disciplinary tribunals police officers charged with misconduct must face. The IAD had leased the space because the rising tide of complaints against officers in the 1990s had resulted in more disciplinary actions and more BORs. Hearings were now happening every day, sometimes two or three running at a time. There was not enough space for this flow of misconduct cases in Parker Center. So the IAD had taken the space in the nearby Bradbury.

To Bosch, the IAD was the only blemish on the building's beauty. Twice he had faced Board of Rights hearings in the Bradbury. Each time he gave his testimony, listened to witnesses and an IAD investigator – once it had been Chastain – report the facts and findings of the case, and then paced the floor beneath the atrium's huge glass skylight while the three captains privately decided his fate. He had come out okay after both hearings and in the process had come to love the Bradbury with its Mexican tile floors, wrought-iron filigree and suspended mail chutes. He had once taken the time to look up its history at the Los Angeles Conservancy offices, and found one of the more intriguing mysteries of Los Angeles: the Bradbury, for all its lasting glory, had been designed by a $5-a-week draftsman. George Wyman had no degree in architecture and no prior credits as a designer when he drew the plans for the building in 1892, yet his design would see fruition in a structure that would last more than a century and cause generations of architects to marvel. To add to the mystery, Wyman never again designed a building of any significance, in Los Angeles or anywhere else.

It was the kind of mystery Bosch liked. The idea of a man leaving his mark with the one shot he's given appealed to him. Across a whole century, Bosch identified with George Wyman. He believed in the one shot. He didn't know if he'd had his yet – it wasn't the kind of thing you knew and understood until you looked back over your life as an old man. But he had the feeling that it was still out there waiting for him. He had yet to take his one shot.

Because of the one-way streets and traffic lights Dellacroce and Rider faced, Bosch and Chastain got to the Bradbury on foot before them. As they approached the heavy glass doors of the entrance, Janis Langwiser got out of a small red sports car that was parked illegally at the curb out front. She was carrying a leather bag on a shoulder strap and a Styrofoam cup with the tag of a tea bag hanging over the lip.

'Hey, I thought we said an hour,' she said good-naturedly.

Bosch looked at his watch. It was an hour and ten minutes since they had talked.

'So you're a lawyer, sue me,' he said, smiling.

He introduced Chastain and gave Langwiser a more detailed rundown on the investigation. By the time he was finished, Rider and Dellacroce had parked their cars in front of Langwiser's car. Bosch tried the doors to the building but they were locked. He got out the key ring and hit the right key on the second try. They entered the atrium of the building and each of them involuntarily looked up, such was the beauty of the place. Above them the atrium skylight was filled with the purples and grays of dawn. Classical music played from hidden speakers. Something haunting and sad but Bosch couldn't place it.

'Barber's "Adagio,"' Langwiser said.

'What?' Bosch said, still looking up.

'The music.'

'Oh.'

A police helicopter streaked across the skylight, heading home to Piper Tech for change of shift. It broke the spell and Bosch brought his eyes down. A uniformed security guard was walking toward them. He was a young black man with close-cropped hair and startling green eyes.

'Can I help you people? The building's closed right now.'

'Police,' Bosch said, pulling out his ID wallet and flipping it open. 'We've got a search warrant here for suite five-oh-five.'

He nodded to Dellacroce, who removed the search warrant from his coat pocket once again and handed it to the guard.

'That's Mr Elias's office,' the guard said.

'We know,' Dellacroce said.

'What's going on?' the guard asked. 'Why do you have to search his place?'

'We can't tell you that right now,' Bosch said. 'We need you to answer a couple questions, though. When's your shift start? Were you here when Mr Elias left last night?'

'Yeah, I was here. I work a six-to-six shift. I watched them leave about eleven last night.'

'Them?'

612

'Yeah, him and a couple other guys. I locked the door right after they went through. The place was empty after that – 'cept for me.'

'Do you know who the other guys were?'

'One was Mr Elias's assistant or a whatchamacallit.'

'Secretary? Clerk?'

'Yeah, clerk. That's it. Like a young student who helped him with the cases.'

'You know his name?'

'Nah, I never asked.'

'Okay, what about the other guy? Who was he?'

'Don't know that one.'

'Had you seen him around here before?'

'Yeah, the last couple nights they left together. And a few times before that I think I saw him going or coming by hisself.'

'Did he have an office here?'

'No, not that I know of.'

'Was he Elias's client?'

'How would I know?'

'A black guy, white guy?'

'Black.'

'What did he look like?'

'Well, I didn't get a real good look at him.'

'You said you've seen him around here before. What did he look like?'

'He was just a normal-looking guy. He . . .'

Bosch was growing impatient but wasn't sure why. The guard seemed to be doing the best he could. It was routine in police work to find witnesses unable to describe people they had gotten a good look at. Bosch took the search warrant out of the guard's hand and handed it back to Dellacroce. Langwiser asked to see it and began reading it while Bosch continued with the guard.

'What's your name?'

'Robert Courtland. I'm on the waiting list for the academy.'

Bosch nodded. Most security guards in this town were waiting for a police job somewhere. The fact that Courtland, a black man, was not already in the academy told Bosch that there was a problem somewhere in his application. The department was going out of its way to attract minorities to the ranks. For Courtland to be wait-listed there had to be something. Bosch guessed he had probably admitted smoking marijuana or didn't meet the minimum educational requirements, maybe even had a juvenile record.

'Close your eyes, Robert.'

'What?'

'Just close your eyes and relax. Think of the man you saw. Tell me what he looks like.'

Courtland did as he was told and after a moment came up with an improved but still sketchy description.

'He's about the same height as Mr Elias. But he had his head shaved. It was slick. He got one of them soul chips, too.'

'Soul chip?'

'You know, like a little beard under his lip.'

He opened his eyes.

'That's it.'

'That's it?' Bosch said in a friendly, cajoling tone. 'Robert, how're you going to make it into the cops? We need more than that. How old was this guy?'

'I don't know. Thirty or forty.'

'That's a help. Only ten years' difference. Was he thin? Fat?'

'Thin but with muscles. You know, the guy was built.'

'I think he's describing Michael Harris,' Rider said.

Bosch looked at her. Harris was the plaintiff in the Black Warrior case.

'It fits,' Rider said. 'The case starts Monday. They were probably working late, getting ready for court.'

Bosch nodded and was about to dismiss Courtland when Langwiser suddenly spoke while still reading the last page of the search warrant.

'I think we have a problem with the warrant.'

Now everyone looked at her.

'Okay, Robert,' Bosch said to Courtland. 'We'll be all right from here. Thanks for your help.'

'You sure? You want me to go up with you, unlock the door or something?'

'No, we have a key. We'll be all right.'

'Okay, then. I'll be in the security office around behind the stairs if you need anything.'

'Thanks.'

Courtland started walking back the way he had come but then stopped and turned around.

'Oh, you know, all five of you better not take the elevator up at once. That's probably too much weight on that old thing.'

'Thanks, Robert,' Bosch said.

He waited until the guard had gone around the staircase and was out of sight before turning back to Langwiser.

'Miss Langwiser, you probably haven't gone out on too many crime scenes before,' he said. 'But here's a tip, never announce that there is a problem with a search warrant in front of somebody who isn't a cop.'

'Oh, shit, I'm sorry. I didn't—'

'What's wrong with the warrant?' Dellacroce said, his voice showing he was upset by the apparent challenge to his work. 'The judge didn't see anything wrong with it. The judge said it was fine.'

Langwiser looked down at the three-page warrant in her hand and waved it, its pages fluttering like a falling pigeon.

'I just think that with a case like this we better be damn sure of what we're doing before we go in there and start opening up files.'

'We have to go into the files,' Bosch said. 'That's where most of the suspects will be.'

'I understand that. But these are confidential files relating to lawsuits against the police department. They contain privileged information that only an attorney and his client should have. Don't you see? It could be argued that by opening a single file you've violated the rights of Elias's clients.'

'All we want is to find the man's killer. We don't care about his pending cases. I hope to Christ that the killer's name isn't in those files and that it isn't a cop. But what if it is and what if in those files Elias kept copies or notes on threats? What if through his own investigations he learned something about somebody that could be a motive for his killing? You see, we need to look at the files.'

'All of that is understandable. But if a judge later rules the search was inappropriate you won't be able to use anything you find up there. You want to run that risk?'

She turned away from them and looked toward the door.

'I have to find a phone and make a call about this,' she said. 'I can't let you open that office yet. Not in good conscience.'

Bosch blew out his breath in exasperation. He silently chastised himself for calling in a lawyer too soon. He should have just done what he knew he had to do and dealt with the consequences later.

'Here.'

He opened his briefcase and handed her his cell phone. He listened as she called the DA's office switchboard and asked to be connected to a prosecutor named David Sheiman, who Bosch knew was the supervisor of the major crimes unit. After she had Sheiman on the line she began summarizing the situation and Bosch continued to listen to make sure she had the details right.

'We're wasting a lot of time standing around, Harry,' Rider whispered to him. 'You want Edgar and me to pick up Harris and have a talk with him about last night?'

Bosch almost nodded his approval but then hesitated as he considered the possible consequences.

Michael Harris was suing fifteen members of the Robbery-Homicide Division in a highly publicized case set to begin trial on Monday. Harris, a car-wash employee with a record of burglary and assault convictions, was seeking $10 million in damages for his claims that members of the RHD had planted evidence against him in the kidnapping and murder of a twelve-year-old girl who was a member of a well-known and wealthy family. Harris claimed the detectives had abducted, held and tortured him over a three-day period in hopes of drawing a confession from him as well as learning the location of the missing girl. The lawsuit alleged that the detectives, frustrated by Harris's unwillingness to admit his part in the crime or lead them to the missing girl, pulled plastic bags over Harris's head and threatened to suffocate him. He further claimed that one detective pushed a sharp instrument – a Black Warrior Number 2 pencil – into his ear, puncturing the ear drum. But Harris never confessed and on the fourth day of the interrogation the girl's body was found decomposing in a vacant lot just one block from his apartment. She had been sexually assaulted and strangled.

The murder became one more in a long line of crimes that gripped public attention in Los Angeles. The victim was a beautiful blonde, blue-eyed girl named Stacey Kincaid. She had been spirited from her bed while she slept in her family's large and seemingly safe Brentwood home. It was the kind of crime that sent a chilling message across the city: Nobody is safe.

As horrible as it was in itself, the murder of the little girl was exponentially magnified by the media. Initially, this was because of who the victim was and where she came from. She was the stepdaughter of Sam

Kincaid, scion of a family that owned more automobile dealerships in Los Angeles County than it was possible to count on two hands. Sam was the son of Jackson Kincaid, the original 'car czar,' who had built the family business from a single Ford dealership his father had passed on to him after World War II. Like Howard Elias after him, Jack Kincaid had seen the merit in local television marketing and in the 1960s became a fixture of late-night TV advertising. On camera, he showed a folksy charm, exuding honesty and friendship. He seemed as reliable and trustworthy as Johnny Carson and he was in the living rooms and bedrooms of Los Angeles just as often. If Los Angeles was seen as an 'autotopia' then Jack Kincaid was certainly seen as its unofficial mayor.

Off camera, the car czar was a calculating businessman who always played both sides of politics and mercilessly drove competitors out of business or at least away from his dealerships. His dynasty grew rapidly, his car lots spreading across the southern California landscape. By the 1980s Jack Kincaid's reign was done and the moniker of car czar was turned over to his son. But the old man remained a force, though a mostly unseen one. And this was never more clear than when Stacey Kincaid disappeared and old Jack returned to TV, this time to appear on newscasts and put up a million-dollar reward for her safe return. It was another surrealistic episode in Los Angeles murder lore. The old man everyone had grown up with on TV was back on once again and tearfully begging for his granddaughter's life.

It was all for naught. The reward and the old man's tears became moot when the girl was found dead by passersby in the vacant lot close to Michael Harris's apartment.

The case went to trial based solely on evidence consisting of Harris's fingerprints being found in the bedroom from which the girl had been abducted and the proximity of the body's disposal to his apartment. The case held the city rapt, playing live every day on *Court TV* and local news programs. Harris's attorney, John Penny, a lawyer as skilled as Elias when it came to manipulating juries, mounted a defense that attacked the body's disposal location as coincidental and the fingerprints – found on one of the girl's schoolbooks – as simply being planted by the LAPD.

All the power and money the Kincaids had amassed over generations was no match against the tide of anti-police sentiment and the racial underpinnings of the case. Harris was black, the Kincaids and the police and prosecutors on the case were white. The case against Harris was tainted beyond repair when Penny elicited what many perceived as a racist comment from Jack Kincaid during testimony about his many dealerships. After Kincaid detailed his many holdings, Penny asked why one of the dealerships was not in South Central Los Angeles. Without hesitation and before the prosecutor could object to the irrelevant question, Kincaid said he would never place a business in an area where the inhabitants had a propensity to riot. He said he made the decision after the Watts riots of 1965 and it was confirmed after the more recent riots of 1992.

The question and answer had little if anything to do with the murder of a twelve-year-old girl but proved to be the pivotal point in the trial. In later interviews jurors said Kincaid's answer was emblematic of the city's deep racial gulf. With that one answer sympathy swayed from the Kincaid family to Harris. The prosecution was doomed.

The jury acquitted Harris in four hours. Penny then turned the case over to his colleague, Howard Elias, for civil proceedings and Harris took his place next to Rodney King in the pantheon of civil rights victims and heroes in South L.A. Most of them deserved such honored status, but some were the creations of lawyers and the media. Whichever Harris was, he was now seeking his payday – a civil rights trial in which $10 million would be just the opening bid.

Despite the verdict and all the attached rhetoric, Bosch didn't believe Harris's claims of innocence or police brutality. One of the detectives Harris specifically accused of brutality was Bosch's former partner, Frankie Sheehan, and Bosch knew Sheehan to be a total professional when dealing with suspects and prisoners. So Bosch simply thought of Harris as a liar and murderer who had walked away from his crime. He would have no qualms about rousting him and taking him downtown for questioning about Howard Elias's murder. But Bosch also knew as he stood there with Rider that if he now brought Harris in, he would run the risk of compounding the alleged wrongs already done to him – at least in the eyes of much of the public and the media. It was a political decision as much as a police decision that he had to make.

'Let me think about this for a second,' he said.

He walked off by himself through the atrium. The case was even more perilous than he had realized. Any misstep could result in disaster – to the case, to the department, to careers. He wondered if Irving had realized all of this when he had chosen Bosch's team for the case. Perhaps, he thought, Irving's compliments were just a front for a real motive – leaving Bosch and his team dangling in the wind. Bosch knew he was now venturing into paranoia. It was unlikely that the deputy chief could have come up with such a plan so quickly. Or that he would even care about Bosch's team with so much else at stake.

Bosch looked up and saw the sky was much brighter now. It would be a sunny and hot day.

'Harry?'

He turned. It was Rider.

'She's off.'

He walked back to the group and Langwiser handed him his phone.

'You're not going to like this,' she said. 'Dave Sheiman wants to bring in a special master to look at the files before you do.'

'Special master?' Dellacroce asked. 'What the hell is that?'

'It's an attorney,' Langwiser said. 'An independent attorney appointed by a judge who will oversee the files. He will be hired to protect the rights of those clients while still giving you people what you need. Hopefully.'

'Shit,' Bosch said, his frustration finally getting the better of him. 'Why don't we just stop the whole thing now and drop the damn case? If the DA's office doesn't care about us clearing it then we won't care either.'

'Detective Bosch, you know it's not like that. Of course we care. We just want to be safe. The warrant you have is still good for searching the office. Sheiman said you can even go through completed case files – which I am sure you need to look at as well. But the special master will have to come in and look at all pending files first. Remember, this person is not an adversary to you. He will give you everything you are entitled to see.'

617

'And when will that be? Next week? Next month?'

'No. Sheiman is going to go to work on that this morning. He'll call Judge Houghton, apprise him of the situation, and see if he has any recommendations for a special master. With any luck, the appointment will be made today and you'll have what you need from the files this afternoon. Tomorrow, at the very latest.'

'Tomorrow at the latest is too late. We need to keep moving on this.'

'Yeah,' Chastain chimed in. 'Don't you know an investigation is like a shark? It's got to keep—'

'All right, Chastain,' Bosch said.

'Look,' Langwiser said. 'I'll make sure Dave understands the urgency of the situation. In the meantime you'll just have to be patient. Now do you want to keep standing down here talking about it or do you want to go up and do what we can in the office?'

Bosch looked at her for a long moment, annoyed by her chiding tone. The moment ended when the phone in his hand rang. It was Edgar and he was whispering. Bosch held a hand over his ear so he could hear.

'I didn't hear that. What?'

'Listen, I'm in the bedroom. There's no phone book in the bed table. I checked both bed tables. It's not here.'

'What?'

'The phone book, it's not here, man.'

Bosch looked at Chastain, who was looking back at him. He turned and walked away, out of earshot of the others. Now he whispered to Edgar.

'You sure?'

'Course I'm sure. I woulda found it if it was here.'

'You were first in the bedroom?'

'Right. First one in. It's not here.'

'You're in the bedroom to the right when you come down the hall.'

'Yeah, Harry. I'm in the right place. It's just not here.'

'Shit.'

'What do you want me to do?'

'Nothing. Continue the search.'

Bosch flipped the phone closed and put it in his pocket. He walked back to the others. He tried to act calm, as if the call had only been a minor annoyance.

'Okay, let's go up and do what we can up there.'

They moved to the elevator, which was an open wrought-iron cage with ornate flourishes and polished brass trim.

'Why don't you take the ladies up first,' Bosch said to Dellacroce. 'We'll come up after. That ought to distribute the weight pretty evenly.'

He took Elias's key ring out of his pocket and handed it to Rider.

'The office key should be on there,' he said. 'And never mind about that other thing with Harris for the time being. Let's see what we've got in the office first.'

'Sure, Harry.'

They got on and Dellacroce pulled the accordion gate closed. The elevator rose with a jerking motion. After it was up one floor and those on it could not see them, Bosch turned to Chastain. The anger and frustration of everything going wrong flooded him then. He dropped his briefcase and with both hands grabbed Chastain by the collar of his jacket. He roughly pushed him against the elevator cage and spoke in a low, dark voice that was full of rage.

'Goddammit, Chastain, I'm only asking this one time. Where's the fucking phone book?'

Chastain's face flushed crimson and his eyes grew wide in shock.

'What? What the fuck are you talking about?'

He brought his hands up to Bosch's and tried to free himself but Bosch maintained the pressure, leaning all of his weight into the other man.

'The phone book in the apartment. I know you took it and I want it back. Right the fuck now.'

Finally, Chastain tore himself loose. His jacket and shirt and tie were wrenched askew. He stepped away from Bosch as if he was scared and adjusted himself. He then pointed a finger at him.

'Stay away from me! You're fucking nuts! I don't have any phone book. You had it. I saw you put it in the goddamn drawer next to the bed.'

Bosch took a step toward him.

'You took it. When I was on the bal—'

'I said stay away! I didn't take it. If it's not there, then somebody came in and took it after we left.'

Bosch stopped. It was an obvious explanation but it hadn't even entered his mind. He had automatically thought of Chastain. He looked down at the tiles, embarrassed by how he'd let an old animosity cloud his judgment. He could hear the elevator gate opening on the fifth floor. He raised his eyes, fixed Chastain with a bloodless stare and pointed at his face.

'I find out otherwise, Chastain, I promise I'll take you apart.'

'Fuck you! I didn't take the book. But I am going to take your badge for this.'

Bosch smiled but not in a way that had any warmth.

'Go ahead. Write your ticket, Chastain. Anytime you can *take* my badge you can have it.'

11

The others were inside Howard Elias's law offices by the time Bosch and Chastain made it up to the fifth floor. The office was essentially three rooms: a reception area with a secretary's desk, a middle room where there was a clerk's desk and two walls of file cabinets, and then the third and largest room, Elias's office.

As Bosch and Chastain moved through the offices the others stood silently and didn't look at them. It was clear that they had heard the commotion in the lobby as they had taken the elevator up. Bosch didn't care about that. He had already put the confrontation with Chastain behind him and was thinking about the search. He was hoping something would be found in the office that would give the investigation a focus, a specific path to follow. He walked through the three rooms making general observations. In the last room he noticed that through the windows behind Elias's large polished wood desk he could see the huge face of Anthony Quinn. It was part of a mural depicting the actor with arms outstretched on the brick wall of a building across the street from the Bradbury.

Rider came into the office behind him. She looked out the window, too.

'You know every time I'm down here and see that I wonder who that is.'

'You don't know?'

'César Chávez?'

'Anthony Quinn. You know, the actor.'

He got a nonresponse from her.

'Before your time, I guess. The mural is called the Pope of Broadway, like he's watching over all the homeless around here.'

'Oh, I see.' She didn't sound impressed. 'How you want to do this?'

Bosch was still staring at the mural. He liked it, even though he had a hard time seeing Anthony Quinn as a Christlike figure. But the mural seemed to capture something about the man, a raw masculine and emotional power. Bosch stepped closer to the window and looked down. He saw the forms of two homeless people sleeping beneath blankets of newspapers in the parking lot beneath the mural. Anthony Quinn's arms were outstretched over them. Bosch nodded. The mural was one of the little things that made him like downtown so much. Just like the Bradbury and Angels Flight. Little pieces of grace were everywhere if you looked.

He turned around. Chastain and Langwiser had entered the room behind Rider.

'I'll work in here. Kiz and Janis, you two take the file room.'

'And what?' Chastain said. 'Me and Del get the secretary's desk?'

'Yeah. While you're going through it, see if you can come up with her name and the name of the intern or clerk. We'll need to talk to them today.'

Chastain nodded but Bosch could see he was annoyed about getting the weakest assignment.

'Tell you what,' Bosch added, 'why don't you go out first and see if you can find some boxes. We're going to be taking a lot of files out of here.'

Chastain left the office without a word. Bosch glanced at Rider and saw her give him a look that told him he was acting like an asshole.

'What?'

'Nothing. I'll be in the file room.'

She left then, leaving just Langwiser and Bosch.

'Everything okay, Detective?'

'Everything's fine. I'm going to get to work now. Do what I can until we hear about your special master.'

'Look, I'm sorry. But you called me out here to advise you and this is what I advise. I still think it is the right way to go.'

'Well, we'll see.'

For most of the next hour Bosch methodically went through Elias's desk, studying the man's belongings, appointment calendar and paperwork. Most of his time was spent reading through a series of notebooks in which Elias had kept reminders to himself, lists of things to do, pencil drawings and general notes from phone calls. Each notebook was dated on the outside cover. It appeared that Elias filled the pages of one book every week or so with his voluminous notations and doodles. Nothing in the books jumped out at Bosch as being pertinent to the investigation. But he also knew that so little about the circumstances of Elias's murder was known that something seeming unimportant in the notebooks at the moment might become important later.

Before starting to page through the most recent notebook, Bosch was interrupted by another call from Edgar.

'Harry, you said there was a message on the phone machine?'

'That's right.'

'There ain't now.'

Bosch leaned back in Elias's chair and closed his eyes.

'Goddammit.'

'Yeah, it's been cleared. I dicked around with it and it's not a tape. Messages are stored on a microchip. The chip was cleared.'

'Okay,' Bosch replied, angrily. 'Continue the search. When you're done, talk to the security people about who's been in and out of that place. See if they've got any video points in the lobby or parking garage. Somebody went in there after I left.'

'What about Chastain? He was with you, wasn't he?'

'I'm not worried about Chastain.'

He flipped the phone closed and got up and went to the window. He hated the feeling growing inside – that he was being worked by the case, rather than the other way around.

He blew out his breath and went back to the desk and the last notebook that Howard Elias had kept. As he paged through, he came across repeated notes regarding someone referred to as 'Parker.' Bosch did not believe this to be a person's real name, but rather a code name for a person inside Parker Center. The notations were mostly lists of questions Elias apparently intended to ask 'Parker,' as well as what looked like notes on conversations with this person. They were mostly in abbreviated form or the lawyer's own version of shorthand and therefore difficult to decipher. But in other instances the notes were clear to Bosch. One notation clearly indicated to Bosch that Elias had a deeply connected source inside Parker Center.

Parker:
Get all 51s – unsustained
1. Sheehan
2. Coblenz
3. Rooker
4. Stanwick

Bosch recognized the names as belonging to four RHD detectives who were among the defendants in the Black Warrior case. Elias wanted the 51 reports – or citizen complaint files – on the four detectives. More specifically, Elias wanted the unsustained files, meaning he was interested in complaints against the four that had been investigated by the IAD but not substantiated. Such unsustained complaints were removed from officers' personnel files as a matter of department policy and were therefore out of reach of a subpoena from a lawyer like Elias. The notation in the notebook told Bosch that Elias somehow knew that there were unsubstantiated prior complaints against the four and that he had a source in Parker Center who had access to the old files on those complaints. The first assumption was not a major leap; all cops had unsubstantiated complaints. It was part of being a cop. But someone with access to that sort of file was different. If Elias had such a source, it was a well-placed source.

One of the last references to Parker in the notebook appeared to be notes of a conversation, which Bosch assumed to have been a phone call to Elias at his desk. It appeared that Elias was losing his source.

Parker won't
jeopardy/exposure
force the issue?

Parker won't what? Bosch wondered. Turn over the files Elias wanted? Did Parker believe that getting the files to Elias would expose him as a source? There wasn't enough there for him to make a conclusion. There wasn't enough for him to understand what 'force the issue' meant either. He wasn't sure what any of the notes might have to do with the killing of Howard Elias. Nevertheless, Bosch was intrigued. One of the department's most vocal and successful critics had a mole inside Parker Center. There was a traitor inside the gate and it was important to know this.

Bosch put the last notebook into his briefcase and wondered if the discoveries he had made through the notes, particularly about Elias's source inside the department, now placed him in the area Janis Langwiser feared might be an infringement of attorney-client privilege. After mulling it over for a few moments he decided not to go out into the file room and ask her for an interpretation. He moved on with the search.

Bosch turned the chair to a side desk that had a personal computer and laser printer set up on it. The machines were off. There were two small drawers in this desk. The top contained the computer keyboard while the bottom contained office supplies with a single manila file on top. Bosch took out the file and opened it. It contained a color printout of a photo of a partially nude woman. The printout had two crease marks indicating it had been folded at one time. The photo itself did not have the technical quality of those in skin magazines found on the newstand. There was an amateurish, badly lit quality to it. The woman in the picture was white and had short, white-blonde hair. She wore thigh-high leather boots with three-inch heels and a G-string, nothing else. She stood with her rear to the camera, one foot up on a chair, her face turned mostly away. There was a tattoo of a ribbon and bow at the center of the small of her back. Bosch also saw at the bottom of the picture a notation that had been printed by hand.

http://www.girlawhirl.com/gina

Bosch knew little about computers but he knew enough to understand he was looking at an Internet address.

'Kiz?' he called.

Rider was the resident computer expert on his team. Before coming to Hollywood Homicide she had worked a fraud unit in Pacific Division. A lot of the work she had done was on computers. She walked in from the file room and he waved her over to the desk.

'How is it going out there?'

'Well, we're just stacking files. She won't let me look through anything until we hear from the special master. I hope Chastain brings back a lot of boxes because we have a – what is that?'

She was looking at the open file and the printout of the blonde woman.

'It was in the drawer. Take a look. It's got an address on it.'

Rider came around the desk and looked down at the printout.

'It's a web page.'

'Right. So how do we get to it and take a look?'

'Let me get in there.'

Bosch got up and Rider sat in front of the computer. Bosch stood behind the chair and watched as she turned the computer on and waited for it to boot up.

'Let's see what Internet provider he's got,' she said. 'Did you see any letterhead around?'

'What?'

'Letterhead. Stationery. Sometimes people put their E-mail address on it. If we know Elias's E-mail address we're halfway there.'

Bosch understood now. He hadn't seen any letterhead during his search.

'Hold on.'

He went out to the reception room and asked Chastain, who was sitting behind the secretary's desk, if he'd seen any stationery. Chastain opened a drawer and pointed to an open box of letterhead stationery. Bosch grabbed a page off the top. Rider had been correct. Elias's E-mail address was printed beneath his postal address on the top center of the page.

Helias@lawyerlink.net

Bosch took the page with him back to Elias's office. When he got there he saw Rider had closed the file that contained the printout of the blonde woman. Bosch realized it must have been embarrassing to her.

'I got it,' he said.

She looked at the page Bosch placed on the desk next to the computer.

'Good. That's the user name. Now we just need his password. He's got the whole computer password protected.'

'Shit.'

'Well,' she said as she began typing, 'most people choose something pretty easy – so even they won't forget.'

She stopped typing and watched the screen. The cursor had turned into an hourglass as it worked. A message then printed across the screen informing Rider she had used an improper password.

'What did you use?' Bosch asked.

'His DOB. You did next of kin, right? What was his wife's name?'

'Millie.'

Rider typed it in and after a few seconds got the same rejection message.

'What about his son?' Bosch asked. 'His name was Martin.'

Rider didn't type anything.

'What's the matter?'

'A lot of these password gates give you three strikes. If you don't get in on the third one they go into automatic lockdown.'

'Forever?'

'No. For however long Elias would have set it at. Could be fifteen minutes or an hour or even longer. Let's think about this for a—'

'V-S-L-A-P-D.'

Rider and Bosch turned. Chastain was in the doorway.

'What?' Bosch asked.

'That's the password. V-S-L-A-P-D. As in Elias versus the LAPD.'

'How do you know that?'

'The secretary wrote it down on the underside of her blotter. Guess she's got to use the computer, too.'

Bosch studied Chastain for a moment.

'Harry?' Rider said. 'Should I?'

'Give it a shot,' Bosch said, still looking at Chastain.

He then turned and watched as his partner typed in the password. The hourglass blinked on and then the screen changed and icon symbols began appearing on a field of blue sky and white clouds.

'We're in,' Rider said.

Bosch glanced back at Chastain.

'Good one.'

He then looked back at the screen and watched as Rider hit keys and maneuvered through the icons, files and programs, all of it meaning little to Bosch and reminding him that he was an anachronism.

'You really ought to learn this stuff, Harry,' Rider said, seeming to know his thoughts. 'It's easier than it looks.'

'Why should I when I've got you? What are you doing anyway?'

'Just having a look around. We'll have to talk to Janis about this. There are a lot of file names corresponding with cases. I don't know if we should open them before—'

'Don't worry about it for now,' Bosch interjected. 'Can you get on the Internet?'

Rider made a few more moves with the mouse and then typed the user name and password into blanks on the screen.

'I'm running lawyerlink,' she said. 'Hopefully the same passwords work and we'll be able to go to that naked lady's web page.'

'What naked lady?' Chastain said.

Bosch picked the file off the desk and handed it unopened to Chastain. He opened it, glanced at the photo and smirked.

Bosch looked back at the screen. Rider was on lawyerlink, using Elias's user name.

'What's that address?'

Chastain read it off to her as she typed. She then hit the enter key and they waited.

'What this is is a singular web page address within a larger web site,' she said. 'What we'll get here is the Gina page.'

'You mean that's her name? Gina?'

'Looks like it.'

As she said this the photo from the printout appeared on the screen. Beneath it was information on what the woman in the photo provided and how to contact her.

I am Mistress Regina. I am a lifestyle dominatrix providing elaborate bondage, humiliation, forced feminization, slave training and golden blessings. Other torments available upon request. Call me now.

Below the block of information there was a phone number, a pager number and an E-mail address. Bosch wrote these down in a notebook he took from his pocket. He then looked back at the screen and saw there was also a blue button with the letter A on it. He was about to ask Rider what the button meant when Chastain made a disdainful sound with his mouth. Bosch turned and looked at him and the Internal Affairs man shook his head.

'The bastard was probably getting his rocks off on his knees with this broad,' Chastain said. 'I wonder if Reverend Tuggins and his pals down at the SCCA knew about that.'

He was referring to an organization called the South Central Churches Association, a group which Tuggins headed and which always seemed to be at Elias's beck and call when he needed to show the media an image of South Central outrage in regard to alleged police misconduct.

'We don't know that he ever even met the woman yet, Chastain,' Bosch said.

'Oh, he met her. Why else did he have this laying around? I tell you,

Bosch, if Elias was into rough trade like that, there's no telling where that could've led. It's a righteous avenue of investigation and you know it.'

'Don't worry, we'll be checking everything out.'

'You're damn right we will.'

'Uh,' Rider said, interrupting. 'There's an audio button.'

Bosch looked at the screen. Rider had the arrow poised over the blue button.

'What do you mean?' he asked.

'I think we can actually hear Mistress Regina.'

She clicked the arrow on the button. The computer then downloaded an audio program and started playing it. A dark and heavy voice came from the computer's speaker.

'This is Mistress Regina. If you come to me I will find the secret of your soul. Together, we will reveal the true subservience through which you will know your rightful identity and attain the release you can find nowhere else. I will mold you into my own. I will own you. I am waiting. Call me now.'

They were all silent for a long moment. Bosch looked at Chastain.

'Does it sound like her?'

'Like who?'

'The woman on tape at the apartment.'

Chastain suddenly realized the possibility and was silent as he thought about this.

'What tape?' Rider asked.

'Can you play it again?' Bosch asked.

Rider clicked the audio button again and asked about the tape once more. Bosch waited until the replay was over.

'A woman left a message on the phone at Elias's apartment. It wasn't his wife. But I don't think it was this voice either.'

He looked at Chastain once more.

'I don't know,' Chastain said. 'Could be. We'll be able to do a comparison in the lab if we need to.'

Bosch hesitated, studying Chastain for any indication that he knew the phone message had been erased. He saw nothing.

'What?' Chastain said, uneasy under Bosch's stare.

'Nothing,' Bosch said.

He turned back and looked at the computer screen.

'You said this was part of a larger web site,' he said to Rider. 'Can we look at that?'

Rider didn't answer. She just went to work on the keyboard. In a few moments the screen changed and they were looking at a graphic which showed a woman's stocking-clad leg bent at the knee and reaching across the screen. Below this it said:

WELCOME TO GIRLAWHIRL
A directory of intimate, sensual and erotic services
in southern California

Below this was a table of contents by which the user could choose listings of women offering a variety of services, from sensual massage to evening escort to female domination. Rider clicked the mouse on this last offering and a new screen was revealed featuring boxes with the names of mistresses followed by an area code prefix.

'It's a goddamn Internet whorehouse,' Chastain said.

Bosch and Rider said nothing. Rider moved the arrow onto the box marked *Mistress Regina*.

'This is your directory,' she said. 'You choose which page you want and click.'

She clicked the mouse and the Regina page appeared again.

'He chose her,' Rider said.

'A white woman,' Chastain said. There was glee in his voice. 'Golden blessings from a white woman. I bet they aren't going to be too pleased about that on the South Side, either.'

Rider turned around and looked sharply at Chastain. She was about to say something when her eyes widened and looked past the IAD detective. Bosch noticed this and turned. Standing in the doorway of the office was Janis Langwiser. Next to her was a woman Bosch recognized from her newspaper photos and television appearances. She was an attractive woman with the smooth coffee-and-cream skin of mixed races.

'Wait a minute,' Bosch said to Langwiser. 'This is a crime investigation. She can't come in here and—'

'Yes, Detective Bosch, she can,' Langwiser said. 'Judge Houghton just appointed her special master on the case. She'll be reviewing the files for us.'

With that the woman Bosch recognized stepped fully into the room, smiled but not warmly and held her hand out to him in order to shake his.

'Detective Bosch,' she said. 'It's good to meet you. I hope we will be able to work together on this. I'm Carla Entrenkin.'

She waited a beat but no one responded. She continued.

'Now the first thing I am going to need is for you and all of your people to vacate these premises.'

12

Outside the front doors of the Bradbury the detectives walked empty-handed to their cars. Bosch was still angry but was cooler now. He walked slowly, allowing Chastain and Dellacroce to get to their car first. As he watched them drive off on their way back up Bunker Hill to California Plaza he opened the passenger door of Kiz's slickback but didn't get in. He bent down and looked in at her as she pulled the seat belt across her lap.

'You go on up, Kiz. I'll meet you up there.'

'You're going to walk it?'

Bosch nodded and looked at his watch. It was eight-thirty.

'I'll take Angels Flight. It should be running again. When you get up there you know what to do. Start everybody knocking on doors.'

'Okay, see you up there. You going to go back up and talk to her again?'

'Entrenkin? Yeah, I think so. Do you still have Elias's keys?'

'Yeah.' She dug them out of her purse and handed them to Bosch. 'Is there something I should know about?'

Bosch paused for a moment.

'Not yet. I'll see you up there.'

Rider started the car. She looked over at him again before putting it into drive.

'Harry, you okay?'

'Yeah, I'm fine.' He nodded. 'It's just the case. First we got Chastain – asshole's always been able to get to me. Now we've got Carla I'mthinkin. It's bad enough we knew she'd be watching the case. Now she's a part of it. I don't like politics, Kiz. I just like putting cases together.'

'I'm not talking about all of that. It's like you've been walking on the sun since we met this morning to pick up the cars in Hollywood. You want to talk about it?'

He almost nodded.

'Maybe later, Kiz,' he said instead. 'We got work to do right now.'

'Whatever, but I'm about to get worried about you, Harry. You need to be straight. If you're distracted, then we're distracted and we aren't going to get anywhere on this thing. That'd be okay most days but on this one you just said it yourself, we're under the glass.'

Bosch nodded again. Her having picked up on his personal turmoil was a testament to her skill as a detective – reading people was always more important than reading clues.

'I hear you, Kiz. I'll straighten up.'

'I copy that.'

'I'll see you up there.'

He slapped the roof of the car and watched her drive off, knowing this would be the time he would normally put a cigarette in his mouth. He didn't. Instead he looked down at the keys in his hand and thought about his next move and how he had to be very careful.

Bosch went back into the Bradbury and as he rode the slow-moving elevator back up he tumbled the keys in his hand and thought about Entrenkin's three separate entries into the case. First as a curious listing in Elias's now missing phone book, then in her capacity as inspector general and now finally a full entrance as a player, the special master who would decide what in Elias's files the investigators would be allowed to see.

Bosch didn't like coincidences. He didn't believe in them. He needed to know what Entrenkin was doing. He believed he had a good idea what that was and intended to confirm it before going any further with the case.

After being delivered to the top floor, Bosch pushed the button that would send the elevator back down to the lobby and got off. The door to Elias's offices was locked and Bosch knocked sharply on the glazed glass, just below the lawyer's name. In a few moments Janis Langwiser opened it. Bosch could see Carla Entrenkin standing a few feet behind her.

'Forget something, Detective Bosch?' Langwiser asked.

'No. But is that your little foreign job down there in the no-park zone? The red one? It was about to get towed. I badged the guy and told him to give me five minutes. But he'll be back.'

'Oh, shit!' She glanced back at Entrenkin as she headed out the door. 'I'll be right back.'

As she moved by him Bosch stepped into the office and closed the door behind him. He then locked it and turned back to Entrenkin.

'Why did you lock that?' she asked. 'Please leave it open.'

'I just thought it might be better if I said what I want to say without anybody interrupting us.'

Entrenkin folded her arms across her chest as if bracing for an attack. He studied her face and got the same vibe he had gotten before, when she had told them all they had to leave. There was a certain stoicism there, propping her up despite some clear pain beneath. She reminded Bosch of another woman he knew only from TV: the Oklahoma law school teacher who was brutalized in Washington by the politicians a few years before during the confirmation of a Supreme Court justice.

'Look, Detective Bosch, I really don't see any other way around this. We have to be careful. We have to think about the case as well as the community. The people have to be reassured that everything possible is being done – that this won't be swept under in the manner they have seen so many times before. I want—'

'Bullshit.'

'Excuse me?'

'You shouldn't be on this case and we both know it.'

'That's what is bullshit. I have the trust of this community. You think they will believe anything you say about this case? Or Irving or the police chief?'

'But you don't have the trust of the cops. And you've got one big conflict of interest, don't you, Inspector General?'

'What are you saying? I think it was rather wise of Judge Houghton to choose me to act as special master. As inspector general I already have a degree of civilian oversight on the case. This just streamlines things instead of adding another person to the mix. He called me. I didn't call him.'

'I'm not talking about that and you know it. I'm talking about a conflict of interest. A reason you shouldn't be anywhere near this case.'

Entrenkin shook her head in an I-don't-understand gesture but her face clearly showed she feared what Bosch knew.

'You know what I'm saying,' Bosch said. 'You and him. Elias. I was in his apartment. Must've been just before you got there. Too bad we missed each other. We could've settled all of this then.'

'I don't know what you're talking about but I was just led to believe by Miss Langwiser that you people waited on warrants before entering his apartment and the office. Are you telling me that is not true?'

Bosch hesitated, realizing he had made a mistake. She could now turn his move away or back on him.

'We had to make sure no one was hurt or in need of help in the apartment,' he said.

'Sure. Right. Just like the cops who jumped the fence at O.J. Simpson's house. Just wanting to make sure everybody was okay.'

She shook her head again.

'The continued arrogance of this department amazes me. From what I had heard about you, Detective Bosch, I expected more.'

'You want to talk about arrogance? You were the one who went in there and removed evidence. The inspector general of the department, the one who polices the police. Now you want to—'

'Evidence of what? I did no such thing!'

'You cleared your message off the phone machine and you took the phone book with your name and numbers in it. I'm betting you had your own key and garage pass. You came in through the garage and nobody saw you. Right after Irving called to tell you Elias was dead. Only Irving didn't know that you and Elias had something going on.'

'That's a nice story. I'd like to see you try to prove any of it.'

Bosch held his hand up. On his palm were Elias's keys.

'Elias's keys,' he said. 'There's a couple on there that don't fit his house or his apartment or his office or his cars. I was thinking of maybe pulling your address from DMV and seeing if they fit your door, Inspector.'

Entrenkin's eyes moved quickly away from the keys. She turned and walked back into Elias's office. Bosch followed and watched as she slowly walked around the desk and sat down. She looked as if she might cry. Bosch knew he had broken her with the keys.

'Did you love him?' he asked.

'What?'

'Did you love—'

'How dare you ask me that?'

'It's my job. There's been a murder. You're involved.'

She turned away from him and looked to her right. She was staring through the window at the painting of Anthony Quinn. Again, the tears appeared to be barely holding back.

'Look, Inspector, can we try to remember one thing? Howard Elias is dead. And believe it or not, I want to get the person who did it. Okay?'

She nodded tentatively. He continued, talking slowly and calmly.

'In order to get this person, I'm going to need to know everything I can about Elias. Not just what I know from television and newspapers and other cops. Not just from what's in his files. I've got to know—'

Out in the reception area someone tried the locked door and then knocked sharply on the glass. Entrenkin got up and went to the door. Bosch waited in Elias's office. He listened as Entrenkin answered the door and spoke to Langwiser.

'Give us a few minutes, please.'

She closed the door without waiting for a response, locked it again and came back to Elias's office, where she took the seat behind the desk. Bosch spoke to her in a voice low enough not to be heard outside of the office.

'I've got to know it all,' he said. 'We both know you are in a position to help. So can't we come to some sort of truce here?'

The first tear fell down Entrenkin's cheek, soon followed by another on the other side. She leaned forward and began opening drawers in the desk.

'Bottom left,' Bosch said from memory of his inventory of the desk.

She opened the drawer and removed the box of tissues. She placed it on her lap, took one tissue and dabbed at her cheeks and eyes. She began to speak.

'It's funny how things change so quickly . . .'

A long silence went by.

'I knew Howard superficially for a number of years. When I was practicing law. It was strictly professional, mostly "How are you"s in the hallways of the federal building. Then when I was appointed inspector general, I knew it was important that I knew the critics of the police department as well as I knew the department. I arranged to meet Howard. We met right here – him sitting right here . . . It went from there. Yes, I loved him . . .'

This confession brought more tears and she pulled out several tissues to take care of them.

'How long were you two . . . together?' Bosch asked.

'About six months. But he loved his wife. He wasn't going to leave her.'

Her face was dry now. She returned the tissue box to its drawer and it seemed as though the clouds that had crossed her face moments before were gone. Bosch could see she had changed. She leaned forward and looked at him. She was all business.

'I'll make a deal with you, Detective Bosch. But only with you. Despite everything . . . I think if you give me your word then I can trust you.'

'Thank you. What is your deal?'

'I will only talk to you. In return I want you to protect me. And by that I mean keep the source of your information confidential. You don't have to worry, nothing I tell you would be admitted in court anyway. You can keep everything I tell you in background. It may help you, it may not.'

Bosch thought about this for a moment.

'I should be treating you as a suspect, not a source.'

'But you know in your gut that it wasn't me.'

He nodded.

'It wasn't a woman's murder,' he said. 'It's got male written all over it.'

'It's got cop written on it, too, doesn't it?'

'Maybe. That's what I'm going to find out – if I could just get to the case and not have to worry about the community and Parker Center politics and everything else.'

'Then do we have an agreement?'

'Before making any agreement like that I have to know something first. Elias had a source inside Parker. Somebody with high access. Somebody who could get him unsustained IAD files. I need—'

'It wasn't me. Believe me, I may have crossed a line when I began a relationship with him. That was my heart, not my head. But I didn't cross the line you are talking about. Never in a hundred years. Contrary to what most of your fellow officers think, my goal is to save and improve the department. Not destroy it.'

Bosch looked at her blankly. She took it as disbelief.

'How would I get him files? I am public enemy number one in that department. If I went in to get files, or even just made a request for them, the word would spread around that building and out into the ranks faster than an earthquake wave.'

Bosch studied her defiant face. He knew she was right. She wouldn't make much of a deep cover source. He nodded.

'Then we have an agreement?' she asked.

'Yes. With one asterisk.'

'And what is that?'

'If you lie one time to me and I find out about it, all bets are off.'

'That is more than acceptable to me. But we can't talk now. I want to finish the files so that you and your people can pursue all leads. Now you know why I want this case solved not only for the sake of the city but for myself. What do you say we meet later? When the files are done.'

'Fine with me.'

As Bosch crossed Broadway fifteen minutes later he could see the garage doors of the Grand Central Market had been rolled up. It was years since he had been in the market, maybe decades. He decided to cut through it to Hill Street and the Angels Flight terminus.

The market was a huge conglomeration of food booths, produce stalls and butcher shops. Vendors sold cheap trinkets and candy from Mexico. And though the doors had just opened and there were more sellers readying for the day than buyers inside, the overwhelming smell of oil and fried food already hung heavy in the air. As he made his way through Bosch picked up pieces of conversations, delivered in staccato snippets of Spanish. He saw a butcher carefully placing the skinned heads of goats on ice in his refrigerated display case next to the neat rows of sliced oxtail. At the far end old men sat at picnic tables, nursing their cups of thick, dark coffee and eating Mexican pastries. Bosch remembered his promise to Edgar to bring doughnuts before they began the canvass. He looked around and found no doughnuts but bought a bag of *churros,* the crisp-fried dough sticks with cinnamon sugar that were the Mexican alternative.

As he came out on the Hill Street side of the market he glanced to his right and saw a man standing in the spot where Baker and Chastain had found the cigarette butts hours earlier. The man had a blood-stained apron wrapped around his waist. He wore a hair net. He snaked his hand in underneath the apron and came out with a pack of smokes.

'Got that right,' Bosch said out loud.

He crossed the street to the Angels Flight arch and waited behind two Asian tourists. The train cars were passing each other at the midpoint on the tracks. He checked the names painted above the doors of each car. Sinai was going up and Olivet was coming down.

A minute later, Bosch followed the tourists as they stepped onto Olivet. He watched as they unknowingly sat on the same bench where Catalina Perez had died about ten hours earlier. The blood had been cleaned away, the wood too dark and old to reveal any stain. He didn't bother telling them the recent history of their spot. He doubted they understood his language anyway.

Bosch took the spot where he had sat before. He yawned again the moment the weight was off his feet. The car jerked and started its ascent. The Asians started taking photos. Eventually they got around to using sign language to ask Bosch to take one of their cameras and take photos of them. He obliged, doing his part for the tourist trade. They then quickly took the camera back and moved to the other end of the car.

He wondered if they had sensed something about him. A danger or maybe a sickness in him. He knew that some people had that power, that they could tell these things. With him, it would not be difficult. It was twenty-four hours since he had slept. He rubbed a hand across his face and it felt like damp stucco. He leaned forward, elbows on his knees, and felt the old pain that he had hoped would never be in his life again. It had been a long time since he had felt so alone, since he had felt like such an outsider in his own city. There was a tightness in his throat and chest now, a feeling of claustrophobia like a shroud about him, even in the open air.

Once more he got the phone out. He checked the battery display and found it almost dead. Enough juice for one more call if he was lucky. He punched in the number for home and waited.

There was one new message. Fearing the battery wouldn't hold, he quickly punched in the playback code and held the phone back up to his ear. But the voice he heard was not Eleanor's. It was the sound of a voice distorted by cellophane wrapped around the receiver and then perforated with a fork.

'Let this one go, Bosch,' the voice said. 'Any man who stands against cops is nothing but a dog and deserves to die like a dog. You do the right thing. You let it go, Bosch. You let it go.'

13

Bosch got to Parker Center twenty-five minutes before he was to meet with Deputy Chief Irving to update him on the investigation. He was alone, having left the other six members of the Elias team to conclude the canvass of the apartment building next to Angels Flight and then to pursue their next assignments. Stopping at the front counter he showed his badge to the uniformed officer and he told the man that he was expecting some information to be called in anonymously to the front desk within the next half-hour. He asked the officer to relay the information to him immediately in Chief Irving's private conference room.

Bosch then took an elevator up to the third floor rather than the sixth, where Irving's office was located. He went down the hall to the Robbery-Homicide Division squad room and found it empty except for four detectives he had called earlier. They were Bates, O'Toole, Engersol and Rooker – the four detectives who had originally handled the call out to the Angels Flight murder scene. They looked suitably bleary-eyed, having been up half the night before the case was turned over to Bosch and his squad. Bosch had rousted them from sleep at nine and given them a half hour to meet him at Parker Center. It had been easy enough to get them in so quickly. Bosch had told them their careers depended on it.

'I don't have a lot of time,' Bosch began as he walked down the main aisle between the rows of desk, locking eyes with the four. Three of the detectives were standing around Rooker, who was seated at his desk. This was a clear giveaway. Whatever decisions had been made out at the scene, when it was only the four of them, Bosch was sure were made by Rooker. He was leader of the pack.

Bosch stayed standing, stopping just outside the informal grouping of the other four. He started telling the story, using his hands in an informal manner, almost like a television news reporter, as if to underline that it was simply a story he was telling, not the threat that he was actually delivering.

'The four of you get the call out,' he said. 'You get out there, push the uniforms back and make a perimeter. Somebody checks the stiffs and lo and behold the DL says one of them is Howard Elias. You then put—'

'There was no driver's license, Bosch,' Rooker said, interrupting. 'Didn't the cap tell you that?'

'Yeah, he told me. But now I'm telling the story. So listen up, Rooker, and shut up. I'm trying to save your ass here and I don't have a lot of time to do it.'

He waited to see if anybody wanted to say anything more.

'So like I said,' he began again, looking directly at Rooker, 'the DL identifies one of the stiffs as Elias. So you four bright guys put your heads together and figure there's a good chance that it was a cop who did this. You figure Elias got what he had coming and more power to the badge who had the guts to put him down. That's when you got stupid. You decided to help out this shooter, this murderer, by staging the robbery. You took off—'

'Bosch, you are full—'

'I said shut up, Rooker! I don't have the time to hear a bunch of bullshit when you know it went down just like I said. You took off the guy's watch and his wallet. Only you fucked up, *Rooker*. You scratched the guy's wrist with the watch. *Post*mortem wound. It's going to come up on the autopsy and that means you four are going to go down the toilet unless it gets contained.'

He paused, waiting to see if Rooker had anything to say now. He didn't.

'Okay, sounds like I have your attention. Anybody want to tell me where the watch and wallet are?'

Another pause while Bosch looked at his watch. It was a quarter to ten. The four RHD men said nothing.

'I didn't think so,' Bosch said, looking from face to face. 'So this is what we're going to do. I meet with Irving in fifteen minutes to give him the overview. He then holds the press conference. If the front desk downstairs doesn't get a call with information as to the location of the gutter or trash can or whatever place this stuff was stashed, then I tell Irving the robbery was staged by people at the crime scene and it goes from there. Good luck to you guys then.'

He scanned their faces again. They showed nothing but anger and defiance. Bosch expected nothing less.

'Personally, I wouldn't mind it going that way, seeing you people get what you got coming. But it will fuck the case – put hair on the cake, taint it beyond repair. So I'm being selfish about it and giving you a chance it makes me sick to give.'

Bosch looked at his watch.

'You've got fourteen minutes now.'

With that he turned and started heading back out through the squad room. Rooker called after him.

'Who are you to judge, Bosch? The guy was a dog. He deserved to die like a dog and who gives a shit? You should do the right thing, Bosch. Let it go.'

As if it was his intention all along, Bosch casually turned behind an empty desk and came back up a smaller aisle toward the foursome. He had recognized the phrasing of the words Rooker had used. His demeanor disguised his growing rage. When he got back to the group, he broke their informal circle and leaned over Rooker's desk, his palms down flat on it.

'Listen to me, Rooker. You call my home again – whether it's to warn me off or to just tell me the weather – and I'll come looking for you. You won't want that.'

Rooker blinked but then raised his hands in surrender.

'Hey, man, I don't know what the fuck you're talk—'

'Save it for somebody you can convince. At least you could've been a man and skipped the cellophane. That's coward shit, boy.'

635

Bosch had hoped that when he got to Irving's conference room there would be at least a few minutes for him to look at his notes and put his thoughts together. But Irving was already seated at the round table, his elbows on the polished surface and the fingertips of both hands touching and forming a steeple in front of his chin.

'Detective, have a seat,' he said as Bosch opened the door. 'Where are the others?'

'Uh,' Bosch said, putting his briefcase down flat on the table. 'They're still in the field. Chief, I was just going to drop my case off and then run down to get a cup of coffee. Can I get you something?'

'No, and you do not have time for coffee. The media calls are starting. They know it was Elias. Somebody leaked. Probably in the coroner's office. So it's about to get crazy. I want to hear what is happening, starting right now. I have to brief the police chief, who will lead a press conference that has been scheduled for eleven. Sit down.'

Bosch took a seat opposite Irving. He had worked a case out of the conference room once before. That seemed like a long time ago but he remembered it as the time he had earned Irving's respect and probably as much trust as the deputy chief was willing to give to anyone else who carried a badge. His eyes moved across the surface of the table and he saw the old cigarette scar that he had left during the investigation of the Concrete Blonde case. That had been a difficult case but it seemed almost routine beside the investigation he was involved in now.

'When are they coming in?' Irving asked.

He still had his fingers together like a steeple. Bosch had read in an interrogation manual that such body language denoted a feeling of superiority.

'Who?'

'The members of your team, Detective. I told you I wanted them here for the briefing and then the press conference.'

'Well, they're not. Coming in. They are continuing the investigation. I thought that it didn't make sense that all seven of us should just drop things to come in here when one of us could easily tell you the status of things.'

Bosch watched angry flares of red explode high on Irving's cheeks.

'Once again we seem to have either a communication problem or the chain of command remains unclear to you. I specifically told you to have your people here.'

'I must've misunderstood, Chief,' Bosch lied. 'I thought the important thing was the investigation. I remembered that you wanted to be brought up to date, not that you wanted everybody here. In fact, I doubt there is enough room in here for everybody. I—'

'The point is I wanted them here. Do your partners have phones?'

'Edgar and Rider?'

'Who else?'

'They have phones but they're dead. We've been running all night. Mine's dead.'

'Then page them. Get them in here.'

Bosch slowly got up and headed to the phone which was on top of the storage cabinet that ran along one wall of the room. He called Rider and

Edgar's pagers, but when he punched in the return number he added an extra seven at the end. This was a long-standing code they used. The extra seven – as in code seven, the radio call for out of service – meant they should take their time in returning the pages, if they returned them at all.

'Okay, Chief,' Bosch said. 'Hopefully, they'll call in. What about Chastain and his people?'

'Never mind them. I want your team back here by eleven for the press conference.'

Bosch moved back to his seat.

'How come?' he asked, though he knew exactly why. 'I thought you said the police chief was going—'

'The chief will lead it. But we want to have a show of force. We want the public to know we have top-notch investigators on this case.'

'You mean top-notch *black* investigators, don't you?'

Bosch and Irving held hard stares for a moment.

'Your job, Detective, is to solve this case and solve it as quickly as you can. You are not to concern yourself with other matters.'

'Well, that's kind of hard to do, Chief, when you are pulling my people out of the field. Can't solve anything quickly if they've got to be here for every dog and pony show you people cook up.'

'That is enough, Detective.'

'They *are* top-notch investigators. And that's what I want to use them for. Not as cannon fodder for the department's race relations. They don't want to be used that way, either. That in itself is ra—'

'*Enough,* I said! I do not have time to debate racism, institutional or otherwise with you, Detective Bosch. We are talking about public perceptions. Suffice it to say that if we mishandle this case or its perceptions from the outside, this city could be burning again by midnight.'

Irving paused to look at his watch.

'I meet the police chief in twenty minutes. Could you please begin to enlighten me with the accomplishments of the investigation up to this point?'

Bosch reached over and opened his briefcase. Before he could reach for his notebook the phone on the cabinet rang. He got up and went to it.

'Remember,' Irving said, 'I want them here by eleven.'

Bosch nodded and picked up the phone. It wasn't Edgar or Rider and he had not expected that it would be.

'This is Cormier downstairs in the lobby. This Bosch?'

'Yeah.'

'You just got a message here. Guy wouldn't give a name. He just said to tell you that what you need is in a trash can in the MetroLink station, First and Hill. It's in a manila envelope. That's it.'

'Okay, thanks.'

He hung up and looked at Irving.

'It was something else.'

Bosch sat back down and took his notebook out of his briefcase along with the clipboard with the crime scene reports, sketches and evidence receipts attached to it. He didn't need any of it to summarize the case but he thought it might be reassuring to Irving to see the accumulation of paper the case was engendering.

'I'm waiting, Detective,' the deputy chief said by way of prompting him.

Bosch looked up from the paperwork.

'Where we are is pretty much point zero. We have a good idea what we have. We don't have much of a handle on the who and why.'

'Then what have we got, Detective?'

'We're going with Elias being the primary target in what looks like an outright assassination.'

Irving brought his head down so that his clasped hands hid his face.

'I know that's not what you want to hear, Chief, but if you want the facts, that's what the facts point to. We have—'

'The last thing Captain Garwood told me was that it looked like a robbery. The man was wearing a thousand-dollar suit, walking through downtown at eleven o'clock at night. His watch and wallet are missing. How can you discount the possibility of a robbery?'

Bosch leaned back and waited. He knew Irving was venting steam. The news Bosch was giving him was guaranteed to put ulcers on his ulcers once the media picked it up and ran.

'The watch and wallet have been located. They weren't stolen.'

'Where?'

Bosch hesitated, though he had already anticipated the question. He hesitated because he was about to lie to a superior on the behalf of four men who did not deserve the benefit of the risk he was taking.

'In his desk drawer at the office. He must've forgotten them when he closed up and headed to his apartment. Or maybe he left them on purpose in case he got robbed.'

Bosch realized he would still need to come up with an explanation in his reports when the autopsy on Elias revealed the postmortem scratches on his wrist. He would have to write it off as having occurred while the body was being manipulated or moved by the investigators.

'Then perhaps it was an armed robber who shot Elias when he did not turn over a wallet,' Irving said, oblivious to Bosch's internal discomfort. 'Perhaps it was a robber who shot first and searched for valuables second.'

'The sequence and manner of the shots suggests otherwise. The sequence suggests a personal tie – rage transmitted from one person to Elias. Whoever did this knew Elias.'

Irving put his hands down on the table and leaned a few inches toward its center. He seemed impatient when he spoke.

'All I am saying is that you cannot completely eliminate these other possible scenarios.'

'That might be true but we're not pursuing those scenarios. I believe it would be a waste of time and I don't have the manpower.'

'I told you I wanted a thorough investigation. I want no stone unturned.'

'Well, we'll get to those stones later. Look, Chief, if you are focusing on this so you can tell the media it might be a robbery, then fine, say it might be. I don't care about what you tell the media. I'm just trying to tell you where we stand and where we're going to be looking.'

'Fine. Proceed.'

He waved a hand in a dismissive gesture.

'We need to look at the man's files and draw up lists of potential suspects. The cops who Elias really nailed in court or vilified in the media over the years. Or both. The grudges. And the cops he would have tried to nail beginning Monday.'

Irving showed no reaction at all. It seemed to Bosch he was already thinking about the next hour, when he and the police chief would go out on a cliff and address the media about such a dangerous case.

'We are being handicapped,' Bosch continued. 'Carla Entrenkin has been appointed by the warrants judge as a special master to oversee the protection of Elias's clients. She's in his office right now and won't let us in.'

'I thought you said you found the man's wallet and watch in the office.'

'I did. That was before Carla showed up and kicked us out.'

'How did she get appointed?'

'She says the judge called her, thought she'd be perfect. She and a deputy from the DA are there. I'm hoping to get the first batch of files this afternoon.'

'Okay, what else?'

'There's something you should know. Before Carla made us leave, we came across a couple things of interest. The first is some notes Elias kept at his desk. I read through them and there were indications that he had a source in here. Parker Center, I mean. A good source, somebody who apparently knew how to find and get access to old files – unsubstantiated IAD investigations. And there were indications of a dispute. The source either couldn't or wouldn't provide something Elias wanted on the Black Warrior thing.'

Irving went quiet for a second, staring at Bosch, processing. When he spoke again his voice was more distant still.

'Was this source identified?'

'Not in what I saw, which wasn't a lot. It was coded.'

'What was it that Elias wanted? Could it be related to the killings?'

'I don't know. If you want me to pursue it as a priority I will. I was thinking that other things would be the priority. The cops he dragged into court in the past, the ones he was going to pull in starting Monday. Also, there was a second thing we found in the office before we got kicked out.'

'What was that?'

'It actually branches into two more avenues of investigation.'

He quickly told Irving about the photo printout of Mistress Regina and the indication that Elias might have been involved in what Chastain had called rough trade. The deputy chief seemed to take a keen interest in this aspect of the investigation and asked Bosch what his plans were in regard to pursuing it.

'I'm planning on attempting to locate and interview the woman, see if Elias ever actually had any contact with her. After that, we see where it goes.'

'And the other branch of investigation this leads to?'

'The family. Whether it was this Regina woman or not, it looks like Elias was a philanderer. There are enough indications in his downtown apartment to suggest this. So if the wife knew about all of this, then we have a motivation right there. Of course, I'm just talking right here. At the moment we have nothing that indicates she even knew, let alone arranged or carried out the kill. It also flies in the face of the psychological read on the killings.'

'Which is what?'

'It doesn't look like the dispassionate work of a hired killer. There is a lot of rage in the killing method. It looks to me like the killer knew Elias and hated him – at least at the moment of the shooting. I would also say it looks like it was a man.'

'How so?'

'The shot up the ass. It was vindictive. Like a rape. Men rape, women don't. So my gut instinct tells me this clears the widow. But my instincts have been wrong. It's still something we have to follow up on. There's the son, too. Like I told you before, he reacted pretty hot when we gave them the news. But we don't really know what his relationship with his father was like. We do know that the kid has been around weapons – we saw a picture in the house.'

Irving pointed a finger of warning at Bosch.

'You be careful with the family,' he said. 'Very careful. That has to be handled with a lot of finesse.'

'It will be.'

'I do not want that blowing up in our faces.'

'It won't.'

Irving checked his watch once more.

'Why have your people not answered the pages?'

'I don't know, Chief. I was just thinking the same thing.'

'Well, page them again. I need to meet with the chief. At eleven I want you and your team in the press conference room.'

'I'd rather get back to work on the case. I've got—'

'That is a direct order, Detective,' Irving said as he stood. 'No debate. You won't have to answer questions but I want your people on hand.'

Bosch picked up the clipboard and threw it back into his open briefcase.

'I'll be there,' he said, though Irving was already through the door.

Bosch sat for a few minutes thinking. He knew Irving would now repackage the information he had given him and deliver it to the police chief. They would put their heads together and then reshape it once more before delivering it to the media.

He looked at his watch. He had a half hour until the press conference. He wondered if that was time enough to get over to the Metrolink station, find Elias's wallet and watch and get back in time. He had to make sure he recovered the dead lawyer's property, particularly because he had already told Irving it was in his possession.

Finally, he decided that there wasn't enough time to do it. He decided to use the time to get coffee and to make a phone call. He walked to the cabinet once more and called his house. Once more the machine picked up. Bosch hung up after hearing his own voice saying no one was home.

14

Bosch decided he would be too nervous waiting until after the press conference and drove over to the MetroLink station at First and Hill. It was only three minutes away and he was pretty sure he could make it back to Parker Center for the start of the press conference. He parked illegally at the curb in front of the entrance to the subway platform. It was one of the few good things about driving a slickback; there was no need to worry about parking tickets. As he got out he removed the baton from the sleeve in the car's door.

He trotted down the escalator and spotted the first trash can next to the automatic doors at the entrance to the station. The way he figured it, Rooker and his partner had left the Angels Flight crime scene with the stolen property and stopped at the first spot they knew they would find a trash can. One waited up top with the car while the other ran down the stairs to get rid of the wallet and watch. So Bosch was confident this first trash can would be the one. It was a large, white rectangular receptacle with the MetroLink symbol painted on its sides. A blue hood on top housed the push door. Bosch quickly lifted it off and looked down. The receptacle was full but there was no manila envelope visible in the debris at top.

Bosch put the hood on the ground and used the baton to stir through the detritus of discarded newspapers, fast-food wrappers and garbage. The can smelled as though it had not been emptied in days, cleaned in months. He came across an empty purse and one old shoe. As he used the baton like an oar to dig deeper, he began to worry that one of the homeless men who populated downtown had beaten him to the can and found the watch and wallet first.

Near the bottom, just before he gave up to try one of the cans further into the station, he saw an envelope smeared with catsup and fished it out with two fingers. He tore it open, careful to take most of the catsup with the discarded end, and looked inside at a brown leather wallet and a gold Cartier watch.

Bosch used the escalator on the way up but this time was content to just ride as he looked in the envelope. The watchband was also gold or gold plated and was the accordion style that slipped over the wrist and hand. Bosch bounced the envelope a bit in his hand in order to move the watch without touching it. He was looking for any fragments of skin that might be caught in the band. He saw nothing.

Once he was back inside the slickback he put on gloves, took the wallet and watch out of the torn envelope and threw the envelope over the seat and to the floor in the back. He then opened the wallet and looked through its partitions. Elias had carried six credit cards in addition to identification and insurance cards. There were small studio-posed photos of his wife and son. In the billfold section there were three credit card receipts and a blank personal check. There was no currency.

Bosch's briefcase was on the seat next to him. He opened it and took out the clipboard, then flipped through it until he found the victim's property report. It detailed everything taken from each victim. Only a quarter had been found in Elias's pockets at the time they were searched by a coroner's assistant.

'You pricks,' Bosch said out loud as he realized that whoever took the wallet had decided to keep whatever cash had been in it. It was unlikely that Elias had been walking to his apartment with only the quarter it would cost him to ride Angels Flight.

Once more he wondered why he was sticking his neck out for people who didn't deserve it. He tried to dismiss the thought, knowing that it was too late to do anything about it, but he couldn't. He was a co-conspirator now. Bosch shook his head in disgust with himself, then put the watch and wallet into separate plastic evidence bags after labeling each one with a white sticker on which he wrote the case number, the date and a time of 6:45 A.M. He then wrote a brief description of each item and the drawer of Elias's desk in which it was found, initialed the corner of each sticker and put the bags into his briefcase.

Bosch looked at his watch before starting the car. He had ten minutes to make it to the press conference room. No sweat.

There were so many members of the media attending the press conference that several were standing outside the door to the police chief's press room, unable to find space inside. Bosch pushed and excused and squeezed his way through them. Inside, he saw the back stage was lined wall to wall with television cameras on tripods, their operators standing behind them. He quickly counted twelve cameras and knew that the story would soon go national. There were eight television stations carrying local news in Los Angeles, including the Spanish-language channel. Every cop knew that if you saw more than eight camera crews at a scene or a press conference then you were talking network attention. You were working something huge, something dangerous.

In the middle of the room, every folding chair was taken by a reporter. There were close to forty, with the TV people clearly identifiable in their nice suits and makeup and the print and radio people just as recognizable as the ones wearing jeans and with ties pulled loose at the neck.

Bosch looked to the front stage and saw a flurry of activity around the podium, which had the LAPD chief's badge affixed. Sound men were taping their equipment to the ever-widening tree of microphones on the podium. One of them was standing directly behind the podium and giving a voice check. Behind and to the side of the podium stood Irving, conferring in whispers with two men in uniform, both wearing lieutenant's stripes. Bosch recognized one of them as Tom O'Rourke, who worked in the media relations unit. The other Bosch did not recognize but assumed he was

Irving's adjutant, Michael Tulin, whose call had awakened Bosch just hours earlier. A fourth man stood on the other side of the podium by himself. He wore a gray suit and Bosch had no idea who he was. There was no sign of the police chief. Not yet. The police chief did not wait for the media to get ready. The media waited for him.

Irving spotted Bosch and signaled him to the front stage. Bosch walked up the three steps and Irving put a hand on his shoulder to usher him into a private huddle out of earshot of the others.

'Where are your people?'

'I haven't heard back from them.'

'That is not acceptable, Detective. I told you to get them in here.'

'All I can say, Chief, is that they must be in the middle of a sensitive interview and didn't want to break the momentum of the situation to call back on my pages. They are reinterviewing Elias's wife and his son. It takes a lot of finesse, especially in a case like—'

'I am not interested in that. I wanted them here, period. At the next press conference you have them here or I will split your team up and send you to three divisions so far apart you will have to take a vacation day to have lunch together.'

Bosch studied Irving's face for a moment.

'I understand, Chief.'

'Good. Remember it. Now we are about to get started here. O'Rourke is going now to get the chief and escort him in. You will not be answering any questions. You do not have to worry about that.'

'Then why am I here? Can I go?'

Irving looked as though he was finally about to curse for the first time in his career, maybe his life. His face was turning red and the muscles of his powerful jaw were at full flex.

'You are here to answer any questions from me or the chief of police. You can leave when I dismiss you.'

Bosch raised his arms in a hands-off fashion and took a step back against the wall to wait for the show to begin. Irving stepped away and conferred briefly with his adjutant and then walked over to the man in the suit. Bosch looked out into the audience. It was hard to see because the overhead TV lights were on. But past the glare he managed to pick out a few faces he knew either personally or from TV. When his eyes finally came to Keisha Russell's he attempted to look away before the *Times* reporter saw him but was too late. Their eyes briefly caught and held, then she nodded once, almost unnoticeably. Bosch did not nod back. He didn't know who might pick up on it. It was never good to acknowledge a reporter in public. So he just held her gaze for a few moments longer and then looked away.

The door to the side of the stage opened and O'Rourke came through and turned so that he could then hold the door open for the chief of police, who entered the room wearing a charcoal gray suit and with a somber look on his face. O'Rourke stepped to the podium and leaned down to the microphone tree. He was much taller than the police chief, for whom the microphones had been set.

'Everybody ready?'

Though a couple of cameramen from the back called out, '*No*' and '*Not yet,*' O'Rourke ignored them.

'The chief has a brief statement about today's events and then he'll field a few questions. But only general details of the case will be released at this time because of the ongoing investigation. Deputy Chief Irving is also here to field questions. Let's maintain some order and we'll get through this quickly and smoothly and everybody will get what they need. Chief?'

O'Rourke stepped aside and the chief of police stepped to the podium. He was an impressive man. Tall, black and handsome, he had spent thirty years on the job in the city and was a skilled media man. He was, however, new to the chief's post, chosen for the job just the summer before after his predecessor, an overweight outsider with no feel for the department and little feel for the community, was dumped in favor of the insider who was striking enough to play himself in a Hollywood movie. The chief gazed out silently at the faces in the room for a moment. The vibe Bosch picked up was that this case and how he handled it would be the chief's first, true test in the job. He was sure the chief had picked up the vibe as well.

'Good morning,' the chief finally said. 'I have disturbing news to report today. The lives of two citizens were taken late last night here in downtown. Catalina Perez and Howard Elias were riding separately on the Angels Flight railroad when they were each shot and killed shortly before eleven o'clock. Most people in this city know of Howard Elias. Revered or not, he was a man who nevertheless was a part of our city, who helped mold our culture. On the other hand, Catalina Perez, like so many of us, was not a famous person or a celebrity. She was just struggling to make a living so that she and her family – a husband and two young children – could live and prosper. She worked as a housekeeper. She worked long days and nights. She was going home to her family when she was slain. I am simply here this morning to assure our citizens that these two murders will not go unanswered or forgotten. You can be assured that we will be working tirelessly on this investigation until we achieve justice for Catalina Perez and Howard Elias.'

Bosch had to admire what the chief was doing. He was packaging both victims as a set, making it seem implausible that Elias was the sole target and Perez just an unlucky traveler in the crossfire. He was slickly attempting to portray them as equal victims of the senseless and often random violence that was the city's cancer.

'At this point, we can't go into too many details because of the investigation. But it can be said that there are leads being followed and we have every belief and hope that the killer or killers will be identified and brought to justice. In the meantime, we ask that the good citizens of Los Angeles remain calm and allow us to do our job. What we need to guard against at this time is jumping to conclusions. We don't want anyone to get hurt. The department, either through me or Deputy Chief Irving or the media relations office, will be providing regular updates on the progress of the case. Information will be provided when it can be released without being detrimental to the investigation or eventual prosecution of suspects.'

The chief took a half step back from the podium to look at O'Rourke, a signal that he was finished. O'Rourke made a move toward the podium but before he had raised a foot there was a loud chorus from the audience of reporters yelling, 'Chief!' And above this din came the deeply resonant voice of one reporter, a voice recognizable to Bosch and everyone else with a television as belonging to Channel 4's Harvey Button.

'Did a cop kill Howard Elias?'

The question caused a momentary pause, then the chorus continued. The chief stepped back to the podium and raised his hands as if trying to calm a pack of dogs.

'Okay, hold on a second. I don't want everybody yelling at me. One at a—'

'Did a cop do this, Chief? Can you answer that or not?'

It was Button again. This time the other reporters remained silent and in doing so fell in behind him, their silence demanding that the chief address the question. It was, after all, the key question. The entire press conference boiled down to one question and one answer.

'At this time,' the chief said, 'I cannot answer that. The case is under investigation. Of course, we all know Howard Elias's record with this department. It would not be good police work if we did not look at ourselves. And we will do that. We are in the process of doing that. But at this point we—'

'Sir, how can the department investigate itself and still have credibility with the community?'

Button again.

'That's a good point, Mr Button. First off, the community can be assured that this investigation will reach its fruition no matter where it leads. The chips will fall where they may. If a police officer is responsible then he or she will be brought to justice. I guarantee it. Secondly, the department is being aided in this investigation by Inspector General Carla Entrenkin, who as you all know is a civilian observer who reports directly to the police commission, the city council and mayor.'

The chief raised his hand to cut off another question from Button.

'I'm not finished, Mr Button. As I said, lastly I would like at this time to introduce Assistant Special Agent in Charge Gilbert Spencer from the Los Angeles field office of the Federal Bureau of Investigation. I have discussed this crime and this investigation with Mr Spencer at length and he has agreed to bring the bureau in to help us. Beginning tomorrow, FBI agents will be working side by side with LAPD detectives in a group effort to bring this investigation to a swift and successful conclusion.'

Bosch tried to show no response as he listened to the chief announce the FBI involvement. He was not shocked by it. He realized it was a good move by the chief and might buy some time in the community. It might even get the case solved, though that was probably a secondary condition in the chief's decision making. He was primarily trying to put out fires before they started. The bureau was a pretty good hose with which to do that. But Bosch was annoyed that he had been left out of the loop and was finding out about the bureau's entry into his case at the same time as Harvey Button and everybody else. He glanced over at Irving, who picked it up on his radar and looked back. They traded glares until Irving looked away to the podium as Spencer took a position behind the microphones.

'I don't have much to say yet,' the bureau man said. 'We will be assigning a team to the investigation. These agents will work with the LAPD detectives and it is our belief that together we will break this case quickly.'

'Will you be investigating the officers in the Black Warrior case?' a reporter called out.

'We will be taking a look at everything but we are not going to be sharing our investigative strategy at this time. From this point, all media inquiries and releases will be handled through the LAPD. The bureau will—'

'Under what authority is the FBI entering the case?' Button asked.

'Under civil rights codes the bureau has the authority to open an investigation to determine if an individual's rights have been violated under color of law.'

'The color of law?'

'By an officer of the law. I am going to turn this over to . . .'

Spencer stepped back from the podium without finishing. He clearly didn't enjoy being in the glare of the media's headlights. The police chief stepped back into place and introduced Irving, who then moved behind the podium and began reading a press release which contained more details of the crime and the investigation. It was still just the basics, nothing anybody could do much with. The statement also mentioned Bosch by name as the detective in charge of the investigation. It also explained why potential conflict of interest with the RHD and scheduling problems with Central Division detectives required a team from Hollywood Division to run the case. Irving then said he could field a few questions, reminding the reporters once again that he would not compromise the investigation by revealing vital information.

'Can you talk more about the focus of the investigation?' a reporter called out ahead of the others.

'The focus is wide-ranging,' Irving said. 'We are looking at everything from police officers who might have held a grudge against Howard Elias to the possibility of the killings being part of a robbery. We—'

'A follow-up,' another reporter barked, knowing that you had to get your question in before the subject finished the last one or you'd never be heard in the ensuing cacophony. 'Was there anything at the crime scene to indicate a robbery?'

'We are not going to discuss details of the crime scene.'

'My information is that there was no watch or wallet on the body.'

Bosch looked at the reporter. He was not a TV man. Bosch could tell that by his rumpled suit. And it did not appear that he was from the *Times* because Keisha Russell was already in the room. Bosch didn't know who he was but he had obviously been leaked the information on the watch and wallet.

Irving paused as if deciding on how much to reveal.

'Your information is correct but incomplete. Mr Elias apparently left his watch and wallet in his desk when he left his office last night. The property was found there today. Of course, that does not preclude attempted robbery as a motive for this crime but it is too early in the investigation and we know too little to make such an assumption at this time.'

Keisha Russell, ever the cool one, had not joined the shouting for attention. She sat calmly with her hand raised, waiting for the others to run out of things to ask and for Irving to call on her. After Irving fielded a few more repetitive questions from the TV people he finally called on her.

'You said Mr Elias's property was found in his office today. Have you

646

searched his office and, if so, what if anything is being done to safeguard the attorney-client privilege that Mr Elias shared with his clients, all of whom are suing the agency that conducted the search of the office.'

'Good question,' Irving replied. 'We have not conducted a full search of the victim's office for the very reason you just mentioned. That is where Inspector General Entrenkin comes into play. She is reviewing files in the victim's office and will turn them over to investigators after she has vetted them for any sort of sensitive information that could possibly fall under attorney-client privilege. This review process was ordered earlier today by the judge who issued search warrants for Howard Elias's office. My understanding is that the watch and wallet were found in or on the victim's desk, very much as if he had simply forgotten them last night when he left work. Now I think that will wrap things up here. We have an investigation to focus on. When there are any further updates we will—'

'One last one,' Russell called out. 'Why has the department gone to twelve and twelves?'

Irving was about to answer but then looked back at the chief of police, who nodded and stepped back to the podium.

'We want to be ready for any eventuality,' he said. 'Going to twelve-hour shifts puts more officers on the street at any given time. We believe the citizens of this city will remain calm and give us time to conduct our investigation, but as a safety precaution I have instituted a readiness plan that includes all officers working twelve hours on and twelve hours off until further notice.'

'Is this the civil disorder response plan that was drawn up after the last riots?' Russell asked. 'When the department was caught flat-footed because it had no plan?'

'It is the plan drawn in 1992, yes.'

He was about to step away from the podium when Russell tossed another curveball.

'Then you are expecting violence.'

It was said as a statement, not a question. The chief returned to the microphones.

'No, Miss, uh, Russell, I am not expecting that. As I said, this is merely precautionary. I am expecting the citizens of this community to act in a calm and responsible manner. Hopefully, the media will act in the same way.'

He waited for one more response from Russell but this time got none. O'Rourke moved forward and leaned in front of the chief to get to the microphones.

'Okay, that's it. There will be copies of Chief Irving's statement down in media relations in about fifteen minutes.'

As the reporters slowly filed out of the room Bosch kept his eyes on the man who had asked the question about the wallet and watch. He was curious to know who he was and what news outlet he worked for. At the logjam at the door the confluence of people brought the man side by side with Button and they started talking. Bosch thought this was odd because he had never seen a print reporter give a TV reporter the time of day.

'Detective?'

647

Bosch turned. The chief of police was standing to his side with his hand out. Bosch instinctively shook it. He had spent nearly twenty-five years in the department to the chief's thirty, yet they had never crossed paths close enough to speak to each other, let alone shake hands.

'Chief.'

'Good to meet you. I want you to know how much we are counting on you and your team. If you need anything don't hesitate to contact my office or to go through Deputy Chief Irving. Anything.'

'Well, at the moment I think we're okay. I appreciate the heads-up on the bureau, though.'

The chief hesitated but only for a moment, apparently discarding Bosch's gripe as unimportant.

'That couldn't be helped. I wasn't sure the bureau was going to become involved until shortly before we started the press conference.'

The chief turned and looked for the FBI man. Spencer was talking with Irving. The chief signaled them over and introduced Bosch to Spencer. Bosch thought he caught a glimmer of disdain on Spencer's face. Bosch did not have a positive record over the years in his dealings with the FBI. He had never dealt directly with Spencer but if he was assistant special agent in charge of the L.A. field office, then he had probably heard of Bosch.

'How are we going to work this, gentlemen?' the chief asked.

'I'll have my people assembled and here at eight tomorrow morning, if you like,' Spencer said.

'Excellent. Chief Irving?'

'Yes, that will be fine. We will be working out of the conference room next to my office. I'll have our team there at eight, we can go over what we've got and take it from there.'

Everybody nodded except for Bosch. He knew he had no say in the matter.

They broke up and headed toward the door the chief had come through. Bosch found himself next to O'Rourke. He asked him if he knew who the reporter was who asked about the watch and wallet.

'Tom Chainey.'

It almost rang a bell with Bosch but not quite.

'He's a reporter?'

'Not really. He was with the *Times* a lot of years ago but now he's TV. He's Harvey Button's producer. He's not pretty enough to go on camera. So they pay him a ton of money to get scoops for Harvey and to tell him what to say and ask. To make him look good. Harvey's got the face and that voice. Chainey's got the brains. Why do you ask? Is there something I can do for you?'

'No. I was just wondering.'

'You mean the question about the wallet and the watch? Well, like I said, Chainey's been around. He's got sources. More than most.'

They moved through the doorway and Bosch turned left to head back to Irving's conference room. He wanted to leave the building but didn't want to wait for an elevator with all of the reporters.

Irving was waiting for him in the conference room. He was sitting in the same spot he had taken before.

'Sorry about the bureau deal,' he said. 'I did not know about it until right before. It was the chief's idea.'

'So I heard. It's probably the smart play.'

He was quiet for a moment, waiting for Irving to make the next move.

'So what I want you to do is have your team finish up the interviews they are involved in now, then everybody gets a good night's sleep, because tomorrow it all starts again.'

Bosch had to stop himself from shaking his head no.

'You mean just shelve everything until the bureau shows up? Chief, this is a homicide – a double homicide. We can't just shut it down and start over tomorrow.'

'I am not talking about shutting anything down. I said finish up what you have going at the moment. Tomorrow we will retrench and regroup and create a new battle plan. I want your people fresh and ready to run.'

'Fine. Whatever.'

But Bosch had no intention of waiting for the bureau. His intention was to continue the investigation, drive it forward and then follow where it led. It didn't matter what Irving said.

'Can I get a key to this room?' Bosch asked. 'We should get the first batch of files from Entrenkin in a little while. We need a secure place for them.'

Irving shifted his weight and reached into his pocket. He removed a key that was unattached to a ring and slid it across the table. Bosch picked it up and started working it onto his own key ring.

'So how many people have a copy of this?' he said. 'Just so I know.'

'You don't have to worry, Detective. No one will be going into this room who is not a member of the team or does not have my permission.'

Bosch nodded even though Irving had not answered his question.

15

As Bosch stepped through the glass doors of Parker Center he saw the beginning of the manufacturing and packaging of a media event. Spread out across the front plaza were a half dozen television crews and reporters ready to transmit stand-up reports as lead-in on the footage from the press conference. Out at the curb was the microwave forest – a line of TV trucks with their microwave transmitters raised high and ready. It was a Saturday, normally the slowest news day of the week. But the murder of Howard Elias was big. The guaranteed lead story and then some. A Saturday morning assignment editor's dream come true. The local stations were going to go live at noon. And then it would begin. The news of Elias's murder would blow through the city like the hottest Santa Ana wind, setting nerves on edge and possibly turning silent frustrations into loud and malevolent actions. The department – and the city, for that matter – was relying on how these young and beautiful people interpreted and delivered the information they had been given. The hope was that their reports would not fan the already smoldering tensions in the community. The hope was that they would show restraint and integrity and common sense, that they would simply report the known facts without any speculation or editorial twisting of the knife. But Bosch knew those hopes had about as much chance as Elias had when he stepped onto Angels Flight little more than twelve hours before.

Bosch took an immediate left and headed to the employee parking lot, careful not to walk into view of any of the cameras. He didn't want to be on the news unless absolutely necessary.

He successfully avoided detection and got to his car. Ten minutes later he parked illegally in front of the Bradbury, pulling in behind yet another TV truck. He looked around as he got out but didn't see the news crew. He guessed that they had walked over to the Angels Flight terminus to tape footage for the story.

After taking the old elevator up to the top floor Bosch pulled back the gate and stepped out onto the landing only to be met by Harvey Button, his producer and a cameraman. There was an uneasy silence as he tried to move around them. Then the producer spoke.

'Uh, Detective Bosch? I'm Tom Chainey from Channel Four.'

'Good for you.'

'I was wondering if we could talk for a few moments about the—'

'No, we can't talk. Have a nice day.'

Bosch managed to get around them and started toward Elias's office. Chainey spoke to his back.

'You sure? We're picking up a lot of information and it would probably do us both a lot of good if we could get it confirmed. We don't want to cause you any problems. It would be better if we could work as a team. You know.'

Bosch stopped and looked back at him.

'No, I don't know,' he said. 'If you want to put unconfirmed information on the air, that's your choice. But I'm not confirming anything. And I already have a team.'

He turned without waiting for a reply and headed toward the door with Howard Elias's name on it. He heard nothing else from Chainey or Button.

When he walked into the office he found Janis Langwiser sitting behind the secretary's desk, looking through a file. Next to the desk there were three cardboard boxes full of files that weren't there before. Langwiser looked up.

'Detective Bosch.'

'Hey. These boxes for me?'

She nodded.

'The first batch. And, hey, that wasn't very nice what you did before.'

'What?'

'Telling me my car was being towed. That was a lie, wasn't it?'

Bosch had completely forgotten.

'Uh, no, not really,' he said. 'You were in a tow-away zone. They would've gotten you.'

He smiled when he knew she knew it was a bullshit cover-up. His face started turning red.

'Look, I had to talk to Inspector Entrenkin alone. I'm sorry.'

Before she could say anything, Carla Entrenkin looked in from the room next door. She, too, was holding a file in her hand. Bosch pointed to the three boxes on the floor.

'Looks like you're making some progress.'

'I hope so. Can I talk to you for a moment in here?'

'Sure. But first, did Channel Four come in here and try to talk to you two?'

'They did,' Langwiser said. 'And Channel Nine was here before them.'

'Did you talk to them?'

Langwiser's eyes darted momentarily toward Entrenkin and then down at the floor. She said nothing.

'I gave a brief statement,' Entrenkin said. 'Something innocuous, just explaining my role. Can we talk in here?'

She stepped back from the doorway and Bosch entered the file room. There was another cardboard box on the desk that was half full of files. Entrenkin closed the door after Bosch entered. She then threw the file she was holding on the clerk's desk, folded her arms and put a stern expression on her face.

'What is it?' Bosch asked.

'Tom Chainey just told me that it was announced at the press conference that How— uh, Mr Elias had left his wallet and watch in his office, in his desk. And I thought that when you people were asked to leave this morning it was clear that—'

'I'm sorry. I forgot.'

651

Bosch put his briefcase down on the desk and opened it. He lifted out the evidence bags containing the wallet and watch.

'I had already bagged them and put them in my case before you came in this morning. I forgot about it and left with them. You want me to put it all back where I found it?'

'No. I just wanted an explanation. And I'm not sure I believe the one you just offered.'

There was a long silence while they stared at each other.

'Was that all you wanted to talk to me about?' Bosch finally asked.

She turned back to the desk and the file she had been looking through.

'I thought our relationship would be better than this.'

'Look,' Bosch said as he closed the briefcase. 'You've got your secrets. You've got to give me mine. The bottom line is Howard Elias wasn't robbed. So we move on from there. Okay?'

'If you are telling me that there were people involved in this investigation who were attempting to tamper with evidence, then—'

'I'm not telling you anything.'

He saw anger flare in her eyes.

'They shouldn't be a part of this department. You know that.'

'That's another battle for another day. I've got more import—'

'You know there are some people who might think there is nothing more important than a police department in which there is no question about the integrity of its members.'

'Sounds like you're giving a press conference, Inspector. I'm going to take those files now. I'll be back for the next batch later.'

He started to turn back to the front room.

'I just thought you were different, that's all,' she said.

He turned back to her.

'You don't know if I'm different because you don't know the first thing about me. I'll talk to you later.'

'There's something else missing.'

Bosch stopped and looked back at her.

'What?'

'Howard Elias was a consummate note taker. He kept a spiral notebook on his desk or with him all the time. His last notebook is missing. You know where that is?'

Bosch came back to the desk and reopened his briefcase. He took the notebook out and tossed it down.

'You won't believe me but I had already put that in my briefcase when you came in and kicked us out.'

'Matter of fact, I do believe you. Did you read it?'

'Parts of it. Also before you showed up.'

She looked at him for a long moment.

'I'll look through it and if it is okay you will have it back later today. Thank you for returning it.'

'You're welcome.'

By the time Bosch got to Philippe's the Original, the others were already there and eating. They had one of the long tables in the back room and were by themselves. He decided to take care of business before waiting in one of the lines at the counter to order.

'How'd it go?' Rider asked as he stepped over the bench and sat next to her.

'Well, I think I definitely was a little too pale for Irving's liking.'

'Well, fuck him,' Edgar said. 'I didn't sign up for this shit.'

'Me, too,' Rider said.

'What are you talking about?' Chastain asked.

'Race relations,' Rider said. 'Typical you can't figure that out.'

'Hey, I—'

'Never mind,' Bosch interjected. 'Let's talk about the case, okay? You first, Chastain. Did you finish the apartment building?'

'Yeah, we finished. Nothing.'

'Except we found out about the woman,' Fuentes said.

'Oh, yeah, right.'

'What woman?'

'The other victim. Catalina Perez. Hold a second.'

Chastain reached down to the bench next to him and came up with a legal tablet. He flipped to the second page and looked at the notes.

'Apartment nine-oh-nine. Perez was the cleaning woman. Came every Friday night. So that's where she was coming from.'

'But she was going up,' Bosch said. 'She didn't work till eleven?'

'No, this is the deal. She works six to ten-thirty, then takes Angels Flight down to the bus stop, catches the bus and goes home. Only on the way down she must've looked in her purse and noticed her notebook, where she keeps her schedule and phone numbers, is missing. She took it out in the apartment last night because her employer, a Mr D. H. Reilly, changed his phone number and gave her the new one. Only she left the notebook on his kitchen table. She had to go back for it so she'd know her schedule. This lady . . .'

He reached to the bench again and pulled up the notebook. It was in a plastic evidence bag.

'. . . I mean, I looked at the schedule. She worked her tail off. She's got gigs every day and a lot of nights. This Reilly guy said Friday nights was the only regular night he could get her for. She did a good job . . .'

'So she was going back up to get her book when she got popped,' Edgar said.

'Looks that way.'

'The old I-O-I-A,' Rider said in a singsong way that was not mirthful in any way.

'What's that?' Chastain asked.

'Nothing.'

They were all silent for a long moment. Bosch was thinking about how leaving that notebook behind had cost Catalina Perez her life. He knew that what Rider had said referred to the inequities of it all – the phrase she began using after a year on the homicide squad to sum up the bad breaks, coincidences and twists of fate that often left people dead.

'Okay, good,' Bosch finally said. 'We now know what everybody was doing on that train. The rest of the building was clean?'

'Nobody heard a thing, nobody saw a thing,' Chastain said.

'You get everybody?'

'No response at four apartments. But they were all on the other side, away from Angels Flight.'

'All right, let those go for now. Kiz, you talk to the wife and son again?'

Rider was chewing her last bite of French dip sandwich and held her finger up until she swallowed.

'Yeah, separately and together. Nothing pulled my trigger. They're both pretty much convinced a cop did it. I didn't—'

'Of course they are,' Chastain interjected.

'Let her talk,' Bosch said.

'I didn't pick up any feel that they knew much about his cases or possible threats. He didn't even keep a home office. I touched on Elias's fidelity and Millie said she believed he was faithful. She said it like that. She "believed." Something about it sounds wrong. I think if there was no doubt she would say he "was" faithful, not that she "believed" he was faithful, know what I mean?'

'So you think she knew?'

'Maybe. But I also think that if she knew then she was the type that would put up with it. There was a lot of social standing in being Howard Elias's wife. Lot of wives in that position make choices. They look the other way on some things to keep the image intact, to keep the life they have intact.'

'What about the son?'

'I think he believed his father was a god. He's hurting.'

Bosch nodded. He respected Rider's interviewing skills. He had seen her in action and knew she was empathic. He also knew he had used her in a way not so dissimilar to the way Irving had wanted to use her during the press conference. He had sent her to do the follow-up interviews because he knew she would be good at it. But also because she was black.

'You ask them the A question?'

'Yeah. They were both at home last night. Neither went out. They're each other's alibi.'

'Great,' Chastain said.

'Okay, Kiz,' Bosch said. 'Anybody else got something they want to bring up?'

Bosch leaned forward on the table so he could look down his side and see every face. No one said anything. He noticed everybody had finished eating their sandwiches.

'Well, I don't know if you've heard anything about the press conference, but the chief called in the cavalry. Tomorrow morning the bureau enters the case. We have a meet at eight in Irving's conference room.'

'Shit,' Chastain said.

'What the hell are they going to do that we can't?' Edgar asked.

'Probably nothing,' Bosch said. 'But his announcing it at the press conference will probably go a long way toward keeping the peace. At least, for now. Anyway, let's worry about that tomorrow when we see how things shake out. We still have the rest of today. Irving gave me an unofficial cease and desist until the agents show up but that's bullshit. I say we keep working.'

'Yeah, we don't want the shark to drown, do we?' Chastain said.

'That's right, Chastain. Now, I know nobody's had much sleep. My thinking is that some of us keep working and knock off early, some of us go home, take a nap and come back in fresh tonight. Any problem with that?'

Again no one said anything.

'All right, this is how we break it up. I've got three boxes of files from Elias's office in my trunk. I want you IAD guys to take them and go back to Irving's conference room. You take the files, pull out names of cops and anybody else to be checked out. I want a chart made up. When we get legit alibis we scratch the names off the chart and move on. I want this ready by the time the bureau arrives tomorrow. When you have it done, then you guys can knock off for the night.'

'And what are you going to be doing?' Chastain asked.

'We're going to run down Elias's secretary and his clerk. Then after that, I'm going home to take a nap. Hopefully. Then tonight we're going to talk to Harris and chase down that Internet thing. I want to know what that's all about before the bureau comes in.'

'You better be careful with Harris.'

'We will. That's one reason we're waiting until tonight. We play it right and the media doesn't even find out we talked to the guy.'

Chastain nodded.

'What about these files you're giving us, they old or new?'

'They're old ones. Entrenkin started on the closed cases.'

'When are we going to see the Black Warrior file? That's the one. The rest of this is bullshit.'

'Hopefully, I'll be picking that up later today. But the rest isn't bullshit. We have to look at every damn file in that office. Because the one we skip is likely to be the one some lawyer shoves up our ass in trial. You understand that? Don't skip anything.'

'I got it.'

'Besides, what do you care so much about the Black Warrior file for? You cleared those guys on it, right?'

'Yeah, so?'

'So what are you going to find in the file other than what you already know? You think you missed something, Chastain?'

'No, but . . .'

'But what?'

'It's the case of the moment. I think there's gotta be something there.'

'Well, we'll see. All in good time. For now stick to the old files and don't skip anything.'

'I told you, we won't. It's just a pain in the ass to know you're wasting time.'

'Welcome to homicide.'

'Yeah, yeah.'

Bosch reached into his pocket and pulled out a small brown bag. It contained several copies of the key Irving had given him that he had had made in Chinatown on his way to the restaurant. He turned the bag over on the center of the table and keys clattered onto the table.

'Everybody take a key. They'll open the door to Irving's conference room. Once the files are in there I want the room locked at all times.'

Everybody reached to the center of the table and took a key except Bosch. He had already put the original on his key ring. He stood up and looked at Chastain.

'Let's go get those files out of my car.'

16

The interviews with the secretary and the clerk were so uneventful that Bosch wished the detectives could have spent the time in their beds sleeping. Tyla Quimby, the secretary, had been out with the flu and holed up in her home in the Crenshaw district for the last week. She had no knowledge of Howard Elias's activities during the days before his death. Aside from exposing Bosch, Edgar and Rider to the flu, she gave the detectives very little. She explained that Elias kept his case strategies and other aspects of his work largely to himself. Her role was primarily opening mail, answering phones, handling walk-in visitors and clients, and paying the office expenses through a small operating account Elias put money into each month. As far as the phone traffic went, she said Elias had a direct private phone line in his office that over the years had become widely known among friends and associates as well as some reporters and even enemies. So she was of little use as far as helping them determine whether Elias had been specifically threatened in the weeks before his murder. The investigators thanked her and left her home, hoping they would not fall victim to her illness.

The clerk, John Babineux, was an equal disappointment. He was able to confirm that it had been he and Michael Harris who had worked until late Friday with Elias. But Babineux said that Harris and Elias had been behind closed doors most of the evening. Babineux, as it turned out, had graduated from the USC law school three months before and was studying for the bar exam at night while clerking for Elias by day. He did his studying in Elias's offices at night because it allowed him access to the law books he needed for memorizing case law and penal codes. It obviously was a better study environment than the crowded apartment near USC he shared with two other law students. Shortly before eleven he had walked out with Elias and Harris because he had felt he had done enough studying for one night. He said he and Harris walked to their cars in a nearby pay lot while Elias walked up Third Street alone toward Hill Street and Angels Flight.

Like Quimby, Babineux described Elias as secretive about his cases and preparation for trial. The clerk said that his responsibility in the last week of work had largely been preparing the transcripts of the many pretrial depositions taken in the Black Warrior case. His job was to download the transcripts and related material onto a laptop computer which would then be taken to court and accessed by Elias when he needed specific references to evidence and testimony during trial.

Babineux could give the detectives no information about specific threats to Elias – at least none that the attorney was taking seriously. He described Elias as extremely upbeat in recent days. He said Elias wholeheartedly believed that he was going to win the Black Warrior case.

'He said it was a slam dunk,' Babineux told the three detectives.

As Bosch drove up Woodrow Wilson Drive toward home he thought about the two interviews and wondered why Elias had been so secretive about the case he was bringing to trial. This didn't fit with his past history of press leaks and sometimes full-scale press conferences as a primary strategy. Elias was being uncharacteristically quiet, yet he was confident in his case, enough to call it a slam dunk.

Bosch hoped the explanation of this would be revealed when he got the Black Warrior file from Entrenkin, hopefully in a few hours. He decided to put thoughts of it aside until then.

Immediately Eleanor came to mind. He thought about the closet in the bedroom. He purposely hadn't checked it before, not sure how he would react if he found she had taken her clothes. He decided he needed to do that now, to get it over with. It would be a good time to do it. He was too tired now to do anything other than crash down onto his bed, regardless of what he found.

But as he came around the last curve he saw Eleanor's car, the beat-up Taurus, parked at the curb in front of their house. She had left the carport open for him. He felt the muscles in his neck and shoulders begin to relax. The tightness in his chest began to ease. She was home.

The house was quiet when he entered. He put his briefcase down on one of the dining room chairs and started stripping off his tie as he moved into the living room. He then moved down the short hallway and looked into the bedroom. The curtains were drawn and the room was dark except for the outline of exterior light around the window. He saw Eleanor's still form under the covers on the bed. Her brown hair was splayed over the pillow.

He moved into the bedroom and quietly took off his clothes, draping them over a chair. He then went back down the hallway to the guest bathroom to take a shower without waking her up. Ten minutes later he slid into the bed next to her. He was on his back, looking through the darkness to the ceiling. He listened to her breathing. He didn't hear the slow, measured breaths of her sleeping that he was used to.

'You awake?' he whispered.

'Mmm-hmm.'

He waited a long moment.

'Where were you, Eleanor?'

'Hollywood Park.'

Bosch didn't say anything. He didn't want to accuse her of lying. Maybe Jardine, the security guy, had simply missed her during his survey of the video screens. He stared at the ceiling, wondering what to say next.

'I know that you called there looking for me,' Eleanor said. 'I knew Tom Jardine in Las Vegas. He used to work at the Flamingo. He lied when you called. He came to me first.'

Bosch closed his eyes and remained silent.

'I'm sorry, Harry, I just didn't want to have to deal with you then.'

'Deal with me?'

'You know what I mean.'

'Not really, Eleanor. How come you didn't answer my message when you got home?'

'What message?'

Bosch realized he had played the message back himself earlier. There wouldn't have been a flashing light on the machine. She would not have heard the message.

'Never mind. When did you get home?'

She lifted her head off the pillow to look at the glowing numbers on the bedside clock.

'Couple hours ago.'

'How'd you do?'

He didn't really care. He just wanted her to keep talking to him.

'All right. Came out a little ahead but I messed up. I missed a big one.'

'What happened?'

'I went with a long shot when I should've stuck with a sure thing.'

'What do you mean?'

'I was dealt a pair of aces but I also had four clubs – ace, three, four, five. So on the draw I broke the pair of aces. I discarded the ace of hearts and went for the deuce, the two of clubs to make the straight flush. They keep a progressive bonus pot going for a straight flush. It was up to about three thousand dollars. That's what I was going for.'

'So what happened?'

'I didn't get the deuce. I didn't even get a club to make a flush. What I got was the ace of spades.'

'Damn.'

'Yeah, I threw down an ace only to get an ace. I stayed in with that but didn't come close. Three tens won it – the pot was about three hundred. So if I had kept the ace of hearts I would have ended up with three aces and been the winner. I blew it. That's when I left.'

Bosch didn't say anything. He thought about the story and wondered if she was trying to say something else. Tossing the ace of hearts, aiming for the bigger pot, failing.

After a few minutes of silence, Eleanor spoke again.

'Were you out on a case? You hadn't been in the bed. I could tell.'

'Yeah, I got a call out.'

'I thought you weren't up on rotation.'

'It's a long story and I don't feel like talking about it. I want to talk about us. Tell me what's going on, Eleanor. We can't . . . this isn't right. Some nights I don't even know where you are or if you are all right. Something's wrong or missing and I don't know what it is.'

She turned and moved under the covers until she was next to him. She put her head down on his chest and brought her hand up to caress the scar on his shoulder.

'Harry . . .'

He waited but she didn't say anything. She moved over on top of him then and started a gentle rocking motion with her hips.

'Eleanor, we need to talk about this.'

He felt her finger glide across his lips, telling him not to speak.

They made love slowly, Bosch's mind a jumble of conflicting thoughts. He loved her, more than he had ever loved anyone. He knew she loved him in some way. Having her in his life had made him feel whole. But at some point he could tell that Eleanor had realized she did not have that feeling. For her there was something missing and the realization that they were on separate planes brought Bosch down as low as he had ever felt.

The feeling of doom had fallen upon the marriage then. During the summer he had caught a series of time-consuming investigations, including a case requiring him to make a week-long trip to New York. While he was gone she went to the poker room at Hollywood Park for the first time. It was out of the boredom of being left alone and the frustration at her lack of success in finding an acceptable job in Los Angeles. She had returned to the cards, doing what she had done when Bosch had found her, and it was at those blue felt tables that she found the thing that was missing.

'Eleanor,' he said when they were finished making love, his arms wrapped around her neck. 'I love you. I don't want to lose you.'

She smothered his mouth with a long kiss and then whispered, 'Go to sleep, darling. Go to sleep.'

'Stay with me,' he said. 'Don't move away until I'm asleep.'

'I won't.'

She held him tighter and he tried for the moment to let everything go. Just for a while, he decided. He would take it all up later. But for now he would sleep.

In a few minutes he was gone, deep into a dream in which he was riding Angels Flight up the tracks to the top of the hill. As the other car came down and passed, he looked in through the windows and saw Eleanor sitting alone. She wasn't looking back at him.

Bosch awoke in a little over an hour. The room was darker, as the light from outside was no longer directly on the windows. He looked around and saw Eleanor was gone from the bed. He sat up and called her name, his voice reminding him of how he had answered the phone that morning.

'I'm here,' she called from the living room.

Bosch pulled on his clothes and left the bedroom. Eleanor was sitting on the couch, wearing the bathrobe he had bought for her at the hotel in Hawaii where they had gone after getting married in Las Vegas.

'Hey,' he said. 'I thought . . . I don't know.'

'You were talking in your sleep. I came out here.'

'What did I say?'

'My name, a few other things that didn't make sense. Something about a fight. Angels fighting.'

He smiled and nodded and sat down in the chair on the other side of the coffee table.

'*Flight,* not fight. You ever been on Angels Flight in downtown?'

'No.'

'It's two train cars. When one goes up the hill, the other goes down. They pass in the middle. I dreamed I was going up and you were in the car going down. We passed in the middle but you wouldn't look at me . . . What do you think it means, that we're going different ways?'

She smiled sadly.

'I guess it means you're the angel. You were going up.'

He didn't smile.

'I have to go back in,' he said. 'This one's going to take up my life for a while. I think.'

'You want to talk about it? Why were you called out?'

He ran the case down for her in about ten minutes. He always liked telling her about his cases. He knew it was a form of ego gratification, but sometimes she made a suggestion that helped or a comment that let him see something he had missed. It was many years since she had been an FBI agent. It was a part of her life that was a distant memory. But he still respected her investigative logic and skills.

'Oh, Harry,' she said when he was done telling the story. 'Why is it always you?'

'It's not always me.'

'Seems like it is. What are you going to do?'

'Same as I always do. I'm going to work the case. All of us are. There's a lot there to work with – they just have to give us the time with it. It's not going to be a quick turn.'

'I know you, they'll throw every roadblock they can think of in front of you. It does no one any good to hook somebody up and bring them in on this. But you'll be the one to do it. You'll bring somebody in no matter if it makes every cop in every division despise you.'

'Every case counts, Eleanor. Every person. I despise people like Elias. He was a suckerfish – making his life off bullshit cases against cops just trying to do their jobs. For the most part, at least. Every now and then he had a legitimate case, I guess. But the point is nobody should get away with what they did. Even if it's a cop who did it. It's not right.'

'I know, Harry.'

She looked away from him, out through the glass doors and past the deck. The sky was turning red. The lights of the city were coming on.

'What's your cigarette count?' he asked just to be saying something.

'I had a couple. You?'

'Still at zero.'

He had smelled the smoke in her hair earlier. He was glad she hadn't lied.

'What happened over at Stocks and Bonds?'

He'd been hesitant about asking. He knew that whatever had happened during the interview had been what sent her to the poker room.

'Same as the others. They'll call if something comes up.'

'I'll go over and talk to Charlie next time I'm at the station.'

Stocks and Bonds was a storefront bail bond agency across from the Hollywood station on Wilcox. Bosch had heard they were looking for a skip tracer, preferably female because a good portion of the bail jumpers out of Hollywood station were prostitutes and a female tracer stood a better chance of running them down. He had gone over and talked to the owner, Charlie Scott, about it and he had agreed to consider Eleanor for the job. Bosch was honest about her background, both good and bad. Former FBI agent on the plus side, convicted felon being the minus. Scott said he didn't believe the criminal record would be a problem – the position did not require a state private investigator's license, which Eleanor could not qualify for with a record. The problem was that he liked his tracers to be armed –

especially a woman – when they went looking for bail jumpers. Bosch didn't share the concern. He knew that most skip tracers were unlicensed to carry weapons but did so anyway. The true art of the craft, though, was never to get close enough to your quarry to make having or not having a weapon a question. The best tracers located their quarry from a safe distance and then called the cops in to make the pickup.

'Don't talk to him, Harry. I think he was just trying to do you a favor but reality hit him between when he told you to send me in and when I arrived. Just let it go.'

'But you'd be good at that.'

'That's beside the point.'

Bosch stood up.

'I've got to get ready.'

He went into the bedroom and stripped off his clothes, took another shower and then dressed in a fresh suit. Eleanor was in the same position on the couch when he came back out to the living room.

'I don't know when I'll be back,' he said, not looking at her. 'We've got a lot to do. Plus the bureau's coming in tomorrow.'

'The bureau?'

'Civil rights. The chief made the call.'

'He thinks it will keep things calm down south.'

'He hopes.'

'Do you have a name of who is coming over?'

'Not really. There was an assistant SAC at the press conference today.'

'What was his name?'

'Gilbert Spencer. But I doubt he'll be involved anymore.'

Eleanor shook her head.

'He's after my time. He probably just came for the show.'

'Yeah. He's supposed to send a team over tomorrow morning.'

'Good luck.'

He looked at her and nodded.

'I don't have the number yet. If you need me just use the pager.'

'Okay, Harry.'

He stood there for a few moments before finally asking her what he wanted to ask all along.

'Are you going to go back?'

She looked back out through the doors.

'I don't know. Maybe.'

'Eleanor . . .'

'Harry, you have your addiction. I have mine.'

'What's that mean?'

'You know that feeling you get when you pull up on a new case? That little thrill you get when you're back in the hunt? You know what I'm talking about. Well, I don't have that anymore. And the closest thing I've found to it is when I pick those five cards up off the felt and see what I've got. It is hard to explain and even harder to understand, but I feel like I'm alive again then, Harry. We're all junkies. It's just different drugs. I wish I had yours, but I don't.'

Bosch just stared at her a moment. He wasn't sure he could say anything without his voice betraying him. He moved to the door, looking back at her once he had it open. He moved through it but then stepped back.

'You break my heart, Eleanor. I always hoped that I could make you feel alive again.'

Eleanor closed her eyes. She looked as though she might cry.

'I'm so sorry, Harry,' she whispered. 'I should never have said that.'

Bosch stepped silently through the door and closed it behind him.

17

Bosch was still feeling emotionally bruised when he got to Howard Elias's office a half hour later. The door was locked and he knocked. He was about to use the keys to open it when he saw movement behind the glazed glass. Carla Entrenkin opened the door and allowed him in. He could tell by the way she appraised him that she noticed he was wearing a different suit.

'I got to take a little break,' he said. 'I think we'll be working a good part of the night. Where's Miss Langwiser?'

'We finished and I sent her home. I said I would wait for you. It's only been a few minutes.'

She led him back to Elias's office and took the seat behind the huge desk. Bosch could see Anthony Quinn through the window though it was getting dark out. He also saw that there were six file cartons on the floor in front of the desk.

'Sorry you were waiting,' he said. 'I thought you were going to page me when you were done.'

'I was about to. I was just sitting here thinking . . .'

Bosch looked at the boxes.

'This is the rest?'

'That's it. Those six are more closed cases. These back here are current cases.'

She rolled her chair back and pointed to the floor behind the desk. Bosch stepped over and looked down. There were two more full boxes.

'This is mostly Michael Harris stuff. Most of it is the police file and depo transcripts. There are also files on lawsuits that haven't proceeded past the initial claims. And there is a file containing general threats and crank mail – I mean unrelated specifically to the Harris case. Mostly just anonymous stuff from racist cowards.'

'Okay. What are you not giving me?'

'I'm holding back only one file. It was his working file. It contains notes on strategy in the Harris case. I don't think you should have that. I believe it goes directly to attorney-client privilege.'

'Strategy?'

'Basically, it's a trial map. Howard liked to chart his trials. He once told me he was like a football coach who designs the plays and what order he will call them in before the game even starts. Howard always knew exactly where he wanted to go during trial. The trial map showed his strategy, what witness came when, when each piece of evidence was to be introduced, things like that. He had the first few questions for every one of his witnesses already written. And he also had his opening statement outlined and in the file.'

'Okay.'

'I can't give it to you. It was the heart of his case and I think whoever the attorney is who inherits the case will want to follow the map. It was a brilliant plan. Therefore, the LAPD shouldn't have it.'

'You think he was going to win?'

'Definitely. I take it you don't?'

Bosch sat down in one of the chairs in front of the desk. Despite having taken the nap, he was still tired and feeling it.

'I don't know the particulars of the case,' he said. 'All I know is Frankie Sheehan. Harris accused him of some of that stuff – you know, with the plastic bag. And I know that's not Frankie.'

'How can you be sure?'

'I can't, I guess. But we go back. Sheehan and I were partners one time. It was a long time ago but you still know people. I know him. I can't see him doing these things. I can't see him letting anybody else do it, either.'

'People change.'

Bosch nodded.

'They do. But usually not at the core.'

'The core?'

'Let me tell you a story. One time Frankie and I brought this kid in. A carjacker. His deal was that first he'd steal a car, any shit can off the street, then he'd go out driving and looking for something nice, something he could take to a chop shop and get a decent amount of bread for. When he saw what he wanted he'd come up behind and at a stop light he'd hit the back end. You know, like a little fender bender, not enough to do much damage. Then the owner of the Mercedes or the Porsche or whatever it was would get out to check. The jacker would get out and just jump into the target car and take off. The owner and the stolen shit can were left behind.'

'I remember when carjacking was the big fad.'

'Yeah, some fad. This guy'd been doing this about three months and making a good amount of money at it. Then one time he hits the back of a Jaguar XJ6 too hard. The little old lady who was driving wasn't wearing her seat belt. She weighs about ninety pounds and she is thrown into the steering wheel. Hits it hard. No air bag. It crushes one lung and sends a rib through the other. She's sittin' there fillin' up with blood and dying when this kid comes up, opens the door and just yanks her out of the car. He leaves her lying on the street and drives off with the Jag.'

'I remember that case. What was that, ten years ago? The media went nuts on it.'

'Yeah. Carjack homicide, one of the first ones. And that's where me and Frankie came in. It was a hot case and we were under pressure. We finally got a line on the kid through a chop shop that Burglary-Auto Theft took down in the Valley. This kid lived over in Venice and when we went to pick him up he saw us coming. Fired a three fifty-seven through the front door after Frankie knocked. Missed him by an inch. Frankie had longer hair back then. The bullet actually went through his hair. The kid went through the back door and we chased him through the neighborhood, calling for

backup on our handhelds as we ran. The radio calls brought the media out –
helicopters, reporters, everything.'

'You got him, right? I remember.'

'We chased him almost all the way through Oakwood. We finally got him
in an abandoned house, a shooting gallery. The hypes went scattering and
he stayed inside. We knew he had the gun and he had already taken a shot
at us. We could've gone in there and blown his shit away and there
wouldn't have been a question. But Frankie went in first and talked the kid
out. It was just him and me and the kid in there. Nobody would've known
or questioned what had happened. But Frankie, he didn't think like that. He
told the kid he knew the lady in the Jag was an accident, that he didn't
mean to kill anybody. He told him he still had a chance at life. Fifteen
minutes earlier the kid tried to kill Frankie, now Frankie was trying to save
the kid's life.'

Bosch stopped for a moment, remembering the moments in the
abandoned house.

'The kid finally stepped out of a closet, holding his hands up. He still had
the gun in his hand. It would have been so easy . . . and so right. But it was
Frankie's call. He was the one who almost took the bullet. But he just went
over and took the gun from the kid and cuffed him. End of story.'

Entrenkin considered the story for a long moment before responding.

'So what you are saying is that because he spared one black man that he
could have easily gotten away with killing, then he would not have tried to
suffocate another black man nearly a decade later.'

Bosch shook his head and frowned.

'No, I'm not saying that. I'm saying that that was just one of the times I
saw Frank Sheehan's core. It was when I knew what he was made of. And
that's why I know the Harris thing is bullshit. He would never have planted
evidence on the guy, he would never have pulled a bag over his head.'

He waited for her to say something but she didn't.

'And I never said anything about the carjacker being black. That had
nothing to do with it. That's just something you bring to the story yourself.'

'I think it was an obvious part that you left out. Maybe if it had been a
white boy in that abandoned house you would never even have thought
about what you could have gotten away with.'

Bosch stared at her a long moment.

'No, I don't think so.'

'Well, it's not worth arguing about. You left something else out of the
story, didn't you?'

'What?'

'A few years later your buddy Sheehan *did* use his gun. And he put a
bunch of bullets into a black man named Wilbert Dobbs. I remember that
case, too.'

'That was a different story and a righteous shoot. Dobbs was a murderer
who drew down on Sheehan. He was cleared by the department, the DA,
everybody.'

'But not a jury of his peers. That was one of Howard's cases. He sued your
friend and he won.'

'It was bullshit. The case went to trial a few months after the Rodney King thing. There was no way a white cop who had shot a black man was going to get a clean verdict in this town back then.'

'Be careful, Detective, you're revealing too much of yourself.'

'Look, what I said was the truth. Deep down, you know it was the truth. How come the moment the truth might be uncomfortable people raise the race card?'

'Let's just drop this, Detective Bosch. You have your belief in your friend and I admire that. I guess we'll see what happens when the lawyer who inherits this case from Howard brings it to trial.'

Bosch nodded and was thankful for the truce. The accusatory discussion had made him feel uncomfortable.

'What else have you held back?' he asked, to try to move on.

'That's pretty much it. Spent all day in here to basically hold one file back.'

She blew her breath out and suddenly seemed very tired.

'You doing okay?' he asked.

'Fine. I think it was good for me to stay busy. I haven't had much time to think about what has happened. I'm sure I will tonight.'

Bosch nodded.

'Any more reporters come around?'

'A couple. I gave them a sound bite and they went on their merry way. They all think the city's going to cut loose over this.'

'What do you think?'

'I think if a cop did this, there's no telling what's going to happen. And if a cop didn't do it, there will be people who just won't believe it. But you already know that.'

Bosch nodded.

'One thing you should know about the trial map.'

'What's that?'

'Despite what you said about Frank Sheehan a moment ago, Howard was out to prove Harris innocent.'

Bosch hiked his shoulders.

'I thought he already was in the criminal trial.'

'No, he was found not guilty. There's a difference. Howard was going to prove his innocence by proving who did it.'

Bosch stared at her a long moment, wondering how he should proceed.

'Does it say in that trial map who that was?'

'No. Like I said, there was just an outline of the opener. But it's in there. He was going to tell the jury that he would deliver the murderer to them. Those were his words. "Deliver the murderer to you." He just didn't write who that was. It would have been a bad opener, if he did. It would give it away to the defense and make for an anticlimactic moment later in trial when he revealed who this person was.'

Bosch was silent as he thought about this. He didn't know how much weight to give what she had told him. Elias was a showman, in and out of court. Revealing a killer in court was Perry Mason stuff. It almost never happened.

'I'm sorry but I probably shouldn't have told you that,' she said.

'Why did you?'

'Because if others knew this was his strategy, it could have been a motive.'

'You mean the real killer of that little girl came back to kill Elias.'

'That's a possibility.'

Bosch nodded.

'Did you read the depos?' he asked.

'No, not enough time. I'm giving all depositions to you because the defense – in this case the city attorney's office – would have been furnished copies. So I'm not giving you something you wouldn't already have access to.'

'What about the computer?'

'I looked through it very quickly. It appears to be depositions and other information out of the public file. Nothing privileged.'

'Okay.'

Bosch started to get up. He was thinking about how many trips down to the car it would take him to move the files.

'Oh, one other thing.'

She reached down to the box on the floor and came up with a manila file. She opened it on the desk, revealing two envelopes. Bosch leaned over the desk to see.

'This was in the Harris stuff. I don't know what it means.'

Both envelopes were addressed to Elias at his office. No return addresses. Both were postmarked Hollywood, one mailed five weeks earlier and the other three weeks earlier.

'There's a single page with a line in each. Nothing that makes sense to me.'

She started opening one of the envelopes.

'Uh . . . ,' Bosch began.

She stopped, holding the envelope in her hand.

'What?'

'I don't know. I was thinking about prints.'

'I already handled these. I'm sorry.'

'Okay, go ahead, I guess.'

She finished opening the envelope, unfolded the page on the desk and turned it so Bosch could read it. There was one typed line at the top of the page.

dot the i humbert humbert

'Humbert Humbert . . . ,' Bosch said.

'It's the name of a character from literature – or what some people consider literature,' Entrenkin said. '*Lolita,* by Nabokov.'

'Right.'

Bosch noticed that a notation had been written in pencil at the bottom of the page.

#2 – 3/12

'That was probably Howard's marking,' Entrenkin said. 'Or someone in his office.'

She opened the next envelope, the more recently mailed of the two, and unfolded the letter. Bosch leaned over again.

license plates prove his innocense

'Looks to me like they're obviously from the same person,' Entrenkin said. 'Also, notice that *innocence* is spelled wrong.'

'Right.'

There was also a pencil notation at the bottom of the page.

#3 – 4/5

Bosch pulled his briefcase up onto his lap and opened it. He took out the evidence envelope that contained the letter Elias had been carrying in his inside suit pocket when gunned down.

'Elias was carrying this when he . . . when he got on Angels Flight. I forgot that the crime scene people gave it to me. It might be good if you are here observing when I open it. It's got the same postmark as those two. It was mailed to him Wednesday. This one I want to preserve for prints.'

He took a pair of rubber gloves out of the cardboard dispenser in his case and put them on. He then carefully removed the letter and opened it. He unfolded a piece of paper similar to the first two. Again there was one line typed on the page.

he knows you know

As Bosch stared at the page he felt the slight flutter in his heart that he knew came with the surge of adrenaline.

'Detective Bosch, what does this mean?'

'I don't know. But I sure wish I had opened it sooner.'

There was no pencil notation on the bottom of the third page. Elias hadn't gotten around to it, apparently.

'It looks like we're missing one,' Bosch said. 'These are marked two and three and this one came after – this one would be four.'

'I know. But I haven't found anything that would be number one. Nothing in the files. Maybe he threw it out, not realizing it meant something until the second one came.'

'Maybe.'

He thought about the letters for a moment. He was mostly going on instinct and premonition, but he felt the charge sustaining in his blood. He felt he had found his focus. This exhilarated him but at the same time he also felt a bit foolish at having unknowingly carried such a potentially key piece of the case around in his briefcase now for about twelve hours.

'Did Howard ever talk to you about this case?' he asked.

'No, we never talked about each other's work,' Entrenkin said. 'We had a rule. You see, we knew that what we were doing was . . . something that wouldn't be understood – the inspector general with one of the department's most vocal and well-known critics.'

'Not to mention him being married and all.'

Her face turned hard.

'Look, what is wrong with you? One minute we're getting along fine and maybe making some progress on this and the next you just want to antagonize me.'

'What's wrong is that I wish you would save the we-knew-it-was-wrong sermon for somebody else. I find it hard to believe you two didn't talk about the LAPD when you were alone up in that apartment.'

Bosch saw pure fire in her eyes.

'Well, I don't give a good goddamn what you find hard to believe, Detective.'

'Look, we made our deal. I'm not going to tell anyone. If I make trouble for you, you can make trouble for me. If I did tell even my partners, you know what they'd say? They'd say I was crazy for not treating you as a suspect. That's what I should be doing but I'm not. I'm flying on pure instinct and that can be scary. So to make up for it I'm looking for any edge or piece of luck or help I can get.'

She was silent a moment before responding.

'I appreciate what you are doing for me, Detective. But I am not lying to you. Howard and I never spoke in detail about his cases or my work with the department. *Never* in detail. The one thing I remember him saying about the Harris case is so vague as to defy interpretation. But if you must know what it was, I will tell you. He told me to brace myself because he was going to blow the department and a few of the city's big shots out of the water on this one. I didn't ask him what he meant.'

'And when was that?'

'That was Tuesday night.'

'Thank you, Inspector.'

Bosch got up and walked around a bit. He found himself at the window staring out at Anthony Quinn in shadows. He looked at his watch and saw it was almost six. He was supposed to rendezvous with Edgar and Rider at seven at the Hollywood station.

'You know what this means, don't you?' he asked, without turning back to Entrenkin.

'What does it mean?'

He turned to her.

'That if Elias was on to something and got close to identifying the killer – the real killer – then it wasn't a cop who put him down.'

She thought a moment and said, 'You're only looking at it from one side.'

'What's the other?'

'Say he was about to go to trial and pull the real killer out of his hat. Conclusively. That would put the lie to the police evidence, wouldn't it? So proving Harris innocent would at the same time prove the cops framed him. If the real killer knew Howard was on to him, yes he could have come after him. But say a cop knew that Howard was going to prove that that cop framed Harris, he could have come at him, too.'

Bosch shook his head.

'It's always the cops with you. Maybe the frame was in place before the cops even showed up.'

He shook his head again, more emphatically, as if warding off a thought. 'I don't know what I'm saying. There was no frame. It's too farfetched.'

Entrenkin watched him for a long moment.

'Whatever you say, Detective. Just never say I didn't warn you.'

Bosch ignored her statement. He looked at the boxes on the floor. For the first time he noticed a two-wheeled trolley leaning against the wall near the door. Entrenkin followed his eyes to it.

'I called the security guy and told him we needed to move some boxes. He brought it up.'

Bosch nodded.

'I guess I better get this stuff to my car. Do you still have the search warrant or did Miss Langwiser take it? I need to fill out the receipt.'

'I have it and I've already catalogued the files. You just need to sign it.'

Bosch nodded and walked over to the trolley. He remembered something and turned back to her.

'What about the file we were looking at when you came in this morning? With the photo in it.'

'What about it? It's in the box there.'

'Well, I mean . . . uh . . . what do you think?'

'I don't know what to think about it. If you're asking me if I believed Howard Elias was involved with that woman I would say no.'

'We asked his wife today if it was possible he was having an affair and she said no, it was not possible.'

'I get your point. But I still think it's impossible. Howard was a well-known man in this city. First of all, he would hardly have to pay for sex. And secondly, he was smart enough to know that he would be vulnerable to extortion from these people if they recognized him.'

'Then what was the file doing in his desk?'

'Like I said, I don't know. It had to be part of a case but I don't know which one. I looked at every file in the office today and didn't find anything that connects to it.'

Bosch just nodded. His mind was already off the file and back on the mystery letters, the last one in particular. His take on it was that it was a warning to Elias. Someone had discovered that the lawyer was in possession of a dangerous piece of information. Bosch was feeling more certain that the investigation, the true investigation, should stem from that note.

'Do you mind if I put on the television now?' Entrenkin said. 'It's six. I want to watch the news.'

Bosch came out of his reverie.

'Sure. Turn it on.'

She moved to a large oak cabinet against the wall opposite the desk and opened the doors. Inside the cabinet were two shelves, each containing a television. Elias apparently liked to watch more than one TV at a time. Probably, Bosch guessed, so he had a better chance of catching all his appearances on newscasts.

Entrenkin hit the power on both sets. As the picture came into focus on the top set, Bosch saw a reporter standing in front of a strip shopping center in which three or four stores were ablaze. Several yards behind the reporter, firefighters worked to contain the blaze but it looked to Bosch as though the buildings were beyond being saved. They were already gutted.

'It's happening,' he said.

'Not again,' Entrenkin said, her voice a scared plea.

18

Bosch turned on KFWB on the car radio while driving into Hollywood. The radio reports were more conservative than the TV news at six. This was because the radio report contained only words, not images.

The bottom-line news was that there was a fire in a strip mall on Normandie, just a few blocks from the intersection of Florence, the intersection that was the flashpoint of the 1992 riots. At that moment it was the only fire burning in South L.A. and there was not yet any confirmation that the fire was an arson linked to protest or anger over the murder of Howard Elias. But every news channel that Bosch and Entrenkin had checked in the office was broadcasting from the mall. Flames filled the screens and the image projected was clear: Los Angeles was burning once again.

'Fucking TV,' he said. 'Excuse my language.'

'What about TV?'

It was Carla Entrenkin. She had talked her way into being taken along for the interview with Harris. Bosch hadn't put up much of a protest. He knew she might help put Harris at ease, if he knew who she was. Bosch knew it was important that Harris be willing to talk to them. He might be the only one to whom Howard Elias had confided the identity of Stacey Kincaid's murderer.

'Overreacting as usual,' Bosch said. 'One fire and they're all there, showing the flames. You know what that does? That's like throwing gasoline on it. It will spread now. People will see that in their living rooms and go outside to see what is happening. Groups will form, things will be said and people won't be able to back down from their anger. One thing will lead to another and we'll have our media-manufactured riot.'

'I give the people a little more credit than that,' Entrenkin responded. 'They know not to trust the TV. Civil unrest occurs when the feelings of overwhelming powerlessness hit critical mass. It has nothing to do with television. It has to do with society not addressing the essential needs of overlooked people.'

Bosch noted that she called it civil unrest instead of rioting. He wondered if calling a riot a riot had become politically incorrect.

'It's about hope, Detective,' she continued. 'Most of the people in the minority communities of Los Angeles have no power, have no money, have no voice. They subsist on hope for these things. And Howard Elias was hope for many of them. A symbol of hope for a day when things will be equal,

672

when their voice will be heard. Of a day when they need not fear the police officers in their community. When you take hope away it leaves a void. Some people fill that up with anger and with violence. To simply blame it on the media is wrong. It's much deeper than that.'

Bosch nodded.

'I understand,' he said. 'At least I think I do. But all I'm saying is the media don't help any by exaggerating things.'

Entrenkin now nodded to his point.

'Somebody once called the media the merchants of chaos.'

'Yeah, well, they got that right.'

'It was Spiro Agnew. Right before he resigned.'

Bosch had no answer for that and decided to drop the conversation. He got his cell phone out of the charger on the floor between the seats and called his home. There was no answer except for the machine and he left a message asking Eleanor to call him. He tried not to show outwardly that he was upset. He called information and got the number for the Hollywood Park poker room again. He called the number, asked for Jardine, the security man, and he was transferred through.

'This is Jardine.'

'This is Detective Bosch from last night. I—'

'She never showed up, pal. At least not on my wa—'

'You can save it, *pal*. She told me that you and she go back to the Flamingo. I understand what you did and it's cool. But I know she's back there now and I want you to give her a message. Tell her to call me on my cell phone as soon as she takes a break. Tell her it's an emergency. You got that, Mister Jardine?'

Bosch stressed the word *mister* so that maybe Jardine would realize he was making a mistake screwing with the LAPD.

'Yeah,' Jardine said. 'I got it.'

'Good.'

Bosch clicked off.

'You know what I remember most about ninety-two?' Entrenkin said. 'One image. A photo that was in the *Times*. The caption was something like "Father and Son Looters" and the picture showed a man leading his four- or five-year-old son out of the smashed-in door of a K-mart or something. And you know what each one was carrying, what they had looted?'

'What?'

'Each one had taken one of those Thigh-Master things. You know, that ridiculous exercise contraption that some television star from the eighties sold late at night on TV.'

Bosch shook his head at the inanity of her image.

'They saw it on TV and so they thought it was valuable,' he said. 'Like Howard Elias.'

She didn't respond and he realized he had been out of line, even if he believed there was something valid in what he had said.

'Sorry . . .'

They drove in silence for a few minutes before Bosch spoke again.

'You know what my image is of ninety-two?'

'What?'

'I was assigned to Hollywood Boulevard. And, as you know, we weren't

673

really supposed to do anything unless we saw people in danger of physical harm. Essentially, this meant that if the looters were orderly about it, we basically weren't going to stop them. It made no – anyway, I was on the Boulevard and I remember a lot of weird things. The Scientologists surrounding their buildings, standing practically shoulder to shoulder and carrying broomsticks, ready to make a stand if needed. The guy who ran the Army surplus store near Highland was in full combat infantry dress and carrying a sniper rifle over his shoulder. He was marching back and forth in front of his store like he was at the gate at Benning . . . People get crazy, the good and the bad. It's day of the locusts.'

'Well, aren't you the well-read detective, Detective Bosch.'

'Not really. I once lived with a woman who taught junior lit at Grant High in the Valley. It was one of the books she taught. I read it then. Anyway, the image that sticks with me from ninety-two is Frederick's of Hollywood.'

'The lingerie place?'

Bosch nodded.

'I pulled up there and the place was swarming. Multiracial, multiage, people who had just lost it. They cleaned that place out in about fifteen minutes. I mean, everything. When they were done I walked in there and there was nothing left. They even stole the manikins. Absolutely nothing but the hangers left on the floor and the chrome display racks . . . and the thing is, all it had been was *underwear*. Four cops get off for beating the shit out of Rodney King on video and people respond by going nuts and stealing underwear. It was so surreal that that's what comes into my head when people bring up the riots. I remember walking around in that empty store.'

'It didn't matter what they took. They were acting out frustrations. It's like the Thigh-Masters. That father and son didn't care what they took. The important thing was that they took something, that in some way they made a statement. They had no use for those things but by taking them they were showing The Man. That's the lesson the father taught his son.'

'It still doesn't make—'

Bosch's phone rang and he opened it. It was Eleanor.

'You winning?' he asked.

He said it with a happy inflection and then immediately realized he had said it in such a way so that his passenger might not surmise what was really going on with his marriage. At once he felt embarrassed and guilty that he would even let what Entrenkin thought or interpreted enter into his relationship with Eleanor.

'Not yet. I just got here.'

'Eleanor, I want you to go home.'

'Harry, we're not going to talk about this now. I—'

'No, I'm not talking about all of that. I think the city . . . have you watched the news?'

'No. I've been coming here.'

'Well, it doesn't look good. The media's lighting the match, Eleanor. And if something happens and the city goes, you're not in a good place to be.'

Bosch took a furtive glance at Entrenkin. He knew he was acting out white paranoia in front of her. Hollywood Park was in Inglewood, a primarily black community. He wanted Eleanor back at their home in the hills where it was safe.

'Harry, I think you're being paranoid. I'll be fine.'

'Eleanor, why take the—'

'Harry, I have to go. They're holding my chair. I'll call you later.'

She hung up then and Bosch said good-bye to a dead line. He dropped the phone onto his lap.

'For what it's worth,' Entrenkin said, 'I think you're being paranoid.'

'That's what she said.'

'I'll tell you right now there are as many blacks as whites, maybe even more, who don't want to see it happen again. Give them the benefit of the doubt, Detective.'

'I guess I don't have a choice.'

The Hollywood Station seemed deserted when Bosch and Entrenkin arrived. There were no patrol cars in the rear lot and when they came through the back door the rear hallway, usually abuzz with activity, was empty. Bosch stuck his head through the open door of the watch office and saw a lone sergeant at a desk. A television mounted on the wall was on. There were no flames on the screen. It showed a news anchor in a studio. The graphic hanging over his shoulder was a photo of Howard Elias. The volume was too low for Bosch to hear what was being said.

'How we doing?' Bosch said to the sergeant.

'Hanging in. For now.'

Bosch knocked twice on the door and headed down the hallway to the detective bureau, Entrenkin following. Rider and Edgar were already there. They had rolled the television out of the lieutenant's office and were watching the same news report. They saw Bosch and Entrenkin and the surprise registered on their faces.

Bosch introduced Entrenkin to Edgar, who had not been in Elias's office that morning. He then asked what the latest news was.

'The city's holding tight, it looks like,' Edgar said. 'Couple fires and that's it. Meantime, they're pretty much making Elias into Saint Howard. Not much said about what an opportunistic asshole he was.'

Bosch glanced at Entrenkin. She showed nothing.

'Well, let's turn it off,' he said. 'We have to talk.'

Bosch brought his partners up to date and showed them the three anonymous notes that had been mailed to Elias. He explained Entrenkin's presence and said he wanted to try to get Harris's cooperation and at the same time eliminate him as a potential suspect in the killings.

'Do we even know where Harris is?' Edgar asked. 'He hasn't shown up on TV that I've seen. Maybe he doesn't even know about Elias.'

'Well, we'll find out. His current address and phone number were in Elias's files. Looks like Elias was putting him up, probably trying to keep him out of trouble before the trial. He's close by – if he's home.'

Bosch got out his notebook and got the phone number. He went to his desk and called it. A man answered.

'Can I speak to Harry?' Bosch said good-naturedly.

'No Harry here, man.'

The phone was hung up.

'Well, somebody's home,' Bosch said to the others. 'Let's go.'

They drove in one car. Harris currently lived in an apartment on Beverly

Boulevard near the CBS complex. Elias had put him into a large complex that wasn't luxurious but was more than nice. And downtown was a straight shot down Beverly.

There was a security door but Harris's name was not on the list of occupants next to the door phone. Bosch had the apartment number but this did not mean anything. The phone codes following occupants' names did not correspond with apartment numbers for security reasons. Bosch called the code number for the building's manager but got no answer.

'Look at this,' Rider said.

She pointed to a listing for E. Howard. Bosch shook his shoulders as if to say it was worth a try and punched in the number. A male voice answered and Bosch thought it was the same voice that had answered his earlier call from the station.

'Michael Harris?'

'Who is it?'

'LAPD. We need to ask you some questions. I—'

'No fucking way. Not without my lawyer here, you don't.'

He hung up. Bosch immediately called back.

'What the fuck you want?'

'In case you don't know it yet, your lawyer is dead. That's why we are here. Now, listen and don't hang up. I have Inspector General Carla Entrenkin here with me. You know who she is? She's going to make sure you are treated well. We just need to—'

'She the watchdog lady, 'sposed to tell when the LAPD is runnin' roughshod?'

'That's her. Hold on.'

Bosch stepped to the side and handed the phone to Entrenkin.

'Tell him he's safe.'

She took the phone, giving Bosch a look that said she now realized why he allowed her to come along. She spoke into the phone while looking at him.

'Michael, this is Carla Entrenkin. You don't have to worry. No one is here to harm you. We need to ask you about Howard Elias, that is all.'

If Harris said anything to her Bosch didn't hear it. The door lock buzzed and Edgar pulled it open. Entrenkin hung up the phone and they all went in.

'The guy's a mutt,' Edgar said. 'I don't know why we're treating him like a saint.'

Entrenkin gave Edgar her look then.

'Yes, you do, Detective Edgar.'

Edgar was sufficiently cowed by her tone.

When Harris opened the door of his fourth-floor apartment he was holding a gun at his side.

'A'right, this is my home,' he announced. 'I don't mean to be threatenin' anybody but I need this for my pers'nal comfort and protection. Otherwise, you ain't comin' in the place, know what I mean?'

Bosch looked at the others, got no read, and looked back at Harris. He tried to contain his fury. Despite what Entrenkin had told him earlier, he still had little doubt that Harris was the murderer of a child. But he knew that what was important at the moment was the current investigation. He

676

had to put his enmity for the man aside in order to extract whatever information he had.

'All right,' he said. 'But you keep that weapon low and at your side. You point it at one of us and we're going to have a big problem. We understand each other?'

'Oh, we understand.'

Harris backed away from the door and let them in by pointing the weapon toward the living room.

'Remember, keep that thing down,' Bosch said sternly.

Harris dropped the gun to his side and they all entered. The apartment was furnished with rental stuff – puffy couch and matching chairs in light blue, cheap faux wood tables and shelves. Pastoral prints were on the walls. There was a cabinet with a television in it. The news was on.

'Have a seat, ladies and gentlemen.'

Harris took one of the big chairs, slumping in it so that the back rose above his head, giving him the appearance of sitting on a throne. Bosch stepped over and turned the television off, then introduced everybody and showed his badge.

'It figure the white man in charge,' Harris said.

Bosch ignored it.

'I take it you know that Howard Elias was murdered last night?' he asked.

''Course I know. Been sittin' here watchin' it all got-damned day.'

'Then why'd you say you wouldn't talk to us without your lawyer if you knew your lawyer was dead?'

'I got more than one lawyer, dumbshit. I also got a crim'nal lawyer and I got a entertainment lawyer. I got lawyers, don't worry. And I'll get another to take Howie's place. I'm gonna need 'em, man, 'specially after they start cuttin' up in South Central. I'mma have my own riot like Rodney. That'll put me on top.'

Bosch could barely follow Harris's line of thought but he understood enough to know Harris was on a power trip at his own community's expense.

'Well, let's talk about your late lawyer, Howard Elias. When was the last time you saw him?'

'Last night, but you already know that, right Chet?'

'Till when?'

'Till we walked out the muthafuckin' door. Are you throwin' down on me, man?'

'What?'

'You in-ter-OH-gating me, man?'

'I'm trying to find out who killed Elias.'

'You did that. You people got him.'

'Well, that's a possibility. That's what we're trying to find out.'

Harris laughed as if what Bosch had said was absurd.

'Yeah, you know that thing they say about the kettle and the pot, that's what that is.'

'We'll see. When did you two part company? You and Howard Elias.'

'When he went to his apartment and I went home.'

'Which was when?'

'I don't know, Chet. Quarter to eleven, eleven a'clock. I don't wear a

677

watch. People tell me the time when I want to know it. They say on the news he got his ass shot at eleven, so we left quarter of.'

'Had he mentioned any threats? Was he afraid of anyone?'

'He wasn't afraida shit. But he knew he was a dead man.'

'What do you mean?'

'You people is what I mean. He knew you would come gunnin' for him someday. Somebody finally did. Prob'ly come for me, too, one day. Tha's why as soon as I get my money I'm splittin' this place. All you cops can have it. And that's all I got to say, Chet.'

'Why do you call me that?'

'Because that's what you are. You're a Chet, Chet.'

Harris's smile was a challenge. Bosch held his gaze for a moment, then turned to Entrenkin and nodded. She took it from there.

'Michael, do you know who I am?'

'Sure, I seen ya on the TV. Just like Mr Elias. I know you.'

'Then you know I am not a police officer. My job is to make sure the police officers in this city are honest and do their jobs the way they should be done.'

Harris snickered.

'You got a lot a work 'head you, lady.'

'I know that, Michael. But the reason I am here is to tell you that I think these three detectives want to do what is right. They want to find the person who killed Howard Elias, whether it is a cop or not. And I want to help them. You should want to help as well. You owe Howard that much. So will you please answer a few more questions?'

Harris looked around the room and at the gun in his hand. It was a Smith & Wesson 9 millimeter with a satin finish. Bosch wondered if Harris would have brandished it in front of them if he knew the murder weapon was a nine. Harris shoved the weapon into the crack between the seat cushion and the arm of the big chair.

'Okay, I guess. But not Chet. I don' talk to white cops or Tom boys. You ask me.'

Entrenkin looked back at Bosch and then back to Harris.

'Michael, I want the detectives to ask the questions. They are better at it than me. But I think it's okay for you to answer.'

Harris shook his head.

'You don't unnerstand, lady. Why should I help these fuckers? These people tortured me for no fucking reason. I ain't got forty percent of my hearing because of the L-A-P-D. I ain't *cop*-erating. Now if you got a question, then *you* ask it.'

'Okay, Michael, that's fine,' Carla said. 'Tell me about last night. What did you and Howard work on?'

'We worked on my testimony. Only you know how the cops call it testi-*lying* on account they never tell the damn truth when it comes to the brothers? Well, I call it my testi-*money* cause the LAPD is going to pay my ass for framin' me and then fuckin' with me. Damn right.'

Bosch picked up the questioning as though Harris had never said he wouldn't speak to him. 'Did Howard tell you that?'

'Sure did, Mr Chet.'

'Did he say he could prove it was a frame?'

'Yeah, 'cause he knew who really done the murder a that little white girl and then put her in the lot near my place. An' it wudn't me. He was goin' to court Monday to start to zonerate me completely and get my money, my man Howard.'

Bosch waited a beat. The next question and answer would be crucial.

'Who?'

'Who what?'

'Who really did the murder? Did he tell you?'

'Nope. He said I didn't need to know. Said it was dangerous to know that shit. But I bet it's in there in his files. He ain't gonna get away again.'

Bosch glanced at Entrenkin.

'Michael, I spent all day with the files. Yes, there are indications that Howard knew who killed Stacey Kincaid but no name was recorded anywhere. Are you sure he never told you a name or gave you any indication of who this person was?'

Harris was momentarily nonplussed. He evidently realized that if Elias went down with the murderer's name kept to himself, his case might have gone down a few notches as well. He would always carry the stigma of being a murderer who got off because a slick defense lawyer knew how to play a jury.

'Goddamn,' he said.

Bosch came over and sat on the corner of the coffee table, so that he could be close to Harris.

'Think hard,' he said. 'You spent a lot of time with him. Who would it be?'

'I don't know,' Harris said defensively. 'Whyn't you ask Pelfry about it, man?'

'Who is Pelfry?'

'Pelfry's his leg man. His investigator.'

'You know his whole name?'

'I think it's somethin' like Jenks or somethin'.'

'Jenks?'

'Yeah, Jenks. Tha's what Howard call him.'

Bosch felt a finger poke his shoulder and he turned to see Entrenkin give him a look. She knew who Pelfry was. He could let it go. Bosch stood up and looked down at Harris.

'You came back here last night after you left Elias?'

'Yeah, sure. Why?'

'Anybody with you? You call anybody?'

'What the fuck is this? You're throwin' down on me, man.'

'It's routine. Relax. We ask everybody where they've been. Where were you?'

'I was here, man. I was beat. I came home and got in my bed. Ain't nobody with me.'

'Okay. Mind if I have a look at your pistola for a second?'

'Jesus Christ, I shoulda known you people weren't on the level. Got-damn.'

He pulled the gun out from the side of the chair cushion and handed it to Bosch. Bosch kept his eyes on Harris's until the gun was safely in his hand. He then studied the weapon and smelled the barrel. He smelled no oil or burned gunpowder. He ejected the cartridge and thumbed out the top bullet. It was a Federal, full metal jacket. A very popular brand and make of ammunition, Bosch knew, and possibly the same brand used in the Angels Flight murders. They wouldn't know until the autopsies. He looked back down at Harris.

'You're a convicted felon, Mr Harris. You realize it is a crime for you to have this weapon?'

'Not in my house, man. I need protection.'

'Anywhere, I'm afraid. This could send you back to prison.'

Harris smiled at him. Bosch could see one of his incisors was gold with a star etched on the front.

'Then take me away, man.'

He raised his arms, offering his wrists for the handcuffs.

'Take me away and watch this muthafuckin' place burn, baby, burn.'

'No. Actually I was thinking of cuttin' you a break, seeing how you've been so helpful tonight. But I'm going to have to keep the weapon. I'd be committing a crime if I left it here with you.'

'Be my guess, Chet. I can always get what I need from my car. Know what I mean?'

He said *Chet* the way some white people say the word *nigger*.

'Sure. I know what you mean.'

They waited for the elevator in silence. Once they were inside and descending Entrenkin spoke.

'Does that gun match?'

'It's the same kind. Ammo might be the same. We'll have the lab check it, but I sort of doubt he would have kept it around if he killed Elias with it. He's not that stupid.'

'What about his car? He said he could get anything from his car.'

'He didn't mean his car car. He meant his crew. His people. Together they're a car, driving somewhere together. It's a saying that comes from county lockup. Eight people to a cell. They call them cars. What about Pelfry? You know him?'

'Jenkins Pelfry. He's a PI. An independent. I think he's got an office over in the Union Law Center in downtown. A lot of the civil rights lawyers use him. Howard was using him on this.'

'We have to talk to him then. Thanks for telling us.'

There was annoyance in Bosch's voice. He looked at his watch. He figured it was too late to try to run down Pelfry.

'Look, it's in the files I gave you,' Entrenkin protested. 'You didn't ask me about it. How was I to know to tell you?'

'You're right. You didn't know.'

'If you want, I could put a call—'

'No, that's okay. We've got it from here, Inspector. Thanks for your help with Harris. We probably wouldn't have gotten up there to see him without you along.'

'You think he had anything to do with the murders?'

'I'm not thinking anything yet.'

'I seriously doubt he's involved.'

Bosch just looked at her, hoping his eyes conveyed that he believed she was treading into areas where she had neither expertise nor a mandate to be.

'We'll give you a ride back,' he said. 'Your car at the Bradbury?'

She nodded. They were crossing the lobby to the doors.

'Detective, I want to be kept apprised of the case and any significant developments.'

'Fine. I'll talk to Chief Irving in the morning and see how he wants to do that. He might prefer to keep you informed himself.'

'I don't want the whitewashed version. I want to hear it from you.'

'Whitewashed? You think that whatever I tell you won't be *white*washed? I'm flattered, Inspector.'

'A poor choice of words. But my point being I would rather hear it from you than after it has been processed by the department's management.'

Bosch looked at her as he held the door.

'I'll remember that.'

19

Kiz Rider had run the telephone number from the Mistress Regina web page through the criss-cross directory contained on a CD-ROM in the squad room computer. The phone was assigned to an address on North Kings Road in West Hollywood. This did not mean that the address would be where they would find the woman, however. Most prostitutes, late-night masseuses and so-called exotic entertainers used elaborate call-forwarding systems to make it hard for law enforcement agencies to find them.

Bosch, Rider and Edgar pulled to the curb at the intersection of Melrose and Kings and Bosch used his phone to call the number. A woman answered after four rings. Bosch went into his act.

'Mistress Regina?'

'Yes, who is this?'

'My name is Harry. I was wondering if you were available tonight?'

'Have we had a session before?'

'No. I saw your web page and thought . . .'

'Thought what?'

'I thought I might want to try a session.'

'How advanced are you?'

'I don't under—'

'What are you into?'

'I'm not sure yet. I'd like to try it out.'

'You know there is no sex, right? No physical contact. I play mind games with people. Nothing illegal.'

'I understand.'

'Do you have a secure phone number that I can call you back at?'

'What do you mean secure?'

'I mean no pay phones!' she said harshly. 'You have to give me a real number.'

Bosch gave her his cell phone number.

'Okay. I'll call you back in one minute. Be there.'

'I will.'

'I will ask for three-six-seven. That is you. You are not a person to me. You do not have a name. You are simply a number.'

'Three-six-seven. I understand.'

He closed the phone and looked at his partners.

'We'll know if it worked in about a minute.'

'You sounded nice and subservient, Harry,' Rider said.

'Thank you. I try my best.'

'You sounded like a cop to me,' Edgar said.

'We'll see.'

Bosch turned the car on, just to be doing something. Rider yawned and then he had to. Then Edgar joined in.

The phone rang. It was Mistress Regina. She asked for him by number.

'You can come to me in one hour. I require a donation of two hundred dollars for a one-hour session. Cash only and in advance. Is that understood?'

'Yes.'

'Yes what?'

'Uh, yes, Mistress Regina.'

'That's very good.'

Bosch looked over at Rider, who was in the front passenger seat, and winked. She smiled back at him.

Regina gave the address and apartment number. Bosch turned the overhead light on and looked over at Rider's notes. The address he had just been given was the same one Rider had but the apartment number was different. He told Regina he would be there and they ended the call.

'It's a go. But not for an hour. She uses a different apartment in the same building.'

'We gonna wait?' Edgar asked.

'Nope. I want to get home and get some sleep.'

Bosch turned the car onto Kings Road and cruised a half block up until they found the address. It was a small apartment building made of wood and stucco. There was no parking anywhere so he pulled into a red zone in front of a fireplug and they got out. He didn't really care if Regina had a front apartment and saw the slickback. They weren't coming to make an arrest. All they wanted was information.

Apartments six and seven were in the back of the building anyway. Their doors were side by side. Bosch guessed the woman who called herself Mistress Regina lived in one apartment and worked in the other. They knocked on the work door.

And got no answer.

Edgar hit the door again, harder, and this time kicked it a couple times as well. Finally, a voice was heard from the other side.

'What is it?'

'Open up. Police.'

Nothing.

'Come on, Regina, we need to ask you some questions. That's all. Open the door or we'll have to break the lock. Then what are you gonna do?'

It was a baseless threat. Bosch knew he had no legal power to do anything if she didn't want to open her door.

Finally, Bosch heard the locks turning and the door opened to reveal the angry face of the woman Bosch recognized from the photo print he had found in Howard Elias's office.

'What do you want? Let me see some ID.'

Bosch badged her.

'Can we come in?'

'You're LAPD? This is West Hollywood, Mister. You're off your turf.'

She pushed the door closed but Edgar reached a strong arm up and stopped it. He pushed it all the way back open and stepped in, a mean look on his face.

'Don't you be closing the door on my face, Mistress Regina.'

Edgar said her name in a tone that indicated that he was subservient to no one. Regina stepped back to allow him space to enter. Bosch and Rider followed him in. They stepped into a dimly lit landing with stairs going up and down from it. Bosch looked down the stairs to his left and saw they retreated into complete darkness. The stairs going up led to a lighted room. He moved to them and started up.

'Hey, you can't just barge in here like this,' Regina said, but the protest was leaving her voice. 'You need a warrant.'

'We don't need anything, Mistress Regina, you invited us in. I'm Harry – or make that three-six-seven. We just talked on the phone, remember?'

She followed them up the stairs. Bosch turned and got his first full look at her. She was wearing a sheer black robe over a leather corset and black silk underwear. She wore black stockings and spike-heeled shoes. Her makeup consisted of dark eye liner and glaring red lipstick. It was a sad caricature of a depressing male fantasy.

'Been a long time since Halloween,' Bosch said. 'Who are you supposed to be?'

Regina ignored the question.

'What are you doing here?'

'We have questions. Sit down. I want to show you a picture.'

Bosch pointed to a black leather couch and the woman reluctantly went to it and sat down. He put his briefcase down on the coffee table and opened it. He nodded slightly to Edgar and started looking for the photo of Elias.

'Hey, where's he going?' Regina cried.

Edgar had moved to another set of stairs that led up to a loft.

'He's insuring our safety by making sure you don't have anybody hiding in the closet,' Bosch said. 'Now take a look at this picture, please.'

He slid the photo across the table and she looked at it without touching it.

'Recognize him?'

'What is this?'

'Do you recognize him?'

'Of course.'

'He a client?'

'Look, I don't have to tell you a fucking thing about—'

'IS HE A CLIENT?' Bosch yelled, silencing her.

Edgar came down from the loft and moved across the living room. He glanced into the alcove kitchen, saw nothing that interested him and went down the stairs to the landing. Bosch then heard his steps on the lower staircase as he descended into the darkness below.

'No, he isn't a client, okay? Now, will you please leave?'

'If he isn't a client then how do you recognize him?'

'What are you talking about? Haven't you been watching TV today?'

'Who is he?'

'He's that guy, the one that got killed on—'

'Harry?'

It was Edgar from below.

'What?'

'I think you ought to come down here a sec.'

Bosch turned to Rider and nodded.

'Take over, Kiz. Talk to her.'

Bosch went down the steps and made the turn in the landing. There was now a glowing red light emanating from the room below. As he came down Bosch saw Edgar was wide-eyed.

'What is it?'

'Check this out.'

As they crossed the room Bosch saw that it was a bedroom. One wall was completely mirrored. Against the opposite wall was a raised hospital-style bed with what looked like plastic sheets and restraints buckled across it. Next to it was a chair and a floor lamp with a red bulb in it.

Edgar led him into a walk-in closet. Another red bulb glowed from the ceiling. There was nothing hanging on the clothes rods running down either side of the closet. But a naked man stood spread-eagled on one side of the closet, his arms up and wrists handcuffed to the clothing rod. The cuffs were gold-plated and had ornate designs on them. The man was blindfolded and had a red ball gag in his mouth. There were red welts caused by fingernail scratches running down his chest. And between his legs a full liter bottle of Coke dangled at the end of a leather strap that was tied in a slipknot around the head of his penis.

'Jesus,' Bosch whispered.

'I asked him if he needed help and he shook his head no. I think he's her customer.'

'Take the gag out.'

Bosch pulled the blindfold up on the man's forehead while Edgar pulled out the gag. The man immediately jerked his face to the right and tried to turn away. He moved his arm and tried to use it to block the view of his face, but his cuffed wrist prevented him from hiding. The man was in his mid-thirties with a good build. It seemed as though he could certainly defend himself against the woman upstairs. If he wanted to.

'Please,' he said in a desperate voice. 'Leave me alone. I'm fine. Just leave me alone.'

'We're the police,' Bosch said. 'Are you sure?'

'Of course, I'm sure. You think if I needed help I wouldn't ask for it? I don't need you here. This is completely consensual and nonsexual. Just leave us alone.'

'Harry,' Edgar said, 'I think we ought to just step the fuck back out of here and forget we ever saw this guy.'

Bosch nodded and they stepped out of the closet. He looked around the room and saw that the chair had clothes draped over it. He went to them and checked the pockets of the pants. He pulled out the wallet and walked to the floor lamp, where he opened it and studied the driver's license in the red glow. He felt Edgar come up behind him and look over his shoulder.

'Recognize the name?'

'No, do you?'

685

Bosch shook his head and closed the wallet. He walked back and returned it to the pocket of the pants.

Rider and Regina were silent as they came back up the steps. Bosch studied Regina and thought he saw a look of pride and a slight smile on her face. She knew that what they had seen down there had shocked them. He glanced at Rider and saw that she, too, had registered the looks on their faces.

'Everything okay?' she asked.

'Everything's fine,' he said.

'What is it?'

Bosch ignored the question and looked at the other woman.

'Where are the keys?'

She put a little pout on her face and reached into her bra. Her hand came out with the tiny cuff key and she held it out to him. Bosch took it and handed it to Edgar.

'Go down and cut him loose. If he wants to stay after that, that's his business.'

'Harry, he said he—'

'I don't care what he said. I said cut him loose. We aren't going to leave here with some guy in shackles down there.'

Edgar went down the stairs while Bosch stared at Regina.

'That's what you get two hundred dollars an hour for?'

'Believe me, they get their money's worth. And, you know, they all come back for more. Hmm, I wonder what it is about men? Maybe you should try me sometime, Detective. Might be kind of fun.'

Bosch stared a long time before breaking away and looking at Rider.

'What've you got, Kiz?'

'Her real name is Virginia Lampley. She says she knows Elias from TV, not as a client. But she says Elias's investigator was here a few weeks ago, asking questions just like us.'

'Pelfry? What did he ask?'

'A bunch of bullshit,' Regina said before Rider could answer. 'He wanted to know if I knew anything about that little girl that was murdered last year. The daughter of the car czar from TV. I told him I didn't know why the hell he was asking me about that. What would I know about it? He tried to get rough but I got rough right back. I don't let men fuck with me. He left. I think somebody put you on the same wild goose chase he was on.'

'Maybe,' Bosch said.

There was silence for a moment. Bosch was distracted by what he had seen in the closet. He couldn't think of what else to ask.

'He's staying.'

It was Edgar. He came up the stairs and handed the cuff key back to Regina. She took it and made a big production out of returning it to her bra, looking at Bosch all the while.

'All right, let's go,' Bosch said.

'Are you sure you don't want to stay for a Coke, Detective?' Virginia Lampley asked, a clever smile on her face.

'We're going,' Bosch said.

They went silently down the steps to the door, Bosch the last in line. On the landing he looked down into the dark room. The glow of the red light

686

was still there and Bosch could see the faint outline of the man sitting on the chair in the corner of the room. His face was in darkness but Bosch could tell the man was looking up at him.

'Don't worry, Detective,' Regina said from behind him. 'I'll take good care of him.'

Bosch turned and looked at her from the door. That smile of hers was back.

20

On the way back to the station Rider repeatedly asked exactly what they had seen in the lower room but neither Bosch nor Edgar told her more than the basic fact that one of Mistress Regina's clients was shackled in the closet. Rider knew there was more to it and kept pressing but she got nowhere.

'The man down there is not important,' Bosch finally said as a means of ending that part of the discussion. 'We still don't know what Elias was doing with her picture and web address. Or for that matter, why he sent Pelfry to her.'

'I think she was lying,' Edgar said. 'She knows the whole story.'

'Maybe,' Bosch said. 'But if she knows the story, why keep it secret now that Elias is dead?'

'Pelfry is the key,' Rider said. 'We should run him down right now.'

'No,' Bosch said. 'Not tonight. It's late and I don't want to talk to Pelfry until we've gone through Elias's files and know what's in them. We master the files, then we brace Pelfry about Mistress Regina and everything else. First thing tomorrow.'

'What about the FBI?' Rider asked.

'We meet the FBI at eight. I'll figure something out by then.'

They drove the rest of the way in silence. Bosch dropped them off at their cars in the Hollywood station parking lot and reminded them to be at Parker Center at eight the following morning. He then parked his slickback but didn't turn in the key because the file cartons from Elias's office were still in the trunk. After locking the car he went to his own car.

He checked the clock as he was pulling out onto Wilcox and saw it was ten-thirty. He knew it was late but he decided to make one last call before going home. As he drove through Laurel Canyon to the Valley, he kept thinking about the man in the walk-in closet and how he had turned his face away, wishing not to be seen. Working homicide for so many years, Bosch could not be surprised anymore by the horrors people inflicted on each other. But the horrors people saved for themselves were a different story.

He took Ventura Boulevard west to Sherman Oaks. It was a busy Saturday night. On the other side of the hill the city could be a tinderbox of tensions but on the main drag in the Valley the bars and coffee shops seemed full. Bosch saw the red-coated valets running to get cars in front of Pinot Bistro and the other upscale restaurants that lined the boulevard. He saw teenagers cruising with the top down. Everyone was oblivious to the seething hatred and anger that churned in other parts of the city – beneath the surface like an undiscovered fault line waiting to open up and swallow all above.

At Kester he turned north and then made a quick turn into a neighborhood of tract houses sandwiched between the boulevard and the Ventura Freeway. The houses were small and with no distinct style. The hiss of the freeway was always present. They were cops' houses except they cost between four and five hundred thousand dollars and few cops could afford them. Bosch's old partner Frankie Sheehan had bought early and bought well. He was sitting on a quarter of a million dollars in equity. His retirement plan, if he made it to retirement.

Bosch pulled to the curb in front of Sheehan's house and left the car running. He got out his phone, looked up Sheehan's number in his phone book, and made the call. Sheehan picked up after two rings, his voice alert. He'd been awake.

'Frankie, it's Harry.'

'My man.'

'I'm out front. Why don't you come out and we'll take a drive.'

'Where to?'

'It doesn't matter.'

Silence.

'Frankie?'

'Okay, give me a couple minutes.'

Bosch put the phone away and reached into his coat pocket for a smoke that wasn't there.

'Damn,' he said.

While he waited he thought about the time he and Sheehan were looking for a drug dealer suspected of having wiped out a rival's operation by going into a rock house with an Uzi and killing everyone in it – six people, customers and dealers alike.

They'd repeatedly pounded on the door of the suspect's apartment but no one answered. They were thinking about their options when Sheehan heard a tiny voice from inside the apartment saying, 'Come in, come in.' They knocked on the door once again and called out that it was the police. They waited and listened. Again the voice called out, 'Come in, come in.'

Bosch tried the knob and it turned. The door was unlocked. Assuming combat stance they entered the apartment only to find it empty – except for a large green parrot in a cage in the living room. And lying right there in full view on a kitchen table was an Uzi submachine gun broken down and ready for cleaning. Bosch walked over to the door and knocked on it once again. The parrot called out, 'Come in, come in.'

A few minutes later, when the suspect returned from the hardware store with the gun oil he needed to finish his work on the Uzi, he was arrested. Ballistics matched the gun to the killings and he was convicted after a judge refused to throw out the fruits of the search. Though the defendant claimed the entry of the apartment was without permission and unlawful, the judge ruled that Bosch and Sheehan were acting in good faith when they acted on the invitation from the parrot. The case was still winding its way through the nation's appellate courts, while the killer remained in jail.

The Jeep's front passenger door opened and Sheehan got into the car.

'When did you get this ride?' he asked.

'When they made me start driving a slickback.'

'Oh, yeah, forgot about that.'

'Yeah, you RHD bigshots don't have to worry about that shit.'

'So, what's up? You got your ass out in the wind on this case, don't you?'

'Yeah, it's out there. How're Margaret and the girls doing?'

'They're all fine. What are we doing? Riding, talking, what?'

'I don't know. Is that Irish place still over on Van Nuys?'

'No, that one's gone. Tell you what, go on up to Oxnard and go right. There's a little sports bar down there.'

Bosch pulled away from the curb and started following the directions.

'I was just thinking about the Polly-wants-an-Uzi case,' he said.

Sheehan laughed.

'That one still cracks me up. I can't believe it's shot the rapids this far. I hear the douche bag's down to one last shot – El Supremo Court.'

'It'll make it. It woulda got shot down by now if it wasn't going to fly – no pun intended.'

'Well, what's it been, eight years? We got our money's worth, even if they do kick him loose.'

'Yeah, six murders, eight years. Sounds fair.'

'Six douche bags.'

'You still like saying douche bag, don't you?'

'Yeah, I'm partial to it. So you didn't come over the hill to talk about parrots and douche bags and old times, did you?'

'No, Frankie. I need to ask you about the Kincaid thing.'

'Why me?'

'Why do you think? You were lead detective.'

'Everything I know is in the files. You should be able to get them. You're lead on Elias.'

'I got 'em. But the files don't always have everything in them.'

Sheehan pointed to a red neon sign and Bosch pulled over. There was a parking place at the curb right outside the bar's door.

'This place is always pretty dead,' Sheehan said. 'Even Saturday nights. I don't know how the guy makes it by. Must be taking numbers or selling weed on the side.'

'Frankie,' Bosch said, 'between you and me, I gotta know about the fingerprints. I don't want to be chasing my tail out there. I mean, I got no reason to doubt you. But I want to know if you heard anything, you know what I mean?'

Sheehan got out of the Cherokee without a word and walked to the door. Bosch watched him go in and then got out himself. Inside, the place was just about empty. Sheehan was sitting at the bar. The bartender was drawing a beer off the tap. Bosch took the stool next to his former partner and said, 'Make it two.'

Bosch took out a twenty and put it on the bar. Sheehan still hadn't looked at him since he had asked the question.

The bartender put down the frosted mugs on napkins that advertised a Superbowl party almost three months before. He took Bosch's twenty and went down to the cash register. In unison Bosch and Sheehan took long pulls on their drinks.

'Ever since O.J.,' Sheehan said.

'What's that?'

'You know what I'm talking about. Ever since the Juice, nothing is solid anymore. No evidence, no cop, nothing. You can take anything you want into a courtroom and there still will be somebody who can tear it to shreds, drop it on the floor and piss on it. Everybody questions everything. Even cops. Even partners.'

Bosch took more of his beer before saying anything.

'I'm sorry, Frankie. I got no reason to doubt you or the prints. It's just that weeding through this Elias stuff, it looks like he was going into court next week with the idea of proving who killed the girl. And he wasn't talking about Harris. Somebody—'

'Who?'

'I don't know. But I'm trying to look at it from his side of things. If he had somebody other than Harris, then how the hell did these prints end up on—'

'Elias was a fucking mutt. And as soon as they get him in the ground I'm gonna go out there one night and do my granddaddy's Irish jig on his grave. Then I'm gonna piss on it and never think about Elias again. All I can say is that it's too fucking bad that Harris wasn't with him on that train. Goddamned murderer. That would have been hitting the quinella, the both of them being put down together.'

Sheehan held his glass up in a toast to Elias's killer and then took a deep swallow. Bosch could almost feel the hate radiating from him.

'So nobody fucked with the scene,' Bosch said. 'The prints are legit.'

'Fucking A legit. The room was sealed by patrol. Nobody went in until I got there. I then watched over everything – we were dealing with the Kincaid family and I knew what that meant. The car czar and heavy contributor to local political coffers. I was on the straight and narrow with everything. The prints were on her schoolbook – a geography book. SID got four fingers on one side and a thumb on the other – as if he had picked the book up by the binding. Those prints were perfect. The guy must've been sweating like a pig when he left 'em because they were grade A perfect.'

He drained his glass and then held it up so the bartender would see he needed a refill.

'I can't believe you can't smoke anymore in a fucking bar in this city,' Sheehan said. 'Fucking douche bags.'

'Yeah.'

'Anyway, we ran everything and Harris pops up. Ex-con, did time for assault, burglary, he's got about as much a legitimate reason for his prints being in her room as I have a chance of winning the lottery – and I don't fucking play. So bingo, we got our man. We go hook him up. Remember, at that time the girl's body hadn't turned up. We were operating on the belief she might still be alive somewhere. We were wrong but we didn't know it at the time. So we hook him up, bring him downtown and put him in the room. Only this motherfucker won't tell us the time of day. Three days and we get nothing. We never even took him to a cell at night. He was in that room seventy-two straight hours. We worked in teams and in shifts and we could not crack his egg. Never gave us jack shit. I tell you what, I'd like to kill the fuck, but I gotta respect him for that. He was the best I ever went against.'

Sheehan took a double gulp from his new beer. Bosch was still only halfway through his first. He was content to let Sheehan talk and tell the story at his own pace without interrupting him with questions.

'On the last day some of the guys lost it a little bit. Did things.'

Bosch closed his eyes. He had been wrong about Sheehan.

'Me, too, Harry.'

He said it matter of factly, as if it felt good to finally say it out loud. He drank more of his beer, turned on his stool and looked about the bar as if seeing it for the first time. There was a TV mounted in a corner. It was tuned to ESPN.

'We're off the record here, right, Harry?'

'Sure.'

Sheehan turned back and leaned toward Bosch in a conspiratorial sort of way.

'What Harris says happened . . . happened. But that doesn't excuse what he did. He rapes and strangles that little girl; we stick a pencil in his ear. Big fucking deal. He gets off and I'm the new Mark Fuhrman – a racist cop who planted evidence. I just wish somebody could tell me how the fuck I could've planted those prints?'

He was getting loud. Luckily, only the bartender was noticing.

'I know,' Bosch said. 'I'm sorry, man. I shouldn't have asked.'

Sheehan went on as if he hadn't heard Bosch.

'I guess I always carried around a set of throw-down prints that belonged to a douche bag I wanted to send away. I then put them on the book – don't ask me how – and *voilà*, we got our douche bag. Only why would I pick Harris to pin it on? I never knew the mutt or had anything to do with him. And there's nobody on this planet that can prove I did because it's not there to be proved.'

'You're right.'

Sheehan shook his head and looked down into his beer.

'I quit caring about shit when that jury came in and said not guilty. When they said I was guilty . . . when they believed that man instead of us.'

Bosch remained silent. He knew that Sheehan had to say his piece.

'We're losing the battle, man. I see that now. It's all a game. The fucking lawyers, what they can do to you. To the evidence. I give up, Harry. I really do. I already decided. It's twenty-five and out for me. I got eight more months and I'm counting the fuckers down. I'm gonna punch out, move on up to Blue Heaven and leave this toilet for all the douche bags.'

'I think that's a good idea, Frankie,' Bosch said quietly.

He couldn't think of what else he could say. He was hurt and stunned by his friend's lapse into a complete state of hate and cynicism. He understood it but was simply surprised by the complete toll it had taken. He was also disappointed in himself and privately embarrassed at how wholeheartedly he had defended Sheehan to Carla Entrenkin.

'I remember on that last day,' Sheehan said. 'I was in there with him. In the room. And I got so fucking angry I just wanted to take my gun out and blow his shit away. But I knew I couldn't. Because he knew where she was. He had the girl!'

Bosch just nodded.

'We had tried everything and got nothing. He broke us before we could break him. It got down to where I was just begging him to tell us. It was embarrassing, Harry.'

'And what did he do?'

'He just stared at me as if I wasn't there. He said nothing. He did nothing. And then . . . then the anger just came over me like . . . like I don't know what. Like it was a bone caught in my throat. Like it never had before. There was a trash can in the corner of the room. I went over and pulled the bag out and just pulled it right down over his fucking head. And I grabbed it around his neck and I held it and I held it and . . .'

Sheehan started crying and trying to finish.

'. . . and they . . . they had to pull me off of him.'

He put his elbows on the bar and pressed the heels of his palms into his eyes. For a long time he didn't move. Bosch saw a drop fall from his chin and into his beer. He reached over and put his hand on his old partner's shoulder.

'It's okay, Frankie.'

Without moving his hands away from his face, Sheehan spoke.

'You see, Harry, I became the very thing that I spent all these years hunting. I wanted to kill him right there and then. I would have if my guys hadn't come in. I'm never going to be able to forget that.'

'It's okay, man.'

Sheehan drank some beer and seemed to recover somewhat.

'After I did what I did, that opened the door. The other guys, they did that thing with the pencil – popped his fucking ear drum. We all became monsters. Like Vietnam, going wild in the villages. We probably would've killed the guy but you know what saved him? The girl. Stacey Kincaid saved him.'

'How's that?'

'They found the body. We got the word and went out to the scene. We left Harris in a cell. Alive. He was lucky the word came when it did.'

He stopped to take another gulp of beer.

'I went out there – just a block from Harris's place. She was pretty much decomposed, the young ones go fast. But I remember how she looked. Like a little angel, her arms out like she was flying . . .'

Bosch remembered the pictures from the newspapers. Stacey Kincaid had been a pretty little girl.

'Harry, leave me alone now,' Sheehan said quietly. 'I'm going to walk back.'

'No, let me give you a ride.'

'No thanks. I'm walking.'

'You sure you're all right?'

'I'm fine. Just a little worked up. That's all. This is going to stay between us, right?'

'Till the end, man.'

Sheehan tried a weak smile. But he still didn't look at Bosch.

'Do me one favor, Hieronymus.'

Bosch remembered when they had been a team. They only used their formal names, Hieronymus and Francis, when they were talking seriously and from the heart.

'Sure, Francis. What?'

'When you catch the guy who did Elias, I don't care if it's a cop or not, shake his hand for me. You tell him he's my hero. But tell him he missed a good chance. Tell him he should've gotten Harris, too.'

A half hour later Bosch opened the door to his home. He found his bed empty. But this time he was too tired to stay awake waiting for Eleanor. He started stripping off his clothes and thinking about his plans for the next day. He finally sat down on the bed ready for sleep and reached for the light. The moment he was in darkness, the phone rang.

He turned the light back on and picked up the phone.

'You bastard.'

A woman's voice – familiar, but he couldn't place it.

'Who is this?'

'Carla Entrenkin, who do you think? Do you really think I wouldn't know what you did?'

'I don't know what you're talking about. What happened?'

'I just watched Channel 4. Your buddy Harvey Button.'

'What did he have?'

'Oh, he blew it up real big. Let's see if I can quote him correctly. "A link between Elias and an Internet prostitution ring was found in Elias's office, a source close to the investigation says. It is believed by this source that Elias may have had liaisons with at least one of the women who advertised her services as a dominatrix on the web site." I think that about sums it up. I hope you are happy.'

'I didn't—'

'Don't bother.'

She hung up. Bosch sat there a long time thinking about what she had said.

'Chastain, you asshole,' he said out loud.

He turned out the light again and dropped back on the bed. He was soon asleep and having the same dream again. He was riding Angels Flight, going up. Only now there was a little blonde girl seated across the aisle from him. She looked at him with sad and empty eyes.

21

Bosch had a surprise waiting for him when he pushed the supply cart stacked with file boxes through the door of Deputy Chief Irving's conference room. It was quarter to eight on Sunday morning. There were six FBI agents already crowded into the room and waiting. The surprise was the lead agent who stepped over to Bosch, his hand out and a smile on his face.

'Harry Bosch,' the man said.

'Roy Lindell,' Bosch replied.

Bosch pushed the cart over to the table and took the man's hand.

'You're on this? What happened to OC?'

'Organized crime was getting boring. Especially after the Tony Aliso case. Hard to top that one, don't you think?'

'Yeah.'

A couple of years earlier they had worked the Aliso murder – the 'Trunk Music' case, according to the local media. Bosch and Lindell had started out as adversaries, but by the time the case was concluded in Las Vegas there was a respect between the two that certainly wasn't shared between the two agencies they worked for. Bosch immediately took Lindell's assignment to the Elias case as a good sign.

'Listen,' Lindell said, 'I think we have a few minutes. You want to grab a cup of coffee and talk about things?'

'Sounds like a plan.'

As they walked down the hall to the elevator they were met by Chastain, who was heading to the conference room. Bosch introduced Lindell.

'You guys going for coffee? I'll come with you.'

'No, that's okay,' Bosch said. 'We've got some stuff to talk about . . . and I don't want it coming out of Harvey Button's mouth on the news later. Know what I mean?'

'I don't know what you're talking about, Bosch.'

Bosch said nothing. Chastain looked at Lindell and then back at Bosch.

'Never mind the coffee,' he said. 'I don't need artificial stimulants, anyway.'

When they were alone at the elevator lobby Bosch warned Lindell about Chastain.

'He's leaking,' he said. 'You see Channel Four last night?'

'The Internet dominatrix thing?'

'Yeah. Six people knew about that. Me, my two partners, Chastain, Carla Entrenkin and Deputy Chief Irving. I can vouch for my partners and I doubt

Entrenkin would leak anything negative about Elias. Either Irving or Chastain talked to Harvey Button. My bet is on Chastain. Irving's been trying to put a clamp on things from the start.'

'Well, was the story bullshit or what?'

'Looks that way. We can't make a connection. Whoever leaked it did it to smear Elias, even things up a bit.'

'I'll watch him. But you know sometimes leaks aren't from the obvious source.'

The elevator opened and Lindell stepped on, leaving Bosch standing there thinking about Irving and whether it was possible that he was the leak.

'You coming?' Lindell asked.

Bosch stepped onto the elevator and pushed the button for the third floor.

'You check the news this morning?' Lindell asked. 'How's it going out there?'

'So far so good. A couple fires last night, but that was about it. No looting and it's pretty quiet now. Supposed to be rain coming in by tomorrow. Maybe that will help.'

They went into the cafeteria and took their coffees to a table. Bosch checked his watch and saw it was five before eight. He looked at Lindell.

'So?'

Lindell laughed.

'So what the fuck. We going to divvy this up or what?'

'Yeah. I got a deal for you, Roy. A good deal.'

'Let's hear it.'

'You can have it. I'll step back and let you run the show. I just want one thing. I want my team to run with the original case. Stacey Kincaid. We'll take the original murder book and review everything RHD did on the case. Then we'll take everything Elias did and go from there.'

Lindell's eyes narrowed their focus as he wondered what this meant. Bosch continued.

'It looks like Elias's plan was to go into court this week and try to prove that Michael Harris didn't kill her. He was going to name her killer and—'

'Who?'

'That's the million-dollar question. We don't know. He was keeping it in his head instead of his files. But that's why I want the case. Because if he had a bead on somebody, that somebody's a pretty good suspect for the Angels Flight murders.'

Lindell looked down at his smoking coffee and was quiet a long moment.

'Sounds like lawyer bullshit to me. Grandstanding. How was he gonna find the killer if you guys on the PD didn't? That is, if the killer really wasn't Michael Harris, like every cop and white person in this town believes.'

Bosch hiked his shoulders.

'Even if he was wrong – even if he was going to name somebody as a smoke screen, it could have made him a target.'

He purposely wasn't telling Lindell everything – particularly about the mystery notes. He wanted the FBI agent to think that Bosch's team would be chasing rainbows while he would be commanding the real investigation.

'So you run with that and I chase down bad cops, is that the deal?'

'Pretty much. Chastain should have a head start for you. First of all, he's the most familiar with the Black Warrior thing. He handled the IAD investigation on it. And—'

'Yeah, but he cleared everybody on it.'

'Maybe he messed up. Or maybe he was told to clear everybody.'

Lindell nodded that he understood the suggestion.

'Also, his crew was supposedly going through Elias's files yesterday and making a list. And I just brought in five more boxes of files. From all of that you'll get a list of guys to talk to. I think you're in good shape.'

'If I'm in such great shape why are you giving this side of things to me?'

''Cause I'm a nice guy.'

'Bosch, you're holding out.'

'I just have a hunch, that's all.'

'That what, Harris really was framed?'

'I don't know. But something wasn't right with the case. I want to find out what it was.'

'So meantime I'm stuck with Chastain and his crew.'

'Yup. That's the deal.'

'Well, what am I going to do with them? You just told me Chastain's a leak.'

'Send them out for coffee and then run away and hide.'

Lindell laughed.

'This is what I would do,' Bosch then added on a serious note. 'I'd put two of them on Elias and two on Perez. You know, doing the paper, managing the evidence, taking the autopsies – which will probably be today anyway. That will keep them busy and out of your way. Regardless of whether it's them or not, you've got to put at least one body on Perez. We've treated her as an also-ran, which she obviously was. But you gotta do the due diligence on it or it can come back on you if you ever go to court and the lawyer asks why Perez wasn't pursued as the primary target.'

'Right, right. We gotta cover all the bases.'

'Right.'

Lindell nodded but said nothing further.

'So come on, do we have a deal?' Bosch prompted.

'Yeah. Sounds like a plan to me. But I want to know what you and your people are doing. You keep in touch.'

'You got it. Oh, and by the way, one of the IAD guys is a Spanish speaker. Fuentes. Put him on Perez.'

Lindell nodded and pushed back from the table. He left his coffee cup there, untouched. Bosch took his with him.

On his way through the anteroom to Irving's conference room, Bosch noticed that the deputy chief's adjutant was not at his desk. He saw a telephone message pad on the blotter and reached down and grabbed it as he passed by. He put it in his pocket and entered the conference room.

Bosch's partners and the IAD men were now in the conference room. Irving was there also. It was very crowded. After some brief introductions the floor was turned over to Bosch, who briefed the newcomers and Irving on the investigation up to that point. He left out specific details about the visit to Virginia Lampley's apartment, making that part of the investigation appear to be at a dead end. He also made no mention at all of his barroom talk with Frankie Sheehan. When he was done he nodded to Irving, who then took the floor. Bosch moved over to the wall and leaned next to a bulletin board Irving had apparently had installed for the investigators to use.

Irving began speaking of the political tensions surrounding the case like a storm pressure cell. He mentioned that protest marches were scheduled that day in front of three of the South End police stations and at Parker Center. He said City Councilman Royal Sparks and Reverend Preston Tuggins were scheduled to be guests that morning on a local meet-the-press type of television show called *Talk of L.A.* He said the chief of police had met with Tuggins and other South Central church leaders the night before to call in markers and urge them to call for calm and restraint from the pulpits during the morning's services.

'We are sitting on a powder keg here, people,' Irving said. 'And the way to defuse it is to solve this case one way or the other . . . quickly.'

While he talked, Bosch took out the phone message pad and wrote on it. He then checked the room to make sure all eyes were on Irving and quietly tore off the top sheet. He reached over and tacked it to the bulletin board and then nonchalantly moved inch by inch down the wall and away from the board. The sheet he had put on the board had Chastain's name on it. In the message section it said: 'Harvey Button called, said thanks for the tip. Will call back later.'

Irving wound up his comments with a mention about the Channel 4 story.

'Someone in this room leaked information to a television reporter yesterday. I am warning you people that we will not have this. That one story was your grace period. One more leak and you people will be the ones under investigation.'

He looked around the room at the LAPD faces, to make sure the message was clear.

'Okay, that is it,' he finally said. 'I will leave you to it. Detective Bosch, Agent Lindell? I would like to be briefed at noon on our progress.'

'No problem, Chief,' Lindell said before Bosch could respond. 'I will be talking to you then.'

Fifteen minutes later Bosch was walking down the hallway to the elevators again. Edgar and Rider were following behind.

'Harry, where are we going?' Edgar asked.

'We'll work out of Hollywood station.'

'What? Doing what? Who is going to run the show?'

'Lindell. I made a deal. He runs the show. We do something else.'

'Suits me,' Edgar said. 'Too many agents and too much brass around here anyway.'

Bosch got to the elevators and pushed the call button.

'What exactly are we doing, Harry?' Rider asked.

He turned and looked at them.

'Starting over,' he said.

22

The squad room was completely empty, which was unusual, even for a Sunday. Under the twelve-and-twelve readiness plan all detectives not assigned to time-critical investigations were to be in uniform and out on the street. The last time such deployment had been instituted was after a major earthquake had rocked the city in 1994. The Elias murder was a social rather than a geologic cataclysm, but its magnitude was just as great.

Bosch carried the box containing Elias's files on the Black Warrior case to what they called the homicide table, a raft of desks pushed up against each other to create a huge boardroom-like table. The section that belonged to team one, Bosch's team, was at the end, near an alcove of file cabinets. He put the box in the middle, where his team's three desks conjoined.

'Dig in,' he said.

'Harry . . . ,' Rider said, not happy with his lack of direction.

'Okay, listen, this is what I want. Kiz, you're going to be master of the ship. Jerry and I will work the field.'

Rider groaned. Master of the ship meant that she was to be the keeper of the facts. She was to become familiar with all facets of the files, a walking compendium of the details of the investigation. Since they were starting off with an entire carton of files, this was a lot of work. It also meant she would not be doing much, if anything, in the way of field investigation. And no detective wants to be stuck in a windowless and empty office all day.

'I know,' Bosch said. 'But I think you are best for it. We've got a ton of stuff here and your mind and your computer will be best for keeping track of it.'

'Next time I get the field.'

'There might not be a next time if we don't do something this time. Let's see what we got here.'

They spent the next ninety minutes going through Elias's files on the Harris case, pointing out specific items to each other when they seemed to warrant attention, other times tossing files back into the box when their importance was not apparent.

Bosch spent his time with the investigative files that Elias had subpoenaed from the LAPD. He had a copy of the entire RHD murder book. Reading the daily investigative summaries turned in by Sheehan and other RHD detectives, Bosch noted that the case seemed initially to be lacking a focus. Stacey Kincaid had been taken from her room in the night, her abductor jimmying the lock on a bedroom window with a screwdriver and then grabbing the girl while she slept. Initially suspecting an inside job, the detectives interviewed the gardeners, the pool man, a local maintenance man, a plumber who had been in the house two weeks earlier, as well as the sanitation men and postal workers who had the route that included the Kincaids' home in Brentwood. Teachers, janitors and even fellow students from Stacey's private school in West Hollywood were interviewed. But the wide net being thrown by Sheehan and his cohorts was pulled in after the lab came up with the fingerprint match between the missing girl's schoolbook and Michael Harris. The case then shifted to a complete focus on locating Harris, taking him into custody and then attempting to make him confess to what he had done with the girl.

The second section of the file also dealt with the crime scene investigation and efforts to connect Harris to the body through scientific analysis and technology. This proved to be a dead end. The girl's body had been found by two homeless men in a vacant lot. The body was naked and badly decomposed after four days. It had apparently been washed after her death and therefore was lacking any significant microscopic evidence that could be analyzed and connected to Harris's apartment or car. Though the girl appeared to have been raped, no bodily fluids belonging to her attacker were recovered. Her clothes were never found. The ligature that had been used to strangle her had been cut away by her killer and that, too, was never found. In the end, the only evidence that connected Harris to the crime was his fingerprints on the book in Stacey's bedroom and the disposal of the body in the vacant lot less than two blocks from his apartment.

Bosch knew that was usually more than enough to win a conviction. He had worked cases in which convictions were won with less evidence. But that was before O.J. Simpson, before juries looked at police in Los Angeles with suspicious and judging eyes.

Bosch was writing a list of things to do and people to be interviewed when Edgar cried out.

'Yahtzee!'

Bosch and Rider looked at him and waited for an explanation.

'Remember the mystery notes?' Edgar said. 'The second or third one said license plates prove he's innocent?'

'Wait a second,' Bosch said.

He opened his briefcase and took out the file containing the notes.

'The third one. "License plates prove his innocense." Came in April five. Innocence spelled wrong.'

'Okay, here's Elias's file on subpoena returns. Got one here dated April fifteen for Hollywood Wax and Shine. That's where Harris worked before they arrested him. It seeks – quote – "copies of all records and receipts of customer orders and billings containing license plate numbers of said customers between the dates of April one and June fifteen of last year." It's gotta be what the note was talking about.'

Bosch leaned back in his chair to think about this.

'This is a subpoena return, right? It was approved.'

'Right.'

'Well, April one and June fifteen, that's seventy-five days. There—'

'Seventy-six days,' Rider corrected.

'Seventy-six days. That would be a lot of receipts. We got none here and there weren't any in the office I saw. There should be boxes of receipts.'

'Maybe he returned them,' Edgar said.

'You said he subpoenaed copies.'

Edgar hiked his shoulders.

'Another thing, why those days?' Bosch asked. 'The murder of the girl was July twelve. Why not subpoena the receipts right up until then?'

'Because he knew what he was looking for,' Rider said. 'Or knew within the parameters of those dates.'

'Knew what?'

They dropped into silence. Bosch's mind was running the puzzle but coming up empty. The license plate clue was still as mysterious as the Mistress Regina lead. Then by joining the two mysteries he came up with something.

'Pelfry again,' he said. 'We need to talk to him.'

He stood up.

'Jerry, get on the phones. See if you can run down Pelfry and set up an interview for as soon as you can get it. I'm going out back for a few minutes.'

Normally, when Bosch told his partners he was going out back it meant he was going outside the building to have a smoke. As he walked toward the rear doorway, Rider called after him.

'Harry, don't do it.'

He waved without turning back.

'Don't worry, I'm not.'

Out in the lot Bosch stood and looked around. He knew he had done some of his best analytical thinking while standing outside smoking. He hoped he could put something together now, without the aid of a smoke. He looked into the sand jar that the station's smokers used and saw a half-smoked cigarette protruding from the sand. There was lipstick on it. He decided he wasn't that desperate yet.

He thought about the mystery notes. He knew because of postmarks and the markings made on the notes by Elias that they had numbers two, three and four, but not the first note. The meaning of the fourth note – the warning Elias was carrying with him – was obvious. The third note they now had a line on, thanks to the subpoena return Edgar had come across. But the second note – Dot the i humbert humbert – still made no sense to Bosch.

He looked at the cigarette protruding from the sand again but once more dismissed it. He remembered he carried no matches or lighter anyway.

It suddenly occurred to him that the one other piece of the puzzle that seemed to stand out as making no sense, at least so far, was the Mistress Regina connection – whatever that was.

Bosch turned and quickly headed back into the station. Edgar and Rider had their heads down and into the paperwork when he came to the table. Bosch immediately began looking through the stacks of files.

'Who has the Mistress Regina file?'

'Over here,' Edgar said.

He handed over the file and Bosch opened it and took out the photo printout of the dominatrix. He then put it down next to one of the mystery notes and tried to make a comparison between the printing on the note and the printing below the photo – the web page address. It was impossible for him to determine if the same hand had printed both lines. He was no expert and there were no obvious anomalies in the printing to make a comparison easy.

When Bosch took his hand off the printout, its top and bottom edges rose an inch off the desk, telling him that at one time the page had been folded top and bottom, as if to be placed in an envelope.

'I think this is the first note,' he said.

Bosch had often found that when he made a logic breakthrough it was like clearing a clog in a drain. The pipe was open and other breaks soon came. It happened now. He saw what he could have and maybe should have seen all along.

'Jerry, call Elias's secretary. Right now. Ask her if he had a color printer in the office. We should have seen this – *I* should have seen it.'

'Seen what?'

'Just make the call.'

Edgar started looking through a notebook for a phone number. Rider got up from her spot and came around next to Bosch. She looked down at the printout. She was now riding on Bosch's wave. She saw where he was going.

'This was the first one,' Bosch said. 'Only he didn't keep the envelope because he probably thought it was crank mail.'

'But it probably was,' Edgar said, the phone to his ear. 'We were there, the woman didn't know the man and didn't know what the hell we—'

He stopped and listened when his line was picked up.

'Mrs Quimby? It is Detective Edgar from yesterday? I have one quick question for you. Do you know if there was a color printer in the office? A printer that could print out stuff from one of the computers. In color.'

He waited and listened, his eyes on Bosch and Rider.

'Thank you, Mrs Quimby.'

He hung up.

'No color printer.'

Bosch nodded and looked down at the printout of Mistress Regina.

'We should have picked up on this yesterday,' Rider said.

Bosch nodded and started to ask Edgar if he had contacted Pelfry, the private investigator, when his pager went off. He cut it off and pulled it off his belt. It was his home number. Eleanor.

'Yeah, I talked to him,' Edgar said. 'He'll meet us at noon at his office. I didn't mention anything about receipts or this Regina. I just said we needed to talk.'

'Okay.'

Bosch picked up his phone and punched in his home number. Eleanor answered after three rings. She sounded either sleepy or sad.

'Eleanor.'

'Harry.'

'Everything all right?'

He slid back into his seat and Rider went back to hers.

'I'm fine . . . I just . . .'

'When did you get in?'

'A little while ago.'

'Did you win?'

'I didn't really play. After you called me there last night . . . I left.'

Bosch leaned forward and put an elbow on the table, a hand against his forehead.

'Well . . . where'd you go?'

'A hotel . . . Harry, I just came back for some clothes and things. I . . .'

'Eleanor?'

There was a long silence on the phone. Bosch heard Edgar say he was going to get some coffee in the watch office. Rider said she'd go along, even though Bosch knew she didn't drink coffee. She had an assortment of herbal teas she kept in the drawer of her desk.

'Harry, it's not right,' Eleanor said.

'What are you talking about, Eleanor?'

Another long moment of silence went by before she answered.

'I was thinking about that movie we saw last year. About the *Titanic.*'

'I remember.'

'And the girl in that. She fell in love with that boy, that she only met right there on the boat. And it was . . . I mean, she loved him so much. So much that at the end she wouldn't leave. She didn't take the lifeboat so she would be with him.'

'I remember, Eleanor.'

He remembered her crying in the seat next to him and his smiling and not being able to understand how a film would affect her in such a way.

'You cried.'

'Yes. It's because everybody wants that kind of love. And, Harry, you deserve that from me. I—'

'No, Eleanor, what you give me is more than—'

'She jumped from a lifeboat *back* onto the *Titanic,* Harry.' She laughed a little bit. But it sounded sad to Bosch. 'I guess nobody can ever top that.'

'You're right. Nobody can. That's why it was a movie. Listen . . . you are all I've ever wanted, Eleanor. You don't have to do anything for me.'

'Yes, I do. I do . . . I love you, Harry. But not enough. You deserve better.'

'Eleanor, no . . . please. I . . .'

'I'm going to go away for a while. Think about things.'

'Will you wait there? I'll be home in fifteen minutes. We can talk about—'

'No, no. That's why I paged. I can't do this in person.'

He could tell she was crying.

'Well, I'm coming up there.'

'I won't be here,' she said urgently. 'I packed the car before I paged you. I knew you'd try to come.'

Bosch put his hand over his eyes. He wanted to be in darkness.

'Where will you be?'

'I'm not sure.'

'Will you call?'

'Yes, I'll call.'

'Are you all right?'

'I'm . . . I'll be fine.'

'Eleanor, I love you. I know I never said that enough but I—'

She made a shushing sound in the phone and he stopped.

'I love you, Harry, but I have to do this.'

703

After a long moment, during which he felt a deep tearing inside, he said, 'Okay, Eleanor.'

The silence that followed was as dark as the inside of a coffin. His coffin.

'Good-bye, Harry,' she finally said. 'I'll see you.'

She hung up. Bosch took his hand away from his face and the phone from his ear. In his mind he saw a swimming pool, its surface as smooth as a blanket on a bed. He remembered a time long before when he had been told his mother was dead and that he was alone in the world. He ran to that pool and dove beneath the calm surface, into its warm water. At the bottom, he screamed until his air was gone and his chest ached. Until he had to choose between staying there and dying, or going up and life.

Bosch now longed for that pool and its warm water. He wanted to scream until his lungs burst inside him.

'Everything okay?'

He looked up. It was Rider and Edgar. Edgar carried a steaming cup of coffee. Rider had a look that said she was concerned or maybe even scared by the look she was seeing on Bosch's face.

'Everything's cool,' Bosch said. 'Everything's fine.'

23

They had ninety minutes to kill before the meeting with Pelfry. Bosch told Edgar to drive over to Hollywood Wax and Shine, on Sunset not far from the station. Edgar pulled to the curb and they sat there watching. Business was slow. Most of the men in orange coveralls who dried and polished the cars for minimum wage and tips were sitting around, drying rags draped over their shoulders, waiting. Most of them stared balefully at the slickback as if the police were to blame.

'I guess people aren't that interested in having their cars washed when they might end up turned over or torched,' Edgar said.

Bosch didn't answer.

'Bet they all wish they were in Michael Harris's shoes,' Edgar continued, staring back at the workers. 'Hell, *I'd* trade three days in an interview room and pencils in my ears to be a millionaire.'

'So then you believe him,' Bosch said.

Bosch hadn't told him about Frankie Sheehan's barroom confession. Edgar was quiet a moment and then nodded.

'Yeah, Harry, I guess I sort of do.'

Bosch wondered how he had been so blind as to not even have considered that the torturing of a suspect could be true. He wondered what it was about Edgar that made him accepting of the suspect's story over the cops'. Was it his experience as a cop or as a black man? Bosch assumed it had to be the latter and it depressed him because it gave Edgar an edge he could never have.

'I'm gonna go in, talk to the manager,' Bosch said. 'Maybe you should stay with the car.'

'Fuck that. They won't touch it.'

They got out and locked the car.

As they walked toward the store Bosch thought about the orange coveralls and wondered if it was coincidence. He guessed that most of the men working at the car wash were ex-cons or fresh out of county lockup – institutions in which they also had to wear orange coveralls.

Inside the store Bosch bought a cup of coffee and asked for the manager. The cashier pointed down a hallway to an open door. On the way down the hall, Edgar said, 'I feel like a Coke but I don't think I can drink a Coke after what I saw last night in that bitch's closet.'

A man was sitting at a desk in the small, windowless office with his feet up on one of the open drawers. He looked up at Bosch and Edgar and said, 'Yes, Officers, what can I do for you?'

Bosch smiled at the man's deduction. He knew he had to be part businessman, part parole officer. Most of the polishers were ex-cons. It was the only job they could get. That meant the manager had seen his share of cops and knew how to pick them out. Either that or he saw them pull up in the slickback.

'We're working a case,' Bosch began. 'The Howard Elias case.'

The manager whistled.

'A few weeks ago he subpoenaed some of your records. Receipts with license plate numbers on them. You know anything about that?'

The manager thought about it for a few moments.

'All I know is that I was the one who had to go through everything and get it copied for his guy.'

'His guy?' Edgar asked.

'Yeah, what do you think, a guy like Elias comes get the stuff himself? He sent somebody. I got his card here.'

He lowered his feet to the floor and opened the desk's pencil drawer. There was a stack of business cards with a rubber band around it. He took it off and looked through the cards and chose one. He showed it to Bosch.

'Pelfry?' Edgar asked.

Bosch nodded.

'Did his guy say exactly what they were looking for in all that stuff?' he asked.

'I don't know. You'd have to ask them. Or, I mean, ask Pelfry.'

'Did Pelfry come back with the stuff yet?'

'No, it was copies, anyway. I mean, he came back but not to bring back the receipts.'

'Then why'd he come back?' Edgar asked.

'He wanted to see one of Michael Harris's old time cards. From when he worked here.'

'Which one?' Edgar asked, a tone of urgency in his voice.

'I don't remember, man. I gave him a copy. You go talk to him and maybe he—'

'Did he have a subpoena for the time card?' Bosch asked.

'No, he just asked for it, you know. I said sure and got it for him. But he gave me the date and you didn't. I don't remember it. Anyway, look, if you want to ask more about this then maybe you better call our lawyer. I'm not going to get involved in talking about stuff I don't—'

'Never mind that stuff,' Bosch said. 'Tell me about Michael Harris.'

'What's to tell? I never had a problem with the guy. He was okay, then they came in and said he killed that little girl. And did things to her. It didn't seem like the guy I knew. But he hadn't been working here that long. Maybe five months.'

'Know where he was before that?' Edgar asked.

'Yeah. Up at Corcoran.'

Corcoran was a state prison near Bakersfield. Bosch thanked the manager and they left. He took a few sips of his coffee but dumped it in a trash can before getting back to the car.

While Bosch waited at the passenger door for it to be unlocked, Edgar went around to his side. He stopped before opening the door.

'Goddammit.'

'What?'

'They wrote shit on the door.'

Bosch came around and looked. Someone had used light blue chalk – the chalk used to write washing instructions on the windshields of clients' cars – to cross out the words *To protect and serve* on the driver's side front fender. Then written in large letters were the words *To murder and maim*. Bosch nodded his approval.

'That's pretty original.'

'Harry, let's go kick some ass.'

'No, Jerry, let it go. You don't want to start something. It might take three days to end it. Like last time. Like Florence and Normandie.'

Edgar sullenly unlocked the car and then opened Bosch's door.

'We're right by the station,' Bosch said after he got in. 'We can go back and spray it off. Or we can use my car.'

'I'd like to use one of those assholes' faces to clean it off.'

After they had the car cleaned up there was still time for them to drive by the lot where Stacey Kincaid's body had been found. It was off Western and was on the way downtown, where they would go to meet Pelfry.

Edgar was silent the whole way there. He had taken the vandalism of the patrol car personally. Bosch didn't mind the silence, though. He used the time to think about Eleanor. He felt guilty because deep down and despite his love for her, he knew that he was feeling a growing relief that their relationship was coming to a head, one way or the other.

'This is it,' Edgar said.

He pulled the car to the curb and they scanned the lot. It was about an acre and bordered on both sides by apartment buildings with banners announcing move-in bonuses and financing. They didn't look like places where people would want to live unless they had no choice. The whole neighborhood had a rundown and desperate feel.

Bosch noticed two old black men sitting on crates in the corner of the lot, under a sprawling and shade-giving eucalyptus tree. He opened the file he'd brought with him and studied the map that charted the location of the body. He estimated that it was less than fifty feet from where the two men were now sitting. He turned pages in the file until he found the incident report which named the two witnesses who reported finding the body.

'I'm getting out,' he said. 'I'm going to go talk to those guys.'

He got out and Edgar did, too. They crossed the lot nonchalantly and approached the two men. As they got closer, Bosch saw sleeping bags and an old Coleman camp stove. Parked against the trunk of the eucalyptus were two supermarket carts filled with clothing, bags of aluminum cans and assorted junk.

'Are you men Rufus Gundy and Andy Mercer?'

'Depends on who's doin' the askin'.'

Bosch showed his badge.

'I wanted to ask a few questions about the body you guys found here last year.'

'Yeah, what took you so long?'

'Are you Mr Gundy or Mr Mercer?'

'I'm Mercer.'

Bosch nodded.

'Why do you say we took so long? Weren't you interviewed by detectives when you found the body?'

'We was interviewed, but not by no detectives. Some wet-eared patrol boy akst us what we knew.'

Bosch nodded. He pointed to the sleeping bags and the camp stove.

'You guys live here?'

'We runnin' a piece of bad luck. We just stayin' till we on our feet again.'

Bosch knew there was nothing in the incident report about the two men living on the lot. The report said they were passing through the lot, looking for cans, when they came across her body. He thought about this and realized what had happened.

'You were living here then, weren't you?'

Neither of them answered.

'You didn't tell the cops that because you thought you might get run off.'

Still no reply.

'So you hid your sleeping bags and your stove and called it in. You told that patrol officer that you were just passing through.'

Finally, Mercer spoke.

'If'n you're so smart, how come you ain't chief yet?'

Bosch laughed.

'Because they're smart enough not to make me chief. So, tell me something, Mr Mercer and Mr Gundy. If you two were sleepin' here during nights back then, you probably would've found that body a lot sooner if it had been here the whole time she was missing, right?'

'Most likely,' Gundy said.

'So somebody probably dumped that body the night before you found it.'

'Could be,' Gundy said.

'Yeah, I'd say that was so,' Mercer added.

'With you two sleeping, what, forty, fifty feet away?'

This time they didn't verbally agree. Bosch stepped over and dropped into a catcher's squat so he was on their eye level.

'Tell me what you men saw that night.'

'We didn't see nothin',' Gundy said adamantly.

'But we heard things,' Mercer said. 'Heard things.'

'What things?'

'A car pull up,' Mercer said. 'A door open, then a trunk. We heard somethin' heavy hit the ground. Then the trunk closed and the door, then the car drive off.'

'You didn't even look?' Edgar asked quickly. He had stepped over and was leaning over, hands on his knees. 'A body gets dumped there fifty feet away and you don't look?'

'No, we don't look,' Mercer retorted. 'People be dumpin' their garbage and whatnot in the field most every night. We never look. We keep our heads down. In the morning we look. We got some nice items time to time from what people throw away. We always wait till mornin' to check out what they throw.'

Bosch nodded that he understood and hoped Edgar would leave the men alone.

'And you never told all of this to the cops?'

'Nope,' Mercer and Gundy said in unison.

'What about anybody else? You ever told it to somebody who could verify this has been the true story all along?'

The men thought about it. Mercer was shaking his head no when Gundy nodded yes.

'The only one we told was Mr Elias's man.'

Bosch glanced at Edgar and then back at Gundy.

'Who's that?'

'His man. The investigator. We told him what we told you. He said Mr Elias was gonna use us in court one day. He said Mr Elias would be takin' care of us.'

'Pelfry?' Edgar asked. 'Was that his name?'

'Could be,' Gundy said. 'I don't know.'

Mercer didn't say anything.

'You guys read the paper today?' Bosch asked. 'See any TV news?'

'On what TV?' Mercer asked.

Bosch just nodded and stood up. They didn't even know Elias was dead.

'How long ago was that when Mr Elias's man talked to you?'

'Be about a month,' Mercer said. 'Somewhere around that.'

Bosch looked at Edgar and nodded that he was done. Edgar nodded back.

'Thanks for your help,' Bosch said. 'Can I buy you guys some dinner?'

He reached into his pocket and pulled out his money. He gave each man a ten. They thanked him politely and he walked away.

As they sped north on Western to Wilshire, Bosch started riffing on what the information from the two homeless men meant.

'Harris is clear,' he said excitedly. 'That's how Elias knew. Because the body was moved. It was dumped there three days after she was dead. And Harris was in custody when it was moved. The best alibi in the world. Elias was going to bring those two old guys into court and put the lie to the LAPD.'

'Yeah, but hold on, Harry,' Edgar said. 'It doesn't clear Harris completely. It could just mean he had an accomplice. You know, who moved the body while he was in lockup.'

'Yeah, then why dump it so close to his apartment and further implicate him? I don't think there's an accomplice. I think it was the real killer. He read in the paper or saw on TV that they had Harris as a suspect and he moved the body to his neighborhood, to be another nail in Harris's coffin.'

'What about the fingerprints? How did Harris's prints get into that nice mansion in Brentwood? Are you goin' along with them being planted by your buddy Sheehan and his team?'

'No, I'm not. There's an explanation. We just don't know it yet. It's what we ask Pel—'

There was a loud explosion as the rear window shattered and glass blasted through the car. Edgar momentarily lost control and the car swerved into the oncoming lanes. There was a chorus of angry horns as Bosch reached over and yanked the wheel right, bringing the car back across the yellow lines.

'What the fuck?' Edgar cried as he finally got the car under control and put on the brakes.

'No!' Bosch yelled. 'Keep going, keep going!'

Bosch grabbed the radio out of the recharge slot on the floor and depressed the transmit button.

'Shots fired, shots fired! Western and Olympic.'

He held the button down as he looked over the backseat and out over the trunk. His eyes scanned the rooftops and windows of the apartment buildings two blocks back. He saw nothing.

'Suspect unknown. Sniper fire on a marked investigative services unit. Request immediate backup. Request air surveillance of rooftops east and west sides of Western. Extreme caution is advised.'

He clicked off the transmit button. While the dispatch operator repeated most of what he had just said to other units, he told Edgar that they had gone far enough and that he could stop.

'I think it came from the East Side,' Bosch said to Edgar. 'Those apartments with the flat roof. I think I heard it in my right ear first.'

Edgar exhaled loudly. His hands were gripped so tight on the steering wheel now that the knuckles were as white as Bosch's.

'You know what?' he said. 'I think I'm never going to drive one of these fucking targets again.'

24

'You guys are late. I was thinkin' about goin' home, already.'

Jenkins Pelfry was a big man, with a barrel chest and a complexion so dark it was hard to make out the lines of his face. He sat on the top of a small secretary's desk in the anteroom of his office suite in the Union Law Center. There was a small television on a credenza to his left. It was tuned to a news channel. The view on the screen was from a helicopter circling a scene somewhere in the city.

Bosch and Edgar had arrived forty minutes late for their noon appointment.

'Sorry, Mr Pelfry,' Bosch said. 'We ran into a little problem on the way over. Appreciate you staying.'

'Lucky for you I lost track of the time. I was watching the tube here. Things are not looking too good at the moment. It's looking a little testy out there.'

He indicated the television with one of his huge hands. Bosch looked again and realized the scene that the helicopter was circling was the scene he and Edgar had just left – the search for the sniper who had taken the shot at their car. On the tube Bosch could see the sidewalks on Western were now crowded with people watching the cops moving from building to building. More officers were arriving on the scene and these new officers were wearing riot helmets.

'These guys oughta just get out of there. They're baitin' the crowd. This isn't good. Just back the hell out, man. Live to fight another day.'

'Tried that last time,' Edgar said. 'Didn't work.'

The three of them watched for a few more moments in silence, then Pelfry reached over and turned off the tube. He looked at his visitors.

'What can I do for you?

Bosch introduced himself and his partner.

'I suppose you know why we're here. We're working the Howard Elias case. And we know you were doin' some work for him on the Black Warrior thing. We could use your help, Mr Pelfry. If we find who did this, we maybe have a shot at cooling this place off.'

Bosch nodded at the blank tube of the television to underline his point.

'You want my help,' Pelfry said. 'Yeah, I worked for Eli – I always called him Eli. But I don't know what I can do for you.'

Bosch looked at Edgar and his partner made a subtle nod of his head.

'Mr Pelfry, our conversation here has to be kept confidential. My partner and I are following an investigative trail that indicates that whoever killed Stacey Kincaid may have also killed your employer. We think Elias got too close to the truth. If you know what he knew, then you could be in danger yourself.'

Pelfry laughed at him – a short, loud snort. Bosch looked at Edgar and then back at Pelfry.

'No offense but that's about the worst pickup line I ever heard,' Pelfry said.

'What are you talking about?'

He pointed at the television once more. Bosch noticed how white the underside of his hand was.

'I told you I been watchin' the news. Channel Four says you guys are already measuring a cell for somebody. One of your own.'

'What are you talking about?'

'They're sweatin' a suspect over at Parker right now.'

'Did they have a name?'

'They didn't say a name but they knew it. They said it was one of the Black Warrior cops. The lead detective, in fact.'

Bosch was dumbfounded. The lead detective was Frankie Sheehan.

'That's impos— can I use your phone?'

'Help yourself. By the way, do you know you have glass in your hair?'

Bosch brushed his hand through his hair while he stepped to the desk and picked up the phone. While he punched in the number of Irving's conference room Pelfry watched. The phone was answered immediately.

'Let me talk to Lindell.'

'This is Lindell.'

'It's Bosch. What's this on Channel Four about a suspect?'

'I know. I'm checking into it. Somebody leaked. All I can say is that I updated Irving and the next thing I know it's on TV. I think he's your leak, not Chas—'

'I don't care about that. What are you saying, it's Sheehan? That's im—'

'I'm not saying that. That's the leak talking and I think the leak is the goddamned deputy chief.'

'Have you brought Sheehan in?'

'Yeah, we got him in here and we're talking to him. Strictly voluntary at this point. He thinks he can talk his way out of the box. We got all day and then some. We'll see if he can.'

'Why Sheehan? Why'd you bring him in?'

'I thought you knew. He was on top of Chastain's list this morning. Elias sued him once before. Five years ago. He shot some asshole while trying to make an arrest on a murder. Put five holes in him. The widow sued and eventually won a hundred grand – even though to me it looked like a righteous shoot. In fact your buddy Chastain was the one who investigated the shoot and cleared him.'

'I remember the case. It *was* a righteous shoot. But that didn't matter to the jury. It was just a little while after Rodney King.'

'Okay, well before it went to trial, Sheehan threatened Elias. During a depo, in front of the lawyers, the widow and, most important, the steno girl. She got it down word for word and it was in the depo which was in the file that Chastain and his people read yesterday. The threat was that Sheehan told Elias that someday when he least expected it, Sheehan was going to come up from behind and put him down like a dog. Words to that effect. Words that describe what happened on Angels Flight pretty good.'

'Come on, that was five years ago. You've got to be kidding me.'

Bosch noticed that both Edgar and Pelfry were watching him intently.

'I know it, Bosch. But then you have this new lawsuit on the Black Warrior thing and who's the lead? Detective Frank Sheehan. On top of that, he uses a nine-millimeter Smith and Wesson. And one other thing, we pulled his file. He's qualified eleven straight years at the range as an expert marksman. And you know the kind of shooting it took on Angels Flight. You take it all into consideration and it puts him at the top of the list of people to talk to. So we're talking to him.'

'The marksman thing is bullshit. They give those pins out like candy at the range. I bet seven or eight out of every ten cops have that ribbon. And eight out of ten cops carry Smith nines. Meantime, Irving – or whoever the leak is – is throwing him to the wolves. Sacrificing him to the media so maybe he can stop the city from burning.'

'He's only a sacrifice if he didn't do it.'

There was a cynical casualness in Lindell's voice that Bosch didn't like.

'You better take it slow,' Bosch said. 'Because I guarantee you Frankie wasn't the shooter.'

'Frankie? You guys friends, are you?'

'We were partners. A long time back.'

'Well, it's funny. He doesn't seem so fond of you now. My guys tell me that the first thing he said when they knocked on his door was "Fuck Harry Bosch." He thinks you ratted him out, man. He doesn't know that we have the threat in the deposition. Or he doesn't remember it.'

Bosch put the phone down on its hook. He was in a daze. Frankie Sheehan believed that Bosch had turned their conversation of the night before against him. He believed Harry had turned him in to the bureau. It made Bosch feel worse than the knowledge that his old partner and friend now sat in an interview room fighting for his life.

'Sounds like you don't agree much with Channel Four,' Pelfry said.

'No, I don't.'

'You know something, I'ma take a wild ass guess here, but I think that glass in your hair means you're the two guys they were talkin' about on TV getting potshotted over on Western.'

'Yeah, what about it?' Edgar asked.

'Well, that's a few blocks from where that Stacey Kincaid girl ended up.'

'Yeah, so?'

'Well, if that's where you were comin' from, then I wonder if you met my two buddies, Rufus and Andy.'

'Yeah, we met 'em and we know all about the body being dumped three days late.'

'You're following my footsteps then.'

'Some of them. We visited Mistress Regina last night, too.'

Bosch was finally out of his daze but hung back and watched Edgar making progress with Pelfry.

'Then this isn't all bullshit what you said about who you think hit Eli?'

'We're here, aren't we?'

'Then what else you want to know? Eli kept his cards close most of the time. Very close to the vest. I never knew for sure which corner of the puzzle I was working, if you know what I mean.'

'Tell us about the license plates,' Bosch said, ending his silence. 'We know you guys pulled seventy-six days' worth of receipts from Hollywood Wax. How come?'

Pelfry looked at them a long moment as if deciding something.

'Come on back,' he finally said.

He led them to the rear office.

'I didn't want you guys back here,' he said. 'But now . . .'

He raised his hands to indicate the boxes covering every horizontal surface in the office. They were short boxes that normally held four six-packs of soda. Stacked in them were bundled receipts with cardboard markers with dates written on them.

'Those are the receipts from Hollywood Wax?' Bosch asked.

'That's right. Eli was going to bring 'em all into court as an exhibit. I was holding 'em here till he needed 'em.'

'What exactly was he going to show with them?'

'I thought you boys knew.'

'We're a little behind you, Mr Pelfry.'

'Jenkins. Or Jenks. Most people call me Jenks. I don't know exactly what alla these receipts meant – remember what I said about Eli not showin' me all the cards in his deck – but I got an idea. See, when he su'peenied these, he gave me a list of license plate numbers on a piecea paper. He said I was to look through alla these and see if any of those numbers on the list turned up on the receipts.'

'Did you?'

'Yeah, took me the better part of a week.'

'Any matches?'

'One match.'

He went over to one of the boxes and stuck his finger into the stack where there was a cardboard marker with the date 6/12 noted on it.

'This one.'

Pelfry pulled out a receipt and took it over to Bosch. Edgar came over and looked as well. The receipt was for a daily special. It identified the car to be washed as a white Volvo wagon. It listed the license plate number and the price of the special – $14.95 plus tax.

'This plate number was on the list Elias gave you,' Bosch said.

'That's right.'

'It was the only match you found.'

'That's what I said.'

'You know whose car this plate is from?'

'Not exactly. Eli didn't tell me to run it. But I got a guess who it belongs to.'

'The Kincaids.'

'Now you're with me.'

Bosch looked at Edgar. He could tell by his partner's face he hadn't made the leap.

'The fingerprints. To prove Harris was innocent beyond any kind of doubt, he had to explain his client's fingerprints on the victim's school-book. If there was no reason or possible legitimate explanation for Harris having been in the Kincaid house and touching the book, then there were two alternative reasons. One, the prints were planted by the cops. Two, Harris touched the book when it was somewhere else, outside of the girl's bedroom.'

Edgar nodded as he understood.

'The Kincaids had their car washed at Hollywood Wax and Shine, where Harris worked. The receipt proves it.'

'Right. All Elias had to do was put the book in the car.'

Bosch turned to the boxes on Pelfry's desk and ticked his finger on the cardboard marker.

'June twelve,' he said. 'That's right around the end of the school year. Kids clear out their lockers. They take all their books home. They're not doing homework anymore so maybe the books lie around in the back of the Volvo.'

'The Volvo goes to the car wash,' Edgar said. 'I'd bet the daily special includes a vacuum, maybe some Armoral on the inside.'

'The washer – the polish man – touches the book when he's working inside the car,' Bosch added. 'There are your prints.'

'The polish man was Harris,' Edgar said. He then looked at Pelfry and said, 'The manager at the car wash said you came back to look at the time cards.'

Pelfry nodded.

'I did. I got a copy of a time card that proves Harris was working at the time that white Volvo came in and got the special. Eli asked me to go over to the car wash and try to finesse that without a su'peenie. I figure the time card was the lynch pin and he didn't want anybody to know about it.'

'Even the judge who signed the subpoenas on the case,' Bosch said. 'He must not have trusted anybody.'

'Looks like with good reason,' Pelfry said.

While Edgar asked Pelfry to show him the time card, Bosch withdrew and tried to think about this latest information. He remembered what Sheehan had said the night before about the fingerprints being so good because the person who had left them had probably been sweating. He understood now that that was not because of nervousness over the crime being committed, but because he was working at the car wash, vacuuming a car when those prints were left on that book. Michael Harris. He was innocent. Truly innocent. Bosch had not been convinced until that moment. And it was astounding to him. He wasn't a dreamer. He knew cops made mistakes and innocent people went to prison. But the mistake here was colossal. An innocent man tortured as cops tried to bully him into confessing to something he had clearly not done. Satisfied they had their man, the police had dropped their investigation and let the real killer slip away – until a civil rights lawyer's investigation found him, a discovery that got the lawyer killed. The chain reaction went even further, pushing the city once more to the brink of self-destruction.

'So then, Mr Pelfry,' Bosch said, 'who killed Stacey Kincaid?'

'It's Jenks. And I don't know. I know it wasn't Michael Harris – ain't no doubt about that. But Eli didn't tell me the other part – if he knew before they got him.'

715

'They?' Bosch asked.

'Whatever.'

'Tell us about Mistress Regina,' Edgar said.

'What's to tell? Eli got a tip, he passed it to me. I checked the broad out and couldn't see any connection. She's just a freak – a dead end. If you guys were there, you know what I mean. I think Eli dropped it after I told him about her.'

Bosch thought a moment and shook his head.

'I don't think so. There's something there.'

'Well, if there is, he didn't tell me about it.'

In the car Bosch called Rider to check in. She said she had completed a review of the files without anything that needed immediate follow-up catching her eye.

'We're going to see the Kincaids,' Bosch said.

'How come so soon?'

'Turns out one of them was Harris's alibi.'

'What?'

Bosch explained the license plate discovery Pelfry and Elias had made.

'One out of four,' she said.

'What do you mean?'

'We now know what one out of four of the mystery notes means.'

'Yeah, I guess so.'

'I was thinking about the first two. I think they're connected and I've got an idea about "dot the i." I'm going to go online and check it out. You know what a hypertext link is?'

'I don't speak that language, Kiz. I still type with two fingers.'

'I know. I'll explain it when you get back here. Maybe I'll know if I have something.'

'Okay. Good luck.'

He was about to hang up.

'Oh, Harry?'

'What?'

'You gotta call from Carla Entrenkin. She said she needed to talk to you. I was going to give her your pager but then I thought you might not want that. She might start paging you every time she gets a wild hair.'

'That's fine. Did she leave a number?'

She gave it to him and they hung up.

'We're going to the Kincaids'?' Edgar asked.

'Yeah, I just decided. Get on the radio and run the plate on that white Volvo. See what name's on it. I've got to make a call.'

Bosch called the number Carla Entrenkin had left and she answered after two rings.

'It's Bosch.'

'Detective . . .'

'You called?'

'Yes, uh, I just wanted to apologize about last night. I was upset at what I saw on the television and . . . and I think I spoke too soon. I've done some checking and I think I was wrong about what I said.'

'You were.'

'Well, I'm sorry.'

'Okay, Inspector, I appreciate you calling. I better—'

'How is the investigation going?'

'It's going. Have you talked to Chief Irving?'

'Yes, I have. He told me that they are questioning Detective Sheehan.'

'Don't hold your breath on that.'

'I'm not. What about what you are pursuing? I was told you are reinvestigating the original case. The murder of Stacey Kincaid.'

'Well, we can now prove Harris didn't do it. You were right about that. Elias was going to go into court and clear him. He didn't do it. We now just have to prove somebody else did. And my money is still on that somebody being the one who also did Elias. I have to go now, Inspector.'

'Will you call me if you make significant progress?'

Bosch thought about this for a few moments. Dealing with Carla Entrenkin somehow gave him the feel of consorting with the enemy.

'Yes,' he finally said. 'I'll call if there is significant progress.'

'Thank you, Detective.'

'Don't mention it.'

25

The Los Angeles car czar and his wife now lived off Mulholland Drive in an exclusive development called The Summit. It was a gated and guarded neighborhood of side-by-side millionaires with spectacular homes that looked down from the Santa Monica Mountains and north across the basin of the San Fernando Valley. The Kincaids had moved from Brentwood to these gated hills after their daughter's murder. It was a move toward security that was too late for the little girl.

Bosch and Edgar had called ahead and were welcomed at the gatehouse. There they were given directions along a curving development road to a huge French Provincial mansion built on a piece of property that must have been the summit of The Summit. A Latina maid answered the door and led them to a living room that was bigger than Bosch's entire house. It had two fireplaces and three distinct groupings of furniture. Bosch wasn't sure what the purpose of this could be. The long northern wall of the room was almost entirely glass. It revealed an expansive view across the Valley. Bosch had a hill house but the difference in views was a couple of thousand feet in altitude and maybe ten million dollars in attitude. The maid told them that the Kincaids would be with them shortly.

Bosch and Edgar stepped to the window, which they were meant to do. The rich kept you waiting so that you could feel free to admire all that they had.

'Jetliner views,' Edgar said.

'What's that?'

'That's what they call it when you're this high up. Jetliner views.'

Bosch nodded. Edgar had sold real estate as a side job with his wife a few years back, until it threatened to turn his police work into a side job.

Bosch could see across the Valley to the Santa Susanna Mountains. He could pick out Oat Mountain above Chatsworth. He remembered going there years before on a field trip from the youth hall. The overall view, however, could not be called beautiful. A heavy layer of smog – especially for April – stretched across the Valley. They were high enough in the Kincaid house to be above it. Or so it seemed.

'I know what you're thinking. It's a million-dollar view of the smog.'

Bosch turned around. A smiling man and a blank-faced woman had entered the living room. Behind them stood a second man in a dark suit. Bosch recognized the first man from TV. Sam Kincaid, the car czar. He was smaller than Bosch expected. More compact. His deep tan was real, not

718

television makeup, and his jet-black hair seemed legitimate. On TV it always looked like a wig. He was wearing a golf shirt like the ones he always wore on his commercials. Like the ones his father had worn when he was the one on the commercials a decade earlier.

The woman was younger than Kincaid by a few years, about forty and well preserved by weekly massages and trips to the salons down on Rodeo Drive. She looked past Bosch and Edgar to the view. She had a vague expression on her face and Bosch immediately realized that Katherine Kincaid had probably not come close to recovering from the loss of her daughter.

'But you know what?' Sam Kincaid continued, smiling. 'I don't mind seeing the smog. My family's been selling cars in this city for three generations. Since nineteen hundred and twenty-eight. That's a lot of years and a lot of cars. That smog out there reminds me of that.'

His statement sounded rehearsed, as if he used it as an opener with all of his guests. He stepped forward with his hand out.

'Sam Kincaid. And my wife, Kate.'

Bosch shook his hand and introduced himself and Edgar. The way Kincaid studied Edgar before shaking his hand made Bosch think that his partner might have been the first black man to set foot in his living room – not counting the ones who were there to serve canapés and take drink orders.

Bosch looked past Kincaid to the man still standing beneath the arch of the entryway. Kincaid noticed and made the last introduction.

'This is D.C. Richter, my chief of security,' Kincaid said. 'I asked him to come up and join us, if you don't mind.'

Bosch was puzzled by the addition of the security man but didn't say anything. He nodded and Richter nodded back. He was about Bosch's age, tall and gaunt and his short graying hair was spiked with gel. Richter also had a small earring, a thin gold hoop on his left ear.

'What can we do for you gentlemen?' Kincaid asked. 'I have to say I'm surprised by this visit. I would have guessed that with everything going on, you two would be out on the street somewhere, trying to keep down the animals.'

There was an awkward silence. Kate Kincaid looked down at the rug.

'We're investigating the death of Howard Elias,' Edgar said. 'And your daughter's.'

'My daughter's? I don't understand what you mean.'

'Why don't we sit down, Mr Kincaid?' Bosch said.

'Sure.'

Kincaid led them to one of the furniture groupings. Two couches faced each other across a glass coffee table. To one side was a fireplace Bosch could almost walk into, to the other was the view. The Kincaids sat on one couch while Bosch and Edgar took the other. Richter stood to the side and behind the couch where the Kincaids sat.

'Let me explain,' Bosch said. 'We are here to inform you that we are reopening the investigation of Stacey's death. We need to start again.'

Both Kincaids opened their mouths into small looks of puzzlement. Bosch continued.

'In the course of investigating the killing Friday night of Howard Elias we

719

have uncovered information that we believe exonerates Michael Harris. We—'

'Impossible,' Sam Kincaid barked. 'Harris was the killer. His fingerprints were found in the house, the old house. You're going to tell me that the Los Angeles Police Department now believes its own people planted this evidence?'

'No, sir, I'm not. I'm telling you that we now have what we think is a reasonable explanation for that evidence.'

'Well, I'd love to hear it.'

Bosch took two folded pieces of paper from his jacket pocket and opened them. One was a photocopy of the car wash receipt Pelfry had found. The other was a photocopy of Harris's time card, also from Pelfry.

'Mrs Kincaid, you drive a white Volvo station wagon with license plate number one-bravo-henry-six-six-eight, correct?'

'No, that's wrong,' Richter answered for her.

Bosch looked up at him for a moment and then back at the woman.

'*Did* you drive this car last summer?'

'I drove a white Volvo station wagon, yes,' she said. 'I don't remember the license number.'

'My family owns eleven dealerships and parts of six more in this county,' her husband said. 'Chevy, Cadillac, Mazda, you name it. Even a Porsche store. But no Volvo franchise. And so what do you know, that's the car she picks. She says it's safer for Stacey and then she ends up . . . anyway.'

Sam Kincaid brought a hand up to cover his lip and held himself still. Bosch waited a moment before pressing on.

'Take my word for it about the plate number. The car was registered to you, Mrs Kincaid. On June twelve last year that car, the Volvo, was washed at Hollywood Wax and Shine on Sunset Boulevard. The person who took the car there asked for the daily special, which included interior vacuuming and polish. Here's the receipt.'

He leaned forward and put it on the coffee table in front of the couple. They both leaned down to look at it. Richter leaned over the back of the couch for a look.

'Does either of you remember doing that?'

'We don't wash our cars,' Sam Kincaid said. 'And we don't go to public car washes. I need a car washed I have it taken to one of my stores. I don't need to pay to—'

'I remember,' his wife said, cutting him off. 'I did it. I took Stacey to the movies at the El Capitan. Where we parked there was construction – a new roof being put on the building next to the garage. When we came out the car had something on it. Like little spots of tar that had blown onto it. It was a white car and it was very noticeable. When I paid the parking attendant I asked him where a car wash was. He told me.'

Kincaid was looking at his wife as if she had just belched at the charity ball.

'So you got the car washed there,' Bosch said.

'Yes. I remember now.'

She looked at her husband and then back at Bosch.

'The receipt says June twelve,' Bosch said. 'How long after the end of school for your daughter was that?'

'It was the next day. It was our way of kicking off the summer. Lunch and the movies. It was a movie about these two guys who can't find a mouse in their house. It was cute . . . The mouse got the better of them.'

Her eyes were on the memory, and on her daughter. They then focused on Bosch once more.

'No more school,' Bosch said. 'Could she have left her books from the last day in the Volvo? Maybe in the back?'

Kate Kincaid slowly nodded.

'Yes. I remember having to tell her at one point during the summer to take the books out of the car. They kept sliding around when I drove. She didn't do it. I finally took them out and put them in her room.'

Bosch leaned forward again and put the other photocopy down for them.

'Michael Harris worked at Hollywood Wax and Shine last summer. That's his time card for the week including June twelve. He worked a full day on the day you brought the Volvo in.'

Sam Kincaid leaned forward again and studied the photocopy.

'You mean all this time we've . . . ,' Kincaid began and then stopped. 'You're saying that he – Harris – vacuumed out the Volvo and in the process touched my stepdaughter's book? Picked it up or whatever, then the book was eventually taken to her bedroom. And after she was taken . . .'

'The police found the prints on it,' Bosch finished. 'Yes, that's now what we think.'

'Why didn't this come out at the trial? Why—'

'Because there was other evidence linking Harris to the murder,' Edgar said. 'The girl's – uh, Stacey – was found less than two blocks from his apartment. That was a strong tie-in. His lawyer decided the tack he had to take was to go after the cops. Taint the fingerprints by tainting the cops. He never went after the truth.'

'And neither did the cops,' Bosch said. 'They had the prints and when the body was found in Harris's neighborhood, that sealed it. You remember, the investigation was emotionally charged from the beginning. It changed at that point when they found the body and it all tied into Harris. It changed from a search for a little girl to a prosecution of a specific target. In between it never was a search for the truth.'

Sam Kincaid seemed shell-shocked.

'All this time,' he said. 'Can you imagine the hate I have built up inside of me for this man? This hate, this utter and complete contempt, has been the only real emotion I've had for the last nine months . . .'

'I understand, sir,' Bosch said. 'But we need to start over now. We need to reinvestigate the case. That was what Howard Elias was doing. We have reason to believe that he knew what I just told you. Only he also knew or had a pretty good idea who the actual killer was. We think that got him killed.'

Sam Kincaid looked surprised.

'But the TV said a little while ago that—'

'The TV's wrong, Mr Kincaid. It's wrong and we're right.'

Kincaid nodded. His eyes wandered out to the view and the smog.

'What do you want from us?' Kate Kincaid said.

'Your help. Your cooperation. I know we are hitting you out of the blue with this so we're not expecting you to drop everything. But as you can tell if you've been watching TV, time isn't something we have a lot of.'

'You have our full cooperation,' Sam Kincaid said. 'And D.C. here can do whatever you need him to do.'

Bosch looked from Kincaid to the security man and then back to Kincaid.

'I don't think that will be necessary. We just have a few more questions for right now and then tomorrow we want to come back and start the case over.'

'Of course. What are your questions?'

'Howard Elias learned what I just told you because of an anonymous note that came in the mail. Do either of you know who that could have come from? Who would have known about the Volvo going to that car wash?'

There was no answer for a long time.

'Just me,' Kate Kincaid said. 'I don't know who else. I don't remember telling anyone I went there. Why would I?'

'Did you send Howard Elias the note?'

'No. Of course not. Why would I help Michael Harris? I thought he was the one who . . . who took my daughter. Now you tell me he is innocent and I think I believe you. But before, no, I wouldn't have lifted a finger to help him.'

Bosch studied her as she spoke. Her eyes moved from the coffee table to the view and then to her hands clasped in front of her. She didn't look at her questioner. Bosch had been reading people in interviews and interrogations for most of his adult life. In that moment he knew she had sent Elias the anonymous note. He just couldn't figure out why. He glanced up again at Richter and saw that the security man was also closely studying the woman. Bosch wondered if he was reading the same thing. He decided to move on.

'The house where this crime took place. The one in Brentwood. Who owns that now?'

'We still own it,' Sam Kincaid said. 'We're not sure what we're going to do with it. Part of us wants to get rid of it and never think of it again. But the other part . . . Stacey was there. She lived half of her life there . . .'

'I understand. What I'd like—'

Bosch's pager went off. He cut it off and continued.

'I'd like to take a look at it, at her room. Tomorrow, if possible. We'll have a search warrant by then. I know you're a busy man, Mr Kincaid. Maybe, Mrs Kincaid, you could meet me there, show me around. Show me Stacey's room. If that won't be too difficult.'

Kate Kincaid looked as if she dreaded the possibility of returning to the Brentwood house. But she nodded her head yes in a disengaged sort of way.

'I'll have D.C. drive her,' Sam Kincaid announced. 'And you can have the run of the place. And you won't need a search warrant. We give you our permission. We have nothing to hide.'

'Sir, I didn't mean to imply that you did. The search warrant will be necessary so there will be no questions later. It is more a protection for us. If something new in the house is found and leads to the real killer, we don't want that person to be able to challenge the evidence on any legal grounds.'

'I understand.'

'And we appreciate you offering the help of Mr Richter but that won't be necessary.' Bosch looked at Kate Kincaid. 'I would prefer it if just you came, Mrs Kincaid. What time would be good?'

While she thought about this Bosch looked down at his pager. The number on it was one of the homicide lines. But there was a 911 added after the phone number. It was code from Kiz Rider: Call immediately.

'Uh, excuse me,' Bosch said. 'It looks like this call is important. Do you have a phone I could use? I have a cell phone in the car but in these hills I'm not sure I'll be able to get—'

'Of course,' Sam Kincaid said. 'Use my office. Go back out to the entry hall and go left. The second door on the left. You'll have privacy. We'll wait here with Detective Edwards.'

Bosch stood.

'It's Edgar,' Edgar said.

'I'm sorry. Detective Edgar.'

As Bosch headed to the entry hall another pager sounded. This time it was Edgar's. He knew it was Rider sending the same message. Edgar looked down at his pager and then at the Kincaids.

'I better go with Detective Bosch.'

'Sounds like something big,' Sam Kincaid offered. 'Hope it's not a riot.'

'Me, too,' Edgar said.

Kincaid's home office would have been able to accommodate the entire Hollywood homicide squad. It was a huge room with towering ceilings and bookcases along two walls that went all the way up to the ceiling. The centerpiece of the room was a desk that would have dwarfed Howard Elias's. It looked as if you could build a nice-sized office *inside* it.

Bosch came around behind it and picked up the phone. Edgar came into the room behind him.

'You get one from Kiz?' Bosch asked.

'Yeah. Something's happening.'

Bosch punched in the number and waited. He noticed that on the desk was a gold-framed photo of Kincaid holding his stepdaughter on his lap. The girl was indeed beautiful. He thought about what Frankie Sheehan had said about her looking like an angel, even in death. He looked away and noticed the computer set up on a worktable to the right of the desk. There was a screen saver on the tube. It showed a variety of different cars racing back and forth across the screen. Edgar noticed it, too.

'The car czar,' Edgar whispered. 'More like the smog wog.'

Rider answered before the first ring was finished.

'It's Bosch.'

'Harry, did you talk to the Kincaids yet?'

'We're here now. We're in the middle of it. What's going—'

'Did you advise them?'

Bosch was silent a moment. When he spoke again his voice was very low.

'Advise them? No. What for, Kiz?'

'Harry, back out of there and come back to the station.'

Bosch had never heard Rider's voice with such a serious tone. He looked at Edgar, who just raised his eyebrows. He was in the dark.

'Okay, Kiz, we're on our way. You want to tell me why?'

'No. I have to show you. I found Stacey Kincaid in afterlife.'

26

Bosch couldn't put his finger on the look he saw on Kizmin Rider's face when he and Edgar returned to the squad room. She sat alone at the homicide table, her laptop in front of her, the glow of the screen reflecting slightly on her dark face. She looked both horrified and energized. Bosch knew the look but didn't have the words for it. She had seen something horrible but at the same time she knew she was going to be able to do something about it.

'Kiz,' Bosch said.

'Sit down. I hope you didn't leave hair on the cake with the Kincaids.'

Bosch pulled out his seat and sat down. Edgar did likewise. The phrase Rider had used referred to making a miscue that tainted a case with constitutional or procedural error. If a suspect asks for a lawyer but then confesses to a crime before the lawyer arrives, there is hair on the cake. The confession is tainted. Likewise, if a suspect is not advised of his rights before questioning, it is unlikely anything he says in that conversation can be used against him later in court.

'Look, neither one was a suspect when we walked in there,' Bosch said. 'There was no reason to advise. We told them the case was open again and asked a few basic questions. Nothing came out of any consequence anyway. We told them Harris has been cleared and that's it. What do you have, Kiz? Maybe you should just show us.'

'Okay, bring your chairs around here. I'll school you.'

They moved their chairs to positions on either side of her. Bosch checked her computer and saw the Mistress Regina web page was on the screen.

'First off, either of you guys know Lisa or Stacey O'Connor in Major Fraud downtown?'

Bosch and Edgar shook their heads.

'They're not sisters. They just have the same last name. They work with Sloane Inglert. You know who she is, right?'

Now they nodded. Inglert was a member of a new computer fraud unit working out of Parker Center. The team, and Inglert in particular, had gotten a lot of play in the media earlier that year when they bagged Brian Fielder, a hacker of international reputation who headed a crew of hackers known as the 'Merry Pranksters.' Fielder's exploits and Inglert's chase of her quarry across the Internet had played in the paper for weeks and were now destined to be filmed by Hollywood.

'All right,' Rider said. 'Well, they're friends of mine from when I worked

Fraud. I called them and they were happy to come in to work this because otherwise they'd have to put on uniforms and work twelve hours tonight.'

'They came here?' Bosch asked.

'No, their office at Parker. Where the real computers are. Anyway, we talked over the phone once they got there. I told them what we had – this web address that we knew was important but at the same time didn't make any sense. I told them about going to Mistress Regina's place and I think I pretty much creeped them out. Anyway, they told me there was a good chance that what we were looking for had nothing to do with Regina herself, just her web page. They said the page could have been hijacked and that we should be looking for a hidden hypertext link somewhere in the image.'

Bosch raised his hands palms up but before he could say anything Rider kept going.

'I know, I know, talk English. I will. I just wanted to take you step by step. Do either of you know anything at all about web pages? Am I making even any basic sense here?'

'Nope,' said Bosch.

'Nada,' said Edgar.

'Okay, then I'll try to keep this simple. We start with the Internet. The Internet is the so-called information superhighway, okay? Thousands and thousands of computer systems all connected by a Telnet system. It is worldwide. On that highway are millions of turnoffs, places to go. These are whole computer networks, web sites, so on and so forth.'

She pointed to Mistress Regina on her computer screen.

'This is an individual web page that is on a web site where there are many other pages. You see this on my computer here but its home, so to speak, is on the larger web site. And that web site resides in an actual, physical piece of equipment – a computer we call the web server. Do you follow me?'

Bosch and Edgar nodded.

'So far,' Bosch said. 'I think.'

'Good. Now the web server may have many, many web sites that it manages and maintains. See, if you wanted to have a Harry Bosch web page you would go to a web server and say put my page on one of your web sites. Do you have one that features morose detectives who never say much of anything to anybody?'

That got a smile from Bosch.

'That's how it works. Often you have like-minded businesses or interests bundled on one site. That's why when you look at this site it's like Sodom and Gomorrah on the Internet. Because like-minded advertisers seek the same sites.'

'Okay,' Bosch said.

'The one thing the web server should provide is security. By that I mean security from anyone hacking in and compromising your page – altering it or crashing it. The problem is, there isn't a whole lot of security out there on these web servers. And if someone can hack into a server they can then assume site-administrator capabilities for a web site and hijack any page on the site.'

'What do you mean, hijack?' Edgar said.

'They can go to a page on the site and use it as a front for their own intentions. Think of it as it is on my screen here. They can come up behind the image you see here and add all kinds of hidden doors and commands, whatever they want. They can then use the page as a gateway to anything they want.'

'And that's what they did with her page?' Bosch asked.

'Exactly. I had O'Connor/O'Connor run a uniform resource locator. In effect they traced this page back to the web server. They checked it out. There are indeed some firewalls – security blocks – but the default passwords are still valid. They, in effect, render the firewalls invalid.'

'You lost me,' Bosch said.

'When a web server is first set up, there are default passwords necessary for first getting inside. In other words, standard log-on names and passwords. Guest/guest, for example. Or administrator/administrator. Once the server is up and running these should be eliminated to prevent compromise but quite often it is forgotten about and these become back doors, ways to sneak in. It was forgotten here. Lisa got in using administrator/administrator. And if she was able to do it, then any hacker worth his salt could have gotten in and then hijacked the Mistress Regina page. And somebody did.'

'What did they do?' Bosch asked.

'They put in a hidden hypertext link. A hot button. When located and pushed, it will take the user to another web site all together.'

'In English,' Edgar said.

Rider thought for a moment.

'Think of it as a tall building – the Empire State building. You are on one floor. The Mistress Regina floor. And you find a hidden button on the wall. You push it and an elevator door you didn't even see before opens and you get on. The elevator takes you to another floor and opens. You step out. You are someplace completely new. But you couldn't have gotten there if you hadn't been on Mistress Regina's floor and stumbled onto that hidden button.'

'Or been told where it was,' Bosch said.

'Exactly,' Rider said. 'Those in the know can go.'

Bosch nodded at her computer.

'Show us.'

'Well, remember, the first note to Elias was the web page address and the image of Regina. The second one said, "dot the i humbert humbert." The mystery writer was simply telling Elias what to do with the web page.'

'Dot the i in Regina?' Edgar asked. 'Click the mouse on the dot?'

'That's what I thought but O'Connor/O'Connor said a hot button can only be hidden behind an image. Something about pixel redefinition that I don't need to get into.'

'So you dot the eye?' Bosch said, pointing to his eye.

'Right.'

She turned to her laptop to which she had attached a mouse. She now moved it with her hand and Bosch watched the arrow on the screen move to Mistress Regina's left eye. Rider double-clicked the mouse button and the screen went blank.

'Okay, we're on that elevator.'

After a few seconds a field of blue sky and clouds appeared on the screen.

Then tiny angels with wings and halos appeared sitting on the clouds. Then a password template appeared.

'Humbert humbert,' Bosch said.

'See, Harry, you get this stuff. You're just acting like you don't.'

She typed in the name humbert in the user name and password slots and the screen went blank once again. A few seconds later there was a welcome message.

WELCOME TO CHARLOTTE'S WEB SITE

Below the message a moving cartoon image formed. A spider crawled along the bottom of the page and then began weaving a web across the screen, shooting back and forth until the web was formed. Then tiny photographic images of young girls' faces appeared in the web, as if caught there. When the image of the web and its captives was complete, the spider took a position at the top of the web.

'This is sick,' Edgar said. 'I'm getting a bad feeling here.'

'It's a pedophile site,' Rider said. With a fingernail she tapped the screen below one of the photos in the web. 'And that is Stacey Kincaid. You click on the photo you like and you get a full spread of photos and videos. It is truly, truly horrible stuff. That poor little angel, she might be better off dead.'

Rider moved the arrow to the photo of the blond girl. It was too small for Bosch to identify the girl as Stacey Kincaid. He wished he could just take Rider's word for it.

'Are you ready for this?' Rider asked. 'I can't run videos on my laptop but the photos give you the idea.'

She didn't wait for a reply and she didn't get one. She double-clicked the mouse and a new screen appeared. A photo appeared on the screen. It was a young girl standing naked in front of a hedge. She was smiling in a forced, seemingly unnatural way. Despite the smile she still had a lost-in-the-woods look on her face. Her hands were on her hips. Bosch could tell it was Stacey Kincaid. He tried to breathe but it felt like his lungs were collapsing. He folded his arms across his chest. Rider started scrolling the screen and a series of photos came up featuring the girl in several poses by herself and then finally with a man. Only the man's naked torso was shown, never his face. The last photos were the girl and the man engaged in various sex acts. Finally, they came to the final photo. It showed Stacey Kincaid in a white dress with little semaphore flags on it. She was waving at the camera. The photo seemed somehow to be the worst one even though it was the most innocent.

'Okay, go back or forward or whatever you do to get that off there,' Bosch said.

He watched Rider move the cursor to a button below the final photo that said HOME on it. It seemed sadly ironic to Bosch that clicking HOME was the way out. Rider clicked the mouse and the screen went back to the spider's web. Bosch pulled his chair back to his spot and dropped down into it. Fatigue and depression suddenly hit him. He wanted to go home and go to sleep and forget everything he knew.

'People are the worst animals,' Rider said. 'They will do anything to each other. Just to indulge their fantasies.'

Bosch got up and walked over to one of the other nearby desks. It belonged to a burglary detective named McGrath. He opened the drawers and started looking through them.

'Harry,' Rider said, 'what are you looking for?'

'A cigarette. I thought Paul kept his smokes in his desk.'

'He used to. I told him to start taking them home with him.'

Bosch looked over at her, his hand still holding one of the drawers.

'You told him that?'

'I didn't want you slipping, Harry.'

Bosch shoved the drawer closed and came back to his chair.

'Thanks a lot, Kizmin. You saved me.'

There wasn't a drop of thanks in the tone he had used.

'You'll get through this, Harry.'

Bosch gave her a look.

'You probably haven't smoked an entire cigarette in your entire life and you're going to tell me about quitting and how I'll get through it?'

'Sorry. I'm just trying to help.'

'Like I said, thanks.'

He looked over at her computer and nodded.

'What else? What are you thinking about? How does that tie in Sam and Kate Kincaid to the point we should've advised them?'

'They had to know about this,' Rider said, amazed that Bosch didn't see what she saw. 'The man in the photos, that's got to be Kincaid.'

'Whoah!' Edgar said. 'How can you say that? You couldn't see the guy's face. We were just talking to the guy and he and his wife are still righteously fucked-up over this.'

It hit Bosch then. When he had first seen the photos on the computer he had thought they were taken by the girl's abductor.

'You're saying these photos are old,' he said. 'That she was abused before she was abducted.'

'I'm saying there probably wasn't an abduction at all. Stacey Kincaid was an abused child. My guess is that her stepfather defiled her and then probably killed her. And that doesn't happen without tacit knowledge, if not approval, by the mother.'

Bosch was silent. Rider had spoken with such fervor and even pain that he couldn't help but wonder if she was talking from some kind of personal experience.

'Look,' Rider said, apparently sensing the skepticism of her partners. 'There was a time that I thought I wanted to move into child sex crimes. This was before I put in for homicide. There was an opening on the endangered-child team in Pacific and the job was mine if I wanted it. They first sent me to Quantico for a two-week training program the bureau puts on once a year on child sex crimes. I lasted eight days. I realized I couldn't hack it. I came back and put in for homicide.'

She stopped there but neither Bosch or Edgar said anything. They knew there was more.

'But before I left,' Rider continued, 'I learned enough to know that most often sexual abuse of children comes from inside the family, relatives or close friends. The boogie monsters who climb through the window and abduct are few and far between.'

'It's still not evidence in this specific case, Kiz,' Bosch said gently. 'This could still be the rare exception. It wasn't Harris who came through the window but this guy.'

He pointed to her computer, though the images of the headless man's assault on Stacey Kincaid were thankfully not on the screen.

'Nobody came through the window,' Rider insisted.

She pulled a file over and opened it. Bosch saw it contained a copy of the protocol from the autopsy of Stacey Kincaid. She leafed through it until she came to the photos. She picked the one she wanted and handed it to Bosch. While he looked at it she started paging through the protocol.

The photo Bosch held was a shot of Stacey Kincaid's body *in situ* – the position and place where it was found. Her arms were spread wide. Sheehan had been right. Her body was darkening with interior decomposition and the face was gaunt, but there was an angelic quality to her in repose. His heart ached from looking at the photos of her tortured and now dead.

'Look at the left knee,' Rider commanded.

He did so. He saw a round dark spot that appeared to be a scab.

'A scab?'

'Right. The protocol calls it premortem by five to six days. It happened before she was abducted. So she had that scab on her knee the entire time she was with her abductor – if there really was one. In the photos on the web site, she has no scab. I can go back in and show you if you like.'

'I'll take your word for it,' Bosch said.

'Yeah,' Edgar added. 'Me, too.'

'So these photos on the web were taken well before she was supposedly kidnapped, well before she was murdered.'

Bosch nodded, then shook his head.

'What?' Rider asked.

'It's just . . . I don't know. Twenty-four hours ago we were working the Elias thing and thinking maybe we were looking for a cop. Now all of this . . .'

'It changes things all right,' Edgar said.

'Wait a minute, if that's Sam Kincaid in those pictures with her, why the hell are they still on that web site? It doesn't make sense that he would risk that.'

'I thought about that,' Rider said. 'There are two possible explanations. One being that he doesn't have editing access to the web site. In other words, he can't take those photos off without going to the site administrator, raising suspicions and exposing himself. The second possibility, and it might be a combination of both, is that he felt he was safe. Harris was fingered as the killer and whether he was convicted or not that was the end of the story.'

'It's still a risk leaving those photos out there to be seen,' Edgar said.

'Who's going to see them?' Rider asked. 'Who's going to tell?'

Her voice was too defensive. She realized this and continued in a calmer tone.

'Don't you see? The people with access to this site are pedophiles. Even if someone recognized Stacey, which is unlikely, what were they going to do?

729

Call the police and say, "Uh, yes, I like fucking children but I don't stand for murdering them. Could you get these photos off our web site?" Not in a million years. Hell, maybe keeping the photos on there was a form of bragging. We don't even know what we have here. Maybe every girl on that site is dead.'

Her voice was growing sharper as she tried to convince them.

'Okay, okay,' Bosch said. 'You make good points, Kiz. Let's stay on our case for now. What is your theory. You think Elias got this far along and it got him killed?'

'Absolutely. We know it did. The fourth note. "He knows you know." Elias went onto the secret web site and was found out.'

'How'd they know he was in there if he had the passwords from the third note?' Edgar asked.

'Good question,' Rider replied. 'I asked the O'Connors the same thing. They did some snooping around after getting into the server. They found a cookie jar on the web site. What that means is that there is a program that captures data about each user who enters the site. It then analyzes the data to determine if someone has entered the site who should not have had access. Even if they have the passwords, their entry is still recorded and a data trail called an Internet protocol address is left behind. It's like fingerprints. The IP, or the cookie, is left on the site you enter. The cookie jar program will then analyze the IP address and match it to a list of known users. If there is no match a flag is raised. The site's manager sees the flag and can trace the intruder. Or he can set up a tripwire program that waits for a return visit from the intruder. When he comes back, the program will attach a tracer which will provide the site manager with the intruder's E-mail address. And once you have that you have the intruder cold. You can identify him then. If it looks like a cop you close the elevator – the page you hijacked and were using as a secret gateway – and you go find a new web page to hijack. But in this case it wasn't a cop. It was a lawyer.'

'And they didn't shut down,' Bosch said. 'They sent someone out to kill him.'

'Right.'

'So you think this is what Elias did,' Bosch said. 'He got these notes in the mail and followed the clues. He stumbled into this web site and set off an alarm. A flag. The response was to kill him.'

'Yes, that would be my interpretation of what we know at this point, particularly in light of the fourth note. "He knows you know." '

Bosch shook his head, confused by his own extrapolations of the story.

'I'm still not getting this. Who is the "they" we're talking about here? That I just accused of murder.'

'The group. The users of the site. The site administrator – which might possibly be Kincaid – picked up on the intruder, realized it was Elias, and dispatched someone to take care of the problem in order to fend off exposure. Whether or not he polled all members of the group first doesn't matter. They are all guilty because the web site is a criminal enterprise.'

Bosch held his hand up to slow her down.

'Slow down. We can leave the group and the bigger picture for the DA to worry about. Stay focused on the killer and Kincaid. We are assuming he was involved in all of this and somehow someone knew about it, then decided to inform Elias instead of the cops. Does that make sense?'

'Sure it does. We just don't know all the details yet. But the notes speak for themselves. They clearly indicate someone tipped Elias to the site, then later warned him that he had been found out.'

Bosch nodded and thought about this for a moment.

'Wait a minute. If he set off a flag, then didn't you just do the same?'

'No. Thanks to the O'Connors. When they were inside the server they added my IP as well as their own to the site's good guy list. No alarms. The operators and users of the site won't know we've been there unless they actually look at their good guy list and notice it has been altered. I think we've got the time to do what we need to do.'

Bosch nodded. He wanted to ask whether what the O'Connors had done had been legal but thought it best not to know.

'So who sent Elias the notes?' he asked instead.

'The wife,' Edgar said. 'I think she got an attack of the guilts and wanted to help Elias rip Sam the car czar a new asshole. She sent the notes.'

'It fits,' Rider said. 'Whoever sent the notes had knowledge of two separate things: Charlotte's Web Site and the car-wash receipts. Actually, a third thing as well: that Elias had tripped an alarm. So my vote goes with the wife, too. What was she like today?'

Bosch spent the next ten minutes updating her on their activities during the day.

'And that's just our work on the case,' Edgar added. 'Harry didn't even tell you how we got the back window of my car shot out.'

'What?'

Edgar told the story and Rider seemed mesmerized by it.

'They catch the shooter?'

'Not that we heard. We didn't wait around.'

'You know, I've never been shot at,' she said. 'Must be a rush.'

'Not the kind you want,' Bosch said. 'I still have questions about all of this Internet stuff.'

'What are they?' Rider said. 'If I can't answer, one of the O'Connors can.'

'No, not technical questions. Logic questions. I still don't understand how and why this stuff is still available for us to look at. I understand what you said about the users all being pedophiles and their seeming feeling of safety, but now we have Elias dead. If they killed him, why the hell didn't they at least move to a new gateway?'

'Maybe they are in the process of trying to do just that. Elias hasn't been dead forty-eight hours.'

'And what about Kincaid? We just told him we are reopening the case. Whether he was in danger of exposure or not, it seems he would have gotten on the computer the minute we left and either contacted the site administrator or tried to crash the site and those pictures himself.'

'Again, maybe it's in process. And even if it is, it's too late. The O'Connors backed everything onto a Zip drive. They can crash the site but we still have it. We'll be able to trace every IP address and take every one of those people – if you consider them people.'

Again the fervor and anger in her voice made Bosch wonder if something about what she had seen on the web site had touched something personal, something deep inside.

'So where do we go from here?' he asked. 'Search warrants?'

'Yep,' Rider said. 'And we bring in the Kincaids. Fuck their big mansion on the hill. We have enough already to bring them in for questioning on the child abuse. We separate them and sweat them in the rooms. We go for the wife and get a confession. Get her to waive spousal privilege and give us her husband, that rat bastard.'

'You're talking about a very powerful and politically connected family.'

'Don't tell me you're afraid of the car czar.'

Bosch checked her look to make sure she was kidding.

'I'm afraid of moving too fast and blowing it. We've got nothing that directly links anybody to Stacey Kincaid or Howard Elias. If we bring mom down here and don't turn her, then we watch the car czar drive away. That's what I'm afraid of, okay?'

Rider nodded.

'She's dying to be turned,' Edgar said. 'Why else send those notes to Elias?'

Bosch put his elbows on the desk and washed his face with his hands as he thought about things. He had to make a decision.

'What about Charlotte's Web Site?' he asked, his face still covered by his hands. 'What do we do with that?'

'We give that to Inglert and the O'Connors,' Rider said. 'They'll jump all over it. Like I said, they'll be able to trace the good guy list to the users. They'll identify them and take them down. We're talking multiple arrests of an Internet pedophile ring. That's just for starters. The DA might want to try to link them all to the homicides.'

'They're probably all over the country,' Edgar said. 'Not just L.A.'

'They might be all over the world but it won't matter. Our people will work with the bureau on it.'

More silence passed by and Bosch finally dropped his hands to the desk. He'd made his decision.

'Okay,' he said. 'You two stay here and work on the search warrants. I want them ready to go tonight, in case we decide to move. We want all weapons, computer equipment – you know what to do. I want warrants for the old house, which they still own, as well as the new house, all cars and Kincaid's office. Also, Jerry, see what you can find out about the security guy.'

'D.C. Richter, will do. What—'

'In fact, on the warrants, write up one for his car.'

'What's the PC?' Rider asked.

Bosch thought a moment. He knew what he wanted but he needed a legal means of getting there.

'Just say that as Kincaid's director of security it is believed that his vehicle may have been used in the commission of crimes relating to Stacey Kincaid.'

'That's not probable cause, Harry.'

'We stick the warrant in with the other ones,' he said. 'Maybe the judge won't care after he's read what is in them. In fact, check the judge list. Let's take these to a woman.'

Rider smiled and said, 'Aren't we sly?'

'What are you going to be doing, Harry?' Edgar asked.

'I'm going downtown to talk to Irving and Lindell, tell them what we got and see how they want to play it.'

Bosch looked at Rider and now saw disappointment.

'Harry, this isn't like you,' she said. 'You know that if you go to Irving he'll take the conservative route. He won't let us move until we've nailed down every possibility.'

Bosch nodded and said, 'Normally, that would be true. But these aren't normal times. He wants to prevent the city from burning. Going with this, and going fast, might be the way. Irving's smart enough to see that.'

'You have too much faith in human nature,' she said.

'What are you talking about?'

'The best way of cooling this city off is to arrest a cop. Irving's already down there with Sheehan in the box. He isn't going to want to hear this, Harry.'

'You think that if you arrest the car czar and say he did Elias that everybody will believe you and be cool,' Edgar added. 'You don't understand. There are people out there who *need* this to be a cop and they won't listen to anything else. Irving's smart enough to see that, too.'

Bosch thought of Sheehan downtown at Parker Center in a room. He was being measured as the department's sacrificial lamb.

'Just work on the warrants,' he said. 'I'll worry about the rest.'

27

Bosch looked out the window and down at the protestors lining the sidewalks in front of Parker Center and across Los Angeles Street. They moved in orderly lines, carrying signs that said 'JUSTICE NOW' on one side and 'JUSTICE FOR HOWARD ELIAS' on the other. The duplication of the signs attested to the careful orchestration of the protest for the benefit of the media. Bosch saw Reverend Preston Tuggins was one of the marchers. As he walked, reporters walked along with him, sticking microphones in front of him and focusing cameras at his face. Bosch didn't see any signs that said anything about Catalina Perez.

'Detective Bosch,' Deputy Chief Irving said from behind him. 'Run it down for us. You've told us what information you've accumulated. Now put it into perspective. Tell us what you think it means.'

Bosch turned around. He looked at Irving, then at Lindell. They were in Irving's office. Irving was ensconced behind his desk, sitting ramrod straight in his full uniform – an indication he would be appearing at a press conference later. Lindell sat in one of the chairs across the desk. Bosch had just recounted for them what Rider had come up with and the steps his team had taken to that point. Irving now wanted his interpretation of it all.

Bosch composed his thoughts as he stepped back to the desk and took the seat next to Lindell.

'I think Sam Kincaid killed his stepdaughter or had something to do with it. There never was an abduction. That was the story he cooked up. Then he got lucky. He caught a big break when those fingerprints happened to point to Harris. After that was discovered he was practically home free.'

'Start at the start.'

'Okay. You start with Kincaid being a pedophile. He married Kate six years ago, probably as a cover. And to get at her daughter. The girl's body was too decomposed for the coroner to determine if there was indication of long-term sexual abuse. But I'm saying there was. And at—'

'The mother knew?'

'I don't know. She found out at some point but *when* that was is the question.'

'Go on. Sorry to interrupt.'

'Something happened last summer. Maybe the girl threatened to tell someone – her mother, if she didn't know yet, or maybe go to authorities. Or maybe Kincaid simply grew tired of her. Pedophiles target a specific age group. They're not interested in children older than their target group.

Stacey Kincaid was about to turn twelve. She may have been too old for her stepfather's . . . tastes. If she was no longer of use to him in that way, she was only a danger to him.'

'This conversation is turning my stomach, Detective. We are talking about an eleven-year-old girl.'

'What do you want me to do about it, Chief? It's turning mine, too. I've seen the pictures.'

'Then move on please.'

'So something happened and he killed her. He hid the body and jimmied the window. He then let events take place. In the morning the mother finds her gone and calls the cops. The abduction story starts to unfold.'

'He then gets lucky,' Lindell said.

'Right. He catches a nice piece of luck. Of all the prints collected in the girl's room and the rest of the house, the computer spits out a match with Michael Harris, ex-convict and all-around dirtbag. RHD was off to the races then. Like they were wearing blinders. They dropped everything and Harris became the only focus. They picked him up and did their thing with him. Only a funny thing happened on the way to a conviction. Harris didn't confess and there was no other evidence to go with those fingerprints. Meantime, Harris's name was leaked to the media. It became known that the cops had a suspect. Kincaid found out where Harris lived – maybe he got it from a friendly cop who was just keeping the parents of the victim informed. However it happened, he knew where Harris lived. He went to the spot where he'd hidden the body and moved it. My guess is that it was in the trunk of a car all along. Probably on one of his car lots. Anyway, he took the body to Harris's neighborhood and dumped it in a trash lot a couple blocks from the suspect's apartment. When it was found the next morning, the cops finally had another piece of evidence – circumstantial as it was – to go with the fingerprints. But all Harris was was a patsy.'

'His prints had been left when he washed Mrs Kincaid's car,' Irving said.

'Right.'

'So what about Elias?' Lindell asked. 'How did he get himself killed?'

'I think Mrs Kincaid did that. By mistake. At some point since she put her daughter in the ground I think she started seeing ghosts. She was feeling guilty about her daughter and maybe tried to make it right. She knew what her husband was capable of, maybe he had even threatened her outright, so she tried to do it on the sly. She started sending anonymous letters to Elias, to help him along. It did. Elias was able to get to the secret web site, Charlotte's Web. Once he saw those pictures of the girl, he knew who the real killer probably was. He was going about it very quietly. But he was going to subpoena Kincaid and spring it on him in court. Only he made a mistake and showed his hand. He left a trail on the web site. Kincaid or the operators of the site learned they had been compromised.'

'They sent out a gun,' Lindell said.

'I seriously doubt it was Kincaid himself. But probably somebody working for him. He's got a security guy working for him. We're checking him out.'

They all sat silent for a long moment. Irving clasped his hands on the desk in front of him. There was nothing on top of it. It was just polished wood.

'You have to cut Sheehan loose,' Bosch said. 'He didn't do it.'

'Don't worry about Sheehan,' Irving said. 'If he's clean he goes home. I want to know how we proceed with Kincaid. It seems so . . .'

Bosch ignored his hesitancy.

'We do what we're doing,' he said. 'We get search warrants signed and ready to go. I'm supposed to meet Mrs Kincaid tomorrow morning at the old house. I go, try to play her, try to get an admission. I think she's fragile, maybe ready to be flipped. Either way, we spring the warrants. We use everybody and hit all places at once – the homes, the cars, the offices. We see what they bring. We also have to pull records on his dealerships. Find out what cars Kincaid was using back in July. Richter, too.'

'Richter?'

'He's the security guy.'

Irving got up and went to the window this time.

'You're talking about a member of a family that helped build this city,' he said. 'The son of Jackson Kincaid.'

'I know that,' Bosch replied. 'The guy's from a powerful family. He's even proprietary about the smog. He looks at it like it's a family accomplishment. But that doesn't matter, Chief. Not after what he's done.'

Irving's eyes dropped and Bosch knew he was looking down at the protest march.

'The city's held together . . .'

He didn't finish. Bosch knew what he was thinking. That those people down on the sidewalks were expecting news of charges being filed – against a cop.

'Where are we with Detective Sheehan?' Irving asked.

Lindell looked at his watch.

'We've been talking to him for six hours now. When I left he had yet to say a single self-incriminating word in regard to the murder of Howard Elias.'

'He previously threatened the victim in the manner in which the victim was killed.'

'That was a long time ago. Plus, it was said in public, in front of witnesses. It's been my experience that people who make threats like that usually don't carry them out. They are blowing off steam most of the time.'

Irving nodded, his face still to the window.

'What about ballistics?' he asked.

'Nothing yet. The autopsy on Elias was supposed to start this afternoon. I sent Detective Chastain over. They'll dig the slugs out and he'll take them over to your firearms people. It will take too long to send them to my people in Washington. But remember, Chief, Sheehan volunteered his gun. He said, "Do the ballistics." Yes, he carries a nine but I kinda think he wouldn't have offered the gun if he didn't know the gun wouldn't match the bullets.'

'And his home?'

'We searched it top to bottom – again, with his permission. Nothing. No other weapons, no hate notes about Elias, nothing.'

'Alibi?'

'Only place he's hurting. He was home alone Friday night.'

'What about his wife?' Bosch asked.

'The wife and kids were up in Bakersfield,' Lindell said. 'Apparently they've been up there a good long time.'

It was one more surprise about Sheehan. Bosch wondered why Sheehan hadn't mentioned it when Bosch had asked about his family.

Irving remained silent and Lindell continued.

'I guess what I'm saying is that we can hold him and wait till tomorrow when we've got the ballistics report to clear him. Or we can hop on Harry's wagon and kick him loose now. But we keep him overnight and the expectations out on the street will just rise that much further . . .'

'And if we release him without explanation we could touch off a riot,' Irving said.

Irving continued to stare at the window, brooding. This time Lindell waited.

'Kick him loose at six,' Irving finally said. 'At the five o'clock briefing I will say he is being released pending further investigation. I can hear the howls already from Preston Tuggins and his people.'

'That's not good enough, Chief,' Bosch said. 'You have to say he's clear. "Pending further investigation?" You might as well say we think he did it but we don't have the evidence to charge him yet.'

Irving wheeled from the window and looked at Bosch.

'Do not dare to tell me what is good enough, Detective. You do your job and I will do mine. Speaking of which, the briefing is in an hour. I want your two partners there for it. I am not going to stand up there with a bunch of white faces behind me and say we are letting a white cop go pending further investigation. I want your people there this time. And absolutely no excuse will be acceptable.'

'They'll be there.'

'Good. Now let's talk about what we will say to the media about the direction the investigation is heading in.'

The press conference was short. This time there was no sign of the chief of police. It was left to Irving to explain that the investigation was continuing and widening. He also said that the police officer who had been interviewed for several hours was being released. This brought an immediate chorus of shouted questions from the reporters. Irving raised his hands as if the action might in some way control the crowd. He was wrong.

'We are not going to turn this into a shouting match,' he barked. 'I will take a handful of questions and that is it. We have an investigation to get back to. We—'

'What do you mean by released, Chief?' Harvey Button called out. 'Are you saying he has been cleared or you just don't have evidence to hold him?'

Irving looked at Button for a moment before answering.

'What I am saying is that the investigation is now moving into other areas.'

'Then Detective Sheehan has been cleared, correct?'

'I am not getting into naming people we talk to.'

'Chief, we all know the name. Why can't you answer the question?'

Bosch thought it was amusing in a cynical sort of way to watch this exchange because Lindell had convinced him it was Irving who had first leaked Frankie Sheehan's name to the media. Now the deputy chief was trying to act insulted that it was out there.

'All I am saying is that the police officer we have talked to provided satisfactory answers at this time. He is going home and that is all I am—'

'What other directions is the investigation going in?' another reporter called out.

'I cannot get into detail,' Irving said. 'Suffice it to say we will be turning over every stone.'

'Can we ask the FBI agent questions?'

Irving glanced back at Lindell, who was standing at the back of the stage next to Bosch, Edgar and Rider. He then looked back at the crowd of lights, cameras and reporters.

'The FBI and the LAPD have decided this will best be handled by funneling information through the police department. If you have a question, ask me.'

'Are other cops being questioned?' Button called out.

Irving had to think again to make sure he put the right words in the right order.

'Yes, police officers are being questioned in a routine manner. At this point there are no police officers that we would classify as suspects.'

'Then you are saying Sheehan is not a suspect.'

Button got him. Irving knew it. He had talked himself into a logic corner. But he took the easy, if not disingenuous, way out.

'No comment.'

'Chief,' Button continued, above the din of other reporters, 'the murders are almost forty-eight hours old. Are you saying there are no solid suspects at this time?'

'We're not going to get into what suspects there may or may not be. Next.'

Irving quickly pointed to another reporter in order to steer things away from Button. The questioning went on for another ten minutes. At one point Bosch looked over at Rider and she gave him a look that said, *What are we doing here?* And Bosch returned a look that answered, *We are wasting our time.*

When it was finally over, Bosch huddled on the stage with Edgar and Rider. They had arrived from Hollywood station just as the press conference had begun and he hadn't had time to talk to them.

'So where are we on the search warrants?' he asked.

'Almost done,' Edgar said. 'It didn't help that we had to come down here for the dog and pony show.'

'I know.'

'Harry, I thought you were going to steer us clear of this stuff,' Rider said.

'I know. It was selfish. Frankie Sheehan is a friend. What they did to him, leaking his name like that, was bullshit. I was hoping that having you two here might add some credibility to the announcement that he was being let go.'

'So you used us the way Irving wanted to yesterday,' she said. 'You wouldn't let him do it but it was okay for yourself.'

Bosch studied her face. He could tell she was genuinely angry at being used in such a way. Bosch knew that it was a betrayal. A small one in his mind, but a betrayal just the same.

'Look, Kiz, we can talk about this later. But like I said, Frankie's a friend. He's now your friend for this. And that could be valuable someday.'

He waited and watched and finally she gave a slight nod. It was over, for now.

'How much more time do you need?' he asked.

'Maybe an hour,' Edgar said. 'Then we've got to find a judge.'

'Why?' Rider said. 'What did Irving say?'

'Irving's sitting on the fence. So I want to have everything ready. I want to be able to move. Tomorrow morning.'

'Tomorrow morning's no problem,' Edgar said.

'Good. Then you two go back and finish up. Get to a judge tonight. Tomorrow we'll—'

'Detective Bosch?'

Bosch turned. Harvey Button and his producer, Tom Chainey, were standing there.

'I can't talk to you,' Bosch said.

'We understand that you have reopened the Stacey Kincaid case,' Chainey said. 'We'd like to talk to you about—'

'Who told you that?' Bosch snapped, anger quickly showing on his face.

'We have a source who—'

'Well, tell your source he's full of shit. No comment.'

A cameraman came up and poked his lens over Button's shoulder. Button raised a microphone.

'Have you exonerated Michael Harris?' Button blurted out.

'I said no comment,' Bosch said. 'Get that out of here.'

Bosch reached to the camera and put his hand over the lens. The cameraman shrieked.

'Don't touch the camera! This is private property.'

'So is my face. Get it away from me. The press conference is over.'

Bosch put his hand on Button's shoulder and forcefully ushered him off the stage. The cameraman followed. So did Chainey, but in a slow, calm way as if daring Bosch to manhandle him as well. Their eyes locked.

'Watch the news tonight, Detective,' Chainey said. 'You might find it interesting.'

'I doubt that,' Bosch said.

Twenty minutes later Bosch was sitting on an empty desk at the mouth of the hallway that led to the RHD interview rooms on the third floor. He was still thinking about the exchange he'd had with Button and Chainey and wondering what they had. He heard one of the doors open and looked up. Frankie Sheehan came down the hallway with Lindell. Bosch's old partner looked drained. His face was slack, his hair unkempt and his clothes – the same ones he had worn the night before in the bar – were disheveled. Bosch slid off the desk and stood up, ready to deflect a physical assault if need be. But Sheehan apparently read his body language and raised his hands, palms forward. He smiled crookedly.

'It's okay, Harry,' Sheehan said, his voice very tired and hoarse. 'Agent Lindell here gave me the scoop. Part of it, at least. It wasn't you who . . . It was myself. You know I forgot all about threatening that douche bag.'

Bosch nodded.

'Come on, Frankie,' he said. 'I'll give you a ride.'

Without thinking too much about it Bosch led him to the main elevators and they headed down to the lobby. They stood side by side, both looking up at the lighted numbers above the door.

'Sorry I doubted you, buddy,' Sheehan said quietly.

'Don't worry about it, buddy. That makes us even.'

'Yeah? How so?'

'Last night when I asked about the prints.'

'You still doubt them?'

'Nope. Not at all.'

In the lobby they went out a side door to the employee parking lot. They were about halfway to the car when Bosch heard a commotion and turned to see several reporters and cameramen moving toward them.

'Don't say anything,' Bosch said quickly. 'Don't say a word to them.'

The initial wave of reporters descended quickly and surrounded them. Bosch could see more coming.

'No comment,' Bosch said. 'No comment.'

But it wasn't Bosch they cared about. They shoved their microphones and cameras at Sheehan's face. His eyes, so tired before, seemed wild now, even scared. Bosch tried to pull his friend through the crowd and to the car. The reporters shouted their questions.

'Detective Sheehan, did you kill Howard Elias?' a woman asked, louder than the others.

'No,' Sheehan said. 'I didn't – I didn't do anything.'

'Did you previously threaten the victim?'

'Look, no comment,' Bosch said before Sheehan could react to the question. 'Do you hear that? No comment. Leave us a—'

'Why were you questioned?'

'Tell us why you were questioned, Detective.'

They were almost there. Some of the reporters had dropped off, realizing they would get nothing. But most of the cameras were staying with them. They could always use the video. Suddenly, Sheehan broke from Bosch's grip and wheeled around on the reporters.

'You want to know why I was questioned? I was questioned because the department needs to sacrifice somebody. To keep the peace. Doesn't matter who it is, as long as they fit the bill. That's where I came in. I fit the—'

Bosch grabbed Sheehan and yanked him away from the microphones.

'Come on, Frankie, forget about them.'

By moving between two parked cars they were able to cut off the clot of reporters and cameramen. Bosch pushed Sheehan quickly to his slickback and opened the door. By the time the reporters followed in single file to the car, Sheehan was inside and safe from the microphones. Bosch went around to his side and got in.

They drove in silence until they were on the 101 Freeway going north. Bosch then glanced over at Sheehan. His eyes were staring ahead.

'You shouldn't have said that, Frankie. You're fanning the fire.'

'I don't give a fuck about the fire. Not anymore.'

Silence returned. They were on the freeway cutting through Hollywood and traffic was light. Bosch could see smoke rising from a fire somewhere to the south and west. He thought about putting KFWB on the radio but decided he didn't want to know what that smoke meant.

'They give you a chance in there to call Margaret?' he asked after a while.

'Nope. They didn't give me a chance to do anything other than confess. I'm sure glad you rode into town and saved the day, Harry. I never did get told what you told 'em but whatever it was it sure saved my ass.'

Bosch knew what Sheehan was asking but he wasn't ready to tell him.

'The media's probably been out to your house,' he said instead. 'Margaret probably got blindsided with this.'

'I got news for you, Harry. Margaret left me eight months ago. Took the girls and moved to Bakersfield. To be near her folks. There's nobody at my house.'

'Sorry, Frankie.'

'I should've told you last night when you asked about them.'

Bosch drove for a little bit, thinking about things.

'Why don't you get some stuff from your place and come stay at my house? The reporters won't find you. Until this blows over.'

'I don't know, Harry. Your house is the size of a box of Girl Scout cookies. I'm already claustrophobic from being in that room all day. Besides, I never met your wife, you know? She's not going to want some stranger sleeping on your couch.'

Bosch looked at the Capitol Records building as the freeway cut past it. It was supposed to resemble a stack of records with a phonograph stylus on top. But like most of Hollywood time had passed it by. They didn't make records anymore. Music came on compact discs. They sold record albums in secondhand stores now. Sometimes all of Hollywood seemed like a secondhand store to Bosch.

'My house got wrecked in the earthquake,' Bosch said. 'It's rebuilt now. I even have a guest room ... and, Frankie, my wife left me, too.'

It felt strange to say it out loud. As if it was some form of confirmation of the death of his marriage.

'Oh, shit, Harry, you guys only got married a year or so ago. When did this happen?'

Bosch looked over at him and then back at the road.

'Recently.'

There were no reporters waiting outside Sheehan's home when they got there twenty minutes later. Bosch said he was going to wait in the car and make some calls while Sheehan got his things. When he was alone he called his house to check for messages, so he wouldn't have to play them in front of Sheehan when they got there. But there were none. He put the phone away and just sat. He wondered if his inviting Sheehan to stay at his house had been a subconscious effort to avoid facing the emptiness of the place. After a while he decided it wasn't. He had lived alone most of his life. He was used to places that were empty. He knew the real shelter of a home was inside yourself.

Light washing across the mirrors caught Bosch's eyes. He checked the side view and saw the lights of a car that was being parked against the curb a block or so back. He doubted it was a reporter. A reporter would have pulled right into Sheehan's driveway, made no effort at concealment. He started thinking about what he wanted to ask Sheehan.

A few minutes later his former partner came out of the house carrying a grocery bag. He opened the back door and tossed it in, then got in up front. He was smiling.

'Margie took all the suitcases,' he said. 'I didn't realize that till tonight.'

They took Beverly Glen up the hill to Mulholland and then took it east to Woodrow Wilson. Bosch usually loved driving Mulholland at night. The curving road, the city lights coming in and out of view. But along the way they drove by The Summit and Bosch studied the gate and thought about the Kincaids somewhere behind it in the safety of their home with jetliner views.

'Frankie, I have to ask you something,' he said.

'Shoot.'

'Back on the Kincaid thing, during the investigation, did you talk to Kincaid much? Sam Kincaid, I mean.'

'Yeah, sure. Guy like that you handled with kid gloves. Him and the old man. You be careful, else it might come back on you.'

'Yeah. So you were pretty much keeping him informed on what was happening?'

'Yeah, pretty much. What about it? You're sounding like those bureau guys who were all over me all day, Harry.'

'Sorry, just asking. Did he call you a lot or did you call him?'

'Both ways. He also had a security guy who was talking to us, staying in touch.'

'D.C. Richter?'

'Yeah, that's him. Harry, you going to tell me what's goin' on or what?'

'In a minute. Let me ask you something first. How much did you tell Kincaid or Richter about Michael Harris, you remember?'

'What do you mean?'

'Look, I'm not saying you did anything wrong. A case like that, you keep the principals involved and informed. So did you go to them and tell them you had brought Harris in on the fingerprints and, you know, that you were smoking him in the rooms?'

'Sure we did. Standard operating procedure.'

'Right. And did you tell them about who Harris was and where he came from, that sort of thing?'

'I suppose I did.'

Bosch let it go for a while. He turned onto Woodrow Wilson and drove the winding road down to the house. He pulled into the carport.

'Hey, this looks nice,' Sheehan said.

Bosch put the car into park but paused before getting out.

'Did you tell the Kincaids or Richter specifically where Harris lived?' he asked.

Sheehan looked over at him.

'What are you telling me?'

'I'm *asking* you. Did you tell any of them where Harris lived?'

'I might have. I don't remember.'

Bosch got out and headed to the kitchen door. Sheehan got his stuff out of the back seat and followed.

'Talk to me, Hieronymus.'

Bosch unlocked the door.

742

'I think you made a mistake.'

He went inside.

'Talk to me, Hieronymus.'

Bosch led Sheehan to the guest room and Sheehan threw his bag onto the bed. Back out in the hall Bosch pointed into the bathroom and headed back into the living room. Sheehan was silent, waiting.

'The toilet handle in that one is broken,' Bosch said, not looking at him. 'You have to hold it down the whole time it's flushing.'

He now looked at his former partner.

'We can explain Harris's fingerprints. He didn't abduct or kill Stacey Kincaid. In fact, we don't even think there was an abduction. Kincaid killed his stepdaughter. He was abusing her and killed her, then staged the abduction scene. He got lucky when the prints on the book tied in Harris. He then used it. We think it was him – or his man, Richter – who dumped the body near Harris's place because he knew where that place was. So think, Francis. I don't want probablys. I need to know if you told Kincaid or his security man where Harris lived.'

Sheehan looked dumbfounded and his eyes wandered to the floor.

'You're saying we were wrong about Harris . . .'

'You guys had blinders on, man. Once those prints came up, you could only see Harris.'

Sheehan kept his eyes on the floor and slowly nodded his head.

'We all make mistakes, Frankie. Sit down and think about what I just asked. What did you tell Kincaid and at what point did you tell him? I'll be right back.'

While he left Sheehan to ponder what he had just been told, Bosch went back down the hall to his bedroom. He stepped in and looked around. It looked the same. He opened the door to the walk-in closet and hit the light. Eleanor's clothes were gone. He looked down at the floor. Her shoes had been cleared out as well. On the rug he saw a little bundle of netting tied with a blue ribbon. He bent down and picked it up. The netting was wrapped around a handful of rice. He remembered that the chapel in Las Vegas had provided the rice bundles as part of the wedding package – for tossing at the happy couple. Eleanor had kept one as a keepsake. Now Bosch wondered if she had mistakenly left it behind or had simply discarded it.

Bosch dropped the bundle into his pocket and turned off the light.

28

Edgar and Rider had rolled the television out of the lieutenant's office and were watching the news when Bosch walked into the squad room after leaving Sheehan at his house. They barely looked up to acknowledge him.

'What?' Bosch asked.

'I guess people didn't like us cutting Sheehan loose,' Edgar said.

'Sporadic looting and arson,' Rider said. 'Nothing like last time. I think we'll make it if we get through this night. We got roving platoons out there and they're coming down on anything that moves.'

'No bullshit like last time,' Edgar added.

Bosch nodded and stared at the TV for a few moments. The screen showed firefighters aiming three-inch hoses into the balling flames pouring through the roof of another strip mall. It was too late to save it. It almost seemed as though it was being done for the media.

'Urban redevelopment,' Edgar said. 'Get rid of all the strip malls.'

'Problem is, they just put strip malls back,' Rider said.

'At least they look better than before,' Edgar said. 'Real problem is the liquor stores. These things always start in the liquor stores. We put a squad out front of every liquor store, no riot.'

'Where are we on the warrants?' Bosch asked.

'We're done,' Rider said. 'We just have to take them over to the judge.'

'Who are you thinking about?'

'Terry Baker. I already called and she said she'd be around.'

'Good. Let's have a look.'

Rider got up and walked over to the homicide table while Edgar stayed behind and continued to watch the television. Stacked neatly at her spot were the search warrant applications. She handed them to Bosch.

'We've got the two houses, all cars, all offices and on Richter we have his car at the time of the killing and his apartment – we threw that in, too,' she said. 'I think we're set.'

Each petition was several pages stapled together. Bosch knew that the first two pages were always standard legalese. He skipped these and quickly read the probable cause statements of each package. Rider and Edgar had done well, though Bosch knew it was likely Rider's doing. She had the best legal mind of the team. Even the PC statements on the proposed search of Richter's apartment and car were going to fly. Using clever language and selected facts from the investigation, the PC statement said the evidence of the case indicated two suspects were involved in the disposal of Stacey

Kincaid's body. And by virtue of the close employer/employee relationship that existed at the time between Sam Kincaid and D.C. Richter, Richter could be considered a second suspect. The petition asked permission to search all vehicles operated or accessible by the two men at the time of the crime. It was a carefully worded tap dance but it would work, Bosch believed. Asking to search all cars 'accessible' by the two men was a masterstroke by Rider. If approved, this essentially would allow them access to any car on any one of the car lots owned by Kincaid because he most certainly had access to those cars.

'Looks good,' Bosch said when he had finished reading. He handed the stack back to Rider. 'Let's get them signed tonight so tomorrow we can move when we want to.'

A search warrant was good for twenty-four hours following approval from a judge. In most cases it could be extended another twenty-four hours with a phone call to the signing judge.

'What about this Richter guy?' Bosch asked then. 'We get anything on him yet?'

'A little,' Edgar said.

He finally got up, turned the sound down on the television and came over to the table.

'Guy was a washout at the academy. This is way back, fall of eighty-one. He then went to one of those bullshit private eye academies in the Valley. Got his state license in eighty-four. Apparently went to work for the Kincaid family after that. He worked his way up to the top, I guess.'

'Why was he a washout?'

'We don't know yet. It's Sunday night, Harry. Nobody's over at the academy. We'll pull the records tomorrow.'

Bosch nodded.

'You check the computer, see if he's got a concealed license?'

'Oh, yeah, we did. He's got a license to carry. He's strapped.'

'With what? Tell me it's a nine.'

'Sorry, Harry. The ATF was closed tonight. We'll get that tomorrow, too. All we know now is that he's got a license to carry a concealed weapon.'

'Okay, remember that, you two. Remember how good the shooter was on Angels Flight.'

Rider and Edgar nodded.

'So you think Richter's doing Kincaid's bidding?' Rider asked.

'Probably. The rich don't get themselves dirty like that. They call the shots, they don't take 'em. Right now I like Richter.'

He looked at his partners a moment. He felt that they were very close to breaking this thing open. They'd know in the next twenty-four hours. He hoped the city could wait that long.

'What else?' he asked.

'You get Sheehan all tucked in?' Rider asked.

Bosch noted the tone of her voice.

'Yeah, he's tucked in. And, uh, look, I apologize about the press conference. Irving wanted you there but I probably could've gotten you out of it. I didn't. I know it wasn't a good move. I apologize.'

'Okay, Harry,' Rider said.

Edgar nodded.

'Anything else before we go?'

Edgar started shaking his head, then said, 'Oh, yeah. Firearms called with an FYI. They took a look at Michael Harris's gun this morning and it looks clean. They said it probably hasn't been fired or cleaned in months, judging by the dust buildup in the barrel. So he's clear.'

'They going to go ahead with it anyway?'

'That's what they were calling for. They got an ASAP from Irving to do Sheehan's gun tomorrow morning as soon as they get the slugs from the autopsy. They wanted to know if you wanted them to go ahead with Harris's piece. I told them they might as well.'

'Good. Anything else?'

Edgar and Rider shook their heads.

'Okay then,' Bosch said. 'Let's go see Judge Baker and then we'll call it a day. I have a feeling tomorrow's gonna be a long one.'

29

It had started to rain. Bosch pulled into his carport and shut off his car. He was looking forward to a couple of beers to take the caffeine edge off his nerves. Judge Baker had served them coffee while she reviewed the search warrant petitions. She had reviewed the search warrants slowly and thoroughly and Bosch had drunk two full cups. In the end, though, she had signed every warrant and Bosch didn't need the caffeine to feel jazzed. The next morning they would be 'hunting and confronting,' as Kiz Rider called it – the put-up or shut-up phase of an investigation, the point where theories and hunches culminated in hard evidence and charges. Or they disintegrated.

Bosch went in through the kitchen door. Besides the beer, he was already thinking about Kate Kincaid and how he would handle her the next day. He was looking forward to it the way a confident quarterback who has digested all the film and known strategies of the opposition looks forward to the next day's game.

The light was already on in the kitchen. Bosch put his briefcase on the counter and opened the refrigerator. There was no beer.

'Shit,' he said.

He knew there had been at least five bottles of Anchor Steam in the refrigerator. He turned and saw the five bottle caps on the counter. He started further into the house.

'Hey, Frankie!' he called. 'Don't tell me you drank everything!'

There was no reply. Bosch moved through the dining room and then the living room. The place appeared as he had left it earlier that evening, as if Sheehan had not made himself at home. He checked the rear deck through the glass doors. The light was off outside and he saw no sign of his former partner. He walked down the hallway and leaned close to the closed door of the guest room. He heard nothing. He looked at his watch. It wasn't yet eleven.

'Frankie?' he whispered.

No reply, only the sound of the rain on the roof. He knocked lightly on the door.

'Frankie?' he said louder.

Still nothing. Bosch reached to the knob and slowly opened the door. The lights were off in the room but light from the hallway cut across the bed and Bosch could see it was not occupied. He flicked the wall switch and a bed table lamp came on. The bag Sheehan had carried his belongings in was empty on the floor. His clothes had been dumped onto the bed in a pile.

Bosch's curiosity turned into a low-grade concern. He quickly moved back into the hallway and made a quick search of his own bedroom and the bathrooms. There was no sign of Sheehan.

Back in the living room Bosch paced about for a few moments wondering what Sheehan might have done. He had no car. It was unlikely he would have tried to walk down the hill into the city and where would he be going anyway? Bosch picked up the phone and hit redial to see if by chance Sheehan had called a cab. It sounded like more than seven tones to Bosch but the redial was so fast he wasn't sure. After one ring the phone was answered by the sleepy voice of a woman.

'Yes?'

'Uh, who is this, please?'

'Who is this?'

'I'm sorry. My name is Detective Harry Bosch of the LAPD. I am trying to trace a call that was made from—'

'Harry, it's Margie Sheehan.'

'Oh . . . Margie . . .'

He realized he should have guessed Sheehan would have called her.

'What's wrong, Harry?'

'Nothing, Margie, nothing. I'm trying to find Frankie and I thought maybe he called a cab or something. I'm sorry to—'

'What do you mean, find him?'

He could read the rising concern in her voice.

'It's nothing to worry about, Margie. He was staying with me tonight and I had to go out. I just got home and he isn't here. I'm just trying to figure out where he went. He talked to you tonight?'

'Earlier.'

'How'd he seem, okay?'

'He told me what they did to him. How they're trying to blame him.'

'No, not anymore. That's why he's staying with me. We got him out of there and he's going to hide out here a few days, till it blows over. I'm really sorry that I woke—'

'He said they'd come back for him.'

'What?'

'He doesn't believe they're going to let him go. He doesn't trust anybody, Harry. In the department. Except you. He knows you're his friend.'

Bosch was silent. He wasn't sure what to say.

'Harry, find him, would you? Then call me back. I don't care what time it is.'

Bosch looked through the glass doors to the deck and from this angle saw something on the deck railing. He stepped over to the wall and flipped on the outside light. He saw five amber beer bottles lined up on the railing.

'Okay, Margie. Give me your number.'

He took the number and was about to hang up when she spoke again.

'Harry, he told me you got married and divorced already.'

'Well, I'm not divorced but . . . you know.'

'Yes, I know. Take care, Harry. Find Francis and then one of you call me back.'

'Okay.'

He put down the phone, opened the slider and went out onto the deck. The beer bottles were empty. He turned to his right and there, lying on the chaise longue, was the body of Francis Sheehan. Hair and blood were splattered on the cushion above his head and on the wall next to the slider.

'Jesus,' Bosch whispered out loud.

He stepped closer. Sheehan's mouth was open. Blood had pooled in it and spilled over his bottom lip. There was a saucer-sized exit wound at the crown of his head. Rain had matted the hair down, exposing the horrible wound even more. Bosch took one step back and looked around the deck planking. He saw a pistol lying just in front of the chaise's front left leg.

Bosch stepped forward again and looked down at his friend's body. He blew his breath out with a loud animal-like sound.

'Frankie,' he whispered.

A question went through his mind but he didn't say it out loud.

Did I do this?

Bosch watched one of the coroner's people close the body bag over Frankie Sheehan's face while the other two held umbrellas. They then put the umbrellas aside and lifted the body onto a gurney, covered it with a green blanket and began wheeling it into the house and toward the front door. Bosch had to be asked to step out of the way. As he watched them head to the front door the crushing weight of the guilt he was feeling took hold again. He looked up into the sky and saw there were no helicopters, thankfully. The notifications and call outs had all been made by landline. No radio reports meant the media had yet to pick up on the suicide of Frankie Sheehan. Bosch knew that the ultimate insult to his former partner would have been for a news chopper to hover over the house and film the body lying on the deck.

'Detective Bosch?'

Bosch turned. Deputy Chief Irving beckoned from the open slider. Bosch went inside and followed Irving to the dining room table. Agent Roy Lindell was already standing there.

'Let us talk about this,' Irving said. 'Patrol is outside with a woman who says she is your neighbor. Adrienne Tegreeny?'

'Yes.'

'Yes what?'

'She lives next door.'

'She said she heard three or four shots from the house earlier tonight. She thought it was you. She did not call the police.'

Bosch just nodded.

'Have you fired weapons in the house or off the deck before?'

Bosch hesitated before answering.

'Chief, this isn't about me. So let's just say that there could be reason for her to have thought it was me.'

'Fine. The point I'm making is that it appears Detective Sheehan was drinking – drinking heavily – and firing his weapon. What is your interpretation of what happened?'

'Interpretation?' Bosch said, staring blankly at the table.

'Accidental or intentional.'

'Oh.'

Bosch almost laughed but held back.

'I don't think there's much of a doubt about it,' he said. 'He killed himself. Suicide.'

'But there is no note.'

'No note, just a lot of beers and wasted shots into the sky. That was his note. That said all he had to say. Cops go out that way all the time.'

'The man had been cut loose. Why do this?'

'Well . . . I think it's pretty clear . . .'

'Then make it clear for *us*, would you please?'

'He called his wife tonight. I talked to her after. She said he might have been cut loose but he thought that it wouldn't last.'

'The ballistics?' Irving asked.

'No, I don't think that's what he meant. I think he knew that there was a need to hook somebody up for this. A cop.'

'And so then he kills himself? That does not sound plausible, Detective.'

'He didn't kill Elias. Or that woman.'

'Right now that is only your opinion. The only fact we have is that it appears this man killed himself the night before the day we would get the ballistics. And you, Detective, talked me into cutting him loose so that he could do it.'

Bosch looked away from Irving and tried to contain the anger that was building inside.

'The weapon,' Irving said. 'An old Beretta twenty-five. Serial number acid-burned. Untraceable, illegal. A throw-down gun. Was it your weapon, Detective Bosch?'

Bosch shook his head.

'Are you sure, Detective? I would like to handle this now, without the need for an internal investigation.'

Bosch looked back at him.

'What are you saying? I gave him the gun so he could kill himself? He was my friend – the only friend he had today. It's not my gun, okay? We stopped by his house so he could get some things. He must've gotten it then. I might have helped him do it but that didn't include giving him the gun.'

Bosch and Irving held each other's stares.

'You're forgetting something, Bosch,' Lindell said, interrupting the moment. 'We searched Sheehan's place today. There was no weapon found there.'

Bosch broke away from Irving and looked at Lindell.

'Then your people missed it,' he said. 'He came here with that gun in his bag because it wasn't mine.'

Bosch moved away from them before he let his anger and frustration get the better of him and he said something that might bring departmental charges. He slid down into one of the stuffed chairs in the living room. He was wet but didn't care about the furniture. He stared blankly out the glass doors.

Irving stepped over but didn't sit down.

'What did you mean when you said you helped him?'

Bosch looked up at him.

'Last night I had a drink with him. He told me things. Told me about how he got carried away with Harris, how the things Harris claimed in his lawsuit – the things he said the cops did to him – were true. All of it was true. You see, he was sure Harris had killed the girl, there was no doubt in him about that. But it bothered him what he had done. He told me that in those moments in the room with Harris that he had lost it. He said he became the very thing he had hunted all these years. A monster. It bothered him a lot. I could see it had been eating at him. Then I come along tonight and drive him home . . .'

Bosch felt the guilt rising up like a tide in his throat. He had not been thinking. He had not seen the obvious. He had been too consumed with the case, with Eleanor and his empty house, with things other than Frankie Sheehan.

'And?' Irving prompted.

'And I knocked down the one thing he believed in all these months, the one thing that kept him safe. I told him we had cleared Michael Harris. I told him he was wrong about Harris and that we could prove it. I didn't think about what it would do to him. I was only thinking about my case.'

'And you think that put him over,' Irving said.

'Something happened to him in that room with Harris. Something bad. He lost his family after that, he lost the case . . . I think the one thread he held on to was his belief that he'd had the right guy. When he found out he was wrong – when I stumbled into his world and told him it was bullshit – the thread snapped.'

'Look, this is bullshit, Bosch,' Lindell said. 'I mean, I respect you and your friendship with this guy, but you aren't seeing what is right here in front of us. The obvious. This guy did himself because he's the guy and he knew we'd come back to him. This suicide is a confession.'

Irving stared at Bosch, waiting for him to come back at Lindell. But Bosch said nothing. He was tired of fighting it.

'I find myself agreeing with Agent Lindell on this,' the deputy chief finally said.

Bosch nodded. He expected as much. They didn't know Sheehan the way Bosch did. He and his former partner had not been close in recent years but they had been close enough at one time for Bosch to know that Lindell and Irving were wrong. It would have been easier for him to agree. It would lift a lot of the guilt off him. But he couldn't agree.

'Give me the morning,' he said instead.

'What?' Irving asked.

'Keep this wrapped up and away from the press for half a day. We proceed with the warrants and the plan for tomorrow morning. Give me time to see what comes up and what Mrs Kincaid says.'

'If she talks.'

'She'll talk. She's dying to talk. Let me have the morning with her. See how things go. If I don't come up with a connection between Kincaid and Elias, then you do what you have to do with Frankie Sheehan. You tell the world what you think you know.'

Irving thought about this for a long moment and then nodded.

'I think that would be the most cautious route,' he said. 'We should have a ballistics report by then as well.'

Bosch nodded his thanks. He looked out through the open doors to the deck again. It was starting to rain harder. He looked at his watch and saw how late it was getting. And he knew what he still needed to do before he could sleep.

30

Bosch felt the obligation to go to Margaret Sheehan in person and tell her what Frankie had done to himself. It didn't matter that the couple had been separated. She and Frankie had been together a long time before that happened. She and their two girls deserved the courtesy of a visit from a friend instead of a stranger's dreadful phone call in the middle of the night. Irving had suggested that the Bakersfield Police Department be prevailed upon to send an officer to the house, but Bosch knew that would be just as clumsy and callous as a phone call. He volunteered to make the drive.

Bosch did prevail upon the Bakersfield cop shop, but only to run down an address for Margaret Sheehan. He could have called her to ask for directions. But that would have been telling her without telling her, an old cop's trick for making the job easier. It would have been cowardly.

The northbound Golden State Freeway was almost deserted, the rain and the hour of night having cleared out all but those motorists with no choice but to be on the road. Most of these were truckers hauling their loads north toward San Francisco and even further or returning empty to the vegetable fields of the midstate to pick up more. The Grapevine – the steep and winding stretch of the freeway up and over the mountains lying north of Los Angeles – was littered with semis that had slid off the roadway or whose drivers had chosen to pull over rather than risk the already treacherous run in the pounding rain. Bosch found that once he cleared this obstacle course and came down out of the mountains that he was finally able to pick up some speed and lost time. As he drove he watched branches of lightning spread across the purple horizon to the east. And he thought about his old partner. He tried to think about old cases and the old Irish jokes that Sheehan used to tell. Anything to keep from thinking about what he had done and Bosch's own guilt and culpability.

He had brought a homemade tape with him and played it on the car stereo. It contained recordings of saxophone pieces Bosch particularly liked. He fast-forwarded until he found the one he wanted. It was Frank Morgan's 'Lullaby.' It was like a sweet and soulful funeral dirge to Bosch, a good-bye and apology to Frankie Sheehan. A good-bye and apology to Eleanor. It went well with the rain. Bosch played it over and over as he drove.

He got to the house where Margaret Sheehan and her two daughters were living before two. There was an outside light still on and light could be seen through the curtains of the front windows. Bosch got the idea that Margie was in there waiting for his call, or maybe for him to show up. He hesitated at the door, wondering about how many times he had made this kind of call, then finally knocked.

When Margie answered the door Bosch was reminded of how there was never any planning for these things. She stared at him for a moment and he thought she didn't recognize him. It had been a lot of years.

'Margie, it's—'

'Harry? Harry Bosch? We just—'

She stopped and put it together. Usually they did.

'Oh, Harry, no. Oh no. Not Francis!'

She brought both hands up to her face. Her mouth was open and she looked like that famous painting of someone on a bridge screaming.

'I'm sorry, Margie. I really am. I think maybe I should come in.'

She was stoic about the whole thing. Bosch gave her the details and then Margie Sheehan made coffee for him so he wouldn't fall asleep on the ride back. That was a cop's wife thinking. In the kitchen Bosch leaned against a counter as she brewed the coffee.

'He called you tonight,' he said.

'Yes, I told you.'

'Tell me how he seemed.'

'Bad. He told me what they did to him. He seemed so . . . betrayed? Is that the right word? I mean, his own people, fellow cops, had taken him in. He was very sad, Harry.'

Bosch nodded.

'He gave his life to that department . . . and this is what they did to him.'

Bosch nodded again.

'Did he say anything about . . .'

He didn't finish.

'About killing himself? No, he didn't say that . . . I read up on police suicide once. Long time ago. In fact, back when Elias sued him the first time over that guy he killed. Frankie got real depressed then and I got scared. I read up on it. And what I read said that when people tell you about it or say they're going to do it, what they are really doing is asking you to stop them.'

Bosch nodded.

'I guess Frankie didn't want to be stopped,' she continued. 'He didn't say anything about it to me.'

She pulled the glass coffeepot out of the brewer and poured some into a mug. She then opened a cabinet and took down a silver Thermos. She started filling it.

'This is for the road home. I don't want you falling asleep on the clothesline.'

'What?'

'I mean the Grapevine. I'm not thinking straight here.'

Bosch stepped over and put his hand on her shoulder. She put the coffee pot down and turned to him to be hugged.

'This last year,' she said. 'Things . . . things just went haywire.'

'I know. He told me.'

She broke away from him and went back to filling the Thermos.

'Margie, I have to ask you something before I head back,' Bosch said.

'They took his gun from him today to run ballistics. He used another. Do you know anything about that one?'

'No. He only had the one he wore on the job. We didn't have other guns. Not with two little girls. When Frankie would come home he'd lock his job gun up in a little safe on the floor of the closet. And only he had the key. I just didn't want any more guns than were required in the house.'

Bosch understood that if it was her edict that there be no more weapons than the one Sheehan was required to carry, then that left a hole. He could have taken a weapon in and hidden it from her – in a spot so obscure even the FBI didn't find it when they searched his house. Maybe it was wrapped in plastic and buried in the yard. Sheehan also could have gotten the weapon after she and the girls moved out and up to Bakersfield. She would never have known about it.

'Okay,' he said, deciding not to pursue it.

'Why, Harry, are they saying it was your gun? Are you in trouble?'

Bosch thought a moment before answering.

'No, Margie, I'm fine. Don't worry about me.'

755

31

The rain continued through Monday morning and slowed Bosch's drive into Brentwood to a frustrating crawl. It wasn't heavy rain, but in Los Angeles any rain at all can paralyze the city. It was one of the mysteries Bosch could never fathom. A city largely defined by the automobile yet full of drivers unable to cope with even a mild inclemency. He listened to KFWB as he drove. There were far more reports of traffic tie-ups than incidents of violence or unrest during the night. Unfortunately, the skies were expected to clear by midday.

He arrived twenty minutes late for his appointment with Kate Kincaid. The house from which Stacey Kincaid had allegedly been kidnapped was a sprawling white ranch house with black shutters and a slate-gray roof. It had a broad green lawn stretching back from the street and a driveway that cut across the front of the house, and then back around to the garage in the side yard. When Bosch pulled in there was a silver Mercedes Benz parked near the covered entryway. The front door of the house was open.

When he got to the threshold Bosch called out a hello and he heard Kate Kincaid's voice telling him to enter. He found her in the living room, sitting on a couch that was covered in a white sheet. All the furniture was covered in this way. The room looked like a meeting of big, heavy ghosts. She noticed Bosch's eyes taking in the room.

'When we moved we didn't take a single piece of furniture,' she said. 'We decided just to start over. No reminders.'

Bosch nodded and then studied her. She was dressed completely in white, with a silk blouse tucked into tailored linen pants. She looked like a ghost herself. Her large black leather purse, which was on the couch next to her, seemed to clash with her outfit and the sheets covering the furniture.

'How are you, Mrs Kincaid?'

'Please call me Kate.'

'Kate then.'

'I am very fine, thank you. Better than I have been in a long, long time. How are you?'

'I'm just so-so today, Kate. I had a bad night. And I don't like it when it rains.'

'I'm sorry to hear that. It does look like you haven't slept.'

'Do you mind if I look around a little bit before we start talking?'

He had a signed search warrant for the house in his briefcase but he didn't want to bring it up yet.

'Please do,' she said. 'Stacey's room is down the hall to your left. First door on the left.'

Bosch left his briefcase on the tiled entryway floor and headed the way she had directed. The furniture in the girl's room was not covered. The white sheets that had covered everything were in piles on the floor. It looked like someone – probably the dead girl's mother – had visited here on occasion. The bed was unmade. The pink bedspread and matching sheets were twisted into a knot – not as if by someone sleeping, but maybe by someone who had lain on the bed and gathered the bedclothes to her chest. It made Bosch feel bad seeing it that way.

Bosch stepped to the middle of the room, keeping his hands in the pockets of his raincoat. He studied the girl's things. There were stuffed animals and dolls, a shelf of picture books. No movie posters, no photos of young television stars or pop singers. It was almost as if the room belonged to a girl much younger than Stacey Kincaid had been at the end. Bosch wondered if the design was her parents' or her own, as if maybe she had thought by holding on to the things of her past she could somehow avoid the horror of the present. The thought made him feel worse than when he had studied the bedclothes.

He noticed a hairbrush on the bureau and saw strands of blond hair caught in it. It made him feel a little easier. He knew that the hair from the brush could be used, if it ever came to the point of connecting evidence – possibly from the trunk of a car – to the dead girl.

He stepped over and looked at the window. It was a slider and he saw the black smudges of fingerprint powder still on the frame. He unlocked the window and pulled it open. There were splinter marks where the latch had supposedly been jimmied with a screwdriver or similar tool.

Bosch looked out through the rain at the backyard. There was a lima bean-shaped pool that was covered with a plastic tarp. Rainwater was collecting on the tarp. Again Bosch thought of the girl. He wondered if she ever dove into the pool to escape and to swim to the bottom to scream.

Past the pool he noticed the hedge that surrounded the back yard. It was ten feet high and insured backyard privacy. Bosch recognized the hedge from the computer images he had seen on the Charlotte's Web Site.

Bosch closed the window. Rain always made him sad. And this day he didn't need it to feel that way. He already had the ghost of Frankie Sheehan in his head, he had a crumbled marriage he didn't have time to think about, and he had haunting thoughts about the little girl with the lost-in-the-woods face.

He took his hand from his pocket to open the closet door. The girl's clothes were still there. Colorful dresses on white plastic hangers. He looked through them until he found the white dress with the little semaphore flags. He remembered that from the web site, too.

He went back out into the hallway and checked the other rooms out. There was what looked like a guest bedroom, which Bosch recognized as the room from the photos on the web page. This was where Stacey Kincaid had been assaulted and filmed. Bosch didn't stay long. Further down the hall were a bathroom, the master suite and another bedroom that had been converted into a library and office.

He went back out to the living room. It did not look as though Kate

Kincaid had moved. He picked up his briefcase and walked into the room to join her.

'I'm a little damp, Mrs Kincaid. All right if I sit down?'

'Of course. And it's Kate.'

'I was thinking that I'd rather keep things on a formal basis for the moment, if you don't mind.'

'Suit yourself, Detective.'

He was angry at her, angry at what had happened in this house and how the secret had been locked away. He had seen enough during his tour of the place to confirm in his own mind what Kizmin Rider had fervently believed the night before.

He sat down on one of the covered chairs across from the couch and put his briefcase on his knees. He opened it and started going through some of the contents, which from her angle Kate Kincaid could not see.

'Did you find something of interest in Stacey's bedroom?'

Bosch stopped what he was doing and looked over the top of the briefcase at her for a moment.

'Not really,' he said. 'I was just getting a feel for the place. I assume it was thoroughly searched before and there isn't anything in there that I could find. Did Stacey like the pool?'

He went back to his work inside the briefcase while she told him what a fine swimmer her daughter had been. Bosch really wasn't doing anything. He was just following an act he had rehearsed in his head all morning.

'She could go up and back without having to come up for air,' Kate Kincaid said.

Bosch closed the case and looked at her. She was smiling at the memory of her daughter. Bosch smiled but without any warmth.

'Mrs Kincaid, how do you spell *innocence?*'

'Excuse me?'

'The word. *Innocence.* How do you spell it?'

'Is this about Stacey? I don't understand. Why are you—'

'Indulge me for a moment. Please. Spell the word.'

'I'm not a good speller. With Stacey I always kept a dictionary in my purse in case she asked about a word. You know, one of those little ones that—'

'Go ahead. Try it.'

She paused to think. The confusion was evident on her face.

'I-double n, I know there's two. I-double n-o-c-e-n-s-e.'

She looked at him and raised her eyebrows in a question. Bosch shook his head and reopened the briefcase.

'Almost,' he said. 'But there's two c's, no s.'

'Darn. I told you.'

She smiled at him. He took something out of the briefcase, closed it and put it down on the floor. He got up and walked across to the couch. He handed her a plastic document envelope. Inside it was one of the anonymous letters that had been sent to Howard Elias.

'Take a look,' he said. 'You spelled it wrong there, too.'

She stared at the letter for a long time and then took a deep breath. She spoke without looking up at Bosch.

'I guess I should have used my little dictionary. But I was in a hurry when I wrote this.'

Bosch felt a lifting inside. He knew then that there would be no fight, no difficulty. This woman had been waiting for this moment. Maybe she knew it was coming. Maybe that was why she had said she felt better than she had in a long, long time.

'I understand,' Bosch said. 'Would you like to talk to me about this, Mrs Kincaid? About everything?'

'Yes,' she said, 'I would.'

Bosch put a fresh battery into the tape recorder, then turned it on and put it down on the coffee table, the microphone pointed up so that it would capture his voice as well as Kate Kincaid's.

'Are you ready?' he asked.

'Yes,' she said.

He then identified himself and said who she was, noted the date, time and location of the interview. He read off a constitutional rights advisement from a printed form he had taken from his briefcase.

'Do you understand these rights as I have just read them?'

'Yes, I do.'

'Do you wish to talk with me, Mrs Kincaid, or do you wish to contact an attorney?'

'No.'

'No what?'

'No attorney. An attorney can't help me. I want to talk.'

This gave Bosch pause. He was thinking about how best to keep hair off the cake.

'Well, I can't give you legal advice. But when you say, "An attorney can't help me," I'm not sure that that is going to constitute a waiver. You see what I mean? Because it is always possible that an attorney could—'

'Detective Bosch, I don't want an attorney. I fully understand my rights and I don't want an attorney.'

'Okay, then I need you to sign this paper at the bottom and then sign again where it says that you do not request an attorney.'

He put the rights form down on the coffee table and watched her sign it. He then took it back and made sure she had signed her own name. He then signed it himself as the witness and put it in one of the slots of the accordion file in the briefcase. He sat back down in the chair and looked at her. He thought for a moment about talking to her about a spousal waiver but decided that could wait. He'd let the district attorney's office handle that – when and if the time came.

'Then I guess this is it,' he said. 'You want to start, Mrs Kincaid, or do you want me to ask you questions?'

He was using her name frequently on purpose – in case the tape was ever played before a jury there would be no misunderstanding of whom the voices belonged to.

'My husband killed my daughter. I guess that's what you want to know first. That's why you are here.'

Bosch froze for a moment and then slowly nodded.

'How do you know this?'

'For a long time it was a suspicion ... then it became my belief based on things I had heard. Eventually, he actually told me. I finally confronted him and he admitted it.'

'What exactly did he tell you?'

'He said that it was an accident – but you don't strangle people by accident. He said she threatened him, said that she was going to tell her friends what he . . . what he and his friends did to her. He said he was trying to stop her, to talk her out of doing it. He said things got out of hand.'

'This occurred where?'

'Right here. In the house.'

'When?'

She gave the date of her daughter's reported abduction. She seemed to understand that Bosch had to ask some questions that had obvious answers. He was building a record.

'Your husband had sexually abused Stacey?'

'Yes.'

'He admitted this to you?'

'Yes.'

She started to cry then and opened her purse for a tissue. Bosch let her alone for a minute. He wondered if she was crying because of grief or guilt or out of relief that the story was finally being told. He thought it was probably a combination of all three.

'Over how long a period was she abused?' he finally asked.

Kate Kincaid dropped the tissue to her lap.

'I don't know. We were married five years before ... before she died. I don't know when it started.'

'When did you become aware of it?'

'I would rather not answer that question, if you don't mind.'

Bosch studied her. Her eyes were downcast. The question was at the foundation of her guilt.

'It's important, Mrs Kincaid.'

'She came to me once.' She got a fresh tissue from her purse for a fresh torrent of tears. 'About a year before . . . She said that he was doing things she didn't think were right . . . At first, I didn't believe her. But I asked him about it anyway. He denied it, of course. And I believed him. I thought it was an adjustment problem. You know, to a stepfather. I thought maybe this was her way of acting out or something.'

'And later?'

She didn't say anything. She looked down at her hands. She pulled her purse onto her lap and held it tightly.

'Mrs Kincaid?'

'And later there were things. Little things. She never wanted me to go out and leave her with him – but she'd never tell me why. Looking back, it is obvious why. It wasn't so obvious then. One time he was taking a long time in her room saying good night. I went to see what was wrong and the door was locked.'

'Did you knock on the door?'

She sat frozen for a long moment before shaking her head no.

'Is that a no?'

Bosch had to ask it for the tape.

'Yes, no. I did not knock.'

Bosch decided to press on. He knew that mothers of incest and molestation victims often didn't see the obvious or take the obvious steps to save their daughters from jeopardy. Now Kate Kincaid lived in a personal hell in which her decision to give up her husband – and herself – to public ridicule and criminal prosecution would always seem like too little too late. She had been right. A lawyer couldn't help her now. No one could.

'Mrs Kincaid, when did you become suspicious of your husband's involvement in your daughter's death?'

'During Michael Harris's trial. You see I believed he did it – Harris. I mean, I just didn't believe that the police would plant fingerprints. Even the prosecutor assured me that it was unlikely that it could be done. So I believed in the case. I wanted to believe. But then during the trial one of the detectives, I think it was Frank Sheehan, was testifying and he said they arrested Michael Harris at the place where he worked.'

'The car wash.'

'Right. He gave the address and the name of the place. And it hit me then. I remembered going to that same car wash with Stacey. I remembered her books were in the car. I told my husband and said we should tell Jim Camp. He was the prosecutor. But Sam talked me out of it. He said the police were sure and he was sure that Michael Harris was the killer. He said if I raised the question the defense would find out and use the information to twist the case. Like with the O.J. case, the truth meant nothing. We'd lose the case. He reminded me that Stacey was found right near Harris's apartment . . . He said he probably saw her with me at the car wash that day and started to stalk us – stalk her. He convinced me . . . and I let it go. I still wasn't sure it wasn't Harris. I did what my husband told me.'

'And Harris got off.'

'Yes.'

Bosch paused for a moment, believing the break was needed before the next question.

'What changed, Mrs Kincaid?' he finally asked. 'What made you send those notes to Howard Elias?'

'My suspicions were never far away. Then one day, a few months ago, I overheard part of a conversation my husband was having with his ... his friend.'

She said the last word as if it was the worst thing you could ever say about anybody.

'Richter?'

'Yes. They thought I wasn't home and I wasn't supposed to be. I was supposed to be at lunch with my girlfriends at the club. Mountaingate. Only I stopped going to lunches with my girlfriends after Stacey ... well, you know, lunches and that sort of thing didn't interest me anymore. So I would tell my husband I was going to lunch but instead I'd go visit Stacey. At the cemetery . . .'

'Okay. I understand.'

'No, I don't think you could understand, Detective Bosch.'

Bosch nodded.

'I'm sorry. You're probably right. Go on, Mrs Kincaid.'

'It was raining on that particular day. Just like today, hard and sad. So I only visited with her for a few minutes. I got back to the house early. I guess

761

they didn't hear me come in because of the rain. But I heard them. They were in his office talking . . . I'd had my suspicions so I went to the door. I didn't make a sound. I stood outside the door and listened.'

Bosch leaned forward. This was the payoff. He'd know in a moment how legitimate she was. He doubted two men involved in the killing of a twelve-year-old girl would sit around reminiscing about it. If Kate Kincaid said that was the case, then Bosch would have to think she was lying.

'What did they say?'

'They weren't talking in sentences. Do you understand? They were just making short comments. I could tell they were talking about girls. Different girls – it was disgusting what they said. I had no idea how organized this all was. I had deluded myself into thinking that if something had happened with Stacey it was a weakness on his part, something he struggled with. I was wrong. These men were organized predators.'

'So you were at the door listening . . . ,' Bosch said by way of getting her back on track.

'They weren't talking to each other. It was like they were commenting. I could tell by how they spoke that they were looking at something. And I could hear the computer – the keyboard and other sounds. Later I would be able to use the computer and find what it was they were looking at. It was young girls, ten, eleven . . .'

'Okay, we'll get back to the computer in a couple of minutes. But let's go back to what you heard. How did this . . . these comments lead you to conclude or know something about Stacey?'

'Because they mentioned her. I heard Richter say, "There she is." And then my husband said her name. The way he said it . . . almost with a longing – it wasn't the way a father or a stepfather would have said it. And then they were quiet. I could tell, they were looking at her. I knew.'

Bosch thought about what he had seen on Rider's computer screen the night before. It was hard for him to imagine Kincaid and Richter sitting in an office together watching the same scenes – and with decidedly different responses to them.

'And then Richter asked my husband if he'd heard from Detective Sheehan. My husband said, "About what?" and Richter said for the payoff for putting Harris's prints on Stacey's book. My husband laughed. He said there was no payoff. He then told Richter what I had told him during the trial, about my having been to that car wash. When he was done telling it, they both laughed and my husband said, and I remember this so clearly, he said, "I've been lucky like that all my life . . ." And that's when I knew. He did it. That they did it.'

'And you decided to help Howard Elias.'

'Yes.'

'Why him? Why didn't you go to the police?'

'Because I knew they'd never charge him. The Kincaids are a powerful family. They believe they are above the law and they are. My husband's father put money into the pockets of every politician in this town. Democrat, Republican, it didn't matter. They all owed him. And besides, that didn't matter. I called Jim Camp and asked him what would happen if they ever found somebody else besides Harris that they thought took Stacey. He told me they'd never be able to try him because of the first case.

All the defense would have to do was point to the first trial and say that last year they thought it was somebody else. That was enough for reasonable doubt right there. So they'd never go ahead with a case.'

Bosch nodded. He knew she was right. Going to trial against Harris put hair on the cake forever after.

'This might be a good point to take a break for a couple minutes,' he said. 'I need to make a phone call.'

Bosch turned the tape recorder off. He got his cell phone out of his briefcase and told Kate Kincaid that he was going to check out the other side of the house while he made his call.

As he walked through the formal dining room and then into the kitchen Bosch called Lindell's cell phone. The FBI agent answered immediately. Bosch spoke quietly, hoping his voice wouldn't carry into the living room.

'This is Bosch. It's a go. We've got a cooperating witness.'

'On tape?'

'On tape. She says her husband killed her daughter.'

'What about Elias?'

'Haven't gotten there yet. I just wanted to get you people going.'

'I'll put out the word.'

'Anybody been seen yet?'

'Not yet. It looks like the husband is still at home.'

'What about Richter? He's involved. She's giving me stuff on him.'

'We're not sure where he is. If he's at his home, he hasn't come out yet. But we'll find him.'

'Happy hunting.'

After disconnecting he stood in the kitchen doorway and looked at Kate Kincaid. Her back was to him and she seemed to be staring at the spot where he had been sitting across from her. She didn't move.

'Okay,' Bosch said, as he came back into the room. 'Can I get you something? A glass of water?'

'No, thank you. I'm fine.'

He turned the tape recorder on and once again identified himself and the subject of the interview. He gave the exact time and date as well.

'You have been advised of your rights, correct, Mrs Kincaid?'

'Yes, I have.'

'Would you like to continue the interview?'

'Yes.'

'You mentioned earlier that you decided to help Howard Elias. Why is that?'

'He was suing on behalf of Michael Harris. I wanted Michael Harris completely exonerated. And I wanted my husband and his friends exposed. I knew the authorities probably wouldn't do it. But I knew Howard Elias was not part of that establishment. He wouldn't be controlled by money and power. Only the truth.'

'Did you ever speak with Mr Elias directly?'

'No. I thought my husband might be watching me. After that day when I heard them, when I knew it was him, it was impossible for me not to be completely repulsed by him. I think he realized I had come to a conclusion. I think he had Richter watch me. Richter or people working for him.'

Bosch realized that Richter could be nearby, having followed her to the house. Lindell had said the security man's whereabouts were currently unknown. He looked at the front door and realized he had left it unlocked.

'So you sent Elias notes.'

'Yes, anonymous. I guess I wanted him to expose these people but leave me out of it . . . I know it was selfish. I was a horrible mother. I guess I had this fantasy that the bad men would be shown to the world without it happening to the bad woman.'

Bosch saw a lot of pain in her eyes as she said it. He waited for the tears to start again but it didn't happen.

'I just have a few more questions at this point,' he said. 'How did you know the web page address and about how to get to the secret site?'

'You mean Charlotte's Web? My husband is not a smart man, Detective Bosch. He is rich, and that always gives the appearance of intellect. He wrote the directions down so he wouldn't have to memorize them and he hid them in his desk. I found them. I know how to use a computer. I went to that awful place . . . I saw Stacey there.'

Again no tears. Bosch was puzzled. Kate Kincaid had dropped her voice into a monotone. She was reciting the story, it seemed, out of duty. But whatever impact it personally had on her was done with and compartmentalized, put away from the surface.

'Do you believe that to be your husband on the images with Stacey?'

'No. I don't know who that was.'

'How can you be sure?'

'My husband has a birthmark. A discoloration on his back. I said he wasn't smart, but he was at least smart enough not to appear on that web site.'

Bosch thought about this. Though he did not doubt Kate Kincaid's story, he also knew that hard evidence backing it up would be needed to prosecute Kincaid. For the same reason she felt she could not bring her story to the authorities, Bosch needed to be able to go into the district attorney's office with Sam Kincaid solidly locked down by the evidence. Right now all he had was a wife saying evil things about her husband. The fact that Kincaid apparently was not the man in the web site images with his stepdaughter was a major loss of corroborative evidence. He thought about the searches. Teams were descending on Kincaid's home and office at that moment. It was Bosch's hope that they would find evidence that would prove his wife's story.

'Your last note to Howard Elias,' he said. 'You warned him. You said your husband knew. Did you mean your husband knew that Elias had found the secret web site?'

'At the time, yes.'

'Why?'

'Because of the way he was acting – on edge, suspicious of me. He asked me if I had been on his computer. It made me think that they must have known someone was poking around. I sent the message, but now I'm not so sure.'

'Why is that? Howard Elias is dead.'

'I'm not sure he did that. He would have told me.'

'What?'

Bosch was thoroughly confused by her logic.

'He would have told me. He told me about Stacey, why wouldn't he tell me about Elias as well? And the fact that you know about the web site. If they thought Elias knew, wouldn't they have closed it down or hidden it somewhere else?'

'Not if they were just going to kill the intruder instead.'

She shook her head. She didn't see it the way Bosch obviously did.

'I still think he would've told me.'

Still confused, Bosch said, 'Wait a minute. Are you talking about the confrontation you mentioned at the start of this interview?'

Bosch's pager went off and he reached down and silenced it without taking his eyes off Kate Kincaid.

'Yes.'

'Well, when was this confrontation?'

'Last night.'

'Last night?'

Bosch was shocked. He had jumped to the conclusion that the confrontation she had mentioned had been weeks or even months earlier.

'Yes. After you left. I knew by the questions you asked that you had probably found my notes to Howard Elias. I knew you would find Charlotte's Web. It was a matter of time.'

Bosch looked down at his pager. The number belonged to Lindell's cell phone. The emergency code 911 was printed on the little screen after it. He looked back up at Kate Kincaid.

'So I finally summoned the courage I didn't have for all those months and years. I confronted him. And he told me. And he laughed at me. He asked me why I cared now since I didn't care while Stacey was alive.'

Now Bosch's cell phone began to ring inside his briefcase. Kate Kincaid slowly stood up.

'I'll let you take that in private.'

As he reached to his briefcase, he watched her pick her purse up and walk across the room in the direction of the hallway to her dead daughter's bedroom. Bosch fumbled with the briefcase's release but eventually got it open and got to the phone. It was Lindell.

'I'm at the house,' the FBI agent said, his voice tight with adrenaline and excitement. 'Kincaid and Richter are here. It's not very pretty.'

'Tell me.'

'They're dead. And it doesn't look like it was an easy ride for them. They were knee-capped, both of them shot in the balls . . . You still with the wife?'

Bosch looked in the direction of the hallway.

'Yes.'

Just as he said it he heard a single popping sound from down the hallway. He knew what it was.

'Better bring her over here,' Lindell said.

'Right.'

Bosch closed the phone and placed it back in the briefcase, his eyes still on the hallway.

'Mrs Kincaid?'

There was no answer. All he heard was the rain.

32

By the time Bosch cleared the scene in Brentwood and got up the hill to The Summit it was almost two o'clock. Driving through the rain on the way he could think only of Kate Kincaid's face. He had gotten to Stacey's room less than ten seconds after hearing the shot, but she was already gone. She had used a twenty-two and placed the muzzle in her mouth, firing the bullet up into her brain. Death was instant. The kick of the gun had knocked it out of her mouth and onto the floor. There was no exit wound, often the case with a twenty-two. She simply appeared as though she was sleeping. She had wrapped herself in the pink blanket that had been used by her daughter. Kate Kincaid looked as though she was serene in death. No mortician would be able to improve on that.

There were several cars and vans parked in front of the Kincaid residence. Bosch had to park so far away that his raincoat was soaked through by the time he got to the door. Lindell was there waiting for him.

'Well, this certainly's turned all to shit,' the FBI agent said by way of greeting.

'Yeah.'

'Should we have seen it coming?'

'I don't know. You never can tell what people are going to do.'

'How'd you leave it over there?'

'The coroner and SID are still there. A couple RHD bulls – they're handling it.'

Lindell nodded.

'I saw what I needed to see. Show me what you have here.'

They went into the house and Lindell led the way to the huge living room where Bosch had sat with the Kincaids the afternoon before. He saw the bodies. Sam Kincaid was in the same spot on the couch where Bosch had last seen him. D.C. Richter was on the floor below the window that looked out across the Valley. There was no jetliner view now. It was just gray. Richter's body was in a pool of blood. Kincaid's blood had seeped into the material covering the couch. There were several technicians working in the room and lights were set up. Bosch saw that numbered plastic markers had been put in place where .22-caliber shells had been located on the floor and other furniture.

'You have the twenty-two over in Brentwood, right?'

'Yeah, that's what she used.'

'You didn't think about searching her before you started talking, huh?'

Bosch looked at the FBI agent and slightly shook his head in annoyance.

'Are you kidding me? It was a voluntary Q&A, man. Maybe you've never done one over there at the bureau, but rule number one is you don't make the subject feel like a *suspect* before you even start. I didn't search and it would have been a mistake if—'

'I know, I know. Sorry I asked. It's just that . . .'

He didn't finish but Bosch knew what he was getting at. He decided to change the subject.

'The old man show up?'

'Jack Kincaid? No, we sent people to him. I hear he is not taking it well. He's calling every politician he ever gave money to. I guess he thinks maybe the city council or the mayor will be able to bring his son back.'

'He knew what his son was. Probably knew all the time. That's why he's making the calls. He doesn't want that to come out.'

'Yeah, well, we'll see about that. We've already found digital video cameras and editing equipment. We'll tie him to Charlotte's Web. I feel confident of that.'

'It won't matter. Where's Chief Irving?'

'On the way.'

Bosch nodded. He stepped close to the couch and bent over, his hands on his knees, to look closely at the dead car czar. His eyes were open and his jaw was set in a final grimace. Lindell had been right when he'd said it had not been an easy ride down. He thought of Kincaid's expression in comparison to his wife's death look. There was no comparison.

'How do you think it went down?' he asked. 'How'd she get the two of them?'

He continued to stare at the body while Lindell spoke.

'Well, you shoot a man in the balls and he's going to be pretty docile. From the blood on them, I'd say that was where they got it first. Once she got past that point, I think she had pretty good control of the situation.'

Bosch nodded.

'Richter wasn't armed?'

'Nope.'

'Anybody find a nine-millimeter around here yet?'

'No, not yet.'

Lindell gave Bosch another *we fucked up* look.

'We need that nine,' Bosch said. 'Mrs Kincaid got them to admit what they did with the girl but they didn't say anything about Elias. We need to find that nine to tie them in and end this thing.'

'Well, we're looking. If anybody finds the nine, we'll be the first to know.'

'You have people on Richter's home, office and car? I'm still putting my money on him being the shooter.'

'Yeah, we're on it but don't count on anything there.'

Bosch tried to read the FBI agent but couldn't. He knew that something was not being said.

'What?'

'Edgar pulled his file from the police academy this morning.'

'Right. He was a washout way back. How come?'

'Turned out the guy was blind in one eye. The left eye. He was trying to make it through with nobody noticing. He did all right until the weapons course. He couldn't shoot for shit on the range. That's how they found out. Then they washed him out.'

Bosch nodded. He thought of the expert shooting that had taken place on Angels Flight and he knew this new information on Richter changed things. He knew it was unlikely Richter could have been the shooter.

His thoughts were disrupted by the muted roar of a helicopter. He looked up at the windows and saw a helicopter from Channel 4 drifting down and hovering outside the house, about fifty yards away. Through the rain Bosch could barely make out the cameraman in the open sliding door.

'Fucking vultures,' Lindell said. 'You'd think the rain would keep them inside.'

He stepped back to the doorway where there was a panel of light switches and other electronic controls. He pushed a round button and kept his finger on it. Bosch heard the whine of an electric motor and watched an automatic window shade drop down over the windows.

'They can't get near this place on the ground,' Bosch said. 'Because of the gates. So the air's their only shot.'

'I don't care. Let's see what they get now.'

Bosch didn't care either. He looked back down at the bodies. Judging by the coloring and the slight odor already apparent in the room, he guessed that the two men had been dead for several hours. He wondered if this meant that Kate Kincaid had been in the house all that time with the bodies or had gone to Brentwood and spent the night in her daughter's bed. He guessed the latter.

'Anybody come up with a TOD?' he asked.

'Yeah. Coroner puts time of death at sometime last night, anywhere from nine to midnight. He said the blood flow indicates they could have been alive as long as a couple hours from first to last bullet. It looks like she wanted some information from them but they didn't want to give it up – at first.'

'Her husband talked. I don't know about Richter – she probably didn't care about him. But her husband told her everything about Stacey. Then, I guess, she finished him. Finished them both. It wasn't her husband with the girl on the web site images. You should get the coroner to take torso photos of Richter and do a comparison. It might have been him.'

Lindell gestured toward the bodies.

'Will do. So what do you think? She did this last night and then what, went up to bed?'

'Probably not. I think she spent the night in the Brentwood house. It looked to me like the girl's bed had been slept in. She had to see me and tell the story before she could finish her plan.'

'The finish being her suicide.'

'Right.'

'That's hard-core, man.'

'Living with her daughter's ghost, what she let happen to her, that was even more hard-core. Suicide was the easy way out.'

'Not if you ask me. Like I keep thinking about Sheehan, man, and wondering. I mean, how dark out could it have been for him to do that?'

'Just hope you never know. Where are my people?'

'Down the hall in the office. They're handling that.'

'I'll be in there.'

Bosch left Lindell then and went down the hall to the office. Edgar and Rider were silently conducting a search. The items they wished to seize were being piled on top of the desk. Bosch nodded his hello and they did the same. A quiet pallor hung over the investigation now. There would be no prosecution, no trial. It would be left to them to explain what had happened. And they all knew the media would be skeptical and the public might not believe them.

Bosch approached the desk. There was a lot of computer equipment with connecting wires. There were boxes of thick disks used for data storage. There was a small video camera and an editing station.

'We've got a lot, Harry,' Rider said. 'We would have had Kincaid cold on the pedo net. He's got a Zip drive with all the images from the secret web site on it. He's got this camera – we think it's what was used to take the videos of Stacey.'

Rider, who was wearing gloves, lifted the camera up to show him.

'It's digital. You take your movie, plug the camera into this dock here and download what you want. Then you upload it on your computer and put it out on the net. All from the privacy of your home. It's literally as easy as—'

She didn't finish. Bosch turned to see what the distraction was and saw Deputy Chief Irving standing in the doorway of the room. Behind him stood Lindell and Irving's adjutant, Lieutenant Tulin. Irving moved into the office and handed his wet raincoat to Tulin. He told him to take it and to wait in another room of the house.

'Which room, Chief?'

'Any room.'

Irving closed the door after Tulin left. That left him, Lindell and Bosch's team in the office. Bosch had an idea what was coming. The fixer was here now. The investigation was about to go through the spin cycle where decisions and public pronouncements would be made based on what best served the department, not the truth. Bosch folded his arms and waited.

'I want to finish this up now,' Irving said. 'Take what you have found and clear out.'

'Chief,' Rider said, 'we still have a lot of the house to cover.'

'I do not care. I want the bodies removed and then I want the police removed.'

'Sir,' she persisted, 'we still haven't found the weapon. We need that weapon to—'

'And you are not going to find it.'

Irving stepped further into the room. He looked around and when his eyes finally came to Bosch's face they stopped.

'I made a mistake listening to you. I hope the city does not have to pay for it.'

Bosch paused a moment before responding. Irving never took his eyes off him.

'Chief, I know that you are thinking in . . . political terms about this. But we have to continue our searches of this house and other locations related to the Kincaids. We need to find the weapon in order to prove that—'

'I just told you, you are not going to find the weapon. Not here or anywhere else related to the Kincaids. All this was, Detective, was a diversion. A diversion that caused three deaths.'

Bosch didn't know what was going on but he felt defensive. He gestured toward the equipment on the desk.

'I wouldn't call this a diversion. Kincaid was involved in a major pedophile ring and we—'

'Your assignment was Angels Flight. I obviously gave you people too much latitude and now here we are.'

'This *is* Angels Flight. That's why we need the weapon. It will tie it all—'

'Damn it, man, we have the weapon! We have had it for twenty-four hours! We *had* the killer as well. *HAD!* We let him go and now we will never get him back.'

Bosch could only stare at him. Irving's face had turned the deep red of anger.

'The ballistics analysis was completed less than an hour ago,' Irving said. 'The three slugs taken from the body of Howard Elias were matched unequivocally to bullets test-fired in the firearms lab from Detective Francis Sheehan's nine-millimeter Smith and Wesson pistol. Detective Sheehan killed those people on that train. End of story. There are those of us who believed in that possibility but were talked out of it. The possibility is now fact but Detective Sheehan is long gone.'

Bosch was speechless and had to work hard to keep his jaw from dropping open.

'You,' he managed to say. 'You're doing this for the old man. For Kincaid. You are –'

Rider grabbed Bosch by the arm to try to stop him from committing career suicide. He shrugged off her grip and pointed in the direction of the living room where the bodies were.

'– selling out one of your own to protect that. How can you do that? How can you make that kind of a deal with them? And with yourself?'

'You are *WRONG!*' Irving yelled back at him. Then, quietly, he said, 'You are wrong and I could crush you for saying what you just said.'

Bosch said nothing. He continued to hold the deputy chief's stare.

'This city expects justice for Howard Elias,' Irving said. 'And for the woman killed with him. You took that away, Detective Bosch. You allowed Sheehan a coward's way out. You took justice away from the people and they are not going to be happy about that. Heaven help us all for that.'

33

The plan was to hold the press conference quickly, while the rain was still falling and could be used as a tool to keep people – angry people – off the streets. The entire investigative team was assembled and lined along the wall at the rear of the stage. The chief of police and the FBI's Gilbert Spencer were to lead the briefing and answer all questions. This was standard operating procedure in highly sensitive situations. The chief and Spencer knew little more than what was on the press release. Therefore, questions about the details of the investigation could be easily and honestly deflected with the *I am not aware of that* or *Not to my knowledge* sort of answer.

O'Rourke, from press relations, did the warm-up, telling the mob of reporters to act responsibly and that the briefing would be short with further information furnished in the days to come. He then introduced the chief of police who took a spot behind the microphones and read from a carefully prepared statement.

'During my short tenure as chief of police I have had the responsibility of presiding over the funeral of police officers who have fallen in the line of duty. I have held the hands of mothers who have lost their children to the senseless violence of this city. But my heart has never been heavier than right now. I have to announce to the people of this great city that we know who killed Howard Elias and Catalina Perez. And it is with deep, deep regret that I report that it was a member of this department. Earlier today ballistics tests and analysis matched the bullets that killed Howard Elias and Catalina Perez to the service weapon used by Detective Francis Sheehan of the Robbery-Homicide Division.'

Bosch looked out across the sea of reporters' faces and saw shock on many of them. The news gave even them pause, for they knew the consequences. The news was the match, they the gasoline. The rain probably wouldn't be enough to put out this fire.

A couple of reporters, probably wire service men, pushed through the standing-room-only crowd and went out the door to be the first to spread the word. The police chief pressed on.

'As many of you know, Sheehan was one of several officers being sued by Howard Elias on behalf of Michael Harris. The investigators on this case believe Sheehan became overwrought with emotions relating to this case and the dissolution of his marriage in recent months. He may have become unbalanced. We may never know because Detective Sheehan took his own life last night, as he understood that it was only a matter of time before he

771

was revealed as the killer. As a police chief, you hope never to have to make a statement such as this. But this department hides nothing from its citizens. The bad must be aired so that we can fully celebrate the good. I know the eight thousand good people of this department join me in apologizing to the families of these two victims as well as to every citizen in this city. And we ask that the good citizens in return react responsibly and calmly to this truly horrible turn of events. Now, I have other announcements but if there are questions relating specifically to this investigation I can take a few at this time.'

Immediately there was a chorus of unintelligible shouts and the chief simply pointed to one of the reporters in the front center. Bosch didn't recognize him.

'How and where did Sheehan kill himself?'

'He was at a friend's home last night. He shot himself. His service weapon had been confiscated for the ballistics exam. He used another weapon, the source of which is still under investigation. It was the investigators' belief that he did not have a weapon at his disposal. They obviously were wrong.'

The cacophony began again but it was coming in behind the booming voice of Harvey Button. His question was clear and it had to be answered.

'Why was this man free? He was a suspect yesterday. Why was he released?'

The chief looked at Button for a long moment before answering.

'You just answered that yourself. He was a suspect. He was not under arrest. We were awaiting the results of the ballistics examination and there was no reason to hold him at that time. At that time there was no evidence with which to charge him. We got that evidence with the ballistics report. Of course, we got it too late.'

'Chief, we all know that the police can hold suspects up to forty-eight hours before charging them. Why wasn't Detective Sheehan held in custody?'

'Frankly, because we were pursuing other avenues of investigation. He was not a full-fledged suspect. He was one of several people we were looking at. We felt there was no reason to hold him. He had satisfactorily answered our questions, he was a member of this department and we did not believe he was going anywhere. We also didn't believe he was suicidal.'

'A follow-up,' Button yelled above the ensuing din. 'Are you saying that his status as a police officer got him the privilege of being released so that he could go home and kill himself?'

'No, Mr Button, that is not what I am saying. I am saying we didn't know for sure it was him until it was too late. We knew today. He was released and he killed himself last night.'

'If he had been a regular citizen – say, a black man like Michael Harris – would he have been allowed to go home last night?'

'I'm not going to dignify that with a response.'

The chief held his hands up to fend off the shouts of other reporters.

'I have other announcements here.'

The reporters continued to shout out questions and O'Rourke stepped forward and shouted louder, threatening to end the news conference and clear the room if there was not quiet. It did the trick. The chief took it from there.

'This announcement is indirectly related to the events I just mentioned. I have the grim duty of also announcing the deaths of Sam Kincaid, Kate Kincaid and Donald Charles Richter, a security specialist who worked for the Kincaids.'

He went on to read from another sheet of paper that described the double murder and suicide, couching the events as the actions of a distraught Kate Kincaid who had let mounting grief over the loss of her daughter get the better of her. No mention was made of her husband's defilement of that daughter or his ongoing pedophilia or involvement in a secret web site dedicated to that perversion. There was also no mention of the ongoing investigation of that site by the bureau and the department's computer fraud team.

Bosch knew it was the old man at work. The original car czar at work, pulling strings to save his family name. Bosch guessed that chits were being called in all over the city. Jackson Kincaid would not allow his son's reputation to be destroyed – along with his own. It might cost him too much business.

When the chief had finished reading from the page there was a smattering of questions.

'If she was distraught, why did she kill her husband?' asked Keisha Russell of the *Times*.

'We'll never know that.'

'And what about the security man, Richter? Why would she kill him if it was about her daughter?'

'Again we're not sure. We are looking into the possibility that he happened to be in the house or happened by when Mrs Kincaid took out the gun and announced the intention of killing herself. There is a strong possibility that both of the men were killed while trying to prevent Mrs Kincaid from doing that. She then left the house and went to their previous home, where the couple had lived with their daughter. She killed herself in the bed where her daughter had slept. It is a very sad situation and our hearts go out to the family and friends of the Kincaids.'

Bosch was disgusted. He almost shook his head but knew that since he was standing against the wall behind the chief such a gesture would be picked up by the cameras and reporters.

'Now, if there is nothing further, I would ask that—'

'Chief,' Button cut in. 'Inspector General Carla Entrenkin has scheduled a press conference at Howard Elias's office in an hour. Do you know what she is going to say and do you have any comment on it?'

'No. Inspector Entrenkin operates independently of this department. She does not answer to me and therefore I have no idea what she'll be saying.'

But by the tone of the chief's voice it was clear that he did not expect whatever Entrenkin was going to say to be positive for the department.

'I want to end this now,' the chief said. 'But before I do, I want to thank the FBI and particularly Special Agent Spencer for the help that was provided. If there is any solace to be found in all of this, it is that the citizens of this community can rest assured that this department is dedicated to weeding out the bad apples, no matter where they might be. This department is also willing to place and accept responsibility for its members' actions without cover-up, no matter what the cost to our pride and reputation. I hope the good citizens of Los Angeles will remember that and accept my sincerest apology. I hope the good citizens of Los Angeles will act calmly and responsibly in reaction to these announcements.'

His last words were drowned out by the scraping of chairs and equipment as the reporters began to get up en masse and move toward the exit doors. There was a story to get out and another press conference to go to.

'Detective Bosch.'

Bosch turned. Irving had come up close to him.

'Any problems with what was announced? Any problems for you or your team?'

Bosch studied the deputy chief's face. The implication was clear. Make any waves and *your* boat will be the one that gets swamped and sinks – and you'd be taking others down with you. *Go along to get along.* The company motto. That's what it should say on the side of the cop cars. Forget about *To protect and serve.*

Bosch slowly shook his head when what he wanted to do was put his hands around Irving's throat.

'No, no problem at all,' he said through a tight jaw.

Irving nodded and instinctively knew it was time to step away.

Bosch saw the exit doors were now clear and headed that way, his head down. He felt that he didn't know anything. His wife, his old friend, his city. Everybody and everything was strange to him. And in that feeling of aloneness he thought he began to understand what it was that Kate Kincaid and Frankie Sheehan were thinking about at the end of the line.

34

Bosch had gone home to watch it all on television. He had his portable typewriter on the coffee table and was leaning over it, typing out the final reports on the investigation with two fingers. He knew he could have given it to Rider to do on her laptop and it would be done in a tenth of the time, but Bosch wanted to write this case summary himself. He had decided to write it exactly the way it had happened – everything, not protecting anyone, the Kincaid family or even himself. He would turn the final package over to Irving and if the deputy chief wanted to rewrite it, edit it or even shred it, then it was up to him. Bosch felt that as long as he told it like it was and put it down on paper there was still a small degree of integrity in that.

He stopped typing and looked at the television when the broadcast broke away from the street reports of sporadic unrest and violence to recap the day's events. There were several outtakes from the press conference – Bosch saw himself standing against the wall behind the police chief, his face giving the lie to everything that was being said. And then the report cut to Carla Entrenkin's press conference in the lobby of the Bradbury. She announced her immediate resignation as inspector general. She said that after she had conferred with the widow of Howard Elias it was decided and agreed upon that she would take over the law practice of the slain attorney.

'I believe that it is in this new role that I can have the most positive effect on reforming this city's police department and rooting out the bad seeds within,' she said. 'Carrying on Howard Elias's work will be an honor as well as a challenge.'

When questioned by the reporters about the Black Warrior case, Entrenkin said that she planned to continue the case with minimal delay. She would ask the presiding judge in the morning to reschedule the start of the trial for the following Monday. By then she would be up to speed on the intricacies of the case and the strategy Howard Elias had been planning to follow. When a reporter suggested that the city would likely go out of its way to settle the case, in light of the day's developments, Entrenkin demurred.

'Like Howard, I don't want to settle this,' she said, looking right at the camera. 'This case deserves a full airing before the public. We will go to trial.'

Great, Bosch thought, as the report ended. It won't rain forever. If a full-blown riot is avoided now, Carla I'mthinkin' would be sure to deliver it the following week.

The broadcast switched to a report on reaction from community leaders to the day's events and the announcements by the chief of police. When Bosch saw the Reverend Preston Tuggins appear on the screen he picked up the remote and switched channels. He caught reports on peaceful candle-light vigils on two other channels and Councilman Royal Sparks on a third before finally finding a broadcast that showed a helicopter shot from above the intersection of Florence and Normandie. The same spot where the 1992 riots flared was packed with a large crowd of protestors. The demonstration – if it could be called that – was peaceful but Bosch knew it was only a matter of time. The rain and the dimming light of the day were not going to hold back the anger. He thought about what Carla Entrenkin had said to him on Saturday night, about anger and violence filling the void left when hope is taken away. He thought about the void that was inside himself now and wondered what he would fill it with.

He turned the sound down and went back to his report. When he was done, he rolled it out of the typewriter and put it in a file folder. He would drop it off the next morning when he got the chance. With the end of the investigation, he and his partners had been assigned to twelve-and-twelve status like everybody else in the department. They were to report in uniform at six o'clock the next morning at the South Bureau command center. They'd be spending the next few days, at a minimum, on the streets, riding the war zone in two-car, eight-cop patrols.

Bosch decided to go to the closet to check out the condition of his uniform. He hadn't worn it in five years – since the earthquake and the last use of the department's emergency response plan. While he was taking it out of its plastic wrap the phone rang and Bosch hurried to answer it, hoping that it might be Eleanor checking in from some place to say she was safe and okay. He grabbed the phone off the night table and sat down on the bed. But it wasn't Eleanor. It was Carla Entrenkin.

'You have my files,' she said.

'What?'

'The files. The Black Warrior case. I'm taking the case. I need the files back.'

'Oh, right. Yeah, I just saw that on the TV.'

There was a silence then that made Bosch uncomfortable. There was something about the woman that Bosch liked, though he seemed to care so little for her cause.

'I guess that was a good move,' he finally said. 'You taking his cases. You worked that out with the widow, huh?'

'I did. And no, I didn't tell her about Howard and me. I didn't see the need to spoil the memories she will have. She's had it rough enough.'

'That was noble of you.'

'Detective . . .'

'What?'

'Nothing. I just don't understand you sometimes.'

'Join the club.'

More silence.

'I have the files here. The whole box. I was just typing out my final report.

776

I'll pack it all up and try to drop it off tomorrow. But I can't be held to it – I'm on patrol until things calm down on the Southside.'

'That will be fine.'

'Are you taking over his office, too? Is that where I should bring everything?'

'Yes. That's the plan. That would be fine.'

Bosch nodded but he knew she couldn't see this.

'Well,' he said. 'Thanks for your help. I don't know if Irving has said anything but the lead to Sheehan came out of the files. One of the old cases. I guess you heard about that.'

'Actually . . . no. But you're welcome, Detective Bosch. I'm curious, though. About Sheehan. He was your former partner . . .'

'Yes. He was.'

'Does all of this seem plausible? That he would first kill Howard and then himself? That woman on the train, too?'

'If you asked me that yesterday I would have said never in a million years. But today I feel like I couldn't read myself let alone anybody else. We have a saying when we can't explain things. The evidence is what it is . . . And we leave it at that.'

Bosch leaned back on the bed and stared up at the ceiling. He held the phone to his ear. After a long moment she spoke.

'But is it possible that there is another interpretation of the evidence?'

She said it slowly, concisely. She was a lawyer. She chose her words well.

'What are you saying, Inspector?'

'It's just Carla now.'

'What are you saying, Carla? What are you asking me?'

'You have to understand, my role is different now. I am now bound by attorney-client ethics. Michael Harris is now my client in a lawsuit against your employer and several of your colleagues. I have to be care—'

'Is there something that clears him? Sheehan? Something you held back before?'

Bosch sat up and now leaned forward. He was staring wide-eyed at nothing. He was all internal, trying to remember something he could have missed. He knew Entrenkin had held back the trial strategy file. There must have been something in there.

'I can't answer your—'

'The strategy file,' Bosch cut in excitedly. 'It was something in there that puts the lie to this. It . . .'

He stopped. What she was suggesting – or the suggestion he was reading in her words – did not make sense. Sheehan's service weapon had been linked to the Angels Flight shootings. There was a ballistics match. Three bullets from the body of Howard Elias, three matches. End of argument, end of case. The evidence is what it is.

That was the hard fact he was up against, yet his gut instinct still told him Sheehan was all wrong for this, that he wouldn't have done it. Yes, he would have gladly danced on Elias's grave but he wouldn't have put the lawyer in that grave. There was a big difference. And Bosch's instincts – though abandoned in light of the facts – were that Frankie Sheehan, no matter what he had done to Michael Harris, was still too good a man at his core to have done the latter. He had killed before, but he was not a killer. Not like that.

'Look,' he said. 'I don't know what you know or think you know, but you've got to help me. I can't—'

'It's there,' she said. 'If you have the files, it's there. I held something back that I was bound to hold back. But part of it was in the public files. If you look, you'll find it. I'm not saying your partner is clear. I'm just saying there was something else here that probably should have been looked at. It wasn't.'

'And that's all you are going to tell me?'

'That's all I can tell you – and even that I shouldn't have.'

Bosch was silent for a moment. He didn't know whether to be angry with her for not telling him specifically what she knew, or just happy that she had given him the clue and the direction.

'All right,' he finally said. 'If it's here I'll find it.'

35

It took Bosch nearly two hours to make his way through the Black Warrior case files. Many of the folders he had opened previously, but some had been viewed by Edgar and Rider or left to others on the squad Irving had put together at Angels Flight less than seventy-two hours earlier. He looked at each file as if he had never seen it before, looking for the thing that had been missed – the telling detail, the boomerang that would change his interpretation of everything and send it in a new direction.

That was the problem with gang-banging a case – putting multiple investigative teams on it. No single pair of eyes saw all of the evidence, all of the leads or even all of the paperwork. Everything was split up. Though one detective was nominally in charge, it was rare that everything crossed his radar screen. Now Bosch had to make sure it did.

He found what he believed he was looking for – and what Carla Entrenkin had hinted at – in the subpoena file, the folder where receipts from the process server were stored. These receipts were received by Howard Elias's office after the subject of the subpoena had been served with the summons to appear for a deposition or as a witness in court. The file was thick with the thin white forms. The stack was in chronological order of service. The first half of the stack consisted of subpoenas for depositions and these dated back several months. The second half of the stack consisted of witness subpoenas for the court case that had been scheduled to start that day. These were summonses to the cops being sued as well as other witnesses.

Bosch remembered that Edgar had looked through this file earlier – he had come across the subpoena for the car wash records. But that discovery must have distracted him from other things in the file. As Bosch looked through the subpoenas another filing caught his eyes as being worthy of a second look. It was a subpoena for Detective John Chastain of the Internal Affairs Division. This was surprising because Chastain had never mentioned any involvement in the lawsuit. Chastain had headed the internal investigation of Michael Harris's allegations that had cleared the RHD detectives of any wrongdoing, so the fact that he had been called wasn't unusual. It would stand to reason that he would be called as a witness in defense of the detectives accused of wrongdoing by Michael Harris. But the fact that Chastain had not told anyone he was a subpoenaed witness for the *plaintiffs* in the lawsuit was. If that had been known he might have been disqualified from the team investigating the murders for the same reason that the RHD bulls had been removed. There was a clear conflict. The subpoena needed explanation. And Bosch's interest in it increased further when he saw that the date of service was Thursday, the day before Elias's murder. But curiosity turned to suspicion when Bosch saw the note handwritten by the process server at the bottom of the subpoena.

Det. Chastain refused acceptance at vehicle. Server placed under wiper.

The note made it very clear that Chastain didn't want any part of the case. And it turned Bosch's attention into a sharp focus. The city could have been burning from Dodger Stadium to the beach and he probably wouldn't have noticed the television now.

He realized as he stared at the subpoena that the subject – Chastain – had been given a specific date and time to appear in court to give testimony. He shuffled through the court subpoenas and realized that they were placed in the file in order of service, not in the order that those summoned would appear in trial. He knew then that by placing them in order according to the appearance dates and times, he would have the chronological order of Elias's case and a better understanding of how he planned the trial.

It took him two minutes to put the subpoenas in the proper order. When he was done, he looked at the documents one by one, envisioning the process of the trial. First Michael Harris would testify. He would tell his story. Next would come Captain John Garwood, head of RHD. Garwood would testify about the investigation, giving the sanitized version. The next subpoena was for Chastain. He would follow Garwood. *Reluctantly* – he had tried to refuse service – he would follow the RHD captain.

Why?

Bosch put the question aside for the moment and began going through the other subpoenas. It became clear that Elias was following an age-old strategy of alternating positive and negative witnesses. He was planning to alternate the testimony of the RHD men, the defendants, with witnesses who would obviously benefit Michael Harris. There was Harris, the doctor who treated his ear, Jenkins Pelfry, his boss at the car wash, the two homeless men who had found Stacey Kincaid's body, and finally Kate Kincaid and Sam Kincaid. It was clear to Bosch that Elias was going to attack the RHD case, expose the torture of Michael Harris and establish his defense of having done nothing wrong. He would then blow the RHD completely out of the water by bringing in Kate Kincaid to detail the car wash connection and the explanation for the fingerprints. Then most likely it would be Sam Kincaid's turn. Elias would use him to expose the Charlotte's Web Site and the horror of Stacey Kincaid's young life. It was clear that the case Elias was going to present to the jury followed the same line of investigation Bosch and his team had followed – that Harris was innocent, that there was an explanation for his fingerprints, and that Sam Kincaid or someone connected to him and the pedo net killed his stepdaughter.

Bosch knew it was a good strategy. He believed Elias would have won the case. He flipped back to the front of the court subpoenas. Chastain was third in line, putting him on the positive side of the alternating strategy – coming after Garwood and before one of the RHD defendants. He was going to be a positive witness for Elias and Harris but he had attempted to refuse being served the subpoena.

Bosch read the name of the service company off the form and called information. It was late but process serving was an odd-hours job. People weren't always served nine to five. A man answered the phone and Bosch, reading from the Chastain subpoena, asked for Steve Vascik.

'He's not here tonight. He's home.'

Bosch identified himself and explained that he was conducting a homicide investigation and needed to talk to Vascik immediately. The man on the other end of the line was reluctant to give out Vascik's phone number but agreed to take Bosch's number and contact Vascik with the message.

After disconnecting the call Bosch got up and paced around his house. He wasn't sure what he had. But he had the fluttering feeling in his stomach that often came when he was on the edge of a breakthrough to something hidden. He was flying on instinct and his instinct told him he was close to something he would soon be able to wrap his hands around.

The phone rang and he grabbed it off the couch and pushed the connect button.

'Mr Vascik?'

'Harry, it's me.'

'Eleanor. Hey, how are you? Are you all right?'

'I'm fine. But I'm not the one in a city about to burn. I've been watching the news.'

'Yeah. It looks bad.'

'I'm sorry it turned out that way, Harry. You told me about Sheehan once. I know you guys were close.'

Bosch realized that she didn't know that the friend's home where Sheehan had killed himself was theirs. He decided not to say anything. He also wished he had call waiting service on his line.

'Eleanor, where are you?'

'I'm back in Vegas.' She gave an unhumorous laugh. 'The car barely made it.'

'At the Flamingo?'

'No . . . I'm somewhere else.'

She didn't want to tell him where and that hurt.

'Is there a number I can call you at?'

'I'm not sure how long I'm going to be here. I just wanted to call and make sure you were okay.'

'Me? Don't worry about me. Are you okay, Eleanor?'

'I'm fine.'

Bosch didn't care about Vascik anymore.

'Do you need anything? What about your car?'

'No. I'm fine. Now that I'm here I'm not worried about the car.'

There was a long moment of silence. Bosch heard one of the electronic sounds that he had once heard somebody call digital bubbles.

'Well,' he finally said, 'can we talk about this?'

'I don't think this is a good time. Let's think about things for a couple of days and then we'll talk. I'll call you, Harry. Be careful.'

'Do you promise? To call?'

'I promise.'

'Okay, Eleanor. I'll wait.'

'Good-bye, Harry.'

She hung up before he could say good-bye. Bosch stood there next to the couch for a long time, thinking about her and what had happened to them.

The phone rang while still in his hand.

'Yes?'

'Detective Bosch? I got a message to call you.'

'Mr Vascik?'

'Yes. From Triple A Process. My boss Shelly said you—'

'Yes, I called.'

Bosch sat down on the couch and pulled a notebook onto his thigh. He took a pen out of his pocket and wrote Vascik's name on the top of a page. Vascik sounded young and white to him. He had some Midwest in his voice.

'How old are you, Steve?'

'I'm twenty-five.'

'You been with Triple A very long?'

'A few months.'

'Okay, last week, on Thursday, you served paper on an LAPD detective named John Chastain, do you remember that?'

'Sure. He didn't want to be served. Most cops I've done don't really care. They're used to it.'

'Right. That's what I wanted to ask you about. When you say he didn't want to be served, what do you mean exactly?'

'Well, the first time I tried to serve him he refused to take the subpoena and walked away. Then when—'

'Wait a minute, go back. When was the first time?'

'It was Thursday morning. I went to the lobby at Parker Center and had the cop at the desk call him and tell him to come down. I didn't say what it was for. It said on the paper he was IAD so I just said I was a citizen with something for him that he needed. He came down and when I said who I was he just backed off and went back to the elevator.'

'What you're saying is that it was like he knew you had a subpoena and even what case it was?'

'Right. Exactly.'

Bosch thought about what he had read in Elias's last notebook. His feuding with a source named 'Parker.'

'Okay, then what?'

'Well, then I went and did some other jobs and I came back about three-thirty and watched the employee lot at Parker. I saw him come out to go home, I guess, and I cut between some cars and ducked down and sort of came up just as he was opening his door. I had my spiel all worked out and told him he was served and said the case number and all of that. He still wouldn't take the paper but that didn't matter because under California law all you—'

'Right, I know. You can't refuse a subpoena once you have been advised that it is a legal, court-ordered subpoena. So what did he do?'

'Well, first he scared the shit out of me. He put his arm under his coat like he was going for his gun or something.'

'Then what?'

'Then he sort of stopped. I guess he thought about what he was doing. He relaxed a little bit but he still wouldn't take the paper. He told me to tell Elias to fuck off. He got in his car and started pulling out. I knew he was served so I just put the paper under his windshield wiper. He drove off with it like that. I don't know what happened to it after that. Could've blown off but it doesn't matter. He was legally served.'

Bosch thought for a moment while Vascik went on about the intricacies of process serving. He finally cut him off.

'Did you know Elias got killed Friday night?'

'Yes, sir. Sure. He was our client. We did all his cases.'

'Well, did you ever think to call the department after he was killed and tell someone about this thing with Chastain?'

'I did,' Vascik answered defensively. 'I called.'

'You called? Who'd you call?'

'I called Parker Center and said I had information. I was transferred to an office and told the guy who answered who I was and that I had some information. He took my name and number and said someone would call me back.'

'Nobody ever did?'

'No, somebody called in like five minutes. Maybe less. Right away. I told him.'

'When was this?'

'Sunday morning. I was out climbing all day Saturday. Up at Vasquez Rocks. I didn't hear about Mr Elias until I read the *Times* on Sunday morning.'

'Do you remember the name of the cop you told this to?'

'I think his name was Edgar but I don't know if that was his first or last name.'

'What about the person who took your call in the first place? Did he give a name?'

'I think he said his name but I forget it. But he did say he was an agent. So maybe it was an FBI guy.'

'Steve, think for a minute. What time did you make this call and when did Edgar call you back? Do you remember?'

Vascik was quiet while he thought about it.

'Well, I didn't get up till about ten 'cause my legs were killing me from the climb. I then kind of lazed around and read the paper. It was all over the front page, so I probably read it right after the sports. And then I called. So maybe about eleven. Thereabouts. And then that Edgar guy called back pretty quick.'

'Thanks, Steve.'

Bosch clicked the phone off. He knew there was no way Edgar had taken a call at Parker Center on Sunday morning at eleven. Edgar had been with Bosch all Sunday morning and most of the rest of the day. And they were on the road, not working out of Parker. Someone had used his partner's name. A cop. Someone inside the investigation had used Edgar's name.

He looked up Lindell's cell phone number and called. Lindell still had it turned on and he answered.

'It's Bosch. You remember Sunday morning, after you and your people came into the case, you spent most of the morning in the conference room with the files, right?'

'Yeah, right.'

'Who was answering the phones?'

'Me mostly. A couple of the others.'

'Did you take a call from a guy said he was a process server?'

'Sounds familiar. But we were getting lots of calls that morning. Reporters and people thinking they knew something. People threatening the cops.'

'A process server named Vascik. Steve Vascik. He said he had some information that might be important.'

'Like I said, it's familiar. What about it, Bosch? I thought this case was over.'

'It is. I'm just checking some loose ends. Who'd you give the call to?'

'I gave those kind of calls – you know, info off the street – to the IAD guys. To keep them busy.'

'Which one did you give the process server to?'

'I don't know, probably Chastain. He was in charge of that group. He might've taken it or told one of the others to call the guy back. See, Irving set up some shitty phones in there. We couldn't transfer one to the other and I wanted the main line free. So we took numbers and passed them on.'

'Okay, thanks, man. Have a nice night.'

'Hey, what is—'

Bosch disconnected before he had to answer any questions. He thought about the information from Lindell. He believed there was a high probability that the call from Vascik had been routed to Chastain himself, who then called back – probably taking the message to his own office for privacy – and posed as Edgar.

Bosch had one more call to make. He opened his phone book and found a number that he had not used in many years. He called Captain John Garwood, head of Robbery-Homicide Division, at home. He knew it was late but he doubted very many people were sleeping in Los Angeles tonight. He thought about what Kiz Rider had said about Garwood reminding her of Boris Karloff and only coming out at night.

Garwood answered after two rings.

'It's Harry Bosch. We need to talk. Tonight.'

'About?'

'John Chastain and the Black Warrior case.'

'I don't want to talk on the phone.'

'Fine. Name the place.'

'Frank Sinatra?'

'How soon?'

'Give me half an hour.'

'I'll be there.'

36

In the long run, Frank Sinatra got ripped off. Decades ago, when the Hollywood Chamber of Commerce put his star down on the sidewalk, they put it on Vine Street rather than on Hollywood Boulevard. The thinking probably was that the Sinatra star would be a draw, people would come down from the boulevard to see it, to take a picture. But if that was the plan, it didn't work. Frank was alone in a spot that probably saw more hypes than tourists. His star was at a crosswalk between two parking lots and next to a residence hotel where you had to convince the security guard to unlock the lobby door if you wanted to go in.

When Bosch had been in RHD years before, the Sinatra star had often been a meeting spot between detectives in the field or between detectives and their snitches. It hadn't surprised Bosch that Garwood had suggested it for their meeting. It was a way of meeting on neutral ground.

By the time Bosch got to the star Garwood was already there. Bosch saw his unmarked Ford LTD in the parking lot. Garwood flashed his lights. Bosch pulled to the curb in front of the hotel and got out. He crossed Vine to the parking lot and got in the front passenger seat. Garwood was wearing a suit, even though called from home. Bosch realized that he had never seen Garwood in anything other than a suit, the tie always pulled tight, the top button of his shirt never undone. Again Bosch thought of Rider's Boris Karloff comment.

'Those fucking cars,' Garwood said, looking across the street at Bosch's slickback. 'I heard about you getting potshotted.'

'Yeah. That wasn't fun.'

'So what brings you out tonight, Harry? How come you're still investigating a case that the chief of police and everybody else has already closed?'

'Because I have a bad feeling about it, Cap. There are loose ends. Things can unravel when you have loose ends.'

'You never could leave things alone. I remember that from when you worked for me. You and your fucking loose ends.'

'So tell me about Chastain.'

Garwood said nothing, just stared ahead through the windshield, and Bosch realized that his former captain was unsure about things.

'We're off the record here, Captain. Like you said, the case is closed. But something about Chastain and Frankie Sheehan bothers me. You should know, a couple nights ago Frankie told me everything. About how he and some of the guys lost it, did things to Michael Harris. He told me all the

Black Warrior stuff was true. And then I made a mistake. I told him that I had cleared Harris. That I could prove he didn't take that girl. And that put the hex on Frankie and later on he did what he did. So when they came up with the ballistics today and said that Frankie did it all, including Angels Flight, I went along to get along. Now I'm not so sure. Now I want all the loose ends tied up and Chastain is one of them. He was subpoenaed for the trial. Nothing unusual about that – he handled the internal investigation of Harris's complaint. But he was subpoenaed by Elias and he didn't tell us. He also tried to duck the service. And that makes it all the more unusual. That tells me he didn't want to be in that courtroom. He didn't want to be on the stand and have Elias asking him questions. I want to know why. There's nothing in Elias's files – at least the files I have access to – that says why. I can't ask Elias and I don't want to ask Chastain yet. So I'm asking you.'

Garwood reached into his pocket and took out a pack of cigarettes. He got one out and lit it, then offered the pack to Bosch.

'No thanks, I'm still off.'

'I decided that I'm a smoker and that's that. Somebody a long time ago told me that it was like destiny or fate. You were a smoker or you weren't, there was nothing you could do about it. You know who that was?'

'Yeah, me.'

Garwood snorted a little and smiled. He took a couple of deep drags and the car filled with smoke. It kicked off the familiar craving in Bosch. He remembered giving Garwood the smoking sermon years before when someone in the squad complained about the cloud of smoke that always hung over the bullpen. He lowered his window a couple of inches.

'Sorry,' Garwood said. 'I know how you feel. Everybody smoking and you can't.'

'It's no problem. You want to talk about Chastain or not?'

One more drag.

'Chastain investigated the complaint. You know that. Before Harris could sue us he had to file a complaint. That went to Chastain. And from what I understood at the time, he made the guy's case. He confirmed it. Fucking Rooker had a pencil in his desk – the tip was broken off and there was blood on it. Kept it like a souvenir or something. Chastain got it with a search warrant and was going to match the blood to Harris.'

Bosch shook his head, at both the stupidity and the arrogance of Rooker. Of the whole department.

'Yeah,' Garwood said, seeming to know what he was thinking. 'So the last thing I heard was that Chastain was going to file departmentals against Sheehan, Rooker, couple of the others, then go to the DA for criminal charges. He was going all the way with this one because that pencil and the blood were hard evidence. He had Rooker at least in the bag.'

'Okay, so what happened.'

'What happened was that the next thing is we get the word that everybody's clear. Chastain filed the case as unfounded.'

Bosch nodded.

'Somebody reached down.'

'You got it.'

'Who?'

'Irving's my guess. But maybe higher. The case was too volatile. If the charges were sustained and there were suspensions, firings, DA charges, whatever, then we start a whole new round of "kick the LAPD" in the press and in the south end with Tuggins and Sparks and everywhere else. Remember, this was a year ago. The new chief had just come on board. It wouldn't be a good way to start out. So somebody reached down. Irving's always been the department fixer. It was probably him. But for something like this, he might have enlisted the chief's okay. That's how Irving survives. He hooks the chief in, then he can't be touched because he has the secrets. Like J. Edgar Hoover and the FBI – but without the dress. I think.'

Bosch nodded.

'What do you think happened to that pencil with the blood on it?' he asked.

'Who knows? Irving's probably using it to write personnel evaluations. Though I'm sure he's washed the blood off it.'

They were silent for a moment as they watched a group of a dozen young men walking north on Vine toward the Boulevard. They were mostly white. In the street light Bosch could see the tattoos covering their arms. Headbangers, probably going up to the stores on the boulevard to replay 1992. A quick memory of Frederick's of Hollywood being looted flashed through his mind.

The group slowed as they passed Bosch's car. They considered whether to do something to the car and then decided against it and moved on.

'Lucky we didn't meet in your car,' Garwood said.

Bosch didn't say anything.

'This place is going to come apart tonight,' Garwood continued. 'I can feel it. Pity the rain stopped.'

'Chastain,' Bosch said, getting back on track. 'Somebody put a cork in him. Complaint unfounded. Then Elias files his suit and eventually subpoenas Chastain. Chastain doesn't want to testify, why?'

'Maybe he takes the oath seriously. He didn't want to lie.'

'There's got to be more than that.'

'Ask him.'

'Elias had a source inside Parker. A leak. I think it was Chastain. I don't mean just on this case. I mean a longtime leak – a direct conduit inside to records, everything. I think it was Chastain.'

'It's funny. A cop who hates cops.'

'Yeah.'

'But if he was Elias's big important conduit, why would Elias put him on the stand and expose him like that?'

That was the question and Bosch had no answer. He was silent for a while, thinking about this. He finally put together the thin beginnings of a theory and said it out loud.

'Elias wouldn't have known Chastain had been corked unless Chastain had told him, right?'

'Right.'

'So just by putting Chastain on the stand and asking him about it would be revealing Chastain as his source.'

Garwood nodded.

'I can see that,' he said. 'Yeah.'

'Even if Chastain sat up there and denied every question, Elias could ask the questions in a way that they would still get the point – and in this case, the truth – across to the jury.'

'It would also make the point at Parker Center,' Garwood said. 'Chastain would be exposed. Question is, why would Elias expose his source? Somebody who had been helping him a hell of a lot over the years. Why would he give that up?'

'Because this was Elias's home run case. The big one that would put him on the national map. It would put him on *Court TV, Sixty Minutes, Larry King* and everything else. It would make him. He would be willing to burn his source for that. Any lawyer would.'

'I see that, too. Yeah.'

The next part was left unsaid. That being the question of what Chastain would do to prevent being publicly burned on the stand. To Bosch the answer was obvious. If he were exposed not only as Elias's source but as the investigator who compromised the internal investigation of Michael Harris's complaint, he would be vilified both inside and outside the department. There would be nowhere for him to go and that would be untenable for a man like Chastain, for any man. Bosch believed Chastain would be willing to kill to prevent that from happening.

'Thanks, Captain,' he said. 'I've got to go.'

'It doesn't matter, you know.'

Bosch looked over at him.

'What?'

'Doesn't matter. The press releases have been made, the press conferences given, the story's out and the city is ready to go like kindling. You think the people in the south end care *which* cop killed Elias? They don't give a shit. They already have what they want. Chastain, Sheehan, doesn't matter. What matters is that a badge did it. And if you go making noise you'll just be adding more fuel to the fire. You bring up Chastain and you bring up the cover-up. A lot of people might get hurt, lose their jobs, all because they wanted to head this off in the first place. You better think about that, Harry. Nobody cares.'

Bosch nodded. He understood the message. Go along to get along.

'I care,' he said.

'Is that enough of a reason?'

'What about Chastain then?'

Garwood had a thin smile on his face. Bosch could see it behind the glowing point of his cigarette.

'I think Chastain deserves whatever he gets. And someday he'll get it.'

Now there was a new message in that. And Bosch thought he understood that as well.

'And what about Frankie Sheehan? What about his reputation?'

'There's that,' Garwood said, nodding. 'Frankie Sheehan was one of my guys . . . but he's dead and his family doesn't live here anymore.'

Bosch said nothing but that answer wasn't acceptable. Sheehan was his friend and partner. Tainting him tainted Bosch himself.

'You know what bothers me?' Garwood asked. 'And maybe you might be able to help me, being that you and Sheehan were partners at one time.'

'What? What bothers you?'

'That gun Sheehan used. That wasn't yours now, was it? I know they asked you that.'

'No, not mine. We had gone by his house on the way to mine. To get clothes and things. He must've picked it up then. The FBI must've missed it when they searched his place.'

Garwood nodded.

'I heard you made notification to his wife. Did you ask her about that? You know, about the gun.'

'I asked. She said she didn't know about any gun but that doesn't—'

'No serial number,' Garwood said, cutting in. 'A throw-down gun, everybody knows that's what that was.'

'Yeah.'

'And that's what bothers me. I knew Sheehan a lot of years. He worked for me a long time and you get to know your guys. I never knew him to be the kind of guy who would have a throw-down . . . I asked some of the other guys – especially the ones that partnered with him since you went to Hollywood. They never knew about a throw-down. What about you, Harry? You worked with him the longest. Did he ever carry an extra piece?'

It hit Bosch then, like a punch in the chest. The kind where you have to keep perfectly still and silent and wait it out until you slowly get your breath back. He had never known Frank Sheehan to carry a throw-down on the job. He was too good for that. And if you were too good to carry one on the job, why have one hidden at home? That question and its obvious answer had been there right in front of him all along. But he had missed it.

Bosch remembered sitting in his car outside Sheehan's house. He remembered the set of headlights he saw in the mirror and the car pulling to the curb down the block. Chastain. He had followed them. To Chastain, Sheehan alive was the only loose end that could cause things to unravel.

He thought of his neighbor's reports of three to four shots being fired at his house. In his mind a drunken cop's suicide was now a calculated murder.

'Motherfucker,' Bosch whispered.

Garwood nodded. He had successfully led Bosch down the road to where he apparently already was.

'Now, do you see how it could have been done?' he asked.

Bosch tried to slow his thoughts and let it come to him. Finally, he nodded.

'Yes, I see now.'

'Good. I'll make a call. I'll have whoever is on duty in the basement let you have a look at the sign-out log. No questions asked. That way you'll be sure.'

Bosch nodded. He reached over and opened the door. He got out without another word and started back toward his car. He was running before he got there. He didn't know why. There was no hurry. It was no longer raining. He just knew he had to keep moving to keep from screaming.

37

Outside of Parker Center there was a candlelight vigil and a funeral procession. Two cardboard caskets – one marked JUSTICE, the other marked HOPE – were being carried aloft by the crowd as they marched back and forth across the front plaza. Others carried signs that said JUSTICE FOR PEOPLE OF ALL COLORS and JUSTICE FOR SOME IS JUSTICE FOR NONE. Above news helicopters circled and on the ground there were at least six news crews that Bosch could see. It was getting close to eleven and all of them were getting ready to put out live reports from the protest front.

At the front door a phalanx of cops in uniforms and riot helmets stood ready to defend the police headquarters if the crowd turned from peaceful demonstration to violence. In 1992 a peaceful demonstration had turned violent and the mob roamed downtown destroying everything in its path. Bosch hurried toward the lobby doors, skirting behind the procession of protesters and through a crack in the human defense line, after holding his badge up high over his head.

Inside, he passed the front counter, which had four cops behind it, also wearing helmets, and went through the elevator lobby and took the stairwell. He went down to the basement level and then followed the hallway to the evidence storage center. He realized as he went through the door into evidence that he hadn't passed a soul since the front counter. The place seemed empty. Under the emergency response plan, all available hands of the A shift were out on the street.

Bosch looked through the wire-mesh window but didn't recognize the man on duty. He was an old vet with a white mustache on a face flushed with gin blossoms. They moved a lot of the old broken-down ones to the basement. This one got off his stool and came to the window.

'So what's the weather like outside? I don't have no windows in here.'

'The weather? It's partly cloudy with a chance of riots.'

'I figured. Tuggins still got his crowd out front?'

'They're there.'

'Yeah, the mutts. Wonder how'd they'd like it if there were no coppers around. See how they'd like life in the jungle then.'

'That's not their point. They want police. They just don't want cops that are killers. Can you blame 'em for that?'

'Yeah, well some people need killing.'

Bosch had nothing to say to that. He didn't even know why he was parrying with this old dog. He looked down at his nameplate. It said HOWDY. Bosch almost laughed. Something about seeing the unexpected name cracked through the tension and anger that had been twisting him all night.

'Fuck you. It's my name.'

'Sorry. I'm not laughing at – it's something else.'

'Sure.'

Howdy pointed over Bosch's shoulder at a little counter with forms on it and pencils tied to strings.

'You want something you gotta fill out the form with the case number.'

'I don't know the case number.'

'Well, we must have a couple million in here. Why don't you take a wild guess?'

'I want to see the log.'

The man nodded.

'Right. You the one Garwood sent over?'

'That's right.'

'Why didn't you say so?'

Bosch didn't answer. Howdy reached below the window to someplace Bosch couldn't see. Then he came up with a clipboard and put it into the pass-through slot beneath the wire mesh.

'How far back you want to look?' he asked.

'I'm not sure,' Bosch said. 'I think just a couple days will do it.'

'There's a week on there. That's all the sign outs. You want sign *outs* not sign *ins*, right?'

'Right.'

Bosch took the clipboard over to the forms counter so he could look at it without Howdy watching what he was doing. He found what he was looking for on the top page. Chastain had checked out an evidence box at seven that morning. Bosch grabbed one of the sign-out forms and a pencil and started filling it out. He noticed as he wrote that the pencil was a Black Warrior No. 2, the first choice of the LAPD.

He took the clipboard and form back to the window and slid them through the slot.

'That box might still be on the go-back cart,' he said. 'It was just checked out this morning.'

'No, it will be back in place. We run a tight ship' – he looked down at the form and the name Bosch had filled out – 'Detective Friendly.'

Bosch nodded and smiled.

'I know you do.'

Howdy walked over and got on a golf cart and then drove away into the bowels of the huge storage room. He was gone less than three minutes before the cart came back into view and he parked it. He carried a pink box with tape on it over to the window, unlocked the mesh window gate and passed the box over to Bosch.

'Detective Friendly, huh? They send you around to the schools to talk to the kids, tell 'em to say no to drugs, stay out of the gang, shit like that?'

'Something like that.'

Howdy winked at Bosch and closed the window gate. Bosch took the box

791

over to one of the partitioned cubicles so he could look through its contents privately.

The box contained evidence from a closed case, the investigation of the shooting of Wilbert Dobbs five years earlier by Detective Francis Sheehan. It had fresh tape sealing it, having just been signed out that morning. Bosch used a little knife he kept on his key chain to cut the tape and open the box. The process of unsealing the box actually took longer than it did for him to find what he was looking for inside it.

Bosch walked through the crowd of protesters as if they weren't even there. He didn't see them or hear their chants of *No justice, no peace.* Some of them yelled insults directly at Bosch but he didn't listen to those either. He knew that you didn't win justice by carrying a sign or a cardboard coffin. You earned it by being on the side of the righteous, by being unswayed from that path. And he knew that true justice was blind to all colors except one: the color of blood.

Bosch opened his briefcase after getting to his car and looked through all the paperwork until he found the call-out sheet he'd had put together on Saturday morning. He called Chastain's pager and punched in the number of his cell phone. He then sat in the car for five minutes, waiting for the callback and watching the protest march. As he watched several of the television crews broke away from their positions and hurried with their equipment toward their vans and he realized that the helicopters were already gone. He sat up straight in his seat. His watch said ten minutes to eleven. He knew that if the media were leaving all at once, and before making their broadcasts, then something must have happened – something big. He flipped on the radio, which was already tuned to KFWB, and caught the middle of a report being delivered in an urgent, quavering voice.

'– out of the truck, then the beating began. Several bystanders attempted to stop the attack but initially the angry mob of youths held them back. The firefighters were pulled into separate knots of attackers and were being assaulted until a platoon of LAPD units stormed the intersection and rescued the victims, who were pulled into the patrol cars and then driven away – to receive medical attention, we assume, at nearby Daniel Freeman Hospital. The fire engine, left behind, had been set ablaze after the mob unsuccessfully tried to turn it over. The police quickly established a perimeter in the area and calmed things. While some of the attackers were arrested, several escaped into the residential neighborhoods bordering Normandie Boul—'

Bosch's phone began ringing. He cut off the radio and flipped the phone open.

'Bosch.'

'It's Chastain, what do you want?'

Bosch could hear lots of voices and radio squawking in the background. Chastain wasn't at home.

'Where are you? We have to talk.'

'Not tonight. I'm on duty. Twelve and twelves, remember?'

'Where are you?'

'In wonderful South L.A.'

'You're A shift? I thought all detectives were B shift.'

'All except IAD. We got the shaft – night shift. Listen, Bosch, I'd love to talk about the schedule but—'

'Where are you? I'll come to you.'

Bosch turned the car's ignition and started backing out of his spot.

'I'm at the Seventy-seventh.'

'I'm on my way. Meet me out front in fifteen minutes.'

'Forget it, Bosch. I'll be swamped. I'm on arrest processing and I hear they're bringing in a dozen mooks who just attacked a fire truck, for chrissakes. These guys were trying to put out a fire in *their* neighborhood and these animals go after them. I tell you, it's un-fucking believable.'

'It never is believable. Be out front in fifteen minutes, Chastain.'

'You're not *listening* to me, Bosch. Things are going to hell out there and Big Blue is about to put down the boots on it. I don't have time to talk. I have to get ready to put people in jail. You want me to stand out front like a target for some mook with a gun? What is this about, Bosch?'

'Frank Sheehan.'

'What about him?'

'Fifteen minutes. Be out there, Chastain, or I'll come find you. You won't want that.'

Chastain started another protest but Bosch closed the phone.

38

It took Bosch twenty-five minutes to get to the Seventy-seventh Street Division station. He was delayed because the 110 Freeway had been closed in all directions by the California Highway Patrol. The freeway was a conduit from downtown to the South Bay area, directly through South L.A. In the last riot, snipers had fired on cars passing through and concrete blocks had been dropped from pedestrian overpasses onto cars below. The CHP was not taking any chances. Motorists were advised to take the circuitous route of the Santa Monica Freeway to the San Diego Freeway and then south. It would take twice as long but it was safer than a run through the expected war zone.

Bosch took surface streets the whole way. Almost all of them were deserted and he never stopped once for a traffic light or stop sign. It was like driving through a ghost town. He knew there were hot spots of looting and arson, but he never passed through them. He thought about the picture the media was projecting compared to what he was seeing. Most of the people were inside, locked down and waiting for this to pass. They were good people waiting out the storm, staring at the television and wondering if that was really their city that was being shown on fire.

The front of the Seventy-seventh station was also strangely empty when Bosch finally pulled up. A police academy bus had been pulled across the entranceway as a guard against drive-by shots and other attacks. But there were no protesters out front and no cops. As Bosch pulled to the no-parking curb in front, Chastain stepped out from the rear of the bus and approached. He was in uniform, his weapon holstered on his hip. He came to Bosch's window and Bosch lowered it.

'Where you been, Bosch, you said fif—'

'I know what I said. Get in.'

'No, Bosch. I'm not going anywhere with you until you tell me what the hell you're doing here. I'm on duty here, remember?'

'I want to talk about Sheehan and the ballistics. About the Wilbert Dobbs case.'

He noticed Chastain take a slight step back from the car. Mentioning Dobbs had landed a punch. Bosch noticed the sharpshooter ribbon on Chastain's uniform below the badge.

'I don't know what you're talking about but the case on Sheehan is closed. He's dead, Elias is dead. Everybody's dead. That's it. Now we have this – the whole city coming apart again.'

'And whose fault is that?'

Chastain stared at him, trying to read him.

'You're not making sense, Bosch. You need to get some sleep. We all do.'

Bosch opened the door and stepped out. Chastain moved back another step and drew his right hand up a little until he hooked his thumb on his belt near his gun. There were unwritten rules of engagement. That was one of them. Bosch was now on deadly ground. He understood this. He was ready.

Bosch turned and swung his car door closed. While Chastain's eyes involuntarily followed that movement, Bosch swiftly reached inside his coat and pulled his pistol out of his holster. He had it pointing at Chastain before the IAD detective could make a move.

'All right, we do it your way. Put your hands on the roof of the car.'

'What the hell are you—'

'PUT YOUR HANDS ON THE CAR!'

Chastain's hands went up.

'Okay, okay . . . easy, Bosch, be easy.'

He moved to the car and put his hands flat on the roof. Bosch came up behind him and took his gun from its holster. He stepped back and put it into his own holster.

'I guess I don't have to check you for a throw-down. You already used yours on Frankie Sheehan, right?'

'What? I have no idea what you are talking about.'

'That's okay.'

Keeping his right hand pressed against Chastain's back, Bosch reached around and took the handcuffs off the man's belt. He pulled one of Chastain's arms behind his back and cuffed his wrist. He then pulled the other arm back and completed the handcuffing.

Bosch walked him around and sat him in the backseat of the slickback opposite the driver's side. He then got back behind the wheel. He took Chastain's gun out of his holster, put it into his briefcase and reholstered his own weapon. Bosch adjusted the rearview mirror so he could quickly see Chastain at a glance and flicked the lock switch which rendered the rear doors inoperable from the inside.

'You stay right there where I can see you. At all times.'

'Fuck you! What the hell do you think you're doing? Where are you taking me?'

Bosch put the car in drive and headed away from the police station. He headed west until he could turn north on Normandie. Almost five minutes went by before he answered Chastain's question.

'We're going to Parker Center,' he said. 'When we get there you're going to tell me about killing Howard Elias, Catalina Perez . . . and Frankie Sheehan.'

Bosch felt anger and bile back up in his throat. He thought about one of the unsaid messages he had received from Garwood. He wanted street justice, and at that moment so did Bosch.

'Fine, we'll go back,' Chastain said. 'But you don't know what you're talking about. You are full of shit! The case is CLOSED, Bosch. Live with it.'

Bosch started reciting the list of Constitutional rights against self-incrimination and then asked Chastain if he understood them.

'Fuck you.'

Bosch pressed on, glancing up at the mirror every few seconds.

'That's okay, you're a cop. No judge in the world would say you didn't understand your rights.'

He waited a moment and checked his prisoner in the mirror one last time before going on.

'You were Elias's source. All these years, you were the guy giving him whatever he needed on whatever case he had. You –'

'Wrong.'

'– sold out the department. You are the lowest of the low, Chastain. Isn't that what you called it before? The lowest of the low? That was you, man, a bottom feeder, a scumbag . . . a motherfucker.'

Bosch saw police barricades across the street ahead. Two hundred yards beyond them he saw flashing blue lights and fire. He realized they were heading toward the hot spot where the firefighters had been attacked and their truck set ablaze.

At the blockade he turned right and started looking north at each intersection he passed through. He was out of his element here. He had never worked an assignment at any of the department's South Central divisions and didn't know the geographic territory well. He knew he could become lost if he strayed too far from Normandie. He gave no indication of this when he checked Chastain in the mirror again.

'You want to talk to me, Chastain? Or play it out?'

'There is nothing to talk about. You are enjoying your last precious moments with a badge. What you're doing here is pure suicide. Like your buddy, Sheehan. You're killing yourself, Bosch.'

Bosch slammed on the brakes and the car swerved to a stop. He drew his weapon and leaned over the seat, pointing it at Chastain's face.

'What did you say?'

Chastain looked genuinely scared. He clearly believed that Bosch was on the edge of losing it.

'Nothing, Bosch, nothing. Just drive. Let's go to Parker and we'll get this all straightened out.'

Bosch slowly dropped back into the driver's seat and started the car moving again. After four blocks he turned north again, hoping to run parallel to the disturbance spot and cut back onto Normandie after they were clear.

'I just came from the basement at Parker,' he said.

He glanced in the mirror to see if that had changed anything in Chastain's face. It hadn't.

'I pulled the package on Wilbert Dobbs. And I looked at the sign-out log. You pulled the package this morning and you took the bullets. You took the bullets from Sheehan's service nine, the bullets he shot Dobbs with five years ago, and you turned three of them into ballistics saying they were the bullets from the Howard Elias autopsy. You set him up to take the fall. But it's your fall, Chastain.'

He checked the mirror. Chastain's face had changed. The news Bosch just delivered had hit like the flat side of a shovel in the face. Bosch moved in for the finish.

'You killed Elias,' he said quietly, finding it hard to pull his eyes away from the mirror and back onto the road. 'He was going to put you on that stand and expose you. He was going to ask you about the true findings of your investigation because you had told him the true findings. Only the case was too big. He knew how high he could go with it and you became expendable. He was going to burn you in order to win the case . . . You lost it, I guess. Or maybe you've always been cold in the blood. But on Friday night you followed him home and when he was getting on Angels Flight, you made your move. You put him down. And then you looked up and there was the woman sitting there. Shit, that must've shocked the hell out of you. I mean, after all, the train car had been sitting there. It was supposed to be empty. But there was Catalina Perez on that bench and you had to put one in her, too. How am I doing, Chastain? I have the story right?'

Chastain didn't answer. Bosch came to an intersection, slowed and looked left. He could see down to the lighted area that was Normandie. He saw no barricades and no blue lights. He turned left and headed that way.

'You lucked out,' he continued. 'The Dobbs case. It fit perfectly. You came across Sheehan's threat in the files and took it from there. You had your patsy. A little research on the case and a little maneuvering here and there and you got to handle the autopsy. That gave you the bullets and all you had to do was switch them. Of course, the coroner's ID markings on the bullets would be different but that discrepancy would only come up if there was a trial, if they took Sheehan to trial.'

'Bosch, shut up! I don't want to hear anymore. I don't—'

'I don't care what you want to hear! You're going to hear this, douche bag. This is Frankie Sheehan talking to you from the grave. You understand that? You had to put it on Sheehan but it wouldn't work if Sheehan ever went to a trial. Because the coroner would testify and he'd say, "Wait a sec, folks, these aren't my marks on these bullets. There's been a switch." So you had no choice. You had to put Sheehan down, too. You followed us last night. I saw your lights. You followed us and then you did Frankie Sheehan. Made it look like a drunken suicide, lots of beers, lots of shots. But I know what you did. You put one in him, then you fired a couple more with his hand wrapped around the gun. You made it all fit, Chastain. But it's all coming apart now.'

Bosch felt his anger overtaking him. He reached up and slapped the mirror so he wouldn't have to look at Chastain's face. He was coming up to Normandie now. The intersection was clear.

'I know the story,' Bosch said. 'I know it. I just have one question. Why did you snitch to Elias all those years? Was he paying you? Or did you just hate cops so much that you'd do whatever you could to nail them any way you could?'

Again there was no answer from the back seat. At the stop sign Bosch looked to his left and could see the blue lights and the flames again. They had circumnavigated the police perimeter. The barricades started a block down and he paused with his foot on the brakes and took in the scene. He could see a line of police cruisers behind the barricades. There was a small liquor store on the corner with the windows shattered and jagged pieces of glass still hanging in the frames. Outside its doors the ground was littered with broken bottles and other debris left by the looters.

'You see that down there, Chastain? All of that? You –'

'Bosch –'

'– did that. That's –'

'– you didn't go far enough!'

'– all on you.'

Picking up on the fear in Chastain's voice, Bosch began turning to his right. In that instant the windshield shattered as a chunk of concrete crashed through it and hit the seat. Through the falling glass Bosch saw the crowd moving toward the car. Young men with dark angry faces, their individualities lost inside the mob. He saw a bottle in midair coming at the car. He saw it all so clearly and with seemingly so much time that he could even read the label. Southern Comfort. His mind began registering some kind of humor or irony in that.

The bottle came through the opening and exploded on the steering wheel, sending a blast of glass and liquid into Bosch's face and eyes. His hands involuntarily came up off the wheel to cover himself too late. His eyes began burning from the alcohol. He heard Chastain begin screaming from the back seat.

'GO! GO! GO!'

And then there were two more explosions of glass as other windows in the car were shattered by missiles of some sort. There was a pounding on the window next to him and the car began to rock violently right to left. He heard someone yanking on the door handle and more glass being shattered all around him. He heard shouts from outside the car, the angry, unintelligible sounds of the mob. And he heard shouts from the back seat, from Chastain. Hands grabbed at him through the broken windows, pulling at his hair and clothes. Bosch slammed his foot down on the gas pedal and yanked the wheel to the left as the car jerked forward. Fighting against the involuntary instincts of his eyes to stay closed, he managed to open them enough to allow a small slice of blurred and painful vision. The car jumped into the deserted lanes of Normandie and he headed toward the barricades. He knew there was safety at the barricades. He kept his hand on the horn all the way and when he got to the barricades he crashed through and only then did he hit the brakes. The car slid into a tailspin and stopped.

Bosch closed his eyes and didn't move. He heard footsteps and shouts but he knew they were cops coming for him this time. He was safe. He reached forward and put the car into park. He opened his door and quickly there were hands there to help him out and the comforting voices of the blue race.

'Are you okay, man? You need paramedics?'

'My eyes.'

'Okay, hold still. We'll get somebody here. Just lean here against the car.'

Bosch listened as one of the officers barked orders into a rover, announcing he had an injured officer needing medical attention. He demanded that attention right now. Bosch had never felt safer than at that moment. He wanted to thank every one of his rescuers. He felt both serene and yet giddy for some reason; like the times he had emerged unscathed from the tunnels in Vietnam. He brought his hands up to his face again and was trying to open one of his eyes. He could feel blood running down the bridge of his nose. He knew he was alive.

'Better leave that alone, man, it doesn't look too good,' one voice said.

'What were you doing out there alone?' demanded another.

Bosch got his left eye open and saw a young black patrolman standing in front of him. A white officer was standing to the right.

'I wasn't.'

He ducked and looked into the back seat of the car. It was empty. He checked the front and it was empty, too. Chastain was gone. Bosch's briefcase was gone. He straightened up and looked back down the street at the mob. He reached up and cleared the blood and booze from his eyes so that he could see better. There were fifteen or twenty men down there, all gathered in a tight group, all looking inward at what was at the center of their undulating mass. Bosch could see sharp, violent movements, legs kicking, fists raised high and then brought down out of sight and into the center.

'Jesus Christ!' the patrolman next to him yelled. 'Is that one of us? They got one of us?'

He didn't wait for Bosch's reply. He brought the rover back up and quickly called for all available units for an officer-needs-assistance call. His voice was frantic, infected with the horror of what he was seeing a block away. The two officers then ran to their patrol cars and the vehicles stormed down the street toward the crowd.

Bosch just watched. And soon the mob changed its form. The object of its attention was no longer on the ground but was rising, being brought up. Soon Bosch could see Chastain's body raised above their heads and held aloft like a trophy being passed by the hands of the victors. His shirt was now badgeless and torn open, his arms were still bound by the handcuffs. One shoe and the accompanying sock were gone and the ivory-white foot stood out like the white bone of a compound fracture through the skin. It was hard to tell from where he stood but Bosch thought Chastain's eyes were open. He could see that his mouth was wide open. Bosch heard the start of a sharp shrieking sound that at first he thought might be the siren of one of the patrol cars racing to the rescue. Then he realized it was Chastain screaming, just before he dropped back into the center of the mob and out of sight.

39

Bosch watched from the barricades as a platoon of patrol officers flooded the intersection and attempted to chase down members of the mob. The body of John Chastain remained sprawled in the street like a sack of laundry that had fallen off a truck. They had checked him and left the body alone once it was determined that the rescue was too late. Soon the media helicopters were overhead and paramedics came and tended to Bosch. He had lacerations on the bridge of his nose and left eyebrow that needed cleaning and stitches but he refused to go to the hospital. They removed the glass and closed the wounds with butterfly bandages. Then they left him alone.

Bosch spent the next period of time – he wasn't sure how long – wandering behind the barricades until a patrol lieutenant finally came to him and said he would have to return to Seventy-seventh Street Division to be interviewed later by the detectives coming in to handle the investigation. The lieutenant said he would have two officers drive him. Bosch numbly nodded and the lieutenant started issuing orders for a car into his rover. Bosch noticed the looted store across the street and behind the lieutenant. The green neon sign said FORTUNE LIQUORS. Bosch said he would be ready in a minute. He stepped away from the lieutenant and walked across the street and into the store.

The store was long and narrow and prior to that night had had three aisles of merchandise. But the shelves had been cleared and overturned by the looters who had stormed through. The debris on the floor was a foot high in most places and the smell of spilled beer and wine was heavy in the place. Bosch carefully stepped to the counter, which had nothing on it but the plastic rings of a liberated six-pack. He leaned over to look behind the counter and almost let out a scream when he saw the small Asian man sitting on the floor, his knees folded up to his chest and his arms folded across them.

They looked at each other for a long moment. The entire side of the man's face was swelling up and coloring. Bosch guessed it had been a bottle that had hit him. He nodded at the man but there was no response.

'You okay?'

The man nodded but didn't look at Bosch.

'You want the paramedics?'

The man shook his head no.

'They take all the cigarettes?'

The man did not respond. Bosch leaned further over and looked under the counter. He saw the cash register – the drawer open – lying on its side on the floor. There were brown bags and matchbooks scattered all over the place. Empty cigarette cartons, too. Placing his body on the counter he was able to reach down and weed through the debris on the floor. But his hunt for a smoke was fruitless.

'Here.'

Bosch raised his eyes to the man sitting on the floor. He was pulling a softpack of Camels out of his pocket. He shook the pack and held it out, the last soldier in it protruding.

'Nah, man, it's your last one. That's okay.'

'No, you have.'

Bosch hesitated.

'You sure?'

'Please.'

Bosch took the cigarette and nodded. He reached down to the floor and picked up a pack of matches.

'Thank you.'

He nodded again to the man and left the store.

Outside, Bosch put the cigarette in his mouth and sucked air through it, tasting it. Savoring it. He opened the matches and lit the cigarette and drew the smoke fully into his lungs and held it there.

'Fuck it,' he said.

He deeply exhaled and watched the smoke disappear. He closed the matchbook and looked at it. One side said FORTUNE LIQUORS and the other said FORTUNE MATCHES. He thumbed open the cover again and read the fortune printed on the inside above the red match heads.

> HAPPY IS THE MAN WHO
> FINDS REFUGE IN HIMSELF

Bosch closed the matchbook and put it in his pocket. He felt something in there and pulled it out. It was the small bag of rice from his wedding. He threw it up into the air a couple of feet and then caught it. He squeezed it tightly in his fist and then put it back into his pocket.

He looked out across the barricades to the intersection where Chastain's body was now covered with a yellow rain poncho from the trunk of one of the patrol cars. A perimeter had been set up within the larger perimeter and an investigation of the death was just beginning.

Bosch thought about Chastain and the terror he must have felt at the end, when the hands of hate reached in and grabbed him. He understood that terror but felt no sympathy. Those hands had begun reaching for him long ago.

A helicopter came down out of the dark sky and landed on Normandie. Doors opened on either side of the craft and Deputy Chief Irvin Irving and Captain John Garwood climbed out, ready to take control and direct the investigation. They walked briskly toward the clot of officers near the body. The air wash from the helicopter had blown a flap of the poncho off the body. Bosch could see Chastain's face staring up at the sky. An officer stepped over and covered him again.

Irving and Garwood were at least fifty yards away from Bosch but they seemed to know of Bosch's presence and at the same time they both looked toward him. He looked back and didn't flinch in his stare. Garwood, still in his perfect suit, gestured toward Bosch with a hand holding a cigarette. There was a knowing smile on his face. Irving finally looked away and focused his attention on the yellow poncho he was walking toward. Bosch knew the score. The fixer was on the job now. He knew how it would be handled and what the official story would be. Chastain would become a department martyr: pulled out of a patrol car by the mob, bound with his own handcuffs and beaten to death, his murder the justification for whatever else happened at the hands of the police this night. In an unspoken way, he would become the trade – Chastain for Elias. His death – broadcast from the mechanical vultures above – would be used to end the riot before it started. But no one would know outside of a few that it had been Chastain who also started it.

Bosch knew he would be co-opted. Irving could get to him. Because he held the only thing that Bosch had left, that he still cared about. His job. He knew Irving would trade that for his silence. And he knew he would take the deal.

40

Bosch's thoughts kept returning to that moment in the car when he had been blinded and he felt the hands reaching and grabbing for him. Through the terror a lucid calmness had come over him and he now found himself almost cherishing the moment. For he had been strangely at peace. In that moment he had found an essential truth. He knew somehow that he would be spared, that the righteous man was beyond the grasp of the fallen.

He thought about Chastain and his final scream, a wail so loud and horrible as to be almost inhuman. It was the sound of fallen angels in their flight to hell. Bosch knew he could never allow himself to forget it.